THE LORD PETER WIMSEY COMPANION

by
Stephan P. Clarke

The Mysterious Press
New York

 For information address The Mysterious Press, 129 West 56th Street, New York, N.Y. 10019.

Photo by Vitelli
Dust jacket illustration and design by John Kovaleski

Library of Congress Catalogue Number: 85-060072
ISBN: 0-89296-850-8 Trade Edition

FIRST EDITION

DEDICATION

This book is dedicated with gratitude and affection to all those who helped me find things or who explained things to me: Particularly Ralph L. Clarke, Philip Scowcroft, Marian Gower, and Thelma Platt, and especially to my daughter, Erin, who helped more than she can ever know.

TO THE READER:

Welcome to The Lord Peter Companion. It is hoped that the present work will add to your enjoyment of the Peter Wimsey stories in some way. There is a good deal of entertainment to be derived from that canon, a fact that is supported by the continued availability of all of the short stories and novels in a variety of editions. There is, in addition, a whole world of witty social commentary and historical record in those tales. Their entertainment value, wit, and social history combine to make them almost universally recognized as works of considerable merit. Critic Howard Haycraft even went so far as to write of Miss Sayers's accomplishments, "Her very errors do her honor."

The canon's entertainment value and wit may be self-evident, but its other qualities are less so. The sheer quantity of material included in the stories to develop verisimilitude for a plot situation is not obvious until one starts to catalogue it all. Only then is the full extent of Miss Sayers's commentary about her society, and Lord Peter's, known. It was an exciting world, but it is now forever gone.

The knowledge that Lord Peter's world has disappeared along with many of those who could explain it has been the motivation for this work. The effort was also urged on by the knowledge that few readers today enjoy the sort of education that Dorothy L. Sayers had. So, what had begun as an attempt to clarify some points of information for myself has grown into the present work. It is based on the assumption that there are many readers who have no personal knowledge of the world before WW II, and who will never have a "classic" Oxford education. Therefore, what began as a personal research exercise became a systematic compilation of all sorts of imformation that pertained to Lord Peter's activities.

This compilation is not complete, nor is it ever likely to be "complete". Even after four years of research with help from all sorts of people, there are items that were identified as needing explanation but which were never located. They may never be, but each reader brings a fresh set of parameters, views, and attitudes, so it is hard to say with precision what might happen as a result of this preliminary effort. Whatever the case, it is hoped that the reader will still find much of value in what follows.

All of that material is addressed to one goal: To make the Peter Wimsey stories accessible to more readers who choose to participate in the stories at some level beyond that of simple entertainment. As with the Sherlock Holmes stories, one does not have to know what a hansom cab is in all its details to enjoy the adventures. So it is with the Lord Peter sotries. However, in each case, the tales assume added depth and dimension when these minor points are made known. Additionally, Miss Sayers enjoyed peppering her stories with a wide variety of quotations and allusions, both literary and historical.

It is also true that knowledge of those references is not necessary to enjoy the stories, yet Miss Sayers used them in such a manner that recognition of them enhances our appreciation of the tales. Nowhere is this more certain than in Clouds of Witness and Gaudy Night. In the former, it will be noted that the plot is both foreshadowed and echoed by chapter heading quotation and others that are sprinkled throughout the text. In Gaudy Night, our understanding of just what happens in the famous proposal and acceptance scene at the end of the last chapter is expanded greatly when one identifies the source of the last clause, "and no hand plucked his velvet sleeve" (item #4748). It explains much and adds great depth of emotion to the whole episode. It also presages the levels of emotional intensity to be found in Busman's Honeymoon.

Other than providing accessibility to the canon, it is hoped that this work will inspire further investigation into the Wimsey adventures. Much biographical material has been prepared of late about MIss Sayers, and there is a growing body of research into the Wimsey canon, but much remains to be done both historically and critically.. It is hoped that the Companion will

help.

To whatever end this collection of notes is put, one objective has been the primary guide during preparation: To demonstrate to this and to successive generations of readers just how marvellous the Peter Wimsey stories are. It is anticipated that the reader will soon come to agree with one of my correspondents during the research: No author would dare put Dorothy L. Sayers into a novel as a character as no reader would ever believe so diversely knowledgeable a person could exist. She did, and we are the better for her efforts to mirror her society so faithfully in what will remain a remarkable achievement in the realm of detective fiction and social commentary.

ACKNOWLEDGEMENTS:

In addition to the persons named in the dedication--to whom I owe a debt of gratitude that can never be repaid properly--many others have earned my heartiest thanks. In particular I should like to recognize the kind assistance of the Rochester Public Library and the Monroe County Library System as well as the reference staff of the Drake Library at the State University College at Brockport, New York.

Special words of thanks are owed to John H. Dirckx, Rutherford Morse, Helen Ketcham, John Morris, Geoffrey Lee, Evelyn A. Herzog, John Gower, Rose Bachem-Alent, Joseph Dunlap, Barbara Dunlap, J. L. Bardolf-Smith, U. H. M. Corner, Thomas Hahn, Waldo Lewis, Mary Cappadonna, Jean Beno, Geoffrey Hinchliffe, Ann Hinchliffe, William Gutsch, Marvin Epstein, Marvin Epstein, Jerold Feldman, D. Donald Cervone, Robert. L. Lauritzen, Louise Goldberg, James P. Devlin, Morris Newman, Richard S. Dirksen, Robert S. Paul, Eunice M. Paul, Elton Francis, Pauline Adams, and

Alexandra Maxwell, Richard Eichorn, Thomas R. Collin, Elizabeth Holmes, Tiffany Hunt, Fred Hutt, John Kuiper, Lowell P. Leland, Frank W. Oakley, Margareta A. Rydbeck, Elizabeth Srinivasagam, Otto Thaler, Penelope Wallace, Ruth Vyse, and Martin Gardner.

The Reverend James Trautwein deserves especial credit for always being the friend to one who was in need frequently. I am also indebted to the Spencerport Central School District for granting me a sabbatical for research. It is, however, to my wife that the greatest debt of thanks is owed. She very patiently put up with me while I worked on the project, and that should easily qualify her for some sort of sainthood.

Stephan P. Clarke
Churchville, NY

The Lord Peter Wimsey Companion

HOW TO USE THIS BOOK:

Each entry in the text is arranged according to basic principles of alphabetization. This system works very well for names, single word entries, and the like, but is not the best arrangement for quotations as the reader is not necessarily going to use the same "key word" as the compiler. The difficulty is immediately obvious: How can the material be made readily available without either a cumbersome collection of cross-references or an index like that found in the typical dictionary of quotations.

The answer is that each entry is numbered consecutively. At the back of the book is an index by short story or novel title. For each short story, every item that relates to that story is listed after its title by entry number. For instance, after the heading for "The Learned Adventure of the Dragon's Head" in the index, the reader will find a list of numbers. Each number identifies an entry in the text which relates to that story. The same applies to novels, but those entries are by chapter or other subdivision, and are not for the work as a whole.

The reader will note that no effort has been made to identify each and every instance in which some person or thing appears. Only the _first_ appearance in each work is listed. Also, some items appear with such regularity that they are not listed specifically at all, but have after their entry only the notation [_passim_].

Any entry that does not have a notation following it is an item provided for the benefit of the reader, but the item itself does _not_ appear anywhere in the texts. _There_ are few such entries, but they are provided as explanations of some other point.

As with any systematic organization, there are exceptions to the general rules:

1. While the English articles have been ignored for alphabetization, no knowledge of foreign languages has been assumed. Therefore, for example, an entry for _"a la bonne heure"_ will be found under _"a"_, _and_ not _under_ some other entry letter.

2. Those entries which appear in the original Greek are all gathered under the heading "Greek passages", item number 2931. Where the Greek has been rendered in the Latin alphabet, follow standard alphabetization practices.

3. Entry items observe British spelling practices where appropriate or necessary to do so. The text follows American practice.

4. All entries beginning with "O" or "Oh" are listed together under "O", those items coming first, the "Oh" items following immediately after.

5. _The Nine Tailors_ and _Busman's Honeymoon_ have unusual chapter identification systems which, for convenience have been rendered in the text as follows:

--for _The Nine Tailors_:

Chapter 1 = "The Bells Are Rung Up"
Chapter 2 = "The Bells in Their Courses"
Chapter 3 = "Mr. Gotobed Is Called Wrong"
Chapter 4 = "Lord Peter Is Called Into the Hunt"
Chapter 5 = "Lord Peter Is Taken From Lead"
Chapter 6 = "Lord Peter Dodges"
Chapter 7 = "Tailor Paul Is Called"
Chapter 8 = "Monsieur Rozier Hunts the Treble Down"
Chapter 9 = "Plain Hunting"
Chapter 10 = "Lord Peter Follows His Course Bell"
Chapter 11 = "Emily Turns Bunter from Behind"
Chapter 12 = "Lord Peter Is Called Wrong"
Chapter 13 = "The Quick Work"
Chapter 14 = "Nobby Goes in Slow"
Chapter 15 = "Will Thoday Goes in Quick"
Chapter 16 = "The Slow Work"
Chapter 17 = "The Dodging"
Chapter 18 = "The Waters Are Called Out"
Chapter 19 = "The Waters Are Called Home"
Chapter 20 = "The Bells Are Rung

Down

--for Busman's Honeymoon:

Prothalamion = P;

Chapters 1 - 20 are numbered in this fashion;

Epithalamion 1 = E1

Epithalamion 2 = E2

Epithalamion 3 = E3

ABBREVIATIONS STANDARDLY USED:

(for the short stories)

[ae] = "Absolutely Elsewhere"

[aq] = "Article in Question"

[bc] = "Bone of Contention"

[cb] = "Cat in the Bag"

[ab] = "Cave of Ali Baba"

[cf] = "Copper Fingers"

[dh] = "Dragon's Head"

[fr] = "Footsteps That Ran"

[hp] = "Haunted Policeman"

[im] = "Image in the Mirror"

[ie] = "Incredible Elopement"

[nf] = "Man With No Face"

[mt] = "Matter of Taste"

[np] = "Necklace of Pearls"

[pj] = "Practical Joker"

[qs] = "Queen's Square"

[ss] = "Stolen Stomach"

[sf] = "Striding Folly"

[t] = "Talboys"

[te] = "Teeth of the Evidence"

[umw] = "Uncle Meleager's Will"

(for the novels)

[WB] = Whose Body?

[CW] = Clouds of Witness

[BC] = The Unpleasantness at the Bellona Club

[FRH] = Five Red Herrings

[UD] = Unnatural Death

[SP] = Strong Poison

[HHC] = Have His Carcase

[MMA] = Murder Must Advertise

[NT] = The Nine Tailors

[GN] = Gaudy Night

[BH] = Busman's Honeymoon

[LPVB] = Lord Peter Views the Body

(for other items)

ca. = circa
ff. = following
p. = page
pp. = pages
* = see also
** = see also (two or more items)
C. = century
l. = a single line of poetry
ll. = two or more lines of poetry
OED = The Oxford English Dictionary

ODQ = The Oxford Dictionary of Quotations

OCCL = The Oxford Companion to Classical Literature

OCEL = The Oxford Companion to English Literature

ms. = manuscript
mss. = manuscripts
b. = born
d. = died
dsp = died without issue
fl. = flourished
s. = succeeded
KJV = King James Version of the Bible
AN = Author's Note [HHC] [GN]
BN = Biographical Note [UD]
P = Prothalamion [BH]
E = Epithalamion [BH]

(A)

1 A. A. -- the Automobile Association of England. In "Cat in the Bag", an A. A. man was assisting with traffic control at an intersection. See also A. A. scout. [cb]

2 A. A. scout -- an employee of the Automobile Association whose duty it was to aid A. A. members--to patrol, to observe police activities and warn of police traps, and to help those in need. When warning motorists of nearby speed traps by positive action, the scouts risked arrest, so they warned them negatively, thus circumventing the law; hence, the saying, "If a patrol does not salute, ask the reason why." The practice of saluting is no longer customary. Scouts used to drive motorcycles with sidecars, but now drive vans and are called patrol men. [UD 20]

3 A. M. S. -- Army Medical Service [WB 8]

4 A la bonne heure! -- French for "Well done!" [CW 13/NT 8]

5 A la guerre comme à la guerre -- French for "in war as in war", or, one must accept things as they are or as they come [UD 6]

6 à la lanterne! -- see Aristocrat! à la lanterne! [UD 3]

7 à la Plato -- see passion à la Plato [BH 13]

8 à merveille -- French for "marvelously" or "perfectly" [CW 5/HHC 7]

9 à propos de bottes -- a French idiom meaning, literally, "speaking of boots". It is also used to mean "by the way", or "for no earthly reason". [UD 21]

10 abandon aloofness . . . -- the "beauty side by side" part appears in Felicia Dorothy Heman's (1793-1835) poem, "The Graves of a Household", in the line:
"They grew in beauty, side by side,
They filled one home with glee;--" [GN 15]

11 Abbé Prévost -- see Prévost d'Exiles, Antoine-François [CW 13]

12 abbey foundation -- Fenchurch St. Paul* was, at one time, a monastic center ruled by an abbot, hence abbey. The original (Norman) church that served the abbey no longer exists, but its foundation supports the church described in the novel. [NT 1]

13 Abbot Martin -- abbot at the monastery at Fenchurch St. Paul*, ca. 1423 [NT 4]

14 Abbot Thomas -- the abbot of the monastery at Fenchurch St. Paul*, ca. 1356-92. It is from a corruption of "abbot" that the bell "Batty Thomas"* gets its name. [NT 1]

15 Abbot, Willy -- the milkman who delivers dairy products to the Sellon* home. It is he who informs the Sellons that PW and HV have moved into Talboys*. [BH 11]

16 Abbott's Bolton -- a fictitious hamlet about fifteen miles North and East of Little Doddering*. The name is probably a corruption of Abbess Roding, Essex. [bc]

17 Abdullahs -- see Turkish Abdullahs [MMA 15]

18 Aberdeen -- in Scotland between the mouths of the Rivers Dee and Don on the North Sea coast. It is the third largest city in Scotland, and is called the "Granite City" for, among other reasons, an old cathedral (14th C. and later) built of granite. It is the seat of a fine university attended by PW's friend, Thomas Macpherson*. [ss]

19 Aberdonian who had lost a sixpence -- PW's search for a clue is compared to such a person. An Aberdonian would come from Aberdeen*, and Scots, being stereotypically known for their frugality, traditionally achieve some special level in that art in Aberdeen. [bc]

20 Aberystwyth -- in Wales, a university town in the county of Dyfed and a seaside resort at the mouth of the River Theidol. Local ruins date from the 13th C. [nf]

21 abode, like Dan, in his breeches -- a typically PW sort of pun. The allusion is taken directly from Judges 5:17, but PW is alluding to the breach in the play of the game

committed by the "fat" player. One is also reminded of Hamlet, I, iv, 15-16,

" . . . it is a custom
more honored in the breech than the
observance".

[MMA 18]

22 aborigines -- used as a somewhat derogatory reference to the locals [HHC 2]

23 ABRACADABRA -- Langley's* yacht. Given its necromantic associations, the name is well chosen. [ie]

24 Abrahams, Moses -- son of Nathan Abrahams* [ss]

25 Abrahams, Nathan -- a diamond merchant in Hatton Garden* to whom PW turns for expert assistance in "Stolen Stomach". Abrahams seems more anxious to get PW married than does his lordship's family, and for very good reason--PW has promised him no small amount of business should that marriage ever take place. In BH we learn that PW has, indeed, gone back to Mr. Abrahams and has obtained a "big solitaire ruby" cut and set exactly to PW's specifications. [ss/BH P]

26 abune -- an obsolete dialectical form of above [FRH 2]

27 Abyssinia -- the African nation now known as Ethiopia. The reference in BH is to one of Benito Mussolini's* few solo military successes, the 1934-6 "war" against the "Lion of Judah", Emperor Haile Selassie, and his spear-throwing tribesmen. Having used air power, tanks, etc., against such opposition, Mussolini had the nerve to gloat over his annexation of that virtually defenseless nation. England struggled to help Selassie, but the French, under Pierre Laval, were frightened off by Hitler and Mussolini, so the League of Nations proved useless once again. Britain couldn't help Selassie alone, so Italy claimed Ethiopia's territories for its new "Roman Empire" in May 7, 1936. [BH P]

28 Academy portraits -- any portrait shown in the Summer Exhibition of the Royal Academy of Arts, Piccadilly, whether done by a member of the Academy or not. The portraits of notable, rich, or beautiful people are shown annually by the Royal Academy of Arts founded in 1768 under the patronage of King George III. Membership is restricted to forty, hence its nickname, "The Forty". [GN 4]

29 accessory after the fact -- one who assists or works with a criminal after the commission of a crime, as in one who knowingly hides a fugitive from justice [FRH 21/NT 16]

30 accessory before the fact -- one who works with a criminal prior to the commission of a crime but without necessarily taking part in the crime itself [NT 16]

31 according to his own lights -- the phrase means to perform to one's capacities, opinions, intellect, etc. [HHC 31]

32 acid drops -- a sweet made of boiled sugar flavored with tartaric acid and made during the mid-1800's and later [HHC 2]

33 ack emma -- the WW I phonetic alphabet for A. M., ante meridiem, before noon [UD 23/HHC 3/MMA 15]

34 aconite[ine] -- a sedative, poisonous, made from the dried tuberous root of monkshood (Aconitum napellus) [SP 1]

35 Acre, Siege of -- the major goal of the Third Crusade was the recapture of Acre, near Haifa, in Israel, which had fallen to Saladin in 1187. The siege lasted from June of 1189 to July 12, 1191. The city finally fell after the long-delayed arrival of Richard I, the Lionheart. [SP 21]

36 Acrobat -- a horse mentioned as racing at 50 to 1 odds. Dian de Momerie* bet on the horse and it won. [MMA 11]

37 acrostics -- word puzzles in which a series of lines or verses are so arranged that certain letters or letter arrangements will form a word or message. Meleager Finch* was fond of them. [umw]

38 Actinax Special Rapid plate -- a well-known manufacturer of filters and dry plates for large format press or studio cameras popular in the 1930's and earlier. In England a full plate became standardized at 6 1/2 x 8 1/2 inches while 5 x 7 and 8 x 10 inches became the standards in the U. S.

By comparison, the "Speed Graphic"

#23 A typical mystical sign using occult symbols around the term "abracadabra".

newspaper photographer's camera used a standard size of 4 x 5 inches. Such large negatives are essential in making even larger prints for advertising, etc., in order to avoid a "grainy" appearance that leaves a rough or pebbly appearance on the print.

The particular plate used had an H & D number of 450. This was an early film speed rating system developed by Ferdinand Hurter (1844-98) and Vero Charles Driffield (1848-1915). Hurter and Driffield, hence H & D, developed a system for measuring photographic sensitivity once uniform film products had been developed, as in the dry plate process. The number rates the "relative speed" of the film.

Such a film speed, an indicator of the amount of light needed to expose a film properly, when coupled with such mechanical factors as shutter speed and _f_-stop ratings, allows uniform picture quality in similar light conditions, a situation that had not previously existed. [MMA 2]

39 acushla -- an Anglo-Irish corruption of a Gaelic phrase meaning "my heart's pulse"; a term of endearment [WB 2/SP 5]

40 acute gastritis -- gastritis is a common stomach ailment caused by an inflammation of the stomach lining by irritation or infection. Acute gastritis involves loss of appetite, a sense of pressure and fullness, nausea, headache, slight temperature, and then vomiting and fatigue. Relief is obtained through elimination of the irritant. [SP 1]

41 _ad infinitum_ -- Latin for "on into infinity"; without discernible end [UD 14]

42 Adam[fireplace, panelling, ceiling, stone stair] -- the references relate to a school of design and architecture originated in the 18th C. by Robert and James Adam. It is characterized by straight lines and surface decorations such as moldings, carved garlands, and medallions. The effect created is one of traditional elegance and understated grandeur. [hp/SP 17/GN 1]

43 adapting a whole quad to an eleven inch double -- altering the size of an advertisement from the full length of a newspaper page covering four columns to one measuring eleven inches in depth covering three columns [nf]

44 Adcock, Mr. -- a cricket-playing member of the staff at Pym's Publicity* who is selected for the scratch team that is to play Brotherhood's* [MMA 10]

45 adders -- any Old World viper. They are venomous, so PW was especially grateful that Bredon* had not captured one. North American adders are commonly thought to be venomous, but are not. [t]

46 Adelaide -- a city in southwestern South Australia on the Gulf of St. Vincent. Mr. Williams's* home was there. [te]

47 Adèle -- Simone Vonderaa's* maid in New York City [CW 16]

48 Adelphi -- a theatre on the Strand in central London dating from 1806. Some of the famous actresses performing there include Madame Céleste, Mrs. Keeley, and Sarah Bernhardt. The theatre has been redecorated, updated, and improved several times, and is still actively involved in London's theatre life. [SP 11/MMA 10]

49 Adelphi drama -- better quality melodrama named for the Adelphi* theatre which made them famous and prospered from them [CW 2]

50 adjective of quality -- a descriptive adjective [CW 2]

51 adjutant stork -- "a gigantic species of stork (_Ciconia argala_) native to India; so-called from its quasi-military gait when walking" (OED) [CW 2]

52 Adolphus -- a name used by Miss Climpson* as a pseudonym for Charles Parker*, her "nephew", when he calls on her at Mrs. Budge's* in Leahampton* [UD 17]

53 advanced artists -- a negative term used to describe any of the cubists, dadaists, or other modern and nonrepresentational artists [np]

54 "advanced" literature -- the Judge is referring to such things as

atheism, anarchy, and free love as "advanced" topics. He might very well have such works as Joyce's Ulysses or Lawrence's Lady Chatterley's Lover in mind. One can almost hear the tone of condescension in his voice. [SP 1]

55 Advertising Agency -- a reference to the adventures recounted in MMA and PW's tenure as a copywriter at Pym's Publicity* [GN 4]

56 aegis -- in WB the word takes on one of its later meanings of protection or defense in the sense of relying on one's reputation [WB 5]

57 Aeneid -- Vergil's* epic recounting the Ulyssean adventures of Aeneas in twelve books. It is designed to honor the birth and growth of the Roman Empire. The story tells of the adventures of Aeneas during his wanderings after the fall of Troy. [GN 8]

58 Aeroplane Girl -- a musical revue of some sort for which parts were being cast by Isaac J. Sullivan*. It is apparently fictitious. [HHC 23]

59 Aesop's bat -- a reference to the fable entitled "The Bat and the Weasels" in which the bat manages to escape an ill fate by confusing the weasels--they are not certain if he is a mouse or a bird. HV is suggesting, in less clichéd form, the confusion over fish or fowl. Interestingly, the moral to the fable is: "Look and see which way the wind blows before you commit yourself." [GN 13]

60 afficher -- French for "to flaunt" or "to parade" oneself [GN 4]

61 Agag . . . Ahasuerus -- the Dowager Duchess* seems to have a penchant for unusual names for her Persian cats. Agag is a biblical character, but here the name applies to one of the Duchess's former pets, a blue Persian cat. Ahasuerus* is, of course, the name of her present feline. Agag was an Amalekite, Ahasuerus a Persian, but such distinctions do not seem to bother Her Grace. [BH E2]

62 Agag-feet -- ghostly or quiet feet. The reference is to I Samuel 15:32. Agag was king of the Amalekites who was killed by Saul. As Agag "came unto him [Saul] delicately", the name is an appropriate reference to a quiet place such as the Bodley*. Also, Agag refers to the dead and than that there is no one quieter. [GN 11]

63 agapemones -- "abodes of love". See item 64. Phoebe Tucker* seems to have meant agapae, "love feasts", from the context, but her choice of words may be a deliberate one as she is implying a negative sense which agapemone has. [GN 2]

64 Agapemonites -- a follower of the Agapemone or "abode of love" institution founded in 1845 at Charlinch in Somerset by Henry James Prince. The cult was communist in nature and held specific religious beliefs at odds with the generally accepted views then and now. The suggestion is one of free love and illicit sex. [UD 11]

65 agitato -- a term usually associated with music in any English language setting. The word is Italian and means "in an agitated state". Mr. Lamplough* uses the term to describe PW. It is not an unreasonable usage given PW's nervous tendencies. [te]

66 Agnes -- head scout (see scout) when HV was a student at Shrewsbury College*. She has since retired from the job. [GN 3]

67 Agroat, John -- usually John o'Groat, as in John o'Groat's House on the coast of Caithness in northern Scotland. The place is popularly held to be the northernmost village in the British Isles. There is no John o'Groat's House there, that being the residue of popular legend, but there is a hotel if one is visiting. Again, as with Jericho*, the reference is to suggest great distance. [NT 4]

68 ague -- a shiver or fit of chills with a related fever. The term is sometimes used by members of PW's family, especially his mother, to refer to his fits of shell shock*. [WB 9]

69 Ah, mon Dieu . . . -- French for "Oh, my goodness (not necessarily my God), that's most difficult. You realize (know) that as the days pass they all seem the same." The "voyons" is used here also as an expression of ennui; "Now then", or "Let's see" does not quite represent the speaker's tone of voice. [CW 5]

70 Ah, mon Dieu! . . . -- French for, "Oh, my God! I knew it." The sentence is meant to convey the idea that the speaker has been convinced for some time, not that she knew it in actual fact. [NT 8]

71 Ah well, as the old pagan said of the gospels -- this is apparently the punch line to a joke or music hall story [CW 2]

72 Ahasuerus -- the Dowager Duchess's pet tom cat, a pampered beast, probably not named for the Old Testament king even though that would be appropriate. The likely reference is to the medieval legend of the Wandering Jew*, called Ahasuerus in some versions, and a more appropriate reference for a tomcat. The name is more a title, something like "exalted one", also suitable for the beast. [BH P]

73 Aholibah -- one of the characters in Charles Algernon Swinburne's The Masque of Queen Bersaba which includes similar short poems spoken by queens of antiquity and mythology. The masque is written in play form, but was not meant to be performed. [BH 16]

74 Ahoy! up she rises. -- PW's version of "Hoo-ray and up she rises" from the anonymous sea chantey, "What Shall We Do with the Drunken Sailor?" [NT 6]

75 Ainsworth, Harrison -- William Harrison Ainsworth (1805-82) was an English magazine editor and publisher, and author of thirty-nine novels of historical fiction, some of which had a rather lurid touch. [bc]

76 Air for [on] a G-string -- Bach's delightful little piece for solo violin as arranged by August Wilhelmj is, in its original form, the "Air for Strings and Continuo" from the Suite in D Major. It is not specified whether the solo or orchestral version was played. [HHC 20]

77 air gun -- a reference to an early exchange between Sherlock Holmes* and Dr. Watson* in "The Final Problem". Watson speaks first:
"'You are afraid of something?' I asked.
'Well, I am.'
'Of what?'
'Of air guns.'"
SH knows that Prof. Moriarty* is after him with one, and one is used against him in "The Adventure of the Empty House". [MMA 17]

78 air raid -- England, and especially London, was subject to air raids throughout much of World War I, but their effect was nothing compared with the devastation of those in WW II. Of the almost 160 raids by airships made during WW I, only 557 people were killed and damage was a relatively modest $7,500,000. Many of the raids were made by the famous Zeppelin dirigibles, but some raids were also carried out by the then huge Gotha and Zeppelin-Staaken "Giant" bombers. [im]

79 Airedale -- a breed of dog, part of the terrier family. They have hard, wiry coats that are dark on the back and sides, tan on the remainder of the body. [SP 16]

80 Airways stock -- an offering mentioned by Freddy Arbuthnot* during conversation with PW. There is no such listing and never has been, but the reference may be to the now defunct Imperial Airways which never made much money. [SP 12]

81 Airy-fairy Lilian -- Mrs. Lefranc's* nickname [HHC 15]

82 Ajaccio -- the capital of Corsica located in the central Western part of that island on the Gulf of Ajaccio [CW 2]

83 Aladdin in the Panto. -- in the late 1800's and after, it became popular to stage pantomimes, but not in dumbshow, of various nursery and folk tales. From the 1860's, Aladdin, drawn from H. J. Byron's burlesque, enjoyed great popularity. It was customary to have women playing the lead roles. [HHC 15]

84 the Albany -- a mansion on Piccadilly* once owned by the Duke of York at the end of the 18th C. The name derives from the Duke's second title, a Gaelic name for the Northern part of Britain. The mansion was divided into bachelor flats and has been since replaced by a street of bachelor flats which retain the name. [CW 2]

85 Albert -- Prince of Saxe-Coburg and Gotha (1819-61), Prince Consort of Queen Victoria* and, during

his lifetime with her, her main counsellor. She never fully recovered from her bereavement over his death. [GN 3]

86 Albert -- Ruddle. Mrs. Ruddle's* son [only?] about whom we know only that he likes to spend his time "a-yarning" with Joe Sellon*. [BH 6]

87 Alcock -- Matthew Gowan's very devoted butler. He is distinctly a Londoner, possibly one with Cockney* connections. [FRH 8]

88 Alcock, Mrs. -- wife of Mr. Alcock, both are in service to Mr. Gowan*. [FRH 15]

89 Aldiborontophoscophornio -- or, correctly, Aldiborotiphoscophornio, a character in Chrononhotonthologos* [MMA 3]

90 Aldine 8vo -- the Divine Comedy as printed in Venice by Aldus Manutius in 1502 as an octavo volume. The Aldine works were considered the Everyman's or Modern Library editions of their day and were very popular. [WB 1]

91 Alexander -- of Macedonia, called "the Great" (356-323 B. C.). He conquered all of the world that was known to him. [BH 16]

92 Alexandra Avenue -- a short street connecting Prince of Wales Drive* with Warriner Gardens and Battersea Park Rd. to the South. The street is at right angles to the southern boundary of Battersea Park* and is almost opposite the main southern entrance to the Park. [WB 3]

93 Alexei Nicholaivitch -- the Russian form of the first and middle names of the only son and heir of Czar Nicholas II. The boy had haemophilia, a condition he inherited from Queen Victoria* through his mother, Victoria's granddaughter, Princess Alix of Hesse. The mutant gene appeared either at the time of Victoria's conception on the X-chromosome from her father, the Duke of Kent, or was a mutation in her own genetic material. [HHC 29]

94 Alexis, Paul -- fully, Paul Alexis Goldschmidt, the unfortunate, romantic young man who is the victim in HHC. He was a gigolo* in the better sense of that word whose world seemed to be a happy and exciting place until he got caught up, naively, in some of its more sordid machinations and got his throat slit. HV found the corpse and thereby comes to begin her career as a detective outside her own works of fiction. The Goldschmidt surname is that of his adoptive parents. In Russia, his name would have been Pavlo Alexeivitch Vorodin. See the genealogical chart in Ch. XXXII. [HHC 3]

95 Alf -- see Thipps, Alfred [WB 6]

96 Alf -- the Boy Scout who led PW et al. to the site of Vera Findlater's* murder. [UD 20]

97 Alford -- there are two possibilities for the location of this community as there are places of that name in Lincolnshire and Somerset. DLS could have had either in mind. [UD 5]

98 Alfred -- Alfred the Great, king of England (Wessex) from 871-899, an "indifferent cook in six letters ending with red." Bunter is still working on his crossword puzzle. Alfred supposedly burned some cakes while in hiding on the lake island of Athelney in 878. The island is in modern Somerset. He had gone there after a particularly ferocious assault by the Danes. [umw]

99 Algy -- likely a reference to Algernon in Oscar Wilde's The Importance of Being Earnest. Algy has a rather youthful, perhaps silly, appearance, perfectly in keeping with Mrs. Ruyslaender's* reaction upon meeting PW. [pj]

100 "Ali Baba and the Forty Thieves" -- the famous tale from the Arabian Nights Entertainments, supposedly told by Scheherazade to her husband, Schahriah, and forming the thematic background for "Cave of Ali Baba". The original story contains the tale of how Ali Baba makes use of the secret words "Open Sesame" to gain great riches. DLS adds an ironic twist to the phrase in her version of the story. [ab]

101 Alice -- either Alice Gibbons or Alice Roach, both friends of Nurse Booth* in their younger days. The name Alice is mentioned in the séance conducted by Miss Climpson*. [SP 17]

102 Alice dusting the White King --

ALFRED THE GREAT

#98 Alfred the Great presented as a bronze statue by H. Thorneycraft set up at Winchester, Alfred's ancient capital.

a reference to Lewis Carroll's* Through the Looking Glass, Ch. 1. When Alice finds several of the chess pieces in the cinders by the fireplace, she dusts the White King because he is so frightfully covered with ashes. [BH 5]

103 Alice in Wonderland -- Lewis Carroll's* delightful fantasy (the full title is Alice's Adventures in Wonderland) published in 1865. Alice, in reality the daughter of one of Carroll's colleagues at Oxford, Alice Liddell (sounds like little), is a little girl who dreams of adventures, wherein she encounters the Cheshire Cat, the Mad Hatter, and other perennially popular characters. [CW 9/MMA 1/ GN 15/BH 13]

104 Alison -- Insp. Macpherson's sister. He would seek her advice in any matters relating to ladies' undergarments. [FRH 5]

105 All About Cocoa -- a pamphlet PW finds when he assumes the late Victor Dean's* office. No reference to it could be found, but it sounds like the typical advertising device, complete with lots of simple drawings or photographs, used by companies to satisfy school children who write, "I am doing a report on cocoa (or whatever), please send me everything you have about this interesting subject." It is, very likely, something DLS remembered from her work as an advertising copywriter. [MMA 1]

106 All-Hallows' Eve/Day -- October 31 and November 1. All-Hallows' Eve, or Halloween, is a remnant of Celtic mythology and is the night when witches and other ghoulish types celebrate the various black rites. Hence, the Night of the Dead would include raising the dead, demons, and other such beings for evil purposes. The following day, All-Hallows' Day, was in Celtic tradition, the New Year's Day and the conclusion of the previous night's evil revels.

In the modern era, the first of November has become All Saints' Day, a general celebration of all the saints that was instituted by Pope Boniface IV in the early 7th C. Therefore, the Day of the Dead is in reference to and in honor of all the saints and martyrs. As with many situations in the Christian church, the distinctions between Christian and pagan are not always sharply defined. [ie]

107 "All honest men, good Melchior" -- the quote is from Torrismond*, I, iv, 43-5. The Duke of Ferrara is speaking to a servant and two courtiers, one of whom is Melchior. [HHC 22]

108 All lovers are lunatics . . . -- perhaps not in those words, but the intimations of those sentiments are to be found throughout Shakespeare's works [CW 13]

109 All other things to their destruction draw -- PW quotes from John Donne's poem, "The Anniversary". [BH 16]

110 All quiet on the Western Front -- a reference to the title of Erich Maria Remarque's 1929 novel, considered by some to be the greatest tale to deal with WW I. PW uses the line to refer to the situation regarding his first-born son in "Haunted Policeman". The phrase is used in similar ways, but not necessarily regarding births, when a situation is no longer tense when it had been so previously. [hp/GN 8]

111 all-stations call -- what Americans know as an APB, an all-points bulletin, a general call to all police units within a certain area [UD 19/ FRH 20]

112 All Souls -- see Oxford Colleges [GN 14]

113 All the kingdoms of the world -- HV is considering Matthew 4:8. Verses 7 and 8 are:

"Jesus said unto him, It is written again, Thou shalt not tempt the Lord thy God.

"Again, the devil taketh him up into an exceeding high mountain, and sheweth him all the Kingdoms of the world, and the glory of them."

The segment of Matthew in question relates the temptations of Jesus by Satan. [GN 23]

114 all the swans of England belonged to the King -- not all the swans in England, but the monarch shares, with the Dyers and Vintners Guilds in The City*, ownership of all swans on the Thames. Every July a "swan-upping" examines and identifies all cygnets as to ownership with colored bands on

their legs to match the bands of their parents. [GN 13]

115 All the villages in the Marne -- while there are many villages in that area with names ending in "y", not all of them do [NT 8]

116 all the world and time -- one is reminded of Andrew Marvell's (1621-78) poem, "To His Coy Mistress", the opening couplet of which is:
"Had we but world enough and time,
This coyness, Lady, were no crime."
[GN 20]

117 All this self-sacrifice -- see Gertrude Rhead [CW 11]

118 Allcock -- Mary Whittaker's* first cousin who lives in Birmingham*. As sole surviving relative, he inherits the remainder of Agatha Dawson's* estate. See the genealogical chart at the end of the novel. [UD 23]

119 Allison, Miss -- Shrewsbury College's* Secretary and Treasurer. She would also be responsible for translating College policies into operating rules and procedures, keeping records, etc. She would be a senior administrator. [GN 5]

120 Almost like being in love -- PW is being too omniscient here. There is a popular song called "Almost Like Being in Love", by Frederick Loewe and Alan Jay Lerner, but it is from the 1947 musical Brigadoon, and that is twelve years after the action in BH. [BH 16]

121 Alopa, Lorenzobodi -- a reference to Lorenzo-Francesco d'Alopa, a 15th C. Florentine printer who began work there in 1484. His works are noted for their ornate capitals and chapter headings and the high quality paper on which they are printed. Among his more notable works are editions of Euripedes' tragedies and the "Argonautica" of Apollonios Rhodius* printed in 1496. [WB 5]

122 alpaca or merino or whatever -- alpaca is a thin wool cloth made from the fine fur of the Peruvian alpaca, a cousin of the llama. Merino is a fabric resembling cashmere but is made from the exceptionally fine fleece of the merino sheep. Again, however, the Duchess is mistaken as Jane Eyre* was to be married in a dress of pearl-colored silk. Later on in BH, HV repeats the Dowager Duchess's* error in Ch. 14. [BH P]

123 Alpine Club -- a more or less social and avocational club devoted to those who share an interest in mountain climbing. Its headquarters are in London. [WB 8]

124 Alps -- normally associated with Switzerland alone, the Alps include ranges throughout central and eastern Europe [SP 15]

125 Alsatian -- another name for the German shepherd dog [GN 12]

126 Always laying down the law -- PW is quoting Peake of Brasenose* from their meeting in the previous chapter [GN 15]

127 Always on the spot like that patent ointment thing -- PW is comparing Parker's punctuality and readiness to some over-the-counter non-prescription preparation, reference unknown. Elliman's Embrocation* is a likely candidate, however, as it is mentioned later on and PW has referred to it in advertisement jargon and it is not unreasonable to associate the two instances. Given DLS's advertising background, one could make a case, but it would be conjecture. [CW 2]

128 amalgam filling -- a tooth filling made of a blend or amalgam of mercury and silver. The exact contents are mercury, 52%; silver, 33%; tin, 12.5%; copper 2%; and zinc, 0.5%. [te]

129 Amalek, children of -- in Genesis 36:12, Amalek is given as the son of Eliphaz and the concubine Timna. In Exodus 17:8-16, right after Moses smote the stone at Meribah* for water, Amalek and his followers come forward to fight with the Israelites and are identified as their perpetual enemy. As long as the Israelites walk in humility before God, they are protected and can defeat the Amalekites. When they act disobediently, they lose. As PW uses the phrase, he means to be in the clutches of one's enemies. I Samuel 15 also relates to the Amalekites. [FRH 19]

130 amber -- the translucent, hard, yellowish-to-brownish fossil resin that polishes well and is used to make

beads and other ornaments. Some of the very best quality amber is found in Poland. [HHC 15]

131 Ambledon Overbrook -- a community about a mile and a half from Pagford* toward Lopsley*. All three towns are fictitious. [BH 18]

132 Ambrose, Mrs. -- a guest who was once caught au naturel by Uncle Roger's* ghost in the new West wing bath at Bredon Hall* [BH E2]

133 ambsace -- a word of seven letters with s in the middle meaning two aces. PW comes up with the word as a help to Bunter* who is apparently given to crossword puzzles. [umw]

134 American Ambassador -- in 1923, the U. S. ambassador to the United Kingdom was Mr. George Harvey. Hence, it was most likely to Mr. Harvey that PW wished to speak. [CW 14]

135 American bar -- a bar set up to make cocktails of various sorts. Even now, cocktails, as known in the U. S., are not well accepted in Britain, and to have had one available, complete with bartenders, at the time of the story would have been quite remarkable. It would also have been an indicator of the social status of the leaders of The Society*. [ab]

136 American cloth -- a flexible cloth enamelled to resemble leather and used as an upholstering material [BC 17]

137 American Consular seal -- Eric Loder* was making a duplicate of it for the purpose of forging a passport. It would be the consul's version of the Great Seal of the U. S., used to authenticate official documents such as passports. [cf]

138 American Embassy -- was and is on Grosvenor Square. In the 1920's the building was at No. 4, but the new embassy, erected in 1960, occupies the entire West side of the Square. [CW 14]

139 Amery, Col. -- a resident of the village near Brough* where PW finally locates Hugh Farren*. [FRH 20]

140 'ammer, 'ammer, 'ammer on the 'ard 'igh road -- PW is quoting from Punch, Vol. XXX, p. 218, of 1856:

"It ain't the 'unting as 'urts 'un, it's the 'ammer, 'ammer, 'ammer along the 'ard 'igh road." [HHC 16]

141 amnesia -- loosely, loss of memory, but there are various types. Anteretrograde am. follows a severe shock or trauma. Robert Duckworthy* fears he may have suffered this form of amnesia. Auditory am. involves only the victim's ability to recognize speech. Retrograde am. involves a loss of all memory of prior events and sometimes the memory of the cause of the amnesia is lost as well. Post-traumatic am. follows an accident and is of variable length, being a guide to the severity of the shock. Any form of amnesia may be partial or general in nature and may not be related to physical trauma in any way. [im]

142 amorino -- a little, decorative cupid [MMA 4]

143 ampelopsis -- a clinging, woody vine. The term is used appropriately by PW to describe blackmailer Paul Melville*. [pj]

144 ampersand -- the "and" symbol: &, &, &, etc. [MMA 8]

145 ampullae -- the plural form of ampulla, also ampul or ampoule; any hermetically sealed vial used to hold solutions to be injected with a hypodermic syringe [UD 2]

146 amyl nitrate -- properly isoamyl nitrate, a vasodilator. When inhaled, it helps blood vessel walls to relax and, thus, lowers blood pressure. Its major use is to relieve the pain of angina pectoris, but it is useful in treating asthma, convulsions, and cyanide poisoning. [BC 19]

147 An eye's an eye for a' that -- the "vague" allusion is to Robert Burns's (1759-96) poem, "A Man's a Man for a' That". The poem is one of the more significant of the 18th C. as it is one of the earliest statements on democracy. [MMA 6]

148 An ill-favored title, but my own --PW is quoting loosely from As You Like It, V, iv, 60: "An ill-favored thing, sir, but mine own." The line is Touchstone's in a conversation with the senior Duke and Jaques. [BH 5]

149 An Inquiry into the Mathematical

Theory of the In and Out of Course -- the title refers to the Rev. Mr. Venables'* fictitious contribution to the literature of the art of change-ringing* [NT 2]

150 Ananias, lied like -- the reference is to Acts 5:1-11. With his wife, Sapphira, he lied to Peter before God and both died. [NT 5]

151 Anastasia -- the illegitimate daughter of Duke Francis Josias* of Saxe-Coburg-Gotha who married Charles Marie Lavannier*. She is not to be confused with the daughter of Czar Nicholas II of Russia. [HHC 32]

152 The Anatomy of Melancholy -- by Robert Burton*, published in 1621. This strange and complex work was originally intended to be a treatise on the then legitimate medical condition called melancholy, one of the problems of which Hamlet complains. Burton analyzes melancholy as a humor, an imbalance of bodily fluids--sound medical thinking in his day--but the work becomes an investigation and commentary regarding his own melancholia. Additionally, the book is larded with quotes from an amazing range of literature and interesting bits of popular information. Stylistically, all is presented in a most clear manner. [GN 21]

153 ancient chain -- from the flue at Talboys*. PW likens it to the more noble chains of office typically worn on ceremonial occasions by mayors and others who hold high public office. [BH 5]

154 Ancient Froth-Blowers -- see Froth Blowers cuff links [UD 4]

155 Ancient Minoan civilization -- the civilization on the island of Crete which successively antedates and coincides with early Greek development [GN 17]

156 And all the powerful kings -- PW's quote is from John Donne's* "Sermon" (LXXIII), "Eternity". [GN 20]

157 And dinner. And dancing. And so to bed. -- the allusion here is to the diary of Samuel Pepys (pronounced peeps) that provides insight into the intimate workings of comfortable 17th C. life in London. Many of his diary entries conclude with phrases almost identical to those cited here. [HHC 16]

158 And he himself has said it -- the Hon. Freddy Arbuthnot is quoting from H. M. S. Pinafore by Gilbert and Sullivan. The line is from a song in Act II:

"He is an Englishman!
For he himself has said it,
And it's greatly to his credit
That he's an Englishman!" [SP 3]

159 And he set the cherubims within -- both of these quotations are from I Kings 6:27 and 7:11 and refer to the description of the temple in Jerusalem as Solomon built it [NT 12]

160 And he that gives us in these days new lords -- see "Contented Man's Morrice" [UD 12]

161 And here's an engine fit for my proceeding -- from Shakespeare's comedy of mistaken identities, The Two Gentlemen of Verona, III, i, 138. The speech is the Duke's. "Engine" simply refers to any sort of mechanical contrivance. [BH 20]

162 And here's to the hound -- see "Drink, Puppy, Drink" [CW 2]

163 And his short minute -- from John Donne's* poem, "A Lecture Upon the Shadow". Lines 25 and 26 of that poem read:

"Love is a growing, or full constant light;
And his first minute, after noone, is night."

The poem addresses love in a way most appropriate to that of Lady Mary* and George Goyles*. [CW 10]

164 And kissed again with tears -- the concept is from a lyric within the long narrative poem by Tennyson*, The Princess. The poem is an "Introductory Song", and the lines are, in part:

"O we fell out I know not why,
And kiss'd again with tears.
And blessings on the falling out
That all the more endears,
When we fall out with those we love
And kiss again with tears!"
[MMA 17]

165 And left him a low, lorn crittur -- the allusion is to Charles Dickens's* David Copperfield, Ch. 3,

where the passage appears as, "I am a lone, lorn creetur, . . . and everythink goes contrairy with me." Mrs. Gummidge is the speaker. [HHC 10]

166 And never has to argue ahead of His data -- PW alludes to Sherlock Holmes's comment in "A Scandal in Bohemia": "It is a capital mistake to theorize before one has data." [NT 13]

167 And she was a fine as a melon -- the reference is to the poem "Daniel", also known as "The Daniel Jazz", by American poet [Nicholas] Vachel Lindsay (1879-1931), the sixth and eighth sections:

"And she was a golden lily in the dew.
And she was as sweet as an apple on the tree,
And she was as fine as a melon in the cornfield,
Gliding and lovely as a ship on the sea . . . ."
"And she prayed to the Lord:--
'Send Gabriel. Send Gabriel.'
King Darius said to the lions;--
'Bite Daniel. Bite Daniel.
Bite him. Bite him. Bite him!'"

The "she" of the poem is Daniel's sweetheart, a person not included in Daniel 6:16-24 wherein the story of the lion's den is recounted. [GN 17]

168 And so-o-o -- PW is performing a mocking imitation of that great radio and TV "art" form, the soap opera and the golden-toned announcer who provided the running commentary between segments. [GN 15]

169 And so to bed. -- see And dinner. And dancing. And so to bed. [HHC 16]

170 And the moral of that is -- from Ch. 9 of Alice in Wonderland*. The line concludes, "Oh, 'tis love, 'tis love, that makes the world go round." [CW 9/BH E2]

171 And these say: "No more now my knight . . ." -- the reference is to William Morris's* "The Judgment of God", ll. 57-61, a poem of considerably masculine attitude that deals with jousts, ladies fair, etc. [GN 17]

172 And you are right and I am right -- PW is quoting from Act I of The Mikado by Gilbert and Sullivan. The song is sung by the noble Lord Pish-Tush early in the act. [SP 8]

173 Anderson -- a friend and business contact whom Sir Reuben Levy* had seen shortly before Levy disappeared. Levy's absence stands to cost Anderson a good bit of money. See also Wyndham's. [WB 2]

174 Anderson, Bob -- one of the Kirdcudbright* and Gatehouse* artists' colony. He enjoys entertaining his friends. [FRH 7]

175 Anderson, Miss; young Mr. -- the children of #174 [FRH 13]

176 Anderson, Mrs. -- wife of Bob Anderson* [FRH 13]

177 Andrews, Mr. -- a photographer in Leahampton*. He is fictitious. [UD 21]

178 Andy -- son of the proprietor of the Anwoth Hotel* whose bicycle is stolen and eventually discovered at Euston Station* in London. He would be the son of Joe Dignam*. [FRH 3]

179 anemones -- the flowers of the large genus Anemone, known for their large, showy flowers [CW 6]

180 Angel -- a pub in Gatehouse-of-Fleet, on the main street of the town. It is a real establishment. [FRH 11]

181 angel roof, decorated -- in older churches where the structural members of the roof were left exposed, it was often the practice to decorate the high open spaces with ornamentation having a heavenly association. Used frequently were carvings or statues of angels, sometimes painted and gilded as described in Exodus and Ezekiel. [WB 4/NT 2]

182 Angleterre -- French for England. Both languages' names for the British Isles reflect the fact that among the early settlers there were the ancient Northern European people called the Angles, hence, "Angleland". [NT 7]

183 Anglican compromise -- the worship service of the Church of England. It is neither Roman Catholic nor low church Protestant, but a compromise between the two. [GN 14]

184 Anglo-Indian liver -- a reference

to the livers of those Englishmen established in India who were notoriously hot-tempered from whiskey and curry. There is a strong connection between livers and whiskey, but curry attacks one's innards more immediately. "Anglo-Indian" is now used to refer to someone of mixed race, but such was not the case in this reference. [SP 20]

185 Anglo-Saxon -- the Old English from which, with extensive alterations, Modern English is derived. As an example, the Lord's Prayer in Old English, set in modern type, begins: "Fæther ure thu the eart on heofonum, si thin nama gehalgod." The "th" sound in Anglo-Saxon was represented by a symbol called the thorn: Þ, þ. As the early printers did not have that form in their type cases and, just as often, to save space on the printed page, they substituted the infrequently used letter "y". Hence, we are still plagued by such monstrous constructions as "Ye Olde Cosye Tea Shoppe", all done in the thought that somehow such kitsch will add to the atmosphere of the place. [GN 3]

186 Angora rabbit -- a breed of rabbit with long, soft, silky fur. They are often bred for show purposes as are Angora cats. [GN 8]

187 Angus -- the booking clerk at the Gatehouse* railway station. Gatehouse is no longer served by trains. [FRH 3]

188 Animals' Hospital -- an otherwise unidentified institution for the care of pets and other animals [MMA 12]

189 The animals went in four by four -- PW sings this version of "One More River" substituting camel for hippopotamus. He also amends that tune, otherwise known as "Noah's Ark", by adding "vive la compagnie", a refrain from the song of that name which is more familiarly known as "Vive l'Amour". The song is an anonymous ditty from the area of Cornwall or Devon. [im]

190 The animals went in two by two -- PW again sings from "One More River to Cross", that anonymous ditty from the West Country. See item 189. [NT 19]

191 Animal, Vegetable, and Mineral -- a game somewhat similar to "20 Questions" wherein "It" selects some item and the players have to take turns asking questions to identify the secret item [np]

192 ankylosing -- the gradual stiffening or fixation of joints resulting from either disease or surgery. If by surgery, the results would be rather more abrupt. [HHC 34]

193 Annie -- see Wilson, Annie [GN 3]

194 Anniversary of the King's Accession -- see King's Accession, Anniversary of [GN 4]

195 Anstruther -- a member of the Bellona Club* [BC 22]

196 antedeluvian monsters -- see Crystal Palace [HHC 4]

197 anthracite stove -- a heater stove designed to burn the harder, less polluting anthracite coal. Such coal, though more expensive than soft coal or peat, became almost essential in urban England to help in the elimination of the yellow "pea-souper" fogs so vividly described in the Sherlock Holmes* stories. The fog, mixed with the noxious sulphur gasses emitted by soft coal, created a singularly unhealthy atmosphere. [SP 8]

198 antic hay on the ruins -- see let the heavens fall [BH 5]

199 anti-grammatical poets -- a negative term used to both describe and to comment upon free verse and other modernist poets [np]

200 antimony -- a brittle, silvery-white, crystalline metalloid commonly used in alloys and in medicine. It is toxic and is used by those murderers who wish to be only slightly more original than those who use arsenic. [CW 6/SP 20]

201 antipyrin -- or antipyrine, a white, crystalline compound used to relieve rheumatism, pain, and fever [HHC 15]

202 anti-vivisection -- literally, against the practice of using live animals for scientific investigation requiring surgery. In a broader sense, the commonly accepted one today, the word applies to any use of animals for

experiments which produce any pain or distress for the animal. [WB 5]

203 Antoine, Mr. -- one of the professional dancers made available to the guests at the Hotel Resplendent in Wilvercombe*. His assistance proves useful to HV during the course of her investigations. [HHC 3]

204 Antonio -- the rich merchant of Shakespeare's The Merchant of Venice [MMA 13]

205 Anwoth -- a hamlet just to the West of Gatehouse*. The two villages are so close together--they are separated only by the Fleet*--that it is a wonder that they are still separate places. [FRH 2]

206 Anwoth Auld Kirk -- or Anwoth Old Church, is located on the western side of Gatehouse-of-Fleet* [FRH 3]

207 Anwoth Hotel -- a favorite of PW, DLS, and the others who inhabit the area around Gatehouse*. It is on Fleet St. and is still open for visits. The local telephone number is 217, and the postal code is DG7 2JT, should one care to make prior arrangements for a stay. The potato scones and ginger cakes** are highly recommended. [FRH 2]

208 anything of that sort -- Parker* and PW are attempting to understand Sir Julian Freke's* explanation of Sir Reuben Levy's visit. Given Sir Reuben's irreproachable reputation and Freke's reputation as a neurologist and surgeon, one suspects that Freke tried to suggest that Levy had noticed the onset of some sort of neurological or psycho-neurological dysfunction. [WB 7]

209 apache language -- the crude, coarse language of the French criminal elements and lower classes. Such language is employed by Jacques Lerouge*. "Apache" is pronounced as "ah-PASH", the French pronunciation of the North American Indian tribe name. [aq]

210 Aphrodite -- the Greek goddess of love, both pure love and lust [BH 10]

211 Apollo Belvedere -- the famous Greek statue of the god Apollo. The "belvedere" part of the title is Italian for "beautiful view", a reference to the Belvedere Gardens where it once stood. [GN 18]

212 Apollo Comes to New York -- a fictitious film starring Varden* [cf]

213 Apollonios Rhodios -- poet and grammarian of Alexandria at about the beginning of the 2nd C. B. C. He was an epic poet of minor accomplishment and is reputed to have subsequently become chief librarian at Alexandria in Egypt. He retired to Rhodes and became a citizen there, hence his surname. The reference is to his epic in the Homeric style, "Argonautica", a version of Jason and the Argonauts, published in Firenze (Florence) in 1496 by Lorenzobodi Alopa*, a less well-known printer of the day. [WB 5]

214 Apollyon -- the Devil, the Angel of the bottomless pit in Revelation 9:11 [ab]

215 apoplexy -- loosely, to be struck dumb or senseless. Medically, apoplexy is more familiarly known as a stroke, a sudden and paralytic attack centered in the brain. The damage done depends on the severity of the attack. [HHC 1]

216 Apostle -- see O SANCTE THOMA [NT 2]

217 Apostles, language of -- see language of the Apostles [ie]

218 Apostle says -- see glass of sound wine [BH 6]

219 apotheosed -- to transform from a lesser thing to a greater one; elevation to a grand rank. PW affects such a change in his nephew's, Viscount St. George's*, view during the excitement of the apartment burglary. [dh]

220 appartement meublé -- French for "a furnished apartment" or "flat" [BH 1]

221 Apple Charlotte -- a fruit purée served as a sort of molded pudding to be served as dessert. Cooking apples are cored, chopped, and cooked until tender. Added to them are apricot jam, sugar, lemon, cinnamon, and butter. This is then reduced to a thick purée and poured into a dish or mold lined with buttered bread. The

whole thing is baked until the bread is brown. It is cooled, unmolded, and served with whipped cream or a custard sauce. [BC 7]

222 Apple of Discord -- from Greek mythology, the famous golden apple on which was inscribed, "For the fairest". Hera, Athene, and Aphrodite all claimed it and were referred to the world's most handsome man, Paris, Prince of Troy. Out of the resulting difficulties evolved the Trojan War; hence, anything that causes extensive discord or ill feeling within a group. [GN 5]

223 Appledore, Mrs. Theophilus -- the unpleasant and obnoxious downstairs neighbor of Mr. Thipps* who is rather bluntly put in her place by a rankled PW [WB 3]

224 Appledore, Theophilus -- the henpecked downstairs neighbor of Mr. Thipps* [WB 3]

225 Applefold -- as Miss Climpson describes the grounds around Rosanna Wrayburn's* house as a veritable Garden of Eden, it is only appropriate that the place should be called Applefold. Also, Miss Wrayburn's reputation as a theatrical beauty and temptress on the stage fits in with the image as well. It is often customary in Europe to name private homes, but the practice never developed popularity in North America. [SP 7]

226 apricot flan -- an apricot tart or pie with no top crust [GN 15]

227 apse -- a usually semicircular protrusion from the side of a church. They are often found in the chancel* behind the altar, thus providing space for a chapel. Fenchurch St. Paul* does not have one. [bc/NT 1]

228 Apuleius -- author of The Golden Ass* [GN 15]

229 Aquarium -- the Aquarium Building at the London Zoo in Regent's Park* [GN 11]

230 aquatints -- an engraving or etching so produced as to appear to have been handtinted [BH E2]

231 Arabian Nights -- or The Thousand and One Nights, a series of stories supposedly told by Scheherazade to her tyrant husband to delay his killing her, as he had done with his earlier brides, after the consummation of their marriage. See also Ali Baba. [UD 15]

232 arbiter elgantiarum--nec pluribus impar -- Latin for a judge of elegance or supreme authority in matters of elegance, not equal to many, a match for the whole world. The phrase was the motto of Louis XIV of France. [UD BN]

233 'Arbottle, Mrs. -- see Harbottle, Mrs. [im]

234 Arbuthnot, the Honorable Freddy -- PW's financial whiz friend who doesn't seem to know much more than the stock market. Like PW, he is a member of the Egotists' Club*, and he rides horses, but any similarites end there. The Hon. Freddy is a comic character who appears intermittently in the canon either to help PW in some way or to round out numbers for a house party.

He is portrayed as an easy-going sort who is most willing to help with PW's schemes even if he doesn't understand what's going on. His most notable scene comes at the end of CW when he, PW, and Parker* celebrate the Duke of Denver's* acquittal in a drunken frolic outside the Houses of Parliament which Insp. Sugg* helps bring to a satisfactory conclusion. Freddy announces his engagement to Rachel Levy* in SP, and is further recognized as a man of cunning in financial matters. By the time of the action in MMA, he and Rachel Levy are married. Later, in GN, HV calls upon his expertise during the course of her investigations. See also Evening Standard. [cf/umw/pj/mt/ie/WB 4/ CW 1/UD 17/SP 1/ MMA 5/GN 11]

235 arc lamps -- especially brilliant electric lights in which an electric current passes between two electrodes in a gaseous atmosphere. Ordinary light bulbs simply heat a filament in a partial vacuum. Such brilliant lights are useful in photography and in the theatre. Bunter* uses them in his photographic work. [WB 4]

236 Archangel Gabriel -- one of the major heavenly angels. Michael is usually considered the chief of the archangels on John Milton's* word in Paradise Lost. The apocryphal Book of

Enoch lists seven archangels: Uriel, Raphael, Raquel, Michael, Sariel, Gabriel, and Jerahmeel, The Koran lists four: Gabriel, Michael, Azrael, and Israfel. Gabriel is given as the one who records Divine decrees and who delivers messages. [UD 21]

237 Archbp's license -- the special license* [BH P]

238 Archie -- a spectator at HV's murder trial [SP 3]

239 architect, little -- see little architect [NT 12]

240 architecture -- the representative periods of English architecture are: Saxon, to 1066; Norman, 1066-1180; Early English, 1160-1310; Decorated, 1300-1380; Perpendicular, 1350-1550; Renaissance (including in its later stages Neo-classical and Georgian), 1550-1840; Victorian, 1837-1901; Early 20th C., 1901-1940; Modern, 1925-present. [references passim]

241 Arden of Feversham -- a play by an unknown author, some say Shakespeare, about Mistress Arden's plot to murder her husband so she can be with her lover, Mosbie. They hire two murderers, their deed is discovered, and they are executed. The story is taken from a real crime that was committed in February of 1550 or 51, as reported in Holinshed's Chronicle. [BH 8]

242 Argentines -- stocks or shares involving a railroading investment venture in Argentina [WB 4]

243 argue ahead of His data -- see And never has to argue ahead of His data . . . . [NT 13]

244 argumentum ad hominem -- Latin for "argument to or against the man", a fallacy of distraction where the person is attacked rather than the ideas which he espouses [GN 17]

245 Ariadne[s] -- the Cretan daughter of King Minos who helped Theseus survive the labyrinth and the Minotaur. She sailed off to the island of Naxos with Theseus, but he abandoned her there. She was later rescued by Dionysus and Theseus paid dearly for his action. [GN 14]

246 Ariadne Adams -- the title of a fictitious novel [GN 11]

247 Ariadne's clue of thread -- the allusion is to Ariadne* and Theseus and how they outwitted King Minos of Crete. Ariadne gave Theseus one end of a piece of string (the clue or clew) while she held the other. Theseus then penetrated the labyrinth, slew the Minotaur, and used the thread to find his way back out of that terrible place. [BH 20]

248 Arisaig -- in the Highlands on the "Road to the Isles" by Loch nan Ceall. It is a scattered village on an inlet of the sea and has a magnificent view of the mountainous Eigg Island to the South of the Isle of Skye*. Tom Drewitt's* telegram confirming Waters'* story was sent from there. [FRH 25]

249 Aristocrat! à la lanterne! -- French for, literally, "Aristocrat! to the lamp post!" The phrase is idiomatic, however, and a closer translation would be, "string him up!" The connection is that a lamp post made a handy gallows when the real thing was not readily available. The allusion is to a famous song of the French Revolution called Ça ira, which, in the refrain, says:

"Oh! it'll go well, it'll go well!
The aristocrats, string them up!"

[UD 3]

250 Aristotle -- the great Greek philosopher (384-322 B. C.), student of Plato, and tutor to Alexander the Great*. In his development as a thinker, Aristotle at first generally accepted Plato's concepts, but eventually developed his own theories, sometimes as extensions of Plato's work, sometimes in opposition to Plato's ideas. He developed the logical argument known as the syllogism*.

His works include On Logic, On Metaphysics, On Natural Philosophy, On Ethics, On Politics, On Rhetoric, and the famous On Poetry and Music, the latter commonly called "The Poetics".

The last work mentioned was developed by DLS into a widely accepted theory of practice for detective fiction readers and writers in her 1935 Oxford lecture, "Aristotle on Detective Fiction". She makes a direct reference to this theory in Ch. 15 of BC, PW's comments there presaging her later speech. Aristotle makes a point of

considering the improbably possible in various places in "The Poetics", and DLS capitalizes on this idea to a much greater extent than Conan Doyle ever did with Sherlock Holmes's comments about it. [WB 3/BC 15/GN 17/BH 13]

251 ark of the Lord -- the wooden coffer containing the tablets of law handed down to Moses by God and kept in the holiest place in the tabernacle [WB 7]

252 Arlen, Michael -- English author (1895-1956) of Armenian birth. He is known for his novel The Green Hat (his most famous), Mayfair, and Young Men in Love*. His work is a mix of farce, sex, and melodrama set in a fantasy London. The works are light and flippant bits of society fluff. [UD 15]

253 'Arley St. -- see Harley St. [BC 8]

254 Armistice -- the end of WW I, 11:00 A. M. on November 11, 1918 [im/BC 1]

255 armoire normande -- French for a free-standing chest or clothes closet of a provincial style typical of Normandy [mt]

256 Armstrong [and his parties] -- the reference is to Major Herbert Rowse Armstrong, of Hay-on-Wye, Breconshire, Wales, who murdered his wife in 1921. It is known that he also tried to poison his rival for legal work in Hay, Oswald Martin, during a series of "tea parties". Martin became suspicious, Mrs. Armstrong was exhumed, and more that three grains* of arsenic* were found in her body. Major Armstrong was hanged in Gloucester Prison on May 31, 1922, the only solicitor ever hanged in Britain. [UD 8/SP 2]

257 Armstrong -- a member of the Egotists' Club* through which he knows PW [cf]

258 Armstrong, Dr. -- probably real, but he was not identified [GN 14]

259 Armstrong, Mr. -- one of the senior members of Pym's Publicity*. He is the copy chief* responsible for the Nutrax* ads. [MMA 3]

260 Armstrong, Betty -- a Shrewsbury College* graduate and a classmate of HV's [GN 1]

261 Armstrong, Nurse -- the alert, thorough, and professional lady who attended Lady Dormer* until that elderly woman died. Her evidence is important to Ann Dorland*. [BC 17]

262 Army -- any references to the Army in the PW stories relate to that branch of the military prior to WW II, and particularly to the Army of WW I. The Regular Army refers to the standing professional force. The men were volunteers and the officers had been to public schools* and either The Royal Military Academy, Woolwich (engineers and artillery), or The Royal Military College, Sandhurst, the latter only existing now. PW was a major in The Rifle Brigade which, like all infantry regiments, included regular, territorial, and New Army battalions. The Territorial Army (a conflation of the old Volunteers, Militia, and Yeomanry) was established pre-War as a reserve. The New Army (Kitchener's Army) was created from the volunteers of 1914-15, and was named for Lord Kitchener, Secretary of State for War.

The New Army was sometimes also known as the Pals Brigades after the practice of whole groups of men with similar geographic or vocational backgrounds signing up together to form a unit. [im/UD BN/passim]

263 army of Napoleon which is popularly reputed to have marched on its stomach -- PW has in mind the popular phrase, "An army marches on its stomach." It is attributed to Napoleon, but remains anonymous in its origin. [FRH 13]

264 arnica -- a tincture derived from the various herbs of the genus Arnica, especially Arnica montana, used as a treatment for sprains, bruises, and contusions [FRH 15/BH 5]

265 A-roving, a-roving, since roving's been my ru-i-in -- Lord Byron says it more eloquently in his poem "So We'll Go No More A-Roving", but PW's lusty rendition of the old anonymous chantey is more in keeping with the spirit of treasures lost and found and other things piratical. The whole song is entitled "The Fair Maid of Amsterdam", and it is just as well he didn't

sing the whole thing as Lord St. George's* mother, the Duchess of Denver*, is every bit as much a prude about such things as PW suggests. The first verse of the song goes:

"In Amsterdam there dwelt a maid,
Mark well what I do say;
In Amsterdam there dwelt a maid,
And she was a mistress of her trade."

Refrain:

"And I'll go no more a-roving
With you fair maid.
A-roving, a-roving, since roving's been my ru-i-in,
I'll go no more a-roving with you fair maid."

There are many verses. [dh]

266 Arramandy, Esteban -- a boy lamed by falling rocks [ie]

267 Arran -- the large island on the West side of the Firth of Clyde. Its southern tip is opposite Ayr*. [FRH 19]

268 arrière-pensée -- French for, "after-thought" [BH 4]

269 arsenic -- the classic poison, favored for generations by real and fictitious poisoners alike. The advances of forensic medicine have led to a decline in its popularity of late.

Arsenic is an elemental metal and is probably not poisonous in its pure state, but as Arsenious oxide it is intensely dangerous. It resembles flour, has little taste, and does not dissolve in water. Large doses bring on a rather violent death in a relatively short time, but weeks may drag on if the poison is administered in smaller doses.

Abdominal pain is noted in almost all cases; the larger the dose, the greater the pain. The larger doses also cause extensive vomiting, wracking pain, and, sometimes, even an acute pain from so slight a thing as the weight of the bedclothes.

A fatal dose depends on the person to whom it is administered and the kind of arsenic used. In England, the sale of arsenic is controlled by the Arsenic Act of 1852, the Pharmacy Act of 1868, and others.

Arsenic is used medicinally and industrially, but is no longer used in weed and rat killing agents or on fly-papers. At the turn of the century, it was common for women to consume tiny amounts of arsenic to keep their complexions white, a suntan being the mark of the working classes. See also grain and Valetta. [UD 19/BC 7/SP 1/HHC 3/GN 4]

270 arsenious acid -- an acid derived from trivalent arsenic [SP 20]

271 Art honest, or a man of many deeds -- the sentence begins, "Isbrand, answer me . . . " and is spoken by Athulf in Death's Jest Book* by T. L. Beddoes*, II, iv, 142-4. [HHC 23]

272 art-linen -- particularly fine linen, done artistically and, possibly, with woven or embroidered embellishments. It is very likely unbleached. The expression suggests an article made more for show than for practical use. [SP 16]

273 The Art of Tomorrow -- a fictitious publication mentioned by Masterman* in reference to the art of Eric Loder* [cf]

274 Artful Dodger -- a character in Charles Dickens's* Oliver Twist and one of the more pleasant members of the gang ruled by Fagin and Bill Sikes [BH 7]

275 Arthur -- P. C. Sellon's son who is described as being a most active two year old [BH 11]

276 article -- the part of speech, "a", "an", or "the". In French, those articles are either masculine, feminine, or neuter, depending upon the noun to which they are linked. One properly trained in the language would never confuse them or their gender. [aq]

277 Arts Club -- probably fictitious. There is an Arts Club, but it is more likely that DLS created this organization. [FRH 1]

278 arums [arum-lily] -- there are several members of the genus Arum, but all have a fleshy flower. Those mentioned in NT have upright white blossoms with yellow stamens. [NT 3/GN 19]

279 As a Tulipant to the Sun . . . -- the quotation is from The Anatomy

of Melancholy*. Tulipant is an archaic form of tulip, not narcissus. [GN 12]

280 as one who hopes against hope -- Mr. Goodacre* is being described in terms of Paul's Epistle to the Romans, 4:18, "Who against hope believin hope . . . ." [BH 6]

281 As Sherlock Holmes said . . . -- see "I think we must look . . ." [GN 8]

282 As Sherlock Holmes says . . . -- see "we shall look imposing enough . . ." [BC 14]

283 As Stevenson says . . . -- R. L. Stevenson may have said it, but so did many others. The ODQ attributes the passage to one Stephen Grellet [1773-1855), but admits its disputed authorship. The passage is usually given as: "I expect to pass through this world but once; any good thing therefore that I can do . . . let me do it now . . . for I shall not pass this way again." [NT 2]

284 as sure as eggs is eggs -- the line is from Dickens's* Pickwick Papers, Ch. 45, in a song rendered by Sam Weller. The subject is the famous highwayman, Dick Turpin:

"And the Bishop says, 'Sure as eggs is eggs
This here's the bold Turpin!'"

[HHC 32]

285 as the rivers in the south -- the reference is to Psalm 126:5 in The Book of Common Prayer; it is 126:4 in the KJV: "Turn again our captivity, O Lord, as the streams of the south." [NT 10]

286 ascendit in coelum -- ascended into heaven. The Latin is in the Roman Catholic Church's former liturgy, but is used everywhere today in the vernacular. The phrase is from the Nicene Creed (see credo). The Widow Etcheverry's* son got to that phrase in his recitation of the Creed before PW, in his guise as wizard, had to help the boy's memory. The Apostle's Creed would more normally be said in conjunction with the Paternoster (Our Father) and Ave Maria*, but the phrase in that case would have been "ascendit ad coelos", "ascended into the heavens". [ie]

287 Ascot -- the town and its famous race track on the A329 route South of Windsor* and Windsor Great Park just to the West of London. The term also applies, loosely, to that great social event, Ascot Week*, the week of the races in June. [GN 3]

288 Ascot Week -- the four-day Royal Meeting in June of each year at Ascot Heath racecourse near Ascot* in Berkshire. The Meeting's races are preceded each day by a Royal procession. The racecourse was inaugurated by Queen Anne on August 11, 1711, and holds races in June, July, September, and October. The Gold Cup Stakes (see Foxlaw won the Gold Cup) is also held during the Royal Meeting. [MMA 1]

289 ash-plant -- a staff or walking stick made from a sapling ash tree. Mr. Payne* carries one and PW does too. A crutch-handled one would have a head shaped like a "T" to allow greater weight to be placed directly downward. [ae/CW 11/HHC 26]

290 ashet -- Scottish dialect for a dish or large, flat plate [FRH 7]

291 Ashton, George -- a resident of Fenchurch St. Paul*, he sees to it that Will Thoday* gets home from Walbeach* after he finds Thoday ill and stranded beside the road. Ashton owns the team of grays that haul PW's car out of the ditch at Frog's Bridge*. He is a churchwarden* at Fenchurch St. Paul. [NT 1]

292 Ashton, Luke -- apparently a DLS lapse. This is the same person referred to earlier as George Ashton. [NT 6]

293 Ashton, Maria -- wife of George/ Luke Ashton** [NT 6]

294 Ask for the old paths . . . -- HV and PW are referring to the Old Testament book of Jeremiah 6:16. They have quoted almost the entire verse. [GN 14]

295 asp -- a small venomous snake of Egypt. It could be either the cerastes or a small African cobra; loosely, any poisonous snake. Asps gained their fame at Cleopatra's bosom. [GN 4]

296 aspidistra -- a large-leaved Asiatic plant of the lily family. It

is prized by indoor gardeners as they do well in the shade. PW prizes them as objects of ridicule. [UD 4/NT 3/ BH 2]

297 aspidistra tonic -- a PW invention [FRH 13]

298 assassin -- the word is from the Arabic hashishin, one who committed murder while under the influence of hashish (marijuana) as part of a political/religious cult. The present word is the English version of the Latin corruption of the Arabic wherein it applied only to members of a fanatic anti-Christian sect. The word has since evolved a broader popular appeal.

299 assizes -- the periodic sessions of English regional superior courts convened to hear both civil and criminal cases. Some larger cities had their own. Assizes no longer exist as such, having been replaced by Crown courts. [CW 3/SP 3/BH E2]

300 assumes superiority though he hath it not -- Mr. Ingleby alludes to Hamlet, III, iv, 160 when Hamlet speaks so rudely to his mother in her chamber:
"Good night; but go not to mine uncle's bed;
Assume a virtue, if you have it not."
The scene is one of the play's more unpleasant ones. [MMA 1]

301 Assyrian wall painting -- a reference to the bas-relief wall decorations--usually executed in glazed, colored brick when outdoors--of the ancient Assyrians which show their warriors with luxuriant and curly beards. [FRH 13]

302 Astor, Lady -- born Nancy Wicher Langhorne in Virginia in 1879, she died in 1964 as Viscountess Astor. Waldorf Astor, 2nd Viscount Astor of Hever Castle (1879-1952), whom she married in 1906, was her second husband. She was elected to the Commons in 1919 when her husband entered the Lords, taking her husband's seat from Plymouth and keeping it until 1945. She was a crusader for temperance, women's and children's welfare, and the antisocialism movement. Noted for her spirited and irreverent attacks on any opponent, she is also remembered as one of England's most colorful and witty public figures. She was the first woman to take her seat in Parliament. [CW 6]

303 astrakhan collar -- the collar of a topcoat or similar garment made from the tightly curled, glossy black fur of the karakul lamb or any wool fabric manufactured to duplicate such lamb's wool [WB 13]

304 astral bodies -- or astral spirits; those who have died and whose souls live among the heavenly bodies or in heaven [SP 16]

305 "At the word, 'I'm murdered,'" -- in one version of T. L. Beddoes' Death's Jest Book**, the quoted words are Isbrand's. The quotation is not included in most "standard" versions of the play, but exists in a fragmentary reworking of the opening to IV, i. [HHC 21]

306 Athalia, Lady -- see Frolic Wind [GN 4]

307 Athulf -- a character in T. L. Beddoes' Death's Jest Book**. The Fool's Tragedy is a subtitle to that play. [SP 8]

308 Atkins, Mr. -- one of the group secretaries* at Pym's Publicity [MMA 2]

309 atrocious wide -- see cricket [MMA 18]

310 'Atry -- a reference to Charles Hatry, a London financier whose bankruptcy lost the savings of many ordinary people who could not afford such a loss [BH 10]

311 Attaboy -- a horse Mrs. Forrest* bet on--she is unsure of the name. That the nag was running at 50 to 1 odds says a great deal about its future and why she couldn't be certain of the name. [UD 7]

312 Attenbury, Lord -- he and his family are long-time friends of the Wimseys despite the fact that he is possessed of a "stupid son" named Abcock* [aq/WB 3/BH 19]

313 Attenbury, Abcock -- Lord Attenbury's "stupid son" who marries a girl known to us only as Sylvia* [aq]

314 Attenbury diamond case -- mentioned in passing in "Practical Joker" and CW, it is the same as the Attenbury emerald case*, PW's first. The confu-

AN ASSYRIAN

#301 An Assyrian from a bas-relief at Ninevah. The original is colored.

sion may be a DLS memory lapse, or the stones may have had a diamond setting. [pj/CW 2]

315 Attenbury emerald case -- a 1921 investigation and PW's first venture into sleuthing. It created a public sensation when PW testified at the trial, according to his uncle, Paul Delagardie* (see the Biographical Note at the beginning of UD). It was during this early and unpublished case that PW first met Charles Parker. This case also accounts for Insp. Sugg's* animosity toward PW in subsequent cases as PW upstaged Sugg in the solution of that case. Attenbury mentions the case in CW, and, by the time of UD, Sugg has apparently forgiven PW as he calls and asks for help in some other unnamed problem. [WB 3/CW 2/UD BN]

316 Attic -- a pun typical of PW. While searching for the attic in Uncle Meleager's* Roman villa, PW comments that an attic is "an un-Attic thing to have in a house like this." PW is probably referring less to the Mediterranean architecture than to the idea of simple elegance, incisive intelligence, and delicate wit, Attic properties and hints of what is to come with the will. [umw]

317 Attorney-General -- the Crown's senior law officer. He is sometimes promoted to Lord Chancellor, the major connection between law, politics, and government. [SP 1]

318 Attwood, Mrs. H. -- the married name of Mary Stokes* [GN 1]

319 Au Bon Bourgeois -- the Soho* restaurant where PW and Parker meet Dr. Carr*, thus beginning their involvement with the events recorded in UD. No such restaurant was located in the indices of the day; however, an Au Petit Riche on Old Compton St. is very nearly the same thing. DLS's favorite was Le Moulin d'Or which used to be on Romilly St. near St. Anne's Church where DLS is buried. The restaurant is now closed. Nevertheless, the Au Bon Bourgeois is likely fictitious. [UD 1]

320 "Au contraire, as the man said . . ." -- a line from a current joke, typical of those in Punch*. A sturdy Briton speaks to an obviously inferior foreigner leaning on the rail of a Channel steamer: "Alors, mon vieux, did your breakfast go down all right?" "Au contraire, it came up." [BC 5]

321 "Au contraire, ma soeur . . ." -- Uncle Paul says, "To the contrary, sister, it is we who are in the way. The time always comes when one learns to distinguish between kissing and loving." Paul Delagardie* is addressing his sister, the Dowager Duchess of Denver*. [BH P]

322 Aubusson carpet -- from a town in central France, long a center for the manufacture of exquisite tapestries and carpets. Many of these products feature scenes of the hunt, designs based on animals, and scenes drawn from the fables of Jean de la Fontaine (see Contes de la Fontaine). PW has such a carpet in his library. [SP 13]

323 Auchenhaye -- a spot roughly halfway between Gatehouse-of-Fleet* and Kirkcudbright* where Mr. and Mrs. McGregor* make their home with their daughter, Helen*. The reference is to a house with a long driveway about one mile South of the A755/A75 junction. It is a farm surrounded by several cottages, one of which is near the road as mentioned. [FRH 11]

324 Audit Office -- the branch of the railway business office responsible for, among other things, ascertaining that all tickets sold are collected and accounted for both in the number of tickets and in the fares collected. [FRH 10]

325 Audley Square -- a little indentation off South Audley St.* where P. C. Burt* was to meet his companion on the next beat over, P. C. Withers*. Instead, however, he meets PW. Wimsey owns a home on Audley Square that is probably modelled on No. 2 Audley Sq., now the University Women's Club. [hp/BH P]

326 August Bank Holiday -- if the action of SP occurs in 1929-30, then the Bank Holiday in question fell on Monday, August 5, 1929. See also Bank Holiday. [SP 10]

327 Augustan -- a person of England's Augustan Age, roughly 1675-1750, or the Neoclassic Age. It was named for the Roman Emperor Augustus (27 B.

C. to 14 A. D.) during whose reign Vergil, Horace, Ovid, and others flourished. The age was marked by a love of words richly and widely used, extensive references to classical literature, and a stylized rhetoric. [GN 15]

328 Augustine, don't chuck that S. -- Parker is apparently handling one of PW's rare volumes too carelessly for the comfort of its owner. Given Parker's interest in theology, it is not unexpected that he would have picked up that particular book. See also St. Augustine. [UD 6]

329 aumbry -- archaic spelling of ambry; a cupboard, closet, etc. Found in a sacristy, an ambry would be used for the storage of vestments, vessels, etc. [bc]

330 Aunt Beatrice -- the pen name of a former Shrewsbury College* student who writes a household hints column for the Daily Mercury* [GN 3]

331 Aunt Emily -- see Emily, Aunt [MMA 6]

332 Aunt Judith -- see "Rosie's Weekly Bits" [BC 7]

333 Aunt Mary -- see Wimsey, Mary and Parker, Mary Wimsey [GN 9]

334 Aunt Sophy -- see Sophy, Aunt [MMA 6]

335 aura -- a subtle emanation emitted from some body, normally human, and possibly connected with some sort of electrical field or discharge. Those who are sensitive to such things claim they have color and resemble halos. A powerful aura may surround a person totally, but they are usually found around the head. Auras are also called nimbuses. [SP 16/MMA 9]

336 Aurora Leigh -- a romance in blank verse by Elizabeth Barrett Browning published in 1856. It is a vehicle for the poet's comments on a variety of social matters of the day. The lines cited are in Book iii, 870ff. [UD 19]

337 Austen, Jane -- whose ability to write amidst distractions is needed by Egotists' Club* members who wish to write letters while within the Club's precincts. Miss Austen (1775-1817) is one of England's great novelists, author of Pride and Prejudice, Sense and Sensibility, and other works. [cf]

338 Austin [7] -- any of the products of the Austin automobile firm of Herbert Austin (1866-1941), England's Henry Ford. The Model 7, a small and extremely popular car, sold for only $225. The company is now a part of British Leyland. [UD 8/FRH 3/MMA 18]

339 Australia -- the former British colony founded, as was Georgia in the U. S., as a penal colony. Emily Dart* goes there with one of her children to avoid bringing scandal to her family. [im]

340 Australia, uncle in -- a favorite mystery and detective story trick is to have a long-lost relative (a twin or a husband will do) return from some faraway place to claim part of an inheritance, to wreak vengeance, or whatever. This person will either explain or confuse the plot, sometimes both. One of the more famous examples of this sort of thing appears in A. A. Milne's The Red House Mystery. [SP 20]

341 Australian's at Lord's -- a reference to the great England vs. Australia cricket* matches held regularly at Lord's* in London and elsewhere, the prize being the famous urn containing "The Ashes". When, in 1882, England lost a challenge to Australia, a mock obituary in The Sporting Times referred to English cricket as having died, the body was to be cremated, and the ashes to be taken to Australia. The following winter an English team, captained by Ivo Bligh, later Lord Darnley, visited Australia with the intention of beating them and recovering the (mythical) "Ashes". This they did, and the ladies (including one who later became Bligh's wife) burned a bail, inserted the ashes into the urn and presented it to Bligh. One version of the story says it was not a bail, but a cricket ball. The urn remained the property of Lord Darnley until his death in 1927, when his widow gave it to the Lord's Museum. It does not change hands because it is not properly a trophy. The England/Australia test matches are still said to be "for the ashes", although the ashes as a trophy are mythical. [NT 1]

342 automatic [pistol] -- PW keeps an

automatic pistol of unknown manufacture in the handkerchief drawer of his bureau. A different one is mentioned as being in the possession of Number One. See also firearms. [dh/ab]

343 Autre temps, autre moeurs -- French for, "Other times, other manners (customs)" [HHC 3]

344 Avalon -- a Celtic word for an earthly paradise to be found in the western seas. It means the "Island of Apples". [FRH 2]

345 Ave Maria -- or Hail Mary, a prayer to the Virgin Mary based on the verses in Luke 1:28ff. The prayer was fixed in its present form by Pope Pius V in the 16th C. [ie]

346 Ave Marias -- small marker cards with the Ave Maria* printed on it along with (probably) some sort of illustration of the Virgin [UD 22]

347 Avenue Kléber -- a street in Paris which runs North and East from the Palais de Chaillot (across the Seine from the Eiffel Tower) to the Arc de Triomphe [CW 17/BH 1]

348 Avernus -- Hell, the infernal regions [NT 11]

349 Aves -- see Ave Maria [ie]

350 "Away, my jolly boys . . ." -- from the anonymous chantey "Rio Grande", slightly misquoted [NT 6]

351 Aylwin, Major -- Gowan's* friend in London who was helping him hide until he healed up and got his beard back into shape [FRH 23]

352 Ayr -- a small city on the Firth of Clyde noted for fishing and excellent resort facilities. The city has strong associations with Robert Burns and is the site of the Brig o' Doon made famous in Burns's "Tam O' Shanter". [FRH 5]

353 Ayrshire -- the former county centered on Ayr* in Scotland. It is now a part of the Strathclyde region. A famous strain of dairy cattle originated there. [FRH 20]

(B)

354 b____[s] -- bastard[s] most likely. The standards for language usage were far more stringent during the 1920's and 30's than they are today. DLS's use of "bloody"* would have raised a few eyebrows as it is. [FRH 11/MMA 18]

355 BB pencil -- a soft lead pencil used for sketching. It allows some control of shading as the lead will smear much like charcoal. [SP 16]

356 B. B. C. -- the British Broadcasting Corporation, the independently owned and controlled broadcasting service in England. Only recently have other independent broadcasters been allowed. It is financed by license fees and operates under a charter from the Postmaster General. [BH 8]

357 B and S -- brandy and soda, the restorative given to Gen. Fentiman* while he was visiting Lady Dormer* [BC 18]

358 B. Litt. -- the abbreviation for the degree bachelor of letters or literature [GN 1]

359 Babcock -- the wine steward at the Bellona Club* [BC 9]

360 "babble of green fields" -- what Falstaff did just before his death as recounted in Henry V, II, iii, 9ff [SP 1]

361 "A babbled of green fields" -- for the location, see preceding entry. The line is spoken by Mistress Quickly during her consideration of Falstaff's whereabouts--heaven or hell--just after the knight's death. She is convinced that he is in heaven, but there remains some doubt. [UD 4]

362 Babel, Tower of -- the famous structure of Genesis 11 that has come to represent any questionably visionary scheme or a confusion of languages. The reference is probably to a Babylonian ziggurat of great size. In WB, PW suggests that both symbolic references apply to Insp. Sugg's* reconstruction of the body in the bath problem. [WB 2]

363 Babel-like [piled] -- a pun on the word confounded or confused. See above. [MMA 11]

364 Babs -- an excited young lady riding in a motorcycle sidecar who happens to witness the restraining of Simpkins*. She wonders, rather loudly, if he is a murderer. [cb]

365 Bacchus -- the ancient Roman version of the Greek Dionysus, the god of wine and inspiration to music and poetry [BH 10]

366 Bach -- Johann Sebastian (1685-1750), the late Baroque composer of prodigious accomplishments, mostly in sacred music. He was known widely in his lifetime as an organist, Georg Phillip Telemann being the foremost composer in the opinion of the day, but it is Bach who is known today while Telemann is relatively obscure. Bach is probably PW's favorite composer, but he shows a thorough appreciation of a wide range of composers. Nevertheless, it is Bach (works unspecified) that is played at the PW-HV wedding. [WB 5 and passim]

367 Bach choir -- the renowned choral group composed of members from throughout Oxford University*. DLS was a member and was extremely fond of the Choir's director, Sir Hugh Percy Allen, the New College organist. The Choir was founded in 1896 and is still an active part of life at Oxford. [GN 3]

368 Bach's Mass in B-minor -- Johann Sebastian Bach's* Mass represents the final maturing of his choral style. It is two-thirds chorus and one-third arias and duets. There are no recitatives or chorales. The Missa (Kyrie and Gloria) were presented to the King of Saxony in 1733, but the rest (Symbolum, Nicenum [Credo], Sanctus, Osanna, Benedictus, Agnus Dei, and Dona nobis pacem) was not assembled until 1748, suggesting to some scholars that the Mass was not written as a unit, but was assembled from various pieces written over a period of time.

Such an assembly procedure would be more in keeping with the Lutheran Protestant ideas of the time than would a Mass prepared in its entirety as a unit. However, there is no question of its great beauty or its standing as perhaps the foremost example of Baroque choral music. [WB 5]

369 bacilluses -- a loose reference to any germ organism; any of the bacteria genus Bacillus, an aerobic, rod-shaped bacterium [WB 9]

370 "Back and side go bare . . ." -- PW is quoting a song from Act II of Gammer Gurton's Needle. The song, not the play, is attributed to William Stevenson (1530?-75), and is a drinking song. All those things go bare if drink is needed. [UD 11]

371 back horses . . . both ways -- see backed [each way] [GN 9]

372 Back Lane -- connects the Herriotting Rd. with Priory Lane in Little Doddering* [bc]

373 backed [each way] -- to bet win, place, and show on a given horse. If the horse places at all, the bettor has to win something, but not always enough to cover the cost of the bets. [MMA 11]

374 backgammon board -- the special board on which the game of backgammon is played. Each player has fifteen pieces resembling checkers, dice, and a dice cup. The object is to move all of one's pieces from the outer table to the inner table and then off the board, moving point to point. Moves are controlled by the throws of the dice. The winner is the first person to remove all pieces from the board. It is more difficult than it looks. [qs]

375 backstroke [set at] -- to raise a bell and set it at a position so that the mouth of the bell is upward and away from the ringer, thus using the greatest extent of the bell's rope. This is done before ringing a peal of bells to allow the ringers to get off to a good start with the bell's weight helping the ringers to establish momentum. [NT 1]

376 Bacon family -- a reference to the family of Sir Francis Bacon, first Baron Verulam and Viscount St. Albans (1561-1626), the famous English essayist, philosopher, lawyer, and man of affairs. He was the son of Sir Nicholas Bacon, Lord Keeper in Queen Elizabeth I's reign. [GN 1]

377 Bacon, Sir Francis -- one of the most brilliant minds of the English Renaissance. While his writing is not of the calibre of Montaigne*, he is

a thoroughly readable and, even today, modern writer whose works considering religion, philosophy, and moral life are especially pertinent while his scientific writings are lucid if no longer valid in their conclusions. See also Bacon family. [GN 3/BH 7]

378 bad King Herod -- see King Herod [ie]

379 Badcock -- a clerk or secretary at Mr. Trigg's* law office [UD 17]

380 badminton -- the familiar indoor or outdoor court game similar in many ways to tennis. It derives from the Indian game of poona and was introduced to England in the later 1800's. The name badminton is from the estate of the 8th Duke of Beaufort who introduced the game to British society. The game score is generally fifteen points, eleven for women's singles, or twenty-one in a game match. Jim Playfair* wears a costume meant to suggest or be an allegory of badminton. [qs]

381 Baedecker -- a travel or tourist guide from Karl Baedecker (1801-59), a printer and publisher of Essen, Germany. His company still finds its name on the highly acclaimed tourist guides. A "baedecker" has also come to mean any sort of a guide or handbook, and not just for travellers. [BH 12]

382 bag[ged] -- stolen, often used in a light or bantering way not intending to suggest any sort of criminal activity [MMA 1/GN 2]

383 bagatelles -- French for "trifles" [BH E1]

384 bags -- slang for pants [FRH 12/ BH 4]

385 Bagstock, Joey -- the quote PW absent-mindedly mumbles is from Dickens's* Dombey and Son, Ch. 7. Its correct form is: "He's tough, ma'am, tough is old J. B. Tough and devilish sly." The "J. B." is Major Joey Bagstock, one of the minor yet colorful characters in the novel. [WB 5]

386 "Bah! the wine she drinks . . ." -- Uncle Paul Delagardie* is quoting from Othello, II, ii, 257, when Iago says, in reference to Desdemona's passion for Othello: "Blessed fig's-end! the wine she drinks is made of grapes: if she had been blessed, she never would have loved the Moor . . . ." [BH P]

387 bailiff's daughter of Islington -- a reference to an anonymous ballad entitled "The Bailiff's Daughter of Islington". The daughter is loved by a local squire's son. After seven years of trials and separation, they are united. This is one of the rarer "happy ending" ballads. [MMA 9]

388 bails -- see cricket [MMA 18]

389 Baines, Dr. -- the physician local to Fenchurch St. Paul*. He is described as a competent man, but somewhat lacking in bedside manner. [NT 1]

390 Baines, Freddy -- a native in the Wilvercombe* area and witness to the fact that the Pollocks* were fishing and did see HV waving on the Thursday that Paul Alexis* was found dead [HHC 10]

391 Bainses -- the Baines family as in #390. They are not on good terms with the Pollock* family. [HHC 10]

392 bairns -- Scots dialect for children [FRH 20]

393 Baiser du Soir -- the brand name of Denis Cathcart's* cologne. It is French for, "Love [carnal] in the Evening", and is apparently fictitious. [CW 2]

394 bait [in an awful] -- used in the sense of being upset as if tormented maliciously [MMA 2]

395 Baker -- a student at Shrewsbury College* [GN 10]

396 Baker, Jack -- the local police constable mentioned in "Talboys" by Mr. Puffett* as being interested in raising peaches for the fair, and therefore, as competitiou to Mr. Puffett for the first prize there. [t]

397 Baker, Ted -- the farmer for whom Dick Twitterton* had worked as a cowman [BH 10]

398 Baker St. -- the site of Sherlock Holmes's* famous flat, but, in WB, the reference is to the underground* station there, near the intersection with Marylebone Rd. [WB 3]

399 Baker St. Irregulars -- PW alludes to the ragtag band of street ur-

chins that Sherlock Holmes* used from time to time to help him gather information. The relationship to the mugs and glassware is most apt. [BH 6]

400 Baldock -- a community on the Great North Road* approximately thirty-five miles North of London in Hertfordshire. The name derives from the Old French, Baldac, for Baghdad. Baldock was founded by the Knights Templars. Of interest there is St. Mary's Church, a 14th C. structure with medieval graffiti. See also motorcycle race. [cb/ae/BH E2]

401 Baldwin, Mr. -- the Baldwins were wealthy steel manufacturers, but Stanley, the Prime Minister, liked to cultivate a rural image as he thought it good for public relations to do so. A part of his rural image campaign was to have himself photographed scratching his pigs' backs on his farm in Bewdley. [BH 18]

402 Balham -- a suburb of London South of Battersea* in the western part of the city [WB 5]

403 Balkan States -- Greece, Albania, Bulgaria, Yugoslavia, and Rumania, or those nations including or bordering on the Balkan Mountains. During the 1920's and 30's they were noted for their instability, a residue of the collapse of the Habsburgs and the Austro-Hungarian Empire, and the outbursts of nationalism among the various ethnic components of that Empire. [HHC 22]

404 "Ballad of Lady Maisry" -- an anonymous Scottish ballad written in thick dialect and telling the story of how Maisry gives her love to a nearby Scottish lord, Lord William, and becomes pregnant by him. Before her pregnancy becomes known, she develops a reputation locally as one who will spurn any who come to court her. When her family realizes the extent of her situation, they burn her to death, but not before she has a chance to notify Lord William. He goes to her and, as she dies, swears vengeance on her entire family and then promises to kill himself by fire as well. The parallels between Mrs. Grimethorpe* and the Duke of Denver* are obvious if not yet quite so extreme. [CW 16]

405 the ballad was right -- see "It is a goosefeather bed!" [BH 2]

406 "Ballade des Pendus" -- or "L'Epitaphe Villon", the French title of François Villon's (1431-?) poem, "Villon's Epitaphe: Ballad of the Hanged". Villon was a brilliant and exceptionally rowdy man who had earned a Master's degree from the Sorbonne before he was twenty-one. The poem cited was inspired by his having been arrested for some connection with a street fight during which a man had been killed (in 1462). He was sentenced to death, but the sentence was commuted to ten years' banishment. Nothing is known of him after 1463. Part of the first stanza reads:

> "Brother men who after us live on,
> harden not your hearts against us,
> for if you have some pity on us poor men,
> the sooner God will show you his mercy . . . .
> Let no one laugh at all our miseries
> but pray to God that He absolves us all." [BH 9]

407 Ballantrae -- a small fishing and boating port on Scotland's West coast, a resort known for fine sand and shingle* beaches and a mild climate year round [FRH 5]

408 Balliol -- one of the colleges of Oxford University* and PW's alma mater. It was founded by John de Baliol, father of John de Baliol, the less than popular and successful king of Scotland from 1292-6, in 1263 as an act of penance. The college has many illustrious members including many statesmen of the past 100 years. It is located on the corner of St. Giles's* and Broad Sts.* in central Oxford. [passim]

409 Balliol Concert -- founded in 1885 by John Farmer (1836-1901), music master at Harrow, then organist at Balliol from 1885. Ernest Walker (1870-1949) worked with Farmer from 1892 and took over from 1900-25. W. H. Harris (1883-1973) of New College ran the concerts from 1925-33 when Thomas Armstrong took responsibility until after WW II. [GN 23]

410 bally -- a sort of all-purpose, reasonably polite adjectival expletive, a euphemism for "bloody"*. It can mean, variously, silly, unusual,

exceptional, etc., depending on the context. PW makes frequent use of it as a sort of gentleman's "damn" as in "Bally well better", or "Bally thing". [passim]

411 "Bally old Homer nodding . . ." -- PW is referring to line 359 of Horace's* Ars Poetica wherein it is written "Indignor quandoque bonus dormitat Homerus" (I am also irritated when the great Homer nods). Nods is used here to mean to have a lapse in style. PW is castigating himself for his lapses in the investigation of the events in his current case. [nf]

412 Ballycastle -- in Ireland's County Antrim in the extreme North of that country and about due West of the tip of the Peninsula of Kintyre. It is on Ballycastle Bay which is sheltered from the North by Rathlin Island. [FRH 21]

413 Balmae -- a small village due South of Kirkcudbright* at the East side of Kirkcudbright Bay* [FRH 21]

414 Bancroft [Mr. Justice] -- the judge who will be the one to hear HV's retrial at the next session of court. Mr. Crofts* at least assumes that Mr. Justice Bancroft will preside. [SP 4]

415 Bancroft [Mrs.] -- Phoebe Tucker's* married name [GN 2]

416 bands -- see cassock and bands [GN 14]

417 Banerjee, Mr. -- a student at Queen's College. See Oxford Colleges. [GN 8]

418 Bank -- the Bank of England* in most cases, but in BC the reference must be to some other bank as the Bank of England has not served private accounts since 1920, when the last such account was closed. It now serves only other banks and the government, and was nationalized in 1946. [aq/BC 6/HHC 11]

419 Bank Holiday -- in the United Kingdom, any one of several days when banks are required to be closed. At the time of the PW stories, the various days, by country, were:
ENGLAND/WALES/IRELAND: Good Friday, Easter Monday, Whit Monday*, 1st Monday in August, Christmas Day, Boxing Day* (or Dec. 27 if the 26th is a Sunday), St. Patrick's Day (Ireland only).
SCOTLAND: Good Friday, 1st Monday in May, 1st Monday in August, Christmas Day, New Year's Day.
The days are considered to be universal days of vacation, and the May and August holidays have been at the end of the month since 1967. Now, of course, the Irish days are quite different, and there have been other alterations as well. [nf/SP 10/GN 14]

420 Bank of England -- the first joint-stock bank in England, founded in 1694 to help the government finance the war with France. Bank of England notes were made legal tender in 1833, and, by 1921, the Bank held a monopoly on note issue. The Bank had become a "central" bank by the end of the 19th C., and was nationalized in 1946. During the 1930's it helped guide and advise the government's financial policies. [aq/mt/HHC 11]

421 Bank of England Notes -- the bank's promise to pay the bearer on demand; a substitute for gold, silver, or other negotiable securities; paper money or currency [mt/BH 5]

422 Banner -- a fictitious newspaper [BC 15/HHC 4]

423 banner position -- newspaper jargon meaning a large or prominent item or location as in "banner headline". The use here suggests that heat had played a major role in the day's news. See also Negretti and Zambra. [nf]

424 bannocks -- unleavened bread of oats or barley baked in flat loaves. In FRH Mrs. Green* is cooking them on a griddle. As they are usually unleavened, this method would be quicker and more convenient than baking them in an oven and should have no particular effect on the finished product. [FRH 7/HHC 1]

425 banns -- the public announcement, now confined to church use, of an impending marriage. The object is to settle any questions concerning the legality of the marriage before the service so as to avoid embarrassment during the sacrament itself as in Jane Eyre. [HHC 12/NT 4]

426 Baptist [stern] -- St. John the

THE BANK OF ENGLAND AND THE ROYAL EXCHANGE.

#420 The Bank of England (left) and the Royal Exchange as PW would have known them.

Baptist. See Feast of St. John the Baptist. [UD 22]

427 Banquo's ghost -- the reference is to the famous scene, III, iv, of Shakespeare's Macbeth after the king has ordered the deaths of Banquo and Fleance. Banquo is killed, but Fleance, his son, escapes. Shortly thereafter, at a dinner Banquo was to have attended, Macbeth sees the dead man's ghost and behaves in a most unkingly manner. Lady Macbeth takes charge and sends everyone home. [GN 4]

428 Bar, below the -- outside the bar or railing that separates the lawyers, judge, jury, etc., from the spectators in a courtroom. Such bars also appear in some legislative chambers; to be in the chamber, but not as a participant in any way. [CW 14]

429 Bar Falling -- this chapter title refers to barometric pressure which, when falling, indicates bad weather ahead. PW's flight across the Atlantic is made all the more dramatic in this chapter when Sir Impey Biggs* explains what PW is doing and then concludes by saying, "My lords, the barometer is falling." The chamber is silent. [CW 15]

430 Barbados -- one of the Lesser Antilles Islands in the Caribbean near Grenada and Martinique. It is the easternmost of the Windward Islands. [SP 1]

431 Barbara -- PW's fiancée prior to WW I. The engagement was broken at the start of the war by "mutual" consent in case PW should suffer any mutilating wounds. His intent was to marry after the war, but Barbara, however, behaved poorly and married another officer in 1916. She did so rather hastily and without telling PW beforehand. PW was understandably hurt and shocked. The situation is especially ironic given the fact that Barbara is the name of the patron saint of artillerymen and of those in danger of sudden death. [UD BN/CW 2]

432 Barbara celarent darii ferio baralipton -- PW is reciting the first line of a 13th C. Latin mnemonic used to help a student of Aristotelian logic remember the form, structure, and order of the various sorts of valid syllogisms*. It is first recorded in William of Sherwood's (ca. 1200-ca. 1271) Introductiones in Logicam. The "poem" continues in part as:

"Barbara, Celarent, Darii, Ferioque, prioris:
Cesare, Camestris, Festino, Baroco, secundae:
Tertia, Darapti, Disamis, Datisi, Felapton, Bocardo, Ferison, habet:
Quarta insuper addit Bramantip, Camenes, Dimaris, Fesapo, Fresison

The device is a coded invention which relies on the vowels and their placement. An "A" anywhere in the underlined parts of the poem stands for a universally absolute affirmative statement such as "All men are mortal"; an "E" represents a universally negative statement such as "No diamonds are soft". An "I" represents a particular affirmative statement such as "Some women are geniuses", while an "O" represents a particular negative statement such as "Some men are not athletes".

To use the system, simply check the word needed and follow the directions in the code. A syllogism in Camestris, then, would have three statements, the first a universal affirmative, the second a universal negative, and a conclusion written as a particular affirmative. If the syllogism is in Barbara, it would also have three statements--the standard for syllogisms--and all of them would be universal affirmatives. Such a syllogism might read:

All diamonds are expensive.
This stone is a diamond.
Therefore, this stone is expensive.

The word baralipton is another and later part of the mnemonic invented by the Scholastic philosophers. It, too, follows the code explained above, but as a syllogism has only three statements, it is necessary to ignore the "O" in the last syllable just as we ignore the "E" in the last syllable of ferioque. Thus, a syllogism in baralipton is an AAI form. As there are 256 different syllogisms, even a mnemonic device might become confusing, so the "poem" includes only those syllogisms that are valid, the rationale being that if the syllogism isn't valid, it isn't meaningful and should be discarded anyway.

As quoted by PW, the passage also

appears in George Farquhar's (1678-1707) play, The Inconstant (1702), II, i, but it is more likely that PW is just reciting something he learned during his school days. Simple forms of the first line of the mnemonic are:

BARBARA: All A is B.
All B is C.
All A is C.

CELARENT: No A is B.
All B is C.
No A is C.

DARII: All A is B.
Some B is C.
Some A is C.

FERIO: No A is B.
Some B is C.
Some A is not C. [SP 11]

433 Barclay's London Lager -- no longer available as it has merged with the Courage brewers [MMA 4]

434 barf -- young Peterkin's* youthful mispronunciation of bath. There is no intention of suggesting the more contemporary vulgarism meaning to vomit. [MMA 17]

435 barf-room -- a "cute" mispronunciation of bathroom. See 434. [GN 11]

436 Bargrennan -- a small village on the River Cree* about eight miles northwest of Newton-Stewart* [FRH 2]

437 Barholm -- a Border keep or castle now in ruins and dating from the 16th C. It is located near Kirkdale* and is a reminder of the incessant border wars between England and Scotland before the Acts of Union of 1707. [FRH 2]

438 Baring, Mr. Alec -- owner of one of Mr. Endicott's* razors [HHC 6]

439 Baring, Dr. Margaret -- warden* at Shrewsbury College*. As Shrewsbury has a warden and a dean*, it must be concluded that at Shrewsbury the warden outranks the dean. [GN 1]

440 "A Barmecide feast, I see." -- PW utters that comment upon entering the dining room at the headquarters of The Society*. The reference is to the "Arabian Nights"* wherein the story of "The Barber's Sixth Brother" tells how a prince of the Barmecide family, rulers of Baghdad before Haroun-al-Raschid (785-809), fed a beggar, Schacabac (the hare-lipped), an imaginary feast from empty dishes, how the beggar went along with the deception, and how he later attacked his entertainer; hence, any imaginarily satisfying situation; unreal, illusory. The irony of PW's allusion becomes clear at the end of the story. Haroun-al-Raschid was the Fifth Caliph of Arabia and was idealized as the glorious ruler of the Arabian Nights Entertainments or The Thousand and One Nights.* [ab]

441 barmy -- full of foam or froth, but in British slang it means crazy, not in full command of one's faculties. The word derives from barm, yeast, hence the froth generated by the yeast. [im/hp]

442 Barnabas -- Dawson. See the genealogical chart at the back of UD [UD 13]

443 Barnes Common -- Barnes is a small community within the London borough of Richmond-upon-Thames. The Common is just South of the Thames and is due North of Richmond Park and Wimbledon Common and the nearby Park now known for tennis. Jessie Haynes's* body was found there. [im]

444 Barnwell, George -- see George Barnwell [BC 10]

445 baron -- the lowest ranking peer in the English system. See also peerage. [CW 14]

446 barrel organ -- a musical instrument generally used by street vendors or entertainers. It has a peg-studded revolving cylinder or drum which, when turned, releases air into pipes through valves activated by the pegs. The result is that characteristically rich, organlike tone. [nf]

447 barrels and wards -- parts of a locking mechanism. The barrel is a hollow tube into which a key is inserted. The wards are the ridges, notches, or whatever, that correspond to a ridge, etc., in the key which, in theory, prevents the use of that lock by anyone who does not have the proper key. [SP 13]

448 Barrett, Elizabeth -- English poet (1806-61) and wife of Robert Browning*. Her Sonnets from the Portuguese are easily her most famous work,

and remain one of the great sonnet sequences of English literature. [GN 3]

449 Barrett, John -- the "Oxford fellow" who gave Hugh Farren* a lift. Barrett had a new Riley* and the ride was one that Farren isn't likely to forget. [FRH 20

450 Barrhill -- a village on the A714 route about eighteen miles northwest of Newton-Stewart* and, formerly, a rail center of minor importance [FRH 2]

451 Barrie, Sir James [Matthew] -- the Scottish playwright (1860-1937) who is most famous for having created Peter Pan (1904), Peter Pan in Kensington Gardens (1906[there is a statue of Peter there now]), and Peter and Wendy (1911), a prose version of the 1904 play. He also wrote The Admirable Crichton (1902) and The Little Minister (1891). Barrie's works include fairies such as the famour Tinker Bell. [NT 9]

452 Barrington, Mr. -- a helpful resident newly arrived in the apartment block where Horace Mountjoy* had lived [MMA 16]

453 Barrington, Arthur -- one of Dian de Momerie's* former lovers who tried, unsuccessfully, to keep up with her crowd and ended his life a suicide [MMA 9]

454 barrister -- a lawyer who may plead in the High Court, Courts of Appeal, and the House of Lords* when it is sitting as a court. Solicitors* may plead in certain lower courts such as magistrates courts and some Crown courts. Any barrister must have gone through his legal training at the Inns of Court*, the only institutions having the right to call a barrister to the bar. The Inns are located in London. [CW 3/GN 4]

455 Barrow, Mr. -- a member of the art department at Pym's Publicity*. It is his illustration for one of Tallboy's* headlines that touches off the "great Nutrax* flap". [MMA 8]

456 Barrow Head -- see Burrow Head [FRH 19]

457 Barrow-in-Furness [grammar school] -- Charles Parker's home town. He is a graduate of the Grammar School there, the equivalent of a secondary school or high school in the U. S. Many of these grammar schools enjoy a reputation almost equal to the public schools*. The grammar schools were founded from the 16th C. onward for the teaching of Latin. The town is located in Cumbria near the Lake District made famous by Wordsworth*. Beatrix Potter, creator of Peter Rabbit, lived in the area. [CW 4/UD 12]

458 Bartlett's Familiar Quotations -- one of the oldest and most famous of such collections of famous quotes, exhaustively indexed and cross-indexed to locate any one of the thousands of quotes from just a word or fragment of the original. It is updated and changed as new editions appear. [MMA 1/BH 12]

459 Barton -- a reporter for the (Evening) Banner* [BC 15]

460 Barton, Miss -- a don at Shrewsbury College* and author of The Position of Women in the Modern State. That book is one of the targets of the malicious poltergeist* that is plaguing Shrewsbury. [GN 2]

461 base coin for a marriage-portion -- literally coins made from non-precious metals used as a part of a bride's dowry. HV is suggesting that she had not been fit or suitable for marriage as she was still so confused and bitter about the result of her affair with Philip Boyes* that she could not be a good wife to PW. [GN 23]

462 Bashan -- see bulls of Bashan [MMA 7]

463 Basque -- either the people or the language native to the western Pyrenees Mountains* on the border between France and Spain. The language is as mysterious as the people who use it as it is related to no other known language. [ie]

464 Bass, bottle of -- one of Britain's larger brewers of beer and ale. At present they are actively involved in the export market to North America. Their products are very smooth, but are darker and heavier than the standard North American brew. [WB 4/UD 8/NT 11/BH 7]

465 Bassanio -- Portia's suitor in The Merchant of Venice, Shakespeare's comedy of about 1596 [MMA 13]

466 bassoon -- a tenor or bass double reed instrument with a long cylindrical body that is doubled for about half its length. The double reed mouthpiece is connected to the body by a thin metal tube. [WB 1]

467 Bateman, H. M. -- a reference to Henry Mayo Bateman (1887-1970), an English designer, artist, and cartoonist who drew for Tatler*, doing caricatures and cartoons. He is noted for a long series of cartoons poking fun at the social gaffes of the middle class types who aspired beyond their abilities. He also drew for Punch* and contributed to most of the leading magazines of his day. [HHC 8]

468 Bates -- one of the servants at Bredon Hall [BH E2]

469 Bates, Hilda -- wife of Capt. Tommy Bates* [SP 12]

470 Bates, Capt. Tommy -- a somewhat tactless houseguest at Duke's Denver during the Christmas festivities in 1929. He seems given to an unneccessary degree of control over his wife's reading material. [SP 12]

471 Batesons -- an elderly and "pleasantly tottering" couple who became fond of HV as a little girl when she made the rounds of house calls with her father, Dr. Vane*. They once owned Talboys*. [BH 1]

472 bath salts -- a mixture designed to both soften and perfume bath water. They usually include some combination of ingredients as sodium bicarbonate, sodium carbonate, starch, talc, and a perfume essence such as violet, rose, gardenia, or PW's favorite, verbena*. [CW 1]

473 bathroom geyser -- a device fitted in the bathroom to heat water automatically by gas whenever the hot water tap is turned on. They were named after the hot springs in Iceland and made a popping noise when they lit themselves. In Miss Climpson's* situation, tenants could put pennies into a metering device which would control the amount of hot water consumed. Some of the earlier models were thought liable to blow up, hence the term "old geyser" (often pronounced geeser) used to describe elderly persons of volatile temperament. [UD 3/BH 13]

474 batsman -- see cricket [MMA 18]

475 battels -- a student's account at a university college from which fees are figured, especially the running account at the buttery* for the supply of milk, cocoa, bread, etc. [GN 6]

476 batten on corpses -- to batten is to fatten or grow prosperous on; an unpleasant image [BC 14]

477 Battersea -- an area of London southwest of the central part of the city and South of the Thames. Formerly a separate administrative area, it is now a part of Wandsworth. It borders Lambeth* which is directly across the Thames from Westminster and the Houses of Parliament. The rapid growth of Battersea dates from the arrival of trains at Clapham Junction in 1845. [WB 1]

478 Battersea Bridge Rd. -- a major South London thoroughfare extending from the South end of Battersea Bridge, West of central London, to Battersea Park Road. [WB 5]

479 Battersea Park -- a refinement of Battersea Fields which had fallen into disrepute because of duels, etc. In 1843, a bill was passed to purchase 360 acres which now include the Festival Pleasure Gardens and a garden for the handicapped. It is due South of Hyde Park across the Thames from Chelsea* and between the Albert Bridge and Chelsea Bridge. [WB 1]

480 Battersea Mystery -- the problem related in WB, PW's first published case. The press coined the name. [CW 1/UD 19]

481 Battery Pool -- an area along the Fleet* where PW, Thomas Macpherson*, and Jock* finally locate Macpherson's bequest after it had been stolen. [ss]

482 Battle of Roncevaux -- see Roncevaux [BH E2]

483 Batty Thomas -- the number seven bell, next to the deepest in tone, was cast in 1338 by Thomas Belleyetere*

of Lynn*, but recast in 1380 by order of Abbot Thomas*. "Batty" is a corruption of Abbot. Its note is D and the bell weighs 30 1/2 hundredweight. Using 112 pounds per hundredweight, the older British standard, she weighs 3,416 pounds. [NT 1]

484 Bay of Biscay -- a large inlet of the Atlantic Ocean bordered on the South by Spain and on the East and northeast by France. It is notorious for a choppy sea state. [ss]

485 bay rum -- a formerly popular aftershave lotion or cologne of a heavy, cloying fragrance. The better versions of the distillate come from the Caribbean area, especially the Virgin Islands. [BH 16]

486 Bayes -- a member of the Egotists' Club* through which he knows PW [cf]

487 "be afraid with any amazement" -- PW is quoting I Peter 3:6, the last part of the verse. That section of the chapter deals with the relationship between husbands and wives. [GN 23]

488 "be sent up again" -- a quotation from LeFanu's* Wylder's Hand, Ch. 48. The "he" in "he was sent up again" refers to the title character, Mark Wylder. [NT 9]

489 "be the earth never so unquiet" -- a further fragment of Psalm 99:1 as found in The Book of Common Prayer [NT 10]

490 "Be thou as chaste as ice . . ." -- the line is from Hamlet, III, i, 142, and that uncomfortable scene between Hamlet and Ophelia wherein he tells her to "Get thee to a nunnery". In SP, PW adapts the line ("Be thou as chaste as ice, as pure as snow, thou shalt not escape calumny.") to suit his purposes. In certain circumstances the Old Bailey* and calumny could be synonymous, a fact well understood by PW. [UD 11/SP 1]

491 Beaconsfield, Lord -- see Disraeli, Benjamin [WB 3]

492 Beaconsfield touch, the -- PW's reference is to the 1st Earl (see Peerage) of Beaconsfield, Benjamin Disraeli*, at whose funeral there was a bunch of primroses from Queen Victoria. On the accompanying card was written, "His favourite flower." PW is thus complimenting Bunter as the buttered eggs are his favorite: " . . . like primroses. The Beaconsfield touch." The earldom is named for a community to the North and West of London. The grave of William Penn is nearby. [umw]

493 beadle[s] -- an administrative officer at Oxford and Cambridge who leads processions carrying a silver mace. Also bedel. [GN 14]

494 beano -- originally the word was printer's slang for a beanfeast, but it now is a reference to any sort of rowdy entertainment leading to a noisy spree [GN 7]

495 Bear -- one of the pubs on the main street in Windle* [SP 16]

496 "beard of Samson was not sacrificed . . ." -- the reference is to what Delilah had done to Samson in the Old Testament book of Judges 16:4-31. She did not shave him as is commonly thought, but had help with that. In any case, the analogy is humorous. If Campbell* is taken as Delilah and Gowan as Samson, the whole thing becomes almost silly. The point is that as Samson's did, Gowan's* hair would grow back and, as the Philistines were punished, so would Gowan's tormentor be punished. [FRH 29]

497 bearer cheque -- a check made payable to "bearer" rather than to a specific person or organization; a check made out to "cash" [UD 21]

498 beargarden -- a popular place in Elizabethan days, it was a sawdust covered ring with a heavy post in the center and with seating around the perimeter of the ring much like an Elizabethan theatre. A bear or bull would be chained to the stake and angry dogs, some bred especially for the "sport", were let out to attack. Betting on the outcome and its ramifications was standard practice. [BC 9/MMA 8]

499 bears -- those who sell stocks, shares, bonds, etc., in anticipation of a decline in market price, possibly from the proverb "selling the bearskin before catching the bear." [WB 4]

500 "A beast, as the schoolboy said, but a just beast." -- the saying is understandably anonymous, but refers to Dr. Temple, Headmaster of Rugby from 1857-69. The correct form of the line omits "as the schoolboy said" and appears as such in SP. [BC 9/SP 2]

501 Beatrice -- one of Annie Wilson's* daughters. Of the two, Beatrice is the elder. Her full name is Beatrice Maud Clarke. [GN 11]

502 Beatrice -- a popular brand of oil stove with two or three burners. The "Florence" model had one burner. [BH 2]

503 Beaumont and Fletcher -- see "Death hath so many doors . . . ." [UD 21]

504 beautiful letter from D.[onne] -- Donne* wrote letters in prose and verse to all sorts of people. Elements of divine and human love were common to many of them, especially after he took holy orders. As the Duchess is notoriously fuzzy about details--including this instance--it is hard to say with certainty just what letter HV has given PW. [BH P]

505 beauty of an ordered life -- this is, perhaps, an allusion to Blaise Pascal's "The serene, silent beauty of a holy life is the most powerful influence in the world, next to the might of the spirit of God," ordered being substituted for holy orders in an understandable lapse of memory [FRH 6]

506 beaux yeux -- French for, literally, "beautiful eyes", but, more generally, "good looks" [SP 5]

507 beaver -- see like young Harry [BH 7]

508 beaverboard -- formerly a tradename like Kleenex, it now refers to any light, thin sheet of paper-covered wood pulp and fibre that has been compressed into a somewhat rigid form. It is used as a building material for lightweight partitions, etc. [MMA 8]

509 beck -- a small brook or stream [CW 16]

510 Beck, Adolf -- in his The Story of Scotland Yard, Sir Basil Thomson, former head of and historian at Scotland Yard*, says, "The Beck case is important in the annals of detective science as having been the motive behind the adoption of fingerprint identification in England." The case involves a con artist who called himself John Smith and who bilked "women of loose character". As Beck bore a superficial resemblance to Smith, Beck was arrested twice and convicted of crimes probably committed by Smith. Even though Beck's character was not above reproach, for having been the victim of a comedy of errors, he was paid £500 by the government but died destitute in Middlesex Hospital in 1909. [WB 2]

511 Beddoes [T. L.] -- Thomas Lovell Beddoes (1798-1850), English author and dramatist. Trained in Zurich and Göttingen in medicine, he lived mostly in Europe. He is author of The Improvisatore, The Bride's Tragedy*, and his most important work, Death's Jest Book*. DLS quotes extensively from his works in HHC, and the morbidity reflected there is typical of his work. [UD 20/HHC AN/BH 14]

512 Bedford -- the county town for Bedfordshire, in the North of that county. It is approximately fifty miles North of London near the River Ouse*. [cb]

513 Bedford, Earl of -- the reference is to the 4th Earl, Francis, 2nd Baron Russell of Thornhaugh and 4th Earl of Bedford (1593-1641), ancestor of the present Dukes of Bedford. The Earl was empowered by Royal Charter to turn the swampy fens* into productive pasture land. Charles I ran out of money to complete the work, but, by 1651, the Old Bedford River (actually a canal) was complete and had been supplemented by the New Bedford River (also a canal), both named for the Earl. It is suggested that the fictitious Thorpe* family fortunes are connected to the real Earl's drainage schemes. [NT 2]

514 Bedford Level -- the flatlands adjacent to the Old and New Bedford Rivers** [NT 18]

515 Bedford Row -- a street running parallel to Gray's Inn Rd.* just to the West of the Inn. It connects Sandland St. on the South with Theobald's Rd. in the North. Many lawyers

have offices there. [UD 17/SP 7/BH 6]

516 bedroom utensil -- the "necessary" or chamber pot. Before indoor plumbing such utensils, usually porcelain, were necessary as a trip to the outhouse or privy at three in the morning in a cold winter's night was something to be avoided if possible. [NT 5]

517 beef-tea -- a drink made from an extract of beef such as boullion or Bovril* [NT 7]

518 Beelzebub -- regardless of who he is taken to mean, he is a powerful source of evil. Matthew refers to him as "prince of the devils", and Milton ranks him second only to Satan himself in Paradise Lost, i, 79. [HHC 18]

519 been in the cart -- see cart [MMA 8]

520 Beerbohm, Max [Sir] -- English essayist and caricaturist (1872-1956). He was a prominent figure in London in his early years and remained notorious for his legendary wit and satirical abilities even after he retired at middle age and moved to Italy. His work is directed mostly at literary mannerisms and social pretenses which he dissects with a polished and ironic wit. See also "Like the man in Max Beerbohm's . . . ." [SP 16]

521 Beesely, Mr. -- an employee of Pym's Publicity* in the printing department, a mediocre cricket* player [MMA 10]

522 Beethoven -- Ludwig van (1770-1827), the great German composer, a student of Haydn's, and one of the leaders of the early Romantic movement. He is perhaps best known for his nine symphonies, but he wrote widely in other forms as well. [HHC 20]

523 beetle -- a wooden bat or flail for domestic tasks such as beating rugs [BC 18]

524 Beetrice -- see Beatrice [BH 2]

525 Beggar's Opera -- a musical play by John Gay (1685-1732), first produced in 1728. Some of the famous characters from the play are Polly Peachum and Captain Macheath. It is the basis of Bertolt Brecht's and Kurt Weill's Threepenny Opera, source of that popular song "Mack the Knife". [WB 10]

526 "begin at the beginning . . ." -- Parker refers to Lewis Carroll's* fantasy masterpiece Alice in Wonderland*, Ch. 7, "Alice's Evidence". The King of Hearts says to Alice, "Begin at the beginning . . . and go on till you come to the end: then stop." It is excellent advice and Aristotle never expressed the concept more succinctly. PW makes use of the same advice in NT. [MMA 5/NT 14]

527 beginning screw -- starting salary [CW 9]

528 "Begone dull care!" -- the line is from an anonymous English poem entitled "Begone Dull Care". The passage in question reads:

"Begone dull care! I prithee begone from me!
Begone dull care, you and I shall never agree."

[BC 3/BH 5]

529 Beit, Miss -- the switchboard operator at Pym's Publicity* [MMA 10]

530 Belchesters' house -- the former owners of the home on Audley Square* that PW bought for a town house to replace the flat at 110A Piccadilly when he and HV were married. It is in this house that PW becomes a father for the first time. [hp/BH P]

531 Belfast -- the capital of Northern Ireland [FRH 5]

532 Belfridge, Col. -- an owner of two of Mr. Endicott's* razors. He's a peppery old gentleman, but good-hearted beneath the gruffness. [HHC 6]

533 Belial-like politeness -- a reference to a fallen angel and helper to Satan who is known for his smoothness of behavior and speech as much as for his falseness of character. He is mentioned in both the Old and New Testaments, but DLS seems to have Milton's* Paradise Lost in mind, especially Book II, lines 106ff. Beginning halfway through line 108 Milton writes:

"On th'other side up rose
Belial, in act more graceful and humane;
A fairer person lost not Heaven; he

seemed
For dignity compos'd and high
exploit:
But all was false and Hollow: though
his Tongue
Dropt Manna, and could make the worse
appear
The better cause . . . ."
The passage is an accurate if, perhaps, unflattering portrait of Sir Impey Biggs'* rhetorical abilities. [CW 14]

534 Bell-Field -- see Tailor Paul [NT 1]

535 bell-inscriptions -- the words included on a bell at the time it is cast [NT 10]

536 bell-tent -- a bell or dome-shaped tent, formerly the Army standard which accommodated eight men. The single, central pole made one-person setup difficult as the pole was heavy, but families and scout groups used surplus tents widely between the wars. Modern light tents had not yet been invented. [HHC 12]

537 Bella -- Mrs. Bill Rumm* [SP 13]

538 Bella Simonetta, La -- see Simonetta, La Bella [WB 3]

539 belle à se suicider -- French for a woman whom might drive one to suicide or over whom one might commit suicide [CW 15]

540 Bellevue [Hotel] -- where PW stays while in Wilvercombe* helping HV investigate the murder of Paul Alexis*. It is another of the posh hotels in that fictitious resort town. [HHC 8]

541 Belleyetere, Thomas -- the founder who cast Batty Thomas* in 1338. There were two men of that name who were active bellfounders in King's Lynn at about that time, one in 1333 and the other in 1440 (approximate dates). DLS had the former in mind, but Batty Thomas is purely fictitious. [NT 1]

542 Bellezzi, David -- the context suggests he is a real photographer as the other references to artists and artwork are to real persons or items, but his existence in fact could not be verified [BH 1]

543 Bellingham, Frank -- a guest at Sir Charles Deverill's* Christmastime costume party. He is dressed as the Red King from Through the Looking Glass* to match his wife's costume as the Red Queen. [qs]

544 Bellingham, Gerda -- wife of Frank Bellingham*, her Red Queen outfit plays an important part in the story [qs]

545 Belloc's scorpion -- Hilaire Belloc (1870-1953) wrote, among other things, two books for children: The Bad Child's Book of Beasts and More Beasts for Worse Children. The books contain short poems for children about various animals, generally in a whimsical manner. "The Scorpion" appears in this collection. It is a quatrain about the dangers of having a scorpion in one's bed. [BH 2]

546 Bellona Club -- one of three clubs to which PW belongs (see also Egotists' and Marlborough Clubs). The name is derived from Bellona, the Roman goddess of war. As Bellona Club the organization is fictitious, but DLS doubtless had the very real Naval and Military Club, 94 Piccadilly, located near PW's flat, in mind. Built in the late 1750's, the town house was formerly home to the Duke of Cambridge, George III's son, and to Lord Palmerston. The Club is sometimes called "The In and Out" in reference to the signs on the driveway gates. The Club is still active. [UD BN/BC 1/SP 8/GN 17]

547 Bellona Club affair -- a reference to the events of BC [SP 8]

548 Belsize-Bradshaw -- the Belsize automobile was manufactured from 1897 to 1925. The Bradshaw model was named for its designer, Granville Bradshaw, and first appeared in 1921, but by 1924 all Belsize products were called Belsize-Bradshaws. The cars were frail and not very reliable. [HHC 33]

549 "The Belvedere" -- the classic Greek statue, Apollo Belvedere* [cf]

550 Belvedere Rd. -- in Eastbourne*, where Mr. Endicott's* former assistant, Plumer, has set up a barber shop. The street is apparently fictitious as officials at Eastbourne could find no reference to it in city records. [HHC 6]

Naval and Military Club, Piccadilly.

#546 The Naval and Military Club, Piccadilly; PW's "Bellona Club".

551 Benares bowl -- a heavy brass bowl manufactured in Benares, India (or one patterned after such a bowl). It was probably intended originally as a cooking vessel of some sort. [BH 2]

552 Bench, on the -- to be a sitting judge in a court of law [SP 10]

553 bend sinister -- or baton, sometimes bar (an incorrect term, but frequently used). A bend is a wide diagonal stripe extending from the upper right to the lower left across an heraldic shield. A baton is basically the same thing, but is reduced in size. Both have traditionally been used as symbols of illegitimacy. [MMA 11]

554 Bendick -- Catherine Freemantle's* married name [GN 3]

555 Benedicite -- Latin for "Bless ye" [ie]

556 Benedictine -- D. O. M. Benedictine, a plant liqueur still brewed in the original place according to the original secret formula developed in 1510 at the Benedictine Abbey of Fécamp in France by Dom Bernardo Vincelli. The letters D. O. M. are an abbreviation for the Latin Deo Optimo Maximo, "To God, most Good, most Great". [GN 2]

557 Benediction -- the blessing that closes a Christian worship service [NT 2]

558 benigne -- Latin for (colloquially), "No thank you." [GN 4]

559 Bennett -- [Enoch] Arnold Bennett (1867-1931), English novelist, journalist, and playwright, author of The Old Wives' Tale, etc. His work remains somewhat popular. [BC 18]

560 Bennett, Abel -- the old gentleman of Princemoor* who is Ann Bennett's* next of kin, and who tells the police how Paul Alexis* came to have 300 gold sovereigns* [HHC 11]

561 Bennett, Ann -- an elderly lady who kept several cats and who, upon her death, leaves all her money to her next of kin with the proviso that the cats be properly cared for [HHC 11]

562 Bentley -- a make of luxury automobile now manufactured by Rolls-Royce* and, in effect, nothing more than a Rolls with a different grille covering for the radiator. At the time of HHC and, probably, MMA, the cars were products of the original W. O. Bentley firm which collapsed in 1931. For £65,000 Rolls-Royce assumed control of the bankrupt firm on July 10, introducing its own version of the Bentley in 1933. [HHC 19/MMA 9]

563 Bentley, Edmund Clerihew -- English detective story writer (novels and short stories), journalist, and humorist (1875-1956). He was called to the bar in 1902. Bentley is best remembered today for his creation of Philip Trent, hero of Trent's Last Case (1913), etc. That novel is frequently cited as one of the greatest of all detective novels. [WB 13/CW]

564 Bentley's, work of Mr. -- Trent's Last Case (see 563). The reference is to the significance of the victim's (Sigsbee Manderson) false teeth. [WB 13]

565 Benton, Dr. -- a dental expert at a hospital near Wimbledon Common*. He works with PW and others in helping to solve the problem in "Teeth of the Evidence". [te]

566 benzene -- a flammable, toxic, liquid aromatic hydrocarbon used as a solvent and cleaning agent among other things. It is frequently used in dry cleaning clothes either alone or in combination with other solvents. [CW 3/FRH 27]

567 Beowulf -- the hero of the great epic poem of the 8th C. or earlier. Its precise origin and author are unknown, but it is linguistically of Northern Germanic or Danish origin. Beowulf recounts the adventures of the title hero and is generally considered the earliest work of English literature as it was brought to England or, perhaps, was composed in England by some of the earliest Northern European invaders to settle the island. [GN 3]

568 Berengaria, S. S. -- launched at Hamburg, Germany, as the Imperator, flagship of the HAPAG line, it came to the Cunard line as the Berengaria as part of Germany's reparations payments after WW I. Always plagued with stability problems, Cunard finally

had to re-work much of the upper superstructure and add tons of ballast to control her tendency to roll too easily. She was the first Cunard liner to be named for a person, the wife of Richard I, Berengaria of Navarre. She never saw England--Richard only spent six months there himself--and saw very little of her husband as he was always off on a crusade. [CW 18]

569 "Berenice" -- a tale by Edgar Allan Poe, first published in the Southern Literary Messenger in 1835. It tells the story of the wildly diseased relationship between Egaeus, a mentally unstable youth, and Berenice. She is mentally normal, but contracts epilepsy. Her disease fascinates Egaeus and the tale centers on it, their relationship and the morbidly horrid events that follow. [NT 17]

570 Beresford, J. D. -- John Davys Beresford (1874-1949), a once-popular English novelist who wrote Jacob Stahl (1911) about a young man growing up. [BC 18]

571 Berger, Célestine -- see Lerouge, Jacques [aq]

572 Berlin, Treaty of -- see Treaty of Berlin [HHC 32]

573 Berman, Louis -- (1893-1946) author of Food and Character (1932), and Glands Regulating Personality: A Study of the Glands of Internal Secretion in Relation to the Types of Human Behavior (1928) [BC 18]

574 Bermondsey -- a section of London on the South side of the Thames and down river from central London [ab]

575 Bert -- Mrs. Ruddle's* son who was delivered by Dr. Vane*. He is fond of "yarning". [BH 1]

576 Bess of Hardwick -- Elizabeth Hardwick (1518-1608), widow of Sir William Cavendish (her second husband) and second wife of George Talbot, 6th Earl of Shrewsbury. She was a tough and proud woman who, through very shrewd dealings tinged with more than a little greed, amassed the then fabulous sum of £60,000 from the inheritances of her husbands' estates. It apparently didn't bother her that she shortchanged several of her stepchildren in the process. She was the daughter of John Hardwick of Hardwick in Derbyshire, and she died on April 13, 1608. See also entries under Shrewsbury. [GN 3]

577 bestrides the clouds and sits and sits . . . -- PW may be alluding to Tennyson's "Sir Galahad". The passage does not seem to be a quotation and PW's "so to speak" supports that idea. "Sir Galahad" has many images that relate to PW's ecstacy. [BH 16]

578 Bet -- see Elizabeth, Miss [CW 11]

579 bête noir -- French for "black beast" in a literal translation; an idiom for a pet aversion, something disliked intensely [NT 2]

580 "Better to reign in hell . . ." -- the line is from John Milton's* Paradise Lost, I, 263, spoken by Satan to Beelzebub upon their arrival in Hell as new landlord and his chief assistant. The preceeding line is almost as famous: "To reign is worth ambition though in Hell." [UD 16]

581 better ways of killing care -- a butt of malmsey is a large barrel of a sweet wine and is not a very good place to drown one's sorrow as the hangover would be monumental. There is also a remote possibility of a reference to George, Duke of Clarence, that "false, fleeting, perjured" peer who was murdered (probably) in the Tower in 1477 by being drowned in a butt of malmsey (supposedly). The exact detail of such events during the Wars of the Roses and the early Tudor era are notoriously fuzzy. [BH 20]

582 Betty -- the central female character in HV's The Fountain-Pen Mystery, the book in progress at the time of HHC [HHC 15]

583 Betty -- see Elizabeth [FRH 8]

584 "Between the joints of the harness" -- see "drawing a bow at a venture" [GN 15]

585 Betwixt and Between -- apparently fictitious as no reference to any play or movie of that title was located. Given the fact that it had had encounters with the censors, one would expect to find some reference. [BC 10]

586 bézique -- a French card game derived from two-handed pinochle. It is still a two-player game and uses a pack of 128 cards: four 32 card packs using A - 7 and ranking A, 10, K, Q, J, 9, 8, 7. The declaration or melding is the same as in pinochle, but with minor differences. Among these is the bézique, a pair consisting of the queen of spades and the jack of diamonds. Such a combination may be doubled, trebled, or quadrupled for a meld score of from 40 to 4500 points. PW and his mother make such a pair when dancing together as their costumes represent the appropriate cards. [qs]

587 bibelot tables -- tables meant to display bibelots or knickknacks [SP 18]

588 bicarbonate of potash -- part of a mixture given to Philip Boyes* by Dr. Grainger* to neutralize whatever was causing Boyes so much distress. It would be a very mild mix meant to absorb excess acid or other irritants without being an irritant itself. [SP 15]

589 bicarb[onate] of soda -- a harmless antacid known to cooks as baking soda [SP 1]

590 bicuspids -- one of eight teeth also known as premolars. There are two relatively sharp points on each tooth designed to rip and tear more than to cut. [te]

591 A Bid for the Throne -- there is a novel by Nora Cranfield called A Bid for a Throne, but it was published after HHC, so one must assume that the entry title is fictitious. [HHC 22]

592 bidding-prayer -- a prayer of entreaty or supplication. The word "bidding", in one of its special sen-senses, means the action of praying itself. [GN 14]

593 Big Ben -- the bell and, by association, the Clock Tower at the Westminster Bridge end of the Houses of Parliament. The tower is 316 feet high and the clock, etc., is named after Sir Benjamin Hall, First Commissioner of Works, and a man of amazing bulk. "Big Ben" is only a familiar name. [CW 14]

594 big loch by the viaduct -- Maggie* is somewhat obscure in this reference, but she probably is speaking of Loch Ken*, a long loch on the River Dee* above Kirkcudbright*. About halfway along the length of the loch it was crossed by the Portpatrick and Wigtownshire Joint Railway between the Parton and Gatehouse stations. The railway no longer exists, but the viaduct, a low structure of steel and masonry, is still there. [ss]

595 big vein in the bend of the elbow -- either the superficial basilic or superficial cephalic veins, whichever is easier to tap [UD 23]

596 Biggars-Whitlow crash -- probably fictitious; it could be any one of many such crashes that periodically occur during times of financial instability [ae]

597 Biggers, Earl Derr -- the American author who, in 1913, published Seven Keys to Baldpate, but who won real fame when he published House Without a Key (1925) in which he introduced that amiable detective, Charlie Chan. [UD 4]

598 Biggleswade -- a village in Bedfordshire approximately forty-five miles North of London on the Great North Rd*. See also motorcycle race. [cb/BH 15]

599 Biggs, Sir Impey -- famous criminal lawyer, barrister*, and friend to the Wimsey family. He provides a variety of services to the family, but none more significant than his defense of the Duke of Denver at the trial in the House of Lords. He can cite all sorts of unusual cases to support or to confuse as needed. He is known affectionately to PW as "Biggy". Biggs is a tall man with a "magnificent build" with "flawless features" on a noble head. The Dowager Duchess* calls him the "handsomest man in England". He is 38 at the time of CW and is a bachelor.

As a barrister he's known to be most careful and is "celebrated for his rhetoric and suave but pitiless dissection of hostile witnesses". He breeds canaries as a hobby and wins prizes with them. He argues HV's defense in SP and owes much of his success there to the alertness and determination of Miss Climpson*. PW hires Biggs to defend William Noakes's* murderer; not that the man is innocent, but because

THE CLOCK TOWER, HOUSES OF PARLIAMENT.

#593 The Clock Tower with "Big Ben" at the Houses of Parliament, Westminster, London.

he deserves proper legal services.
Sir Impey is fictitious, but one is reminded in many ways of the real Sir Edward Marshall Hall, also a tall man of imposing appearance who was noted for his rhetorical excellence as well. [pj/WB 2/CW 2/SP 1/BH E1]

600 bilge -- technically, the area between the inner and outer hulls of a ship, but the word is loosely used to refer to anything of little value or worthless. The slang derives from the idea that the air and water in a bilge are usually stagnant and foul. [nf]

601 Bill -- one of the two burglars who attempt to steal Viscount St. George's* copy of the Cosmographia Universalis* for Wilberforce Pope*. PW catches him in the act and arranges for his arrest. See also Rumm, Bill. [dh]

602 Bill -- one of the movers who help remove the furniture from Talboys* as PW and HV helplessly watch. They did not know that Noakes* had borrowed money against it. [BH 19]

603 Bill [Jenkins] -- son of the gatekeeper at Bredon Hall*, Duke's Denver* [BH E2]

604 Billings, Mr. -- mentioned as having a noteworthy moustache which young Roger Wimsey* has duplicated with part of his breakfast egg [t]

605 billy-doos -- a deliberate corruption of the French billets-doux, love letters [MMA 4]

606 Bilt, Mrs. -- an unidentified situation mentioned as "that silly affair". No clarification is given. [cf]

607 bingled -- see shingled or bingled [FRH 13]

608 Binns, Mr. -- a young employee of Pym's Publicity* who works in vouchers* and has quite a reputation as a dart thrower [MMA 6]

609 Binns, Bouncible -- one of the medical student acquaintances of Mr. Piggott* who is not further identified. [WB 10]

610 bird which has no feet -- the swallow or martlet in heraldic representation. Popular misconception has it in some places even today that swallows have no feet or, at least, cannot land on the ground. In heraldry, the martlet is the symbol of the fourth son from the assumption that by the time the first sons have claimed their inheritances, there will be nothing left for a fourth son "to land on". [BC 7]

611 biretta -- a square cap with points worn fore and aft and side to side. It has three or four stiff, upright pieces extending from the center to the points. There is usually a pompom in the center where the upright projections converge. They are worn by Anglican and Roman Catholic clerics. [bc]

612 Birkett -- the showroom clerk at Sparkes and Crisp* in Glasgow [FRH 28]

613 Birkett, Mr. -- a department chief at Crichton's* advertising agency [nf]

614 Birmingham -- a major manufacturing and industrial center approximately 115 miles northwest of London. It is sometimes thought of as "Britain's Second City". [cb/UD 23]

615 biscuits -- something more on the order of what North Americans would call a cracker [nf/MMA 1]

616 Bishop of Rome -- the Pope. He is also the head of state for the Vatican. In 1929-30, the pope was Pius XI, Achille Ambrogio Damiano Ratti (1857-1939). He was elevated to the Papacy in 1922, and is most remembered as having signed the Lateran Treaty (February 11, 1929) with Benito Mussolini* which established the Vatican as a separate state. [NT 3]

617 bits [whiskery] -- wisps of whiskers on the jaws as in a "bit" of something, a small amount [HHC 11]

618 bitter[s] -- a very dry ale, heavily hopped, popular in Britain. In BH, the reference is to stomach medicine. [UD 12/FRH 7/MMA 12/NT 11/BH 15]

619 bizzom -- a form of snoop; it is drawn from various slang words derived from "busy-body", etc. The definition is derived from the context as the word was not listed elsewhere. [BH 15]

620 black and hideous flag -- a refer-

ence to the practice of flying a black flag to announce an execution. Perhaps the most famous literary example of this appears in Thomas Hardy's Tess of the D'Urbervilles, the next to the last paragraph: "Upon the cornice of the tower a tall staff was fixed. Their eyes were riveted on it. A few minutes after the hour had struck something moved slowly up the staff, and extended itself upon the breeze. It was a black flag." [UD 23]

621 black but comely -- a reference to The Song of Solomon 1:5. "I am black, but comely, O ye daughters of Jerusalem . . . ." [BH 4]

622 black-coated brigade -- the phrase usually applies to the clergy in a rather deprecatory manner, but it is used here to refer to office workers [HHC 1]

623 black draught -- a laxative or purgative. The OED lists its ingredients as an "infusion of senna with sulphate of magnesia and extract of liquorice". Its mention in the works of Thackeray and Mrs. Braddon indicate that it was well-known for quite a while. [bc]

624 Black Faced Ram -- the restaurant or pub that hosted the Plumbers' and Glaziers' Ball [WB 6]

625 black frost -- or killing frost, so-called because it leaves no telltale white deposit of ice on any affected vegetation [CW 15]

626 black habit -- the black and distinctive attire worn by the various religious orders for women [UD 19]

627 "Black he stood as night . . ." -- PW is quoting from Milton's* Paradise Lost, II, 670-71:

"black it stood as night
Fierce as ten furies, terrible as hell,
And shook a dreadful dart; what seemed his head
The likeness of a kingly crown had on."

The description is of Satan. [BH 8]

628 Black holes of Calcutta -- a loose reference to the one cell at Fort William, Calcutta, India, into which 146 Europeans were locked for a night in 1756 on the order of Suraja Dowla. Only twenty-three survived the ordeal because of the cramped and suffocating conditions. Dowla was the Nawab of Bengal who had captured the fort. The prison room was just eighteen by fifteen feet. The story originated with John Holwell (1711-98), a member of the British council at Bengal. [MMA 1]

629 Black Lass -- one of the bird dogs on the estates at Denver*. She is a setter. It is disclosed that she had to be put away some six months prior to the action in WB because of her age. [WB 9]

630 Black Magic -- evil magic involving spells, conjuring spirits, the Black Mass, etc., all designed to honor or gain the power of Satan. Standish Wetherall* uses the superstitious beliefs of his Basque* neighbors to keep them away from his house, convincing them that his wife is under the influence of such magic. [ie]

631 The Black Mask -- a pulp magazine of great importance in the development of mystery and detective fiction. Founded by H. L. Mencken and George Jean Nathan, it published a full range of adventure fiction. It is especially noted for its encouragement of the tough guy or hard-boiled school of detective fiction through the publication of the works of Dashiell Hammett, Erle Stanley Gardner, and Raymond Chandler. It ceased publication in 1953. [UD 20]

632 Black Ralph of Herriotting -- hanged on November 9, 1674, for the murder of George Winter*. The place of execution is marked by Dead Man's Post*. The whole affair is fictitious. [bc]

633 Black Rod -- the short title of The Gentleman Usher of the Black Rod* [CW 14]

634 Black Spider -- an overly evil villain in an unidentified (if real) adventure thriller read by Ginger Joe Potts*. The name is typical of those wildly unprincipled characters who people pulp novels and Saturday afternoon movie serials and the more contemporary soap opera. [MMA 19]

635 black treacle cure -- to cure a ham or bacon with heavy black mo-

lasses (treacle) instead of some less pungently flavored sugar; sugar cures being one of the more popular curing processes for pork [UD 6]

636 Blackbeard [Captain] -- the nickname of the audacious and cruel West Indies pirate, Edward Teach or Thatch, master of the ship Queen Anne's Revenge. He was killed in 1718 by a Royal Navy officer in hand-to-hand combat during an engagement off the coast of North Carolina where he had been bullying the locals. He is the subject of all sorts of tales, of which "Dragon's Head" is DLS's contribution to the canon. He is supposed to have left a fabulous treasure which has never been found. Cuthbert Conyers's* cache may have been a part of that larger hoarde. PW helps locate at least that part of the larger mass of riches. [dh]

637 blackbeetles -- cockroaches, which are not beetles at all [BH 3]

638 Blackfriars, Lord -- an owner of two of Mr. Endicott's* razors. He committed suicide after his wife bankrupted and jilted him. The razors were given to his manservant. [HHC 6]

639 Blackfriars subway -- the subway, an underground walkway, not any sort of railroad, at the northern end of Blackfriars Bridge at the corner of Queen Victoria St. [MMA 17]

640 blackguard -- an evil person, one showing baseness and lack of moral decency. The word is pronounced as if it were spelled "blaggard". [bc/ss/SP 5]

641 Blackhall Rd. -- a curved, North-South street in Oxford that connects Keble Rd. with Museum Rd. [GN 18]

642 Blackpool -- a resort town in Lancashire, North of Liverpool* and on the Irish Sea [GN 14]

643 Blackraven Wood -- a fictitious wood where P. C. Sellon* is located. It is a favorite spot for "ramblers and children". [BH 12]

644 Blackshirts -- a catch-all name for Fascists of any variety that derives from Mussolini's troops who wore black shirts as did Hitler's SS (Schutz-staffel) [GN 11]

645 Blackthorne, Johnny -- Miss Clara Whittaker's* groom before Ben Cobling* assumed the job [UD 12]

646 Blackwater -- a river in Essex with a large estuary North of the Thames at the head of which stands the town of Maldon. The coastline is irregular with salt marshes and inlets ideal for smuggling activities. [MMA 7]

647 Blackwell's -- Oxford's famous booksellers on Broad St [GN 10]

648 Blackwood -- the Procurator-Fiscal* has the latest issue of Blackwood's Edinburgh Magazine, a monthly started in 1817 by William Blackwood (1776-1834). Thomas de Quincey was an early contributor. Its contents generally include biographies, memories, short stories, military and social history, travel, and poetry. [FRH 27]

649 Blades, Sgt. -- a police officer who helps Supt. Kirk* from time to time during the investigation of the murder of William Noakes* [BH 7]

650 Blaggs -- a soup manufacturer for whom Pym's Publicity* does the advertising. The firm is fictitious. [MMA 10]

651 Blake, Sexton -- a serial detective character who first appeared on December 20, 1893, in an adventure story called "The Missing Millionaire". Created by Harry Blyth, the stories became tremendously popular and are still being written. Nearly 200 authors have produced Blake's approximately 4000 stories. He resides, as does Sherlock Holmes*, on Baker St.; has a "Watson" named Tinker, a boy; and a landlady named Mrs. Bardell. Both the Viscount St. George* and Ginger Potts* seem familiar with Blake's adventures, and one suspects that PW knows them too. [dh/CW 7/MMA 6]

652 blanc-mange -- a molded gelatine dessert made with milk and usually sweetened and flavored in some way [FRH 21]

653 Blankshires -- a cover-up name for any county regiment. It is a term used because it looks better on a page than does ______shires. After 1881, regiments in general were named for

counties, so the term is handy if one wishes to avoid any specific identification, thus avoiding any favoritism or embarrassment. [ie]

654 blatherskites -- a noisy, talkative fellow, from the U. S. colloquialism "bletherskite". The word was made popular through the Scottish song "Maggie Lauder", widely sung during the Revolutionary War (the War for American Independence). [WB 7]

655 blazon -- the technical description applied to an heraldic coat of arms; the coat of arms itself [GN 17]

656 bleeder -- a variant form of bloody*; a bloody person, an awful person [BH 8]

657 bleedin' -- a variant form of bloody*; to behave in an awful manner [bh]

658 Blessed St. James of Compostella -- also St. James the Greater and one of the original apostles, brother of John. Martyred in Jerusalem in 43 A. D., St. James has been associated by legend (dating from the 9th C.) with Spain where he was supposed to have preached before his death. His body was supposedly taken to Compostella in northwestern Spain. He is the patron saint of Spain. [ie]

659 blew the gaff -- slang for "spilled the beans", to talk to the police after an arrest; to talk with the police about a matter under investigation in such a way as to uncover things for the police that they might not have found in other ways [NT 2]

660 blighter -- British slang for any person or thing of "baleful influence or atmospheric or invisible origin" (OED); any negative or malignant influence. It may also be used in such a way that it has the opposite of its usual meaning, thus becoming a term of affection. [pj/dh/nf/ab/CW 15/SP 5/GN 8]

661 blighty one -- the reference is to a German shell which landed near and almost killed Robert Duckworthy*. The term is WW I slang for a wound that required being shipped back to England and derives from the Hindustani word for home, "<u>bilayati</u>". [im]

662 Blindfold Bill -- see Rumm, Bill [SP 13]

663 b[l]istered about the orbits -- bistre is a brown pigment prepared from soot, so Boyes'* eyes had such rings around them, thus suggesting that he was tired or ill. The orbits are the bony sockets which contain and protect the eyeballs. [SP 10]

664 bloater -- the OED considers this a nearly vulgar term applied to the result of the process for curing herrings, leaving them soft and only half dried. The fish are left on dry salt for one day and then are smoked from one to four days, depending on how long they are to be stored; the fish prepared in this manner. [CW 2]

665 bloater-paste -- a sort of sandwich spread made from bloaters* as one would use tuna to make a tunafish salad sandwich [FRH 22]

666 block makers -- those persons in a print shop who transfer artwork from a sketch to a metal plate on a wooden block that can be used in the printing process [MMA 4]

667 blocking -- see cricket [MMA 18]

668 block -- one of the two bottom horizontal beams that support the rest of the framework from which a bell is hung. On one block the slider* is attached. On the other, the slider's free end is set to shift back and forth as the stay* hits it at each end of a bell's swing. [NT 3]

669 Blodgett, Willy -- he endures PW's wrath from the lectern for having pinched his sister while PW was reading the Scriptures. The incident is notable for showing how well PW knows the people of Duke's Denver* even though he spends most of his time elsewhere. [BH E2]

670 blood groups -- the four identified groups into which mammalian blood can be divided. They are "A", "B", "AB", and "O". The positive and negative Rhesus (Rh) factors further aid identification as each of the four groups may be either positive or negative. [GN 17]

671 "Blood, though it sleep . . ." -- see <u>The Widow's Tears</u> [UD 6]

672 bloody -- an English all-purpose expletive and intensifier as in "bloody well better". It is considered vulgar and would not generally be used in polite company. It is derived from the oath, "Christ's Blood", and would, therefore, be thought blasphemous. [pj/bc/dh/CW 18/BC 15/FRH 1/HHC 11/MMA 8]

673 bloody steak/footprints -- bloody here simply means to be suffused with blood as in a rare beefsteak or in footprints with blood in or near them. PW is very careful in the latter instance to point out just which usage he has in mind, the adjective or the expletive, as Helen, Duchess of Denver*, is very much a prude about such things. [CW 2/UD 14]

674 bloody Welshman -- Mr. Pomfret* is referring to the fact that Jones is one of the most common of all surnames in Wales (and elsewhere for that matter). See also #3662. [GN 19]

675 Bloomsbury -- a district in central London focused on the University of London and Russell Square. Dr. Hartman* lives there, Mrs. Grimethorpe* is housed in a hotel in the area, and Mary Whittaker* studied at the Royal Free Hospital* which is located there as is the Peveril* Hotel. PW calls himself a "Bloomsbury" in reference to the fact that the area has a noted Bohemian* character, but it is also a most pleasant residential location.

It has long been known for its literary and musical residents--HV and Philip Boyes* lived in the area and HV maintained an apartment there after Boyes' death. Pym's Publicity* keeps offices there, so much of the action of MMA is centered there. Will and Mary Thoday** tried to renew their marriage vows at Bloomsbury's St. Andrew's* church.

The area figures so prominently in DLS's tales because she lived there (see Gt. James St.) for many years. [cf/aq/fr/hp/WB 10/CW 19/UD 17/SP 2/HHC 18/MMA 2/NT 13/GN 20]

676 "Blossoms of the honey-sweet . . . ." -- what is given in at least some editions as "menuphar" should be "nenuphar", the water lily or lotus, used formerly to produce a flavored syrup. The allusion at least derives from the early part of Book IX of the Odyssey, the tale of the land of the Lotus-eaters*. It may be that DLS, trusting her memory, has blended parts of Tennyson's "The Lotus-eaters" with parts of Shelley's "Oedipus Tyrannus". The switch from nenuphar to menuphar could likely be the result of her own sense of euphony. [HHC 4]

677 blot on the 'scutcheon -- any person or thing that brings the family name into disrepute or dishonor. It is also, perhaps, an allusion to a play (a tragedy in three acts) by Robert Browning* that was first performed in 1843 at the Covent Garden Theatre. The play was named A Blot in the 'Scutcheon and involves love, honor, error, and death. [WB 9]

678 The blot upon the paper's rim . . . . -- PW is playing with lines from Wordsworth's* "Peter Bell", lines 240-2, which read:

"A primrose by a river's brim
A yellow primrose was to him,
And it was nothing more." [CW 13]

679 blotto -- slang for drunk to the point of insensibility [GN 8]

680 blown -- out of breath, winded; normally applied to horses [HHC 16]

681 "Blue Danube" -- the waltz by Johann Strauss II (1825-99). It was written in 1867 and may well be the most famous of all the Viennese waltzes. [HHC 3]

682 Blue Dragon -- the neighborhood pub near the Fentiman* flat in Finsbury Park*. It is fictitious. The nearest "Blue" anything pub would be the Blue Lion on Gray's Inn Rd.* [BC 7]

683 Blue Gate Close -- PW's address in Kirkcudbright* just off the High St. there. A close is a narrow street or alley leading from a main street into a courtyard or central area of a group of homes or flats which surround it. In reality, the address is Green Gate Close and may still be seen. [FRH 5]

684 blue-pencil -- a publishing term (jargon) meaning to delete or to censor, from the practice of editors who used a blue grease pencil to correct proofs and copy [MMA 4]

685 blue pill -- the OED calls it "a pill of anti-bilious operation". Such pills have not been available for many years. [bc]

686 Blue River Trout [truite bleu] -- a European river trout which turns a rich, deep blue when cooked (the skin only, not the flesh). To be served properly, the fish must be alive until they are ready for the pot. They are then killed, gutted, and dropped into a bouillon which has a high vinegar content. They are cooked rapidly and are served with melted butter or hollandaise sauce. [UD 1]

687 Blue Room -- one of the salons at Bredon Hall*. It houses some china that the Dowager Duchess* is anxious to show to HV, so they take tea there. [BH E2]

688 Blue Train -- the nightly luxury train, a sleeping car express, of the Paris, Lyon, and Mediterranean Railway which rushed passengers from Paris to the Côte d'Azur and Riviera* areas of France's southern coast. [SP 13]

689 Bluebeard -- the legendary collector and murderer of wives. Often ascribed to the "Arabian Nights"*, he is a later invention who has had, unfortunately, his imitators in real life. [HHC 12]

690 Bluebeard's Chamber -- the fairy tale from the collection of French academician Charles Perrault*, translated into English by Robert Samber. It is a tale with an Oriental setting of the infamous Bluebeard* who wishes to marry Fatima. He gives her the key to a room (the Chamber) and goes away, having instructed her not to enter that room. She does, of course, enter the room and finds the corpses of his former wives. The phrase refers to any such situation where curiosity gets the better of discretion. The allusion is especially and ironically appropriate for Matthew Gowan*. [FRH 15]

691 bluebottle -- any sort of blowfly of an irridescent blue color. They make a loud buzzing noise when flying. [MMA 15]

692 blueing the lot -- "blueing" is racing slang for losing money on horse races. The term derives from the marks bookies place in their record books. [GN 9]

693 bluestocking -- a woman with intellectual or literary interests. The term derives from the "Blue Stocking Society", ca. 1750. A group of women started the club to have something to do other than play cards. The name comes from the dress of one Benjamin Stillingfleet who wore blue worsted stockings rather than black silk ones. [BH P]

694 bluggy -- a child's euphemism for bloody*, derived from mispronunciation [GN 21]

695 bluidy -- Scots dialect for bloody* [FRH 1]

696 Blundell, Ann -- one of Supt. Blundell's* daughters [NT 6]

697 Blundell, Betty -- one of Supt. Blundell's* daughters [NT 6]

698 Blundell, Mrs. -- Supt. Blundell's* wife [NT 18]

699 Blundell, Supt. -- of Leamholt*. The ranking local investigative officer who is in charge of the mystery of the battered corpse in the churchyard at Fenchurch St. Paul*. He is presented as an intelligent and capable man, and PW seems to enjoy working with him. [NT 4]

700 Blunt -- a resident of Paggleham*, possibly deceased. Aggie Twitterton* lives in the cottage he used to own. [BH 1]

701 Board -- the Board of Directors at Pym's Publicity*. They would be the general governing and policy making group for the company. [MMA 3]

702 Board of Guardians -- the supervisory committee for a local workhouse. Thomas Frobisher-Pym* is a member of such a board. [bc]

703 board-school -- an elementary school run by a school board elected by the ratepayers under the Education Act of 1870. Education to the age of twelve became compulsory for all children in 1876, and the school boards coordinated the existing church and national schools, building more schools where necessary. These later schools became known as the board-schools and have nothing to do with boarding; they

were meant simply to provide free schooling. They were taken over by the State in 1902. [MMA 3]

704 "The boast of heraldry . . ." -- Supt. Kirk* is quoting from the ninth stanza of Thomas Gray's (1716-71) "Elegy Written in a Country Churchyard":

"The boast of heraldry, the pomp of power
And all that beauty, all that wealth e'er gave
Awaits alike the inevitable hour:
The paths of glory lead but to the grave."

The lines are 33-6. [BH 7]

705 boat train -- any train which connects with one of the cross-Channel ferries or which allows connection with a passenger boat in other service [te]

706 boat train to Folkestone -- a train from London to Folkestone, Kent, from where one may connect with cross-Channel steamers to Boulogne, Calais, and Ostend. There are two stations in Folkestone, one at the harbor for quick connections. [CW 9]

707 Bob [Bancroft] -- Phoebe Tucker's* husband, an archaeologist [GN 1]

708 bob -- British slang for shilling*. See British Monetary Units. [passim]

709 bob -- a style of short haircut for women and children, popular during the 1920's and 30's [passim]

710 bob[s] -- a change-ringing* method for producing certain changes that create longer peals* [NT 1]

711 bobbed -- see bob, item 709 [CW 9 and passim]

712 Bobbie -- see Anderson, Bob [FRH 6]

713 bobby -- the common and affectionate nickname for a British Police Constable. The name derives from Sir Robert Peel, founder of the English police as they are known today. Peel put the London Metropolitan Police to work in 1829. [ae/hp/HHC 19/NT 2]

714 Boccace, John -- see Boccaccio [bc]

715 Boccaccio, Giovanni -- Italian novelist, poet, and storyteller (1313?-75). He was a contemporary of Dante* and Petrarch, and he knew them both. His works have provided inspiration for Chaucer, Shakespeare, and Keats, among others. He is most noted for the Decameron, a series of tales in celebration of life, love, and beauty. There are ten tales told by ten people, one each on a ten-day trip; hence, the title. The stories were written between 1348 and 1358, and are rather overplayed for their naughtiness. [bc/GN 15]

716 Boche -- the word is the French corruption of the German word for a square-headed nail, a caboche. Hence, a square-head, a derisive term applied to the Germans in both World Wars. The word alludes, perhaps, to the effect created by the helmet worn by German troops in those wars. [NT 8]

717 Boddy jackets -- unknown as such to any naval or life-saving services in the U. K. or the U. S. British Rail Sealink services suggest that it might be "body" jacket, an enclosed stretcher carried on some ships, but that is only a supposition. [CW 13]

718 "Bodies in Blazing Garages . . ." -- the first of these allusions is to the case detailed in "Teeth of the Evidence". The other references are obscure enough to defy positive identification. See also Rouse and Furnace cases. [NT 18]

719 Bodleian -- see Bodley [GN 7]

720 Bodley -- the Bodleian Library, named for Sir Thomas Bodley [1545-1613), a Fellow of Merton College, who was the library's personal benefactor after he retired from public life. The "library" then was a vast empty room as most of its books and furnishings had been sold off during the reign of Edward IV. Bodley started a new flow of books that has not stopped since then, so that the Bodleian now has some four and a half million volumes on some seventy miles of shelves located in several interconnected buildings. The main entry is through the Proscholium, the Divinity School vestibule. Books may not be signed out by anyone--even Charles I and Oliver Cromwell* were refused.

#720 A rendering of the interior of the Bodleian Library, Oxford, ca. 1910.

See also Duke Humphrey. [GN 6]

721 Boer -- the Boer War (1899-1902), common name for the war between Great Britain and the combined forces of the Orange Free State and the Transvaal Republic in South Africa. Boers refers to South Africans of Dutch descent. [BC 1/HHC 8]

722 bog -- wet, spongy ground too soft to bear the weight of any substantial body and composed of decaying vegetation. Bogs can act very much like quicksand if sufficiently wet. [CW 4]

723 bogey [round against] -- one over par for a hole in golf. To play a round against bogey means to play against your average for that course in an attempt to match or equal that average. The expression is chiefly British. [FRH 4]

724 Bohemia[n] -- the central European source of gypsies. The word Bohemian has since been applied to artists, poets, and others who seem to survive without visible means of support. [SP 8]

725 boiled shirt -- a stiff evening dress shirt with starched front and cuffs and a stiff collar worn with black or white tie in PW's day, now only with a white tie [MMA 12]

726 boiled sweets -- brittle, hard candies made from sugar, flavorings and colorings as is peanut brittle [MMA 4]

727 the Bois -- the Bois de Boulogne, probably the most important park in Paris and certainly one of the largest. It features seven lakes, race tracks, a tennis stadium, a polo field, a children's zoo, and other attractions. [CW 18]

728 "Bolingbroke: 'Call forth Bagot . . . .'" -- see <u>King Richard II</u> [CW 14]

729 Bolshevist[vik] -- a member of the political group that survived the Russian Revolution; not a Menshevik. Later, the term came to refer to any follower of Lenin and his theories of Communism; more generally, any follower of the Marxist-Leninist theories of social and governmental reform. Philip Boyes* was not a Bolshevist. Mrs. Chipperley-James* has confused HV with Lady Mary Wimsey* who was engaged for a time to George Goyles* who was a Bolshevist. [CW 2/SP 8/HHC 5/BH P]

730 Bolshevik days -- from the time of the Bolshevik revolutions in Russia in 1917. All through the 1920's and 30's revolutions deposed most of Europe's royal families or at least restricted severely their powers. The reference is suggested by PW when he adjusts Frank Bellingham's* crown on his costume as the Red King from <u>Through the Looking Glass</u>*. The irony of the comment is lost until one reflects on the story's conclusion. [qs]

731 Bolshevism -- the activities of Bolshevists* or any behavior which seems to go counter to the accepted Establishment norms [UD 5]

732 bolt -- the projectile fired from a crossbow. Such bolts are thicker and shorter than arrows, and are delivered with great force--they are known to have pierced armor during battles in the Middle Ages. [GN 6]

733 Bolter, Jack -- an errand boy at Pym's Publicity* [MMA 7]

734 Bom-Bom -- the Wimsey family puppy [t]

735 bombardon -- a bass tuba, but not a Sousaphone. The tuba's bell opens upward, making it most suitable for PW's prank. [MMA 4]

736 Bombay -- capital of Maharashtra state, India; the nation's second most populous city. "The Gateway to India", an English triumphal arch, still stands overlooking the harbor. [HHC 6]

737 bombazine -- a silk fabric of a twill weave, dyed black [GN 1]

738 bombinating -- buzzing, droning [GN 15]

739 <u>bon-papa</u> -- French for grandfather in a familiar sense such as grandpa or granddad. The formal sense would be <u>grand-père</u>. [NT 8]

740 <u>bona fides</u> -- Latin for good faith or honest intentions; recommendations [WB 5/HHC 10/BH 2]

741 Bond St. -- Mrs. Forrest* is referring to the Underground

station at the intersection of Oxford* and Davies Sts., near New Bond St. That station is called Bond St. It would mean that PW, if he took that route, would have a longer walk than if he left his Piccadilly* flat and walked directly to South Audley St.* In other instances, the reference is to the West End* thoroughfare called Bond St., a blending of Old and New Bond Streets. They connect Piccadilly with Oxford St. [UD 15/HHC 8/GN 3]

742 Bone, Zedekiah -- a man sometimes seen in the company of William Grimethorpe* when the latter visits Stapley* [CW 11]

743 boned -- to seize as to steal. The word is slang, origins unknown, but seems to relate to how a dog seizes a bone with quickness and firmness. [WB 5]

744 Bones, Sparkey -- an otherwise unidentified criminal, a friend of Nobby Cranton's* [NT 14]

745 bonhomous soul . . . baby elephant -- a genial, good-natured person with that sort of curiosity related by Rudyard Kipling in his story, "The Elephant's Child"* [MMA 3]

746 Boniface, old Professor -- the ninety-seven year old, almost deaf, and practically gaga don who has exhausted Miss Martin* as she had to scream at him to be heard [GN 1]

747 bonne à tout faire -- French for "maid of all work" [NT 7]

748 bonne fortune -- French for good fortune or luck. Note that it is feminine, a holdover from the medieval and earlier portrayals of fortune as a fickle woman, often an empress. [CW 5]

749 bonnet -- British English for the hood of a car [mt]

750 bonté d'âme -- French for goodness (or kindness, benevolence, etc.) of soul [BH 16]

751 Bonzo dog -- a famous cartoon character between the two World Wars. Bonzo was a fat puppy with big eyes, the canine equivalent of Felix the Cat. While it is difficult to verify its presence in Piccadilly* as part of an advertising gimmick, it is safe to assume that if DLS says it was there, it was there as she would have been alert to such things. The puppy was created by G. E. Studdy. See 752. [CW 19]

752 Bonzo vase -- a vase fashioned to resemble the comical puppy mentioned in 751. Studdy's drawings of the pup first appeared in The Sketch on November 8, 1922. [BH 5]

753 The Book of Common Prayer -- the prayer book of the Church of England. It contains aids to devotion such as psalms, collects, and epistles, the services for various rites and sacraments, and, sometimes, Hymns A & M*. The one commonly used in PW's day would have been Cranmer's in its final version of 1662. It was developed from the Sarum breviary as reissued in 1541. It underwent revision in 1928 and has been further revised since then. [SP 6]

754 Book of the Fortnight -- a fictitious book club [GN 11]

755 Book of the Moment -- a fictitious book club [GN 11]

756 book of the words -- that part of The Book of Common Prayer* containing the Scriptures. George Herbert (1593-1633) referred to "The book of books", the Scriptures, in A Priest to the Temple, Ch. 4. [NT 5]

757 Booth, Miss Caroline [Lucy] -- the nurse and attendant to Rosanna Wrayburn* who is so interested in spiritualism that Miss Climpson* is able to manipulate Miss Booth to obtain the vital information that PW so desperately needs to prove HV's innocence. [SP 16]

758 Booth, G. -- Nurse Booth's* nephew, probably the son of her older brother, Tom. Miss Climpson* wonders if he survived WW I. [SP 17]

759 Booth, Thomas -- Nurse Booth's* older brother [SP 17]

760 Bootle -- HV's agent. He would handle the details of getting her books published and of keeping track of copyrights and royalties. His fee is usually 10%, a more or less standard fee for agents. [HHC 15]

761 border company [gobony] -- a term from heraldry. A border is a

decoration around the perimeter of an heraldic shield. Company is a single row of squares of two alternating colors. Such a decoration on a coat of arms signifies that the bearer is illegitimate. [MMA 11]

762 Border Country -- the territory through which the English-Scottish border runs. Sometimes called the "Debatable Lands" because they were fought over so often between the 13th and 16th centuries. The territory is not limited to the land, however, and includes the coastal area from Gretna at the head of Solway Firth to Port Patrick*. [FRH 3]

763 Border history, darker side of -- PW's mental meanderings on the subject of garlic and vampires have brought him to the general subject of blood, a great deal of which was spilled in the area through which he is driving. The Border "disputes" account for most of it, but there was a good deal of religious persecution as well. [FRH 2]

764 Border keep -- one of the many heavily fortified border castles, remnants of the Border Wars common before the Acts of Union of 1707 joined England and Scotland [FRH 2]

765 Borgan -- a small village or hamlet between Larg and Clauchaneasy** on the A714 route from Newton-Stewart to Girvan** [FRH 2]

766 Borgue -- a village just North of Brighouse Bay* on the B727 route to the South and West of Kirkcudbright* [FRH 19]

767 Boris -- a poet who is reciting one of his poems over the din at the Kropotky's* gathering [SP 8]

768 Boris -- an alias used by the mysterious writer of the cipher letters addressed to Paul Alexis*. The alias was chosen to suggest authenticity for the fake revolution. [HHC 29]

769 Botanical Gardens -- those in Oxford* are across High St. from Magdalen College [GN 20]

770 bottle of fizz -- champagne [MMA 13]

771 bottles and half-bottles -- see laws about bottles and half-bottles [HHC 15]

772 Botticelli Nativity -- it is probable that DLS had in mind Sandro Botticelli's (1444?-1510) painting of 1500. In that Nativity there are figures supported by angels and an allegorical inscription considered by most critics to be Botticelli's comment about the execution of Savonarola and two of his followers by the Florentines. The artist was a follower of that famous and fiery preacher. The devils appear at the bottom of the painting--there are at least five of them--and seem oddly out of place until one considers the painting as a mystical vision of the Apocalypse. [GN 14]

773 botulism -- the acute and sometimes fatal food poisoning caused by botulin, the secretions of the spore-forming bacterium Clostridium botulinum [SP 10]

774 Boudet's -- a cafe or restaurant on the corner of the Rue de la Paix* and the Rue August Leopold* in Paris's Opera Quarter. Parker retires there after discovering when the diamond and emerald cat-shaped good-luck pin was purchased. The establishment is apparently fictitious as it is not listed anywhere. It may, however, have been a small place known to DLS, but its existence could not be verified. [CW 5]

775 Boul' Mich' -- the Boulevard Saint Michel in central Paris which runs North and East from southern Paris to the Ile de la Cité, site of the Cathedral of Notre Dame and the Palais de Justice. It traverses the heart of the student quarter. [CW 5]

776 Boulestin's -- the restaurant where PW meets Pamela Dean* for dinner on the Friday evening when he begins his masquerade as Harlequin. It is located at 25 Southampton St., London, WC2. [MMA 4]

777 Boulter's Mews -- a fictitious place. Bott's Mews is the closest thing in reality. [BC 16]

778 Bounce -- a Danish dog owned by Alexander Pope*; also the name of the pet pooch at the Anwoth Hotel* [FRH 11]

779 boundary -- see cricket [MMA 18]

780 bounded in a nutshell -- PW alludes to Hamlet's comment, "O God, I could be bounded in a nutshell and count myself a king of infinite space, were it not that I have bad dreams." (II, ii, 246) Talboys is PW's nutshell, and he does have "bad dreams", remnants of his bouts with shellshock following WW I. [BH 19]

781 Bourbons -- the French and Spanish royal families. In France, if one ignores the Revolution and Empire, they ruled in an unbroken line from Henri IV in 1589 to Louis Philippe whose reign ended in 1848, a turbulent and, at times, exotic period of 259 years. The Spanish Bourbons flourish today in the person of King Juan Carlos who re-established the monarchy there after the interruption by dictator Francisco Franco. [HHC 32]

782 Bourne's -- formerly Bourne & Hollingsworth, one of the famous department stores on Oxford St.* in London. It is no longer in business. [SP 20]

783 Bournemouth -- a famous Channel coast seaside resort in Dorset, due West of Southampton on Poole Bay. Miss Climpson* mentions that she met a spiritualist there once when on vacation. [UD 10/SP 16]

784 Bournemouth Murder -- the newspapers' reference phrase for the case of the murder of Irene May Wilkins by Thomas Henry Allaway on December 22, 1921. Miss Wilkins had advertised for a position as a cook. Allaway answered the ad, she appeared for an interview, Allaway attempted to rape her, she resisted, and he killed her. In addition to witnesses who had seen the two together, much emphasis was placed on the car, a Mercedes belonging to the family for which Allaway was chauffeur.
The car had new Dunlop "Magnum" tires, the same tread pattern as found beside the body. Mr. Justice Avory,* known as a "hanging judge" heard the case in July of 1922, and Allaway was hanged in August of that year. [CW 3]

785 Bovril -- the famous British meat extract still sold in its familiar squat bottle. It can be mixed with water to make a drink or can be added to soups, sandwiches, etc. It was advertised intensely between the Wars. As it says on the label, "The warming beefy drink, good and nourishing at any time of day." Add hot water to one teaspoonful to make a cup. [BC 18]

786 bow drawn at a venture -- see drawing a bow at a venture [GN 15]

787 bow or stroke -- in rowing, the "bow" is that oarsman's position closest to the bow of the shell. The "stroke" sits nearest the stern and calls the "stroke" or "beat" for the other oarsmen is there is no coxswain. [GN 11]

788 bowler -- see cricket [MMA 10]

789 bowler hat -- a derby; a stiff felt hat with a dome-shaped crown and a nearly round brim [UD 20/HHC 11/MMA 7/BH 6]

790 Bowler, Miss -- Hilary Thorpe's* English teacher or "mistress" of whom Hilary is fond [NT 3]

791 box border -- a low, clipped hedge of boxwood shrubs used as a garden or walkway boundary or border. An evergreen, the one mentioned in CW is probably Buxus sempervirens and is also called boxwood. [CW 2]

792 box-room -- a small room for the storage of boxes, luggage, and other impedimenta. Such rooms are frequently located under the stairways or in a part of an attic, as under the eaves. [WB 6]

793 boxed -- newspaper parlance for framing a notice or special headline with heavy black lines or, in some cases, a decorative border [im]

794 boxed the compass -- to name the thirty-two points of the compass in their proper order, or, more loosely, to make a good effort at confusing and, thereby, losing one who is following. To do so usually requires a number of quick and devious maneuvers. [HHC 30]

795 Boxing Day -- the first weekday after Christmas, so named from the tradition of presenting boxed gifts to the postman, employees, etc.; it is now widely observed as a holiday [SP 12/NT 19]

796 Boyes, Rev. Arthur -- father of Philip Boyes* and pastor to an unnamed parish relatively close to London. He is a most decent man who seems as distressed over HV's plight as he is about his son's death. Wimsey is genuinely impressed and pleased by Mr. Boyes' cooperative attitude. [SP 6]

797 Boyes, Philip -- the victim of arsenical poisoning in SP. It is assumed that HV, his live-in mistress at one time, killed him and she is tried for his death in that story. Boyes is described as a very handsome man to whom any woman might become attached. He appears, however, to be more attractive in his physical person than in any other way. He appears not to be able to handle his personal affairs at all well. [SP 1/HHC 3]

798 Boys' Friend Library -- a quite extensive series of books for adolescents published in the early years of this century and usually bound in leather-backed cloth. Number 74, for instance, is L. J. Beeston's The Airship's Quest, a thriller about a lost race in South America. Heavily romantic-adventure oriented, they would be just the thing for Viscount St. George* in his younger days. [dh]

799 Bracey, Miss -- HV's secretary. We are given no description of her, but the indication is that she and HV have a good working relationship to the point that she loans HV some money to travel with. [GN 11/BH 14]

800 Bracket -- a footman at the Duke of Denver's* London residence [MMA 11]

801 Bradenham ham -- manufactured in Chippenham, a Wiltshire market town, from the 14th C. and still one of England's largest cattle markets. The Bradenham is a dry-salt cured ham that has been further treated to a costly process of curing with molasses and spices. The exact process is said to be known to only two people at the Wiltshire Bacon Company, the only producers of the hams. [UD 6]

802 Bradford -- "that stupid Bradford woman", the Dowager Duchess of Medway's* reference to Disraeli's* paramour. At the time, the Duchess had been interested in the P. M. for herself. [aq]

803 Brahmin [high caste] -- a Hindu of the highest rank and of a pale tan or beige skin coloring. The skin would be considered dark only in comparison to a Northern European. [UD 11]

804 Braithwaite, Slinger [Slinker] -- a party-throwing member of the de Momerie* crowd who leads the party-crashing assault on the Mayfair* home of the Duke of Denver*. [MMA 11]

805 Bramah -- a lock with moving parts invented by Joseph Bramah (1748-1814), an English inventor. His refinements on lock mechanisms were considered particularly secure in their day. [SP 13]

806 Bramah, Ernest -- see Wallet of Kai Lung [BH 7]

807 Brameld [John Wager] -- brother of William Brameld (see Rockingham) who became known for his excellent landscapes, flowers, and figures executed on pottery. Brameld died in 1851. [BH E2]

808 Bramhill, Mr. Justice -- the judge who sentenced Deacon* and Cranton* to jail for their parts in the theft of the Wilbraham emeralds*. The justice is fictitious. The only judge whose name is close was Mr. Justice George Bramwell, Baron Bramwell, but he retired from the bench in 1881, well before the actions for which Deacon and Cranton were jailed. [NT 5]

809 bran-tub -- a tub or barrel filled with bran in which small wrapped toys are hidden. The children search through this and choose a toy by feel only. It is a common device at parties and money-raising events. [MMA 4]

810 brandy [Napoleon] -- a somewhat snobbish identification for certain finer brandies, a rather obvious advertising ploy. It is curious that DLS should have chosen to repeat the device anywhere except in "Matter of Taste" where reference is made to the Imperial seal having been blown into the bottle's glass, that being the only indication of true Napoleon brandy, or brandy that had been in the Emperor's cellars at some time. The year 1800 suggests that PW might just have had some in WB, so his anguish

at Bunter's thoroughness of method in Chapter 9 is more than justified. Bunter* learns well, for later, in CW, he admonishes Lady Mary* not to snort it as PW would be "distressed" to think that any of it should be wasted. Her reply is not given. [aq/mt/WB 9/CW 7]

811 Brasenose College -- the name comes from a large brazen door-knocker at the college gate that depicts a lion's head with a prominent nose. The knocker is now above the head table in the main hall. See Oxford Colleges. [GN AN]

812 brass eagle -- in churches that have both a pulpit and a lectern, as do most Anglican churches, it seems popular to have a large stylized eagle support the lectern with its head, back and outstretched wings [BH E2]

813 brass plate [set up my] -- Thomas Macpherson* uses the phrase to mean that when he is a practicing M. D., the brass plate will indicate that he is licensed and ready to open his practice. The phrase could apply to any professional about to open offices. It corresponds to "hanging out a shingle" in the U. S. [ss]

814 brass-rags [parted] -- a slang expression meaning to quarrel or to be at odds [BH 18]

815 Brave New World -- a satirical novel by English writer Aldous Huxley (1894-1963). The novel is a foreshadowing of where Huxley thinks the world is headed. It was written in 1932 and remains popular. The title is an ironic reference to Shakespeare's The Tempest, V, i, 183. [GN 1]

816 Bravo case -- or the Balham mystery, the curious case of the death of Charles Delaunay Turner Bravo of poisoning by antimony* in most curious circumstances. It is most likely that he was killed by his wife's odd "friend", a Mrs. Cox, by poisoning his bedside water with enough antimony to do in a regiment. The case seems to have provided DLS with ideas for SP as there are several notable similarities. The case involves marital and extra-marital discord, a confused death suspected of being suicide, and the suicide is thought to be related to the marital problems. A verdict of without "sufficient evidence to fix the guilt upon any person or persons" was returned. Note the absence of "unknown" in reference to the persons. There is even a questionable bottle of burgundy that was absolved of complicity. [SP 20]

817 brazen mouth -- the reference is to the fact that bells are cast in bronze. The phrase is also a common poetic expression. [NT 3]

818 break up the images -- the English Civil War and the Protectorate were all workings of the Puritans under Oliver Cromwell*. During that time, 1649-60, many statues of Jesus, the Virgin Mary, and the saints, stained glass windows, and other religious and liturgical items similarly associated were destroyed as being too close to the practices of Roman Catholicism which was anathema to the Puritans. [NT 3]

819 Bream's Buildings -- London, EC4, is a street that links Chancery Lane with Fetter Lane [MMA 13]

820 Breck, Alan -- a creation of R. L. Stevenson who appears in Kidnapped and Catriona. Breck does indeed have to struggle and fight until he finally escapes to the Continent in the latter novel, a sequel to the former. The second novel's title is pronounced ka-tree-na with emphasis on the second syllable as it would be in Gaelic. [HHC 13]

821 "Bred an' bawn in a briar-patch, Brer Fox" -- PW is quoting from Joel Chandler Harris's (1848-1908) "Tar Baby Story" from Uncle Remus: Legends of the Old Plantation. This does not suggest that PW is treating Mr. MacBride with any degree of respect. [BH 6]

822 Bredon, Death -- PW's middle names. They are pronounced as deeth and breeduhn. PW uses them as a first and last name in MMA to establish a cover identity while he works at Pym's Publicity*. See also "summer time on Bredon". [mt/MMA 1]

823 Bredon Hall -- acquired in the 1300's when Gerald, the 5th Baron Wimsey, married Margaret, daughter and heiress of Sir Thomas Bredon. It has been the chief residence of the Wim-

seys ever since. For a more complete consideration of the family history, see C. W. Scott-Giles's The Wimsey Family. See also Denver and Duke's Denver. [BH E2]

824 Bredon Letters -- some family letters, not further identified. One is reminded of the famous Paston Letters of the 15th C., a collection of rather commonplace letters among the members of a well-to-do family of Norfolk*. The letters are important today for their insights into the day-to-day life of the era. [BH E2]

825 "The breezes are blowing--a race, a race!" -- PW is quoting from ll. 23-4 of R. H. Barham's "The Legend of Hamilton Tighe". See Tighe, Hamilton. [UD 12]

826 brekker -- a slang term for breakfast [ss]

827 Brennerton -- one of the fictitious communities created by DLS for HHC [HHC 2]

828 Brennerton Farm -- Will Coffin's* farm [HHC 3]

829 Brewer -- a reference to one of the reference volumes produced by the Rev. Ebenezer Cobham Brewer (1810-97). Among these works are The Dictionary of Phrase and Fable and The Reader's Handbook. From the context, the Dictionary is the most likely candidate. [MMA 3]

830 brick -- see dropped a brick [MMA 11]

831 brick [be a] -- slang or colloquial English for a good fellow or one of good quality; a supporter or follower [WB 8]

832 Bricklayer's Arms -- a pub in Stapley*, perhaps named for one in London's West End* behind the Churchill Hotel in the Portman Square area just North of Oxford St.* The London one is now about 160 years old. There is also a no-longer-used railroad locomotive service area South of Tower Bridge that is known by that name. [CW 11]

833 Brickmaker's Arms -- a fictitious pub* [MMA 16]

834 bridal raptures of Pentecost -- a reference to the nuptial union of the Holy Ghost with the Disciples to create the Christian church. [UD 22]

835 brides-in-the-bath -- a reference to the famous Brides in the Bath Case involving George Joseph Smith. It came to light in 1915. Smith would woo a lady, marry her for the insurance money in the policy he took out on her, have wills drawn in each other's favor, buy a bathtub, and drown his new wife in the new tub. This was accomplished by making certain that the tub was shorter than the lady. Smith would then offer a pedicure while she was bathing, grab her ankles and jerk her forward. The back of the hapless victim's head would hit the edge of the tub, stunning her just as she gasped for air from the surprise of it all. This created the impression of her having either slipped or blacked out, hitting her head and, thus, drowning.

Physicians were not suspicious enough to do a thorough investigation although several expressed their curiosity about how such a young and healthy woman could die in so odd a fashion. Smith moved from town to town, changed his name, and, eventually, had killed at least three women. He was caught only when people began to notice the similarities, unusual as they were, among the three deaths. Investigations followed and Smith was finally identified positively on February 1, 1915, and was arrested on the minor charge of falsifying information on a marriage certificate. 150 witnesses had to testify to secure conviction on a murder charge, but it was done. Smith was hanged at Maidstone jail after a rejected appeal. [WB 10 and passim]

836 The Bride's Tragedy -- a play by T. L. Beddoes* recounting the love of Hesperus for Floribel whom he has promised to marry. However, Lord Ernest, Hesperus's father, is greatly in debt to the Duke, so the Duke's son, Orlando, hatches a plot to imprison Lord Ernest and then offer him freedom if he can convince Hesperus to marry Olivia, the Duke's daughter, thus eliminating the debt. This Hesperus eventually agrees to do, but he kills Floribel just before the wedding to Olivia.

The murder is discovered and what had begun and an innocent plot to help

old friends becomes a sordid bloodbath. Beddoes claims to have worked his plot from that of a ballad by a Mr. Gilbert called "Minor's Tragedy", supposedly a reworking of an old Oxford murder: A student at an Oxford college marries a beautiful young girl, but neither family knows of it. While separated during a vacation, he is introduced to another young woman who also becomes his bride. Just before his second marriage he returns to Oxford and murders his first wife at a lonely spot on Divinity Walk and buries her there. The crime remains hidden until his deathbed confession. Upon revelation of the crime, Divinity Walk was abandoned and eventually demolished. [HHC 5]

837 bridge -- the most popular card game in the English speaking world. It evolved from the British card game of Whist. From 1904, it was called Auction Bridge, and, from 1926, it has been called Contract Bridge. In the latter, bidding establishes the right to name the trump suit, a process that involves a variety of conventions which are dependent upon the bidding system being used. The aim is to win the exact number of tricks bid or called.

The four suits are ranked according to their relative strength in the game. From the weakest they are: Clubs, Diamonds, Hearts, and Spades. If "No Trump" is called, the bidder is declaring that he is willing to play allowing the highest card played on any trick to be the winner, regardless of suit if that card follows the suit led. No Trump outranks Spakes in bidding and scoring. A game is 100 points.

Winning two out of three games is called a rubber, after which partners are usually switched. A team having won a game toward the rubber is "vulnerable". This status affects later scoring, but not the play. If a team takes all the tricks but one, they have scored a "small slam"; to take all of the tricks is a "slam" or "grand slam". Bonus points are earned for such feats.

Bridge requires four players, two against two as teams. Whichever person makes the last and highest bid is the declarer, his partner becomes the "dummy". The declarer plays both his and the dummy's, the latter's hand laid out on the table for all to see. Bridge is a subtle and complicated game. Its basics can be learned in an evening, but people have spent a lifetime trying to master it. It is like chess or backgammon in that regard.

In "Queen's Square", PW and friends are playing contract bridge during which a bid of four spades, meaning that the declarer intends to take a total of ten of the thirteen possible tricks with spades as trump. Another player, an opponent, doubles the bid, meaning that he does not think the bid can be made. Such a move is an effective psychological weapon, but, if accurate, also affects strongly the resultant scoring. DLS makes reference to bridge in many of the chapter titles in BC. [qs/BC/HHC 18/MMA 6]

838 Bridge and Bottle -- a pub* in Stapley*. Its name is a corruption of Bridge Embattled, a stone bridge with decorative battlements or crenellations. The term is an heraldic one in nature and describes the scene on the pub's sign. [CW 11]

839 bridge-coat -- not the heavy, calf-length wool topcoats known and loved by naval officers, but a decorative fashion accessory worn by ladies. Individual styles may vary, but they are generally not meant to close in front. Such jackets are worn over simpler dresses which often have fairly low-cut fronts and backs. One suspects that Mrs. Goodacre's dress is not of the daring kind though. [BH 15]

840 Bridges -- the poet-laureate, Robert Bridges (1844-1930), a student at Eton and Oxford. The bulk of Bridges' work was done at about the turn of the century. [GN 3]

841 The Bridget Tea Shop -- the scene of one of Robert Duckworthy's* most unnerving doppleganger* experiences. PW also visits there in his search for a solution to the unhappy Duckworthy's dilemma. The shop is located in the Hatton Garden* area of London. It is unknown if such a shop existed, but it is doubtful. [im]

842 brief [hold no] -- to be impartial or to be without prejudice in some matter [WB 6]

843 briefless barrister -- a lawyer without a client [CW 10]

844 brig -- Scots dialect for bridge [FRH 2]

845 Brig of Dee -- a small village about two and a half miles southwest of Castle Douglas* [FRH 5]

846 Briggs -- a former attendant at the Bellona Club*. He has left his employment there at the time of BC. [BC 4]

847 Briggs -- a barber in Holborn (Hatton Garden*) mentioned by Robert Duckworthy* and visited by PW in that same story [im]

848 Briggs -- the police constable who detains Simpson* during an investigation. He is not otherwise detailed. [cb]

849 Briggs, C. I. -- a student at Shrewsbury College* [GN 7]

850 Briggs, Eliza -- see Madame Brigette [CW 17]

851 Briggs, John -- gardener to Rosanna Wrayburn and witness to her will [SP 19]

852 Brighouse Bay -- the small bay due West of Kirkcudbright* Bay and also situated on a North-South axis [FRH 13]

853 Bright, Mrs. -- a ground-floor resident of HV's apartment building who saw Philip Boyes* arrive at 9:25 P. M. In England the ground floor is what would be the first floor in the U. S., while the first floor in England is the second floor in the U. S., etc. [SP 1]

854 Bright, William -- a travelling barber fallen on hard times. The name is an alias, a fact justified in part by the observation that he is not a competent barber. He is one of the chief suspects in HHC as that plot develops. [HHC 8]

855 Bright Young Things -- the standard label for the young society set that rose to prominence during the 1920's in England and the U. S. Included under that epithet would be Scott and Zelda Fitzgerald, the Mountbattens, T. S. Eliot, Gertrude Stein, the Duff Coopers, Virginia Woolf, and Evelyn Waugh. These people are not to be confused with the gin-drinking, Charleston-dancing crowds of followers; the Bright Young Things were the intellectual leaders of that movement; its spokesmen. [SP 5/MMA3]

856 Brighteye -- a horse Mrs. Forrest* bet on--she is unsure of the animal's name. At 50 to 1 odds, there is little hope in the venture. [UD 7]

857 "Bright-eyed after swallowing a wingless biped" -- a clue in the crossword puzzle PW works on as he waits to speak to a theatrical agent. It is one of those curious and maddening clues typical of English puzzles and suggests Plato's definition of man in his Politicus (The Statesman), §266. Thomas Carlyle uses the same definition in his Sartor Resartus, Book I, Ch. 3. In Plato's work, young Socrates is debating with The Stranger when, near the end of the section, we find, "seeing that the human race falls into the same division with the feathered creatures and no others, we must again divide the biped into featherless and feathered . . . ." [HHC 23]

858 Brighton -- a fashionable seacoast resort approximately fifty miles due South of London, made popular by the Prince Regent who was later George IV. It is noted for its pier and wide variety of entertainments. [cb/WB 13/GN 14/BH P]

859 Brillat-Savarin, Anthelme -- the French magistrate and writer (1755-1826) who is best remembered for his writings on gastronomy, especially La Physiologie du Goût (The Physiology of Taste), which is concerned with the pleasures of eating and drinking. The work is presented in a lengthy and charming series of anecdotes, aphorisms and observations. [UD 7]

860 brilliantine -- a cosmetic preparation used by men during the early part of this century to make their hair shine [WB 2/UD 21/HHC 1]

861 "Bring me flesh and bring me wine" -- the opening line of the third stanza of the Christmas carol "Good King Wenceslas"* [qs]

862 bring the pole up in three -- the standard technique for propelling

a punt*, viz: Stand on the rear platform of the punt facing forward and 1) drop the pole through the hands to the right of the boat until it touches the bottom of the river, 2) push the pole until its end is reached, working hand over hand to the top, 3) allow the pole to rise under its own buoyancy, using it as a rudder at the same time. The process is repeated as necessary. [GN 15]

863 bringing not peace but a sword -- the line alludes to Matthew 10: 34, Jesus's instructions to His disciples: "Think not that I am come to send peace on earth: I came not to send peace but a sword." [GN 22]

864 Brinvilliers, Marquise de -- the famous French multiple murderess, Marie Madelaine d'Aubray (1630-76). She used a preparation called aqua tofana, the exact contents of which are unknown, but it worked very well. A popular subject for authors, she is featured in some detail in the letters of one of her contemporaries, Marie de Rabutin-Chantal, Marquise de Sévigné. The quote PW cites appears in her letter to her daughter on July 22, 1676, a Wednesday. Madame de Sévigné wrote: "Let me entertain you with a little more of the history of La Brinvilliers. She died as she lived, that is to say, very resolutely. She entered the place where she expected to have been put to the torture, and on seeing three buckets of water she said, 'What! All that water for a little person like me? They must intend to drown me for considering my small size they can never hope to make me drink so much.'"

Torture proved unnecessary as she confessed to the murders of her father, sister, and two brothers, all in 1670. It is reputed that she visited hospitals to test her poisons on the sick in the guise of cheering them up. Her nonchalance led eventually to her capture, trial, and execution. She was beheaded and the corpse was burned on Friday, July 17, 1676, in Paris. Sir Arthur Conan Doyle* used the quote in his short story "The Leather Funnel" where it appears as "All that water must have been brought here for the purpose of drowning me, Monsieur. You have no idea, I trust, of making a person of my small stature swallow it all." The water would have been forced down her throat, perhaps by means of the leather funnel mentioned above. [UD 19]

865 Briquet, Monsieur -- the proprietor of the jewelry shop where Charles Parker found the mate to the diamond and platinum cat found on the grounds at Riddlesdale Lodge*. The shop is located on the Rue de la Paix* and is fictitious. [CW 5]

866 Britannica, Encyclopedia -- see Encyclopedia Britannica [np]

867 British East Africa -- the area including what are now Kenya, Uganda, and Tanzania (formerly Tanganyika and Zanzibar), all of which were parts of the British Empire until after World War II. [HHC 6]

868 British Journal of Photography -- a highly regarded publication from its inception in 1854. It appeals to the full range of professional uses as well as to the advanced amateur. Bunter* reads it, an indication of his level of photographic expertise. [SP 20]

869 British Monetary Units -- items common in PW's day included the farthing (withdrawn in the '30's), ¼d; halfpenny (ha'penny), ½d; penny (copper), 1d (from the Latin denarii); three penny bit, 3d; six penny bit, 6d; shilling (bob; 1/ or 1s), 12d; florin, 2s or 24d; half a crown, 2/6; ten shillings (a note, not a coin), 10/ or 10s; one pound ("quid", a note), £1 or 20 shillings; five pounds ("fiver", a note), £5 or 100s. The guinea was not a unit of currency, but was the value of £1 and 1s found on quoted statements of professional accounts. The gold sovereign was withdrawn from circulation in WW I. The pound (£) and its symbol derive from the Latin libra, while the shilling (s) derives from the Latin solidi.

During the time frame of the PW stories, the pound fluctuated around U. S. $4.00, making the shilling worth about $.20 U. S. British currency, while retaining the old names, is now on a decimal system with the pound valued at 100 pence, not at 240 pence as in PW's day. [passim]

870 British Museum -- described as the

#870 The British Museum, London.

"richest and most varied collection of treasures in the world", it was founded in 1753 by Act of Parliament. The nucleus of the collection is the priceless manuscript collection of Sir Robert Cotton. The Royal Library, founded by Henry VII, was added to it in 1757. That addition made the Museum the beneficiary of the compulsory copyright rule which gives it a free copy of every book printed in England. It was, until recently, the largest and most comprehensive museum/library in the world, but the two functions are now separate. [UD 3/HHC 30/MMA 10]

871 Brittany -- the area of France that occupies the broad peninsula that juts into the Atlantic Ocean at the mouth of the English Channel [BH 19]

872 Brixton -- a residential area in Greater London which was, during WW I, the home of Robert Duckworth's* mother. It is South of central London and about three miles South of the Thames River. [im/HHC 30]

873 Broad St. -- in Oxford, one of the East-West main streets of the old part of the city. It extends from Cornmarket to Parker Rd. [GN 12]

874 Broad Walk -- an East-West path that separates Merton Fields and Christ Church Meadow in the old part of Oxford [GN 13]

875 broadcast -- the word is being used in its original sense of "to spread seeds widely over prepared ground". The modern application to radio and television is a later use that has overshadowed the original meaning. [MMA 5]

876 Broadmoor -- an asylum for the criminally insane in southeastern Berkshire. Robert Duckworthy*, in PW's consideration, is in danger of spending the rest of his life there if PW can't solve the poor man's dilemma. [im/UD 7/BC 18/NT 14]

877 Brobdingnagian corkscrew -- a very large one. The phrase is used in reference to one of Mr. Puffett's* chimney cleaning tools. The allusion is to Brobdingnag, the second stop in Lemuel Gulliver's travels as related by Jonathan Swift. The people there are all as tall as steeples and everything is proportionally large. [BH 4]

878 Brocken spectres -- an apparently enormous shadow, the size of which is partly the illusion of the viewer who assumes that the shadow is as far away as some other distant object. The name relates to a phenomenon at Brocken Mountain in Germany when a low sun casts shadows of persons or objects on clouds that are below the person or object whose shadow is cast. The peak is the highest of the Harz range in Saxony, and is famous also as the scene of a witches' sabbath on the eve of May 1st, the feast of Walpurgis. <u>Walpurgisnacht</u> is an event that would not be without spectres in its own right. There is a powerful description of a Brocken spectre in one of Thomas DeQuincey's opium dreams in <u>Confessions of an English Opium Eater</u>. [WB 12]

879 Brocklebury, Sir Ralph -- PW is on his way to attend a sale of Brocklebury's books when he is interrupted by a call from his mother informing him of the corpse in Mr. Thipps's* bathtub. The sale is apparently fictitious, the only sale that seems appropriate being one at Christie's, that of one R. Brocklebank on 10-11 July, 1923, but that seems a bit late for DLS to have included it in her manuscript, although it is a possibility. [WB 1]

880 Brodribb -- a former Shrewsbury College* student who has gone "absolutely potty on some new kind of religion". [GN 2]

881 broke prison -- colloquial English for escaped from prison [NT 2]

882 bromide -- any commonplace or trite comment or remark; a worn phrase [ie/GN 8]

883 bromide -- a sedative, probably potassium bromide [UD 1]

884 bromide prints -- enlargements. The name is taken from the active chemical base, a silver bromide emulsion, used in coating the paper [WB 5]

885 Brontë College -- a fictitious institution. The name is meant simply to be suggestive of Yorkshire and the Brontë family of writers, but the only colleges in Yorkshire at the time were Leeds (1904), Sheffield

(1905), and Hull (1927). [GN 2]

886 Brontës -- Charlotte, Anne, and Emily, the eminent Victorian novelists and poets. Charlotte wrote Jane Eyre, and Emily wrote Wuthering Heights, two of the most famous of all the Victorian novels. [GN 3]

887 brooch spire -- a sharply rising, round church spire erected on a square tower. They are common in Essex. The word is more commonly spelled "broach". [BH 18]

888 Brooke, Rupert -- son of a Rugby master and educated at Rugby and King's College, Cambridge (1887-1915). He first published poetry in 1911, but his death during WW I, while on active service, ended what had started to be a career of exceptional promise. [BH 12]

889 Brooklands -- the world's first specially designed speedway for motor racing built in 1906-7 near Weybridge, Surrey [cb/UD 19]

890 Brooks of Sheffield -- a character in Dickens's* David Copperfield. Brooks is invented by Mr. Murdstone to identify David to Quinnion, and appears in Ch. 2. [CW 11]

891 brother's keeper -- see my brother's keeper

892 Brotherhood, Ltd. -- "that extremely old-fashioned and religiously minded firm who manufacture boiled sweets* and nonalcoholic liquors." It is famous in sports literature for having fielded the cricket* team that PW helps defeat. The firm is a DLS invention. [MMA 4]

893 Brotherton -- the tenant upstairs over Dr. Hartman's* flat. He is a gas company inspector and a very jealous husband. [fr]

894 Brotherton, Maddalena -- the beautiful wife of the tenant over Dr. Hartman's* flat. She is murdered with a six-inch spiral skewer. [fr]

895 Brough -- a small community on the A66 route to the South and East of Carlisle* in Cumbria. Nearby is the ruin of the 11th C. Brough Castle, once home to the 13th Baron Clifford (1435-61), nicknamed "The Butcher" for his ferociousness during the Wars of the Roses. The area is renowned for its scenery and excellent walking trails. [FRH 20]

896 brought his bell up -- see raising a bell [NT 1]

897 Brown, Dr. -- the physician who attends Rosanna Wrayburn* [SP 18]

898 Brown, Miss H. -- a student at Shrewsbury College* [GN 6]

899 Brown, Mr. -- owner of a drug store on Southampton Row* in London, very near HV's Doughty St.* flat [SP 1]

900 Brown, Mr. -- a Queen's College (see Oxford Colleges) student who "helps" his friends by letting them into the college through his room when they are out after hours [GN 8]

901 Brown, Mrs. -- the name of a fictitious person used by Parker to illustrate a point in discussing the HV case with PW [SP 5]

902 Brown, Alice -- see "It was a robber's daughter . . ." [BH 18]

903 Brown, Capability -- the name of Lancelot Brown (1715-83), a landscape architect, among other things, who revolted against formal French and Italian gardens, choosing naturalistic landscape gardening which featured rolling lawns, streams, clumps of trees with accent pieces of Gothic or Classical architecture for variety. He designed the grounds of Blenheim Palace, home of the Dukes of Marlborough, thereby gaining most favorable attention for his work. [dh]

904 Brown, Henry -- husband of Jane Hubbard* and Philip Boyes' grandfather [SP 11]

905 Brown, J. -- the alias used by Matthew Gowan* while in London [FRH 16]

906 Brown, Julia -- daughter of Henry and Jane Hubbard Brown**, wife of the Rev. Arthur Boyes* and mother to Philip Boyes* [SP 11]

907 Brown, Susan [Aunt] -- Robert Duckworthy's* aunt. See also Dart. [im]

908 Browne, Sir Thomas -- see Religio Medici [GN 15]

909 Browning [Robert] -- the great English Victorian dramatist and poet (1812-89), remembered now only for his poetry. Perhaps the most famous of his efforts are the dramatic monologues, those playlike poems which include the often-anthologized "My Last Duchess". With Tennyson he is in the forefront of the Victorian poets. His plays are best forgotten. [CW 9/BH 16]

910 Browning, Elizabeth Barrett* -- the English poet and wife of Robert Browning* (1806-61). She is mostly remembered for her Sonnets From the Portuguese (1850), but her work was quite extensive beyond that fine creation, the most popular sonnet sequence since Elizabethan times. [UD 19]

911 Browning's poem -- the allusion is to the poem "One Way of Love" (1855), especially to the second of its three stanzas:

"How many a month I strove to suit
These stubborn fingers to the lute!
Today I venture all I know.
She will not hear music? So!
Break the string; fold music's wing:
Suppose Pauline had bade me sing!"

[MMA 7]

912 Brownlow -- a mechanic and garage owner at Fenchurch St. Peter* who can be called on, if needed, to assist with the repairs to Mrs. Merdle's* front axle [NT 2]

913 Brownlow St. -- a short street connecting Sandland St. with High Holborn*. Mr. Pond* would have to walk down Bedford Row* to Sandland, down Brownlow, and then a few short blocks to the Chancery Lane* underground station. [SP 14]

914 Brownrigg-Fortescue, Mr., K. C.* -- one of the defense attorneys working with Sir Impey Biggs* in the case of the Duke of Denver* [CW 14]

915 Brown-Séquard [Charles Édouard] -- a French physician and physiologist (1817-94), and one of the founders of the modern science of endocrinology. His contributions to neurophysiology, especially in relation to the spinal nerves have been considered important. The Brown-Séquard syndrome is a reaction to a spinal lesion first described by him wherein a lesion on one side of the nerve bundle causes paralysis on that side, but a loss of sensation mostly on the opposite side. [WB 2]

916 Broxford -- a fictitious community near Paggleham* where Mr. Noakes* maintains a radio business. Noakes travels frequently between the two towns. [BH 1]

917 Broxford and Pagford Gazette -- a fictitious newspaper that sends a reporter to cover William Noakes's* funeral [BH 19]

918 Brummagem handles -- or brummagem; of cheap or inferior quality. Brummagem is a dialectical form of Birmingham*. [GN 19]

919 Brunswick Square -- a square just North of Guilford St.* and at the West end of Coram's Fields* in London. [HHC 30]

920 Brushwood Cross -- a fictitious place in Warwickshire [UD 11]

921 Brutus -- the best of Julius Caesar's friends to stab him to curb his ambition. He is central to Shakespeare's Julius Caesar. [HHC 23]

922 Bryant, Elsie -- Mrs. Wilbraham's* maid. She is too talkative about her mistress's possessions. [NT 5]

923 bucked as hell -- a common slang expression meaning elated [NT 7]

924 bucket-shop -- an illegal betting parlor. The word is of U. S. derivation and referred originally to speculation in grain commodities at the Chicago Board of Trade. [MMA 10]

925 "Buckingham and the clock" -- in Richard III, IV, ii, 111ff. The reference is to the scene when Buckingham, formerly Richard's "other self" realizes that the king is now plotting against him. The final lines of the scene are:

"O, let me think on Hastings, and be gone
To Brecknock, while my fearful head is on!"

Good advice! The clock relates to the conversation between Richard and Buckingham wherein the king keeps asking what time it is and becomes increasingly annoyed as Buckingham keeps asking for promised rewards instead of giving a simple answer. [HHC 23]

926 Buckingham Palace -- built in 1703

#926 Buckingham Palace, the sovereign's official residence in London.

as a home for the Duke of Buckingham, it was first used as a royal residence by George III who bought it as Buckingham House in 1762. George IV had the famous architect John Nash alter it, but he and his successor, William IV, both died before the work was done. The first monarch to occupy the building as Buckingham Palace was Queen Victoria*. It was she who added the present front which encloses the large forecourt. This front faces The Mall and the Victoria Memorial. Above the forecourt entrance is the famous balcony where the royal family appears on special occasions. [CW 14/MMA 2]

927 buckshee -- from the Hindu bakhsis (alms), and used in Britain to mean a gratuity or windfall; free or freely acquired [HHC 11]

928 Budge, Mrs. Hamilton -- owner of the rooming house, Fairview, in Leahampton* where Miss Climpson* stays while doing the investigative work PW needs to have done there [UD 4]

929 budget -- an obsolete word, now only dialectical, for a leather wallet or note case, etc. [FRH 13]

930 Buff Orpington -- see Orpington [BH 15]

931 buffets -- leather coverings fitted over the striking ends of the clappers to produce a muted to dulled tone from the bell [NT 3]

932 Buffs -- the official title of the unit was The Buffs (1st East Kent) Regiment, originally the 3rd Foot, raised about 1660. The title comes from the color of the facings on cuffs, collars, etc., now only worn with mess kit (dress uniform). It provided sixteen batallions during WW I. At the outset, the 1st (regular) battalion was a part of the 16th Infantry Brigade, 6th Division in the 3rd Corps, BEF, and saw active service from September, 1914. Robert Duckworthy* was a member of the Regiment. [im]

933 buhl -- or boulle, a cabinetmaker's term for inlaid decoration of tortoiseshell, yellow and white metal, ivory, etc. [SP 18]

934 Bulfinch, Mr. -- husband of Grace Bulfinch*. He is a proponent of the "don't get involved" school of thought in civic matters. Fortunately for HV and PW, Grace is not. [SP 10]

935 Bulfinch, Mrs. Grace Montague -- barmaid at the Nine Rings Pub* on Gray's Inn Rd.* prior to her marriage to Mr. Bulfinch*. It was she who observed Philip Boyes* consume a white powder and who accounted for the missing ten minutes after he left HV's apartment. [SP 10]

936 bulge -- in one of its senses it means to have an advantage over someone. If Lord St. George* should die, PW would become heir to the estate and titles, something he does not want. [GN 8]

937 bull -- or bullseye, the center of the target, the exact thing [MMA 11]

938 bull -- a stock market expression applied to those times when prices are on the rise, probably from the idea of bulling or forcing activity; boldness [WB 5]

939 The Bull -- a hostelry in Brough* where PW stopped in his search for Hugh Farren*. DLS probably noted the place as she and her husband journeyed from London or Witham to Galloway*. [FRH 20]

940 Bull & Dog -- possibly a real pub, but under the circumstances, probably fictitious [MMA 16]

941 bull terrier -- a short-haired terrier originated in England by crossing terriers with bulldogs [CW 4]

942 bullocks -- young and/or castrated bulls [NT 7]

943 bulls of Basan -- see bulls of Bashan [BH 14]

944 bulls of Bashan -- an interesting allusion to several references in the Old Testament, especially to Psalm 22:11-14. The psalm is a vivid picture of a crucifixion and opens with the famous line found later in Matthew 27:46, "My God, my God, why hast thou forsaken me?" The cattle of Bashan, especially the bulls, are always mentioned as being robust and large. Basan or Bashan was a kingdom beyond the Jordan River. It and its king, Og, were conquered by the Israelites under Moses (Numbers 21:33). [MMA 7]

945 Bulteel's, Mr. -- the "best" stationery shop in Windle* [SP 16]

946 Bultridge, Mr. -- headmaster of the preparatory school attended by the Viscount St. George* [dh]

947 bum-sucking -- a particularly vulgar expression referring to the posterior. It implies a noxious effort to curry favor. [BH 15]

948 bumpers -- see cricket [MMA 18]

949 bumping races -- a type of English university boat race for narrow waterways. A boat "bumps" another from behind and they exchange places for the next race. [GN 13]

950 Bunbury's Breakfast Bran -- a cereal product created by DLS for use in MMA [MMA 4]

951 Bunbury's Whole Meal Flour -- a product created by DLS for use in MMA [MMA 3]

952 bung-full -- a bung is the filling hole on the side of a barrel; hence, to be "bung-full" is to be as full as is possible, full to the point of overflowing. [SP 22]

953 Bungo -- a codes and ciphers expert and friend of PW's who is attached to the Foreign Office* in some sort of espionage work. The name is a nickname. [HHC 26]

954 bunk [do a] -- slang for "to make an escape" [GN 10/BH 6]

955 Bunn and Fishett -- the name of a fictitious safemaking firm. The name derives from three real firms: English lockmakers Chubb, still in business, and French safe and fire cabinetmakers Fichet and Bauche, now in business as Fichet-Bauche for the English sales. [ab]

956 Bunnett in F -- Edward Bunnett's (d. 1923) Magnificat and Nunc Dimittis in F (1867), a popular staple for small 19th C. choirs, rural or otherwise [BH 5]

957 Bunsen burner -- a device for the burning of propane or other fuel gases in a laboratory. It consists of a tube supported vertically with an air draft regulator at the base of the tube just below the point where the gas feed line is attached. Its value is that it supplies a very hot, clean, odorless blue flame. [BC 17]

958 Bunt, Sir Roger -- he is a "coster* millionaire" caterer who prefers a beer and pipe. He won £200,000 in a Sunday Shriek* contest. He comes to know PW through their membership in the Egotists' Club*. [cf]

959 Bunter, Mervyn [Sergeant, WW I] -- PW's uncommonly capable man. His accomplishment include cooking, running a household, photography, a knowledge of wines, and so sufficient an understanding of bibliophilia that PW sometimes sends him to auctions in his stead. He makes superb coffee, is almost absolutely unflappable, and is "seagreen incorruptible"*. When PW tells him about the body in Mr. Thipps' tub, Bunter responds, "Indeed, my lord? That's very gratifying", but when he learns that Mrs. Ruddle* had dusted the Cockburn port so lovingly carried to Talboys*, he explodes in anger. It is unlikely that PW could have a more enthusiastic or capable "Watson".

Bunter was PW's sergeant in WW I, but does not join PW as valet until January of 1919. He actively assumes supervision of PW's convalescence from shell shock after the war, and signs of his affection for PW show in several of the stories. PW's affection for Bunter is shown most strongly in BH.

We learn of some of Bunter's talents in NT when it is disclosed that he does music-hall* imitations, and his toast to the bride and groom in BH is a masterpiece.

Before the War, Bunter had been a footman in the home of Sir John Sanderton*.

Bunter appears in about half of the short stories and in all of the novels, but his role is quite small in in UD, MMA, and GN. [WB 1 and passim]

960 Bunter, Mrs. -- Bunter's mother who lives near Maidstone in Kent. In CW she is mentioned as being 75 years of age, but in BH she is given as being in her 80's; precisely, she would be 87. Bunter writes to her regularly, and she seems to follow her son's adventures with alert pride. [CW 4/BH P]

961 Bunthorne -- a WW I comrade of PW who is not futher identified [bc]

962 Bunyan, John -- English Puritan

#959 Glyn Houston as Bunter in the BBC production of CW. BBC copyright photograph.

writer (1628-88), he was the son of a tinsmith and was a tinsmith himself. He wrote many religious works, the most famous being Pilgrim's Progress*. [bc]

963 Buol's -- a cafe frequented by Oxford undergraduates which no longer exists [GN 14]

964 Burberry -- commonly known as a trench coat, it was first manufactured in 1856 by Thomas Burberry. The name Burberry is first reputed to have been used by Edward VII. The company called them raincoats. The term trench coat came about as a result of WW I and their extensive use as part of the equipment for the military. [CW 3/UD 11/FRH 7/MMA 4]

965 Burd Ellen -- the reference is to a Scottish legend that forms the basis of several ballads. A sister of Childe Roland (Rowland) is rescued by him from captivity by faeries in a castle in Elfland with help from Merlin. A burd is a young maiden, and a childe is a young man or a knight in training. Maria Morano* is Burd Ellen to PW's Childe Roland. The assumption on Armstrong's* part is that PW will rescue Miss Morano in an equally successful manner. [cf]

966 Burdock, Aldine -- the son of Squire Burdock* who was killed in WW I [bc]

967 Burdock, Diana -- Martin Burdock's* pretty, young wife [bc]

968 Burdock, Haviland -- Squire Burdock's* youngest son. He had had words with Tom Frobisher-Pym* which had led to hard feelings between them, and his greed had led to some unprincipled and sacreligious behavior, just as his father apparently knew it would. [bc]

969 Burdock, Martin -- son of Squire Burdock* and estranged from his father at the opening of the story. It appears that the squire knew his sons well when he wrote his will, playing on their greed for one grand post mortem debacle. [bc]

970 Burdock, Simon [Squire] -- a sour character who seemed to dislike his entire family. Following his death, his corpse wanders all over the parish and his will has made it into the "bone of contention" of the title. [bc]

971 Burdock, Winnie -- Haviland Burdock's* gambling wife [bc]

972 Burglars in Bucks -- a not very satisfying nonmurder novel by G. D. H. and M. I. Cole*. Among their better works are The Murder at Crome House and Death in the Quarry for novels, and a short story collection entitles Superintendent Wilson's Holiday. [FRH 27]

973 burgle -- burglar, a proper word, came first, but the verb "to burgle" is a back-formation developed for its comic effect as much as for any other reason [MMA 6]

974 burgundy, sealing up that bottle of -- a reference to the Bravo* case [SP 22]

975 Burial Service -- the service for the Burial of the Dead as found in The Book of Common Prayer [NT 5]

976 buried in Munster -- Cuthbert Conyers'* clue to the location of his buried treasure. In the story there are three Munsters to consider: Münster in Germany, Munster in Ireland, and Sebastian Munster*, author of the Cosmographia Universalis. The actual location of the treasure is only obliquely related to one of the three. [dh]

977 Burke -- the taxi driver who took Philip Boyes* from Guilford St.* to Woburn Sq.*, the site of Norman Urquhart's home [SP 1]

978 Burke, Edmund -- one of England's great orators and Members of Parliament (1729-97). His speeches "On American Taxation" and "On Conciliation with the Colonies", with those delivered during the impeachment of Warren Hastings, are still considered great models of rhetorical excellence. [UD 12]

979 Burke and Hare -- William Burke and William Hare were the famous Edinburgh murderers and grave robbers (resurrectionists) who sold bodies to medical schools. The verb "to burke" is to quiet something, to hush it up, frequently by smothering, a favorite tactic of Mr. Burke's when graves to be

robbed were scarce or when the practice became too dangerous. In their later career they abandoned grave robbing all together in favor of the less strenuous process of murder by suffocation. In the end their greed caught up with them and Burke was hanged on January 28, 1829. Hare turned King's evidence and disappeared after his release. Burke was flayed after his death, and the hide was tanned for sale by enterprising entrepreneurs in one-inch squares. One suspects that he would have approved. [UD 8]

980 burking -- suppressing information as above. Burke had become so expert at it that he gave his name to the process. [GN 23]

981 Burleigh Bldg. [House] -- one of the original buildings at Shrewsbury College* and named for Sir William Cecil, Lord Burleigh*, Lord Treasurer for Queen Elizabeth I and, for a time, her chief minister. In the novel, the building has entered a new phase of existence as a dormitory for students. [GN 1]

982 Burleigh, Lord [of] -- William Cecil, Lord Burleigh or Burghley (1520-98). Lord Treasurer and chief minister to Queen Elizabeth I, he enjoyed a long career of service to the Tudor monarchs. St. George's* allusion is to R. B. Sheridan's (1751-1816) comedy, The Critic, which includes a scene with Burleigh and others of Elizabeth's advisers just before the arrival of the Spanish Armada. Much of his job in that scene is to pace and nod his head as if involved with the cares of his duties. See also Lord of Burleigh. [GN 21/BH P]

983 Burlington Arcade -- built in 1819 as an enclosed shopping arcade, it still serves that function. Connecting Piccadilly* with Burlington Gardens, it is still famous for its collection of boutiques and shops with a myriad of delightful and tasteful items to purchase. The beadle* still locks the gates at either end on nights and weekends. [HHC 4/BH P]

984 Burmese idols -- Buddhism being the religion of Burma, these idols would be representations of the Buddha [GN 19]

985 burn[s] -- a Scottish term for a small stream or brook. A "wee" burn would be an especially small one. [ss/FRH 2]

986 Burne-Jones -- Sir Edward Coley Burne-Jones (1833-98), a prominent painter of the Romantic school and a friend of the Rossetti's and William Morris*, both of whom were a part of the famous pre-Raphaelite school*. One of Burne-Jones's more famous works is a painting of King Cophetua*. He is also known for his stained glass and other decorative work. [FRH 6]

987 burnt his [her] boats -- a proverbial expression in the same vein as "burning his bridges", the idea being that one has advanced without leaving any means of retreat if one is needed [CW 16/HHC 32]

988 Burrow Head -- the tip of the Machars Peninsula that separates Wigtown Bay* from Luce Bay [FRH 19]

989 Burrows, Miss -- librarian and a don* at Shrewsbury College [GN 5]

990 Burt, Alfred -- the young police officer to whom PW unwinds after the birth of his first son, Bredon, and for whom PW helps solve the problem in "Haunted Policeman" [hp]

991 Burton, Robert -- the English scholar (1577-1640) of Brasenose* and Christ Church* colleges, cleric, and author of The Anatomy of Melancholy*, a respository for his life's learning as he interpreted it [GN 2]

992 Bury Fen -- apparently fictitious and intended to be in keeping with the nature of the locality [NT 18]

993 'bus -- either an abbreviated form of omnibus, a public passenger carrier, or slang for a car or motorcycle [BC 9/CW 10/FRH 3/HHC 19]

994 'busman's holiday -- doing on one's vacation what is usually done as an occupation, thereby negating the intent of the vacation [WB 6]

995 "A busman's honeymoon." -- HV starts a chain of suggestions that instantly includes Supt. Kirk* and PW. The allusion is to Lord Byron's* long poem, Childe Harold's Pilgrimage, published between 1812 and 1818. The passage in question is:

"He heard it but he heeded not--
his eyes
Were with his heart, and that was far
away;
He reck'd not of the life he lost nor
prize
But where his rude hut by the Danube
lay,
There were his young barbarians all
at play
There was their Dacian mother--he,
their sire,
Butcher'd to make a Roman holiday."
(CXLI) The idea proceeds from Roman holiday to busman's holiday to busman's honeymoon, a natural progression given HV's love of word-play. [BH 7]

996 bust-up -- a fight or rough fracas [MMA 2]

997 "Busy old fool, unruly sun . . ." -- PW quotes from John Donne's poem, "The Sun Rising", line one, the opening of one of Donne's most metaphysical love poems. It continues:
"Why dost thou thus,
Through windows, and through curtains
call on us?
Must to thy motions lovers seasons
run? [BH 4]

998 but and ben -- a but is a kitchen or living quarters of a two-room cottage. A ben is the inner room or parlor of such a cottage. Both terms are Scottish dialect. [FRH 3]

999 "But do consider what an excellent thing sleep is . . ." -- the quotation is from Thomas Dekker's* The Guls Hornebooke (1609), a satirical and ironical attack on the manners of the fops of his day through a series of instructions on how to be obvious in public through obnoxious behavior. [GN 15]

1000 "But for the Bride-bed . . ." -- from Michael Drayton's* The Muses' Elizium, "The Eighth Nimphall" of 1630. [BH 2]

1001 "But how I caught it . . ." -- a part of the opening speech of Shakespeare's Merchant of Venice*, I, i, 3-5. The speaker is Antonio. The first two lines are:
"In sooth, I know not why I am so
sad.
It wearies me, you say it wearies
you;" [UD 1]

1002 "But, however entrancing it is to wander unchecked . . ." -- see The Wallet of Kai-Lung [SP 4/BH 7]

1003 but it isn't the lunatic, the lover or the poet, is it? -- see the lunatic, the lover or the poet . . . . . [BH P]

1004 "But man walks in a vain shadow" -- the reference is to Psalm 39:7 as it appears in The Book of Common Prayer. It is verse seven in the Coverdale Psalter and is part of the Matins service for the eighth day of the month if that day is not a Sunday or a feast day which have special readings that supercede the regular ones. [CW 11]

1005 "But what to me, my love . . ." -- the words are apparently PW's as he waxes eloquently apprehensive [BH 3]

1006 Buthie, Uncle -- a nickname that Freddy Arbuthnot* applies to himself. It is meant as a sarcastic reference to some agony column writer. [SP 12]

1007 Butler, Samuel -- (1612-80), author of Hudibras*. He enjoyed the favor of Charles II in the form of awards and pensions, but appears to have died a pauper. His style is most distinctive and suits his satirical ends admirably. [UD 5]

1008 buttery -- a room at a college where students may buy food, etc., and have it charged to their accounts at the college. Such a room is usually connected to or is near to the pantry. [GN 1]

1009 buttinskis -- a deliberate attempt to sound comically Russian, but the origin of the word is unknown. It refers to one who butts in, a nosey person. [MMA 4]

1010 buttle -- a verb created to explain what it is that a butler does: he buttles. The original intent may have been humorous, but it is a sometimes useful verb that summarizes neatly all of the duties of a butler even if it does so in a vague manner. [WB 9]

1011 buttresses [flying] -- exterior supports on large Gothic buildings that look like huge half-arches. They

help carry the weight of the roof and walls, thus leaving the interior of the building less cluttered and more spacious. The use of flying buttresses also allowed the great height that is typical of such buildings. [NT 2]

1012 bwoan -- Yorkshire dialect for bone [CW 12]

1013 "By the pricking of my thumbs, Something wicked this way comes. -- the line is not evil as given. The line is delivered by the second witch in Macbeth, IV, i, 44-5, just prior to Macbeth's entry when he is shown the apparitions which outline his eventual fate. [UD 2]

1014 by a long chalk -- see long chalk [im/UD 3/BC 3]

1015 byes -- see cricket [MMA 18]

1016 Byron -- George Gordon, Lord Byron, 6th Baron Byron (1788-1824), the great English Romantic poet whose beautiful poetry was often criticized for offending contemporary morality. His poetry was thought tame, however, when compared with his personal life. His often wild behavior--he kept a bear while at Cambridge to circumvent the University's rule against keeping a dog--eventually led him to brand English society as hypocritical and he left the country in 1816, spending the rest of his life in Europe.

He died in Greece, but was brought home for burial in Nottinghamshire. Among his great works are Childe Harold's Pilgrimage, "She Walks in Beauty", "The Destruction of Sennacherib", "The Prisoner of Chillon", and the earthy and sarcastic Don Juan. [MMA 19/BH 1]

1017 Byronic [blighter] -- a reference to Lord Byron's* extravagant good looks or to his equally extravagant and scandalous love affairs when the "blighter" is appended. If behavior is intended obviously, then the "blighter" is sometimes omitted. [CW 5/GN 8]

(C)

1018 C. C. S. -- Casualty Clearing Station, WW I's advance hospitals in the Corps area able to do emergency surgery and patching up prior to evacuation to general hospitals in the rear echelons. British troops had to be shipped home only for convalescence. Robert Duckworthy* was treated at one near Ytres* in late 1917. [im]

1019 C. I. D. -- the Criminal Investigation Department. It is normally thought of in connection with Scotland Yard*, but any police force may have one. [ae/NT 10]

1020 C____y -- an unidentifiable village along the Marne River in France [NT 8]

1021 cabala -- or kabbalah and qabbalah, the oral tradition of the Jews. The word derives from the Hebrew word for "traditions", and was employed during the Middle Ages to refer to the World of Souls. The cabalists, or rabbis, who guarded the cabala were thought to have some special secret or magical powers. [im]

1022 cabalistic -- see cabala [CW 13]

1023 cabinet photo -- a photograph somewhat larger than a visiting card, on similar to a wallet-sized photo of today. The name derives from the special cases or "cabinets", built to store and display such photos. [SP 17]

1024 cadaveric lividity, rigidity -- the color and stiffness state of a corpse. Lividity refers especially to discoloration from bruises. [WB 2]

1025 cabriolet -- either a light, two-wheeled carriage with a folding hood or rain shelter, or a convertible coupe automobile [HHC 25]

1026 cadet -- a younger brother [WB 9]

1027 Caesar's sacrifice -- the reference is to Julius Caesar, II, ii, 38-43, especially to 42-43:

"Caesar should be a beast without a heart,
If he should stay at home to-day for fear."

The scene is the one where a sacrifice has been done from which to foretell

the future and the animal killed was found to have no heart. Shakespeare always knew the precise moment to include a lurid touch. [GN 4]

1028 Caesar's wife -- not a reference to Shakespeare, but to Plutarch's Life of Julius Caesar, X, 6, where it is written that, "Caesar's wife must be above suspicion." When Pompeia, Caesar's second wife, became linked in name only with Clodius, Caesar divorced her. He did not believe her guilty, but felt that his wife must not even come under suspicion. [SP 21]

1029 Caesarian operation -- PW's jest in response to Mr. Venables'* concerns over the confusion attendant upon the financial relationships between the government and the Church of England. The joke rests upon the fact that a separation is in order and that the Caesar of "Render unto" is a title derived from Julius Caesar whose name has come to identify the Caesarian or surgical removal of the fetus from the womb, a somewhat different but analogous sort of separation. [NT 9]

1030 Caesars -- see fourteen-fold sneer of the Caesars [GN 12/BH 19]

1031 café au lait -- a half and half mixture of coffee and milk. The milk is sometimes scalded and the brew is usually very sweet. [CW 1/BC 13]

1032 café-cognac -- coffee with cognac brandy added, an excellent evening relaxer [CW 5]

1033 cage -- the openwork metal box used to convey passengers in older elevators before the safety regulations required an enclosed conveyance which is now called a car [MMA 4]

1034 Cairnderry -- a collection of a few cottages on the A714 route about three miles northwest of Bargrennan* [FRH 2]

1035 Cairnsmuir -- or Cairnsmuir of Fleet, a 2331 ft. mountain about ten miles North of Creetown* made famous by John Buchan in his adventure novel The Thirty-nine Steps [FRH 2]

1036 Caius College -- one of the several colleges which comprise Cambridge University. The full name is Gonville and Caius (pronounced as keys) College, the names referring to Edmund Gonville who founded the college in 1348, and to Dr. John Caius who expanded the endowment in 1557. The college is at the junction of Trinity Lane and King's Parade in Cambridge. [NT 2]

1037 Calais -- a major Channel port in northern France near the border with Belgium on the English Channel. The cross-Channel ferries to Dover depart from there. [ae]

1038 calamine lotion -- a mixture of zinc and ferric oxides used as a lotion to treat skin irritations such as poison ivy, insect bites, etc. [HHC 24]

1039 Calendar -- the record of graduates, the colleges, degrees, honors, and other information as kept at Oxford by the university and by the separate registrars [GN 14]

1040 California Poppy -- a cologne of the cheaper dime-store variety [UD 20]

1041 Caligari, Dr. -- the 1919 German expressionist horror film written and directed by Robert Wiene. The full title is The Cabinet of Dr. Caligari, and the film starred Werner Kraus as the mad physician. It is considered by some to be the first "art" film. Robert Duckworthy* mentions it. [im]

1042 call her in the middle -- see 704 (an entry, not an item number) [NT 1]

1043 calling clubs -- see bridge [fr]

1044 Cally Lodge -- a place about a mile southwest of Gatehouse*, now enclosed in park lands. Named for Cally House, it is a smaller place for sheltering hunting parties in the hills. Cally House is now an excellent hotel. [FRH 4]

1045 calomel -- mercurous chloride used as a purgative or as a fungicide. The difference between three and nine grains is significant, two and a half grains being the usual dosage as a purgative. The nine grains dose would be fatal in someone already weak or ill and would at least cause great discomfort in anyone else. [UD 5]

1046 Cambrai -- a town in France almost due South of Lille about 50 miles, and about 25 miles from the Bel-

gian border. Robert Duckworthy* fought there in WW I. [im]

1047 Cambridge -- a university city founded in the 12th C. on a site first settled by the Romans. The University there is a collection of colleges, the eldest of which is Peterhouse (1281). Also found there are Queens', Trinity (the largest), Magdalene, King's, and Christ's colleges among others. Langley* is identified as a young Cambridge ethnologist, but it is not mentioned with which college he is affiliated. Sir Julian Freke* is a graduate of Caius College*. [ie/WB 8/CW 15/FRH 5/HHC 10/GN 11]

1048 Cambridge Circus -- the name for the intersection of Charing Cross Rd. and Shaftesbury Avenue**. It is North and slightly West of Trafalgar Square. [SP 14]

1049 Cambridgeshire -- now a county bounded by Norfolk, Suffolk, Bedfordshire, Northamptonshire, and Lincolnshire. From the geographical references that can be drawn from NT, that novel's action in PW's time was probably in the area of Norfolk and the Isle of Ely**. In the 1970's, a drive to streamline and simplify local governments combined and rearranged many counties. [NT]

1050 cambrioleur -- an Anglicized French word for burglar, thief, or safe-cracker [NT 8]

1051 the camel and the needle's eye -- "It is easier for a camel to go through the eye of a needle, than for a rich man to enter into the kingdom of God." Matthew 19:24. [BH 14]

1052 Camembert -- a cheese first made in the village of Camembert, Normandy, France. It is a creamy, mold-ripened cheese that softens in the middle as it matures. It is a favorite mild accompaniment to fruit after dinner. [WB 5]

1053 Camera -- see Radcliffe Camera [GN 23]

1054 Cameron, Dr. -- the local physician who pronounces Sandy Campbell* dead at the place where his body was discovered. His pronouncements about the cause of death and about the advancement of <u>rigor</u> <u>mortis</u> prove to be accurate. [FRH 2]

1055 camomile -- see not a chameleon [BH P]

1056 Camorra[rist] -- a secret criminal organization or a member of such an organization. It was formed in Naples, Italy, in about 1820. The word now means any such criminal group if in lower-case letters. PW indicates that he does not like detective or police stories which deal with such things. [nf]

1057 campanology -- the art and science of ringing bells in a pleasing and artistically meaningful way as distinguished from simply ringing a bell for some purpose [NT 1]

1058 Campbell, Archie -- Viscount St. George's* bookmaker. In England such men operate openly and legally, the opposite of most places in the U. S. [GN 10]

1059 Campbell, Sandy -- the moderately talented and obnoxiously short-tempered artist who becomes the victim in FRH. Like E. C. Bentley's* Sigsbee Manderson, Campbell is the perfect victim; one is <u>almost</u> forced to regret that his <u>killer is</u> finally apprehended. [FRH 1]

1060 Camperdown, Miss -- a Shrewsbury College* student who, in spite of spending all her time doing everything except studying, manages to earn her B. A. with first class honors [GN 12]

1061 Campostella, Blessed St. James of -- see Blessed St. James of Compostella [ie]

1062 Campshott, Muriel -- a Shrewsbury College* graduate known, unwillingly, to HV [GN 1]

1063 <u>Can the Dead Speak?</u> -- the book <u>Miss Booth*</u> is <u>reading</u> when Miss Climpson* meets her. It was published by the Spiritualist Press*, one of several books published by that company. on that general topic between the World Wars. [SP 16]

1064 Can you tell me, rosy fingered Aurora . . . -- PW has lapsed into typically poetic phrases, apparently of his own creation. Aurora refers to the dawn. [BH 14]

1065 Canary Islands -- formerly known as

the Fortunate Islands, the Canaries are off the northwest coast of Africa and comprise two provinces of Spain. The seven major islands in the chain are Hierro, La Palma, Gomera, Tenerife, Gran Canaria, Fuerteventura, and Lanzarote. [dh]

1066 Cannibal Islands -- probably a reference to the South Pacific, especially the area around Fiji and New Guinea where cannibalism and head hunting were practiced until recent times. [BH 11]

1067 canon -- one of a body of dignitaries attached to a cathedral or collegiate church. The Rev. Mr. Weeks is one*. [bc/MMA 12]

1068 Canon Law -- the law of the church. It is separate and distinct from Civil Law, but there may be overlapping in some areas as with divorce. [GN 17]

1069 canoodling -- the gerund form of the rather unusual verb "to canoodle", a slang term, origins obscure, which means to fondle or caress endearingly or to persuade to do so [UD 2]

1070 can't come home -- a bell cannot return to its "home" position until the proper sequences of changes have been rung that would allow the bell to return home as a natural result of the changes rung [NT 9]

1071 Canterbury, Archbishop of -- the senior archbishop and religious adviser to the Queen who is head of the Church of England in its various forms (Anglican, Episcopalian, etc.). He is Primate of the Church of England and, in that capacity, only he may annoint and crown an English monarch. [WB 9/UD 19/NT 13]

1072 canting -- affected language built on the understanding of some special concept or bit of jargon; in this case, a pun on a religious phrase [NT 4]

1073 cantoris side -- the North side of a church, especially that half of the choir on the North or precentor's* side of the chancel in any church laid out on an East-West axis liturgically speaking. The builders might not be able to put the altar at the East end of the building, but, liturgically, the altar is always at the East end no matter where it is geographically. [NT 4]

1074 Captain Cuttle -- see "When found, make note of." [BH 7]

1075 carat -- a carat is equal to one-twenty-fourth pure gold in an alloy of some sort. One carat is equal to 4.1666% pure gold. Fifteen carat gold, as in Paul Alexis's cigarette case, would be 62.49% pure gold. Twenty-four carat is pure gold, but most jewelry items are in the fourteen to eighteen carat range, twenty-two carat being the highest gold content usually available other than in ingots as there would not be enough alloy material to protect the gold's shape and design. [HHC 4]

1076 carbolic soap -- a particularly strong disinfectant soap used in hospitals, morgues, etc., to help assure thorough cleanliness. The soap is made with phenol, a caustic poison acid present in coal and wood tar. [WB 2]

1077 Carcassonne -- the ancient walled city in the southern part of France's Languedoc region [GN 4]

1078 card of the Last Supper -- a small card with what would probably be a poor reproduction of da Vinci's "The Last Supper" printed on it. The reverse would likely have a Gospel message of some sort, something appropriate to the Eucharist. [UD 22]

1079 card-sharper -- a card cheat or trickster. The term is not used to suggest skill alone, but carries with it the idea of intentional deceit. PW is one as needed, having learned the art from an Army compatriot while serving near Ypres* in WW I. Denis Cathcart* is one as well, but to less noble ends than PW. [pj/CW 18]

1080 Cardinal Wolsey's . . . pet -- it is known that goldfish, a kind of carp, can grow to great size and live long lives, a 400 year old fish is a strain on credulity. The emphasis is on the fact that Wolsey founded Christ Church (then Cardinal) College. It was taken over by Henry VIII and given its present name after Wolsey's fall from the king's favor. [GN 8]

1081 Cardinals -- a type of trout fishing fly and one of the more popular ones. The fly may be tied for either wet or dry use, making it most flexible. It was, along with the March Browns, Royal Coachmen, etc., among the top ten or so flies used by fly fishermen. [FRH 1]

1082 Cardoness Castle -- on the coast road* (A75) just beyond Gatehouse* and before Mossyard*. It would be the remains of one of the ancient Border Keeps*. [FRH 2]

1083 Carency -- a village in Artois, about seven miles North-northwest of Arras. Robert Fentiman* served near there. It would not have been near the front line after the Canadian Corps captured Vimy Ridge in April of 1917. [BC 9]

1084 Carey, Mr. -- of the Red Farm, one of the few locals along the coast road to Wilvercombe* to have telephone service. HV* starts to go there in an effort to get help to deal with the corpse she has found. [HHC 2]

1085 Carfax -- the intersection of Queen, Cornmarket, High, and St. Aldate's Sts. in the old section of Oxford [GN 18]

1086 Carisbrooke, Bishop of -- a distant and fictitious relative of both PW and Mrs. Appledore*. The bishop is described by the latter as "always being taken in by imposters", but one suspects that she doesn't recognize charity when she sees it. Carisbrooke is a small town on the Isle of Wight, but it is not the location of a bishopric, and there is no listing of such a bishop in Crockford's*.

1087 Carlisle -- pronounced as carlile, the city is near the Scottish border and is one of the busier agricultural and industrial centers in the North of England. It was once a Roman camp, Luguvalium, and ruins and sites dating from then as well as from later eras are to be found there. The city is inland, just to the East of Solway Firth, and remains a major railway junction. [FRH 8]

1088 Carlton -- the Carlton Club at 69 St. James's Place between Piccadilly* and Pall Mall. It originated as Arthur's and was founded in 1832 by the Duke of Wellington. [HHC 28/MMA 14]

1089 Carlyle -- Thomas (1795-1881), the great Scottish essayist and historian who is noted especially for his work in translating Goëthe into English and for his history of the French Revolution and of the life of Frederick the Great. _The History of the French Revolution_ was destroyed accidentally while still in manuscript, but Carlyle rewrote the entire thing, much from memory, and published it in 1837. [GN 1/ BH 7]

1090 Carmelite House -- PW goes there to obtain the name of a photographer whose picture (i. e., his work) was being run in the _Evening News_* which is published from Carmelite House. DLS locates it "in Fleet St.*", a catch-all name for the publishing industry in Britain which is located in large part on or near that street. The Carmelite Order once had religious houses in that area, and there are still streets named Carmelite and Whitefriars on the South side of Fleet St. The _Daily Mail_* is still published there and at New Carmelite House as was the _Evening News_ until 1980, when it became the _Evening News and Standard_. Carmelite House is headquarters now for the Rothermere Press Group and is on the Victoria Embankment*. [im]

1091 Carmichael -- one of Dian de Momerie's* former lovers, now deceased [MMA 9]

1092 carminative -- an aid to the expulsion of gas from the lower digestive tract [MMA 12]

1093 Carnaby, Billy -- an actor with whom Mrs. Lefranc* had worked. On his last night he took all his money, threw a party for everyone, and then committed suicide. [HHC 15]

1094 Carola -- Annie Wilson's* younger daughter [GN 11]

1095 Carolus -- the name of a bell at Fenchurch St. Paul* in the late 1600's. The name refers to Charles (_Carolus_ in Latin) II who was restored to the throne in 1660. [NT 4]

1096 carotid -- either of the two large arteries located on each side of the neck [HHC 21]

1097 _carpe diem_ -- Latin for make the

the most of today. The reference is to Horace's*, "carpe diem quam minimum credula postero", or enjoy today and don't trust what tomorrow may bring. The lines appear in his Odes, I, xi, 8. [HHC 13]

1098 Carr, Dr. Edward -- the young physician whose remarkable tale at the beginning of UD starts PW and Parker* off on that adventure. He proves to be a competent physician, but he is somewhat lacking in gratitude. [UD 1]

1099 carriage forward -- the Wimsey's luggage is to be sent on and the costs will be paid by the receiver [BH E1]

1100 Carrick -- the coastline along Wigtown and Fleet** Bays and opposite the Fleet Islands* [FRH 17]

1101 Carrie -- the head or senior scout* at Shrewsbury College* [GN 16]

1102 carrion flesh -- see why they rather choose to have a weight . . . [BH 18]

1103 Carroll, Lewis -- the pseudonym of Charles Lutwidge Dodgson (1832-98) who lectured in mathematics and logic at Oxford from 1855 to 1881. He is most famous for Alice's Adventures in Wonderland and Through the Looking Glass, but his work in mathematics and logid remain popular and in print. The best version of the Alice stories are those illustrated by John Tenniel, and for anyone interested in pursuing them carefully, Martin Gardner's The Annotated Alice is essential. The stories are often passed off as for children only, but they offer a full range of sophisticated, subtle complexities for adults, too. [MMA 4/ BH 13]

1104 Carroll, didn't make themselves too Lewis -- the reference is not to Carroll* himself, but to the nonsense works he wrote and suggests that the costumes themselves were not too overdone [qs]

1105 Carruthers necklace -- see The Society [ab]

1106 carrying figure -- the number remaining to be "carried" over to the next column when adding a column of figures [NT 10]

1107 Carstairs, Joan -- a guest at Sir Charles Deverill's* costume party. Her costume is meant to represent a diabolo*. [qs]

1108 cart [been in the] -- having been in trouble, a reference to the cart formerly used to transport criminals to execution or to expose offenders to public ridicule and embarrassment [MMA 8]

1109 Carter Paterson -- the largest firm of moving/removal agents in England [BH 7]

1110 Cartwright -- a friend of Viscount St. George's* to whom the Viscount owes money [GN 10]

1111 Casabianca -- Joan Carstairs* characterizes James Playfair* as "looking like Casabianca", a reference to Giacomo Casabianca, son of the French flag captain at the Battle of the Nile in 1798, who stood his assigned post even after his father's death and who also died in the line of duty. The boy's heroism is immortalized in Felicia Hemans'* poem, "Casabianca", which begins, "The boy stood on the burning deck". The hyperbole is appreciated in context, but the irony is not. [qs]

1112 cascading thirds of the Queen's Change -- the sound produced when bells are rung in thirds* according to a pattern now known as the Queen's Change, an allusion to the fact that Queen Elizabeth I was making a royal progress past St. Michael's, Cornhill, heard that ring and liked it, so it was named in her honor. A Queen's Change can be rung on any standard number of bells. [NT 1]

1113 Cassandra-like cry -- Cassandra, daughter of King Priam of Troy, was beloved of Apollo, but she refused him, so he rendered his gift of prophecy useless to her by making one and all ignore her prognostications. She prophesied how Troy would fall, but was ignored then, too. [BH 15]

1114 cassock [and bands] -- a long, loosely fitted garment, generally black, except for cardinals or the pope, worn by clerics or lay persons engaged in church work. The bands are

the extension of the collar that hangs down the front of a clerical or academical gown. Depending on the nature of the accoutrements, the bands may or may not be synonymous with the stole. [bc/GN 14]

1115 cast[s] [trout] -- fishing line leaders, the segment of slightly lighter line which joins the hook or fly to the main length of the fishing line [FRH 2/NT 6]

1116 "cast into outer darkness" -- see "many shall come . . ." [SP 13]

1117 cast porcelain fillings -- see porcelain fillings [te]

1118 "cast your bread upon the waters" -- the allusion is to Ecclesiastes 11:1, "Cast thy bread upon the waters: for thou shalt find it after many days." The chapter deals with man's inability to know the will of God. [SP 6]

1119 Castle, the -- see Castle Douglas [FRH 5]

1120 Castle Douglas -- a town to the North and East of Kirkcudbright* and founded in the 18th C. It is an agricultural and cattle-oriented community. Just to the West is Threave Castle, a 14th C. stronghold of one branch of the Douglas clan, hence the name of the town. The castle was rendered useless by the Covenanters, a violently anti-Catholic group of Presbyterians, in 1640. [FRH 3]

1121 Castle Kennedy -- a stop on the rail line from Girvan* to Stranraer* [FRH 5]

1122 The Castle of Otranto -- the Gothic novel by Horace Walpole (1717-97), published in 1764. It is a story of castles, princes, usurped thrones, damsels in distress, ghosts, and a happily-ever-after ending. With Anne Radcliffe's Mysteries of Udolpho (1794), it gave rise to the Gothic mystery subgenre that continues with Jane Eyre, Laura, Rebecca, and others of that type. [FRH 15]

1123 Castramont -- a hamlet about three miles North and West of Gatehouse* and located in a wooded area alongside the Fleet* [FRH 27]

1124 Cat! -- just after his talk with Mrs. Appledore*, PW applies that term to her. It is a distinctly negative one that refers to a woman who says mean things about another woman behind her back. [WB 3]

1125 cat[amaran] -- someone who is seen to be stern, inflexible, troublesome, demanding, backbiting, or condescending, especially a woman. It is a colloquial term in no way related to the boat. [WB 3/NT 6]

1126 Cat and Fiddle -- the pub/inn at Walbeach* where PW and Bunter stop for lunch after having robbed His Majesty's Mails. The place is obviously known to PW as he states that its "port is remarkable and the claret not to be despised". Such is warm praise indeed from PW. [NT 7]

1127 Cat St. -- correctly Catte St., it extends from Parks Rd. to High St. in Oxford [GN 12]

1128 cat laugh -- see make a cat laugh [GN 20/BH 7]

1129 cat's pyjamas -- a slang phrase indicating intense approval or desirability. It is one of many such nonsense phrases common during the 1920's and 30's that involved some part of the animal kingdom and some article of clothing as in caterpillar's boots. There seems to be a connection between the animal and the article of clothing. Cats sleep a great deal, caterpillars have many feet, etc., and other examples of such phrases follow the pattern. [GN 15]

1130 Catalogue of the Ships -- see Homer's catalogue of the ships [ie]

1131 catapult -- a slingshot, not the medieval siege machine. It is probable that the concept of a small, lightweight, handheld weapon antedates the war machine. [MMA 5]

1132 catchpenny -- a device designed to get the money of those too ignorant to know better; an intellectual scam [GN 1]

1133 catechism -- usually used in the religious sense, but, generally, any set of questions put as a test [FRH 8]

1134 caterpillar's boots -- see cat's

pyjamas [MMA 3]

1135 Cathcart, Capt. Denis -- the vain, handsome, and unhappy victim in CW. Engaged to Lady Mary Wimsey*, they do not love each other. He loves Simone Vonderaa* and Mary loves George Goyles*, or at least they think they love those people. Theirs would have been, at best, an alliance of convenience. While Cathcart's death is unfortunate and wasteful, it does serve to prevent a series of events from unfolding as they had been orginally planned, and that proves to be valuable. [CW 1]

1136 Cathcart, Miss Lydia -- Denis Cathcart's maiden aunt into whose care he had been given when left an orphan at age eighteen. As with everyone in England then, Denis could not come of age until he was twenty-one, so Miss Cathcart controlled his finances for that interim. [CW 1]

1137 Cathedral -- in CW the reference is to York Minster* [CW 11]

1138 Cathedral -- Salisbury Cathedral, built ca. 1220, featuring the tallest tower and spire in England (404'), particularly lavish decoration on the West front, and a clock dating from 1386 which may be the oldest clock in the world. It has no dial and chimes the hours. See also Close. [WB 5]

1139 Cathedral Close -- see Close [WB 5]

1140 Catherine-wheel -- a wheel with spikes projecting from the circumference or a popular spinning fireworks piece. The name refers to the legend of the device used to martyr St. Catherine who is said to have been tied to a revolving spiked wheel, flogged, and then beheaded. She supposedly lived in Alexandria, ca. 310, but no reference to her antedates the 10th C. [MMA 18]

1141 Catholic doctrine [sound] -- following the basic teachings of the universal Catholic church, the Anglican, Orthodox, and Roman Communions, as opposed to any sort of nonconformist* or cult approach. Miss Climpson* is suggesting strict adherence to the teachings of the Church of England. [UD 4]

1142 catkins -- the yellow catkins mentioned are the long yellow flowers of the willow tree. Several trees have similar flowers, and children use them to taunt each other, using them as worms. [NT 3]

1143 catspaw, innocent -- one who is used by another as a fool or dupe from the fable of the monkey that used a cat's paw to draw chestnuts from a fire [WB 5/NT 10]

1144 Cattermole, Violet -- one of Shrewsbury College's* students, she is plagued by a series of problems in her personal life which HV helps her straighten out [GN 5]

1145 Cattery [my or The] -- PW's nickname for the organization he supports to hire single women to ferret out those who would bilk, abuse, scandalize, or otherwise defraud other women. The goal is to bring as many of the miscreants to justice as possible. Miss Climpson* supervises its operations and handles some of the more delicate matters for PW. On matters of less importance or in matters of specialization, she or any of the other women employed there may help with aspects of an investigation that PW, Bunter, or Parker could not handle themselves. The group has the superficial appearance of a secretarial service, but its members rarely do any of that sort of work. [SP 5]

1146 Catullus -- Gaius Valerius Catullus (84? B. C. - 54? B. C.), a Roman poet and master of many shorter verse forms. He is noted particularly for the poems in which he celebrated his love for Lesbia who was, in reality, one Clodia, sister of Publius Clodius, an enemy of Cicero. At one point PW is in pursuit of a manuscript version of some of the poet's works for inclusion in his collection of incunabula*. [dh/ss]

1147 Caucasus -- the short mountain range in the northern Middle East that extends from the Black to the Caspian Seas through Russia along the northern borders of Turkey and Iran. [SP 15]

1148 Caudry -- about eight miles East and South of Cambrai* in northern France near the Belgian border. It was

#1135 Anthony Ainley as Denis Cathcart (left) and David Langton as the Duke of Denver in the BBC production of CW. BBC copyright photo.

behind the German lines on the Western Front until late in 1918. Robert Duckworthy* mentions that he saw action there and at Cambrai*. Caudry is also near where PW was, according to his uncle, Paul Delagardie*, "blown up and buried in a shell-hole" in 1918. That experience left PW with "a bad nervous breakdown, lasting, on and off, for two years". (The quotations are from Paul Delagardie's "Biographical Note" in UD.) [GN 17]

1149 caught at cover point -- see cricket [MMA 18]

1150 caught at mid-on -- see cricket [MMA 18]

1151 cautioned the witness -- equivalent to being read one's rights--"You have the right to remain silent", etc.--in the U. S. It is interesting to note that this practice was in force some fifty years before a similar practice was begun in the U. S. [WB 6]

1152 Cave Canem -- Latin for "beware the dog". The reference is to a famous mosaic in the ruins at Pompeii that features a viscious dog and the above inscription. [umw]

1153 Cavendish Square -- a large square at the southern end of Harley St.* and just North of Oxford St.*. It is slightly to the West of Oxford Circus. General Fentiman* meets George Fentiman* there quite by accident on November 10, 1927. [BC 8]

1154 caviar -- the eggs or roe of salmon, lumpfish, sturgeon, or other large fish, cleaned, seasoned, and salted. It is considered a delicacy and is served as an appetizer, the roe of sturgeon from Iran or Russia being considered the finest. Such caviar is exclusively black (some others are red). At one point PW asks his dentist not to use too much oil of cloves so as not to blight the taste of the caviar. Ryland Vaughan* is seen eating some with a pickle fork, an act that speaks volumes about his character. [te/SP 8]

1155 Cawthorne -- a Police Constable working with Insp. Sugg* at the scene of the discovery of the naked corpse in the bathtub [WB 3]

1156 Caxton, William -- (1422?-91) was the first English printer. Apprenticed to a mercer in London, he became engaged in business and diplomacy in the Low Countries and France where he began translating various French romances. He began his printing career in the early 1470's, probably in Cologne, Germany. From 1477 to 1491, he issued nearly eighty books, many of them his own translations from French, at his press in Westminster. He enjoyed the favor of Kings Edward IV, Richard III, and Henry VII. In addition to his work as a printer, his translations helped form 15th C. English prose style. [WB 1/CW 4]

1157 Cay-day-verric Rigeedity -- cadaveric rigidity. The P. C. is having difficulty with the medical terms. See rigor mortis. [FRH 25]

1158 ce blond cadet -- French for, "the blond younger son of the English ducal family" [BH 3]

1159 ce grand homme -- French for, "this great man, this famous man" [WB 11]

1160 "Ce n'est pas rigolo . . ." -- French for, "It's no joke being a gigolo*." [HHC 7]

1161 Cedric -- one of the errand boys at Pym's Publicity* [MMA 6]

1162 cellarman -- the worker at a pub or restaurant who is responsible for the proper care of the bottles and kegs of beer, ale, porter, stout, and wine as are served in such an establishment. Temperature control and proper handling of the kegs and bottles is essential if the flavors are to be maintained. [NT 11]

1163 Cemetery Company -- the organization in charge of the various business aspects of running a cemetery, such as with the sale of plots and the maintenance of the grounds [BC 13]

1164 Cenotaph -- in general, a cenotaph is a tomb or monument erected to a person or persons whose bodies are elsewhere. Specifically, the Cenotaph is the very simple monument in Whitehall*, not far from either Downing St. or the Houses of Parliament, and is a memorial to honor Britain's war dead from WW I to the present. The monument was designed by Sir Edward Lutyens and is inscribed with only three words:

Thenne beganne agayne the bataylle of the one par
te/And of the other Eneas ascryed to theym and
sayd . Lordes why doo ye fyghte/ Ye knowe well
that the couuenaunte ys deuysed and made/ That Tur:
nus and I shall fyghte for you alle/

Thenne beganne agayne the bataylle of the one parte/And of the other Eneas ascryed to theym and sayd. Lordes why doo ye fyghte/ Ye knowe well that the couuenante ys deuysed and made/That Turnus and I shall fyghte for you alle/

FACSIMILE OF PART OF CAXTON'S "ÆNEID" (REDUCED)

With the same passage in modern type.

#1156

THE CENOTAPH AND WHITEHALL.

#1164 The Cenotaph, Whitehall, Westminster, London.

"The Glorious Dead". [BC 1/MMA 19]

1165 Central -- one of the tea shops in Windle* frequented by Miss Climpson* in her search for the nurse/companion to Rosanna Wrayburn* [SP 16]

1166 Central News -- the second oldest news agency in England, established in 1863 to deal with national news. Reuters* had been well established for foreign news by 1860. In 1870, Reuters moved into the national news field, so Central News began covering foreign news in 1871. They remain in competition, and both are based in London. [CW 15]

1167 Central Police Station -- in Glasgow it is on Turnbull St. in the southeast section of the central city, not far from Glasgow Green [FRH 10]

1168 Central Station -- a British Rail station and a Merseyrail subway stop about a half mile South of the Lime St. station, the present main rail terminus for Liverpool. It originally served Liverpool's rail patrons who needed to travel to the South and East of the city. [UD 11]

1169 Cerberus -- the multiheaded dog of Greek mythology, the watchdog of Hades. PW uses the term to describe one of Insp. Sugg's* subordinates, but uses the term elsewhere to refer to anyone in an official position. [WB 3/UD 15]

1170 ceremonial of potter -- as in "to potter or putter about"; fussing in small, seemingly meaningless stages, to dawdle [BH 4]

1171 "Certainly there is no happiness . . ." -- from _Religio Medici_*. See "'strange and _mystical_' _transmigration of silk worms_". [GN 15]

1172 Certifying Surgeon -- under the various Factory and Workshops Acts of this century, this surgeon, now called a Medical Officer of Health, would be concerned with health and safety in places of employment. He is, generally speaking, another type of public health official. [UD 3]

1173 Certorari and Return -- the Certiorari is Latin (literally to be certified) for a writ used to call up the records of a lower court. The Return is the submission of that writ to the judge or other person in authority who demanded it. [CW 14]

1174 cervical vertebrae -- the backbone segments of the neck between the shoulders and the base of the skull [WB 6]

1175 _"C'est bien, embrasse moi . . ."_ -- French for, "Very well, kiss me . . . be careful! you're mussing my hair . . . Come now, be serious." [BH 19]

1176 _"C'est cela que cherche monsieur?"_ -- French for, "Is this what you've been looking for, sir?" [CW 16]

1177 _c'est inoui_ -- French for, "that's incredible (shocking, outrageous)" [HHC 15]

1178 _"C'est parfait . . ."_ -- French for, "That's perfect--all my congratulations, my lord . . .". [aq]

1179 _"C'est un homme précieux."_ -- French for, "He is an invaluable man." [WB 11]

1180 _"C'est un morceau . . ."_ -- French for, "That's a very impressive piece (i. e. poem)." [NT 8]

1181 _"c'est un saint . . ."_ -- French for, "he is a saint who performs miracles! We pray for him, Natasha and I, every day. Don't we, dear?" [WB 11]

1182 _"C'est Venus . . ."_ -- French for, "It is the goddess Venus herself fastened on her prey." The line is from Racine's (1639-99) play, _Phèdre_, I, iii. [CW 18]

1183 _"C'est vrai."_ -- French for, "That's true." [NT 8]

1184 _cette franchise_ -- French for, "this frankness (candor)". [BH 19]

1185 _"Cette femme te sera . . . ."_ -- Uncle Paul Delagardie's* French for, "This woman will be a staff for you to lean upon. Until now she has known only the pain of love; you will teach her its delights. She will find in you unexpected refinements that she will know how to appreciate. But most important, my friend, she is not weak-headed. She is not a feather-brained or silly young woman, she has a healthy intelligence and she likes to solve

problems in her head. You do not need to be submissive, she will not be grateful for it (will be annoyed with it). Even less, do not cajole her, she might change her mind. She needs to be convinced; I am persuaded that she will show herself to be magnanimous. Make an effort to restrain the giddiness of a fiery heart--or at least reserve it for moments of conjugal intimacy where it is not out of place and might serve a useful purpose. In all other circumstances, make use of that ability to reason which you do not entirely lack. At your ages it is necessary to be precise; one may no longer settle a situation by giving up the reins of restraint or by screaming. Be firm, in order to inspire the respect of your wife; by allowing her her own thoughts, you will be providing her with the best means of not becoming bored." [BH 19]

1186 Ch. de Fer de L'Ouest -- Chemin de Fer . . . . The literal translation from the French is, "The Iron Road of the West", but it is actually the name of a famous prenationalization railway. PW boards one of its trains in a rather unorthodox manner. See Paris-Evreux express. [mt]

1187 chablis -- any of the various white wines of the Burgundy region of France. They tend to be quite dry. [ae]

1188 Chablis Moutonne -- the seventh ranked of the fourteen major chablis* vineyards. A tiny vineyard of slightly more than three acres, it is located just North of the village of Chablis. It would take an extremely well-educated palate to recognize La Moutonne for what it is instead of picking it as one of the more famous Chablis varieties. Chablis vineyards are located South and East of Paris in the vicinity of Auxerre. [mt/UD 1]

1189 chair of state -- the throne from which the monarch reads the speech outlining the government's proposals for the session of Parliament being opened. It reverts to chair of state when the Lord High Steward* occupies it for some reason as the monarch's official representative. [CW 14]

1190 chaise -- a single-horse carriage for one or two people and fitted with a sunshade roof [BH 12]

1191 chalk, by a long -- see long chalk [im/UD 3/BC 3]

1192 Challoner, Dick -- also known as "Tin Tummy" in reference to WW I wounds, he is a member of the Bellona Club* [BC 2]

1193 Challoner, Mr. -- Harriet Vane's literary agent, the person who arranges contracts with publishers, etc., all for a fee. That she has need of such services indicates her level of success as relatively few writers have need of or can afford an agent. [SP 2]

1194 Chambers' Dictionary -- like Chambers' Encyclopedia, a publication of the firm of W. and R. Chambers, Edinburgh. Both publications are regularly updated and reissued. [HHC 22]

1195 Chamberlain and Levine -- Clarence D. Chamberlain and Charles A. Levine flew the Atlantic on June 4, 1927, and were feted in England and on the Continent, especially in Germany, where they landed. Their goal had been Berlin, but they landed 108 miles away in Eiselben. Their aircraft was a Bellanca monoplane, the "Columbia". [UD 19]

1196 Chamberlain, Joseph -- one of England's greatest political leaders of the early 20th C. (1836-1914). He was a liberal who supported Conservative governments, was against home rule for Ireland, but had an enlightened colonial policy for West Africa. He was the main influence behind the Workmen's Compensation Act of 1897. The reference to a rare orchid comes from his habit of wearing one regularly, giving him something of a dandified appearance. His two famous sons were Austen and Neville Chamberlain. [WB 1]

1197 Chambers, Mrs. Helen -- a new resident in Kirkcudbright* at the time of Sandy Campbell's* death [FRH 8]

1198 Chambers, Sir William -- an English architect (1726-96) who practiced a refined classical style but who also designed various structures in an Oriental rococo manner. He designed several Oriental buildings for Kew Gardens*, among them a Chinese pagoda which may still be seen. He also designed the gold Royal State Coach which

is still used for coronations. Duke's Denver* has one of his pagodas as well. [dh/BH E2]

1199 Chambertin -- a classic Grand Cru burgundy, meaty and considered by many to be the best Burgundy in its good years. It is an excellent choice to accompany the perdrix aux choux* PW enjoys with guests. [BC 11]

1200 chameleon -- see "not a chameleon . . ." [BH P]

1201 chamois leather -- an especially soft leather from the hide of the chamois (Rupicapra rupicapra) or of sheep. It is ideal for drying or wiping down easily marred surfaces such as those on automobiles. Synthetic ones are used mostly today although the real thing is still available. [NT 2]

1202 champagne -- the champagne country is an area straddling the River Marne just to the East of Paris and is noted for producing some of the very best sparkling wines that the world has to offer. The market city of Epernay is in the center of the district. [CW 15]

1203 Champs-Elysées -- the major avenue in Paris extending from the Arc du Triomphe to the Place de la Concorde [BH 14]

1204 chancel -- that part of the church including the choir and sanctuary. As older churches tend to be laid out on an East-West axis for liturgical reasons, the chancel will be at the eastern end of the church. It is often raised above the level of the nave and its steps make a convenient platform from which the clergyman can conduct weddings and other services. [NT 1/ BH P]

1205 Chancellor -- the position at Oxford is now largely ceremonial, filled by some eminent public figure who is elected to the post for life [GN 1]

1206 Chancellor, Lord -- originally a royal chaplain on his way to becoming a bishop, but, following the appointment of Sir Thomas More in 1529, laymen have usually held the job, invariably after 1625. The Lord Chancellor presides over the House of Lords*, is head of the English judiciary, and must, therefore, be a lawyer. The job is an appointment and is, therefore, related to the party in power, but the appointment cannot be a purely political one. [dh/aq/CW 6/ BH 7]

1207 chancery -- a slang term describing the position of a head when held under an adversary's arm to be beaten. The position prevents an adequate defense. The term derives from the tight control with which the former Courts of Chancery held any property. Miss Quick* demonstrates such a hold to Bredon Wimsey*, much to his chagrin. [t]

1208 Chancery Lane -- a major North-South street in Holborn*. The buildings of Staple Inn* and the Public Record Office are on its East side, Lincoln's Inn is on the West. It joins the Strand* on the South where that street joins Fleet St.*, and joins High Holborn on its northern end. It gets its name from a grant of land from Henry III to his Lord Chancellor*, the Bishop of Chichester, in 1227. [SP 14]

1209 Chancery Lane Station -- the subway (underground) station at the corner of High Holborn and Gray's Inn Rd.* opposite the junction with Chancery Lane* [SP 20]

1210 'Change -- see Stock Exchange [WB 4]

1211 change-ringing -- the art and science of ringing a set (peal*) of swinging bells to produce changes* or rhythmic permutations in the striking order of the bells, thus creating a melodic and mathematical series of sounds--the sequence of bells rung is determined mathematically so as to produce a melodic effect when rung in that sequence [NT 1]

1212 changelings [legerdemain of] -- a baby exchanged for another at infancy. The references are to Sir Thomas Browne's Religio Medici*. See "'strange and mystical' transmigration of silk worms . . .". [GN 15]

1213 changes -- the different orders in which a set or peal of bells may be rung. With three bells six changes are possible if the first is repeated

Public Record Office, Chancery Lane.

#1208 Chancery Lane and the Public Record Office

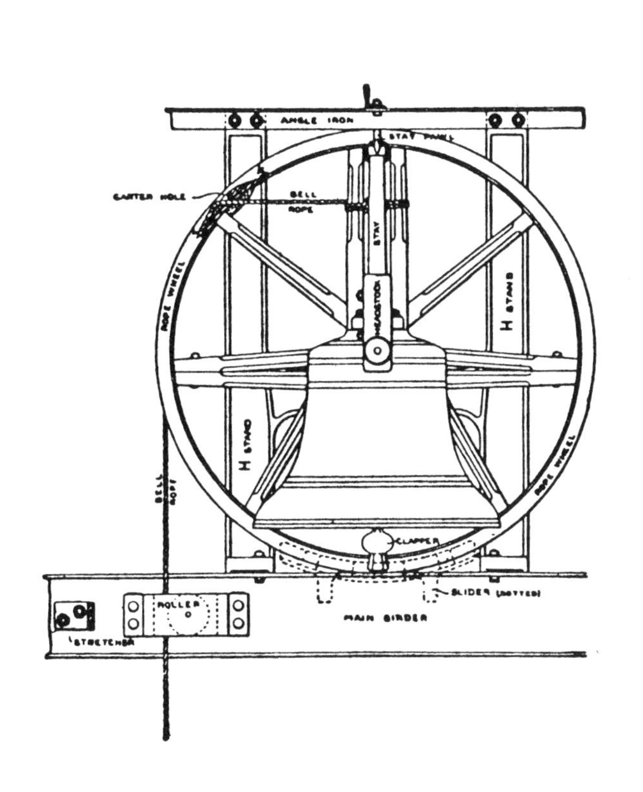

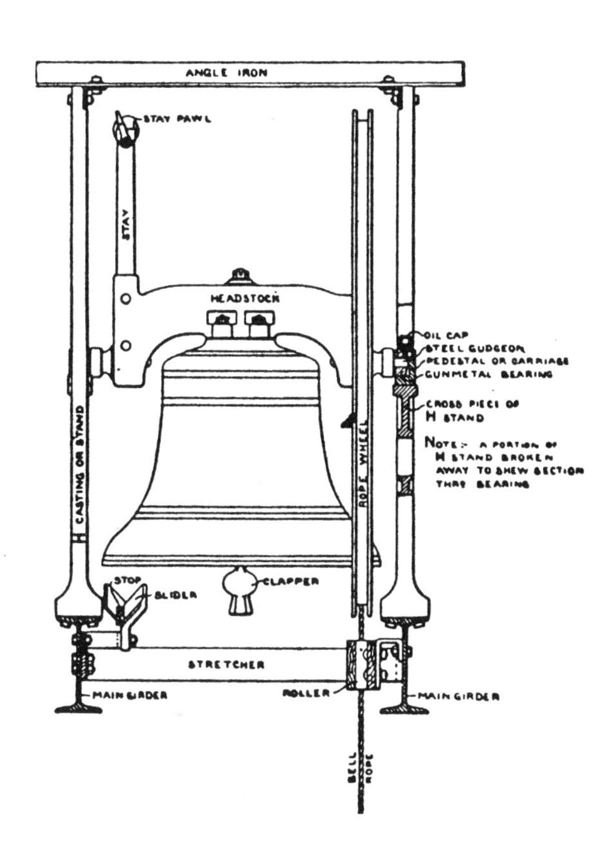

#1211 Two views of a bell hung for change-ringing. Reproduced by permission of Macmillan Publishers, Ltd., from Grove's Dictionary of Music and Musicians, 5th Ed.

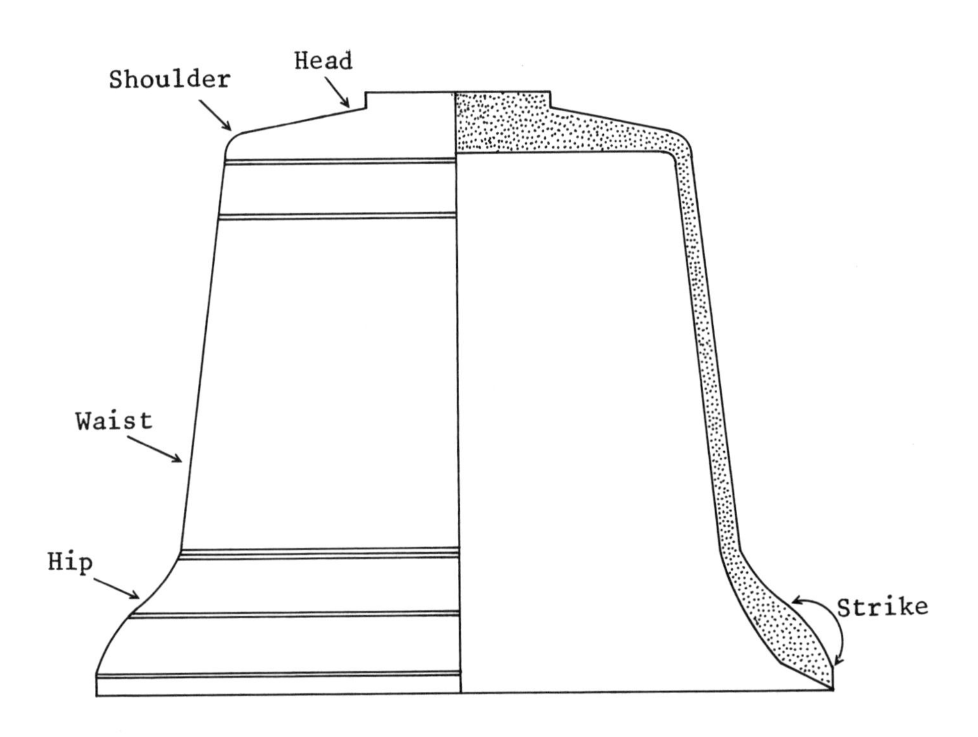

#1211 The diagram of a bell as cast for use in change-ringing. Illustration by John D. Kovaleski.

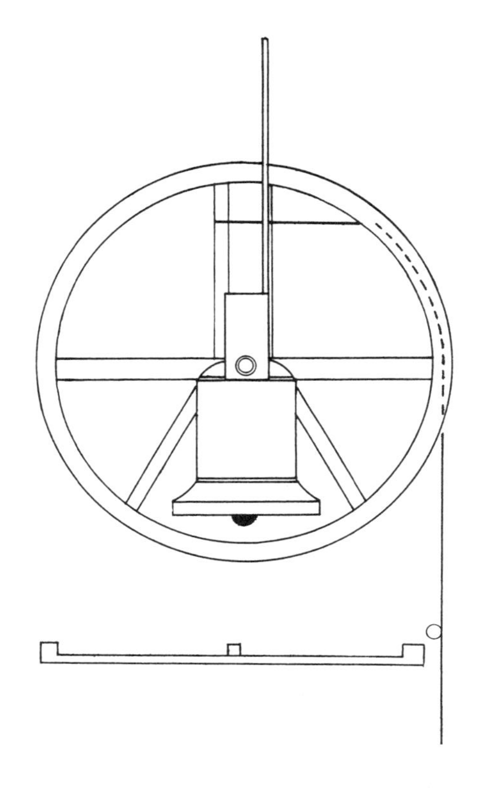

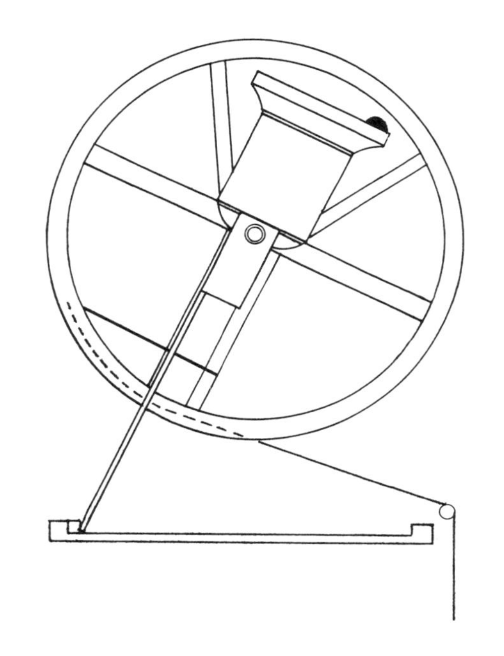

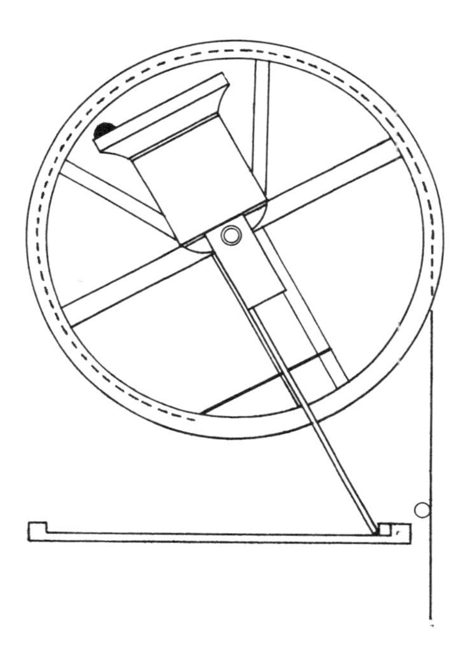

#1211

The three standard positions of a wheel-hung bell as used in change-ringing. The first position shows the bell at rest with the mouth down. The second position has the bell in the "raised" position ready to begin a touch or peal. The third position shows the bell in position to strike the first note. It would then return to the second position for the second note, etc., until stopped in the at rest position. Illustration by John D. Kovaleski.

as the last. If there are twelve bells, there would be approximately 480 million changes and would require about thirty-eight years to complete ringing them all. [NT 1]

1214 chantry -- a chapel endowed for the purpose of chanting Masses, usually for the founder of the abbey or church. The chantry at Fenchurch St. Paul* was removed to make room for the organ. The church at Duke's Denver* has one with canopied tombs which HV supposes to be for various ancestral Wimseys. [NT 2/BH E2]

1215 Chantycleer Restaurong -- Mr. Watchett* thinks the French speak better English in the unidentifiable restaurant than Yorkshiremen do. [CW 11]

1216 the chap who leapt into the gulf -- see leapt into the gulf [BH 14]

1217 Chapel -- the usual designation for some church that is not affiliated with the Church of England. See also item 1218. [NT 3/BH 9]

1218 Chapel -- in colleges some form of daily worship service is provided in observance of the rites of the Church of England, attendance being generally mandatory unless otherwise stipulated in the college's charter. For those schools that are nondenominational, as Shrewsbury College* is, some sort of service is still provided on a daily basis. [GN 5]

1219 Chapel St. -- there are two Chapel Sts. in central London, one near Paddington Station, the other in Knightsbridge, but neither is anywhere near Great James St. where DLS places it. This is apparently another tactic for making certain that real people or places cannot be harmed by coincidences in her fiction. [NT 16]

1220 Chaplin, Charlie -- the great English movie comedian, Charles Spencer Chaplin (1889-1977), famous for such productions as The Kid (1919), The Gold Rush (1926), City Lights (1931), and Limelight (1952). Miss Climpson* finds that he always makes her laugh. Chaplin was knighted by Queen Elizabeth II in 1975. [SP 5]

1221 Chapman, George -- (1559?-1634?), English poet, dramatist, and translator of Homer, Petrarch, Musaeus, Hesiod, and Juvenal. He is most remembered for his famous translation of Homer's Iliad and Odyssey immortalized in John Keats' poem, "On First Looking Into Chapman's Homer". Highly regarded as a scholar, he may be the "rival poet" of Shakespeare's sonnets. [UD 6]

1222 char -- short for charwoman or charlady, a cleaning woman [WB 9]

1223 charabanc -- a long bus used for sightseeing, the seats of which may be tiered to give everyone a good view. They may be either horse drawn or motor driven. In the later works, the reference is almost certainly to motor coaches, the older term not yet having been dropped. See also sharrer. [bc/MMA 15/GN 11]

1224 charades -- a parlor game where "It" selects a word, phrase, title, etc., or may draw one from a hat, and then has to act out the clues syllable by syllable, or by whole words, for the others to guess. From the clues, the others must attempt to determine the whole item. The same game, but done in pantomime, is called "dumb crambo". [np]

1225 Charing Cross -- refers usually to the train station situated in The Strand between Westminster and The City. It is named after one of the crosses erected by Edward I to mark the resting places of the body of his first wife, Eleanor, daughter of Fernando III, King of Castile, on its way to burial in Westminster Abbey after her death in Harby, Nottinghamshire. The cross was originally in Trafalgar Square on the site of the statue of Charles I, and a replica now stands in the forecourt of the station. [UD 9/HHC 30/MMA 15]

1226 Charing Cross Hospital -- the one PW visited was at Charing Cross*, built in 1831 from designs by Decimus Burton. The hospital is now on Fulham Palace Rd. in quarters erected in 1973. [CW 8]

1227 Charing Cross Rd. -- the street, a major London thoroughfare, that begins at Charing Cross* and which runs northerly to Oxford St. after which it becomes Tottenham Court Rd. The word "charing" is a form of "chare", mean-

a turning back or coming around again of time, either sense being appropriate to either the deceased queen, and in a sense, to the railway terminus as well. [CW 7/BC 10]

1228 Charing Cross Underground Station -- the London subway (underground) station that serves Charing Cross* and the train terminal there. This station has since been renamed Embankment Station, but both names often appear on Underground maps. [BC 8]

1229 charioteer of Delphi -- the famous Greek bronze statue of a charioteer victorious at Delphi's Pythian Games in 474 B. C. when the team of Polyzolos, brother of Gelon, Tyrant of Syracuse, won the laurel garland. The statue may be seen in the Delphi museum. It was discovered in 1896 near the Temple of Apollo in Delphi. [CW 3]

1230 Charis -- one of the professional dancers at the Hotel Resplendent at Wilvercombe* [HHC 7]

1231 Charlemagne -- (742-814), king of the Franks from 768, and Holy Roman Emperor from 800. During the Middle Ages his real exploits were expanded greatly in many of the great _chansons de geste_, most notably in the _Chanson de Roland_*. See also Roland [BH E2]

1232 Charles I -- the second of the Stuart monarchs, son of James I, he ruled from 1625 to January 30th, 1649, when he was beheaded by the Puritans under Oliver Cromwell*. [GN 3]

1233 Charles II -- king of England and son of Charles I*. Technically, he was king from the instant of his father's death, but he did not become king until the Restoration on May 25, 1660, when he returned to England from exile, stepping ashore at Dover. [CW 5]

1234 _Charley's Aunt_ -- Brandon Thomas's farce first produced in 1892 and still successfully revived from time to time [BH 18]

1235 Charlotte -- the youngest of the seven offspring of Charles Marie Levannier and Anastasia**. She supposedly had a morganatic marriage with Czar Nicholas I of Russia. The Czar did marry a Charlotte, but she was the daughter of Frederick William III of Prussia and the marriage was in 1817. [HHC 32]

1236 Charlotte Ann -- see Clarke, Charlotte Ann [GN 20]

1237 Charlotte-Louise of Prussia -- see Charlotte [HHC 29]

1238 chased -- ornamented with hammered indentations made with tools not having a cutting edge; usually applied to finely detailed metal objects and ornaments; to groove or indent [WB 2]

1239 chaste -- pure or straightforward in design as used to describe the silver tray on which PW's breakfast is brought to him [BC 13]

1240 _Chat en diamants (Dessin C-5)_ -- French for, "_cat of (in) diamonds_ (Design C-5)" [CW 5]

1241 Chateau Margaux -- see Margaux [HHC 4]

1242 Chateau Thierry -- a town in the department* of the Aisne on the River Marne about forty-five miles to the East and North of Paris. It was intermittently involved in action throughout WW I. [NT 8]

1243 Chateau Yquem -- the great sauternes chateau of the Bordeaux region. Its wine was classified as a First Great Growth in 1855, a rank created for that wine alone. The Chateau's output is small and is sold as Chateau d'Yquem. It is a sweet, smooth, rich gold and has no serious rivals. [mt/CW 6]

1244 Chatteris -- a thriving market town at the junction of the A141 and A142 routes just West of the Old and New Bedford Rivers** about sixteen miles North of Cambridge [NT 18/BH E2]

1245 Chatterton -- Thomas (1752-70), an English poet remembered mostly for his invented archaic poems. He became despondent after being exposed as a hoax and was left a pauper. He committed suicide with arsenic at age seventeen. [GN 17]

1246 cheese soufflé -- a basic soufflé flavored with grated cheese, probably something on the order of a sharp cheddar, so the flavor of the cheese will be noted in the finished product [FRH 5]

A QUEEN ELEANOR CROSS

After the death of his wife Eleanor, Edward I caused a memorial cross to be set up at each place where her funeral procession had stopped on its way to London. There were originally seven crosses. Of the three that still exist, the Geddington cross is the best preserved. It consists of three stories and stands on a platform of eight steps.

#1225 A Queen Eleanor cross. There were originally seven such crosses. Of the three that remain, the Geddington cross, shown above, is the best preserved. It consists of three stories on a base of eight steps.

CHARLEMAGNE

Lateran Museum, Rome

A mosaic picture, made during the lifetime of Charlemagne, and probably a fair likeness of him.

#1231 A mosaic of Charlemagne in the Lateran Museum, Rome. It was made during his lifetime and is reputed to be a fair likeness of him.

1247 Chelsea -- the Royal Borough of Kensington and Chelsea. It is that area of West London directly across the Thames from Battersea*. The area has been home to such people as Sir (Saint) Thomas More, Erasmus, the pre-Raphaelite artists, Oscar Wilde, Thomas Carlyle*, the Sitwells, and others. It has swung from a center of cosmopolitanism to raffishness and back again. Chelsea is sometimes used to refer to the "modern" attitude of women being involved in the arts, something not being met kindly in all circles, especially since, in the time of BC, Chelsea was not in one of its cosmopolitan attitudes. [WB 9/BC 7]

1248 Chelsea buns -- originated in Chelsea* in the 18th C. The original firm that made them had royal patronage until it closed in 1830. The buns are similar to Danish pastries: slices of sweet dough are rolled up around currants, peel, and sugar, baked and coated with honey, and eaten, often with butter. [MMA 2]

1249 Chelsea pauper -- the person who matched the description of the man found in Mr. Thipps'* bathtub before he was cleaned up and shaved. See also workhouse. [WB 10]

1250 Chelsea tea-shop affair -- DLS is apparently having some fun with the reader here. The suggestion seems to be that we should recall the famous Thompson-Bywaters case (see Thompson case) of 1922, in which some prominent testimony regarded a conversation in a tea-shop. PW connects Sir Impey Biggs* to that case, but that fictitious barrister* is related to it only in DLS's imagination. Sir Henry Curtis-Bennett, K. C., led the defense for Mrs. Thompson, while Cecil Whitely, K. C., defended Bywaters. Medical testimony--quite unspectacular--was provided by Dr. Sir Bernard Spilsbury*. The trial was precisely the sort of situation that Sir Impey seems to like best, but its outcome leads one to suspect that even his talents would have been challenged. [WB 2]

1251 Chelsea workhouse -- a workhouse* located in Chelsea* [WB 9]

1252 chemist [shop] -- the druggist or his shop [SP 1/MMA 12]

1253 Cher -- see Cherwell [GN 1]

1254 cherub blue -- see cherubim [WB 7]

1255 cherubim -- sometimes cherubin, one of the angelic orders usually presented as cute little children, chubby, with stubby wings. Their aerodynamics suggest that they were designed by whomever designed the bumblebee--it doesn't seem possible that they could fly. The ch is pronounced as in church, not as a "k". Cherubims are of the second, or next to the lowest, of the nine orders of heavenly beings, and can be depicted (as in early Christian art) as either blue or red. [WB 7/NT 2]

1256 Cherwell -- one of the two rivers in Oxford. The Thames, called the Isis* while in Oxford's precincts, is on the West side of the city, the Cherwell in on the East. They meet on the South edge of the Christ Church College Meadow. The boathouses for the punts* are on the Thames at the confluence of the two rivers. Cherwell is pronounced "charwool". [GN 11]

1257 Cheshire cat[s] -- the fabulous beast of Alice in Wonderland that could disappear until only its smile remained. It appears (or disappears) in Ch. 6. There is no satisfactory explanation of where Carroll got the allusion to Cheshire, but some have attempted a relation to the fact that Cheshire cheeses were once molded in the shape of cats and to the preponderance of rampant lion inn signs in that county. Cheshire in this case may also be a corruption of the French "chasseur", or hunter. [FRH 15/HHC 31]

1258 chess -- an ancient game of confused origin played in its present form for about the past 400 years. It is played by two persons using "armies" of sixteen pieces per player. One army is usually white, the other black, but any two contrasting colors will do. Each player has a king, the central figure; a queen, the most mobile and powerful piece; two bishops; two knights; and two rooks, or castles. In addition, each player has eight pawns or soldiers.

The game is played on a checkered board of 64 squares, and the queen always begins play on a square of her own

#1257 A picture of the Cheshire cat by John Tenniel, the original illustrator for the "Alice" stories.

color. The other pieces are arranged by convention around her position. The object of the game is to capture the opponent's king, or so move that his king cannot move without being captured. The game's basic rules are simple, but the intricacies of strategy are immensely complex and can take a lifetime to master. The pieces can be of any design, but the Staunton* design is the closest to a standard, its being the pattern for most commercially available chess sets. [qs/sf/BC 20/ GN 19]

1259 Chesterfield -- a davenport or sofa having arms of the same height as the back and usually being tufted deeply, giving the appearance of rich comfort. They suggest massiveness, weight, and substance. The word chesterfield has come into common use and is no longer capitalized. [WB 2/ CW 6/SP 13]

1260 Chesterton, Mr. -- Gilbert Keith Chesterton (1874-1936), English essayist, novelist, poet, and short story writer known particularly for his Father Brown detective stories in recent times, but he had a much broader appeal in letters while he was alive and writing. DLS admired him greatly and succeeded him as President of the Detection Club. [ss/CW 9/FRH 22]

1261 Chesterton says . . . -- the allusion is to Ch. 3, The Great Victorian Poets, wherein Chesterton* takes Swinburne to task for the lines PW cites and calls them the worst couplet ever written in English. GKC may have overstated the case a bit. [FRH 22]

1262 Mr. Chesterton's definition of a nice Jew -- PW refers to Nathan Abrahams* in this allusion. Chesterton, notoriously opinionated, said, "The poor Jews were nice, the rich were nasty." The problem of anti-Semitism is rampant in GKC's work, and DLS was not immune to his influences. In his "The Problem of Zionism" in The New Jerusalem, he says, "There are good, honourable, and magnanimous Jews of every type and rank . . . ," but he goes on to say that he prefers the revolutionary Jew to the plutocratic one. He explains that a revolutionary Jew would leave England while the plutocratic one would not. [ss]

1263 cheval-glass -- a large, full-length mirror mounted in a free-standing frame in such a way that the mirror can be tilted easily [SP 18]

1264 Chevalier des Grieux -- see Manon Lescaut [CW 18]

1265 chevalier d'industrie -- French for, "swindler" or "sharper", one who lives by his wits [MMA 19]

1266 chevaux de frise -- spikes installed on the top of a wall or paling. They are not necessarily meant to be ornamental. [CW 3]

1267 Cheyne Walk -- the famous residential walk, a westward extension of the Chelsea Embankment, along the North shore of the Thames opposite Battersea*. Many famous writers have had addresses on Cheyne Walk, and the area remains a fashionable address. It occupies much of what once was the estate of Sir (Saint) Thomas More. PW's uncle, Paul Delagardie*, keeps a home there, address unspecified. [BH P]

1268 chianti -- the wine local to Florence. Poorer grades can be quite raw and rough, but the better grades of the wine can hold up favorably to other robust red wines. [BC 21]

1269 chiaroscuro -- the treatment of light and dark areas of a painting, the evaluation of which is done without regard to the colors employed [FRH 2]

1270 Chicago Ring -- see Groot, Phineas E. [cf]

1271 Chief Constable -- the senior police officer in a county or borough police establishment. In NT he is addressed as "Colonel", a reference to previously held military rank, and not to any police rank. See police ranks. [sf/UD 19/FRH 5/HHC 25/ NT 6/BH 11]

1272 Chief Engineer at 2LO -- PW pestered him concerning the oscillation of radio waves, thereby uncovering the Ploffsky* gang of anarchists and their code. See also 2LO. [aq]

1273 children of Amalek -- see Amalek, children of [FRH 19]

1274 children of Israel -- the twelve

tribes of Israel, the Jews; the moneylenders Saint George* owes [GN 9]

1275 Children's Encyclopedia -- edited by Arthur Mee and published by the Educational Book Co., Ltd., Tallis House, Whitefriars, London, in ten volumes. There were numerous editions and revisions between the Wars. [MMA 1]

1276 Children's Service -- an informal service for children that has no special order of worship laid down [NT 12]

1277 Chillingford, Lord Humphrey -- see The Trail of the Purple Python [HHC 15]

1278 Chilperic, Miss -- Shrewsbury College's* youngest don*, she is anticipating marriage herself, but finds time to be a bridesmaid for HV [GN 5/BH P]

1279 Chilterns -- the Chiltern Hills, a small range through Buckinghamshire to the West of London [GN 3]

1280 chimaera[s] -- a beast from Greek mythology, it has a fire-breathing lion's head on a goat's body with a serpent's tail. It is symbolic of any mental fabrication or unattainable dream. [GN 15]

1281 chime -- a type of rhyme, in this case between two words that are in nearly the same place in successive lines, but which are not end rhymes [GN 11]

1282 chimney-stack -- a collection of several chimneys grouped for support and convenience and usually topped by some more or less ornate earthenware or terra-cotta tubes, called pots, which serve as deflectors to help force the smoke to rise as well as for decoration. [WB 4]

1283 China, mess-up there -- the reference is unclear, but probably relates to the Japanese invasion of China, especially Manchuria, and to the bombing of Shanghai, both in 1930-31 and after. [HHC 28]

1284 Chinese business, this -- the reference is to the bloody confrontations between the various political factions in China following the death of Sun Yat Sen in 1925. With Mao Tse-tung and his followers on one side and Chiang Kai-shek on the other, there was much bloodshed and deprivation throughout the land that continued until well after the communist takeover more than twenty years later. [UD 5]

1285 Chinese precepts, five great -- as Buddhism moved from India, it took hold in China. The precepts, then, are basically Buddhist, but are complimentary to the teachings of Confucius and Lao-Tzu. They are: 1) To abstain from taking life, 2) To abstain from taking what is not given, 3) To abstain from going wrong about sensuous pleasure, 4) To abstain from false speech, 5) To abstain from intoxicants as tending to cloud the mind. [CW 13]

1286 Chippendale -- a school of elegantly restrained design named for English cabinetmaker Thomas Chippendale who flourished in the mid-18th C. The lines of the furniture are gracefully curved, but the relief carving often borders on the extravagant. Nevertheless, while suggestive of the rococo influences, his work never became that florid. [BH P]

1287 Chipping Barnet -- a community approximately six miles North of London's western sections. See motorcycle race. [cb]

1288 chips -- what would be called French fries in the U. S. However, what PW has ordered to go with his steak are the larger, thicker fries sometimes listed on menus as steak fries. [FRH 7]

1289 Chitty, William Girdlestone -- a "detestable poisoner" uncovered by PW, whose evidence leads to Chitty's being hanged [aq]

1290 chloroform -- a colorless, toxic, volatile, heavy liquid of peculiar odor and a sweetish taste used generally as an anesthetic. Dr. Grainger* used it in the prescription for Philip Boyes* to calm Boyes' stomach and to help relieve his pain. [UD 19/SP 1]

1291 chloroform burns -- chloroform has a drying effect on the skin, so a large quantity, when used, coupled with the post mortem conditions of Vera Findlater's* body, could lead to the suspicion of a sunburnlike problem. [UD 21]

1292 chlorryform -- the deliberate mis-spelling of chloroform* to suggest semi-literate speech [im]

1293 choc. -- a slang abbreviation for chocolate that would be pronounced as the short form is spelled [SP 3]

1294 choice between hanging either my brother or my sister -- PW refers to his situation in CW [GN 17]

1295 choir -- a group of angels. As birds travel in flocks, angels are grouped in choirs. [NT 2]

1296 choke -- the device on an automobile that controls the air flow into the carburetor to permit easy starting from cold. If not properly adjusted, the car will not operate well, if at all. They used to be operated by hand, but are now automatically controlled for optimum engine firing. [HHC 29]

1297 cholera -- an acute infection centering on the small intestine in most cases. Diarrhea, vomiting, reduced urine output, and cramps are all symptoms. It is caused by the ingestion of the comma bacillus through impure drinking water. It may be fatal if not properly treated with bed rest and sodium bicarbonate in particular. Innoculation is helpful in almost all cases. [SP 9]

1298 Christ Church -- an Oxford college founded by Cardinal Wolsey, but finally established by Henry VIII in 1546 after Wolsey's fall from the King's grace. John Locke, John Wesley, and William Gladstone are among its graduates. Its precincts also include the cathedral of Oxford which is the College's chapel, an unusual arrangement. Tom Freeborn* and the Duke of Denver* are graduates, and Lord Saint George is enrolled there. [CW 1/GN 8]

1299 Christ Church Cathedral -- the chapel of Christ Church College and Oxford's cathedral, the building dates from about 1200, but some parts antedate that. See also Oxford Colleges. [GN 8]

1300 Christ Church College -- see Christ Church and Oxford Colleges [GN AN]

1301 Christ Church Meadow -- in the South of Oxford, it is triangular in shape, the apex in the South at the confluence of the rivers Thames (Isis*) and Cherwell* [GN 11]

1302 Christchurch -- in Dorsetshire (Hampshire before 1974) on the Channel coast. It is an old town dating from at least Norman times. It is the home town of the Gotobed girls. [UD 10]

1303 Christie's -- the famous art auctioneers at No. 8 King St., just South of Piccadilly* between St. James St. and St. James's Square. [UD 15]

1304 Christmas carol -- the Dowager Duchess* could be thinking of any one of several, but the leading choices would have to be either the Lutheran carol "Away in a Manger" or the old anonymous carol, "The Snow Lay on the Ground". The former carol opens with:

"Away in a manger, no crib for a bed,
The little Lord Jesus lay down his sweet head;
The stars in the heavens looked down where he lay,
The little Lord Jesus asleep in the hay."

[BH P]

1305 chrome yellow -- a rich, yellow-gold hue made from lead chromate [FRH 2]

1306 chromium tubes -- a reference to the influence of modern design using such tubes, especially from Germany and France, on basic items such as chairs and tables. One suspects that the Duchess has in mind such designers as Marcel Breuer and Walter Gropius, and, especially, the famous Barcelona chair of Ludwig Miës van der Rohe which was introduced in 1929. [BH P]

1307 Chronicle -- a morning paper which contains an article about "a very singular little burglary" which Bunter suggests to PW for his breakfast reading. It was the Daily Chronicle until 1930 when it amalgamated with the Daily News as the News Chronicle which ceased publication in 1960, a victim of newspaper groupings. [WB 5]

1308 Chronique d'un Cadet de Coutras -- a book found among Denis Cathcart's* personal items upon his death. It is by a minor French author, Abel

THE WESTERN ENTRANCE AND BELL TOWER, FROM TOM QUAD.

#1298 Christ Church College, Oxford, the western entrance and bell tower from Tom Quad.

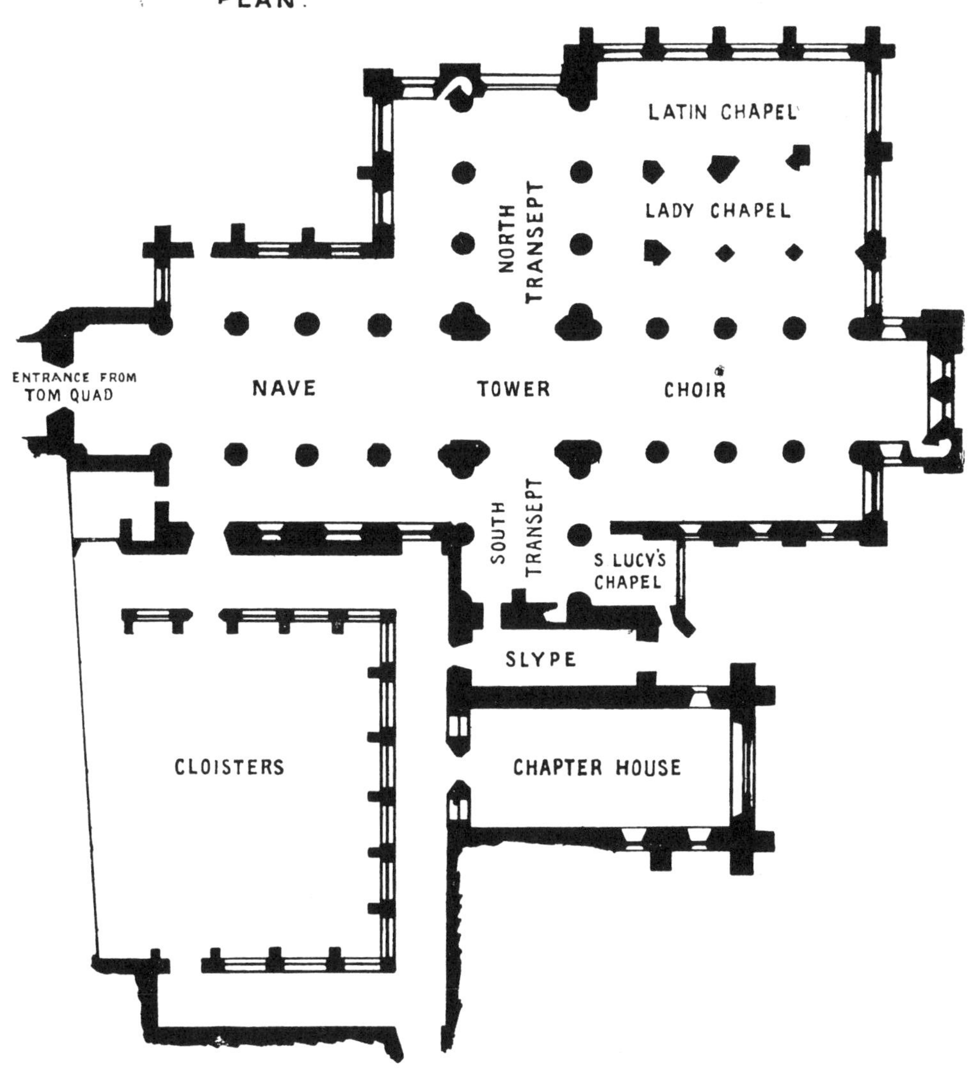

#1299 Floorplan for Christ Church, Oxford.

THE ROOF OF THE NAVE.

#1299 A rendering of the ornate vaulting of the roof of the nave of Christ Church, Oxford.

Hermant (1862-1950). A naturalistic novelist and bitingly sarcastic critic, he was elected to the French Academy in 1927, but was excluded from that august group, disgraced, and imprisoned for his pro-Nazi sympathies during WW II. The book's naturalistic (extreme realism) style is probably what prompted PW's comment, "tut, tut, Charles". The book and its author are now all but forgotten. [CW 2]

1309 Chrononhotonthologos -- King of Queerummania who, with Aldiborontiphoscophornio* and Rigdum-Funnidos, are central to the action of Chrononhotonthologos, a play by Henry Carey first produced in 1734. It is a burlesque of contemporary drama and is subtitled: "The Most Tragical Tragedy that ever was Tragediz'd by any Company of Tragedians". [MMA 3]

1310 chryselephantine -- made of gold and ivory [cf]

1311 Chrysler [70] -- Henry Strachan's* automobile. As Chrysler never manufactured cars in England, one must assume that it was an American import. The 70 series of cars was widely sold in the U. S. in the 1920's and was one of the heavier, larger sedans. It must also be assumed that right-hand drive modifications had been made for British driving practices. The 70's engine was large, so he should have had a great deal of trouble crank-starting it. The model of Chrysler automobile is not mentioned in MMA. [FRH 21/MMA 9]

1312 "Chuck the ball back to me . . ." -- a reference to cricket*, the playing ground boundaries of which are usually a circle or an oval [GN 17]

1313 chuckerout -- slang for doorman or attendant; a bouncer [MMA 11]

1314 Church Music Fund -- Paggleham's fund for the purchase of music and the maintenance of the organ, robes, etc. [BH 5]

1315 Church of Rome -- the Roman Catholic Church, so-called because its headquarters is in the Vatican in Rome. The distinction was made after the Western, or Roman, Church, split from the Eastern, or Orthodox, Church in 1054 when the Pope and the Patriarch mutually excommunicated each other's churches. The differences center on Papal Supremacy, clerical celibacy, and certain questions of theology and creed. [WB 1]

1316 Church Restoration Fund -- at Denver, the fund to repair and restore the Church, and especially its angel roof*. Mr. Thipps* was engaged as architect for the job. The fund is an indication of the difficulties faced in many English communities where the church buildings are ancient masonry with intricate woodwork and other ornamentation, the maintenance of which is prohibitively expensive when workers with the appropriate skills can be found to do it [WB 6]

1317 churchwarden -- a layman and parish officer responsible for parish properties and alms. The office is peculiar to the Church of England. [NT 4]

1318 churched -- the process of churching--a woman's public appearance in church to give thanks after childbirth. It follows particular Anglican rituals. [NT 12]

1319 cider -- not to be confused with the fresh apple squeezings enjoyed every autumn in North America, English cider is a light golden color and may be powerfully alcoholic. The drink is fruity and refreshing, but not quite in the same league as the Pol Roger* 1926 to which P. C. Burt* compares it. [hp]

1320 cigarette card -- a small card with a picture of some famous real or fictitious person given away in cigarette packs. They were widely collected and traded before WW II much as are chewing gum (bubblegum) cards today. [UD 18/HHC 16]

1321 cigars -- see Trichinopoly, Villar y Villar (Villar Villar), or Corona Corona

1322 cigarettes -- see Sobranie

1323 cinch -- used in the sense of a certainty, to have a tight hold on [WB 4]

1324 cipher -- a secret writing system wherein a certain letter or number is substituted in some way for some other letter or number. This is opposed to a code which functions much like a dictionary where the word to be hid-

den is represented by some combination of letters or numbers, or both. Ciphers work on a letter by letter system of some sort while codes work on a word by word system. [ab/HHC 16]

1325 cipher lock -- a locking mechanism similar to a modern combination lock. PW has such a lock with a code word or key word of "unreliability". The mechanism is described as a "three alphabet thirteen letter lock by Bunn and Fishett*" which seals the safe he has built in his Lambeth* flat while doing undercover work. Such a lock would be formidable indeed without either the key word or large quantities of explosives. [ab]

1326 Circassian slaves -- Caucasians from Russia who do not speak a language of Indo-European origin. Caucasian slaves were highly sought after for Moslem harems because of their light complexion. A "white slave" trade still exists in North Africa. [GN 18]

1327 Circe -- a character in Greek mythology, a daughter of Helios. By Odysseus she was mother of Telegonus. Circe was the enchantress of the isle of Aeaea who turned Odysseus' men into swine, but Odysseus protects himself with the herb moly given to him by Hermes. She releases the wanderers after a year. [MMA 9]

1328 Circle train -- the Underground* route that makes a complete circle around London and which makes connections with other lines [WB 3/BC 10]

1329 circs. -- a slang abbreviation for circumstances that would have been pronounced as written in the brief form [BC 18]

1330 circularize the laundries -- to send a descriptive flier around to various laundries asking for information about laundry marks, etc., found on personal objects belonging to those not otherwise identified [MMA 15]

1331 cist-graves of Theotokou -- a grave made of upright stone slabs and covered with other slabs, or, sometimes, a grave hollowed out in rock. This site, near the modern Volos, in Thessaly, Greece, dates from the Greek Dark Age (11th-9th centuries B. C.). [GN 3]

1332 Citroen -- a make of automobile manufactured in France and still available. The company tends to specialize in small automobiles and racers. The modern cars are technically innovative. [CW 13]

1333 The City -- the area of London within its ancient boundaries and dating from as early as 43 A. D. It maintains a separate governmental structure within greater London. It was and is the center of British business and economy. The City is about a square mile in size and extends from Tower of London to Blackfriars Bridge on the South, then North to Ludgate and Newgate, East to Aldersgate, North again to the Roman fort, East to Cripplegate, Moorgate, and Bishopsgate, then South to Aldgate and back to the Tower. Enclosed within these precincts are the Bank of England, the Royal Exchange, St. Paul's Cathedral, Billingsgate Market, Mansion House*, and the Old Bailey among other famous landmarks. The City is also used metaphorically to refer to Britain's center of business. [passim]

1334 city man -- the word city should be capitalized as it refers to The City* as well as to Sir Reuben Levy's status in the financial world headquartered there [WB 2]

1335 city of dreadful night [day] -- PW has in mind James Thomson's (1834-82) poem, "The City of Dreadful Night":

"The City is of Night; perchance of Death,
But certainly of Night."

The reflection on advertising is not a favorable one. Thomson's poem has a nightmare setting in London, doubtless inspired by his wanderings as an insomniac. It symbolized the spiritual wasteland of modern lives as T. S. Eliot has done in more recent times. [MMA 11]

1336 City of Light -- a nickname for Paris, France [BC 13]

1337 civil debts contracted elsewhere -- the law in Scotland is written in such a way (in Northern Ireland, too) that when leave is asked of a judge to serve process in Scotland and it appears to him that there may be a

concurrent remedy in that place, he must have regard to the cost and convenience of proceedings in the district or place of residence of the person on whom it is sought to serve the process, and particularly to the powers and jurisdiction of the sheriffs' courts or small debts (claims) courts. [BH 10]

1338 Clairmont, Claire -- Claire (Clara Mary Jane) Clairmont (1789-1879) was William Godwin's stepdaughter and accompanied Mary Godwin when she ran off with Percy Shelley. Claire met Lord Byron through the Shelleys and became his mistress for at least three years. Their daughter, Allegra, was born in 1817, placed in a convent in 1821, and died there from a fever in 1822. Miss Clairmont's description of Byron's features is most accurate. [BH 1]

1339 clapping -- more properly clappering, a serious situation arising when the bell is raised incorrectly, putting the clapper on the wrong side so that it swings in opposition to, rather than in tandem with, the bell itself. Should this happen, the clapper could crack the bell. The situation is analogous to a head-on automobile collision where the speed of the impact is the sum of the speeds of the two cars and is, therefore, more dangerous than one car hitting a stationary object. [NT 4]

1340 Clarendon Bldg. -- built from 1711 to 1713, it allowed the Oxford University Press to move out of the Sheldonian Theatre into its own building, where it remained until 1830. The building is now a part of the Bodleian Library* even though the OUP still has a Delegates Meeting Room there. It is named for Edward Hyde, 1st Earl of Clarendon, and a former Chancellor* of Oxford (1660-67) who gave the building to the University. [GN 12]

1341 Clarendon caps -- capital letters in the Clarendon style, a thick-faced and condensed type design. The font's name derives from the Clarendon Press at Oxford. The types that PW purchased would look like this:

S M L A D 0 1 2 3 4 5

[FRH 28]

1342 claret -- any of the dry red table wines from the Bordeaux region of France [ae/CW 9/HHC 4]

1343 claret cup -- one is properly made of claret*, soda, fruit juices, fresh herbs, and, perhaps, cucumber slices. A "dubious" one would have, most likely, only the wine and club soda, and possibly a poor wine at that. It is always a mistake to use cheap and inferior wines in the assumption that the taste will be masked by the other ingredients. [BC 16]

1344 Clarion -- a fictitious newspaper [HHC 4]

1345 Clark, Tom -- a groundskeeper at the Gatehouse* golf club [FRH 17]

1346 Clarke, Charlotte Ann -- Annie Wilson's* real name [GN 20]

1347 Clauchaneasy -- a village on the A714 route between Larg* and Bargrennan* [FRH 5]

1348 clean copy -- to a book collector the term means that the book is free from serious flaws, is sound, intact, and unstained [dh]

1349 clean shirt on Friday -- in the days of detachable collars and cuffs, it was customary to wear one shirt for several days, the clean cuffs and collars giving the impression of a fresh shirt daily. One must remember that permanent press fabrics were still in the future at this time. [MMA 8]

1350 Clegg's Temperance Hostel -- a "cheap and comfortable" place in Wilvercombe* suggested to HV by Insp. Umplety*. She opts not to stay there. [HHC 3]

1351 Clement -- Clement VII, Pope from 1523-34. It was in his lap that the Henry VIII and Catherine of Aragon divorce question was placed by Cardinal Wolsey. However, as he was virtually a prisoner of Catherine's nephew, the Holy Roman Emperor, the outcome of the divorce proceedings was never in much question. See also the Emperor. [GN 17]

1352 Cleopatra's duodenum -- PW's reference to the various specimens on display in the jars in Dr. Hartman's laboratory [fr]

1353 Cleopatra's Needle -- on the Vic-

toria Embankment* just below Waterloo Bridge. It was presented to Great Britain in 1819 by Mehmet Ali, a viceroy of Egypt and has no connection with Cleopatra whatsoever. It was one of a pair of obelisks erected at Heliopolis some 3500 years ago. Its twin is in New York's Central Park. [MMA 17]

1354 clerestory above the arcading -- an arcade is a series of columns and arches inside a building and above which is often found a row of windows, the clerestory windows, which are also above any sort of lean-to roof and which illuminate that upper level or clerestory [NT 1]

1355 clerical felt -- the dark gray or black felt hat, probably a homburg, suitable for a cleric of Mr. Venables'* position [NT 3]

1356 clerk -- a legal or secretarial aide or paraprofessional. A solicitor's* clerk (pronounced in England as clark) may do research, draft documents, etc., but only under the supervision of a solicitor.

1357 Clerk of the Assizes -- the clerk of the court; one of the minor court officials. His duties would include swearing in witnesses and jurors, and asking the jury for its verdict on any and all charges. [SP 3]

1358 Clerk of the Crown in Chancery -- usually the Permanent Secretary (there are several) to the Lord Chancellor*. The office dates from the 14th C. and deals mostly with the administration of the Crown's dealings with Parliament, including receiving grants of honors, commissions to judges and justices of the peace, and Speakers' warrants for Parliamentary elections and their returns. [CW 14]

1359 Clerk to the House of Lords -- an official who keeps the records of and handles the general day to day business of the upper house of Parliament. For the Duke of Denver's* trial he would be responsible for the smooth operation of that House while it functions as a court as well as seeing to it that proper transcripts of the trial are prepared. [CW 14]

1360 Clerkenwell -- an area of central London northeast of and adjacent to The City. It centers on Clerkenwell Rd. between the Finsbury and Holborn areas. Frank Crutchley* has a girl friend there. [BC 21/BH 18]

1361 Climpson, Miss Alexandra Katherine [Kitty] -- she is introduced in UD as PW's assistant in charge of investigating all those things which he, Bunter, or Scotland Yard would bungle or find closed to them by reason either of their gender, their social status, or their official status. She is exceptionally competent and resourceful, and is probably one of the world's most energetic letter writers and conversationalists. Her strong sense of moral worth and justice are instrumental in winning a retrial for HV, thus providing PW with the chance to save HV's life. She later indulges in an "orgy of teas", thereby helping PW establish the real motive for Philip Boyes'* murder. She heads a "secretarial bureau" for PW, but they rarely do any typing or shorthand as it is a cover for investigative work, the typists being called upon from time to time to help. In other areas, PW can rely upon her help when he has a touchy situation to unravel as in the case of Polly Mason's* difficulties in BH. In all, Miss Climpson is a quite remarkable woman for her day in that she has been given the opportunity to use her talents in a way that is suitable to her employer and that is most appropriate to her station in life. She is indeed fortunate. [UD 4/SP 1/GN 5/BH P]

1362 Clinic -- the new Clinic planned by Dr. Penberthy* to study rejuvenation by gland transplants. See Dr. Voronoff. [BC 16]

1363 Clints of Dromore -- the flinty rock outcroppings and jagged hills to the West of Gatehouse-of-Fleet* just before Creetown* [FRH 3]

1364 clock in -- or "punch in", to record one's arrival at work with a time card and clock device [MMA 5]

1365 clock incident -- the reference is to Ch. 1 of GN wherein Vera Mollison* comments on the value of clocks as a source of alibis. This all parallels A. E. W. Mason's use of clocks in his _The House of the Arrow_ (1924). [GN 3]

1366 cloisonné -- an oriental art where a design is created in relief on a metal object such as a vase, the design usually being worked in either brass or precious metal wires. Enamel is then filled in to color the design and is fired to a permanent hardness. The finished product is then buffed to a lustrous shine, the wire relief being flush with the enamelled surface. [BH P]

1367 cloistered -- used to mean protected or sheltered as in a medieval monastery or convent [NT 2]

1368 Cloot, Mr. Adrian -- a fictitious critic [GN 11]

1369 Clos-Vougeôt -- a classic red wine of the Côte de Nuits, Nuits St. Georges area, and a member of the Burgundy family of wines [mt]

1370 close -- close-mouthed, not talkative [NT 6]

1371 Close -- the walled square built to protect the houses of the clergy adjacent to a cathedral or abbey. The one in Salisbury* is adjacent to the Cathedral and was built before the city. It is the largest and finest Medieval cathedral close in England. Entered through Medieval gates, the Close contains the Bishop's Palace and the Deanery, both as old as the Close itself. [WB 5]

1372 to close him down -- Mr. Lugg* is referring to Mr. Noakes's casket. Even with embalming, the corpse would be unpleasant, having been left so long after death before receiving the attentions of a mortician. [BH 10]

1373 cloth of gold -- see gold lamé [BH P]

1374 Clothing Club -- in an area as poor as that of Fenchurch St. Paul*, such a club would be most helpful to quite a few people. Also, since the locals were all well-known to one another in the parish, the Club's work would be less like charity and more like expected "hand-me-downs" in a family. Their collection, repair, and distribution for free or for a modest price was a particularly useful activity in the 1930's period of economic depression. [NT 6]

1375 Cloud Cuckoo-land -- or Nephelococcygia, Aristophanes' imaginary city in the air built by birds. It appears in the great Greek dramatist's play, The Birds, and has come to represent any such imaginary location no matter how strongly connected to factual reality. [MMA 11/GN AN]

1376 Clouds of Witness -- the title of the second DLS novel is taken from Hebrews 12:1: "Wherefore seeing we also are compassed about with so great a cloud of witnesses, let us lay aside every weight, and the sin which doth so easily beset us, and let us run with patience the race that is set before us." In terms of the allegorical nature of this novel, the second verse is even more interesting when applied to the events and conclusion of the story: "Looking unto Jesus the author and finisher of our faith; who for the joy that was set before him endured the cross, despising the shame, and is set down at the right hand of the throne of God." [CW]

1377 cloves, oil of -- a light, clean oil heavily scented with an extract from cloves. It is frequently and generally used in dental work and for the treatment of minor tooth pains for short periods. [te]

1378 club -- any one of those to which PW belongs--Marlborough*, Bellona*, or Egotists'*. [WB 4/CW 11]

1379 Club -- the Gatehouse Golf Club about a mile North of the village. It has nine holes and Henry Strachan* is the secretary. The Club is real, Strachan is not. [FRH 4]

1380 Club Secretary -- see Captain Culyer [BC 2]

1381 clue -- or clew, a ball of yarn or thread used as a guide out of a maze or difficulty. The modern application of the word as a bit of information needed to help solve a problem is a derivation from the earlier meaning. [CW 12]

1382 The Clue of the Crimson Star -- a Sexton Blake* adventure being read by Ginger Potts*. It was not issued in standard book format, and, if real, existed as some sort of "dime novel" or magazine serial. There were so many authors and titles involved with the Sexton Blake phenomenon that this par-

ticular title could not be verified. DLS was a fan of them, so it could be a real title. [MMA 6]

1383 Cluer, Judge -- His Honor, Judge Albert Rowland Cluer (1852-1942) presided over a variety of English courts during his career, retiring from the bench at the Whitechapel County Court. [CW 19]

1384 Clumps -- or clubs, a game of two teams. A member of each team meets with the "captain" and is given the name of some item. Each team then works on its "member", who may not speak, to discover the identity of the item. The first team to do so is the winner. [np]

1385 Clumps -- one of PW's friends from his espionage days who works in the Foreign Office*. The name is either a nickname or a cute corruption of some sort of unclassified code name. [HHC 26]

1386 coach [verb] -- while a tutor is a regular instructor attached to an Oxford college, a coach instructs students of one discipline in his subject area for a fee. His clients would not be restricted to any particular college. [GN 1]

1387 coast-guard service -- originally a part of the Customs Service with duties directed at preventing smuggling, hence the Preventive Service. It was transferred to the Admiralty in 1856 for service as a general police force along the coast that could be pressed into defensive service if needed. It was reorganized in 1921. [MMA 5]

1388 coast-road -- the road, the A75, from Gatehouse-of-Fleet* to Creetown*. It is an impressively beautiful eighteen mile stretch which once had itself recommended to Queen Victoria by Thomas Carlyle as the finest stretch of road in the kingdom. [FRH 2]

1389 cob -- a short-legged horse, usually stocky and with an artificially high gait [HHC 16]

1390 cobalt -- a bright, rich shade of blue of the middle ranges [FRH 2]

1391 Cobbleigh, Arthur -- the name on the Army identification disc found at the home of Jean and Suzanne Legros**. The "real" Cobbleigh had been from near Dartford*. [NT 12]

1392 Cobbley, Jim -- the Empire Free-Trader* on the inquest jury for Paul Alexis'* death who held out for a murder verdict, but who was outvoted for suicide [HHC 21]

1393 Cobley, Uncle Tom -- or Cobbleigh, a character mentioned in "Widdicombe Fair", an anonymous ballad. The ballad's speaker wants to go to the Widdicombe Fair with a group of friends, "Old Uncle Tom Cobbleigh and all". [SP 20]

1394 Cobling, Ben -- Clara Whittaker's* groom for forty years and from whom PW and Parker learn about the Dawson family tree. He is a genial old soul who genuinely welcomes PW and the chance to tell old stories to fresh ears. See the genealogical chart at the end of UD for a summary of his information. [UD 11]

1395 Cobling, Mrs. -- Ben Cobling's* wife and hostess to PW and Parker for a visit while they stay in Crofton* [UD 12]

1396 cocaine -- a bitter, crystalline narcotic derived from coca leaves. The use of and trafficking in this drug are central to the action of MMA. The cocaine alkaloid, a discovery of the German chemist Albert Niemann (1840-1921), was first isolated at Göttingen, Germany, but Niemann did not see much use for or application for his discovery. [HHC 15/MMA 5/GN 19]

1397 Cochran, Miss Mary [Sally] -- a neighbor of PW's in Kirkcudbright* whom Bunter helps with various chores. His kindness is more from a sense of propriety than anything else--he just doesn't think that women should have to do certain jobs. See also Miss Selby. [FRH 5]

1398 Cock Tavern -- Ye Olde Cock Tavern is on Fleet St.* near the Law Courts*. It dates from the 17th C. and was known to Dickens and Thackeray among others. [MMA 12]

1399 cockatoo -- any of the Australian parrots known for their showy plumage, especially their ornate head feathers or crests [HHC 8]

1400 Cockburn [1868, 1896, 1908] -- Cockburn's is an old and established import house for the fortified wines of Spain and Portugal, especially sherry and port*. PW enjoys fine wines, and, from the context of the various stories, one may assume safely that he keeps some of Cockburn's finest ports in his cellar. It is unusual for such wines to have a vintage year unless the products of that year are of exceptional quality. It follows, then, that when Mrs. Ruddle* unpacks, dusts, and sets upright some thirty bottles of a Cockburn 1896, that Bunter's rage is justified. It is essential that the sediment in a bottle of port not be disturbed before the bottle is decanted. [WB 9/BC 3/BH 15]

1401 Cocker, according to -- the reference is to Edward Cocker (1631-75), a London teacher of writing and arithmetic. His arithmetic text enjoyed great popularity and gave rise to the expression cited here. A modern parallel would be "according to Hoyle". [BC 7/NT 7]

1402 cockney -- a native or permanent resident of that part of London, especially The City*, which is within the hearing range of the "Bow Bells" of St. Mary-le-Bow, Cheapside. It also refers to the distinctive dialect of those persons. The dialect is noted for dropping the "h" sound and for its colorfully rhyming slang. In a looser sense it may refer to innocent "city slickers" who have gotten dangerously far from their regular milieu. [im/CW 11/UD 18]

1403 cockscomb -- the lurid red appendage on a rooster's head; a jester's cockscomb is the multipeaked cap with bells in its points much favored by medieval jesters. Some of the academic caps used at Oxford (not so much today) are soft and are given to assuming unusual shapes when blown in the wind. [GN 1]

1404 cocktails -- mixed drinks other than something with soda or tonic, such as a Manhattan or a Rob Roy. They are still something of a novelty in England as they have never been fully accepted as they have been in the U. S. [np]

1405 cocoa-nut matting -- door mats and larger pieces used in areas of heavy traffic. Noted for their durability, they are made of dried cocoanut husks, the heavy fibrous material that surrounds and protects the smaller, rounded nut within. [NT 2]

1406 "Codlin is the friend, not Short" -- a reference to characters from Dickens's Old Curiosity Shop, a pair of travelling showmen who perform a Punch and Judy show. Codlin is rather sour; Short is cheerful. The line HV uses is Codlin's, and is addressed to Little Nell in Ch. 19. [GN 10]

1407 coefficient of spherical curvature -- along with his comments "go all Eddington"* and "Fitzgerald contractions"*, Parker is further showing his knowledge of physics in his citation of some of the mathematical elements involved in the study of space and its presumably curved structure [ae]

1408 coffee except in bottles -- Camp Coffee, an oily mixture of coffee, chicory, and sugar, mixed with hot water. It was the only thing available of an instant nature before WW II. The label has a picture of a kilted Scotsman at an outpost of Empire being served by a native. It is still sold. [BH 4]

1409 coffee mill -- or grinder. Before instant or preground coffee, one bought beans and ground them in a small mill. The noise made, however, is not usually quite like purring. [BH 16]

1410 Coffin, Will -- a resident of Brennerton* whom HV sought out in the hope of using a telephone. He did not have one. [HHC 2]

1411 coffin-stool -- a support for one end of a coffin such as might be used in a church or funeral parlor [GN 19]

1412 Cognac -- after the town and region in Western France known for its particularly fine brandy. If seen with a lower case "c", one is dealing with some other brandy meant to resemble in some way the real thing. While not necessarily a spurious product, cognac must be selected with care, while Cognac is of a uniformly high quality. [SP 15]

1413 Cohen & Gold, Messrs. -- manufacturers of electrical fittings on Farringdon St.* in London. We may assume the firm is fictitious as Her Majesty's Registry of Companies holds no listing for the firm. [sf]

1414 coign of vantage -- a position of advantage; in reference to the bathing dresses, the phrase refers to displaying one's wares to too great an advantage [GN 12]

1415 coke -- slang for cocaine* [MMA 9]

1416 coke-house -- a storage place or bin for the coke (see furnace-coke) used to heat the church at Fenchurch St. Paul* [NT 2]

1417 Coke, Mr. -- probably a reference to Mr. A. J. Cook, a mineworkers' leader and secretary to what was then called The Mineworkers' Federation. It is now called The National Union of Miners. The reference requires someone far to the left of center, and Cook was considered a Communist in the early 1920's. [CW 7]

1418 Coke, Sir Edward -- an English barrister* (1552-1634) and judge who eventually rose to the position of chief justice of Common Pleas and of the King's Bench. His fame as an author is derived from his legal Reports and Institutes. [UD 10]

1419 Colburn, Miss -- a student at Shrewsbury College* [GN 6]

1420 cold-house -- a glass-covered frame under which plants can be induced to germinate before they might otherwise do so. The glass traps solar energy that heats the soil, speeds germination, and protects the seedlings from cold or late frost. [BH 4]

1421 Cole -- a reference to G[eorge] D[ouglas] H[oward] Cole (1890-1951) and M[argaret] I[sabel] [Postgate] Cole (b. 1893), a husband and wife team who authored more than thirty detective novels as well as work in economics and biography. Their novels are considered uneven, especially in their later efforts. [FRH 27]

1422 Cole, Mr. -- one of the more senior members of the staff at Pym's Publicity*, he is in charge of the Harrogate Brothers* soap account as group-manager* [MMA 4]

1423 Cole, Mr. -- one of the partners in the law firm of Grimsby and Cole*. PW interviews him to gather information about Philip Boyes*. [SP 16]

1424 Cole, John -- the itinerant founder who cast John*, the number three bell at Fenchurch St. Paul*. Such a founder was active in the Hampshire and Sussex area ca. 1573-92. John was supposedly cast in 1557 which is pre-Cole, but, no doubt, DLS adjusted the dates here intentionally to use Cole's name for verisimilitude. [NT 4]

1425 Colegrove, Dr. -- the Chelsea* workhouse* physician who attended the man later found as a nude corpse in Mr. Thipps's* bathtub [WB 12]

1426 Colfin -- a small village about three miles from Port Patrick* and to the East [FRH 5]

1427 colis postal -- French for postal packet or parcel post [CW 5]

1428 Coliseum [The London] -- a theatre on St. Martin's Lane just North of Charing Cross and Trafalgar Square. It was a famous music hall until 1931, when it became a theatre. [WB 4/UD 11]

1429 collar, put on a clean -- see clean shirt on Friday [t]

1430 A colleague, as Sherlock Holmes would say . . . -- the reference is to Ch. 3 of The Hound of the Baskervilles when Holmes exclaims, "Excellent! This is a colleague, Watson, after our own heart." The comment congratulates Dr. Mortimer for having observed some cigar ash, thus enabling Holmes to estimate how long a man had stood at a given place. [NT 9]

1431 collect -- a short prayer, the content of which varies from Sunday to Sunday and for saint's days. It is comprised of an invocation, a petition, and a conclusion, and usually refers to the prayer that precedes the Scripture Lesson in the Eucharist. [NT 12]

1432 College of Arms -- the organization that is still responsible for the identification, authentication, and creation of coats of arms. The

College is now also responsible for helping supervise and execute the major functions of a royal court (weddings, funerals, coronations, protocol for state visits, etc.). The Earl Marshal is head of the College at present. The English kings of arms (the highest ranking members of the College) are Garter, Norroy and Ulster, and Clarenceux. Next in rank are the heralds: Windsor, Chester, York, Lancaster, Richmond, and Somerset. The pursuivants follow and are: Rouge Croix, Blue Mantle, Rouge Dragon, and Portcullis.

Scotland has the Lord Lyon King of Arms; three heralds, Rothesay, Albany, and Marchmont; and three pursuivants, Unicorn, Kintyre, and Carrick. A king of arms is the ranking officer for an heraldic district, and is followed in rank by the other officers as listed above. Their jobs are now largely ceremonial in nature, although there is a renewed interest in armorial grants and coats of arms, over which the College of Arms has jurisdiction. [CW 14]

1433 College debates -- debating has long been a staple of the academic life at Oxford as is shown in the long and healthy life of the Oxford Union (see Union). [GN 5]

1434 College oven -- the college kitchens are the modernized version of Wolsey's original design for Christ Church College [GN 8]

1435 College Youths -- fully, the Ancient Society of College Youths, founded in 1634. Fabian Stedman* had joined the group by 1664. It is considered the senior secular change-ringing group, the "Ancient" in the group's title having been added, in part, to reflect that fact. On April 27, 1868, the Society rang a peal of 15,840 Kent Treble Bob Majors* at Bethnal Green in nine hours and twelve minutes, but a different group ran 18,240 of the same at Mottram in 1922 in eleven hours and thirteen minutes, a record that was still standing after PW's help in that notable ring at Fenchurch St. Paul*.

Of interest in the Bethnal Green peal is that the ringers were locked in the St. Matthew's bell tower for the duration of their feat, but the peal was not rung on bells as heavy as those at Fenchurch St. Paul. The name "College Youths" may have derived from the College of the Holy Spirit and St. Mary that was destroyed by fire in 1666. That college had a ring of six bells and was supposedly founded by Sir Richard (Dick) Whittington, London's most famous Lord Mayor. [NT 1]

1436 collie-shangie -- Scots dialect for a noisy quarrel, a loud howling and yelling as dogs might do, but the expression (sometimes appearing as a single word) usually applies to a human fracas [FRH 7]

1437 Collins -- a police officer sent to question Bertha Gotobed's* fiancé, John Ironsides, a railway employee [UD 6]

1438 Collins, Mr. -- a handwriting expert at Scotland Yard used by PW and Parker to ascertain with certainty that General Fentiman had, in fact, written the notes on the letter paper PW found at the Bellona Club* [BC 8]

1439 Collins, Dorothy -- a Shrewsbury College* graduate and classmate of HV's [GN 1]

1440 Collins, Wilkie -- William Wilkie Collins (1824-89), an English author and novelist, friend of Charles Dickens*, and creator of such famous early detective and mystery works as _The Woman in White_ (1860), _Armadale_ (1866), and _The Moonstone_ (1868). The latter work is still regarded as one of the greatest of all detective novels. Collins's plots are known for their complexity mixed with a remarkable clarity. [UD 22/FRH 15/GN 9]

1441 Colney Hatch -- a small community East of Finchley* and North of Hampstead*. The references are to the lunatic asylum which was founded there in 1851, and was then the best and largest in Europe. The name, which had come, like Bedlam and Borstal (see old Borstalian), to describe the type of institution rather than any particular one, was changed in 1937 to Friern. It closed in 1982. [hp/HHC 26]

1442 Colomb -- the reference is to Paul Colomb, Vicomte de Batines, author of the _Bibliografica dantesca_, Prato (near Florence), 1845-6 [WB 1]

1443 Colonel -- a member of the Ego-

tists' Club* who is not further identified. He is well known to PW and, from the context, appears to be one of the club's officers. The Chief Constable* for the area including Fenchurch St. Paul* is also addressed as Colonel, a reference to his former military rank, and not to his status as a police officer. [MMA 19/NT 19]

1444 Colonial Office -- its origins date back to the Councils of Trade and Plantations in the late 1600's, but it dates as a separate office only from 1854. It administered all elements of government in the colonies. In 1966, the Commonwealth Office was formed, a merger of the Colonial Office and the Commonwealth Relations Office. [HHC 6]

1445 colophon -- a printer's mark of identification which furnishes information about the source of a book. Early books usually have the colophon at the end, later ones at the beginning of the book. Colophons may also include information about the author, designer, illustrator, type style, paper, even the publisher himself. In those cases where the printer also makes his own paper, the colophon will appear as a watermark in the paper itself, but this is rare. [WB 1]

1446 Colosseum -- the major gladiatorial combat arena in ancient Rome, a good portion of which is still standing despite more recent problems with heavy traffic vibrations and air pollution [GN 6]

1447 colour-screens -- or gelatin photographic filters, their function being to increase the contrast between different colors. A yellow screen placed over the camera's lens would darken the image of the purplish ink in the letter found on Paul Alexis's* body. This principle is widely used to render otherwise ruined photographs or documents visible or legible to a usable degree. [HHC 26]

1448 Columbine -- a character in the old _Commedia dell' arte_ plays of Italy. _Young and lovely_, she is supposed to be invisible to mortal eyes. Her lover is usually Harlequin*, but is also sometimes Pierrot*, depending on the story being told. She is a popular costume ball figure. [qs]

1449 "come and go on lissome . . ." -- PW is quoting Rupert Brooke's* poem, "The Old Vicarage, Grantchester". Brooke wrote:

"Curates, long dust will come and go
On lissome, clerical, printless toe;
And oft between the boughs is seen
The sly shade of a Rural Dean."

1450 "Come hether friend . . ." -- from "The Sixth Dialogue" of _The French Garden: for English Ladyes and Gentlewomen to walke in or a sommer dayes labour_, by Pierre Erondell*, printed in London in 1605. The passage deals extensively with a consideration of the moral/social responsibilities of the "gentle-born". The part omitted by DLS in the quote considers the evil of too much sleep. [GN 9]

1451 "Come unto these Yellow Sands" -- by Henry Purcell*, a song from _The Tempest_ or _The Enchanted Island_ (Z631), a semiopera patterned after Shakespeare's play and first performed in about 1695. The lyrics appear as "Ariel's Song" in Shakespeare in I, ii, 378ff. [CW 4]

1452 "Come tell me now . . ." -- from T. L. Beddoes'* _The Brides' Tragedy_*, IV, iii, 61-2. The lines are in a speech of Hesperus's after he has killed Floribel. A servant notices a large ruby ring and comments on it. Hesperus misinterprets the comment and has a verbal outburst, the result of his feelings of shattered love and guilt. The confusion is clarified and Hesperus gives the ring to the servant. [HHC 9]

1453 comerlongme -- a dialectical expression for "come along with me" [HHC 4]

1454 _Comet_ -- a fictitious newspaper [HHC 4]

1455 coming into the straight -- or straightaway, a racing allusion [NT 5]

1456 _comme ça_ -- French for "so", or "just like that" [HHC 7]

1457 _commissaire de police_ -- French for Commissioner of Police, an office akin to chief of police or a police superintendent [NT 8]

1458 Commission -- the formal warrant

or instrument passing the authority to perform some act from the person or agency who holds that authority to the person or agency who is to exercise it. Such a Commission passed the authority from the Crown to the Lord High Steward* for the purpose of arranging the trial of the Duke of Denver* in the House of Lords*. [CW 5]

1459 Commission Agent -- one who carries out a specific transaction for a percentage of the fees or earnings involved. The term can apply to any sort of transaction, including hiring someone to place bets with bookmakers. [UD 7/HHC 31]

1460 commissionaire -- an attendant such as a doorman [BC 5/HHC 4/MMA 15]

1461 Committee -- the supervisory group at the Bellona Club* which makes the Club's rules and to which the various operating officers must make their regular reports; a sort of board of governors elected from the membership [BC 2]

1462 commoner's gown -- a short academic gown worn by commoners*. It appears as though someone had taken an ordinary academic gown and had cut it off at about knee length. [GN 5]

1463 commoner -- an Oxford student who is not a scholar; a nonscholarship student who, as a consequence, is required to wear a distinctive short gown to advertise that fact. The gowns differ from college to college within the University. [GN 1]

1464 Commons, House of -- the lower house of Britain's bicameral legislature. Unlike the Lords*, members of the Commons must be elected to office. At present, the Commons holds the bulk of Britain's political power, the last vestiges of real power held by the House of Lords having been removed with the Parliament Act of 1911, but the Lords do have delaying power which, sometimes, can be decisive. [MMA 10]

1465 commercial traveller -- a travelling salesman [sf]

1466 Communion vessels -- the various cruets, chalices, etc., necessary to administer the Sacrament of Communion [NT 2]

1467 Communism -- when spelled with a capital "C", the reference is to the Marxist-Leninist doctrine of political, social, and economic revolution to create a classless society featuring common ownership of all means of production and livelihood. More realistically, however, it is socialism* as practiced in Communist countries. In that guise it is usually spelled with a lower case "c". [CW 7]

1468 communistic in a literary way -- a reference to the common practice among university and literary circles during the 1920's and 30's of expressing sympathy toward the theories of Communism and Socialism. There was a great deal of rhetoric expended on the subject and there were some significant economic changes as a result, but most people were content to talk about it, usually in vague terms that suggested some sort of Utopia. [MMA 3]

1469 Comphrey, George -- a cousin of Lady Shale's* [np]

1470 "company of spearmen . . ." -- PW alludes to a musical setting for Psalm 68, especially to verse 30, which, in the KJV, is, "Rebuke the company of spearmen, the multitude of the bulls, with the calves of the poeple, till every one submit himself with pieces of silver: scatter thou the people that delight in war." [BH 5]

1471 Compline, Mr. -- the coroner* mentioned as living in Leamholt* [NT 3]

1472 <u>compos mentis</u> -- Latin for of sound mind; in one's "right mind" [UD 17]

1473 <u>comte</u> -- the French equivalent of count, an aristocrat of the middle ranks, but, nevertheless, one demanding of considerable attention in those countries where such titles are recognized [mt]

1474 Comte de Rueil -- the fictitious inventor of a formula for poison gas which he wishes to sell to the British government because he hates the French Republic and because he needs the money. PW functions as an agent for the British defense establishment in their efforts to purchase the formula. PW has functioned in such a capacity more than once, diplomatic errands

#1464 The House of Commons, Westminster.

being mentioned in several stories, and it is uncertain whether those activities are an offshoot of his detective work, or vice versa. The Comte hosts a fabulous wine-tasting with an excellent dinner to identify the real PW from among the imposters, all of whom want the formula. [mt]

1475 Conan Doyle -- see Doyle, Sir Arthur Conan [BC 18/SP 3]

1476 Conan Doyle and the black man -- the Dowager Duchess is referring to the case of George Edalji, the half-caste son of a minister. He was convicted of maiming horses and was imprisoned in 1903. In 1906, Doyle* proved Edalji innocent and identified the real culprit. Nevertheless, no one was ever charged, and Edalji was never given any reparation for his three years in prison. [SP 3]

1477 conceited, metaphysical conclusion -- see A very conceited metaphysical conclusion [GN 18]

1478 Concerto in D Minor -- by J. S. Bach* for two violins, S. 1043. This is the only Bach concerto for two solo violins. [GN 23]

1479 conchy -- WW I slang for conscientious objector [CW 13]

1480 concierge -- a caretaker for a block of flats in France [CW 5]

1481 "Confess, or to the dungeon . . ." -- the lines are from II, iii, 232, an exchange between Thorwald and Duke Melveric in Death's Jest Book by T. L. Beddoes**, and are spoken as the Duke reveals to all that he has returned from the Crusades while removing his disguise. [HHC 19]

1482 Confessio Amantis -- the foremost English poem of John Gower (1330?-1408). Caxton's* version of 1483 follows the second version of the poem as dedicated to Henry IV. Chaucer and Gower were good friends, Chaucer calling him "moral Gower". The Confessio is a series of tales and uses some of the same stories that appear in The Canterbury Tales. The vehicle of the Confessio is a priest of Venus illustrating a consideration of the seven deadly sins with one or more stories. [CW 4]

1483 confession box and hassock -- the hassock is the padded rail on which the penitent kneels during confession; the priest listening to the confession would be in the "box", a telephone booth sort of apparatus designed to mask the penitent from the priest in an effort to assure anonymity and completeness of confession [UD 22]

1484 Confessions -- see 1) rudeness, and 2) St. Augustine [MMA 15]

1485 confitures -- French for jams, preserves, etc. [mt]

1486 conjuring banter -- PW's assortment of Greek and Latin phrases used to frighten the ignorant locals in "Incredible Elopement". Among these phrases are: "poluphloisboio thalasses", Greek for "the loud-roaring sea", a typical Homeric epithet; "ne plus ultra", Latin for, "the utmost attainable", or "extreme perfection", and "valete", also Latin for, "farewell". The Latin "plaudite" means "applaud", or "may it please you". The latter two are standard exit words for Roman actors, suitable phrases for the histrionics involved. [ie]

1487 connaisseur -- French for, "expert" in the sense of being a professional as opposed to a connoisseur which suggests amateur status [HHC 7]

1488 Connaught Rooms -- at 61-5 Great Queen St., WC2, it is a restaurant specializing in private dining facilities, and is just around the corner from Kingsway Hall* [MMA 12]

1489 Connington -- J. J., the pseudonym of Alfred Walter Stewart (1880-1947), Scottish scientist and detective story author who created Sir Clinton Driffield. Stewart was educated at Glasgow, Marburg, and at the University College, London. He also wrote various technical volumes relating to chemistry. He is frequently mentioned in the company of such other authors as Freeman and Crofts**, high praise indeed. See also The Two Ticket Puzzle. [FRH 27]

1490 Connoisseur -- established in 1901, it is a magazine for colletors, scholars, and dealers in antiques and art, now published by the National Magazine Co., Ltd. [MMA 10]

1491 Consecration, Prayer of -- see

Prayer of Consecration [UD 22]

1492 consecutive fifths of Tittums -- when bells are rung in a fifths pattern, a small bell is rung between the strikes of two larger bells, thus creating a distinctive ti-tum-ti-tum-ti-tum, hence, Tittums. Fifths refers to the sequence in which the bells are rung, the change-ringing* pattern. [NT 1]

1493 Conservative -- in England, the political group also known as the Tories. The official title since 1909 has been the Conservative and Unionist Party. Benjamin Disraeli and Stanley Baldwin were, perhaps, its most influential leaders. The party tends to support a more cautious, middle-class orientation. [BC 18/HHC 8]

1494 conservatory -- a relatively large and probably ornate greenhouse attached to the main house. It would be a year-round source of herbs and flowers for the house and might even serve as a sort of informal sitting room for an afternoon tea as the light atmosphere and exotic plants would provide a pleasant background. [CW 1]

1495 consommé marmite -- a clear broth cooked and served in an earthenware pot. Often called petite marmite, it is usually served with toast points spread with bone marrow and other such delicacies. [mt]

1496 Consommé Polonais -- a clear broth soup made of chicken stock flavored with wine and various vegetables, served hot, and garnished with crumbled egg yolk [WB 4]

1497 Constable Z15 -- the P. C. at Stapley* who overheard William Grimethorpe* threaten some unknown person while drinking at the Pig and Whistle* [CW 11]

1498 constables -- see Police Ranks [WB 1 and passim]

1499 The Constant Nymph -- a novel (1924) by Margaret Kennedy (1896-1967), an English author of a series of popular novels. The entry title was a bestseller and chronicles the various activities of the Albert Sanger family. The nymph of the title is Teresa Sanger, the fifteen year old daughter who faces the challenges of love and fidelity. [NT 3]

1500 Constantinople -- now Istanbul, the famous and ancient Byzantine (now Turkish) city astride the southern end of the Bosporous on the coast of the Sea of Marmara. It is known and loved by detective story fans as one terminus of the fabled Orient Express. [WB 3]

1501 Constitutional Developments -- one of Miss Hillyard's* lecture series in the Shrewsbury College* history program. It is noted for its unchanging content and unending dullness. [GN 2]

1502 A contempt for money . . . -- PW creates his own version of I Timothy 6:10: "For the love of money is the root of all evil: which while some coveted after, they have erred from the faith, and pierced themselves through with many sorrows." [HHC 21]

1503 "Contented Man's Morrice" -- a poem by George Wither*. A morrice --usually morris--is a colorful costumed dance, often in cap and bells. The reference is to the religious and legal upheaval following the return of Charles II to the throne in 1660. At that time those who did not swear fealty to the king and to the Church of England could not hold public office, and there had been a great shift from Puritan to Monarchial government. [UD 17]

1504 Contes de la Fontaine -- an exquisite volume in PW's library with hand-colored illustrations by Fragonard*. The work contains tales from other sources such as Boccaccio* in which characters have been more sharply drawn to create smoother tales. The stories are not noted for meeting the standards of Victorian decorum. [aq]

1505 contralto -- the lowest of the standard divisions of the female voice when identified for singing purposes. HV is one, and DLS sang contralto in the Bach Choir* in 1914-15. [GN 19]

1506 controls -- the spiritual persons, or whatever, that are thought to to control or regulate the actions and words of a medium during a séance [SP 16]

1507 convinced Disraelian -- see Disraelian school of thought [NT 6]

1508 Conybeare -- Parker is referring to Frederick Cornwallis Conybeare (1856-1924), an Armenian scholar, BA from Oxford in 1879, who worked extensively comparing ancient Greek and Armenian texts of the various classics. He was also a noted Church historian. Parker is reading some of his work on the textual criticism of the New Testament. [WB 7]

1509 Conyers, Cuthbert -- also known as "Cut-throat", the fictional ancestor of Dr. Conyers*. He settled at Yelsall Manor in 1732 after a nefarious career that is supposed to have included dealings with the pirate Blackbeard*. Dr. Conyers was one of many who had hoped to find Cuthbert's treasure, supposedly "buried in Munster*". PW's work is instrumental in locating the treasure. [dh]

1510 Conyers, Dr. -- the master of Yelsall Manor and an elderly and eminent cancer researcher so in need of funds that he has sold some of his ancient library to obtain the money. He is the recipient of PW's beneficent activities. [dh]

1511 Cook [stomach] -- John Parsons Cook died on November 20, 1855, probably of strychnine* given to him by Dr. Palmer*. Cook's death was the last in an amazing string of murders of which Palmer is most certainly guilty. The reference to his stomach comes from the fact that when it was removed for examination, all sorts of indecent and inept attempts were made to prevent the examination. The eventual analysis itself will never be recorded as one of science's great triumphs as Cook had been stuffed full of strychnine, but the analysts found no trace of it. [UD 8/BC 13]

1512 Cook, Nell -- see "Nell Cook under the paving stone" [BH 4]

1513 Cooke -- a student at Shrewsbury College* who is commented upon for having "scrubby friends" [GN 18]

1514 Coomberland -- Cumberland, now Cumbria, one of the two counties in Northern England on the border with Scotland [CW 3]

1515 cop -- a slang term meaning to catch. A copper, therefore, is a policeman. "Fair cop" means to be caught fairly, not to be the victim of a trap. Jacques Sans-culotte* is admitting that PW has caught him with his linguistic pants down. The term "no cop" is also used to mean "no catch" in the sense that it is nothing special to the recipient, but could be of real value to the police. [aq/ab/GN 7]

1516 copal medium -- a resin mixed with oil paints to allow better control of their plasticity [FRH 2]

1517 Copernicus -- Nicolas Koppernik (1473-1543), the Prussian-Polish canon of Frauenberg and formulator of the theory that the planets orbit the sun. His theory is in diametrical opposition to the older, accepted in his day, Ptolemaic theory of an Earth-centered universe. His astronomical observations were published in De revolutionibus in 1543. [BH 12]

1518 Cophetua -- a legendary African king who did not care for women until he saw a beggar maid dressed in gray. He fell in love with her and they lived quietly and happily thereafter. The poem appears in Percy's Reliques of Ancient English Poetry of 1765. References to the story appear in Shakespeare and Tennyson. The king chased the maiden, but PW will not "chase" HV as he has too much respect and love for her to do so. Eiluned Price* is correct, she will have to send for him. [FRH 6/SP 23/HHC 13/ GN 12]

1519 coping-stone -- or capstone, the crowning or final touch in some situation or action from the fact that such a stone is the last one set in place and is often needed to hold the others in place [CW 2]

1520 Copley, Mr. Frederick -- an older member of the Pym's Publicity* copywriting staff, he does not choose to associate with the others there very frequently. He has the unenviable position of being able to foretell unpleasant consequences of actions taken by his colleagues without their ever believing him; the office Cassandra*.

1521 Copley, Mrs. -- wife of Mr. Copley*, she is not pleased when he

arrives home late from work without having telephoned her to warn her of the delay. He suffers as a result. [MMA 8]

1522 copped that packet -- a slang term for one person's taking the punishment intended for another [MMA 7]

1523 copper -- a slang term for either a policeman or a British penny. See also British Monetary Units. [nf/ GN 8]

1524 copper -- a large laundry kettle and the fire under it, the kettle's metallic content providing a name for the whole apparatus [NT 8]

1525 copper sulphate -- a blue crystalline chemical necessary to the process of electroplating [cf]

1526 Coppins, Mrs. -- the lady whom Mrs. Gates* accuses of vulgar ostentation in her choice of a wreath for Sir Henry Thorpe's* funeral. One can't help feeling that the objection relates more to the fact that Mrs. Coppins is a Nonconformist. [NT 6]

1527 copy chief -- normally called a Creative Director today, he is the principal person in the Creative Department of an advertising agency. In DLS's day, he would have been a copywriter, hence the title. He is responsible for the standard of work produced by all the artists and writers in the department. There may also be an Art Director in which case the supervisory functions would be shared. [MMA 8]

1528 copying ink -- heavy permanent ink used for making final entries in a ledger, etc. [GN 5]

1529 Coqcigrues -- the word appears in Charles Kingsley's The Water Babies, Ch. 8. The 1911 Larousse defines the word as either a fanciful beast or an idle tale. Therefore, the coming of the Coqcigrues would mean the same as "till hell freezes over", something that we never expect to happen. [GN 4]

1530 cor lumme [coo lumme] -- a Cockney utterance derived from "God love me", an all-purpose expletive [MMA 10]

1531 corbel -- some sort of device, plain or ornamental, that projects from a wall and is meant to support a weight. They would be used in connection with hammer-beams*. The ones in Fenchurch St. Paul* are decorated with carvings of cherubs' heads. See also grotesque from a Gothic corbel. [CW 15/NT 2]

1532 Coriolanus -- the title hero of Shakespeare's play of that name, ca. 1608, based on a story in North's translation of Plutarch's Lives. Coriolanus leads the Romans in a mighty victory over the Volscians and is hailed by Rome as a hero. It is proposed that he be made a consul, but his arrogance toward and contempt for the rabble turns everyone against him and he is banished. As revenge he sides with his former enemies and lays seige to Rome. Eventually he wins terms favorable to the Volscians, but his mother persuades him to betray them and the Volscians murder him. [BH E3]

1533 Cork -- either Ireland's southernmost county or the city and county seat of Cork. The area was noted for the harbor of Queenstown, now Cobh, formerly a stop for transatlantic steamers. [HHC 11]

1534 corked -- wine whose flavor has been tainted by the odor of an unsound or moldy cork. It is unfit to drink. [BC 22]

1535 Cormorant Press -- see Drew, Mr. [MMA 8]

1536 corn -- wheat, oats, barley, rye, etc., but not, in this context, sweet corn or maize; a catch-all term for the major cereal grains [NT 3]

1537 Corner House -- superior to the other Lyons* tea shops, Bertha Gotobed* was employed at one in North London near Epping Forest at the time of her death. There were four in London, the one near Piccadilly is spread over several floors, and Bunter almost loses a quarry there in that maze of serving areas. [UD 6/HHC 4/MMA 2]

1538 Cornwall -- the southwesternmost English county extending from just West of Plymouth to Land's End and including among its sights Tintagel and Penzance. Mrs. Grimethorpe's* family are located there, one of the remaining strongholds of Celtic influence in

Britain. [CW 19]

1539 Corona Corona -- a kind of cigar manufactured by various companies. It is round, straight, and has a bluntly rounded end. The better ones are made from highest quality Cuban tobacco. La Corona is one of the more famous brands. [WB 4]

1540 coroner -- a public official one of whose duties is to investigate any death not certified by a physician and to refer to the police if the death is suspected of not being the result of natural causes [passim]

1541 Corot -- Jean Baptiste Camille Corot (1796-1875), the renowned French landscape painter [WB 5/FRH 22]

1542 The Corpse on the Mat -- by Milward Kennedy*. It is a cleverly written work, but its somewhat strained plot built around two mirror-image apartment houses situated side-by-side and connected on some floors is flawed. This is not considered one of Kennedy's best works. The Murderer of Sleep, a later novel, probably holds that distinction. [FRH 27]

1543 Corporation Dump -- the dump for the City and Corporation of Oxford. We learn in GN that no matter how glorious the name may sound, a dump by any other name . . . . [GN AN]

1544 Corpus -- the college, Corpus Christi College, Oxford, that may have been attended by the clergyman that PW has remembered from his youth [BH 5]

1545 Corpus, pious pelican of -- see pious pelican of Corpus [GN 13]

1546 Corpus Christi -- a special feast day to honor the Eucharist, it is the Thursday after Trinity Sunday, the sixtieth day after Easter. The day became a universal feast day during the pontifical reign of Urban IV (1261-64) [UD 22]

1547 corpus delicti -- the body of the crime, that is, sufficient proof that a crime has been committed. One does not necessarily need a body to prove that murder has been done if enough other evidence exists to allow the coroner's jury to return a verdict of foul play. [HHC 21]

1548 correspondences -- communication, however done (as with rappings, voices, Ouija boards, etc.), with spirits of deceased or absent persons [SP 16]

1549 Corsica, wilds of -- a Mediterranean island about 105 miles southeast of France, part of the administrative district of Provence-Côte d'Azur-Corse [Corsica]. Most of the island is hills with some low mountains, and is well-suited to the sheep ranches and vineyards which cover them. The climate is mild year round and the scenery is extravagantly craggy. It would no longer be fair to call Corsica wild, but it would have appeared so to PW in the 1920's. [CW 1]

1550 Corton Burgundy -- fine burgundies from the area of the Bois de Corton near the village of Aloxe-Corton in the Côte de Beaune in eastern central France. There are several Corton burgundies, even two with Grand Cru appellations. The red Grand Cru is Le Corton, the white is Corton-Charlemagne. The particular wine is not specified. [SP 1]

1551 cosh -- a stout stick or a rod of wood or metal, sometimes covered with leather continued into a flexible handle. When swung with force, it makes a formidable weapon for incapacitating someone. [MMA 7]

1552 Cosmographia Universalis -- a combination of astronomy and general geography, basically a German approach, published in 1544 in Basel. It provides much information about Germany, some on Europe generally, but very little about the rest of the world. It was written by Sebastian Munster* and figures prominently in "Dragon's Head". The full correct title is: Cosmographei oder Beschreibung aller Länder stetten. [dh]

1553 cossack -- in some editions of MMA and BH the text is printed in such a way that someone is wearing one. The feat would be a difficult one at best because a cossack is a member of a Russian military class under the czars. A cassock is meant. They are ankle-length coats or outer garments with close-fitting sleeves. They are usually black and are worn by the clergy and some lay people. If one eliminates the

typographical error, the only other reason for such an error is the deliberate misuse for a humorous effect. Such a fad was popular during the 1920's in some literary circles. [MMA 4/BH 15]

1554 coster -- a fruit or vegetable peddler, short for costermonger. The term derives from costard, a kind of apple. [UD 23]

1555 Cotswold slate -- the Cotswold area of England (to the North of the Thames and Cirencester) has long been known for its limestone building blocks and exceptionally fine limestone roofing slabs [GN 1]

1556 cottage -- a loaf of special shape with a smaller loaf on top of a larger one [BH 4]

1557 Cotterill, Wilfred -- one of Pym's Publicity's* errand boys. He had a bloody nose on the afternoon of Victor Dean's* death and slept through the whole fracas. [MMA 10]

1558 cotton-reel -- a spool for cotton thread [UD 7]

1559 Council School -- see London County Council School (L. C. C. School). Julian Perkins* is a teacher at one. In a broader sense, any of the publicly supported schools run by a local government authority as opposed to a public school* which is privately owned and run. [HHC 24/MMA 10]

1560 counterfoils -- a detachable stub used as a receipt or for record keeping as with lottery or theatre tickets and checks [MMA 1]

1561 counterpoint -- a term used by Gerard Manley Hopkins* to identify a line of verse wherein a formal metre and a sprung rhythm* coexist [GN 13]

1562 counterpoint -- or polyphony, the mixture of two separate melodies into a single harmonic work. The device is typical of Bach's work. [GN 19]

1563 counterpoise -- a counterbalance weight [NT 3]

1564 Countess of Essex -- Frances Howard, later Countess of Somerset. Described by some as a junior edition of Lady Macbeth, she refused to allow her first husband, Robert Devereux, 3rd Earl of Essex, to consummate their marriage, divorced him, arranged the poisoning of Sir Thomas Overbury*, and eventually married Robert Carr, Earl of Somerset. She died of cancer after a term of six years in the Tower of London which she served with her husband, Somerset, but became estranged from him and was an outcast from court. He died in 1646, the last Earl of Essex, and his title reverted to the Crown. It was, however, later recreated. [GN 7]

1565 country-house cricket -- cricket* based at a "stately home" that had its own grounds and, often, an excellent team featuring amateur or professional players. Competitors were drawn from all over, frequently from among the wandering teams such as the famous I Zingari (The Gypsies) that had no "home" field. Such cricket flourished in the late 19th and early 20th centuries. After WW I it declined through lack of servants and private groundsmen. [MMA 10]

1566 County -- a reference to Norfolk*, site of the holdings of the mythical Dukes of Denver. There is, however, the ancient Duchy of Norfolk, still prominent in England, that was created for Thomas Mowbray who died in Italy in 1399. The Howard family, the present Dukes of Norfolk and relatives of the Mowbrays, date their peerage from John Howard who assumed the title ca. 1430. Since that time, the Dukes of Norfolk have been prominent in English politics, not always successfully --Katherine Howard, a niece of Thomas, the 2nd Duke, married Henry VIII in 1540 and was beheaded for treason in 1542. More recently, the Dukes of Norfolk have served as hereditary Earl Marshals for the highest state occasions. [BH P]

1567 County Council -- the elected governing body in each of England's counties. The governing system dates from the Local Government Act of 1888, amended in 1972 to create new boundaries and a merging of counties and districts. [HHC 20]

1568 County Histories -- a reference to the Victoria County Histories dedicated to Queen Victoria. Each county prepared its own history, a survey from

prehistory to the present arranged chronologically. Among the first to be completed was the volume for Hampshire, published in 1900. Some have been reprinted recently. [BH E2]

1569 County Scholarship -- a university scholarship provided by a county council. Scholarships from various sources, even from the colleges themselves, have long been a common feature of British university life. [GN 11]

1570 coup de théâtre -- French for an unexpected and spectacular turn of events; a stage trick [MMA 8]

1571 a couple of twos -- see cricket [MMA 18]

1572 Courier -- a fictitious newspaper [HHC 4]

1573 course[s] -- the successive shifting of the order in which a bell is struck in a series of changes* as established according to a mathematically derived system. The number of changes in a course is determined by the method being rung. The number of courses in a part may vary as well. In Holt's Ten-Part Peal (Grandsire Triples*)* there are five courses in each part for a total of fifty courses in the peal. [NT 1]

1574 course bell -- the bell that sets the hunting course for a section of a touch or peal [NT 1]

1575 Course [and Part] Ends -- a specific number of changes, the number depending on the method being rung, is a course. A course end is the last change* in that course. A part is composed of several courses, the last one of which becomes the Part End. [NT 1]

1576 Court Windlesham helicopter plans -- this reminds one of Conan Doyle's "Bruce-Partington Plans" and is just as fictitious. See also The Society. [ab]

1577 Courts of Love [medieval] -- an institution said to have existed in Provence and Languedoc in France and established to pass judgment on questions or problems of gallantry and chivalry. It relates especially to the code of conduct created by Eleanor of Aquitaine (ca. 1122-1204), wife of Henry II of England and mother of kings Richard I and John. The convention was spread throughout Western Europe through her patronage of troubadours, and holds that a knight will devote himself to a lady of great beauty who may be married or not, but who remains chaste so their love cannot be consummated. He performs brave deeds for her while she ignores him. The consequences of failing to remain chaste are seen in the story of Arthur, Lancelot, Guinevere and Mordred. [GN 1]

1578 Covent Garden [Market] -- the third theatre, built in 1858, to be located on the Bow St. site. The theatre is the principal center in England for opera, both English and Italian, and is located adjacent to what was, until recently, the center of London's fruit and vegetable trade, the Covent Garden Market. The area was originally a convent garden which was acquired by the Russell family (the Dukes of Bedford) during the reign of Henry VIII and was developed in the 17th C. The area is located in London's West End*, just North of The Strand*. [ab/im/MMA 4]

1579 Coventry -- the resilient and modern cathedral city in central England, home of the new cathedral, automobile manufacturing and bicycle factories, and the most famous equestrienne in history, Lady Godiva, wife of Leofric, Earl of Mercia, who started Coventry's growth as a center of commerce and industry. As a center for engineering and manufacture 900 years later, Coventry was savagely attacked by bombs on the night of November 14, 1940, but has now been rebuilt. [SP 14]

1580 Coventry St. -- a street about two blocks long that extends from the East side of Piccadilly Circus* eastward to New Coventry St. and on to Leicester Square* [MMA 2]

1581 cover point -- see cricket [MMA 18]

1582 covert-coat -- a coat made from a durable twilled fabric woven usually of mixed-color yarns. Such coats are sometimes waterproofed. [CW 1]

1583 Covert Corner -- an excellent name for a fictitious village or road junction in Warwickshire [UD 11]

1584 Cow and Pump -- the pub where PW, as Mr. Bredon, claims to have taken honors throwing darts. Its location, if real, remains elusive. This is the only mention of PW's expertise at darts. [MMA 6]

1585 cow-pats -- manure "patties" in a pasture [GN 19]

1586 coward enough to deny -- this and the subsequent references to cocks crowing, etc., are all allusions to the disciple Peter, who, as Christ foretold, denied Jesus three times before the roosters crowed to announce the morning [GN 14]

1587 Cowley, Mr. -- an employee of Crichton's* advertising agency. He is a motorcycle racing fan and provides further proof that Coreggio Plant* did not take all the tours he claimed to have taken. [nf]

1588 cowslip wine -- wine made from the blossoms of the cowslip (Primula veris). Similar plants are known in North America as well. The leaves of the plant are good as a springtime cooked green as are dandelions, but just the young and tender leaves. [NT 6]

1589 to cox -- to function as a coxswain; the steersman who shouts the rhythm, the only person in the shell who is looking forward [GN 12]

1590 Cox's Charing Cross branch -- Cox and Co. is a London banking firm headquartered at 6 Pall Mall. It is now a part of Lloyd's Bank but retains its separate identity as army agents. It is famous in detective literature as the repository of Dr. Watson's famous tin dispatch-box which is supposed to contain several Sherlock Holmes adventures thought too lurid for publication. [CW 2]

1591 cracked heels -- a crack or split on the back side of a horse's hoof. As such a crack would affect the tender part of the hoof called the frog, it would also tend to make the animal behave as if lame. [SP 12]

1592 cracker mottoes -- the slips of paper with sayings or bits of poetry written on them and hidden in lightly explosive party favors called crackers. They come apart when the ends are pulled, thus exposing the gift (often a paper hat) and motto. There is only enough explosive in one to make a mess of the paper wrapping and expose the contents. They are a common Christmas or birthday party favor. The British variety has a cardboard pull fastened to the detonating device while those in the U. S. (where still available legally) use string. Sir Septimus Shale* is noted as being particularly fond of them. [np]

1593 crackling -- what is left after the lard has been removed from pig fat, the crisp skin on roast pork. It is considered by some to be a delicacy. [GN 17]

1594 the Cracow monster [monstrum hoc Cracoviae] -- a human anomaly who supposedly had webbed and clawed hands and feet, a tail, a nose resembling a tail, and animal-like heads at the elbow and knee joints and at each breast. It also had eyes in its abdomen. There is little wonder that it held such fascination for Viscount St. George* who, at age ten, is unlikely to have encountered such things previously. PW refers to it as "that distressing infant". [dh]

1595 Craig -- an exhibitor at the Glasgow Exhibition*. He is fictitious as presented here. [FRH 12]

1596 Craig, Bobby -- a schoolmate of Myra* Strachan. They fought and Myra got a black eye, but she bloodied his nose. She is quite proud of the encounter. [FRH 4]

1597 Craig, Mrs. -- a prominent local spiritualist in Windle*. She is not regarded highly by the other residents of the boarding house where Miss Climpson* is staying, but Miss Booth* regards her talents as extraordinary. [SP 16]

1598 Craikes, Insp. -- the police inspector from Stapley* who begins the official investigation into the death of Denis Cathcart*. He is not pleased when Charles Parker* and PW "interfere" with his work. [CW 1]

1599 cramoisie -- spelled variously depending on its national usage; the French, English, and Scots all had their own spellings. Cramoisie is a scarlet cloth. See also "My love was

#1594 "That distressing infant", the Cracow Monster, from an illustration done in the 1600's.

clad in black velvet . . .". [qs]

1600 Cranton, Col. -- host at a tennis party attended by Mrs. Morecambe* [HHC 20]

1601 Cranton, Nobby -- the likeable thief who, while working with Deacon*, is caught and jailed as part of the Wilbraham* emeralds case [NT 2]

1602 crashing social bricks -- an extreme form of dropped a brick* [GN 12]

1603 Crate Mystery -- the murder mystery which occupies Parker's attention for the first half of BC. His successful solution of that crime earns him his promotion to Chief Inspector (see Police Ranks). [BC 12]

1604 Craven, Dr. James -- a physician in the area around Gt. Pagford and Paggleham** who serves, when needed, as police surgeon* to the local constabulary [BH 7]

1605 Craven St. -- a street running from Charing Cross* along the West side of Charing Cross Station to the Victoria Embankment in Westminster* [WB 10]

1606 Crawford, Rev. -- the Evangelical preacher who holds forth in Judd St.* His preaching is recommended highly to Bunter by Hannah Westlock*. [SP 9]

1607 Cream, Neill -- Dr. Thomas Neill Cream was hanged on June 3, 1892, for the motiveless murders of several prostitutes in the Lambeth* area of London in 1891-2. He was a bizarre man who followed the same general methods in each of his murders. [UD 19]

1608 crease -- see cricket [MMA 18]

1609 crease-patting -- see cricket [MMA 18]

1610 Crédit Lyonnais -- a major French joint-stock or incorporated commercial banking firm that is prominent in international banking circles [CW 3]

1611 Credo -- Latin for, "I believe", and, therefore, a statement of beliefs. There are various ones in use, but the one in question is the Nicene Creed, the basic statement of faith evolved at the Council of Nicaea under the Emperor Constantine in 325 A. D., and is a basic statement of orthodox belief. [ie]

1612 credo quia impossibile -- Latin for, "I believe it because it is impossible". As Certum est quia impossibile est, "It is certain because it is impossible", the same concept appears in the De Carne Christi of Tertullian (A. D. ca. 160-ca. 225), one of the greatest of the early Christian writers to use Latin. [WB 8/SP 20/ MMA 15]

1613 Cree -- the River Cree flows South and East from an area of small lochs and hills about thirty miles northwest of Newton-Stewart*. It empties into the West branch of Wigtown Bay. [FRH 2]

1614 Creech, Mr. -- the victim in "Striding Folly". He is a rich businessman of questionable scruples who plays chess* weekly with Mr. Mellilow*. [sf]

1615 Creeside -- a collection of a few cottages on the A714 route about four and a half miles northwest of Bargrennan* [FRH 2]

1616 Creethorpe, Lady Hermione -- a "very redoubtable virgin", and a formidable opponent for any who would cross her. She is not about to put up with anything she does not approve of. However, she dances well and was PW's partner when playing bridge* for small sums of money. She speaks her mind and does so clearly, regardless of current social attitudes. At Sir Charles Deverill's* Christmas costume party she comes as the queen of clubs, referring to herself as the Old Maid*. [qs]

1617 Creetown -- a small port on the estuary of the River Cree* and on Wigtown Bay about halfwayy between Gatehouse-of-Fleet* and Newton Stewart* [FRH 2]

1618 cremation authorities -- the governmental agency that grants permission to cremate a corpse. It requires the signatures of two physicians, one close to the case who can state that there is nothing suspicious involved. The other signatory must be some sort of public health official. Standard burials require only one sig-

nature on the death certificate. [UD 3]

1619 crenellated moulding -- an ornamental molding meant to look like the battlements of a castle [NT 2]

1620 crêpe-de-Chine -- the phrase is from the French and means crepe from China; a fine, soft fabric of a crinkled texture and used for either under or outer garments [CW 2/GN 8]

1621 cretonne -- an unglazed cotton or linen fabric of great strength used mostly for curtains and upholstery [SP 17]

1622 Crewe -- in Cheshire, West central England. It was a London and North Western Railway junction built in 1837 and later chosen as the site for the LNWR workshops around which the town grew. Crewe locomotives were famous for 100 years. [FRH 14]

1623 crib -- slang for either a place to live or a place of work [NT 14]

1624 cribbed, cabined and confined as Hamlet says -- Miss Climpson* is confused. Macbeth says:

"But now I am cabined, cribbed [hampered], confined, bound in
To saucy [sharp] doubts and fears."

The reference is to his unsuccessful attempt to kill both Banquo and Fleance when the murderers inform him that Fleance has escaped their trap. The passage appears in III, iv, 24-5, shortly before the famous banquet scene. [UD 3]

1625 "Crichton's for Admirable Advertising" -- the motto of Messrs. Crichton, Ltd.*, a Hatton Garden* advertising firm. The motto is a pun on James Barrie's* play, <u>The Admirable Crichton</u>, and on the real James "The Admirable" Crichton, a 16th C. scholar and swordsman who was killed in a brawl in Mantua, Italy. In the play, the servant, Crichton, becomes master when shipwrecked with the family he serves. He remains so until they are saved. Crichton is said as cry-ton. [nf/im]

1626 Crichton Ltd., Messrs. -- an advertising firm located in Hatton Garden*, London. Among their employees are Coreggio Plant* and Robert Duckworthy*. The former is a victim of murder, the latter of confusion. Duckworthy started in the packing department and later became a checker for outdoor displays. [nf/im]

1627 cricket -- a game for two teams of eleven, popular in the U. K. as is baseball in the U. S. The bowler, a pitcher in baseball, aims the ball (about nine inches in circumference and made of red leather over a twine and cork core) at a wicket nine inches wide and twenty-eight inches high consisting of three ash stumps so placed that the ball cannot pass between them. His object is to displace the bails, small pieces of wood placed across the stumps, and the batsman tries to stop his doing so by using a bat that is not more than thirty-eight inches long and four and a quarter inches wide which is made of straight-grained willow. There are two wickets, one at each end of a twenty-two yard long "pitch", and a batsman from the batting team stands at each.

The bowler bowls from one end six times, and then another bowler bowls from the other end six times, etc., At each change, "over" is called, and the fielders move over to their reciprocal positions, the wicket keeper (a catcher in baseball) changing ends as well. The ball must be "delivered" (leave the bowler's hands) while he still has a part of one foot behind the "bowling crease" (a white line drawn level with the wicket) or the umpire will shout "No Ball" and the batsman can hit as he likes and cannot be given out, bowled, or caught.

The bowler can bowl fast or slow, a leg-break (with counter-clockwise spin to make the ball veer to the left on striking the ground), an off-break, a googly (an off-break with leg-break action), a spinner which swerves, a lob with a high trajectory, a yorker striking the ground at the batsman's feet, or a bumper striking the ground early and bouncing high. If he bowls "wide" or out of the batsman's reach, a run is credited to the batting team unless the batsman hits it. The bowler is responsible for placing the fielders and takes the credit for a fallen wicket.

Each fielding position has a name. That behind the batsman being the

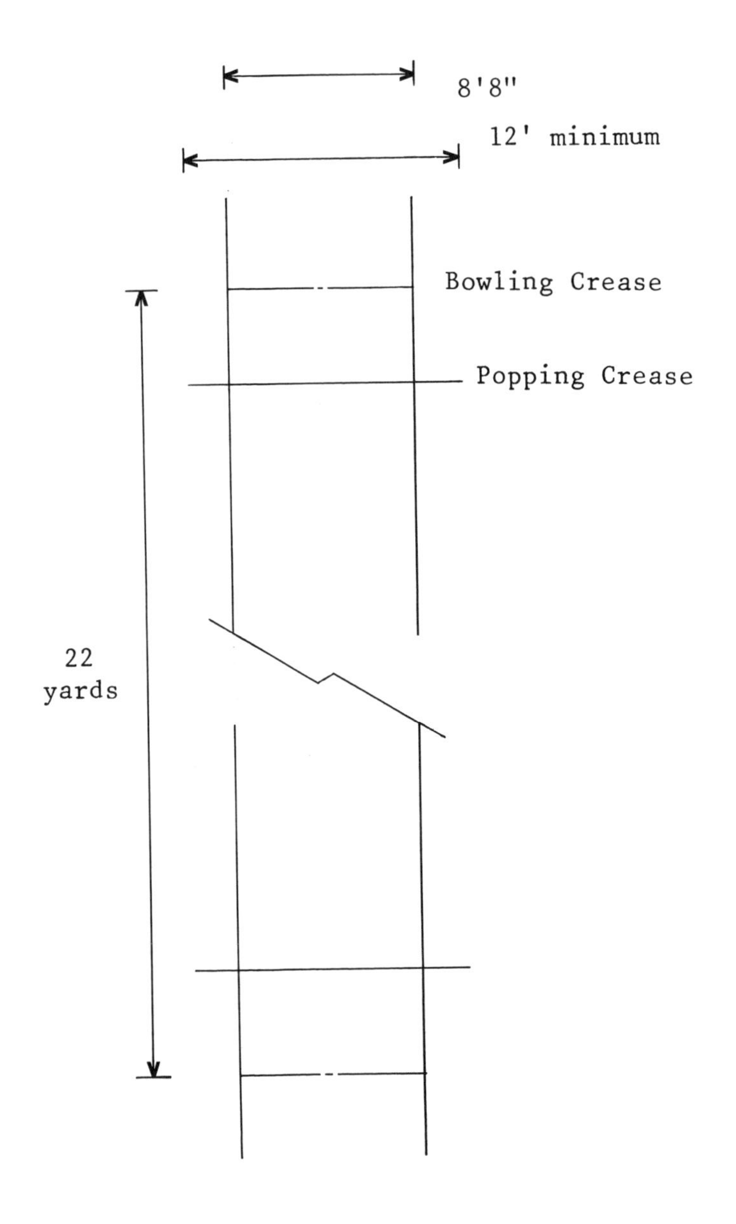

#1627 A typical cricket oval layout with placement of the bowler and the fielders. Allowing some latitude for individual situations, the players' assigned areas are indicated by the solid lines. Illustration by John D. Kovaleski.

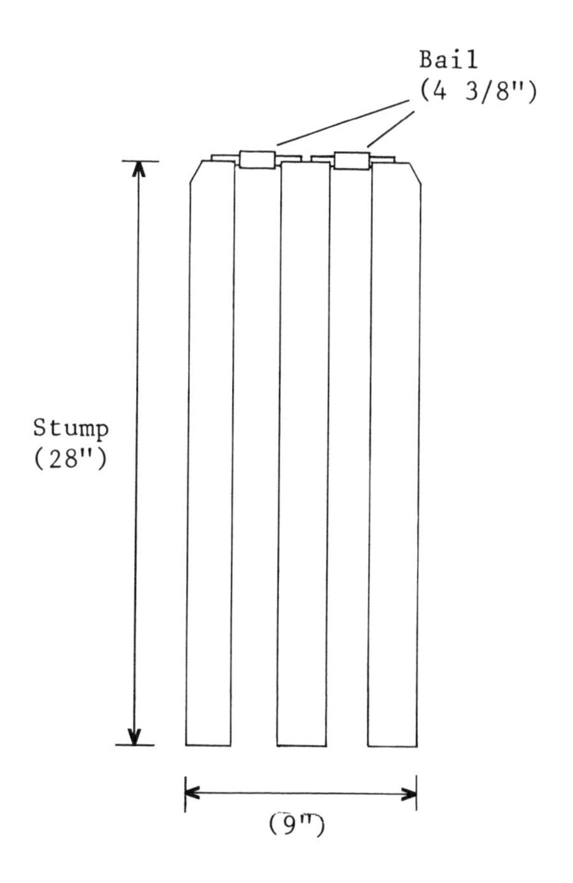

#1627 A wicket; the three "stumps" and two "bails" that the batsman attempts to defend. Illustration by John D. Kovaleski.

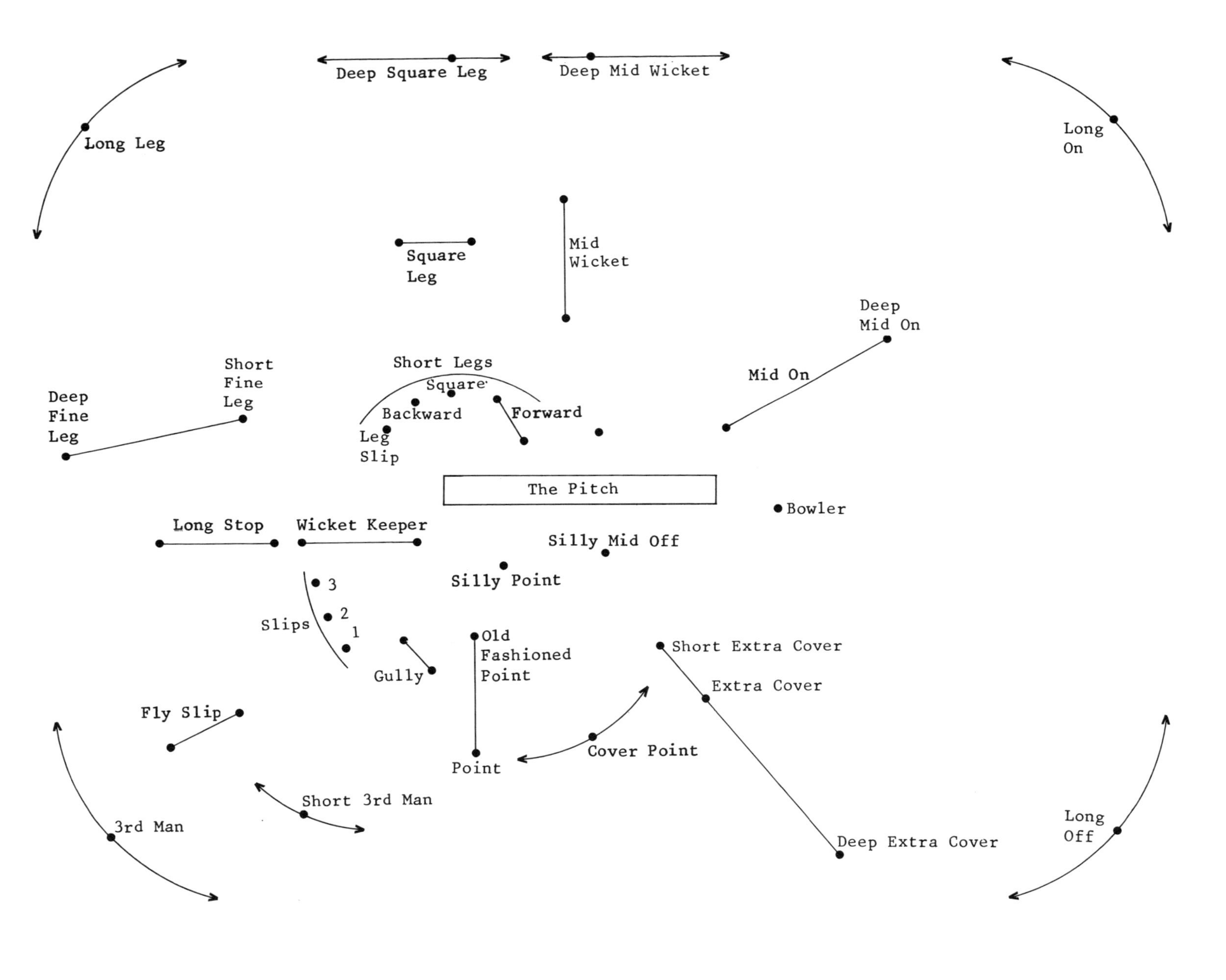

#1627 The layout and dimensions of a cricket pitch. Illustration by John D. Kovaleski.

wicket keeper who puts on protective gloves and "buckles on his pads" like the batsman. He can be reinforced for fast bowling by a long stop. As many as three or more slips may stand to the batsman's right rear. Cover point stands on a level with the batsman and mid off on a level with the bowler. Opposite them on the "leg" side are, respectively, "square leg" (where one of the two umpires also stands), and mid-on. There are many other possible positions (see the field chart). The other umpire stands behind the bowler's wicket. A position closer to the batsman is qualified by the term "silly". If placed a long way away, the fielder is said to be in "the deep field" (in the expectation of a high hitting stroke).

After each ball is bowled, the two batsmen may run to change places one or more times, scoring each time: a "run" if the ball has been hit, a "bye" if it has not, or a "leg bye" if it has hit the batsman's body. A batsman is "out" and takes no further part in that innings if: a) a bail is displaced by the ball in bowling, or by the batsman, or by a held or thrown ball when the batsman is not at the wicket ("stumped" or "run out"), b) a ball is caught after it has been hit and before it touches the ground, c) if the ball is prevented from striking the wicket by part of the batsman's person other than his hand or his bat ("leg before wicket", or "lbw").

If the batsman is thought to be out, any player can appeal to the umpire by shouting, "How's that?" and the appropriate umpire must shake his head or raise his index finger. The umpire's decision may not be questioned.

When the batsman first comes in, he places his bat on the "popping crease", the white line about four feet in front of the wicket, behind which he must keep foot contact or he will be "stumped", and he will "take guard" (meaning that the umpire will give him the position of his bat relative to the wicket). He may, for example, ask for "centre", or "middle and leg" (covering the middle and leg stumps), depending on his style of batting. He may also, as baseball players do, pat the ground to smooth the pitch. An uneven pitch may cause the ball to "bump". A worn and dry pitch may be called a "fast wicket", a damp one may be called a "sticky wicket".

Batting strategy includes defensive play (to stone-wall or "block") without scoring until he "gets his eye in". To "hit for two" means to hit hard enough to change places twice before the ball is returned, thus leaving the batsman where he started from. If he runs an odd number, the other batsman has to take the bowling unless it is the end of an over. If the fielders return the ball to either wicket too quickly for the batsman, and if that wicket is unoccupied, the batsman closest to it is "run out". The batsman can "hit all round the wicket" (in all directions), he can "pull" or "hook" the ball to "leg" or his left, or he can "cut" it (suggesting only a slight change of direction) through the slips (a fielding position) or square on the off side. A hit to the boundary (of the playing area, a distance which is variable) must be signalled by the umpire; it is worth four runs, six if it crosses the boundary without touching the ground.

A successful batsman may make his "century" (100 runs in one innings). PW accomplished this twice in succession, a notable feat. On the other hand, he may be out for nothing, known jestingly as a "duck's egg", a "duck", or a "quack-quack".

Each team has an innings when the whole team bats in sequence, completed after ten wickets have fallen, one man being left "not out" or "carrying out his bat". Each team may have one or two innings per match, the number being decided before play begins. The match in MMA (Ch. 18) is scheduled to last from 10 A. M. to 6:30 P. M., including the break. The start is frequently later, but the end (when "stumps are drawn") will be decided by the umpires if the light fails. If the second team to bat scores insufficient runs, it may be required to "follow on" (bat again) to see if it will lose by an innings. The winning team, provided the loser has finished batting, is that team which has scored the most runs in aggregate. A team can "declare" (voluntarily finish its batting) if the

captain feels that by so doing he will save enough time to dismiss the other team and, thus, avoid a "drawn game" (one won by neither side).

Cricket players used to observe a strict standard of personal behavior and dress. The typical "uniform" consisted of white flannel trousers, white open-necked shirts, and optional white sweater with a single colored band at the V-neck opening, and a cap in the team's colors. PW wore Oxford's "cricket blue". [HHC 12/MMA 10 and 18/ GN 14]

1628 cricket blue -- one gets a "blue" at Oxford or Cambridge when one represents one University against the other at various sports, of which cricket* is one. Players are then privileged to wear a special cap, dark blue at Oxford and light blue at Cambridge. [GN 14]

1629 cricket screen -- see screen [MMA 18]

1630 Crickett, Mrs. -- housekeeper for George and Sheila Fentiman* [BC 7]

1631 Cricklewood -- a community in the northwestern suburbs of London near Wembley, the location of a dance hall not further identified [nf]

1632 Cri -- see Criterion Bar [im]

1633 Crime King -- an oriental "villainous doctor" who can be none but the archest of all archvillains, Dr. Fu Manchu. As DLS, in the Detection Club oath, made special negative reference to the use of Chinamen, it is no surprise to have her poking fun at Sax Rohmer's evil genius. Fu Manchu is more ambitious than Prof. Moriarty*, and the Dr. has a better sense of fair play as well. [MMA 7]

1634 crime passionel -- "crime of passion". The expression in French for crimes committed in the heat of the moment, not necessarily a lovers' problem, and can be pleaded in mitigation of sentence in France. [CW 10]

1635 Crimea -- the Crimean War of 1854-56 between Russia and the combined forces of Turkey, England, France, and Sardinia. Out of this war came Tennyson's famous poem, "The Charge of the Light Brigade", which commemorates one of the bravest if most confused and devastating cavalry charges in history. [BC 1]

1636 Crimplesham and Wicks -- fictitious solicitors* located on Milford Hill, a real street in East central Salisbury*. PW is distracted to them by the pince-nez* found on the nude corpse found in Mr. Thipps's* bathtub. [WB 5]

1637 Crimplesham, Thomas -- the elderly solicitor* who answers PW's advertisement inquiring about some pince-nez* found on a nude corpse. The glasses do belong to Mr. Crimplesham, but the connection is a red herring. [WB 5]

1638 crimson lake -- a dark, reddish hue derived originally from the lac or gum-lac resin from whence shellac is obtained as well [FRH 2]

1639 Crippen and LeNeve -- the reference is to Dr. Hawley Harvey Crippen and Ethel LeNeve. Dr. Crippen was a rather mousy little man who was dominated by his wife who sang in music halls as Belle Elmore and who was less than faithful to him. The doctor's attention was diverted to a typist, Ethel LeNeve. Crippen murdered Belle with hyoscine*, chopped her up, and buried her in the cellar. He then started showing up in public with Ethel who wore some of Belle's jewelry. Suspicion aroused, Crippen invented different stories and, just as suspicion was dying down, he tried to escape to Canada as John Philo Robinson with Ethel disguised--not too convincingly--as a boy. Crippen was arrested aboard the S. S. Montrose in the first case of the use of telegraphy to catch a fleeing criminal. Crippen was tried and convicted in October of 1910. Miss LeNeve was acquitted. [BC 20]

1640 Crisp, Mr. -- one of the partners for whom Sparkes and Crisp* is named [FRH 28]

1641 Critch -- one of the competitors for the first prize for best peaches at the local fair. Mr. Puffett suggests that he might be the one who raided Puffett's orchard in an effort to prevent his winning that prize. [t]

1642 Criterion Bar -- a Victorian building at Piccadilly Circus*

#1628 Cricket at Oxford as PW would have known it.

featuring pavilion roofs. Originally a hotel and restaurant, it no longer serves those functions. The Criterion Theatre is also in the block. It opened in 1874, and was among the first to be lit electrically. It is mostly underground. [nf/im/MMA 2]

1643 The Critic -- a comedy by Richard Brinsley Sheridan (1751-1816). In act three of the play within the play, much is made of Lord Burleigh* wandering on and off stage without saying anything, only shaking his head. One stage direction reads: "Burleigh comes forward, shakes his head, and exits." [BH 4]

1644 critic on the hearth -- a pun on Dickens's Christmas story, The Cricket on the Hearth. In that story, Dot, the cricket (a good luck symbol) on the hearth, chirps when all is going well. [GN 17]

1645 Crockford -- fully, Crockford's Clerical Directory, an annual reference for facts about the Church of England and its clergy. It was first published in 1857. [UD 11]

1646 crofter -- a Scottish tenant farmer [FRH 2]

1647 Crofton -- a fictitious village. There are many villages in Warwickshire with "croft" in the name somewhere, but it is quite impossible to determine which one DLS might have had in mind. [UD 8]

1648 Croftover Magna -- a village twelve miles from Crofton* and a former home and place of business of Mr. Thomas Probyn*. It is fictitious, but may have been suggested by Crofton Magna. [UD 12]

1649 Crofts, Dr. -- a local physician from Baldock* who comes to William Grimbold's* home functioning as police surgeon [ae]

1650 Crofts, Mr. -- a partner in Crofts and Cooper*, solicitors*, who handled HV's defense during her trial for murder. One is not convinced of his belief in her innocence. [SP 4]

1651 Crofts and Cooper -- the firm of solicitors* who handled HV's defense during her trial for the murder of Philip Boyes*. They had the foresight to hire Impey Biggs* to argue the case in court. [SP 4]

1652 Crofts, Freeman Wills -- an Irish railway engineer (i. e. civil engineer, not locomotive engineer) (1879-1957) who also became a writer of detective stories featuring Insp. French. In 1939, he was elected a Fellow of the Royal Society of Arts (FRSA). Crofts is perhaps most remembered for his first novel, The Cask, a straightforward yet complex puzzle involving intricate problems in timetable movements, etc., written in 1920. [FRH 21]

1653 Cromwell, Oliver -- the Puritan leader (1599-1658) of the English Civil War and ruler of the country as Lord Protector from 1653 until his death. His son was unable to retain control and the royalists brought Charles II back from exile in 1660, returning the country to its traditional monarchical system, but with marked changes in the distribution of power in favor of Parliament. [NT 7]

1654 Cromwell Rd. -- a major thoroughfare due South of Kensington Gardens leading West past the Victoria and Albert and the Natural History Museums which are next door to each other at the corner of Cromwell and Exhibition Rds. [MMA 15]

1655 Cromwell's men -- a reference to Oliver Cromwell* and the Commonwealth (1649-60) that period between the execution of King Charles I and the Restoration of King Charles II. During this period many church decorations were destroyed if Cromwell and his minions thought they were too popish*. [NT 2]

1656 Crookes' glasses -- an early form of polarized sunglasses of superior quality that are no longer manufactured [FRH 10]

1657 Cropper, Mrs. Evelyn -- see Gotobed, Evelyn [UD 6]

1658 Crosbie and Plump -- solicitors* with offices located in the Bloomsbury* section of London. They employ Robert Ferguson*. [ss]

1659 Cross, Johnnie -- the man whom Will Thoday* attempted to save when the sluice gates collapsed killing both men [NT 19]

By Charles Lucy, R.A.

Oliver Cromwell

#1653

1660 Crossley [Mr. Justice] -- the "severe" judge who heard HV's trial for murder, the judge that PW describes as "A beast, but a just beast"*. He will be remembered in the annals of crime fiction for the marvellous digression during his summation to the jury about the proper way to make an omelette. It has been suggested that DLS may have had in mind Mr. Justice Avory who was known as a hanging judge. Descriptions of the two men are almost identical. Avory is described as icy, not known for a sense of mercy, and concerned only with legal considerations. He also liked to sit with his eyes closed assuming an air of unconcern until someone made an error. He sat from 1910 until his death in 1935. [SP 4]

1661 Crowder, Thomas -- a Crichton's* advertising agency artist who painted an oil portrait of murder victim Coreggio Plant*. PW liked the painting (its technique, not the subject) so well that he bought it. [nf]

1662 crown[ed] -- the replacement of some or all of the outer part of a tooth above the gum with an artificial, sculpted substitute, usually gold for molars because it is less brittle than porcelain or the standard mercury-silver amalgam. Crowns are used in areas larger than what would be called a "cavity" in normal circumstances. [HHC 34]

1663 Crown -- a fictitious pub in Paglesham* [t/BH 7]

1664 crown and anchor -- a gambling game played with dice on which those symbols are marked. The reference suggests a trivial offence and may allude to some old bylaw. [BH 11]

1665 Crown Derby -- (pronounced as darby) a particularly fine, soft paste porcelain manufactured at Derby in Derbyshire from 1756 when William Derby founded the factory. If the Crown Derby is used in its strict sense, the piece would have to have been made between 1770 and 1890 when that phrase was a correct technical descriptor. Before 1770, the product was simply Derby ware; after 1890, the pieces were called Royal Crown Derby by command of Queen Victoria. The products were originally imitative of wares from the Meissen and Chelsea works. [UD 4/BH E3]

1666 Crow's Beach -- a fictitious location on England's South coast. DLS might have had either Brighton or Bournemouth in mind as either will fit her general geographical description. [UD 19]

1667 Croydon -- a suburb in South London where Mr. Tallboy* is supposed to live. The airport facility there was London's major air terminal before WW II, but was replaced by Gatwick. Gatwick and Heathrow are now London's major commercial air terminals. [fr/MMA 8/GN 21]

1668 crucified upside-down -- St. Peter was supposedly crucified in that manner at his own request because he did not feel worthy enough to be crucified as Jesus had been. The process would certainly cure any lack of blood to the brain as it is the removal of so much blood from the skull that is partly the cause of death in the standard form of crucifixion. [CW 12]

1669 cruel as the grave -- the reference is to the Song of Solomon (or Song of Songs)* 8:6: "Set me as a seal upon thine heart, as a seal upon thine arm: for love is as strong as death; jealousy is cruel as the grave: the coals thereof are coals of fire which hath a most vehement flame." [fr/UD 16]

1670 cruet -- a vessel, usually of glass, with a stopper and a pouring lip used for serving condiments at the table [UD 1/BH 9]

1671 Cruives of Cree -- salmon traps on the River Cree*. The cruives were set in the middle of dams, much used as bridges for crossing rivers, and were widely known local landmarks at one time. [FRH 28]

1672 Crump, Mrs. -- the head charlady* at Pym's Publicity* [MMA 4]

1673 crumpets -- a sort of pancake or dropscone about the size of an English muffin made with yeast, flour, milk, and salt. They are "baked" on top of the stove in a frying pan using buttered crumpet forms. If crumpet forms are not available, they may be prepared as one would prepare pancakes.

[BC 7/SP 9]

1674 Crusoe fashion -- after being shipwrecked, Robinson Crusoe swam back to the hulk many times to float supplies, material, anything useful, from it with which to make his island home more comfortable. His goal was to rescue as much as he could before storms and currents on the reef destroyed the vessel totally. [SP 8]

1675 crusted -- usually referring to the fine material deposited in the bottle as a wine ages which is also called lees or dregs in a barrel, as in crusted port. By extension, it refers to anything antiquated or venerable. The reference to crusted old tawny, a kind of port, suggest set in its ways, traditional, perhaps even reactionary. [WB 7/CW 9]

1676 crutch-handle[stick with] -- a cane with a handle resembling the letter "T" as opposed to the more traditional straight stick or one with a rounded head. Such a stick would provide a firmer support for someone who depended heavily upon the cane for assistance and did not have it as a showpiece. [BC 6]

1677 Crutchley, Frank -- the ambitious and hard-working gardener who tends the grounds at Talboys*. He is among the many locals whose trust has been abused by William Noakes*. [BH 5]

1678 "Cry havoc! . . ." -- the line is from Shakespeare's Julius Caesar, III, i, 273, and usually appears as, "Cry, 'Havoc!' and let slip the dogs of war." It comes from Antony's soliloquy after Brutus has agreed to let him speak at Caesar's funeral. [FRH 22]

1679 Crystal Palace -- the glass structure made famous by the Great Exhibition of 1851. It was designed by Sir Joseph Paxton. After the Exhibition, the building was moved from Hyde Park to Sydenham in South London. It was mostly destroyed by fire on December 1, 1936, and the remainder was torn down in 1941 to prevent its being used as a landmark for bombers raiding London. The "antediluvian monsters" are almost the only remnants of the original Exhibition and Palace. They are the brightly colored, huge dinosaurs of a sort on an island in the middle and on the sides of the lake at the Sydenham site. [BC 3/HHC4]

1680 "The crystal springs . . ." -- the lines are from Christopher Marlowe's (1564-1593) play, Tamburlaine the Great, Part II, II, iv. Zenocrate is the daughter of the Sultan of Egypt and wife of Tamburlaine. The speech is part of a long elegy that Tamburlaine delivers to Zenocrate just before her death, and the line, "To entertain divine Zenocrate" is repeated as a sort of refrain. [GN 19]

1681 Cuban heel -- a straight, moderately high heel fashionable in the 1930's [GN 21]

1682 cubist electrical fittings -- cubism is an art movement originating in Paris in the early 20th C. which emphasizes basic geometrical shapes and was totally nonrepresentational. Such an electrical fixture would, therefore, be totally geometrical in design, and probably very simple as well. [np]

1683 cuckoo in the nest -- cuckoos lay their eggs in other birds' nests and then abandon them for the other birds to raise. The young of the "adoptive" parents usually die in the process. [MMA 21]

1684 cucumber frame -- a cold frame* for starting cucumbers [MMA 6]

1685 cui bono -- Latin for, "whom will it benefit", a guide to the guilty person [BC 20/BH 13]

1686 cuisine bourgeoise -- French for common home cooking [NT 8]

1687 cullies -- someone or something that imposes upon another; "con" artists; also a term of endearment like "old rogue" [GN 15]

1688 Culpepper, Mr. -- a not very well-liked student of Queen's College. See Oxford Colleges. [GN 8]

1689 Culyer, Captain -- a member and Secretary of the Bellona Club*. As Secretary he would oversee the day-to-day operations of the Club. [BC 2]

1690 Cumberland ham -- the hams prepared according to the traditions of Cumbria in northwest England [FRH 20]

1691 Cummings, Mr. -- proprietor of the

#1679 The Crystal Palace.

tobacco shop in Old Broad St.* where PW realized that he has tipped his hand regarding the drug smuggling business in MMA [MMA 17]

1692 Cummings, John -- Sir Julian Freke's* manservant [WB 9]

1693 Cummins -- the Munns's* neighbor lady and something of a snoop [BC 18]

1694 Cunningham -- physician and teacher at St. Luke's Hospital*, and a colleague of Sir Julian Freke* [WB 10]

1695 Cup Final -- the final match of the Football Association Cup competition, an elimination tournament open to all English football teams, though in its early days at least one Scottish team competed. The Cup has been competed for annually in peacetime since 1872 and, since 1923, the final has been played at Wembley Stadium. [GN 11]

1696 curare -- a South American poison extracted from the _Strychnos toxifera_. It is a powerful muscle relaxant with important medical uses. It is also very readily fatal. [UD 19]

1697 curate[s] -- a clergyman, either one in charge of a parish or one who assists a rector* or a vicar* [BC 20/BH E2]

1698 _curé_ -- French for a parish priest [NT 8]

1699 "Curioser and curioser" -- the line is Alice's from Ch. 2 of _Alice in Wonderland_* [BC 7/FRH 15/NT 10]

1700 _Curiosity Killed the Cat_ -- a title HV gives to Salcombe Hardy* to help get rid of him. It is supposedly the title of her next book, but it is more of a jab at Hardy's pesty snooping, one he chooses to ignore. The allusion is to the old adage, "Curiosity killed the cat", to which Hardy seems to respond, "But satisfaction brought him back." [BH 13]

1701 Currency Notes -- Bank of England* notes or paper money; legal tender [MMA 17]

1702 curry -- a dish (sauce or relish) heavily spiced with curry (a powdered mixture of cumin, coriander, tumeric, and other aromatic and powerful spices) and served with rice, meat or fish, and, often, with a wide selection of condiments such as raisins, shredded coconut, and chutney. It varies in potency from pleasantly spicy to self-abusive. [WB 5]

1703 cut off the joint -- meat sliced from some large roasted piece such as a leg or haunch [UD 1]

1704 cut the leather -- see cricket [MMA 18]

1705 Cuthbert -- Bredon's* grass snake. PW and Bredon use the animal to inflict justice upon Miss Quirk*. For a snake it is treated well, being housed in a cloth sack perched atop its own hot-water bottle. [t]

1706 cutting . . .the off -- see cricket [MMA 18]

1707 Cuttle, Capt. -- see "When found, make note of . . ." [BH 7]

1708 cyanide [of potassium] -- a notoriously deadly and fast-acting poison [cf/UD 21]

1709 Cyril -- one of the errand boys employed by Pym's Publicity* [MMA 10]

1710 Czecho-Slovakian pretended to swim the Channel -- there were several swimmers who pretended or attempted to do so in the late spring and summer of 1927, not all of whom were identified as to nationality [UD 19]

(D)

1711 D. 1234 -- a Police Constable's badge number [SP 1]

1712 D. Sci. Cantab. -- Doctor of Science, Cantabrigiensis, Latin for Cambridge. Oxford and Cambridge still print their diplomas in Latin. [WB 5]

1713 D. S. O. -- the Distinguished Service Order. It is awarded to officers in any branch of Great Britain's military for good service. It consists of two gold bars decorated with bas relief oak leaves between which is suspended a ribbon of red with narrow blue borders. From this is suspended a Maltese cross with rounded ends. The cross is white enamel on gold, in the center of which is a green laurel wreath on gold surrounding a red field on which appears a gold imperial crown. PW earned his DSO for some "recklessly good intelligence work behind the German front" in WW I. [UD BN]

1714 d. s. p. -- the genealogical abbreviation for the Latin decessit sine prole, "died without issue" or childless [GN 8]

1715 D. T. -- delirium tremens. PW suggests that conflicting aspects of the problems leave him feeling as though he had "a kind of mental D. T." The condition is marked by a shaking, frenzied confusion. [WB 5]

1716 d'Aumale, Duc -- Henri, the fourth of the five sons of Louis Phillipe* [HHC 32]

1717 "Da mihi basia mille, deinde centum . . ." -- Latin for, "Kiss me a thousand times o'er, then a hundred . . .". The line is from Catullus's* poem titled "Love is All":

"Let us, Lesbia darling, still
Live our life, and love our fill;
Heeding not a jot, howe'er
Churlish dotards chide or stare!
Suns go down, but 'tis to rise
Brighter in the morning skies;
But when sets our little light,
We must sleep in endless night.
A thousand kisses grant me sweet;
With a hundred these complete;
Lip me a thousand more, and then
Another hundred give again.
A thousand add to these, anon
A hundred more, then hurry one
Kiss after kiss without cessation
Until we lose all calculation;
So envy shall not mar our blisses
By numbering up our tale of kisses."

The translation is by Theodor Martin. Robert Herrick* uses much the same lines in his poem (in English) "To Anthea: Ah, My Anthea!" [BH 1]

1718 da Soto, Luis -- the orchestra leader at the Winter Gardens* in Wilvercombe*. He is a vain, slick, jealous sort of person. [HHC 10]

1719 daffodils -- also narcissus, a popular spring flower having bright green foliage and flowers resembling trumpet bells. The trumpet is traditionally yellow and may have either yellow or white petals. They grown from bulbs. Later varieties have different colors, but yellow or yellow and white remain the standard. [NT 3]

1720 dago -- a derogatory term applied to the Latin peoples. It is used by Det. Insp. Winterbottom* in reference to an Italian suspect. [nf/HHC 6]

1721 Daily Express -- one of London's leading morning papers, founded in 1900 with Independent/Conservative political leanings which remain [FRH 19/SP 12]

1722 Daily Flashlight -- a fictitious newspaper [GN 10]

1723 Daily Headline -- a fictitious newspaper being sued for libel by Sugar Toobin* [GN 11]

1724 Daily Mail -- one of London's several daily morning papers. Founded in 1896 by Lord Northcliffe, it is politically Independent/Conservative. [WB 5/FRH 19]

1725 Daily Mercury -- a fictitious newspaper [GN 3]

1726 Daily Message -- a fictitious newspaper [HHC 15]

1727 Daily Mirror -- one of several of London's morning dailies. It is headquartered on Fetter and New Fetter Lanes in the Holborn* section. It remains one of England's major papers and one of its most highly circulated news publications. Founded in 1903 by Lord Northcliffe, it is a tabloid sheet known in England as a "sex and scandal"

paper with left-wing political attitudes. [CW 11]

1728 daily physical jerks -- the morning calisthenics conducted at Pym's Publicity* for the benefit of the errand boys [MMA 3]

1729 Daily Telegraph -- founded in 1855, it is one of London's major papers. It tends to be Conservative in nature. [GN 10]

1730 Daily Tidings -- a fictitious newspaper, possibly referring to the Daily Mail* [UD 20]

1731 Daily Trumpet -- a fictitious newspaper [CW 14/GN 10]

1732 Daily Views -- a fictitious newspaper, possibly a reference to the Daily Mirror* [UD 20/BC 15]

1733 Daily Wire -- a fictitious newspaper which may be a reference to the Daily Telegraph* [UD 20]

1734 Daily Yell -- Uncle Meleager Finch* once won a £10 prize from this paper for having solved a crossword puzzle it ran. Both he and the paper are fictitious. [umw/UD 6/BC 15]

1735 Daimler -- an early automobile named for its inventor, Gottlieb Wilhelm Daimler (1834-1900), who, with Karl Benz, was one of the major developers of the internal combustion engine. Daimler, Benz, and, later, Emil Jellinek formed the Daimler-Benz Company in Germany to produce Daimler and Benz autos. A separate company was established in Coventry*, and Daimler was on the board of both. The two companies developed separately, however.
The products of both companies are noted for their excellence of design and craftsmanship, their superb handling characteristics, and the luxury their appointments. Their price tags are equal to their degree of excellence. British Daimlers were used by the Royal family until the early 1950's and PW has owned at least nine of them, all named Mrs. Merdle*. Among PW's Daimlers is a Twin Six model which he drives fast and well, a habit which unnerves both Parker* and HV, and he metamorphoses into his portrayal of Death Bredon in the back seat of a Daimler saloon (large sedan), but it is not stated whether it is his or not. [te/UD 6/FRH 4/SP 21/HHC 4/MMA 19/BH 1]

1736 Dairyfields -- manufacturers of Green Pastures margarine among other fictitious products. Their advertising is done by Pym's Publicity*. [MMA 1]

1737 Dalbeattie -- a community about five miles East of Castle Douglas* on the Urr Water [FRH 13]

1738 Dallmeyer, Dahlia -- the decapitated victim in "Cat in the Bag". She was a famous actress (fictitious) who ruined her husband and was unfaithful to him. The story is reminiscent of Crippen and LeNeve*, and, in both instances, the husband seems to have had the last word. [cb]

1739 Dalmellington -- a village on the A713 route at its junction with the B741 route between New Galloway* and Ayr*. The town is twenty-two miles northwest of New Galloway and fifteen miles southeast of Ayr. [FRH 14]

1740 Dalziel, Sergeant -- one of the investigators involved with the death of Sandy Campbell*. He is the senior official present when the murder scene is first examined before the body is removed. He proves to be a very thoughtful and tenacious policeman. [FRH 2]

1741 Dan -- see abode like Dan [MMA 18]

1742 Danaë's shower -- a reference to the story from Greek mythology of the daughter of King Acrisius of Argos. An oracle foretold that her son would kill the king, so he locked her up in a bronze tower, but she was "visited" by Zeus in a golden shower. She later bore Perseus who accidentally fulfilled the oracle's prophecy. [NT 3]

1743 Danbury -- an officer in PW's unit who was killed, apparently at the same time that PW was buried alive at Caudry* in 1918 [GN 17]

1744 The Dance of Machabree -- by John Boccace (see Boccaccio). A copy of this work was examined by PW while perusing Squire Burdock's* library. Boccaccio never wrote any piece with this name, but he did write a long work entitled De Casibus Vivorum Illustrium, stories of great men who suffered great

misfortunes. In that light it is very similar to the dance of death concept in that both observe death as the great and inevitable leveller of all men both great and small. Dances celebrating death were staged to reinforce the idea of man's earthly vulnerability and of death's omnipresence.

A later author, John Lydgate, took large parts of the De Casibus to form his Fall of Princes, published during the 1430's. It is a poem of some 36,365 lines. When Richard Tottel reprinted the Fall in 1554, he added an appendix, "The daunce of Machabree". Apparently Squire Burdock has at least that part of Tottel's reprint of the Fall, and it justifiably arouses PW's instincts as a book collector, especially in its deplorable state. The Fall and the Dance of Death have both been edited and published in the 20th C. by the Early English Text Society of London. [bc]

1745 dance Sir Roger -- see Sir Roger [qs]

1746 Danegeld -- a tax imposed at the end of the 10th C. or in the early 11th C. to raise money to buy off the Danish raiders so as to protect England. The Normans, lovers of precedent, continued it as a land tax after conquering England in 1066. [BH 18]

1747 Dane, Clemence -- pseudonym of Winifred Ashton (1888-1965), an English novelist, dramatist, and poet. The pen name refers to London's St. Clement Danes church. Miss Climpson* is most likely referring to one of Miss Dane's earliest works, Regiment of Women, a devastating study of a girls' school. [UD 8]

1748 Daniel, mother of -- see mother of Daniel [GN 17]

1749 Daniel come to judgment -- the words are Shylock's in The Merchant of Venice*, IV, i, 223 [BH 18]

1750 Daniels, Mr. -- one of the more senior staff members at Pym's Publicity*. He is a group manager* in charge of several of the firm's accounts. [MMA 1]

1751 Daniels business -- the reference is to the death of a nurse, Miss May Daniels, while on vacation near Boulogne, France, in March of 1927. There was some confusion about the death, but there seems to have been no determination of foul play. [UD 19]

1752 Danse Macabre -- considered by some to be one of the poorer works of Camille Saint-Saens*, it remains well known on concert programs for its having been accurately titled. PW uses the piece in recorded form to help support his conjuring act. [ie]

1753 danseuse -- a dancer, usually of ballet, but, in this case, of a kind of dance both less classical and more ancient [MMA 4]

1754 Dante -- the great Italian poet (1265-1321), Dante Alighieri. He was the first writer of importance to compose works in his native tongue. Author of The Divine Comedy* and La Vita Nuova, he remains a powerful influence on Western culture. DLS taught herself Medieval Italian so she could translate The Divine Comedy into English, a work that was near completion at her death in 1957. Her friend, Barbara Reynolds, finished the Paradiso for her. Of note in DLS's translation is that it retained Dante's verse structure, the Italian terza rima, the only translation to do so. [WB 1/ BC 18]

1755 Dante painted an angel -- while he is remembered for his literary impact on western culture, exceeded only by the Bible and Shakespeare, Dante* did study painting and music and had the great painter Giotto as one of his friends [BC 18]

1756 Danvers, Mr. -- a fellow student and friend of the Viscount St. George's* at Christ Church* College, Oxford [GN 9]

1757 Darby and Joan pair -- a common and kindly phrase applied to an attached couple, usually elderly and often of reduced circumstances. The source of the phrase is uncertain, but seems to have first appeared in some anonymous verses first printed in Gentleman's Magazine of 1735 (V, 153). [BH 1]

1758 "Dark and true and tender is the North" -- line 80 from the "Introductory Song" of Tennyson's The Princess. In full, the passage is:

"O tell her, Swallow, thou that know-

DANTE ALIGHIERI

From a fresco, somewhat restored, ascribed to the contemporary artist, Giotto. In the National Museum, Florence.

#1754 Dante Alighieri, after a fresco by Giotto in the National Museum, Florence.

est each,
That bright and fierce and fickle is the South,
And dark and true and tender is the North." [GN 8]

1759 dark as Egypt -- see darkness was Egyptian [BH 19]

1760 dark-room -- a room especially constructed without windows, or with windows blacked out, and with a light-proof doorway. It is so arranged for the safe handling of light-sensitive photographic materials before and during processing. The photographer sees with the aid of a red light of a type that will not affect the films, papers, and chemicals. [GN 16]

1761 darkening counsel -- confusing the explanation or advice. The concept seems to originate in Job 38:2 and elsewhere in that Old Testament book, at least as expressed as in the citation here. [GN 14]

1762 darkness was Egyptian -- the allusion is to Exodus 10:22: "And Moses stretched forth his hand toward heaven; and there was a thick darkness in all the land of Egypt three days." This occurs just before the judgment of the firstborn and the Passover. The suggestion is of a darkness somehow beyond the norm, a foreboding of evil or of God's wrath. [MMA 9]

1763 Darley -- a village between Lesston Hoe and Wilvercombe**. It is fictitious. [HHC 2]

1764 Darley Halt -- a train stop between Lesston Hoe and Wilvercombe**. It is fictitious. [HHC 2]

1765 Darling -- manufacturers of the "Non-Collapsible Towel Horse" and other commodities. It is fictitious. [MMA 1]

1766 Dart -- the family name of three sisters: Susan, Hester, and Emily. Susan became Susan Brown*, Hester became Hester Duckworthy*, and Emily remained unmarried. Emily was the mother of Robert Duckworthy*, but Hester raised the boy as her own. [im]

1767 Dartford -- a village on the South bank of the Thames between Maidstone and London and about halfway between the two. Deacon had travelled not quite fifteen miles in the two days following his escape from prison. [NT 12]

1768 Dartmoor [prison] -- the maximum security prison on Dartmoor at Princeton. It was originally built to house prisoners of the Napoleonic Wars, the foundation being laid in 1806. It became a prison for criminals in the mid-1800's and has since developed a worldwide reputation as a tough stronghold. [BC 18/NT 5]

1769 Datchett -- a farmer in Great Pagford or Paggleham** [BH 11]

1770 daurna -- a deliberate misspelling by DLS to indicate the Scots dialectical pronunciation for dare not [ss]

1771 David -- the second king of Israel and the youngest son of Jesse of the tribe of Judah. He slew Goliath. The reference to David having danced before the ark of the Lord* is a pun on the name of David Wicks and the Biblical king. It was the latter who danced before the ark as told in II Samuel 6:14ff. PW mentions all this "wildly" because he is rapidly becoming aware of the fact that the whole business of the pince-nez* is a red herring and that, consequently, he has wasted a good deal of time. [WB 7]

1772 David and Beersheba--or do I mean Daniel? -- the Dowager Duchess* is confused. Beersheba is a place, "well of the oath", twenty-seven miles southwest of Hebron on the border of the Southern Desert. She has in mind Bathsheba, the Hittite wife of Uriah, who was loved by David. David ordered Uriah, his captain, into a dangerous battle situation where he was killed. David then married Bathsheba who bore him Solomon. David followed Saul as the second king of Israel. What the Duchess probably has attempted to recall is the story of David and Jonathan. Jonathan was Saul's son and the two boys were the closest of friends. The Old Testament books of I and II Samuel recount the whole story. The hero Daniel, of lion's den fame, has nothing to do with David in any way. [SP 1]

1773 David and Goliath -- the reference is to the famous Old Testament story found in I Samuel 17:31-58.

[MMA 5]

1774 David Copperfield -- a novel by Charles Dickens* published in serial form in 1849-50. Dickens called it his favorite novel. In some ways it is also his autobiography. The story recounts the life of the title character and hero, and we meet many memorable characters along the way such as Peggotty, Aunt Betsy Trotwood, Wilkins Micawber, and the vile Uriah Heep. [CW 3]

1775 Dawson -- see the genealogical chart at the end of UD [UD 4]

1776 Dawson, Agatha -- the first of several victims in UD. Born in 1852, she died, unnaturally, in 1925. A spinster by choice, she impresses one as a person who is very much in control of her life and who intended to maintain that control for as long as she could. [UD 4]

1777 Dawson, Rev. Hallelujah -- Agatha Dawson's* second cousin, a Black from the West Indies. He is a mild and gentle man of distressed financial condition to whom Miss Dawson had been paying an allowance. He does not quite live up to the fiery qualities his first name suggests. [UD 11]

1778 Dawson, Simon -- Agatha Dawson's* great uncle, he was last heard of as being in the West Indies [UD 12]

1779 Day of Judgment -- in Christian theology the day when all persons will be raised in their flesh to face the judgment of God [GN 14]

1780 Day of the Dead -- see All-Hallow's Eve/Day [ie]

1781 deFramboise-Douillet, Mme. -- see Framboise-Douillet [MMA 11]

1782 deJoinville, Prince -- François (1818-1900), third son of the five born to Louis Philippe* and his wife, Maria, daughter of the King of Naples. He served with the Union forces under General McClellan in the American Civil War (1861-65) while in exile from France. He wrote extensively in his later years on topics in history and the French navy. [HHC 32]

1783 "De la Vanité" -- an essay by Michèle de Montaigne (1533-92), one of the world's great essayists. Its content was inspired by the Old Testament book of Ecclesiastes, 1:2. [GN 13]

1784 deMomerie, Dian -- the central figure of the group of drugs, sex, and alcohol fiends who descend upon Major Milligan's* home every weekend for their orgy--their effor to overcome their ennui which is terminal in Dian's case. She becomes infatuated with PW in his guise as Bredon disguised as the harlequin, but she is later found dead in a wood near Maidenhead*; her throat had been cut. [MMA 3]

1785 de mortuis -- in full, de mortuis nil nisi bonum, Latin for "of the dead say nothing but good" [MMA 3/ BH 7]

1786 "De Novis Insulis" -- the chapter title of one chapter in Sebastian Munster's* Cosmographia Universalis*. It means "Concerning the New Islands", and Cuthbert Conyers* certainly intended the title as a pun. All this figures prominently in one of PW's more amusing cases. [dh]

1787 de Reszkes -- a brand of cigarette used by Paul Alexis*. They were an English brand made of Virginia tobacco and had a rather snob-appeal market until they disappeared in about 1950. [HHC 4]

1788 deVine, Miss [Helen?] -- a newly arrived Research fellow attached to Shrewsbury College*. She is a scholar whose specialty is National Finance under the Tudors, and who is working as a recipient of Shrewsbury's Jane Barraclough Fellowship--all of which is fictitious. She becomes a rather unexpected and helpful confidante for HV while she sorts out her feelings for PW. The name Helen may be her own, but it may also be an allusion attached to her in the circumstances described in GN 18. She later is one of HV's bridesmaids. [GN 1/BH P]

1789 Deacon, Jeff -- the butler at the Red House*, and Mary Russell Thoday's* first husband. His theft of the Wilbraham* emeralds led to his imprisonment and eventual death after his escape. He is portrayed as a thoroughly despicable person. [NT 2]

1790 dead cert, straight from the stables -- race course jargon for an

absolute certainty; information directly from the jockey or trainer [SP 21]

1791 dead sea apples -- see dead sea fruit [GN 21]

1792 dead sea fruit -- the apples of Sodom which traditionally are lovely in appearance, but are ashes or smoke within. Supposedly they grew beside the Dead Sea and are referred to by Josephus and Tacitus, among others, who may have had in mind gall nuts produced by an insect, the Cynips insana. [UD 16]

1793 Dead Man's Post -- a fictitious location on the commons area between Little Doddering and Frimpton**. It is the place where Black Ralph of Herriotting* murdered George Winter and was hanged in chains for having done so. [bc]

1794 Dead Man's Walk -- a path adjacent to Merton College and along the northern edge of Merton Fields in Oxford [GN 13]

1795 deaf as an adder -- PW is alluding to The Book of Common Prayer* and its quote from Psalm 58:4-5: "Even like the deaf adder that stoppeth her ears; Which refuseth to hear the voice of the charmer: charm he never so wisely." The statement is accurate also. As far as is known now, snakes are deaf to airborne sound as humans know it. It is uncertain, but they may be sensitive to vibrations picked up through the ground. [MMA 13]

1796 deal -- the wood of some fir or pine tree [NT 4]

1707 deal table -- a heavy table made of fir or pine planks seven to nine inches wide by up to three inches thick [SP 4/BH 2]

1798 Dean -- the senior administrator at a college or cathedral [GN 1/BH P]

1799 Dean, Pamela -- sister of the murder victim in MMA, she cooperates generously with PW during his investigation into her brother's death. She eventually marries Mr. Willis* of the Pym's* staff. [MMA 2]

1800 Dean, Victor -- a former member of the staff at Pym's Publicity* who had died about a week prior to the opening of the action in MMA. He was a thoroughly unpleasant sort of person whose murder is as well justified as a murder ever can be. [MMA 1]

1801 Dear Brutus -- a play by Sir James M. Barrie, written in 1917. The title refers to Shakespeare's Julius Caesar, I, ii, 139-40. One character in Barrie's play, Purdie, is given to phrases beginning with "Hold on to", especially in Act III. PW seems to have him in mind. [fr]

1802 Dear Dizzy -- the common nickname for the former Prime Minister, Benjamin Disraeli*, of whom the Dowager Duchess of Medway* was fond [aq]

1803 Dear Lillian -- PW's attempt to emulate verbally the characters in movies who can write one thing while saying something else or who recite the letters they write for the benefit of the viewer. He is, in fact, asking his mother to get Sir Impey Biggs* and come to Riddlesdale Lodge* as soon as possible to start work on the Duke's defense. [CW 3]

1804 "Dearly beloved brethren" -- the opening of a standard invocational prayer in many Christian services of worship [NT 2]

1805 Death -- PW's second name. It is pronounced to rhyme with teeth to avoid any unpleasant associations. [UD BN/MMA 1]

1806 Death by Misadventure -- a coroner's verdict in the U. S. would more likely bring in a ruling of Accidental Death [te/CW 1]

1807 death grip -- the vicelike grip of a corpse, usually coming with the onset of rigor mortis*; that Victor Dean* should have such a firm grip so soon after death is highly unlikely, especially as he was on a flight of stairs and would instinctively have tried to save himself if possible, thus releasing the book from his grasp. Yet, it is possible that such a grasp could be established if death was instantaneous, but it remains unlikely even if possible. [HHC 1/MMA 5]

1808 "Death has so many doors to let out life." -- the line is from The Custom of the Country (ca. 1620), a bawdy romantic drama by Fletcher and Massinger, not Beaumont as stated in

UD. The line comes from II, ii, and it echoes one of DLS's maxims: "It is fortunate for the mystery monger that, whereas up to the present there is only one known way of getting born, there are endless ways of getting killed." [UD 21]

1809 Death in the Pot -- the novel HV is working on at the time of Philip Boyes'* death. As Boyes died of arsenical poisoning and as the novel centered on that very method of murder, her work contributed greatly to he problems at her trial for Boyes' death. Of interest is the fact that she finished writing it in jail, and it was being published during her trial. A better aid to publicity is hard to imagine, even if it is a somewhat drastic situation upon which to capitalize. [SP 6]

1810 Death 'twixt Wind and Water -- the novel that HV has in progress during the action of GN. [GN 11/BH P]

1811 "The death was certainly sudden . ." -- see Paterson, Dr. James [UD 1]

1812 Death-watch -- any of a group of insects which make a ticking sound and which are the object of the superstition that to hear one means that someone has died nearby. The same has been said of crickets. [GN 17]

1813 "Death, where is thy sting" -- see "Oh death! where is thy sting?" [MMA 1]

1814 Death's Jest Book -- or the Fool's Tragedy, by T. L. Beddoes*, was published after the author's death in 1850, and is considered his best work. The story is one of murder, revenge, political intrigue, superstition, and the macabre, all of which are elements of Beddoes' work. There are duels, charnel-house scenes, scenes of raising the dead, treachery, fratricide, suicide, and enough murder to gladden the heart of any "B" grade movie producer. Every principal character is dead by the end of the play, the last one being taken to his grave while still alive, escorted by the ghost of the play's first murder victim. Despite all of this carnage, there are some excellent examples of blank verse and some notable lyrics, but even they are replete with much graveyard imagery.

The characters are: Melveric, Duke of Münsterberg; Adalmar and Athulf, his sons; Wolfram, a knight, and Isbrand, the court fool, also brothers; T[h]orwald, a governor in the Duke's absence; Siegfried, a conspirator; Ziba, a Moorish sorcerer; Sibylla, a lady; and Amala, T[h]orwald's daughter. There is a record of an actual Duke of Münsterberg (in Silesia) having been stabbed to death by the court fool, the most complete account of which appears in Karl Friedrich Flögel's Geschicte der Hofnarren, Leignitz und Leipzig, 1789, Ch. 12. It is from this version that it appears Beddoes drew the basics of his plot. [UD 20/SP 8/HHC 3]

1815 Debrett -- the reference is to the Peerage of England, Scotland, and Ireland, first published in 1802 by John Debrett. It is now issued annually. The firm undertakes to do genealogical work for private individuals both in the U. S. and the U. K. [HHC 4]

1816 debagging Culpepper -- to pull down Mr. Culpepper's pants (bags) in public as a practical joke, the intent of which is to cause acute embarrassment [GN 8]

1817 Decameron -- see Boccaccio, Giovanni [CW 5]

1818 decani side -- the term derives from Fenchurch St. Paul's prior existence as an abbey church. "Decani" is the side of the chancel* where the Dean's chair was located, or the South side. In the Middle Ages the choir was in two groups, thus allowing much of the Mass to be sung in a responsive (question and answer) manner or antiphonally. See also #1073. [NT 3]

1819 deckle-edge -- most high quality paper is made one sheet at a time. The frame used to make the sheet leaves a somewhat rougher edge than would be found on machine-made papers. The gilt edging would frame the writing surface as a decoration and would be added late in the manufacturing process. [MMA 7]

1820 decree absolute -- the final divorce decree which terminates the marriage. It is given only after a period of separation. [UD 15]

1821 decline jusjurandum -- Wilberforce

Pope* asks the Viscount St. George to decline the word (it means to swear an oath). The word is an exception and is, therefore, a common trick question on Latin tests. The word has to be treated as two words, not one. Latin requires the declention of nouns, pronouns, and adjectives, but only English pronouns require such special consideration. [dh]

1822 Dee -- a short river flowing via Loch Ken* and Kirkcudbright* into Solway Firth [FRH 1]

1823 deed box -- a light metal box for the safe storage of valuable papers. They sometimes have simple locks to slow those who might pry. By "safe storage" is meant keeping the papers safe from mice, insects, etc. Deed boxes are not meant to be burglarproof or fireproof. [SP 10]

1824 deed of gift -- a legal undertaking to make a gift or regular gifts by deed of covenant. They are particularly useful for persons who wish to dispose of their property before their death and, thus, avoid probate, inheritance taxes, etc. While a deed of gift in the U. S. does not have the authority of a warranty deed, when properly executed it has full legal weight and would be difficult to circumvent. [SP 7]

1825 Deed of Trust -- see Trust deeds [SP 14]

1826 deep field -- see cricket [MMA 18]

1827 "The deep waters have gone over us . . ." -- a misquotation from Psalms 69 and 124. In the KJV, the verse is 69:2: "I am come into deep waters, where the floods overflow me." The second part of the allusion probably relates to Psalm 124:4: "Then the waters had overwhelmed us, the stream had gone over our soul." [NT 19]

1828 "Defeat thy favour . . ." -- this quotation is from Othello, I, iii, 341, Iago's speech to Roderigo which begins, "It is merely a lust of blood and a permission of the will." [NT 5]

1829 Dekker, Thomas -- English playwright and essayist (1570-1632). Most of his plays have been lost, but The Honest Whore and The Shoemaker's Holiday are among those that survived. Of his prose works, it is The Wonder-Ful Yeare of 1603 and The Gulls Horn-book that are best remembered. [GN 15]

1830 Delagardie, Honoria Lucasta -- in some editions her middle name is given as "Lucaster", a typographical error. She is the Dowager Duchess of Denver as her husband, Mortimer G. B. Wimsey, the 15th Duke, died as the result of a fall from his horse during a hunt in 1911, leaving her son, Gerald, as the 16th Duke. His wife, Helen,*, then became the Duchess, so his mother became the Dowager Duchess to differentiate between the two ladies. Her other children are PW and Lady Mary*.

She appears in only a few of the short stories, but figures notably in WB, CW, and SP. The best portrait of her appears in BH where her delightful personality is shown to excellent effect. She is a bright, alert, and friendly person who is always in good spirits and ready for whatever comes her way. She is known as Lucy to her intimates, and has an amazing range of diverse social contacts which PW does not hesitate to use if he needs to do so, especially her friends at Scotland Yard*.

She attends HV's trial as a favor to PW, but when he announces that he is engaged to HV, it is the Dowager Duchess who does the most to assist HV in her transition to a life of wealth and ease in an ancient ducal family. It is her innate graciousness mixed with a sometimes overly honest bluntness that seems to endear her most to her fans.

Her humor is often unconscious as it arises from her fuzzy memory--she often misquotes or confuses allusions, but she can be incisive in her observations about people and it is that incisiveness that also contributes to her humor. Throughout she remains witty, practical, and sometimes fuzzy, but she is always supportive of her children when they need her. One would soon learn to put great value on her friendship. [qs/WB 1/CW 3/SP 1/BH P]

1831 Delagardie, Paul Austin -- PW's uncle, brother to Honoria Lucasta Delagardie* Wimsey, PW's mother. Uncle Paul has had as much, if not more, to

do with PW's education and upbringing as his father, and PW relies on his advice in several instances. DLS "asked" him to prepare a biography of PW which appears in UD as an introductory element. His most extensive appearance is in BH where he becomes for us the concerned, loving, worldly, and ascerbic uncle who knows PW well enough to trust his judgment in selecting a wife, and who envies PW the choice he has made. He is portrayed as the sort of uncle that anyone would enjoy having as a relative. [UD BN/BH P]

1832 Delaprime -- a young lady jilted by Martin Burdock* [bc]

1833 Dell, Ethel, M. -- the maiden and pen names of Ethel Mary Savage (1881-1939). She was an English novelist who wrote such things as The Way of an Eagle (1912), known for their appeal to what would have been called, at the time, literary passion. She invented the male variety known as the "strong silent" type. [BC 20/MMA 7]

1834 deltoids -- the muscles, triangular in shape, which cover the shoulder joints and function to raise the arm laterally [SP 17]

1835 dem'd total -- the elegant alternative to "damned". Baroness Orczy created Sir Percy Blakeney, the Scarlet Pimpernel, perhaps literature's most famous user of that word: "Is he in heaven or is he in hell, that dem'd elusive Pimpernel." [BC 7]

1836 demon -- the basic form of solitaire or patience, also called Demon Patience and other local names. Twenty-eight cards are dealt into seven piles, one card in the left pile, seven in the right, with two, three, four, etc., in the intervening piles. The top card of each pile is face up, the rest are face down. The object is to get all the cards into play either in the original piles or in foundation piles which align the cards by rank in their suits. [BC 20]

1837 dene-holes -- found usually in Essex and Kent, they are sixty to eighty feet deep, vertical, and have horizontal passages and chambers at the bottom. The name is probably a corruption of "Dane holes" as it is assumed that the Danes dug them for reasons now unknown. [NT 5]

1838 deniges -- from the French verb dénigrer, to disparage. PW has Anglicized the word. [GN 4]

1839 Denmark, Prince of -- Shakespeare's Hamlet [UD 5]

1840 Dennis, Jack -- an errand boy at Pym's Publicity* [MMA 10]

1841 Dennison, Beryl -- a distant relative of Lady Shale* [np]

1842 Dennison, Mr. -- he is noted in the Gatehouse-of-Fleet* area for having caught a large fish in the Minnoch* near where Sandy Campbell* was killed. The fish was caught about a year before Campbell's death. [FRH 2]

1843 Dennison, Richard -- a distant relative of Lady Shale* [np]

1844 Denver -- Gerald, the Duke of Denver, PW's brother. See Wimsey, Gerald Christian. [MMA 11/BH P]

1845 Denver -- a real village in Norfolk about two miles South of Downham Market*, and about fifteen miles South of King's Lynn. It is not to be confused with Duke's Denver* which is fictitious. DLS used the name of the real Denver as the source of the Wimsey family title, but chose to locate the family seat about fifteen miles away and just a few miles South of Swaffham which is East and North of Downham Market. A more thorough consideration of this whole study of names and locations appears in C. W. Scott-Giles's The Wimsey Family. [passim]

1846 Denver, Dowager Duchess of -- see Delagardie, Honoria Lucasta [passim]

1847 Denver Ducis -- Duke's Denver* [BH E2]

1848 Denver Sluice -- the adjustable barrier across the Great Ouse just above where it is joined by the Old and New Bedford Rivers**. A series of gates and channels assists in the removal of water from the fenlands by preventing the waters from back-flooding up the Great Ouse River. This sluice is near Denver* and Downham Market* in western Norfolk. [NT 2]

1849 department -- a French unit of local government akin to a county

in England. The Dept. of the Marne and of Seine-et-Marne are adjacent to each other and border on the eastern edge of Paris. They were in the front lines during some of WW I. The French form of the word is département. [NT 7]

1850 Derby -- the famous Epsom Derby, pronounced as darby, an annual horse race in England, founded in 1780 by the 12th Earl of Derby. It is for three year olds and is usually run at Epsom on the Wednesday before or the second Wednesday after Whit-Sunday*. In 1932 (see MMA [notes]), the race was in early June and was won by April the Fifth. Dastur was second, and Miracle was third in a field of twenty-one horses. [HHC 16/MMA 1/GN 3]

1851 Derby -- see Crown Derby [BH E2]

1852 des Grieux, Chevalier -- see Manon Lescaut [CW 18]

1853 des histoires -- French for, "difficulties", "unpleasant scenes" [CW 16]

1854 Desdemona -- see Stupid and dangerous, like . . . [FRH 6]

1855 "Detection in Fact and Fiction" -- the title of HV's speech to the Junior Common Room* of Shrewsbury College* while in residence there during the action of GN.

One is reminded of DLS's speech, "Aristotle on Detective Fiction", given at Oxford in March of 1935, roughly the same time as the action of GN. That essay remains one of the best considerations of the structure of the detective story ever penned. [GN 7]

1856 detective turns out to be the villain -- it is hard to know just what PW might have had in mind here as there are all sorts of stories that have used the "least likely person" approach. Some of the more famous of these are Israel Zangwill's The Big Bow Mystery, Gaston Leroux's The Mystery of the Yellow Room, or, even, Agatha Christie's The Mystery of Roger Ackroyd.

There is no question that DLS was being deliberately vague here as she did not believe in revealing the endings to specific novels unless there was a particular reason for doing so as in her essay, "Aristotle on Detective Fiction" (see above). [MMA 13]

1857 détraqué -- French for "unhinged", or "crazed"; "out of touch" [HHC 15]

1858 Devant -- see Maskelyne and Devant stunts [ie/te/hp]

1859 Deverill, Sir Charles -- the host of the Christmastime party to which all guests come dressed as a representation of some game. He is dressed as a Mahjong* set. It is at this party that Charmian Grayle is murdered. [qs]

1860 Deverill, Lady Charles -- wife of Sir Charles Deverill* [qs]

1861 The devil is always ready to quote scripture . . . -- Helen, Duchess of Denver*, shows some acquaintance with Shakespeare when she alludes to his The Merchant of Venice, I, iii, 99, "The devil can cite scripture for his purpose." The line is Antonio's and continues:

"An evil soul producing holy witness
Is like a villain with a smiling cheek,
A goodly apple rotten at the heart:
O, what a goodly outside falsehood hath!" [SP 12]

1862 Devil's Flat Iron -- the local name for the large rock outcropping on which HV found Paul Alexis' body [HHC 4]

1863 Devon apples -- apples from Devonshire which has a gentle climate well suited to growing fruit [MMA 4]

1864 Dewsbury, Lord -- Minister for Foreign Affairs. He is mentioned by Sir Reuben Levy* in his diary as having been a dinner guest in the Levy home. He is fictitious. [WB 5]

1865 Dewsby -- head of the Scotland Yard fingerprint department. He is fictitious. [UD 23]

1866 diabolo -- a balance game requiring skill and dexterity. It consists of two sticks, one held in each hand, the outer ends being joined by a string or thread on which one balances a spool or spindle resembling two cones joined at the point. The object is to move the balanced spool around so as to do tricks with it. Joan Carstairs* wore a costume meant to suggest a diabolo. [qs]

1867 diagrammatic furniture -- steel or wood furniture of the Bauhaus or Breuer style as it was introduced and made popular during the 1920's and 30's. Much of the furniture remains in vogue today. Not all of the designs provide comfort, and the term's negative tone in context reflects this. [np]

1868 Diana -- Col. Belfridge's* best spaniel bitch, mother of Stamford Royal [HHC 8]

1869 diatonic scale -- the standard musical scale of eight tones, either major or minor, and without chromatic deviation [SP 8]

1870 Dickens, Charles -- the great Victorian novelist (1812-70) quoted from or alluded to by PW and others throughout the canon. Among his greatest works are David Copperfield, A Tale of Two Cities, and Great Expectations. [passim]

1871 Dickensian good fare -- among other talents, Dickens* had great descriptive powers, especially regarding the magnificent Victorian dinners, and particularly those celebrating Christmas. To this day, a Dickensian feast suggests great quantities of perfectly prepared food in a convivial atmosphere. [np]

1872 dickey -- touchy, unhealthy, weakened, a slang word [NT 10]

1873 Dickie -- one of the revellers at the first de Momerie* crowd party attended by PW as Harlequin. He is sober enough to attempt to dissuade PW from diving off the fountain into its receiving basin. [MMA 4]

1874 Dictionary of Quotations -- most likely a reference to The Oxford Dictionary of Quotations, a collection of over 40,000 cross-indexed quotations that is continually refined and expanded with each new edition. It is published by the Oxford University Press. [MMA 19]

1875 diddle[d] -- to hoax, fool, or swindle; to elude a pursuer by a series of zigzags and "duck and weave" movements [BC 14/HHC 26/ BH P]

1876 "died because they never knew" -- the lines are from Hilaire Belloc's (1870-1953) poem, "The Python" that appears in More Beasts for Worse Children. The verse goes:

"I had an aunt in Yucatan
Who bought a Python from a man
And kept it for a pet.
She died because she never knew
These simple little rules and few;--
The Snake is living yet." [UD 15]

1877 diethylsulphonmethylethylmethane -- perhaps more commonly known as methyl sulphonal or trional. It is a crystalline, non-narcotic, hypnotic and sedative that is stronger than sulphonal. It has since been withdrawn from the market because of its toxicity. [UD 19]

1878 Digg's Drove -- "drove" is a word for a path along which cattle are regularly driven. The location of Digg's Drove is unspecified other than as being in the parish of Fenchurch St. Stephen* which borders on Fenchurch St. Paul*. [NT 2]

1879 digitalin -- a drug compounded from the leaves and seeds of the common foxglove. It is a white, crystalline steroid used as a powerful and potentially fatal heart stimulant and as a diuretic. [BC 14]

1880 Dignam, Joe -- proprietor of the Anwoth Hotel*, Kirkcudbright*. He is a real person at whose hotel DLS stayed on summer vacations. [FRH Foreword]

1881 "Dilly Song" -- a Cornish folk song and a variant of the song called "The Ten Commandments". The song is done in two voices, the first saying, "Come and I will sing to you." The second voice responds, "What will you sing to me?" Then the first continues, "I will sing you one-e-ry." "What is your one-e-ry?" "One and one is all alone and ever more shall be so." The line "Five are the flamboys under the pole" (or "boat" in some versions) is from the fifth verse of the song. [CW 13]

1882 Dimity -- the number six bell in the ring at Fenchurch St. Paul* She weighs about 3/4 ton and is tuned to ring E. She was cast in 1883. [NT 1]

1883 Dimsworthy, Mrs. "Freak" -- a houseguest at Duke's Denver* during the Christmas holidays in 1929.

Tact and intelligence do not seem to be among her strong points. [SP 12]

1884 Dinglewood, Marchioness of -- she had an eight-string necklace of pearls stolen during the "Jewel Song"* in Faust* while attending a performance at the Covent Garden Theatre*. See also The Society. [ab]

1885 Dinglewood, Marquis of -- husband of the marchioness mentioned above of whom we know no more [ab]

1886 Diogenes -- of Sinōpe in the 4th C., B. C. He is the principal voice of Cynic philosophy which sought to achieve freedom from wants and desires through a simple life and repudiation of civilized customs. He is said to have searched in daylight with a lantern for an honest man. [SP 20]

1887 Directoire -- Directory, the government that ruled France from November 3, 1795 to November 9, 1799. It was overthrown by Napoleon's coup. In its later days it was marked by avarice and corruption. See also merveilleuse. [mt]

1888 Directory of Directors -- one of the books PW finds when he assumes the late Victor Dean's* office. It is a list of the directors of joint stock companies in the U. K. It has been published by T. Skinner since 1880. [MMA 1]

1889 disabuse -- to free from error or fallacy. A valuable proposition for Insp. Sugg*. [WB 6]

1890 disarmament -- in the era following WW I, one of the foremost ideas was to avoid war at any cost, so disarmament was popular everywhere outside of Germany [GN 4]

1891 discovered a plot -- perhaps a reference to the information obtained during a Scotland Yard raid on the Russian Trade delegation offices in London which gave proof of espionage and subversive activities in England. The raid took place on May 12, 1927. [UD 19]

1892 disestablishment and disendowment -- the former is the withdrawal of state patronage and control from a church or other religious body. The latter refers to stripping away special financial considerations afforded by the state to the official church in exchange for some other form of aid. Such actions, as done in Wales in 1914 and 1920 when the Welsh Disestablishment and Church Temporalities Acts were passed, strip a church body of state control and of much of its former financial foundation. Mr. Venables* expresses deep concern about these problems and the need for revision in England. [NT 9]

1893 diseuse -- French for, "great speaker"; in this case, female [NT 8]

1894 Disraeli, Benjamin -- a major forming hand of the modern Conservative Party, and one of the Commons' most brilliant parliamentarians (1804-81). Disraeli served as Prime Minister in 1868 and from 1874-80. He was created 1st Earl of Beaconsfield by Queen Victoria in 1878. [aq/umw]

1895 Disraeli [dear] -- the Dowager Duchess's allusion is uncertain, however, in a speech delivered on July 28, 1871, Disraeli referred to apologies as accounting only "for that which they do not alter", a thought which applies to this particular encounter between HV and Helen, Duchess of Denver*. [BH P]

1896 Disraelian school of thought -- a reference to the polish and gentility of Benjamin Disraeli* who was noted for being polite to a fault. His extreme politeness infuriated many, but Queen Victoria loved it. [NT 6]

1897 distemper -- a paint using a water base with size for hardening and used for wall decoration; tempera [GN 6]

1898 District Messenger -- also district messenger, an employee of The District Messenger & Theatre Ticket Co., Ltd. The firm provided messengers to meet trains, take charge of luggage, act as guides, deliver messages, etc., at hourly and daily rates. It was a separate company that functioned as an auxiliary to the old Telegraph Co. before it was taken over and phased out by the Post Office, and in that capacity the messengers also delivered telegrams within a particular postal area. Their functions are now largely being assumed by Securicor, a security

firm. The original District Messenger Co. was headquartered at 100 St. Martin's Lane and had branch offices at 91 and 194 Piccadilly, among other places. [UD 23/BC 8/NT 16]

1899 ditching -- see hedging and ditching

1900 diver tram -- one that "dived" into a tunnel down the middle of Kingsway*, passing under The Strand*, and emerging on the Embankment*. They generally plied the route between Holborn* and Westminster*, but were done away with in 1952 at about the time the last London trams ran. Part of the tunnel still exists as an underpass. Such a tram would provide Parker with one of the fastest routes from his lodgings to Scotland Yard. A "diver" is also slang for a pickpocket, so a "diver tram" might not be illogical in that sense either, especially during rush hour. [UD 6]

1901 Dives in what's-his-name -- dives is Latin for "rich man", and the word is used to mean that as well as to function as a name of sorts for the otherwise nameless rich man in the story of Lazarus and the rich man in Luke 16:19-31. The word "Dives" appears in the Vulgate version, but not in the King James Version. [GN 9]

1902 _The Divine Comedy_ -- Dante's* epic poem composed over a span of several years and completed just before his death in 1321. The poem is broken into cantos of which there are 100. After a single introductory canto, there are three groups of thirty-three cantos each, one group for Hell, "The Inferno"; one for Purgatory, "The Purgatorio"; and one for heaven, "The Paradiso". His description of the universe and his theology are based on the ideas of St. Thomas Aquinas almost totally, but the beauty of the poetry and the universality of the poem's concepts are far more important today than any of its doctrinal content. [WB 1]

1903 divine Sarah -- Sarah Bernhardt [Bernard] (1845-1923), one of the world's first great actresses in the sense that she was adored around the world, not just in some specific place. She began training at the age of thirteen, played at the _Comédie Française_, and then toured the world in triumph. She is best remembered, by those who saw her, for her voice which was described as a "golden bell". [CW 10]

1904 the Divorce -- the one arranged by Henry VIII to dispose conveniently of his first wife, Catherine of Aragon. That divorce precipitated the arrival of the Protestant Reformation in England with a vengeance. [GN 17]

1905 dixie -- from Hindi and related languages, a _degachi_, or iron pot or kettle, used especially by soldiers to make tea or stew [HHC 12]

1906 Dixmude -- a town in West Flanders, Belgium, about fifteen miles South of Ostend on the coast [NT 8]

1907 Dixon Mann -- John Dixon Mann was a Manchester* physician, born in 1840, who wrote _Forensic Medicine and Toxicology_, published in 1893 with a sixth edition as late as 1922. This book inspired and provided plots for many of the English writers of detective fiction during the Golden Years of the 1920's and 30's. It is a warehouse of information about all sorts of crimes and is liberally illustrated with legal cases and their connection with the work of the forensic pathologist. [WB 2/BC 15/FRH 25/SP 20]

1908 djibbah -- or djubbah, a loose Arabic outer garment or gown worn like a coat, open in front, and having sleeves extending nearly to the wrists [GN 3]

1909 Do cats eat rats? -- in Ch. 1 of _Alice in Wonderland_, Alice asks: "'But do cats eat bats, I wonder?' And here Alice began to get rather sleepy, and went on saying to herself, in a dreamy sort of way, 'Do cats eat bats? . . . and sometimes, 'Do bats eat cats?'" [HHC 16]

1910 "'Do I look like it?' said the Knave . . . ." -- PW is quoting from Ch. 12 of _Alice in Wonderland_. The quotation is a response to the King's query, "You can't swim, can you?" [HHC 25]

1911 do our dooties in the station . . . -- Mr. Lavender is not quoting Scriptures, but he is quoting, after a fashion, The Catechism in _The Book of Common Prayer_ where the line is written: "To learn and labor truly to

get mine own living, and to do my duty in that state of life, unto which it shall please God to call me." [NT 4]

1912 do the thing that's nearest -- the allusion is to Charles Kingsley's (1819-91) "Ode to the North-east Wind":

"What we can we will be,
Honest Englishmen.
Do the work that's nearest,
Though it's dull at whiles,
Helping, when we meet them,
Lame dogs over stiles." [BH 11]

1913 "Do ye ken John Peel?" -- from the poem "John Peel", by John Woodcock Graves (1795-1886). The poem deals with fox hunting and Peel's excellence as a hunter. [UD 12]

1914 Dodd, Ephraim -- sexton of the local Anglican parish church who accompanies the vicar* and the waits* to Sir Charles Deverill's* Christmas-time party [qs]

1915 Doddering-in-the-Dumps -- one of PW's creations, the name of his invented country village [hp]

1916 Doddering Priory -- a religious ruin in Little Doddering* that is described as "more ancient" than the neighboring church. As the church has a Norman apse*, the priory may date from Saxon times. [bc]

1917 dodge [dodging] -- a change-ringing maneuver in which a bell is shifted, or dodged, from its normal ascending or descending order in a course* to one place in the opposite direction, and is then, in the next round, returned to the position it would have had had it not shifted [NT 1]

1918 Does a livelier iris . . . -- PW assaults some otherwise famous lines from Tennyson's* "Locksley Hall":

"In the Spring a livelier iris
changes on the burnish'd dove;
In the Spring a young man's fancy
lightly turns to thoughts of
love."

They are lines number 19 and 20 in the poem. [SP 8]

1919 Dog and Gun -- the pub in the unnamed village (perhaps Kirkby Stephen) near Brough*. It was here that PW finally caught up with Hugh Farren*. [FRH 20]

1920 dog collar -- the stiff white collar worn by many clerics [UD 11]

1921 Dog-faced Dick -- a fictitious gangster of the excessively evil variety popular in the early crime movies, especially the melodramatic serials [MMA 11]

1922 dog with two tails about it -- excited in the extreme, a proverbial expression [HHC 7]

1923 "Dogs and children always know . . ." -- a phrase of unknown origin suggesting that dogs and children are somehow aware of good or evil intentions before those intentions are made known, a dangerous and patently false assumption [HHC 21]

1924 "dogs eat Jezebel" -- the reference is to II Kings 9:30-7, especially verse 36 which relates to Jezebel's violent death [CW 4]

1925 Dogsbody Dan -- a criminal mentioned by Parker while trying to figure out who might have assaulted him [MMA 7]

1926 doing evil that good may come -- the allusion is to Romans 3:8. Paul condemns the idea that any sin can glorify God. PW refers to the idea because Noakes* was cheap and did not keep his chimney swept (evil) that his murderer was captured (good). [BH 20]

1927 Doings, Mrs. -- PW's reference to Michael Waters's* landlady, Mrs. McLeod*, when he had forgotten her name momentarily [FRH 7]

1928 Dolby, Mark -- a grocer in Stapley* with whom William Grimethorpe* had done business [CW 11]

1929 dole [on the] -- receiving national assistance payments; similar to being on welfare in the U. S. [HHC 21]

1930 dolichocephalic -- descriptive of of a long head with a cranial index (the ratio of a head's maximum breadth to its maximum height multiplied by 100) of less than 75 [MMA 15]

1931 Domestic Economy -- the term formerly used to identify what is now called Home Economics [GN 2]

1932 domina -- Latin for "lady" used here in its academic sense to mean a female don or one who has

achieved academic rank at Oxford or another University. It would be the proper form of address used in Latin inscriptions on diplomas, etc. PW refers to HV in such a way in BH to indicate to her that he will treat her as an investigative and intellectual equal despite her "alarming plunge into wifeliness". [GN 1/BH 7]

1933 dominoes -- the ancient game played with rectangular tiles that are marked with every possible combination of numbers that can be rolled with a pair of dice plus a set of "bones" or playing pieces that have a blank or zero at one end. Standard sets go up to the double six bone, but there are larger sets available. Many variations on the game exist. [BC 20/FRH 27]

1934 Dominique -- daughter of the owner of the posada* [ie]

1935 don -- a title applying to the fellows of an older university [GN 1/BH P]

1936 Don Juan -- the legendary, profligate, and young Spanish nobleman; a synonym for one who is obsessed with the pursuit of women regardless of how the woman feels about it. The Don's great appearances in literature and music include G. B. Shaw's Man and Superman, the "Don Juan in Hell" segment, Mozart's opera Don Giovanni, and Richard Strauss's tone poem, Don Juan. Lord Byron's sixteen canto, 16,000-line poem, Don Juan, is only loosely based on the Spanish nobleman. The Don first appeared in 1630 in Tirso de Molina's El Burlador de Sevilla. [SP 8/NT 7]

1937 Don Quixote -- that brilliant picaresque novel by Miguel de Cervantes Saavedra that recounts the zany and mad adventures of the title hero, Don Quixote. The book is profound in its observations and insights, and eventually attains that rarest of literary accomplishments, the fusion of comedy and tragedy. However, the book's innate good humor is retained throughout. It has had great and prolonged influence on the development of the modern novel. [UD 11]

1938 Donaldson -- an exhibitor at the Glasgow Exhibition*. He is fictitious as presented here. [FRH 12]

1939 donjon keep -- the massive central tower or innermost fortification in old castles, especially the Norman ones. The White Tower in the Tower of London is a much modified donjon keep, improved to make it habitable in keeping with the advances in society's demands for comfort. .[BH E2]

1940 Donne, John [old] -- the great English poet and theologian (1571? -1631) who wrote satires, elegies, lyrics, and sermons which are among the best of the 17th C. His sonnet,"Death be not proud" is ranked among his very best and is still widely anthologized. He was a metaphysical poet, and, as such, his early secular verse can be, at time, rather straightforwardly candid. From 1621 until his death he was Dean of St. Paul's Cathedral in London. [CW 10/NT 5/GN 15/BH P]

1941 Donne's ecstatic couple -- the allusion is to John Donne's* poem, "The Ecstacy":

"And whilst our souls negotiate there
We like sepulchral statues lay;
All day, the same our postures were,
And we said nothing, all the day."

[BH 14]

1942 Donnington, Alf -- landlord at the Red Cow in Fenchurch St. Paul**. He rings the number six bell, Dimity*, in the local change-ringing* group. He is also the foreman at the coroner's inquest into the matter of the body found buried without authority in the churchyard. [NT 1]

1943 Donnington, B. -- a churchwarden* at Fenchurch St. Paul* in 1887. He is remembered in the inscription on the number five bell, Jubilee*. [NT 4]

1944 Don't worry. I'm sure something will turn up. -- words like this do appear in Ch. 11 of David Copperfield by Charles Dickens*: "I have known him [Mr. Micawber*] come home to supper with a flood of tears, and a declaration that nothing was now left but a jail; and go to bed making a calculation of the expense of putting bow-windows to the house, 'in case anything turned up,' which was his favorite expression." [BH 9]

1945 Doomsday -- day of judgment or of reckoning. The word also applies to the record of lands in England ordered drawn by William the Conqueror in

1086, the Domesday Book. The document is now in the Public Record Office in London. In the word's former meaning it is sometimes loosely interpreted as a reckoning to be met in some distant future. [ss]

1946 Doon -- Loch Doon, approximately twenty-one miles due North of Creetown* on the Dumfries and Galloway border with what is now County Strathclyde, formerly Ayrshire (from whence come the famous dairy cattle). [FRH 7]

1947 door-sneck -- northern British dialect for door latch. To sneck is a verb, but as with so many words in common usage, it became convenient to use the verb as a noun for the thing doing the work. [ss]

1948 Doppelgänger -- a ghost, demon, or spirit that is the double of a living person. Its appearance, as Robert Duckworthy* thought he had experienced it, is supposed to warn of one's imminent death. Translated literally from the German, the word means "double walker". [im]

1949 Dora -- the nickname for the Defense of the Realm Act of 1914, which restricted many liberties; any sort of artificially or externally legislated conscience [HHC 21]

1950 Dorchester -- the county seat for Dorset, it was founded by the Romans as Durnovaria. It is famous in literature as the center of Thomas Hardy's "Wessex". Hardy lived in Dorset and featured Dorchester as Casterbridge. [UD 20]

1951 Doré and Cie., Messrs. -- the London company for which Olga Kohn* was working as a model. As known by the entry name, the firm were high fashion ladies' couturiers. Firms using the Doré name are still in business in London. [HHC 22]

1952 Doris -- one of the professional dancers at the Hotel Resplendent at Wilvercombe* [HHC 7]

1953 Dorking -- the location of Meleager Finch's* Roman villa and the scene of detective fiction's purest puzzle plot. It is about twenty-three miles South of London. [umw]

1954 Dorland, Ann -- the rather too plain companion of Lady Felicity Dormer*. Her romantic susceptibilities have left her with much insecurity and unhappiness, but PW manages to help her smooth things out and get her life in order. She eventually begins a relationship with Major Robert Fentiman*. [BC 3]

1955 Dormer, Lady Felicity -- sister of General Fentiman, and wife of the late Sir Henry Dormer, Bart.*, button millionaire. When she and her brother die within hours of each other and when the time of his death becomes of the greatest importance to her legatees, the real nature of the story's unpleasantness becomes evident. [BC 2]

1956 Dormer, Sir Henry, Bart. -- husband, deceased at the time of BC, of Lady Felicity Dormer* who made his fortune in the button manufacturing business and who was awarded the rank of baronet (Bart.) for his efforts. A baronetcy ranks above a knight and below a baron. [BC 3]

1957 Dorset -- a county on England's southern coast between Devon and Hampshire [HHC 6]

1958 "Dost thou know what reputation is?" -- Ferdinand, Duke of Calabria, addresses his sister, the Duchess, with these lines in a speech in John Webster's (1580?-1625?) The Duchess of Malfi, III, ii. The speech is an accusation and lament about the Duchess's consideration for reputation. Webster was the closest of Shakespeare's contemporaries to approaching the Bard in dramatic intensity and skill. The Duchess (ca. 1614) is a bloody play of love betrayed, revenge, and death. [BH 9]

1959 dottle[s] -- the plugs from the bottoms of pipes consisting of unburned tobacco, tar, and nicotine. They are usually hard and dry. [HHC 12]

1960 Double Anastigmat and supplementary lenses -- the most superior type of lens available to Bunter at the time (early 1920's). It was particularly expensive for its time by today's standards, but provided the sharpest images in the best exposure time then available. The supplementary lenses were for close-up work. [WB 2]

1961 double dodge -- see dodge [NT 1]

1962 double those four spades -- see bridge [qs]

1963 doubles -- DLS's name for a set of changes* rung on five bells, the tenor (#6) being rung last or "behind" in each change [NT 10]

1964 doubting Thomas -- the apostle Thomas who, in John 20:25, refuses to believe that Christ has risen until he sees the nail marks. Thomas's name is now used to indicate anyone who refuses to believe without extensive proof. [WB 10/MMA 5]

1965 Dougal, Major -- he found Sandy Campbell's* body in the Minnoch* [FRH 2]

1966 Doughty St. [No. 100] -- a North-South street parallel to Gray's Inn Rd.* and a block to the West of that major street. It connects Rogers St. and Mecklenburgh Sq. Number 100 is the location of HV's flat after her split with Philip Boyes*. There never has been a No. 100, but likely real candidates are Nos. 29, 30, or 31, now rather decayed. DLS knew the area well. [SP 1]

1967 Douglas -- a brand of motorcycle manufactured in England during the first half of the century. The 349cc. model was used as a racing bike as early as 1913 when it successfully competed in the International Six Days Trial. For its time it was an important and powerful machine. George Goyles* has a 1914 model with a dark gray sidecar that he had planned to use when eloping with Lady Mary Wimsey* [cb/CW 3]

1968 Douglas, James -- a book reviewer for the Express*. He is most likely fictitious, but one cannot be certain as DLS did not precisely identify which newspaper she had in mind, and there were several. [SP 12]

1969 Doulton, Mr. -- the harbor-master* at Kirkcudbright* [FRH 13]

1970 Dover -- the famous Channel port of great historic significance. It is near the famous White Cliffs [chalk) on England's Channel coast. [UD 20]

1971 Dover St. -- a short street which runs North from Piccadilly* to Grafton and which is West of and parallel to Bond St. On this short street was located General Fentiman's* flat, a short walk from the Bellona Club* for a younger man in better health. [BC 2]

1972 Dowager Duchess of Denver -- see Delagardie, Honoria Lucasta [passim]

1973 Dowager Duchess of Medway -- see Medway, Dowager Duchess of [aq]

1974 Dower House, Denver Castle -- the Dowager Duchess's* home on the grounds of Denver Castle at Duke's Denver*. It is on the opposite side of the Park grounds from Bredon Hall*, and is "impeccable Inigo Jones*". [WB 3/BH 19]

1975 "Down in Demerara" -- the nonsense song, many verses and versions are extant, sung so heartily by the group in the Talboys* parlor. It is an anonymous English folk song to the tune of "The Old Gray Mare". Other versions involve Abe Lincoln coming out of the wilderness, the Queen's Navy not being what it used to be, and the old gray mare getting lost in the wilderness. [BH 5]

1976 Downham Market -- a market town in Norfolk ten miles South of King's Lynn. The real Denver* is about two miles farther to the South. PW says the fictitious Denver is about fifteen miles beyond Downham Market near Swaffham. [BH E2]

1977 Dowson -- an elderly and hard of hearing lawyer who is working with Sir Impey Biggs* on the case of Quangle and Hamper v. Truth*. [CW 10]

1978 Doyle, Sir Arthur Conan -- English author, physician, and spiritualist (1859-1930), famous for the creation of Sherlock Holmes, Dr. Watson, and Prof. Moriarty. [BC 18/SP 3/BH 10]

1979 Dr. Caligari -- see Caligari, Dr. [im]

1980 Dr. en Méd. Paris -- Doctor of Medicine, degree awarded at the University of Paris (the Sorbonne), founded in the 12th C. [WB 8]

1981 "Dr. Livingstone, I presume?" -- Sir Henry Morton Stanley's famous greeting to Dr. David Livingstone at

Ujiji, Tanganyika. The remark, understatement at its best, is found in Ch. 11 of Stanley's How I Found Livingstone. [HHC 16]

1982 Dr. Owen's porch -- on the church of St. Mary the Virgin, facing High St. in Oxford. It is an Italian Baroque porch designed by Nicholas Stone and given to the church in 1637 by Dr. Morgan Owen, Bishop of Llandaff. [GN 14]

1983 Dragon -- a fictitious pub just around the corner from Mrs. Lefranc's* boarding house in Wilvercombe*. She finds its proximity most convenient. [HHC 15]

1984 dragoons -- soldiers who operated as cavalry and who carried a short musket; now, any sort of cavalry unit [dh]

1985 drain -- a reference to any of the engineered drainage ditches in the fen* country [NT 1]

1986 drains -- sewers, a reference to the niceties of indoor plumbing. We who are accustomed to modern conveniences must remember that Talboys is about 380 years old. Any sort of indoor plumbing would have been a novelty when it was built. [BH P]

1987 Drake, Sylvia -- a Shrewsbury College* graduate known to HV. She apparently worked a longer time than is usual to earn her degree. [GN 1]

1988 Drake's Spinney -- a copse or small wood with undergrowth named for one of its previous owners and located near Wilvercombe* [HHC 16]

1989 dratted regulations -- see Judges' Rules [NT 9]

1990 draughts -- checkers, a cousin to chess*, and in some respects almost as profound [BC 20]

1991 draw stumps -- see cricket [MMA 18]

1992 drawing -- or pulling in some uses; to arrange the dampers in a stove or flue so as to have the fire burn more efficiently without smoking the room [NT 6]

1993 drawing a bow at a venture -- the allusion is to I Kings 22:34 in the story of the Battle of Ramoth-gilead and the defeat and death of Ahab. The passage is: "And a certain man drew a bow at a venture, and smote the king of Israel between the joints of the harness: wherefore he said unto the driver of his chariot, Turn thine hand and carry me out of the host; for I am wounded." Tallboy's* use of such a phrase is most prophetic. The passage continues in verse 37 as: "So the king died, and was brought to Samaria; and they buried the king in Samaria." [MMA 20]

1994 drawing-pin -- a thumbtack [HHC 12]

1995 Drayton, Michael -- English poet (1563-1631) and, like Shakespeare, from Warwickshire. He was workmanlike, versatile, and exceptionally skillful, not to mention prolific. He is today, however, remembered for only a few of his works. Many critics consider Drayton the last true Elizabethan poet, a position more often accorded to Milton*. [GN 7/BH 2]

1996 dree his own weird -- Scots dialect for suffer his own fate [FRH 1]

1997 Dresden shepherdess -- a statue of a shepherdess made of Dresden porcelain which is highly prized by collectors and is most valuable. Dresden is one common name for porcelain products made in Meissen, Germany. The very best products from that works were made prior to 1760. [BH P]

1998 Dreux -- a stopover point on the route of the Chemin de fer de l'Ouest*. It is a small city about forty-six miles West of Paris. [mt]

1999 Drew, Mr. -- a representative from the Cormorant Press with which Pym's Publicity* does business. Apparently Pym's does not have an extensive print shop of its own and contracts with the Cormorant Press for work when its own staff is overloaded. Both Mr. Drew and the Cormorant Press are fictitious. [MMA 8]

2000 Drewitt, Tom -- an old college friend of Michael Waters's* with whom Waters goes sailing. The outing is marked only by its unpleasantness for Waters. [FRH 19]

2001 Drews -- Parker* is referring to Arthur Drews (1865-1935), a German anti-Christian apologist who identified God and the world in "concrete monism". He claimed that true religion is based solely on reason, not on history, and he challenged the physical reality of Christ (He was either a spirit in another's body, or was some sort of phantasm). He was what might be called a 20th C. Gnostic. DLS is known to have been quite familiar with Drews' works. [WB 7]

2002 drills -- an agricultural machine for cutting a furrow, planting seeds, fertilizing and covering them all in one operation [CW 11]

2003 drills, electric -- PW is probably referring to the pneumatic drills that are supplied with air from pumps driven by portable gas or diesel-electric generators. Their noise level closely approaches the decibel level of the threshold of pain. [FRH 22]

2004 "Drink, Puppy, Drink" -- a poem by George John Whyte-Melville (1821-78) in celebration of a puppy's future as a hound for the hunt [CW 2]

2005 drive a wedge into it like one o'clock -- to drive a wedge into something with ease, origin unknown [SP 15]

2006 Driver, Stephen -- the mysterious worker who shows up in Fenchurch St. Paul*, works there for a few days, and then disappears. His identity and whereabouts are eventually discovered. [NT 4]

2007 Dromore -- a hamlet to the North of the Clints of Dromore* [FRH 3]

2008 dropped a brick -- to have committed a serious social blunder [UD 5/MMA 11]

2009 drove -- see Digg's Drove [NT 2]

2010 drum head court martial -- a summary treatment of offenses while in action and held around an upturned drum. The capstan, however, is also called a drum, so the court martial could also be held there if necessary, but, since drummers were formerly used to sound quarters on ships, the more usual definition would be preferred. [t]

2011 Drumbrain -- a hamlet, more likely a cottage or two, on the A714 route between Bargrennan and Barrhill**. It is not shown on the Ordnance Survey 1:50,000 maps of Galloway, but is probably about two or three miles beyond Creeside* toward Barrhill. [FRH 2]

2012 Drummer -- from the context, he is apparently Salcombe Hardy's* editor at the Evening Views* office [nf]

2013 drums -- the circular, often carved stone discs or cylinders which, when placed on top of each other, form the elements of a pillar [NT 1]

2014 "Drunk as a lord?" -- the expression "drunk as a lord" can be traced back as far as Somer's Tracts, vii, 184, of 1659. One of the more notable examples of such behavior is found in Philip Herbert, 9th Earl of Pembroke, who died in 1683 at the age of thirty, the result of too much drunken and riotous living. The cited quote is from Judge Cluer*. [CW 19]

2015 Drury, Mr. Garrick -- the stage name of Obadiah Potts, a fictitious actor who is killed in the non-PW story, "Blood Sacrifice". His names are taken from David Garrick (1717-79), the famous actor, and from the Drury Lane Theatre where Garrick is known to have performed. [GN 11]

2016 Drury Lane -- a major street which connects High Holborn* and Aldwych. Several theatres called Drury Lane have been located there, but a theatre of that name is now located at the corner of Catherine and Russell Sts. [MMA 19]

2017 Dryden, John -- English poet, critic, and dramatist (1631-1700), author of Absalom and Achitophel, The Hind and the Panther, and Religio Laia, among other works [BH 1]

2018 du, de, la, les, de l'apostrophe -- PW is being cute. This recitation of various French articles is in keeping with the tenor of their search and with their use of language at the moment [HHC 16]

2019 Dubois, M. -- M. Rozier's* predecessor as commissaire de police* at Chateau-Thierry* [NT 8]

2020 Ducange's Late Latin Dictionary -- the reference is to Charles Du Fresne, Sieur DuCange's (1610-88) Glossarium ad Scriptores Mediae et Infimae Latinitatis (1678), a work practically indispensable to those who study medieval Latin as it is in many ways quite different from classical Latin. The book is still in print. [GN 5]

2021 Duchess [of Denver] -- the wife of the 16th Duke, Gerald, and PW's sister-in-law for whom he has an active dislike. See Wimsey, Helen. [dh/CW 1/MMA 11/GN 9]

2022 The Duchess of Malfi -- see "Dost thou know what reputation is?" [BH 9]

2023 Duchy of Lancaster -- see Lancaster, Duchy of [UD 14]

2024 Duckworthy, Alfred -- the adoptive father of Robert Duckworthy* [im]

2025 Duckworthy, Hester -- the adoptive mother of Robert Duckworthy*. See also Dart. [im]

2026 Duckworthy, Richard -- the twin brother of Robert Duckworthy*, the doppelgänger* that Robert has come to fear so completely. This evil twin causes great consternation for Robert and provides an entertaining diversion for PW. [im]

2027 Duckworthy, Robert -- the confused victim of mistaken identity who is nicknamed "Ginger" because of his remarkably red hair [im]

2028 Dudden, Joe -- a member of the parish at Lopsley* who had put the sundial together using one of the chimney pots that William Noakes* had sold from Talboys* [BH 14]

2029 Dudden, Tom -- the auctioneer at Great Pagford* who sold the furniture and other goods from Talboys* that had been signed over to William Noakes* [BH 10]

2030 Duggins -- his boy and Hubbard* prayed over Squire Burdock's body while the latter lay in state [bc]

2031 "The Duke drained a dipper . . ." -- this misquotation is from Stephen Leacock's "Gertrude the Governess: or, Simple Seventeen" which is found in his Nonsense Novels. The exact quotation is: As the door of the library closed upon Ronald, the Earl sank into a chair. His face changed. It was no longer that of the haughty nobleman, but that of the hunted criminal. 'He must marry the girl,' he muttered. 'Soon she will know all. Tutchemoff has escaped from Siberia. He knows and will tell. The whole of the mines pass to her, this property with it, and I--but enough.' He rose, walked to the sideboard, drained a dipper full of gin and bitters, and became again a highbred English gentleman." This joyous nonsense involves love, wills, disinheritance over misplaced lover, and angry heirs who fling themselves upon horses and ride, "madly off in all directions". [GN 17]

2032 Duke Humphrey -- also Humphrey, Duke of Gloucester (1390-1447), brother to Henry V. The original library room for the Bodleian Library (see Bodley) was built over the Divinity School by Duke Humphrey and it is still known by his name in his honor. The original collection housed there was largely dispersed in fits of reformatory zeal during the reign of Edward IV (1547-53) and was not restored until Bodley* did so (1602ff). [GN 7]

2033 Duke of Denver -- used principally in reference to Gerald, the 16th Duke, PW's brother. See also Wimsey, Gerald Christian. [passim]

2034 Duke of Kent -- see Kent, Duke of [GN 3]

2035 Duke of Wellington . . . skellington -- this line is from one of E. C. Bentley's* clerihews, a form of humorous verse invented by Bentley. The poem is in four lines, rhymes aabb, and concerns the person named in the first line. [BH 4]

2036 Duke's Denver -- or Denver, the fictitious village about fifteen miles northeast of the real Denver*. Bredon Hall*, ducal seat of the Wimseys, is located near here and is also fictitious. See C. W. Scott-Giles's The Wimsey Family for a complete explanation of the whole Wimsey family history and that of Duke's Denver as well. [passim]

2037 "Duke's son, cook's son . . ." -- PW is quoting from Rudyard Kip-

ling's (1865-1936) poem, "The Absent Minded Beggar". The lines are usually set as:

"Duke's son--cook's son--son of a hundred kings--
(Fifty-thousand horse and foot going to Table Bay!)"

[FRH 22]

2038 dulcimer -- a wire-stringed instrument played with light hammers. It is an ancient instrument popular with folk musicians throughout much of Western and Eurasian culture. [SP 13]

2039 Dumas, Alexandre -- Dumas the elder (1802-70), the prolific French author of such great romances as *The Three Musketeers* and *The Count of Monte Cristo* who remains popular for the excitement and drama of his tales despite the fact they are often careless and unperceptive. [UD 7]

2040 dumb crambo -- a variety of charades where one team attempts to guess the subject word by acting it, having been told what it rhymes with. Speaking is not allowed. Failure is met with hisses, success by applause, and the team with the fewest failures wins. [np]

2041 Dumbleton -- Mr. Tallboy's alma mater. It is a fictitious public school*. [MMA 10]

2042 Dumfries -- county town for Dumfriesshire, and royal burgh of medieval origin on the River Nith. Poet Robert Burns* lived there from 1791-96, and much of his life is memorialized there. The town is located a short distance North of the eastern end of Solway Firth not far from Kirkcudbright*. Burns is buried in the mausoleum at St. Michael's churchyard in Dumfries. [ss/FRH 3]

2043 dun -- to demand payment of a debt forcefully or noisily [GN 9]

2044 Duncan, P. C. Charlie -- the young constable who wants so much to be of help in the Campbell* investigation. It is his interview with the press that causes him great difficulty with his superiors, but which brings about some unexpected results useful in the case. [FRH 18]

2045 Dunlop -- a brand of automobile motorcycle and bicycle tire still manufactured and widely available in the U. K., Europe, and North America [CW 3/UD 20/FRH 10]

2046 *The Dunlop Book* -- subtitled *The Motorist's Guide, Counsellor, and Friend*, by E. J. Burrow of E. J. Burrow and Co., Publishers, Cheltenham, and E. R. Cross and A. J. Wilson, published by A. J. Wilson & Co., of London, in 1919 with a second edition in 1920. Dunlop also sponsored a variety of maps and traveller's guides, none of which remains in print. A copy of *The Dunlop Book* owned by PW was being read by Robert Duckworthy*. [im]

2047 Dunragit -- a stop on the rail line from Girvan* to Stranraer* [FRH 5]

2048 Dupin -- Edgar Allan Poe's* creation, C. Auguste Dupin, the central figure and detective hero of such great Poe stories as "The Murders in the Rue Morgue" and "The Purloined Letter". He is the first detective in fiction. [SP 8]

2049 durance -- imprisonment [MMA 6]

2050 dust-bin -- garbage can [BC 18/ [HHC 10]

2051 *Dusk and Shiver* -- a fictitious novel [GN 11]

2052 dust of kings and queens -- PW is speaking poetically of the fragments of ivory dust that are all that remain of the chess* pieces which include pieces called kings and queens [GN 21]

2053 dust-sheets -- the large fabric sheets used to cover furniture, etc., when a house is to be closed for some lengthy time [MMA 10]

2054 duster -- a dusting cloth or brush [MMA 4]

2055 Dutch doll -- a wooden doll, crudely painted and very popular prior to WW I. It was jointed, the limbs being joined with string, and painted in brilliant colors with staring eyes and large scarlet discs on its cheeks. They gave rise to a series of children's books such as *Golliwog and the Dutch Dolls*, and to the expression "painted dolls". [BC 17]

2056 Dutch oven -- a large, heavy, usu-

ally iron cooking utensil with a heavy lid. They were designed to be used either on top of the stove or in the oven, but the earliest models were meant to be set in a fire's coals. Lids on such early models sometimes had rims around the perimeter of the top to hold more coals, thus providing uniform heat overall. [MMA 9]

2057 Dutch uncle -- Dutch in this case is more likely a corruption of "Deutsch", or German, and refers to anyone who rebukes from a standpoint of moral excellence whether it is an earned or deserved position or not; one who lectures from the standpoint of too sober religiosity [MMA 5]

2058 Dutchmen -- the engineers who, directed by Vermuyden*, drained the fens* according to the demands of the 4th Earl of Bedford* [NT 7]

2059 Dwight, Penelope -- a friend of Hilary Thorpe's* [NT 9]

2060 Dyer, Mr. and Mrs. -- occupants above the flat occupied by HV and Philip Boyes*, and witnesses to the argument that led to their separation [SP 1]

2061 dying elephants -- Dr. Lamplough* is referring to the old myth of some fabulously rich elephant's graveyard, a place where all dying elephants are supposed to go, and which is supposed to contain tons of beautiful ivory [te]

2062 Dykes -- the police officer who interviews George Fentiman* and who, thus, frightened George into his nervous breakdown [BC 18]

2063 Dykesey -- a fictitious community in the fen* country near Fenchurch St. Paul* that has train service. It is about ten miles West of Fenchurch St. Paul. [NT 2]

2064 Dykesey Viaduct -- the railway bridge across the Thirty-foot Drain* at Little Dykesey*. It is about ten miles West of Fenchurch St. Paul*. [NT 2]

2065 dyspepsia [peptic] -- upset stomach, indigestion [HHC 3/NT 5]

(E)

2066 E minor -- in music, a key of one sharp, diatonically the same as G major [GN 19]

2067 E really is the most frequently recurring letter . . . . -- it is, and it is the most frequently used letter in most Indo-European languages [HHC 26]

2068 Eagles, P. C. -- the constable who, with Sgt. Lumley*, trails Hector Puncheon* as he follows that mysterious man in evening clothes [MMA 15]

2069 eagles of Varus -- see Varus [BH 14]

2070 Ealing -- a suburb West of London on the North side of the Thames [HHC 6]

2071 Earith Bridge -- or Earith, a Cambridgeshire village at the junction of the River Ouse and the Old and New Bedford Rivers** near where DLS spent her childhood. Her father, Henry Sayers, was rector* of the parish of Bluntisham-cum-Earith from 1897 to 1917. [NT 2]

2072 Earl of Galloway -- see Galloway, Earl of [FRH 22]

2073 Earl of Shrewsbury -- see Shrewsbury, Earl of [GN 3]

2074 Earl of Strathallen and Begg -- see Strathallen and Begg, Earl of [CW 14]

2075 Earl Spencer -- see Spencer, George John [WB 1]

2076 Early Celebration -- a celebration of the Eucharist before breakfast [NT 6]

2077 early-closing day -- through much of the century it has been the custom in England and in the U. S. to set aside one day in the week when the various shops, etc., would close at noon or thereabouts. Mercenary considerations have generally ended the practice in the U. S., but not in England. [HHC 2]

2078 Early English -- an early Gothic architectural style preceding Decorated and Perpendicular, and following the Norman Romanesque. Examples

would date from the 13th and 14th centuries. The style includes elements of all the styles, but is not strictly patterned after any of them. See architecture. [NT 1]

2079 Early English -- a catchall name that, depending on who uses it, can include anything following Old English (Anglo-Saxon) through Early Middle English. HV and Miss Lydgate appear to be using the term to refer to English as it was used between the Anglo-Saxon period and the time of Chaucer, a period of about 250 years. [GN 5]

2080 Early Service -- the same as Early Celebration* [NT 1]

2081 "Earth hath not anything" -- usually written as "Earth has not anything to show more fair", it is the opening line of Wordsworth's* sonnet, "Composed Upon Westminster Bridge", written in 1802 [MMA 4]

2082 East Anglia is famous -- East Anglia, one of the original ancient English kingdoms, gives its name now to East central England--Norfolk, Suffolk, Cambridgeshire, etc., and the area is, indeed, famous for its parish churches, both for architectural variety and for interior decoration [NT 1]

2083 East Anglian -- an allusion to one of the original seven Anglo-Saxon kingdoms (Northumbria, Mercia, East Anglia, Wessex, Essex, Kent, and Sussex). It is still used to identify persons from the geographical area centered on Norfolk and Suffolk. [HHC 12]

2084 East End -- of London. The area around the docks and markets, center of the various ethnic enclaves, slums, and the opposite in nature and attitude of the West End*. [FRH 18/SP 13]

2085 East Felpham -- a fictitious place described as a "lonely spot on the coast". There is a Felpham near Bognor Regis and Littlehampton, but no separate town of East Felpham. In addition, there are no long rock spurs in that area as DLS describes. [nf]

2086 East Indies -- the Southeast Asian islands that include New Guinea, Sumatra, and Borneo, plus thousands of smaller islands [UD 12]

2087 East Level Waterways Commission -- a fictitious agency [NT 7]

2088 Eastbourne -- a town in East Sussex known as a resort since 1780 when four of George III's children spent a summer holiday there. There are magnificent beaches, promenades, and other attractions, plus a wide range of accommodations available now. [HHC 6/MMA 10]

2089 Easter term -- the second of the three segments of the school year at Oxford or Cambridge. Oxford more generally uses the phrase Hilary term, but either will do. The term extends into the spring months. [GN 4]

2090 Eaton Socon -- a community approximately fifty miles North of London's Westminster area. See also motorcycle race. [cb]

2091 Ecclesiastical Commissioners -- an office, now called Church Commissioners, dating from 1836. Their function is to manage the civil affairs of the church of England. They would be involved with the collection of tithes* among their other duties. [GN 3]

2092 _echter_ -- German for "genuine". PW uses the term in reference to _Schloss Johannisberger_* wine [mt]

2093 _éclaircissement_ -- French for "clearing up" as in a mystery; elucidation, explanation [bc]

2094 eclipse -- at the end of the last chapter of UD, PW and Parker* discuss the odd appearance of the day and Parker reminds him that it is the scheduled full solar eclipse. That event was visible in parts of England between, roughly, six and eight in the morning on June 29th, 1927. [UD 23]

2095 "Eclogue for the Marriage of the Earl of Somerset" -- an eclogue is a form of pastoral poem employing shepherds and shepherdesses in a bucolic setting and was a popular convention in the 17th C. [BH E3]

2096 "Ecstasy on the Letter Z" -- see Vrilovitch's "Ecstasy on the Letter Z" [SP 8]

2097 ectoplastic materialisations -- or

ectoplasmic, the materialization of spirits of the deceased or absent [SP 16]

2098 Eddington, go all -- the reference is to Sir Charles Stanley Eddington (1882-1944), a British physicist and astronomer. Parker is trying to calm PW down and get him off the speed of light idea. Parker seems to be well-read in contemporary theories of physics. [ae]

2099 Eden, garden of -- a paradise, a beautiful place. The allusion is to Genesis 2:8-17. [SP 16]

2100 Edinburgh -- the capital of Scotland. An ancient and beautiful city built on hills, crags, and in the valleys, it is the seat of government and an arts and education center of unique accomplishment. [FRH 1/HHC 3]

2101 Edinburgh granite -- much of northern England and Scotland features outcroppings of extremely ancient rock, and the city of Edinburgh is built on and around such outcroppings [BH 7]

2102 edizione rarissima -- Italian for "an extremely rare edition". The term is used to refer to the Naples folio* of the Divine Comedy* printed in 1477. [WB 1]

2103 Edward, the late King -- Edward the Seventh. See King Edward. [UD 3]

2104 Edwardian chairs -- chairs made during the reign of Edward VII (see King Edward), a period of somewhat modified Victorian influence [BH 2]

2105 Edwards, Joan [Teddy] -- a don* and the science tutor at Shrewsbury College* who receives a description of the Wimsey-Vane wedding from Miss Letitia Martin*, one of HV's bridesmaids [GN 12/BH P]

2106 Edwards, Mrs. -- a parishoner at Fenchurch St. Paul* who was to be churched* on the Sunday afternoon when PW had solved the riddle of the code [NT 12]

2107 Edwards, Susan -- a former member of the parish at Fenchurch St. Paul*, she is now buried on the North side of the churchyard [NT 4]

2108 Egerton, Capt. Francis -- an old customer of Mr. Endicott's* who bought a dozen of that barber's fine razors [HHC 6]

2109 eggs is eggs -- see as sure as eggs is eggs [HHC 32]

2110 Eglamore, Sir -- see Sir Eglamore [UD BN]

2111 Egotists' Club -- one of the clubs to which PW belongs (see also Bellona Club and Marlborough Club). As given it is fictitious, but DLS most certainly had in mind the Eccentric's Club, now located on Ryder St., London, just South of Piccadilly* and near Piccadilly Circus*. DLS describes it as "one of the most genial places in London". [cf/mt/UD BN/MMA 19/GN 4]

2112 eiderdown -- a comforter or spread filled with the smallest and softest feathers from particular breeds of Scandanavian ducks. Such comforters are especially good insulation as they are light and retain heat well. [NT 2]

2113 eight -- see one or two over the eight [SP 10]

2114 18 shillings -- a pound (£) was twenty shillings, or 240 pence, so eighteen shillings would have been 216 pence, or, roughly, $3.60 U. S., at the time. See British Monetary Units. [CW 7]

2115 eighteen stone -- a stone is equivalent to fourteen pounds avoirdupois, so the constable weighs about 252 pounds [CW 2]

2116 1837 -- the year Queen Victoria succeeded to the throne [UD 14]

2117 840 -- the number of changes* in the touch*. The same applies to other such number references (as 704). [NT 13]

2118 8vo -- octavo, a symbol of the printing trade indicating a single sheet of paper printed, folded, and cut so as to make eight pages of text. The finished page size can vary from five by eight inches to six by nine inches. [WB 1]

2119 eights -- a racing shell (rowboat) having a crew of eight oarsmen and a coxswain to call the beat of the stroke. Such boats do not resemble ordinary rowboats as they are made long

and narrow for racing purposes. [GN 12]

2120 Eine Kleine Nachtmusik -- W. A. Mozart's* famous piece for string orchestra, "A Little Night Music", K. 525, in four movements. It lasts about fifteen minutes. [HHC 20]

2121 "Elbow: What is't your worship . . ." -- the quote is from Shakespeare's Measure for Measure, II, i, 192ff. [BH 11]

2122 electric hare -- DLS refers to the introduction of greyhound racing to that racing emporium by the British Greyhound Racing Assoc. It was the first such racing ever held in London. The use of live hares is not legal and has not been so for many years. See also The White City. [UD 19]

2123 Electrical Company -- an unnamed concern meant to symbolize unwanted progress as far as Mr. Mellilow* is concerned [sf]

2124 electric drills -- see drills, electric [FRH 22]

2125 electros -- electrotyping, a method of duplicating an original by making a copper plate from a mold of the original. The method is used frequently for making cheap reproduction of expensive or rare originals. They are usually not very sharp or clear in their details. [dh]

2126 Elephant -- fully, The Elephant & Castle Theatre, located at the northern end of New Kent Road, just South of the Blackfriars area and East of Lambeth in southern London. The present theatre opened in August of 1902 and became a cinema in 1928. The name derives from a public house located at the junction of six main roads in Southwark*. The pub gave its name to the junction and, thence, to the theatre. [BC 10]

2127 Elephant's Child -- one of PW's nicknames as employed by his sister, Mary*. The reference is to Rudyard Kipling's Just So Stories and "The Elephant's Child". In that story, the young elephant is described as being "full of insatiable curiosity". Mary feels the name appropriate because of PW's habit of asking questions that are variously described as being "silly", "idiotic", and "undignified". [aq]

2128 elephantiasis -- an infestation of tissues by filarial worms which causes an enlargement and thickening of the infected tissues, usually a limb or the scrotum [MMA 1]

2129 11 inch double -- used by DLS to mean the same as a half-page double column of newsprint or advertising material [MMA 1]

2130 elevenses -- the morning tea break at or about eleven A. M. [MMA 1]

2131 Elf-Land, King of -- the fairy tale character of Northern European origin who appears in tales written as recently as those of Hans Christian Andersen. Elves traditionally live underground, their hill homes often being round or mound-shaped. There may be a connection to prehistoric burial mounds and the sort of evil spirit or mischievous spirit lore that has built up around such sites. [FRH 2]

2132 Eliot, T. S. -- Thomas Stearns Eliot (1888-1965), American-born poet and dramatist who later became a British citizen. His two most famous works are probably "The Waste Land" and Murder in the Cathedral, the latter having been written for the Canterbury Cathedral Festival in 1935. DLS's The Zeal of Thy House was written for that festival series as well. Eliot's "The Hollow Men", a poem mixing rhyme with parts of the liturgy (1925), considers the spiritual vacuum of 20th C. man. [BH 19]

2133 elliptical -- the Dowager Duchess* uses the term to describe PW's explanation for Mr. Thipps's* arrest, suggesting thereby that he was being too vague or unclear for her. Grammatically, the term suggest the omission or information that is not supposed to be essential for complete understanding. [WB 3]

2134 Elizabeth -- Matthew Gowan's* maid, Betty. She provides PW with some good information through Bunter's machinations. [FRH 8]

2135 Elizabeth I -- see Queen Elizabeth [NT 4/GN 3]

2136 Elizabeth, Miss [Bet] -- surnamed

Dobbin; waitress and maid at the Rose and Crown* in Stapley* [CW 11]

2137 Elizabethan, being so -- the suggestion here is of naughty or bawdy behavior [WB 6]

2138 Elizabethan wit [to argue like an] -- as is popularly evidenced in Shakespeare's work, among others, great fun was had with language through puns and other types of word play. The practice is also typical of the metaphysical poets. Such language use was widely encouraged in all levels of society, but especially among the educated classes as college training emphasized the adroit use of language, even going so far as to require a logical disputation or logical defense of a formal thesis orally defended before all who wished to ask questions of the person presenting it. The extremes of rhetorical fencing could be quite amazing, and such word play was carried on after college training. To be accused of arguing in such a manner might carry with it the negative sense of attempting to evade the issue by losing it in rhetorical maneuvering. [GN 4]

2139 Elkbottom, Mr. -- author of Modern Verse-Forms. Both he and his book are fictitious. His work is attacked by Miss Lydgate* in her work on prosody*. [GN 5]

2140 Ellangowan Hotel -- in Creetown*. Mr. Millar of that hospitable establishment helped DLS with the preparation of various details around Creetown. See the "Foreward" to FRH. [FRH 28]

2141 Ellen -- a maid at Riddlesdale Lodge* [CW 15]

2142 Elliman's embrocation -- sometimes known as Elliman's Rub, it is a liniment for application to sore muscles or places on the back or at joints; wherever strain has left its effects. It helps by warming the afflicted area. [CW 6]

2143 Elliott-Fisher typewriter -- a fictitious product [MMA 1]

2144 Ellis Island -- where immigrants to the U. S. were processed during the first half of the 20th C. Cabin passengers would not have gone there, but would simply have cleared customs at the pier. However, as PW did not have all the proper papers, he needed to get special clearance from the U. S. ambassador* to avoid having to face a period of quarantine when he arrived in New York City. [CW 14]

2145 elm -- an exceptionally hard wood and, of importance in the fen* country, having an extremely slow rate of rot or decay [NT 4]

2146 Elsfield -- an outlying village to the northeast of Oxford [GN 19]

2147 Ely -- the famous medieval cathedral city on the Great Ouse* in Cambridgeshire. The name means "eel island", a reference to the dietary staple of the Saxons who lived there. The place once was an island and later the center of a separate administrative district called the Isle of Ely. The cathedral was begun in 1083. Henry Weldon* lives near Ely. [HHC 12]

2148 elytra -- the sound-making appendages found on some beetles [GN 17]

2149 Embankment -- the Victoria Embankment, along the North side of the Thames from Westminster Bridge to Blackfriars Bridge, is a wide, tree-lined thoroughfare completed in 1870, which exactly follows the bank of the Thames and incorporates the District underground railway. It provides a number of shelters and other attractions for members of the mendicant class. Where the street forms a "T" with Westminster Bridge St. just opposite the Clock Tower of the Houses of Parliament, it can be closed off quite easily. [hp/CW 19/SP 8/MMA 7]

2150 embolism -- the sudden blocking of a blood vessel by some object such as a clot or an air bubble [UD 23]

2151 Emerson, Dr. -- the physician who examined Victor Dean* after his fall and who declared Dean dead of a contusion on the right temple and of a broken neck [MMA 2]

2152 Emily -- Holliday*, the Venables'* maid [NT 1]

2153 Emily -- a Shrewsbury College* scout* [GN 7]

2154 Emily, Aunt -- Ginger Potts's aunt

who had owned a cat since dispatched by the boy and his slingshot [MMA 6]

2155 emollient diet -- a soothing, soft, probably bland diet [WB 5]

2156 Emperor -- a standard and popular variety of daffodil* [NT 3]

2157 the Emperor -- Charles V, von Hapsburg, the Holy Roman Emperor and, in theory if not in fact, the most powerful of all Christian monarchs. He was the nephew of Catherine of Aragon by her sister, Juana. Family honor being a strong tie, when Catherine appealed to Charles for help in the question of her divorce from Henry VIII, he offered it. The result was the divorce not only of Henry from Catherine, but the Church of England from the Roman Catholic Church and the consequent centuries of religious hatred and turmoil. [GN 17]

2158 Emperor of Japan -- in 1932 it was Hirohito (b. 1901); who has reigned as Emperor of Japan since December 25, 1926 [HHC 33/NT 13]

2159 Empire Free-Trader -- a believer in free trade, the practical expression of the Adam Smith policy of laissez-faire within the Empire as it existed before WW II. The free-trade policy, or let business compete and survive as best it can, did not apply to other nations outside the Empire. In actuality, it was more on the order of giving preferential treatment to countries of the Empire, and imposing trade sanctions and tariffs on all others. [HHC 21]

2160 Empress -- a standard and popular variety of daffodil* [NT 3]

2161 emptying the bedroom water-bottle -- a reference to the Bravo* case. See also water-bottle. [SP 21]

2162 ems -- units of measure of print spacing equal to the width of the letter "M" which, with "W", is the biggest letter in any uniform type set. The measure varies according to the point size of the type as an em in pica will be larger than an em in elite, etc. [MMA 8]

2163 en prise -- French for, "exposed", or in danger of capture, a term often employed in chess* [sf/GN 17]

2164 Encaenia procession -- the procession prior to Oxford's major degree-granting ceremony held on the Wednesday following the end of Trinity term* in early July. The name dates from the dedication of the Sheldonian Theatre* in 1669, and is the last part to survive from the medieval ceremony of granting degrees. The ceremonies are still conducted in Latin. [GN 1]

2165 encephalitis, lethargic -- PW is referring to encephalitis lethargica, an epidemic of a viral encephalitis that followed WW I and which was prevalent for about the next ten years or so. The cause was never determined even though it was associated with influenza*. Symptoms included apathy, double vision, extreme muscular weakness, and the other symptoms associated with what is loosely called "sleeping sickness". This specific strain of the disease seems to have disappeared.

Encephalitis of any kind (there are several) involves an inflammation of the brain leading to drowsiness, a slowing down of mental faculties, headache, fever, and even, in severe cases, delirium convulsions, and death. Encephalitis may be caused by either a virus or parasites. [WB 7]

2166 Enchanter -- one of Satan's many names [NT 3]

2167 Encyclopedia Britannica -- one of the major established English language encyclopedias, and the oldest of those now in production in English. First published serially between 1768 and 1771 in three volumes, it has grown continuously ever since. Among scholars the Eleventh Edition (1910-11, 28 vols.) is still remembered and sought for its excellent articles on the arts and letters, especially Elder Olson's consideration of prosody*. [np]

2168 Endicott -- the elderly, retired, and amazingly retentive barber who had operated one of the West End's* most exclusive tonsorial parlors [HHC 4]

2169 Endicott, Mrs. -- wife of the barber mentioned above. She was not at home when PW called. [HHC 6]

2170 Endicott's Special Tonic -- if, as Mr. Endicott* claims, his tonic

does help prevent baldness, it would have to be special as nothing short of hair transplants or gene splicing will prevent that problem. The attendant scalp massaging would, however, help, regardless of the tonic used. [HHC 6]

2171 Endymion -- in Greek mythology, the most beautiful man and beloved of Phoebe* [GN 15]

2172 enfin, on apprend . . . -- French for, "eventually, one learns not to think about it" [WB 11]

2173 Enfin, du courage! -- French for, "At last, some courage! Kiss me, my dear. All the same, I will find some way to please you. Well? What do you wish? Say so then. I want you." [BH 3]

2174 Engaged Label -- a "Do Not Disturb" sign [GN 7]

2175 England's supremacy challenged at Wimbledon -- it was so challenged in 1927 by American Helen Wills, known as the greatest woman lawn tennis player of her day [UD 19]

2176 "England, with all thy faults . . ." -- PW is quoting line 206 of English poet William Cowper's (1743-1809) "The Task", book ii, "The Time-Piece" [NT 14]

2177 English novel that had an explanation of the Playfair cipher -- DLS probably had in mind Rhodes's* Peril at Cranberry Hall, published by Dodd Mead in 1930 [HHC 33]

2178 English Prosody -- the title of Miss Lydgate's* massive study of poetical techniques from Beowulf to Bridges** [GN 4]

2179 English rose -- see Pembroke [GN 4]

2180 entailed -- the limiting of an inheritance to a specified line of heirs so that it cannot be otherwise distributed or bequeathed. It applies especially to land (property). [bc/t/UD 14/BH 1]

2181 "Enter into your heritage" -- see "be afraid with any amazement" [GN 23]

2182 "Enter Richmond . . ." -- it is actually "Enter Gloucester . . ." in Richard III, III, vii [HHC 23]

2183 entrain -- French for, "high spirits", "verve" [HHC 7]

2184 Entwhistle, Rev. Melchisedek -- a Victorian benefactor of some importance to Shrewsbury College* whose plaster bust is destroyed during the rampages of the College's poltergeist. The loss of the bust is cheered by the Dean. [GN 9]

2185 epicene -- a word used to indicate a person lacking the characteristics of either sex [UD 15/BC 10/SP 15/GN 22]

2186 Epictetus -- the Roman stoic philosopher (ca. 60-140 A. D.) whose work is known to us mostly through his Lectures. A freed slave, his catch words were endure and abstain. He shows great faith in the will to overcome life's problems. Hence, given the problem in UD, the reference to will is a noteworthy one. [UD 19]

2187 Epicurean enjoyment -- a reference to the philosophy of Epicurus (341-270 B. C.) which holds, in part, that the chief good is found in the enjoyment of sensual pleasures, particularly those of the table [HHC 13]

2188 Epimetheus -- brother to Prometheus*, Epimetheus's name means "afterthought". It is he who fell victim to Zeus's gift of Pandora and her "box of troubles". [GN 1]

2189 Epistle and Gospel -- for June 24, the Feast of St. John the Baptist, they are Isaiah 40:1-11 and Luke 1:57 ff. These date from 1549 and the first English language prayer book in the Sarum Rite which, after the Reformation, became the dominant rite. [UD 22]

2190 Epistle to the Galatians -- see Galatians, Epistle to [WB 7]

2191 Epistle to the Hebrews -- see Hebrews, Epistle to [CW 5]

2192 epithalamion -- a song composed in honor of a bride and bridegroom [BH 3]

2193 epithet -- any adjective, title, or nickname expressing a real quality, sometimes used to indicate a negative attitude and frequently disparaging [nf]

2194 Epping Forest -- was bought by The City of London for its residents as there is no room in The City for a large park. The Forest's 6000 acres of tranquility northeast of the East End* of London are still a true forest, but are open to the general public. Fallow deer still wander there, not far from Queen Elizabeth's hunting lodge. [UD 6]

2195 Erebus -- primeval darkness, chaos; hence, hell. The allusion is to Greek mythology. The word also appears as Herebus. [NT 3]

2196 "Ergo omnis longo solvit se Teucria luctu" -- the quote is from Vergil's Aeneid*, Book II, 26, and reads, "So all of Troy was loosed from its long distress . . .". The passage is appropriate as it is delivered when PW presents Martha* with the medicine needed to release Alice Wetherall* from her long, medically induced imprisonment. It is part of the famous passage in which Aeneas describes to Dido's court the ruse of the wooden horse, telling how it was built, of the men concealed in it, and how the Greeks sailed their ships to the deserted beach behind the Isle of Tenedos. [ie]

2197 Erith, Lord -- PW sent for the catalogue for Lord Erith's library sale, but his lack of enthusiasm, even in light of his concern with the investigation at hand, suggests that he was not as impressed with that collection as he had been with the Brocklebury* offerings. His lordship and the sale are both fictitious. There is, however, a place called Erith, formerly in Kent, now a part of Greater London, which could have been DLS's inspiration. [WB 5]

2198 'Erne Bay -- Herne Bay, almost due North of Canterbury on the North coast of Kent. It is the first of the several scenes of Smith's brides-in-the-bath* murders. [BH 5]

2199 Eroica Symphony -- Ludwig van Beethoven's third symphony in E-flat major, Opus 55, published in October of 1806. This is the symphony that was supposedly dedicated to Napoleon Bonaparte until Beethoven heard that the Little Corporal had declared himself an emperor. It was subsequently dedicated to Franz Joseph Max, Prince Lobkowitz, an important Beethoven benefactor. [HHC 19]

2200 Erondell, Pierre -- he flourished ca. 1586-1609 as an author of various textbooks of French. The typical arrangement was to have an introductory segment about French grammar and pronunciation, some exercises, and then a series of lectures or dialogues with a page of text in English faced on the right by the matching page of text in French. Erondell authored several such books. [GN 9]

2201 Errinyes, avenging -- or Erinyes, Furies, Eumenides, and Semnai. They are primeval beings born of the blood of the mutilated Uranus. They are avengers of crime, usually those against the ties of kinship. (OCCL) [UD 5]

2202 Eructavit cor meum -- Latin for, "My heart cast it forth". The reference is to Psalm 44:2, especially the concluding phrase of that verse, "cast them out". (KJV) [BH 5]

2203 Esau, hands of -- see Jacob's voice [WB 2]

2204 Esmeralda -- PW's nickname for the little girl he hires to guard Mrs. Merdle* outside the Mission House* in Stepney* while he confers with the Rev. Hallelujah Dawson*. The name is, perhaps, a reference to The Hunchback of Notre Dame. [UD 13]

2205 Esmeralda Hyacinth -- Bill Rumm's* young daughter who pesters PW into singing "Nazareth"* [SP 13]

2206 esq. -- the abbreviation for esquire, a social grade ranking immediately below knight. The title is now used only in writing to address or refer to gentlemen or professional men in their private capacity. [ie/ WB 8]

2207 Esquimaux -- a variant spelling for Eskimos [UD 11]

2208 Essex -- an English county, in ancient times a kingdom. It is East of London and to the North of the Thames estuary. DLS had a home in Witham in mid-Essex at 24 Newland St., not far from Roslyn House, the base of the Dorothy L. Sayers Society. Essex is not a "shire" or share of a former

kingdom as is, for instance, its neighboring county of Hertfordshire which was part of the ancient kingdom of Mercia. [bc/np/MMA 5/GN 11]

2209 Essex -- most likely a reference to Robert Devereux, 2nd Earl of Essex, who was the favorite of Elizabeth I. He was beheaded in 1601 for attempting to overthrow her government. [GN 1]

2210 Essex, Countess of -- see Countess of Essex [GN 7]

2211 Essex County Constabulary -- the county police force for Essex* [BH 11]

2212 Established [Church or way] -- the Church of England or its authorized methods for conducting the various rites, services, and sacraments as opposed to those of other denominations [CW 9/BH 5]

2213 Establishment -- a church recognized by a state as the official religion, especially the Church of England, or any permanently established force or organization, particularly in government and church affairs [bc]

2214 estaminet -- French for "taproom", a cafe or smoking room may also be meant [NT 8]

2215 Et avec ça que nous somme . . . -- French for, "Even with that we are of a good family--but, alas, sir, in Russia, as you know, that isn't worth much because of the insults, the atrocities. In short . . . ." [WB 11]

2216 et ego in Arcadia -- Latin for, "I, too, have been in Arcadia", an expression in favor of broad-mindedness as used in this instance. It refers to a region of ideal happiness, but figuratively means, "I know all about it". Mr. Hancock is not shocked in the least by anything Boccaccio has to say. [bc]

2217 et iterum venturus est -- Latin for, "and he shall come again", a passage from the Nicene Creed* portion of Bach's B-minor Mass*. Since this passage is treated musically with its own phrase, it is reasonable for PW to be singing just that portion. [WB 6]

2218 Et ma joli colombe -- additional verses of the dirty French ditty PW sings frequently in BH, "La caill', la tourterelle". This is one of those instances where a translation is of no use whatever. Either one knows what the song is about or one doesn't, there is no translation that will make much sense of the lyrics as the whole song is idiomatic innuendo. [BH 15]

2219 Et responsum est ab omnibus . . . -- Latin for, "And the response from everyone is: He (it) has not been found." It appears in Thomas deQuincey's "Supplementary Paper on Murder, Considered as One of the Fine Arts". The us, a, um endings refer to the masculine, feminine, and neuter endings possible for inventus, but do not appear in the quote's source. [NT 6]

2220 Et tot millia millies quot sunt sidera caelo . . . -- Latin for, "And a thousand times as many thousands as there are stars in the skies . . .". See "Da mihi basia . . .". [BH 1]

2221 Etcheverry, Widow -- her son was the first to contact PW in the latter's guise as a great and wise magician [ie]

2222 Etheridge, Miss -- one of the guests at the boarding house where Miss Climpson* stays in Windle* [SP 18]

2223 Ethiopian could change his skin -- the allusion is to Jeremiah 13:23: "Can the Ethiopian change his skin, or the Leopard his spots." The rhinoceros reference is PW's slight variation on the Biblical original. The Ethiopian also figures in Rudyard Kipling's Just So Stories wherein Kipling considers "How the Leopard Got His Spots" and "How the Rhinoceros Got His Skin". [GN 18]

2224 the Ethiopian shall stay black -- see entry 2223 [BH 7]

2225 Etoile -- the Place de l'Étoile in Paris, now the Place Charles DeGaulle. It is the traffic circle at the West end of the Champs-Elysées at the center of which is the Arc de Triomphe. [CW 13]

2226 Eton -- the reference is to the school there as, in fact, the town would probably not exist without it. In essence, Eton is an extension of Windsor as the school is only about a thousand yards from Windsor Castle on

the North side of the Thames. Eton was founded by Henry IV in 1440 as a school to prepare students for King's College, Cambridge, and has always been a major training ground for the aristocracy. PW is an alumnus. [WB 1/UD BN/FRH 28/HHC 3/MMA 10/GN 11/BH 1]

2227 Euphelia serves to grace . . . -- PW quotes from Matthew Prior's (1664-1721) "An Ode, 'The Merchant to Secure His Treasure'" [BH 18]

2228 Euripedes -- PW quotes at length from the Greek and Roman classical writers to support his act as a wizard. Euripedes (480-406 B. C.) is one of the three great Attic tragedians known to us. He wrote some eighty or ninety plays of which eighteen tragedies survive, including Medea and The Trojan Women. He is noted for his portrayal of exceptional female characters. A chorus is a group of actors representing the local people in the play who comment on or question the actors or the action of the play. In the early tragedies, their role was of great significance and some choruses are rather lengthy. [ie]

2229 Euroclydon -- Mr. Venables* and PW are quoting from Acts 27:14, the story of Paul's journey to Rome: "But not long after there arose against it a tempestuous wind called Euroclydon". The word appears only in that verse and nowhere else in antiquity or the Scriptures, and translates, roughly, as "East wind billows". It is, perhaps, a corruption of Euraquilo, Greek for a stormy wind from the northeast or north-northeast. [NT 19]

2230 Euston -- Euston Station, the huge railway terminus in Northern London just to the East of Regent's Park. The terminus was built in the late 1830's by the London and Birmingham Ry. in Euston Square, named after Lord Euston who owned the land. It has been rebuilt in recent times. [BC 8]

2231 Euston Road -- essentially a continuation of Marylebone Rd. that begins at Great Portland St. and continues on to Gray's Inn Rd.* [cf]

2232 Evangelical [theology] -- that set of Protestant Christian attitudes or principles which hold that salvation depends upon 1) faith in the atoning death of Jesus, 2) personal conversion, 3) familiarity with the Scriptures, 4) preaching as opposed to ritual. [BC 8/SP 9]

2233 Evangelist, John -- St. John, the Disciple, also known as St. John the Divine [NT 4]

2234 Eve of St. John -- June 23rd. See Feast of St. John [UD 23]

2235 Evening Banner -- a fictitious newspaper, but DLS may have had the Evening Standard in mind [CW 14/UD 14/BC 1/MMA 1]

2236 Evening Comet -- the fictitious evening version of the Morning Star* [MMA 12]

2237 Evening News -- a politically Conservative paper founded in 1881, but no longer published. It was taken over by the Evening Standard during the post-WW II drive to consolidate newspapers into chains. [nf/im]

2238 Evening Views -- a fictitious paper for which Salcombe Hardy* works [nf/UD 6]

2239 Evening Wire -- a fictitious London paper that reports PW's feat of having successfully named seventeen wines correctly to vintage years while blindfolded, thus winning a bet from Freddy Arbuthnot* at the Egotists' Club [mt]

2240 Evensong -- the standard Sunday evening worship service in the Anglican church [WB 5]

2241 Everard -- a character in HV's book, Death 'twixt Wind and Water. She refers to him as a "wart". [GN 19]

2242 Eversharp -- the brand name of one of the earliest and most famous mechanical pencils. The name, for a while, came to refer to all such pencils, but that practice does not seem to have endured, very likely a victim of the ball-point pen. [MMA 10]

2243 "Every cock will crow . . ." -- an old proverb used here to suggest that perhaps PW and Reggie Pomfret* are roosters on the same dung hill, so to speak, and that is a dangerous arrangement in most barnyards [GN 19]

2244 every third word type -- some ciphers hide the message by burying the text in a predetermined se-

quence in some other innocent text that the sender hopes will not arouse suspicion. One is reminded of the every third word message in Conan Doyle's* "The Gloria Scott". [NT 9]

2245 "Everyone suddenly burst out singing . . ." -- the line recalled is from Siegfried Sassoon's "Everyone Sang". Later lines from the poem are:
"The song was wordless;
The singing will never be done."
[BH 5]

2246 Evesham -- located in Worcester on the River Avon, downstream from Shakespeare's Stratford and to the North and West of London. It is an agricultural town famous for the fruit grown in the region. It is given as the home of Susan Brown*, aunt of murder suspect Robert Duckworthy*. [im]

2247 Évreux -- a small city approximately sixty miles West of Paris. See Paris-Évreux Express [mt]

2248 Evvie -- one of Will and Mary Thoday's* two daughters [NT 6]

2249 ewer -- a vase-shaped pitcher or jug of indeterminate size [NT 14]

2250 Ewigkeit -- German for "eternity". It is used to suggest "unknown blackness". [GN 10]

2251 ex abundantia cautelae -- Latin for, "out of excessive caution (hesitation)" [CW 6]

2252 ex cathedra pronouncements -- from the (bishop's) chair; hence, any absolute or authoritative statement. Cathedra is the root word of cathedral, those churches which serve a bishop as his diocesan headquarters, the location of a bishop's throne, e. g. Rome, Canterbury, York, London, New York, Cleveland, Moscow, etc. [FRH 25]

2253 ex hypothesi -- Latin for, "by hypothesis" [SP 5]

2254 Examination Schools -- the building at Oxford wherein students take their final examinations for their B. A. degrees. Designed by T. G. Johnson after Elizabethan and Jacobean models, the building is a series of huge and imposing rooms. When not being used for exams, the building is used for lectures, meetings, etc. [GN 12]

2255 "except in the Hesperides" -- HV is quoting from Shakespeare's Love's Labor's Lost, IV, iii, 340-41:
"For valor, is not Love a Hercules,
Still climbing trees in the Hesperides."
The speech is Berowne's and refers to the eleventh of Hercules' twelve labors, gathering the golden apples from the tree in the garde of the Hesperides, sisters who, in Greek mythology, lived far away in the West, near the Atlas Mountains in Northern Africa. [GN 12]

2256 Exchange -- the central telephone switchboard for a given area, controlled by operators. Before direct dialling, operators had to assist with all telephone calls made. [ae/UD 6]

2257 executor -- a person named in a will to be responsible for supervising the terms of that will and to make certain that its provisions are carried out [passim]

2258 executrix -- a female executor* of a will [CW 1/SP 7/BH 19]

2259 exeunt omnes -- Latin for, "all go out", "exit"; usually a theatrical direction at the end of a scene [UD 8]

2260 Exhibition -- in "Haunted Policeman" the reference is probably to the British Empire Exhibition of 1924, held at Wembley. The reference in BC is too vague to allow positive identification. [hp/BC 10]

2261 Exhibition -- the major Glasgow art exhibit that attracted so much attention among the artists of Kirkcudbright* and Gatehouse* was probably the Royal Glasgow Institute show held during the summer of 1930. The Times of London's art critic, in a September 27th review printed on the 29th, penned what may be one of the great criticisms of all time: "Unconscious humor is provided by Mr. John B. Souter in "Imagery", which might be taken to represent the forcing upon a reluctant Southron* of a winged haggis." It is a pity that the author of so devastating and marvellous a line should remain anonymous. [FRH 5]

2262 exhumation order -- the legal order required to remove a body from its grave once it has been interred there. Such an order is difficult

to obtain. [WB 10]

2263 experience of women -- see Dr. Watson [BH 18]

2264 explore every stone -- usually the expressions are "explore every avenue" and "leave no stone unturned". Being a firm opponent of clichés, perhaps PW decided to be unique. [NT 7]

2265 Express -- the reference is to Glasgow's Scottish Daily Express, a morning paper. In SP the reference is probably to the Daily Express*. [FRH 19/SP 12]

2266 Express Dairy -- the Express Dairy ran a chain of light lunch establishments at one of which Parker* lunches while on his search for the solicitor* in the Holborn* area who might have advised someone on the new Property Act of 1926*. [UD 17]

2267 extravasation of blood -- the forcing of blood from its proper channel either into the surrounding tissue or from the body [NT 4]

2268 The Eye of Osiris -- first published in 1911 as The Vanishing Man. Archaeologist John Bellingham disappears and then reappears, completely transformed to conceal his murder. While the method of discovery wouldn't impress anyone today, it was most extraordinary and unique in 1911. The novel is by R. Austin Freeman*. [FRH 27]

2269 eye-wash -- military slang for a good appearance which is only superficial [GN 17]

(F)

2270 f.16 at 1/5 second -- the "f" number indicates the size of the opening in the iris of a camera's lens. The larger the number, the smaller the hole, f.16 being one of the smallest apertures standardly available (the smallest on most lenses, although some go down to f.22). Such a small aperture at the relatively long exposure time of 1/5th second would expose a high speed film without the use of a flash and would allow both close and distant objects to be in sharp focus. [MMA 2]

2271 F---e -- a French expletive, demurely deleted. There are two or three possible competitors for use here, but foutre seems the most appropriate. Foutre translates loosely to "stuff it" in the crudest sense possible and is never used in reference to one's turkey. Foutre also serves as the French equivalent of the CLASSIC English obscenity. [mt]

2272 F. O. -- the abbreviation for the Foreign Office* [BH P]

2273 F. R. C. P. -- Fellow of the Royal College of Physicians, London. Founded by Thomas Linacre, a physician to Henry VIII, by letters patent* signed September 23, 1518, by Cardinal Wolsey, the College had the exclusive right to test and to license physicians in London and within seven miles of it. Such license has not been needed since the passage of the Medical Act of 1858. The College (not one in any teaching sense as with Oxford) elects members more as an honor for outstanding work or research. A Fellow is a member of the College. [WB 8]

2274 F. R. C. S. -- Fellow of the Royal College of Surgeons. A member of that College, founded in 1800. The College issues recommendations regarding the training of surgeons, honors noteworthy work in surgery and surgical techniques or in research, and still exercises the privileges granted by its Royal Charter in the examination and licensing of surgeons. [WB 8]

2275 face-fungus -- slang for a beard [NT 10]

2276 faced a fence -- refers to horseback riding and the hunt, working

up the courage to take a horse over an obstacle of any sort [BH 14]

2277 factory end of the pitch -- see cricket [MMA 18]

2278 fag -- a slang term for cigarette [SP 5/MMA 16/NT 2]

2279 fag round [fagging] -- to struggle around to, a slang expression [FRH 4/MMA 2]

2280 fagged -- tired, worn out [BH 10]

2281 Faggott, Tom -- owner of a pea-shooter and an office errand boy at Pym's Publicity* [MMA 6]

2282 Fagin -- ruler of the gang of petty thieves and pickpockets in Charles Dickens's Oliver Twist [BH 7]

2283 Faguet, Emile -- a noted French literary critic (1847-1916) and professor during the 1890's and early 20th C. André Gide (1869-1950) condemned Faguet as unperceptive. Faguet is the author of Lit. du XVIIe siècle (Literature of the 17th Century). [umw]

2284 "Fain would I change that note . . ." -- an anonymous lyric found in Tobias Hume's (?-1645) The First Part of Ayres, French, Pollish, and others together . . ., London, 1605. The last part of the second verse is:

"Fair house of joy and bliss
Where truest pleasure is,
I do adore thee.
I know thee what thou are,
I serve thee with my heart
And fall before thee."

Song CXII thus differs from DLS's version in GN. [GN 19]

2285 "Faint heart never won . . ." -- PW could be referring to Robert Burns's poem, "To Dr. Blacklock" where he wrote:

"Come Firm Resolve, take thou the van,
Thou stalk o' carl-hemp in man!
And let us mind, faint heart ne'er wan
A lady fair;
Wha does the utmost he can,
Will whyles do mair."

The "faint heart" idea also appears in Gilbert and Sullivan's Iolanthe, Act II, in a trio near the end of that act:

"Faint heart never won fair lady!
Nothing venture, nothing win--
Blood is thick, but water's thin--
In for a penny, in for a pound
It's love that makes the world go round!"

Either reference is appropriate here. [SP 5]

2286 "Fainter by day . . ." -- PW is quoting from Alfred, Lord Tennyson's poem, "The Holy Grail", ll. 472-74. Sir Galahad is describing how it led him on and what he endured to obtain the Holy Grail*. [BC 13]

2287 fair cop -- slang for "a clean catch", or "caught in the act" [aq/ab/GN 7]

2288 Fair Isle -- a kind of knitting in many colors and intricate horizontal patterns originating in Fair Isle in the Shetlands. The sweaters are available as pullovers and as cardigans [SP 8/BH 4]

2289 Fairview -- the name of the guest house in Leahampton* where Miss Climpson* stays while investigating matters there for PW [UD 4]

2290 faisan rôti -- roast pheasant; with pommes Byron*, the main course in PW's dinner with Ann Dorland* [BC 21]

2291 Faith, of the -- the Roman Catholic faith. Langley* is questioned about his religious beliefs by Martha*. [ie]

2292 faithful hound -- a reference, fateful it seems for PW, to Odysseus' return to Ithaca when he is instantly recognized by his old dog, Argus [CW 4]

2293 Falbae -- a farm due North of Creetown* on the moors South of the Cairnsmore of Fleet* in the vicinity of some abandoned lead mines [FRH 14]

2294 Fall of Troy -- the ancient walled city in Asia Minor that fell several times, the most notable fall being described by Homer in The Iliad [GN 17]

2295 Falstaff -- a London pub or tavern frequented by Salcombe Hardy*. It is one place where PW can expect to find him. The name honors that fat soldier created by Shakespeare and who figures prominently in The Merry Wives of Windsor, Henry IV, Parts

I and II, and Henry V. PW is known to visit the pub as well. DLS visited the place with her husband-to-be in 1926, but it is now occupied by an outlet of the Pizzaland chain who only maintain a "Falstaff Tap" in the basement. [nf/ BC 19]

2296 fame outlasting gilded monuments -- Supt. Kirk* alludes to Shakespeare's Sonnet 55:

"Not marble, nor the gilded monuments
Of princes, shall outlive this powerful rhyme."

[BH 12]

2297 Famille Rose jar -- Famille Rose is the European name for a spectacular type of decoration on Chinese vases of the Ch'ing (Manchu) Dynasty (1644-1912). The particular jars in question were developed at the imperial kilns at Ching-te-chen under the supervision of T'ang-Ying (1736-49), and featured an elaborate range of opaque glazes, especially a carmine glaze derived from gold. Such jars, vases, and other ornamental ware, if authentic, are extremely valuable. [UD 7/ BH E2]

2298 Family -- Mrs. Gates* speaks here with a capital "F" to indicate that she is thinking of the family with whom she is in service [NT 6]

2299 fan tracery -- the pillars in churches, etc., using Perpendicular architecture often open outward into arches in a manner resembling an open fan. The tracery is ornamental carving on the surface of the "fan's" stonework. In the screen* at Fenchurch St. Paul* the tracery would be carved into the wood of the screen and would be openwork, not just surface carving. The design is an extension of patterns developed in Gothic architecture. [NT 2]

2300 fantods -- a variant of fantad, or to make restless, nervous, or uncomfortable without necessity of a reason; from fantastic [NT 14]

2301 Farley's Footwear -- a company created by DLS [MMA 3]

2302 Farquharson -- an exhibitor at the Glasgow Exhibition*. This may be Joseph (1846-1935) who did some Scottish landscapes. [FRH 12]

2303 Farrar, Dean -- the reference is to Frederick William Farrar (1831-1905), English novelist and theologian born in Bombay, India. He was a master at Harrow and Headmaster at Marlborough College. He eventually became Dean of Canterbury, hence PW's reference to Dean Farrar. He wrote several school stories noted mostly for their high content of virtue and religion patterned after the duty, honor, country tenets of Dr. Thomas Arnold who is considered the founder of the modern English public school* systerm. The quote PW cites is typical of the style of language in Farrar's books where even the bullies have that aristocratic air to their speech, and is probably from one of Farrar's books such as Eric or Little by Little, his best known school stories. The novels appeared in the 1850's and 60's. [SP 5]

2304 Farren, Gilda -- the wife of Hugh Farren*, a lovely and sensitive woman who serves as a sort of mother-confessor to Sandy Campbell*. This enrages her husband's jealousy, but she is sufficiently independent to want to lead a life of her own. She is, in her own right, an accomplished artist in textiles. [FRH 1]

2305 Farren, Hugh -- one of the prominent members of the Gatehouse* and Kirkcudbright* artists' colony, he is jealous of Sandy Campbell* and is not known to be very level-headed in his marital dealings. [FRH 1]

2306 farriery -- the art or establishment of a farrier; one who shoes horses. The term farrier is also used to refer to a horse doctor or veterinarian as well. [bc]

2307 Farringdon, Lionel -- once engaged to Miss Cattermole*, he comes under attack by the voracious Miss Flaxman* [GN 5]

2308 Farringdon St. -- at the intersection with Fleet St.*, New Bridge St. becomes Farringdon St. which continues North, eventually becoming Farringdon Rd. [sf]

2309 Fascist[i] -- the followers of Benito Mussolini*, Fascists, and leading Italian government figures from 1922 to 1943. The name derives from the ancient Roman badge of magisterial

power, the fasces, a bundle of rods wrapped around an axe. Mussolini adopted the symbol during his term of power. [nf]

2310 fashing masel the noo -- Scottish dialect for "vexing (irritating) myself now" [FRH 21]

2311 fat-headed hero -- see detective turn out to be the villain [MMA 13]

2312 fatal error of theorizing ahead of my data -- see theorizing ahead of my data [GN 15]

2313 "Fate has vanquished me" -- see "not you but Fate has vanquished me" [GN 4]

2314 Father Christmas -- another name for Santa Claus [BC 22]

2315 "Father, I cannot tell a lie . . ." -- a remark attributed to George Washington by Parson Weems in his biography of America's first president. It alludes to the incident of the hatchet and the cherry tree during Washington's youth. [MMA 6]

2316 The father weakens, but the governor is firm -- the reference is to Richard Brinsley Sheridan's (1751-1816) The Critic, a comic attack on sentimental drama and on the viscious literary criticism of the day. Sheridan's satire involves an unscrupulous author who writes a sentimental tragedy called The Spanish Armada and invites the vicious critics to a rehearsal of it, thus providing a vehicle to ridicule the play, the author, and the critics. The quote is from that satirized play and refers to the father of Tilburnia who is the governor of Tilbury Fort and concerns his reaction to her love for a Spanish prisoner there. See also Lord Burleigh. [CW 13]

2317 Father William -- see Old Father William [HHC 2]

2318 fatigue -- the English equivalent of "KP" as punishment [GN 17].

2319 Faulkner, Dr. -- the pathologist sent by Scotland Yard to examine Vera Findlater's* body [UD 21]

2320 Faust -- a legendary figure, probably based on one Georg Faust (1480?-1538?). Christopher Marlowe and J. W. von Goëthe are the authors of the two most famous versions of the Faust legend, but in "Cave of Ali Baba", the reference is to Charles Gounod's opera, Faust, which is based on Goëthe's work. In that play Faust is presented as a man who seeks all experience more than all knowledge and, to gain his goal, promises his soul to Mephistopheles. At the end, however, Faust is saved and transported to heaven because even though he has committed crimes and has made agreements with the devil, his divine spark of curiosity led him to those actions. Therefore, mankind's activities are positive despite any negative consequences. Gounod's opera premiered in Paris in 1859, and remains popular. See also "Jewel Song" in Faust. [ab]

2321 Faustus -- see Faust. The Dowager Duchess* has him confused with Manichaeus (see Manichee) [CW 9]

2322 Fawkes, Guy -- see Gunpowder Plot [t]

2323 Faversham burglary -- see The Society [ab]

2324 Fear not him that killeth -- Parker* alludes to Matthew 10:28: "And fear not them which kill the body, but are not able to kill the soul: but rather fear him which is able to destroy both soul and body in hell." [MMA 15]

2325 fear to tread -- see where the lords of creation fear to tread [BH 10]

2326 Fearney, Miss -- am employee of Pym's Publicity* [MMA 10]

2327 Feast of All Fools -- April Fools' Day, April 1st, the day when fools are celebrated instead of saints. The custom survives from the celebration of pagan rites held at the spring equinox. [GN 4]

2328 Feast of St. John -- on June 24th. This would be the feast day of St. John the Baptist, the prophet who prepared the way for the coming of the Messiah. He baptized Christ, was later arrested and, eventually, was beheaded for Salome at Herod's order. It was John who called for repentance to prepare for Christ's coming and was an ascetic who directed his work against worldliness. [UD 19]

2329 "The feast with gluttonous delays . . ." -- Donne's "An Epithalamion on the Lady Elizabeth and Count Palatine" is one of several such poetic celebrations of a marriage that he wrote. It is not known in each case to whom the poem was addressed. [BH 3]

2330 the Feathers -- an otherwise unidentifed inn or pub [sf]

2331 Featherstone, Mr. -- a former client of Mr. Murbles's* who, in his will, left Murbles a dozen bottles of an 1847 port. Rather than drink the great wine himself, Featherstone had saved it, feeling that, "no pleasure ever came up to the anticipation". By the time it was set out for consumption--in 1923--it was no longer drinkable. [CW 10]

2332 Featherstone, Mrs. -- a rather intelligent lady who is able to discuss what she has read with at least some insight, a trait that makes her rather notable given some of the rest of the company at the Christmas gathering at Duke's Denver* in 1929. [SP 12]

2333 febrile diseases -- those related to or resulting from high external temperature or fever [WB 2]

2334 Fedora -- the control* used by Nurse Booth* during her séances with Mrs. Craig* [SP 17]

2335 Felix -- PW is being clever. Felix is Latin for happy, but is often associated with felis, Latin for cat. Through the words' similarities, especially as pronounced, the switch from one word to the other is an easy one. Felix, named for the cartoon cat, is also the resident mouser at the Anwoth Hotel*. [CW 11/FRH 11]

2336 fell down in the second lead -- to make an error during the changes* of the second lead* [NT 1]

2337 Fellow[s] -- a senior member of a college in England who is attached to that college in either a teaching or in a research capacity, but who need not be a graduate of that college. A fellow is a distinguished graduate selected to join a faculty for some special expertise he or she might have. They are commonly called "dons". [GN 1/BH 19]

2338 felo-de-se -- Late Latin for suicide, now Anglicized [GN 8]

2339 "The female of the species . . ." Supt. Kirk* is quoting from Rudyard Kipling's* "The Female of the Species":

"When the Hymalayan peasant meets the he-bear in his pride,
He shouts to scare the monster, who will often turn aside.
But the she-bear thus accosted rends the peasant tooth and nail
For the female of the species is more deadly than the male."

[BH 8]

2340 femoral artery -- the major artery in the thigh [UD 23]

2341 fen country -- fens are lowlands that would be mud flats or under water if not drained. In England, they are found around the Wash* extending through West Norfolk, Cambridgeshire, and South Lincolnshire. The whole area is drained by a series of canals and ditches which have left the land very fertile. This drainage feat was mostly accomplished by the Dutch engineer Cornelius Vermuyden in the 17th C. and has been improved in later years. [HHC 12/NT 2]

2342 Fen Drainage Board -- a fictitious agency [NT 7]

2343 fence -- one who disposes of stolen property as an agent for the thief and for a large percentage of the value of the goods disposed of [GN 9]

2344 Fenchurch, Dr. -- the police surgeon in Wilvercombe* who performs the autopsy on Paul Alexis* [HHC 3]

2345 Fenchurch St. Paul -- the church and the community are fictitious places patterned after the places of DLS's girlhood in the fen country*. She grew up in Christchurch and Bluntisham, and knew the area intimately. [NT 1]

2346 Fenchurch St. Peter -- the fictitious parish to the southeast of Fenchurch St. Paul*. It boasts a garage and the closest police constable in the vicinity of Fenchurch St. Paul. [NT 2]

2347 Fenchurch St. Stephen -- the fictitious community built around the

parish church of St. Stephen, the first Christian martyr. It is about five miles to the southwest of Fenchurch St. Paul*. [NT 1]

2348 the Fender -- the small enclosure on the St. Giles or East side of St. John's College, Oxford. DLS is probably referring to the walled area on St. Giles's St. just outside the College. The area used to be used for political gatherings. [GN 12]

2349 fender, gas ring in the -- a gas burner inside the fender, the decorative metal barrier meant to protect the floors and rugs from falling ashes or coals in a fireplace. As the time of year in question is June, there would not have been a fire to keep things warm, hence the gas ring. [SP 1]

2350 Fenimore Cooper -- James Fenimore Cooper (1789-1851), the American novelist of The Last of the Mohicans and The Leatherstocking Tales fame. His adventure stories deal with plots unfolding in what was, at the time of the American Revolution and shortly thereafter, the frontier. Many tales unfold in what is now central and western New York State. [WB 10]

2351 Fentiman, General Arthur -- the central figure in and cause of The Unpleasantness at the Bellona Club. It is distressing enough that he is discovered dead in his favorite chair on the evening of Armistice Day, but the Club's decorum is soundly shaken when it is learned that the old gentleman had been murdered, that his corpse had been tampered with, and that knowledge of the exact time of his death was essential to settle the terms of his sister's will. [BC 1]

2352 Fentiman, Captain George -- the younger of General Fentiman's* grandsons, George is the shell-shocked, nervous young man who has difficulty accepting having his wife work to support him, and who, during an attack of nerves, falsely confesses to his grandfather's murder. His brother is Major Robert Fentiman*. [BC 1]

2353 Fentiman, Major Robert -- brother of George*, Robert is the matter-of-fact, professional military man. His behavior at the Bellona Club* regarding his grandfather's death might make one question his ethical discernment, but he does manage to redeem himself. [BC 2]

2354 Fentiman, Sheila -- George Fentiman's* loving and sympathetic wife who struggles to help keep George's nerves under control and who also works to provide money for their existence [BC 1]

2355 Feodora -- the name inscribed on a photograph carried by Paul Alexis* [HHC 21]

2356 Ferguson, John -- a fictitious landscape and figure painter who, at the time of the action in FRH, is not on good terms with his wife and has separated from her. He is also in the group who have quarrelled with Sandy Campbell*. [FRH 1]

2357 Ferguson, Joseph Alexander -- great-uncle to Thomas Macpherson*, he is an eccentric, reclusive old man who, at age ninety-five, decided that he did not want to deal with the problems of declining health and committed suicide, leaving his entire alimentary canal from the esophagus South to his great-nephew, a medical student. At his death, the organs were put in a jar and delivered. These items are central to one of DLS's more bizarre stories. [ss]

2358 Ferguson, Mrs. -- the wife of John Ferguson* [FRH 3]

2359 Ferguson, Robert -- the only remaining relative of Joseph Ferguson* who is upset because he received only £500 as residuary legatee of the old man's will. The cause for the elderly man's dislike of young Robert is amply documented in the goings on in the story. [ss]

2360 Ferrara's -- a fictitious restaurant suggestive of the real Frascati's* [GN 4]

2361 Ferrars, Earl -- also spelled Ferrers. The reference is to Laurence Ferrars, 4th Earl Ferrars and Viscount Tamworth. He had a great and often uncontrollable temper which some ascribed to madness. As a result, one John Johnson, steward and long time family servant, was appointed as a trustee for the Earl. When Johnson refused to dishonor his required duties and give the Earl money whenever he

wanted it, his lordship flew into a rage and shot the elderly steward. Ferrars pled insanity, but couldn't convince the House of Lords at his trial that he was insane at the time of the shooting. He was convicted, sentenced to be hanged, drawn and quartered, and was executed at Tyburn on May 5, 1760, on a new gallows erected especially for the occasion, the last peer to be hanged publicly. His major complaint was that he had to be hanged at Tyburn where the common criminals were executed, but the new gallows helped appease his wounded pride. A contemporary account of the whole affair is presented in the Annual Register of 1760. Of note is the fact that there is no appeal to a verdict from a trial in the Lords. [CW 2]

2362 ferrets -- long, slender, small and vicious members of the European polecat family. They can be domesticated to a point and trained to hunt rats, rabbits, and other small, burrowing game. The word ferret also applies to one who searches diligently. [SP 8]

2363 fettled -- prepared, made fit for use [GN 11]

2364 feudal privilege -- a reference to the droit de seigneur, the medieval right of a lord to deflower a bride on the first night [CW 4].

2365 Ffolliott, Mr. -- a London rare book dealer who specialized in classical authors. Both he and the shop PW visits are most likely fictitious, but shops like his are readily found in London. [dh]

2366 Fichley -- see Finchley. The entry spelling is a typographical error in some editions. [BC 6]

2367 fiddle and cocaine -- the allusion is to Sherlock Holmes's two main methods for spending time while not on a case: playing his Stradivarius violin (he is asserted by Watson to be a concert quality performer), or injecting himself with a solution of cocaine [BH 13]

2368 fiddle will shatter glass -- see periods of vibration [NT 20]

2369 field at mid on -- a cricket* term. Fielding in cricket is the same as in baseball, the goal being to prevent the scoring of runs within the rules of the game. "Mid on" is a fielding position equidistant from the batsman and the bowler. See cricket. [MMA 18]

2370 field crossed over -- see cricket [MMA 18]

2371 field sable -- an heraldic term for a black background on a coat of arms. See Wimsey arms. [GN 15]

2372 Fielding, Mrs. -- Arthur Prendergast's lover [te]

2373 Fiennes, Ulric -- another sculptor friend of Marjorie Phelps. He is the source of irritation in the Schlitzers' marital discord. [BC 10]

2374 Fiesole -- a small Italian city just to the northeast of Florence in Tuscany. It is the retirement home of Thomas Probyn*. [UD 12]

2375 fifteen-carat gold -- see carat [HHC 4]

2376 "Fifteen men on a dead man's chest, etc." -- PW is quoting from Ch. 1 of Treasure Island by Robert Louis Stevenson. The quote would certainly be well known to his nephew, the Viscount St. George*, and is also most appropriate for the occasion. However, substituting a bottle of Johnny Walker* for one of rum is PW's idea and is perfectly in keeping with his tastes as pirate rum would not have met his standards. [dh]

2377 15 stone -- 210 pounds, Supt. Kirk's weight [BH 7]

2378 fifteen thousand eight hundred and forty Kent Treble Bob Majors -- a challenge for even experienced ringers! Nine hours may be a conservative estimate as the College Youths* rang such a peal* in 1868, but they used lighter bells. [NT 1]

2379 15th ____shires -- the unidentifiable British military unit in which Denis Cathcart* has been commissioned to serve in WW I. It is likely that DLS wished to avoid any positive unit identification because of Cathcart's later activities as a card sharper. [CW 5]

2380 Fifth Chapter of the Book of the Prophet Jeremiah -- the passages

PW reads are all from Jeremiah 5. That chapter deals with the universal corruption and idolatry found in Jerusalem. [BH E2]

2381 50 guineas -- an amount equal to £52/10 (shillings). See British Monetary Units. At $4.00 U. S. to the pound, that would equal about $210, a not overly modest price for the times considering that one could buy an automobile for a bit more. [FRH 21]

2382 fifty-three, nineteen, four -- the Viscount St. George* is listing off the checks he has written by their amount. In this case it is fifty-three pounds, nineteen shillings, and four pence, or about $216 U. S. See British Monetary Units. [GN 10]

2383 Filet de Sole -- sole baked to a delicate doneness after the bones have been removed. It is the fish course for PW's dinner with Ann Dorland*. [BC 21]

2384 filthy expressions, Sally -- PW is addressing Salcombe Hardy* concerning the latter's use (or misuse) of English. DLS had a particular hatred for standard newspaper writing, calling it "telegraphic journalese", and considered it a poor substitute for English. Her epithet comes from the reporter's habit of inventing words or misusing words to save space or to create a cheap effect. She believed such misuses of the language could be excused only in telegrams and used PW to chastise Hardy and, thereby, all guilty reporters. [nf]

2385 Final Reading -- the final (third) formal presentation of a bill in Parliament before it goes for Royal Assent and becomes an Act [UD 18]

2386 final Schools -- those tests with which a student concludes a college career in England, and upon which the awarding of the B. A. degree rests. The term is primarily associated with Oxford. [UD BN]

2387 Finch, Meleager -- the talented maker of crossword puzzles and acrostics whose will becomes the object of an amazing search. If his niece fails to solve a particular puzzle, his estate will go to the Primrose League*, a fate that would greatly upset Miss Marryat's* Socialist political tendencies. For additional notes to the solution of the puzzle, see Puzzle Clues. [umw]

2388 Finchley -- a northern suburb of London, approximately eight miles North of Westminster. See also motor cycle race. [cb/BC 6/MMA 15]

2389 Findlater, Mrs. -- a lady in the Leahampton* church work party and mother of Vera Findlater* [UD 5]

2390 Findlater, Vera -- the youngest daughter of Mrs. Findlater* and a friend of Mary Whittaker*. She becomes the last victim in UD. [UD 5]

2391 Finnart Bay -- on the East side of the mouth of Loch Ryan* at the mouth of the Glen App [FRH 25]

2392 Finsbury, Michael -- the lawyer/detective in Robert Louis Stevenson's The Wrong Box. The story involves shipping a body from place to place to prevent discovery of the death. Despite the macabre situation, the story is absurdly and improbably zany. The plot involves a tontine, an early "insurance" scheme, the proceeds of which will go to either Joseph or Masterman Finsbury. It is they who hide the body. Michael tries to track it down. Stevenson's stepson, Lloyd Osbourne, collaborated with RLS on the story. [WB 13/HHC 13]

2393 Finsbury Park -- a residential area due North of the Tower of London and East of Hampstead Heath. The Park itself is at the junction of Seven Sisters Rd. and Green Lane. George and Sheila Fentiman** live in the area. [BC 7]

2394 Finsbury Park murder -- the newspapers' name for the situation surrounding the death of Dahlia Dallmeyer*. The park is real, the murder is not. [cb]

2395 firearms -- PW usually does not carry them, but he is known to have an automatic pistol in his bedroom and he also owns an undescribed revolver [dh/ab]

2396 first and last terms of the progression -- see terms [BH 20]

2397 First Class Honours -- the highest level of accomplishment of the Bachelor of Arts degree at a university

[UD BN]

2398 first floor -- in North America, the second floor. The first floor in America is called the ground floor in England, so the second floor is the first, the third the second, and so on. [WB 6/SP 20/HHC 32/GN 11]

2399 First in English -- having earned First Class Honours* in English--whether literature or linguistics is not specified, but literature is probably meant [GN 1]

2400 First in Greats -- having earned First Class Honours* in "Greats" which is the final degree examination at Oxford, known as "Tripos" at Cambridge [GN 12]

2401 First Lesson -- a reading from the Old Testament at Anglican matins. The Second Lesson would be from the New Testament. The lessons are different every day and are set in the Church calendar with the intention of covering as much of the Bible as is possible during the year. Special feast days have appropriate lessons. [BH E2]

2402 "First, Lucus mortis . . ." -- the passage is from LeFanu's* Wylder's Hand, Ch. 48, where the mad Uncle Lorne is again encountered. The "places" mentioned are all fictitious ones related to darkness and death, hell, etc. [NT 9]

2403 first over -- see cricket [MMA 18]

2404 first return -- railway jargon for a first class, round-trip ticket [FRH 14]

2405 first single -- railway jargon for a first class, one-way ticket [FRH 14]

2406 first time his features had ever been prized -- see prized above rubies [BH P]

2407 first water -- the highest degree of clarity and lustre for a precious stone, especially a diamond; loosely, anything of noteworthy magnitude. [FRH 15]

2408 fish have gold in their mouths -- see most fish have . . . [MMA 14]

2409 Fisherman's Arms -- a pub just outside Windle* on the bus route from the guesthouse where Miss Climpson* is staying to Rosanna Wrayburn's home [SP 16]

2410 Fishmonger's Gazette -- as presented, a fictitious journal. There was a Fish Trades Gazette which DLS may have had in mind, but it is not the magazine Mr. Tallboy needed. [MMA 10]

2411 Fishy Ness -- a fictitious place [HHC 13]

2412 Fitzgerald contractions -- a reference to the theories of Irish physicist George Francis FitzGerald [1851-1901) who hypothesized the foreshortening of moving bodies. Parker* is trying to get PW to be more reasonable in his considerations regarding the mysterious events of "Absolutely Elsewhere". Parker appears well-read in the then modern theories of physics. [ae]

2413 five aces -- in poker*, the best possible hand, but possible only when there are wild cards in use. Otherwise, the best hand would be a royal flush (A-K-Q-J-10). [WB 3]

2414 "Five are the flamboys . . ." -- see "Dilly Song" [CW 13]

2415 Five Elms -- see Mr. Vickery [BH 1]

2416 5-metre yacht -- the International Rule classifies yachts not by length alone, but by a system which takes into consideration such things as beam, amount of sail area carried, etc., and converts this information into a rating system. For example, the twelve metre yachts used for the famous America's Cup races are not necessarily thirty-nine feet long. [HHC 9]

2417 five-minute bell -- the bell rung to announce that divine service will begin in five minutes [NT 2]

2418 5 point type -- a point in printing is a unit of type equal to 0.01384 inch. Five point type, therefore, would be a font 0.0692 inch high.

This is five point type.

Since such tiny types are fragile, PW would have to be very careful not to break them when he struck the impressions. [FRH 28]

2419 five rows of ermine -- an unknown rank. A duke has four rows of

ermine on each side of the robe, the most markings on the robe of any peer. One suspects that DLS, knowing that there are five degrees of the peerage*, assumed that a baron would have one ermine bar and that a duke would have five. They do not. Barons have two, viscounts two and a half, earls have three, marquises have three and a half, dukes four. [CW 14]

2420 five--seventeen--six -- five pounds, seventeen shillings, and six pence, an amount just short of $30 U. S. See British Monetary Units. [qs]

2421 five shilling piece -- a crown, which is no longer minted except to commemorate such things as Royal weddings. See British Monetary Units. [np]

2422 five third singles -- railway jargon for five third class, one-way tickets [FRH 14]

2423 five up and three to play -- golf jargon meaning that one player has won five holes of the eight, thereby winning the match [FRH 7]

2424 five wickets down -- from cricket* and meaning that five batsmen are out, leaving five wickets to fall. The eleventh wicket falls automatically as two batsmen are required to carry on an innings. Batsman and wicket are here being used essentially as synonyms. In baseball the situation would be equivalent to having the bases loaded in the bottom of the ninth inning, two men out, and a 3-2 count on the batter who knows that he has to score all four possible runs to win the game. [GN 17]

2425 5XX -- a radio station operated from 1925 by the BBC* at Daventry in Warwickshire. PW claims the Ploffsky gang* of anarchists used the station for some of their activities. The 500 to 600 mile range would, today, suggest a short wave service, but 5XX was, in fact, operated with a long wave transmitter. One must remember that the airwaves were far from crowded in 1925, and the signals could travel much further without interference than is possible today. [aq]

2426 "fix a vacant stare" -- this quotation is from Alfred, Lord Tennyson's poem, "Lady Clara Vere de Vere", ll. 47-8. The last four lines of the stanza read:

"You held your course without remorse,
To make him trust his modest worth,
And, last, you fixed a vacant stare,
And slew him with your noble birth."

HV uses the line to query PW about his interview with Reggie Pomfret*. [GN 20]

2427 fixing of the seals -- see seals, fixing of the [CW 5]

2428 fizz -- see bottle of fizz [MMA 13]

2429 Flackett -- the "old" and rich former Shrewsbury College* student who is suggested as a possible source for a donation to provide "first-class" coffee for the College rather than a tankful of tropical fish [GN 2]

2430 flagged, passage being -- paved with flagstones [ae]

2431 flake white -- one of the several white oil paints available to artists and indispensable to their work when blending, shading, or cutting the pure colors as they come from the tube [FRH 26]

2432 Flamborough College -- a fictitious college. See Brontë College. [GN 1]

2433 flan -- see apricot flan [GN 15]

2434 Flanagan -- the maiden name of Campbell's* mother [FRH 1]

2435 Flanagan, Walter -- a resident of Kirkcudbright* who has a wooden leg, the result of wounds suffered during WW I [FRH 8]

2436 Flanders -- the area of northern France and southern Belgium where Flemish is still spoken and where most of the fighting on the Western Front of WW I took place. While never an independent state in the full sense of the words, the controlling house of Flanders exercised much political clout from the 9th to the 15th centuries. [GN 11]

2437 Flanders -- the area of the Western Front where PW saw action as a major during WW I

2438 Flanders poppy -- the vermilion poppy, symbol of the WW I dead and, now, of all war dead. It is a strong visual reference to the famous poem by John McCrae, "In Flanders Fields", first published in Punch* in December of 1915. McCrae died in 1918. [BC 12]

2439 flannel -- a fabric of wool or cotton, twilled or worsted, and napped slightly. It is used widely for all sorts of things from winter sheets to trousers. [UD 3]

2440 Flannel to Unmarried Mothers -- there is no record of any such organization. It is likely a PW creation to add flavor to the conversation. [UD 3]

2441 "Flat, stale, or stale, flat" -- in Hamlet's famous "O! that this too too solid flesh would melt" soliloquy, I, ii, 129ff., the lines are:

"How weary, stale, flat, and unprofitable
Seem to me all the uses of this world."

Note that the word is "uses", not "curses" or "courses" as Mr. Ingleby* says. [MMA 19]

2442 flattie -- a slang derivative of "flatfoot", a demeaning description of a policeman [NT 14]

2443 Flavel -- a parishoner at Fenchurch St. Paul* whose banns* are almost lost by Mr. Venables* [NT 4]

2444 Flaxman, Catherine -- a Second Year scholar* at Shrewsbury College* who is known as a rather insatiable chaser after other girls' boyfriends [GN 5]

2445 flea in his ear -- to be sent away with a sharp reproach or rebuff [HHC 20]

2446 "Fleat Heraclitus an rideat Democritus?" -- the passage HV reads provides a translation. Burton's Anatomy has that much to say for itself, at least the style is clear even if the text is massive. [GN 21]

2447 Fleeming, Jimmy -- a poacher and friend of Jock Graham's* near Bargrennan*. He and Graham sometimes poach together. [FRH 22]

2448 the Fleet -- the Water (River) of Fleet which flows southward to Wigtown Bay. Gatehouse-of-Fleet* is just above the mouth of the river. [ss/FRH 3]

2449 Fleet St. -- headquarters of most of the various major English newspapers are located along this half-mile street situated in central London. It connects the East end of The Strand* with The City*. The street gets its name from the Fleet River which has been paved over since the 17th C. It has become synonymous with the newspaper business in England. [im/HHC 11/MMA 12/BH 19]

2450 Fleetwhite, Mr. -- he and his library are fictitious. At the sale of the library it is noted that a copy of the Confessio Amantis* as printed by Caxton* came up for bid. [CW 4]

2451 Fleming, James -- the Duke of Denver's* manservant at Riddlesdale Lodge*. It is unfortunate for the Duke that Fleming did his duties so well when under stress. [CW 1]

2452 Fleming, James -- see "The Sandyford Mystery" [BH 13]

2453 Fleming, Marjory -- see Marjory Fleming's turkey [GN 1]

2454 Fletcher, Colonel -- a Crofton* resident who was fond of the annual hunt and who worked with Miss Clara Whittaker* to keep the Crofton Hunt* going during WW I [UD 11]

2455 flex -- a flexible electrical cord as an extension cord [qs/te/WB 12]

2456 Flibbertigibbet -- see "foul fiend Flibbertigibbet" [BH 18]

2457 Flim [Flimsy] -- a nickname for PW used by the doctor (unnamed) who delivers Wimsey's first child, Bredon*. The name derives from PW's days at Eton*. [hp]

2458 flimsies -- carbon copies on onionskin paper, a thin but tough paper suited for making up to twenty copies so the typist does not have to hit the keys with such force to get a clean copy [MMA 1]

2459 floater [perfectly providential] -- a serendipitous wanderer who fits conveniently into the plan devised by PW to entrap Major Fentiman [BC 14]

St. Paul's from Fleet Street.

#2449 Fleet St. with St. Paul's Cathedral in the background. The view is looking East.

2460 Flops -- the nickname for one of PW's contacts at the Foreign Office* [HHC 28]

2461 florin -- see British Monetary Units for other units of currency. A coin called a florin was first minted in Florence in 1252, its name being derived from the flower on it. In the reign of Edward III, two coins, also called leopards and double leopards, worth three and six shillings, were minted that were called florins. Any modern references to florins would be to those coins minted after 1842 and worth two shillings. [HHC 30/MMA 1]

2462 floury potato -- a properly boiled or baked potato should be dry and crumbly, like flour, never soggy or lumpy. The flesh should mash easily with a fork. [NT 6]

2463 fly -- a light passenger carriage drawn by a horse [bc]

2464 Fly-Catcher -- an otherwise unidentified criminal, a friend of Nobby Cranton's* [NT 14]

2465 foliated column head -- the top of a pillar or column decorated with leaves [NT 2]

2466 folio -- the word has a variety of meanings, the most important being a large piece of paper folded once to form four pages. It can also mean the simplest form of a book or it can refer to a standard book size (the largest), being thirteen or more inches in height. [dh/WB 1]

2467 Folio Chaucer -- as important as Chaucer is in English literature, it is impossible to determine which one DLS might have had in mind. However, it is pleasant to think that DLS might have blessed the Shrewsbury College* library with one of Caxton's* edition of the Canterbury Tales, printed in 1478 on 374 leaves. [GN 6]

2468 Folio Dante -- the edition of the Divine Comedy* (1481) was scheduled as the first illustrated Dante*, but printer Nicolo di Lorenzo had great difficulty with the use of copperplate engravings, so only nineteen of the thirty-four illustrations were ever done, none appearing in the Purgatorio or Paradiso. Of the nineteen included, the first is invariably cut off by the binder as it was printed in the wrong place. [WB 1]

2469 Folkestone -- a Channel port and seaside resort in Kent [CW 9/UD 20/BC 13]

2470 "Follow the knave . . ." -- from Shakespeare's King Henry VI, Part II, II, i, 156. The line is Gloucester's. [BH 18]

2471 follow-on -- in cricket*, a team captain has the option of having the opposing team bat two successive innings rather than alternating as is usually done if the side batting second has scored "x" fewer runs than the side batting first. Depending on how long the match is, "x" can be 75, 100, 150 or 200 runs and has varied in cricket history. In this particular case it would be 150, so PW needed to score at least 90 runs in order to save the situation. [GN 17]

2472 the Folly -- a stone tower on the grounds of Striding Hall*. It has smooth sides, an inner spiral staircase, and is the center of much attention as it provides even the title of the story in which it appears. It resembles a rook, or castle, in a chess* set. [sf]

2473 Folly Bridge -- the St. Aldate's/Abingdon Rd. bridge across the Thames in Southern Oxford. The bridge dates from at least the 1200's, but was rebuilt by Ebenezer Perry in 1825-27. [GN 14]

2474 font -- baptismal font. In Anglican practice they are always in the back of the church away from the altar. [NT 1]

2475 "Fool, hypocrite, villain--man!" -- see George Barnwell [BH 15]

2476 "Fool, would thy virtue . . ." -- from I, iv, 66-7 of T. L. Beddoes' Death's Jest Book**. The lines are spoken by Duke Melveric to Wolfram. The men are both in love with Sibylla and Melveric has tried to kill Wolfram to have her for himself. Wolfram discovers the plot only to hear that Melveric has been captured by Saracens (the setting here is Egypt). Wolfram rushes off, saves Melveric, forgives him, only to have Melveric kill him with a Saracen sword. [HHC 13]

2477 Fool's Tragedy -- a subtitle for Death's Jest Book* [SP 8]

2478 foolscap -- a size of paper, usually thirteen by sixteen inches [MMA 10]

2479 foot-muff -- an insulated foot-warmer large enough to hold both feet [NT 10]

2480 football -- usually soccer, as here, but the term may also apply to Rugby [WB 7]

2481 Football Club -- no particular one is specified. A club provides the players and equipment, organizes match-matches, owns or provides the playing ground, and takes the gate receipts. [FRH 24]

2482 footer -- slang for football* [dh]

2483 footman -- in the 20th C., a household servant used to run errands, answer the door, wait on table, etc. [hp]

2484 footprints in Niagara -- Parker* exaggerates. Even London at its wettest cannot quite match the flow of water over Niagara Falls [WB 4]

2485 "for any pains of death . . ." -- from the service for the Burial of the Dead in The Book of Common Prayer* at that point in the service when the body is being lowered into the grave [NT 5]

2486 "for better, for worse" -- part of the traditional marriage service, the giving of the troth [HHC 11]

2487 "For His mercies shall endure . . ." -- Mr. Puffett is quoting from the old hymn, "Let Us with A Gladsome Mind", found in The Parish Choir of 1850 and elsewhere. The lyrics are John Milton's* reworking of Psalm 136. The music is by W. H. Monk (1823-89). The hymn is a short one, the first verse of which is:

"Let us with a gladsome mind
Praise the Lord for he is kind:
For his mercies shall endure,
Ever faithful, ever sure."

The section after the colon is a refrain for all verses. [BH 8]

2488 "For man walketh in a vain shadow . . ." -- the correct form for the passage is: "For man walketh in a vain shadow, and disquieteth himself in vain: he heapeth up riches, and cannot tell who shall gather them." The verse is from Psalm 39:7 as it appears in The Book of Common Prayer. [BC 3]

2489 "For, to speak in a word . . ." from Burton's* Anatomy of Melancholy* [GN 20]

2490 "For what we are about to receive . . ." -- the opening line of a standard blessing said before any meal [NT 1]

2491 Forbes, Nurse -- she followed Nurse Philliter* in service to Agatha Dawson*. She is spoken of as being most competent. [UD 5]

2492 forbye -- Scots dialect for "besides" [FRH 10]

2493 the Force -- the English police constabulary generally, not to be confused with the Metropolitan Police Force at New Scotland Yard*. The training and promotion steps of the county forces are almost identical to those of the Yard, but the various forces are separate and distinct units. They do, however, work closely with one another. [nf]

2494 Ford [pre-War] -- the British version of Henry Ford's ubiquitous automobile [BH 1]

2495 Ford, Christine -- Lady Levy's* maiden name [WB 2]

2496 Ford, Mr. H. -- the alias used by Hugh Farren* on his walkabout through northern England [FRH 20]

2497 Ford, John -- see "Why, how now friend!" [BH 12]

2498 Fordyce, Stephen -- he assisted Sir James Lubbock* in the analysis of Philip Boyes'* body in their search for arsenic. It was found in large quantities. [SP 2]

2499 Foreign Office -- since 1968, the Foreign and Commonwealth Office, it is the office of the Secretary of State for Foreign Affairs. From 1920, the staff could be required to serve at home or abroad in the diplomatic corps and in the consular service. [HHC 26]

2500 Forensic Medicine and Toxicology

-- see Dixon Mann [FRH 25]

2501 "Forewarned is forearmed" -- this famous precept appears in two equally famous places, in Don Quixote*, Part II, Ch. 17, and in Benjamin Franklin's Poor Richard's Almanac for 1736. It is undoubtedly more ancient than either of those sources. [SP 12/MMA 14]

2502 Forged Decretals -- a reference to the second part of canon law. These false decrees and decisions aim to establish the validity of the early papal claim to spiritual and temporal authority. Some date from as late as the 10th C., but most are much earlier, usually from the first three centuries A. D. [GN 17]

2503 forgot to lay the four blows -- to make the blows or strikes required in the fourth place in the change at the bob* [NT 1]

2504 Forked Lightning -- a racing dog, breed not specified, but probably a greyhound [MMA 12]

2505 formalin -- or Formalin, a trade name for an aqueous solution of formaldehyde and a small quantity of methanol. It is used as a preservative and disinfectant. [BC 13]

2506 Formamint lozenge -- the brand name of a cough drop or lozenge popular in England before WW II [WB 6]

2507 forme, lock the -- see lock the forme [MMA 8]

2508 Forrest, Mrs. -- the mysterious woman connected to the death of Bertha Gotobed* by a £5 note found in the dead girl's belongings. Until Miss Climpson* goes to work, Mrs. Forrest's real identity remains unknown to PW and Parker*. [UD 7]

2509 Forsyte, James -- a character in John Galsworthy's The Man of Property and In Chancery, the first two novels (1906 and 1920) of The Forsyte Saga. He is the father of Soames Forsyte. [GN 10]

2510 Fortescue, Miss -- a former student at Shrewsbury College* [GN 2]

2511 Fortescue, Sneep -- a fictitious person (publisher?) mentioned as having distinct anti-Fascist feelings [GN 11]

2512 fortnit -- dialectical English for fortunate, not fortnight [NT 3]

2513 Fortnum and Mason [Fortnum's] -- the small but luxurious department store founded in 1707 where the clerks still wear morning coats and striped trousers. It is famous for its gastronomically amazing groceries, but cigars, chocolates, clothing, perfume, mink-lined raincoats, porcelains, stationery, kitchen appliances, etc., are also available there as are the services of a hairdressing salon and a restaurant. They will prepare a picnic for two or 6000. [UD 7/BH 1]

2514 Fortunate Islands -- see Canary Islands [dh]

2515 Forty-eight, one of the -- a reference to J. S. Bach's forty-eight preludes and fugues as published in Das Wohltemperiertes Clavier (The Well-Tempered Clavier). The collection appeared in 1722 and 1744 with twenty-four preludes and their attendant fugues in each, one set for each of the twenty-four major and minor keys. [SP 13]

2516 '47 port -- importer unspecified. A great wine, but hardly able to survive until the mid-1920's, a span of eighty years. It might well survive fifty, but twenty to thirty years is considered ideal in most cases. [CW 10]

2517 Foster, Sgt. -- the unmarried and morally rigid police officer who is Joe Sellon's* immediate superior in the local constabulary. It is Foster's rigidity that contributes in part to Sellon's dilemma in that Sellon does not feel able to confide in Foster at the very time when he should have done so. [BH 11]

2518 fou' as a puggie -- drunk as a monkey, an obsolete dialectical phrase equivalent to the American expression "drunk as a skunk", or "stinking drunk"; a notable excess in any case [FRH 25]

2519 "foul fiend Flibbertigibbet" -- Edgar's speech from King Lear*, III, iv, 120ff., the "mad" scene. This quote is the opening volley of what has come to be known as the "Shakespeare

match" between PW and Supt. Kirk* [BH 18]

2520 foulard [navy sprigged] -- a silk fabric, lightweight, and of a plain or twill weave. It is often used to make neckties. [GN 21]

2521 Foulis, Rev. Nathaniel -- his license plates were stolen by George Goyles* in his silly attempt to get away from Riddlesdale Lodge* [CW 3]

2522 foundation of the world -- given the context and PW's later comment about the turtle soup being a "trifle out of key", the reference may be to The Book of Common Prayer, Psalm 82:5, "all the foundations of the earth are out of course." [BH 17]

2523 foundry metal -- a tougher lead alloy than monotype*. It has greater concentrations of antimony, zinc, and other metals. The types PW purchases, while cast in foundry metal, were probably cast by the monotype machine in the print shop where he purchased them. It is not regularly used any more, having been replaced by photographic typesetting systems in all but the smallest operations. [FRH 28]

2524 fount -- or font, a particular style or design of type [MMA 8]

2525 The Fountain Pen Mystery -- the detective story that HV has in progress during the action of HHC. PW and the other events engaging her attention at that time distract her enough that she makes very little progress in any notable sense. [HHC 1]

2526 four-ale bar -- a bar that sold a quart of ale for four pence (about one and a half new pence). By the late 1920's one suspects that the price was more than 4d. The current (1983) price is over 50 pence for a pint of beer. The name is sometimes also given as "Four-Ale". [FRH 20/SP 10/BH 14]

2527 four fours -- see cricket [MMA 18]

2528 four-in-hand -- the standard long necktie. They are wide at one end, narrow at the other, with the wide end so hanging as to cover the narrow one. Such a tie is properly tied with a Windsor slipknot to maintain symmetry at the knot to make certain that it hangs properly when worn. [HHC 11]

2529 four inches of copy -- the amount of words, pictures, etc., that will fit in a space one newspaper column wide (that varies from paper to paper) by four inches long [MMA 3]

2530 four quarters -- the quarter-hour chimes as struck by a clock. Each quarter is successively longer than the one just played until, on the hour, the whole tune is played, then the chimes are struck for the hour. [NT 2]

2531 four rows of moth-eaten ermine -- a reference to the four rows of fur which distinguishes a duke's robes from those of other peers* [GN 8]

2532 "Four Sons of Aymon" -- part of the Charlemagne cycle of medieval French romances or tales (chansons de geste). This tale tells of the four sons of Count Aymon of Dordogne against whom the emperor makes war for their insubordination. The war continues until Charlemagne is encouraged to make peace. He pardons the four if Renaud promises to go to Palestine to fight the Saracens. Renaud, the eldest son, does so, has further adventures, and later becomes a hermit. As Rinaldo (or Roland), he appears in Orlando Furioso, Orlando Innamorato, and Jerusalem Delivered, poems by, respectively, Ariosto (1532), Boiardo (late 1400's), and Tasso (1581). PW is after Caxton's* folio* of 1489. The descriptor "unique" is appropriate for this edition as Caxton translated the works himself and his prose style had extensive influence in the 15th and 16th centuries. [WB 1]

2533 four spades -- see bridge [qs]

2534 a four was signalled -- see cricket [MMA 18]

2535 four wickets having fallen -- see cricket [MMA 18]

2536 fourteen-fold sneer of the Caesars -- a reference to the sculptures on the steps of the Sheldonian Theatre, Oxford. They are heads and were not, originally, intended to represent anyone in particular. [GN 12]

2537 fourteen hands -- a hand is a unit of measure equal to four inches

that is usually applied to horses. The animal's height is from the ground to the shoulder, so at fourteen hands it would be four feet eight inches tall. [HHC 16]

2538 fourteenth century manuscript of Justinian -- an unclear reference, but the manuscript may be the same one mentioned in "Stolen Stomach". See also Justinian. [BC 3]

2539 fourth cervical vertebra -- the fourth vertebra down from the skull in the neck. There are five cervical vertebrae. [MMA 2]

2540 Fourth Commandment -- "Remember the sabbath day, to keep it holy." The whole list appears in Exodus 20 and Deuteronomy 5. [NT 12]

2541 fourth dimension -- following the standard dimensions of length, breadth, and depth, the fourth is time, especially when considered in a space-time continuum [im]

2542 fourth form -- roughly equivalent to the tenth grade in a U. S. high school [UD 23]

2543 fourths -- the fourth position in the changing sequence. In rounds* the fourth position is occupied by the fourth bell, but during a change pattern, depending on which one is used, almost any other bell could occupy the fourths position.. [NT 1]

2544 Fourways -- the name of Henry Weldon's* farm near Leamhurst* [HHC 22]

2545 Fowler, Miss -- a Shrewsbury College student [GN 7]

2546 Fox-and-Hounds -- the pleasant inn at Crofton* where PW and Parker* stay to interview old Ben Cobling* [UD 11]

2547 Foxe's Book of Martyrs -- a copy was in Squire Burdock's* library when examined by PW in "Bone of Contention". Written by John Foxe, it was first published in English in 1563. The book is a strong indictment against papists although it deals with Church history and, especially, martyrs of all ages. [bc]

2548 foxglove -- the source of digitalis*, it is a common garden and wild flower [BC 15]

2549 Foxlaw won the Gold Cup -- the Gold Cup is a famous race at Ascot*, a part of June's Royal Ascot Meeting, and was begun in 1807. The race is two and a half miles and is open to all ages. DLS correctly identifies Foxlaw as the winner for 1927. [UD 19]

2550 fox trot -- a ballroom dance originated in the United States in the early 20th C. and popularized by Vernon and Irene Castle. Many variations on the basic 4/4 step have been developed over the years. [qs]

2551 Fra Angelico Annunciation -- "had strayed from the office for March 25", the Feast of the Annunciation of Our Lady (the Virgin Mary), the day that is celebrated as the date on which the archangel Gabriel told Mary that she would bear Jesus. The card would probably be a poor reproduction of Fra Angelico's famous painting, perhaps as large as four inches by six inches, but more likely about the size of a wallet-size photo. [UD 22]

2552 Fragonard, Jean Honoré -- a French painter (1732-1806) whose work is of the rococo period, but which also reflects Rousseau's primitive naturalism. Illustrator of PW's copy of the Contes de la Fontaine*, his work would add greatly to the book's value. [aq]

2553 Fragment -- see the individual quotations as each one is taken from a different fragmentary bit of Beddoes'* work. There is no one work with the title Fragment. [HHC 11]

2554 Framboise-Douillet, Mme. de -- a guest at the party given by the Duke of Denver* in his London home. PW is sent to get her an ice*. [MMA 11]

2555 Francis Josias -- Duke of Saxe-Coburg-Gotha (1678-1735) and a fictitious one at that. The little German duchies of Saxe, Coburg, Gotha, Saalfield, etc., eventually were organized, along with some other territories, into the German state of Thuringia, since absorbed into East Germany. At no time was there a Duke Francis Josias, supposed ancestor of Paul Alexis*. [HHC 32]

2556 Franco-Prussian War -- that little contre-temps between France and Prussia in 1870-71. In fairness, it

must be said that both sides sought the war, but Prince Otto von Bismarck was in no small way responsible for starting it. He moved to put a Hohenzollern on the throne of Spain and then edited a telegram from the French ambassador to make it appear that the ambassador had been rude to the Kaiser, Wilhelm I. France declared war on July 18, 1870, just as Bismarck had expected them to do. After the Battle at Sedan, on September 1, Napoleon III was taken prisoner; Paris came under siege on September 20. On January 18, 1871, the German Empire was created with Wilhelm in charge. This creation was declared, in of all places, in the palace at Versailles! Paris surrendered on January 28, 1871, thus ending the horrible and gruelling siege where even the elephants in the Paris zoo were slaughtered for food. Bismarck achieved his immediate goal of unifying Germany under Prussian domination, but the long-term effect was to set the stage for World Wars I and II. [HHC 32]

2557 francs -- the plural of franc, the official unit of currency in France [CW 5]

2558 François, M. -- owner of apartments in Paris to whom Denis Cathcart* had made regular payments. Cathcart was not living in the apartment at the times when he made the payments. [CW 13]

2559 frangipani -- a scent derived from the flower of the red jasmine, a tropical plant [SP 18]

2560 Frank -- one of the public who has come to observe HV's trial for murder. He doesn't think she looks like a murderess. [SP 3]

2561 Frankau, Gilbert -- an English popular novelist (1884-1952) who is perhaps best known for World Without End (1943) [UD 3]

2562 Franklin -- the Dowager Duchess's* personal servant, Miss Franklin is important in the Duchess's household, but has the misfortune to dislike cats. Therefore, the Duchess's cat, Ahasuerus*, instinctively pesters the poor woman. He manages to inflict damage on almost everyone, Bunter included. [BH P]

2563 Frascati's -- was located at 26-32 Oxford St., near Tottenham Court Road. The restaurant no longer exists. [MMA 8]

2564 fratchet[t]y -- a dialectical adjective, possibly onomatopoetic, meaning to grate or to scold; to be bad-tempered [NT 6/BH 8]

2565 Frayle, Mrs. Tommy -- one of the guests at Lady Swaffham's* luncheon [WB 7]

2566 Fred -- a servant at the Bellona Club* [BC 5]

2567 Fred -- the barber whose help is enlisted by PW, indirectly, to obtain some hair trimmings from a suspect [SP 21]

2568 Frederick -- Dawson. See the genealogical chart at the end of UD [UD 13]

2569 free -- used here in the sense of having been granted the liberty of a place without interference [NT 7]

2570 Free State -- the Irish Free State was established as a dominion on December 6, 1921, when Ireland was partitioned, creating the present area of Northern Ireland and what has since become (on April 18, 1949) the independent country of Eire [CW 9]

2571 Free Trade[r] -- see Empire Free Trade [HHC 22/NT 11]

2572 free warren [right of] -- the right to hunt small game in a place especially set aside for that purpose [MMA 6]

2573 Freebody -- see Brodribb [GN 2]

2574 Freeborn, Thomas -- Tommy to the Duke of Denver*. It was Freeborn's letter to Denver exposing Denis Cathcart* as a card sharper* that started the chain of events that led to Denver's trial in the House of Lords on a charge of murder. [CW 1]

2575 freehold -- a piece of property held absolutely for as long as the owner wishes by right of purchase or inheritance and not, like a leasehold, merely for a specified number of years [sf]

2576 freeman -- see free, a person with such liberties [GN 2]

2577 Freeman, Mr. -- one of the staff at Pym's Publicity* [MMA 2]

2578 Freeman, Mr. Austin -- R. Austin Freeman (1862-1943), an M. D. born in London and trained as a surgeon. He was a close friend of Sir Arthur Conan Doyle*. His life after age thirty was plagued by medical problems, so he wrote. His creation, Dr. John Evelyn Thorndyke, is a major contribution to the literature of mystery and detective fiction. A forensic pathologist and barrister*, Dr. Thorndyke's stories were so carefully crafted that that fictional character and his work were accepted sources of inspiration and ideas for police investigations. [UD 21/BC 18/FRH 27]

2579 Freemantle, Catherine -- the brilliant Shrewsbury College* scholar who had married a farmer and ruined herself intellectually and physically when the farming business went bad. This is a rather unflattering portrait of DLS's former schoolmate, Doreen Wallace, and the portrayal drawn strained their relationship thereafter. [GN 3]

2580 Freemantle, Mrs. -- wife of an eminent railway director in The City* known for her unintentional humor deriving from the mistakes she makes when discussing the world of finance of which she is quite ignorant; a sort of business world edition of Mrs. Malaprop. [WB 7]

2581 Freemason -- a member of a Masonic Lodge, the Free and Accepted Masons, the secret fraternal organization [NT 14]

2582 Freke, Edward Curzon, Esq. -- Sir Julian Freke's* father [WB 8]

2583 Freke, Sir Julian -- a famous surgeon and "distinguished neurologist with a highly individual point of view" who figures prominently in WB. A biography of this fictitious person can be found in Ch. 8 of the novel in the form of his Who's Who* entry. Freke Rd., South of Battersea Park*, may be inspiration for the name, but see also #7085. [WB 1/UD 4]

2584 Freke, publications of Sir Julian -- a list is provided in the Who's Who entry mentioned in 2583 [WB 8]

2585 French, Insp. -- the famous Scotland Yard* detective created by Freeman Wills Crofts*. He is renowned for his ability to crack ingeniously difficult timetable puzzles as in Sir John Magill's Last Journey. He appears in a variety of other novels as well. [HHC 33]

2586 French heel -- a two or three inch curved high heel on ladies' dress shoes [GN 21]

2587 French Revolution -- see Carlyle and "sea-green incorruptible" [BH 7]

2588 Frensham pearls -- see The Society [ab]

2589 fresh -- unsalted when applied to butter, uncured when applied to pork or other meats [MMA 3]

2590 Fresher -- a first-year student at an English college; a freshman [GN 1]

2591 Freudian -- a reference to any of the works or theories of the Viennese founder of modern psychological theory, Sigmund Freud (1856-1939) [BC 20]

2592 frichtened -- a deliberate misspelling meant to represent Scots dialect for frightened [ss]

2593 Frimpton -- a hamlet nine miles North of Little Doddering*. It is the home of Major Daniel Lumsden*. The name is a corruption of Frinton, Essex, but, as spelled in the story, the place is fictitious. [bc]

2594 frisson -- French for, "shudder" as in "blood-curdling" or "the creeps" [SP 12]

2595 Frith, Messrs. -- a real firm of photographers on Wardour St.* who took the picture of Olga Kohn carried by Paul Alexis*. The firm was noted for its post cards during the 1930's. [HHC 22]

2596 Frith St. -- a North-South street in Soho* which connects Shaftesbury Ave.* on the South with Soho Sq. [SP 14]

2597 Frivolity -- a fictitious theatre, probably a music hall [MMA 19]

2598 Frobisher, Col. -- his identity is not clear from the context,

but he is probably Fentiman's commanding officer [BC 18]

2599 Frobisher-Pym, Agatha -- wife of Thomas Frobisher-Pym* and hostess to PW [bc]

2600 Frobisher-Pym, Thomas -- a rather down-to-earth, Low Church* farmer, magistrate for Little Doddering*, and host to PW [bc]

2601 Frog's Bridge -- a fictitious bridge over the Thirty-foot Drain* just West of Russell's Bridge. Its danger lies in the fact that it terminates on the South side of the Drain in a right-angle intersection that is not properly guarded so as to prevent cars from going into a ditch. [NT 1]

2602 Frogglesham -- a fictitious community in the fen* country [NT 16]

2603 Frolic Wind -- a novel, later dramatized, by Richard Oke, published in January of 1930. The story involves four spinsters, one of whom is Lady Athaliah, who held a house party at Pagnell Bois, the family estate. The guests are all "modern" celebrities, two of whom fall in love. Their romance is dampened when Lady Athaliah dies and her hoard of pornographic "treasures" is discovered in her "tower", and the rather bitterly witty book ends in a vision of a sort of Armageddon. [GN 4]

2604 from hand to mouth -- see he lives from hand to mouth [MMA 15]

2605 from lead to hinder place -- following a hunting course* [NT 1]

2606 "From lilies and languors . . ." -- the lines are from Swinburne's* poem, "Dolores" (ix), and read:
"Change in a trice
The lilies and languors of virtue
For the raptures and roses of vice." [FRH 22]

2607 "From noise of Scare-fires . . ." -- from Robert Herrick's* short poem, "The Bell Man". The remaining two lines are:
"Past one aclock, and almost two,
My Masters all, Good day to you."
[GN 16]

2608 "From such a ditch as this . . ." -- PW is parodying the first line of V, i, in The Merchant of Venice:
"The moon shines bright: in such a night as this
When the sweet wind did gently kiss the trees . . . ."
[CW 3]

2609 Froth Blowers [cuff links/anthem] -- a friendly society much like the Lions or Rotary who gather for mutual protection such as with insurance, for vacation plans, and for charitable activities. The cuff links would have the membership insignia on them. In his biography of DLS, James Brabazon describes the group as a "beer-drinker's union", commenting that DLS belonged and wore the group's lapel pin. [ab/BC 6]

2610 frowst -- a slang word from Harrow School, origin otherwise unknown, derived from students' universal passion for sleeping late whenever possible. It means to relax, lounge, be lazy, etc. [GN 12]

2611 fugal form -- relating to the art and nature of the construction of the fugue, a complex polyphonic form contrapuntally developed [SP 13]

2612 fugal passage, intricate -- PW is tapping out an unidentified passage from a fugue, probably one of Bach's* [BC 3]

2613 full academicals -- the cap, gown, and hood, etc., that comprise academic regalia and including a dark skirt and stockings and a white blouse for the ladies [GN 1]

2614 full close -- or full stop; a period, used in the sense of having exhausted the idea. [GN 11]

2615 full house -- three of a kind and a pair, a powerful poker* hand ranking after a straight flush and four of a kind [WB 3]

2616 full marks -- a perfect score or high grade [NT 7]

2617 full organ -- an unclear term as it will vary from instrument to instrument, depending on the number of manuals and stops it has. At Fenchurch St. Paul*, that would mean two or three keyboards and the foot pedals. Depending on the stops used, that could make a great demand on the windchest and whoever has to keep it up to pressure.

[NT 2]

2618 fumed oak settles -- straight-backed benches made of oak with a decorated finish fashionable in the 1930's [SP 16]

2619 Furnace Case -- the reference is to the murder charged to Samuel James Furnace, 39, a builder and decorator of Crogsland Rd., Chalk Farm. A corpse, assumed to be that of Furnace, was found burned to death while seated at Furnace's desk at 30 Hawley Crescent, Chalk Farm Rd., Camden Town (a London suburb North of Regent's Park*) on January 3, 1933. Upon closer examination, death was found to have been caused by three bullet wounds to the chest. It was later determined that the body was actually that of twenty-four year old Walter Spatchett, a rent collector. Furnace was arrested at Southend while trying to hide there, and was charged with the murder, but he drank hydrochloric acid on January 15, and died on January 17.

It was never absolutely determined how Furnace got the acid while in jail. In his confession it came out that Spatchett's death was an accident, the burning having been done to try to cover up the accident, thus making it look like a suicide. The Britannic Assurance Co. of Birmingham held insurance polices on both Furnace and Spatchett. They refused to pay Furnace's because of his suicide, but they paid his widow a sympathy sum. Spatchett's policy was honored in full. [te]

2620 furnace-coke -- or coke, the burnable residue of coal left after heating coal without air to drive off the volatile elements [NT 2]

2621 Furse -- probably Charles Wellington Furse (1868-1904), an English portrait and figure painter influenced by Whistler and Sargent*. A less likely candidate is Charles A. Furse (fl. 1891), but only one show was given by him and he is a much less significant painter. [BH E2]

2622 fused porcelain fillings -- see porcelain fillings [te]

(G)

2623 G. C. V. O. -- the abbreviation for the rank of Knight Grand Cross of the Royal Victorian Order, the highest rank in that Order. First established in 1896, it is awarded for important or personal services to the sovereign or to the Royal Family. Membership is unlimited and is granted exclusively by the sovereign in any one of the five ranks or classes. [WB 8]

2624 G. M. C. -- Britain's General Medical Council. According to Salcombe Hardy*, the Council was being annoyed continually by unnamed persons who wrote to the daily papers about medical problems, especially about glands (see Dr. Voronoff). [BC 16]

2625 G natural -- PW is telling HV that she needs to drop the sharp and sing the note G [GN 19]

2626 G. P. -- general practitioner. A physician who does not specialize in a particular branch of medicine. Dr. Hartman* and Dr. Vane* were both G. P.'s. [BC 16]

2627 G. P. -- Grand Passion, or "Pash", a strong infatuation for someone, usually Platonic as in a doglike devotion [GN 2]

2628 Gable, Clark -- the great Hollywood movie actor (1901-60), often called "The King". He played in a wide range of films from Gone With the Wind (1939) to It Happened One Night (1934). [BH 16]

2629 Gabriel, Archangel -- see Archangel Gabriel [UD 21]

2630 gadflies -- any of the various flies that are found among livestock [BH 9]

2631 gaff, blew the -- see blew the gaff [NT 2]

2632 Gainsborough -- Thomas (1727-88), the English painter of a variety of works, but who is popularly remembered for his "Blue Boy". His portraits are noted for their faithful rendering of English society in his day and for his masterful handling of colors. [BH E2]

2633 gaiter -- a type of patch of leather or heavy fabric wrapped

around a tire as a temporary repair. It was wrapped around once and tied. Used in the early days of motoring when rubber was scarce, they are not now used legally. [CW 3]

2634 gaiters [leather] -- leg wrappings similar to the upper part of a pair of boots. Mr. Cobling* uses them, a long pair wrapped from the instep to just below the knee, to protect his legs. [UD 12]

2635 Galahad -- son of Lancelot and Elaine in Malory's Le Morte d'Arthur. His immaculate purity allows him, of all the Round Table knights, to succeed in his quest for the Holy Grail. See also "Lead and I follow". [UD 11/BH 16]

2636 "Galahad will sit down in Merlin's seat" -- PW is quoting loosely from Tennyson's* "The Holy Grail", l. 181, from The Idylls of the King: "That Galahad would sit down in Merlin's chair." It is when Galahad sits in that chair that the Round Table is granted a vision of the Holy Grail. [BH 7]

2637 Galatians, Epistle to the -- St. Paul's letter to the church group centered in the Roman province of Galatia, Asia Minor, near what is now the Turkish city of Ankara. It is concerned with the controversy of what, if any, part of Jewish custom, tradiditon, and law was binding upon the new Christians. Central was the necessity of circumcision as essential for salvation. Paul wrote that such practices did not matter because justification, that is salvation, was dependent solely on faith. [WB 7]

2638 gallery -- a balcony running lengthwise of the nave on either or both sides. Fenchurch St. Paul* had galleries on both sides, but, since they were not part of the original edifice, Mr. Venables* had them removed. Also, he didn't need the seating space. [NT 2]

2639 Gallic in their audacity and restraint -- Mrs. Featherstone's* polite way of saying "blunt and rather risqué" [SP 12]

2640 Galileo -- Galileo Galilei (1564-1642), Italian scientist and philosopher. PW is referring to his trial for heresy before the Inquisition on a charge of having publicly supported and proclaimed the truth of Copernicus's pronouncements on the nature of the physical universe which had been branded as heretical by the Church. He recanted his views in order to be allowed to live and work. [GN 17]

2641 Gallio[s] -- a reference to the proconsul of Achaia, a brother of Seneca, mentioned in Acts 18. Gallio has since come into English as a term of reproach for one who helps start trouble and who then does little or nothing to stop it, observing from a distance in amusement generated by disinterest in the outcome. [MMA 10]

2642 The Gallovidian -- a local magazine for the Southern counties of Scotland that deals with the area's social and artistic life [FRH 7]

2643 Galloway -- a general term referring to the Scottish lowlands area between Dumfries and Wigtown along the Northern shore of Solway Firth. It is the scene for most of the action of FRH. [FRH 1]

2644 Galloway Arms -- a licensed restaurant in Newton-Stewart* where PW has dinner with Insp. Macpherson*. It is apparently fictitious. [FRH 13]

2645 Galloway, Earl of -- at the time of FRH it was the 12th Earl, Sir Randolph Algernon Ronald Stewart, Lord Garlies in Scotland, Baron Garlies in England (1892-1978, s. 1920). Earl Galloway had a long and distinguished career including service as a J. P. and as Lord Lieutenant of the Stewartry of Kirkcudbrightshire from 1932. He was succeeded by his son, the 13th Earl, Randolph Keith Reginald. The family is descended from Sir John Stewart and the hereditary Lord High Stewards of Scotland. [FRH 22]

2646 Galsworthy -- John (1867-1933), English novelist and playwright. He is famous for social satire in his portrayal of the British upper classes in such works as The Forsyte Saga. [BC 18/GN 14]

2647 galumph [ed/ing] -- a portmanteau word invented by Lewis Carroll* and first appearing in his mock epic poem, "Jabberwocky", l. 20, in Through

the Looking Glass. The word is possibly a blend of gallop and triumphant. [FRH 5/GN 11]

2648 Gamaliel -- a Pharisee, a member of that ancient Jewish sect noted for their strict observance of the law and by their pious sanctity, who convinced the Jews not to slay the Apostles. He was president of the Sanhedrin, the "Supreme Court" or council, and he raised the apostle Paul (brought up at his feet). See Acts 5:34 and 22:3. [MMA 1]

2649 gamin -- a street urchin, especially a streetwise child [aq]

2650 Gammy Pluck -- Parker hazards a guess as to what well-known criminal delivered the letter to Cranton*. As "gammy" means bad, and as "pluck" means boldness or courage, the name is likely a nickname for a notorious evil-doer. [NT 14]

2651 gamp [green] -- a large umbrella named for Sarah Gamp in Dickens's* Martin Chuzzlewit. She is a nurse who carries a large umbrella. [HHC 11]

2652 Gamp, Mrs. -- Sarah Gamp, a nurse in Dickens's* Martin Chuzzlewit, who exhibits some typically Dickensian speech habits, but "rubbidge" is still a common dialectical word in the West of England and John Donne* uses it in his "Progresse of the Sourle, 2nd Anniversary". Her name survives as in entry 2651. [GN 3]

2653 Gander, Gaffer -- the resident "old-timer" in Darley*. He would know everything that went on there as he had retired to the job of local observer. [HHC 26]

2654 gaol[ed] -- British English for jail[ed] [passim]

2655 a garden, as Bacon observes -- the observation is made by Sir Francis Bacon* in his essay, "Of Gardens" [GN 20]

2656 Garden, Cremorna -- the stage name of Rosanna Wrayburn*. It is taken from Cremorne Gardens, once located in Chelsea*, but closed in 1877 because, according to the OCEL, it "became notorious for irregularities". How appropriate! [SP 6]

2657 "A garden is a lovesome thing . . ." -- HV is quoting from Thomas Edward Brown's (1830-97) poem, "My Garden" [BH 4]

2658 garden label -- a small plaque on a support used to identify plants in a garden before they have reached sufficient growth that their identity is obvious (if it is obvious). Simpler versions are just a stick to which the seed packet is attached. [BH 4]

2659 Garden Quad -- an area on the grounds of Somerville College* [GN 18]

2660 Gare de Lyon -- a Paris railway terminus of moderate size in terms of the number of passengers served daily. It handles trains arriving from or departing to the South of France. [mt]

2661 Gare des Invalides -- a small railway station in South central Paris with connections to the South and West of Paris. PW departs from there for Verneuil-sur-Eure*. The reference to the station's size relates to the numbers of passengers served, not the physical plant. [mt]

2662 Gare Saint-Lazare -- in terms of the numbers of passengers served, this is the largest terminus in Paris. It is located in northwest Paris and has the shortest connections to Cherbourg and LeHavre. PW arrives there from LeHavre. [mt/aq]

2663 Garfield, Dr. Herbert -- the physician who narrowly escapes death under the wheels of a subway train at the South Kensington* Station* when he is clutched at by a man who has tripped. The fallen man is killed. [MMA 15]

2664 Gargantuan Colour-Talkies, Ltd. -- a fictitious movie-making firm [GN 11]

2665 gargoyle -- hideous monsters serving as decorative rain spouts, etc., on older buildings, especially Gothic cathedrals. There are those who claim that rather than being mere ornamentation that the superstitious workmen in the Middle Ages carved them to ward off evil spirits. [CW 6]

2666 Garland, Leila -- the gold-digging former girlfriend of Paul Alexis*. She first asks, "What's in it for me?",

before doing anything. [HHC 7]

2667 Garlic Mews -- Dian de Momerie's* London address; she has a maisonette* there. The address is fictitious. There is a Garlick Hill near the Mansion House in The City*, but it hardly seems likely that she would maintain a flat there as it is too far from the life that she "enjoys" leading. [MMA 5]

2668 Garrett -- see Maunder and Garrett [BH 5]

2669 Garrett, Mr. -- one of the quieter members of the staff at Pym's Publicity* [MMA 1]

2670 Garstairs, Miss -- headmistress at Hilary Thorpe's* school [NT 19]

2671 garsong -- a somewhat overdone attempt to reproduce the elusive French adenoidal diphthong as in garçon [NT 8]

2672 Garter King-of-Arms -- see College of Arms [CW 14]

2673 Garter Ribbon -- the blue sash or other ribbons of the Order of the Garter, England's premier order of chivalry dating from about 1344. The sovereign is the chief officer and membership is restricted to a certain number. The order's motto, "Honi soit qui mal y pense" or "Shame to him who thinks evil of it", is an allusion to an incident when the Countess of Salisbury was dancing with the king, lost her garter, and discovered that the king had picked it up and put it on his own leg. The motto was uttered when some present reacted churlishly to his gesture, so the king's comment has come to be the Order's motto as well as a phrase long associated with the monarchy. [BH E2]

2674 Garvice, Charles -- an English writer (d. 1920) who is the author of such bland items as Her Heart's Desire, Just a Girl, and others [WB 5]

2675 Gas-Filled Bulbs -- an exposé masquerading as a novel. It is fictitious. [GN 11]

2676 gas ring -- a small, one or two burner device for cooking light meals or for boiling water, a gas-fired hot plate [FRH 1/SP 1]

2677 gas works [squat majesty of the] -- the five gas tanks that expanded or retracted vertically, thereby indicating how full they are, the top of the tank being a gauge against the support framework on its outside. They are long-standing fixtures of a gas works near the Kennington Oval* in London. [MMA 18]

2678 gasper -- slang for cigarette [bc/MMA 1]

2679 Gasperettes -- a fictitious brand of cigarette invented by DLS [MMA 15]

2680 Gaston -- DLS lists him as the natural son of Louis-Philippe*, but that king has no son of that name. He would be Paul Alexis's great-grandfather in the fictitious genealogy DLS created. [HHC 32]

2681 gastritis, acute -- see acute gastritis [SP 1]

2682 gate, gaein off that -- Scottish dialect for "going off that way" [FRH 7]

2683 gated -- Oxford slang for being confined to the area of one's college as punishment for some offense [GN 7]

2684 Gatehouse-of-[the]Fleet -- founded circa 1760, it is a small town located above the estuary of the Water of Fleet* near the 15th C. tower of Cardoness Castle. It is a former cotton town and is central to some of the work of both Robert Burns and Sir Walter Scott. The town houses much of the artists' colony which centers on Kirkcudbright*. [ss/FRH 1]

2685 Gates, [H]'Arry -- a worker who helped Joe Dudden* install the sundial at Lopsley* that incorporated one of the chimney pots from Talboys* that William Noakes* sold [BH 14]

2686 Gates, Mrs. -- the ramrod straight and intimidatingly correct housekeeper at the Thorpe home, Red House, in Fenchurch St. Paul* [NT 2]

2687 Gatti's -- a restaurant frequented by Major Robert Fentiman* and the location of one of his encounters with the elusive Mr. Oliver*. The restaurant was originally a music hall or vaudeville theatre on Villiers Street, underneath Charing Cross Station*. It eventually became the establishment

mentioned. It ended its career at 436 The Strand. It no longer exists. [BC 6]

2688 Gaude -- the treble, or number one, bell at Fenchurch St. Paul*. It is the lightest, weighing a bit less than two-fifths of a ton, and has the highest tone, a C. She was cast in 1666. [NT 2]

2689 "Gaude, Gaudy, Domini in Laude" -- Latin for, "Rejoice, Gaudy, in praising the Lord", the inscription on the treble bell, Gaude*. The inscription is a canting* or punning motto that plays on the similarities of "gaude" and the family name Gaudy. The inscription is in Roman letters and appears as: GAVDE•GAUDY•DÑI•IN•LAUDE• MDCLXVI. [NT 4]

2690 Gaudeamus Igitur -- the title of a student song dating from the 13th C., "Gaudeamus igitur, juvenes dum sumus . . ." which translates as "Let us live then and be glad while we are young . . .". Brahms uses the tune in a sweeping melody that comes toward the end of his Academic Festival Overture, and Mario Lanza recorded a famous version of the song as it appears in Sigmund Romberg's The Student Prince.

2691 gaudy -- a festival of rejoicing, a grand feast or entertainment frequently held on an annual basis by a college to commemorate some event in the college's history. In some ways a gaudy resembles a "homecoming" at an American college as both feature similar events. Nevertheless, a gaudy has a flavor of its own that is peculiar to English colleges, regardless of external similarities. [GN 1]

2692 Gaudy [under old] -- on the South or right side of the nave in front of the chapel where the Gaudy family are buried [NT 3]

2693 Gaudy family -- residents of Fenchurch St. Paul* until the time of Elizabeth I*, but the family is extinct in the area at the time of the story. That their tombs are inside the church gives some indication of their great importance in the area. [NT 2]

2694 gauntlets -- stout gloves of leather or fabric used in driving, fencing, riding, etc. They cover the hand and much of the forearm as well. [CW 3]

2695 gave you the office -- did you the favor, gave you help. Office is used here to mean duty or service. [NT 5]

2696 gazetted -- published in the London Gazette as having attained a particular rank or level. Used here to indicate that PW had only recently attained the rank of major. [GN 17]

2697 Geary -- the blacksmith who served the needs of the farmers in the area around Darley* [HHC 12]

2698 gee -- a child's word for horse [CW 10/HHC 16]

2699 gees and tables -- see item 2698. The implication here is that Winifred Burdock* has a gambling problem. [bc]

2700 gelignite -- a type of dynamite in which the adsorbent base is kaolin, often mixed with wood pulp, the explosive being nitro-glycerine [NT 8]

2701 gendarme -- a French policeman [NT 8]

2702 gêne -- French for "an annoyance", a bother or inconvenience [SP 14]

2703 General Confession -- that part of the Anglican Eucharist that, as its name implies, is a confession in generalities rather than of specific things. It appears early in the service. [NT 2]

2704 Geneva -- see League of Nations [NT 7]

2705 genie -- or jinn, one of a class of Moslem spirits inhabiting the earth, having supernatural powers, and being able to assume different forms. They often take human form to serve whoever summons them; hence, metaphorically, something supernatural, mysterious, or magical. [WB 10]

2706 Gentile -- not Jewish in the sense of not being one of the Children of Israel, and used here in the sense of ethnic origin [SP 12]

2707 gentleman -- a man of "gentle" birth or an educated man who accepts his social obligations; a vague indicator of relatively exalted social status [NT 4]

2708 Gentleman Jim -- a criminal mentioned by Parker* while trying to to figure out who might have assaulted him [MMA 7]

2709 Gentleman Usher of the Black Rod -- so called because of the black rod or wand of office that is topped with a golden lion in repose. Whoever it happens to be, he is a servant of the Order of the Garter and is usher to both the House of Lords, where he keeps order and attends to the peers, and to the Order of the Garter, where he is the doorkeeper . All peers impeached for any crime are given to him for custody. He is also Chief Gentleman Usher of the Lord Chamberlain's part of the Royal Household. [CW 14]

2710 Gentleman's Special Pickle -- an apparently excellent condiment even if fictitious, but DLS does not tell us more about it [HHC 6]

2711 Gentlemen, you are all wrong. -- when PW makes that pronouncement, he brings to mind the poem "The Blind Men and the Elephant", by American poet John Godfrey Saxe (1816-87) wherein six blind "Hindoos" are shown an elephant. None of them examined the whole beast, yet all proceeded to define "elephant" from their examinations. The next to the last stanza states:

"And so these men of Indostan
Disputed loud and long,
Each in his own opinion
Exceeding stiff and strong,
Though each was partly in the right
And all were in the wrong!"

[FRH 26]

2712 Geoffrey -- Miss Layton's* boy-friend whom she protects jealously from the clutches of Miss Flaxman* [GN 7]

2713 George, Mr. Lloyd -- see Lloyd George [HHC 26]

2714 George -- an engine-driver (locomotive engineer) invented by PW to people some of his storytelling [FRH 13]

2715 George -- uncle to Jem, the blacksmith's helper at Darley* [HHC 16]

2716 George -- one of the movers who help remove the furniture from Talboys* [BH 19]

2717 George -- the one-eyed patron of the Crown pub in Paggleham* [BH 10]

2718 George -- Tom Puffett's* son-in-law [BH 8]

2719 the George -- a highly regarded inn in Stamford* at 71 St. Martin's St. It is a 17th C. coaching inn with a walled monastic garden and forty-seven rooms. [HHC 8]

2720 the George -- a fictitious pub in Leahampton* where Parker*, PW, and Sir Charles Pillington* retire for lunch during their search for Mary Whittaker*. The pub's name probably refers to some one of the first four kings named George, or, possibly, to St. George, England's patron saint. Inns are not named for reigning monarchs. [UD 19]

2721 George V -- King of England and the United Kingdom, etc., from 1910-36, and sovereign during the action of most of the PW stories and all of the novels [CW 14]

2722 George and Dragon -- a reference to the reverse side of the gold sovereign (see British Monetary Units), first issued in 1817 during the reign of George III whose portrait would have been on the obverse (front). As the monarchs change, the royal face would be changed as soon as more coins were minted after a new reign had begun. The coins in question were ordered in 1816, designed by Pistrucci, and first issued in 1817. They were the first issue of sovereigns in modern times. They were withdrawn from circulation in 1914 at the start of WW I and were not minted after 1917 at the suspension of gold coinage. They are no longer circulated, but the Royal Mint has struck sovereigns to mark such events as coronations or for other special purposes. [HHC 31]

2723 George Barnwell -- The History of, or, The London Merchant, by George Lillo (1693-1739), first produced in 1731. The play is a famous prose domestic tragedy. It is drawn from the ballad "George Barnwell" which recounts how Barnwell is seduced by and infatuated with a courtesan, Millwood. He robs his employer and even murders his uncle for her and they are both eventu-

ally executed. It was highly popular and successful in England and Europe. PW and Marjorie Phelps* see a production of the play at the Elephant and Castle* shortly before that famous theatre turned to showing movies instead. DLS uses a quote from the play as a chapter heading for Ch. 15 of BH. [BC 10/BH 15]

2724 georgette -- usually capitalized, it is a brand name for a thin, strong fabric of crepe* [GN 1]

2725 Georgian -- reflective of architectural and interior design style common during the reigns of the first four Georges, roughly 1714-1830 [WB 5/GN 4]

2726 Gerald -- either the Duke of Denver* or his son, the Viscount St. George* when addressed by their family or friends informally [CW 1 and passim]

2727 "German female . . . who enjoyed seeing people die" -- the reference is uncertain, but two women fit the description well. One, Gesina Gottfried, executed at Bremen in 1828, poisoned her children, her brother, a husband or two, and several lovers, the exact number of people being unknown. A better candidate for the dishonor is Anna Maria Zwanziger who was described by one judge as a person who "trembled with pleasure and gazed upon the white powder (arsenic*) with eager eyes beaming with rapture". She, too, was executed in the mid 1800's. [SP 5]

2728 Germans has a revolution -- see revolution [NT 8]

2729 German shells -- probably small calibre artillery shells that Cathcart* could have kept as war souvenirs [CW 5]

2730 Gerrard St. -- in London, it is parallel to and South of Shaftesbury Avenue* between Wardour St. and Newport Place. It is into Newport Place and Newport Court that George Goyles disappears on his way to Charing Cross Road* after assaulting PW. The location is just East of Piccadilly Circus* and is the site of the Detection Club (at No. 31 Gerrard St.) which DLS helped found. [CW 7]

2731 Gertrude -- Nurse Booth's* older sister [SP 17]

2732 Gertrude -- one of Shrewsbury College's* scouts* [GN 8]

2733 Gertrude's Rhead's observation, "All this self-sacrifice is a sad mistake!" -- the reference is to Act III of the Arnold Bennett and E. Knoblock play, Milestones (1912). Rhead is a character in the play who utters the quoted sentiment. [CW 11]

2734 getting up -- arriving in London. Regardless of the direction travelled, one "goes up" to London. [CW 9]

2735 Gherkins -- a nickname for the Viscount St. George* [GN 9]

2736 Gibbons, Alice -- see Alice [SP 17]

2737 gibus -- an opera hat of the collapsible variety [MMA 6]

2738 Giddens, Mrs. -- a resident of Little Doddering* who owns a white donkey [bc]

2739 Giddings, Eliza -- an "ungrateful old wretch" who complained about the lack of plums in her Christmas plum pudding*. There is also a reference to a Giddings lease, but it is not clear if it involves Mrs. Giddings or not. [NT 6/9]

2740 Giddy, Mr. -- a Paggleham* local who owns property near the church [BH 19]

2741 Gidea Park -- a small community about fifteen miles northeast of central London [MMA 4]

2742 gigolo -- loosely, a man living off the earnings of a woman; more specifically, a male dancer or escort. It is this latter sense that is meant in HHC. [HHC 3]

2743 gigue -- a usually lively piece of dance music in two sections or strains, each of which is repeated for the full piece. They often function as the last movement of an 18th C. suite. The English equivalent is "jig". [GN 19]

2744 Gilbert and Sullivan -- see Gilbertian [BH 8]

2745 Gilbertian -- a reference to Sir William Schwenk Gilbert (1836-1911) who, with Sir Arthur Sullivan

(1842-1900), did the famous "Savoy Operas". The allusion is to Gilbert's fondness for absurd plots such as that sequence in The Mikado where the Lord High Executioner is a former convict who may not execute anyone until he has somehow managed to cut off his own head. [GN 5]

2746 gilded dens of infamy -- Salcombe Hardy* attests to PW's honor by saying that PW would not take a young lady to such a place. The comment is made when Miss Twitterton* hesitates to accept PW's invitation to lunch. [nf]

2747 Giles, Sir Warburton -- a surgeon and cancer specialist who was formerly chief to Dr. Carr. He had performed surgery on Agatha Dawson*. He is fictitious. [UD 1]

2748 Gillian -- one of Viscount St. George's* female acquaintances. She visits him in the hospital while he recovers from his automobile accident. [GN 10]

2749 Gilmour St. -- the station stop in Paisley* and just to the West of Glasgow. This was one of the area's many stations. [FRH 10]

2750 "Gin a body . . ." -- PW is being extravagant in his rendition of Robert Burns's lyric poem "Coming Through the Rye":

"Gin a body meet a body
Coming through the rye;
Gin a body kiss a body,
Need a body cry?" [WB 2]

2751 Ginger -- Robert Duckworthy's* nickname [im]

2752 ginger beer -- a concoction popular in England with no exact equivalent in the U. S. It would be a sort of noncarbonated ginger ale, but with a much stronger flavor. It is nonalcoholic. [SP 1]

2753 ginger cakes -- slices of cake made from ginger, molasses, eggs, flour, butter, brown sugar, baking powder, and lemon rind [FRH 3]

2754 Girgashites -- see Hivites [BH E2]

2755 The Girl Who Gave All -- the title of the book in which Luis da Soto* found Paul Alexis's* letter to Leila Garland* about his imperial heritage. Dozens of titles have girls giving all sorts of things, but not their all; apparently a fictitious title. [HHC 32]

2756 Girvan -- a fishing and boating community on the West coast of Scotland about half way between Ayr* and the mouth of Loch Ryan* [FRH 5]

2757 gitana -- Spanish for "gypsy (female) [umw]

2758 giuoco piano -- one of the oldest of the standard openings for pawns in chess*, and dating from at least the early 16th C. It features a quiet pawn opening for white, thus allowing players who are unknown to each other a chance to "size each other up". It is still considered a good opening maneuver, but is not as popular as it once was. The opening is presented in chess notation as:

1. P-K4; P-K4
2. N-KB3; N-QB3
3. B-B4; B-B4 [sf]

2759 give and hazard all we have -- the reference is to The Merchant of Venice, II, vii, 16ff. PW alludes to what the Prince of Morocco reads on the lead casket in Portia's home. [BH 18]

2760 Give him his drink -- the line is reminiscent of V, ii, 294, of Hamlet when Claudius tries to persuade Hamlet to drink the poisoned wine: "Give him the cup." Even if unintentional, the unconscious use of that line is entirely in keeping with the story at this point. [BH 18]

2761 Give me a good stupid horse -- Edgar Wallace* not only wrote an amazing quantity of adventure fiction, he also kept a stable of race horses which contributed to his financial difficulties. One can appreciate his desire to have a predictable, hardworking animal rather than a nervous prima donna. [GN 12]

2762 Give me just a country cottage -- PW declaims verses of his own creation [BH 5]

2763 glacé -- having a glossy surface [NT 6]

2764 "The gladsome light of Jurisprudence." -- the line is from Sir Edward Coke's* Institutes: Commentary

Upon Littleton, in the epilogue. [UD 10]

2765 Gladstone collar -- a collar that is left turned up. It has almost no collar points and leaves exposed the part of the necktie that goes around the neck. [HHC 11]

2766 Gladys -- the Prendergast household servant. See also Horrocks, Gladys. [te/WB 1]

2767 Glaisher, Supt. -- the supervising police officer in the Wilvercombe* area. See Police Ranks. [HHC 3]

2768 Glaister -- John Glaister, Sr., author of several medical books, but DLS has his Text Book of Medical Jurisprudence, Toxicology, and Public Health, first published in 1902, in mind. John Glaister, Jr., has since updated many of his father's works. [WB 2/BC 15/FRH 6]

2769 glands -- see Dr. Voronoff [BC 19]

2770 Glasgow -- a major Scottish industrial center on the banks of the Firth of Clyde and just South of Loch Lomond. By today's roads, it is forty-two miles West of Edinburgh. Glasgow is particularly noted for shipping and shipbuilding, and is Scotland's largest city at present and Great Britain's third largest. It is an important industrial center for other heavy industries than shipbuilding. The city has strong links with its medieval past, and its university was Scotland's second, after the one in Edinburgh. [ss/FRH 1]

2771 Glasgow Bank -- there may be or may have been a bank of that name, but no reference to one of that exact title could be found. DLS very likely created a plausible name to avoid any confusion with some real institution, a practice she commonly uses. [ss]

2772 Glasgow Bulletin -- a fictitious newspaper [FRH 3]

2773 Glasgow Clarion -- a fictitious newspaper [FRH 18]

2774 glass-blowers cat is bompstable --Parker's* wandering nonsense as he drifts off to sleep, and the closest to "stream-of-consciousness" writing style that DLS ever comes in the canon. [CW 6]

2775 glass of sound wine -- the allusion is to I Timothy 5:23: "Drink no longer water, but use a little wine for thy stomach's sake and thine often infirmities." The Apostle in this case is James, author of the first letter to Timothy. Paul wrote the second one. [BH 6]

2776 the glass is going back -- an expectation of rain; the lower the reading of a barometer, the worse the weather; the higher the reading, the better the weather [bc/ss]

2777 glebe -- land belonging to a parish church allotted to the parish priest and from which he derives revenue [HHC 16/NT 2]

2778 glee(s) -- a song form popular in the 18th C. featuring parts scored for three or more voices and no accompaniment [CW 4]

2779 Glegg's Folly -- a home at which PW found evidence to hang prisoner William Girdlestone Chitty*. It is fictitious. [aq]

2780 Glen -- a small village about three and a half miles West of Gatehouse* [FRH 21]

2781 Glen Trool -- a forested area now enclosed in the Galloway Forest Park [FRH 7]

2782 Glenwhilly -- a stop on the rail line between Girvan* and Stranraer* [FRH 5]

2783 Glibbery, Mr. [K. C. *] -- one of the defense attorneys working with Sir Impey Biggs* during the trial of the Duke of Denver* [CW 14]

2784 "glitter is the gold" -- PW is wide of the mark here. He may have been referring either to The Merchant of Venice, II, vii, 66, "All that glisters is not gold", from the poem in the "Golden Casket" that Portia presents. There is also a similar line in Thomas Gray's "Ode on the Death of a Favorite Cat", "Nor all, that glisters, gold." [HHC 31]

2785 gloamin' -- see Waiting for kisses in the gloamin'?" [BH 15]

2786 Globe edition -- of the works of

William Shakespeare, edited by W. G. Clark and W. Aldis Wright. It was published by Macmillan as part of their "Globe Library" in 1866 in 1075pp. [MMA 1]

2787 "Glory, glory, glory" -- probably a reference to hymn 455 in the Salvation Army Hymn Book with words attributed to Lowell Mason:
"Glory, glory Hallelujah, I have given my all to God
And now I have full salvation through the Precious Blood."
The third glory in the citation might have been a bit of confusion with "Holy, Holy, Holy, Lord God Almighty". The conclusion that Bill Rumm* is a member of the Salvation Army is a safe one in this instance as he appears at the PW-HV wedding in a uniform of that organization. [SP 13]

2788 glottis -- the space between the vocal folds in the throat just behind the "Adam's apple" [HHC 21]

2789 Gloucester Gate -- one of the many Nash* structures formerly found in Regent's Park*. On the Outer Circle Rd. in the northeast corner, it comprised part of the elegant collection of gates and town houses which bordered almost two-thirds of the Park's perimeter. Its name remains. [BC 8]

2790 Gloy -- a well-known brand of paste in a conical bottle. It has a screw-on lid with an applicator brush incorporated into it, and both were made of wood. They are now metal. In England, "Gloy" is a trade name that has become so well-known that it has become synonymous with paste as "Kleenex" has become synonymous with tissues. [GN 10]

2791 Glyn, Mrs. Elinor -- the Canadian novelist and writer of romantic tales (1864-1944) who created the concept of "It"* which was all the rage during the later 1920's before the Depression. [UD 15/MMA 7]

2792 go in first -- see cricket [MMA 18]

2793 go off the rails a bit -- normally an expression indicating a serious deviation from the norm, but PW uses it here only to suggest a degree of childish rebellion [SP 6]

2794 "Go round about her and tell the towers thereof." -- PW is quoting from Psalm 48:11 in The Book of Common Prayer. With slight differences it is verse 12 in the King James Version of the Bible. [GN 23]

2795 "Go tell that witty fellow . . ." -- Queen Elizabeth's comment is typical of her conversational sallies. She spoke her mind openly and clearly so as to leave no doubt about her feelings. [GN 18]

2796 "Go to Bed, sweet Muse" -- a song by Robert Jones (15??-16??) as presented in Ultimum Vale (1605). The song title is also the first line of the song. The lines "Love is a fancy, Love is a frenzy" are from the second verse of the same song, number III in the collection. The lyricist is unknown. [GN 19]

2797 go to the boundary -- see cricket [MMA 18]

2798 Gobbersleigh, Lord -- a fictitious newspaper magnate [GN 11]

2799 Gobbo, Lancelot -- see Lancelot Gobbo [UD 22]

2800 goblin page boy -- see Lay of the Last Minstrel [CW 3]

2801 "God is gone up with a merry noise" -- from Psalm 47:5 in The Book of Common Prayer. It concludes: "and the Lord with the sound of the trump." The KJV reads: "God is gone up with a shout, the Lord with the sound of a trumpet." [NT 2]

2802 "God knows in what part of the world . . ." -- from John Donne's* Easter evening sermon of 1626, Sermon XXI in Fifty Sermons, but the quotation is a loose one. The sermon reads: "God that knowes in which Boxe of his Cabinet all this seed Pearle lies, in what corner of the world every atome, every graine of every man's dust sleeps, shall re-collect that dust, and then re-inanimate that man, and that is the accomplishment of all." [NT 5]

2803 "God made the integers . . ." -- Miss Stevens is quoting Leopold Kronecker (1823-91), a German mathematician and theoretician, from Jahresbericht der Deutschen Mathematiker Vereinigung, Book II. Kronecker made significant contributions to algebraic

number theory and wanted to eliminate analysis from mathematics to whatever extent possible. [GN 2]

2804 God makes power -- an oblique reference to Psalm 62:11. The next verse also applies: "Also unto thee, O Lord, belongeth mercy: for thou renderest to every man according to his work." [BH 20]

2805 "God moves in mysterious ways" the hymn proposed by Mr. Russell* is "God Moves in a Mysterious Way", one of the Olney Hymns by William Cowper (pronounced cooper)(1731-1800). The collection was published in 1779. The first verse of the suggested hymn is:

"God moves in a mysterious way
His wonders to perform;
He plants his footsteps in the sea,
And rides upon the storm."

The hymn remains popular throughout the various Protestant sects. [NT 4]

2806 God on the Seventh Day -- the day God rested after the Creation. Any such analogy is, perhaps, a bit overstated. [GN 9]

2807 "God Save the King" -- or Queen, depending on the gender of the current sovereign. The song is the national anthem of Great Britain and the remaining colonies. [HHC 19]

2808 "God send each man at his end" -- a variant form of the tenth and last stanza of the anonymous English ballad, "The Three Ravens". Other versions give the verses as:

"God send every gentleman
Such hounds, such hawkes, and such a leman!"

A "leman" is a lover or paramour. [CW 18]

2809 God's law and Caesar's -- the Rev. Mr. Tredgold* is encountering the same problem as considered in Matthew 22:15-22 which contains the famous line, "Render unto Caesar that which is Caesar's; and unto God the things that are God's." Mr. Tredgold opts to observe God's law since it takes precedence. [UD 19]

2810 God's time -- or solar time as opposed to daylight-saving time [BH 14]

2811 Godfrey, Sir Edmund Berry -- a magistrate and victim of an unsolved murder discovered on October 17, 1678. The crime had extensive implications for the precariously situated Roman Catholic community in England. One Titus Oates, an anti-Catholic rabble-rouser, used Godfrey's death to further rumors of another Popish Plot. Laws were enacted against Catholics who were imprisoned, excluded from Parliament, and victimized in other ways as well. The result of all of this was the furor between James II and Parliament, the succession of William and Mary, and the permanent alteration of the course of English history. [GN 7]

2812 Godfrey, Jack [John P.] -- a resident of Fenchurch St. Paul* and a regular bell ringer. He handles the number seven bell, Batty Thomas*. [NT 1]

2813 gold brocade -- see gold lamé [BH P]

2814 Gold Cup -- see Foxlaw won the Gold Cup [UD 19]

2815 Gold Flake[s] -- a famous cigarette manufactured by the Wills Co. of Bristol, now a part of the Imperial Group of companies. The cigarettes were then sold in yellow packets with cigarette cards* at twenty cigarettes to the pack for a shilling*. [FRH 2/ HHC 16]

2816 gold in their mouths -- see most fish have gold in their mouths [MMA 14]

2817 gold lamé -- a brocaded fabric given a glittering appearance by the combination of some typical fabric fibre with tinsel threads, in this case, of gold [BH P]

2818 Gold Standard -- the policy of having the paper currency changeable on demand for gold at the current value of that metal so that gold is in free circulation as an exchange medium. There are no trading restrictions on gold under this system. Great Britain went on the Gold Standard in 1821 and was the first country to do so in modern times. It discontinued the standard on September 21, 1931. [HHC 31]

2819 Goldberg -- an acquaintance of

Freddy Arbuthnot's* who is also involved in The City's* financial business. See 2820 also. [SP 12]

2820 the Goldbergs -- friends of Sir Reuben Levy* who had recommended Simpson* to the financier as a butler. The man was hired shortly before Levy's disappearance and death. [WB 5]

2821 golden ass -- the reference is to a lengthy Latin romance called "Metamorphoses" or "The Golden Ass". It is best known under the latter title and was written by Lucius Apuleius in about 155 A. D. The story is a narrative by Lucius, a Greek who, while on a trip, sees the sorceress wife of his host change herself into an owl. He desires to do the same, but a servant brings the wrong ointment and Lucius becomes an ass, falls prey to some bandits, and becomes the abused and beaten victim of them and of other owners. He is eventually returned to human form by a favor of the goddess Isis after eating a garland of roses and being initiated into her rites, a popular form of Eastern mysticism common in Rome at the time. The most famous story in the narrative is the beautiful "Cupid and Psyche". The work was translated into English in its entirety for the first time in the 16th C. "The Golden Ass" was not Apuleius's title, but was given to the work by St. Augustine*. [WB 3]

2822 Golden Legend -- also known as Golden Legends, Legenda aurea, Legenda sanctorum, or Lives of the Saints by the Blessed James of Voragine*. The work is an anthology of spiritually uplifting tales about the lives of saints, and is not intended to be either fiction or history; only the slightest historical accuracy may be assumed. The readings are arranged for the Christian liturgical year, beginning with the pre-Christmas season of Advent, and having special readings for selected feast days. The book was widely popular in the 13th and 14th centuries, and over 500 copies from 150 editions are known (an astronomical figure for the times). In England, Caxton* printed the first English version in 1483. The work fell into disfavor when its purpose was lost sight of. DeVoragine intended only to spread the idea that God helps those who show Him love even if the use of miracles is necessary, and deVoragine freely altered the facts to illustrate his point. By the 16th C. the book had fallen from favor and use. PW is after the third edition in English as printed by Wynkyn de Worde* in 1493. [WB 1]

2823 golden mean -- a philosophical concept drawn from Aristotle's* Nichomachean Ethics, an extensive treatise on ethical theory. The basic idea is to avoid the extremes of a situation and find the middle path, the "golden mean", that is morally and ethically correct. PW suggests to Insp. Sugg* that it would be a good idea for him to follow the golden mean. [WB 3]

2824 Golden Spur -- a standard and popular variety of daffodil [NT 3]

2825 Golder's Green -- see Golder's Green Cemetery [CW 2/UD 18]

2826 Golder's Green Cemetery -- Golder's Green is a northerly section of Hampstead Heath*, part of which contains a cemetery. The community is a quiet residential one as are Hampstead and the surrounding suburbs. Coreggio Plant* and Denis Cathcart* are buried there. [nf/CW 2]

2827 Goldschmidt [Paul Alexis] -- see Alexis, Paul. Goldschmidt is the name of the family that adopted the boy after his escape from Russia. [HHC 4]

2828 Goldstein, Rachel -- prospective daughter-in-law for Nathan Abrahams* and bride for Moses Abrahams*. She is a pretty girl who seems assured of a warm welcome into the Abrahams family. [ss]

2829 Golem -- a supernatural creature created in the 16th C. by a cabalistic (see cabala) rabbi of the Prague Ghetto, Judah Lowe or Loew. The Golem is both a representative of the collective psyche of the Ghetto, its soul, so to speak, but it is various elements of an individual's soul or psyche as well. He is freedom from restraint and must be mastered. Robert Duckworthy* would have been both terrified and fascinated by the concept. One of the more recent considerations of the Golem is in Gustave Meyrink's expressionist novel of 1913-14 called The Golem. [im]

2830 Gomorrah -- one of two cities, Sodom being the other, destroyed by God for their wickedness in the days of Lot and Abraham. For a complete account see Genesis 13, 18, and 19. However, in "No Face", the speaker has confused Gomorrah with Camorra*. [nf]

2831 The Gondoliers -- a Gilbert and Sullivan comic opera subtitled "The King of Barataria". It opened to rave reviews on December 7, 1889. [HHC 30]

2832 "gone over" to the Scarlet Woman -- also Scarlet Whore as mentioned in Revelations 17:6. Protestants have used the image to refer to Roman Catholoicism. The phrase here means to transfer from Protestantism to Roman Catholicism. [UD 12]

2833 Gooch -- an agricultural products salesman of Stapley* from whom William Grimethorpe* bought two drills* [CW 11]

2834 Good baiting at the Bull -- a pun on bull baiting or bear baiting (see beargarden). To bait also means to give food or shelter to an animal when travelling; hence, to stop for food and rest while on a journey. [FRH 20]

2835 "Good gracious! How very tenacious!" -- see St. Gengulphus [FRH 7]

2836 "Good Judge" mixture -- a fictitious smoking tobacco [MMA 3]

2837 "Good King Wenceslas" -- a Christmas carol written by John Mason Neale in the 19th C. based on an improbable legend related to Saint and Duke Vaclav or Wenzel of Bohemia, a descendant of the Přemyslid dynasty. He was born about 907 and died by his brother's hand in 929. He was a Christian ruler, but no authentication of the story in the carol is known. [qs/NT 19]

2838 "Good night sweet Prince . . ." -- from Hamlet, V, ii, 370. The line continues, "And flights of angels sing thee to thy rest." The speech is Horatio's just as Hamlet dies. [CW 14]

2839 good Samaritan -- a reference to the Parable of the Good Samaritan in Luke 10:30 [NT 6]

2840 good stick, but a bad crutch -- a proverbial phrase meaning that the thing in question is a good helper, but cannot be relied upon for full support [NT 5]

2841 Goodacre, Rev. Simon -- the vicar* at Paggleham*. He is a kindly gentleman, knowledgeable, and genuinely sympathetic to the needs of his parishoners. PW induces his High Church* leanings from the fact that he wears a Roman vest* and has an otherwise unidentifiable emblem on his watch chain. [BH 5]

2842 Goodge St. -- a short street just North of Oxford St.*, running roughly West to East from Mortimer St. to Tottenham Court Rd.* [WB 6]

2843 Goodrich, Mr. -- the man who owns the property on which Hinks's Lane is located [HHC 12]

2844 Goodrich, Squire -- one of the first in the Wilvercombe* area to own an auto, in about 1900; perhaps the same person as #2843 [HHC 16]

2845 Goodwin, Mrs. -- the Dean's* secretary at Shrewsbury College*, and mother of a fragile child to whom she is frequently called for extended periods of time when he is ill [GN 5]

2846 googly [ies] -- see cricket [MMA 1]

2847 goose-girl -- a fairly young woman in a fairy tale who tends geese. Traditionally such girls are lovely beneath their rags and bring much happiness to the lucky man who marries one. PW thinks that Thomas Crowder* is engaged to marry such a girl, or is at least trying to save enough money to marry her. A goose is also a talisman for marital felicity. [nf]

2848 gooseberry -- a chaperon, especially one who acts to aid the lovers rather than performing the typical role of a chaperon; a go-between [HHC 20]

2849 Gordian knot -- the knot of Gordias, king of Phrygia and father of Midas of golden touch fame, that was so artfully tied that legend arose that whoever untied the knot would rule all of Asia. Alexander the Great is supposed to have cut the knot with his sword and he did go on to rule all of

the then known world. PW's analogy is to the knotty situation he finds himself in upon the discovery of William Noakes's* corpse. [BH 7]

2850 Gordon, Clarence -- the lisping sales representative who travels for Moss and Gordon* in Glasgow*. It is his schedule that provides PW with a major part of the solution to the timetable problem in the story. [FRH 22]

2851 gorgons -- the three ugly sisters, Stheno, Euryale, and Medusa, of Greek mythology. Medusa is the only mortal one, but "her glance that turns one to stone" made her the most famous. Supposedly their hair was mixed with serpents, their hand were made of brass, their bodies were covered with hard scales, and their teeth resembled boars' tusks. Some versions have it that all three had glances that could turn one to stone. [GN 10/BH 1]

2852 Gorgonzola -- an Italian blue cheese, usually made from cow's milk [WB 1]

2853 Gorleston bank robbery -- see The Society [ab]

2854 gorse -- furze, low spiny evergreen shrubs with bright yellow flowers in the spring [FRH 11]

2855 Gosling -- the police superintendent at Ripley* who helps PW and Parker* trace the movements of George Goyles*. See also Police Ranks. [CW 6]

2856 Gospel of Nicodemus -- or "The Acts of Pilate", an archetypal part of the New Testament that dates from about the 5th C. It is an elaborate and rather fanciful recounting of the trial of Jesus, the supposed conversion of the Sanhedrin on learning of Jesus' Ascension into Heaven, and other events not recounted elsewhere. It also names the two thieves (Dismas and Gesta) who were crucified with Jesus, Pilates' wife (Procla), the centurion (Longinus), and others. [NT 1]

2857 Gospels, women in the -- see women in the Gospels [BC 16]

2858 gossip-shop -- a typical nickname for a newspaper office [nf]

2859 got me by the short hairs -- see short hairs [GN 9]

2860 got the wind up -- to become upset to a marked degree [MMA 10]

2861 got up regardless -- artificially and elaborately dressed without regard to expense [MMA 2]

2862 Goth -- colloquial for a person lacking in culture and refinement; a barbarian ranking just above a Vandal as Goths are apparently just uncultured while Vandals are destructive. PW is being rather harsh on Parker* who is, naturally, more concerned with the basics of the investigation. [UD 6]

2863 Gothic lettering -- the heavy black-letter script of the Middle Ages: est anima ei9 cū ea: mitigauitq; deliniuit
blandicijs: et pergens ad emor prēm

[NT 1]

2864 Gothic Theseus -- a latter day Theseus as in a Gothic novel. Amongst other things, Theseus found his help into and out of the maze of the Minotaur and slew the monster, all with the aid of a ball of string provided by Ariadne. In a Gothic novel one would expect melodrama, high adventure, and a heroine in need of being rescued, often from her own lack of thought, the rescue being effected by her "Theseus". [CW 12]

2865 Gotobed, Mrs. -- mother of Bertha and Evelyn Gotobed** [UD 10]

2866 Gotobed, Bertha -- maid at the home of Agatha Dawson*, she is the second victim in the story. She dies about a year after leaving the employment of that household after a dispute over some broken crockery. [UD 4]

2867 Gotobed, Dick -- son of the sexton at Fenchurch St. Paul*, Harry Gotobed*. He assists his father with some of the more difficult jobs, such as gravedigging. [NT 3]

2868 Gotobed, Evelyn -- maid in the home of Agatha Dawson* who leaves that employment when her sister is dismissed for breaking a teapot. She subsequently marries and moves to Canada. [UD 4]

2869 Gotobed, Harry -- the sexton at Fenchurch St. Paul*, he succeeded

Hezekiah Lavender* to the job. In the local change-ringing* society he pulls the number four bell, Jericho*. [NT 1]

2870 Goudy [Bold and 24 point] -- these type references are to the work of Frederick William Goudy (1865-1947), an American printer and type designer. He wrote four books on type design, printed exceptionally fine books on his own presses, and designed more than 100 typefaces, a feat unmatched in the history of typography.

This is Goudy Bold type.

This is Goudy 24 point type.

[MMA 8]

2871 Goudy, Insp. -- a police officer who saved a child from drowning. See Police Ranks. [BH 11]

2872 Gourock -- a village at the mouth of the River Clyde and at the head of the Firth of Clyde. It is twenty-six miles West of Glasgow* and forty-three miles North of Ayr*. [FRH 19]

2873 the Government -- the collective personification of whatever party happens to be in power at a given time in England [CW 7]

2874 Governor [old] -- Sir Charles Thorpe* [NT 3]

2875 Governor -- St. George's* father, the Duke of Denver*. See also Wimsey, Gerald Christian [GN 8]

2876 Gov'ment time -- a slighting reference to daylight-saving time [BH 14]

2877 gov'nor -- used in reference to Freddy Arbuthnot's* father. It will more often appear as "guv'nor". [WB 4]

2878 Gowan, Matthew -- one of the prominent and successful artists in the Gatehouse* and Kirkcudbright* colony whose character is based on the real artist Edward A. Hornel (1884-1933). Hornel was rather reclusive and rebuffed DLS when she attempted to meet him one summer. DLS got her revenge on him by writing him into FRH as Gowan and making him the butt of Campbell's* beard-cutting bad humor. Gowan's house in the novel is Hornel's "Broughton House" on High St. in Kirkcudbright which is now an art gallery and home of the Hornel Trust. The fictitious Gowan, at age 46, is one of the oldest members of the colony, specializes in landscapes and figures, and is noted for the luxuriant beard which is sacrificed. [FRH 1]

2879 Goyles, George -- a "modern thinking" member of the Soviet Club and a leading speaker for that group. He and Lady Mary* have become quite close and, in CW, actually plan to elope, but the death of Denis Cathcart* prevents their doing so. The events which follow, including Goyles's attempt on PW's life, end Mary's infatuation with him. Miss Tarrant* describes him as "quite young", but that he has attracted a good deal of attention from Governmental authorities. One hopes that his politics are in better shape than his personal affairs. [umw/CW 7]

2880 Gracchi -- the sons of Tiberius Sempronius Gracchus, a Roman praetor, and his wife, Cornelia. The sons were Tiberius Sempronius and Gaius Sempronius. Their mother, the daughter of Scipio Africanus, is even today remembered as a model of womanly virtue and excellence in motherhood. Both sons died as a result of their attempts to treat the peasants fairly but at the expense of wealthy landowners. [GN 3]

2881 Grace -- one of the hopefuls in the office of talent agent Isaac Sullivan* [HHC 23]

2882 Grace and Lambelet -- referred to as masters of the art of false perspective, but they were not further identifiable; presumably fictitious [hp]

2883 Graham, Jock -- one of the Gatehouse* and Kirkcudbright* artists' colony, a devil-may-care sort of person who is fond of playing jokes on and otherwise irritating Sandy Campbell's notoriously short temper [FRH 1]

2884 Graham, Mr. -- Squire Burdock's* long-time solicitor* [bc]

2885 grain -- the smallest unit of weight in avoirdupois, troy, or apothecaries' systems of measurement. In avoirdupois there are 7000 grains in a pound, 5760 in the others. There-

fore, nine grains of calomel* would be 0.018747 ounce, a significant quantity, possibly fatal if added in error to a preparation already having calomel in it. By comparison, there are five grains of aspirin in a standard tablet, or 0.010405 ounce. Two or three grains of arsenic can be a fatal dose. [BC 7/ UD 18/SP 2]

2886 Grainger -- a member in residence at the Bellona Club* who is in poor health [BC 1]

2887 Grainger, Dr. -- the nearest physician available to treat Philip Boyes* when his last and fatal gastric attack struck. Taking the various symptoms into account, Dr. Grainger diagnosed acute gastritis* and treated Boyes accordingly. [SP 1]

2888 gramophone -- originally a trademark, but now an old-fashioned word for a record player [ab/SP 13/ HHC 12]

2889 gran -- coarse, poorly refined, granular white sugar as opposed to fine or caster sugar [BH 2]

2890 Grand Duke -- in Russian and some other aristocratic hierarchies, a noble who ranks above a duke but below a prince [HHC 29]

2891 Grand Duke Dmitri -- the reference is to the Grand Duke Dmitri Pavlovich, cousin to Czar Nicholas II, and a possible heir presumptive. It was he, along with Prince Yusupov, two members of the Duma, and a Dr. Stanislas Lazovert, who killed the "mad monk" Gregory Rasputin. [HHC 32]

2892 Grand National Sweep -- or Sweepstakes, a reference to the lottery draws on the Grand National Steeplechase held in March of every year at Aintree, near Liverpool. The course is four and a half miles long and has thirty jumps. Lotteries were then illegal and, so, were organized outside of England,as in Dublin or Malta. [HHC 12]

2893 Grand Panjandrum -- created by Samuel Foote (1720-77) as part of some nonsense he composed to test the memory of the famous actor, Charles Macklin. It is a mock title for any imaginary person of great power and pretension. [UD 9/GN 20]

2894 Grand Stand at Ascot -- the central viewing stand at the Ascot Race Course, a great place to view the race if tickets are available. See also Ascot week. [MMA 11]

2895 <u>Grande Paresse</u> -- PW's derisive term for French express train service. It means, "deluxe slowness (laziness)". See also item 2896. [mt]

2896 <u>Grande Vitesse</u> -- French for, "deluxe, high-speed service" in reference to passenger trains, an express train [mt]

2897 Grandsire [Triples, Major, etc.] -- Grandsire (pronounced grandser) is one of the oldest methods of change-ringing*, and originated in about 1640. It is the simplest method for ringing on an odd number of bells, and is a variation of the Plain Bob. "Triples" would be ringing on seven bells, the eighth or tenor bell being rung last in each change. "Major" refers to ringing in Grandsire on all eight bells. [NT 1]

2898 Grant, Air Pilot -- the pilot of PW's flight from New York to Whitehaven*, England, en route to London. Not the commonplace event it is now, the two men were in an open cockpit plane over the North Atlantic and at the worst possible time of year. Grant is possibly a reference to Lt. Vernon F. Grant, USN, winner of the Curtiss Marine Trophy for seaplane races among others. It might have been logical to have used one in this situation, but he did not. As the real Grant received wide attention at the time, it is not unreasonalble to suggest that DLS incorporated his name for an extra touch of verisimilitude. [BW 15]

2899 Grant, Miss -- the mysterious and handsome lady who visited the lawyer, Mr. Trigg*; an alias of Mary Whittaker [UD 18]

2900 Grant, Miss -- the schoolmistress in Paggleham* who has all the school children attend William Noakes* funeral [BH 19]

2901 grass [English] -- asparagus in its green form as opposed to the French who grow it covered with dirt to keep it white [UD 14]

2902 grass-widower -- a phrase of uncertain origin meaning one who lives apart from his wife. Mr. Ferguson* is one. The phrase implies a temporary separation; one who is "put out to grass" like a horse resting. [FRH 3]

2903 grave-bands -- either the bandages which are sometimes used to wrap a corpse (no longer a common practice), or an allusion to the unbreakable fetters of the grave [GN 12]

2904 gravel-rash -- light abrasions caused by a fall on gravel or any other loose, rough surface. Runners who fall on cinder tracks are especially plagued by this situation. [FRH 21]

2905 gravelled -- hindered in the sense of stuck, stranded [HHC 16/GN 3]

2906 Graves, Mr. -- Sir Reuben Levy's* valet [WB 4]

2907 Grayle, Charmian -- the unintentional victim of murder. Her reputation is as something of a man-chaser, and she seems to enjoy some success in her pursuits before her death. She is killed at Sir Charles Deverill's* Christmastime costume party where she had represented the White Queen from Through the Looking Glass*. That costume had a great deal to do with the solution of the puzzle surrounding her death. [qs]

2908 Gray's Elegy -- see "The boast of heraldry" [BH 7]

2909 Gray's Inn -- located in Holborn* on lands originally granted to Reginald de Grey, Justiciar of Chester, in 1294. Grey, in turn, allowed a part of the land to be used, for a fee, as quarters for law students. It is one of the Inns of Court*. [UD 14]

2910 Gray's Inn Rd. -- a major London street which begins at High Holborn* near Gray's Inn* and proceeds to Euston Rd. at a northwesterly angle. Many lawyers have offices along this street. [UD 17/SP 10]

2911 Grayson, Mr. -- an employee of Pym's Publicity* who refuses to function as wicket-keeper* for the coming match against Brotherhood's*. He lost a tooth in a previous match, so his refusal is not just capricious. [MMA 10]

2912 Great Change -- spiritualist jargon for death; the complete separation of the soul from the body [SP 18]

2913 Great Flim -- see Flim [UD BN]

2914 the great "It" -- see "It" [UD 15]

2915 Great James St. -- a short street in Bloomsbury* which runs North from Theobalds Rd. toward Coram's Fields. It begins not far from Gray's Inn*. Dr. Hartman's* kitchen has a view out on to that street. The doctor's flat is DLS's own maisonette* at No. 24. She had moved into a second floor flat in 1921, and, when she married in 1926, the Flemings took the flat above as well. DLS maintained that address until the 1940's. The story says that the street is little and sordid, but it dates from the early 1700's and features a number of fine Georgian* architectural elements. The building has since been combined with No. 23 and now houses offices. [fr/NT 16]

2916 Great Leam -- a fictitious river with similarities to both the Nene and the Great Ouse** [NT 16]

2917 Great North Road -- now known as the A-1 route, it is a major road North toward Leeds, Newcastle, and Edinburgh. See also motorcycle race. [ae/cb/BH E2]

2918 Great Ormond St. -- in Bloomsbury* where it connects Southampton Row with Lamb's Conduit St. just South of Coram's Fields and East of the British Museum*. A postman mentioned in "Footsteps That Ran" lives there as does Insp. Charles Parker*, at No. 12A. After his marriage to Lady Mary*, the flat is enlarged into a maisonette* (the top two flats), which PW uses as a cover address during MMA. The house would be similar to No. 12 which still exists. [fr/WB 5/CW 14/BC 13/MMA 1]

2919 Great Pagford -- home of Drs. Vane and Jellyband**, it is fictitious but typical of villages in that part of England [T/BH P]

2920 Great Plague -- a reference to the ravaging pestilence of the bubonic plague that began its devastation of Europe in December of 1347. It entered

Italy from the Black Sea, having travelled overland on the silk routes from China and India. The area of modern Hungary was the only large area of Europe that remained somehow immune. In the years 1348-50, almost all of Europe was overrun and the population was probably cut by as much as one-third to one-half. Florence became involved in early 1348. [SP 18]

2921 Great Portland St. -- a major North-South street which connects Oxford St.* near Oxford Circus to the Southeast corner of Regent's Park where it intersects with Marylebone Rd., Euston Rd., and Albany St. The fictitious automobile dealership for which George Fentiman* works is located on it, but at an unspecified point. [BC 8]

2922 Great Queen St. -- beginning at the East end of Long Acre*, it connects Drury Lane with Kingsway*. Benson's offices, where DLS worked, was on the corner of Kingsway and Great Queen St. [HHC 30/MMA 12]

2923 Great Rebellion -- the English Civil War, 1642-8. See Oliver Cromwell. [NT 4]

2924 Great Seal -- the sovereign's chief seal, it is used to authenticate various documents of importance such as proclamations, treaties, etc. It is always circular and double-sided, one side showing the sovereign in full regalia and enthroned, the other showing the sovereign mounted. [CW 14]

2925 Great Tom -- see Tom Tower [GN 11]

2926 Great War -- World War I. While exceeded in magnitude by WW II, the name was appropriate at the time. [FRH 1/HHC 8]

2927 Great Wimpole St. -- a fictitious combination of Wimpole St. and Great Windmill St. [BC 19]

2928 "a greater than he, which is my lady of Shrewsbury" -- Sir Francis Bacon* wrote those words "To the King, touching Peacham's Business, etc.," on January 31, 1614. He stated, "I have not been unprofitable in helping to discover and examine, within these few days, a late patent, by surreption obtained from your Majesty, of the greatest forest in England, worth 30,000£, under colour of a defective title, for a matter of 400£. The person must be named, because the patent must be questioned. It is a great person, my lord of Shrewsbury; or rather, as I think, a greater than he, which is my lady of Shrewsbury." [GN 3]

2929 "The greater the sin, the greater the sacrifice . . . ." DLS has probably summarized various ideas from the Summa Theologica of St. Thomas Aquinas, Q. 84, "Sacrifice". In that work we find, "The greater a person is, the greater the honor due to him." There is, later, a reference to all "being obliged to offer to God a devout mind . . . ." [GN 17]

2930 Greats -- see First in Greats [GN 5]

2931 Greek passages:

κυμάτων ἀνηριθμον γέλασμα -- the line is from Aeschylus's Prometheus Bound, 88. The better translations seem to agree with PW's which emphasizes the sound of the waves instead of their visual qualities. The Herbert Weir Smith translation reads, "Multitudinous laughter of the waves of the ocean," but PW's "innumerable laughter of the sea" reads more smoothly. [nf]

ὂν και μν ὂν -- the allusion is to Aristotle's Metaphysics and translates as "being and nonbeing". Aristotle considers the concept at length in that work, and Christopher Marlowe quotes the phrase in Doctor Faustus, I, i, 2, in one of Faustus's speeches. [umw/GN 3]

ὦ πέπον, ει μεν γαρ πόλεμον περι τονδε φυγοντε . . . -- these lines are from Homer's* Iliad, book 12, 11. 322-25, and are a part of an exchange between two Trojans, Sarpedon and Glauchos. The former is suggesting that they cannot live forever, so they may as well attack. The lines PW quotes are translated by Robert Fitzgerald as:

"Ah, cousin, could we but survive this war
to live forever, deathless, without age,
I would not ever go again into battle,
nor would I send you there for honor's sake!" [ie]

ψευδε̃ λελειν ὧσ δεῖ -- this passage translates as "saying false things

as it is necessary", and is probably from Aristotle's Metaphysics [GN 17]

2932 Greely, Mr. -- the manager of the Hotel Resplendent in Wilvercombe* [HHC 5]

2933 Green, Dr. -- a physician who attended Philip Boyes* during his university days (which university is unspecified) for a gastric condition [SP 1]

2934 Green, Mrs. -- Campbell's* char-lady/housekeeper [FRH 3]

2935 greengrocer -- one who sells fruits and vegetables. Mrs. Harbottle* is one. [im/FRH 12]

2936 Green Lion -- the inn at Shelly Head* where PW and Parker* stayed while investigating Vera Findlater's* murder [UD 21]

2937 Green Park -- an addition to St. James's Park made by Charles II in 1667. The restored Stuart monarch liked to take early morning walks along a path that is now known as Constitution Hill. The modern effect of the two parks, combined, is to face Buckingham Palace with lush parkland which is now open to the public. PW's London flat (before his marriage to HV) is across Green Park from the Palace. [WB 1/CW 1/BC 4] .

2938 Green Pastures -- a play by Marc [us] Connelly, an American dramatist (b. 1890), produced and published in 1930. It won the Pulitzer Prize for drama for that year. It presents Old Testament history in terms of the southern Blacks' anthropomorphic understanding of God and Heaven. [MMA 1]

2939 green room -- a room in a theatre, not necessarily green, where the actors wait before a play and between the scenes when they are on stage [SP 18]

2940 Greenaway's Gadget -- given as one of PW's favorite trout fishing flies, it is unknown by that name. DLS describes it as a large, fuzzy, artificial lure for larger trout and sea trout. She may have had Greenwell's Glory, a common fly, in mind, but she may also have known a one-of-a-kind fly of that name. [ss]

2941 "Greensleeves" -- a ballad dating from at least 1584, but it is probably much older than that. It has been attributed to Henry VIII by some, but it is still generally considered anonymous. [GN 19]

2942 Greenwich controlled clock -- a clock set and maintained to the national standard clock kept at the Royal Observatory at Greenwich, just Southeast of London. In the U. S., radio station WWV, run by the National Bureau of Standards, broadcasts a time signal twenty-four hours a day, thus allowing radio and television stations and others in the need to maintain uniform times. [MMA 16]

2943 Gregory [Old] -- a very odd and distant relative of the Wimseys descended from a Duke of the time of William and Mary. His ghost lives on in Bredon Hall and says nothing to anyone. PW tells HV that she should be flattered that he had "ventured out so early in the day" for a visitor. [BH E2]

2944 Gregory, Mr. -- one of the staff at Pym's Publicity* who is usually on the scratch team* they field for cricket*, but who is unable to participate in the match against Brotherhoods* [MMA 10]

2945 Grenfell, Mr. -- one of the Wilvercombe* locals from about two generation back (ca. the 1880's) [HHC 16]

2946 grey powder -- gray fingerprint dust, a mixture of mercury and charcoal powder [MMA 6]

2947 grid -- a piece of paper or card-stock punched with holes or slots meant to be read in a certain sequence. When placed over an otherwise innocent-looking letter, the secret message appears when the grid is read properly. [NT 9]

2948 the Grid -- short for the National Grid, the pattern of electrical cables, transformers, and substations used to distribute electricity throughout Great Britain [sf]

2949 Grider's Hole -- home of the Grimethorpes*, a small farm about two and a half miles from Riddlesdale Lodge* and due North of Riddlesdale. It is a stark and desolate place which

strongly reflects the character of the moor on which it is located and of the man who owns it. [CW 4]

2950 gridiron -- not an American football field, but the grate over the coals on which something is cooked, the earlier ones being a grid made of iron slats. See St. Thingummy. [MMA 4/ BH E2]

2951 griffin -- a mythological beast with the head and wings of an eagle and the body and hindquarters of a lion [GN 13]

2952 Griffin -- see Temple Bar [MMA 12]

2953 griffon, toy -- any of a breed of miniature sporting dogs with long heads, downy undercoats, and more harsh and wiry outer coats, as with a toy fox terrier [WB 11]

2954 Griggs, Miss -- an employee of Pym's Publicity* who is not otherwise identified [MMA 6]

2955 Griggs of Walbeach -- the Bass* bottlers at Walbeach*. The firm is fictitious. [NT 11]

2956 Grill Room -- the precise location is not specified, but it is probably at the Bellevue Hotel in Wilvercombe* where PW is staying [HHC 29]

2957 Grimbold, Dr. -- the Scotland Yard* physician who worked with Sir Julian Freke* on the autopsy of the naked corpse of the man found in Mr. Thipps's* bathtub. He is also present at the exhumation in Ch. 12. He is fictitious. [WB 6]

2958 Grimbold, Mr. -- a member of the Outdoor Publicity Department at Pym's Publicity* who serves as an umpire at the famous Pym's-Brotherhoods cricket* match. He is described as elderly and impassive. [MMA 18]

2959 Grimbold, Harcourt -- nephew of William Grimbold* and accessory to murder [ae]

2960 Grimbold, Neville -- William Grimbold's* nephew, and a man of questionable moral character [ae]

2961 Grimbold, William -- the victim of murder, he was a moneylender, hard and shrewd, but known to be loving and kind to his two nephews, Harcourt and Neville Grimbold** [ae]

2962 Grimes, Col. -- an owner of one of Mr. Endicott's* razors who lost it in the retreat over the Marne* in 1918 [HHC 6]

2963 Grimethorpe, William -- a harsh, rough, obnoxious man of about forty-five years who is built like a bull terrier. Noted mostly for a foul temper lit by a short fuse, he is thoroughly unlikeable. His main manner of dealing with people is a mix of bullying, physical violence, and threats. He is abusive of his wife, the help, his daughter, and everyone else. [CW 4]

2964 Grimethorpe, Mrs. William -- the much-abused wife of the violent-tempered farmer and neighbor to the Duke of Denver* at Riddlesdale Lodge*. PW considers her to be surpassingly beautiful despite the conditions in which she lives. At the end of CW she has made her escape from the farm, but one wonders about her child as she is not mentioned specifically at that time. [CW 4]

2965 Grimsby and Cole, Messrs. -- the publishers of Philip Boyes'* works. They are fictitious. [SP 6]

2966 Grinch, Joe -- the sexton at Little Doddering* [bc]

2967 Grinders -- rocks near the scene of Paul Alexis's* death. They are in an area of strong currents and high tides, making them particularly dangerous to mariners. The place is fictitious. [HHC 2]

2968 Groot -- an old man and the hermit of Whemmeling Fell*. PW gathers some information of questionable value from him. [CW 11]

2969 Groot, Phineas E. -- of the "Chicago Ring" mentioned by Varden*. The "Ring" is a fictitious band of desperadoes. [cf]

2970 Grosvenor Square -- located in the Mayfair* section of London's West End*, the Square was laid out in 1695 and has been associated usually with a leisurely, gracious, and wealthy life. PW and HV have a town house just to the South in Audley Square*. [hp]

2971 grotesque from a Gothic corbel -- a curious or fantastic decoration on the support for an arch or buttress which protrudes from a wall. See corbel. [CW 15]

2972 group manager -- a group director. Such a manager would oversee the work of a number of Account Executives, those persons in charge of a particular client's campaigns, or, if he is in a creative department, he would oversee, as above, the work of several copywriters and artists. [MMA 8]

2973 group secretary -- a secretary usually employed in the creative department of an advertising agency, often assigned to specific campaigns or clients [MMA 8]

2974 grouse -- any one of a number of feathered game birds of the family Tetraonidae which have plump bodies and plumage usually less brilliant than that of pheasants [CW 6]

2975 The Grove -- the name given to the Dawson/Whittaker home on Wellington Ave. in Leahampton* [UD 4]

2976 grues -- the frights or creeps; derived from gruesome [NT 17]

2977 Grummidge, Lady Marjorie -- recipient of a letter from Helen, Duchess of Denver, which explains just how upset Helen was at the way PW's marriage to HV was conducted [BH P]

2978 Gruyère -- originally from that district in Switzerland, it is a pale yellow, firmly textured cheese which may or may not have holes in it and which is made from whole milk [WB 5]

2979 Gryll Court -- the home of Edward Curzon Freke, Esq.*, father of Sir Julian Freke*. See also item 2980. [WB 8]

2980 Gryllingham -- the location of Gryll Court*, and possibly a pun on Gryll from Spenser's Faerie Queen, II, xii, 86. Gryll is a human magically turned into a pig by Acrasia and kept in her Bower of Bliss. He complains when returned to human form. [WB 8]

2981 guano, liquid -- a fertilizer, in this case some sort of liquid preparation, made from the excrement of sea birds. It is very high in nitrogen. [FRH 13]

2982 guard-book -- rather like a scrapbook in which is kept all of the past advertisements done for a particular firm. These are kept for historical purposes as well as to avoid duplicating earlier efforts in other campaigns. [MMA 1]

2983 guard's van -- what North American railroad practice calls a caboose. However, in European practice they are also used with passenger trains wherein they resemble a baggage car. The guard corresponds to the conductor, but also performs some of the brakeman's duties as well. [FRH 10]

2984 Gubbins, Miss -- a former Shrewsbury College* student only vaguely known to HV [GN 1]

2985 Gubbins, Mr. -- the vicar's* warden*, one of the ranking lay officers in an Anglican parish, at Darley*. He had gained some notoriety as a winner of the Grand National Sweepstakes*. [HHC 12]

2986 Gubbins, Eve -- Rosanna Wrayburn's* housekeeper, and a witness to her will [SP 19]

2987 Gudgeon, Harry -- landlord at the Crown pub in Paggleham* [BH 10]

2988 gudgeons -- the bearings on either end of a beam from which a bell is suspended. They rest in sockets in the bell support frame and would require heavy grease to withstand the heat from friction and the heavy wear. [NT 3]

2989 guichet -- French for a ticket-seller's cage or a ticket-taker's booth at a turnstile or other entrance gate. The reference is to a baggage and ticket check counter at a railroad station. [aq]

2990 Guildford -- a town in Surrey and its traditional county seat. It is a thriving market and residential community visited by Miss Climpson* while she is staying in Leahampton*. [UD 22]

2991 Guildford St. -- a typographical error for Guilford St.* [NT 16]

2992 Guilford St. -- in Bloomsbury*, it connects Russell Square* with

Gray's Inn Rd.* Jacques Lerouge* lives on it at some unspecified number. [aq/SP 1/HHC 30/NT 16/GN 4]

2993 guinea -- originally a gold coin worth twenty-one shillings (one pound and one shilling), so named after the African origin of its gold. It would have been worth a bit more than $4.25 U. S. during the time of the PW stories. PW turned down the copy of Catullus at thirteen guineas (about $54.00) because of its poor condition. See British Monetary Units. [dh]

2994 Guinness -- the famous Dublin brewers of a full range of beers. They produce Harp Ale as well as the internationally famous Guinness Stout, a dark, heavy-bodied brew made with roasted malt and a high percentage of hops. It is stout which, most likely, Mr. Piggin* has ordered. The Stout's famous slogan is, "Guinness Is Good for You", often illustrated with the toucan introduced to the campaign by DLS. [UD 12/SP 1/MMA 12]

2995 Gulliver, Dorcas -- Bertha Gotobed's landlady. She identifies the girl's body for the police. [UD 6]

2996 Gunbury St. Walters -- near Duke's Denver* and just as fictitious [WB 6]

2997 Gunner, Mrs. -- the Parker* household cook [MMA 17]

2998 Gunpowder Plot -- a conspiracy led by Robert Catesby and a few Roman Catholic followers. They planned to destroy the British government on November 5, 1605, by blowing up the Houses of Parliament when James I was speaking to a joint session at the opening of Parliament. Guy Fawkes was to fire the gunpowder, but he was caught on Nov. 4. The plot's failure is still celebrated on November 5 as Guy Fawkes' Day and, as a continuing tradition, the Beefeaters, or Yeomen Extraordinary of the Guard, search the Houses of Parliament prior to each instance when the sovereign is scheduled to open Parliament. [t]

2999 Gunpowder Treason -- see item 2998 [t]

3000 Gurney, Tom -- another Wilvercombe* fisherman with whom old Esdras Pollock* is feuding. Pollock steals lobsters from Gurney's pots as revenge. [HHC 27]

3001 gut -- the silken thread obtained from the intestines of silkworms killed before they begin to spin their cocoons. The thread is dried and used in the manufacture of fishing tackle. [FRH 1]

3002 gutter -- a candle is said to gutter when it has burned a channel down its center along the wick and through which molten wax pours out. The effect can be caused by a too-long wick or by too rapid burning. [ie]

3003 Guy's -- one of five hospitals founded in London between 1720 and 1745. Guy's was founded in 1722 and is named for its benefactor, Thomas Guy (1644-1724). It remains a major medical center, a vast 1000-bed facility, and is located South of the Thames near London Bridge and Southwark Cathedral. Nurse Philliter* had been trained there. [WB 12/UD 4/BH 12]

3004 Guy Fawkes -- see Gunpowder Plot [t/BC 2/GN 4]

3005 Gwyn, Nell -- Eleanor Gwynn (1650-87), an English actress who managed to conquer King Charles II when she delivered the witty epilogue to <u>Tyrannic Love or The Royal Martyr</u> by Dryden*. She became the king's mistress, bore him two sons, lived extravagantly, and outlasted him by two years. His dying request that Nell not "starve" assured her a comfortable pension. It is suggested that she may have induced Charles to found the Chelsea Hospital. [SP 11]

3006 gyves -- fetters [BH 20]

(H)

3007 H & D number 450 -- see Actinax Special Rapid Plate [MMA 2]

3008 H. M. -- abbreviation for headmistress, the senior official at a girls' school [NT 9]

3009 H. M. S. Pinafore -- along with such perennial favorites as The Mikado and The Pirates of Penzance, one of the more popular operas by Gilbert and Sullivan, the brilliant team famous for their light, satirical, witty operas called Savoy Operas because most of the later productions were staged at the Savoy Theatre. See Savoy. [CW 5/SP 3]

3010 H. T. lead -- high tension lead, the high voltage line from the coil or magneto to the starter motor [HHC 12]

3011 H. T. & V. latch key -- the company was real, but no longer exists [MMA 5]

3012 "Ha! well! what next?" -- from T. L. Beddoes' The Second Brother**, I, i, 254-56. The lines are spoken by Marcello, a brother of the Duke of Ferrara, to Ezril, a Jew who has just brought the news that the Duke is dying after a fall from his horse. [HHC 31]

3013 Haagedorn, Mr. -- a group manager* for Pym's Publicity* who is in charge of Sopo and related products [MMA 10]

3014 Habeas Corpus -- such writs date from the 13th C., but became fully formalized in Acts of 1679 and 1816. The Acts guarantee the subjects' right to a free trial and to freedom from arrest or imprisonment without reasonable cause. [UD 19/HHC 31]

3015 habile comme tout pour la toilette -- French for, "[she is] clever as anything at dressing" [CW 16]

3016 Hackett -- one of PW's soldiers at Caudry*. He helped Padgett* dig PW out of the collapsed trench where he had been buried alive. [GN 17]

3017 Had he looked on the wine . . . -- Supt. Kirk* alludes to Proverbs 23:31. Verse 29 asks, "Who hath woe", etc., and verses 30-32 respond:

"They that tarry long at the wine;
they that go to seek mixed wine.
"Look not thou upon the wine when it is red, when it giveth his colour in the cup, when it moveth itself aright.
"At the last it biteth like a serpent, and stingeth like an adder." [BH 12]

3018 "Had we but world enough and time . . ." -- the first line of Andrew Marvell's poem, "To His Coy Mistress", a delightful argument against the virtues of chastity. The poem was written in 1681. [MMA 16/BH 12]

3019 haemophilia -- or hemophilia, the hereditary tendency to uncontrollable bleeding caused by the absence of what is called the "clotting factor". Fibrinogen is the natural aid to clotting present in nonhemophiliacs, but Vitamin K, found in green vegetables, is a natural aid to clotting that, along with certain drugs, is being investigated as a source of help for hemophiliacs. [HHC 34]

3020 hag-ridden -- troubled by nightmares [GN 8]

3021 Haig -- the famous and excellent Scotch whiskey, available worldwide, typically in the U. S. in the firm's unusual triangular "pinch bottle" [BH 6]

3022 "Hail, shrine of blood!" -- from T. L. Beddoes' The Brides' Tragedy**, II, vi, 36. The speech continues:

"in double shadows veiled,
Where the Tartarian blossoms shed their poison
And load the air with wicked impulses;
Hail, leafless shade, hallowed to sacriledge,
Altar of death!" [HHC 26]

3023 hair dresser to the White Queen -- in Lewis Carroll's Through the Looking Glass, Ch. 5, Alice helps the White Queen adjust her coiffure. The description of the event goes: "It would have been all the better as it seemed to Alice, if she had got some

#3023 Alice adjusting hairpins for the White Queen in a drawing by John Tenniel.

one else to dress her, she was so dreadfully untidy. 'Every single thing's crooked,' Alice thought to herself, 'and she's all over pins!--May I put your shawl straight for you?' she added aloud." [GN 1]

3024 hair in papers -- a method of waving the hair wherein wisps of hair are curled around pieces of paper and left overnight. In the morning the wave has set by body heat, the papers are removed, and the hair is combed out and arranged. This is not a type of home permanent; these did not arrive in England until the 1950's. [MMA 8]

3025 Halcock -- see Alcock [FRH 8]

3026 half a yard wide to leg -- see cricket [MMA 18]

3027 half-[a] crown -- a British coin worth two and a half shillings* [dh/WB 10/UD 13/MMA 1]

3028 half-double -- half of a newspaper page covering two columns [MMA 1]

3029 half turn -- see turn [NT 13]

3030 half-penny points -- an extremely modest bit of gambling, the loser paying a half-penny (see British Monetary Units) per point of score he loses by, rather like playing bridge for a quarter of a penny a point in the U. S. Even defeat by some outrageous score would amount to a small sum per rubber. [FRH 27]

3031 the Hall -- see Striding Hall [sf]

3032 the Hall -- see Bredon Hall [BH E2]

3033 Hall & Knight's Algebra -- a text by Sinclair Hall and Samuel Ratcliffe Knight, Elementary Algebra, was published by Macmillan in 1885 and went through many editions. [NT 7]

3034 Hall Building -- one of the major buildings on the Shrewsbury College* campus [GN 21]

3035 halitus -- an aroma, vapors from something [HHC 1]

3036 "Hallelujah Chorus" -- that stirring choral segment of G. F. Handel's oratorio, The Messiah. The Paggleham* church choir tackled it for their Harvest Festival in 1935, probably in September. [BH 5]

3037 Halls -- the music halls; vaudeville houses [WB 9 and passim]

3038 Halos -- see tumulus at Halos [GN 3]

3039 halves, too many wee -- a colloquial reference to a measure of drink as a half pint of ale or cider (alcoholic). The specific beverage is not mentioned, only that he had consumed too much of it [FRH 7]

3040 Haman, hanged higher than -- Haman, the Agagite of whom we learn in Esther 3ff., was hanged from a gallows some seventy-five feet high (fifty cubits, and a cubit is equal to about eighteen inches). [NT 20]

3041 Hambledon -- an artist of major stature compared to Sandy Campbell*. Campbell's obituary as an artist was written by one of Hambledon's followers. [FRH 22]

3042 hames -- points on the lower sides of a horse collar to which are attached the traces from the vehicle being pulled [bc]

3043 Hamlet -- William Shakespeare's famous tragedy, written sometime before 1603, and based on events related in Saxo-Grammaticus and Belleforest. It is basically a story of murder and revenge, but only superficially, as the main concern of the play is with the consequences of actions in a moral universe. There are many parallels to the Old Testament book of Job. [FRH 22/MMA 19/BH 9]

3044 Hamlet's aunt -- also his mother, Gertrude. When the elder Hamlet died, Gertrude married his brother, Claudius, thus becoming aunt and mother to her son, Hamlet. [GN 3]

3045 hammer of God [like the parson in Chesterton's story] -- the reference is to G. K. Chesterton's* (1874-1936) Father Brown, a Roman Catholic priest who appears as the detective in a series of stories, one of which is entitled, "The Hammer of God", wherein the murderer is a parson who kills his evil brother. [BH 13]

3046 hammer-beam -- a short beam that protrudes from a wall at the base

of a main rafter in a roof. It takes the place of an unsightly tie-beam by supporting the angle of the rafter. Such construction techniques are frequently found in association with carved angels and the hammer-beam itself would rest on a corbel* [NT 2]

3047 Hammond, Albert -- Matthew Gowan's chauffeur. He is devoted to his master's well-being. [FRH 8]

3048 Hammond [old] -- an Oxford proffessor noted for his lack of sartorial expertise [GN 1]

3049 "Hammond out-Graced Grace" -- a reference to the fact that in May of 1927, Walter Hammond equalled cricket* great W. G. Grace's feat of scoring 1000 runs in May. Hammond scored 1042 runs to Grace's 1016. [UD 19]

3050 Hamperly, Mr. -- an employee of Pym's Publicity* who is not otherwise identified [MMA 6]

3051 Hampshire -- the southern coastal county of England which includes Winchester, Southampton, Portsmouth, and the Isle of Wight. It is the home county of the Dowager Duchess of Denver*, and is the setting for much of the action of UD. [CW 4/UD 1]

3052 Hampstead -- a respectable residential area of North London flavored by intellectuals and rich socialists, and is the meeting place of The Society* [ab/UD 18/MMA 8]

3053 Hampstead Heath -- public open land near Hampstead famous for its natural beauty and for its recreations much enjoyed by Londoners; hence, the phrase 'Appy 'Ampstead. The Surrey Hills and all of London are visible from the higher elevations of the park. [ab/UD 18/BC 3]

3054 Hamsey -- a community to the East and South of Little Doddering* that is fictitious. Its name is a corruption of Ramsey, a small town in Essex. [bc]

3055 Hamworthy -- the butler at William Grimbold's* home who discovered his master's body [ae]

3056 Hancock, Miss -- the parish priest's daughter who, with her mother, was locked in the vestry* by ruffians bent on disrupting the all-night prayer vigil for Squire Burdock* [bc]

3057 Hancock, Mr. -- a resident of Great Pagford* who has automobiles for rent and who runs a taxi service from his garage [BH 5]

3058 Hancock, Mrs. -- the parish priest's wife who was locked in the vestry* during the prayer vigil for Squire Burdock* [bc]

3059 Hancock, Rev. --host to Haviland Burdock* and Little Doddering's* current vicar*. He is thought to be a bit too High Church* by many of the locals. [bc]

3060 Hand Court -- a very short North-South street connecting High Holborn* with Sandland St. on the northern side of High Holborn between Southampton Row and Gray's Inn Rd.** [SP 14]

3061 hand of a murderer which no perfume of Arabia -- Bunter compares himself to Lady Macbeth, something of an exaggeration, in the sleep-walking scene, V, i, 56, of Macbeth, when the Lady says: "All the perfumes of Arabia will not sweeten this little hand." [NT 11]

3062 handbells -- small, handheld bells used for practice in change-ringing and other musical performances, one bell held in each hand [NT 1]

3063 Handel, George Frideric -- the great composer (1685-1759) who was born in Germany, but who settled in England in 1712. He is ranked with Bach as the greatest composer of the late Baroque era. He wrote extensively and produced thirty-nine operas, several oratorios, and a wide range of secular and sacred music. [HHC 20]

3064 hanged man -- a reference to an actual hanging, not a reference to the Tarot card called "The Hanged Man", although there are some similarities [MMA 9]

3065 "The hangman with his gardener's gloves . . ." -- PW quotes Oscar Wilde's "The Ballad of Reading Gaol", I, 14. The poem was written in 1898 and is considered one of his more notable works. [BH E3]

3066 Hankin, Mr. -- one of the more

ON HAMPSTEAD HEATH.

#3053 Hampstead Heath in the 1920's.

senior members of the staff at Pym's Publicity*. He is a copy chief*, and, as such, would have extensive authority over the final works produced by Pym's. [MMA 1]

3067 Hannah Brown -- the tramp merchant vessel to which Jim Thoday* is assigned as mate. She is owned by Lampson & Blake of Hull**, and is as fictitious as the firm that owns her. [NT 6]

3068 Hanover Square -- a square just South of Oxford St.* and between New Bond and Regent Streets**. St. George's* church is located on the South side. [HHC 4/BH P]

3069 Hanson's -- see Hanson & Hanson, Messrs. [SP 14]

3070 Hanson & Hanson, Messrs. -- a law firm to which Norman Urquhart* had to send some papers that Miss Murchison* appeared to have some difficulty typing. There is no such firm now, and it is most likely fictitious. [SP 14]

3071 Hants. -- the postal abbreviation for Hampshire. Derived from the Saxon Hamtun (as in Southampton), Hamptonscire was first recognized as an entity ca. 757. There was no standarized spelling at the time and it is recorded in William the Conqueror's Domesday Book as Hantescire. Thus, the modern county has, as its postal abbreviation, an allusion to a variant spelling of its more ancient name. The Hampshire Regiment, however, was abbreviated to Hamps. [UD 4]

3072 Harbottle, Mrs. -- the elderly greengrocer* who provides PW with some of the information he needs to solve Robert Duckworthy's* dilemma [im]

3073 harbour-master -- the person in charge of the various services in a harbor such as determining who unloads where and when, who docks, who anchors out, etc. [FRH 13]

3074 Hardraw, John -- the gamekeeper at Riddlesdale Lodge*. He is responsible for the upkeep and integrity of the approximately twenty acres that go with the lodge. He would also be responsible for fending off poachers. [CW 1]

3075 Hardraw, Mrs. John -- wife of the gamekeeper at Riddlesdale Lodge* [CW 3]

3076 Hardwick, Bess of -- see Bess of Hardwick [GN 3]

3077 Hardy, Chief Insp. -- a colleague of Parker's* at Scotland Yard* [ae]

3078 Hardy rods -- formerly the Rolls-Royce of fly-fishing rods, usually of hand-crafted bamboo. Hardy still produces excellent fly-fishing equipment, but nowhere as extensively as before WW II. [FRH 1]

3079 Hardy, Salcombe -- one of PW's friends and sometime aide or information source. He is a reporter for various papers, depending on the story. He is known as "Sally" to his friends and is usually covering a crime story of some sort. He is a heavy-drinking, friendly sort, but he can be a pest. PW and HV both show that they can handle him competently in BH. [nf/BC 15/SP 1/HHC 4/BH 13]

3080 Hardy, Thomas -- English naturalistic novelist and poet (1840-1928) who was born in Dorset (the Wessex of his novels). In such works as Far from the Madding Crowd, Return of the Native, and Jude the Obscure, Hardy expounded upon his theory of man which saw him as subject to forces he could neither control nor understand. Parker* mentions reading his works. [UD 5/BC 18]

3081 hares, starting two -- see starting two hares [WB 5/UD 6]

3082 Harkaway -- the alias taken by Simon Dawson* while living in the West Indies* on the island of Trinidad* [UD 13]

3083 "Hark! hark! the lark at heaven's gate sings" -- the line PW uses to greet the morning is from Shakespeare's Cymbeline, II, iii, 22, and is one of his more famous songs [BC 14]

3084 Harlech -- where Philip Boyes* and Ryland Vaughan* spent a short vacation. The town is on Tremadoc Bay in Wales, and is dominated by Harlech Castle, built by Edward I (ca. 1283) to insure keeping the area under his control after defeating Llwellyn ap Gruffydd to gain that control. There are famous views of the Bay and of the

Snowdonia Mountains to be enjoyed. The castle figured prominently in the Wars of the Roses and during the Civil War. [SP 1]

3085 Harlequin -- a horse mentioned as having paid off at odds of 100 to 1 [MMA 11]

3086 Harley St. -- famous as a center for physicians in London. Physicians there cater to a wealthy clientele and their services are priced accordingly. Harley St. is a North-South street running between Cavendish Square and Marylebone Rd. It is roughly parallel to Baker and Wimpole Sts. which are farther to the West. Drs. Lamplough, Freke, Carr, Penberthy, and Garfield** all have offices (surgeries) there in the various stories. [te/ WB 1/UD 23/BC 4/MMA 4]

3087 harmonium -- a reed organ or keyboard wind instrument wherein the wind blows against a set of metal reeds which vibrate and produce a musical sound. The wind is supplied by foot-pedals that drive a bellows. [SP 13]

3088 Harper, Miss -- a former Shrewsbury College* student who is typing the manuscript for Miss Lydgate's book on English prosody* [GN 3]

3089 Harper's Cut -- part of the fen* drainage system. It is fictitious, but typical of the area. [NT 7]

3090 harpies -- mythological beasts depicted as great birds with the heads of women. They are associated with the dead and their souls, and the idea that the souls of the dead try to capture those of the living. Aeneas encounters them at the Strophades Islands in Book III of Vergil's <u>Aeneid</u>. [GN 8]

3091 harpsichord -- an early keyboard instrument commonly used in the 17th and 18th centuries. Its main distinction from the piano is that it plucks the strings while a piano hits them, thus creating completely separate tone and resonance characteristics. Minor differences include such things as frequent use of dual keyboards, and a reversal of key colors. Unlike a piano, it cannot play loud or soft; hence the need for separate keyboards, although there are single manual instruments. [WB 3]

3092 Harriet -- Dawson Whittaker, Agatha Dawson's* sister. See the genealogical chart at the back of UD. [UD 8]

3093 Harringay, Mr. -- a houseguest at Duke's Denver* during the Christmas festivities of 1929. He is in some way connected with The City*. [SP 12]

3094 Harris, Mr. -- one of the Pym's Publicity* staff who is responsible for Outdoor Advertising [MMA 4]

3095 Harris, Mrs. -- she is the fictitious friend invented by Mrs. Gamp* in Dickens's* <u>Martin Chuzzlewit</u> [BC 12]

3096 Harris tweed -- a tweed of exceptional quality that is still hand-woven in the Outer Hebrides islands of Scotland. It is a particularly popular fabric for sports clothing, hunting jackets, Norfolk suits*, etc. [BH 16]

3097 Harrison's -- the Dowager Duchess* is helping PW and HV furnish their Audley Square* home and has made some purchases from this firm, specialists in antique furniture. There may have been such a firm, but no record of its ever having existed could be located. [BH P]

3098 Harrogate Bros. -- a DLS creation for the accountants at Pym's Publicity* [MMA 1]

3099 Harrow -- the Harrow School at Harrow-on-the-Hill, Middlesex, was founded and endowed by John Lyon (1514?-91) under letters patent* and a charter from Queen Elizabeth I. Lord Byron, Sir Robert Peel, and Sir Winston Churchill are among its more distinguished graduates. Archery is a sport particularly important to Harrow, having been especially encouraged since 1684. PW is "famous" for having led Eton's cricketers in a singular match in which Harrow was soundly defeated in the annual event which started in 1805. It is usually played at Lord's Cricket Ground and, before 1914, when PW played, was a great social occasion. [WB 8/UD BN/FRH 5/MMA 10/GN 11]

3100 Harry -- see like young Harry [BH 7]

3101 Harry -- a former boyfriend of Nurse Booth* to whom she was seriously attached, but whom she never mar-

ried. His spirit is manipulated by Miss Climpson*, figuring in the famous séances in which she discovers the information that PW needs. [SP 17]

3102 Harry -- the lift, or elevator, operator in the building that houses Pym's Publicity* [MMA 4]

3103 Harry -- see Strachan, Henry [FRH 4]

3104 Hart -- a Hertfordshire police constable [BH 11]

3105 Hartford, Nina -- the rather large lady who comes to the costume party in a swimming dress and carrying a ball to represent the game of water polo in keeping with the party's games theme [qs]

3106 Hartlepool, Lady -- a lady with whom Mrs. Weldon* had visited the Riviera*, but who is deceased at the time of this story [HHC 5]

3107 Hartley, Major -- an owner of two of Mr. Endicott's* razors [HHC 6]

3108 Hartley, Miss -- one of the employees at Pym's Publicity* [MMA 7]

3109 Hartman, Dr. -- a physician who figures prominently in "Footsteps That Ran". With PW's permission, Bunter is helping him by doing photographic work which will be a part of his research into vitamin deficiencies. [fr]

3110 Harvest Festival -- a festival staged in the fall, usually in September, to celebrate the harvest. It is traditional in many English churches and in some American ones as well. [NT 3]

3111 "Has it gone twelve?" -- from IV, iv, 7-8, in T. L. Beddoes' Death's Jest Book**. Isbrand poses the question to Siegfried, who responds. The reference is to their plot to stage a coup and disrupt the wedding of Amala to Adalmar, but they don't know that Athulf has just killed the groom, his brother. [HHC 27]

3112 "hated to be touching" -- see item 3999, "Like the man in Max Beerbohm's story . . ." [SP 16]

3113 Hatfield -- a community in Hertfordshire about twenty miles North of London's West End* on the Great North Road*. See Motorcycle Race. [cb/BH E2]

3114 Hatton Garden -- a street in London named for Sir Christopher Hatton, a favorite of Elizabeth I, to whom she gave the gardens of Ely Place, palace of the Bishops of Ely, during a vacancy in the see. The area is known today as the center of the diamond trade in London, located to the North of Holborn. [ss/nf/im]

3115 hause-bone -- the spine. The hause is the neck, from the Scots dialectical "hause", a narrow neck of land connecting two larger summits. It also refers to the tube[s] at the bow of a ship through which the anchor rope or chain passes; the hause-pipe. The allusion is to the anonymous ballad, "The Twa Corbies". [HHC 1]

3116 Haut Brion -- since the splash is a "great crimson" one, there might be cause for curiosity as all of the various Haut Brion wines are from the Graves district which is most noted for its white wines. However, the Chateau Haut Brion and its more recent imitations are all excellent reds which can easily compete with those of Pauillac and Margaux. [UD 14]

3117 Have His Carcase -- the title and subsequent references to this title phrase are an allusion to Dickens's* Pickwick Papers, Ch. 43ff., the segment that details Mr. Weller's imprisonment for debt. In Ch. 43, Weller says, "The have-his-carcase, next to perpetual motion, is vun of the blessedest things as was ever made." DLS and Mr. Weller have alluded to the Writs of Habeas Corpus*, developed from the early 13th C., which insure a defendant's presence in court, the regular attendance of jurors, and prevents illegal imprisonment. The Habeas Corpus Act of 1679 was meant to guarantee the right of the accused to a free trial, but applied only to criminal charges. The H. C. Act of 1816 extended that right to other charges as well. These acts established the idea that no one may be tried in absentia. In HHC, the title also relates to the fact that a coroner's jury usually can't make a ruling unless there is a "carcase" indicating a death has occurred.

"Carcase" in this sense means corpus delicti, the body of the crime. One need not have the entire corpse, just proof that a crime has been committed. Thus, until Paul Alexis's* body, or some portion of it, had been recovered, no verdict as to cause of death could be given as no admissable proof of death was provided. [HHC]

3118 Have-His-Carcase-Act -- see Have His Carcase and Habeas Corpus [HHC 4]

3119 Havre -- LeHavre, the major French port on the Bay of the Seine almost due southeast of Southampton*. It is the home port for many French transatlantic lines and was also the first stop for English liners outbound for New York and elsewhere. [BC 11]

3120 Hawkeye -- one is not certain if DLS just chose a suitable name for an alert detective or if she meant to suggest that Ginger Potts* might also have read any of James Fenimore Cooper's novels that feature Natty Bumppo who is known variously as "Deerslayer" or "Hawkeye" in the five Leather-Stocking Tales. [MMA 7]

3121 Hawkins, Mr. -- news editor of the Morning Star* to whom Hector Puncheon* goes with his discovery of cocaine*. He is fictitious. [MMA 12]

3122 Hawkshaw the detective -- a creation of Tom Taylor, Hawkshaw appears in Taylor's melodrama, The Ticket-of-Leave Man, which opened in London and New York in 1863. It is the first significant appearance of a detective in a play. Cecil Henry Bullivant made a novel of the play in 1935, so DLS must have had the play version in mind for UD. See also Who Put Back the Clock. [UD 2/BH 14]

3123 hay -- see or some hay . . . [SP 5]

3124 Hay, Ian -- the pseudonym of Sir John Hay Beith (1876-1952), an English writer and soldier known for his humorous novels which often concern themselves with boys' boarding schools. The most famous is A Safety Match of 1911. See "He maun ha' gotten a rare fricht . . .".

3125 Haydock, Eve -- a history student at Shrewsbury College* [GN 7]

3126 Haymarket -- a street in central London connecting Piccadilly Circus with Pall Mall* [HHC 30]

3127 Haynes, Miss Jessie -- the young woman supposedly murdered by Robert Duckworthy* [im]

3128 hayrick -- a hay stack, especially one built regularly with a ridged top [HHC 26]

3129 Hazlemere -- or Haslemere, a center for craftsmen in iron, glass, wood, etc., and for an internationally known music festival. It is in southwest Surrey near Hampshire. [UD 20]

3130 hazard all we have -- see give and hazard all we have [BH 18]

3131 He belonged to a family -- see never shot a fox [WB 11]

3132 "He denies it, said the King" -- the reference is to Ch. 11 of Lewis Carroll's Alice in Wonderland**, and the somehow bizarrely logical trial segment entitled, "Who Stole the Tarts?" [MMA 17]

3133 "he for God only . . ." -- the line is from Milton's* Paradise Lost where the creation of Adam and Eve is considered. The passage reads:

"He for God only, she for God in him:
His fair large front and eye sublime declared
Absolute rule."

The quotation is from lines 295-7. Compare this to Miss Climpson's* earlier comments about jealousy. The lines suggest a dangerous attitude toward life and religion in that "he", Adam, may relate to God, but that "she", Eve, may relate only to Adam, and we know how that arrangement developed. [UD 16/SP 4]

3134 "He had not reached the time to babble of green fields . . ." -- see babble of green fields [SP 1]

3135 "He is a righteous judge . . ." -- Mr. Venables* is paraphrasing Psalm 7:12 as it appears in The Book of Common Prayer: "God is a righteous Judge, strong and patient: and God is provoked every day." The KJV is 7:11: "God judgeth the righteous, and God is angry with the wicked every day." [NT 20]

3136 "He is faithful that promised" --

the line is from the Epistle to the Hebrews* 10:23, Mr. Featherstone's* reminder to himself that God will keep his word. [CW 10]

3137 "He's tough, sir, tough . . ." -- see Bagstock, Joey [WB 5]

3138 "He is well paid that is well satisfied." -- the reference is to Portia's speech in The Merchant of Venice*, IV, i, 415. [BH 18]

3139 "He lives from hand to mouth . . ." -- in some editions lives is printed lies. An old proverb, it refers to living marginally. [MMA 15]

3140 "He maun ha' gotten a rare fricht . . ." -- the quote is from Ch. 11 of Ian Hay's* The First Hundred Thousand (1915), and is taken from a discussion of barracks life and the problems of vermin. The soldiers' blankets were put through some sort of sterilizer to kill the lice which, of course, did no such thing. In an undated American edition we find the following exchange between two soldiers:

Ogg (examining his blanket): "They're a' there yet. See!"
Hogg (an optimist): "Aye; but they must have gotten an awfu' fricht!"

One suspects that some editor who did not know enough to leave the passage alone is responsible for the switch from "maun" to "must", etc., but the spirit of the comment has survived. [FRH 9]

3141 "He rode upon the cherubims . . ." -- a reference to either Psalm 18:10 or II Samuel 22:11, most likely the former as it appears in The Book of Common Prayer. [NT 2]

3142 "He said, dear mother . . ." -- from T. L. Beddoes' The Bride's Tragedy**, III, ii, 55-7. Floribel speaks of her expectation of marrying Hesperus. The lines are presented as an innocent case of a bride's nervousness and are, as such, an intensely ironic bit of foreboding. [HHC 5]

3143 "He sitteth between . . ." -- Psalm 99:1: "The Lord reigneth; let the people tremble: He sitteth between the cherubims; let the earth be moved." in the KJV, but PW and Mr. Venables* are using The Book of Common Prayer. [NT 10]

3144 "He that questioneth much . . ." -- the selection is taken, with some freedoms, from Sir Francis Bacon's essay "Of Discourse" (1597) [GN 17]

3145 "He whispers, he hisses . . ." -- this quote is from a sermon by John Donne* preached at the Earl of Bridgewater's house at the marriage of his daughter on November 19, 1629. Donne's words are an adaptation of ideas from Isaiah 5:26: "And he will lift up an ensign to the nations from far, and will hiss unto them from the end of the earth: and, behold, they shall come with speed swiftly." "Hiss" is better translated as "whistle". The sermon is one of a group first published in 1629 as Fifty Sermons. [NT 5]

3146 Head of the College -- the Warden* of Shrewsbury College* [BH P]

3147 Headington -- a suburb of Oxford, formerly the home of C. S. Lewis, about three miles East of the old central part of the city on the A40 route toward London [GN 1]

3148 Headington Hill -- the Headington Rd. between Headington* and central Oxford descends to become St. Clement's St., crosses the Magdalen Bridge, and then becomes High St. [GN 1]

3149 Hearn, Mr. -- the grocer at Darley*. He has a telephone that HV uses to summon help with the corpse that she has found. [HHC 2]

3150 "Heart of oak are our ships" -- the line is from a poem, "Heart of Oak", by David Garrick (1717-79), written in 1759, and set to music by William Boyce. PW is apparently playing a word association game while investigating. [UD 6]

3151 Heath -- see Hampstead Heath [ab]

3152 Heath-Warburton, Erica -- an apparently fictitious writer [CW 7]

3153 Heathbury -- the fictitious local market center for Lesston Hoe, Wilvercombe**, and the surrounding villages. On a Thursday, market day, that is where most of the local population can be found. [HHC 2]

3154 Hébert, Prof. -- a witness at the

trial of the Duke of Denver* who explained Denis Cathcart's* promising career as a diplomat in pre-War Paris [CW 15]

3155 Hebrews, Epistle to the -- a New Testament book wrongly ascribed to St. Paul before A. D. 70, presented in the form of a synagogue address. It has two purposes: 1) to confirm Jewish Christians in the belief that Judaism was at an end because of Christ, the fulfillment of the Law, and 2) to prevent professed believers from lapsing back into Judaism. The book is essentially a contrast between the good things of Judaism and the better things of Christianity. [CW 5]

3156 Hector -- son of Priam, King of Troy, by Hecuba, and brother to Paris*. He is considered the most heroic and valiant of the Trojans. He was killed by Achilles as revenge for Hector's having killed Patroclus, Achilles' friend. [GN 18]

3157 hedging and ditching -- making or repairing hedges and ditches. Insp. Sugg* threatens to turn to such a life in lieu of the pursuit of crime, suggesting a simpler and more basic form of labor requiring less thought, and we learn in NT that he has done so. Hedging and ditching do require, however, a good bit of knowledge and skill if they are to be done properly and well. [WB 3/HHC 22]

3158 Helen -- MacGregor, the girl who witnessed the fight between Campbell* and Gowan* [FRH 11]

3159 Helen -- see Wimsey, Helen, Duchess of Denver [passim]

3160 _Helix pomatia_ -- an edible snail about two inches long with a thin, yellowish-brown shell that is often banded. The species, mostly limited to Europe, is a member of the largest group of land snails, the _Helicidae_, and has been considered a food delicacy since Roman times. [UD 1]

3161 Hell-fire Club -- an association of young hoodlums known for recklessness and profligacy. Centered in and around London in the early 1700's, the most famous club was founded in about 1745 by Sir Francis Dashwood. That group held meetings in a ruined Cistercian abbey on the Thames near Medmenham. The club was also known as the Franciscans after its founder. Orgies also took place at West Wycombe. [bc]

3162 Hell gapes -- in medieval drama and art, Hell, or the entrance to it, is often depicted as a huge, gaping, fire-belching mouth set in a hideously ugly head, as in DLS's play, _The Devil to Pay_ [NT 3]

3163 hell-hounds -- reporters. The reference is to Cerberus, the three-headed dog that guards the entrance to Hades in Greek mythology. In Vergil's _Aeneid_, the Sibyl gives the dog a cake laced with poppies and honey to allow safe passage. In this case, Bunter is the Sibyl, the newsman is the Hound, and PW and HV constitute Vergil. The cake is the little news tidbit. [BH P]

3164 helmet wreath -- the decorative wreath surrounding the top of a helmet located above the shield itself in a coat of arms. See Wimsey arms. [GN 15]

3165 helots -- a serf or slave, from Helots, the slave class of ancient Sparta. The word is here used to mean the symbiotic relationship between two people or a person and a company, etc., where one serves as a slave to the other. [FRH 20]

3166 "Help, Jehan!" -- see "The Rosamunde" [NT 17]

3167 Hemans, Mrs. -- hostess of the dance HV attends in Oxford, and a friend of some years' standing [GN 7]

3168 Hemans, Felicia [Dorothea] -- _née_ Browne (1793-1835), a popular author, especially in the U. S. Her poem, "Casabianca"*, was for years a staple for those who would declaim heroically. [BH 7]

3169 hemlock for the Dean -- an allusion to the means by which Socrates committed suicide as is described in Plato's _Phaedo_. It was the means used against those who had committed serious crimes against the state in ancient Greece. [GN 9]

3170 Henderson -- a former Shrewsbury College* student who has "gone" nudist. Comment is made about her be-

#3162 A "hell-mouth" from a Medieval play.

ing so brown. [GN 2]

3171 Henley, Insp. -- a member of the Baldock* police force. PW and Insp. Parker* assist him in the solution to the murder of William Grimbold*. [ae]

3172 henna -- a reddish-brown dye obtained from the leaves of the henna plant [Lawsonia inermis], an Old World tropical shrub. The dye is used chiefly to color hair. [SP 18]

3173 Henry -- in Queen Mab, the vigil-keeper who watches over Ianthe's body while Queen Mab shows her spirit a vision of the world [GN 15]

3174 Henry -- assistant to Mr. Merryweather*, the Seahampton* barber [HHC 8]

3175 Henry -- See Wimsey, Henry [BH E2]

3176 Henry IV -- king of England from 1399 to 1413. He forced his cousin, Richard II, to abdicate, mostly as a result of Richard's treatment of Henry during a 1398 quarrel with the Duke of Norfolk that led to Henry's being exiled and his lands confiscated by Richard. Henry spent his reign securing the crown he had taken by force. This is the King Henry of Shakespeare's Henry IV, Parts I and II, which feature the popular Prince Hal and Falstaff. [CW 5]

3177 Henry VIII -- the second Tudor king of England (1509-47), born in 1491, the second son of Henry VII, and subject of one of Shakespeare's histories. Gerald, the Duke of Denver*, is described as resembling the young Henry VIII, sturdy and conventional. Miss Martin* repeats this and amplifies it by saying that Denver looks, "rather like Henry VIII, debloated and debearded and brought up to date". The monarch's naval policy is the subject of Miss Cattermole's* paper in GN. He is, perhaps, more famous for his divorce difficulties with Rome and the resultant schism and dissolution of the Catholic monasteries to the benefit of the Royal Exchequer. [WB 9/UD 14/GN 9/BH P]

3178 Hensman -- the grocer at Fenchurch St. Paul*. It is probably his son who is ill at the time of Sir Henry Thorpe's death. [NT 3]

3179 Henty -- George Alfred (1832-1902), an English author who is best remembered as a writer of boys' stories [WB 10]

3180 Hepplewater, Tasker -- a fictitious author [GN 11].

3181 "Her feet beneath her petticoat . . ." -- PW is quoting from Sir John Suckling's (1609-42) "Ballad: Upon a Wedding", stanza 8. The sentence quoted continues, "Like little mice stole in and out,/As if they feared the light". [BH 4]

3182 Her Grace -- the proper formal way to refer to the Duchess of Denver or to any other duchess [BH P]

3183 Her life has had some smatch of honor in it -- PW is referring to Aggie Twitterton's* having gotten HV's title right on the first try. He alludes to Julius Caesar, V, v, 45ff:
"Thou art a fellow of good respect;
Thy life hath had some smatch of
honor in it."
Brutus addresses Strato just before he has Strato help him commit suicide. [BH 2]

3184 Heraclitan universe -- a reference to the philosophy of Heraclitus of Ephesus (ca. 500 B. C.) who wrote, in Concerning Nature, that all things are in a state of flux and that the mind has a false perception of permanence in the world. His rather negative view of things led to his being called "the weeping philosopher". [GN 2]

3185 Herald -- officially the Daily Herald, a morning paper which contains a "rather ill-written" attack on the aristocracy which Bunter suggests that PW would enjoy because of its unconscious humor. The paper was founded in 1912, became the organ of the Labour Party and, in 1964, metamorphosed into a politically independent paper called The Sun. It was a part of the Odhams-Newnes Group of papers. [WB 5]

3186 heralds -- see College of Arms [CW 15]

3187 "Here we go round the mulberry bush . . ." -- PW refers to the nursery song [HHC 17]

3188 "Here we go round the prickly pear

. . ." -- the quotation is from T. S. Eliot's* "The Hollow Men", section V. It is Eliot's version of the preceeding entry. [BH 19]

3189 Hermitage -- a community in the Rhone valley of France known for its classic dark red wine. It is a blended wine, not produced from a single grape variety as are the Bordeaux and the Burgundies. With Chateauneuf-du-Pape it is the most important of the red wines of the Côtes-du-Rhone. [BH 17]

3190 heroin -- a powerful narcotic made from morphine, but more potent than the parent drug [MMA 11]

3191 Herrick, Robert -- an English poet (1591-1674) noted for the easy erudition and lightness of his verse. The title of one of his poems, "To Live Merrily, and to Trust to Good Verses", might easily be his motto. Perhaps his most famous poem is "To the Virgins, to Make Much of Time". [GN 16]

3192 Herridge, Mabel -- a friend of Nurse Booth's* who married and went to India. Her name is mentioned during two of the séances conducted by Miss Climpson*. [SP 17]

3193 Herriotting -- a community to the northeast of Little Doddering*. The name is a corruption of Margaretting, Essex, but Herriotting is fictitious. [bc]

3194 Herrogate Bros. -- a fictitious manufacturer of soaps; as given here, probably a typographical error for Harrogate*. [MMA 4]

3195 Hertfordshire -- see Herts. [BH E2]

3196 Herts. -- the official post office abbreviation for Hertfordshire, the county on London's northern border between Essex and Buckinghamshire [BC 18/BH P]

3197 Hesperides -- see except in the Hesperides [GN 12]

3198 Hewitt, Mr. -- an optician of Stapley* with whom William Grimethorpe* had done business [CW 11]

3199 hexameters [Latin] -- a line of poetry having six feet or divisions into which the line is broken when analyzing the pattern of stressed and unstressed syllables. [GN 8]

3200 Hide and Seek -- the ever-popular childrens' game where all but "It" hide. When the search begins, the first one found by "It", if "It" gets back to "home base" first, is the next "It". [np]

3201 "hides a multitude of sins" -- the line is from I Peter 4:8: "And above all things have fervent charity among yourselves: for charity shall cover the multitude of sins" [HHC 31]

3202 Higgins, Prof. -- an otherwise unidentified fictitious member of the faculty of an unnamed Oxford college. He likes HV's detective novels.

3203 the High -- High St., Oxford [GN 8]

3204 High [at the] -- see High Table [GN 2]

3205 High Altar -- the central altar in a church as opposed to any side altars such as might be found in a Lady Chapel* [UD 19]

3206 High Church -- those in the Church of England who put great emphasis on church authority and ritual, including all of the ornate robes and regalia [bc/CW 14/UD 19/SP 4/BH 5]

3207 High St. -- the main street in Kirkcudbright* [FRH 1]

3208 High St. -- the main street in Windle* [SP 16]

3209 High Table -- in most English college Common Rooms there is a dais across one end with a table set at right angles to those on the main floor at which are seated the dean or warden, senior dons, honored guests, etc., for meals and meetings; the head table [GN 2]

3210 High Wycombe -- a town on the A40 route to the East of the Chiltern Hills and just North of the Thames at a point roughly halfway between London and Oxford [GN 1]

3211 "Hikers' Column -- hiking was a national rage in England between the Wars and was in no way connected with hitchhiking as the true hiker would never "hitch" a ride. The column mentioned could have been any one of many that were popular at the time that

#3203 High St., Oxford, as PW would have known it during his college days.

offered hints on the care of equipment and people, the latest gadgetry, etc. [HHC 1]

3212 Hilary Term -- Hilar was a doctor of the Church and bishop of Poitiers who died in 367. His festival is January 13 in England and lends its name to a High Court session as well as to the university term at Oxford and elsewhere. The Quarter Sessions* are four times during the year when criminal charges are heard. [SP 5]

3213 Hilda -- the wife of Capt. Tommy Bates* [SP 12]

3214 Hill 60 -- a hill near Ypres* where Col. Marchbanks'* son was killed in WW I [BC 1]

3215 Hillside View -- the guest house where Miss Climpson* stays during her visit to Windle* [SP 16]

3216 Hillyard, Miss -- one of the dons at Shrewsbury College* who is not noted as being particularly alert to the emotional needs of others and who has achieved a certain notoriety for her dull lectures. See #1501. [GN 1]

3217 Himalayas -- the Asian mountain range extending along the Indo-Chinese border. Many of the world's highest peaks are located there. [SP 15]

3218 hinder bells -- those of deeper tone, the ones rung last if following through the scale from high to low tones [NT 1]

3219 Hinkins, Mr. -- the second cab driver to be interviewed by Mr. Murbles* and PW regarding General Fentiman's* movements on November 10th [BC 8]

3220 Hinkins, E. -- a churchwarden* at Fenchurch St. Paul* in 1887. He is remembered in the inscription on the number five bell there, Jubilee*. [NT 4]

3221 Hinkins, Joe [Joseph] -- the Venables'* gardener and general handyman. He rings the number five bell, Jubilee*, in the local change-ringing* group. He had been gardener's boy or helper at the Red House* at the time of the theft of the Wilbraham emeralds*. [NT 1]

3222 Hinks -- the Bible-reading scoundrel for whom Hinks's Lane* was named [HHC 12]

3223 Hinks's Lane -- a dirt lane not far from where Paul Alexis* was found dead and between that point and Wilvercombe* [HHC 10]

3224 Hinksey -- a suburb bordering on Oxford's southwest side [GN 21]

3225 hip-baths -- a small, portable bathtub that allows only partial submersion of the lower half of the body that provides a sort of glorified sponge-bath. They do not invite one to dawdle or luxuriate in their comfort. [BH 5]

3226 hip yoke -- an unpleated section of fabric fitted around the hips from the waist. To this is attached a skirt of some fullness, often pleated. The style was popular during the late 1920's and 30's and still appears from time to time in what is called a peasant skirt (variation). [GN 8]

3227 His Majesty -- George V, who ruled from 1910-36 [CW 12]

3228 His Majesty's bounty -- Cranton* is referring to his term of imprisonment, not to some sort of welfare [NT 10]

3229 His Majesty's coroners -- see coroner [BH 10]

3230 His Majesty's Mails -- the postal service was a governmental agency and, as such, was a service of the Crown [NT 7]

3231 hissing -- short for "hissing-stock", objects of scorn and derision. The term suggests something more extremely negative than "laughing-stock". [BH 13]

3232 <u>Historical Review</u> -- probably a reference to the <u>English Historical Review</u>. Under the entry heading, however, there is no journal which would relate to the material being considered. [GN 17]

3233 History first -- first class honors in some branch of history (ancient, medieval, modern, etc.), earned as a result of the exams taken for an Oxford or Cambridge B. A. degree [GN 7]

3234 <u>History of the Bells of Fenchurch</u>

St. Paul -- like the church, the book is fictitious [NT 2]

3235 Hitchcock, Louisa -- a parishoner at Fenchurch St. Paul* [NT 19]

3236 Hitlerite Berlin -- GN was written and published shortly after Hitler's assumption of power in Germany. HV's visit was slightly before. [GN 4]

3237 Hivites . . . Perizzites . . . Girgashites -- the names first appear in Genesis 10:16-17 and 13:7. The first reference is to the Hivites and Girgashites in the "begats". The Perizzites figure in the story of the separation of Abram and Lot. [BH E2]

3238 Ho Bryon -- Samuel Pepys'* phonetic spelling of Haut Brion* [UD 14]

3239 hoarding[s] -- any advertisement, etc., placed on a temporary fence used to enclose a construction site. The fence is called a hoarding, so the bills posted there assumed the name as well. Robert Duckworthy* was responsible for checking hoardings posted by Crichton's*, his employers. Hoardings, as fences, have a minor significance in the murderer's plottings in FRH. [im/FRH 28/MMA 21]

3240 hob, left on the -- to leave a pot or other utensil standing beside the coals or lit burner to keep warm. A hob is an iron plate attached to the grate of a fireplace on which such a pot can be left standing. [FRH 27/ SP 19]

3241 Hobart, Bobby -- a friend of Marjorie Phelps* who apparently fancies himself an artist but who, to use her word, "daubs" rather than paints [BC 10]

3242 Hobbs, Jack -- one of England's premier cricket* players (batsman) between the Wars. Sir John Berry Hobbs (1882-1963) commanded much attention in worldwide cricket circles from 1905 to 1934. He was a superlative batsman and a capable cover fieldsman. Queen Elizabeth II knighted him in 1953. [MMA 10]

3243 hobby-horse -- a toy horse in either of two configurations: one is the figure of a horse worn about the waist to give the appearance of a horse and rider, the other is a stick with a representation of a horse's head at one end. Both have reins to add to the illusion. Mr. Vibart* seems to have one of the latter to add to his costume as a polo* player. [qs]

3244 hobnailed liver -- a liver covered with hobnail-like lumps, the result of too much drink. HV is using the term to refer to a hangover and a cure for that malady. [GN 8]

3245 hock -- the English shortened form of the German Hochheimer; used to denote any Rhine wine, it does not apply to Moselles. Since Johannisbergers are not Moselles, but are Rieslings, they are also hocks. Hocks tend to be an "aristocratic" wine with a powerful bouquet and a full body. They vary widely in the degree of sweetness. [mt]

3246 Hodges, Mr. -- a student at Queen's College. See Oxford Colleges. [GN 8]

3247 Hodges, Mrs. -- the charlady who serves the office building occupied by Norman Urquhart's* law firm, among others [SP 14]

3248 Hodges, Mrs. -- a friend of Mrs. Ruddle's* at Paggleham* to whom Mrs. Ruddle goes to complain of PW's unusual behavior [BH 4]

3249 Hodges, Sir James -- until Hodges' death he was PW's physician, possibly a neurologist, and he treated PW's shell shock*. He is fictitious. [WB 11]

3250 Hodgson, Mr. -- a fictitious solicitor* of Leahampton* who handled Agatha Dawson's* legal affairs after she relieved Mr. Probyn* of that responsibility [UD 17]

3251 Hogarthian -- a reference to the drawings of William Hogarth (1697-1764), English painter and engraver known for such satirical and narrative endeavors as The Harlot's Progress, The Rake's Progress, etc. [SP 20]

3252 Hogben -- a farmer near Leamhurst* who, by virtue of his hay baler, knows most of the farmers in that area [HHC 22]

3253 Hoggarty, William -- a gardener to Sir Charles Deverill* [qs]

BRIBING A VOTER

(By Hogarth)

#3251

3254 hogged mane -- a short cut mane, often arranged to have what hair that remains stand erect [UD 12]

3255 The hoist with his own petard touch . . . -- the reference is to Hamlet, III, iv, 207. Hamlet switches letters with Rosencrantz and Guildenstern so they will be killed in his stead when they arrive in England. PW has in mind to accomplish much the same sort of thing with his two imposters when writing a letter admitting himself to the home of the Comte de Rueil*. A petard was a bomb or mine used to blow down castle walls and gates during sieges. [mt]

3256 Holborn -- a street beginning at New Oxford St. and ending at the Old Bailey* on the western perimeter of The City*; also, the area of London on either side of that street including the Inns of Court*. Many law offices are located there. [UD 17/SP 20/HHC 30]

3257 Holborn Empire -- the famous theatre located at 242 High Holborn until destroyed by bombs in 1941. It was a famous music hall that sometimes staged matinees. PW visited the Empire particularly to see performances by George Robey*, a famous comedian also mentioned by P. C. Burt*. Timothy Watchett* has promised to take his wife to that well-known Holborn landmark, but has not done so yet. [ie/hp/CW 11/GN 8]

3258 Holborn Tube Station -- the subway (underground) station at the southeast Corner of the intersection of Kingsway* and High Holborn* [MMA 4]

3259 hold no brief -- see brief [WB 6]

3260 hole and corner fashion -- done in secret, private; contemptuous of public knowledge [MMA 10]

3261 holiday -- vacation [CW 10]

3262 Holliday, Jackie and Fred -- children in the parish of Fenchurch St. Paul* who quarrelled in church over some prayer books they had been given [NT 9]

3263 Holliday, Emily -- the Venables'* maid. She has the distinction of being one of the two women who ever, to our knowledge, cause Bunter to lose his temper. She is a niece of Bob Russell's* and a distant relative of Mary Russell Thoday's*. [NT 1]

3264 Holliday, Miss Evelyn -- a parishoner at Fenchurch St. Paul* [NT 19]

3265 Holliday, Obadiah -- a parishoner at Fenchurch St. Paul* [NT 19]

3266 "Hollow, hollow, hollow . . ." -- from Tennyson's "The Passing of Arthur", the concluding idyll of The Idylls of the King. The reference is to line 37, but ll. 30-37 explain the allusion. The words are part of what Sir Gawain's ghost shreiks in Arthur's dream before the last battle when all but Arthur, Bedivere, and Mordred are killed. Arthur then kills Mordred, Bedivere throws Excalibur into the lake, and then Arthur is carried off to Avalon. All of this is related by Sir Bedivere who is the last of Arthur's knights to survive. [SP 20]

3267 "The Hollow Men" -- see T. S. Eliot [BH 19]

3268 Holloway Gaol -- opened in 1853 as a home for waywards and had both male and female residents until 1903. Other than Ruth Ellis, the last woman to be hanged in England, the most famous resident of the place is HV. The prison is on Parkhurst Rd., Holloway, two miles due North of Bloomsbury*. [SP 4]

3269 Holmes, Sherlock -- certainly the best known and perhaps greatest of all the fictional detectives. An invention of Sir Arthur Conan Doyle*, Holmes has been the model against which all subsequent amateur detectives have been judged. While Edgar Allan Poe* may have invented the detective story, Doyle, through Holmes, made it the popular literary form it is today. PW frequently alludes to or quotes from the Holmes canon, and Dr. Watson is mentioned often as well. It is obvious that PW enjoys and relates to the adventures of "the Master" fictional detective. [passim]

3270 Holport -- a fictitious fen-town to the North of Fenchurch St. Paul* [NT 2]

3271 Holt's Ten-part Peal -- a peal* as composed by John Holt (1726-56), a prolific composer of peals and a leader

in their ringing. He was particularly fond of the Grandsire* methods and the peal mentioned here is Grandsire Triples done in ten parts of five courses to each part. [NT 2]

3272 Holy Grail -- the cup used by Jesus at the Last Supper and the elusive goal of the quest by King Arthur's knights (Galahad, Percival, and Bors) [BC 13]

3273 Holy Relic -- any part of or possession of a saint or holy person that remains after that person's death or canonization. Especially venerated are items in any way associated with martyrs. Martha* relies on one. [ie]

3274 Holy Season -- Eastertime, the holiest and most significant of the Christian religious seasons [ie]

3275 Holy Sepulchre -- the tomb belonging to Joseph of Arimathea where Jesus was buried for the time between His Crucifixion on Good Friday and His Resurrection on Easter Sunday. As the Dowager Duchess* is uncertain just what she has in mind here, it is difficult to ascertain her thoughts. None of the gospels mentions specifically any reference to stars in relation to the Holy Sepulchre, so whatever it is she has in mind (fuzzily), it is either the invention of later authors or is a total bit of confusion on her part. [BH P]

3276 Holywell -- a street in central Oxford, an extension of Broad St. and, after a ninety degree turn to the South, it becomes Longwall St. [GN 9]

3277 Home and Colonial -- a chain of grocery stores now owned by Allied Suppliers who also now own Lipton's, the Home and Colonial's major competition. The chain was begun by Julius Drew in 1878 to eliminate the middleman and prospered until after WW II. Drew retired at age thirty-three to build himself a Norman castle, Castle Drogo, in Devonshire. Drew was a descendant of the knight Dru or Drogo who came to England with William the Conqueror. [BH 4]

3278 Home Office -- the office headed by the Home Secretary* [BC 11]

3279 Home page -- that part of the paper dealing with national news rather than international or local news [MMA 4]

3280 Home Rule -- the rule of a geographical entity by the people who live there although it may be short of complete sovereignty. Foreign affairs and defense are usually reserved by the sovereign power. It was offered to Ireland by Great Britain, but was rejected by Ulster. [FRH 1]

3281 Home Secretary -- the Secretary of State for Home (i. e. internal) Affairs. He advises the sovereign on domestic matters and administers the prisons, police, registration of aliens and the care of children, among other duties. [WB 12]

3282 Home Students -- fully, the Society of Oxford Home-Students, set up in 1879 under the aegis of the Association for the Education of Women in Oxford to provide for those women who arrived at Oxford to study without having a link with a college or a residential hall. The Society became St. Anne's Society in 1942, a College in 1952, and became fully accredited in 1959. [GN 2]

3283 Homer -- the Greek poet and author of The Iliad and The Odyssey. PW declaims passages from the former, the history of the Trojan War, to support his guise as a wizard. [ie]

3284 Homer nods -- see Bally old Homer nodding [BH 5]

3285 Homer's Catalogue of the Ships -- referred to by PW, the passage is in The Iliad, book ii, ll. 484-785, and is exactly that, a list of the Greek ships that set out against Troy, who commanded them, etc. [ie]

3286 Hong Kong -- the British Crown Colony on the southeast coast of China opposite the southern tip of Taiwan. The present colony dates, as a colony, from 1843, but acquisition of the island came in 1841. Kowloon Peninsula was added in 1860, and other areas were added in 1898. A "Crown Colony" is one that is unable to exist independently and is governed through the Foreign Office* directly from England. Other Crown Colonies include Gibraltar and the Falkland Islands. [NT 6]

3287 Honor Mods -- the mods* exam taken in anticipation of special recognition in one's academic field. The exam is beyond that required for a B. A. degree. [GN 7]

3288 hood [academic] -- the decorative "collar" that is suspended from the neck down the wearer's back. The colors and trimmings on it identify the college or university that conferred the degree and the academic area in which the degree was granted. The hood's length and ornateness indicate the degree: three feet for a bachelor, three and a half feet for a master, and four feet for a doctor. These modern hoods, while no longer resembling their ancestors to any great extent, are direct descendants of the hoods on a monk's habit and were formerly used as umbrellas, sun shades, or book bags as need required. [GN 1/BH 19]

3289 hood [of a car] -- in England, the convertible top of a car. The covering over the engine compartment would be the bonnet. [NT 18]

3290 Hoogstraten, Samuel Dircksz van -- a Dutch painter (1627-78) of Rembrandt's school who was also interested in trompe l'oeil (deceptive two-dimensional paintings with amazing three-dimensional properties), and perspective or peep-show boxes. His works are on display at London's National Gallery* and elsewhere. [hp]

3291 hook round to leg -- see cricket [MMA 18]

3292 hoop -- a metal or wooden circle of varying sizes, probably originally a barrel hoop, rooled along the street and pushed and controlled by a stick held by a child who runs alongside. The trick is to keep the hoop moving fast enough to prevent its falling over without getting it going so fast that it goes out of control. [NT 5]

3293 Hope-Wilmington Case -- see The Society [ab]

3294 Hopkins -- a police constable from Leahampton* who assists with the investigation of Vera Findlater's* murder [UD 20]

3295 Hopkins, Gerard Manley -- English Victorian poet (1844-89), a graduate, like PW, of Balliol*. His poetry is marked by a strongly religious flavor resulting from his conversion to the Church of Rome in 1866. [GN 10]

3296 Horace -- Quintus Horatius Flaccus (65-8 B. C.), one of the great Augustan poets and author of various odes, satires, and epistles. He is remembered also by modern critics for his Ars Poetica. His satire is of the gentler sort as opposed to the more vicious satires of Juvenal. His influence on English poetry is so pervasive as to be hard to judge. [BH 8]

3297 Hordell -- a physician called in by Dr. Baines* to assist in the treatment of Sir Henry Thorpe* [NT 3]

3298 horizontal rule -- a rule for the placement of letters in or reading them from a Playfair cipher. The rule stipulates that letters being enciphered that fall in the same row as the same letter in the enciphering grid are replaced by the letter to the right. [HHC 28]

3299 Hornby, Mr. -- one of the employees at Pym's Publicity* [MMA 6]

3300 Horner, Dr. -- Sir James Lubbock's* assistant [BC 13]

3301 Horrocks -- the male secretary and resident Cerberus* in the office of Isaac Sullivan*. He keeps a humorous running battle going with Insp. Umpelty* over whether the Insp. will ever get to see Sullivan. [HHC 23]

3302 Horrocks, Gladys -- Mr. Thipps's* servant girl who left the bathroom window open thus allowing someone to deposit a nude corpse in the bathtub [WB 1]

3303 Horseshoe Pass -- in North Wales just above Llangollen on the A542 route. The name accurately describes the torturous twist the road must take to clear the obstacles in the terrain. [UD 2]

3304 "horti conclusi, fontes signati" -- this reference, cited by John Donne in the quotation on the title page of the novel, is from the Song of Songs (or Solomon), 4:12, in the Vulgate version. In the KJV it is given as: "A garden inclosed [the Hebrew is "barred"] is my sister, my spouse; a spring shut up, a fountain sealed."

[GN 13]

3305 the Hospital -- see St. Luke's Hospital [WB 1]

3306 Host -- or host, the bread used in the Sacrament of Communion [UD 19]

3307 hot toddy -- a hot drink of sugar, spices, water and some sort of alcoholic beverage such as rum or whiskey. Properly prepared they are very good and will do wonders for insomnia victims. [NT 10]

3308 Hotel Bellevue -- see Bellevue [HHC 11]

3309 Hotel Gigantic -- while there may be such a hotel "somewhere-or-other on the Continent", the context suggests that neither HV nor PW had a particular hotel in mind [BH 2]

3310 Hôtel Meurice -- a deluxe Paris hotel at 228 Rue de Rivoli. It has 212 rooms, most with bath, and is called the hôtel of kings because so many have stayed there. It is opposite the Jardin des Tuileries and is between the Rue Castiglione and the Rue D'Alger. [CW 1/BC 13]

3311 Hôtel Saumon d'or -- the Golden Salmon Hotel at the Plâce de la Madeleine in Verneuil-sur-Eure*, France. It is the destination marked on the luggage of one of the PW look-alikes. As of this writing it is still open. [nt]

3312 Houdin, M. duBois-Gobey -- a witness at the trial of the Duke of Denver* who remembers a card sharping* incident involving Denis Cathcart* and himself [CW 15]

3313 hough -- Scots dialect for the shin or lower leg of beef cattle, used mainly for stewing or as flavoring for stocks and soups. It would be called the shank in the U. S. [FRH 5]

3314 Hound of Heaven -- the reference is to Francis Thompson's poem (1893), a richly exotic work telling of a soul's flight from God. O'Conor's A Study of Francis Thompson's "Hound of Heaven" (1912, p. 7) states, "As the hound follows the hare, never ceasing in its running, ever drawing nearer in the chase . . . so does God follow the fleeing soul by his [sic] Divine grace." [MMA 20]

3315 "hounds of spring" -- a reference to Algernon Charles Swinburne's (1837-1909) Atalanta in Calydon, a verse drama in the fashion of ancient Greece. The lines cited are from an early chorus and honors Atalanta as "Maiden most perfect, lady of light . . .", another accurate clue of things to come. [CW 4]

3316 houri[s] -- a Persian word that made its way into English by way of the French. It refers to the beautiful maidens who provide one of the pleasures of the Moslem paradise. PW's sofa in his library is described as suggesting the embrace of these lovely creatures. [WB 2/MMA 3]

3317 House -- the House of Commons. See Parliament, Houses of [BH E1]

3318 house [get in to the last] -- a phrase used to mean becoming a part of the audience for the last show at a theatre [im]

3319 House blazer -- the jacket denoting membership of a particular college, in this case of Christ Church College, known colloquially as "The House". It would have a crest or badge of the college on the pocket. [GN 18]

3320 House [kitchen] -- [the kitchen of] Christ Church College, Oxford [CW 1/GN 9]

3321 The House of Exile -- see Waln, Nora [NT 7]

3322 House of Commons -- see Commons, House of; Terrace, House of Commons; and Parliament, Houses of [MMA 10]

3323 House of Lords -- see Lords, House of; peers, trial by, and Parliament, Houses of [CW 11/NT 11]

3324 the House of Lords made the gesture of stooping to conquer -- a reference to the efforts in May and June of 1927 to once again "reform" the House of Lords to further limit and control that House. The reform measures were not accepted. [UD 19]

3325 House of Lords' veto -- the Duchess of Medway* says that all sense went out of society with the Parliament Act of 1911 which, for all time,

took from the House of Lords the absolute veto power it had held over all legislation originated in the Commons. [aq]

3326 "Household Column" -- Aunt Beatrice's fictitious helpful hints column in the Daily Messenger* [GN 3]

3327 Household Gods -- for an explanation of this chapter title, see both Lares and Penates [BH 4]

3328 Houses of Parliament -- see Parliament [CW 19]

3329 Housman, A[lfred] E[dward] -- English poet and classical scholar (1859-1936) at Cambridge University. His lyrics are noted for their economy and simplicity. He is most remembered for A Shropshire Lad* (1896). [SP 20/ BH E3]

3330 Housman, L[aurence] -- English novelist, dramatist, and artist (1865-1959), brother of A. E. Housman*. He is famous for his highly acclaimed plays grouped under the title Victoria Regina. [UD 15]

3331 "How all occasions do inform against me!" -- "And spur my dull revenge!" The speech is Hamlet's from IV, iv, 32-3. [GN 3]

3332 "How are the mighty fallen!" -- PW is quoting II Samuel 1:19 and 1:23, the story of Saul and Jonathan [GN 17]

3333 "how doth my lady? What, sweeting . . ." -- PW quotes Petruchio in IV, iii, 36 of Shakespeare's The Taming of the Shrew. "How fares my Kate? What, sweeting, all amort?" It is an interesting choice of plays and characters for PW to use to address HV. "Amort" means depressed. [GN 21]

3334 "How I despise . . ." -- the opening lines of a soliloquy spoken by Isbrand immediately after the exit of Siegfried in T. L. Beddoes' Death's Jest Book**, V, ii, 46-7. The lines are usually given as:

"How I despise
All you mere men of muscle!"

[HHC 12]

3335 "How many leagues to Babylon?" -- or:

"How many miles to Babylon?
Threescore miles and ten."

These are the first two lines of a song in the 1805 Songs for the Nursery. [HHC 16]

3336 How's that? -- see cricket [MMA 18]

3337 "'How wonderful,' says the poet . . ." -- the line is from Percy Shelley's* The Daemon of the World, I, i, or Queen Mab, I, i. [GN 15]

3338 howd toong -- Yorkshire dialect for hold your tongue [CW 12]

3339 "However entrancing it is to wander . . ." -- PW has quoted exactly from "The Story of Hien" in The Golden Hours of Kai Lung by Ernest Bramah [Smith]. See also Wallet of Kai Lung. [BH 7]

3340 Hubbard -- a person prevented from praying over Squire Burdock's* coffin as he was locked in the church's furnace room. He is the publican at the Red Cow*. [bc]

3341 Hubbard, Jane -- daughter of John Hubbard* and Philip Boyes's* grandmother [SP 11]

3342 Hubbard, John -- the common ancestor of Philip Boyes* and Norman Urquhart*. See Ch. 11 of SP for genealogical details. [SP 11]

3343 Hubbard, Mary -- daughter of John Hubbard* and ancestor of Norman Urquhart* [SP 11]

3344 Hubbard, Rosanna -- the maiden name of Rosanna Wrayburn* who is also Cremorna Garden*. She is great aunt to Norman Urquhart* and Philip Boyes*. [SP 11]

3345 Hubert, Sir -- a character in Thomas Morton's (1764?-1838) comedy, A Cure for the Heartache (1797). The phrase HV uses is, in its context, "Approbation from Sir Hubert Stanley is praise indeed." [GN 15]

3346 Hudibras -- a satire written in octosyllabic couplets. It is divided into three sections, each section consisting of three cantos. The story is incomplete, so it is likely that Butler* intended to write at least one more section. The satire is set up as a mock-heroic poem modelled after Don Quixote. The poem's purpose is to ridicule the hypocrisy of the Presbyterians and Independents which it does

quite thoroughly. [UD 5]

3347 Hudson, Miss -- a student at Shrewsbury College* [GN 5]

3348 hue and cry -- the great noise and fuss generated by the open public search for felons, formerly required by law in that if one heard such a search going on, one was obligated to join and help. A comic, almost fairy-tale version of a hue and cry is found in Thomas Hardy's short story, "The Three Strangers". [UD 20/FRH 9]

3349 Hughie -- the "idiot great-nephew" of Mirabelle, Countess of Severn and Thames*, who "bungled" a gentlemanly attempt at divorce [BH P]

3350 Huitres Musgrave -- oysters baked with bacon and served with a lemon wedge. It is the appetizer part of the dinner PW has with Ann Dorland*. [BC 21]

3351 Hull -- officially the city's name is Kingston-upon-Hull. It is England's third largest port after London and Liverpool, and is northeast England's main port, at the confluence of the rivers Humber and Hull. [NT 6]

3352 Humber -- a brand of bicycle first manufactured in the 1870's. It is no longer made. [FRH 10]

3353 Hume, Tobias -- see "Fain would I change that note . . ." [GN 19]

3354 humpty -- a plump, soft, floor cushion, stuffed seat, or large pillow used for sitting or as a footstool. They are also called "dumpties" by association. [GN 17]

3355 Humpty-Dumpty's method -- the allusion is to Ch. 6 of Through the Looking Glass by Lewis Carroll. Alice is talking with the famous egg and he's always one or two answers behind her questions. The conversational style is unique, but makes sense after a while. [HHC 16]

3356 hunchback in the story -- Quasi modo is the hunchbacked character in The Hunchback of Notre Dame by Victor Hugo. He is a bell-ringer who lives in the towers and on the parapets of the great cathedral. One is struck by the analogy of the Quasimodo, Esmerelda, Frollo, and Phoebus love interest in that great novel with the Freke*, Levy*, Ford* confusions in WB. However, Freke lacks Quasimodo's virtue. [WB 13]

3357 "A hundred years hence, or, it may be, more." -- the speech is Isbrand's in V, iv, 267-8, of T. L. Beddoes' Death's Jest Book**. Isbrand has usurped Duke Melveric's throne and has, in turn, been stabbed by one of Melveric's followers, thus restoring Melveric to the throne of the duchy. The lines are part of Isbrand's death speech. [HHC 32]

3358 hunt -- see hunting course [NT 2]

3359 Hunt Ball -- a dance held by a fox hunting society (called a Hunt) for members and their guests. Fox hunting is a popular sport in all parts of Great Britain and Ireland. [MMA 3]

3360 hunt the slipper -- a game wherein "It" tosses a slipper into a circle of players saying "Cobbler, cobbler, mend my shoe. Have it done by half past two." The players then hide the slipper, passing it amongst themselves while "It" tries to guess who has it. When he or she is successful, the person caught holding the shoe becomes "It" for the next round. [np]

3361 Hunter, Sir Henry -- a friend of Mr. Mellilow*, and one who is opposed to Mr. Creech's* plans for electrification of the area [sf]

3362 hunting course -- to alter the position of a bell in successive changes so that its position is moved from first to last or from last to first (hunting up or down). If a ring of four bells is in use, plain hunting would be:

1 2 3 4
2 1 4 3
2 4 1 3
4 2 3 1

The shifting of the first bell would continue until it was back ringing in the first place. [NT 2]

3363 hunting up [down] -- see hunting course [NT 2]

3364 Huntingdon -- now a part of Cambridgeshire, Huntingdon was a county town on the Great Ouse (see Ouse) of some antiquity. Oliver Cromwell* was born there, his record of baptism being at All Saints' Church. The grammar school that he and Samuel

Pepys attended is now a Cromwell museum. [BH E2]

3365 Huntingdonshire -- formerly an English county centered on the town of Huntingdon*. The county was absorbed by Cambridgeshire during the reorganization of local government in the 1970's. [HHC 12]

3366 hurdles -- a temporary length of fence resembling a farm gate used to set up pastures or to form safety barriers where permanent fencing is not needed. They are often of woven sticks and twigs. One is used as a stretcher for the body found in Lady Thorpe's* grave. [CW 4/NT 3]

3367 Hurley, Kate -- one of Nurse Booth's* college friends at the Maidstone Ladies College*. The name is mentioned during the séance conducted by Miss Climpson*. [SP 17]

3368 Hurlford -- now a suburb of Kilmarnock to the North and East of Ayr*, and formerly a stop on the rail line from Dumfries* to Glasgow* [FRH 10]

3369 Huxley, Julian -- English essayist and zoologist (b. 1887), brother of Aldous Huxley. Among other things, he is the author of Essays of a Biologist and What Dare I Think. [BC 18]

3370 Hybla honey -- particularly fine honey from the town of Hybla in Sicily [BC 10]

3371 "Hybrias the Cretan" -- a once popular ballad by J. W. Elliot. While perhaps "strong, he-man stuff", it was appropriate for the audience and seems rather tame by contemporary standards. [BH 5]

3372 Hyde Park -- annexed and created as a royal park by Henry VIII and improved by Elizabeth I, it was opened as a public park in the 17th C. It is the largest of London's three major parks: Hyde, Regent's, and Green/St. James's. Hyde Park continues into Kensington Gardens with the famous statue of Peter Pan, and includes the Serpentine*, a large lake, riding paths, and the famous shrine of free speech, Speakers' Corner. [im/CW 4/UD 5/HHC 30]

3373 Hyde Park Corner -- the southeast corner of Hyde Park*, closest to Green Park* and Buckingham Palace* [WB 4/CW 8/MMA 20]

3374 hydra[s] -- a mythological monster of Greek legend. It had at least nine heads, but if one were cut off, two more would grow in its place. It lived near Lake Lerna in the Peloponnese. Hercules, with the help of Iolaus, killed it as one of his twelve labors. [BH 1]

3375 hydrocyanic acid [gas] -- also known as prussic acid when in solution with water, it is extremely toxic, condenses to an unstable liquid at 25.6°C, is flammable in the air, and may explode. It is loosely referred to as cyanide [gas]. [BC 15/UD 19]

3376 hydros -- hotels that offer water baths or cures, mineral water drinks, etc.; a spa [UD 3]

3377 Hymn 373 -- in Hymns Ancient and Modern (see Hymns A&M) the cited hymn is a setting for William Cowper's "God moves in a mysterious way"* [NT 5]

3378 Hymns A & M -- Hymns Ancient and Modern. From its appearance in 1861, the standard Church of England hymnal; by 1950, one-hundred million copies had been sold. A second edition appeared in 1904 and various supplements and emendations have appeared regularly. [NT 4]

3379 hyoscine -- also known as scopalomine, it is extracted from plants such as henbane and is used as a truth serum, sedative, etc. It is thick, colorless, and has a syrupy consistency. It works slowly, but a sufficiently large dosage would be fatal. [te/SP 8]

3380 hypertrophy -- exaggerated growth or development. The word usually applies to limbs or organs, but PW applies it to his imagination [bc]

3381 Hypnerotomachia -- the full title is Hypnerotomachia Poliphili (The Dream of Poliphilo, and allegorical novel by Francesco Colonna, written in 1467 and printed in Venice in 1499 by the famous Aldus Manutius. The quality of the printing plus the 192 woodcuts makes the book one of the major later works of incunabula* and a prize

Scale of ½ Mile

Hyde Park and Kensington Gardens.

#3372-3

for any serious collector of such works as PW is. PW bids on it just to force Skrymes* to overbid and, thereby, to fleece himself. As PW already had a copy, he had no need for the one Skrymes wanted, but enjoyed a touch of sheer perversity for the fun of it. [ss]

3382 hypo -- see hyposulfite [qs]

3383 hypodermic -- PW alludes to Sherlock Holmes's sometime practice of injecting a solution of cocaine to help himself while away the hours between cases when his mind did not have the proper stimulation [HHC 4]

3384 hypostasis -- the settling of blood in the various parts and organs of the body after death [BH 12]

3385 hyposulfite -- or sodium thiosulfate, a photographic fixing agent also called hypo. It is white, translucent, and crystalline until mixed with water. [fr]

(I)

3386 I agree with Dryden -- see Dryden, John, and Johnson, Samuel [BH 1]

3387 I am as black as Belloc's scorpion -- see Belloc's scorpion [BH 2]

3388 I am coming, my own, my sweep. PW plays loose with Tennyson's* Maud, Part I, "She is coming, my own, my sweet." His choice is, perhaps, encouraged by the garden setting he shares with HV and the similar setting in Tennyson's poem. [BH 4]

3389 I am no orator as Bunter is -- PW alludes to Julius Caesar, III, ii, 221ff. The line is Mark Antony's and refers to Brutus's earlier speech over Caesar's body. [BH 3]

3390 "I am the Queen Aholibah" -- see Aholibah [BH 16]

3391 "I am tame; pronounce" -- this is Hamlet's (III, ii, 322) and is, fully, "I am tame, sir: pronounce" and is addressed to Guildenstern in a mocking way just as PW's eyes mock HV [GN 15]

3392 "I am the Resurrection and the Life" -- from John 11:25, part of the usual service of the Burial of the Dead and alluded to in the committal of the body to the ground in that service in The Book of Common Prayer [NT 5]

3393 "I am striving to take into public life . . ." -- see Lady Astor. This is typical of Lady Astor's blunt public comments. [CW 6]

3394 "I attempt from Love's Fever to Fly" -- a song by Henry Purcell* from the semi-opera The Indian Queen (Z630), first performed in London's Drury Lane Theatre in 1695. [CW 4]

3395 "I [have] been a-courtin' Mary Jane . . ." -- the first reference to Ilkley Moor, a real place in Yorkshire near the town of Ilkley. The song, an adaptation of the hymn tune "Cranbrook", is something of a "national song" in Yorkshire. Mary Jane was in the first choir to sing it. [CW 12]

3396 "I can't get out, said the starling . . ." -- PW quotes Laurence

Sterne's (1713-68) A Sentimental Journey, "The Passport. The Hotel at Paris": "'I can't get out, I can't get out', said the starling." [BH E3]

3397 I can't overthrow cities and burn the population -- Parker's* reminder to PW about the limitations of police work are reminiscent of the Assyrian King Ashurnasirpal II (883-859 B. C.) who laid waste to conquered lands and destroyed populations with the relentless savagery of a sadistic fury. [MMA 15]

3398 "I could not love thee, Bob . . ." -- the line is from Richard Lovelace's (1618-58) poem, "To Lucasta, Going to the Wars", and is correctly written as:

"I could not love thee (Dear) so much,
Lov'd I not Honour more."

[FRH 13]

3399 I didn't examine them, à la Dr. Thorndyke . . . -- HV is alluding to R. Austin Freeman's* Dr. Thorndyke* short story, "The Apparition of Burling Court". The clear glass will simply allow the candle flame to appear right side up while a lens will invert the image as in a camera. [HHC 9]

3400 "I dwell among the untrodden ways . . ." -- PW is paraphrasing Wordsworth's* poem "She Dwelt Among the Untrodden Ways". That poem, one of the six "Lucy" poems, opens:

"She dwelt among the untrodden ways
Beside the springs of Dove
A maid whom there were none to praise
And very few to love;"

The poem concludes with:

"She lived unknown and few could know
When Lucy ceased to be;
But she is in her grave, and oh,
The difference to me!"

The passage is a perfect foreshadowing of Bertha Gotobed's* fate. [UD 6]

3401 "I followed the gleam." -- Bunter is paraphrasing Tennyson's* poem, "Merlin and the Gleam", lines 9-10:

"I am Merlin
Who follow the Gleam."

However, Bunter might very well have had the poem's third stanza in mind:

"A demon vexed me,
The light retreated,
The landskip darkened,
The melody deadened,
The Master whispered,
'Follow the Gleam.'"

We must assume that Bunter uses "gleam" to refer to any elusive goal, and not as Tennyson intended the usage. [UD 11]

3402 I gloat, as Stalky says. -- a reference to Rudyard Kipling's* Stalky and Co., Ch. 1, wherein appears the line, "I gloat! Hear me gloat!" [FRH 13]

3403 I had served nearly seven years -- Freddy Arbuthnot* is alluding to Genesis 29:20 specifically, and to Genesis 29:1 to 31:10, the story of Jacob's years at Haran with Laban, his marriage with Leah and Rachel, and his trials during that time. The cited passage is: "And Jacob served seven years for Rachel; and they seemed unto him but a few days, for the love he had to her." The story shows the severe discipline and covetousness to which Jacob was subjected by Laban as a method of purging from Jacob one undesireable element of his character to purify it and to teach him to rely on simple faith in the love of God. As Jacob had no "bride price" to pay Laban, he offered to work seven years for her hand in marriage. [SP 12]

3404 I happened to find out that a young woman . . . -- PW summarizes the plot of UD [GN 17]

3405 "I have fought with the beasts at Ephesus . . ." -- the line is from I Corinthians 15:32 and deals with the order of resurrections [NT 5]

3406 I have locked my heart in a silver box . . . -- this is PW's version of some lines from an anonymous ballad called "Waly, Waly", and is usually presented as:

"I had lock'd my heart in a caseo' gowd,
An pinn'd it wi' a siller pin."

[SP 3]

3407 I hope your rabbit dies. -- it is unclear what PW might have in mind with this comment, but he is certainly being inconsequential and it has nothing to do with pregnancy tests as, under the circumstances, that sort of thing would not have been mentioned, even jokingly [HHC 12]

3408 I know a man's a man for a' that

-- the reference is to Robert Burns's poem, "For a' that and a' that". The phrase appears, beginning at "a man's", exactly as PW says it and also appears fragmentally throughout the poem as a sort of refrain. [MMA 13]

3409 "I know not whether . . ." -- the passage is the first four lines of a fragment of poetry entitled "Evening Brook" by T. L. Beddoes*. The last two lines are:
"When the least moon has silver on't
no larger
Than the pure white of Hebe's
pinkish nail."
[HHC 28]

3410 "I know not why I am so sad." -- the full line is: "In sooth I know not why I am so sad", I, i, 1 of The Merchant of Venice*. See also "But how I caught it . . ." [MMA 13]

3411 "I know thou art religious . . ." from Titus Andronicus, V, i, 74-7. The lines are spoken by the Moor, Aaron. The play was first performed in 1594, and Shakespeare's part in its authorship is uncertain. The play is one of revenge by Andronicus for the atrocities committed against his daughter, Lavinia. The speech is part of Aaron's dialogue with Lucius, a son to Titus, which concerns oaths and their keeping. [UD 22]

3412 "I know two things about a horse . . ." -- an anonymous author in The Week-End Book is attributed with:
"I know two things about a horse,
And one of them is rather coarse."
[HHC 16]

3413 "I know what is and what has been" -- see "In the Room" [BH 7]

3414 I see nothing at all. -- the allusion is to the Sherlock Holmes canon, "The Adventure of the Devil's Foot", from His Last Bow. Dr. Leon Sterndale, in response to the news that Holmes had followed him, says, "I saw no one." To that Holmes replies, "That is what you may expect to see when I follow you." A great "Sherlockismus". [SP 20]

3415 "I sing but as the throstle sings . . ." -- PW responds to a compliment about his storytelling abilities with this quote from J. W. von Goëthe's romance, Wilhelm Meister's Apprenticeship. In Thomas Carlyle's translation the verse is:
"I sing but as the linnet sings,
That on the green bough dwelleth,
A rich reward his music brings
As from his heart it swelleth . . ."
The song is sung by an elderly harp player who composed the song to earn a glass of wine. PW seems content with the praise his story brings. Similar lines also appear in Goëthe's "Der Sänger". [nf]

3416 "I tell thee all, I can no more." -- HV is alluding to Lewis Carroll's Through the Looking Glass, Ch. 8, where the line appears as, "I give the all, I can no more." Alice is alluding to Thomas More's love lyric, "My Heart and Lute", which begins, "I give thee all--I can no more--". PW uses the line as well. [HHC 4/NT 15]

3417 "I thank goodness and the grace . . ." -- the verse continues:
"And made me, in these Christian
days,
A happy English child."
The lines are from a hymn entitled "A Child's Hymn of Praise" and is from Hymns for Infant Minds by Ann and Jane Taylor, and dates from the early 1800's. [WB 3]

3418 "I think it was the cat" -- from Act II of H. M. S. Pinafore* by Gilbert and Sullivan. The line, "It was the cat!", is spoken by Dick Deadeye as Ralph Rackstraw, the able seaman, is about to elope with Josephine, Capt. Corcoran's daughter. [CW 5]

3419 "I think we must ask for amnesty in that direction" -- Sherlock Holmes actually says, "We must have an amnesty in that direction, I think," in the last paragraph of "Silver Blaze" [GN 8]

3420 "I thought as much,/It was a little--window cleaner." -- the reference is apparently to a duet between Patience and Angela from Act I of Gilbert and Sullivan's comic opera Patience, wherein the second verse of the item quoted appears as, "He was a little boy!" [fr]

3421 "I thought so once, but now I know it." -- PW is quoting the

second (last) line of John Gay's (1685-1732) "My Own Epitaph":

"Life is a jest; and all things show it.
I thought so once; but now I know it." [BH 14]

3422 "I want to be happy" -- the first line of the chorus of the song by the same name. The first line of the song is, "I'm a very ordinary man." The song appeared in the 1925 production of No, No, Nanette, and was composed by Vincent Youmans with lyrics by Irving Caesar. Youmans is perhaps more famous for "Tea for Two". [np]

3423 "I weep for you the Walrus said . . ." -- PW is quoting from Lewis Carroll's poem, "The Walrus and the Carpenter", found in Ch. 4 of Through the Looking Glass:

"'I weep for you,' the Walrus said:
'I deeply sympathize.'
With sobs and tears he sorted out
Those of largest size,
Holding his pocket-handerchief
Before his streaming eyes."

This is all the Walrus's carrying-on as he sets out to eat the oysters he invited along. [UD 8]

3424 "I weep, I know not why." -- this line is a misquotation that should read, "To weep, yet scarce know why . . ." and is from Thomas Moore's (1779-1852) poem, "The Blue Stocking, VI" in his Miscellaneous Poems. The full citation is:

"To sigh, yet feel no pain;
To weep, yet scarce know why;
To sport an hour with Beauty's chain,
Then throw it idly by." [MMA 19]

3425 "I will be bloody, bold and resolute . . ." -- less the "I will", the line was first spoken by the second apparition in Macbeth, IV, i, 79, as Macbeth watches. To have Queen Victoria use the same phrase seems out of character for her. Certainly no such utterance is credited to her that could be found. More than likely, PW is relying on that old stalwart of sexual innuendo and the beginning of any number of jokes, "As the actress said to the bishop . . .". [UD 19]

3426 "I will be good." -- PW echoes the words of Queen Victoria when, as Princess Victoria, she spoke those famous words to her tutor, Baroness Lehzen. The date was March 11, 1830, and the comment came when she first realized how close she was to the throne and how important her lessons were and would be. The statement is in reference to her continued effort to do well with her studies, but is especially significant in what it foretells of her character and of her resolve to do well in general. The Viscount St. George* uses the sentence too, but one is suspicious of his sincerity if he was conscious of the quote. [FRH 26/GN 18]

3427 "I'd have it be understood . . ." -- PW is quoting a bell motto dating from 1782 that is on "the treble [bell] of the parish church, Buckingham," according to John Camp's Bell Ringing. The motto is also quoted in Arthur L. Humphreys' The House, The Garden, The Steeple (1906). [NT 1]

3428 "I'd rather be alive than not." -- a popular idea expressed variously, but DLS seems to have been in error when she attributed the line to G. K. Chesterton*. It is actually from Graham R. Tomson's (the pen name of Rosamund Marriott Watson) "The Optimist" where it functions as the last line of each of the poem's four stanzas. DLS has altered the line to fit the circumstances as the original is, "We'd rather be alive than not." [FRH 15]

3429 I'll go no more a-sleuthing -- this is PW's version of "A-roving, a-roving"* [HHC 31]

3430 I'll have to come clean . . . -- an excruciatingly poor attempt at humor, but interesting for the reference to "patent washer". It is to be remembered that in 1930, even wringer washers were relatively scarce in much of the world, the automatic washer, as known today, as yet uninvented. [NT 10]

3431 "I'll talk a word with this same learnèd Theban." -- the line is Lear's from the famous "mad scene" of King Lear, III, iv, 162. [BH 18]

3432 I'm coward enough -- see coward enough to deny [GN 14]

3433 I've known a murderer to sleep . . . -- PW alludes to the events

recorded in FRH [BH 8]

3434 I've stopped one, two, three, four earths -- a hunting metaphor meaning to block off a quarry's possible refuges. PW suggests thereby that he is making progress with his investigation. [SP 8]

3435 Iago -- the masterful villain of Shakespeare's Othello [HHC 23/GN 1]

3436 Ianthe -- the name of P. B. Shelley's* daughter by his first wife, Harriet, but referring here to the young woman in his Queen Mab to whom the fairy, Mab, grants a vision of the world [GN 15]

3437 ice -- ice cream, a British usage [ab/MMA 11/GN 1]

3438 Iceland -- the independent island republic about 180 miles East of Greenland and bordering the South side of the Arctic Circle. The island is located on the mid-Atlantic ridge, and is volcanic in origin. Weather patterns affecting England would pass over Iceland first. [FRH 13]

3439 "If I were on Greenland's coast" -- this misquotation is from John Gay's (1685-1732) The Beggar's Opera, first produced in 1728, Act I, scene xii, the first stanza of an air sung by Macheath and Polly Peachum. Macheath sings:

"Were I laid on Greenland's coast,
And in my arms embraced my lass;
Warm amidst eternal frost,
Too soon the half year's night would pass."

One of Polly's lines later in the song serves also as its title: "Over the Hills and Far Away". [BH 13]

3440 "If it were done . . ." -- the line is from Macbeth, I, vii, 1:

"If it were done when 'tis done, then 'twere well
It were done quickly: if assassination
Could trammel up the consequence, and catch
With his surcease success; that but this blow
Might be the be-all and the end-all here . . . ."

The lines are Macbeth's soliloquy wherein he questions strongly his intent to kill Duncan. [HHC 21]

3441 "If my love swears . . ." -- from Shakespeare's sonnet 138, but the line usually appears as:

"When my love swears that she is made of truth
I do believe her, though I know she lies."

The last two lines of the sonnet are:

"Therefore I lie with her and she with me,
And in our faults by lies we flatter'd be." [CW 18]

3442 "If the shout of them that triumph . . ." -- PW is quoting from hymn 228 (Hymns A & M*), "Jerusalem the Golden" by J. M. Neale as translated from the French of Bernard of Cluny. The "If" that begins this citation is PW's addition. [NT 11]

3443 "If thine eye be single . . ." -- the allusion is to either Matthew 6:22, the Sermon on the Mount, or to Luke 11:34, the passage about hiding one's light under a bushel. The passage in Matthew is: "The light of the body is the eye: if therefore thine eye be single, thy whole body shall be full of light." [GN 4]

3444 "If you have tears" -- the line is from Julius Caesar, III, ii, 173:

"If you have tears, prepare to shed them now."

The line is part of the famous funeral oration delivered by Mark Antony. [MMA 19]

3445 Iffley -- a southern suburb of Oxford [GN 15]

3446 Ikey-Mo -- the nickname for Clarence Gordon*. It is short for Isaac Moses; indicative of a Jew. [FRH 29]

3447 Il m'aime--un peu--beaucoup -- French for, "He loves me--a little --a lot". HV continues, "passionately --madly . . . not at all. He loves me --". [BH 18]

3448 Il ne sait pas vivre . . . . -- Uncle Paul Delagardie* says, "Confound Peter! He doesn't know how to live. But I wish I were between his sheets." [BH P]

3449 il n'est que sensible . . . -- Uncle Paul Delagardie's French for, "he is only sensitive and passa-

bly sensual. He has more need of you than you of him, so be generous--his is a personality that one would have a hard time trying to pamper too much. He feels the need to give of himself--to unburden himself (to get things "off his chest"); certainly you will not refuse him this modest pleasure. Coldness, affectation itself, is a killer; he doesn't know how to assert himself against it, the struggle (effort) is repugnant to him. All that you know already--pardon me! I find you extremely understanding and I believe that his well-being is dear to us both. With that, he is a merchant of happiness to whom ill will comes in return; I hope that you will find in him that which will give you pleasure. You have only to be happy to keep him happy; he doesn't bear the sufferings of others very well. Accept, my dear niece, my most sincere good wishes." [BH 19]

3450 il tenait son lit . . . -- French for, "he keeps to his bed like a Grand Monarch (Louis XIV) and conducts himself there like a great Turk (a sexual reference) [BH 3]

3451 Il y a des femmes . . . -- Uncle Paul Delagardie's* French for, "There are those women who have a genius . . . the genius of love." The last phrase is the Dowager Duchess's*.

3452 Ilfracombe -- a seaside resort on Devon's North coast which features a charming harbor and lots of rocky cliffs [HHC 17]

3453 Ill-gotten goods never thrive -- the paragraph of Biblical allusions that opens as cited here refers to Job 20, Zophar's second discourse against Job, and to Psalm 109:10-11. [BH 10]

3454 illuminated missal -- a missal with hand-done capitals, rubrics, and other ornamentation, often intensely complex in its beauty. Such illuminated books were hand-done and were relatively common in the early days of printing--the incunabular period of which PW is so fond. Production expenses eventually became so prohibitive that the practice has been almost unknown in the time since the printing press. [GN 14]

3455 imbrangled -- or embrangled; confused, entangled, etc. Onomatopoetically, it is the perfect word to describe what happens when a bell ringer gets "lost" midcourse. [NT 1]

3456 imitation très difficile -- French for, "a very difficult imitation" --PW's description of his transformation into the perfect "Lounge Lizard"*. Bunter, in one of his more Jeeves*-like moments, has no difficulty in suggesting the perfect outfit for PW to wear. [HHC 31]

3457 the immortal bones obey control -- PW's mind is wandering, distracted by love, so it is hard to determine just where his thoughts may have wandered to, but, in this case, they may be with Milton's Paradise Lost, IX:913-16:

> " . . . I feel
> The link of nature draw me: Flesh of Flesh,
> Bone of my Bone thou art, and from thy State
> Mine never shall be parted, bliss or woe."

Adam is addressing Eve. [BH 16]

3458 Imperial Crown -- the crown of Russia, an Empire under the Czars (or Tsars) as it was a huge geographical area encompassing many peoples, both requirements of an empire [HHC 5]

3459 Imperial Tokay -- a rich, silky smooth, and very sweet wine of Hungary, probably an Aszu, the sweetest of the Tokays and almost a liqueur. Emperor Franz Josef used it as a gift to Queen Victoria, and some Polish rulers kept bottles of it for as long as 200 years. None of it is known to remain. [mt]

3460 impluvium -- Latin for a basin or pool used to gather rainwater from the roof. Meleager Finch's* is a small version intended only as a decorative device. [umw]

3461 importance of being earnest -- an allusion to Oscar Wilde's play of the same name. Its reference is not lost here as Miss Marryat* is the perfect Jack in sad need of becoming Ernest for a while. [umw]

3462 in -- see out quick/in slow [NT 13]

3463 In a Balcony -- DLS has quoted lines 905-9 from Browning's* fragment of a play in verse. Critic Arlo Bates writes that, "The great motiv of In a Balcony is the awakening of the inmost consciousness of Constance to the greatness of the love of Norbert and her quick response to that call which this perception makes to her highest and most feminine nature . . ." This is analogous to the PW-HV relationship as it has unfolded from its beginnings in SP. [BH 16]

3464 "In a flash at a trumpet crash . . ." -- PW is quoting, choppily, from the end of Gerard Manley Hopkins' (1844-89) poem, "That Nature is a Heraclitan Fire and of The comfort of the Resurrection", lines 20-22:

"In a flash, at a trumpet crash,
I am all at once what Christ is,| since
he was what I am, and
This Jack, joke, poor potsherd,| patch
matchwood, immortal diamond
Is immortal diamond." (1888)

[NT 5]

3465 in aeternum floreant -- Latin for, "may they flourish eternally" [GN AN]

3466 In convertendo -- the Latin opening of the 126th Psalm: "When the Lord turned . . ." [NT 10]

3467 "In one word hear, what soon they all shall hear . . ." -- the speech is Isbrand's in V, i, 34-6 of T. L. Beddoes' Death's Jest Book**. The preceeding sentence is:

"Tomorrow is the greatest fool I know,
Excepting those that put their trust in him." [HHC 29]

3468 IN•PIAM•MEMORIAM•RICARDI•THORPE . . . -- Latin for, "In pious (reverent) memory of Richard Thorpe, Knight, Lord now lettest thy servant depart in peace", Luke 2:29. It is also the text for Simeon's canticle. See also "Puzzle Clues". [NT 4]

3469 In re R. v. Vane -- the standard abbreviations used in court documents meaning, "In the matter of", or "Concerning the matter of the Crown (R. = Rex or Regina, depending on the gender of the monarch) versus [Harriet] Vane". Norman Urquhart* would know immediately the purpose of PW's visit from that note. [SP 7]

3470 "In silence and in tears" -- the reference is to Lord Byron's* poem, "When We Two Parted", but the lines are correctly written as:

"When we two parted
In silence and tears . . ."

[MMA 19]

3471 in situ -- Latin for, "in its original place" or "as it was found" [GN 16]

3472 in statu quo -- Latin for, "in the same state as formerly" [BH 7]

3473 "In that Deep Midnight of the Mind" -- the line is from Lord Byron's* work and is from Domestic Pieces (1816). The poem is one of two entitled "Stanzas to Augusta", she being his half-sister. The first two of eleven stanzas are:

"When all around grew drear and dark
And reason half withheld her ray,
And hope but shed a dying spark
Which more misled my lonely way;

In that deep midnight of the mind
And that internal strife of heart
When dreading to be deem'd too kind,
The weak despair--the cold depart . . . . [MMA 19]

3474 "In the midst of life we are in death." -- Mr. Lavender* is quoting from the First Anthem in the Sacrament of the Burial of the Dead in The Book of Common Prayer. [NT 2]

3475 "In the Room" -- a poem by James Thomson (1834-82). It is typical of his work, being rather dreamlike and melancholy in its tone. [BH 7]

3476 in vacuo -- Latin for, "in a vacuum", or "isolated" [CW 18]

3477 In vino veritas -- Latin for, "In wine there is truth". The phrase usually means that wine will loosen a tongue to speak the truth, but here it means that whoever can identify the wines correctly will be the real PW. [mt]

3478 inaccurate major premise -- the major premise is the first term or statement in a logical argument (see syllogism). If it is wrong, inaccurate, or incomplete, then the conclusion cannot be true. Even if some

accident should happen to make the conclusion true, it cannot be accepted as such until the premises are stated properly. [HHC 21]

3479 incisor -- one of eight teeth in the front of the mouth, four on top and four below, used for cutting and biting. They are not pointed. [te]

3480 incubus -- an evil spirit; something oppressively burdensome [t]

3481 incunabula -- books produced prior to 1501. PW collects them and is known to be an expert in the field. [ss]

3482 india rubber -- a rubber artists' eraser [SP 16/MMA 1]

3483 india rubber boots -- also India rubber; boots coated with or having soles of barely refined natural rubber; farmers' work boots [WB 4]

3484 Indian colonel -- an officer, in this case British, who served in the Indian Army which was, until 1947, under the King as Emperor of India, but was separate and distinct from other British forces [WB 5]

3485 Indian hemp -- marijuana, _Cannabis sativa_, or hashish. It was known in ancient times for the effects that have gained so much attention since the 1960's. [CW 4]

3486 Indian Regiment -- an army regiment raised in India with mainly native components, but with officers mostly from Britain. Major Robert Fentiman* was attached to such a regiment. [BC 3]

3487 infallibility -- in Roman Catholicism, doctrine has it that the pope is incapable of error in defining church attitudes in the areas of faith and morals. The doctrine in its modern form dates from 1870. [UD 19/BC 16]

3488 infernal machine and magnesium -- PW addresses Bunter about the photographic apparatus he uses. The magnesium refers to the flash powder as flash bulbs or electronic flash units were unknown at the time. [WB 3]

3489 influenza -- known variously as flu or grippe, it is a highly contagious, often debilitating disease caused by a virus. It frequently reaches epidemic form throughout the winter months. The disease usually runs a specific course and lasts a predictable amount of time, depending on the variety of virus involved. The symptoms include headache, chills, backache, fever, and general discomfort. Robert Duckworthy* describes the additional difficulties he encountered as a result of the flu; the reference in WB probably being to the great international pandemic of the Spanish flu in 1918. The flu is a prominent feature of NT, and the Chief Constable in BH is prevented from doing his job as he should like because of it. [im/WB 6/SP 7/NT 1/BH 11]

3490 Information, Ministry of -- George Goyles* lost a job there because of his Socialist* leanings. The ministry, under Lord Beaverbrook, operated from February to November of 1918, and employed such luminaries as Lord Northcliffe and Rudyard Kipling. [CW 9]

3491 Ingeniouser and ingeniouser -- PW has created his own version of "curioser and curioser"* [FRH 25]

3492 Ingersoll [watch] -- a brand of inexpensive watch formerly available world-wide, but not now so widely distributed [FRH 2/BH 11]

3493 _Inghilterra_ -- Italian for England. See also _Angleterre_. [GN 9]

3494 Ingleby, Mr. -- a copywriter for Pym's Publicity*. He is a likeable sort, has a puckish wit, and plays cricket* middling well. He and PW get along together nicely. [MMA 1]

3495 inglenook -- a corner by a fireplace [CW 4]

3496 _The Ingoldsby Legends_ -- a series of humorous narratives in prose and verse written by the Reverend Richard Harris Barham (1788-1845). During the mid 1800's they were immensely popular even though some thought them irreverent.

3497 initial S -- see Scoot [WB 4]

3498 initial W -- Magdalen College* was founded by William of Waynfleet in 1458, hence the "W" on the barge [GN 13]

3499 innocently waking to a new day -- Bunter's allusion, if he meant

one, is veiled, but is reminiscent of Wordsworth's "Ode, Intimations of Immortality", section xi, ll. 95-6:
"The innocent brightness of a newborn day
Is lovely yet . . ." [NT 11]

3500 Inns of Chancery -- including Staple*, Barnard's, and Furnival's, were subordinate to the great Inns of Court*. At first they supplied housing for Chancery clerks and only later provided training for solicitors and attorneys. They were eventually absorbed by the Inns of Court.

3501 Inns of Court -- the four corporations or societies which, in England, have sole authority to call candidates to the bar. They are all in London and consist of Gray's Inn, Lincoln's Inn, and the Inner and Middle Temples. The Outer Temple has long since been dissolved. See also The Temple, and Inns of Chancery.

3502 inquest -- a formal, judicial hearing, presided over by a coroner*, the purpose of which is to present to a coroner's jury information regarding unexplained deaths. It is then the responsibility of the jury to determine if the case is criminal or not. If criminal action is found to be involved, the case is then given to the police for investigation and possible prosecution. [passim]

3503 Inquisition -- a court, The Holy Office, established to investigate heresies and other offenses against the Roman Catholic Church. It was instituted by Pope Gregory IX in 1235, and torture was approved for use by Pope Innocent IV in 1252. Inquisitions were held in most European countries, but it was most common in southern Europe. Spain did not finally put an end to it until 1834. [BH P]

3504 inrigger -- a rowing boat having oarlocks on the gunwales as opposed to those on an outrigger* [GN 15]

3505 insinuate yourself, snakelike -- PW alludes to that considerably more evil insinuator, Satan, as he appears to tempt Eve in the garden of Eden, Genesis 3:1 ff. We may assume that PW sees Bunter not as the writhing serpent of loathsome nature, but as the beautiful and subtle creature that existed prior to God's curse. [SP 8]

3506 Inspector -- see Police Ranks

3507 Instructions for Parish Priests -- see Myrc, John [NT 3]

3508 "Intercranial Haemorrhage" -- a subheading in Taylor's* Medical Jurisprudence [BH 12]

3509 interlocutor -- a conversationalist, especially one who directs the conversation by questioning or implying questions to draw information from those to whom he is speaking [WB 4]

3510 "Internationale" -- see Third International [CW 12]

3511 interval -- the difference in pitch between notes in music [SP 8]

3512 invalided home -- to be wounded with enough severity to prevent any further immediate participation in the hostilities, thus allowing one to be sent home to England [NT 2]

3513 Inverness [cape] -- or inverness, after the city in Scotland. It is a coat or rain cloak having a loose belt, a cape around the shoulders, and a round collar. Sherlock Holmes is popularly pictured wearing one. [SP 16/BH 12]

3514 invigilator -- a supervisor at an examination; a proctor [GN 6]

3515 invocation -- a prayer calling for divine guidance and supervision, usually opening a worship service. In a general sense, the word may apply to any prayer of that sort wherever it appears in the service of worship. [NT 12]

3516 ipecacuanha -- also ipecac, an alkaline from a creeping South American vine (Cephalis ipecacuanha) of the madder family from which the agent emetine is extracted. It induces vomiting. [CW 6]

3517 ipsissima verba -- Latin for, "the very words", or "the exact words" [SP 10]

3518 ipso facto -- Latin for, "by that very fact" [UD 8]

3519 Ireland, Henry -- William Henry

Ireland (1777-1835) an English forger of Shakespearean manuscripts, etc., whose Vortigern and Rowena was such a failure that it led to his exposure as a fraud [GN 17]

3520 Irish Sweep -- the nickname of the Irish Hospital Sweepstakes, the world's largest lottery. It has been run annually since 1930, and is based on drawings connected to the Lincolnshire Handicap, the Cambridgeshire, and the Irish Derby horse races. The "Sweep" is set up to help finance Irish hospitals. [HHC 24/MMA 4]

3521 iron pineapple -- the allusion is to Eden Phillpotts'* story, "The Iron Pineapple", not a work of pure detection. DLS included the story in the "Mystery and Horror" section of her The Second Omnibus of Crime; high praise indeed. [BH 13]

3522 Ironsides, John -- Bertha Gotobed's* fiancé, a clerk on the Southern Railway* [UD 6]

3523 irregular establishment -- having a mistress, keeping an apartment for the purpose of lovers' trysts [CW 5]

3524 Is this the city . . . -- PW's raptures allude to Lamentations 2:15 in the first sentence, "All that pass by clap their hands at thee; they hiss and wag their head at the daughter of Jerusalem, saying, Is this the city that men call the perfection of beauty, The joy of the whole earth?" The second sentence is a combination of Isaiah 33:1 and II Kings 13:14. The whole point of the outburst is a somewhat sarcastic consideration of the empty rooms the mourners have returned to. [BH 19]

3525 "Is there yet any that is left . . ." -- PW alludes to II Samuel 9:1-2: "And David said, Is there yet any that is left of the house of Saul, that I may shew him kindness for Jonathon's sake"/And there was of the house of Saul a servant whose name was Ziba . . . ." [GN 20]

3526 "Is thy servant a dog . . ." -- HV is quoting from II Kings 8:13 with the pronoun "he" altered to "she". The section from which the quote is taken relates Elisha's prediction that Hazael would reign over Syria. [GN 21]

3527 Isaacson, Miss -- a student at Shrewsbury College* [GN 6]

3528 Isaiah -- the Old Testament prophet who is remembered most in the Christian church for his prediction of the coming of Christ and His blessing of the Gentiles. He also gives a clear discussion of the concept of grace. [BH 9]

3529 Ishmaels -- outcasts from society. The reference is to Ishmael, a son of Abraham by Hagar and, by allusion, an outcast; a descendant of Ishmael, as the Arabs claim to be. [WB 3]

3530 Isis -- the Thames when it is passing through Oxford. The name derives from the Latin for Thames: Thamesis, hence "Isis" from the Latin ending. [GN 1]

3531 Isle of Ely -- see Ely [HHC 17]

3532 "The isles may be glad" -- Psalm 97:1: "The Lord reigneth; let the earth rejoice; let the multitude of the isles be glad thereof" is the KJV. PW and the rector are, of course, using the Coverdale version as found in The Book of Common Prayer. [NT 10]

3533 Isles of Fleet -- Murray's Isles, Ardwell Island, and Barlocco Island, all located just to the South of the confluence of the Fleet and Wigtown Bays [FRH 17]

3534 "It" -- a concept created by Elinor Glyn* in her novel, It. The word was used to refer to that special magnetism which attracted both sexes. Physical attraction was required, beauty was not. Clara Bow, the famous silent movie actress, had "It", but, then, so did a stallion named "Rex". The craze ended with the advent of talkies when it became clear that Miss Bow had a thick Brooklyn accent. Perhaps Mrs. Glyn's inspiration came from Rudyard Kipling's Traffic and Discoveries, Mrs. Bathurst where he wrote: "'Tisn't beauty, so to speak, nor good talk necessarily. It's just IT. Some women'll stay in a man's memory if they once walked down a street." [UD 15]

3536 "It does those things . . ." -- PW is paraphrasing the text of the General Confession* in the services of Morning Prayer in The Book of Common Prayer. The passage is given there as:

"We have left undone those things which we ought to have done; And we have done those things which we ought not to have done; And there is no health in us." [GN 4]

3537 It is a beautiful description . . . -- Mr. Venables'* description is a reflection of his preoccupation with the three Psalms (92, 99, and 126) that provide the text of the code that he and PW broke. [NT 12]

3538 "It is a frightful plight . . ." -- from LeFanu's* Wylder's Hand, Ch. 48 [NT 14]

3539 It is a goosefeather bed! -- HV is referring to "Raggle Taggle Gypsies, O" (or, sometimes, wraggle). It is a variant form of the poem called "The Gypsy Laddie", both being anonymous humorous ballads. HV is thinking of the last two stanzas of the poem in which we find (in the first title listed):

"Last night you slept on a goose-feather bed,
With sheet turned down so bravely, O!
And to-night you'll sleep in a cold open field
Along with the wraggle-taggle gypsies, O!" [BH 2]

3540 It is like the taste of a passion . . . -- PW may well have the Donne poem "A Lecture Upon the Shadow" in mind. His reference to the wine parallels closely the mood of the poem and the opening quote for Ch. 10. See "And his short minute". [CW 10]

3541 It is possible, but . . . -- PW alludes to Aristotle's* Poetics, "A likely impossibility is always preferable to an unconvincing possibility." This subject was a favorite of DLS's and appears as a central point in her essay (originally delivered as a speech at Oxford in March of 1935), "Aristotle on Detective Fiction". While much of the essay is done with tongue planted firmly in cheek, it remains worthy of careful study. [BH 13]

3542 "It is the little rift within the lute . . ." -- the allusion is to Tennyson's* "Merlin and Vivien", 11. 388-9. [BH 12]

3543 it says in the Bible -- Insp. Umpelty* is confused. It is not the Bible where that idea appears, but in William Congreve's (1670-1729) play (a tragedy), The Mourning Bride. The play has many famous lines--Act I opens with "Music has charms to sooth a savage breast", and Act III, viii, closes with:

"Heaven has no rage, like love to hatred turn'd,
Nor Hell a fury, like a woman scorn'd." [HHC 10]

3544 It waited with her . . . -- see its evil spirit cast out [BH E3]

3545 "It was a robber's daughter . . ." -- PW is quoting the first two lines of one of W. S. Gilbert's Bab Ballads, "Gentle Alice Brown". The first stanza concludes:

"Her mother was a foolish, weak, but amiable old thing;
But it isn't of her parents that I'm going for to sing."

The ballad tells of Alice's love for a local gentleman, but her love horrifies her parents and the local priest. Mr. Brown murders Alice's love, and "Mrs. Brown dissected him before she went to bed". The ballad was first published in Fun, May 23, 1868. [BH 18]

3546 It's a Far, Far Butter Thing -- this delightful pun refers to Sydney Carton's speech as he approaches the guillotine and his death in Ch. 15, the last chapter, of Charles Dickens's A Tale of Two Cities. The paragraph ends the book and reads:

"'It is a far, far better thing that I do than I have ever done; it is a far, far better rest that I go to than I have ever known.'" [MMA 2]

3547 "it's a wise child . . ." -- the line is an inversion of a line in The Merchant of Venice, II, ii, 83, where Launcelot Gobbo, Shylock's clown, addresses Old Gobbo, his father. The line reads: "Nay, indeed, if you had your eyes, you might fail the knowing of me: it is a wise father that knows his own child." [WB 3]

3548 Ita -- Latin, short for ita est, "it is so", or "just so" [GN 22]

3549 "Italian Concerto" -- by J. S. Bach*. It is in F major, S971, for solo harpsichord. It was first published in 1735 as part of Vol. 2 of the Clavier-Übung, and is named for the

composer's use of the form and style of the early 18th C. Italian instrumental concerto form. [SP 13]

3550 Italiano -- used as a derogatory ethnic slur by Det. Insp. Winterbottom* in reference to a suspect [nf]

3551 Ithaca -- in Greece, the home of Odysseus of Homer's The Odyssey. It is an island between Cephalonia and the West coast of northern Greece in the Ionian Sea. [GN 1]

3552 'Itler -- Mr. Padgett's cockney* pronunciation of Hitler [GN 6]

3553 its evil spirit cast out -- the allusion is to Matthew 12:43-4 (also Luke 11:24-6), the parable of the swept and garnished house: "When the unclean spirit is gone out of a man, he walketh through dry places and findeth none./Then he saith, I will return into my house from whence I came out; and when he is come, he findeth it empty, swept, and garnished." [BH E3]

(J)

3554 J pen -- a common broad-tipped desk pen with a brass nib* [BC 6]

3555 JCR -- see Junior Common Room [GN 1]

3556 "J. D." portrait -- this set of initials on the back of a photograph is a typographical error which should read "R. D." [im]

3557 Jabez -- one of Mr. Grimethorpe's* workers, he tends the dogs among other duties [CW 4]

3558 Jack -- other than Robert Templeton*, the central character in HV's novel, The Fountain-Pen Mystery, the book in progress at the time of HHC [HHC 15]

3559 Jack -- one of the movers who help remove the furniture from Talboys* to help settle Noakes's* debts [BH 19]

3560 Jack Sprat and his wife -- a reference to the nursery rhyme, "Jack Sprat could eat no fat . . .", etc., as it appeared in John Clarke's Paroemiologia Anglo-Latina of 1639 [BH 14]

3561 Jack the Giant Killer -- a nursery tale of unknown Northern European origin [CW 11]

3562 jackdaws -- the European grackle, a smaller relative of the crow marked by an irridescent head and neck [GN 1]

3563 Jackson -- the source of the new fuses needed to remedy the prank of the poltergeist*. He (she?) is not mentioned elsewhere. Did DLS perhaps mean Mullins? [GN 9]

3564 Jacob -- the Jacob who is son of Isaac and Rebecca in Genesis. It is he who falsely obtained his father's deathbed blessing by impersonating his twin, Esau. [BH E2]

3565 Jacob's voice -- see the story in Genesis 27 and the preceeding entry. The reference is to any sort of duplicity or hypocrisy where one assumes a guise to obtain a gift or blessing meant for another. The specific reference is to Genesis 27:22: "And Jacob wnet near unto Isaac, his father,; and he felt him, and said, The

voice is Jacob's voice, but the hands are the hands of Esau." PW is gently twitting Bunter for so rapidly responding to an offer to buy some new photography equipment with some unexpected profits from Bunter's astute bidding for PW at the Brocklebury* book sale. [WB 2]

3566 Jaeger -- Mr. Murbles'* dressing gown is from Jaeger, that famous Regent St.* clothing firm known for its knitwear [CW 16]

3567 jaeger -- a dressing gown patterned after those available at Jaeger's* [GN 6]

3568 Jake -- one of the hired hands at William Grimethorpe's* farm [CW 12]

3569 Jake of Dead Man's Bush -- a fictitious movie about Australian bushmen starring Varden* [cf]

3570 Jakes, Sgt. -- a police officer of the Hertfordshire* constabulary assigned to the Pagford/Paggleham** area [BH 11]

3571 jalousies -- a French form of Venetian blinds [mt]

3572 jam for the fielders -- to make the job "sweet", i. e. easy for the fielders [MMA 10]

3573 jam roll -- a jelly roll with jam substituted--a thin sheet of cake with jam spread over it and then rolled into a log with the jam inside. It is then cut into slices for eating. [MMA 12]

3574 Jamboree Jellies -- one of the fictitious accounts handled by Pym's Publicity*. It is a particular favorite of Mr. Copley's*. [MMA 8]

3575 James -- a servant at the Egotists' Club* [GN 4]

3576 James -- a footman at Duke's Denver* who later appears in the Dowager Duchess's household and from whom PW learns of Bunter's toast to the newlyweds. That toast, slightly modified, appears in BH, Ch. 3. [SP 12/BH 3]

3577 James, Mrs. Chipperly -- an acquaintance of the Wimsey family who, in a letter to a friend, expresses her astonishment that PW has wed HV [BH P]

3578 James I -- also James VI of Scotland. When Elizabeth I died in 1603, she was succeeded by James, son of Mary, Queen of Scots, who was the next in the line of succession. At that time he already ruled Scotland as James VI. He ruled both countries until 1625. His successors continued to rule both countries (except during the Interregnum, 1649-60), but the union of the two nations did not occur officially until 1707 with the creation of Great Britain. [NT 4]

3579 James, Henry -- (1843-1916), the American novelist and short story writer famous for Washington Square, The Turn of the Screw, and other works which emphasize strong moral themes and the relationship between innocence and experience in an impeccable technique. His works also have a strong psychological overtone. [BC 18]

3580 Jameson, [Margaret] Storm -- English novelist (b. 1897) who often uses a Yorkshire setting as in The Lonely Ship, The Voyage Home, and A Richer Dust, published from 1927-31. [BC 18]

3581 Jamieson, Sir Maxwell -- the Chief Constable* for Kirkcudbrightshire* and Wigtownshire*. When PW reconstructs the crime, Sir Maxwell suffers the fate of being cast as Campbell's* corpse. [FRH 5]

3582 Jane Barraclough Fellowship -- a fictitious fellowship given by Shrewsbury College*, itself fictitious, to Miss de Vine* to help her continue her research without financial concern [GN 1]

3583 Jane Eyre -- the heroine of Charlotte Brontë's novel of the same name. The novel follows the traditions of the Gothic romance as established by Ann Radcliffe and Horace Walpole, but it is to that subgenre what the Sherlock Holmes canon is to the detective story--it may not be the first, but it holds the position as the definitive work. Daphne Du Maurier's Rebecca (1938) and Vera Caspary's Laura (1942) are the modern masterpieces of the form. [BH P]

3584 Japan, Emperor of -- see Emperor of Japan [HHC 33]

3585 jape, rather a -- a joke or bit of amusement. Jape is a Middle English word relating to a mocking attack on something. [SP 13/HHC 34]

3586 "Je connaissais Manon . . ." -- French for, "I knew Manon: Why distress myself so for a misfortune which I ought to have foreseen?" The reference is to a passage in Book II of Manon Lescaut*. [CW 17]

3587 "Je me suis couché . . ." -- from Montaigne's essay, "De la Vanité"* where, translated from the French, we find: "I have gone to bed a thousand times in my own home, imagining that someone would betray me and slaughter me that very night . . . ." [GN 13]

3588 Je ne suis pas femme . . . -- French for, "I am not a woman to endure great vexation (tedium, annoyance, disagreement). That is understandable, isn't it?" [CW 16]

3589 Je suis de votre avis. -- French for, "I am of your opinion." [NT 8]

3590 Je suis fou. -- French for, "I am mad (insane)"; Cathcart* completes the sentence with "de douleur", or "with misery". [CW 13]

3591 "Jealousy is as cruel as the grave" -- see Song of Songs and "cruel as the grave" [UD 16]

3592 Jean -- probably a farm hand at the Legros* farm [NT 7]

3593 Jeanie -- a scrub girl and household helper for the Farrens* [FRH 6]

3594 Jeeves, talk like -- the reference is to that always correct, always unflappable, always resourceful butler and valet who appears in many of P. G. Wodehouse's stories. It is not unreasonable to consider Bunter a member of the Jeeves school of behavior. [SP 20]

3595 "Jeffries of a judge" [old] -- a reference to George, 1st Baron Jeffries (1644-89). He is notorious as a hanging judge, and for his brutality as the judge who presided over the "Bloody Assizes" of 1685, the trials of the supporters of the defeated Duke of Monmouth's Rebellion. The Duke had attempted, in 1685, to remove James II from the throne. Some 300 of the Duke's followers were said to have been executed and 1000 sent as slaves to the North American plantations. In 1688, the attempt by William of Orange to remove James was successful, and Judge Jeffries died in the Tower. [SP 1]

3596 Jehoshaphat, Great -- an allusion to II Chronicles 17:12: "And Jehoshaphat waxed great exceedingly." His greatness came because he followed, enforced, and spread the word of God and lived in God's grace. It is likely that the expression has remained popular as it is a harmless expletive and has an interesting and comical sound. W. C. Fields used it and others like it to avoid overzealous censors in the early days of motion pictures. [FRH 27]

3597 Jellyband, Dr. -- one of the locals mentioned by Mr. Puffett* as being interested in raising peaches for the fair, and, therefore, as competition to Puffett's bid for the first prize [t]

3598 Jellyfield, Dr. -- the local physician who serves the Pagglehum* area at the time of BH. One wonders if, perhaps, DLS slipped here (see Dr. Jellyband) as the doctor would probably be the same one in both "Talboys" and BH, there being only seven years between the two stories (1935-42). It is, therefore, possible that Drs. Jellyfield and Jellyband are one and the same person, and, as Jellyfield appeared first, he is probably the physician in question. The error may be the result of Mr. Puffett's consternation. [BH 2]

3599 Jem -- old Esdras Pollock's* grandson who had made the trip to Cork, Ireland, on "business". He verified the sighting of the body of Paul Alexis* and of HV's frantic waving. He is fussy about how his shirt collars are ironed. [HHC 21]

3600 Jem -- the blacksmith's helper at Darley* [HHC 16]

3601 Jem -- a barkeeper/waiter at the Rose and Crown* in Stapley* [CW 11]

3602 Jemima -- a name PW uses to address a cow while attempting to

drive through Leamholt* on a market day [NT 7]

3603 jemmy -- a crowbar or pry-bar [BH 8]

3604 Jenkins, P. C. -- an otherwise unidentified police officer [te]

3605 Jenkins -- the gatekeeper at Bredon Hall*, Duke's Denver*. He and his wife are long-time servants to the Wimsey family. [BH E2]

3606 Jenkins, Frank -- the honest district messenger* hired by Jim Thoday* to return a motorbike to the agency from which it was rented [NT 16]

3607 Jenkinses -- Broxford* residents who attend William Noakes's* funeral [BH 19]

3608 Jenks, Mr. -- a representative of the Whifflet's* cigarette firm. He is not otherwise identified. [MMA 16]

3609 Jenkyn, Mr. -- a "youngish and agreeable don" whom HV had met. He is a pro-Proctor* residing at Magdalen College*. See Oxford colleges. [GN 11]

3610 Jenkyn, Nurse -- one of the nurses hired to care for PW's new son, Bredon Delagardie Peter* [hp]

3611 Jeremiah -- the Old Testament prophet and author of the Book of Jeremiah and, probably, of Lamentations as well. He has been aptly called "the prophet of the decline and fall of the Jewish monarchy", and he died for those prophecies. During his lifetime he suffered as many true prophets have suffered: No one believed him. Mr. Copley* is a prophet of the Jeremiah school. PW reads from Jeremiah extensively in BH E2. [MMA 8/BH 9]

3612 Jericho -- a reference to the ancient Palestinian city, perhaps the oldest inhabited place in the world. The suggestion is of great distance, however, not great age, and refers, loosely, to a remote place. The later reference is to the flattened walls of Jericho which appears in Joshua 6:20. [NT 20]

3613 Jermyn St. -- a street in Westminster* that is parallel to and South of Piccadilly* from St. James's St. to Haymarket. Harcourt and Neville Grimbold** have an apartment at some unspecified number on this street which is still a major shopping thoroughfare. [ae/HHC 4]

3614 Jerry[kins] -- a nickname for Viscount St. George* [dh/GN 9/ BH P]

3615 Jerusalem, my happy home! -- PW addresses his almost empty home in terms of the Holy City as recounted in the famous hymn, "Jerusalem, my happy home!", based on the works of St. Augustine. The first verse of the hymn is: "Jerusalem, my happy home, When shall I come to thee? When shall my sorrows have an end? Thy joys when shall I see?" [BH 19]

3616 Jessop, P. C. -- one of the constables who had the beat outside PW's Audley Square* home prior to P. C. Burt* [hp]

3617 Jesuit[ical] -- a member of or pertaining to the Society of Jesus, founded by St. Ignatius Loyola in 1533. The reference in WB is to any sort of weasel-wording or logical legerdemain, equivocation, etc., practices traditionally ascribed to the Jesuits who held that the end justifies the means. The usage stems from the order's frequent practice of mentally reserving the truth, practices refined during the Counter-Reformation (ca. 1540ff.), a movement they were largely responsible for implementing. [WB 2/ UD 4]

3618 Jesus -- Jesus College. See Oxford Colleges. [GN 14]

3619 Jewel Song in Faust -- the Marchioness of Dinglewood* has her pearl necklace stolen during a performance of Gounod's opera at the point when Marguerite sings the song cited here. It begins, "Ah, the joy past compare,/ these jewels bright to wear . . .". Irony abounds here. Marguerite is young and fancies that the jewels make her of regal importance, but the Marchioness is older and is wearing fake jewels, having pawned the real ones to avert financial difficulty. [ab]

3620 jew's harp -- a small mouth-held musical instrument played by plucking its metal tongue with a finger. The mouth and nasal cavities

provide a resonating chamber and some control of the sounds created. [MMA 8]

3621 "The Jews have no dealings with the Samaritans." -- PW is quoting the Gospel of John, 4:9, the story of Jesus and the Samaritan woman at Jacob's well. He is referring to the tendency for Oxford's colleges to be entities unto themselves on the one hand and to the natural rivalry which might develop between two ancient schools that exist in such close proximity as do Balliol and Trinity**. [FRH 19]

3622 Jeyes' Fluid -- a disinfectant used on the premises at Pym's Publicity*. The product is still in common use. [MMA 4]

3623 jiggot -- the Scottish form of the French gigot, leg of lamb or mutton [FRH 21]

3624 Jiggs, Mr. -- a catch-all name for any criminal, probably PW's variation on the old phrase "the jig is up", used when catching or being caught in any questionable activity [cf]

3625 Jim -- one of the offspring of PW's acquaintance at Oxford, Peake of Brasenose [GN 14]

3626 Jim -- the landlord of the Crown* pub who is accused by a thin patron of selling beer with a funny taste [BH 10]

3627 Jim -- an otherwise unidentified husband of a friend of HV's [BH 19]

3628 Jimmy -- the son of George Willis* who is Paggleham's* grocer [BH 4]

3629 jimmy o'goblins -- slang for sovereigns*. The OED suggests the origin is with a bit of rhyming slang as in sov-rin with gob-lin. It is unclear where the jimmy comes in as the coins had nothing to do with either of the kings named James. They were first minted by Henry VII. [HHC 11]

3630 Jinny -- see Puffett, Jinny [t/BH 8]

3631 jip -- a term used to suggest pain of an intense nature. The word is onomatopoetic in origin, like yip, yipe, ouch, etc. [te]

3632 Joan -- an otherwise unidentified member of the Wimsey family in 1587 [BH E2]

3633 Jock -- the husband of the housekeeper, Maggie*. He displays the stereotypical Scots concern for finances with a vengeance. [ss]

3634 Jock, young -- the lad who saw Campbell's* painting along the Minnoch* at about ten and again at eleven on the morning of the day the artist was found dead [FRH 11]

3635 Jocks -- Scotsmen, an affectionate nickname from the Scottish for John [FRH 1]

3636 Jocund Day -- the title of a fictitious novel which alludes to Romeo and Juliet, III, v, 9:

"Night's candles are burnt out, and jocund day
Stands tiptoe on the misty mountain tops." [GN 11]

3637 Joe -- the bartender, perhaps also the owner, of the White Swan* in Covent Garden* [MMA 12]

3638 Joey -- the name of a parrot once owned by a parson much to that man's good fortune [MMA 12]

3639 Joey -- the Thoday's* gray African parrot [NT 11]

3640 Johannisberger -- one of a family of great German white wines of the Rhine valley. See also Schloss Johannisberger. [mt]

3641 John -- the number three bell at Fenchurch St. Paul*, it weighs eight hundredweight, or just less than a half ton. It is tuned to strike A, and was cast in 1557. [NT 1]

3642 John, Augustus -- a celebrated English portrait painter (1879-1961), known for his flamboyant personality. His subjects include Dylan Thomas, G. B. Shaw, James Joyce, and Queen Elizabeth II. [WB 5]

3643 John Begg, a peg of -- a shot of "Blue Cap", Scotch whiskey manufactured by John Begg, Ltd., Glasgow [CW 14]

3644 John Bull -- a British weekly begun in 1906 and edited by Horatio Bottomley. Located at 92 Long Acre*, it lasted until after WW II. It also ran a competition paper, Bullets, and offered prizes. [UD 3]

3645 John Citizen -- a fictitious publication, though there was a weekly paper called Citizen. The headline, "Ninety-six Murderers at Large", actually appeared, but in the daily press. [UD 19]

3646 John Evangelist -- see Evangelist, John [NT 4]

3647 Johnnie -- the name by which Henry Weldon* addresses the bartender at the Resplendent in Wilvercombe*. Given Weldon's miserable abuse of people and language, it is probably not the man's name. [HHC 12]

3648 Johnny Walker -- a premium Scotch whiskey which still enjoys great popularity in both the Red and Black Label brands. It was introduced in 1820. [BC 7/MMA 12]

3649 Johnson -- the Thorpe* family chauffeur at Fenchurch St. Paul* [NT 2]

3650 Johnson, Mrs. -- one of the staff at Pym's Publicity*, she is in charge of the errand boys, the first-aid cupboard, and Dispatching, that branch of the agency responsible for getting the right ad layout to the right publication or distributor at the right time [MMA 6]

3651 Johnson, Superintendent -- the ranking police officer (see Police Ranks) assigned to investigate the death of Gharmian Grayle*. He welcomes the assistance of PW in his work. [qs]

3652 Johnson, James -- a waiter at the Rose and Crown* at Stapley*. It was he who let Mr. Grimethorpe* back into the inn early in the morning on October 14th. [CW 11]

3653 Johnson, Jeremiah -- a parishoner at Fenchurch St. Paul* [NT 19]

3654 Johnson, Samuel -- or Dr. Johnson (1709-1784), English essayist, poet, and lexicographer who, through James Boswell's biography of him, remains one of the central literary figures of the 18th C. Johnson was, perhaps, one of the world's great conversationalists, and the comment alluded to in BH (see Old Johnson) is typical of the sort of remark he is noted for. [BH 1]

3655 joint(s) -- a large piece of meat, as a leg of mutton, for roasting [GN 8]

3656 Joliffe -- Little Doddering's* undertaker [bc]

3657 Jollop's Concentrated Lactobeef Tablets for Travellers -- a DLS concoction created for MMA [MMA 4]

3658 Jolly Roger -- the black flag of a pirate vessel. There were variations on the size and design of the flag, but most had some sort of skull and crossbones device represented on them. [t]

3659 Jones [Miss] -- a student at Shrewsbury College* [GN 6]

3660 Jones, Mr. -- a member of the staff at Pym's Publicity* [MMA 1]

3661 Jones, Mr. -- the curate* at the church in Duke's Denver* [BH E2]

3662 Jones, Mr., of Jesus -- PW's name for Reggie Pomfret*. The name Jones and Jesus College have strong associations with the Welsh. [GN 14]

3663 Jones, E. B. C. -- probably a reference to Emily Beatrix Coursolles Jones (1893-1966), author of Helen and Felicia (1928), and Morning and Cloud, works of "women's" literature [BC 18]

3664 Jones, Inigo -- an architect and designer of court masques (1573-1652) who had extensive influence on English architecture. He did the Banqueting House in Whitehall, St. Paul's Church, and the piazza in the old Covent Garden, among others. The present St. Paul's Cathedral was designed by Christopher Wren after the Great Fire of 1666 destroyed the one on which Jones had worked. [BH E2]

3665 Jones, Sir William -- one of Mr. Endicott's* former customers [HHC 6]

3666 Jones, Sergeant -- station sergeant and P. C. Burt's* immediate superior [hp]

3667 jonquils -- a spring flower grown from bulbs (Narcissus jonquilla). It has clustered yellow or white flowers noted for their fragrance. [NT 7]

3668 Jonson, Ben -- see "O no, there is no end . . ." [GN 22]

3669 Jordan -- the river of Biblical and spiritual fame. It flows South from Lebanon along the eastern border of Israel into the Salt or Dead Sea [BH 1]

3670 Jordan, P. C. -- a police officer of the Hertfordshire constabulary who is fictitious [BH 11]

3671 Journals of this House -- the journals or records of the House of Lords, the originals of which are kept in the Victoria Tower of the Parliament Building [CW 12]

3672 Jove -- the poetical equivalent of Jupiter, chief of the Roman gods. Used in such expressions as "by Jove", it has become an acceptable expletive. [passim]

3673 Jowett Lodge -- the gatekeeper's home on the Jowett Walk* side of Shrewsbury College* [GN 5]

3674 Jowett Walk -- a street in the old central part of Oxford that runs parallel to Holywell St. and connects Mansfield and St. Cross Rds. It is on the North side of Jowett Walk, smack in the middle of the Balliol* Cricket Ground that DLS placed her fictitious Shrewsbury College*. The walk is named for the former Master of Balliol, Benjamin Jowett (1870-93 as Master), about whom it was written:

"Here come I, my name is Jowett;
There's no knowledge but I know it.
I am the Master of this college
What I don't know isn't knowledge."

[GN 1]

3675 Joyce -- the reference is to the great Irish writer, James Joyce (1882-1941). His more important works include the short story collection, Dubliners, which contains some of the 20th century's most magnificent and subtle language, and the novels, A Portrait of the Artist as a Young Man, Ulysses, and Finnegan's Wake. Joyce came to use the "stream of consciousness" writing technique more and more as his career progressed. The first novel mentioned is generally orthodox in style, but somewhat difficult. Ulysses is more experimental, especially the last section, while Finnegan's Wake is totally experimental. His influence on other writers is extensive, particularly upon William Faulkner in the U. S. Joyce plays with punctuation and word forms, and, what caused him the greatest problem in the publication of his works, he used language that some considered obscene. U. S. censorship of Ulysses, published in Paris in 1922, was not discontinued until December of 1933. [CW 7]

3676 Juan -- PW's servant and Spanish/Basque translator who helps PW with the magic act developed to impress the superstitious locals [ie]

3677 Jubilate•Deo•Omnis•Terra -- the inscription on the shoulder* of Jubilee*. It is the Latin text for Psalm 100:1: "Make a joyful noise unto the Lord all ye lands." [NT 4]

3678 Jubilee -- the number five bell at Fenchurch St. Paul*, she weighs about half a ton and is tuned to ring F#. She was cast in 1887. [NT 2]

3679 Judd, Arthur and Mary -- parishioners at Fenchurch St. Paul* [NT 19]

3680 Judd St. -- a part of the thoroughfare which, when considered with Hunter St., Brunswick Square, and Grenville St., connects Euston Rd. on the North with Guilford St.* on the South. The northern end of Judd St. is opposite St. Pancras Station. [SP 9/HHC 30]

3681 Judgment Day -- the Christian theological doctrine that holds to the inevitability of the Second Coming of Christ to judge all people of all ages. At that time, each soul is to be resurrected with its body as in life to face judgment. [NT 16]

3682 "Judgment of Paris" -- the title of one of Ann Dorland's* paintings. The reference is to the incident from Greek mythology wherein the Trojan, Paris, is forced to choose from among Hera, Athena, and Aphrodite which of them is fairest. He chooses Aphrodite who helps him carry off Helen, thus starting the Trojan War. This series of events is not related by Homer, and the subject of the painting is hardly unique to Miss Dorland. [BC 17]

3683 Judges' Rules -- a code regulating

the conduct of the Police, especially in such matters as the questioning of witnesses, the taking of voluntary confessions or other statements from the accused, and the charging of suspects. The Rules were first formulated in 1912, and have since been modified by directives from the Home Office* and with the approval of the Lord Chief Justice, hence, Judges' Rules. [FRH 7/NT 5/BH 9]

3684 Judkins, Mr. -- the judge who is friendly to the idea of keeping pubs open until 11:00 P. M. on weekdays [SP 10]

3685 Judson -- a member of the Egotists' Club* known to PW [cf]

3686 Judson, Luke -- a parishoner at Fenchurch St. Paul* [NT 19]

3687 jug -- slang for jail [SP 8]

3688 jug and bottle -- the service offered by a public house to people who do not drink on the premises but who bring their own jugs and bottles to be filled. This is called the "off-license" trade. [SP 10/HHC 15]

3689 juggins[es] -- person[s] who are easily duped, a possible derivative of the surname Juggins, but the exact origin remains unknown [GN 8]

3690 ju-jitsu -- a Japanese martial art for personal encounters not usually involving weapons, now commonly called judo. PW uses it when Brotherton* attempts to escape. [fr]

3691 jujubes -- (pronounced as joo-joobs) a chewy, fruit-flavored gumdrop or lozenge. The reference is to the Formamint* lozenges used by the coroner*. The word jujube is a thorough corruption of the Greek word zizyphus, a plant with an edible fruit which, depending on the species, may resemble in flavor anything from a cherry to an almond. The North African variety, the lotos mentioned in Homer's Odyssey, is mildly narcotic. [WB 6]

3692 Jukes -- formerly a porter at Shrewsbury College* who was fired for petty theft and who is caught in an effort to extort blackmail payments from Reggie Pomfret* [GN 8]

3693 Jukes, Mr. -- a member of The Society* who introduces PW to that group. Jukes is known to them as No. 37. [ab]

3694 Jukes, Mrs. -- wife to the porter in item 3692. She cares for Annie* Wilson's children while Annie is at work at Shrewsbury College*. [GN 3]

3695 Julius Caesar -- Shakespeare's tragedy of political intrigue based on North's translation of Plutarch's Lives. Ambition and conspiracy are the mainstays of the play which probably dates from 1599. [UD 10]

3696 jumper -- a sweater or loose jacket made of wool and usually knitted [CW 9]

3697 Junior Censor -- the assistant to the Censor, that college official charged with supervision of noncollegiate or "unattached" students at Oxford*. As Lord St. George* is attached to a college, his "interview" must have had to do with some of his highjinks in other regards. [GN 8]

3698 Junior Common Room [JCR] -- the students' social hall at an English college [GN 1]

3699 Junior High -- the Junior [or students'] High Table, usually reserved for the senior students at an English college [GN 13]

3700 Jupiter Tonans -- Jupiter the Thunderer, one of his many guises. It is interesting to note that Bunter can sound like that. [BH 15]

3701 jusjurandum -- see decline jusjurandum [dh]

3702 "Just so, they crossed . . . ." -- from The Second Brother* by T. L. Beddoes*, I, i, 247. The line is spoken to Marcello, a brother to the Duke of Ferrara, by Ezril, a Jew, in describing the ducal palace and its frenzy after the accident that threw the Duke from his horse and which is to prove fatal. [HHC 30]

3703 Justinian -- a vague reference to a work that PW had purchased at some earlier auction. In all probability the reference is to Justinian I, emperor of Constantinople (527-65), who was famous for his code of Roman

laws (*Corpus Juris Civilis*), in four parts, and for building St. Sophia. The manuscript in the allusion is probably all or some part of the *Corpus*. [ss/BC 3]

(K)

3704 K. C. -- King's Counsel, a barrister* who becomes known for his experience and ability is appointed King's (Queen's when the sovereign is female) Counsel and may charge higher fees and may have the assistance of junior counsel [pj/CW 14]

3705 K. C. B. -- the abbreviation for Knight Commander of the Bath, the second of three ranks in the Order of the Bath, an order of chivalry. The name derives from the bath which concluded the extensive preparations for the conferral of the honor and which precedes the installation ceremony. It dates from 1399 and is one of Great Britain's more prestigious honorary orders. [WB 8]

3706 K. C. V. O. -- the abbreviation for Knight Commander of the Royal Victorian Order, the next to highest rank of that Order. Established in 1896, it is awarded for important or personal service to the sovereign or to the royal family. Membership is unlimited and is granted exclusively by the sovereign in any one of five classes or ranks. [WB 8]

3707 Kt. -- or kt., the abbreviation for knight [WB 8]

3708 Kai Lung -- see *Wallet of Kai Lung* [CW 1/SP 4/GN 15/BH 7]

3709 kail -- Scots dialectical variant of kale, an edible member of the cabbage family which has wrinkled leaves but does not form a tight head [ss]

3710 Kamchatka -- the large Siberian peninsula between the Bering Sea and the Sea of Okhotsk. From its tip spread the Kurile Islands which are strung along to the northern island of Japan, Hokkaido. [FRH 25]

3711 *Kamerad* -- German for comrade. Used by German soldiers in WW I when hoping for quarter. PW uses the phrase "Hi! Kamerad" when, for the second time, he is left trussed up in the torture chamber. His goal is to have his captors leave him with some sort of light as he wishes to study their torture machines. [ab]

3712 Kathleen -- Margaret Selby's*

married sister visited by the Misses Selby and Cochran* during their trip to Glasgow to see the art exhibition [FRH 7]

3713 Katie -- a patron of the Crown* pub in Paggleham* who has a morbid curiosity--she wants to see William Noakes's* corpse before the inquest. The corpse is in a back room of the pub as the coroner's inquest is to be held there. [BH 10]

3714 Kaulfussia amelloides -- a variety of aster, a common and popular garden flower [GN 20]

3715 Kaye-Smith, Sheila -- an English regional novelist (1887-1956) who centered her work on Sussex. Among her works are Sussex Gorse and Joanna Godden. [UD 5]

3716 Keats, John -- English poet and letter writer (1795-1821) of the Romantic period most remembered for his exquisitely beautiful longer poems such as Endymion, The Eve of St. Agnes, The Fall of Hyperion, and others. However, when he chose to do so, he could write equally sophisticated and beautiful shorter pieces such as "To Autumn", and "This Living Hand". [GN 14]

3717 Keble -- one of Oxford University's colleges. See Oxford Colleges. [BH 5]

3718 keep -- a strongly fortified defensive position; the most heavily fortified part of a castle. See also Border Keep. [FRH 2/BH E2]

3719 keep stroak of time . . . -- follow the stroke or beat as established for the touch or peal**. The rhythm or beat would work out in change-ringing* as in any other music. [NT 1]

3720 Kelmscott Morrises -- a reference to the printing work of William Morris* at the Kelmscott Press, started at Hammersmith in 1890. The press issued only fifty-three books, but the ornamental letters, typography, and paper make copies of these works most valuable as they are masterworks of the printer's art. From the context it is suggested that the Shrewsbury College copies were of Morris's own writings, not some of the other material he published. [GN 6]

3721 Kenilworth, Lord -- otherwise unidentified, he sent a wreath to Lady Thorpe's* funeral. It was placed inside the hearse. He is fictitious. [NT 6]

3722 Kennedy [Milward] -- pseudonym of Milward Rodon Kennedy Burge (1894-1968), English author, reviewer, and civil servant. Kennedy wrote some twenty novels of mystery and detection during the 1930's, 40's, and 50's. Death to the Rescue (1931) and The Murderer of Sleep (1932) are considered among his better works. [FRH 27]

3723 Kensington -- a wealthy residential district in the West of London around Kensington Gardens (see Hyde Park) where the foreign embassies and the museums are located [BC 7/HHC 20/MMA 15/NT 4]

3724 Kensitite -- a follower of John Kensit (1853-1902), a strongly anti-Church of England Protestant nihilist who opposed ritualism and what he perceived as a Romanizing movement within the Church of England [bc]

3725 Kent -- one of the original "kingdoms" in England and, hence, does not have the suffix "shire". It borders on the southeast corner of the greater London area. [UD 16]

3726 Kent, Duke of -- Edward Augustus, Duke of Kent (1767-1820), fourth son of George III and father of Queen Victoria. He was never known as an intellectual powerhouse. [GN 3]

3727 Kent Treble Bob Major -- one of a class of dodging* or bobbing methods wherein the treble bell has a dodging course* instead of a plain one. Kent is an identifying name only and differentiates one form from another--such as Oxford Treble Bob Minor. Treble refers to the bell that follows the dodging course (see treble), and bob refers to the course followed. Major indicates that the method requires eight bells. Minor requires six. [NT 1]

3728 Kestrel, Leon -- Master Mummer, or actor, and something of a quick change artist and con man. He is not connected to E. Phillips Oppenheim's 1905 novel, The Master Mummer, but is apparently some other character of the

period. [WB 6]

3729 Kew -- the residential village near Kew Gardens* to the South and West of London. It is the home of Mr. Postlethwaite*. [BC 11]

3730 Kew Gardens -- officially, the Royal Botanical Gardens in the parish of Kew, the municipality of Richmond, Surrey. It is on the South side of the Thames, about seven miles West of London. One may see there some of the work of Sir William Chambers*, architect for the famous Chinese pagoda located there. [dh]

3731 key of seven sharps -- the modern composer may be Scriabin, but it is impossible to tell with certainty who DLS may have had in mind. The key is either C# major or A# minor as both have seven sharps. [BC 3]

3732 key-word -- when scrambling the alphabet for cipher work, some word is chosen, preferably without any duplicate letters. The first letters of the new alphabet are those of the key word, the remainder of the alphabet being left in its normal order. This scrambled alphabet can then be arranged in various ways to encipher plaintext messages. The recipient needs the keyword and the method of encipherment to decipher the message. [HHC 26]

3733 Keynes, Mr. -- John Maynard Keynes was 1st Baron Keynes of Tilton (1883-1946), Great Britain's most influential modern economist. From January to June of 1919, he was principal representative from the Treasury to the Paris Peace Conference. He resigned in June because of his opposition to the reparations clauses of the Versailles Treaty. It was his position that the defeated nations could not pay those reparations because they were bankrupt. The payments did, in fact, contribute to Hitler's later rise to power as they had exacted such a hardship on the German people and economy during the postwar years that Hitler could capitalize on that suffering as a base upon which to build much of his popular support. [BH 8]

3734 Khartoum -- capital of the Sudan in eastern Africa. The reference is in a limerick recited by PW which is by the Very Rev. W. R. Inge, former Dean of St. Paul's, London [BC 10]

3735 kidney [a gentleman of Peter's] -- temperament, class, sort, etc., a slang term [GN 13]

3736 Kidwelly poisoning case -- the popular press name for the case of R. v. Harold Greenwood, a solicitor accused of poisoning his wife. He was acquitted after a now-famous speech by his defense attorney, Sir Edward Marshall-Hall (1858-1929), at the Carmarthen Assizes. Kidwelly is on Carmarthen Bay, Wales. Mabel Greenwood had a history of poor health, mostly heart trouble, so when she was taken ill in early 1919, her physician treated her for her heart problem. When she died on January 16, 1919, he signed her death certificate without hesitation. A short while later, Harold married a Gladys Jones, a considerably younger woman with whom he had been having an affair for some time, even before Mabel's death. Suspicions were aroused and Mabel was exhumed at 3:00 A. M. on April 17, 1920, following which it was learned that she had consumed a fatal dose of arsenic just before her death. Greenwood was arrested and tried for her murder. During the trial it was revealed that he had purchased a ten gallon tin of Eureka weedkiller from a firm in Scotland. Eureka was a brand of sodium arsenide (60% arsenic), a particularly soluble pink powder that becomes perfectly clear and deep red in liquid form. It is virtually tasteless. Mrs. Greenwood had had red wine with the last meal she ate. However, others had consumed wine at the meal also; but the information that saved Greenwood's neck from the noose was probably the incompetence of the attending physician who seemed to have confused opium and morphine and who kept bismuth and Fowler's arsenic solutions (almost identical in appearance) side-by-side on the shelf of his apothecary closet. The defense attorney (Marshall-Hall) played on these difficulties of evidence and Greenwood was acquitted. The trial created quite a furor, especially in the matter and method of physicians keeping their own pharmacies. [SP 1]

3737 Kilkenny cats -- the OCEL relates that during one of the various

#3730 The Pagoda, Kew Gardens.

Irish rebellions ca. 1800, Kilkenny was garrisoned by Hessian soldiers who enjoyed tying two cats' tails together, hanging them over a clothesline, and then watching them fight until one or both of them were dead. When discovered, their officers ordered a halt to the practice, but it continued. One day a surprise inspection almost caught the cats midfight. A trooper cut the tails with his sabre and, later, explained to the officer that the cats had eaten each other with the exception of their tails so furious was their fight. [FRH 13]

3738 Kilmarnock -- a small city to the North of and slightly East of Ayr*. It has strong associations with Scotland's national bard, Robert Burns*. [FRH 10]

3739 Kimberley -- a city in central South Africa noted as a diamond mining center. Henry Ruyslaender* was returning from there when his wife approached PW for help. [pj]

3740 "Kind hearts are more than coronets" -- the line is from Tennyson's "Lady Clara Vere de Vere", stanza vii (line 55):

"Howe'er it be, it seems to be,
'Tis only noble to be good.
Kind hearts are more than coronets,
And simple faith than Norman blood."

The poem is an assault on the false pride of a long lineage. [HHC 21/BH 11]

3741 kind heart, which, despite the poet -- see item 3740 [NT 7]

3742 Kinder, Kirche, Küche -- German for, "children, church, and cooking", the traditional spheres of "womanly" activity [GN 22]

3743 kine -- the archaic plural of cow [CW 4]

3744 King and Queen -- in 1931, the time of HHC, they were George V and Queen Mary. A delightful story is told of how the officers of the Cunard steamship company approached H. M. King George for permission to name their next liner after "England's greatest Queen." They had in mind, of course, Queen Victoria as her name would continue their tradition of "ia" suffixes on the names of all their vessels. His Majesty, however, is reputed to have said, "My wife will be most flattered!" The ship was named Queen Mary, but it should be noted, though, that Her Majesty's full name was Victoria Mary. [HHC 5]

3745 King Charles' Head -- Charles I was beheaded on January 30, 1649, but the allusion here is to Charles Dickens's David Copperfield, Ch. 14. The amiable simpleton, Mr. Dick, has an obsession about the King's head, just as Potty Peake* has one about hanging. [NT 9]

3746 King Cophetua -- see Cophetua [GN 12]

3747 "King Darius said to the lions . . . " -- see "And she was as fine as a melon . . ." [GN 17]

3748 "King Death has asses' ears with a vengeance" -- this is PW's version of a line from T. L. Beddoes' Death's Jest Book**. See "Take thou this flower . . ." [HHC 34]

3749 King Dick Spanner -- a wrench manufactured by the King Dick tool company. They are excellent tools and use a bulldog as their trademark. [FRH 13]

3750 King Edward, the late -- Edward VII (1841-1910), the eldest son of Queen Victoria*. He succeeded her in 1901. [UD 3]

3751 King Henry -- the reference is to Henry VIII, father of Queen Elizabeth I, founder of the Church of England, and despoiler of Roman Catholic cloisters in England between the years 1535-40 during what is known as the Dissolution of the Monasteries under the direction of Thomas Cromwell, vicar-general. [NT 2]

3752 King Henry -- see "A babbled of green fields" [UD 4]

3753 King Herod -- or Herod the Great, king of Judea from 40-4 B. C. It was at his order that the slaughter of the innocents was carried out, thus forcing Joseph and Mary and the infant Jesus to flee to Egypt. [ie]

3754 King James I -- see James I [NT 2]

3755 King Lear -- Shakespeare's tragic hero of 1606. The play of that

name investigates the follies of an unwise old man who divided his kingdom among his daughters before his death in a test of love. The eventual results leave Lear mad from rage and maltreatment at the hands of his daughters Goneril and Regan, the two who had promised their love the loudest and who eventually do each other in. Cordelia, the loving daughter, is hanged by the evil Edmund, supposed Earl of Gloucester, and Lear dies of grief. The play is Shakespeare's chief investigation into the folly of old age, although he considers the problem elsewhere. [BH 18]

3756 King of Elf-Land -- see Elf-Land, King of [FRH 2]

3757 King Richard II -- the opening quote for this chapter is from IV, i, 1-6 of the cited history drawn from the life of Richard II, king of England from 1377-99 when he was "induced" to abdicate. See also Henry IV. [CW 14]

3758 King's Accession, Anniversary of -- the King would have been H. M. King George V, and the anniversary of his accession to the throne was May 6. That is not the date of his coronation, but is the date he officially became king upon the death of Edward VII. [GN 4]

3759 King's Cross -- one of the major railway termini in North London, built by the Great Northern Railway Co. for connections up the eastern side of Great Britain to Edinburgh and beyond. In 1922 it became, with the Liverpool St. Station, one of the termini of the London Northeastern Ry., and is now part of the Eastern Region of British Rail. It is adjacent to St. Pancras Station. [MMA 8/NT 17]

3760 King's Evidence -- to come to agree to testify against others with whom you were engaged in illegal activities in return for special consideration or a reduced sentence [MMA 20]

3761 King's Fenton -- a small town on the Yorkshire dales. It is fictitious. DLS did not know that area well, so it is difficult to tell which, if any, town she might have had in mind. [CW 3]

3762 King's Head -- a fictitious pub used by DLS. There are hundreds of real pubs by that name, but we may be certain that this one is fictitious as DLS carefully avoided using real places if there might be any chance of embarrassment resulting from it. [MMA 17]

3763 King's Mill -- the weir and rapids on the Cherwell* just beyond Parson's Pleasure*. Together they form an unforgettable challenge to punters and canoeists alike. [GN 11]

3764 kings-of-arms -- see College of Arms [CW 14]

3765 king's pawn to king's fourth -- a move in chess* involving the pawn directly in front of the king which is moved to a position three places in front of the king. On its first move, a pawn may move either one or two places. Therefore, counting the spaces occupied by both the king and the pawn, the pawn has moved from the second square to the fourth square. [sf]

3766 King's Proctor -- the representative of the court (canon or civil) appointed to oversee whatever his letters of proxy require of him. A Proctor is similar to an attorney, but his power is limited by these same letters of proxy. In this case, the King's Proctor would be an officer of a civil court responsible for keeping the court apprised of any relevant doings in "Mrs. Forrest's"* divorce suit before the divorce becomes final. [UD 15]

3767 King's Restoration -- May 29, 1660, a Tuesday, the date on which Charles II was restored to the throne of England after the Interregnum. Technically, he was king from the instant of his father's death on Tuesday, January 30, 1649, but his reign is usually dated from the 1660 date of his return to English soil. [NT 4]

3768 King's Robing Room -- approximately adjacent to the Royal Entrance at the base of the Victoria Tower in the Houses of Parliament*. The room is richly decorated with badges of sovereigns and frescoes of the legend of King Arthur. [CW 14]

3769 kings of arms -- see College of Arms [CW 15]

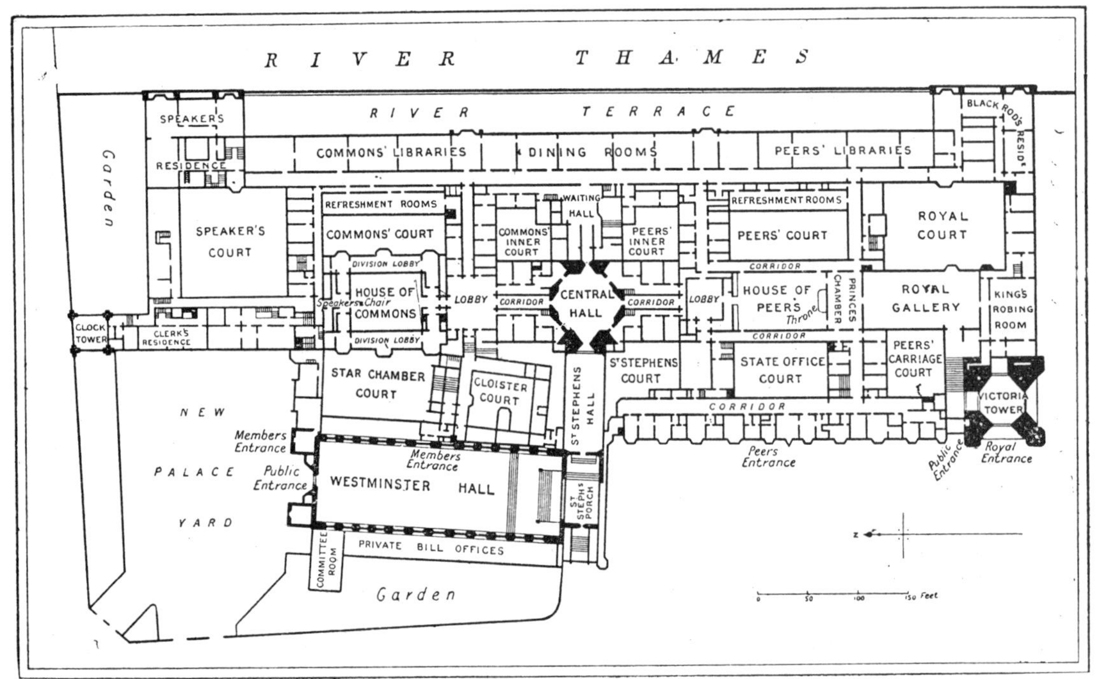

THE HOUSES OF PARLIAMENT.

#3768

3770 Kings of the Kukuanas -- the petrified remains of previous rulers of Kukuanaland. They and their country were created by H. Rider Haggard in King Solomon's Mines. [UD 11]

3771 Kingsley [welcomed the wild north-easter] -- PW is alluding to Charles Kingsley's (1819-75) "Ode to the North-East Wind", which begins:

"Welcome, wild North-easter!
Shame it is to see
Odes to every zephyr
Ne'er a verse to thee."

See also "do the thing that's nearest". [NT 1/BH 11]

3772 Kingsway -- a major thoroughfare in central London joining Holborn with Aldwych. DLS worked at Benson's advertising agency which was at 75 Kingsway in Kingsway Hall*. [HHC 30/MMA 12]

3773 Kingsway Hall -- on Kingsway*, it is a concert hall where gramophone recordings were made in the 1930's. It is now the West London Mission of the Methodist Church. [MMA 12]

3774 Kintyre -- the long peninsula to the West of the Isle of Arran [FRH 19]

3775 Kipling, Rudyard -- English poet and author (1865-1936), sometimes styled as the voice of the Victorian Empire. His output is vigorous and often dialectical, reflecting backgrounds set in India, New England, and Sussex in such works as The Jungle Book and Captains Courageous. [BH 8]

3776 kipper -- either a herring or salmon, usually a herring, that has been split and cleaned, then cured by salting and smoking [ab/FRH 7/SP 8]

3777 Kirk, Supt. -- the local police superintendent (see Police Ranks) who supervises the investigation into the death of William Noakes*. He, PW, and HV come to enjoy each other's antics with their game of speaking in quotations in an effort to see who can stump whom. It is to Kirk's very great credit that he can hold his own with PW and HV in that game as his educational background is no match for theirs. He is a hard-working man for whom PW seems to develop a sincere liking. [BH 7]

3778 Kirkcudbright -- the county town for Kircudbrightshire* in southwest Scotland. It is just above the River Dee's estuary and features 18th C. homes, wide streets, and the 16th C. McClellan's Castle. The town and the river's estuary are located on the northern end of Kirkcudbright Bay at the mouth of Solway Firth. The area remains a center of artists of all sorts and figures prominently in FRH. The name is pronounced as kur-coo-bree and is accented on the second syllable; it derives from kirk Cuthbert or church of Cuthbert (i. e. St. Cuthbert). [ss/FRH 1]

3779 Kirkcudbrightshire -- the mid-section of what is now the county of Dumfries and Galloway. It extended from the coast North to a point about opposite Loch Doon and from the River Cree* East to Maxwelltown. The southern border is Solway Firth. [ss/FRH 5]

3780 Kirkdale -- a small village along the Coast Road* between Gatehouse-of-Fleet* and Creetown*. The Coast Road is now identified as the A75 route. [FRH 2]

3781 Kirkgunzeon -- a small village to the North and East of Dalbeattie* [FRH 13]

3782 Kirkwall -- on the island of Mainland in the Orkneys in the far North of Scotland. It is the county town and features structures dating from the 12th C. [FRH 1]

3783 kirkyard -- churchyard [FRH 2]

3784 Kiss the Book -- loosely, swearing an oath in court, but, now, and for many years past, it has been considered adequate merely to hold the Bible while swearing such an oath. Such kisses used to be required before the relatively modern concern with hygiene and the spread of disease. [SP 20/NT 4]

3785 Kittle Cattle -- a Nutrax* headline. Kittle is a dialectical word meaning sensitive, ticklish, even skittish [MMA 4]

3786 Kitty -- see Climpson, Miss Alexandra Katherine [SP 16]

3787 Kitty -- a young and loving wife who speaks briefly about her husband's dangerous swimming habits [nf]

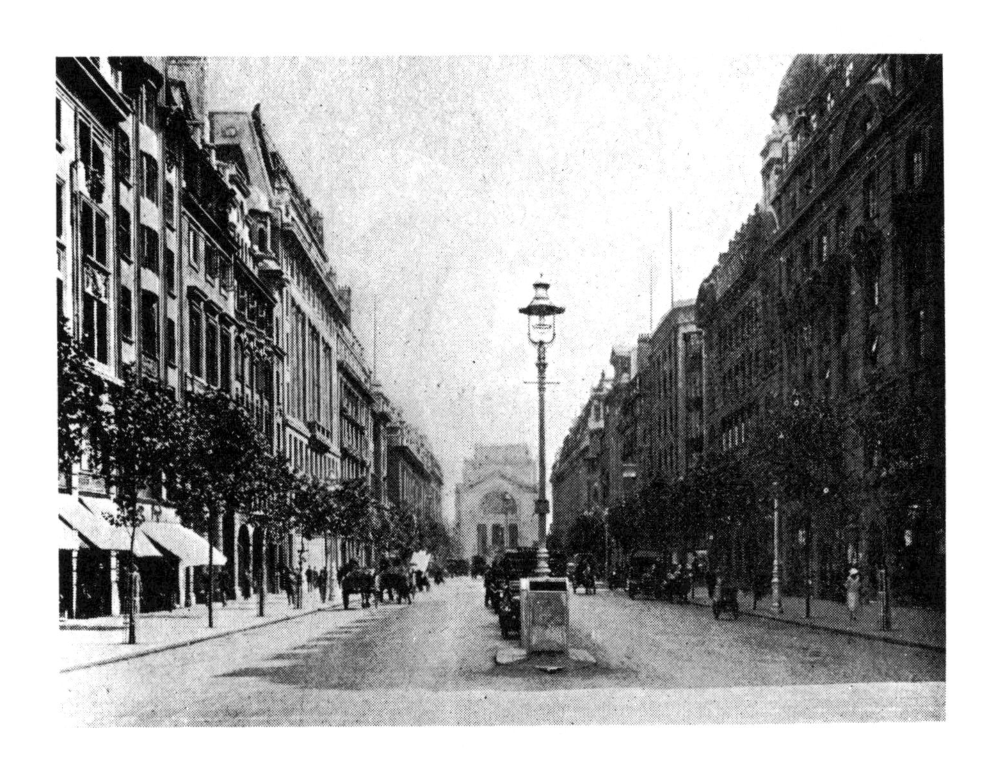

KINGSWAY, LOOKING SOUTH.

#3772 Kingsway, looking South, as DLS might have known it when working for Benson's.

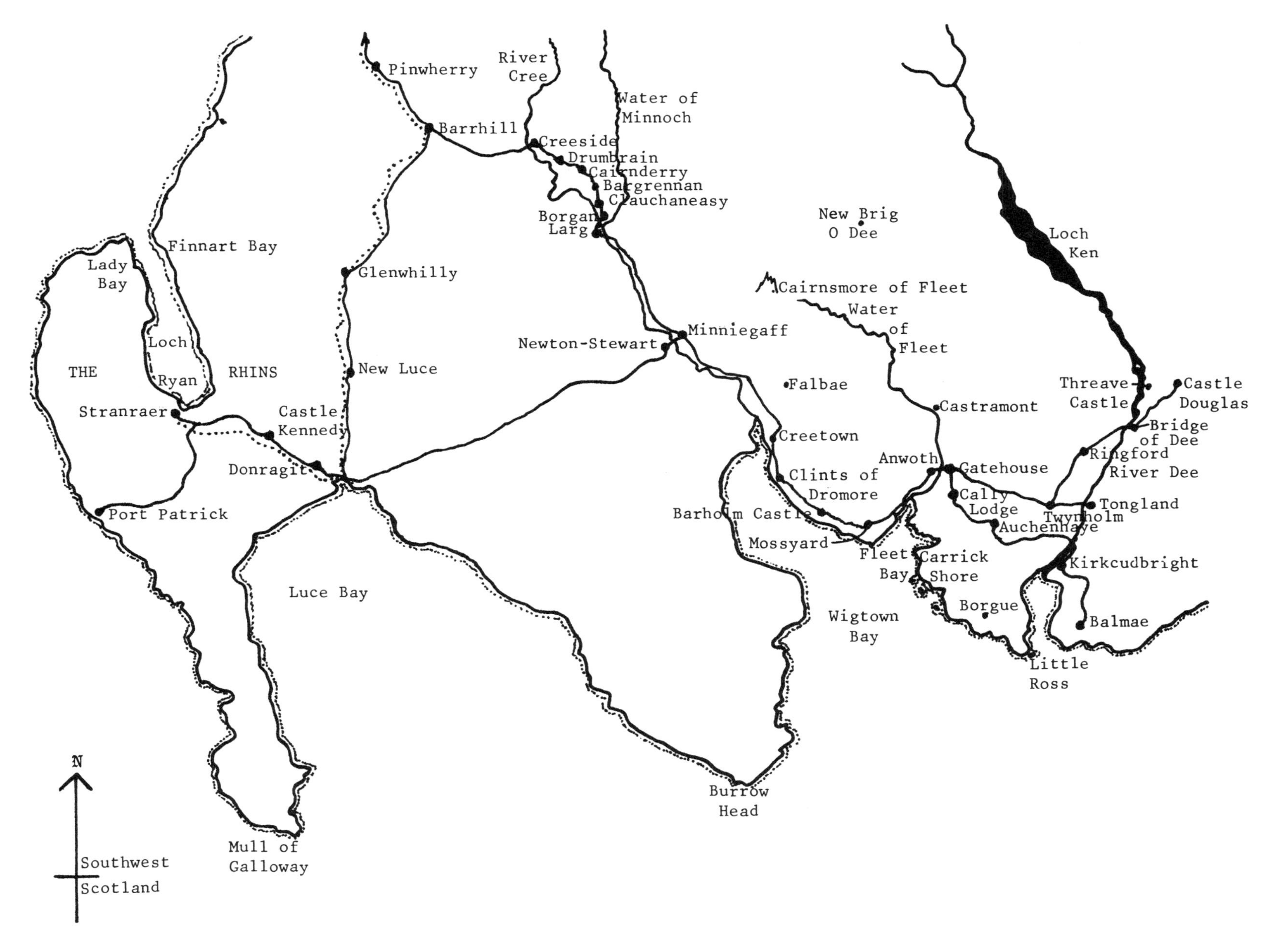
Pinwherry
River
Cree
Water of
Minnoch
Barrhill
Creeside
Drumbrain
Cairnderry
Bargrennan
Clauchaneasy
Borgan
Larg
New Brig
O Dee
Loch
Ken
Finnart Bay
Lady
Bay
Glenwhilly
Cairnsmore of Fleet
Water
of
Fleet
Loch
Ryan
THE
RHINS
New Luce
Newton-Stewart
Minniegaff
Falbae
Stranraer
Castle
Kennedy
Castramont
Threave
Castle
Castle
Douglas
Bridge
of Dee
Creetown
Donragit
Anwoth
Gatehouse
Ringford
River Dee
Clints of
Dromore
Cally
Lodge
Tongland
Twynholm
Auchenhaye
Port Patrick
Barholm Castle
Mossyard
Fleet
Bay
Carrick
Shore
Kirkcudbright
Luce Bay
Borgue
Wigtown
Bay
Balmae
Little
Ross
Burrow
Head
N
Southwest
Scotland
Mull of
Galloway

#3778

3788 Klassika Corsets -- an account handled by Pym's Publicity*. The product is fictitious. [MMA 10]

3789 knight in the ballad -- the outlandish knight in question is Sir Thomas in Richard Harris Barham's "The Knight and the Lady". While on one of his outings to collect specimens of flora and fauna, he falls into a stream and drowns. When recovered, the clothing is found to be full of eels which prove to be most delicious. Lady Jane, his not quite grief-stricken widow (she has been entertaining on the side), decides that it is better to have the eels than a properly buried husband, so she orders him thrown back into the stream to trap another catch of the delectable squirmers. [FRH 7]

3790 Knight of Grace -- see Order of St. John of Jerusalem [WB 8]

3791 knock-up -- to pay someone a visit for the purpose of arousing them from sleep. For other visits one would "look up". [GN 12/BH 2]

3792 Knockeans -- a hamlet just to the East of Creetown* [FRH 21]

3793 Knockout Wally -- a criminal mentioned by Parker* while trying to figure out who might have assaulted him [MMA 7]

3794 known another horse -- Polly Flinders*, another PW mount [HHC 27]

3795 "knows't thou the land where blooms the citron flower?" -- PW refers to the early lines of "Mignon", a poem by Johann Wolfgang von Goëthe which dates from his trip to Italy, a journey which influenced him greatly. The poem is written from the feminine point of view, making it an unusual item in the Goëthe canon. The subsequent honeymoon reference is to Italy, a favorite European honeymoon spot. [UD 12]

3796 knuckle[-duster] -- brass knuckles, a device for protecting the attacker's hand while increasing significantly the damage done to the person attacked [MMA 7]

3797 Kohn, Olga -- the professional model whose photograph Paul Alexis* had. However, he thought she was the lovely "Feodora", an exiled princess who awaited his arrival in Russia for their marriage and their joint effort to restore the monarch there. [HHC 22]

3798 Komisarjevsky -- Theodore Komisarjevsky, a Russian-born English theatrical designer (1882-1954) of great influence. His aluminum set designs for a 1933 production of Macbeth were controversial. [GN 8]

3799 Komski -- a fictitious artist with whom Marjorie Phelps* almost consented to live. She discovered later that he was a bully. [BC 16]

3800 kow-tow -- any almost reflex-action gesture of obeisance. The word is from the Oriental, especially Japanese, posture assumed before the shogun or emperor wherein one went down on one's knees, put one's buttocks against the heels and the forehead against the floor. Such position was maintained until the termination of the audience, which one hoped would be short, or until motioned to relax. The position is an effective deterrent to assassins as it is difficult to assault someone from that posture. [CW 9]

3801 Kraska -- the reference to the fingernails apparently relates to a beautician or some sort of cosmetic preparation, now unknown if real [UD 7]

3802 Krasky, Capt. Stefan Ivanovich -- Paul Alexis' grandfather in the fictitious genealogy [HHC 32]

3803 Kropotky, Nina -- Madame Kropotky welcomes PW to Bohemia* on his tour with Marjorie Phelps*. She is impressed and pleased that PW expresses admiration, however equivocal, for the musical work being performed as he arrives. [SP 8]

3804 Kropotky, Vanya -- PW's host on his first stop on the tour of Bohemia* in his search for Ryland Vaughan* [SP 8]

3805 Kropp -- not a typographical error for Krupp, the famous German steel firm, but one suspects that it is they whom DLS had in mind as the firm of Kropp is unknown [HHC 6]

3806 Kruschean feelings -- the reference is to Kruschean Salts which were added to water and drunk for the

#3789 An illustration from the edition of 1864, New York, for "The Knight and the Lady".

relief of pains and for a general toning up. Widely advertised before WW II to give one "that Kruschean feeling", they are not now available. [CW 6]

3807 Ku Klux Klan -- the American organization that spreads bigotry and racist and religious hatred under the guise of patriotism. It was formed in the Confederate states near the end of the American Civil War, was outlawed by Congress in 1871, and still exists. [nf/MMA 5]

3808 Kukuanas -- see Kings of the Kukuanas [UD 11]

(L)

3809 L. B. & S. C. Electric Railway -- the first electrically powered line of the London, Brighton, and South Coast Railway which was opened in 1904 and included the Victoria-Crystal Palace Line. This reference dates the novel prior to November, 1922, as the railways were merged in 1923, the L. B. & S. C. becoming part of the Southern Railway. [WB 5]

3810 l. b. w. -- see cricket [MMA 18]

3811 L. C. C. regulation -- one of many London County Council regulations for fire safety. The L. C. C. (now absorbed into the Greater London Council) incorporated such regulations into their building bylaws. Other localities made their own bylaws until about 1960, when the Building Regulations replaced them. [MMA 7]

3812 L. C. C. School -- a London County Council School. Schools in England are run on a county basis by the County Council* through Education Committees. They would be public schools in the same sense as in North America--open to all. [HHC 24]

3813 L. M. S. -- the London, Midland, and Scottish Railway Co., the amalgamation in 1923 of the London and North Western, the Midland, the Caledonian, and other smaller companies. It is, since 1948, a part of British Rail. [FRH 5]

3814 L. N. E. R. -- the London and North Eastern Railway, an amalgamation of the Great Northern, Great Eastern, and other smaller companies. It was created in 1923 and is now a part of British Rail. See North-Eastern. [NT 2]

3815 _l'amour_ -- French for "love", or "passion". Used here it suggests the rather shallow sort imagined by those who do not have the real thing. [HHC 15]

3816 _L'Anneau d'Améthyst_ -- a book found among Denis Cathcart's* personal items. It is the last of four volumes by Anatole France in his _Histoire Contemporaine_ published between 1896 and 1901. The title refers to an amethyst ring worn by a bishop whose

see two rival clerics vie for at his death. [CW 2]

3817 l'Enclos, Ninon de -- or de Lenclos, a name taken by Anne L'enclos (1620-1705), a Frenchwoman known for her beauty and wit, both of which she kept to a very advanced age. Molière and Voltaire frequented her salon, and she had many famous lovers. [HHC 32]

3818 "La caill', la tourterelle . . ." --PW is singing a dirty little French ditty which means absolutely nothing at all when translated into English:
 "The quail, the turtledove
 And the pretty partridge
 Beside my blonde (female intended)
 How pleasant, pleasant, pleasant,
 Beside my blonde--"
The song is a jolly, well-known bit of vulgarity, the details of which are lost in translation. It is surprising that Mr. MacBride* knows enough to be scandalized. [BH 7]

3819 "la femme jalouse de l'oeuvre" -- French for, "the wife jealous of the (husband's) work" [BH 18]

3820 La Fontaine, Jean de -- French poet (1621-95) whose fables are models of polished language used to imply a worldly-wise, everyday moral code. They remain perennially popular. See Contes de la Fontaine. [aq]

3821 La Rotisserie de la Reine Pédaque -- a book found among Denis Cathcart's* personal effects. It is a philosophical romance by Anatole France published in 1893, and features the predictable mixture (for Cathcart) of a confused man's life, in this case a priest, and a beautiful but loose woman who, indirectly, is the cause of his death. See also Manon Lescaut. [CW 2]

3822 Laban [old] -- he was, indeed, "a bit of a tough". He was a patriarch of Mesopotamia, covetous and shrewd, not to mention shifty. His behavior toward Jacob was not what we today would think of as honorable. See Genesis 29:1 to 31:10 for the full story. [SP 12]

3823 Labour -- see Labour Party [CW 9]

3824 Labour Party -- a British political party claiming to represent the working classes. Its roots are traced to 1869, but it did not gain any power until the election of 1906, when James Ramsay MacDonald, Philip Snowden, and others were returned to Parliament as members of a unified political party. The Labour Party has strong socialist leanings. It displaced the Liberals as the radical party of two-party government and first came to power in 1924. [CW 9]

3825 laddered -- see stocking ladders [HHC 5]

3826 Ladies' Compartment -- in the bygone days of greater gentility, a separate compartment in a railway carriage was reserved for use by single or unaccompanied ladies [FRH 7]

3827 The ladies. God bless them. -- Supt. Kirk* may be alluding to Mark Twain's after-dinner speech, "The Ladies", a humorous response to a toast proposed at the 1872 Anniversary Festival of the Scottish Corporation of London [BH 7]

3828 Ladies' Room -- many London clubs --most until recently--did not allow women on their premises. Those that did quite often had special areas set aside for the ladies or other nonmembers who were guests. [GN 4]

3829 lady-altar -- an altar dedicated to the Virgin Mary, as in a Lady Chapel* [NT 2]

3830 Lady Athaliah's tower -- see Frolic Wind [GN 4]

3831 Lady Bay -- the local name for one of the small bays at the mouth of Loch Ryan. It is just opposite and below Finnart Bay*. [FRH 19]

3832 "Lady, by yonder blessed moon I swear." -- PW is quoting from the famous "balcony scene" of Romeo and Juliet, II, ii, 107. Juliet's equally famous response is (l. 109), "O! swear not by the moon, the inconstant moon . . . ." A few sentences later PW adds line 108, "That tips with silver all these fruit-tree tops." [BH 16]

3833 Lady Chapel -- a chapel dedicated to the Virgin Mary. It is generally at one's right when facing the main altar. [UD 22]

3834 "The lady doth protest too much,

methinks." -- from Hamlet, III, ii, 240, during the famous play within a play scene [UD 5]

3835 "Lady Head" -- a totally incorrect reference to the warden or to the headmistress at a ladies' school or college. To use such a phrase would expose either one's ignorance, prejudice, or both. [GN 4]

3836 "Lady Maisry, Ballad of" -- see "Ballad of Lady Maisry" [CW 16]

3837 Lady of Shalott -- see Shalott, Lady of [t/FRH 6]

3838 Lady Somebody -- see beautiful letter from D[onne] [BH P]

3839 Lady Susan -- one of the Wimsey family ghosts in residence at Bredon Hall. PW is supposed to have tipped his hat to her on the terrace one day. [BH E2]

3840 Lafit[t]e -- a reference to the Chateau Lafite or Lafite-Rothschild near the village of Pauillac in the Commune of the Haut Médoc. It produces what is considered to be France's best Bordeaux wine, and possibly the world's best such wine. It is a dry red. A Lafite '75 mentioned was one of the great vintages of the last century. The Lafite '76 mentioned is apparently not the real thing. [mt/CW 10/UD 6]

3841 lag -- slang for an ex-convict [NT 2]

3842 Laincolonne -- a Frenchman's attempt to pronounce Lincoln [NT 8]

3843 laisser-aller -- French for, "unlimited freedom" or "lack of restraint" [GN 7]

3844 Lamb and Flag -- a long, narrow pub on St. Giles St., Oxford. It has long been popular. [GN 12]

3845 Lamb's Conduit St. -- a street which connects Guilford St.* with Theobald's Rd.* in the northern section of Holborn*. Its name is drawn from an ancient water supply to Holborn built by William Lamb. As Parker* lives on Gt. Ormond St.*, to which Lamb's Conduit is at right angles, it is a fast route for him to use to get to Kingsway* to catch a diver tram* to Westminster. Part of the street is now barred to traffic and serves as a pedestrian walkway. [UD 6/SP 9/HHC 30]

3846 Lambard [old] -- an archaeologist whose conclusions regarding ancient funerary rites were being contradicted by Phoebe Tucker* and her husband, Bob*. Lambard is apparently fictitious. [GN 1]

3847 Lambert, Bishop -- head of the Orinoco Mission* and friend of PW. Lambert would be the bishop's own name and not that of his see. From the description, he is apparently retired from active field work and serves as the Mission's liaison in London. He is also fictitious. [UD 12]

3848 Lambeth -- a section of London on the South side of the Thames directly across from Westminster and the Houses of Parliament. It derives its name from Lambeth Palace, seat of the Archbishop of Canterbury when he is in London. The Palace is a 700 year old residence adjacent to Archbishop's Park. PW lives in Lambeth during his period of undercover work spent penetrating "The Society". [ab]

3849 Lamentations -- the Old Testament book by the prophet Jeremiah which follows the book of Jeremiah. It relates God's love for the Jewish people whom he is punishing for their transgressions. Supt. Kirk* is punning on the word and its relationship with the other prophecies mentioned. [BH 9]

3850 lammed -- soundly struck, hit, or thrashed [FRH 23]

3851 lamp lighter [up it like a] -- to go up something quickly. Lamplighters had to move quickly from light to light in a relatively short period of time, get up it, light it, and go on to the next one. The fuel could not be wasted in daylight, but the lamps needed to be lit before darkness fell, so rapidity of movement was essential. Most of them carried little step-stools to reach the wicks easier. With the coming of gas, a pilot light allowed control with a switch operated by a long stick. [HHC 30]

3852 lampblack -- a pigment made from soot or any residue from incompletely burned carbonaceous material. PW or Bunter would find use for it in lifting fingerprints off of light-col-

ored or clear objects. [WB 3]

3853 Lamplough, Mr. -- PW's dentist and helper in the case of faked murder and real arson who is also Arthur Prendergast's* dentist [te]

3854 lampisterie -- French for a reading or waiting room,as in a train station [mt]

3855 Lampson and Blake -- owners of Jim Thoday's* ship, the Hannah Brown*. The firm is located in Hull* and is fictitious, as is the ship. There was, however, a company called Lamport and Holt of which DLS could have known and drawn upon for inspiration for her company. [NT 6]

3856 Lancaster, Duchy of -- the dukedom of Henry of Bolingbroke which passed to the Crown when he became Henry IV in 1399. Since that time the sovereign has retained the duchy as a separate and distinct entity which pays its revenues to the Crown for the management of its personal expenses. [UD 14]

3857 Lancaster, "Spot" -- a member of the de Momerie crowd who fancies an attachment to Dian de Momerie. His nickname reflects negatively on his personality. [MMA 9]

3858 Lancelot and Guinevere -- the allusion is to Tennyson's* Idylls of the King, in either "The Coming of Arthur" or "Lancelot and Elaine", and seems to have mixed the two passages cited. In the former, Guinevere's eyes fall when they meet Arthur's (l. 469), and in the latter, Guinevere's eyes are lifted up to Lancelot's and dwell there (ll. 83-5). It would be easy to confuse them. [BH 9]

3859 Lancelot Gobbo -- "between conscience and fiend". He is a clownish servant in II, ii, 16ff., in The Merchant of Venice*, who is given to playing all sorts of word games. [UD 22]

3860 lancet -- a narrow, often tall, window, sharply pointed at the top [NT 2]

3861 Landru -- Henri Desiré Landru, the French "Bluebeard", a lonely hearts killer who is known to have disposed of at least eleven victims, but no one is certain how. The Duchess is a bit confused in that Landru's oven had only a few unrecognizable bone fragments in it. He was guillotined on February 23, 1922. [SP 1]

3862 Langley -- a young ethnologist and a professor of that subject at a Cambridge* college. His observations allow PW to concoct a series of mystifying acts to rescue Alice Wetherall* from her husband's hideous tortures. [ie]

3863 language of the Apostles -- Greek. The various New Testament books of the Apostles have come to us in Greek. [ie]

3864 Language Special -- a course of study in language in some way limited to a "special" area, in this case, philology* [GN 7]

3865 Lar -- see Lares [BH 4]

3866 Lares -- plural of Lar, a household god in ancient Rome, one to a home. They were protective spirits, often deified ancestors, sometimes a hero, especially if connected to the family in some way. [GN 17]

3867 Larg -- a farm at the union of the Minnoch and the Cree** near Galloway Forest State Park and South of Bargrennan on the A714 [FRH 2]

3868 Larne -- in Northern Ireland across the North Channel and due West of Stranraer*. It is the Irish terminal of the Stranraer to Larne auto and passenger ferry service. [FRH 5]

3869 The Last Days of Pompeii -- a novel published in 1834 and written by Edward Bulwer-Lytton. The action centers on a love story unfolding just before the eruption of Vesuvius that destroys Pompeii. The book gives a reasonably accurate picture of Roman life at the time. [WB 10]

3870 "Last night you slept in a goosefeather bed . . ." -- see "It is a goosefeather bed!" [BH 1]

3871 "Last of all the woman died also" -- HV is reading from Matthew 22:27, Jesus's answer to the Sadducees. She may also be reading Mark 12:22 or Luke 20:32 as the line appears in all three places. [HHC 16]

3872 "The last refuge and surest reme-

dy . . ." -- from Burton's Anatomy of Melancholy** [GN 23]

3873 Last Supper, card of -- see card of Last Supper [UD 22]

3874 Laszlo -- Philip Laszlo de Lombos (1869-1937), member of the Royal Society of Portrait Painters and widely regarded for his portraits of Edward VII, Lords Haldane and Roberts, Theodore Roosevelt, and others [BH E2]

3875 latch, on the -- shut, but not locked [FRH 3]

3876 Late Perpendicular -- see Perpendicular [NT 1]

3877 Latouche, Abbé -- a cleric local to the area near the Legros* farm near Chateau-Thierry*. It was he who reported the stranger at the farm to the proper authorities. [NT 8]

3878 Latymer Scholar -- one of the named scholarships at Shrewsbury College*, it is fictitious. Like the Rhodes Scholarships for American students at Oxford, such named scholarships are usually valuable and are awarded on a basis of academic potential and need. PW donates £250 to that scholarship's fund during the wedding festivities in BH. [GN 12/BH P]

3879 laudanum -- a Latin word referring to opium, any of its derivatives, or a tincture of it. Opium was introduced to Western medicine by the Swiss alchemist, Paracelsus (1493?-1541). It was he who applied the word laudanum (most highly praised) to his concoction of opium, gold, and pearls. The British physician, Thomas Sydenham (1624-89), perfected the tincture of opium, naming it after Paracelsus's brew. [BH 13]

3880 Laugh, lover, laugh. This is the end of the journey . . . -- the words are PW's, but he seems to be alluding to Shakespeare's song from Twelfth Night, II, iii, 40ff: "O mistress mine! where are you roaming?" wherein one reads: "Journeys end in lovers meeting." [BH 3]

3881 laurels -- aromatic leaves of the shrub or tree Laurus nobilis, native to the Mediterranean area. It is also called the bay tree and is the source of bay leaves as used in cooking. From the ancient practice of awarding wreaths of laurel as an honor, we obtain the phrase "covered with laurels" as an indication of great accomplishment. Because of the mild climate, laurel can be grown in England, too. [ss/NT 20]

3882 Laurieston Rd. -- the A 762 route from Tongland North to New Galloway* by way of Ringford. Laurieston is about seven miles North of Kirkcudbright*. [FRH 14].

3883 Lauriston -- a typograhical error in some editions. See 3882. [FRH 25]

3884 laurustinus -- also laurustine, a shrub (Viburnum tinus) of the honeysuckle family. It has fragrant pink or white flowers. [dh]

3885 lavabo -- a wash basin with a tank and spigot above for water storage. It is handy for those places where indoor plumbing is incomplete for whatever reason. In a more general sense the term applies to a closet-sized private washroom, a small (tiny) lavatory. [SP 14]

3886 lave -- rest, remainder [FRH 24]

3887 Lavender, Hezekiah -- the elderly former sexton at Fenchurch St. Paul* who rings Tailor Paul, the tenor or deepest tone bell. He is the acknowledged leader of the bell ringers and, even though too old to be sexton, he retains the right to ring his bell for deaths and funerals. [NT 1]

3888 Law and the Prophets -- PW is being slightly irreverent here. He is likening Mr. Hankin's* discourse to a reading from the Old Testament Scriptures, specifically to introductory passages of the Anglican Eucharist. The intent is to suggest, simply, that PW is paying especially close attention. [MMA 1]

3889 law calf -- the more durable, uniformly light-brown calf bindings of law books used in preference to the sheepskin bindings more common in the U. S. Law bindings do not wear as well as other bindings, but the books are not used as rigorously as some other reference volumes might be. [CW 10]

3890 Law Courts -- the Royal Courts of Justice on The Strand* near Chancery Lane* dating from 1874-82 and

built to replace the originals in Westminster*. There are more than twenty courtrooms. [MMA 12]

3891 law of chivalry -- the rules of behavior and propriety, the purpose of which, if observed by all parties, is to allow all persons to enjoy themselves comfortably. They are an outgrowth of, but not a part of chivalry in the Medieval sense as practiced by the courts of love*. [GN 14]

3892 Lawrence, D. H. -- David Herbert Lawrence (1885-1930), English novelist, essayist, poet, and short story writer. In 1912, he eloped with and married Frieda von Richtofen, sister of Manfred, the Red Baron of WW I air warfare fame. Lawrence is considered a great if inconsistent writer. His novel, Lady Chatterley's Lover, and his collection of poems, Pansies, were both banned as obscene at various times. In The Plumed Serpent he explains his theories about the Nietzschean superman. He is probably best remembered for his short stories and his critical work, Studies in Classical American Literature.

Lawrence held some rather unusual ideas regarding philosophy and psychology which found their way into his writing. At times he becomes so involved in the ideas and their attendant symbolism that he becomes obscure and vague. Despite those flaws, Lawrence will be remembered as one of the greatest of the writers of the early 20th C. [CW 7/BC 18/SP 8]

3893 laws about bottles and half-bottles -- a reference to the licensing laws included in the Defense of the Realm Act of 1914. The law allows licensed bars, etc., to sell liquor for consumption "on premises" or, during normal business hours, to sell package goods for consumption "off premises". The specific reference to bottles and half-bottles is unclear, but may, perhaps, refer to wine. [HHC 15]

3894 "The Lay of the Last Minstrel" -- written in 1805 by Sir Walter Scott, it is a narrative poem telling of Lady Margaret of Branksome Hall, beloved of Baron Henry of Cranstown, and how the Baron overcomes a feud to win Margaret. The story is based on an old Border legend of the Goblin Gilpin Horner and is written as a lay, or short narrative lyric meant to be sung by a minstrel. [CW 3]

3895 lay the blows behind -- make the blows or strikes behind or after the bells that are dodging* at that time and in preparation for his own dodge into the eighth or last place in that change and before hunting down* [NT 1]

3896 Layton, Miss -- a Shrewsbury College* third-year student who is expected to earn a first in English [GN 7]

3897 Lazarus -- brother of Mary and Martha of Bethany. It is recorded in John 11:43 that Jesus raised Lazarus from the dead after four days, considered to be Jesus' greatest miracle. [ie]

3898 "Le Carillon" -- see Verhaeren [NT 8]

3899 LeFanu, J[oseph] Sheridan -- Irish author (1814-73) of stories of mystery and the supernatural. He is best and rightly remembered for Uncle Silas: A Tale of Bartram Haugh. He has been ranked with Wilkie Collins, but the comparison cannot stand close scrutiny. Wylder's Hand is not one of LeFanu's better works. HV spends some time researching his works preparatory to writing about him as an excuse for her presence at Shrewsbury College*. This somewhat parallels DLS's own infatuation with Wilkie Collins's work. A projected study of Collins' detective fiction was begun, but DLS never found time to complete it. LeFanu's name is pronounced as if spelled leff-new, with the accent on the first syllable. [NT 9/GN 7]

3900 Le Havre -- see Havre [BH 2]

3901 Le Queux -- William [T.] Le Queux (1864-1927), English author of novels, etc., featuring mystery, crime, and international intrigue. The name rhymes with le-cue. [BC 18]

3902 Leach, Mrs. -- the mother of a noisy infant with whom she attended the inquest into the mysterious corpse found in Fenchurch St. Paul*. She is a parishoner there. [NT 4]

3903 lead, get off the -- to get off the hook, to be released from

whatever usually or presently "leads" or controls one's life. A dog's leash is also called a lead. [HHC 1]

3904 Lead and I follow as Sir Galahad says. -- the reference is to Tennyson's The Idylls of the King, "Gareth and Lynette", line 726. [UD 11]

3905 leaderettes -- additional small headlines below the main headline in a major news story and before the first paragraph of the story itself [CW 14]

3906 leading-strings -- the OED identifies them as "strings with which children used to be guided and supported when learning to walk"; hence, figuratively, to be childish or dependent [MMA 6]

3907 lead[s] -- the front position in each change, or the bell that rings in that position. The lead end is the change upon which a pattern of changes* is designed beginning with rounds*. After twelve changes the order would return to rounds, but for variation the thirteenth change is bobbed to become 1-3-5-2-6-4, the new lead end. The whole course of Plain Bob Minor consists of 5 leads, each of twelve changes, making sixty changes without repetition. [NT 1]

3908 leads -- the lead panels that make up the roofing material on the roof of the belltower at Fenchurch St. Paul*. Lead was often used as a roofing material as it is soft, easily worked, and durable. [NT 2]

3909 League for the Encouragement of Matrimonial Fitness -- one of Sadie Schuster-Slatt's* unnatural selection organizations. Such outfits have been popular for years, even becoming cultural staples in those countries where arranged marriages are common, but the perverse natural intelligence of the population has prevented their general acceptance. [GN 3]

3910 League of Nations -- one of the outgrowths of WW I and a predecessor in concept of the present United Nations. The League became operative on January 16, 1920, with headquarters in Geneva, Switzerland. The U. S. never joined and other countries either entered late, left early, or were expelled so that the League never managed to function with any efficacy. It dissolved itself and transferred its assets to the U. N. in April of 1946. [FRH 1/HHC 22/NT 16/BH P]

3911 Leahampton -- this fictitious community is definitely located in Hampshire, but is likely not Winchester as no cathedral is mentioned. Petersfield, Farnborough, Basingstoke, Andover, Eastleigh, and Aldershot are all possibilities, but positive association is impossible. The name is likely a combination of Eastleigh and Southampton spelled with a bit of poetic license. [UD 4]

3912 Leahampton Mercury -- the local newspaper for the Leahampton* area. It is fictitious. [UD 20]

3913 leam -- an old word for drain* and DLS employs it in the name of some of her fictitious communities

3914 Leamholt -- one of the Cambridgeshire* communities of NT. It is fictitious as presented here, but has many of the qualities of March*, a community on the A141 route fourteen miles East of Peterborough. See also leam. [NT 1]

3915 Leamhurst -- the fictitious village near which Henry Weldon* farmed the place he inherited from his father, George. It is supposedly located near Ely* in what is now Cambridgeshire*, then Huntingdonshire or the Isle of Ely, then separate counties; it could be identified with Earith. See Earith Bridge and leam. See also #7173. [HHC 17]

3916 lean and hungry look -- an allusion to Shakespeare's Julius Caesar, I, ii, 193:

"Yond Cassius has a lean and hungry look;
He thinks too much: such men are dangerous."

The phrase now refers to any sort of scheming and plotting of a nefarious sort. [GN 18]

3917 leapt into the gulf -- HV is thinking of Macaulay's long narrative poem, "Horatius", stanza LIX, which recounts the story of how Horatius and two friends held off an invading force while Roman citizens wrecked the only bridge across the Tiber. Just before the bridge fell, the two

friends escaped across, but Horatius was forced to jump into the torrent and swim to safety in full armor. There is much patriotic sentiment. The exchange between HV and PW that follows the citation here is to the poem's emphasis on all of Rome's citizens working together against a common enemy, but, in England, a peer or the relative of one, is more effective, especially in distracting the newshounds. Macauley's poem is probably based on Livy's history of Rome, Ab Urbe Condita Libri, Book II, x. [BH 14]

3918 leather -- to beat someone as with a leather belt or strap [HHC 27]

3919 "Leave me, O Love . . ." -- Sir Philip Sidney's* Sonnet CX from Astrophel and Stella, according to some editions. Other scholars do not include this sonnet with that group. The lines quoted are numbers one through eight, the sonnet's octave. [GN 11]

3920 leaven -- see Truth in advertising is like leaven . . . [MMA 5]

3921 Leblanc, Madame -- Mrs. Leblanc, the day housekeeper for Denis Cathcart's* Paris apartment [CW 5]

3922 Ledbury, Ambrose -- one of Ann Dorland's* pre-Penberthy* crushes [BC 16]

3923 Lee, Tony -- Charmian Grayle's* latest conquest who escorts her to Sir Charles Deverill's* costume party as the White King from Through the Looking Glass*. She comes as the White Queen. [qs]

3924 Leeds -- a wool center in the Middle Ages, Leeds has grown to the point where, in the 19th and 20th centuries, it has become a world center for textiles and ready-to-wear clothing. It is 194 miles North of London in West Yorkshire. [HHC 32]

3925 "left talking" like the hero of Man and Superman -- the hero is Jack Tanner in G. B. Shaw's (1856-1950) comedy of 1903. He is "left talking" in the famous Don Juan in Hell sequence midway through the play. [GN 21]

3926 Lefranc, Mrs. -- owner of the boarding house where Paul Alexis* and, later, HV take a room. Mrs. Lefranc is a tough, shrewd, sentimental woman who isn't about to be duped by anyone. See also #81. [HHC 10]

3927 leg[-break] -- see cricket [MMA 18]

3928 leg-pull -- as in pulling one's leg; a joke, teasing, etc. [MMA 20]

3929 Leger, the [St. Leger] -- a famous horse race, the oldest of the five classic flat course races run annually in England. It is named after the Yorkshire landowner, Anthony St. Leger, was first run in 1776, and except for some wartime interruptions, has been run on the Town Moor Course at Doncaster during the September race week ever since. Formerly it was a great social occasion. The other classic races are The Derby and The Oaks, run at Epsom; and the 1000 and the 2000 Guineas races run at Newmarket*. [FRH 13]

3930 Leggatt, Mr. -- one of the tenants at Duke's Denver who seems to be having difficulties with a mortgage [BH E2]

3931 Legitimation -- during the 1920's this issue was of vital interest to the peerage. By the Legitimacy Act of 1926, children could be legitimized by the subsequent marriage of their unmarried parents, but such legitimation offered no claim with regard to succession in those instances where hereditary titles might be involved. This denial of claim may be the Prohibition DLS is referring to, but it is uncertain. [CW 14]

3932 Legros, Jean -- the name provided for the body found at Fenchurch St. Paul*. It is an alias. Legros is the husband of Suzanne, and father of Pierre, Marie and a baby. [NT 8]

3933 Legros, Pierre -- Suzanne's* grandfather, an elderly man who refused to leave his farm even though the world had collapsed around it during WW I. It is to her credit that Suzanne stayed with the old gentleman and helped him keep the farm. [NT 8]

3934 lei -- plural of leu, the official Rumanian unit of currency [CW 5]

3935 Leicester -- an ancient city North of Oxford on a direct route from Manchester* to London by rail. To the

Romans, the city was Ratae Coritanorum, but by the time of the Domesday Book in 1086, it was listed as Ledecestre. Part of the Roman town is still extant as the Jewry Wall. Simon de Montfort and Thomas, Cardinal Wolsey are two of history's famous figures associated with Leicester. [WB 6]

3936 Leicester Square -- a square with a garden in the center located in London's West End* and a short distance from a home built there in the 17th C. by the Earl of Leicester, a nephew of Robert Dudley who was also an Earl of Leicester and Queen Elizabeth's favorite [MMA 2]

3937 Leicester Square tube station -- the subway (Underground) station in central London located at the intersection of Charing Cross Rd.* and Cranbourn St. on the southeast corner and a block East of Leicester Square*. [HHC 30]

3938 Leider ohne Worter -- or, correctly, lieder; "Songs Without Words". Mendelssohn* wrote a series of such short piano pieces in the Romantic style. [HHC 20]

3939 lemon yellow -- the light, bright yellow that the name suggests [FRH 2]

3940 lemur -- an arboreal animal resembling monkeys but distinct from them. They are noted for their large eyes, soft, wooly fur, and long, furry tails. PW has one as a familiar and pet while in his disguise as a wizard. [ie]

3941 Leopard -- see "too vulgar big" [HHC 19]

3942 leprosy -- the chronic degenerative disease caused by the bacillus Mycobacterium leprae. It is no longer the feared problem it once was. [BC 20]

3943 Leptosiphon hybridus -- a variety of phlox, a common and popular garden flower [GN 20]

3944 Lerouge, Jacques -- thief, safecracker, and female impersonator (Célestine Berger) who attempts to steal diamonds from the Dowager Duchess of Medway*. PW's nickname for him is Jacques "Sans-culotte"*, a reference to his female impersonations. [aq]

3945 lerve -- a deliberate misspelling of love to express contempt for the popular novelette variety [BH P]

3946 les beaux yeux de la cassette . . . -- French for, "the beautiful eyes of Uncle Peter's money box", but it means that the invitation is an attempt to guarantee that Uncle Peter isn't told anything that will shut off Saint George's supply of additional funds [GN 9]

3947 les forces vitales -- see métier d'époux [BH 19]

3948 Lesser Redpoll -- a type of finch, the males having a distinguishing red cap [GN 1]

3949 lesson -- the Scripture Lesson [NT 5]

3950 Lesston Hoe -- a fictitious town on the southwest coast of England [HHC 1]

3951 "Let everything that hath breath" -- see "Praise Him in the cymbals" [NT 2]

3952 "Let pass the justice of God" -- the line is from The Count of Monte Cristo (1844) by Alexandre Dumas, père*, Ch. LXVI, and refers to the execution of Mme. de Winter [UD 7]

3953 Let the bell that the Treble turns from behind -- each bell moves in and out of various positions during the ringing of a peal. In this case, the treble* bell is moving into the last place (behind) so the bell that is there has to move someplace else in the changing sequence, to be turned out as it were. [NT 11]

3954 Let the extortioner -- see "Ill-gotten goods never thrive . . ." [BH 10]

3955 "Let the galled jade wince . . ." -- from Hamlet, III, ii, 252, near the end of the play within a play scene wherein it states: "We that have free souls, it touches us not: let the galled jade wince, our withers are unwrung." A galled jade applies to a horse that has been chafed by the saddle and refers to Claudius's reaction to the play he has watched at a point just before the player king is murdered. [UD 5/GN 4]

3956 let the heavens fall and tread the

antic hay on the ruins -- HV is alluding to Christopher Marlowe's (1654-93) play, Edward II, I, i, 59:
"My men, like satyrs grazing on the lawns,
Shall with their goat-feet dance antic hay." [BH 5]

3957 "Let time pass; it helps more than reasoning." -- HV attributes this to Queen Elizabeth I in GN, Ch. 9, and there is no reason to dispute this citation. [sf/GN 9]

3958 "Let us beget a temperance . . ." the line is from Hamlet, III, ii, 7-9, the famous "advice to the players" speech, "Speak the speech, I pray you . . . ." [BH 6]

3959 "Let Zion's children" -- the "elaborate passage of Bach"* which PW whistles after the discovery of Goyles's entry into the grounds of Riddlesdale Lodge* during the night when Denis Cathcart* died. That the passage is "elaborate" is something of an understatement. It is taken from "Sing Ye to the Lord" (Singet Dem Herrn), BWV 225, a motet* for double choir.

The piece in question uses two standard SATB groups with the cited part of the text interwoven between the two for some twenty-four pages of the score. The whole text is:
"Sing to the Lord a new made song,
let the saints in congregation sing and praise Him,
Israel rejoice in him that made thee.
Let Zion's children be joyful in their King,
and let them praise His holy name.
Let them with timbrel and with harp sing his praises."

It is interesting that Bach chose this particular passage for a complex bit of work which he constantly makes more important as the piece progresses. The passages are from Psalms 148 and 150, and were probably performed first on May 12, 1727, at the birthday celebration of Friedrich Augustus, "The Strong", Elector of Saxony, although it may have been introduced at St. Thomas's, Leipzig, on New Year's Day, 1727. [CW 3]

3960 lethargic encephalitis -- see encephalitis, lethargic [WB 7]

3961 Letter from Göttingen -- see "Send him back again . . ." [HHC 8]

3962 letter-press -- anything printed on a press where the letters are individually set by hand or machine as opposed to offset printing or some other photographic method [NT 2]

3963 Letters of a Self-Made Merchant to His Son -- the book found on Sir Reuben Levy's* nightstand. It was written by George Horace Lorimer (1867-1937), an American editor and author. Lorimer's keen understanding of the reading tastes of the American middle class saved the Saturday Evening Post magazine from extinction and he was a pioneer in the subgenre of business fiction. His books are strong arguments for rugged individualism and include the title for this entry and the sequels More Letters (etc.), Jack Spurlock--Prodigal, and Old Gorgon Graham, which were not as successful. The Letters were serialized in the Post and then, in 1904, began a long history in editions such as the one that Sir Reuben was reading before his death. The letters were written, supposedly, by John, "Old Gorgon", Graham, head of the House of Graham & Co., pork processors in Chicago, to his son, Pierrepoint. [WB 4]

3964 letters patent -- papers issued by a government granting special rights, privileges, or restrictions

3965 Levannier, Charles Marie -- a fictitious member of the French legation to the court of the equally fictitious Duke Francis Josias of Saxe-Coburg-Gotha*. Levannier married the Duke's illegitimate daughter, Anastasia. [HHC 32]

3696 level -- used throughout East Anglia* to refer to a drainage system, as in 100-Foot Level, a 100-foot wide drainage ditch [HHC 22/NT passim]

3967 level-crossing -- the grade-level intersection of a highway and a rail line. Before the rapid growth of auto travel, it was sometimes the practice to leave the gates closed to vehicular traffic at rail crossings. The automatic safety devices are a relatively recent invention. [HHC 2]

3968 Levett, Mr. -- the Home Secretary's* representative at the exhumation of Sir Reuben Levy's body

[WB 12]

3969 Levly, Rachel -- a typographical error in some editions, see item number 3975 [MMA 5]

3970 Levy -- the fictitious moneylender to whom the Viscount St. George* has turned for financial help while at college. It is an archetypal Jewish name often used by DLS for moneylenders. [GN 9]

3971 Levy [old] -- a reference to Sir Reuben Levy* [SP 12]

3972 Levy, Lady Christine -- née Ford, the wife of Sir Reuben Levy*. Born into the Hampshire Fords, she and her husband were known to the Wimseys for many years as friends. When Lady Levy has to identify her husband's remains, it is the Dowager Duchess of Denver* to whom she turns for companionship and support through the ordeal. [WB 2]

3973 Levy, Levy, & Levy -- the fictitious firm to which William Noakes* owes £900, capital and interest. They hired Macdonald & Abrahams* to get the money. No one in Pagglehem* realized the nature of Noakes's* dealings, so the demand for such a sum of money came as a surprise. [BH 6]

3974 Levy of Portman Square, Mr. -- Sir Reuben's* uncle. See also Portman Square. [WB 6]

3975 Levy, Rachel -- daughter of Sir Reuben and Lady Christine Levy**. She and Freddy Arbuthnot* manage to overcome their differences in religion and their engagement is announced in SP, seven years after they were first linked romantically. The delay results from the need to overcome those religious difficulties. [WB 4/SP 12/MMA 5]

3976 Levy, Sir Reuben -- a very straightforward and honest London financier who is murdered. He and his wife have long been friends to the Wimseys, and PW and the Dowager Duchess figure prominently in the solution to Sir Reuben's disappearance and death. [WB 2]

3977 Lewis and Short, Messrs. -- Charlton T. Lewis and Charles Short, compilers of a highly regarded Latin-English dictionary published in 1879 and used by the Viscount St. George* to help him deal with the Cosmographia Universalis*. The work is still in print, a highly useful compilation of derivations and citations of places where particular words and phrases are used in other works. [dh]

3978 li -- an obsolete abbreviation for libre, or pounds; hence, "ii li tenterhooks*" becomes two pounds of tenterhooks [BH E2]

3979 Liberty's -- founded in 1875 by Arthur Liberty, the shop is known for its excellent silks and other fine fabrics. While still reflecting an aura of the 1920's, Liberty's today has a wide line of goods from silks to wallpaper to bronzes. [WB 3]

3980 Liberty tie -- one of HV's ties or scarves borrowed by PW to complete the necessary touches on a costume. As ladies' fashions had a strongly masculine air at the time, the effect would have been quite Bohemian*. See also item 3979, the source of HV's tie. [hp]

3981 library -- PW's library at 110A Piccadilly is described as "one of the most delightful bachelor rooms in London". Its scheme is black and primrose (pale yellow) and features exquisitely comfortable furniture, a grand piano, and a magnificent collection of incunabula*. [WB 2]

3982 library subscription -- before free public libraries became widely available, libraries were founded and maintained by "subscription" or paid membership [SP 12]

3983 "License my roving hands . . ." -- HV is quoting lines 25-6 of John Donne's poem, "To His Mistress Going to Bed." The short work is one of Donne's more explicit efforts. [BH 17]

3984 licensing hour -- the 5000+ pubs in London are regulated by strict licensing and opening regulations. The usual operating hours are from 11:00 A. M. to 3:00 P. M. and from 5:30 to 11:00 P. M. There may be local variations of as much as a half hour. Ten or fifteen minutes prior to closing, the barman or publican will warn patrons so they can order that last drink legally. On Sunday the typical hours are from noon to 2:30 P. M. and from 7:30 to 10:30 P. M. if the establishment is open at all.

[SP 10]

3985 li-chee -- or litchi or leechee, the oval fruit of the Litchi chinensis, a member of the soapberry family. The fruit's flesh is edible fresh or dried and is very sweet. When fresh, the flesh is white with a faint pinkish cast. When dried, it is black. [HHC 16]

3986 Liddell, Mr. -- a local at Duke's Denver* who sometimes stops by Bredon Hall* to use the library [BH E2]

3987 Liebfraumilch -- rather a catchall name for a pleasant wine from Germany. It may come from any one of several German wine-producing areas, and most is quite mild and semisweet. It is an excellent companion for fish. [BC 7]

3988 life preserver -- slang for either a cosh* or a woven leather pouch filled with shot and fixed with a leather handle [SP 1]

3989 Liffey, Mrs. -- the owner of the boarding house at Windle* where Miss Climpson* stays [SP 18]

3990 "The Light of Africa" -- a diamond necklace of 115 stones stolen from Mrs. Ruyslaender*. Diamonds certainly are the light of Africa, but the name's resemblance to the real diamond, now a part of the British Crown Jewels (The Star of Africa) is not lost. [pj]

3991 "lighten our darkness . . ." -- the opening of the third collect* of Evening Prayer in The Book of Common Prayer: "Lighten our darkness, we beseech thee, O Lord; and by thy great mercy defend us from all perils and dangers of this night." [NT 19]

3992 lights -- see according to his own lights [HHC 31]

3993 like a dog with two tails -- see dog with two tails [HHC 7]

3994 Like charity, he never fails. -- Miss Martin* is alluding to I Corinthians 13:8. The chapter is a short one and is often committed to memory as it is one of the most beautiful passages in the New Testament. The first verse is: "Though I speak with the tongues of man and of angels, and have not charity, I am become as sounding brass or a tinkling cymbal." [GN 6]

3995 "Like Niobe, all Tears." -- PW is quoting from Hamlet, I, ii, 149, and both he and Shakespeare are alluding to the Greek legend of the boastful Niobe who so angered the gods that they killed eleven of her twelve children because of her boasting about them. They changed her into stone afterward, but she still wept, water running down the stone. She is a popular subject for fountains. [MMA 13]

3996 "Like Summer Tempest came her Tears" -- the line is, indeed, Tennyson's*, and appears as the "Introductory Song" in The Princess (see also "Tears, Idle Tears). The passage is:

"Rose a nurse of ninety years,
Set his child upon her knee--
Like summer tempest came her tears--
'Sweet, my child, I live for
thee.'" [MMA 13]

3997 Like that horrid man who pretended to be a landscape painter -- the reference is to Tennyson's* "The Lord of Burleigh", ll. 7 and 79-80. The poem is a narrative that describes at length both the events that PW remembers. [SP 4]

3998 like the lady in Maeterlinck -- see Maeterlinck [BC 18]

3999 Like the man in Max Beerbohm's story . . . -- the allusion is to Beerbohm's* short story "A. V. Laider" (1914) in which Beerbohm has the narrator remark, inwardly, "I had wished to be convincing, not touching. I can't bear to be called touching." The story can be found in Seven Men and Two Others, published by the Oxford University Press in their series The World's Classics, in which it is Volume 610. [SP 16]

4000 like the people in the Psalms, I lay traps -- PW is probably referring to Psalm 69:22: "Let their table become a snare before them: and that which should have been for their welfare, let it become a trap." The song continues (verse 27): "Add iniquity unto their iniquity: and let them not come into thy righteousness." [UD 6]

4001 like the poet Wordsworth, he heard it and rejoiced -- the reference

is to William Wordsworth's (1770-1850) poem, "To the Cuckoo: O Blithe New-comer!":

"O blithe new-comer! I have heard,
I hear thee and rejoice.
O Cuckoo! Shall I call thee bird,
Or but a wandering voice?"

[UD 9/BH 7]

4002 like the ranks of Tuscany -- see Tuscany, like the ranks of [FRH 28]

4003 like young Harry with his beaver on -- the allusion is to King Henry IV, Part I, IV, i, 104ff:

"I saw young Harry with his beaver on
His cuisses on his thighs, gallantly armed,
Rise from his ground like feathered Mercury."

The lines are Sir Richard Vernon's speech in that play. A beaver is a helmet, and cuisses are partial armor for the thighs (front and side only). [BH 7]

4004 "The Lilacs" -- the name of William Grimethorpe's* home [ae]

4005 Lillo, George -- see George Barnwell [BH 15]

4006 Limehouse -- a section of eastern London adjacent to the docks and Limehouse Basin and Limehouse Cut, East of the City* along Commercial Rd. as it becomes East India Dock Rd. at the junction of Burdett Rd. The area has strong associations with any sort of criminal activity one would care to pursue, especially in fiction. [MMA 7]

4007 limelight -- loosely, in the center of things, receiving all attention. The term is from the early theatrical lighting device wherein a mixture of oxygen and hydrogen was burned to render a small piece of lime incandescent, a mirror directing the light. [WB 5]

4008 limerick -- a rigidly structured bit of light verse in five lines. Lines one, two, and five must rhyme according to one scheme, while lines three and four must rhyme according to a second scheme. All lines follow a rigid pattern of metrical structure. Edward Lear (1812-88) wrote many nonsense limericks such as:

"There was an old man with a beard,
Who said it is just as I feared!--
Two Owls and a Hen,
Four Larks and a Wren,
Have all built their nests in my beard!"

While many limericks are suitable for and enjoyed by children, many more are not. PW has chosen to share one of the latter with the landlord at the Anwoth Hotel*. [FRH 7/MMA 1]

4009 Lincoln Imp -- the original of the Imp from which the door-knocker is copied will be found in the Angel Choir of Lincoln Cathedral. It is a grotesque carving of an imp with long ears and only one leg showing; it is sitting on the other leg. Imp is used here in its original sense as being a small, evil being or demon. [HHC 22]

4010 Lincoln's Inn -- one of the great Inns of Court*, Lincoln's was probably named for Henry de Lacy, 3rd Earl of Lincoln, who resided there during the time of Edward I. As an Inn of Court, it dates from 1310. [UD 17/BC 3]

4011 Lincolnshire -- the large English county that borders along The Wash* and the North Sea. It centers on Lincoln, an ancient cathedral city. See also Lincoln Imp. [bc/NT 7]

4012 Lind, James -- Scottish physician and naval surgeon whose studies aboard ship in 1749 (not 1755 as DLS states) led to the publication of A Treatise on Scurvy in 1753. He related his use of lemons and oranges in the successful treatment of scurvy, or vitamin C deficiency. However, it was not until 1795 that Sir Gilbert Blane's work convinced the British Admiralty to issue lime juice to all Naval vessels, the limes actually being lemons. From this comes the sobriquet "limey" for Englishmen. [fr]

4013 line and wash -- black line drawings that have been shaded or colored with diluted ink or water color [FRH 7]

4014 line by line like Euclid -- constructing a step by step series of propositions as one does when solving a problem in geometry, the object being to arrive at a single, logically inescapable conclusion proving whatever it was that one has set out to prove [HHC 26]

4015 Line upon line . . . -- the reference is to Isaiah 28:10 and 13: "For precept must be upon precept, precept upon precept; line upon line, line upon line; here a little, and there a little." [BH 9]

4016 Lion St. -- a short North-South street connecting High Holborn* with Theobald's Rd.* It is a typographical error in some editions for Red Lion St., item #5638. [SP 20]

4017 lions of Oriel -- a reference to the heraldic crest of Oriel College, Oxford. See also Oxford Colleges. [GN 13]

4018 liripipe [sleeves] -- pendulous, full, as on an academic robe or a minister's gown [GN 12]

4019 Lister Professor of Medicine -- a special and honorary chair of medicine named for the great English surgeon, Joseph Lister (1827-1912). It is not known who, if anyone, DLS had in mind as there is no faculty of medicine at Oxford, only a Nuffield Professor of Clinical Medicine. Therefore, the chair and its occupant must be fictitious. [GN 5]

4020 Listerine -- the world-famous mouthwash. Amber in color and strong in flavor, it was, for many years, available wrapped in a khaki-colored paper tube, the wrapping being almost as famous as the product. It is still available widely. [BC 19]

4021 literary executor -- an executor specified in one's will to supervise one's publishing career after one has died. A literary executor may be the same as the executor for the rest of the estate, but it is usually a person who had a knowledge of or expertise in such matters. [SP 7]

4022 _Litterae Humaniores_ -- Latin for the humanities as in literature, arts, and the classics [GN 14]

4023 "Little and grisly, or bony and big . . ." -- the lines are from a song sung by skeletal figures of a dance of death (see The Dance of Machabree) in V, iv, 15-18, of T. L. Beddoes' _Death's Jest Book_**. The song is sung in a ruined Gothic cathedral at midnight. The first two lines of the quote refer to those who have died. [HHC 3]

4024 little architect -- Thipps, the poor soul who found the nude corpse in his bathtub, thus starting PW on the events recorded in WB. See also Thipps, Alfred. [NT 12]

4025 _Little Arthur's England_ -- fully _Little Arthur's History of England_ by Lady Maria Dundas Graham Callcott (1785-1842). The book is a children's history of England first published in 1835 but still in print as late as 1937 in yet another "new" edition. Lady Callcott wrote a series of "Little Arthur" histories. [NT 7]

4026 Little Dancing Men -- a reference to the stick-figure code in Conan Doyle's* "The Adventure of the Dancing Men". The story is interesting for its code, but it is not one of Sherlock Holmes's* more brilliant cases. [NT 10]

4027 Little Doddering -- a fictitious community in Essex* as presented in the story, but it is a deliberate corruption of the name Doddinghurst, a real Essex town. It provides the setting for a contested will dispute with overtones of Burke and Hare*. The ghostly goings-on are also reminiscent of at least two of the popular ghost stories told in Pluckley, Kent, a village that boasts of at least twelve resident spooks. [bc]

4028 Little Dorrit -- the nickname of Amy Dorrit, heroine of Charles Dickens's* novel, _Little Dorrit_*. She is known for her open kindness and beauty of character. The "Little" relates to her small size. [UD 6]

4029 _Little Dorrit_ -- Charles Dickens's novel, serialized in 1857-58, that relates the financial struggles of the Dorrit family both in and out of the Marshalsea Debtor's Prison. The characterization of the heroine (see item 4028) is especially memorable, but the book has not worn well when compared to some of the other Dickens novels. See also Mrs. Merdle.

4030 little-ease -- a place of confinement that is narrow and uncomfortable. There is one in the Tower of London. It is also a name for a stocks or pillory. [BH E2]

4031 Little Flower -- Paul Alexis's* nickname for Mrs. Weldon* [HHC 5]

4032 Little James St. [No. 103] -- a fictitious address [NT 4]

4033 A little knowledge is a dangerous thing -- the almost correct quotation is from Alexander Pope's* "An Essay on Criticism", l. 215. The rest of the sentence is:

"Drink deep, or taste not the Pierian spring:
There shallow draughts intoxicate the brain,
And drinking largely sobers us again."

PW is also correct in reminding Supt. Kirk* that the word is "learning" in the line cited, not "knowledge" as is misquoted. That error is a common one. [BH 9]

4034 Little Percy -- for whatever reason, Percy, as a given name, has long been used in contempt. The most famous and offensive Percy is probably Sir Percy Blakeney, the quintessential fop in Baroness Orczy's The Scarlet Pimpernel. An unhappy member of PW's WW I unit called PW "Little Percy", but lived to regret it. [GN 17]

4035 lived to wear a coronet -- see Alfred, Lord Tennyson and "Kind hearts . . ." [BH 11]

4036 liver fluke -- a type of worm, such as the Fasciola hepatica, that invade mammalian livers, especially those of sheep; a parasite [GN 2]

4037 Liverpool -- a major seaport, second only to Southampton*, and the third largest city in England. It is located on the River Mersey on the North central part of England's West coast. [nf/WB 10/CW 3/UD 11]

4038 Liverpool Assizes -- see assizes [CW 3]

4039 Liverpool Street -- a short street in London between Bishopsgate and Blomfield on to which the Liverpool St. Station (train terminal) fronts. It is the station to which DLS refers in MMA. A pub on the street and a post office near it are mentioned in NT. [MMA 4/NT 9]

4040 Livinsky -- a "Russian type" actress recommended to Maurice Vavasour* by Isaac Sullivan's* talent agency [HHC 23]

4041 Liz -- either Mrs. Timothy Watchett* or Mrs. Ezra Wilderspin* [CW 11/NT 4]

4042 Lizzie's girls -- from the context, apparently a reference to the children of the daughter of the woman speaking. She is frightened by the prospect of some "Ripper" type and the resultant horrors, the possibilities of which are suggested at the beginning of the story. [nf]

4043 Lloyd George, Mr. -- David Lloyd George (1863-1945), British statesman born in Wales. He was Prime Minister from 1916-22, and played a leading role in creating the Versailles Treaty. His work also led to the creation of the Irish Free State. He was elevated to an earldom in 1945. See Lord George Pension. [HHC 26]

4044 Lloyds Bank -- where Mr. Grimethorpe* had his accounts in Stapley*, and where Paul Alexis* has his accounts in Wilvercombe*. The firm is a large and respected international banking house headquartered at 71 Lombard St., London, and has branch offices throughout Great Britain. It is one of the five major British banks, acts as agent for the British Army, and has worldwide connections. It is in no way related to Lloyd's Insurance or to Lloyd's Shipping. [CW 11/UD 7/SP 14/HHC 10]

4045 lob -- see cricket [MMA 3]

4046 Lob's Pond -- also Cob's or Hob's Pond; a jail or lockup. Lob also means a country fellow, a bumpkin, clown, or goblin. Both references are appropriate when considered in light of PW's predicament at the end of the chapter. [CW 11]

4047 lobster mayonnaise -- usually an appetizer. The cold, cooked lobster is seasoned with lemon juice, olive oil, salt, pepper (white) or Tabasco, shallots, and herbs. Drain after marinating, mix with mayonnaise, and serve on lettuce. Top the mixture with additional mayonnaise and decorate with more chunks of lobster, tomatoes, hard-boiled egg slices, etc. It should be accompanied by a light, dry white wine. [BC 7]

4048 lobster pots -- the underwater traps made of wood and netting used to trap lobsters in such a way as to assure they stay alive and unharmed [HHC 17]

4049 lobster's dress shirt -- the sartorial equivalent of the caterpillar's foot gear, another expression of approval in the extreme [MMA 5]

4050 Local Government Act of 1888 -- this Act provided a revolutionary change in the basis of local government in England. Administrative authority was taken away from the justices of the peace and was given to local elected county councils. The justices, however, retained all of their former "powers, duties, and liabilities of justices of the peace as conservators of the peace." [CW 14]

4051 Loch Ryan -- the large loch in the West of Dumfries and Galloway which opens out into the North or St. Patrick's Channel. Stranraer* is at the foot of Loch Ryan. [FRH 19]

4052 Loch Skerrow -- a roughly shield-shaped loch about eight miles North of Gatehouse-of-Fleet*. The loch eventually empties into the Little Water of Fleet. [FRH 3]

4053 Loch Trool -- a small lake roughly nine miles North of Newton-Stewart* and about four miles northeast of Bargrennan. It is now inside the Galloway Forest Park. [FRH 3]

4054 Loch Whyneon -- listed as Loch Whinyeon when it is listed at all. It is about six miles northeast of Gatehouse-of-Fleet. [ss]

4055 Lochinvar -- see Young Lochinvar [CW 9]

4056 lock -- see cipher lock [cb/ab]

4057 lock the forme -- the forme is a wood and metal frame of various sizes into which the letters and print blocks are placed, squared up, and then forced into a rigid unit by a series of opposing wedges called quoins. Such a locked-up form prevents the various small pieces of type from shifting during the printing or proof-making processes. [MMA 8]

4058 Locke, W. J. -- William John Locke (1863-1930), an English popular novelist who is best remembered for The Beloved Vagabond which centers on a Bohemian wanderer. [BC 18]

4059 locomotor ataxy -- lack of control of voluntary muscle movements. It is a typical symptom of.various nervous disorders. [MMA 1]

4060 locum tenens -- a substitute or deputy. The Latin phrase is usually applied to members of the professions, especially clergymen and doctors, and not to blue-collar workers. [MMA 5]

4061 Loder, Eric P. -- the fictitious wealthy New York sculptor and psychopath introduced to the story by Varden*. Loder worked in metals. [cf]

4062 lodge in a garden of cucumbers -- the reference is to Isaiah 1:8: "And the daughter of Zion is left as a cottage in a vineyard, as a lodge in a garden of cucumbers, as a beseiged city." "Lodge" is used here to mean a small tent or hut of a temporary nature, perhaps even an arbor or some temporary covering as for a watchman. The image conveys desolation as that following defeat. [CW 13/GN 17]

4063 Loeb edition -- a reference to the Loeb Classical Library of Greek and Latin authors which give the original text on one page and the translation on the facing page. The Library was started by James Loeb (1867-1933), a Harvard-educated American banker. [CW 13]

4064 Logan, Cuthbert -- a reporter for a morning paper who is covering HV's trial for murder. He is described as a writer of vivid pictures that sometimes approach that level of quality called distinguished. [SP 3]

4065 logaoedic rhythm -- a deliberate mixing of metrical feet in poetry, often a mixture of dactyls and trochees. It was used by Gerard Manley Hopkins* as an extension of his version of sprung rhythm*. [GN 13]

4066 loggia -- a roofed, open gallery along the side of a building; a covered walkway, usually rather ornamental in its architecture [GN 18]

4067 Lohengrin -- Richard Wagner's famous opera, first performed in 1850, that recounts the story of Lohen-

grin, the son of Percival, as told by Wolfram of Eschenbach, ca. 1200-20, in his "Parzifal". Lohengrin is the story with the swan boats, and a favorite tale among opera lovers, probably apocryphal, tells of a nervous stagehand who, upon hearing the cue music, sent the swan boat off without Lohengrin in it. The tenor singing Lohengrin (which tenor varies, but the story has been told of Joseph Tichatschek [1807-86], the first tenor to sing the role) is supposed to have turned to the stagehand and inquired, nonchalantly, "When does the next swan leave?" The familiar "Wedding March", often referred to as "Here Comes the Bride", is from this opera. See also "Wedding March". [NT 17/BH P]

4068 Lombard St. -- a short street in the center of The City* beginning in front of the Bank of England and continuing East to Gracechurch St. [WB 4]

4069 Lombroso -- the reference is to Cesare Lombroso, the Italian criminal anthropologist and proponent of the idea that there is such a thing as the "criminal man", a particular type of human who can be identified as a criminal. His most famous work is L'Uomo Deliquente. English author Joseph Conrad, in his novel The Secret Agent, wrote, "Lombroso is an ass," a fairly accurate summary of his modern reputation. [GN 5]

4070 London and East Anglia Bank -- as given, fictitious. There was a London and Eastern Bank, but it failed in 1857. [NT 6]

4071 London and Westminster -- a bank having a branch in Seahampton* where Abel Bennett* had Paul Alexis's* bank notes checked. It was formed in 1834, London's first joint stock bank after the Bank Charter Act of 1833. The Bank of England had held a monopoly until that date. Following a variety of mergers it became The National Westminster Bank. [HHC 11]

4072 The Londoner -- the reference is unknown. The nearest titles that fit the times are London Opinions and London Mail; both were weeklies. [UD 18]

4073 Long Acre -- a street North of and roughly parallel to The Stand*, it connects St. Martin's and Drury Lanes, forming the northern boundary of Covent Garden* at about the halfway point of its length [HHC 30/MMA 12]

4074 long and short of it -- a common phrase meaning, "the whole situation being considered", which appears in a variety of places not the least of which is Shakespeare's The Merry Wives of Windsor, II, ii, 60. [SP 13/NT 2]

4075 long chalk, by a -- a great deal. In the U. S. the equivalent would be "by a long shot". The British phrase refers to keeping score in a game of darts; leading by a long chalk or large score, scoring being done in chalk. [im/UD 3/BC 3]

4076 Long Drove -- a road in the parish of Fenchurch St. Paul*. See also Diggs's Drove for "drove". [NT 3]

4077 long-headed -- having the capacity for calculation and forethought carefully intelligent [FRH 28]

4078 long in the tooth -- a colloquial expression for one who is aging; past one's prime. It is of recent origin, ca. 1910, and is taken from horses whose teeth indicate their age because, like those of other herbivores,, they never stop growing. [BH 10]

4079 Long Marston -- a road leading from Headington Rd. to the northeast toward Marston* [GN 19]

4080 long-stop -- see cricket [MMA 18]

4081 Long Wall St. -- in Oxford, it is at right angles to High St. and curves 90° to the left to become Holywell St. [GN 1]

4082 Longfellow -- Henry Wadsworth Longfellow (1807-82), American poet known for "Evangeline", "Paul Revere's Ride", "The Song of Hiawatha", and many others. His is one of the better known and loved efforts of the 19th C. New England poets. [BH 11]

4083 loofah[s] -- any one of several Old World vines having a gourdlike fruit, the fibrous part of which, when dried, becomes spongelike. It is also called a vegetable sponge and is used in the bath. Parker compares his

breakfast kippers to them as prepared by his housekeeper/cook. [CW 4/UD 6]

4084 Looking-Glass Country -- an allusion, like those that follow it in the text, to Lewis Carroll's Through the Looking-Glass, Ch. 2, "The Garden of Live Flowers". The action takes place on a chess board according to basic chess moves. The line, "Takes all the running . . . to stay in the same place", is spoken by the Red Queen to Alice near the end of the chapter. The picture reference is to the famous illustrations by John Tenniel. [NT 9]

4085 Lopsley -- a fictitious town about thirty miles from Pagglehame*, probably in the Chilterns. It is there that PW locates the first of the chimney pots that William Noakes* had sold from Talboys. [t/BH 14]

4086 Lord Attenbury -- see Attenbury, Lord [aq/WB 3/BH 19]

4087 Lord Byron -- George Gordon, Lord Byron (1788-1824), the great English poet, author of Childe Harold's Pilgrimage, Don Juan, and a multitude of shorter verses including "She Walks in Beauty" and "When We Two Parted". See also Byron. [BH 7]

4088 Lord Chancellor -- see Chancellor, Lord [CW 6/BH 7]

4089 Lord George Pension -- Lloyd George's* old-age pension bill became law in 1908 when Lloyd George was Chancellor of the Exchequer. At that time, some 572,000 people over age 70 became eligible to receive five shillings per week (about $1.00 at the time) at a cost to the government of some six million pounds. [NT 4]

4090 Lord High Investigator -- Marjorie Phelps's* nickname for PW. It is, rather appropriately when one considers the light, bantering nature of the conversation, rather like Pooh-bah in Gilbert and Sullivan's The Mikado. Pooh-bah's title is "Lord High Everything Else". [SP 8]

4091 Lord High Steward -- see Steward, Lord High [CW 5]

4092 Lord in Glory -- an inn wherein PW spent the night before arriving at Riddlesdale Lodge* to begin the investigation into the death of Denis Cathcart* [CW 2]

4093 Lord Mayor of London -- The City*, that is. The other areas of London have their own councils and other elected officials. Compared to the others, though, the Lord Mayor controls a time-honored political position of some significance that dates from a Charter granted by King John in 1215. The City's twenty-five wards elect 178 members to the Court of Common Council, 153 Councilmen, and twenty-five aldermen. The mayor is chosen from among those persons who have served at least one term as sheriff and is installed on the second Saturday in November for a one-year term. [CW 14/MMA 19]

4094 Lord Melbourne, dictum of -- the reference is to William Lamb, Viscount Melbourne (1779-1848), Queen Victoria's first prime minister and mentor, who seems to have spoken in dicta. While the reference is unclear, one of his comments has particular bearing in this allusion: "Things have come to a pretty pass when religion is allowed to invade the sphere of private life." [CW 2]

4095 Lord of Burleigh -- or Burghley. William Cecil, Baron Burleigh of Burleigh, was a politician of great power (1520-98) who served Edward, Mary, and Elizabeth I in a variety of positions from adviser to secretary of state to Lord High Treasurer. He was a conservative, tactful, somewhat Puritanical man who could be patronising in such a way that those so treated enjoyed it. See also Burleigh, Lord of. [BH 1]

4096 Lord Protector -- Oliver Cromwell's* title while he ruled England after the Civil War and during the Interregnum [NT 7]

4097 "Lord Randal" -- or Randall, one of many anonymous ballads surviving in the oral tradition until written down at some relatively recent time. Many were first printed in 1765 in Percy's Reliques of Ancient English Poetry. Most, but not all, of these ballads deal with a death or murder and have unhappy or tragic endings. "Lord Randal" is one of the better known such ballads and appears frequently with such others as "Sir Patrick Spens" and

"Barbara Allen". [SP 1]

4098 Lord Roger -- see Wimsey, Lord Roger [BH E2]

4099 Lord St. George -- see Viscount St. George [BH P]

4100 Lord Warden -- a hotel in Dover that did not reopen after WW II as it is no longer necessary to spend a night recovering from the Channel crossing. The name was derived from the title of the Lord Warden of the Cinque Ports, ports once important in the wars against the French, the harbors of which are now mostly dry, the result of dropping sea level. The ports are Hastings, Romney, Hythe, Dover, and Sandwich. Winchelsea and Rye were added later. The present Lord Warden is Queen Elizabeth the Queen Mother. [BH P]

4102 Lord's -- the famous cricket* ground at St. John's Wood, London, named not after the aristocracy, but after Thomas Lord, its original owner. It is, perhaps, the most famous cricket ground in the world, and is home ground to the Middlesex County and Marylebone Cricket Clubs. The latter of those was, until recently, the governing body of the sport. The international competitions, or Test Matches, are played here as well as at the Oval* and other places. The MCC museum at Lord's is to cricket what the Hall of Fame at Cooperstown, N. Y., is to baseball in the U. S. [MMA 18/GN 11]

4103 Lords, House of -- the upper house of Great Britain's Parliament*. Those members of the Wimsey family who had titles would have had seats there and would continue to do so for as long as there are male heirs to the title. PW's title, "Lord" is a courtesy title granted to younger sons, not a rank, and would not entitle him to a seat in the Lords as he was a commoner. Trials by peers as in CW have not been possible since 1948. [aq/CW 11/NT 11]

4104 lords with white staves -- see white staves [CW 12]

4105 Lorenzo, Nicolo di -- an early Florentine printer who worked in the late 15th C. Among other things, he attempted the first illustrated Divine Comedy*, but only nineteen of the planned 100 illustrations were ever included. See also Folio Dante. [WB 1]

4106 Lorenzo's glove -- see "murder'd Lorenzo's glove" [BH 4]

4107 lorry -- British English for truck [HHC 10/NT 2]

4108 losh -- an expletive used as a substitute for "Lord" [FRH 23]

4109 Lothario -- a heartless libertine. A character of that name appears in Nicholas Rowe's The Fair Penitent, in Cervantes' Don Quixote, and in Goëthe's Wilhelm Meister. The character's name has entered the language to refer to any cruel love. [BH 18]

4110 lotos-eater -- a reference to Homer's Odyssey, ix, and the Lotophagi, or eaters of a fruit that caused all who ate it to lose all interest in returning home. Tennyson wrote a famous poem, "The Lotos-Eaters", in reference to that famous Homeric episode. The place that Homer had in mind is on the coast of North Africa where, according to Ernle Bradford's Ulysses Found, there is a hallucinogenic plant used regularly by the natives there. The plant is a relative of the jujube*. The descriptor "lotos-eater" has come to refer to any who partake of a substance to escape reality. [BH 7]

4111 Lottery Act -- one of several such acts (e. g. 1709, 1712) that made private lotteries illegal. Government lotteries followed in 1826. Lotteries were again made legal in 1960. [MMA 16]

4112 Loughborough -- a town in Leicestershire of ancient origin, and now famous for the John Taylor* bell foundry located there in 1858 [NT 4]

4113 Louis-Philippe -- the "Citizen King" of France from 1830-48 (1773-1850). His was an uneasy reign between revolutions. He is given as great-great-grandfather to Paul Alexis* in the fake genealogy in Ch. 32 of HHC. His five sons were Ferdinand, Louis, François, Henri, and Antoine. Gaston, listed in that fake genealogy, supposedly comes between François and Henri. [HHC 32]

4114 Louis Quinze Saloon -- a room at the Resplendent* decorated after the manner popular during the reign of

#4103 The House of Lords, Westminster.

Louis XV of France who ruled from 1715 to 1754. The style tends to be rococo. [HHC 24]

4115 Louise -- the fictitious grandmother of Paul Alexis* [HHC 32]

4116 Lounge Lizard -- that disagreeably overdone sort who hangs about the lobbies of resort hotels and watering-holes looking for either naive, rich, young things to exploit, or rich, old things who know they're being exploited and who don't care; a term of disapprobation for those slick and sleek specialists in indoor activities. [HHC 31]

4117 Lovat tweeds [lovats] -- usually a bluish or greenish tweed in rough and smooth finishes. Other color blends would be available. The fabric obtains its colors from the inclusion of threads dyed with a vegetable dye, so the finished fabric is subdued in tone. It is named in honor of Lord Lovat who designed the fabric for hunting clothes. [HHC 26/BH 4]

4118 "Love? Do I love?" -- the quotation is from II, i, 38-46, of T. L. Beddoes' <u>The Second Brother</u>**. An attendant is speaking to Valeria in the consideration of the attendant's own love in response to Valeria's comments on that subject. [BH 14]

4119 "Love in Bloom" -- the song made famous as Jack Benny's theme song on radio and on television. The song is pretty, but its fame rests on the comedian's deliberate mistreatment of it as a part of his image as a violin "virtuoso". The tune was composed by Ralph Rainger, lyrics by Leo Robin, and was introduced by Bing Crosby in the Paramount movie <u>She Loves Me Not</u>. It became a major hit of 1934-5. [GN 15]

4120 "Love is a fancy, love is a frenzy" -- see "Go to Bed, sweet Muse" [GN 19]

4121 to love one only and cleave to her -- see Round Table rule [BH 10]

4122 lovers in that Stroheim film -- the reference is to Erich von Stroheim's film masterpiece, <u>Greed</u>, taken from Frank Norris's novel, <u>McTeague</u>. The names of the lovers are Trina and Mac, and were played in the film by Zasu Pitts and Jean Hersholt. [GN 17]

4123 Low -- see Low Church [NT 2]

4124 Low Church -- those of the Anglican church who hold evangelical views and who lay less emphasis on the Sacraments and on church authority. [bc]

4125 Lower Regent St. -- Regent St.* from Piccadilly Circus* South to Waterloo Place [WB 1]

4126 Lubbock, Dr. [Sir James] -- PW's "analytical assistant" or analytical chemistry research resource. He is probably based on Dr. Sir Bernard Spilsbury*. Lubbock is called as an expert witness in HV's murder trial, and he assists with the analysis of organs taken from the mysterious corpse found in the churchyard at Fenchurch St. Paul*. [CW 4/UD 19/BC 7/SP 1/NT 4]

4127 Lubbock, Lady -- wife of Sir James Lubbock*, they invite PW to tea in BC. He accepts and spends a pleasant two hours with them. [BC 7]

4128 <u>Lucarnia</u>, S. S. -- the ship by which PW sent sworn statements and depositions to England while he flew back to testify at his brother's trial. Lloyd's Register of Shipping has no listing for such a vessel, so it is, therefore, assumed to be fictitious. [CW 15]

4129 Lucerne -- or lucerne; alfalfa, a fodder grass for cattle [bc/NT 7]

4130 Lucina -- the title of a group sculpted in gold by Eric Loder* [cf]

4131 Lucy -- the name by which the Dowager Duchess of Denver* is known to her closer friends [WB 12]

4132 Lucy -- a name by which Nurse Booth* is addressed on the back of a photograph [SP 17]

4133 Ludgate 6000 -- the apparently fictitious telephone number of the <u>Morning Star</u>* [HHC 3]

4134 Lugg, Mr. George -- the undertaker at Paggleham* [BH 9]

4135 Luke XII:6 -- "Are not five sparrows sold for two farthings, and not one of them is forgotten before God?" The verse is from Jesus's warn-

ing of the leaven of the Pharisees. [NT 5]

4136 lumbago -- rheumatism of the lumbar region of the spine [BH E2]

4137 Lumley, Sgt. -- the "morose" officer who helps Parker* with the later investigations of MMA [MMA 12]

4138 Lumsden, Major Daniel -- PW's WW I friend who lost a leg during the War. He resides at Frimpton*, and is PW's host for dinner and reminiscences. [bc]

4139 Lumsden, Mrs. Daniel -- the wife of Major Lumsden* [bc]

4140 Luna -- the moon. Cuthbert Conyers* was playing with the terms of astrology, making puns about the nature of his hidden treasure. The moon and Cancer are associated with silver, but Cuthbert was more concerned with the effect of moonlight on his lake and the "new" islands it contained. [dh]

4141 the lunatic, the lover or the poet -- HV refers to the David Belezzi* photograph of PW kept by his mother with an allusion to Shakespeare's A Midsummer-Night's Dream, V, i, 7:
"The lunatic, the lover, and the poet
Are of imagination all compact."
[BH P]

4142 Lunch Edition of the Evening Banner -- a very early afternoon edition of that fictitious paper [MMA 4]

4143 Lundy, Mr. -- landlord at the Three Feathers* pub in Darley* [HHC 12]

4144 Luton -- a town in Bedfordshire northwest of London about thirty miles [UD 9]

4145 lych-gate -- or lich-gate, a covered gateway to a churchyard under which a corpse or coffin is put to await the clergyman [NT 1]

4146 Lydgate, Miss -- HV's former tutor at Shrewsbury College*. She is working on a scholarly study of English prosody* and HV helps her get it together in a form suitable for the printers. DLS characterizes her with greatest care, creating a person whom, one suspects, it would be a great pleasure to know. She is a bridesmaid for HV in BH. [GN 1/BH P]

4147 Ly-doh -- Lido deliberately misspelled to reflect the mispronunciation. A reference to any swimming and sunbathing area named for the one outside Venice. [BH 4]

4148 Lympsey -- a fictitious community near Leamholt* [NT 16]

4149 Lympsey Fen -- a fictitious fen in the western fen country* [NT 6]

4150 Lymptree -- a fictitious town to the northwest of Little Doddering* in Essex [bc]

4151 Lyndhurst, Sylvia -- a fictitious person invented by PW to meet his needs during an interview with Mrs. Forrest*. She is supposedly his first cousin while in his guise as Mr. Templeton*. [UD 7]

4152 Lyndhurst, Major -- Sylvia's philandering husband, a further PW invention to serve the same need as Sylvia [UD 7]

4153 Lynn -- in Norfolk*, the reference is to King's Lynn, a city at the mouth of the Great Ouse on the Wash*. King's Lynn is an ancient market town, port, and industrial center important in the manufacture of glass. [NT 1]

4154 Lynn, Ralph -- (1882-1962) an actor who, with Tom Walls (1883-1949), was in a comedic duo who made the Aldwych Theatre (on Aldwych just off the Strand*) famous for what came to be known as the "Aldwych farces". The plays were written by Henry Ben Travers, and their fame lasted from about 1919 to 1933, making the Aldwych one of London's most popular theatres between the Wars. Some of the farces, such as Rookery Nook, are still revived from time to time. [MMA 1/BH 14]

4155 Lyons -- a chain of tea shops popular throughout England mainly because they were both cheap and clean. They did not serve heavy meals. A few are left, but many have fallen victim to fast food marketing techniques. [CW 19/UD 6/SP 16]

4156 Lyon's Inn -- see "throat they cut from ear to ear" [HHC 1]

4157 Lysol -- the household cleaner and disinfectant still generally

available in containers that PW would recognize instantly [FRH 23]

4158 Lyttleton -- a hairdresser (barber) in Seahampton* where William Bright* had applied for work [HHC 17]

(M)

4159 M. A. -- Master of Arts. Mr. Venables* has an M. A. from Caius College*, Cambridge* [NT 2]

4160 M. A. gown -- an academic gown between knee and ankle in length and worn open in front. It has full sleeves and velvet panels down the front on either side of the opening. [GN 5]

4161 M.I. -- those branches of the War Office (now the Army Department of the Ministry of Defense) which come under the Director of Military Intelligence (except M.I. 5, the security service; and M.I. 6, the secret service which come directly under the Prime Minister). PW is probably connected to M.I. 6 which works closely with the Foreign Office*. M.I. 5 works closely with the Home Office* and the police. [BH P]

4162 _ma foi_ -- French for, "my faith", or, loosely, "indeed", or "upon my word" [HHC 7]

4163 Mabel -- Col. Belfridge's* housekeeper/cook [HHC 8]

4164 Mabel -- the manicurist whose help PW enlists to obtain samples of Norman Urquhart's* hair and fingernails [SP 21]

4165 Macaulay, Rose [Dame] -- English novelist (1889-1958). The early works to which PW refers were recognized for their wit and mild satire, and include _Potterism_, _Told by an Idiot_ and _Crewe Train_. [BC 20]

4166 _Macbeth_ -- Shakespeare's version of the life of Macbeth, king of Scotland from 1040-57. He succeeded Duncan I, "the Gracious", and was followed by Lulach, "the Simple", who reigned only a few months. There is little semblance of actual history in Shakespeare's play, written in 1605 or '06, and it appears that one of its main goals was to please the new king, James I, who also reigned as James VI of Scotland. There are many sections of the play that were certain to have pleased His Majesty. _Macbeth_ is one of the shorter tragedies, is intensely unified, and ranks with _Hamlet_, _Lear_, and _Othello_ as among Shakespeare's

greatest plays. [UD 2/SP 9/BH 17]

4167 "Macbeth has murdered sleep" -- a slight variation on the famous sleep speech right after Macbeth has murdered Duncan, II, ii, 36-40, in Macbeth* [BC 18/MMA 5]

4168 MacBride, Mr. -- the "financial" person who calls at Talboys looking for William Noakes*. It is through MacBride's intervention that we learn of Noakes's financial difficulties. [BH 5]

4169 MacDonald, Ramsay -- James Ramsay MacDonald (1866-1937), Prime Minister of Great Britain in 1923-4 and 1929-31 (Labour*) and from 1931-35 (National Government). MacDonald is remembered mostly for his successes in foreign affairs, including the Dawes Plan and the Young Plan, but he also rode the economic storm when Britain went off the Gold Standard* in 1931. [MMA 19]

4170 Macdonald & Abrahams -- a fictitious firm of solicitors* with offices on Bedford Row*. PW refers to them as "That clannish old North British firm". [BH 6]

4171 Macgregor, Helen -- a typographical error in some editions as her name is Mcgregor. See Helen. [FRH 25]

4172 Machiavelli -- Nicolo Machiavelli (1469-1527), the Italian (Florentine) statesman and philosopher of the art of statecraft. He is best remembered for The Prince (1513), the famous political treatise including such ideas as cruelty may be mercy in disguise, or that it is safer to be feared than loved. His basic idea is that the survival of the state justifies whatever means are necessary to insure that survival, and that public and private ethical and moral standards are not the same. [GN 15]

4173 Mackenzie, Sir Andrew -- a friend of the Wimsey family and mentioned by DLS as head of Scotland Yard*. He is fictitious. The real head of the Yard for most of the 1920's was Sir William T. F. Horwood, Brig. Gen., K. C. B., D. S. O., who served in that post from April of 1920 to November of 1928. He was succeeded in the post by Lord Byng of Vimy who retired in October of 1931. He was, in turn succeeded by Marshal of the Royal Air Force, Lord Trenchard. [WB 9/CW 7/UD 6]

4174 MacKenzie, [Sir] Compton -- English essayist, novelist, and nonfiction writer (1883-1972) who was knighted in 1952. His novels include The Four Winds of Love and Aegean Memories. [BC 18]

4175 Macpherson, Insp. -- one of Kirkcudbright's* senior police officials who helps supervise the investigation into the death of Sandy Campbell* [FRH 6]

4176 Macpherson, Jessie -- see "The Sandyford Murder" [BH 13]

4177 Macpherson, Thomas -- PW's young friend in medical school with whom he fishes when in Scotland, and for whom he rescues a most considerable legacy from an unusually curious fate [ss]

4178 MacStewart, Dougal -- a usurious moneylender whose "generosity" is destroying the financial situation of George and Sheila Fentiman**. The name is a DLS creation and is absurd in reference to any clan. [BC 7]

4179 Mad as a March Hare -- a traditional saying based on the antics of jack hares during mating season. It is also reminiscent of Alice in Wonderland, Ch. 7, "A Mad Tea Party", wherein we find the March Hare who is quite mad also. [NT 5]

4180 Madame Brigette -- a beauty specialist and perfumer of New Bond St.* who provided services in those specialties to Denis Cathcart* [CW 17]

4181 Madame Crystal -- see "Susie's Snippets" [SP 21]

4182 "Madame, je vous en félicite" -- French for, "Madame, I congratulate you." [WB 11]

4183 Madame Tussaud's -- the famous museum of persons preserved as wax sculptures. The collection was founded in Paris in 1770 and moved to England in 1802. Its permanent home in London was founded in 1835. It is perhaps most notorious for the Chamber of Horrors and the reconstruction of famous crimes displayed there. It may be visited at Marylebone Rd., near Regent's Park, not far from Baker St.

[SP 3]

4184 "Madame, we're strangers . . ." -- From T. L. Beddoes' The Bride's Tragedy**, II, ii, 178-80. The speech is Hesperus's to Floribel during some verbal love-play, and concludes:

" . . . as fair, as delicate. O heaven!
To think of it. But she was innocent,
Innocent, innocent."

There seems to have been good cause for DLS to have omitted this portion of the speech. [HHC 20]

4185 Madden, Miss -- the very correct and, to her employer, very irritatingly accurate secretary who is not amused by his mental meanderings [FRH 28]

4186 Maddison -- the police detective assigned to follow Ann Dorland* [BC 18]

4187 madeira -- the rich, amber-colored dessert wine from the island of Madeira [GN 7/BH 6]

4188 made free -- see free [NT 7]

4189 The Madonna -- the Virgin Mary in any artistic or literary representation [ie]

4190 "Madonna and Child" -- the title of one of Ann Dorland's* paintings and one which Parker* considers "an abominable blasphemy" [BC 17]

4191 Madras muslin -- a light-weight open-weave, cotton fabric with some sort of heavy striped design and usually used for curtains. The fabric was originally made in Madras, India, but the term now applies to any similar fabric patterned after the original. [BC 7]

4192 Maeterlinck [like the lady in] -- the reference is to Maurice Maeterlinck (1862-1949), a leader in the Belgian and French symbolist schools of literature. PW is not apparently referring to any of Maeterlinck's drama, for which he is most famous, but to a collection of essays entitled The Treasure of the Humble in which appears "The Tragedy in Daily Life". PW seems to have blended two sentences that are in close proximity to each other into one concept that he remembers not quite accurately. The first sentence is, "Is it while I flee before a naked sword that my existence touches its most interesting point?" The second is, "Indeed, when I go to a theatre . . . I am shown a deceived husband killing his wife . . . ." [BC 18]

4193 Mafeking year -- the reference is to the relief of the siege of Mafeking, May 17, 1900, during the Boer War. It was a military feat for the British who held the place against the Boers with only 1300 men under Col. Baden-Powell, later the founder of the Boy Scout movement. [HHC 16]

4194 Magdalen Bridge -- the bridge by which High St. crosses the River Cherwell* beside Magdalen College* [GN 1]

4195 Magdalen College -- one of the early Oxford Colleges, established in 1458 by William of Waynfleet (1395?-1486), Bishop of Winchester and Lord Chancellor of England. The College lies outside of what was Medieval Oxford and is situated on magnificent grounds of 100 acres of parks, meadows, and uniformly beautiful college buildings. Facing Oxford's High St. and bordered on the East by the River Cherwell*, the college is in southeastern central Oxford. Madgalen is pronounced as "maud-lin", with the accent on the first syllable. The name is an allusion to Mary Magdalen (Luke 8:2). The Rev. Simon Goodacre* is an alumnus. See also Oxford Colleges. [HHC 6/GN AN/BH 5]

4196 Magdalen lilies -- a reference to the Magdalen College* coat of arms which, in heraldic parlance, is described as "Lozengy ermine and sable, on a chief of the second three lilies argent slipped and seeded or." [GN 13]

4197 Magdalen May-Day -- a hymn is sung from the top of the college's Tower every May-Day at 6:00 A. M., a tradition of great antiquity. The Tower, built in 1452-1505, is the college's chapel bell tower and is on High St.* near the Magdalen Bridge*. [GN 1]

4198 Magdalen Tower -- the tall, square tower on the High St.* front of Magdalen College* which dominates Oxford in the vicinity of Magdalen Bridge* [GN 1]

#4194 Magdalen Bridge and Tower, Oxford, ca. 1910.

4199 Maggie -- Thomas Macpherson's housekeeper [ss]

4200 Maggs, Billy -- he, with his unnamed brother, is suspected of having stolen Mr. Puffett's prize peaches to prevent Puffett from winning a prize at the local fair. Maggs is the local blacksmith. [t]

4301 Maggs, Dr. -- the police surgeon, otherwise unidentified, who works with PW in the matter of the corpse in the burned garage [te]

4202 Maggs, Joey -- son of Billy Maggs* who unwittingly tells Bredon Wimsey* some information that allows PW to solve the mystery of Mr. Puffett's missing peaches [t]

4203 maggot -- used here in the archaic sense of an odd notion or whim [dh]

4204 magneto -- the electrical spark generating apparatus used on automobiles, but no longer in the U. S. [BC 8/FRH 3]

4205 Magnifical -- a hotel mentioned without specifying its location, but it is most likely Southampton*. PW and Mrs. Ruyslaender work together there to solve a most embarrassing problem she has gotten into. [pj]

4206 Magnolia -- an unspecified product for which Pym's Publicity* does the advertising. See also Muggins's Magnolia Face Cream. [MMA 1]

4207 _magnum opus_ -- Latin for, "great work" [UD 19/GN 3]

4208 Mahjongg -- or Mah Jongg/Jong. This is an ancient Chinese game that enjoyed "fad" status in the 1920's and early 1930's, but which never remained popular in the West. A game set consists of 144 tiles. There are three suits of 36 tiles each called characters, circles, and bamboos; 28 honors tiles, four each of Red Dragon, White Dragon, Green Dragon, East Wind, North Wind, South Wind, and West Wind. The remaining eight tiles consist of the four seasons and four flowers. The game is of the rummy family, using the tiles instead of cards. Start of play is controlled by a roll of dice. Players attempt to assemble matching groups of tiles called chows, pungs, or kongs. Flowers and seasons are bonus tiles. Only bonus tiles, pungs, and kongs count in scoring and the winner is said "to woo". Sir Charles Deverill* is wearing a costume meant to represent a Mahjongg set. [qs]

4209 Mahlstick Club -- a mahlstick, or maulstick, is a rod with a padded, leather-covered end used by artists as a surface upon which to balance their brush or hand while doing fine work or lettering; hence, an appropriate name for a club devoted to the interests of artists. It is fictitious as presented, but sounds like the Beefsteak Club on Irving St., London; any similarities being conjectural. [FRH 8]

4210 Mahon, Patrick [and the chopper] -- the reference is to the particularly brutal murder of Emily Beilby Kay, 25, by Patrick Herbert Mahon, 35, at the Officer's Bungalow, a former Coast Guard residence on Pevensey Bay near Eastbourne*. Miss Kay, pregnant with Mahon's child, argued with him on or about April 15, 1924. During the argument she fell and struck her head forcefully, but in his anger Mahon strangled her as well. He then dismembered the body and put most of it in a trunk, but hid the head and most of the internal organs. He even went so far as to burn and boil some of the flesh. Mahon seems to have been attempting to obtain Miss Kay's money. Later, while the corpse was still in the cottage, locked in the trunk in a bedroom, Mahon lured Primrose Duncan to the place, but she had no knowledge of the prior events until after Mahon's arrest. Dr. Sir Bernard Spilsbury* gave the medical evidence and Mr. Justice Avory heard the case. Mahon was found guilty and was hanged at Wandsworth Prison on September 3, 1924. [HHC 33]

4211 Maida Vale -- a suburb of London to the North of Paddington and Kensington* [MMA 20]

4212 Maidenhead -- a residential town on the Thames West of Windsor known for its fine summer boating. Dian de Momerie's* body was found in a woods near there. [MMA 19]

4213 Maidstone -- in Kent, the county town located at the confluence of the rivers Medway and Len. Bunter's mother lives near Maidstone. It is

also the site of H. M.'s Prison on Lower Boxley Rd., near the train station. [CW 4/SP 17/NT 2]

4214 Maidstone Ladies' College -- a fictitious institution. The name suggests Cheltenham Ladies' College, the only English school having that combination of words in its name. [SP 17]

4215 Mainwaring, Lady -- an acquaintance of the Dowager Duchess* who had an artificially overstuffed daughter whom she had hoped to marry to Sir Julian Freke* [WB 3]

4216 *Mais je te répète que je ne les ai pas . . .* -- French for, "But I repeat, I haven't got them, . . . Come, come. It was indeed you who took them, wasn't it? Well then, how do you expect me to have them?"
"Why no, no, I gave them to you up there before going to look for the newspapers."
"I assure you not. In short, it's obvious. I've looked everywhere, damn it! You didn't give me anything, nothing, nothing at all."
"But since I told you to go and register the luggage, how could it be that I didn't give you back the tickets? Do you take me for an imbecile? Go on! I'm not that stupid! But look at the time! The train leaves at 11:20. Look a bit at least."
"But I have looked everywhere--my vest, nothing! My jacket, nothing! My topcoat--nothing! Nothing! Nothing! It is you--" The argument is interrupted at this point. [aq]

4217 *Mais je vous en prie* -- French for, "Don't mention it." [WB 11]

4218 *Mais oui, je l'ai vu, ce monsieur-là* -- French for, "Oh yes, I have seen this man." [CW 5]

4219 *Mais priez dieu que tous nous veuille absoudre.* -- French for, "But pray (i. e. please) God that we all be granted absolution." [BH 19]

4220 *Mais quel tact, mon dieu! . . .* -- French for, "My Lord! what tact! Do you know then who I am?" [BH 4]

4221 *Mais si quelqu'un venoit de la part de Cassandre . . .* -- this quotation is from Pierre de Ronsard's (1524-85) sonnet*, "To His Valet", the first line of which is, *"Je vais lire en trois jours l'Iliade d'Homere"*, translated by C. H. Page as, "I want three days to read the *Iliad* through". The poem is sonnet 51 in *"Pièces retranchées des Amours"* (1560), and is considered one of Ronsard's finest as well as one of the best expressions of the spirit of the Renaissance: love of life, learning, and love. It first appeared in Ronsard's *Continuation des Amours* (1555).
The lines quoted are ll. 9-11 which Page renders as:

"Ah! but--if any one should come from
Cassandre,
Admit him quickly! Be no loiterer,
But come and make brave for his
receiving . . . ."

M. Antoine* seems to have come to know HV well. [HHC 15]

4222 maisonette -- an apartment on two or more floors made from two apartments, sometimes side by side, sometimes one over the other. The word is taken from the French and means, literally, "little house". Parker and Lady Mary make one at 12A Great Ormond St.* after their marriage, and DLS had one on Great James St.* [MMA 5]

4223 Maitland Buildings -- one of the buildings on the campus of Somerville College*. [GN 18]

4224 major -- the lowest rank of field officer in the army. Field officers (majors through colonels) come between general officers and subalterns (lieutenants through captains). PW held this rank during his later service in WW I. [WB 8]

4225 Majuba -- General Colley and 648 British troops were killed at Majuba in the Transvaal by Boers who were angered by P. M. Gladstone's failure to reverse Disraeli's annexation of that South African territory. These events of 1881 led to an attempt at magnanimous behavior by Gladstone which was interpreted by the Boers as a retreat. [BC 1]

4226 make a cat laugh -- the line is, "It would have made a cat laugh", and it appears in James Robinson Planché's (1796-1880) *Extravaganzas* (1879), in *The Queen of the Frogs*, I, iv. [GN 20/BH 7]

4227 make a galled jade wince -- see "let the galled jade wince" [GN 4]

4228 "Make her a goodly chapilet . . ." -- these are lines from Michael Drayton's* The Idea: The Shepheard's Garland Fashioned in Nine Eclogues, or Rowland's Sacrifice to the Nine Muses. Specifically, they appear in the "Third Eclogue", a portion of which is called "Song to Beta". The "Song" is in twelve stanzas, the sixth of which reads:

"Make her a goodly chapilet of azur'd Columbine,
And wreath about her Coronet with sweetest Eglantine:
Bedeck our Beta all with lillies,
And the dayntie Daffadillies,
With Roses damask, white, and red, and fairest flower delice,
With Cowslips of Jerusalem, and cloves of Paradice." [GN 20]

4229 Malacca walking stick -- one of several that PW owns, but he likes this one best for sleuthing as it is marked off in inches and has a heavy silver knob on top, making it both a handy tool and a weapon. He refers to it as "the gentleman scout's vademecum". [WB 1/BC 4]

4230 maladetta -- Italian for, "bad luck, annoyance, turmoil" [SP 18]

4231 Malden -- a small residential community South of Wimbledon in outer London's southwestern region [BC 9]

4232 malice aforethought -- see "of his malice aforethought" [CW 1]

4233 malice prepense -- malice aforethought; an evil planned prior to its execution [BH 9]

4234 Mallow, Miss -- a parishoner of Fenchurch St. Paul* who was fond of decorating the pulpit, lectern, etc. etc., with greenery at Eastertime. The practice does seem, as Mrs. Venables* points out, a bit absurd if not downright pagan. [NT 3]

4235 "malt does more than Milton can" -- the line is from poem 62 of A. E. Housman's* A Shropshire Lad. It opens with the famous, "Terence, this is stupid stuff", and lines 19-24 are:

"Oh many a peer of England brews
Livelier liquor than the muse,
And malt does more than Milton can
To justify God's ways to man.
Ale, man, ale's the stuff to drink
For fellows whom it hurts to think:"

Houseman, in turn, was alluding to Book I, line 26 of Milton's Paradise Lost wherein the poet is explaining why he wrote the great epic. [HHC 14]

4236 Maltogene -- a fictitious concoction advertised by Pym's Publicity* [MMA 4]

4237 Malus aspidistriensis -- the much maligned common aspidistra* [BH 16]

4238 Maman, dites-moi -- PW carols this tune in "a husky light tenor" on his way to the bath. The song is an example of a bergerette (literally, "little shepherdess"), a light folk tune that is artificially pastoral in character, and was especially popular in the 18th C. Later versions often affected an 18th C. manner. This particular bergerette is an anonymous ditty beginning:

"Mother please explain
What is love?
Won't you tell me . . . ."

The lyric is artificial in tone and is rather suggestive as translated by Sigmund Spaeth. [umw]

4239 Mammy -- one of the hopefuls in the office of talent agent Isaac Sullivan* [HHC 23]

4240 "a man's a man for a' that" -- see "I know a man's a man for a' that" [MMA 13]

4241 man of business -- a lawyer, one who supervises one's business affairs in all their legal technicalities [BC 3/SP 10]

4242 a man of infinite-resource-and-sagacity -- the English classic to which PW refers is Rudyard Kipling's Just So Stories; especially to "How the Camel Got His Hump". [WB 5]

4243 The Man of Property -- the title of the first (1906) of John Galsworthy's* novels that comprise The Forsyte Saga. The "man" in the novel's title is Soames Forsyte, a purely materialistic person who is more concerned with things than with people. [GN 6]

4244 "The man of upright soul . . ." --

Horace* had a good deal to say about upright souls and humours placid, the lines here being PW's corruption of Horace, probably from Odes I, xxii [BH 8]

4245 Man proposes and God disposes -- the line is taken from Thomas à Kempis's (1380-1471) Imitatio Christi, Ch. 1, section xix, and is written there as, "Nam homo proponit, sed Deus disposit", the translation being as the citation above, but with a "but" in place of the "and" [NT 1]

4246 "The man that asked questions on Friday . . . ." -- this is the Basque equivalent, apparently, of "curiosity killed the cat". Note that there is no suggestion of satisfaction having any recuperative or restorative powers included as the quote is presented here. [ie]

4247 "Man that is born of woman . . ." -- from the Service for the Burial of the Dead in The Book of Common Prayer [NT 5]

4248 "man walketh in a vain shadow" -- see "For man walketh . . ." [BC 3]

4249 "a man where nae man should be" -- from an old Scottish song of unknown authorship entitled "Our Goodman". The line is from the twenty-first stanza of that song and includes:

"And there he spy'd a sturdy man,
Where nae man should be."

The song tells of a man being cuckolded by his wife in a devious question and answer format. [GN 7]

4250 The Man Who Never Laughed Again -- this poem appears as part of the "October" section of William Morris's* long poetic group, The Earthly Paradise. His prefatory argument for the poem states: "A certain man, who from rich had become poor, having been taken by one of his former friends to a fair house, was shown strange things there, and dwelt there a while among a company of doleful men; but these in the end dying, and he desiring above all things to know their story, so it happened that he at last learned it to his own cost." [NT 11]

4251 Manchester -- a major shipping and textile manufacturing center just to the East of Liverpool. There are major art galleries there, so a show at one would be important to Thomas Crowder's* career. PW attended that show and later purchased some of Crowder's work. [nf/WB 2/UD 18/HHC 14/GN 1]

4252 mandarin -- a public official at any one of nine levels of rank during the Chinese Empire [GN 6]

4253 Mandragorae dedurunt odorem -- Latin for, "Mandrake gives off a scent." See mandrake. [GN 20]

4254 mandrake -- a Southern European and Mediterranean member of the nightshade family, the root of which was superstitiously credited with human qualities as it often resembles the lower half of a human body. More practically, it is dried and used as an aphrodisiac or soporific. Since it was thought that uprooting a mandrake would cause death because it gave a terrible shriek, cords were looped around them and a dog; the dog was chased to uproot the plant, and the animal was then supposed to die. It didn't. [CW 9]

4255 mangle -- a device for extracting excess water from washed clothing by passing the garments through tangential parallel rollers; a wringer [HHC 25]

4256 mangel-wurzel -- see mangold [SP 15/NT 18]

4257 mangold -- another name for the mangel-wurzel or large beet used as fodder for cattle or to add moisture to fodder [bc]

4258 Manichee -- a follower of Manes, a 3rd C. A. D. Persian who taught a form of religious dualism including a release of the spirit from matter through self-denial. St. Augustine of Hippo* was a follower of this sect before his conversion even though his mother had been Christian. The sect had influence on Christianity through the 13th C. when the Church worked actively to eradicate it. The founder is also known as Mani or Manichaeus. [CW 9]

4259 the Manor -- the Whittaker/Dawson horse farm in Crofton*. Clara Whittaker* ran the farm while Agatha Dawson* ran the house. [UD 11]

4260 Manon Lescaut -- a novel, volume

seven of the Memoirs and Adventures of a Man of Quality (nobleman), by Antoine-François Prévost d'Exiles* (1657-1763). The first six volumes are of little note, but Manon is considered brilliant. The story tells how the chevalier Des Grieux loves Manon Lescaut, a beautiful and amoral innocent destined to become a mistress to everyone in society. Des Grieux, an aristocrat's son, has a future of great promise, but, in falling passionately in love with Manon, he has cursed that future. The story of how the love unfolds is set against the corrupt society of Paris where money is all-important.

Des Grieux's driving passion causes his family to disown him and he is left without money. Because he is an aristocrat, he cannot work for a living; so he turns to card-sharping which, in turn, leads to debt and then to murder. His virtue is destroyed as his passion comes to rule his life, and the couple come to ruin each other. PW sees Des Grieux in Cathcart* and finds Manon in Simone Vonderaa*. [CW 2]

4261 Mansfield, Katherine -- the pseudonym of Kathleen Mansfield Beauchamp Murry (1888-1923). Born in New Zealand, she led an unhappy early life and died of tuberculosis at age 35. She is famous for her sensitive stories written in the "slice of life" style. [BC 18]

4262 Mansfield Lane -- DLS wrote, "For the purpose of this book (GN), Mansfield Lane is deemed to run from Mansfield Road to St. Cross Road, behind Shrewsbury College and somewhere about the junction between the Balliol and Merton Cricket grounds as they stand at present (ca. 1935)." [GN 1]

4263 Mansfield Road -- it extends from Holywell St.* to South Parks Rd. in a North-South direction [GN 1]

4264 Mansion House -- in the City* directly across the street from the Bank of England*. It is the official residence of the Lord Mayor of London. Built from 1739-52, it is the only private residence in the kingdom to have a Court of Justice with cells in the basement as the Lord Mayor is the Chief Magistrate of The City. [WB 13]

4265 mantelpiece -- Parker* is described as being seated and as having his feet on the mantelpiece, mormally a difficult if not impossible feat. However, the term also applies to those much smaller fireplaces never meant to burn wood, but which are designed to have small gas burners installed. The mantel on such smaller fireplaces is only about two or two and a half feet high, so Parker could be quite comfortable. [WB 7]

4266 mantle -- a cloak [BH 19]

4267 many evil men is as quick as monkeys -- see unjust steward [NT 4]

4268 "many shall come . . . cast into outer darkness" -- Bill Rumm* is running together a series of phrases from the parable of the Marriage Feast found in Matthew 22:1-14. [SP 13]

4269 Marathon -- the name of a fictitious film starring Varden* [cf]

4270 Marble Arch -- designed by John Nash at the command of George IV in 1828, it was originally intended to be the gateway to Buckingham Palace. Too late it was found to be too narrow for the State Coach, so it was moved to its present location in Hyde Park* facing Bayswater Rd. at the northeast corner of the Park. It occupies a position near where the Tyburn* gallows stood from 1571-1783. The area was the scene of public executions for over 500 years.

4271 March -- in the fen country*, a large railway junction on the River Nene just East of Peterborough. The church Mrs. Venables* has in mind is that of St. Wendreda which has a double hammer-beam* roof with 120 angels and a devil in four tiers. The unusual thing about this angel roof is that the angels are "in flight", their wings are open rather than being folded back as if at rest. [NT 2/ BH E2]

4272 March Brown -- a fly used in trout fishing. As it is tied as a fly or as a nymph and is used, depending on how it is tied, for either wet or dry fly fishing, it has become one of the mainstays of any basic fly fishing lure collection. [FRH 1]

THE MARBLE ARCH.

#4270 The Marble Arch, Hyde Park, London.

4273 March Hare -- see Mad as a March Hare [NT 5]

4274 Marchbanks, Col. -- a friend of PW and the entire Wimsey family, he is a houseguest at Riddlesdale Lodge* at the time of Denis Cathcart's* death. Marchbanks shows skill in bridge* and billiards, and enjoys the hunt (for bird, not foxes). He annually gives a dinner at the Bellona Club* on November 11 to honor the memory of his son who was killed in WW I, and is sufficiently upset by General Fentiman's* death in the Club's precincts that he helps PW solve that case. [pj/CW 1/BC 1]

4275 Marchbanks, Mrs. -- another houseguest at Riddlesdale Lodge* with her husband, the Colonel [CW 1]

4276 Marchbanks, young -- Col. Marchbanks'* son in whose memory the Colonel gives a dinner at the Bellona Club* each November 11. He was killed near Ypres* in WW I. [BC 1]

4277 marchioness -- the wife of a marquis* or a peer in her own right if her title is inherited. Her position in the peerage is of the second rank, just below dukes and duchesses. See also Peerage. [ab]

4278 mare's nest -- a red herring; something false, illusory, or in the manner of a deliberate hoax [HHC 19]

4279 mare's nest full of cockatrice's eggs -- as a mare's nest is a hoax, or something false, and as a cockatrice is a mythological serpent possibly related to the basilisk, a beast said to be able to kill merely by looking at its prey, the reference is dubious at best. Also, since basilisks are said to be hatched from cock's eggs, an accomplishment of note in itself, we have further evidence of the curious falseness of the subject; in short, a boondoggle. [BH 12]

4280 Marfa -- Stefan's wife. See Mr. Petrovinsky. [hp]

4281 Margate [Beach] -- a town about twenty miles northeast of Dover on the Channel in Kent. It is known for its nine miles of sandy beach and an amusement park. It is a favorite summer's day trip for Londoners. [cb/GN 12/BH 6]

4282 Margaux -- one of the great first growth chateaux of Bordeaux. It is known particularly for its delicate and fine perfume, a characteristic of finer wines. However, only the wealthy can today enjoy such a claret with any frequency. [BC 9/HHC 4]

4283 Maria -- Mrs. Luke Ashton*, a member of the parish of Fenchurch St. Paul* [NT 6]

4284 Marie -- the daughter of Jean and Suzanne Legros** [NT 7]

4285 Marincetti -- a prime suspect in the murder of Maddalena Brotherton* as he had attempted to attack her a few days before her death [fr]

4286 Marjory Fleming's turkey -- Margaret [Marjory] Fleming (1803-11) was the daughter of James Fleming of Kirkcaldy, Scotland. She was a literary prodigy and was the favorite of Sir Walter Scott who delighted in playing with her. She wrote poems and kept a diary. The turkey reference is to an epitaph she wrote for three young turkeys:

"A direful death indeed they had
That would put any parent mad;
But she [their mother] was more than usual calm,
She did not give a single dam."

[GN 1]

4287 market place -- the reference is to Market Place just North of Oxford St.* which connects Great Castle and Eastcastle Sts. [WB 10]

4288 Market Square -- one of the central squares in Wilvercombe* [HHC 19]

4289 Marketing Board -- one of the control and supervision boards of the Ministry of Agriculture and Fisheries, now (since 1955) including Food. It is the same as item #4448. [GN 3]

4290 Markham, Mr. -- a resident of Leahampton* who has earned the wrath of the church ladies' work group for his condescending attitude [UD 16]

4291 marks -- plural of mark, the official German unit of currency [CW 5]

4292 Marlborough -- a reference to Marlborough College, founded in

1843, one of England's best-known public schools*. It is located at Marlborough in Wiltshire. [MMA 10]

4293 Marlborough Club -- one of the three clubs to which PW belongs. It was at 52 Pall Mall opposite the entrance to Marlborough House and was established in 1869. It was functioning in PW's heyday, but does not now exist. See also Bellona Club and Egotists' Club. [WB 4/UD BN/MMA 19]

4294 Marlborough St. -- the Police Station on Great Marlborough St., a short street running East-West from Regent St. to Poland St., just South of Oxford St. in Mayfair* [mt]

4295 marlin spike -- an iron tool resembling a large awl, used to separate strands of rope for splicing. They served as handy weapons for close combat during brawls, mutinies, etc. [t]

4296 Marne -- see department [NT 7]

4297 Marne, Retreat over the -- see Retreat over the Marne [HHC 6]

4298 Marne, Third Battle of the -- M. Rozier* is strictly correct as there were no troops of any sort in that battle as it never took place. One suspects that he meant Aisne, not Marne, along which much of the bloodiest trench warfare of WW I was fought. [NT 8]

4299 marocain -- a heavier silk fabric of excellent quality and with a dull finish favored by older ladies [GN 3]

4300 marquee -- a large, often ornate and colorful, tent set up to shelter a party, reception, etc. [MMA 11]

4301 marquis[ate] -- a peer who, in England, is of the second rank, just below a duke and above an earl. See Peerage. [ab/UD 19]

4302 Marriott, Sylvia -- a close friend of HV's and a character witness for her at her trial for murder. PW interviews Miss Marriott during his investigation of Philip Boyes' death and he impresses her favorably. She later tells HV that she will send for Peter and marry him. Harriet denies this, but events prove otherwise. [SP 1]

4303 marrow-bones -- any bones used for soup, etc., and having the marrow --considered by some to be a delicacy-- intact in the center. The term is used here to suggest a shuddering that penetrates as deep as is possible. [NT 1]

4304 marrowfat pea -- a particularly large variety of pea. In "Necklace of Pearls", the necklace of the title consists of twenty-one pearls, each the size of a marrowfat pea, or, roughly, eight to ten millimeters in diameter and perfectly matched. Their loss would be a justifiable cause for concern. [np]

4305 Marryat, Hannah -- the "intense young woman with the badly bobbed hair and the brogues". She is Meleager Finch's* niece, and it is she who must find a later will in order to get her uncle's money and prevent it from going to the Primrose League*, a fate she dearly hopes to circumvent. [umw]

4306 Marsh's Test -- one of the standard tests for determining the presence of arsenic or antimony in a given substance. The apparatus is set up as shown in the illustration. At a point between the flask and the narrow end of the exit tube is a section of cotton and calcium chloride to dry the gas from the flask. Metallic zinc and dilute (1:8) sulphuric acid are put in the flask, the reaction removing all air from it. When the air is gone, a lighted bunsen burner is placed under the exit tube about an inch from the narrowed escape end of that tube for about a half hour before any of the suspected material is poured into the flask. This allows determination of the purity of the reagents in use.

The suspect material is then poured into the flask at regular intervals, bit by bit, over a period of an hour or so. If arsenic is present a nut-brown deposit will form inside the glass tube toward the narrow end and about an inch from the flame. If there is a great deal of arsenic, the deposit will be a shiny black with brown margins. The deposit is decomposed arsine gas (AsH_3) which results from the interaction of the contents of the flask and the heat applied to them. The gas at the narrow exit end of the tube, if it is arsenuretted hydrogen, will have a marked garliclike odor which will reveal even

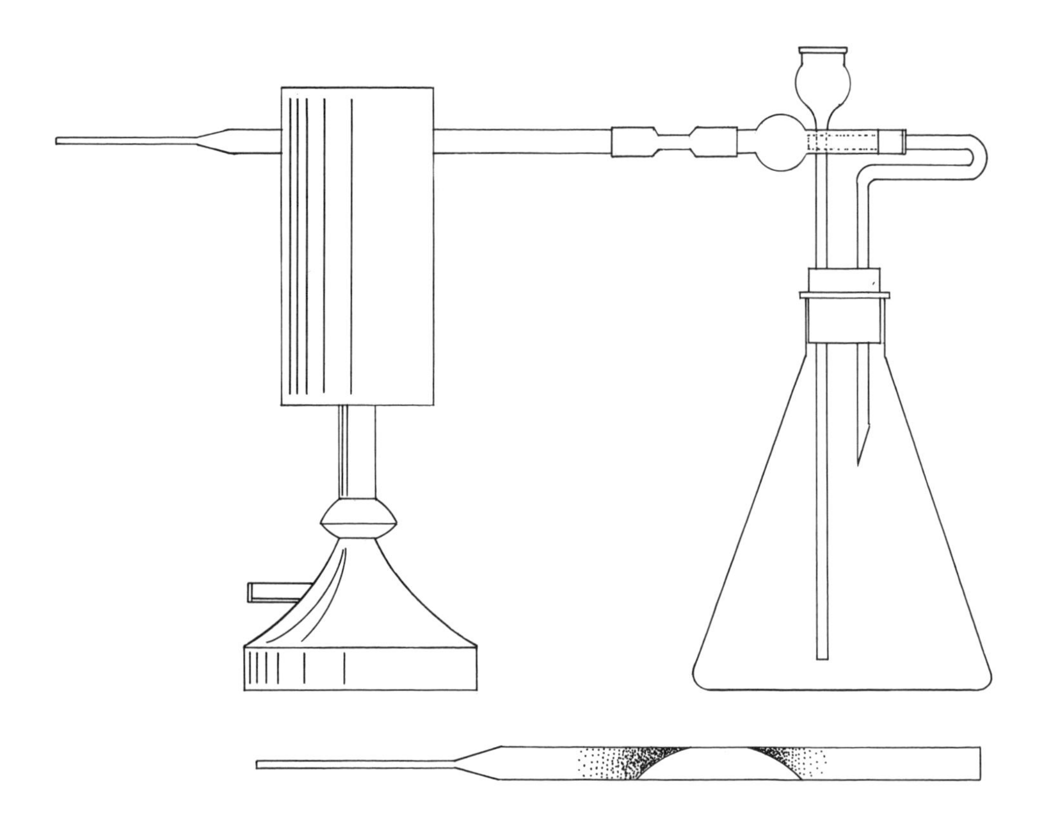

#4306 Apparatus set up for a Marsh's Test. The Bunsen burner and exit tube are at left, the flask for reagents and suspect material at right. The tube at bottom shows how arsenic or antimony would be deposited above the flame of the Bunsen burner if present in the suspect material. The metallic deposit would be inside the glass tubing. Illustration by John D. Kovaleski.

minute traces of arsenic. The test can also be used for some other metallic poisons in addition to arsenic and antimony. [BC 7/SP 20]

4307 Marston -- a Queen's College student recognized by Reggie Pomfret* for his ability to act [GN 8]

4308 Marston -- a suburb in the northeast of Oxford [GN 19]

4309 Martell [Three-Star] -- a famous brand of brandy produced by one of the great cognac shippers just North of the Gironde estuary on the coast of the Bay of Biscay. They produce some of the finest champagne cognac brandies. The Three-Star appellation designates the area of Cognac where the grapes were grown, the choicest having the most stars. [SP 10/HHC 12]

4310 Martha -- an old woman who is servant to Standish and Alice Wetherall**. Her love for her mistress and her ignorance of PW's conjuring abilities allows PW to use Martha to save Alice from her horrible captivity. [ie]

4311 Martha -- an otherwise unidentified person in residence at Shrewsbury College*. The context suggests that, perhaps, one of the scouts* is being addressed. [GN 10]

4312 Martha -- a reference to Luke 10:38-42, one who does all the unpleasant things, or an intentional malapropism for "martyr" [BC 15]

4313 Martin -- Major Armstrong's rival solicitor* and intended victim. Armstrong's persistence in attempting to poison Martin with scones, however, not chocolates, led to his being hanged on May 31, 1922. [UD 18]

4314 Martin, Haviland -- the mysterious camper at Hinks's Lane*. His alibi is too tight and his dark glasses make him too suspicious, and with good reason. The name is an alias. [HHC 10]

4315 Martin, Letitia -- the Dean of Shrewsbury College*, Oxford. Her quarters are in the New Quad. She and HV have a high regard for one another that is strengthened by their work on the poltergeist* problem. She is a bridesmaid for HV. [GN 1/BH P]

4316 Martinmas -- or Martlemas, November 11, the day of commemoration for St. Martin of Tours, ca. 371, the patron saint of tavern keepers. In England it was, formerly, the time for hiring servants and slaughtering cattle. [HHC 26]

4317 martlets of Worcester -- a reference to the heraldic crest of Worcester College, Oxford, which displays prominently such birds. See also bird which has no feet and Oxford Colleges. [GN 13]

4318 Martyr's Memorial -- in Oxford in the center of Magdalen St., a southerly continuation of St. Giles's St., just outside Balliol's* West front, is a memorial to honor Cranmer, Latimer, and Ridley, the Protestant reformers who were martyred (burned in 1555-6) at Oxford. The monument was erected in 1841-3. [GN 14/BH 19]

4319 Marvell, Andrew -- English poet (1621-78) and supporter of Oliver Cromwell and John Milton. After the Restoration he joined Parliament and became a violently satirical politician who attacked one and all, including the King. [BH 12]

4320 Mary -- see Wimsey, Lady Mary [BH P]

4321 Marya -- a singer who dislikes interruptions. She is performing at the Kropotky's* gathering, a bad place to avoid interruptions. [SP 8]

4322 Marylebone -- the district of London centering on Marylebone Rd.* See also Tyburn. [CW 6]

4323 Marylebone Rd. -- a major thoroughfare in North central London that runs from Edgeware Rd. in the West to the intersection with Albany and Great Portland Streets in the East. For part of its length it runs roughly parallel to the southern boundary of Regents' Park*. The name is pronounced as marl-buhn, the emphasis being on the first syllable and is derived from the Marylebone district of London which was named for St. Mary le Bourne. The street was developed as a choice residential area in 1756. Today, among other attractions along its length, are Madame Tussaud's Wax Works, the Planetarium, and the Royal Academy of Music. Baker St.*, famous for its association with Sherlock Holmes*, crosses Maryle-

#4318 The Martyr's Memorial, Oxford.

bone St. to the South of Regent's Park*. See also Tyburn.

4324 the mask of night was on his face -- the reference is to Romeo and Juliet, II, ii, 85. Supt. Kirk* is blushing at PW's too obvious reference to the conjugal bed when the embarrassed policeman thinks of Juliet's speech:

"Thou know'st the mask of night is on my face,
Else would a maiden blush bepaint my cheek . . ."

[BH 12]

4325 Maskelyne and Devant [stunt, contraption] -- John Nevil Maskelyne (1839-1917) and his partner from 1904 to 1915, David Devant (1868-1941), were noted particularly for their magical illusions, levitations, disappearances, etc. Devant's real name was David Wighton. Maskelyne gained great fame after he uncovered the Davenport Brothers as fraudulent spiritualists. He and Devant published Our Magic (1911), an important work about magic and a major source concerning magic theory. PW enlists Mr. Devant's help to manufacture a disintegrating cabinet to assist in his conjuring in "Incredible Elopement", and PW refers to his dentist's drill stand as a Maskelyne and Devant contraption in that it has hidden compartments and other devices that a magician's cabinet might have. [ie/te/hp]

4326 Mason, A[lfred] E[dward] W[oodley] -- English playwright and author of many works of mystery and detection (1865-1948). He created Inspector Hanaud, a rather comic French detective, who appears in such classics as At the Villa Rose (1910) and The House of the Arrow (1924). The incident DLS had in mind appears in the latter work. [GN 3]

4327 Mason, Polly -- Frank Crutchley's* fiancée who eventually finds herself pregnant and abandoned to her fate. HV, Miss Climpson*, and PW step in to help her cope with her problem. [BH 10]

4328 Massey, Joe -- the sluice-keeper at the Van Leyden's Sluice* whose job has made him overly loquacious when a visitor happens by [NT 18]

4329 Massey's baby -- an infant who died about a week after Lady Thorpe*, on or about January 7 or 8, 1930 [NT 4]

4330 Massingbird St. -- a street in Manchester* on which William Bright* claims he once had a barber shop. The Legal Department of the Greater Manchester Council states that their records show no such street as having existed in this century, nor does it appear that there ever was such a street in Manchester. [HHC 14]

4331 Master of Balliol -- the chief academic officer, called either principal, warden, or master, of Balliol College*. In 1935, the time of the action in GN, the master was A. D. Lindsay, M. A. [GN 14]

4332 Master of the Workhouse -- the official in charge of a workhouse* [WB 12]

4333 Masterman -- a "cubist" poet who is a member of the Egotists' Club. He is not otherwise identified and is fictitious. [cf]

4334 masticated -- chewed; an unusual term to apply to fingernails, but suggesting that they were thoroughly bitten [WB 2]

4335 mat, on the -- another form of "on the carpet"; to be scolded or to be given a dressing-down [FRH 1]

4336 Materia Medica -- it is hard to be sure what volume Parker* saw as Materia Medica is something of a catch-all title and appears as the title or some part of it in many medical reference books such as Hale-White's Materia Medica, Pharmacy, Pharmacology and Therapeutics, or W. W. Krueger's Elementary Materia Medica. Generally, however, Materia Medica refers to a national bibliography of articles, reviews, etc., regarding medical texts, journals, dissertations, learned papers, and other such reports. [BC 15]

4337 matins -- the normal Anglican service for a Sunday morning but without Holy Communion [NT 4/BH 5]

4338 Matron -- the lady in charge of the nursing staff and the various housekeeping requirements in a hospital or any other public institution [UD 4/GN 10]

4339 Matthew -- see Wimsey, Matthew [BH E2]

4340 Matthews -- an attendant at the Bellona Club* who is ill with the flu at the time of the story [BC 4]

4341 Mauchline -- a town about ten miles from Ayr* to the East and North. It is a junction of the rail routes to Glasgow from Stranraer* in the West and from Dumfries in the East. [FRH 10]

4342 Maunder and Garrett -- the reference is to George Mursell Garrett (1834-97), an English organist and composer who wrote many anthems and services popular for more than a generation, and to John Henry Maunder (1858-1920), an English composer, organist, and choirmaster whose work is strongly sentimental. Among Maunder's works is the famous cantata _From Olivet to Calvary_. PW's allusion to the "company of spearmen" (Psalm 68:30, KJV) is to one of their joint efforts to prepare a musical setting for the psalms. Pointing refers to the ways the words of the Psalms are set to the chants in Anglican worship. [BH 5]

4343 _Maxima reverentia_ -- the phrase shows PW's ability to get Wilberforce Pope to watch his language and insult him at the same time. The words are Latin for, "show greatest or most reverence", a reminder to Pope to delete his expletives in the presence of the young Viscount St. George*. [dh]

4344 Maxwelltown -- a suburb to the West of Dumfries formerly on the rail route from Kirkcudbright* and Castle Douglas* [FRH 10]

4345 May-Day -- May first, a traditional date for celebrating the rites of spring, a leftover from pagan rites that will still frequently include Maypoles and other remnants of fertility rites. See also Magdalen May-Day. [GN 1]

4346 May we ne'er lack a friend . . . -- see Swiveller, Dick [UD 6/HHC 11]

4347 Maybole -- a town on the rail line and about halfway between Girvan* and Ayr* [FRH 10]

4348 Mayfair -- the area of London bounded by Piccadilly, Regent St., Oxford St., and Park Lane which used to be a fashionable place to live. It is now offices and expensive flats, and includes Old and New Bond Streets**. [BC 8/FRH 18/MMA 11/GN 2]

4349 Maybrick, Florence Elizabeth Chandler -- Flossie Chandler (1862-1941), of Mobile, Alabama, married Liverpool cotton broker James Maybrick in 1881. He died on May 11, 1889. On May 14, Flossie was arrested for his murder by arsenical poisoning. No case has caused greater uproar at the time it was tried that the notorious "Maybrick Case". Florence claimed to have used arsenic for her complexion, a common practice, and James seems to have had some sort of abnormal fixation for poisons. He had a favorite "pick-me-up" several times a day which contained ever-increasing doses of arsenic. Toxicologists had a battle over the case and never could agree as to what killed him. In addition, the judge, Mr. Justice James Fitzjames Stephen, had had a stroke and was incompetent in his summation to the jury. Florence was found guilty and sentenced to hang, but public outrage was so great that the sentence was commuted to life in prison. She was released on parole in 1914, and returned to the U. S., eventually settling in South Kent, Connecticut, as Mrs. Chandler, in 1917. She lived there as something of a recluse, her true identity hidden until her death in 1941. [SP 20]

4350 McAdam -- a fisherman present at the McClellan Arms* who pulled Campbell* out of his fight with Waters* while PW handled the latter [FRH 1]

4351 McAllister, Mr. -- group-secretary* at Pym's Publicity*, he works with the Dairyfields, Ltd., accounts and speaks with a marked Scottish accent [MMA 10]

4352 McClellan Arms -- most likely a reference to the Selkirk Arms*. In some editions McClellan is wrongly spelled McClennan. [FRH 1]

4353 McDonald, Marcus -- a bedridden resident of Kirkcudbright* [FRH 8]

4354 McGeoch -- a customer at the McClellan Arms* at the time of the Campbell-Waters fight [FRH 1]

4355 McGregor, George -- Helen's* father. Mrs. McGregor suggests that he spoils his daughter. [FRH 11]

4356 McGregor, Mrs. -- Helen's* mother, a lady who is concerned about her daughter's behavior [FRH 11]

4357 McHardy, Rabbie -- one of the residents of Gatehouse-of-Fleet* [FRH 3]

4358 McLeod, Mrs. -- Waters's* landlady or housekeeper [FRH 1]

4359 McSkimming -- the railway porter at Girvan* who suffered acute appendicitis complicated by peritonitis* and who, therefore, was unable to help Sgt. Dalziel*, PW, and the others who were investigating Campbell's* death as they attempted to track down the movements of the man in the gray suit [FRH 10]

4360 McTaggart, Jimmy -- a friend of Jock's* who has a gun Jock wishes to borrow for the purpose of hunting seagulls--not all seagulls, just a particular one, but he is willing to sacrifice as many as necessary to find that one [ss]

4361 McWhan, James -- the undertaker responsible for preparing Campbell* for burial [FRH 13]

4362 meâ culpâ -- Latin for, "my fault" or "I am to blame" [GN 8]

4363 Mead, Mrs. Marion -- the mysterious wounded lady who called Mr. Trigg* to make a will; an alias of Miss Grant* [UD 18]

4364 Meadow Buildings -- part of Christ Church College on that College's South side. The buildings (1863) are Victorian/Venetian Gothic and include the visitors' entrance to the College. [GN 13]

4365 Meakers, Mrs. -- housekeeper for Meleager Finch* who provides the last clue to the whereabouts of her employer's last will [umw]

4366 meanness of fifty-thousand Scotch Jews -- excessive stinginess [NT 5]

4367 Measure for Measure -- a "black" comedy by William Shakespeare, probably first performed in 1604 as part of the celebration of the arrival of James VI of Scotland to assume the throne as James I of England. The play is a "black" comedy in that it leaves some serious questions on the nature of love and moral behavior only superficially considered and uncomfortably so. [BH 11]

4368 meat, funny kind of -- the Dowager Duchess* is trying to think of kosher, anything ritually declared fit to use according to Jewish dietary laws [WB 3]

4369 Mecklenburgh Square -- with Brunswick Square, it forms an East and West garden on either side of Coram Fields Playground on the North side of Guilford St.* in Bloomsbury*. HV has an apartment there. See also Wimsey, Harriet Vane. [SP 5/GN 1]

4370 Medes -- natives of Media in ancient Persia [HHC 1]

4371 Medical Jurisprudence -- see Taylor [BH 12]

4372 Medical Officer of Health -- a doctor employed by the local authorities, now commonly called a Community Physician, who provides medical advice and services to a local authority or government [UD 3]

4373 Medical Referee -- under the Workmen's Compensation Act of 1897, the MR or Deputy MR is a medical practitioner of not less than five years' standing which includes experience and qualifications as, perhaps, a coroner or Medical Officer of Health*. In the situation in UD, the MR must be satisfied that the application for cremation is made by a properly authorized person such as an executor or a nearest living relative, and that the death is in no way suspicious. He is one of two signatories on any application for cremation. [UD 3]

4374 Medlicott's Bank -- a fictitious financial institution in which Mr. Crimplesham* is a shareholder [WB 5]

4375 Medusa head -- Medusa was the only mortal one of the Gorgons*, the amazingly ugly daughters of Phorcys and Ceto, children of Pontus and Ge. As Mrs. Grimethorpe* is anything but ugly, DLS could have had in mind either that Medusa was beautiful before Athene made her ugly for her dalliance with Poseidon, or that the Gorgons were sometimes portrayed as beautiful in death. This

latter is apt as Mrs. Grimethorpe is figuratively dead as long as she stays at Grider's Hole*. [CW 4]

4376 Medway -- the Duke of, who, when he died, left his duchess the opportunity to seek out Benjamin Disraeli*, but "Dear Dizzy"* was otherwise occupied with "that stupid Bradford woman"*. The Duke and Duchess of Medway are fictitious. [aq]

4377 Medway, Dowager Duchess of -- the rather "Marlborough House set" friend of the Wimsey family for whom PW saves some exquisite diamonds from theft. See also item 4376. [aq]

4378 meeting the wind -- the flood and tidewaters are all flowing outward against the wind at the moment, but the situation will change when the tide reverses and flows in with the wind, adding its force to the tidal flow [NT 19]

4379 Megatherium Scandal -- a reference to the collapse of the Megatherium Trust* [HHC 6]

4380 Megatherium Trust -- a fictitious financial operation. DLS avoided using real names if there was any chance of embarrassment to real persons or firms. The word "megatherium" is from the Greek and means, literally, a "great wild beast", but refers to a fossil quadruped. [SP 11]

4381 meiosis -- or litotes, intentional understatement for humorous or satirical effect [BH 6]

4382 Mélanie [Krasky] -- given as Paul Alexis's mother in the fake genealogy in HHC [HHC 32]

4383 Melbourne, dictum of Lord -- see Lord Melbourne, dictum of [CW 2]

4384 Melville, Paul -- Mrs. Ruyslaender's* distant relative by marriage, turned thief and blackmailer. He is unmasked by PW. [pj]

4385 Mellilow, Mr. -- the chess*-playing innocent and dupe whose adventures form the basis of the story which is focused on his weekly game of chess with Mr. Creech* [sf]

4386 Mellilow on Pawn-Play -- the title of a fictitious work written by Mr. Mellilow* [sf]

4387 Mellon, Cdr. -- a naval officer who had two of Mr. Endicott's* razors, but lost them when "his ship was blown up and sank with all hands" [HHC 6]

4388 Member of Council -- the College Council or governing body [GN 1]

4389 The Memoirs of Sherlock Holmes -- the second collection of short stories involving the great detective. Published in 1894, it contains "Silver Blaze", "The Musgrave Ritual", "The Greek Interpreter", and "The Final Problem", among others. It was the last story mentioned in which Doyle killed Holmes only to outrage his reading public so much that he was forced to resurrect the great detective for many more adventures. [CW 13]

4390 "Men have died and worms have eaten them . . ." -- PW is paraphrasing, rather loosely, Rosalind's line from As You Like It, IV, i, 107, "Men have died from time to time and worms have eaten them, but not for love." The speech is a demonstration of Rosalind as perceptive realist. The rest of PW's line is an inversion of the old proverb, "The early bird gets the worm." [GN 16]

4391 Mendelian factors -- factors relating to the work of the Austrian botanist and monk, Gregor Johann Mendel (1822-84) the founder of the modern study of genetics and inherited traits. While abbot at Brünn, Mendel worked out his theories from experiments cross-fertilizing edible peas. [GN 1]

4392 Mendelssohn -- [Jakob-Ludwig] Felix Mendelssohn [-Bartholdy] was a German composer and conductor (1809-1847) who was instrumental in starting the revival of Bach's work in the mid-1800's. He is also know as the composer of St. Paul and Elijah, both oratorios; a variety of symphonies, The Hebrides Overture, incidental music for Shakespeare's A Midsummer-Night's Dream, and a host of smaller works. See also Wedding March. [SP 13/HHC 20/BH P]

4393 Lady Mendip -- a guest at the Duke of Denver's garden party when it is crashed by the de Momerie* crowd. Her ladyship must have family connections in Somerset as the Mendip Hills, famous for their old lead mines, are

there in the vicinity of Cheddar and Wells. She is fictitious. [MMA 11]

4394 Mentonne [tone/ton] -- a town and commune in France approximately thirteen miles North of Nice. It is a famous winter and health resort in the Department of the Alpes-Maritimes founded in the 10th C. Lady Levy* was vacationing there when her husband disappeared. [WB 2/BH P]

4395 Mepal Wash -- the village of Mepal is North of Cambridge* on the New Bedford River*. The area between the New and Old Bedford Rivers is called the Wash as it is meant to be flooded to relieve pressure on the drainage system as needed. Hence, Mepal Wash is that section of The Wash near Mepal. [NT 2]

4396 mephitical -- foul-smelling, stinking [SP 8]

4397 Merchant of Venice -- Shakespeare's comedy of about 1596. The story is an ancient one, first printed in the Gesta Romanorum of the 1470's. It is a tangled tale of love and justice centering on the adventures of Antonio, Portia, Bassanio, Shylock the moneylender, and Jessica, Shylock's daughter. [UD 1/BH 12]

4398 Mercury -- the Roman equivalent of Hermes, son of Zeus and Maia, inventor of the lyre and, most notably, messenger to the gods. He was the god of luck and wealth and the patron of merchants, thieves, and travellers. [NT 19]

4399 Mercury -- the Roman god (see item 4398) of whom there is a statue--the present one a 1928 replacement of the 17th C. original--in the pond located in the center of the Christ Church College Quadrangle. The pond was the reservoir for the College at one time. The statue's name, by association, has become the name of the pond as well. [GN 8]

4400 mercury powder -- a powder made from mercury and either charcoal or powdered chalk or talc and used to obtain fingerprints. The dark powder is used on glass and light surfaces, the light on dark surfaces. [FRH 13/MMA 6]

4401 Merdle, Mrs. -- any one of PW's nine Daimlers* named for the wife of the swindling financier in Charles Dickens's Little Dorrit**. She liked to think of herself as fashionable, and that would be a suitable way for PW to think of his cars. Also, PW says he chose the name because "she was averse to row," and that certainly applies to both Mrs. Merdles. The Daimler in BH is identified as the ninth Mrs. Merdle, a large sedan. [SP 6 and passim]

4402 mere -- a sheet of standing water [NT 19]

4403 mere -- a boundary or property line [BH 18]

4404 Mere Wash -- a fictitious area in the fen country* [NT 16]

4405 Meribah -- strife. The word originally appears in Exodus 17:7, Numbers 20:13 and 27:14, Deuteronomy 32:51 and 33:8, and Psalm 81:7. It is associated with the rock at Horeb where Moses struck the stone to get water for the Israelites during their wanderings. Hence, the waters of strife, most apt considering where PW finds himself at the end of the chapter. It is also PW's nickname for the granite war memorial in Stapley from which a stream of water flows without Moses' help. [CW 11]

4406 meringues -- shells made of whipped egg whites and sugar, dried in an oven, paired, with whipped cream between [BC 7/GN 8]

4407 Merlin's seat -- see "Galahad will sit down in Merlin's seat" [BH 8]

4408 Merridew -- a stablehand and general helper for Thomas Frobisher-Pym* [bc]

4409 Merriman's End -- described by DLS as a cul-de-sac off South Audley St.*, there is no such place [hp]

4410 Merritt's -- the funeral parlor responsible for handling General Fentiman's* memorial service and burial. There is/was an H. E. Merrett Funeral Directors, 519 Hackney Rd., London, but this in nowhere near Shepherd Market*. The firm is apparently a DLS fabrication. [BC 5]

4411 Merryweather -- the Seahampton*

barber who had Col. Belfridge's* Endicott* razors. The Col. had given them to his gardener who, in turn, had given them to Merryweather, his brother-in-law. [HHC 8]

4412 Merryweather -- a parishoner in Fenchurch St. Paul* whose health is poor [NT 3]

4413 Merryweather -- a "rascally old poacher" on the Wimsey estates at Duke's Denver* to whom PW took a fancy as a young lad [BH P]

4414 Merton -- the college, Merton College, Oxford, that may have been attended by the clergyman that PW has remembered from his youth as having been a great baritone [BH 5]

4415 Merton Grove -- part of the parks, gardens, and meadows of Oxford, and just South of Merton College [GN 13]

4416 Merton St. -- an East-West street roughly parallel to and South of High St. in Oxford [GN 13]

4417 merveilleuse -- French for, "marvellous" or "wonderful". In this sense, however, it is used to refer to a follower of high fashion during the Directoire*. The reference is to a Renault* automobile as "all bonnet* and no body", a punning allusion to the period's typically huge and elaborate hats. [mt]

4418 Mesopotamia -- a long, narrow island in the River Cherwell*. The name alludes to Babylonia and means the land "between the [Tigris and Euphrates] rivers", often thought of as the "birthplace" of Western civilization. The name is a typical Oxford joke as the land in question is nothing pretentious, being, as it is, located between a narrow stretch of the Cherwell and an old mill stream. [GN 11]

4419 metaphysics -- the science which is concerned with the complexities of life from first principles. The 17th C. metaphysical poets, the school of John Donne and his followers, saw metaphysics as a means to analyze, somewhat psychologically, the emotions of religion and love, a consideration of the obscurities of the universe in terms with which they all could deal. Such dealings often involved complex metaphors called conceits. [MMA 2]

4420 Metcalf, Clarence -- the head errand-boy at Pym's Publicity* [MMA 7]

4421 Meteyard, Miss -- one of the copywriters at Pym's Publicity* with whom PW works. Like DLS, she is a Somerville College* graduate who chose to work "in advertising". Her name is pronounced as meet-yard, and is a variation on metewand, a measuring rod, and is used here as a standard of measurement or estimation. [MMA 1]

4422 Methodists -- followers of the Protestant denomination that has evolved from the teachings of John and Charles Wesley in England in the 1700's. Methodism emphasizes free grace and the individual's responsibilities. [CW 2]

4423 methylated -- methylated spirits, alcohol rendered unpalatable and poisonous by the addition of methanol, pyroxylic spirits, and coloring. It is so treated as it is unfit for human consumption and is not subject to the duties payable on drinkable alcohol. [NT 11]

4424 métier d'époux . . . une vie reglée . . . -- French for, "husbandly duties . . . a regular life (i. e. ordered) . . . too emotional . . . the vital forces". To Uncle Paul Delagardie*, this latter certainly refers to the sex drive. [BH 19]

4425 metol-quinol -- an old trade name (Metol) for a photographic developing agent [BC 5]

4426 metre -- the rhythmic pattern found in most, but not all, poetry [GN 11]

4427 Metropolitan and Counties Bank -- a fictitious institution. DLS may have had in mind the London and Counties Bank founded in 1836. [MMA 8]

4428 meublés -- French for, "movables", household goods and furniture [SP 11]

4429 mews -- a street or yard of stables with living quarters for the grooms [SP 8]

4430 Meyer-Lübke -- Wilhelm Meyer-Lübke (1861-1936) was a Swiss philologist and author of a variety of dic-

tionaries and works on philology. He is perhaps best known for his Romanisches etymologisches Wörterbuch and Grammatik der romanischen Sprachen in four volumes. His specialty was the study of the evolution of the Romance languages from the Vulgar Latin. [GN 12]

4431 mezzotint -- a print taken from a hand-engraved copper plate on which light rubbing was done to shade off the contrast by giving a range of tones between black and white [dh]

4432 Micawber, Mr. Wilkins -- a popular character in Charles Dickens's David Copperfield. He is famous for his "mercurial and impecunious" nature (OCEL). He is alluded to by PW as something of a model upon which Dr. Hartman's* fortunes seem to be based. [fr/HHC 7/BH 9]

4433 Michaelmas -- September 29, the Festival of St. Michael and All Angels. Michael is the leader of the angelic armies of God. In England it is one of the four "quarter days" when rents are due, the day when magistrates are elected, and it also lends its name to a period of time of work or service such as the Michaelmas term in the courts and universities. In universities it is the first of the three major college terms or divisions of the school year. [UD 12/SP 5/HHC 2/GN 4/ BH P]

4434 Michelin -- a brand of automobile tire manufactured in France. The company still publishes a series of famous travel guides. [UD 20]

4435 miching mallecho -- probably from the Spanish malhecho, the line being from Shakespeare's Hamlet, III, ii, 148. It apparently means making secret and insidious mischief. [UD 2]

4436 Micky -- the name of PW's pet lemur* [ie]

4437 mid-on -- see cricket [MMA 10]

4438 Mid-Summer Day -- June 24, the feast of the Nativity of St. John the Baptist. Its name derives from its long association with solar ceremonies including the summer solstice. The date is Dorcas Gulliver's* birthday. [UD 6]

4439 middle -- in change-ringing, the word is applied to a specific type of dodging* maneuver [NT 1]

4440 middle and off -- see cricket [MMA 18]

4441 Middleton's Practical Astrology -- see Practical Astrology [dh]

4442 midges -- a catch-name for any small, biting, two-winged fly of the family Chironomidae. They are often described as greatly irritating. [HHC 1]

4443 Midhurst, standing for -- Abcock Attenbury* wants to become the member of Parliament* for that district in West Sussex. His candidacy is not highly regarded. [aq]

4444 milady -- the term is from French, but is not a title of rank, just an equivalent for my lady or lady [CW 5]

4445 milestone -- a stone or concrete marker indicating the mileage to the next town or place of significance [NT 2]

4446 Milford Hill -- a continuation of Milford St. which leads eastward from the center of Salisbury*. It houses the offices of the solicitors* Crimplesham and Wicks. The street is real but the firm is not. [WB 5]

4447 mild and bitter -- a roughly 50/50 mix of bitter, or strongly hopped ale, with mild, a lightly hopped ale, to achieve a drink that has some of the properties of both. One can approximate this in the U. S. by mixing a bottle of Guinness stout with Harp ale in equal proportions. The result is a very dark ale flavored rather mildly for those who haven't acquired the taste for the Guinness straight. See also bitter. [HHC 12/ BH 10]

4448 Milk Board -- one of the control and supervision boards of the Ministry of Agriculture and Fisheries, now, since 1955, it includes Food. [GN 3]

4449 milk pudding -- milk baked with sweetened carbohydrate such as rice, tapioca, sago, pasta, or bread for feeding the infirm, young children, or those whose digestion is impaired [UD 2]

4450 Millbanks, Lilian -- the Senior Student* at Shrewsbury College* [GN 7]

4451 Miller, Mr. -- a director at Pym's Publicity* who, in Mr. Tallboy's* opinion, does not play cricket well, but is chosen for the team in deference to his position [MMA 10]

4452 Milligan, John P. -- the London representative of the Milligan railroad and shipping company on Lombard St.* in The City* just South of the Bank of England*. He is an American millionaire, and both he and the firm are fictitious. [WB 4]

4453 Milligan, Major Tod -- an integral part of the dope smuggling and distribution operation under investigation in MMA, he is a bit too greedy for his own good as it brings about his timely and violent death. The party house he runs on Friday and Saturday evenings is the focal point of the de Momerie* crowd. [MMA 5]

4454 mills -- boxing matches or bouts [NT 1]

4455 mills of God -- the phrase appears in Friedrich von Logan's (1605-55) Sinngedichte, III, ii, 24, as translated by H. W. Longfellow:
"Though the mills of God grind slowly,
yet they grind exceeding small;
Though with patience He stands waiting, with
exactness grinds He all."
[BH 13]

4456 Milly -- Mrs. Henry Strachan*, a rather nervous and giggly sort of woman [FRH 4]

4457 Milton, John -- the great English Puritan poet and essayist (1608-74), author of Paradise Lost and Paradise Regained, great epic poems; "L'Allegro" and "Il Penseroso"; Samson Agonistes; and Areopagitica. A Puritan, Milton was a humanist too, so he was often at odds with official Puritan dogma. [UD 15/BH 8]

4458 Milton's remark about Eve -- see "he for God only" [UD 16]

4459 "The mind most effectively works . . ." -- from Burton's The Anatomy of Melancholy** [GN 12]

4460 Ministry of Information -- see Information, Ministry of [CW 9]

4461 Minni[e]gaff -- a small village across the Cree* from Newton-Stewart*, and joined to it by a bridge of granite built in 1813 to replace one swept away by a flood [FRH 2]

4462 Minnoch -- the Water of Minnoch which rises in what is now the Galloway Forest Park and which joins the River Cree* at a point just above Larg*. Sandy Campbell's* body was found along the Minnoch. [FRH 2]

4463 Minster Hotel -- there is no record of any such hotel ever having existed in Salisbury*. However, the Cathedral Hotel and the Red Lion Hotel are both on Minster St., and the former hotel is geographically appropriate. [WB 5]

4464 minstrels of Portland Place -- the BBC's* orchestra. The BBC headquarters is at Broadcasting House on Portland Place*. In the 1930's it was still common to have live studio orchestras for radio concerts, dance music, and background music for the various live drama and comedy presentations. [BH 16]

4465 Mint -- the Royal Mint. Mints have operated in England and Great Britain from at least Anglo-Saxon times. From about 1299 to 1811, the Mint was located in The City* as a function of the London minters. In 1811, the Mint moved to the Tower of London and all Mint activities centered there, branches being established in Commonwealth countries as needed. The Mint has been in Llantrisant, Wales, since December of 1968, and has produced the decimal coinage now used. [HHC 11]

4466 Mirabelle, Countess of Severn and Thames -- a fictitious relative by marriage of the Wimseys [BH P]

4467 mirror [last] -- a reference to the result of a Marsh's Test* for. arsenic (or antimony) [BC 7]

4468 Mirror Hall -- see Strand Corner House [im]

4469 Misadventure, Death by -- see Death by Misadventure [CW 1]

4470 misereres -- or miserere seats or misericord seats, the name of a

peculiar arrangement in medieval choir stalls. Since the monks were not allowed to sit down yet might become tired during the long Masses, a compromise was reached in the miserere seat. These seats could be raised to provide a shelf of sorts upon which one could prop one's derriere to achieve some relief. The word miserere comes from the Latin for "be merciful", the opening plea in several of the Psalms in the Vulgate*, especially Psalm 50. The suggestion is one of subtle monkish humor. [bc/NT 2]

4471 missal -- a prayer book. The 14th C. missal mentioned would have been a Roman Catholic guide to the responses necessary for celebrating the Mass throughout the year. For the GN reference, see illuminated missal. [ss/GN 14]

4472 Mission House -- a London center of the Tabernacle Mission* located in Stepney*. The Rev. Mr. Hallelujah Dawson* is staying there while in London. [UD 13]

4473 Mission Settlement -- the organization, a slum mission supported by Miss Climpson's* church, is the one for which she was soliciting contributions while trying to help PW solve the mystery of Vera Findlater's* death. Her work almost causes her own death. [UD 22]

4474 Mitcham, Mrs. -- Lady Dormer's* proper and efficient housekeeper [BC 17]

4475 "Mithradates he died old" -- the reference is to A. E. Housman's* A Shropshire Lad*, poem 62, line 76. The segment to which PW alludes is:

"They put arsenic in his meat
And stared aghast to watch him eat;
They poured strychnine in his cup
And shook to see him drink it up:
They shook, they stared as white's their shirt:
Them it was their poison hurt.
--I tell the tale that I heard told.
Mithradates, he died old."

The point of this reference is that Mithradates had, by ingesting small amounts of poisons over a period of time, developed a tolerance for them. He was, thus, able to consume large quantities without harm. [SP 22]

4476 Mitre -- an Oxford inn famous from the 13th C., the existing building dating from the 17th C. It was formerly a coaching inn owned by Lincoln College since 1523, but PW would be highly distressed to learn that the College has taken over the rooms as dormitory space, and the dining room has been sold out to a steak house chain. [GN 15/BH P]

4477 mitred -- wearing a mitre, that pointed headgear used especially by abbots and bishops [NT 2]

4478 mixed grill -- an assortment of broiled (grilled indoors) meats, the nature and variety of which would be determined by availability and household preference [CW 9]

4479 mix mustard -- until relatively recently when "prepared" mustard became available, it was purchased dry as a flourlike powder and mixed with water to the desired strength. It was also mixed with mayonnaise. The English firm of Colman's still provides mustard in the dry form. See also Mustard Club. [FRH 2]

4480 Mock Turtle -- a fictitious book by the fictitious author, Tasker Hepplewater. The allusion is to Lewis Carroll's Alice in Wonderland**, chapters 9 and 10, where the Mock Turtle appears. Mock turtle soup is made with veal instead of green turtle. [GN 11]

4481 Modern Verse-Forms -- Mr. Elkbottom's* book of prosody*. It is fictitious. [GN 5]

4482 Moderns -- precisely what PW means by this term is unknown, but we may safely assume that he had in mind such composers as Arnold Schoenberg, Alban Berg, Heitor Villa-Lobos, Leoš Janáček, Ralph Vaughan Williams, Igor Stravinsky, William Walton, Frederick Delius, and Alexander Scriabin, among others. [SP 13]

4483 Mods -- an Oxford slang term referring to the First Public Examination for the B. A. degree. The name derives from the Moderator or College official who conducts the examination. [GN 5]

4484 modulations -- the musically correct progression from one key to some other key, usually through a

cascade of notes, the difficulty of which depends upon the keys involved [GN 19]

4485 Moffatt, P. C. -- a police constable known to PW. He encounters PW outside of Dian de Momerie's* flat after his lordship had taken her home. PW's appearance in the harlequin suit understandably gives the constable a moment's pause. [MMA 9]

4486 Moggeridge -- a whole family clan in Wilvercombe* including, among others, Arthur, Polly, Rosie, Billy, Susie, Fanny, David, Jenny, and her baby, Charles. [HHC 10]

4487 Moggeridge, Billy -- Esdras Pollock's* brother-in-law and a member of one of Wilvercombe's* less cooperative fishing families [HHC 25]

4488 Moggeridge, Mrs. -- a younger member of the Moggeridge* family [HHC 25]

4489 Mohammedan -- a follower of the Islamic faith and its prophet, Mohammed [FRH 15]

4490 moithered -- or moidered; confused or perplexed, fatigued, etc. [BH 9]

4491 Mollison, Vera -- a classmate of HV's at Shrewsbury College* [GN 1]

4492 mon Dieu -- French for, literally, "my God!", but idiomatically it can mean, "my goodness", "dear me", etc. It is a sort of all-purpose expletive suitable for all levels of society. [WB 11/HHC 7]

4493 Mon Souci -- the name given to the estate of the Comte de Rueil*. In contrast to one of Frederick the Great's homes, "Sans Souci", it means "my care", "worry", or "anxiety", and is frequently used in reference to monetary worries. The chateau showed the result of these worries in its neglect. [mt]

4494 money for jam -- money for doing little or nothing [ab]

4495 Monica -- daughter of the Hon. Mrs. Trumpe-Harte who had worked hard to bring Monica to PW's attention [BH P]

4496 monk's stalls -- where the monks half sat and half stood when singing their offices. See office book and misereres. [NT 2]

4497 monocle -- a single eyeglass that may or may not have a metal rim. PW has one that Parker describes as "powerful" and which PW claims is "jolly useful when you want to take a good squint at somethin' and look like a bally fool at the same time". [WB 1]

4498 monomania -- excessive concentration on one idea or group of ideas to the point that many become so obsessed with those ideas as to become unbalanced mentally [SP 7/MMA 16]

4499 monomark -- a system of letters, sometimes also numbers, used to identify property, etc. The system was invented by William Morris*. Persons would register their property and affix an identification code to it. Then, if it was lost or stolen, it could be traced to its owner with ease. [UD 3]

4500 monotype castings -- Monotype is a trademark for a machine and process that casts and sets letters and numbers in a lead alloy. The castings would not be the right hardness for the use PW intends to make of them. Such castings are no longer used widely, having been replaced by photographic methods. [FRH 28]

4501 Monstrum hoc Cracoviae -- see Cracow Monster [dh]

4502 Montague, Walter -- the owner of Riddlesdale Lodge* from whom the Duke of Denver* had rented it for the shooting season. Montague is in the U. S. throughout the action of the novel and never appears other than to be mentioned in passing. [CW 1]

4503 Montague, Miss Grace -- see Bulfinch, Mrs. Grace Montague [SP 10]

4504 Monte [Carlo] -- the Hon. Freddy Arbuthnot* testified that he had been taken at cards there once in one of the famous gaming clubs, the major business in that part of Monaco, the tiny principality on France's Mediterranean coast near Italy. It is mentioned in passing that an eccentric third cousin of the Wimseys' lives a reclusive life there. [CW 1/MMA 11/

#4501 The Monument.

BH P]

4505 Montessori -- Maria Montessori (1870-1952), Italian physician and educator who espoused self-education for children through development of the child's initiative, sense of liberty, and through special developmental games and exercises. [FRH 7]

4506 Montrachet -- the greatest of the white wines of the Burgunday area, pronounced mon-rah-shay. They are from either Puligny or Chassagne. The Chevalier Montrachet and the Montrachet-Ainé were, and in the case of the Chevalier still is, of the first growth and among the very best white wines that France has to offer. PW and Freddy Arbuthnot* enjoy a 1908 vintage in WB. [mt/WB 4]

4507 The Monument -- a pillar designed by Christopher Wren and Robert Hooke to commemorate the Great Fire of 1666. It is located just to the East of the North end of London Bridge and is 202 feet high. It was built between 1671 and 1677. The height supposedly equals the distance from its base to the place in Pudding Lane where the fire began on September 2, 1666. [MMA 5]

4508 Moody, Miss -- a parishoner at Paggleham* who does "clack on" when given the opportunity [BH 8]

4509 _Moonlight_ -- Beethoven's* famous "_Moonlight_ Sonata", more correctly identified as Sonata in C-sharp Minor, "_Sonata quasi una fantasia_", Op. 27, No. 2 (1801). The sonata was published in Vienna in March of 1802, and was introduced in the _Allgemeine Musikalische Zeitung_ on June 30, 1802. The name "Moonlight" was coined by Ludwig Rellstab who connected the music with a moonlight ride across Lake Lucerne. [HHC 20]

4510 moors -- or heath; any tract of unenclosed land, usually considered waste land, which may be marked with marshes or bogs. It may also be an area reserved especially for shooting/hunting. In 1883, Grant Allen's _Colin Clout's Calendar_ stated: "In Yorkshire a moor means a high stretch of undulating heath-covered rock . . ." All of the senses of the word seem to apply to CW. [CW 1]

4511 Moor of Venice -- Othello, the Black tragic hero of Shakespeare's play, _Othello_. PW alludes to Othello because of all the charcoal he has on his face from figuring out Uncle Meleager Finch's* crossword puzzle. [umw]

4512 Morano, Maria -- the perfect model for any sculptor, she was Eric Loder's mistress and model, but she eventually becomes a silver-plated sofa [cf]

4513 Morecambe, Alfred -- one of the major plotters of HHC, he is the "real" person behind the characterizations of Mr. Field, William Bright, Mr. Vavasour, and William Simpson. It is his slightly hunched appearance, reminiscent of Richard III that helps tie his various characters together. [HHC 20]

4514 Morecambe, Mrs. -- wife of Alfred and a resident of Kensington*, driver of the Bentley who gave Haviland Martin* a ride into Wilvercombe*, she is the guest of the Rev. and Mrs. Trevor. She often stays with them at Heathbury Vicarage. [HHC 20]

4515 Moreton -- the barber on the Esplanade* in Wilvercombe* [HHC 14]

4516 Morgan -- a type of automobile called a runabout and mentioned variously. Originally a three-wheeled auto that was constructed more closely to the lines of a motorcycle with a cabin on it, the car had a two-cylinder engine and a three-wheel frame, two wheels in front, one in back. They were built at Malvern from 1906 to '51. Four-wheel cars were built from 1936 to the present using standard automobile engines and designs. Robert Duckworthy* probably would have driven one of the three-wheeled versions as did Haviland Martin*. [im/HHC 10]

4517 morganatic -- the marriage of a member of royalty to a commoner with the understanding that any offspring of the marriage cannot succeed to titles or entitlements. The rank of the inferior partner in the marriage also remains unchanged. Such a marriage was proposed to King Edward VIII as a possible solution to his marriage crisis with Wallis Simpson, but was rejected as an alternative. [HHC 32]

4518 Moriarty -- Sherlock Holmes's* archenemy who dies with Holmes at the Reichenbach Falls in Switzerland in Sir Arthur Conan Doyle's short story, "The Final Problem". Doyle later had to recant and provide Holmes with a miraculous resurrection, but Moriarty was not so fortunate. The evil genius, the Napoleon of Crime, must be content now to live in the language as a name for any particularly evil, criminous ringleader. Doyle's original was a mathematical genius who became the head of organized crime in England. He does not fare so well in DLS's reference to him. [ab/WB 9/BC 1/MMA 17]

4519 *Moriturus* -- Latin for, "I who am about to die", an allusion to "*Ave Caesar, morituri te salutant*" (Hail Caesar, we who are about to die salute you), the salute of the gladiators before the games began. [BH 14]

4520 Morley's *Canzonets for Two Voices* -- Thomas Morley's (1557-?1603) *The First Booke of Canzonets to Two Voices* was published in London in 1595. The canzonet, lyrics anonymous, sung by PW and HV in the antique shop, has the first two lines given, and concludes:

"Doth walk the woods so dainty
Gathering sweet violets and cowslips plenty
The birds enamored sing and praise my Flora:
Lo, here a new Aurora."

A canzonet is a little song. [GN 19]

4521 *Morning Post* -- a newspaper founded in 1772 and absorbed by the *Daily Telegraph* in 1937, both papers being editorially Conservative in their politics [ab/WB 5/CW 2/BC 1]

4522 *Morning Star* -- the real paper of that name has and had Communist leanings and was once known as the *Daily Worker*. As presented in the PW canon, however, the paper is fictitious, but DLS may have had the *Morning Post** in mind. [*passim*]

4523 *Morning Yell* -- a fictitious newspaper [cf]

4524 Moro, Antonio -- Anthonis Mor Van Dashorst (ca. 1517-67), a Dutch painter often known by the Spanish version of his name as in this entry citation. He was a noted painter of nobility known to have been in England as he painted a portrait of Queen Mary I in 1554. [BH E2]

4525 Morpheus -- the Greek god of dreams [BC 12/MMA 9]

4526 morphine [phia] -- an addictive alkaloid narcotic derived from opium. It was isolated by the German chemist Friedrich Sertürner in 1806.

4527 Morphology -- usually not capitalized. It is used here in reference to the study of morphemes, the smallest units of language. Morphology attempts to describe word formation in language through a study of inflection, derivation, and development. [GN 21]

4528 Morris -- the "Bolshevik wallah*" as Parker* calls him. He is the fictitious person who is knowledgeable about the Russian menace in England. He could have been attached to either Scotland Yard or to the Security Service (see M. I.) had he been a real person. [HHC 19]

4529 Morris -- one of the products, model unspecified, of Morris Motors, Ltd.; either the Morris Oxford or the Morris Cowley. The Morris Oxford, first manufactured in 1912, brought the company its initial great success and the firm eventually evolved into one of the largest mass production companies in England. Its founder, William Richard Morris (1877-1963), 1st Viscount Nuffield, is remembered as a great public benefactor, having endowed several research institutions in medicine and social research. The firm is now a part of British Leyland. [FRH 3/HHC 1/NT 18]

4530 morris about -- to dance or play about in a careless, frolicsome, and, perhaps, dangerous manner. The term derives from the medieval morris dances. A contemporary version of a morris dance is Percy Grainger's popular piano solo, "Country Gardens". [NT 2]

4531 Morris chair -- a large easy chair with an adjustable back and removable cushions designed by William Morris* [SP 8]

4532 Morris, William -- distinguished poet, artist, decorator, printer, and socialist (1834-96), his interior

designs changed the tastes of the English public. He helped create the modern English concept of socialism, and designed various type fonts and ornamental letters for the exceptional work done by the Kelmscott Press, products that are still eagerly sought by bibliophiles. [WB 6/NT 11/GN 17/BH 6]

4533 Morrison -- a porter who provides police with important evidence in their search for George Goyles*. Morrison's illness is slowing down the search. From the context it is not clear whether Morrison is a doorkeeper of some other kind of porter at Marylebone Station, London. [CW 7]

4534 Morrison case -- see The Society [ab]

4535 Morrison, Walter -- the head ploughman* on Henry Weldon's* farm [HHC 22]

4536 Morse signals -- any method of mechanical, electrical, auditory, or visual communication using Samuel F. B. Morse's dot and dash code [ab]

4537 mort -- many; origin obscure [BH 4]

4538 mortarboards -- the flat-topped hats with tassels worn as part of the academic regalia when full academicals* are worn [GN 1]

4539 mortice [mortise] lock -- a lock inserted into a cavity hollowed into the door itself. Most modern house locks are of this variety. [BH 18]

4540 Mortimer -- a local involved with Squire Burdock's* meandering corpse, he loans an extra pair of horses to Joliffe* for the latter's hearse [bc]

4541 Mortimer -- see Wimsey, Mortimer [BH E2]

4542 Mortimer St. -- a street running for several blocks in an easterly direction from Regent St.* to Cleveland St. North of Oxford St.* [WB 10]

4543 Morton -- a footman at the Dower House, Duke's Denver* [BH E2]

4544 Moses, five books of -- the Pentateuch or Torah--Genesis, Exodus, Leviticus, Numbers, and Deuteronomy--the first five books of the Old Testament [CW 13]

4545 Moses, Mr. -- one of the suspects in disguise as a "harmless Jew" salesman and chess* opponent for Mr. Mellilow* [sf]

4546 Moss & Gordon -- most probably a fictitious ladies' wear firm as Clarence Gordon* is a figure of mild ridicule and DLS avoided such practice when real people or firms were involved [FRH 22]

4547 Moss & Isaacs -- a company to whom William Noakes* mortgaged the household furniture from Talboys. The firm is fictitious. [BH 18]

4548 Mossyard Farm -- on the Coast Rd.* just beyond Gatehouse-of-Fleet at Mossyard [FRH 2]

4549 "most fish have gold in their mouths . . ." -- PW alludes to the Miracle of the Tribute Money in Matthew 17:24-7. Jesus says to Peter: "Go thou to the sea and cast an hook, and take up the fish that first cometh up; and when thou has opened his mouth, thou shalt find a piece of money." A version of this story appears in Mark 12:13-17 and includes the famous "Render unto Caesar the things that are Caesar's, and to God the things that are God's." [MMA 14]

4550 motet -- a polyphonic choral composition on a sacred text, usually _a capella_. They were often, but not _exclusively_, prepared for religious services.

4551 mother of Daniel -- HV refers to the Biblical prophet, Daniel, of lion's den fame, who was taken to Babylon as a captive of King Nebuchadnezzar to be trained as a servant of the court so that when he became an adult he could serve as a learned adviser. Thus, his mother would have felt great fear for her child. HV further suggests this in the context. [GN 17]

4552 Mother Goose -- nursery tales and poems published by John Newbery in the mid-1700's. Perrault's _Contes de ma mère l'Oye_ was Newbery's _source_, but _the name Mother_ Goose is more ancient than that. [BH 7]

4553 Mother Siegel's Syrup -- or, correctly, Mother Siegels Syrup. In one of that product's snappier advertisements of 1918-19 we find:

MOTHER SIEGELS SYRUP

is excellent for indigestion,
Pain after eating,
Biliousness, Languor, Headaches, Acidity;
Because it assists the organs of digestion
--stomach, liver, and bowels--
to do their work perfectly
Take it after meals!
[HHC 23]

4554 motley -- the ragged or patched suit of a clown or jester, often now presented, as on a harlequin, as a diamond patch pattern, and as often in black and white [SP 5]

4555 mottoes -- see cracker mottoes [np]

4556 motorcycle race -- the famous race from "Cat in the Bag" starts at Paddington Station, London, and proceeds North from there to Finchley, Chipping Barnet, Hatfield, Baldock, Biggleswade, Tempsford, and ending at Eaton Socon**. The race between Simpkins and Walters** began between Hatfield and Baldock. These are real towns which exist along the Great North Road, now called the A1 route, which runs between London and Edinburgh. [cb]

4557 motorcycles -- the brands listed in the canon are: Norton, Scott Flying Squirrel, and Douglas. For details, see the particular brand name entry.

4558 motor-lorry -- British English for a motor truck, especially if open or low-sided [im]

4559 motor people -- an automobile dealership [BH 8]

4560 mould -- a variant of mold and dialectical English for earth, dirt, but especially that earth rich in humus and, therefore, particularly suited for gardening [t]

4561 _moules marinièrs_ -- mussels. It is unclear exactly how these mussels were prepared, but the recipes agree generally on cooking the cleaned raw mussels in butter, herbs, white wine, shallots or onions, and over a high flame. When the mussels are open fully, half the shell is removed, the cooking sauce is poured over them and sprinkled with parsley. Sometimes a _Velouté_ sauce is used as well to make _moules à la Normande_, a variation on the basic recipe. [BC 9]

4562 mountebank -- a snake-oil salesman, a purveyor of quack cures and remedies of a high alcoholic content; a "con" artist. The term derives from the practice of such salesmen in mounting a bench to sell his wares. [MMA 11/GN 16]

4563 Mountjoy, Horace -- the name of Hector Puncheon's mysterious person in evening clothes. He dies horribly under the wheels of a subway train at the South Kensington Station*. [MMA 15]

4564 Mountweazle, Lord -- a Wimsey houseguest to whom George Goyles* was once "unnecessarily rude". His lordship is fictitious. [CW 9]

4565 _mouton_ -- French for sheep. There is nothing of the cute and cuddly suggested. [HHC 15]

4566 moving like chessmen upon their alloted squares -- the allusion may be to the basic structure of Lewis Carroll's _Through the Looking Glass_**, the entire plot of which is centered on chess moves, and most of the characters are chess pieces [BH 5]

4567 Mozart -- Wolfgang Amadeus Mozart (1756-91), Austrian composer and child prodigy of enormous talent and accomplishment. In his short life he composed over 600 works, including three of the world's greatest operas: _Don Giovanni_, _The Marriage of Figaro_, and _The Magic Flute_. [HHC 20]

4568 much ado about nothing -- a common phrase made famous by Shakespeare through his comedy of that title, a favorite known for its witty word play. The plot is typically Shakespearean in that it has confused lovers using confused identities. [MMA 13/BH E1]

4569 "much learning hath made thee mad" -- the quotation is from Acts 26:24: "And as he thus spake for himself, Festus said with a loud voice, Paul, thou art beside thyself; much learning doth make thee mad.
"But he said, I am not mad, most noble Festus; but speak forth the words of truth and soberness." [GN 6]

4570 much of a muchness -- PW is think-

ing of Alice in Wonderland*, but the phrase did not originate there. The words also appear in George Eliot's Daniel Deronda, Book 4, Ch. 31, and in Sir John Vanbrugh's The Provok'd Husband, I, i. PW alludes to Ch. 7 of Carroll's* work, "A Mad Tea Party", wherein the Dormouse, when pinched to awakeness by the Hatter, says, "you known you say things are 'much of a muchness'--did you ever see such a thing as a drawing of a muchness!" The phrase is still a common one in England and equates to the phrase, "six of one and half a dozen of the other", no discernible difference. [MMA 4/NT 12]

4571 Muffet, Miss -- the central figure in the nursery rhyme "Little Miss Muffet"; she is frightened by a spider [HHC 4]

4572 muffled peal -- a peal* rung with leather covers on the clappers to create a dulled tone. The practice of muting bells, drums, etc., in respect for the dead is an ancient one. [NT 3]

4573 mufti -- in civilian clothes, not in any particular uniform [HHC 4/MMA 18]

4574 Muggins, Bill -- a member of the parish of Lopsley*, about thirty miles from Paggleham* where PW and HV spend an idyllic afternoon [BH 14]

4575 Muggins's Magnolia Face Cream -- a fictitious product created by DLS to be advertised by the equally fictitious Pym's Publicity* [MMA 11]

4576 Muggleton's -- one of the advertising clients handled by Pym's Publicity* [MMA 10]

4577 Muirkirk -- a village at the junction of the A70 and A723 routes about twenty-five miles to the East and North of Ayr* [FRH 14]

4578 mules -- a ladies' slipper covering only the toe area, the rest of the sides and heel being open [HHC 15]

4579 mulier vel meretrix . . . -- Latin for, "woman or whore, the fellowship of which has been absolutely forbidden to Christians." DLS has not quite correctly remembered the Oxford University "Statutes". Her reference is to Titulus XV, "De Moribus Conformandis", Section 3, "De Domibus Oppidanorum non frequentandis", which translates as: "Of (Concerning) Customs Which Must Be Observed", Section 3, "Of (Concerning) Domicles (Residences) of the City Not to be Frequented". In that section is written: "Academici vero omnes abstineant ab aedibus infames seu suspectas Mulieres vel Meretrices alentibus aut recipientibus; quarum consortio Christianis prorsus interdictus est." That passage translates as: "Members of the college shall abstain from domiciles which maintain disreputable or suspect women or whores, or receiving the same; association with whom is absolutely forbidden to Christians." The statute dates from 1636 with revision in 1838, and was in effect when DLS attended Somerville and as late as 1942. As undergraduate behavior was rigidly enforced at that time, DLS has not exaggerated here at all. However, there is no rule of that sort among the University Statutes any longer. [GN 12]

4580 The Mull -- The Mull of Galloway, the name for the headland of the peninsula that is part of the Rinns of Galloway; the double-ended prominence at the western end of Dumfries and Galloway on the North or St. Patrick's Channel between Scotland and Ireland. A mull is a headland around which an estuary curves. [FRH 19]

4581 Mullins -- the Jowett Lodge* porter at Shrewsbury College* [GN 5]

4582 Mullins, Joe -- a resident of the parish of Fenchurch St. Paul* [NT 2]

4583 Munnings -- Sir Alfred James Munnings (1878-1959), English artist who specialized in painting horses and hunting and racing scenes. He was president of the Royal Academy from 1944-49. [BH E2]

4584 Munns, Joe -- husband of George Fentiman's* landlady. He is a rather thoughtless lout, but he does attempt to be accommodating. [BC 18]

4585 Munns, Primrose -- wife of above and owner of the building that houses the Fentiman's* flat. She is not portrayed as too cooperative, sympathetic, or intelligent. [BC 7]

4586 Munns, Mrs. -- Parker's* day lady,

cook, and housekeeper while alone at his Great Ormond St.* flat [WB 5]

4587 Munster, Sebastian -- a 16th C. German astronomer and general geographer who made important contributions to the early efforts of descriptive and regional geography. He is author of the Cosmographia Universalis*. [dh]

4588 mural tablet -- a plaque or tablet placed on the wall inside a church to commemorate people buried there or elsewhere [NT 1]

4589 Murbles, John -- the elderly and delightfully Victorian Wimsey family solicitor* who regularly provides legal advice to PW and who plays a significant role in the trial of the Duke of Denver*for murder. He keeps rooms at the Inns of Court* and will not have a telephone there. He does, however, keep a superb wine cellar. In UD, he is exposed to some considerable personal danger as he helps PW untangle the legal technicalities of that story, but his regimen is generally less exciting. Murbles handles the Fentiman* family affairs as well, and PW turns to him to have a will drawn for himself and HV. Given Mr. Murbles' experiences with wills, PW's instructions to him to make the PW-HV will as ironclad as possible will result in as absolute a document as is conceivable. It is to be noted that no one normally addresses him as anything other than Mr. Murbles or sir. [CW 2/UD 6/BC 3/BH P]

4590 Murchison, Miss Joan -- the employee from PW's "cattery"* sent to observe the doings at Norman Urquhart's* law office. She is a most alert and enterprising woman who enters into the spirit of PW's investigation with great verve. It is later learned that she has been married for a year and that she is no longer in PW's employ. [SP 10/GN 13]

4591 Murder at Smutty Nose -- see Pearson, Edmund [UD 8]

4592 Murder Bay -- HV's nickname for the place where she found Paul Alexis's* body [HHC 3]

4593 Murder by Degrees -- the detective novel completed by HV just prior to her walking tour [HHC 1]

4594 Murder Must Advertise [notes] -- an interesting dilemma arises with the dating of events in MMA. The book was published in early February, 1933, which means that the action of the story takes place from May to July of 1933. PW was born in 1890, but she gives his age as 42. Hence, DLS is writing about events that have not yet taken place. This perhaps helps explain the almost surrealistic nature of the scenes with PW as Harlequin as he "seduces" Dian de Momerie* (note the symbolism of the pennywhistle and of Harlequin as "forbidden fruit").

In these sequences, PW as Death Bredon who is masquerading as Harlequin, a situation has been created that is twice removed from reality. It is a psychological game which, if maintained, is a dangerous one, almost as dangerous as the drug "games" being investigated.

The dates confusion also complicates the identification of elements within specific events mentioned. For instance, the Epsom Derby mentioned is real, but DLS could not have known what horses would be running or which one would win, and consideration of events from 1932 is not valid as a reference framework for the story either.

An explanation for all of this is that DLS worked on MMA while doing research for NT, thus creating a chronological mess. However, the consensus of opinion is that MMA is set in the summer of 1933, a hot one as in the book, and because of the precocity of young Charles Peter--even Wimseys and their relatives are not known to talk that well at age one! A purely speculative rationale for this chronological confusion is that because the story and its events are particularly sordid and evil, yet could be readily associated with real people and places, DLS retained the "time distraction" to insure that no such connection could be made--a reverse of the ploy used in FRH when all but the murder itself was so firmly rooted in reality. DLS enjoyed her work at Benson's (Pym's Publicity* in MMA) and would want to be especially careful not to offend or harm the agency or the people there in any way.

Another consideration is that DLS has used the surrealistic approach to further support her obviously strong

condemnation of the then current version of the "drug culture" that existed within the "bright young thing"* crowd of the day. The most surreal elements of the novel are those involving direct contact with that movement. Less surreal, but nonetheless out of touch with reality, is the advertising world of Pym's Publicity*, which only comes into the real world at the end of the cricket* match when PW drops his restrained manner of play and bats like the "Flim"* of Oxford fame, thus exposing his real identity for all who are alert enough to see it. Even Dean's and Tallboy's** deaths are not "real" events in the full sense of real. A new copywriter and a shilling for the wreath put Dean out of mind for most, and Tallboy is only the poor victim of a late night auto accident--another shilling, another wreath, another new employee, and no sense of loss. PW and Parker are the only central characters who fully realize the nature of what has happened.

MMA thus becomes a damning comment on the hollowness of modern society as Joseph Conrad and T. S. Eliot have defined it in Heart of Darkness and in "The Waste Land" or "The Hollow Men."

Lastly, it is possible that MMA was published sooner than DLS had expected, thus confusing any time-delay she might have included to insure that the story sounded "timely". Even so, the earlier considerations of surrealism are significant parts of the story now whether DLS intended them to be there or not.

4595 murdered Lorenzo's glove -- the allusion is to John Keats' poem "Isabella" (1820), a melodramatic effort recounting the love of Lorenzo for Isabella and how her brothers kill him. She finds the body, takes the head, and hides it in a pot under a basil plant. The verses in question are in XLVII and read:

"Soon she turn'd up a soiled glove, whereon
Her silk had play'd in purple phantasies.
She kissed it with a lip more chill than stone,
And put it in her bosom, where it dries."

Keats' story is from Boccaccio's Decameron, the Fourth Day, Fifth Story, Filomena's tale of Lisabetta and Lorenzo. [BH 4]

4596 The Murderer's Vade Mecum -- or 101 Ways of Causing Sudden Death. PW's "cute" threat to write such a book comes to fruition as it is listed in his Who's Who entry as one of his publications. PW should have had no trouble finding suitable examples and it is no surprise to read Parker's* resigned, "Oh well," in response to PW's threat to write the book. [UD 14]

4597 Murdoch, Wullie -- or Willie, the owner and publican at the McClellan Arms* where Campbell and Waters** have their fight [FRH 1]

4598 Murgatroyd, Miss -- a church worker in Leahampton* [UD 5]

4599 Muriel -- a person's name overheard by HV as she investigates the lounge at the Hotel Resplendent in Wilvercombe* [HHC 3]

4600 Murphy, Mr. -- Mr. Murbles's* noisy Irish barrister* friend at Staple Inn* who has a telephone, something that Mr. Murbles's Victorian attitudes have not yet allowed him [CW 16]

4601 Murray -- a banker, native of Kirkwall*, who was in the McClellan Arms* at the time of the Campbell-Waters** fight [FRH 1]

4602 Murray Arms -- on the High St. in Gatehouse-of-Fleet*. Now owned by the Best Western chain of hotels, they accept several charge cards. There are twenty-six rooms and the hotel remains a popular local hostelry. [FRH 11]

4603 Murray, Davie -- a neighbor of Thomas Macpherson's* who has some cattle which apparently get out from time to time and do damage to Macpherson's garden [ss]

4604 Mus. Doc. -- Doctor of Music, a degree in musical theory or performance equivalent to a Ph. D. in some other area [GN 1]

4605 Museum Rd. -- an East-West street in Oxford that connects St. Giles' St. with Parks Rd. [GN 12]

4606 mushroom clubs -- those that spring up seemingly overnight, flourish a while, and then disappear just as quickly as they appear

[HHC 5]

4607 music hall -- the British equivalent of vaudeville [NT 7]

4608 Musical Chairs -- the children's game where one chair less than the number of players is placed for their use in the game. Music is played while the players march around the chairs. When the music stops, all scramble for a seat, one person being left out. A chair is removed and the process is repeated until only one person survives as the "winner". [np]

4609 musquash -- muskrat or the fur of muskrats made into a coat, cape, or other garment for a woman to wear. Musquash is the Algonquin Indian name for the muskrat. Mrs. Forrest* wears a muskrat coat. [UD 7]

4610 Mussolini -- Benito Mussolini (1883-1945), the swaggering Fascist* dictator of Italy from 1922 to 1943. Called Il Duce, he tried to collaborate with Adolf Hitler, but was out of his league. [MMA 1/NT 13/BH P]

4611 Mussolini to organize trade conditions -- Mussolini* did have extensive influence on the Italian economy, being especially remembered for getting the trains to run on time. As in Germany, however, much of his economic "revitalization" was built around building a war machine. [MMA 1]

4612 mustard, mix -- see mix mustard [FRH 2]

4613 Mustard Club -- DLS is having a bit of fun with her readers here as she was one of the guiding lights of the Mustard Club advertising scheme during her time as a copywriter at Benson's. The Club was developed for Colman's mustard, a brand still available today--it is dry and comes in a mustard-yellow metal box--and was led by the fictitious Baron de Beef. Other officers included Miss Di Gester, Lord Bacon, Signor Spaghetti, etc. The Club had a specific set of "Rules" as well, all of which were designed to get people to eat mustard or bathe in it when ill.

Not content with all that, the campaign featured little mysteries, adventures, games, puzzles, and other entertainments, all starring members of the Mustard Club. The Club was patterned after some sort of hybrid cross between a social club and a secret society, but was open to anyone who used mustard.

Among the Club's publications was The Recipe Book of the Mustard Club which contains some excellent recipes. For 3d in stamps, one could even join the O. M. B., the Order of the Mustard Bath, and receive a pin to wear.

All this joyous nonsense sold a great deal of mustard after it began in the fall of 1926. It was an instant success and the sales of mustard soared by as much as 50%! [MMA 19]

4614 mustard plaster -- a concoction thicker than an ointment and containing ground mustard seed. It is meant to apply heat and to bring the blood to the area to which it is applied. [BH E2]

4615 mutton -- sheep after being butchered and prepared for the table. The English language generally has two names for its commonly eaten meats: one, usually Anglo-Saxon in origin, is used to name the animal when on the hoof; the other, usually a French derivative, describes the same animal when prepared for eating as in sheep/mutton, deer/venison, calf/veal, and pig/pork. [WB 10/BC 5/MMA 4]

4616 mutual friend -- an allusion to Charles Dickens's* novel of 1864-65, Our Mutual Friend [MMA 14]

4617 "My back aches and a drowsy numbness . . ." -- PW, in the spirit of the "let's swap allusions" game with HV, is rendering his own version of the first two lines of Keats' "Ode to a Nightingale", composed in early May of 1819 [HHC 16]

4618 my brother's keeper -- an allusion to the famous passage in Genesis 4:9 that recounts the fist murder: "And the Lord said unto Cain, Where is Abel thy brother? And he said, I know not: Am I my brother's keeper?" [GN 7]

4619 "My Canary Has Circles Under His Eyes" -- the name of a "hot" dance tune first recorded in 1931. In London a group called the Waldorfians cut the record, but in the U. S. it was recorded by a group led by Lawrence Welk. [HHC 30]

4620 "My ear is open like a greedy shark . . ." -- the line is from John Keats' sonnet, undated but published in 1817, entitled, after the poem's first line, "Light feet, dark violet eyes, and parted hair". It is a youthful work as the entry citation might suggest. The quoted lines are the last two of the poem. [GN 14]

4621 "My gracious silence . . ." -- the allusion is to Shakespeare's Coriolanus*, II, i, 192 [BH E3]

4622 "My life upon't some miser . . ." -- from T. L. Beddoes' The Brides' Tragedy**, III, iii, 173-76. The lines are Hubert's, spoken to a huntsman just as they come upon Hesperus finishing the task of burying Floribel whom he has just murdered. Hubert and the huntsman have mistaken Hesperus for a miser burying his gold and undertake to see the cache for themselves. [HHC 10]

4623 "My lips kissed dumb . . ." -- see Aholibah [BH 16]

4624 "My love was clad in black velvet . . ." -- PW quotes these lines from an anonymous ballad entitled "Jamie Douglas". The Oxford Book of Ballads gives the passage as:

"My gude lord in the black velvet,
And I mysel' in cramasie."

PW's version of the quote is addressed to Lady Hermione Creethorpe* whose vanity is pleased by his attentions. See also cramoisie. [qs]

4625 "My sad hurt it shall releeve." from Michael Drayton's* poem, "The Shepherd's Sirena", ll. 65ff. [GN 13]

4626 "My snow white horses foam and fret . . ." -- PW is misquoting from Matthew Arnold's (1822-88) poem, "The Forsaken Merman", line 21: "The wild white horses foam and fret." The poem was written in 1849. [BH 16]

4627 "My text is taken . . ." -- a formula introduction to a sermon or homily and usually referring to the source in the Scriptures from whence inspiration was derived. The phrase is a sort of liturgical soporific to many, but not to Gaffer Gander*. The remainder of the comment, "Now God the Father", introduces the benediction which closes the service. [HHC 26]

4628 "my true love hath my heart" -- from Sir Philip Sidney's The Arcadia, a pastoral romance in verse. PW has quoted part of the first line (the title as well) of a famous song from book iii of that romance. It continues:

". . . and I have his,
By just exchange one for the other giv'n;
I hold his dear, and mine he cannot miss,
There never was a better bargain driv'n."

HV quotes the cited line later in that same chapter. [BH 16]

4629 Myra -- Henry Strachan's* daughter. From her conversation and obvious tomboy tendencies, one would put her age at about ten. [FRH 4]

4630 Myrc, John -- or Mirc (fl. ca. 1400) was an English Austin canon and prior of the Canons Regular at Littleshall Abbey, Shropshire. The group followed a rule somewhat more relaxed than that of the Benedictines. Various of his works survive, including sermons, but his Instructions for Parish Priests -- an English poem in rhyming couplets for the instruction of priests in their various duties--is the one DLS cites. The passage quoted concerns commination, the recital of Divine threatenings against sinners, an office read after the Litany on Ash Wednesday and at other times. Myrc is remembered as a superstitious man, but his writings remain an important source of information about Church life in the early 15th C. [NT 3]

4631 myrmidons -- from Greek mythology, people created from ants. PW uses the term to refer to some police constables who will escort him on his visit to Dr. Conyers*. A myrmidon is one who works faithfully and who carries out orders without question, and PW uses it to refer to the uniformed police at other times. [dh/FRH 3]

4632 Mystofilms Ltd. -- Varden's* employer when he starred in Jake of Dead Man's Bush* [cf]

(N)

4633 N. C. O. -- the abbreviation for noncommissioned officer, any enlisted person of the rank of lance corporal or higher. Bunter was PW's N. C. O. in WW I, an enlisted aide to a commissioned officer. [BC 7]

4634 N. S. P. C. A. -- the standard abbreviation for the National (now Royal) Society for the Prevention of Cruelty to Animals [SP 10]

4635 N'ayez pas peur, je m'en charge -- French for, "Don't worry, I'll see to it." [HHC 7]

4636 Nadgett, Mr. -- the A. A.* point man [cb]

4637 "Naggin at a feller as is six-foot three" -- part of an old music hall ditty which runs:

"It's a great big shame and if she belonged to me
I'd show 'er what to do!
Putting on a fellow what is six foot three
And 'er only four foot two!
They 'adn't been married not an hour or so
When underneath 'er thumb went Jim.
Isn't it a pity that the likes of 'er
Should put upon the likes of 'im."
[GN 17]

4638 name block -- a wooden block with a metal plate affixed to one surface, the metal plate having a standard word or headline permanently set in types of various sizes as needed [MMA 4]

4639 Nancy Belle [steward of] -- PW alludes to W. S. Gilbert's rollicking "The Yarn of the Nancy Belle" of 1866 in which the lone survivor of a wreck in the Indian Ocean tells how he and his former shipmates cannibalized each other. PW has taken some liberties, though, as the captain was shot and the purser and steward were not specifically mentioned by job title. [MMA 21]

4640 Naples folio of 1477 -- the first edition of Dante's Divine Comedy with commentary and the first to print Boccaccio's life of Dante. The edition is both rare and desirable, the only copy known in the U. S. being at the Huntingdon Library. [WB 1]

4641 Naples yellow -- a dull, creamy, brick-yellow to yellow-gold color [FRH 7]

4642 Napoleon -- Napoleon Bonaparte, emperor of France from 1804 to 1815. See also brandy and perfect Napoleon. [WB 3 and passim]

4643 Napoleon of Crime -- see Moriarty, Professor [MMA 15]

4644 narcissi -- see pheasant-eye narcissi [NT 3]

4645 nark -- a spy employed by the police. PW is one in "Cave of Ali Baba". The word may derive from the Romany word nak, or nose, hence snoop. [MMA 7]

4646 nasturtiums -- a widely cultivated ornamental flower. The word is used for comic effect as a substitute for aspersions. [BC 13/MMA 1]

4647 Natasha -- the name of Ledbury's* girl friend and, perhaps, model. She goes with him when he leaves England for Poland. [BC 16]

4648 Natasha -- the old peasant woman who brought Paul Alexis* out of Russia at the time of the Revolution* [HHC 5]

4649 National -- one of the pre-WW II radio programs available from the BBC*. It provided the same basic content for all stations that carried it. Later it was called the Home Service, but is now called Radio 4. See also Regional. [BH 9]

4650 National Finance under the Tudors -- the financial haggling between the Tudors and Parliament, especially during the reigns of Henry VII and VIII at the beginning of that dynasty, are of intense interest to any historian who intends to understand the growth of Parliament and the decline of the power of the monarchy. The Tudor period is one of the pivotal points in that development. [GN 1]

4651 National Gallery -- not to be confused with the National Portrait Gallery which is nearby, the National Gallery is a museum of art in Trafalgar Square. Its collection contains some 4500 works, a number so vast that fewer than half can be displayed

at any one time. Originally opened in 1838, the Gallery has grown continually since. [ab/hp]

4652 National Press -- the various papers designed to serve all of Great Britain rather than some part of it, and taken collectively [HHC 24]

4653 Natural History Museum -- on Cromwell Rd. in South Kensington, the collection of about 40 million specimens now housed there includes representatives of all sorts of flora and fauna from dinosaur skeletons to an extensive exhibit on human biology. The museum is open daily at ten, Sundays at 2:30 P. M., almost every day of the year. It is an outgrowth of the British Museum which became a separate entity in 1880. [MMA 15]

4654 "nature, red in tooth and claw . . ." -- Bunter is described with lines from Tennyson's* "In Memoriam", LVI:15. The quote is exact up to "claw", the rest of the sentence being DLS's. [BH 15]

4655 Nautical Almanack -- a joint publication of the U. S. and Royal Navies, it lists information of tides, currents, channel markings, etc., of interest to sailors. It is updated regularly to account for the various geophysical and human changes that alter its accuracy. [HHC 3]

4656 nave -- the main part of a church, the area where the congregation sits [NT 2]

4657 navy sprigged foulard -- see foulard [GN 21]

4658 navvy -- an unskilled worker; from navigator, a name given to the workmen who built the canals in the 18th C. [GN 3/BH 7]

4659 nayles -- nails, in an obsolete spelling [BH E2]

4660 "Nazareth" -- a sacred song by French composer Charles Gounod (1818-93) that enjoyed immense popularity in Victorian England and somewhat later. It ran through dozens of editions after its introduction in the 1860's. [SP 13]

4661 neaps -- tides of a minimum height which occur around the first and third quarters of the moon; the opposite of springs* [HHC 1]

4662 neat whiskey -- straight, no ice or water [SP 20]

4663 ne plus ultra -- see conjuring banter [ie]

4664 Nebuchadnezzar -- the greatest Assyrian king, he ruled from 604-561 B. C. PW's son has to eat his tea on all fours like Nebuchadnezzar who, according to Daniel 4, "did eat grass as oxen". Nebuchadnezzar is the king who conquered Jerusalem and carried the Jews into captivity at Babylon in July of 586 B. C. after a siege of nineteen months. [t]

4665 Nec saevior ulla pestis -- Latin for, "no pestilence more savage". See tristus haud illis . . . . [GN 22]

4666 Necropolis -- literally a city of the dead, a cemetery [BC 13]

4667 necrosis -- the pathological death of living tissue in any plant or animal [te]

4668 Needham Market -- a town in Suffolk about eight miles northwest of Ipswich [NT 2]

4669 needs must and all that -- fully, "needs must when the devil drives", meaning that the circumstances leave no option, a colloquial expression [NT 14/GN 20]

4670 Negretti and Zambra -- well-known and widely respected makers of scientific instruments and photographic equipment, the company was formed in 1850 by Enrico A. L. Negretti (1818-79) and Joseph W. Zambra (1822-97). Among their early accomplishments was the creation of the Fitzroy gun barometer built to withstand the heavy gunfire aboard naval vessels, and supplying Charles Darwin with deep-sea equipment for his voyage aboard the H. M. S. Beagle. The firm also served as the official photographers at the Crystal Palace Exhibition*.

The firm's most famous and historic address was 38 Holborn Viaduct, London, and was occupied from November of 1869 to May of 1941 when it was destroyed by German bombs. The company also had offices on Regent St.* from 1862 to 1965. It is presently located in Aylesbury, Bucks., and is manufacturing micro-chip products for the com-

#4653 The Natural History Museum.

puter industry. They no longer manufacture meteorological instruments. During the earlier part of the century they did provide weather forecasts for the London press, and later, for the BBC*. The Evening News and Daily Mail even good-naturedly satirized the company name in cartoons whenever the weather was newsworthy. From the 1920's through 1935, Mr. A. C. Whatley did the daily forecasts. Such forecasts are now done by the Meteorological Office. [nf]

4671 Nell Cook under the paving stone -- the reference is to R. H. Barham's "Nell Cook!--Legend of the 'Dark Entry'", one of the Ingoldsby Legends*. In that poem is told the story of Ellen Bean, cook to a canon in Canterbury during the reign of Henry VIII and prior to the Reformation. The canon becomes host to his "niece", but Ellen, known familiarly as Nell Cook, thought, "They were a little less than 'kin', and rather more than 'kind'." Nell frowned on their frolics and killed them with a poisoned pie. She disappeared and the monks claimed ignorance, but later screams are heard from under a back door paving stone. The screams last for a while and then die out, but a hundred years later a skeleton of a woman is found there during some renovations. [BH 4]

4672 Nellie -- a Shrewsbury College* scout* who looks after Miss deVine's* rooms among others [GN 21]

4673 Nellie -- Lady Dormer's* housemaid, she is young and cooperative [BC 17]

4674 Nelson -- Horatio, Viscount Nelson (1758-1805), famous English naval hero and the Admiral who won the Battle of Trafalgar with daring tactics, but was killed there. He was born in Burnham Thorpe, Norfolk. The Dowager Duchess* has in mind, perhaps, either version of Nelson's last words: "Thank God, I have done my duty", or "Kiss me, Hardy", probably the latter. His flagship, the H. M. S. Victory, could fire a broadside every 80 seconds and is now on display at Portsmouth. [CW 9]

4675 Nene Outfall Cut -- the mouth of the Nene River, about eight miles West of the mouth of the Great Ouse, periodically dredged to keep it clear [NT 16]

4676 Nero -- the Roman emperor (54-68 A. D.), notorious for his brutality and passion for self-advertisement. He was, however, accomplished in a variety of the arts providing at least a little justification for his deathbed comment, "What an artist dies in me!" He was an active persecutor of the early Christians. [SP 17]

4677 Nestlé's baby -- an infant used by the candy and dairy products company to advertise certain of its products. It is difficult to verify its presence in Piccadilly Circus*, but DLS would have been acutely aware of such things, so we may assume that there was, indeed, such an infant in an ad there. [CW 19]

4678 nettle [rash] -- a weed of the genus Urtica having fine prickers or hairs which cause a blisterlike rash when they come in contact with the skin. The rash resembles the plant's sting, but is caused by an allergy. [SP 9/NT 9]

4679 neuralgia pain -- acute pain along one or more standard nerve routes. Such pains can be quite violently painful. [UD 8]

4680 neurasthenia -- a term describing such symptoms as fatigue, worry, a sense of inadequacy, headache, and sensitivity to light and noise. These symptoms are usually indicative of a more serious condition. Captain George Fentiman's* symptoms are the outward manifestations of shellshock*. [BC 2]

4681 never shot a fox -- a comment about PW's upper-class status. The Wimseys hunt foxes with hounds for sport. [WB 11]

4682 New Arlesford -- in Hampshire*, a picturesque market town near the River Itchen [UD 20]

4683 New Army -- see Army

4684 New Bedford River -- built in 1649-51 to supplement the drainage provided by the Old Bedford River*, it is also known as the Hundred-Foot Drain, and is sluice-free and tidal [NT 2]

4685 New Bond St. -- with Old Bond St. it connects Piccadilly* with Ox-

THE NELSON MONUMENT, TRAFALGAR SQUARE, LONDON

#4674 The Nelson Monument, Trafalgar Square, London.

ford St.* just West of Regent St.* [CW 17]

4686 New Bridge -- a wing connecting the Tudor Building and the North Annexe at Shrewsbury College* [GN 5]

4687 New Brig o'Dee -- on some maps as Upper Brig o'Dee, it is a point about seven miles from New Galloway* and about eleven miles from Newton-Stewart* on the A712 route where it crosses the Black Water of Dee [FRH 20]

4688 New Century Dictionary -- a famous two-volume dictionary of English published in 1927 in N. Y. and London by D. Appleton-Century Co. [MMA 10]

4689 New College -- see Oxford Colleges. The roses on the heraldic shield are the English roses. [GN AN and 13]

4690 New College Lane -- a meandering street that connects Catte St.* to High St. in Oxford. The street is New College Lane only from Catte St. to the point adjacent to the South wing of New College where it becomes Queen's Lane to High St., as it skirts the perimeter of Queen's College on the North and East. [GN 23]

4691 New Cut -- now known as The Cut*, it runs from Waterloo Rd. to Blackfriars Rd. The Waterloo Rd. end is near Waterloo Station and the Old Vic Theatre. Robert Duckworthy* was born somewhere in the vicinity of New Cut, an area known at the time as a fruit- and vegetable-sellers market. [im]

4692 New Cut [Outfall] -- a reference to the channel that was cut to assist the water of the fictitious River Wale to flow out into the Wash* [NT 18]

4693 New Cut -- a channel connecting the Cherwell and Isis** Rivers just North of their natural confluence in South Oxford [GN 13]

4694 New Forest -- in Hampshire*, the forest was reserved by the Norman kings as a royal hunting preserve. It is still kept in its original state and is administered by a forestry commission. The Forest covers some 90,000 acres, two-thirds of which are open to the public. In addition to the forested areas, there are heaths, bogs, pasturage, ponds, farms, small old churches, and thatched cottages that all suggest earlier centuries. Wild animals have the right of way on Forest roads, and law forbids the public feeding them. [CW 7]

4695 New Galloway -- a town on the Water of Ken at the North end of Loch Ken about eighteen miles North of Gatehouse-of-Fleet [FRH 2]

4696 New Jerusalem -- Bill Rumm* is referring to the Revelation of St. John the Divine, 21:2. It is one of seven "new" things that will follow the Last Judgment. [SP 13]

4697 New Luce -- a stop on the rail line between Girvan* and Stranraer* [FRH 5]

4698 new physics -- the physics of outer space and nuclear energy, all of which was still "new" in the 1930's [GN 2]

4699 new Property act -- see Property Act of 1925 [UD 14]

4700 New Psychology -- that of Freud and the subsequent variant teachings of Adler, Jung, and others [GN 14]

4701 New Quad -- one of the two open areas in Shrewsbury College* enclosed on four sides by buildings; a "court" at Cambridge [GN 1]

4702 New York -- the references are always to New York City, not to New York State. Standish and Hiram Wetherall** have homes there and Simone Vonderaa* moved there after ending her liason with Denis Cathcart*. [ie/CW 16]

4703 New Zealanders -- PW and Freddie Arbuthnot* are off to watch a cricket* match somewhere out of London. A New Zealand team toured England in 1927, but it is not clear just what match DLS might have had in mind. [UD 17]

4704 Newbolt, Mr. -- an employee of Pym's Publicity* who is not otherwise identified [MMA 6]

4705 Newcastle -- probably Newcastle-upon-Tyne, county seat for county Tyne and Wear in the northeast of England [UD 20]

4706 Newcombe [Farmer] -- the farmer who works the land adjacent to Hinks's Lane*. He keeps horses on the land at the time of HHC, but is not noted for the care he gives to his hedge fences. [HHC 12]

4707 Newgate fringe -- a fringe of beard worn under the chin (OED). PW suggests he should grow one to look more serious or perhaps more detectival. The prison no longer exists, having been torn down in 1902-03. The Central Criminal Court (the Old Bailey) now stands on the site. [pj]

4708 Newland, Miss -- the Latymer Scholar* at Shrewsbury College* who seems favored to earn First Class Honors with her degree [GN 12]

4709 Newmarket -- the headquarters, in Suffolk, of British horse racing since the days of James I. It is home of the Jockey Club, which controls British horse racing, and The National Stud, a 500-acre farm run by the Horserace Betting Levy Board. Henry Weldon* visits there often. [UD 7/HHC 22]

4710 Newport Court -- see Gerrard St. [CW 9]

4711 News of the World -- a London Sunday newspaper typical of the mass appeal or tabloid papers which emphasize gossip, lurid crime, sex, and scandal. In that regard it is one of the more sensational English papers and has the world's largest Sunday circulation. Founded in 1843, its politics are Liberal-Independent. [CW 4/UD 4/ BC 18/SP 10]

4712 newspapers -- some papers mentioned in the PW canon are real, but many are fictitious. Some of their names are rather silly, perhaps reflecting DLS's dislike of "telegraphic journalese" as a poor substitute for English. When a particular title is not important to the verisimilitude of the story, DLS apparently thought that any title would do and often had some fun with them.

4713 Newton, Waffles -- one of PW's sometimes useful newspaper friends who is one of the reporters assigned to HV's trial for murder [BC 16/SP 1]

4714 Newton-Carberry business -- the reference is apparently fictitious and relates to one of PW's escapades for the Foreign Office. No details are given. [HHC 28]

4715 Newton-Stewart -- an agricultural town on the River Cree* known for its long thriving cattle market. It figures prominently in the comings and goings in FRH. [FRH 2]

4716 Newton's apple -- popular history has it that Sir Isaac Newton was inspired to his theories of gravitation and motion when an apple fell on his head [GN 19/BH 8]

4717 Niagara -- see footprints in Niagara [WB 4]

4718 nib -- the point of a pen, especially that part which comes in contact with the paper [BC 6]

4719 "nice Jew" -- see Mr. Chesterton's definition of a nice Jew [ss]

4720 Nicodemus, Gospel of -- see Gospel of Nicodemus [NT 1]

4721 Nicholas I -- Tsar (or Czar) of Russia from 1825 to 1855. He was born in 1796. Known as the Iron Czar, it was he who ruled at the outbreak of the Crimean War, but he died before its conclusion. He was the third son of Paul I and came to the throne only after his older brothers had relinquished their claims to it. [HHC 29]

4722 Nicolaevna [Nicole] -- the supposed offspring of Czar Nicholas I and Charlotte**. They are given as Paul Alexis's great-grandparents, so Nicole is his grandmother. [HHC 32]

4723 Nicotina -- a goddess of recent creation, she honors tobacco and is revered widely [BH 15]

4724 Niersteiner '23 -- a wine produced at Nierstein on the Rhine in the Rheinhessen region of Germany. It is a superb Rhine wine in just about any year. [GN 9]

4725 Night of the Dead -- see All-Hallows Eve/Day [ie]

4726 nightly hundred and one -- see Tom Tower [GN 11]

4727 "Night's candles are burnt out." -- PW is quoting from Romeo and Juliet, III, v, 9-10. The line concludes:

"and jocund day
Stands tiptoe on the misty mountain

tops." [BH 7]

4728 nimbus -- a halo or disc representing a radiance around the head of a divine or sacred being. They were also used in pictorial versions of medieval kings as a reflection of the theory of the Divine Right of kings. [bc]

4729 9A, Park Lane -- the address of Sir Reuben Levy*. It is a particularly fashionable address along the eastern boundary of Hyde Park*. See also Park Lane. [WB 2]

4730 nine familiar spirits -- nine is three time three, an especially potent number in magic and numerology. Therefore, a magician with nine familiar spirits (magical helpers) would be seen as particularly powerful. [ie]

4731 950 guineas -- or £997/10. In the currency of the day, that was about $3990 U. S., easily three or four times the average annual salary of a working person of the 1930's, so it is no wonder that Miss Climpson* was left speechless. [BH P]

4732 Nine Rings -- the fictitious pub on Gray's Inn Rd. where Philip Boyes* went after his unsuccessful interview with HV. It was in this pub that Boyes took some medication and was observed doing so by Mrs. Bulfinch* who reports her observations to PW and Parker*. [SP 10]

4733 nine tailors -- tailors is a corruption of tellers, or strokes, meant to tell of someone's death as rung on a parish church bell. Nine tailors are rung for a man, followed by one stroke for each year of his age, then the bell is tolled in mourning. The tailors are rung in groups of three. The process is the same for women except that six tailors are rung instead of nine. It is such bell ringing that inspired John Donne's famous "Meditation 17: The Tolling of the Bells" and its famous, "therefore never send to know for whom the bell tolls; it tolls for thee." [NT 1]

4734 19 'bus -- the omnibus serving the 19 route in central London. The route runs from Gray's Inn Rd. through Soho, Piccadilly, to Hyde Park Corner and on into Knightsbridge and Brompton to Battersea. This would be the perfect bus for Parker* to use to get from his flat to PW's. [WB 1]

4735 1918 adjustment -- to Queen Anne's Bounty*. See also tithe. [NT 9]

4736 1914 -- the year Denis Cathcart* joined the army and the year that saw the start of WW I. The War was the result of a long series of events, but the assassination of Archduke Franz Ferdinand in June of that year provided the excuse needed to start the hostilities. [CW 1]

4737 1925 Act -- the Act of Parliament that further defined the process for the collection and distribution of Church of England tithes* as a function of Queen Anne's Bounty* [NT 19]

4738 Nineteenth-Century Pamphlets -- a reference to some forgeries by one Thomas James Wise (1859-1937), a bibliographer and editor whose reputation was called into serious question when it was learned that a number of pamphlets about 19th C. subjects, authenticated on Wise's authority, were actually forgeries. [GN 17]

4739 9:30 post -- a creation of DLS to suit the story. Times referred to collections, not deliveries, and a letter that late would certainly have been delivered at one of the morning deliveries. [MMA 7]

4740 96 'bus -- a weekdays-only bus which runs East-West through the middle of London along Piccadilly, The Strand, past the Bank of England, etc. [WB 4]

4741 Nippy -- a waitress in one of the J. Lyons & Co. restaurants (see Lyons). The word is a trademark of the company first used in 1924, and the waitresses wore special uniforms. Nippies have recently been reintroduced by Lyons. [UD 6]

4742 no beauty without measure -- HV refers to the Neoclassic or Augustan passion for perfection in the form of all things; the golden mean [GN 15]

4743 no bell for a daily Celebration -- PW didn't hear the bell that would call to worship, but, more significantly, he didn't hear the bells that are rung three times at specific points during a celebration of the Eucharist.

[BH 5]

4744 no better than you [we] should be [ought to be] -- a variation on "she is no better than she should be"* [CW 18/BH 1]

4745 "no bon" -- a PW mixture of French and English meaning, "no good" [MMA 5]

4746 No flies on that young lady -- a colloquial expression referring to HV's businesslike and industrious attitude, rather like "a rolling stone gathers no moss". [HHC 4]

4747 no fury like a woman scorned -- see "it says in the Bible . . ." [HHC 10]

4748 no hand plucked his velvet sleeve -- this reference is to Book IV, Chapter 71, of Baldesar Castiglione's The Book of the Courtier (Il libro del cortegiano, 1528), one of the great masterpieces of Italian Renaissance literature. Given the circumstances of DLS's allusion, the context is important: "Having spoken thus far with such vehemence that he seemed almost transported and beside himself, Bembo remained silent and still, keeping his eyes turned toward heaven, as if in a daze; when signora Emilía, who with the others had been listening to his comments most attentively, plucked him by the hem of his robe and, shaking him a bit, said, 'Take care, messer Pietro, that with these thoughts your soul, too, does not foresake your body.'"
"'Madam,' replied messer Pietro, 'that would not be the first miracle Love has wrought in me.'" [GN 23]

4749 No lily on my cheek . . . -- PW is quoting freely from John Keats' La Belle Dame Sans Merci, ll. 9-12. Given correctly they are:

"I see a lily on thy brow,
With anguish moist and fever dew;
And on thy cheek a fading rose
Fast withereth too."

The title of the poem, "The Fair Lady Without Pity", is from a medieval poem by Alain Chartier. Keats' poem was written in April of 1819. [SP 8]

4750 no more spirit than the Queen of Sheba -- see Sheba, no more spirit than [BC 13]

4751 No one can bathe in the same river -- a proverbial expression. HV is suggesting that things change constantly, that nothing remains unchanged forever. [GN 1]

4752 no trumps -- see bridge

4753 No weapon, no suicide--that was the law . . . -- the part of the passage following the dash appears in Daniel and Esther of the Old Testament and is usually followed by, "which altereth (or changeth) not." This is not a quote, but is a reference to the fact that once a law had been given it could not be retracted as the king's word had gone forth and could not be broken. The Jews perceived the Medes and Persians as closely connected and the two were virtually one from the time of Cyrus on (550 B. C.). [HHC 1]

4754 Noah's Ark -- the famous floating zoo of Genesis, chapters 6 - 8. It is given as being 450-feet long by 75-feet wide and had at least three decks. Models of it remain favorite toys. The phrase is used to describe the Tolbooth* in Kirkcudbright*. [FRH 7]

4755 Noakes, William -- the previous owner of Talboys* from whom PW and HV have purchased that home. He is the victim of the murder that so confused their honeymoon. He owns a radio (wireless) shop and is involved in all sorts of shady deals financially. He is presented as a grasping, miserly man who uses and abuses everyone with equal harshness. [BH P]

4756 nobbut -- Yorkshire English dialect for "nothing but" [CW 11]

4757 noblesse oblige -- an expression borrowed from the French which means, literally, that nobility obligates. The phrase has come to mean that honorable, generous, and responsible behavior is the duty of those associated with high rank or birth. [WB 2/HHC 11]

4758 "Nobody; I myself; farewell." -- the line is from Othello, V, ii, 124. Emilia asks, "O who hath done this deed?"* The answer is the line cited here and is Desdemona's. She is faithful and protects Othello to the death. It is the answer to the quotation cited at the opening of Ch. I. [CW 18]

4759 "Nobody ever tells me anything." -- the line is, "Nobody tells me anything." It is spoken by James Forsyte in John Galsworthy's* The Man of Property, part I, Ch. I, the first (1906) segment of his The Forsyte Saga. [GN 10]

4760 "the noiseless tenor of our way" -- Mr. Venables* is alluding to Thomas Gray's (1716-71) poem, "Elegy Written in a Country Churchyard", wherein he wrote (stanza 19):

"Far from the madding crowd's ignoble strife,
Their sober wishes never learn'd to stray;
Along the cool sequester'd vale of life
They kept the noiseless tenor of their way." [NT 4]

4761 +NOLI+ESSE+INCREDULUS+SED+FIDELIS+ -- Latin for, "Be not faithless but believing", a line that appears in John 20:27. It is addressed by Jesus to the Apostle Thomas and is the inscription on the number seven bell, Batty Thomas*, at Fenchurch St. Paul*. [NT 2]

4762 non sequitur -- Latin for, "it does not follow", an illogical or fallacious conclusion [BC 18]

4763 non-stop lift -- a somewhat difficult yo-yo* trick [MMA 17]

4764 Nonconformists -- those who refuse to conform to the teachings of the Church of England. Included were Congregationalists, Baptists, Methodists, Unitarians, and Presbyterians. All of these groups were, at one time or another, subject to penal law when religion was a political matter, but in 1688 the Toleration Act was passed. Full religious freedom was granted in the late 19th C. [bc/UD 13/HHC 17/NT 6]

4765 "None sit in doors . . ." -- from T. L. Beddoes' The Second Brother: A Tragedy**, I, i, 7-10 [HHC 2]

4766 noomony -- Yorkshire dialect for pneumonia [CW 12]

4767 "Norbert: 'Explain not . . .'" -- see In a Balcony [BH 16]

4768 Norfolk -- an English county North and East of London, bounded by Suffolk, Cambridgeshire, and Lincolnshire, and by The Wash* and the North Sea. It is the location of the ancestral home of the Wimseys. See also Duke's Denver, Wimsey genealogy, and fen. [dh/BC 5/SP 22/HHC 12/MMA 19]

4769 Norfolk suit -- a two-piece wool suit. The jacket is loose fitting with a belt across the back, and has vertical expansion pleats on the shoulders. The pants are knickerbockers, often worn with heavy wool stockings and stout walking shoes. There is also often a suede or leather patch on the shoulder (right or left depending on the owner's preference) to help provide stability when shooting. [CW 11]

4770 Norgate, William -- the secretary to Sir Septimus Shale* [np]

4771 Norman, P. C. -- a constable whose thumb was sprained when he was knocked off his bicycle by a Great Dane [BH 11]

4772 Norman foundation -- the church at Fenchurch St. Paul* was originally an abbey built in Norman times (ca. 1066-1200), and the remains of that abbey church and a few stones marking the site of the old cloister could still be seen to the East and South of the existing chancel [NT 1]

4773 Normania -- PW and Bunter cross the Channel aboard her. While the name is reminiscent of the Cunard liners because of the "ia" suffix, there has never been a vessel of that name. See also item 4774. [aq]

4774 Normannia -- Lloyd's Register of Shipping lists several ships of that name, but the one in question, and probably the one DLS had in mind with item 4773, was built in 1911 in Glasgow by the Fairfield Company expressly for the London and South Western Railway's cross-Channel service. She was a relatively small ship of 1567 tons, and not the best choice for the faint of stomach. [CW 13]

4775 North Annexe -- one of the buildings on the campus of Shrewsbury College* [GN 5]

4776 North-Eastern -- the London and North-Eastern Railway system which was founded by Act of Parliament on January 1, 1923. The inevitable amalgamation of several smaller companies

into one large one was a direct result of increasing road transport and of railroad grouping during WW I. The other companies so formed at the same time were: Southern, and London Midland and Scottish. With the exception of a period of time during WW II, those companies remained until January 1, 1948, when they were nationalized as British Rail. See #3814. [CW 2]

4777 North Fellcote -- where the Rev. Mr. Foulis's license plates were stolen from his motorcycle, make not specified. The place is fictitious as presented by DLS, and, as she did not know the Yorkshire dales well, it is futile to attempt to ascribe the name to some real locality. [CW 3]

4778 North-Herts Advertiser -- a fictitious newspaper that sends a reporter to cover William Noakes's funeral. The closest title in reality is the North-Herts Mid-Week Gazette. [BH 19]

4779 North Riding -- a former administrative district in Yorkshire. There were three such divisions, the North, East, and West Ridings. The word "riding" derives from the Old English and Old Norse meaning a third part. Yorkshire was the only county to make continued active use of the distinction into the present, but they disappeared in 1974 with local government reorganization. [CW 1]

4780 Northallerton -- a town about thirty-two miles North and West of York in North Yorkshire which, in 1923, was the county town for the North Riding* of Yorkshire. It features several 18th C. homes and a fine 12th to 15th C. church. It is a thriving railway and market town. [CW 2]

4781 Northanger Abbey -- a novel by Jane Austen published in 1818 to ridicule the then popular Gothic romances of Anne Radcliffe and Horace Walpole. The heroine is Catherine Morland who, in her mind, invents a gruesome tale around the man she hopes will be her father-in-law. Her humiliation in these events forms one high point of the story. The reference is to anyone who allows the mind to take over and invent intrigue where there is none. [CW 4]

4782 Northbury Hall -- mentioned as the home of Mr. Fleetwhite*. It is apparently fictitious. [CW 4]

4783 Northerners -- residents of that area of northern England around the Pennine Mountains: Yorkshire, Lancashire, Cumbria, Durham, and Northumberland [CW 11]

4784 Norton -- an overhead valve motorcycle built in England and prominent in racing circles during the 1920's and 30's, and usually of the 500cc engine size. The "Manx" model was most famous. [cb]

4785 nosey-parker[ing] -- a snoop or snooping. The OED gives Compton MacKenzie's Carnival (1912) as the earliest printed use of the phrase. [MMA 2/BH 15]

4786 nostalgie de la banlieue . . . -- French for, "a yearning for the country . . . for the muck and mire", but not likely a reference to gardening [MMA 3]

4787 not a chameleon to smell any sweeter -- the Dowager Duchess* is correct as far as she goes, but what Shakespeare really said (in Henry IV, Part I, II, iv, 394) was: "For though the camomile, the more it is trodden on the faster it grows, yet youth, the more it is wasted the sooner it wears." The Duchess's fuzzy memory is playing its usual tricks here. [BH P]

4788 "Not faint Canaries but ambrosial . . ." -- the line is from John Donne's* "Elegie XVIII", "Love's Progresse", ll. 51-2:

"Upon the Islands fortunate we fall,
Not faynte Canaries, but Ambrosiall
. . ."

See also Canary Islands. [BH 3]

4789 "Not for him . . ." -- the speech is Ziba's (the Moorish sorcerer) in IV, iii, 320-7 of Death's Jest Book by T. L. Beddoes**. Ziba has sold a fake potion to Athulf who wanted to commit suicide; it is not fatal. The sentence concludes:

" . . . and swallowed
A draught, that may depress and shake his powers
Until he sleeps awhile; then all is o'er." [HHC 14]

4790 "not its fellow in the universe --

Mr. Murbles* is referring to the North Star as alluded to by Caesar in Julius Caesar, III, i, 60-3:

"But I am constant as the northern star,
Of whose true-fixed and resting quality
There is no fellow in the firmament."
[CW 10]

4791 "Not love, quoth he, but vanity . . ." -- the line is from [James Henry] Leigh Hunt's (1784-1859) poem, "The Glove and the Lions", and is an exact quote. [BH 7]

4792 not proven -- known as "that bastard verdict", a nickname given to it by Sir Walter Scott at the end of a trial when the jury did not return the guilty verdict he thought it should have, it is the third option available to a Scottish jury: 1) not guilty, 2) not proven, 3) guilty. The not proven verdict is available to a jury if it feels that the prosecution has not adequately proved guilt. It suggests that the jury is saying, "We think you are guilty, but the prosecution did not prove so adequately, so don't get caught again." Such a verdict does not provide much comfort, however, as it carries the stigma of doubt. There is no suggestion of innocence at all, just insufficient proof of guilt. When PW uses the phrase in BC (Ch. 21) in reference to English law he is speaking generally as no such verdict is available to an English court. H. W. Fowler in his Modern English Usage suggests that the only place where "proven" is correct is in reference to this verdict; all other situations require "proved". [CW 3/BC 21/SP 10]

4793 not serpentine at all, as the Bible advises -- in Matthew 10:16 it is written, "Behold, I send you forth as sheep in the midst of wolves: be you therefore wise as serpents, and harmless as doves." The verse suggests a skeptical attitude only, and nothing of the usual evil symbolism is implied. [UD 4]

4794 "not the first nor the second that presents itself" -- in reference to taxis, PW is quoting Sherlock Holmes in his directions to Dr. Watson as they prepare to leave London to elude Prof. Moriarty*. The quotation appears in "The Final Problem". [MMA 17]

4795 "Not there, not there, my child." -- the line is from Felicia Dorothea Hemans's* poem, "The Better Land" [BH 7]

4796 ". . . not you but Fate has vanquished me." -- the reference is to Sir Walter Scott's (1771-1832) "The Lay of the Last Minstrel", Canto Fifth, stanza xxvi, line 410. The line, exactly as quoted here (with a capital "n", however) is spoken by the Lady of Branksome Hall when it becomes apparent that Lord Cranstoun and the fair Margaret will wed after all. [GN 4]

4797 Notable British Trials -- originally Notable Scottish and Notable English Trials, a series of over 100 titles, most were published between 1900 and 1920 by William Hodge of Edinburgh. The contents range from Mary Queen of Scots (1586) to the present. [SP 20]

4798 note-case -- a gentleman's leather billfold designed to be carried, usually, in the breast pocket of a suit or sport coat [BC 5]

4799 notes -- see Bank of England notes [mt]

4800 Notes on the Collection of Incunabula -- one of PW's publications. See also incunabula and The Murderer's Vade Mecum. [UD BN/NT 1]

4801 "Nothing in life became him . . ." -- the line is from Macbeth, I, iv, 7ff. The speech is Malcolm's in reference to the execution of the traitorous Thane of Cawdor. The lines are:

"Nothing in his life
Became him like the leaving it; he died
As one that had been studied in his death
To throw away the dearest thing he owned
As 'twere a careless trifle."
[FRH 2/MMA 3]

4802 "Nothing new under the sun" -- the reference is to Ecclesiastes 1:9: "The thing that hath been, it is that which shall be; and that which is done is that which shall be done: and there is no new thing under the sun." PW expresses the commonly held belief that Solomon wrote Ecclesiastes, but there is considerable scholarly doubt on that

point. It appears to have been written later than Solomon's day. [UD 3]

4803 nothing should more deeply have offended -- see like the poet Wordsworth [BH 7]

4804 Notting Dale -- Parker's destination early in UD as he attempts to track down "an elusive anonymous letterwriter". The name is a deliberate corruption of Notting Hill, a district immediately adjacent to the northwest corner of Kensington Gardens* in western metropolitan London. [UD 3]

4805 Nottingham -- a city in the East Midlands; the county town of Nottinghamshire in mid-central England. The city is famous in trade, legend, and sports. It is the home of Players cigarettes, the Raleigh bicycle, world-renowned lace and woolen goods, and "Boots the Chemists", Britain's largest chain of drug stores. Robin Hood the legendary outlaw of Sherwood Forest, plied his trade in the Nottingham area, having supposedly lived at some time during the reign of Richard I (1189-99), but that is uncertain at best. [SP 11/GN 19]

4806 Nous menons une vie assez mouvementée." -- French for, "We lead a rather eventful life." [BH 18]

4807 "Now you see how this dragon egg of ours" -- the speech is Isbrand's in addressing Siegfried in Death's Jest Book by T. L. Beddoes**, II, iv, 1-2 [HHC 33]

4808 nowt's -- Yorkshire dialect for, "nothing is" [CW 11]

4809 Nubian Venus -- a Black Venus from Nubia, an ancient kingdom between Egypt and Ethiopia [BH 5]

4810 Nugget -- a common brand of shoe polish still available in flat tins of brown, black, tan, etc. [SP 16]

4811 "Num" -- Latin for, "query"; a question, or, simply, "what?" It expects a negative response. [GN 4]

4812 number plates -- automobile number plates. These serve the same function as license plates as used in the United States and Canada [CW 3]

4813 "Nun gehn wir wo der Tudelsack . . ." -- German for, "Now we go where the bagpipes (go or lead) . . .", from J. S. Bach's* Mer Hahn en neue Oberkeet ("Now We Have a New Squire"), his burlesque cantata, BWV 212, also known as the "Peasant Cantata". The line is more usually "Wir gehn nun wo der Tudelsack . . .". "Tudelsack" has also been translated--very loosely-- as "hurdy gurdy".

The whole thing is a celebration of the arrival of a new squire to take charge of his inherited properties and is one of Bach's rare joke or burlesque cantatas. The passage cited is from the final duet, and the German used is a dialect of Upper Saxony, so "Oberkeet" translates as "authority" or, more loosely, as "the brass hat", or "boss".

The piece was written to celebrate the succession of Carl Heinrich von Dieskau, Chamberlain of the Saxon Exchequer, to the lordship of the manors Klein Zschocher and Knauthahn, villages near Leipzig, on August 30, 1742. The libretto was written by Christian Friedrich Henrici under the pseudonym Picander, not by Bach, and is in the Upper Saxon patois. [MMA 11]

4814 Nuremburg Chronicle -- a copy is in Squire Burdock's* library, and PW finds the Squire's will in it. The book is one of many such chronicles printed in Europe as late as the 1700's that recorded fact, fiction, history, and myth and treated it all equally. Despite their questionable accuracy, they have proved useful as sourcebooks for actual events which could later be verified in other ways. The particular chronicle was probably the one published in 1493, a folio copy of which is in the Magdalen College Library, Cambridge*. [bc]

4815 The Nursing Times -- a highly regarded professional journal for nurses and those in allied professions which was established in 1905. It is now published by Macmillan Journals, Ltd. [MMA 10]

4816 Nutrax -- a fictitious patent nerve medicine advertised through the offices of Pym's Publicity*. The weekly ads for it held the key to much of the mystery of the drug smuggling operation being investigated by PW as Death Bredon. [MMA 1]

4817 nux vomica -- the seed, poison-

ous, of the Asiatic tree, Strychnos nux-vomica, which contains, among other toxins, strychnine*. It is a stimulant to the central nervous system. [BC 15]

(O)

4818 O. C. Directories -- a reference to the telephone directories. O. C. is a military abbreviation for Officer Commanding, but is used here to refer, loosely, to the man in charge of directories. [MMA 16]

4819 o. h. v. -- the abbreviation for overhead valve as in an internal combustion engine, and is applied to a Norton* motorcycle [cb]

4820 O. U. C. C. -- the abbreviation for the Oxford University Cricket Club. PW is one of its more famous members. [BH 5]

4821 O. U. D. S. -- the abbreviation for the Oxford University dramatic society, a highly regarded organization with high standards of performance [GN 8]

4822 O felix culpa! -- Latin for, "O fault most fortunate!" The allusion is to St. Augustine's comment on the Fall from Grace (Adam and Eve) which concludes, " . . . quae talem ac tantum meruit habere Redemptorem", or " . . . which has deserved to have such and so mighty a Redeemer." [BH 17]

4823 "O ho! here's royal booty . . ." -- the lines are from a fragmentary segment of a projected Act V of T. L. Beddoes' The Second Brother**. The lines are numbers 32-3 of V, i, and are spoken by a Venetian citizen to Ezril, a Jew and advisor to Duke Marcello of Ferrara. [HHC 17]

4824 "O horror, horror, horror . . ." -- PW is scrambling quotations, a favorite game of his during idle chatter. The "O horror" part is probably his version of the Ghost's lament in Hamlet when he discloses his murder to the Prince in I, v, 80: "O, horrible! O, horrible! most horrible!" The "tongue nor heart" fragment is from A Midsummer-Night's Dream, IV, i, 218ff, when Bottom awakens from his "dream" and says, "The eye of man hath not heard, the ear of man hath not seen, man's hand is not able to taste, his tongue to conceive, nor his heart to report, what my dream was." The "goose-look" phrase is from Macbeth, V, iii, 12, when Macbeth addresses the

servant who brings the news of Malcolm's army, "Where got'st thou that goose look?" [FRH 22]

4825 "O Inspiration, solitary child . . ." -- PW is alluding, inaccurately, to Milton's "L'Allegro", ll. 109-10:

"Or sweetest Shakespeare, Fancy's child,
Warble his native wood-notes wild."

In the context of the poem, Milton is suggesting that Shakespeare's verse is free and natural like a bird's song in contrast to Ben Jonson's more allusive and "learned" work. [UD 19]

4826 O les beaux jours que ce siècle de fer -- French for, "O those beautiful days of that age of iron." Miss Millbanks* has slipped into French, appropriately enough, to refer to chivalry and the knights of romantic literature, a genre strongly associated with the French tradition in literature. [GN 7]

4827 "O my deare Cloris be not sad . . ." -- the line is from Michael Drayton's* The Muses' Elizium, "The Fourth Nimphall", of 1630. Mertilla is addressing Cloris and continues:

"Let not thy noble thoughts descend
So low as their affections;
Whom neither counsell can amend,
Nor yet the Gods corrections."

[GN 7]

4828 "O no, there is no end . . ." -- the passage is from III, vii, of The Spanish Tragedy by Thomas Kyd (?1557-?95), a popular blank verse tragedy first acted in 1592. DLS's notation that Ben Jonson (1572-1637) is the author alludes to the fact that Jonson apparently revised the play to some considerable length in which form it was very popular. [GN 22]

4829 "O, now, for ever farewell the tranquil mind!" -- PW has selected segments of Othello's speech, III, iii, 346ff, delivered after the famous handkerchief scene, wherein Iago seals Desdemona's fate in Othello's eyes [HHC 31]

4830 O SANCTE THOMA -- Latin for, "O HOLY THOMAS", a bit of ecclesiastical vanity, perhaps, as the reference could be either to the Apostle (Doubting) Thomas, or to the abbot buried beneath the carvings [NT 2]

4831 "O say, what are you weeping for?" -- this line is from a children's rondel dating from the 1920's or earlier which ran for several verses:

"O Mary is a-weeping, a-weeping, a-weeping,
O Mary is a-weeping on this bright summer's day.
O say, what are you weeping for, a-weeping for, a-weeping for?"
(etc.)
"I'm weeping for my true love . . ."
(etc.)

[MMA 19]

4832 "O take a pilgrim home!" -- "Bullets", short satirical jabs in John Bull*, took the form of the joke cited here [MMA 6]

4833 O Turpitude . . . -- despite PW's citation of "Wimsey's Standard Poets, with emendations by Thingummy", he is reciting a corrupted version of William Cowper's (1731-1800), "Verses Supposed to be Written by Alexander Selkirk". Selkirk (1676-1721) was the inspiration for Daniel Defoe's Robinson Crusoe. Cowper's poem states:

"I am monarch of all I survey,
My right there is none to dispute;
From the centre all round to the sea
I am lord of the fowl and the brute.
Oh, solitude! where are the charms
That sages have seen in thy face?
Better dwell in the midst of alarms,
Than reign in this horrible place."

Note how the last two lines seem to echo Milton's Paradise Lost. Selkirk was a sailor whose adventures inspired many, but Defoe's story remains the most famous result of those inspirations. [UD 23]

4834 "O well-knit Samson!" -- from Shakespeare's Love's Labours Lost, I, ii, 77-9. The lines are spoken by Armado to Moth. [GN 9]

4835 "O, who hath done this deed?" -- from Othello, V, ii, 123. Emilia speaks in response to Desdemona's dying comment: "A guiltless death I die." The exchange provides an interesting clue to the entire set of circumstances in CW. The answer to the cited quote is the heading for Ch. 17 in CW. [CW 1]

4836 "O ye gods! render me worthy . . ." -- the line is addressed to Portia by Brutus in Julius Caesar, II, i, 302-3 [BH 10]

4837 "O'er moor and fen . . ." -- PW is quoting from John Henry, Cardinal Newman's hymn, "Lead, Kindly Light", line 15 [BC 14]

4838 "Oh death! where is thy sting?" -- HV is quoting Paul's first Epistle to the Corinthians, 15:55. Verses 54-58 (the end of the chapter) are concerned with the final victory over death. [HHC 16/MMA 1]

4839 "Oh dry those tears" -- the line is from a popular drawing-room ballad, author unknown, which ran, "Oh Dry those tears, Clouds will be sunshine tomorrow." The entry item is also the ballad's title. [MMA 19]

4840 "Oh, frabjous day!" -- the reference is to Lewis Carroll's* "Jabberwockey" from Through the Looking Glass. In the circumstances, PW is most apt in his choice of lines to quote, but, then, PW is a veritable Carroll scholar as he quotes from all over that master of nonsense's works. [umw/BH 4]

4841 "Oh ho, my friend!" -- see Lob's pond [CW 11]

4842 "Oh, I am changing, changing, fearfully changing." -- the lines are spoken by Athulf in Death's Jest Book by T. L. Beddoes**. Athulf, called Sibald in one version of the play, is the son of Melveric, Duke of Münsterberg. He says the lines quoted in IV, iii, 372-3, just after he has killed his brother in order to marry Amala to whom his brother was engaged. The word "fearfully" in DLS's quotation is "dreadfully" in most versions of the play. [SP 8]

4843 "Oh Sammy, Sammy, why vorn't there an alleybi?" -- the line is Mr. Weller's* in Ch. 33 of Charles Dickens' Pickwick Papers [UD 16]

4844 the oak -- the outer door to a room in reference to the wood from which it was made; usually university slang. See also sported oak. [UD 14]

4845 Oakapple, Lord -- the fictitious Chancellor* who dedicates the new library at Shrewsbury College* [GN 4]

4846 oakum -- loosely twisted hemp or jute impregnated with tar and used to caulk seams or pack joints. The reference in SP is to one of the traditional activities of prison inmates. [SP 12]

4847 Oban -- a town and fishing port to the North and West of Glasgow on the Sound of Kerrera. It is the center of the Western Highlands tourist industry. [FRH 25]

4848 obelisks -- Leila Garland uses this word when she means odalisques, concubines in a harem [HHC 15]

4849 obscure morbid condition -- some undiagnosed or unnoticed disease condition [UD 2]

4850 obscurum per obscuriora -- a Latin phrase meaning to explain an obscure thing with a thing that is even more obscure than the first; a non-explanation in most instances [NT 10]

4851 observation bell -- the bell that all others follow, or "observe", during the ringing of a touch or peal** [NT 10]

4852 obviate halation -- the arrangement of materials and processes to prevent the spread of light beyond its proper boundaries. As Bunter uses the phrase, he is describing a dissolvable opaque backing on photographic plates that is light sensitive. [qs]

4853 Och aye -- Scots dialect for "ah", or "oh yes" [ss]

4854 octave -- the interval between two notes, one of which is half the frequency of the other. This interval is divided into the eight-note octave scale which has twelve notes if the semitones are included. [SP 8]

4855 octave -- any eight-line stanza, but the word is more usually applied to the first eight lines of a sonnet in the Italian form which is rhymed abba/abba and poses a problem or makes a statement which is addressed in the sonnet's last six lines, the sestet [GN 11]

4856 oculist -- an eye doctor, either an opthalmologist who must be an M. D., or an optometrist who is licensed, but who is not an M. D. and who may not perform surgery or prescribe

drugs [WB 6]

4857 Oddenino's -- a restaurant PW suggests that he and Marjorie Phelps* visit. It was at 56/62 Regent St. just off Piccadilly Circus, but it no longer exists. They instead opt to dine with friends after a show. [BC 10]

4858 The Odes of Horace -- a collection of famous lyrics written in various meters by Quintus Horatius Flaccus (65-8 B. C.), a contemporary of Vergil*. He is considered one of the greatest of the Roman poets because of the perfection of his poetic form, his sincerity and frankness of expression, his urbanity, humor, and good sense. He pictures Roman society clearly. His influence on English poetry is especially reflected in some of the work of Pope* and Milton*.

An ode is a usually serious poem of some length devoted to the contemplation of some aspect of life. Henry Shale* carries a copy of Horace's _Odes_. [np]

4859 odsbodikins -- a mild oath corrupted from "God's (od's) body". The origin is "od", a shortened form of God that became popular about 1600 as an exclamatory substitute for the profanation of God's name. [WB 7]

4860 _oeuf_ -- French for egg [CW 13]

4861 _oeuvre_ -- French for work or action as in opus [CW 13]

4862 "Of his malice aforethought" -- this quote is the chapter heading for Ch. 1 of CW, and is the standard phrasing for part of an indictment. An excellent definition of this legal idiom is found in R. v. Serne and Goldfinch, 1887: "The definition of murder is unlawful homicide with malice aforethought; and the words 'malice aforethought' are technical. You must not therefore construe them, or suppose that they can be construed, by the ordinary rules of language. The words have to be construed according to a long series of decided cases, which have given them meanings different from those which might be supposed. One of these meanings is the killing of another person by an act done with the intent to commit a felony. Another meaning is an act done with the knowledge that the act will probably cause the death of some person . . . ." [CW 1]

4863 off break -- see cricket [MMA 18]

4864 off[-side] -- see cricket [MMA 18]

4865 office book -- not a prayer book, but a collection of all the anthems, prayers, etc., that are used at a particular office on a particular day with all of the necessary guides for each worship service. It is a "how to" manual for each of the day's services with the corrections and changes if the day happens to be a special feast day, etc. Office books are often called breviaries. The offices included will always be matins and vespers and, frequently, lauds, prime, terse, sext, none, and compline. [UD 22]

4866 "Often when they were gone to Bed . . ." -- this quotation is a bit confusing in that from its beginning to "middle of the room" is not Turner's at all, but is a quote from Henry More (one of the Cambridge Platonists) in his _Continuation of the Collection [of Joseph Glanvil] or, an Addition of Some Few More Remarkable and True Stories of Apparitions and Witchcraft_, London, 1688. The quotation is almost all of episode twelve, page Ii4. The section of the quotation following the ellipses is William Turner's only contribution to the passage. The Turner in question is probably Sir William Turner, English teacher and anatomist (1832-1916). [GN 6]

4867 O'Halloran, Mr. -- there are two Mr. O'Halloran's, the younger of whom is something of a jokester much to P. C. Burt's* dismay [hp]

4868 OI-0101 -- the automobile plate number of Mrs. Morecambe's* Bentley* [HHC 20]

4869 oil cake -- a type of cattle feed. When the oil is pressed from cotton seed or soy beans, a flat pancake of husks, pulp, and oil remains. This is excellent additive bulk for cattle fodder as it helps their hide and fur, and is also a rich source of nutrients for lactating cows. The hard cakes are broken up with a hammer and added to whatever other feed is being used. [FRH 4]

4870 'Olborn Empire -- see Holborn Empire [hp/CW 11]

4871 Old Age Pension -- see Lord George Pension [HHC 26]

4872 Old Anderson -- see Wyndham's, Anderson of [WB 4]

4873 Old Bailey -- since 1907, London's Central Criminal Court and scene of some of England's most famous trials. The name derives from the word "ballium", the circuit of defences of a castle, later an open space for guards and watchmen. Londoners, through the corruption of use and mispronunciation, changed it to "bailey". The Old Bailey is the name of the street derived from such an area by the City wall where the Central Criminal Court was built, so the Court, too, became Old Bailey. [CW 14/UD 14/SP 1/BH P]

4874 Old Bank dyke -- a weak part of the dyke and drainage system in the fen country* [NT 16]

4875 Old Bank Sluice -- a fictitious place, given the context of the story, but it is typical of the sluices in the fen country* [NT 16]

4876 Old Bedford River -- a canal dug by the Dutch engineer Vermuyden, hired by the 4th Earl of Bedford* to drain the fens* by cutting off a loop of the Great Ouse River. It was sluiced to prevent backwash when the tides came in. The idea worked for a while until so much water had been drained off that the land sank below sea level and, eventually, pumping stations were required to remove the excess water. [NT 2]

4877 "Old benevolent man." -- from T. L. Beddoes' The Second Brother**, II, ii, 94. Orazio, youngest brother of the late Duke of Ferrara, is begging Ezril, an advisor to the new Duke, for permission to see him. The new Duke, Marcello, the second brother, has banished Orazio from Ferrara for his past behavior. [HHC 6]

4878 Old Borstalian -- Mr. Tallboy is being particularly snobbish and cruel in this reference. The Borstal System is an English juvenile correction program for young men which emphasizes individual treatment and the rehabilitation of youngsters. Tallboy is suggesting that Mr. Smayle is a "graduate" of that correction system who would be so ignorantly oblivious of his background that he would wear the "school" colors in public on a necktie as one might wear an Eton* tie. [MMA 10]

4879 Old Bridge -- a geographical location, fictitious, in Hertfordshire (see Herts.). The structure crosses the River Pagg which is equally fictitious. [BH 11]

4880 Old Broad St. -- intersects with Threadneedle St. at the Stock Exchange** and goes in a northerly direction to Liverpool St. at the Liverpool St. Station. PW is thinking of Mr. Tallboy's* connection with the Stock Exchange. Later we learn that the tobacconist's shop where all of Tallboy's letters are delivered is on that street. [MMA 17]

4881 Old Father William -- an allusion to Robert Southey's (1774-1843) poem, "The Old Man's Comforts, and how he Gained Them". In that poem the line, "You are old Father William, the young man cried", is repeated throughout. In HHC, however, HV has Lewis Carroll's parody of Southey's poem in mind. The parody appears in Ch. 5 of Alice in Wonderland. [HHC 2]

4882 Old Hall -- a building on the grounds of Somerville College* [GN 18]

4883 The old house was Harriet's companion -- see "its evil spirit cast out" [BH E3]

4884 Old Hundredth -- a tune known to many as The Doxology, but originally associated with the Sternhold and Hopkins Psalter of 1562 as the musical setting of Psalm 100. The tune has had various other sets of words, including the words from Daye's Psalter of 1560 which uses William Kethe's lyric which begins, "All people that on earth do dwell". [bc]

4885 Old Johnson -- probably Dr. Samuel Johnson (1709-84), lexicographer, man of letters, and subject of Boswell's Life of Dr. Samuel Johnson. While the precise reference is uncertain, an appropriate candidate would be, "Depend upon it, Sir, when a man

THE CENTRAL CRIMINAL COURT, OLD BAILEY.

#4873 The Central Criminal Court, Old Bailey, London.

knows he is to be hanged in a fortnight, it concentrates his mind wonderfully." The sentiment appears in the Life, Vol. 3, in the entry for September 19, 1777. [BH E3]

4886 The Old Maid -- the odd queen left at the end of the card game of the same name. However, the queens of clubs and spades are often designated--one or the other--as "old maid". Lady Hermione Creethorpe* is dressed as a queen of clubs and refers to herself by that card's sometime designation. [qs]

4887 Old Man Kangaroo -- HV's reference is to "Sing-Song of Old Man Kangaroo" from Rudyard Kipling's Just So Stories [GN 8]

4888 Old Man of Thermopylae -- a reference to a limerick in Edward Lear's One Hundred Nonsense Pictures and Rhymes:

"There was an old man of Thermopylae
Who never did anything properly;
But they said, 'If you choose
To boil eggs in your shoes,
You shall never remain in Thermopylae.'" [GN 10]

4889 "old man sitting on a gate" -- see "versifying after the manner of the . . ." [FRH 13]

4890 Old Market -- the market near the fairgrounds at Wilvercombe*. It is separate and distinct from Market Square. [HHC 32]

4891 Old Mossy-face -- George Fentiman's* nervously irreverent nickname for his grandfather, General Fentiman* [BC 1]

4892 Old Quad -- one of the two open areas in Shrewsbury College* [GN 1]

4893 Old School Ties -- the neckties, usually striped, demonstrating an affiliation with a public school or university. The ties are also worn to indicate membership in clubs, societies and military units and regiments. [GN 11]

4894 Old Simon -- see Dawson, Simon [UD 12]

4895 Oldham's -- mentioned as having been destroyed during a bombing raid on January 28, 1918. The raid occurred on a Monday between nine and ten in the evening and was aimed particularly at London. Forty-seven were killed and 169 were injured in that raid. Of that number, thirty-eight were killed and eighty-five were injured when a single 660-pound bomb, dropped by a German Zeppelin-Staaken "Giant" bomber, exploded in the basement of the Odham's, not Oldham's, Press printing works, the basement of which was being used as an air raid shelter for about 500 people. The building is on Long Acre*. [im]

4896 oleograph -- a chromolithograph printed in oil colors; an inexpensive print [fr]

4897 Oleroso of 1847 -- or oloroso, a sherry of great roundness and richness when mature. It is naturally dry, but is usually sweetened for sale as cream sherry. [SP 1]

4898 Olga -- see Schlitzers [BC 10]

4899 olive-branch -- the reference is to Genesis 8:11, but it's a leaf there, not a whole branch. The dove sent out by Noah brought the olive leaf back, thus signifying that the flood waters had subsided. [NT 20]

4900 Oliver -- a reference to the dashing but more cautious hero and friend of Roland* in The Song of Roland*. The name is applied aptly to Parker* here. [BC 8]

4901 Oliver, Mr. -- the mysterious caller who said that General Fentiman* would be away all night on the night before he was discovered dead [BC 6]

4902 Oliver Twist -- the perenially popular novel by Charles Dickens* which recounts the adventures of young Oliver, first in the workhouse, then at the hands of Bill Sykes, Fagin, Nancy, and, at last free from his misery [BC 13]

4903 Olympian humour -- good luck; serendipity; a sense that Providence or the Fates are smiling on one's ventures at the moment [CW 5]

4904 Olympic -- a London theatre in existence from 1805 to 1899. It was built from timber taken from the old French warship, Ville de Paris. It burned down in 1849 and was rebuilt.

It featured, variously, plays, operas, and musical extravaganzas. Located in the Aldwych area, it was torn down at the turn of the century to allow rebuilding of that area. [SP 11]

4905 Olympus -- Mt. Olympus, home of the Greek gods, is located in northern Thessaly, not far from the Aegean Sea [UD 6]

4906 OM -- or Om, a Hindu mystic holy word regarded as a summary of all truth. It is also the first word of the Buddhist formula, "om mani padme hum", regarded as having special religious sanctity. [UD 11]

4907 omnibus -- a public conveyance, a bus* [FRH 24/SP 16]

4908 on remand -- a form of arrest that allows investigations to take place. One may be "remanded" only before the case is heard; it is a form of arrest to allow investigations pending trial. There is no need for a guilty plea. When the case has been heard, the guilty party can be "bound over", or put on probation, on promise of good behavior. If he disobeys the terms of probation, he will be brought back to court for sentencing; otherwise the sentence is suspended. [MMA 15]

4909 "One cried, 'God bless us!'" -- the speech is in Macbeth, II, ii, 28-9, and appears in Macbeth's report to Lady Macbeth about the murder of Duncan. The reference is to the sleepers in the next room, Duncan's sons, who cry out in their sleep while Macbeth murders their father. [BH 17]

4910 "One halfpennyworth of bread . . ." -- the line is from King Henry IV, Part I, II, iv, 591, and in full is: "O monstrous! but one halfpennyworth of bread to this intolerable deal of sack!" The line is Prince Hal's upon reading one of Falstaff's bills for food wherein sack (dry sherry wine) accounts for more than half of the total and bread for only a halfpenny. [GN 10]

4911 100 guineas -- the amount PW pays for Thomas Crowder's* portrait of Coreggio Plant*. The amount works out to about £105 or, roughly, U. S. $420 in the values of the day. [nf]

4912 186,000 miles a second -- the speed of light and the speed at which Neville Grimbold* would have had to have travelled if he had not employed the ruse of the telephone call. [ae]

4913 150 women students, in excess of the limit ordained by statute -- a University Statute of 1927 limited women undergraduates to 150 each for Somerville and St. Hilda's, and 160 each for Lady Margaret Hall and St. Hugh's. Therefore, Shrewsbury would have been within the limits by that Statute, but Shrewsbury's limit is not known. [GN AN]

4914 110A Piccadilly -- PW's London address prior to his marriage to HV. He lives on the second floor, third floor in the U. S., in a flat opposite Green Park* on a site formerly occupied by an unsuccessful commercial enterprise. After Holmes's archetypal digs at 221B Baker St., PW's 110A Piccadilly address is perhaps the most famous address in detective fiction. [passim]

4915 £129,17s,8d -- the price William Grimethorpe* paid for his two agricultural drills*. The sum equates approximately with $520 U. S. in the day's currency, about $7,000.00 today. [CW 11]

4916 one or two over the eight -- drunk. In WW I, eight beers were considered the limit for sobriety. [SP 10]

4917 one step into the path of wrongdoing makes the next one easier -- one is reminded of Thomas De Quincy's "On Murder Considered as One of the Fine Arts": "If once a man indulges himself in murder, very soon he comes to think little of robbing; and from robbing he comes next to drinking and Sabbath-breaking, and from that to incivility and procrastination." [SP 1]

4918 onionisation -- built up in layers as an onion is [BH 4]

4919 "Only a man with a criminal enterprise desires to establish an alibi." -- the words are Sherlock Holmes's in "The Adventure of Wisteria Lodge": "It was Garcia, then, who had an enterprise, and apparently a criminal enterprise, in hand that night in the course of which he met his death. I say 'criminal' because only a man

with a criminal enterprise desires to establish an alibi." [HHC 34]

4920 Onoto -- a fountain pen with a gold casing found among Denis Cathcart's* possessions. In a medium price range, the pens are still available. [CW 2]

4921 oojahs -- a slang word of unknown origin referring to sweets or other delicacies; "goodies" [GN 8]

4922 "Open Sesame" -- the voice command to PW's fabulous safe in "Cave of Ali Baba" as used by Ali Baba in the Arabian Nights* story. See also voice identification and "Ali Baba and the Forty Thieves". [ab]

4923 Oppenheim, E[dward] Phillips -- an English mystery and adventure story writer (1866-1946) who produced 116 novels and 39 short story collections. He was enormously successful and his popularity brought him great wealth. His stories concentrate on plot with little attention paid to the niceties of characterization. [MMA 7]

4924 "or some hay. There is nothing like it . . ." -- PW is alluding to Lewis Carroll's Through the Looking Glass**, Ch. 7, when the King says, "There is nothing like eating hay when you're faint." [SP 5]

4925 Orange Free State -- a political subdivision of the Union, now the Republic, of South Africa, settled by Boers in 1836-7. The Dowager Duchess's commentary about colors is a reference to the Irish with green being associated with St. Patrick and the Roman Catholics while orange is the color of the Protestants and the Orange Society, named for William of Orange. [CW 9]

4926 orangery -- a large greenhouse designed for raising citrus fruit trees in climates where they could not otherwise be grown [BH E2]

4927 Order of St. John of Jerusalem -- the Grand Priory in the British Realm of the Venerable Order of the Hospital of St. John of Jerusalem (1888) was introduced to recognize effort in the fields of hopital and ambulance work is highly regarded for that effort. The title "Knight of Grace" is one of six classes or ranks in the Order. In Europe it dates back to about 1113 and is, with the Knights Templar, one of the most important of the early orders of knighthood, combining charitable and military service. Also known as the Knights of Malta, the group gained fame in detective fiction through Dashiell Hammett's novel, The Maltese Falcon. See also St. John of Jerusalem. [WB 8]

4928 Oriel, lions of -- see lions of Oriel and Oxford Colleges [GN 13]

4929 oriel windows -- large bay windows projecting from their surrounding wall and supported by a corbel[s] or bracket[s] [HHC 8]

4930 Oriental [Café] -- the tea shop in Windle* where Miss Climpson* finally meets Nurse Booth*; also a tea shop in Wilvercombe*. DLS may have had in mind the excellent Kardomah chain of tea shops and cafés. They are still in existence. As "Oriental", however, they are fictitious. [SP 16/HHC 32]

4931 orifan -- apparently a trade name for an expensive perfume now unknown if real. Mrs. Forrest* wears this aroma a bit too heavily to be in good taste. [UD 7]

4932 oriflamme -- from the medieval Latin aurea flamma, golden flame, a reference to a banner of flag inspiring devotion, to a brightly colored banner, or to both [BH 16]

4933 Origen -- one of the early Greek fathers (ca. 185-235) of the Church, he wrote extensively and was head of the catechetical school in Alexandria Caesaria. He combined Christian doctrine with his own observations which were rejected by the Church. [WB 12]

4934 Orinoco Mission -- a fictitious mission which sounds most plausible as its name accurately indicates the locale it supposedly serves in northern South America. At the time of the story, however, that area fell within the area of the Diocese of Trinidad and Tobago under the direction, in 1927, of Bishop A. H. Anstey. [UD 12]

4935 orkerd one -- a deliberate misspelling of awkward to indicate dialectical speech [BH 5]

4936 Ormerod, Mr. -- the head of Crich-

ton's* copy department. As such, he would supervise the preparation of the textual material for their advertisements. [nf]

4937 Ormond, P. C. -- one of the constables in Wilvercombe* [HHC 20]

4938 Ormsby, Old -- a member of the Bellona Club* who is seen only once and then only in reference to his snoring, supposedly quite sonorous [BC 1]

4939 'Ornby, Mr. -- see Hornby, Mr. [MMA 6]

4940 Orpington -- a town in northwestern Kent* to the South and East of London and now part of the Greater London Borough of Bromley. It is in a rich agricultural area specializing in fruit and poultry. The Orpington (Buff and otherwise) breed originated there. The Buffs are colored as their name suggests and they lay an egg that has a shell of a tan or cream color. They are large, docile, and showy birds, are excellent for meat, and are easy to keep. [UD 16]

4941 Orsino -- see Twelfth Night [BH 18]

4942 Ossian -- a series of Gaelic poems were ascribed to the ancient bard by one James Macpherson who claimed to have found the poems in the Highlands. The poems are highly eclectic, but are mostly Macpherson's work. [GN 17]

4943 Ostend -- a Belgian port on the North Sea from whence one could take a boat or ferry to the English coastal ports [NT 8]

4944 ostler -- a variation of hostler, one who cares for horses and mules as at an inn or stable [CW 11]

4945 Ostrander, Isabel -- an American writer (1883-1924) of detective novels from 1915 to 1927. She used her own name and a variety of pseudonyms. She is one of the founders of the "Had I But Known" school of mystery (NOT detective) fiction. [BC 18]

4946 "Other things are all very well in their way . . ." -- the lines are spoken by Mr. Waterbrook in Ch. 25 of David Copperfield* by Charles Dickens* [CW 3]

4947 Ottawa Conference -- the July, 1932, meeting in Ottawa, Canada, of the Dominions with the government of Great Britain to settle differences in trade and financial policies after the abandonment of the gold standard in 1931. The object was to unify the Imperial trade and finance situations to bolster domestic economies during the Depression. [GN 4]

4948 Ouija board -- the trade name for a rectangular board with a planchette* or sliding pointer. The board is marked on one side only with the alphabet, numbers, the words yes and no, and other symbols. It is said that those who are sensitive to the spirit world can communicate with the spirits quite easily using such a board. The boards enjoyed a great vogue during the 1920's and 30's, but are not much used any longer. They are now marketed by the Parker Bros. Co. in the U. S. and are still available for purchase. [SP 16]

4949 "Our ancestors are very good kind of folks . . ." -- from Richard Brinsley Sheridan's (1751-1816) comedy, The Rivals*, IV, i. [UD 13]

4950 Our [Blessed] Lady -- the Virgin Mary [ie]

4951 Our Dumb Friends -- the Our Dumb Friends League existed, but is now part of The Blue Cross, an animal welfare organization not to be confused with the Blue Cross/Blue Shield insurance programs in the U. S. which are strictly for humans. Such charitable organizations were common during the 1930's, but most have now amalgamated with other groups into larger, nationally oriented service charities. [UD 3]

4952 "Our mouths shall shew forth Thy Praise." -- a variation on Psalm 51:15 in the KJV: ". . . my mouth shall shew forth thy praise." The quote appears on the plaque honoring the great New Year's ring. [NT 10]

4953 "Our wills are ours to make them thine." -- Alfred, Lord Tennyson* wrote the line at line 16 of the prologue to his long collection of poems regarding the death of A. H. Hallam, "In Memoriam". The series of poems reflects Tennyson's changing reaction to the death of Hallam, a change that

begins at a sense of profound loss and moves to a sense of spiritual unity and love of God. The work ends cheerfully. [UD 9]

4954 Ouse [Great] -- a river in central eastern England that takes a long, meandering course from a spot in Northampton to the North of Oxford, through Cambridge and Norfolk, across the fens, finally emptying into The Wash* just North of King's Lynn. The river's name is pronounced to rhyme with ooze. [NT 11]

4955 out -- see cricket [MMA 18]

4956 out -- see out quick/in slow [NT 13]

4957 "Out of the deep, O Lord, out of the deep" -- the allusion is to Psalm 130:1 as it appears in The Book of Common Prayer [NT 19]

4958 out quick/in slow -- a maneuver in Stedman's* system where a bell moves from the 4-5 position to the 1-2-3 position and back again according to specific rules [NT 13]

4959 outburst of murder at Moscow -- DLS seems to have had in mind an instance of highly controversial political executions reported from Riga, then in the independent nation of Latvia, to The Times in June of 1927. Former Prince Paul Dolgorukoff and nineteen others, already incarcerated for suspicion of anti-Bolshevist activity, were executed by order of the OGPU, predecessor of the present KGB, the state security police, and without benefit of trial. The charges that led to the executions related to the bombing of a Communist social club in Russia. There remains a good deal of suspicion regarding the deaths of the twenty, all of whom were members of the pre-Revolution Russian aristocracy, and the Soviet government seems to have exhibited considerable interest in world opinion after the fact. [UD 19]

4960 outhouse -- an outbuilding, not a latrine [NT 8]

4961 outlandish knight in the ballad -- see knight in the ballad [FRH 7]

4962 outlines -- the squiggly shapes used in shorthand [MMA 1]

4963 outrides -- a reference to Gerard Manley Hopkins' prosody where lines are run-on, chopped up, and otherwise made difficult [GN 13]

4964 outrigger -- a small rowing boat designed for less than four oars with oarlocks or rowlocks projecting outward from the side of the boat on metal brackets [GN 11]

4965 Outside only! -- meaning that one had to sit on the upper deck of the bus which, in the earlier part of the century, was open to the elements [CW 15]

4966 Outside Publicity -- that branch of Pym's Publicity* responsible for billboards, the large posters on buses, etc. [MMA 3]

4967 the Oval -- the Kennington Oval, home ground for the Surrey County Cricket Club team in South London. It dates from 1845. [MMA 18]

4968 over -- see cricket [MMA 18]

4969 Over -- a tiny village in Cambridgeshire* just East of St. Ives and Huntingdon [NT 2]

4970 over the falls -- one of the more ornate tricks to be done with a yo-yo and requires careful timing [MMA 17]

4971 Overbury, Sir Thomas -- he died on September 15, 1613, a prisoner in the Tower of London, the result of poison administered to him there through the machinations of Frances Howard, Countess of Essex* and Robert Carr, Duke of Somerset. The three had a hetero-homosexual triangle going that sometimes involved James I. Carr, however, was an illiterate lump, though handsome, and was suitable only for stud service. His stupidity eventually landed him and, by this time his wife, the former Countess of Essex, in the Tower under sentence of death. Neither was beheaded, but they did serve six years in prison there. Overbury was murdered for his interference in the relationship between Carr and Howard. [GN 7]

4972 overmantel -- an ornamental work of wood and carving, often with a mirror, over the mantle of a fireplace. The suggestion is that the shelves on the overmantel had some sort of velvet hangings or coverings rather more typi-

cal of a Victorian parlor. [NT 1]

4973 Overstrand Mansions -- a fictitious street in London. One suspects that DLS meant Queen Caroline Mansions*. [WB 13]

4974 overthrow [a bell] -- various sorts of damage could be done when a bell is allowed to exceed the maximum arc of swing it is intended to make. The stay* (meant to prevent such a happening) or slider* could be broken which would render the bell useless for change-ringing* until repairs are made. [NT 1]

4975 Owen, Thomas -- a fictitious Birmingham* jeweller, he stole some jewelry from PW's car and hid it at Paddington Station*. Simpkins* was supposed to be carrying it, not the grisly package he actually took. [cb]

4976 Owen's porch -- see Dr. Owen's porch [GN 14]

4977 Oxford -- the city and manufacturing center roughly 56 miles North and West of London which is probably most famous for the university located there [CW 11/HHC 3/NT 3/GN 1]

4978 Oxford and Cambridge Club -- located in London and open to membership to those who have graduated from either university. It is located on Pall Mall* in the vicinity of Marlborough House and St. James's Palace. [WB 8]

4979 Oxford Colleges -- Oxford is a university made up of several distinct colleges, each of which is a separate entity which, for the sake of convenience and mutual support, adheres to the policies of the encompassing University. The situation is analogous to the fifty separate states of the United States functioning together within the framework of the Federal government. The colleges are, in order of their founding: University College, 1249; Balliol, 1263; Merton, 1264; St. Edmund Hall, ca. 1278; Exeter, 1314; Oriel, 1326; Queen's, 1340; New College, 1379; Lincoln, 1427; All Souls, post-graduate, 1438; Magdalen, 1458; Brasenose, 1509; Corpus Christi, 1517; Christ Church, 1546; Trinity, 1554; St. John's, 1555; Jesus, 1571; Wadham, 1612; Pembroke, 1624; Worcester, 1714; Keble, 1870; Hertford, 1874; Lady Margaret Hall, 1878; Somerville (DLS's alma mater), 1879; St. Hugh's, 1886; St. Anne's, 1893, St. Hilda's, 1893; St. Peter's, 1929; Nuffield, 1937; St. Anthony's, 1950; St. Catherine's, 1962; Linacre House, post-graduate society, 1962.

In addition, there are five halls which cater to specific religious groups: Regent's Park College, Baptist, 1810; Mansfield, Congregational, 1885; Campion, Society of Jesus, 1896; St. Benet's Hall, Benedictine, 1897; Greyfriar's, Franciscan, 1910.

4980 Oxford decided that women were dangerous -- likely a reference to the heated debate in the spring of 1927 to consider limiting the number of women students to be admitted to the University. The debate had started in March. See #4913. [UD 19]

4981 Oxford hood -- see hood [BH 19]

4982 Oxford in 1911 -- PW is known to have been an excellent cricketer as the Pym's/Brotherhood's match indicates, and he did play for Oxford. He would have been twenty-one during 1911. [MMA 18]

4983 Oxford marmalade -- an orange marmalade distinguished from the others by the addition of black treacle (molasses) and chopped crystalline ginger [WB 5]

4984 Oxford St. -- a major East-West street in central London. It starts at the Marble Arch* of Hyde Park* and continues to the intersection of Charing Cross Rd. where it changes to New Oxford St. [WB 6/MMA 16]

4985 Oxford University -- its colleges provide alma maters for PW, HV, and DLS. Organized as a _studium generale_ in the late 1100's, probably by students who migrated from Paris, the University has remained of great importance since that time. It was incorporated in 1571. Along with Cambridge University*, Oxford ranks as one of England's two great institutions of higher learning and is one of the foremost universities of the world. It is located in the Thames valley to the northwest of London. Its name is derived from oxen ford, a place where cattle could safely ford the Thames at

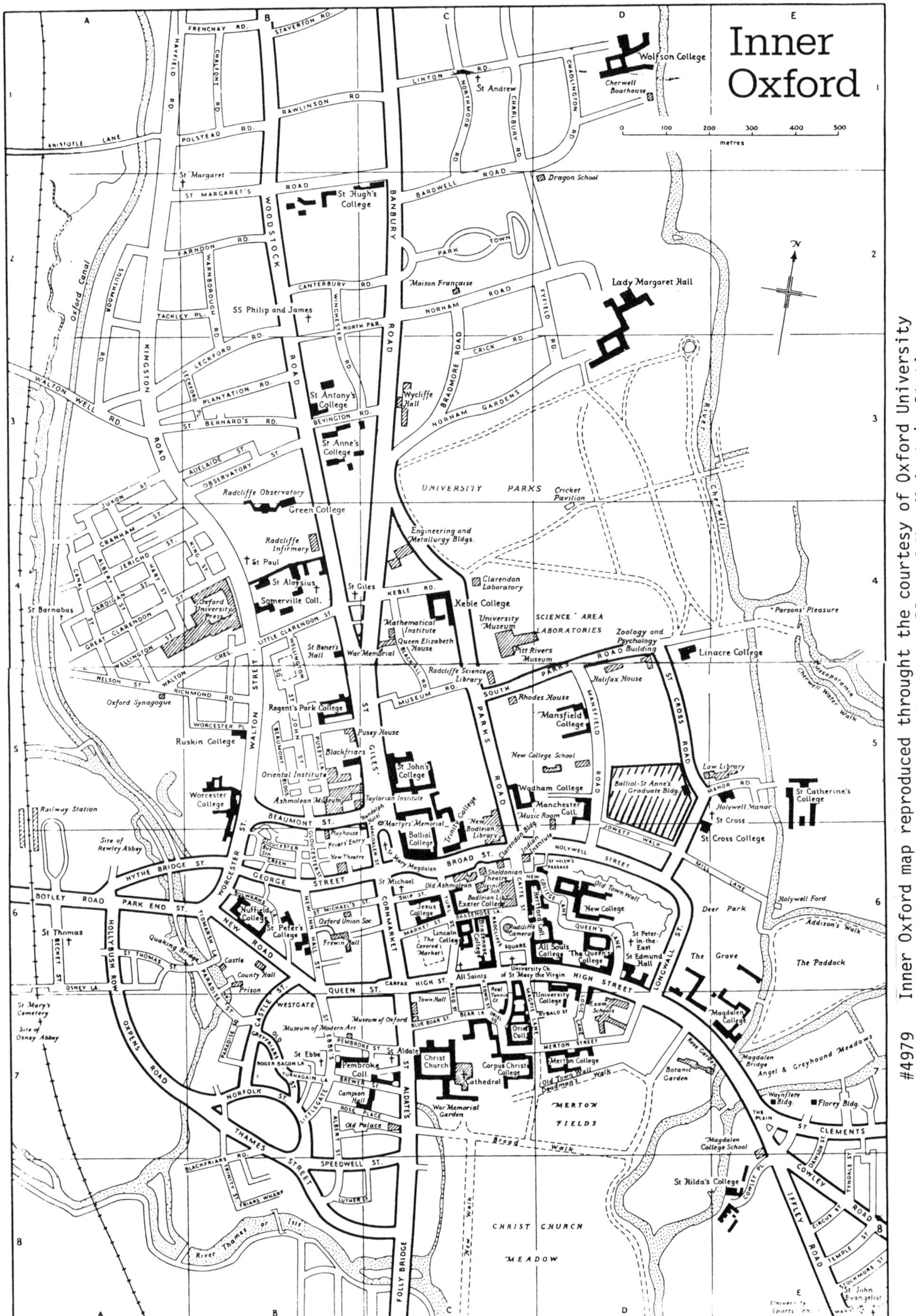

#4979 Inner Oxford map reproduced throught the courtesy of Oxford University Press with the permission of the Controller of Her Majesty's Stationery Office, Crown copyright reserved.

OXFORD STREET.

#4984 Oxford St., London, in the 1920's.

most times of the year, a fact recorded on the city's heraldic arms. [WB 5/UD 19/FRH 5/HHC 3/GN 1/BH P]

4986 Oxford University Press -- the prestigious and internationally regarded printing arm of Oxford University. It is located on Kingston Rd., across the street from DLS's alma mater, Somerville College. [GN 3]

4987 Oxhey, the earth opened at -- Oxhey is near Watford, to the North and West of London in Hertfordshire. On June 14, 1927, a hole developed mysteriously in front of numbers 63 and 65 Kingsfield Rd. In a short time it had expanded to leave a pit some thirty feet in diameter and eighty feet deep. It was theorized that an underground stream had shifted its course, thus leading to the near disaster. [UD 19]

4988 "Oysters have beards . . ." -- an oyster's beard is the gills or breathing apparatus. While the oyster may "wag" its beard in a physical sense, it is in no way capable of wagging it in the sense PW means as to talk; chin wag, a slang term. [NT 16]

(P)

4989 p. b. policeman -- applied to P. C. Burt*, it stands for "poor bloody" (see bloody) policeman. This is a PW original adaptation from the WW I expression "poor bloody infantry" which was commonly abbreviated to P. B. I. [hp]

4990 PLM express -- an express train of the former French railroad, the Paris, Lyon and Mediterranean. In January of 1938, this railroad joined the others in the nationalization of French railroads into the Société Nationale des Chemins de fer Français (SNCF). [BC 13]

4991 P. M. -- post mortem as used here [BC 16]

4992 Paddington -- Station, a train terminus of the Great Western Railway in northwest London. See Motorcycle Race. [cb]

4993 paddy-paw -- hand. The allusion is to "The Beginning of the Armadillos" from Rudyard Kipling's* Just So Stories. [pj]

4994 Padgett -- the porter who, with his wife, occupies the St. Cross Lodge at Shrewsbury College*. He is known to PW as Corporal Padgett, one of the soldiers who helped dig PW out of the collapsed entrenchment after the shell burst that buried him alive at Caudry*. Padgett shows a great fondness for PW. [GN 3]

4995 Pagford Parva -- a fictitious Hertfordshire community. It was part of the immediate area of HV's childhood as her father, Dr. Vane*, served patients in that area. [BH 1]

4996 Pagg -- a fictitious Hertfordshire river [BH 12]

4997 Paggleham -- a fictitious Hertfordshire hamlet known to HV from her childhood. It is the village near which Talboys* is located. [BH 1]

4998 pair-oar skiff -- a skiff or small rowboat propelled by a single pair of oars pulled by a single oarsman [GN 15]

4999 Paisley -- a suburb of Glasgow to the South and West of that city. The fabric design for shawls,

neckties, etc., is named for this city, but the design originated in Kashmir. [FRH 10]

5000 Palais de Danse -- the phrase applies to a popular dance hall with partners for hire, this one being located near Cricklewood* [nf]

5001 Palais de Justice -- in Paris, the central criminal court on the Ile de la Cité [aq]

5002 Pall Mall -- the center of London club life, it derives its name from "paille maille", an early French predecessor of croquet. It runs between and is parallel to Piccadilly and The Mall. The latter replaced it as the royal croquet area; The Mall is now the capital's ceremonial street to and from Buckingham Palace. Pall Mall is North of The Mall and connects St. James's Palace with Trafalgar Square. [CW 8/UD 17]

5003 Palladian front -- the front of Bredon Hall* is designed after the principles of the Italian architect Andrea Palladio (1518-80) who created his own school of design after classical ideals; hence, the Renaissance Neo-classical school of architecture. [BH E2]

5004 Palladium -- the London Palladium is on Argyll St., and opened in 1910. At the time Robert Fentiman* takes Ann Dorland* there, it had long been known for spectacular revues. HV attends a show there with Reggie Pomfret*. [BC 23/GN 11]

5005 Pallambra -- a London music hall mentioned by PW, but there is no such place. The name cited is probably a combination of Alhambra and Palladium as either would be appropriate, but the Palladium is chronologically more likely as it opened in 1910 while the Alhambra had reached its peak before then. [umw]

5006 Pallas -- Pallas Athena, Greek goddess of wisdom; mentioned by Poe at various points in his poem, "The Raven" [UD 14]

5007 Palm Sunday -- the Sunday before Easter when Jesus entered Jerusalem on an ass [NT 3]

5008 Palmer -- the reference is to Dr. William Palmer of Rugeley who may have poisoned as many as sixteen people including four of his legitimate children and one illegitimate child. He is known to have been connected to at least half a dozen murders including those of his wife and alcoholic brother. He was finally indicted for those two murders, was tried, found guilty, and executed on June 14, 1856. [UD 8/BC 13/SP 20]

5009 Palmerston, Lord -- Henry John Temple, 3rd Viscount Palmerston (1784-1865), Prime Minister of Great Britain from 1855-58 and from 1859-65. He is remembered for his energetic and blustering approach to the problems of British foreign policy and was once referred to by Queen Victoria as "that dreadful old man". His statue stands in Parliament Square*, adjacent to the Houses of Parliament where he served for nearly sixty years. [CW 19]

5010 palmistry -- the art of character analysis or fortunetelling based upon a study of the lines and other markings on the palms [np]

5011 pampas-grass -- Cortaderia argentea, a tall grass with feathery plumes native to South America. It is sometimes grown as an ornamental filler in gardens or is dried and used as an indoor ornament. [BH 4]

5012 Pan -- the Greek god of flocks and shepherds, usually presented as partly goatlike. He invented the musical pipe of seven reeds with which he is closely associated. In the OCCL it is stated that, "Pan was reputed to be the cause of sudden groundless fear, especially that felt by travellers in remote and desolate places, known in consequence as Panic fear." [MMA 9]

5013 Panama hat -- a lightweight hat of natural hand-plaited straw, frequently having a colorful band at the base of the crown. They are presently returning to fashion. [WB 10]

5014 panama straw -- same as item 5013 [UD 18]

5015 Pandarus -- see Uncle Pandarus [BH P]

5016 Pantaloon -- PW refers to the abuse that Pantaloon could expect. He was a stock character, the old man, buffoon, merchant, father, or guardian to the beautiful young Columbine, and

was constantly subject to all sorts of comic abuse that would kill most people. PW is mocking The Society* when he says that he will talk more freely if he is not threatened with torture. He is comparing their methods with those more likely to have been used by the Marx brothers. [ab]

5017 pantiles -- tiles of a coarse nature that in their usual double curve configuration are used as roofing tiles, one curve overlapping the next tile. In their less common single curve style, they were usually used to line ditches, etc., but could also be used as roofing tiles. [HHC 32]

5018 Panto -- see Aladdin in the Panto [HHC 15]

5019 pantry -- a butler's pantry, a room usually located between the kitchen and the dining room and organized to hold silver, linens, etc., and to provide a place for the butler to arrange a meal for serving, to decant wine, and to perform related household duties [ae]

5020 Pattison, Dr. -- a guest at Sir Charles Deverill's* Christmastime costume party. He examines Charmian Grayle* and determines that her death was by strangulation. [qs]

5021 paperfile -- a filing cabinet or "file" [MMA 1]

5022 papiers d'identité -- French for identity papers [mt]

5023 Papist -- a follower of the teachings of the Roman Catholic Church. The term is usually derogatory in tone. [UD 12]

5024 par. -- slang for paragraph [BC 1]

5025 par-roasted -- incompletely or partially roasted [NT 18]

5026 parable of the swept and garnished house -- the reference is to the Gospel of Matthew, 12:43-5, which deals with the worthlessness of self-reformation [BC 16]

5027 Paradise Lost -- not a reference to Milton's epic poem, but to the poet's inspiration, the eviction from Eden as recounted in Genesis [BH 4]

5028 paraffin -- British English for kerosene [BH 3]

5029 paraffin-oil stove -- a small stove fueled by paraffin* [NT 19]

5030 parapet -- a low wall rising above the point where the roof joins the side walls of a structure [WB 4/MMA 5]

5031 parclose -- a screen or divider; the screen that separates a side chapel from the choir [NT 2]

5032 Parents' Match -- a cricket* match between fathers and sons relative to a particular school [GN 14]

5033 Parfitts [Mr. and Mrs.] -- Miss Climpson* thinks this couple may be selling a home on Wellington Ave.* in Leahampton* [UD 5]

5034 Paris -- the famous and handsome prince of Troy who abducted Helen, Queen of Sparta, thus precipitating the Trojan War [GN 8]

5035 Paris, Treaty of -- see Treaty of Paris [HHC 32]

5036 Paris-Évreux Express -- DLS states that PW boarded this express train with the intent of getting off at Verneuil after an intermediate stop at Dreux. Such a connection would be difficult. DLS is correct in the Paris-Dreux-Verneuil connection, but Évreux is about twenty-eight miles North and East of Verneuil, and Dreux is not on the Paris-Évreux line. Perhaps she read the wrong line on the timetable. [mt]

5037 Paris in 1815 -- Louis XVIII assumed the throne of France in 1814 as a constitutional monarch under the charter of June 4, 1814. There was an understandable rush to restore the aristocracy by the emigrés. When, however, Napoleon returned from Elba in 1815, Paris became rather hysterical. The "Little Corporal's" return was, in part, encouraged by reaction against the policies of this new aristocracy. Political intrigue became a way of life that, in a sense, lasted until after the Franco-Prussian War*. [HHC 32]

5038 Parish Room -- a church hall of some sort near the rectory at Fenchurch St. Paul* used for transacting parish business [NT 4]

5039 the Park -- Battersea Park*, 200 acres on the South bank of the Thames reclaimed from former marsh land

at the suggestion of Thomas Cubitt in 1843 [WB 1]

5040 Park Lane -- possibly the most fashionable address in London during the 1920's and 30's, it runs the full length of the East end of Hyde Park* from the Marble Arch to Hyde Park Corner. The Dowager Duchess of Medway* and Sir Reuben Levy* have homes there, and PW's Piccadilly and South Audley St. addresses are very close by. Now there are mostly hotels and offices there. [aq/WB 2]

5041 Park St. -- the taxi driver has become flustered during the questioning. He means Parkway which leads directly away from Gloucester Gate at the northeast corner of Regent's Park*. [BC 8]

5042 Parker, Charles -- PW's long-time friend and associate, an officer at Scotland Yard* who eventually marries PW's sister, Lady Mary Wimsey*. PW and Parker have a strong friendship and a caring one, and it is interesting to note that Parker has a healthy career when PW isn't around to assist.

Parker's rank is Detective-Inspector in aq, cb, dh (see Police Ranks), and Inspector in fr. His rank is not mentioned in ab and he was not aware of PW's undercover activities as he thought PW was dead. Concurrent with his resurrection, PW presents Parker with the whole of The Society* to arrest. By the time of im, Parker is Chief Inspector, the rank he holds in ae and bc.

In WB, the first novel, Parker is apparently new to the plainclothes forces as his rank is not mentioned at all. He takes the case when his work to find Sir Reuben Levy* connects with Sugg's* corpse and after Sugg has botched the case. In CW, Parker's rank is given as Detective-Inspector and he works with PW to extricate the Duke of Denver* from his encounter with an indictment for murder. It is at this time that he realizes that he is in love with Lady Mary. PW is especially delighted by this news given the romantic messes Mary has been in, and encourages Parker's pursuit of her.

In UD, PW and Parker are again working together and he is still a Det. Insp. No mention is made of Lady Mary. Parker's chief function seems to be to clear the way for PW's activities. During the action of BC, Parker is promoted to Chief Inspector for his work on the "Crate Murder"*, an adventure that does not involve PW and was not recorded by DLS. Parker remains generally in the background here as in UD. More attention is given to PW's forcing Parker's actions regarding Lady Mary than to any detective work he does in SP. He is a bit more prominent than in the earlier three works, but not much more. The marriage proposal is not approved by the Ducal family, but PW smoothes things out for the lovebirds and they are married by the time of the action in HHC, two years later. The wedding probably took place in the spring of 1930.

In HHC Parker is merely PW's London "agent" who serves as host for Insp. Umpelty* when he travels up to London. He fills a similar role in FRH.

When the action of MMA takes place, Parker and Lady Mary have two children, Charles Peter and Mary Lucasta. Parker's role here is an interesting one in that he takes a bone-breaking blow meant for PW and clears away some potentially embarrassing complications that arise as a result of PW's dual life as himself and as Death Bredon. The action of NT partly antedates Parker's marriage to Lady Mary, but he is in the background anyway, only being identified as working with the C. I. D. He does help, but only late in the novel.

Prior to the action of GN Parker is working on the "difficulties" in a case in the North of England and does not appear in his own right. Parker and Lady Mary are, of course, in attendance at PW's marriage to HV, but not, apparently, in any capacity other than as guests. [passim]

5043 Parker, Charles Peter -- or "Peterkin", the eldest of the two children born to PW's best friend, Charles Parker*, and to his sister, Lady Mary. He is given as being three years of age at the time of this novel. [MMA 5]

5044 Parker, Lady Mary -- see Wimsey, Lady Mary [MMA 5]

5045 Parker, Mary Lucasta -- the second child of Charles and Lady Mary

#5042 Mark Eden as Charles Parker in the BBC production of MMA. BBC copyright photograph.

Parker. She is named Mary after her mother and Lucasta for her grandmother, the Dowager Duchess of Denver*. [MMA 5]

5046 parkin -- a kind of gingerbread made with oatmeal and molasses [GN 1]

5047 Parks -- the University Parks, an extensive range of flower gardens, playing fields, and copses of trees and shrubs, both familiar and exotic, located on the East side of Oxford University's grounds on both sides of the Cherwell* [GN 12]

5048 Parliament, Houses of -- the bicameral legislative body of Great Britain, consisting of the House of Commons and the House of Lords. Over the centuries the Lords' powers have been reduced to discussing and delaying legislation. The Wimseys are involved through the House of Lords as the Duke of Denver would have a seat there. Commons has the bulk of the power today. The story of the creation of Parliament antedates King John and the Magna Charta of 1215. Its growth is a story, at first, of the struggle between an absolute monarchy and nobles who had to provide the men and funds for any wars to be fought; this control of the purse strings approach brought more and more power to Parliament until the modern situation of a constitutional monarchy with Parliament in complete control eventually came about after the Restoration in 1660. The building housing Parliament is not, technically, Parliament Building, but is the Palace of Westminster. [aq/CW 19]

5049 Parliament Square -- the square to the right of the Houses of Parliament if one stands facing the Clock Tower. Laid out in 1750, there are now statues of Palmerston*, Churchill*, and Smuts, among others. PW and Parker hold quite a celebration there and Insp. Sugg*, of all people, is the one who prevents their celebration from becoming an embarrassment. [CW 19]

5050 parma violet[s] -- a type of violet, _Viola odorata sempervirens_, especially cultivated for its fragrant blossoms; any aromatic cosmetic preparation made from them [WB 1/HHC 24]

5051 parricides -- those who murder parents or close relatives. One suspects that Mrs. Munns* meant paramour. [BC 18]

5052 parritch -- Scots dialect for porridge [ss]

5053 Parry -- Sir Charles Herbert Hastings Parry (1848-1918), English composer and musicologist. He wrote various orchestral works, but he was most successful with his choral endeavors. He was influenced strongly by Richard Wagner. Parry was knighted in 1898, and was elevated to a baronetcy in 1902 at the coronation of Edward VII. [BC 3]

5054 Parsee -- a follower of Zoroastrian religious beliefs. Originally from ancient Persia, they are now located near Bombay, India. [UD 20]

5055 parsnip wine -- a wine made from chopped parsnips, sugar, water and yeast. It can be quite potent. [BH 2]

5056 Parson's Pleasure -- a swimming hole for those men who prefer not to wear swimming trunks. It is on the Cherwell down an extension of Parks Rd. past Linacre College. [GN 11]

5057 Parsons, Miss -- the Warden's secretary at Shrewsbury College* [GN 5]

5058 Part Ends -- see course ends [NT 3]

5059 Parthenon -- the ancient temple of Athena on the Acropolis in Athens, or at least what's left of it. The friezes are in the British Museum, part of it was blown up, and the remainder is now suffering from noise and air pollution. [GN 6]

5060 Parthenon Frieze -- the heroic bas-relief sculptures from either end of the pediments on the Parthenon*. They may now be seen in the British Museum. These are the famous Elgin Marbles named for Lord Elgin who bought them from the Turks. [GN 7]

5061 particle -- a unit of speech and grammar that somehow limits or controls. Most articles, interjections, prepositions, adverbs, and conjunctions are particles. [GN 4]

5062 _partie carrée_ -- French for, _literally_, "a square party", or idomatically, "a double date" [BH 10]

THE HOUSES OF PARLIAMENT AND WESTMINSTER ABBEY

#5048 The Houses of Parliament and Westminster Abbey.

#5056 Parson's Pleasure, Oxford, as PW might have known it, ca. 1910.

5063 "Parting is such sweet sorrow" -- from Romeo and Juliet, II, ii, 184, at the end of the balcony scene as Romeo departs [BH 18]

5064 Parton, Miss -- one of the two secretaries for the copywriting staff at Pym's Publicity* [MMA 1]

5065 Parturiunt montes -- the reference is to Horace's Ars Poetica, 139: "Parturient montes, nascetur ridiculus mus", or, "The mountains will labor to bring forth a single, laughable mouse." [BH 4]

5066 Pas du tout. Il m'aime . . . -- see Il m'aime . . . [BH 18]

5067 pash -- a slang term used in girls' schools meaning a passion as in infatuation with; noted attraction to or regard for a senior girl or teacher [UD 8]

5068 pass in a crowd with a push -- an expression meaning to be satisfactory, but not in any way special. Whatever it is, it "will do". [NT 3]

5069 Passion-flower Pie -- the title of a fictitious novel by Mrs. Snell-Wilmington* [GN 11]

5070 passing strokes -- the tolling of a bell to signal the passing or death of the old year or of someone who had died. See also nine tailors. [NT 1]

5071 passion à la Plato -- an allusion to Platonic love quoted from Bunthorne's song in Act I of Gilbert and Sullivan's* Patience: "Passion à la Plato for a bashful young potato or a not-too-French french bean;" aspidistras too, à la PW. [BH 13]

5072 The Passion Streak -- a fictitous movie starring Varden* [cf]

5073 Passionément--à la folie -- see Il m'aime [BH 18]

5074 passmen -- a university student who studies for a "pass" degree as opposed to an "honors" degree is called a passman; a student who takes a degree without academic distinction [GN 8]

5075 pastille -- a small pill or piece of candy. It is sometimes used, as in "Incredible Elopement" to refer to any such small item, in this case, a piece of incense. [ie]

5076 Pate, Ellen -- one of Nurse Booth's* college friends at the Maidstone Ladies' College*. The name is mentioned during Miss Climpson's séance. [SP 17]

5077 Paternoster -- the Lord's Prayer. The name derives from the first two words of the prayer in Latin. [ie]

5078 Paters -- see Paternoster [ie]

5079 Paterson, Carter -- see Carter Paterson [BH 7]

5080 Paterson, Dr. James -- a neighbor of Dr. Pritchard's* who was asked to certify the cause of death for Pritchard's mother-in-law, Mrs. Taylor, a service he refused to perform. Instead, he wrote to Mr. James Struthers, Registrar (of births, deaths, marriages, etc.) that: "The death was certainly sudden, unexpected, and to me mysterious." [UD 1]

5081 path of light is curved -- this is one of the discoveries of physics in the early 20th C., a result of the quantum physics studies of Planck, Hertz, Einstein, and others. Such forces as gravity and magnetic fields seem to cause the curving. [SP 5]

5082 patience -- another name for the card games collectively called solitaire [BC 20]

5083 "Patience and shuffle the cards" -- the line is from Miguel de Cervantes' Don Quixote*, Part II, Ch. 23, and is said by Durandarte in response to the recital of the prophecy from Merlin that Don Quixote would disenchant Durandarte and the others held in the cave of Montesinos. The full line is, "And if that may not be, then, O my cousin, I say 'patience, and shuffle the cards.'" [UD 11]

5084 the Patriarch -- the elder Mr. Ferguson's* stomach. PW is teasing Robert Ferguson* as much as he can. [ss]

5085 Patriarch -- an allusion to Tailor Paul*. PW is addressing the bell in his thoughts. [NT 5]

5086 patronising and Lord of Burleigh -- see Lord of Burleigh [BH P]

5087 Patty, Miss -- a character played by Mary Stokes* in her class's Second Year play* [GN 1]

5088 "Pause there, Morocco." -- the line is from The Merchant of Venice, II, vii, 24. The Prince of Morocco is speaking to himself as he considers which of Portia's three caskets to choose. The lines continue, "And weigh thy value with an even hand!" PW is cautioning himself to pause and weigh his evidence. [HHC 21]

5089 pavement artists -- itinerants who draw pictures on the sidewalks in the expectation that passers-by will leave donations in appreciation of their work [NT 10]

5090 Pavlo Alexeivitch -- Paul Alexis's* first and middle names in Anglicized Russian [HHC 29]

5091 pax -- Latin for, "peace". Colloquially in English, the term has come to mean "I surrender" in the vein of saying "uncle". [UD 6]

5092 Pax Academica -- Latin for, "the peace of academica", or world peace through knowledge and understanding [GN 2]

5093 pay-ah -- pair, a deliberate phonetic spelling to reflect pronunciation; the Victorian manner of calling for a "carriage and pair" (of horses) [bc]

5094 Payne, Mr. -- an enraged client of Mr. Grimbold's* [ae]

5095 pea-souper -- one of what formerly plagued London, a dense, pea-soup yellow fog. The fog is entirely a natural phenomenon, but the pea-soup effect was the contribution of all the fireplaces, furnaces, and stoves, etc., that burned a low grade of high sulfur coal. The mixture of fog, smoke, and coal gas created the characteristic dense, yellowish, choking sulfuric atmosphere. Cleaner air standards and better fuels have eliminated the pea-souper. [WB 11]

5096 Peabody -- see Brodribb [GN 2]

5097 Peabody's -- a cereal manufacturer whose accounts for advertising are with Pym's*. The firm is fictitious. [MMA 3]

5098 "Peace ho! the moon sleeps with Endymion" -- the line is Portia's in V, i, 109-10 of The Merchant of Venice* [BH 12]

5099 Peace Treaty -- the Treaty of Versailles that concluded WW I, exacted war reparations, "established guilt" for the war, and laid the foundations for WW II [BH 8]

5100 Peagreen Incorruptible -- a nickname given to Sir Reuben Levy*. See also seagreen incorruptible. [WB 3]

5101 Peake of Brasenose -- an acquaintaince of PW's from their mutual college days. For Brasenose, see Oxford Colleges. [GN 14]

5102 Peake, Potty [Orris] -- Horace Peake is the mentally deficient man who lurks around the church at Fenchurch St. Paul*. He sees much, but is unable to present it in any way that is meaningful to others. He tends pigs and pumps the bellows that fill the windchest* on the organ in the church. The job was a hard one prior to electric motors and blowers. [NT 2]

5103 peal -- 5040 changes* or more rung in succession. Less than that number is a touch*. [NT 2]

5104 Pearson, Edmund L[ester] -- an American chronicler of true crime (1880-1937) famous for Studies in Crime (1924), a collection of eight cases including the Lizzie Borden and the Hauptmann/Lindbergh trials. He also wrote More Studies in Murder, Five Murders, and various other essays. His work, including Murder at Smutty Nose, was highly regarded, but is no longer considered as highly as that of William Roughead and William Bolitho who wrote in a similar vein. The volume Murder at Smutty Nose and Other Murders appeared in 1926 as a supplement to Studies in Murder. The title story relates a particularly brutal double murder in 1873 on the island of Smutty Nose, one of the Isles of Shoals, just off the Maine-New Hampshire border not far from Portsmouth, N. H. [UD 8]

5105 Peasgood, Mrs. -- a church worker in Leahampton* [UD 5]

5106 pêche Melba -- a dessert created to honor the famous singer, Nellie Melba. It consists of a peach half with vanilla ice cream on top, all covered with Melba sauce, a concoction of raspberry purée and currant jelly. [BC 18]

5107 Pecksniff, Mr. -- a character in Charles Dickens's* Martin Chuzzlewit. He is an architect and a thorough hypocrite. [bc]

5108 Peerage -- the aristocracy of Great Britain and Ireland. The ranking is as follows:

1. dukes and duchesses
2. marquesses and marchionesses
3. earls and countesses
4. viscounts and viscountesses
5. barons and baronesses

Royalty is not included in the Peerage when the term "peer" is used in this sense.

Royalty includes the King or Queen (not both at once), the Prince of Wales (when there is one), other princes, the princesses, and Dukes of the Blood Royal (they are presently only Gloucester and Kent, but formerly included Windsor, a title created for Edward VIII when he abdicated but which died with him).

Peerages can be inherited, as is the Duke of Denver's, or can be created for the life of the holder. [passim]

5109 peers, trial by -- in England has two meanings: 1) any person has the right to a trial by a jury of his peers in the sense of equals, but, 2) until 1948, peers, in the sense of the aristocracy (as above), had the right to be tried by the House of Lords, but only in criminal cases. The only drawback was that there could be no appeal; the verdict is final and binding. [CW 13]

5110 peg -- see tightened a peg [HHC 3]

5111 peg out -- the reference is to board games such as cribbage where one moves a peg or marker to help keep score. To "peg out" is to end a game and its scoring and, colloquially, it refers to someone having died. [CW 12]

5112 peggle[s] -- a local name for the fruit of the hawthorn bush. If it can be induced to ferment, it can be made into a wine of sorts. [NT 6]

5113 Pegler, Gen. -- the deceased husband of Mrs. Pegler* [SP 18]

5114 Pegler, Mrs. -- the "stout, pussy* old lady, with a long tongue" who is staying at the guest house in Windle where Miss Climpson* is staying. She has strong opinions on most things and does not hesitate to share them. [SP 16]

5115 Peigne en écaille et diamants -- French for, "comb of tortoise shell and diamonds" [CW 5]

5116 pelican in the wilderness -- the allusion is to Psalm 102:6, the Psalm for the afflicted to cry to the Lord [BC 18]

5117 pelota -- Spanish for, "ball", but it refers to a game played in a court known more commonly as jai alai [ie]

5118 Pembroke [rose and thistle] -- the arms of Pembroke College, Oxford, include the English or Tudor rose and the thistle of Scotland, heraldic floral emblems that allude to the Earl of Pembroke (English) and King James I (Scottish) who were, respectively, Chancellor of Oxford and Founder (even if only honorarily) of the College [GN 13]

5119 Pembroke College Fours, 1883 -- the reference is to that college's participation in the four-man boat races of that year. Which Pembroke College is open to speculation as there is one at both Oxford and Cambridge. [SP 17]

5120 Pemming, Mrs. -- Sir Reuben Levy's* cook [WB 4]

5121 Penates -- ancient Roman deities who guarded the state and the household. They were something like personifications of natural forces whose duty it was to bring wealth and plenty to those who worshipped. [GN 17]

5122 Penberthy, Dr. Walter -- the retired Army surgeon and member of the Bellona Club* who attends to the medical needs of the Club's members and who has offices (a surgery) on Harley St.* He is particularly interested in the effects of glands on human beings. See also Voronoff, Dr. [BC 1]

5123 Pendennis [illustrations to] -- a novel by William Makepeace Thackeray published serially from 1848 to 1850. Part of the action of the story is set in a university, illustrations for which were published in

the magazine serial entries for the novel. [GN 1]

5124 penny/pence -- pence is the plural of penny, a copper coin and now the smallest regularly minted denomination now in use. It would be worth just a bit more than its U. S. counterpart. See British Monetary Units. [passim]

5125 Penny-farthing St. -- or Pennyfarthing St., a small sidestreet off Milford St. in Salisbury*. DLS locates it off Milford Hill, a minor memory lapse as Milford Hill is an extension of Milford St. [WB 5]

5126 penny whistle -- a cheap, hence penny, shrill pipe or whistle with holes for finger stops to allow simple tunes to be played [MMA 19]

5127 Pentecost -- the second most important Christian festival (after Easter) which celebrates the descent of the Holy Spirit to the Apostles on the day of Pentecost, the fiftieth day after Easter. It coincides with the Jewish Festival of Weeks and with the delivering of the tablets of law to Moses. See also bridal raptures of Pentecost. [UD 22]

5128 People who live in glass skylights -- PW's variation on the old adage that "People who live in glass houses shouldn't throw stones." The adage dates from at least 1640 when it is first recorded as being in print. [MMA 5]

5129 Peplets -- an aid to digestion invented by DLS for use here [MMA 5]

5130 Pepper's ghost -- a stage illusion first performed by one Mr. Pepper. The actual figure is brightly illuminated out of sight of the audience, and the image is reflected upward on to a column of smoke issuing from the illusion's apparatus. [GN 19]

5131 Peppercorn, Jacob -- Miss Chilperic's* fiancé who is subjected--in absentia--to a scathing blast from Miss Hillyard who is not impressed with his scholarship [GN 18]

5132 Pepys -- Samuel Pepys (pronounced as peeps), the famous English naval administrator and diarist (1633-1703) whose firsthand account of the Great Fire remains one of the best accounts of that grand conflagration. The reference to Ho Bryon* is his own phonetic spelling. [UD 14]

5133 per impossibile -- Italian for by or through some impossibility [GN 4]

5134 percer le coeur -- French for, "to stab (to break) my heart" [CW 13]

5135 perceras le coeur -- French for, "will break my heart" [CW 13]

5136 perdrix aux choux -- a rich and hearty game dish which is constructed around a partridge (perdrix) and cabbage (choux) prepared as a casserole. When complete, the cabbage is put on a large platter with the partridge on top. A sauce of game stock, wine, and cornstarch is generally served with it. [BC 11]

5137 perfect Napoleon -- one who shows great initiative and command of self in dealing with new, difficult, or sensitive issues while, at the same time, creating an aura of strength and perseverance. PW describes Mrs. Thipps* with that phrase. [WB 3]

5138 perfume of Arabia -- see hand of a murderer [NT 11]

5139 periods of vibration -- the length in time of the cycle which is the inverse of the number of cycles per second (frequency) generated by a vibrating body such as a bell, violin string, or column of air in a musical instrument. Such vibrations, the basic vibration and any harmonics it may generate, can shatter glass. Singers have been known to do so. [NT 20]

5140 peritonitis -- an inflammation of the peritoneum or membrane lining the abdominal cavity and enclosing the viscera. Before penicillin and the other drugs of that nature, such an inflammation was considered far more dangerous than at present, but it is still a dangerous situation. [WB 7/FRH 14/SP 1]

5141 periwinkle -- a trailing or woody evergreen herb of the dogbane family. It is widely used as a ground cover and has the added benefit of pretty little blue or white flowers. [NT 3]

5142 Perizzites -- see Hivites [BH E2]

5143 Perkins -- the porter at Staple Inn* [CW 16]

5144 Perkins, John -- attorney and a coroner* for Hertfordshire who convenes the Coroner's Court to investigate the death of William Noakes*. He is fictitious. [BH 10]

5145 Perkins, Julian -- the frightened little hiker with a myriad of health problems who, because of an accident, becomes an irritating red-herring for PW, HV, and Insp. Umpelty* [HHC 2]

5146 Perkins, Nathaniel -- a notable sportsman who lived in Fenchurch St. Paul* [NT 1]

5147 permis de séjour -- French for a form of a certificate of registration, a sort of visa to cover an extended or special visit [mt]

5148 Perpendicular -- an architectural style of the 14th-16th centuries that is mainly an extension of and a refinement (simplification) of the Gothic style. Perpendicular is marked by an emphasis on vertical lines with very little use of curves, and it forces to one's attention the treatment of windows and roofs. The former became quite large, the latter very ornate, especially on the inside. See architecture. [NT 1]

5149 perry -- the extracted juice of pears, fermented to induce an alcoholic content [MMA 5]

5150 Perry, Miss -- a student at Shrewsbury College* [GN 16]

5151 Persians -- inhabitants of that area of southwestern Asia now known as Iran; a large, long-haired breed of show cat [HHC 1/BH E2]

5152 persona grata -- Latin for a "welcome person" [dh]

5153 The Personal Equation -- a book by Louis Berman* and published in London and New York by Century in 1925. It deals with health and personal improvement. [BC 18]

5154 Peruvians -- shares in a Peruvian oil venture that showed a sudden and unaccountable surge of activity at the time of Sir Reuben Levy's death [WB 5]

5155 Peter the Hermit -- PW refers to Peter of Amiens (1050-1115), a gentleman of Picardy who had been a soldier, then a monk. He is remembered for having preached the First Crusade and for having been present on that Crusade. He was a hermit mostly in the sense of having withdrawm from secular life to become a monk. [SP 15]

5156 Peter, what a rock you are! --the name Peter comes from the Greek petros, rock, and St. Peter was called "the Rock" by Jesus who said that, "upon this Rock I will build my church". The second part of HV's comment (The shadow of a great rock . . .) is from Isaiah 32:2 where Isaiah tells of Christ's coming in terms both of a promise and of a warning. [GN 14]

5157 Peter's hands -- the reference is to Matthew 16:19, in part, when Jesus gives Peter "the keys of the kingdom of heaven". The hell part is HV's addition referring to her own uncertainty now that she has to face the reality of marriage to PW. It is to be noted that PW is proud that he had inherited the Wimsey hands. [BH 1]

5158 Peter's Pot -- a particularly nasty bog* near Grider's Hole* which almost claims PW's life [CW 4]

5159 Petering Friars -- a cluster of houses approximately seven miles northwest of Little Doddering* [bc]

5160 Peterkin -- see Parker, Charles Peter [MMA 17]

5161 Peterson, old John -- a ninety-two year old artist resident of Kirkcudbright* [FRH 8]

5162 petite saucisse -- French for, "little sausage", cocktail frankfurter in more modern parlance [GN 11]

5163 petitio elenchi -- some editions have eleuchi, a typographical error. The phrase is Latin for, "begging the point in dispute", a logical fallacy wherein one attempts to avoid the point being argued while, at the same time, trying to refute it. The fallacy is a form of circularity and comes as a result of this confusing mess since avoidance usually means never dealing with the problem directly if the opponent isn't clever enough to keep the argument on topic. [HHC 21]

5164 petits-fours -- small French decorated pastries coated with frostings and filled with jellies, etc. [BC 16]

5165 petrol gas light -- a lamp consisting of a fuel reservoir under pressure, a mantle, and a glass shade. It burns gasoline and gives off a very white light. [FRH 27]

5166 Petronius -- Gaius Petronius Arbiter (d. 65 A. D.) a friend of the emperor Nero and his "director of the pleasures of the imperial court" (OCEL). His prose satirical romance, The Satyricon*, is considered by some to contain passages which would more than justify PW's reaction: "Rather a lively author." Mrs. Ruyslaender* has a locket from her lover with an inscription from Petronius on it. Quite understandably, she would rather her husband didn't see it. [pj]

5167 Petrovitch -- owner of the stable over which Vanya and Nina Kropotky* live [SP 8]

5168 Petrovinsky, Mr. -- PW's assumed name while portraying a Bohemian* character. Confusion over the pronunciation of the name leads to his being called Stefan and Mr. Whiskey. [hp]

5169 Petrovna -- a "Russian type" actress recommended to Maurice Vavasour* by Isaac Sullivan's* talent agency [HHC 23]

5170 Pettican, Mrs. -- Norman Urquhart's* cook at his Woburn Square home [SP 1]

5171 Pettifer -- a member of the Egotists' Club* known to PW [cf]

5172 Pettigrew-Robinson, Mr. -- a house guest at Riddlesdale Lodge*. He is quite put out at having to be a party to accommodating Charles Parker*, especially when Parker asks him not to help in the investigation of Denis Cathcart's* death. He is further ruffled when called upon to testify at the Duke's trial in the House of Lords. Later, PW refers to him as "that infernal fellow" for having tried out some wine of dubious origin while trying to pass it off as a Lafite '76*. [CW 1/ [UD 6]

5173 Pettigrew-Robinson, Mrs. -- wife to the above, and also a guest at Riddlesdale Lodge*. She talks fast and has rather marked opinions on some subjects which sometimes causes others to work to avoid her. She particularly dislikes Lady Mary's "modern" ways, preferring the Duchess of Denver* for company, a preference that speaks volumes about her. She is not too fond of PW, either. [CW 1]

5174 Peugeot -- a long-established French automobile builder dating from well before 1900. It features small cars and racers, but has built other types as well. PW, in 1926, was well-advised to choose one for speed. [mt]

5175 Peveril Hotel -- a fictitious place, but, by association with Sir Walter Scott, DLS might have been thinking of the Ivanhoe Hotel on Bloomsbury St. which is still open. The "Peveril" reference is to Scott's novel, Peveril of the Peak, published in 1822. [UD 18]

5176 Pharmacopoeia -- the British Pharmacopoeia of the General Council of Medical Education and Registration, a standard master list of drugs, etc., is probably what Parker* has consulted. [BC 15]

5177 pheasant-eye narcissi -- the narcissus is a flower akin to the daffodil*, but is smaller and usually white. Both flowers' blossoms have the same general shape and they both grow from bulbs. Pheasant-eye is a descriptor for the bright center of the flower. [NT 3]

5178 Phelps, Miss Marjorie -- PW's Chelsea* artist friend and confidante. She is a sculptress and is quite talented. PW regards her work highly and is genuinely flattered when she shows him a figurine of himself that she had done. Their relationship seems quite genuine and open, but ends abruptly in any romantic sense when she realizes PW's feelings for HV. They remain friends, though. She is his "key" to the Bohemian life in London in SP. [BC 10/SP 8]

5179 phenacetin -- or acetophenetidin, a white, crystalline painkiller [HHC 5/MMA 8]

5180 Philistine -- a crass, materially oriented, prosaic person, often

without a sense of artistic or intellectual values [BC 17/MMA 18]

5181 Phillips -- a resident of Dumfries* who supposedly owned two of Matthew Gowan's* paintings which were to be returned to Gowan for an unspecified reason [FRH 8]

5182 Philliter, Nurse -- Agatha Dawson's* attendant who becomes engaged to Dr. Carr*. She is relieved of her duties after a dispute with Miss Whittaker*. [UD 4]

5183 philology -- in general, the study of literature and such related areas as linguistics (historical and comparative) and speech with the intent of helping illuminate cultural history [GN 7]

5184 Philpots, Dr. -- a friend of Mr. Crimplesham* who lives in Balham* where Crimplesham lost his pince-nez* [WB 5]

5185 Philpotts -- a WW I comrade of PW's [bc]

5186 Philpotts -- PW's Greek teacher, probably at Eton* [nf]

5187 Philpotts, Eden -- or Phillpotts, an English novelist (1862-1960), poet, dramatist, and short story writer who was born in India, but who spent most of his life in Devon. Of his works, the most notable are The Red Redmaynes and The Grey Room. Perhaps more notable was his encouragement and support for Agatha Christie in her early career. See also iron pineapple. [BH 13]

5188 Phoebe -- mythologically associated with the moon, Phoebe continues to cast Endymion* into perpetual sleep. She then comes to him every night and embraces him. Both Drayton and Keats** tell the story in poetic form. [GN 15]

5189 phoenix -- the mythological gold and red bird which, every 500 years, builds a funeral pyre on which it dies, a new bird arising from the ashes [GN 13]

5190 Phyllis -- one of the hopefuls in the office of talent agent Isaac Sullivan* [HHC 23]

5191 The Physiological Bases of the Conscience -- the latest book by Sir Julian Freke*. PW is interested in Freke's ideas, but his theology, or lack of it, bothers PW greatly. See Ch. 8 of WB for a list of Freke's other publications, all of which are as fictitious as he is. [WB 5]

5192 Picard, Jean-Marie -- Suzanne Legros'* fiancé. He was killed in WW I before their wedding. [NT 8]

5193 Piccadilly -- a major thoroughfare in London which runs from Hyde Park Corner* to Piccadilly Circus. PW lives at number 110A, across from Green Park*, when he is in town. His flat would be on the third floor by U. S. reckoning, on a site formerly occupied by an unidentified commercial enterprise. The name, Piccadilly, is derived from a sort of ruffled collar called "piccadils" or "piccadillies" made popular and sold there by Robert Baker in the 1500's. They often appear in paintings of Elizabethan court figures. [mt/WB 1/CW 8/UD 1/BC 4/FRH 8/SP 6/ HHC 6/GN 4/BH E1]

5194 Piccadilly Circus -- the London traffic circle where Piccadilly*, Haymarket, Regent Sts. and Shaftesbury Avenue all intersect. The center of the circle is adorned with a statue of Eros dedicated to the philanthropist, Lord Shaftesbury. [CW 11/FRH 9]

5195 Piccadilly merry-go-round -- an apt description of Piccadilly Circus, especially in heavy traffic [MMA 2]

5196 Piccadilly Tube station -- the Underground (subway) station located in central London at Piccadilly Circus [nf/SP 8]

5197 Pickering -- an artist on the staff at Pym's Publicity* [MMA 19]

5198 Pickled Gherkins -- a nickname for the Viscount St. George* [dh]

5199 Pickwick Papers -- a novel by Charles Dickens* published serially from 1836-37. Its immediate success made Dickens famous. The title refers to the fact that the book is structured as a series of letters and other papers that relate the activities of members of the Pickwick Club, named for the group's founder, Samuel Pickwick. The Club contains many of Dickens's best-known characters. [UD 16]

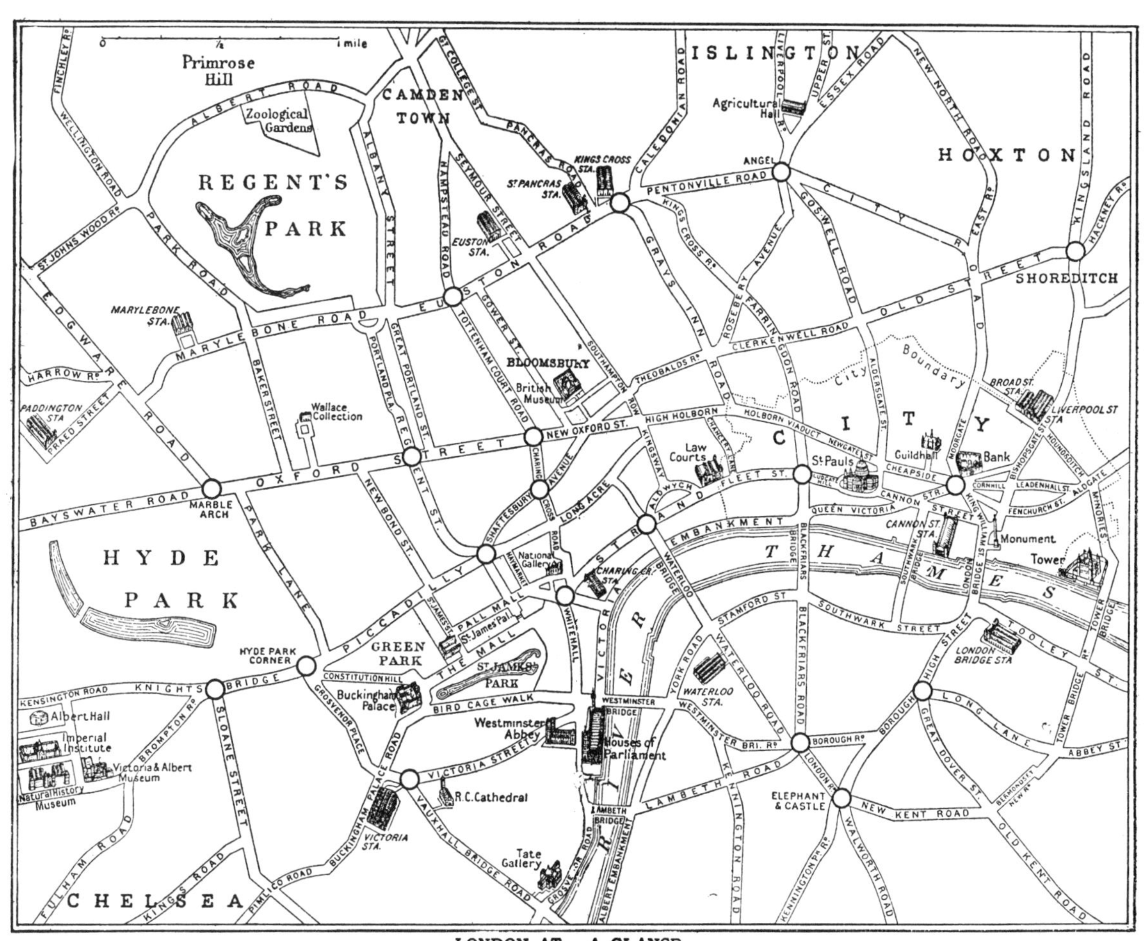

LONDON AT A GLANCE.
Showing the Principal Buildings, **Chief** Thoroughfares, Railway Termini, etc.
The Circles denote the intersections of the principal omnibus and traffic routes.

#5193

5200 Pickwickian sense -- any usually negative or derogatory word or phrase which, in their complete context, are not as negative as they seem at first. Thus, when PW says he has eloped with another man's wife, he is not speaking literally in that he has only helped her escape a horrid imprisonment and has done so as honorably as the circumstances permit. The reference is to an exchange between Mr. Pickwick and Mr. Blotton in Ch. 1 of Pickwick Papers*. [ie]

5201 Picture Exhibition -- see the second entry for Exhibition [FRH 19]

5202 Picture News -- a PW name used to refer to any one of London's tabloid newspapers. Bunter is somehow supposed to make himself look like a photographer from such a paper. [BC 5]

5203 picture-palace -- a movie theatre. The phrase derives from the practice of making the early theatres very ornate. [BH 4]

5204 pieces de conviction -- a French legal phrase meaning evidence or material to be used against the accused as one would consider the English phrase material evidence [BC 14]

5205 pièd à terre -- French for, "foot on the ground", a temporary lodging, a place to spend the night [CW 5]

5206 Pierre -- the nine-year-old son of Jean and Suzanne Legros** [NT 17]

5207 Pierrot -- a commedia dell' arte character popular also in mime. He is usually young, tall, and wears a loose white outfit with large buttons, white makeup, and a conical white cap. He is something of a lover and a clown, and usually pursues either Pierrette or Columbine*. All of these characters are popular for costume parties or masked balls. [qs]

5208 Pig and Whistle -- a fictitious pub in Stapley*, known to have been visited by William Grimethorpe*. It is also a fictitious pub in Great Pagford*. [CW 11/BH 7]

5209 pig-like -- from the phrase "to bleed like a stuck (i. e. butchered) pig". The reference is to draining the blood from the carcase of slaughtered animals. [GN 21]

5210 pigeon -- PW uses carrier pigeons as part of his system of communication with the real world while he is in disguise to penetrate The Society* [ab]

5211 pigeon [that's his] -- the word is used here to mean "his own concern" or "business" [nf]

5212 Piggin, Mr. -- landlord at the Fox-and-Hounds* in Crofton* [UD 11]

5213 Piggin, Mrs. -- wife of Mr. Piggin as above [UD 11]

5214 Piggott -- an otherwise unidentified resident of Paggleham* [BH 4]

5215 Piggott, Mr. -- the elder one is an upholsterer in Liverpool and the father of a medical student enrolled in Sir Julian Freke's* anatomy class. It is this younger Mr. Piggott that PW and Parker* question about Freke's anatomy classes. [WB 10]

5216 Piggott and Piggott -- of Liverpool, they are the upholsterers with which the elder Mr. Piggott* is connected [WB 10]

5217 pike staff -- the long wooden handle of a pike or early form of bayonet. It was used by foot soldiers and was convenient for helping to unhorse cavalry. To be as plain as one is to be easily seen. [UD 23]

5218 Pilate -- see wash our hands like Pilate [GN 17]

5219 Pilgrim's Progress -- by John Bunyan*; a copy was found in Squire Burdock's* library when PW investigated it. Part I recounts the adventures of Christian's trip to the Celestial City in dream-allegory form. Part II deals with Christian's wife and children and their trip to the Celestial City. [bc/WB 3/CW 4]

5220 pillar box -- a hollow pillar about five feet tall, erected in a public place, containing a letter box or receptacle for posting letters (OED); a mailbox [UD 4]

5221 pillboxes -- the old-fashioned drum-shaped paper boxes with card-

board lids made to hold pills. The U. S. version was more apt to be a rectangular box with a sliding drawer. Glass bottles have replaced them both. PW and Bunter find them useful for storing small bits of evidence. [WB 3]

5222 Pillington -- a fictitious community in the Pagford/Paggleham** area [BH 11]

5223 Pillington, Sir Charles -- Chief Constable for Hampshire who assists PW in his search for Mary Whittaker*. He is apparently fictitious. [UD 19]

5224 pilsener -- a light beer named for its place of origin in the vicinity of Pilsen, Czechoslovakia [MMA 4]

5225 Pimlico -- an area in central London on the North side of the Thames in the vicinity of Vauxhall Bridge. It is adjacent to Westminster*. Miss Climpson* has a flat there on St. George's Square*. [hp/UD 3]

5226 Pimlico Pet -- as Pimlico was not one of the choicer London suburbs, the Misses Parton and Rossiter** are being somewhat derisive. The name is meant to suggest a playboy dandy, a phoney swell. [MMA 2]

5227 pince-nez -- eyeglasses which clamp on to the bridge of the wearer's nose, the nose-piece of the glasses being a spring. They have no bows to hook over the ears, but do have some sort of safety cord to catch them if they should fall off. The corpse in Mr. Thipps's* bathtub is wearing a rather ornate pair, but they are an afterthought. Mr. Murbles* owns and uses a pair regularly, as does the Rev. Mr. Boyes. [ie/WB 1/CW 10/SP 6]

5228 Pinchley, Mr. -- a cricket-playing member of the staff at Pym's Publicity* who is selected for the scratch team chosen to play against Brotherhood's* [MMA 10]

5229 Pincian Gardens -- the famous public gardens in the North of Rome near the Piazza di Spagna, the Spanish Steps, and the garden of the Villa Borghese. The hotel in question is probably the Parco Dei Principi. [GN 11]

5230 pineal -- the body or gland at the back of the base of the brain [BC 16]

5231 pineapple -- see iron pineapple [BH 13]

5232 Pinker, P. C. -- one of the constables who had the beat outside PW's Audley Square* home prior to P. C. Burt* [hp]

5233 Pink Sisket -- a trout fly invented by PW expressly for the purpose of trapping a nonangler in a lie [ss]

5234 Pink 'Un -- a nickname for England's Sporting Times, a newspaper so named because of the pink paper on which it is printed. Its appearance in church would understandably raise the more conservative eyebrows. [bc]

5235 Pinmore -- a stop on the rail line between Girvan* and Stranraer* [FRH 5]

5236 pious pelican of Corpus -- a reference to the heraldic crest of Corpus Christi College, Oxford, a pelican with a bowed head from the legend that it piously took blood from its breast to feed its young [GN 13]

5237 Pinwherry -- a stop on the rail line between Girvan* and Stranraer* [FRH 5]

5238 pip -- something that annoys or irritates; a vexation [MMA 2]

5239 pipe-clay -- see white linen and pipe-clay [GN 14]

5240 pipemma -- or pip emma. PW's dentist is using the WW I phonetic alphabet for the letters "P" and "M" for post meridiem, the correct form to use when in conjunction with a specific hour. [te]

5241 Piper -- a WW I comrade of PW's [bc]

5242 Piper -- the Bellona Club's* hall porter [BC 5]

5243 Piper Parritch -- the fictitious canned porridge being readied for market by Peabody's* [MMA 3]

5244 pippin -- an apple, often referring to a high quality dessert apple, usually yellow-green with red markings. Colloquially, someone or something that is highly admired. In

the reference to Miss Clara Whittaker*, both meanings apply figuratively. [UD 12]

5245 piscina -- a basin with a drain, usually found in a sacristy, set aside for emptying the water used in washing sacred vessels [bc/NT 2]

5246 pitch -- see cricket [MMA 18/ GN 17]

5247 pituitary -- the complex gland attached by a stalk to the base of the brain. It controls a whole range of bodily functions in humans including growth, the production of milk, and the rate of excretion by the kidneys. [BC 16]

5248 *pius* -- Latin for, "pious"; respectful of one's parents or of God [GN 17]

5249 *Placet* -- see *Placetne, magistra?* [GN 23]

5250 *Placetne, magistra?* -- Latin for, "Does it please you, mistress?" without expecting the answer to be either yes or no. PW is addressing HV in formal, academic Latin. The verb *placeo* was used in decrees from the Roman Senate as in, "It pleases the people and the Senate of Rome . . . ." "*Magistra*" is the feminine equivalent of master, as in Master of Arts. As Oxford degrees are written in Latin, the gender question is important. PW's proposal asks HV to forsake the security of Oxford for the emotionally more dangerous life in marriage. Her answer, "*Placet*", means, "It pleases me." See also no hand plucked . . . . [GN 23]

5251 "A plague on both your houses" -- the line is Mercutio's just before he dies in *Romeo and Juliet*, III, i, 112 [FRH 1]

5252 plaice -- a large European flatfish [UD 17]

5253 plain -- changes of a hunting nature that take a bell only from a given position to a position next to it as in: 1 2 4 3 6 5
1 2 3 4 5 6
Such a process will produce twice as many changes as there are bells. [NT 9]

5254 planchette -- a pointer device used with a Ouija board*. It may be in either of two common forms: one is a heart-shaped piece of wood or plastic with little wheels (casters) at the broad end and a pencil at the pointed end with which to write the spirit-induced messages. Miss Climpson* and Nurse Booth* use that variety. The second type is the same shape, but has three padded feet and is moved to point out the messages on the board.

5255 Planck's constant -- German physicist Max Karl E. L. Planck's 1901 contribution to modern physics is his introduction to quantum mechanics of the constant "h" which equals 6.62 X 10^{-34} erg seconds. The constant explains how the radiant energy in the cavity of a body has a distribution of frequency that is a function of the temperature of that body. His work led to the conclusion that energy exists in discrete *quanta*, a radical departure from previous thought in physics. [GN 2]

5256 Plant, Coreggio -- the murder victim in "Man With No Face" and an employee of the publicity firm of Crichton, Ltd.* of Holborn* [nf]

5257 plastic surgery -- to alter the appearance of any part of the body by surgically adding to, deleting from, or rearranging the skin, musculature, fatty tissues, or skeletal structure either for reconstructive or cosmetic purposes. While it is possible to create new fingerprints artificially through surgery, it is difficult and often not permanent. R. Austin Freeman, the author who created Dr. Thorndyke, even managed to creat temporary artificial fingerprints to prove that it could be done. Police agencies around the world have not been pleased with either accomplishment. [ab]

5258 plate [enlarge them on] -- a photographic plate, probably a glass one coated with light-sensitive chemicals in a gelatinous suspension, can be exposed in such a way as to create an enlargement of an object by taking a close-up picture of it [WB 2]

5259 platinum -- a heavy, precious, metallic element. It does not corrode, does conduct electricity, and is malleable. More precious than gold, it is used widely in jewelry. When refined and polished, it resembles sil-

ver. [CW 5]

5260 "The Plattner Experiment" -- the reference is to H. G. Wells's short story, but the correct title is "The Plattner Story" [im]

5261 Plato -- the famous Greek philosopher (ca. 427-347 B. C.) and student of Socrates. It is through Plato's dialogues that we have any knowledge of his great teacher in any detail as Socrates never wrote down any of his conversations. Plato's greatest writings are probably The Republic, The Apology, and The Symposium. [GN 17/BH 13]

5262 platonic archetypes, dim -- DLS is alluding to Plato's* "Allegory of the Cave" from Book VII of The Republic which deals with such concepts as truth and reality. The concept of an archetype is from the ancient Greek and is basic to the works of Plato. [MMA 11]

5263 plaudite -- see conjuring banter [ie]

5264 Plautus -- Titus Maccus (or Maccius) Plautus (254-184 B. C.) who, with Seneca, is considered one of Rome's two greatest playwrights, but only twenty or his 130 plays are known to have survived. Fortunately, all of them are known to be authentic works of his. Those plays known are adaptations of earlier Greek works from writers such as Menander. Plautus is considered the creator of Miles Gloriosus, the braggart soldier, in his play of that name. Plautus has had extensive influence on English drama as Shakespeare's A Comedy of Errors and Dryden's Amphitryon are only two of the more famous reworkings of Plautus's material. Ben Jonson made extensive use of Plautus's plots and devices.

5265 Players -- a popular brand of cigarette in England, it is available throughout much of North America as well [BH 10]

5266 Playfair -- a cipher invented by Charles Wheatstone in 1853-4. The cipher's name, Playfair, is a reference to Lyon Playfair, 1st Baron Playfair of St. Andrews, Wheatstone's friend, who did much to make Wheatstone's cipher known. It is the first true digraphic cipher and operates as outlined in HHC. For further information, read David Kahn's The Codebreakers, Macmillan, 1967, pp. 198ff. [HHC 26]

5267 Playfair, James -- a guest at Sir Charles Deverill's* party whose costume was meant to represent badminton*. He is one of the targets of Charmian Grayle's obvious flirting. [qs]

5268 plenipotentiary -- a diplomat invested with the full power to transact any business to which he has been assigned [WB 5]

5269 "plenteously bringing out good works . . ." -- the passage is "Stir up, we beseech thee, O Lord, the wills of thy faithful people; that they, plenteously bringing forth the fruit of thy good works, may of thee be plenteously rewarded." It is found in The Book of Common Prayer* for the 25th Sunday after Trinity, near the end of Pentecost* and the end of the church year. Following Pentecost would be the first Sunday in Advent, thus starting the Christmas season and the church year. [SP 6]

5270 plinth -- a stone support. Often carved for decorative purposes, this one is not. [GN 1]

5271 Ploffsky Gang -- the anarchist conspirators unmasked by PW. The case was not recorded and is only mentioned here in passing. [aq]

5272 plough in Schools -- to fail the Schools* examinations [GN 7]

5273 ploughman -- or plowman, the person who guides the team and directs the plow; generically, a farm worker [HHC 22]

5274 Pluck -- see Gammy Pluck [NT 14]

5275 plum pudding -- the traditional dessert for an English Christmas dinner. It is a mixture of suet, flour, spices, brandy, bread crumbs, sugar, eggs, milk, and dried or candied fruits. The mixture is steamed for many hours and is then served under flaming brandy. [np/SP 12/NT 9]

5276 Plumbers' and Glaziers' Ball -- a social event, probably annual, sponsored jointly by the guilds (unions) stated. It is probably fictitious. [WB 6]

5277 Plumer -- an assistant to Mr. Endicott* before Endicott retired. The name is derived from one who deals in plumes or feathers. [HHC 6]

5278 plummet -- a plumb line or plumb bob, something used to measure a depth or to keep a straight vertical line [NT 6]

5279 Plunkett -- the Frobisher-Pym's* gardener and handyman. He is given to "attacks" of various sorts related to his advanced age. He is the first to report seeing the "death coach". His wife is Sarah; his children are Alf and Elsie. [bc]

5280 Plunkett, Alf -- see 5279 [bc]

5281 Plunkett, Elsie -- see 5279 [bc]

5282 Plunkett, Sarah -- see 5279 [bc]

5283 plus-fours -- knickerbockers four inches longer in the length of material, thus enabling them to overhang the knee fastener. Fashionable in the 1920's and 30's for golf, they are regaining some popularity among golfers today. [FRH 7/HHC 1]

5284 Pluto, that new planet -- discovered by Clyde W. Tombaugh in 1930, Pluto is the ninth and most recently discovered planet in the solar system. Its mean distance from the sun is 3670 million miles, and it requires 248 years to orbit the sun once. [np]

5285 Plymouth Brethren -- a religious group that developed in about 1830 in Plymouth, England. They believe in Christ, but have no creed or official organization of the clergy. [BH 11]

5286 pocket propelling pencil -- see propelling pencil [MMA 7]

5287 Poe -- Edgar Allan Poe (1809-49), American poet, critic, essayist, and short story writer. He is credited with being the "Father of the Detective Story" and may have a strong claim at a similar title for science fiction as well. He created the detective C. Auguste Dupin who appears in several of his better stories. The classic tales of detection are: "The Murders in the Rue Morgue", 1841; "The Mystery of Marie Rôget", 1842; "The Gold Bug", 1843; "The Purloined Letter", 1844; and "Thou Art the Man", 1844. In those five stories Poe laid down guidelines for almost every sort of detective-mystery-thriller fiction, the only additions of significance being R. Austin Freeman's "inverted" story where we read about the crime and then its detection, and Agatha Christie's masterpiece, The Murder of Roger Ackroyd. [FRH 22/NT 17]

5288 poet ungrammatically observes -- see There, as the poet . . . . [BH 9]

5289 Poggleton-on-the-Marsh -- a fictitious place invented by PW for the purpose of filling out an explanation he presents to Lady Swaffham* [WB 7]

5290 pogrom -- an organized massacre of helpless people from the Russian word describing action taken against the Jews. PW's description of the work he and Miss Climpson* are doing against moneylenders and other unscrupulous types hardly qualifies as a pogrom. [UD 3]

5291 Pogson's farm -- Major Lumsden* had to go there to explain away rumors of a ghost [bc]

5292 point [chance to] -- see cricket [MMA 18]

5293 Point, Jack -- the strolling jester in Gilbert and Sullivan's* The Yeomen of the Guard. He is known for his puns, quips, etc. [SP 5]

5294 point-device -- too meticulous, with too much attention to detail; an archaic term [ab/BC 5]

5295 point-duty -- traffic control at an intersection [HHC 2]

5296 pointed arcading -- a series of interconnected arches, the tops of which come to a point as opposed to being rounded [NT 2]

5297 Pointer and Winken -- the fictitious law firm that bought out Mr. Probyn's* offices in Croftover Magna* [UD 12]

5298 pointing -- see Maunder and Garrett [BH 5]

5299 poker -- any of hundreds of variations of this card game, popular around the world. PW plays it in "Practical Joker". The hands, in straight poker, rank: 1) straight flush, five cards in sequence in the same suit; 2) four of a kind; 3) full

house, three or a kind and a pair; 4) flush, any five cards of the same suit; 5) straight, any five cards in sequence if they are not of the same suit; 6) three of a kind; 7) two pairs; 8) one pair; 9) high card. If wild cards are used, five of a kind beats a straight flush. [pj/MMA 14]

5300 Pol Roger, 1926 -- Pol Roger is one of the great champagne houses of Epernay, France. It is an excellent champagne, but is not, in some marketing theories, of the same quality as Dom Perignon from Moët et Chandon, also of Epernay, or of Taittinger's Comtes de Champagne from Reims, the other major champagne production center. The date refers to the vintage. As with most white wines, champagnes are best when drunk young as they do not age all that well. [hp]

5301 Police Ranks -- starting at the bottom and working up, they are:
1. Police Constable (P. C.) or Detective Constable
2. Sergeant or Detective Sergeant
3. Inspector or Detective Inspector
4. Chief Inspector or Detective Chief Inspector
5. Superintendent or Detective Superintendent
6. Chief Superintendent or Detective Chief Superintendent

Following this, if an officer is in the London Metropolitan Police (Scotland Yard), the rank proceeds to Deputy Assistant Commissioner (now Commander), Assistant Commissioner, Deputy Commissioner, and Commissioner.

In the English and Welsh County Police Forces, the ranks following the above listing are: Assistant Chief Constable, Deputy Chief Constable, and Chief Constable.

The decision as to whether an officer proceeds through the regular ranks or through the detective ranks depends on tests and aptitude. The detective ranks supply the famous C. I. D.*, the Criminal Investigation Department. Charles Parker* is variously listed as Inspector, Detective Inspector, and as Chief Inspector. Such variety is possible in that the system has a built-in preference for movement back and forth among the ranks to allow the officers to acquire experience and versatility. Such movement can enhance promotion chances.

5302 Police Surgeon -- a doctor attached to and working with a specific police group as with a county constabulary. It would be his responsibility to investigate any situation involving injury or death that also required police investigation. He would examine the corpse _in situ_, pronounce it dead, and cooperate with the court of inquest when it is necessary to convene one. [UD 3/BH 7]

5303 Policeman's Lot -- this chapter heading title refers to Gilbert and Sullivan's opera, _The Pirates of Penzance_, and a song from _Act II_:

"When a felon's not engaged in his employment--
Or maturing his felonious little plans--
His capacity for innocent enjoyment--
Is just as great as any honest man's--
Our feelings we with difficulty smother--
When constabulary duty's to be done--
Ah, take one consideration with another--
A policeman's lot is not a happy one."

There is an equally apt second verse. [BH 11]

5304 polished morocco -- a fine leather made from sumac tanned goatskin and highly prized by book binders and book lovers for its beauty and durability. Being polished simply imparts a smooth, glossy finish as opposed to a rougher, natural one. [WB 4]

5305 poll -- either the crown of a hat or the top of the head and nape of the neck considered together [MMA 4]

5306 Pollock -- a Wilvercombe fishing family [HHC 10]

5307 Pollock, Esdras -- the ornery old patriarch of the fishing family of that name that lives near Wilvercombe*. His namesake in the Apocrypha recorded angelic visions and revelations, something that this fisherman is not likely to do even if he had seen all the angels and the other wonderful things. [HHC 10]

5308 Pollock, Granpa -- probably Esdras Pollock* [HHC 25]

5309 Pollock, Mrs. -- a younger member of one of Wilvercombe's* extended fishing families [HHC 25]

5310 Pollock, Mrs. -- probably Esdras Pollock's* wife [HHC 25]

5311 Polly -- see Wimsey, Mary [CW 2/ MMA 5]

5312 Polly -- Ashton, daughter of Luke and Maria Ashton of Fenchurch St. Paul**. It is she who tells of Rosie Thoday's* tale of ghosts in the churchyard. [NT 6]

5313 Polly -- the woman, not further identified, who is staying with Nobby Cranton* as his nurse [NT 10]

5314 Polly -- see Mason, Polly [BH 10]

5315 Polly Flinders -- PW's alert and able mount, she has, nevertheless, a mind of her own and refuses to stop at Dead Man's Post*. She is owned by Mr. Frobisher-Pym*. [bc]

5316 polo -- an ancient ball game played from horseback. The word derives from the Tibetan word pulu, meaning ball, but the game probably originated in the Middle East at about the beginning of the Christian era. The game is played by two teams of four mounted men each who use a mallet to hit a ball into the opponent's net. The team with the most points wins. [qs/GN 10]

5317 poltergeist -- a noisy, mischievous, and often destructive ghost or spirit [SP 16/GN 4]

5318 poluphloisboio thalasses -- see conjuring banter [ie]

5319 Polwhistle, Mr. -- the garage owner and mechanic in Darley* who did repair work for Haviland Martin* [HHC 12]

5320 Polynesian -- an inhabitant of the isles of Polynesia in the central South Pacific [UD 13]

5321 Pomfret, Giles -- a guest at the Christmastime party hosted by Sir Charles Deverill*. Pomfret is notable in that he chose as his costume a billiard table with a green lampshade as a hat. He was at once both conspicuous and uncomfortable. [qs]

5322 Pomfret, Reggie -- "that fair-faced goop at Queen's" who figures too prominently in the social life at Shrewsbury College*. He develops an ill-considered crush on HV and tries to take out his frustrations on PW who helps him finally to settle down. [GN 7]

5323 Pommery -- fully Pommery & Greno, one of the great French champagnes of Reims, in the extreme North of the central champagne area [SP 19]

5324 pommes Byron -- baked potatoes from which the flesh has been removed and fried in butter and salt and pepper. The flesh is replaced and baked with a topping of heavy cream and Parmesan cheese. [BC 21]

5325 Pommerais, Edmund de la -- a Parisian physician who, in the 1860's, murdered both his mother-in-law and his former mistress, Madame de Pauw, solely for profit. It is the ex-mistress, perhaps, who is one of history's more compliant victims. Induced by de la Pommerais to feign an illness to collect on an insurance settlement, she wrote a letter outlining her faked ills. He then killed her with an overdose of digitalis (see digitalin). He attempted, however, to claim the insurance money too precipitately, thereby arousing suspicion. He was guillotined. [WB 10]

5326 Pond, Mr. -- the rather old-fashioned but thoroughly efficient and honorable chief clerk in Norman Urquhart's* law office [SP 13]

5327 Pongo[celli] -- the control* contacted after Harry* during the first séance conducted by Miss Climpson*. He was an Italian Renaissance acrobat of questionable morality who redeemed himself by tending an abandoned child during the Great Plague in Florence (ca. 1348). He died as a result of his act of mercy as he contracted the plague himself. [SP 17]

5328 ponies -- a pony is British slang for £25, a rather considerable sum in 1927--almost $100 U. S. in the money of the day. Given that $1000 was not an unreasonable annual salary, it is no surprise that Parker* hesitated to bet with PW. [dh/UD 6]

5329 Pontius Pilate -- the most famous Procurator of Judea who found his troubles with the Jews over the fate of Jesus to be his most perplexing case [BC 18]

5330 pony trap -- a light, two-wheeled carriage pulled by a pony [cb]

5331 "A poor soul sat sighing" -- a song sung by Desdemona in Othello, IV, iii, 41ff. The song is not original with Shakespeare, but he makes it fit the play by having the forsaken lover a woman--it is a man in other extant versions. The ballad was apparently a popular one, well known to Shakespeare's audiences. [MMA 19]

5332 Popcorn St. -- a fictitious street in the western London suburb of Kensington* [HHC 20]

5333 Pope -- PW met with Pius XI, pontiff from 1922 to 1939. See also Bishop of Rome. [BH P]

5334 Pope is infallible -- see infallibility [BC 16]

5335 Pope -- Alexander Pope (1688-1744) is a famous English poet of great metrical skill. Among his famous works are "An Essay on Criticism", "The Rape of the Lock", and his translations of Homer's The Iliad and The Odyssey. His work brought him financial security, a remarkable thing for a poet in almost any age. His work is noted for its extensive use of the heroic couplet, two lines of iambic pentameter (decasyllabics), rhymed, and having the meaning of the first line completed in the second. His work is generally either hated or loved with little emotion in between, but it is widely quoted for its wit by both its supporters and its detractors. [CW 9/BH 9]

5336 Pope, Wilberforce -- a plump, bald man in his thirties whose greed and ignorance convince PW that he's after the Cosmographia Universalis* for more than sentimental reasons [dh]

5337 Poperinghe -- a town in Belgium eight miles West of Ypres*. During WW I it was a British communication and leave center. PW, having fought not far from there, would certainly have known the town. Being close to the front, the burning stables reference is probably PW's memory of the result of a stray shell or of one of the German bombing raids. [CW 11]

5338 Popham -- a WW I comrade of PW's who "went off his rocker" (shell shock*?) and was sent home by PW. At the time of the story he is living in Lincolnshire*. [bc]

5339 popish -- a detracting term for anything Roman Catholic used by those who do not practice that faith [SP 17/NT 2]

5340 Popoffsky blighters -- Henry Weldon's* name for Russians or other East Europeans. The appellation is intended to be funny. [HHC 12]

5341 Poppaea -- Poppaea Sabina, wife of the future emperor Otho. She was claimed by Nero as his second wife when his first, Octavia, died. Nero murdered his mother, Agrippina, for Poppaea's sake. She, in turn, supposedly died (A. D. 65) from a kick by Nero. [SP 17]

5342 Poppelhinkin, Mrs. J. -- identified only as the president of the fictitious League for the Encouragement of Matrimonial Fitness* [GN 3]

5343 porcelain fillings -- as used here the term suggest crowns rather than fillings. Fused porcelain is a layer of porcelain bonded to a metal crown underneath. "Cast" porcelain is a misnomer technically, but reflects the process whereby the crown is made. An impression of the tooth is taken, lined with metal foil, and a porcelain crown is "cast" in the mold. The impression medium and foil are removed, leaving a crown to be bonded to the roots of the tooth. It might be superficially difficult to tell them apart, but a forensic odontologist with adequate X-ray equipment could not be fooled. [te]

5344 Porchester, Mrs. -- an acquaintance of the Dowager Duchess of Denver's* [WB 3]

5345 porcupines -- the child means concubines. The two are equally dangerous even if the danger is of different orders, so the child's confusion is understandable. Solomon is supposed to have had 300 concubines. [UD 3]

5346 Porlock -- a servant in the London home of the Duke of Denver* [MMA 11]

5347 port -- according to the Anglo-Portuguese Treaty of 1916, it is, "A fortified wine produced in the delimited Douro region and exported through the Bar of Oporto." Nothing else may be sold in England or the U. S. as Port unless it carries some qualifier such

New York State Port, etc. Fortified in the Treaty means to add brandy to the wine before all the sugar is fermented out. Among the more famous brand names are Warre's, Cockburn's, Sandeman's, Harvey's, and Croft. [WB 9/passim]

5348 Port Meadow -- a pasture, often flooded by the Thames, to the West and North of Oxford. It is owned by the Freemen of Oxford and is a rather desolate place. [GN 19]

5349 Port Patrick -- or Portpatrick, a coastal town about thirty-five miles West of Gatehouse-of-Fleet* on the North Channel [FRH 2]

5350 Porter, Mr. -- Viscount St. George's* history teacher at Mr. Bultridge's* school [dh]

5351 porter's lodge -- the porter's office at the main entrance to some place the admission to which is restricted. In Oxford colleges the porter is something of a sentry, handyman, and confidant for the members of that college. [GN 1]

5352 Portia's caskets -- the reference is to The Merchant of Venice in which the heroine, Portia, places her portrait in one of three caskets. One is gold, one silver, and one lead. The process of choosing occupies the end of Act II and the beginning of Act III of the play. Portia's first suitors choose wrongly. Bassanio, who loves her, chooses correctly and they are wed. [FRH 25]

5353 Portland Place -- the major North-South street that connects Park Crescent on the South side of Regent's Park* with Langham Place and thence to Regent St.* The BBC's Broadcasting House is located on Portland Place. [BH 16]

5354 Portman Square -- a smart residential area just North of Oxford St. and between Baker and Gloucester Sts. in the West End*. It is the location of the elder Mr. Levy's and of Lady Dormer's* homes. [WB 6/BC 2]

5355 portmanteau -- a large leather suitcase that opens into two compartments [WB 3/NT 2]

5356 "The portrait of a blinking idiot" -- HV quotes from The Merchant of Venice, II, ix, 54. The line is the Prince of Arragon's when he opens the silver casket and does not find Portia's portrait. [GN 10]

5357 Portsmouth -- the center of British Navy activity; shipping and naval industry have been located there for centuries, but it dates as a royal dockyard and as England's chief naval port since the days of Henry VIII. The city is East of Southampton on the Solent. [UD 23]

5358 posada -- Spanish for an inn or a hotel [ie]

5359 The Position of Women in the Modern State -- a book, fictitious, by Miss Barton* [GN 5]

5360 Positivists -- followers of the philosophy of the Frenchman Auguste Comte (1798-1857). Positivism excludes metaphysics and revealed religion and focuses attention on a religion of humanity based on sociological ethics and history. Comte outlines his principles in his Cours de Philosophie Positive (1830-42). [GN 2]

5361 post occasio calva -- Latin for, "opportunity's bald behind". The expression relates to references in Marlowe and Dekker, but the former's The Jew of Malta, V, ii, has, "Begin, betimes; Occasion's bald behind; Slip not thine opportunity." The meaning being that one needs to act when opportunity presents itself because to wait is to deny one's self the chance to grasp that opportunity. When one is faced with a bald opportunity, there is nothing left to grasp, one is too late. [GN 4]

5362 Post Office -- the English Post Office system runs the mails and a banking service for small savers among other services. It has been, since 1969, a semi-independent business operation with only some governmental control. Prior to that it was fully controlled by the government as a governmental service. [GN 10]

5363 post-office near Liverpool Street -- the office in question is on the corner of South Place and Dominion St., about three blocks West of the Liverpool St. station [NT 9]

5364 poste restante -- general delivery service; a post office address

from which the recipient has to collect the mail in person [CW 2/NT 7]

5365 postern -- a private rear gate [GN 7]

5366 Postlethwaite, Mr. -- the gentleman accosted by Major Fentiman* who mistook him for the mysterious Mr. Oliver*. The incident takes place in Southampton*. [BC 11]

5367 potato scones -- a small cake made of flour, baking soda, cream of tartar, butter or bacon fat, mashed potatoes, salt, and milk [FRH 3]

5368 pothooks -- a reference to the various symbols and markings for contractions used in old Latin texts. Pothooks are the heavy metal hooks from which pots are hung in large kitchen work areas. The analogy rests on the fact that the markings do resemble the hooks, and look less like an apostrophe (') than a cedilla (¸). In GN the reference is to Miss Lydgate's* new method of scansion* for English poetry which uses alphabets and odd little marks (the pothooks). The reference in BH does mean the hooks from which the pots are hung, the only place in the canon where the term is so used. [dh/GN 13/BH 8]

5369 potmen -- waiters in a pub or bar [CW 11]

5370 potted meats -- finely ground meats used as a spread on crackers or bread. A pâté is a refined version of a potted meat. [MMA 11]

5371 potter -- see ceremonial of potter [BH 4]

5372 Potter's Lode -- DLS's name for Popham's Eau, a drain or canal named for Sir John Popham, Lord Chief Justice under James I*. It cuts off the bend through Upwell of the Nene River's old bed. Potter's Lode does the same thing for the fictitious River Wale in Fenchurch St. Paul*. [NT 2]

5373 Potter's Lode Bank -- the dyke* marking the course of Potter's Lode* [NT 19]

5374 Potts -- the innkeeper at the Feathers* [sf]

5375 Potts fracture -- PW wonders if Robert Ferguson's* broken kneecap is an example of one. It is not. A Potts fracture involves the lower part of the fibula, the smaller and outer of the lower leg bones, at a point just above the ankle. It will also include damage to the larger bone, the tibia, to the extent of bone chipping or ligament damage. The fracture was named for Percival Potts, a British surgeon of the 18th C. [ss]

5376 Potts, Bert -- the second of the three Potts boys, age 16. He is Ginger's* brother. [MMA 7]

5377 Potts, Ginger Joe -- one of the office errand boys at Pym's Publicity*. He is fourteen and a half, reads detective fiction voraciously, and proves to be an able "Watson" for PW during his investigations at the agency. His full name is Joseph L. Potts. [MMA 7]

5378 Potts, Wally -- the eldest of the three Potts boys, he is a police constable [MMA 7]

5379 pouffe -- a very soft, stuffed piece of furniture rather Moorish in appearance; same as a humpty* [BC 7/GN 7]

5380 poulet en casserole -- French for, "chicken casserole", an easy dish to prepare and very tasty [SP 1]

5381 Poultry News -- there is one, but it is in Pakistan. No such publication in England could be located, but DLS may have had in mind either of the periodicals Poultry or Poultry World. [UD 6]

5382 pour porter bonheur -- French for, "for bringing good luck" [CW 5]

5383 pour s'amuser -- French for, "for one's amusement" [HHC 7]

5384 pour ses beaux yeax', a-t'il ajouté en riant . . . -- French for, "for her beautiful eyes, he added, laughing. Ah, sir, he is a saint, a veritable saint." Some editions spell riant incorrectly as raint. [WB 11]

5385 pouter-pigeon -- a domestic pigeon capable of inflating its chest for courting rituals, fights, etc. [FRH 26/GN 13]

5386 power of attorney -- a document granting certain limited rights for someone to act in one's behalf if incapacitated or if away from home for

an extended period of time. Such rights might include endorsing checks or conducting other minor legal or business affairs. [UD 10/SP 14]

5387 "The power of perpetuating our property . . ." -- see Reflections on the Revolution in France [UD 12]

5388 Practical Astrology -- a book by astrologer John Middleton, an octavo volume and his only known work. DLS says it was published in 1678, but the Stationer's Office lists it as having been published in 1679. The discrepancy could be between the printing and registering dates. [dh]

5389 "Praise Him in the cymbals" -- this line and those that follow are from Psalm 150, the last of the Psalms, as presented in The Book of Common Prayer. It is only slightly different in the KJV. [NT 2]

5390 "Praise Him upon the well-tuned cymbals" -- see item 5389 [NT 2]

5391 praise him with faint damns -- PW reverses Alexander Pope's* line in the "Epistle to Dr. Arbuthnot", line 201:

"Damn with faint praise, assent with civil leer
And, without sneering, teach the rest to sneer . . . ."

[MMA 3]

5392 Praslin, Duc de -- the reference is to the fascinating crime of passion that rocked Paris and all of France in August of 1847 when M. le Duc viciously and clumsily murdered his wife, Fanny. The duc, Charles Louis-Theobald, was a weak and timid man who had been bullied by his wife, a woman quite a bit larger than himself. Henriette Deluzy-Desports, the governess, was the third angle in the triangle. A combination of the wife's bullying, the governess's bewitching beauty, and the duc's weaknesses led to the sordid crime. He died on August 24, 1847, the day of his wife's funeral, six days after her murder and six days after he had taken the arsenic that eventually killed him. There seems to be no question of murder in his case as suicide was the only option open to him other than the guillotine. The case is strikingly similar to that of Crippen* and LeNeve not many years later. [SP 5]

5393 Pratt, Young Wally [Walter] -- one of the bell-ringers at Fenchurch St. Paul*, he is the least experienced and least assured of the group as he has not yet learned to concentrate as is required of change-ringers. He pulls the number three bell, John*. [NT 1]

5394 Prayer-book -- the marriage ceremony in The Book of Common Prayer. It contains the word "obey" for the bride to say which has long been a point of contention. The 1928 Prayer Book does not have "obey". [BH P]

5395 Prayer of Consecration -- in the Eucharist, the long prayer to consecrate the Host prior to communion [UD 22]

5396 pre-Raphaelite -- the Pre-Raphaelite Brotherhood was formed in 1850 with the goal of returning to the techniques of art and literature as they theorized them to have existed before the time of Raphael (Raffaello Sanzio or Santi, 1483-1520, of Urbino, Italy), an artist of great fame who is noted for his madonnas. The Brotherhood consisted of William Holman Hunt, John Everett Millais, James Collinson, Dante Gabriel Rossetti, William Michael Rossetti, Thomas Woolner, and Frederick George Stephens. Several others joined or became hangers-on as the group gained importance and notoriety. [FRH 6]

5397 pré-sale -- young sheep fattened in meadows by the sea. The seaside pasturage adds a particularly prized flavor to the meat. The phrase is French for, "pre-salted". [mt]

5398 Precentor -- a high-ranking cleric just below the Dean of a cathedral; now, however, a minor canon among whom he usually takes precedence [WB 7]

5399 précis -- a short summary of some longer work. Technically, it should use the longer work's words and style and should not be more than one-quarter to one-third the length of the original. [SP 14]

5400 Prefect of Police for the Quartier -- the Chief of Police for one of Paris's administrative districts [CW 5]

5401 premières -- French for, "first

class" passenger coaches [mt]

5402 Prendergast, Arthur -- the dentist who attempts to arrange for his own disappearance in a clever manner, but he is not clever enough [te]

5403 Prendergast, Mrs. -- the somewhat possessive and jealous wife of the dentist above [te]

5404 present [brought his weapon to the] -- Bunter is holding the fireplace poker in the military "present arms" position as if he were saluting an inspecting officer [t]

5405 Presbyter, John -- or Prester John, the legendary Christian king of the Middle Ages who is usually associated with Ethiopia or Abyssinia [NT 4]

5406 Presbyterian -- a follower of one of the churches that evolved from Calvinism; the national church of Scotland [GN 2]

5407 presbytery -- another word for rectory or parsonage; a minister's residence [ie]

5408 Prescott, Lavinia -- a friend of George Comphrey's* who is not otherwise identified [np]

5409 Preservatives in Food (Restrictions) Act -- a 1926 Act that defined what preservatives could be used in what foods and to what extent [MMA 1]

5410 Preston -- Miss Climpson's* wait was at the Preston in Lancashire on the Ribble River North of Liverpool [SP 16]

5411 Preston, Sir Lucius, the R. A. -- an artist and uncle to the younger O'Halloran*. The "R. A." stands for the Royal Academy of Arts, founded in 1786 under the patronage of George III. Its membership is limited to forty, membership becoming available only when one of the forty dies. [hp]

5412 Press Association Exchange Telegraph -- established in 1868 mostly as a stock exchange ticker with news items, it now also functions as a domestic news agency that features factual news and features while retaining its monopoly on news from the floor of the Stock Exchange. Every news bulletin broadcast in the 1920's and 30's was prefaced by the "Copyright" heading found at the beginning of this chapter. [CW 15]

5413 press-gang -- gangs of roving naval recruiters under the command of an officer. They did not bother to ask first if the person being recruited had any desire to be considered for the honor. [UD 13]

5414 pretty quick on the drop -- a reference to death by hanging. The hangman determines the "drop", the distance the body needs to fall to make death as close to instantaneous as is possible. He determines this by experimenting with a sandbag equal in weight to the person to be executed. Properly done, the death is the result of a broken neck, not of strangulation nor of decapitation. [NT 14]

5415 Prévost d'Exiles, Antoine-François -- a French author (1697-1763) also known as the abbé Prévost, reminding us of his periods as a Jesuit novice and as a Benedictine priest and as chaplain to the Prince de Conti. In and out of trouble, exile, and Roman Catholicism, he finally settled down in 1742 to a quiet life as a professional hack writer. His too many mistresses and too little money left him at the mercy of whomever would buy what he wrote or translated. His only work of merit is Manon Lescaut*, a somewhat autobiographical work considered by some critics to be brilliant. [CW 13]

5416 Price, Eiluned -- a close friend of HV's and a character witness for her at HV's trial for murder. PW interviews Miss Price during his investigations to free HV of murder charges for the death of Philip Boyes*. PW impresses her and she predicts that he will marry Harriet. [SP 1]

5417 Price, Mabel -- Sir Reuben Levy's* kitchen maid [WB 4]

5418 pricking this little touch -- working out the details of a short touch* of Kent Treble Bob Major* [NT 9]

5419 Prière de ne pas brutaliser la machine. -- French for, "Pray (i. e. please as in you are requested) do not brutalise (abuse) the machine." [BH 14]

5420 Priest, Jack -- a police constable

#5415 The Abbé Prévost from a portrait engraved in 1746.

at Fenchurch St. Peter*, the closest police officer to Fenchurch St. Paul* [NT 2]

5421 Primrose -- Mrs. Munns's* Christian name [BC 18]

5422 Primrose Dalliance -- a fictitious novel the title of which alludes to Hamlet, I, iii, 50: "Himself the primrose path of dalliance treads" [GN 11]

5423 Primrose League -- formed in 1883 in memory of Lord Beaconsfield (see Disraeli, Benjamin) for the maintenance of conservative principles. The anniversary of Beaconsfield's death (April 19) is celebrated as "Primrose Day". Meleager Finch* intended to leave all of his money to the League if his niece, Hannah Marryat*, an avowed Socialist, couldn't find a later will leaving it to her and her mother. Meleager considers the League "fatuous" at best, but chose it because it would be particularly upsetting to Miss Marryat if they got the money. The League's name is an allusion to the fact that Queen Victoria sent primroses to Disraeli's funeral saying that they were his favorite flower, something nobody else knew and many doubted. [umw]

5424 prince [arbitrary] -- the Archbishop of Canterbury* is a prince in the sense of being the primate of the Church of England, a prince of the Church. However, PW is merely referring to his power to grant the Thodays a special marriage license, a power restricted to the Archbishop of Canterbury. [NT 13]

5425 Prince Florizel of Bohemia -- PW is probably referring to the Prince's speech in The Winter's Tale, IV, iv, 547-51, by William Shakespeare. The passage is:

"But as the unthought-on accident is guilty
To what we wildly do, so we profess
Ourselves to be the slaves of chance and flies
Of every wind that blows."

The speech is in response to Camillo's plan to help Florizel elope with Perdita to Sicily, a plan which Florizel has most anxiously sought from Camillo. [UD 1]

5426 Prince of Denmark -- Shakespeare's Hamlet [UD 5]

5427 Prince of Ruritania -- see Ruritania [GN 4]

5428 Prince of Wales -- at the time of CW it would have been Prince Edward who later became Edward VIII and who abdicated in 1936 to marry the American divorcée, Wallis Warfield Simpson. The reference in BH is to Edward VII, Victoria's son, and holder of the record for longest tenure as Prince of Wales. [CW 9/BH 4]

5429 Prince of Wales Rd. -- listed now as Prince of Wales Drive, it extends from Battersea Bridge Rd. along the South edge of Battersea Park to Queen's Circle on Queenstown Rd. in a roughly East-West direction. [WB 1]

5430 Princemoor -- a fictitious community, probably a combination of Princetown* and Dartmoor [HHC 15]

5431 Princess of China -- Aladdin's wife in some versions of the story. He marries a sultan's daughter in others. [HHC 15]

5432 Princeton St. -- a short street in Bloomsbury* that connects Red Lion Square* with Bedford Row* [SP 13]

5433 Princetown -- the town closest to Dartmoor Prison* in Devon [NT 4]

5434 principal boy -- the chief character in the modern pantomime (not dumbshow), and traditionally played by a woman as in Peter Pan. Some popular principal boys of the 1880's included Harriet Vernon, Nellie Stewart, and Queenie Leighton. [HHC 15]

5435 principals of the angel-roof -- the main rafters of the angel-roof which are usually carved and decorated in their own right [NT 2]

5436 Pringle, Tommy -- a medical student friend of Mr. Piggott's* (the younger) [WB 10]

5437 Priory Lane -- one of Little Doddering's* two main thoroughfares [bc]

5438 Prisoner at the Bar -- this was the standard format for a sentence of death as pronounced in an English court. The judge traditionally wore a black cap when pronouncing such a sentence. [BH E3]

5439 Prisoner's Aid Society -- it is not now listed as a charitable organization, but several such groups were founded under the Discharged Prisoner's Aid Act of 1862. Their function was to look after dependents and to help find work for discharged prisoners. Such functions are now handled by various state-sponsored services such as the probation service. [BH P]

5440 Pritchard, Dr. Edward William -- an English surgeon, born in 1825 and hanged in Glasgow on July 28, 1865, for the murders by poison of his wife and her mother. His MD degree was purchased in Erlangen, Germany, _in absentia_, so he had no legal right to the title of doctor. The poisons he used included antimony*, tartar emetic* and aconite*, with opium thrown in for good measure. [CW 6/UD 1]

5441 Pritchard, Mr. -- the lawyer of Lincoln's Inn* who handled Lady Dormer's* legal affairs and who represented Ann Dorland in the confusion following her aunt's death. He is presented as a very proper man who tenaciously protects his client. [BC 3]

5442 Pritchard, Mr. -- an owner of one of Mr. Endicott's* razors who suffered the amazing experience of having been attacked with it by his manservant [HHC 6]

5443 _Private Lives_ -- a comedy of happy and witty dialogue, considered a minor theatrical classic and written by Noel Coward (1899-1973). The play was first produced in 1930. [GN 21]

5444 privateer -- an armed private vessel commissioned to attack the commercial and military vessels of some other country or countries; sometimes suggested as the forerunner of modern commercial practices [UD 13]

5445 Privy Council -- the sovereign's private advisory council, it dates from the 14th C. after the earlier King's Council evolved into Parliament. This once informal council still has important administrative functions as it issues various Orders in Council, those orders issued by Royal Prerogative but which may not substantially alter the law. [GN 3]

5446 Privy Stair -- a stair that allowed a sovereign secret access to the royal apartments, but the one at Talboys* leads to the bathroom, the "privy". [t/BH 4]

5447 prized above rubies -- PW echoes the famous lines from Proverbs 31:10 where it is written, "Who can find a virtuous woman? for her price is far above rubies." [BH P]

5448 pro-Proctor -- an assistant to a Proctor* [GN AN]

5449 _pro tem._ -- the abbreviation for the Latin _pro tempore_, for the time being, temporarily [CW 5]

5450 probate -- the official proving of a will as authenticated and valid [umw]

5451 Probyn, Mr. Thomas -- Agatha Dawson's* solicitor* for many years. He lived in Croftover Magna* and had his office there. He retired to Italy. [UD 12]

5452 Proctor -- a Fellow of an Oxford college who is elected to the position for a period of one year. Among his duties is the supervision of University discipline in the town. A Proctor is the last person a miscreant student wants to meet. [GN 12]

5453 Proctor's bull-dogs -- assistants to a Proctor* who do any necessary running. They are usually college servants and have to be respectful of the quarry. The name is applied to them in reference to a bulldog's tenacious fighting spirit. [GN 12]

5454 Proctorial Rules for Mixed Parties -- those University rules applying to the requirements for chaperones, the allowances for what sorts of food and drink to be permitted, the hours to be observed, etc., at any given mixed party [GN 7]

5455 Procurator-Fiscal -- a Scottish public servant, a public prosecutor of a given area who also performs some of the duties of a coroner. He is appointed by the sheriff or magistrates. The term originates from his earlier function of collecting the fines, etc., levied by the various courts he served. He also now initiates the prosecution of crimes. [FRH 2]

5456 prog[gins] -- slang for Proctor* [GN 12]

5457 Prometheus -- in Greek mythology the son of a Titan who made mankind from clay and whose name means "forethought". Zeus attempted to deprive man of fire, but Prometheus stole it and gave it to man, teaching man many of his arts as well. Later, for refusing to tell Zeus an important secret regarding the marriage of Peleus and Thetis, Prometheus was chained to a rock in the Caucasus Mountains where an eagle ate his liver every day, the organ being restored every night so the torment could continue. His brother was Epimetheus*. [GN 1]

5458 proof -- see pulls [MMA 4]

5459 Propaganda Society -- apparently a branch of or at least connected with the Soviet Club* and for which Lady Mary Wimsey* and Miss Tarrant* had done work. Lady Mary was the Society's secretary for six months. [CW 7]

5460 propelling pencil -- a mechanical pencil with replaceable leads [MMA 7]

5461 proper Bank of England note -- Mr. Goodacre isn't suggesting that he has been dealing with counterfeit ones, only that he doesn't see notes of that much financial significance very often as £10 was a considerable sum of money in 1935. [BH 5]

5462 Property Act of 1925 -- properly the Administration of Estates Act of 1925 and the other legislation associated with it which became operative on January 1, 1926, and which did not make it uncertain if great-nieces inherited on intestacy. They do inherit, and DLS seems to have gotten this all wrong! [UD 14]

5463 Prosodic elements -- see prosody [GN 3]

5464 prosody -- the study of the technical elements of poetry: meter, rhyme, rhythm, stanza forms, etc. as they apply to the poem as a whole unit [GN 4]

5465 Protestant appearance -- Miss Climpson* claims that Parker* has such an appearance, but what there is that distinguishes a Protestant from anyone else is elusive at best [UD 22]

5466 Protestantism -- the faith of those who protest against the errors of the Church of Rome. In this sense, the Church of England lies between Roman Catholicism and Protestantism in that it rejects the leadership of the Pope, the intermediation of the saints, and the doctrine of purgatory, but shares most other beliefs of Roman Catholicism. [UD 5]

5467 prothalamion -- a New Latin (i. e. medieval) word with Greek roots meaning "a song to celebrate a marriage" [BH P]

5468 Prout, Mr. -- the photographer for Pym's Publicity* who manages to create a stir one day when he arrives at work wearing a black shirt [MMA 1]

5469 "provided for" -- the phrase is identified as being Mr. Micawber's by Tommie Traddles in Ch. 28 of David Copperfield [HHC 7]

5470 Provost -- the Scottish equivalent of mayor [FRH 7]

5471 Provost of Flamborough -- the chief administrator at Flamborough College*, a position formerly held by Miss de Vine* [GN 1]

5472 Prunella -- written in 1904 by Laurence Housman* and Harley Granville-Barker, the play is a light bit of fluff reminiscent of the work of James Barrie*. It was not a popular success. [UD 15]

5473 prussic acid -- see hydrocyanic acid [BC 15/SP 1/BH 14]

5474 psaltery -- a string instrument resembling a zither. It is very ancient. [SP 13]

5475 Psychical Research Society -- a group founded in England in 1882, the first of such groups devoted to the study of parapsychology and psychical phenomena [SP 16]

5476 P't-être qu' m'sieur a bouté les billets . . . -- French for:
"Perhaps, sir, you have stuffed the tickets into your pants."
"Triple idiot! I ask you, have you ever heard of anyone putting tickets in his pants? Never--"
"Do you say so? There's a pretty

mess! Well, young man; wearing a false collar doesn't give you the right to insult people."

The verb a bouté is an unusual choice. It is the past tense of bouter which is normally only used in set phrases and means to throw out by physical force as in Jeanne d'Arc a bouté les Anglais loin de France (Joan of Arc threw [or drove] the English out of France.). The verb is strictly French argot today, but survives in English as the root for "buttress", to push or bear against. DLS's use of the argot probably dates from her stay at the school in Les Roches, France, in 1919-20. [aq]

5477 public convenience -- a public toilet [FRH 28]

5478 Public Health, Ministry of -- following passage of the Public Health Act of 1848, the General Board of Health was created, eventually becoming the Ministry of Health in 1919. Neville Harcourt* is mentioned as being an official for that Ministry. It governs the workmen's compensation, social security, and the various health insurance programs run by the government for the public. [ae]

5479 Public Health Committee -- a group organized under a County Council* and charged with the supervision of local public health situations, regulations, etc. [HHC 21]

5480 public-house -- or pub; an inn, tavern, or saloon [SP 5/MMA 16]

5481 public place within the meaning of the act -- the phrase, "a place within the meaning of the Act", appears in the Betting Acts of 1853 and 1906. It is probably the latter, the Street Betting Act, that is meant. Another Act was under consideration in 1934, and many have been passed since. [MMA 1]

5482 public school [education/English] -- in England, a private boarding school that would teach a non-regional English such as Eton, Harrow. etc. Such private schools arose as early as the 1400's, but increased in number greatly during the 19th C. to meet the needs of a growing and ever increasingly affluent middle class and of an empire in need of administrators of high integrity. The oldest school is Winchester, dating from 1382. There are now more than 250 such schools in Great Britain and the Commonwealth. [WB 11/FRH 5/MMA 3]

5483 public school tradition -- the ideal that demands chivalrous protection of the ladies as well as standing up to and confronting any sort of bullying. A modern code of chivalry and honor, it includes a more severe ostracism for cheating than for some instances of murder. [CW 4]

5484 publican -- the keeper of a public house* or tavern [bc/SP 1]

5485 Publications of Sir Julian Freke -- all of the publications listed for the Who's Who* entry for Sir Julian Freke* in Ch. 7 of WB are fictitious [WB 7]

5486 "publish and be damned" -- a phrase made famous when the Duke of Wellington (1769-1852) supposedly uttered it when he was threatened with having some injurious material published about him; the Duke was a notorious ladies' man [MMA 20]

5487 Puddley-in-the-Rut -- one of PW's names for a fictitious country village [hp]

5488 Puddock, Mr. Ted -- a resident of Paggleham* and a patron of the Crown pub there [BH 10]

5489 Puffett, Jinny -- Mr. Tom Puffett's* daughter. She is married, but her married surname is not given. It is she who keeps Mr. Puffett on his toes as he has to be careful of her moods as she is pregnant with her fourth child. Her husband's name is George. [t/BH 8]

5490 Puffett, Tom -- a neighbor of PW's who raises prize peaches as a hobby. He is a builder by profession but serves the area as a general handyman, sweeping chimneys and doing other odd jobs as needed. PW helps him solve the case of the peaches stolen from his orchard in return for some of the favors he has done for PW. Peter is also anxious to clear his son, Bredon, of any guilt as Bredon is a prime suspect in the great peach theft. Puffett is described as a widower. [t/BH 4]

5491 Puffin cigarettes -- a fictitious brand [MMA 15]

5492 puggie -- see fou' as a puggie [FRH 25]

5493 pukka -- a variant of pucka, an Anglo-Indian word meaning of full weight, the genuine article, etc. [CW 3/HHC 4/MMA 3]

5494 pull[s] -- in printing, to make sample copies of matter set in type for the purpose of proofreading. The proofs are pulled from the inked type one at a time and by hand. The verb can double as a noun as well. The same terms are used when printing works of art such as lithographs and serigraphs. U. S. practice usually has "proof" function as the noun. [MMA 1]

5495 pulled a proof -- see pull[s] [MMA 4]

5496 pulled the plug on it -- on older toilets the water tank for storage of the water for flushing was mounted on the wall some distance above the bowl. The flushing mechanism was activated by a pull chain, hence, pulling the plug, thus allowing the water to perform its flushing action. The process is essentially the same today. [GN 2]

5497 Pullman Restaurant Car -- a railroad car complete with facilities for the storage, preparation, and serving of food to passengers while the train is under way. The Pullman reference indicates that the railroad has either purchased or leased the car from the Pullman Company that manufactured it as the name "Pullman" is a registered trademark. [FRH 10]

5498 pumps -- as worn by Denis Cathcart* the evening of his death, they are a dress shoe not held on by laces or ties, but by friction of light pressure agains the heel and toe. They are often made of patent leather with satin or grosgrain trim. [CW 1]

5499 Punch -- a famous British humorous weekly magazine which was first issued in 1841. The periodical is noted for its sharp wit, excellent cartoons, and its biting political and social satire. [BC 1/GN 11/BH 14]

5500 punch in the wind -- to strike someone so as "to knock the wind out of them" [MMA 4]

5501 Puncheon, Hector -- the "nonentity" and reporter for the Morning Star*. He is fictitious. It is his work that helps force the events of MMA to their eventual climax, but he pays dearly for his efforts with a hard blow to the head while trying to follow a suspect through the Natural History Museum*. He shows up, doggedly, at Talboys* for a story, but HV manages to intimidate him with some of her four-legged rural friends. [MMA 12/BH 13]

5502 punnet[s] -- a small, square basket supposed to hold one pound of soft fruits or vegetables [MMA 12]

5503 punt[s] -- long, narrow, flat-bottomed boats propelled either by poles or paddles, traditionally by the former. One end of a punt slopes, the other has a flat deck. Whether a person is a graduate of Oxford or of Cambridge can be determined by which end of the punt he stands in while punting as Oxford students punt from the sloping end while Cambridge students punt from the deck end. [GN 11/BH P]

5504 Punter-Smith suicide -- a reference to the death of one of the followers of the drugs, alcohol, and sex crowd led by Dian de Momerie* and Major Tod Milligan*. The situation is fictitious and no details are given. [MMA 3]

5505 Purcell, Henry -- an English composer (1659-95) of great skill who wrote widely in both sacred and secular forms. He wrote one small-scale grand opera, Dido and Aeneas, but is best remembered for his choral and string music. He was organist at Westminster Abbey from 1679 until his death.

5506 Purcellish -- see Purcell, Henry [CW 4]

5507 pure -- the laws governing the contents of foods, words used to advertise those contents, etc., are still as strict as they were in DLS's day if not more so. To the average consumer they have no real meaning. [MMA 3]

5508 purgatory -- a place where souls go to suffer to expiate venial transgressions or to undergo penalties for mortal sins before entering heaven according to the Roman Catholic faith. It is not a place of probation

#5503 Punting on the Cherwell, Oxford, as PW and HV might have known it.

because those in purgatory are guaranteed of heaven, but are not pure enough to get there at the instant of death; hence, and place of punishment at suffering in preparation for something better.

5509 "The Purloined Letter" -- Edgar Allan Poe's* short story of 1844 wherein the object being sought is hidden in the most obvious place it could be. The tale is the original detective as secret agent story. [FRH 22]

5510 push-cycle -- a bicycle as distinguished from a motorcycle [FRH 2/HHC 10/NT 3]

5511 puss-in-the-corner -- a children's game. One stands in the center and attempts to capture one of the "dens" or "bases" while the other move around. Several variations on the game are known. [WB 7]

5512 pussies [silvery] -- pussy-willows as with the North American Salix discolor [NT 3]

5513 pussy old lady -- a common English phrase meaning an elderly woman who is soft and engaging, but who has sharp claws ready for use at any time [SP 16]

5514 pussychology -- psychology with an exaggerated pronunciation of the Greek letter psi (Ψ, ψ) which is a combination of the "p" and "s" sounds, the "p" being almost silent. [BH 8]

5515 put his crime off to a more convenient season -- Insp. Umpelty* is confused again. Shakespeare did not write that idea, St. Luke did. It appears in the Acts of the Apostles, 24:25: "Go thy way for this time; when I have a convenient season, I will call for thee." The reference is to the Roman governor, Felix, and his reaction to St. Paul's presentation on righteousness, temperence, and the judgment to come. [HHC 10]

5516 put on a clean collar -- see collar, put on a clean [t]

5517 put[s] the wind up -- to become alarmed, to be in a "funk", or to cause to become so agitated. The phrase is a slang expression conveying both of these ideas. [HHC 3]

5518 putting her hair in papers -- see hair in papers [MMA 8]

5519 Puzzle Clues -- the following are references to and additional explanations for the crossword puzzle created by Meleager Finch*.

Clues Across:

X.2: see the opening verses of Ecclesiastes

IV.3: the parable is in Matthew 9:16, Mark 2:21, and Luke 5:36 and deals with new doctrine on old prejudices

I.4: "most unkindest cut", Julius Caesar, III, ii, 188. "Cut" is also a pun on secant when it is used as an adjective.

XI.5: Pussyfoot: William Eugene Johnson, an early 20th C. prohibition propagandist and indefatigable, catlike pursuer of lawbreakers as a special officer of the U. S. Indian Service. He is credited with over 4000 convictions.

VI.9: Karroo -- a vast plateau in the South of the Republic of South Africa

VII.10: Much Ado About Nothing, Shakespeare

I.11: Pleas + e. Pleas stops too short to be the polite plea, please.

I.13: AE, the pseudonym for Irish poet and artist George William Russell (1867-1935)

I.15: Damon. In the original legend he puts himself up as bail for Phythias (Phintias) and would be executed if his friend did not return

Clues Down:

1.I: verst, a Russian unit of linear measure, about two-thirds of a mile

4.III: Nunc Dimittis, the canticle of Simeon, Luke 2:29-32

4.III: Magnificat, the hymn of the Virgin Mary, Luke 1:46-55

14.III: HM, His or Her Majesty

1.IV: gitana, Spanish for gypsy (female)

1.V: King Phalaris, an ancient tyrant king who roasted criminals in a brazen bull

11:V: Sehon--the spelling of Sihon as found in the Vulgate. He was king of the Amorites. See Numbers 21:21, Deuteronomy 1:4 and 2:26,

and Psalms 135 and 136.
12.VI: NID which backward is din; also a nest, perhaps in reference to shore birds
9.VIII: Admetus who persuaded his wife to die for him, but Heracles returned her to him
6.IX: guano, the dung of bats, birds, etc. It is rich in nitrogen and is excellent fertilizer
2.X: vel, Latin for an indefinite either/or construction as in either this or that is the correct answer
11.XI: awned, adjective, appendages forming the beard on wheat, corn, etc.
1.XIII: Di, Diana of the Ephesians. See Acts 19:34.
4.XIII: Versicles, a reading of verses, frequently from the Psalms and led by the pastor or priest. A response is usually expected.
11.XV: Astra = star [umw]

5520 Pygmalion -- a legendary king of Cyprus who fell in love with a statue (Ovid claims Pygmalion sculpted it himself). He prayed to Aphrodite to give him a wife like the statue and she gave the statue life. He married it/her. G. B. Shaw drew inspiration for his play, Pygmalion, from this story and Lerner and Loewe based their musical, My Fair Lady, on Shaw's play. [CW 13]

5521 pyjamas -- PW wears mauve or primrose silk ones and has a mauve dressing gown [aq/pj]

5522 Pyke, George -- one of the errand boys at Pym's Publicity* [MMA 7]

5523 Pyke, Miss -- the Classical tutor at Shrewsbury College* [GN 3]

5524 Pym, Mr. -- the owner of Pym's Publicity* [MMA 3]

5525 Pym's Publicity, Ltd. -- the very believable advertising agency created by DLS to use as a setting for MMA. After Oxford, DLS spent some time teaching in England and France but, in 1923, at age 30, she got the job she had always wanted at Benson's, later Ogilvy, Benson & Mather, and now Ogilvy & Mather, the advertising agency. It is upon her experiences at Benson's that she drew for MMA. The famous spiral staircase was a real fixture of the Kingsway* offices of Benson's, but the present firm of Ogilvy & Mather is no longer located there. [MMA 2]

5526 pyorrhoea -- an inflammation of the gums and teeth sockets which leads to a loosening and potential loss of teeth [te/BH E2]

5527 pyramids -- probably a facetious reference to Clarke's Pyramid Nightlights, the best-known brand and highly advertised before the coming of electric lights. A diplomatic crisis was signalled by "the lights burning all night at the Foreign Office" as is said in novels, and it is likely that Lord St. George* would be quite familiar with such phrases. In the spirit of the word-play in GN, it is a small step to the reference here. [GN 21]

5528 Pyrenees -- a 260-mile mountain range that separates France from Spain and which has a high point of just over 11,000 feet. It is the homeland of the Basques* and was so isolated that Standish Wetherall* could expect to achieve relative separation from European civilization there. He could also expect to encounter Langley* when the latter came there to do his research on the Basque language. [ie/bc]

5529 pyro [stains] -- a photographic developing agent, and the oldest of the commonly used chemicals for that purpose. It oxidizes too rapidly so, after 1930, it was replaced by other agents as they became available. Bunter uses it in some of the earlier stories and it does stain. [fr/BC 5]

5530 Pytchley [the] -- a famous pack of foxhounds that hunts between Rugby* and Northampton. The pack may date as far back as the reign of Henry III, 1216-72. The name is pronounced to rhyme with "pie". [HHC 12]

DOWN THIS STAIRCASE
was precipitated to his death with malice
aforethought and for the gratification of all
who appreciate the fine art of murder
VICTOR DEAN OF PYM'S PUBLICITY
25 MAY MCMXXXIII
"Murder must advertise"
THIS TABLET WAS UNVEILED A.D.1950 BY DOROTHY L.SAYERS M.A.

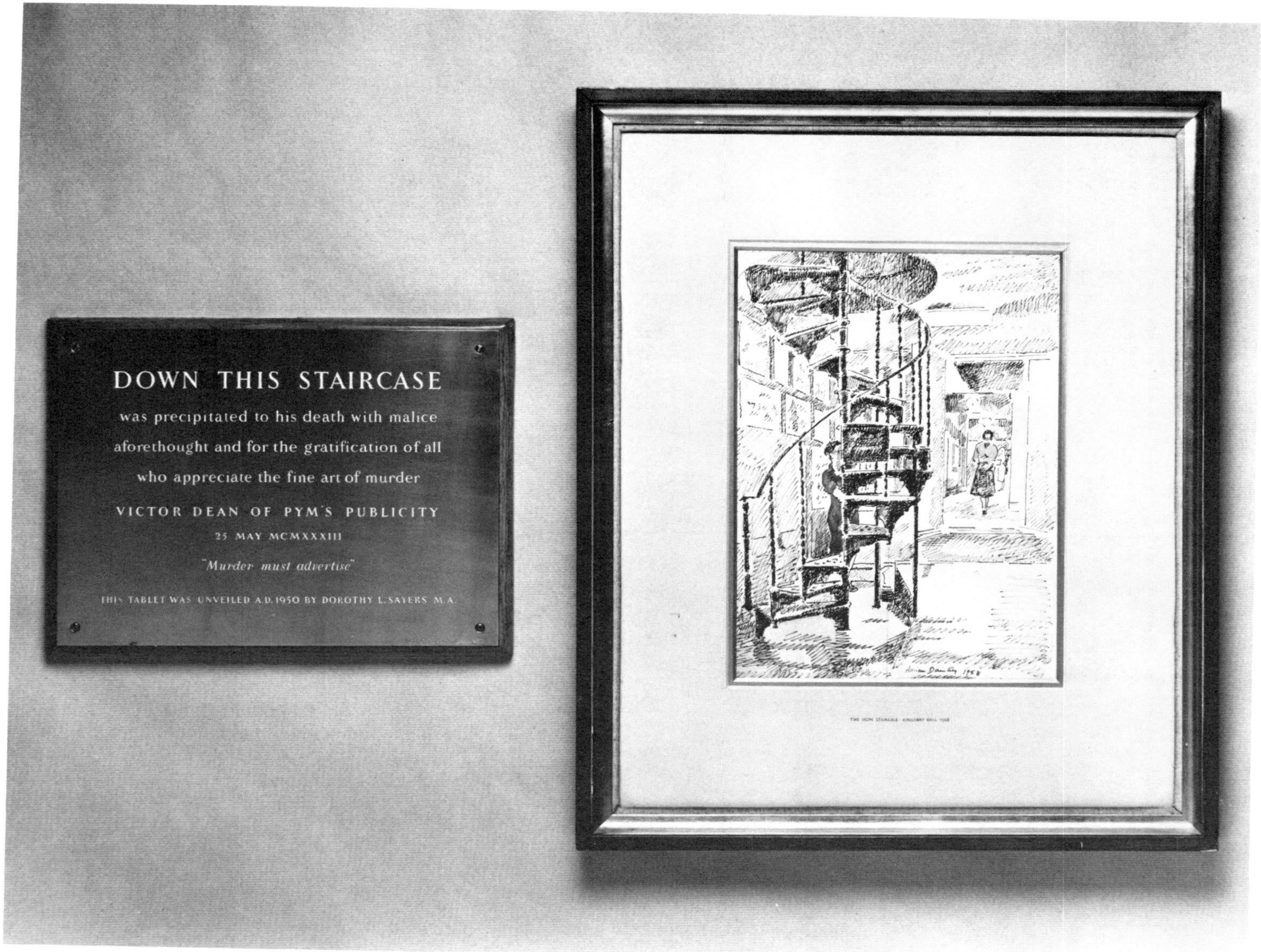

#5525 This plaque, dated 1950, commemorating MMA and DLS's association with the S. H. Benson advertising firm was formerly in their offices at Kingsway Hall. The rendering of the famous iron staircase, a real fixture of the Kingsway offices, is by Adrian Daintrey and is dated 1958. Photograph courtesy Ogilvy and Mather, London.

(Q)

5531 Q. C. -- the abbreviation for Queen's Counsel. See King's Counsel (K. C.).

5532 Q. E. D. -- the abbreviation for the Latin, "quod erat demonstrandum", "which was to be demonstrated" [WB 3]

5533 Qu'il fait bon dormi -- see "Et ma joli colombe" [BH 16]

5534 quâ -- Latin for, "in the capacity of" or "in the character of" [SP 6]

5535 quack-quack -- see cricket [MMA 18]

5536 Quaecunque honesta -- Latin for, "whatever is honest (or upright)". It is the motto of the school attended by Mrs. Pettigrew-Robinson*. The line is reminiscent of St. Paul in Philippians 4:8, but does not appear there in the Latin form of this entry's heading. [CW 2]

5537 quagga -- "a South African quadruped in six letters, beginning with Q". The word was sought by Bunter to complete a crossword puzzle. The quagga was an equine mammal, extinct since about 1875, and was related to the zebra, but only the front half had any stripes. [umw]

5538 Quai d'Orléans -- one of several streets which run roughly parallel to the Seine in Paris [mt]

5539 Quain's Dictionary of Medicine -- Sir Richard Quain's A Dictionary of Medicine with sections in general pathology, general therapeutics, hygiene, and the diseases peculiar to women and children. Quain was the editor. The volume was published in 1816 pp. by Longmans Green in editions dated 1882, 1894, and 1902. [BC 17]

5540 quaint metaphysical people -- a reference to the metaphysical poets of the 17th C., including Donne and Cowley. Their work is noted for its "witty conceits", fantastic imagery, and sexual innuendo. Frequently their poetry puns on ideas for effect or to provide a double meaning either sacred or secular in the pattern of the Song of Songs*. One example of this punning is with the word "die" which may mean either death or a sexual climax and its aftermath. [CW 9]

5541 Quaker meeting-house -- the Quakers, officially the Society of Friends, do not have churches. Their places of worship are correctly known as Meeting Houses. [HHC 12]

5542 Quangle & Hamper v. Truth -- the case on which Sir Impey Biggs* is working immediately prior to his involvement with the Duke of Denver's* trial in the House of Lords*. The case considers the problem of a patent medicine and false advertising claims and is fictitious. [CW 10]

5543 quarter-day -- one of the four days per year when rents are due, courts go into session, etc., in England [BH 7]

5544 Quarter Sessions -- one of the four quarterly sessions of the law courts held locally and superior to magistrates courts, now superseded by Crown Courts. Appeals were heard by the Court of Criminal Appeal. [NT 7]

5545 Quartermain, Alan -- or Allan, the name of the hero of some of H. Rider Haggard's romantic adventure novels of the late 1800's. Quartermain appears in King Solomon's Mines and Allan Quartermain. [UD 11]

5546 quarter-turned -- the bells in a ring have to be turned from time to time so the clapper isn't striking the same spot all the time. Without such turning, the bell would be knocked out of tune and, thus, be irreparably damaged in time. To prevent this, the bells are turned so that no one striking spot wears more than another. [NT 3]

5547 quatrain -- any collection of four lines of verse meant to function together in some way [HHC 17]

5548 Que donneriez-vous, belle . . . -- more verses to "La caille, la tourterelle"*. These lines do not make any sense when translated either. [BH 16]

5549 Que voulez-vous? -- French for, "What do you want?" It is used here idiomatically to mean something like "What can I say?" or "What can you expect?" [HHC 7/NT 8]

5550 Queen Anne coffee pot -- an item in the Queen Anne design is going to feature simplicity of style and a reliance upon gracefully interconnecting curves. It is a gentle, smooth style, but is intricate in its apparent simplicity. [BC 13]

5551 Queen Anne Chinoiserie -- furniture in the fashion made popular during the reign of Queen Anne and decorated with Chinese motifs. Such furniture is usually finished in black lacquer with stencilled oriental designs applied over it in gold and brilliant colors muted in the stencilling process. [BH E2]

5552 Queen Anne's Bounty -- a fund, established by Queen Anne in 1704, for the relief of the poorer Anglican clergy. The money came from annates, payments for the first year's income of a benefice after the appointment of a new bishop, and from tenths (tithes*). This money had been paid to the Pope before the Reformation and, later, was diverted to the Crown acting as Head of the Church by the Act of Annates of 1532 (Henry VIII). The fund later received grants from Parliament and from private benefactors. The "Bounty" augmented the livings of poorer clergy by capital grants and repairs. The Queen Anne's Bounty is now a part of the income of the Church Commissioners. See also tithe. [NT 9]

5553 Queen Caroline Mansions -- a group of apartment buildings opposite Battersea Park* on Prince of Wales Rd.* The buildings, most likely fictitious, apparently commanded a fine view of the Park. Number 59 is the home of Alfred Thipps*, discoverer of the naked body in his bathtub. [WB 1]

5554 Queen Elizabeth -- the "Virgin Queen" of England from 1558 to 1603, she was the daughter of Henry VIII by Anne Boleyn. Born in 1533, her childhood was unhappy and precarious after her mother's beheading at 9:00 A. M. on May 19, 1536. It was not until after the deaths of Edward VI and Mary I (Bloody Mary) that Elizabeth finally became queen at the age of 25. She reigned for forty-five of England's most glorious years. [CW 5/NT 2/GN 3/ BH E2]

5555 Queen Elizabeth Building -- one of the major academic buildings on the campus of Shrewsbury College* [GN 5]

5556 Queen Elizabeth . . . slept here in the usual way -- an allusion to Elizabeth I's fondness for touring England in what was known as a Royal Progress. Such a Progress meant going from estate to estate and living like the Queen she was whether her host could afford her or not. Her arrival was welcomed as a great honor--which it was--but her departure was more often welcomed by a great sigh of financial relief. [BH E2]

5557 Queen of Hearts (in Alice) -- the reference is to Lewis Carroll's <u>Alice in Wonderland</u> and to the Red Queen who is always shouting, "Off with their heads!" The phrase is used to describe William Grimbold as being externally fierce but gentle underneath. Both he and the Queen bluster a good deal. The line is also applied to Hugh Farren. [ae/FRH 12]

5558 Queen Mary -- her Gracious Majesty was the wife of King George V who ruled from 1910 to 1936. Queen Mary (1867-1953) was the only daughter of the Duke of Teck and was grandmother to the present Queen, Elizabeth II. [NT 6]

5559 Queen of Sheba -- see Sheba, no more spirit than [BC 13]

5560 Queen stands on a square of her own color -- in chess*, the white queen always begins play on a white square, the black queen on a black one. This concept is essential for solving the murder of Charmian Grayle*. [qs]

5561 Queen Victoria -- see Victoria [UD 14/GN 3]

5562 Queen's Change -- see cascading thirds of [NT 1]

5563 Queen's College -- see Oxford Colleges [GN AN]

5564 Queen's Drawing Rooms -- regular events where ladies decked out in trains and ostrich feathers were presented <u>en masse</u> to the Queen, usually at <u>St. James's</u> Palace. Over 1000 ladies might be present, and those attending for the first time, thus entering Society, were debutantes. The Queen's Garden Parties have replaced

them, but, as Society is no longer of such significance, formal presentations are not made. [MMA 11]

5565 Queen's Jubilee -- the Queen is Victoria, and the Jubilee is that of 1887, the celebration of Victoria's fiftieth year as queen. It is customary to celebrate a jubilee for every twenty-five years of a reign. The next closest queen is Anne, but she did not have a jubilee. [NT 1]

5566 Queen's Square -- Dr. Emerson's* address is just East of Southampton Row off Great Ormond St.* [MMA 2]

5567 Queer St. -- to be in difficulty or in difficult straits, a slang term corrupted from Carey St., London, site of the Bankruptcy Court [ie/ WB 9/CW 12]

5568 Quelle folie--mais quel geste! -- French for, "What madness--but what a gesture!" "Gesture" is used here in the sense of "beau geste", a particularly marvellous act of some sort that often suggests a sacrifice. [BH 14]

5569 Quelle histoire sanglante! -- French for, "What a bloody story (history)!" [NT 8]

5570 Quelle scie, mon dieu, quelle scie! -- French for, "What a bore, my lord, what a bore!" "Bore" might also be read as "nuisance" or "bother". [BH 6]

5571 Qu'est-ce-que je vous ai dit? -- French for, "What did I tell you? The impetuosity is found." Antoine* is referring to an earlier remark he had made to HV that when she found the right partner she would be a marvellous dancer. [HHC 12]

5572 quid -- a slang term for a British pound (£). See British Monetary Units. [HHC 11/MMA 1]

5573 Quint, Humphrey -- a fictitious author [GN 11]

5574 Quirk, Miss -- a friend of PW's sister-in-law, Helen, the Duchess of Denver*, who visits PW and HV for a country vacation. Her holiday is more exciting that she had anticipated thanks to the jokes of PW and his eldest son, Bredon*, as abetted by Cuthbert*. Miss Quirk's theories on child-rearing border on the absurd, and she deserves everything she gets for attempting to force them on the Wimseys. [t]

5575 quod -- prison, a slang term [passim]

5576 Quod semper, quod ubique, quod ab omnibus -- Latin for, "What always, what everywhere, what by all men [is believed]." The full sentence appears in the Commonitorium, ii, of St. Vincent of Lerins (fl. 400-450 A. D.) as given in the citation with the addition of "creditum est". [BH 5]

5577 Quoi encore? Voyons-- -- French for, "What else? Let me see--". [CW 5]

5578 quoiting -- playing quoits or tossing rings of flattened iron or of rope toward a post or pole for scoring. It is rather like horseshoes. [FRH 7]

5579 the Quorn -- one of England's most famous foxhound packs, prominent since 1753. The kennels are at Quorndon Hall in Quorndon, near Melton Mowbray in Leicestershire. [HHC 12]

5580 quysshons -- an archaic spelling for cushions. In 1587, spelling was anything but exact; however, the citation is spelled in a manner typical of the time. [BH E2]

(R)

5581 R. A. C. see Royal Automobile Club [cb/CW 14]

5582 R. T. O. -- the abbreviation for Railway Transport Officer, an officer at a railway station who helped troops in trouble, issued any necessary emergency papers, and who would help a soldier avoid trouble with his unit if unavoidably delayed [im]

5583 rabbit dies -- see I hope your rabbit dies [HHC 12]

5584 Rabelaisian -- an allusion to the literary style of François Rabelais (1454?-1553) which is marked by coarse, boisterous humor [MMA 9]

5585 Rachel, Miss -- see Levy, Rachel [WB 4]

5586 Racine -- the French tragic dramatist, Jean Racine (1639-99), author of such works as Andromaque, Bérénice, Iphegénie, and Phèdre. He ranks with Corneille and Molière as one of the great French playwrights. [CW 18]

5587 racing news -- the reference is probably to the series of races held at Ascot* in June during Royal Ascot Week [SP 10]

5588 Radcliffe Camera -- a part of Oxford's immense library system, it is a reading room and repository for 600,000 volumes. The structure is a large dome built from 1737 to 1749 from a bequest by Dr. John Radcliffe, a physician to Queen Anne. It is on Radcliffe Square in central Oxford*. [GN 11]

5589 Radcliffe Square -- in central Oxford*, the Radcliffe Camera* is in its center. It is bounded on the North by the Bodleian Library, on the East by Hertford and All Souls Colleges and on the South by the University Church of St. Mary the Virgin. Brasenose College is on the West. [GN 11]

5590 Radder -- a nickname for the Radcliffe Camera* [GN 12]

5591 Radical -- never a recognized political party in England, they were associated with the extremists of the Liberal party. After 1914, many of them joined the Labour party. The Radicals were interested mostly in social and parliamentary reform, much of which had been achieved by 1914. [HHC 26]

5592 Radio for Amateurs -- the magazine Sam Tabbitt* was reading while waiting for an errand to do at Pym's*. There was an Amateur Radio magazine, but the entry citation is fictitous. [MMA 10]

5593 Raffles -- the reference is to what many consider to be the finest thief in any collection of stories about rogues. A. J. Raffles was created by E. W. Hornung and the character became popular immediately. He dresses well, has expensive tastes, enjoys good company, exercises a razor wit, is a famous cricketer, and steals to support his lifestyle. His "Watson" is a journalist named Bunny. [WB 11]

5594 rag[s] -- slang for practical jokes [CW 18/GN 5]

5595 Raikes, Mr. -- a resident of the Paggleham* area who raises birds (chickens?) and who has complained to the police about having lost some of them (to poachers?) [BH 11]

5596 rails -- see go off the rails a bit [SP 6]

5597 "raised a spiritual body" -- the reference is to I Corinthians 15:44 [NT 5]

5598 raising a bell -- bells are hung with their mouths, the open part, down, but in change-ringing* it is necessary to start the touch* or peal* with the mouths up. As the bell swings round once to come to rest with the mouth up against the opposite stay, the clapper will strike the bell once in the natural way to give a true tone. [NT 1]

5599 rajah -- an Indian or Malay chief or prince; a title of noble rank in Hindu culture [HHC 9/MMA 7]

5600 rake's progress -- a reference to a series of engravings by William Hogarth (1697-1764) entitled, "The Rake's Progress", a social commentary on the evils of a dissolute life. To an extent they are humourous, but have been used for generations as weapons for moral didactics. There is a companion series called "The Harlot's

THE
RADCLIFFE.

#5588 The Radcliffe Camera ca. 1910.

Progress" which pictures a woman's downfall. [GN 7]

5601 Raleigh -- a brand of bicycle still widely available in England and the U. S. They presently cost from £70 to £1000 depending on the model, the latter being a top racing model. Prices in the 1930's were about a tenth of that listed. [FRH 10]

5602 Ramage's -- a fictitous barbershop in Lesston Hoe* where William Bright* was employed for a short time [HHC 14]

5603 Ramborough -- a fictitious location. See Shelly Head. [UD 20]

5604 ran like the Red Queen -- a reference to Through the Looking Glass, Ch. 2, when Alice and the Red Queen have to run as fast as they can just to keep their place [BH 18]

5605 Ranelagh -- famous gardens which opened in 1742. They were purchased by the Royal Hospital (home of the Chelsea Pensioners) in 1805. The gardens are renowned and host the Chelsea Flower Show every May. [MMA 11]

5606 rang the bell -- the bus or trolley conductor's signal that he is about to get under way again [CW 5]

5607 rang up -- telephoned in British English [WB 7]

5608 rangé -- French for "neat", orderly or tidy [CW 18]

5609 Ratcliffe, the Hon. Henry -- owner of one of Mr. Endicott's* razors. The razor was destroyed by his sister and some friends who used it to cut out stage scenery! [HHC 6]

5610 rates and taxes -- rates are taxes on property levied by a local government for the funding of local services. Taxes are levied by the central government for national purposes. [NT 10]

5611 ratepayers -- see rates and taxes [UD 3/HHC 13]

5612 Raven never flitting -- PW is referring to lines 103-4 of Poe's* curious poem, "The Raven", published in 1845 and subsequently revised several times by Poe. It enjoys continued popularity. [UD 14]

5613 Rawlinson -- a young clerk* in the employ of Mr. Graham*, a solicitor* from Herriotting*. Rawlinson was supposed to pray over Squire Burdock*, but was prevented from doing so by practical jokers who locked him in the furnace room of the church. [bc]

5614 Raymond -- a spiritualist manifesto written by Sir Oliver Joseph Lodge, an eminent scientist and avocational spiritualist in England at the turn of the century and later. It purports to prove that his son, Raymond, was "alive" and happy in the spirit world. Raymond Lodge was killed near Ypres in September of 1915, and the book was published at the end of 1916. The volume is divided into three parts: The first is a brief biography of Raymond, the second details the sittings (séances) where Sir Oliver received his information, and, last, "scientific" information regarding life after death. [SP 17]

5615 reach-me-down -- either a second-hand or a ready-made garment; off the rack clothing [HHC 14]

5616 Reading -- an industrial and university town in Berkshire about 25 miles southeast of Oxford. It is Hackett's* home. [GN 17]

5617 reading History -- one "reads" a subject at an English university. It is the equivalent of expressing an academic major at an American university. [GN 1]

5618 "Reading maketh a full man . . ." -- PW, HV, and Supt. Kirk* are quoting parts of one sentence from Francis Bacon's* essay, "Of Studies". [BH 7]

5619 "The real sting of this episode lay in its tail" -- PW refers to Revelations 9:10 which tells of the locusts loosed by the fifth angel: "And they had tails like unto scorpions, and there were stings in their tails: and their power was to hurt men five months." [FRH 15]

5620 The real tragedy is not the conflict of good with evil -- DLS seems to have Spinoza's Ethics in mind. In the Elwes translation, Part IV, proposition xvii, he writes: "the true knowledge of good and evil stirs up conflict in the soul." In proposition xxxvii we find: "he who . . . under

#5604 Alice and the Red Queen from an illustration by John Tenniel.

emotion . . . endeavors to cause others to love what he loves himself . . . is . . . hateful especially to those who take delight in something different."

Under proposition lxv is found: "A good which prevents our enjoyment of a greater good is in reality an evil . . . we may . . . pursue the lesser evil as though it were the greater good and shun the lesser good, which would be the cause of the greater evil." It is this latter quotation that seems closest to DLS's ideas. [GN 17]

5621 reaper and binder -- a baler, a machine that cuts the grain crop, threshes it, and bales the hay or straw in a single operation. In more recent models it will also kick the bound bale into a trailing wagon to further ease the work. [HHC 22]

5622 rear brake -- a rear brake van or baggage car. U. S. practice traditionally places such cars between the locomotive and the first of the passenger cars. In a freight train, a caboose is required as the last car of the train for any trips outside the yards. [FRH 10]

5623 "The reason no man knows . . ." -- the lines are from Christopher Marlowe's (1564-93) "Hero and Leander", the First Sestiad,. ll. 173-4. The verse segment is, beginning at line 167:

"It lies not in our power to love, or hate,
For will in us is over-rul'd by fate.
When two are stripped, long ere the course begin,
We wish that one should lose, the other win;
And one especially do we affect
Of two gold ingots, like in each respect
The reason no man knows; let it suffice
What we behold is censured by our eyes.
Where both deliberate, the love is slight;
Who ever loved that loved not at first sight?"

[GN 19]

5624 receive the sacrament -- see Sacrament [to a dying parishoner] [NT 2]

5625 <u>recherché</u> -- French for,"unusual", sought out with care, exquisite, or choice [HHC 4]

5626 <u>Record</u> -- a newspaper mentioned which cannot be identified as no location is given in the story. It is, however, probably safe to say that it is fictitious. [sf]

5627 Recorder -- a magistrate or judge having criminal and civil jurisdiction in The City* where he is still appointed by the aldermen. Elsewhere, he is appointed by the Crown. [CW 14]

5628 recovery of civil debts contracted elsewhere . . . -- see civil debts contracted elsewhere [BH 10]

5629 rector -- a clergyman in charge of a parish who formerly had possession of all its rights, tithes, etc. His income, which used to be from such sources, is now paid by the Church Commissioners in the same way as a vicar*. [NT 3]

5630 recusant -- one who refuses to obey the directions of established authority, especially a Roman Catholic who refused to attend Church of England services, a statutory offense from 1570 to 1791 [GN 3]

5631 Red -- PW's catch-all nickname for socialists, communists, and, most likely, quite a few other non-Tory* political persuasions as well [umw]

5632 Red Cow -- a pub in or near Little Doddering* where Hubbard* is the publican* [bc]

5633 Red Cow -- an inn in the village of Fenchurch St. Paul*. The other is The Wheatsheaf*. [NT 1]

5634 Red Farm -- the Carey homestead between Lesston Hoe and Wilvercombe**. It is one of the few places along the coast road between those two villages that has a telephone. [HHC 2]

5635 red herring[s] -- loosely, any device meant to distract and confuse. The phrase derives from the ancient practice of dragging dead fish, etc., behind one's self to mask personal scents while escaping from jail, slavery, serfdom, or whatever. The object being to use the riper scent of the fish to cover one's own ripe scent. In terms of logic, the fallacy is one of the divisions of distraction.

[FRH 12/BH 3]

5636 Red House -- named for the red bricks from which it was made, it is the home of the Thorpe family in Fenchurch St. Paul* [NT 2]

5637 Red Lion Square -- a small square in Bloomsbury* just South of Theobald's Rd.* [SP 13]

5638 Red Lion St. -- in Holborn*, it connects Theobald's Rd.* with Holborn between Southampton Row and Gray's Inn Rd.** [HHC 30]

5639 Red Queen -- see ran like the Red Queen [BH 18]

5640 red Russian -- the communists as opposed to the "white" Russians, the unsuccessful opponents of communism under Lenin in the Russian Revolution [CW 9]

5641 Red Sea [divided like] -- the reference is to the parting of the Red Sea by Moses as recounted in Exodus in 14:21-31 [MMA 10]

5642 red tape -- bureaucratic operation, especially if marked by delay or inactivity. The term is drawn from the red ribbon formerly used to bind legal documents in England when cutting the red tape was a literal process. [WB 6]

5643 reely -- a deliberate misspelling of really to overemphasize the pronunciation [WB 1]

5644 <u>Reflections on the Revolution in France</u> -- by Edmund Burke* was published in 1790. In it Burke supports the right of hereditary succession and repudiates those who would claim that the English king owes his throne solely to the whim of the people. The quote in UD relates to a part of this argument. He concludes, generally, with the idea that the French should have revised and reformed their monarchy, not to have destroyed it. [UD 12]

5645 reflex -- reference to either a twin lens or single lens camera that is equipped with mirrors so that the photographer sees exactly the same image as will be exposed on the film. Other forms of viewfinder are less accurate and may cause ruined photographs as a result of the problem of parallax. [CW 19]

5646 Reformation polemical pamphlets -- theological pamphlets addressed to the refutation of the errors of the Church first published during the Reformation (16th C.). The Christian church overhauled itself violently, thus leading to the institution of Protestantism and the resultant growth of various Protestant sects. The overhauling was prompted by errors that many felt demanded change and correction. [GN 14]

5647 refractory subaltern -- a stubborn or unmanageable junior officer; one of the rank of captain, lieutenant, or second lieutenant [fr]

5648 Reg. v. Pritchard -- see Pritchard, Dr. Edward William. The citation is a legal abbreviation meaning The Crown versus Pritchard. Reg. would be the abbreviation for Regina as Victoria was on the throne at the time of Pritchard's trial. [UD 1]

5649 Regent Square -- a small square in Bloomsbury* between Judd St. and Gray's Inn Rd.** North of Coram's Fields* [HHC 22]

5650 Regent St. -- a major thoroughfare designed by John Nash and named for the Prince Regent. Beginning at Piccadilly Circus* it makes a long, sweeping, ninety degree turn to the North and West, crossing Oxford St. at Oxford Circus, continuing on to Cavendish St., just South of Regent's Park. From there to Regent's Park the street is known as Portland Place*.

Regent St. is the location of many of London's department stores and fashionable shops. Liberty*, Jaeger*, Aquascutum, Austin Reed, and Garrard, the Queen's jeweler (responsible for the upkeep of the Crown Jewels), are all located here. [WB 1/UD 7]

5651 Regent's Canal -- the canal which joins the Grand Union Canal of 1793 to the Thames at Limehouse in the middle of the vast London docks area. The canal, dating from 1820, skirts Regent's Park and the Zoo, hence its name. [BC 18]

5652 Regent's Park -- the large North London park laid out generally according to plans prepared by John Nash (1752-1835). The Park now houses the London Zoo, Queen Mary's Garden, and other attractions. The Park's name

is drawn from the Prince Regent, later George IV, who was responsible for the Park and its elegant surrounding homes [BC 8/BH 1]

5653 régime of bread and circuses -- an allusion to the ancient late Roman practice of handing out free bread to the masses and of providing all sorts of games--as at the Circus Maximus or the Coliseum -- to keep the populace happy. At Brotherhood's*, such practices could have a double effect--they would help encourage loyalty to the company and it is a useful device still employed in many companies for keeping out trade unions. [MMA 8]

5654 regimental tie -- a necktie with the colors of a regiment or other military unit usually arranged in diagonal stripes. Such neckwear is not restricted to the Army as any military unit or branch may have such a tie and they are common among other organizations as well. [BH 7]

5655 Regional -- a BBC* radio service which, as the name implies, varied from region to region (Midland, Scottish, Welsh, etc.). It is no longer broadcast. See also National. [BH 9]

5656 Registrar['s Office] -- the General Register Office headed by the Registrar-General is meant. The local offices record births, deaths, and marriages, and civil marriages may be performed there. The resulting documentation is stored at the GRO at St. Catherine's House, 10 Kingsway, London, where copies may be obtained. Registration has been compulsory since 1837. [UD 1/BH P]

5657 Regular Army -- see Army [passim]

5658 Reith, Sir John -- John Charles Walsham Reith, 1st Baron Reith of Stonehaven, (B. 1889). Reith became general manager of the BBC* in 1922, managing director in 1923, and was the first director-general in 1927, a post he held until 1938 when he became chairman of Imperial Airways, later BOAC. He later held a variety of telecommunications and transport positions of importance. [BH 16]

5659 relativity -- the theories of time and space, gravity, and the equivalence of energy with mass accelerated to the square of the speed of light ($E=mc^2$) as propounded by Albert Einstein in his special and general theories of relativity. [np/HHC 31]

5660 Religio Medici -- the eclectic confessions of Christian faith by Sir Thomas Browne (1605-82) first published with the author's approval in 1643. Earlier editions were not so authorized. The work is a collection of opinions, essays, and prayers originally written for Browne's own use and not intended for publication. [GN 15]

5661 remand -- see on remand [MMA 15]

5662 remembrance day -- usually Remembrance Day, the day when Britain honors her war dead. Originally meant to honor the dead of WW I, it now honors all war dead from WW I to the present. It is observed on the Sunday nearest November 11, when WW I ended on the Western Front. The two-minute silence is now observed as part of that day's worship service. [BC 1]

5663 Renault -- a French automobile manufacturing firm dating from 1898. It is noted for the broad range of engine and automobile types manufactured during its long history. [mt/UD 7]

5664 Render unto Caesar -- the text appears in Matthew 22:21, Mark 12:17, and Luke 20:25 [NT 9]

5665 Rennie -- a police constable in Wilvercombe* who gets into trouble by being too free with information regarding the progress of the investigation into the death of Paul Alexis* [HHC 20]

5666 rentes -- French for any sort of yearly income from stocks, bonds, etc.; dividends [CW 5]

5667 Republican -- the political bent of an ill-paid French porter. Use of the term suggests a degree of radicalism, opposition to the government, support for trade unions, and other similar attitudes. [aq]

5668 res angusta -- Latin for narrow, straitened, or confined circumstances, a clerical joke referring to the grave. Mr. Venables' car is small and difficult to get out of. [NT 1]

5669 reservation -- Mr. Hancock* has gotten permission from his bishop

to set aside part of the Eucharistic host for private administration [bc]

5670 reserved his defense -- before any person accused of a serious crime can be brought to trial in England, a preliminary hearing (committal proceedings) must be held to determine if there is a case to prosecute or not. The accused need not defend himself at this time and may choose to "reserve his defense" if remanded for trial in a higher court. [MMA 19]

5671 residuary legatee -- that person specified in a will to get whatever is left after the other bequests have been made [ss/SP 13]

5672 residue -- the remainder of an estate after the debts, charges, bequests, etc., have been satisfied [SP 19]

5673 Resplendent [Hotel] -- Wilvercombe's* largest and among its best hotels. HV stays there during the early part of her stay in Wilvercombe. As presented, it is fictitious, but is typical of many such resort hotels in England and elsewhere. [HHC 3]

5674 Responsions -- the first of three annual examinations which lead to the BA degree at Oxford, familiarly called "Smalls". The Cambridge term is "Little Go". [GN 5]

5675 rest-gown -- a lounge gown, loose-fitting, for informal evening wear; a hostess gown today [SP 16]

5676 Restoration Drama -- the theatre during the reign of Charles II after his Restoration to the monarchy in 1660. The drama was noted for its bawdy puns and word play, especially in the works of Dryden, Congreve, and Farquhar, but the term has been applied to any work written in the vein of the Restoration plays. [GN 4]

5677 Restoration figure -- a lady who possesses ample physical charms such as those portrayed by Rubens, etc. [qs]

5678 Restoration Fund -- a fund to do work on the church in Darley* [HHC 12]

5679 Retreat over the Marne -- the reference in both instances is to the retreat of May, 1918, following the Third Battle of the Aisne, a German offensive [HHC 6/NT 8]

5680 Reubenssohn -- the producer for the movie Apollo Comes to New York, starring Varden*. All are fictitious. [cf]

5681 Reuter -- the Reuters News Agency, one of the world's largest news-gathering organizations, it dates in a primitive form from 1849. In 1858, it started operation in a form that would be recognizable as a modern press agency. It is now international in scope. [CW 15]

5682 Revito -- a product invented by DLS [MMA 4]

5683 Revolution -- the Bolshevik Revolution of October, 1917, that overthrew the Czar and established, eventually, the beginnings of the present system of communism under Vladimir I. Lenin [HHC 4]

5684 revolution [German] -- after WW I, actually beginning on November 10, 1918, the Imperial government collapsed when the Kaiser abdicated and fled his country. What followed was a series of maneuvers that eventually created the Weimar Republic which, in turn, collapsed in 1933 under the onslaught of Adolf Hitler and the Nazis. The Weimar Republic was a weak coalition of the army and various political factions whose only apparent point of agreement was the desire to prevent a Bolshevik takeover like that in Russia. [NT 8]

5685 revue airs -- songs from dramatic presentations consisting of a series of disconnected scenes and often of a satirical nature [CW 3]

5686 Rhead, Gertrude -- see Gertrude Rhead's observation [CW 11]

5687 rheumatic fever -- an acutely painful inflammation of the muscle in and around the joints and of the joints themselves. The disease also attacks the heart valves. It usually attacks children and young adults, but is not exclusive. [NT 10]

5688 rheumatism -- any of several diseases, such as inflammation of the muscles, tendons, joints, etc., causing varying degrees of discomfort and disability. It can be fatal if it involves heart tissues. [WB 10/CW 12]

5689 Rhinns of Kells -- sometimes

rinns. A mountainous area about twenty miles North of Creetown*. The word rhinn may be derived from the Greek for nose, as prominence, "rhis" or "rhinos", nostril or nose. Whatever the derivation, it is now used to apply to a sawback ridge of mountains like the knobs of the vertebrae down someone's spine. [FRH 2]

5690 Rhode, John -- pseudonym of Cecil John Charles Street (1884-1964), English mystery novelist credited with 140 mysteries. He also wrote as Miles Burton. He is particularly noted as a master of carefully contrived, baffling plots, a trait he apparently shared with DLS when she constructed HHC as he helped her with the cipher therein. Some of his early novels deal with the Bolsheviks, the drug menace, and reconstructions of earlier real crimes in a fictional setting. [HHC 33]

5691 rhoomatick -- rheumatism* in Yorkshire dialect [CW 12]

5692 rhubarb tart -- a pie that is filled with cooked, chopped, and sweetened rhubarb stalks. The leaves are never used as they are toxic to humans. [FRH 7]

5693 ribbed vault -- a reference to the roof over the chancel, a vault being an arched roof. The ribs are decorative structural supports which are named for the ribs in a skeleton, which they resemble [NT 2]

5694 ribbon-building -- a housing development built along a main road. The practice is no longer permitted. [GN 14]

5695 Rich as Sneezes -- a variant of the old phrase, "Rich as Croesus". Croesus (ca. 550 B. C.) was king of Lydia and was famous for his great wealth. He lost his wealth and his empire when he attacked Cyrus of Persia in 546 B. C. He almost lost his life as a result of that attack, but a timely fit of humility saved him and Cyrus made him an adviser. [SP 9]

5696 Richard -- the eldest of Phoebe Tucker's* children [GN 1]

5697 Richard III -- the last Plantagenet king and ultimate loser in the Wars of the Roses. He usurped the throne upon his brother's death in 1483, and is remembered mostly for the mysterious disappearance of the Princes in the Tower, the young Edward V and Richard, Duke of York. Both of these boys were murdered, but it is not known upon whose orders; there are many who feel Richard has been wrongly accused. He died at the Battle of Bosworth Field on August 22, 1485, by the forces of Henry Tudor, later Henry VII. Richard is presented by Shakespeare as every bit as evil and hunchbacked as the Tudor propaganda would have us believe, yet Richard III remains one of the more popular history plays. Its accuracy does, however, leave many questions for the serious student of the enigmatic monarch, the last of the House of York. [CW 5/HHC 23/GN 1]

5698 Richardson, Dorothy -- English stream-of-consciousness novelist (1873-1957). Her works emphasize feminine sensibility. [BC 18]

5699 Richmond -- a residential area located to the West of London on the Thames. The area centers on Richmond Green, once a site of Tudor jousting matches. With the advancement of the railroads, the area became a prosperous Victorian community. Robert Fentiman* is presented as having rooms there. [BC 9/MMA 4]

5700 Richmonds, quite a little boom in -- PW's comment relates to Shakespeare's Richard III, V, iv:

"I think there be six Richmonds in the field:
Five have I slain to-day instead of him."

Richmond is Henry, Earl of Richmond, or Henry Tudor, later Henry VII, the man who was responsible for the fall of Richard III at the Battle of Bosworth Field on August 22, 1485. A Richmond, then, is a fresh opponent or an inexhaustible adversary. [mt]

5701 ricks -- a stack of hay or straw. Such stacks will ignite by spontaneous combustion if piled or baled when wet. [NT 18]

5702 Ridd, River -- a little river, about a half mile from Grider's Hole* when walking there from Riddlesdale Lodge*. It is fictitious, but there is a River Nidd in the area. [CW 4]

5703 Riddle-me-right, and riddle-me-ree. -- apparently a reference to

l. 159 of "The Witches' Frolic" from The Ingoldsby Legends*. The line is given there as: "Now riddle me, riddle me right, Madge Gray". [SP 20]

5704 Riddlesdale --- the community in North Yorkshire near where the Duke of Denver* had rented a hunting lodge for the fall season. The location is fictitious. [CW 1]

5705 Riddlesdale Lodge -- the name of the Yorkshire hunting lodge rented for the fall hunting season by the Duke of Denver*. It is here that the unhappy events of CW begin with the death of Denis Cathcart*. It is a large building with comfortable quarters for several couples and servants. It is fictitious. [CW 1]

5706 Riddlesdale Mystery -- the newspapers' catch-name for the problems centered on the death of Denis Cathcart* [UD 2]

5707 Rigby, Diana -- a mutual acquaintance of Freddy Arbuthnot* and PW. It was while waiting for her to appear at her own wedding that Freddy, in bored desperation, started reading the pew Bible from whence he got the inspiration to use the Jacob and Rachel story in Genesis (29ff) to obtain Rachel Levy's* hand in marriage. See also, "I had served nearly seven years . . . ." [SP 12]

5708 right, wrong -- in change-ringing* the terms refer to specific dodging* maneuvers [NT 3]

5709 rigmarole -- from the obsolete "ragman role", a long list or catalogue, meaning any sort of confused and confusing, meaningless chatter. PW is past master of the art as a part of his idiot aristocrat guise. [WB 4]

5710 rigor [mortis] -- the temporary stiffening or rigidity of the muscles after death. The onset and departure of the phenomenon depend on a multitude of variables so use of the presence or absence of rigor as a measure of how long a body has been dead is at best tricky. [passim]

5711 Riley -- a car manufactured in Britain from 1898 to 1969. One sports version marketed from 1923 to 1928 cost £450 and could go 70 mph. [FRH 20]

5712 Rimmon, bow down in the House of -- the reference is to II Kings 5:18: "In this thing the Lord pardon thy servant, that when my master goeth into the house (temple) of Rimmon to worship there, and he leaneth on my hand, and I bow down myself in the house of Rimmon, the Lord pardon thy servant in this thing." Rimmon is identical with the Assyrian storm god Ramman. The expression has come to mean following a practice that is morally repugnant when one does not wish to do so, but must for some reason. It is interesting to note that the Lord does pardon his servant in verse 19. [SP 16]

5713 Ringwood, Sir Harry -- a former customer of Mr. Endicott's* who bought two of that barber's razors for his son, Ringwood junior [HHC 6]

5714 Ringwood, young Mr. -- son of Sir Harry, he studied at Magdalen College* and then entered the foreign service through the Colonial Office* [HHC 6]

5715 "Rio Grande" -- an anonymous folk song, it is a sea chantey or sailors' work song [BH 5]

5716 Ripley -- a fictitious town that coincidentally suggests the real Ripley in North Yorkshire [CW 3]

5717 Ritz -- a particularly deluxe hotel and restaurant in Piccadilly*. Sir Reuben Levy was known to have dined there with friends shortly before his disappearance. The hotel opened in 1905 and was noted at the time for the opulence of its Louis XVI gilded and marble decor. It is named for Swiss hotelier Cesar Ritz and is frequented by PW as it is not far from his flat. [WB 2]

5718 The Rivals -- a comedy by English dramatist Richard Brinsley Sheridan (1751-1816). The play centers on a romantic confusion provided by the marvellous Mrs. Malaprop. Everyone lives happily ever after. [UD 13]

5719 River of the Water of Life -- Bill Rumm* is referring to the Revelation of St. John the Divine, 22:1: "And he shewed me a pure river of water of life, clear as crystal proceeding out of the throne of God and of the Lamb." [SP 13]

5720 River Wale -- a fictitious River, but DLS has stated that she had in mind the real Rivers Nene and Great Ouse [NT 2]

5721 Riverside Dr. -- a parklike thoroughfare in New York City known for its stately homes and magnificent public buildings. Hiram Wetherall* at one time owned a home there. The street is parallel to the Hudson River in the northwestern section of Manhattan, beginning at 72nd St. In some ways it is a more prestigious address than Park Avenue. [ie]

5722 Riviera -- the Italian and French Mediterranean coastal resort area extending from LaSpezia, Italy, westward to Hyères, France, and including Monte Carlo, Nice, and Cannes. Bill Rumm* pronounces it as Rivereera. [CW 5/SP 13/HHC 13/GN 9]

5723 Roach, Alice -- see Alice [SP 17]

5724 Road-House -- it should not be capitalized. The reference is to any of a type, fashionable at the time, of roadside restaurants licensed for dancing and the sale of alcohol. The term is rather old-fashioned now. As they were usually found in the countryside, they catered to motorists, then considered somewhat dashing and naughty. [ae]

5725 Rob -- landlord at the Anwoth Hotel* in Gatehouse-of-Fleet*. In reality this was Joe Dignam, DLS's good friend (see the Foreward to FRH). It is unknown why she used the name Rob here as she uses Joe elsewhere. [FRH 7]

5726 rob Peter to pay all -- Viscount St. George* puns on the old proverb, "rob Peter to pay Paul". It dates from at least the 12th C. in similar forms. In John Wycliffe's Works, Vol. 3, p. 174 (1383), we find, "How should God approve that you rob Peter and give this robbery to Paul in the name of Christ." By 1440, the line has been shortened to the popular phrase now known. [GN 10]

5727 Roberson's -- the source of John Ferguson's* art supplies. It is Roberson & Co., Artists Colour Makers, 77 Park Way, London. They are still manufacturing artists' supplies. [FRH 3]

5728 Roberts, Mr. -- owner(?) of the Crown* pub. Perhaps Sellon* is confused here. See also #2987. [BH 7]

5729 Robertson -- Parker is referring to Archibald Robertson (1853-1931) who was bishop of Exeter and a noted New Testament Scholar. A graduate of Trinity College, Oxford, his fame rests on his studies of Athanasius and Augustine of Hippo*. He is considered the principle Athanasian scholar of his time. DLS is known to have been quite familiar with his work. [WB 7]

5730 Robertson, Supt. -- the fictitious superintendent (see Police Ranks) of police at Glasgow* who helps matters along by providing assistance in the locating of the various suspects, in this case Waters* [FRH 19]

5731 Robey, George -- English comedian, writer, watercolor painter, and amateur Egyptologist (1869-1954). He is known mostly for his rollicking music-hall humor and was known as the "Prime Minister of Mirth". He was knighted for his services during WW I. PW goes to see one of his performances and refers to a part of one of his acts. Miss Climpson* states that she does not care for Robey's performing. [ie/BC 18/SP 15]

5732 Robinson -- Mr. Pettigrew-Robinson* [CW 18]

5733 Robinson, Arthur -- the history scholar who chose to ignore some evidence that disproved his thesis in a major paper and whose reputation was, as a result, destroyed when Miss de Vine* exposed his dishonesty. His wife is the Shrewsbury College* scout*, Annie Wilson (see Annie). [GN 19]

5734 Robinson, Heath -- William Heath Robinson (1872-1944) was an English cartoonist and book illustrator. His cartoons showed fantastic machinery using yards of knotted string and appeared in the Illustrated London News and in the Strand Magazine, among others. He also illustrated the works of many famous authors. Rube Goldberg's contraptions would be an approximate U. S. equivalent. [FRH 13]

5735 Roc's eggs -- as usually presented, a mythical bird of Arabian origin that is apparently first mentioned in the Arabian Nights* story

of Sinbad. The bird is probably a reference to a giant ostrich, the Aepyornis, that lived on the island of Madagascar until it became extinct in the 1660's. Arab traders and other sailors used to use the birds' eggs as storage containers. PW is suggesting that there is no limit to what he would do for HV. [GN 19]

5736 Rochester, Mr. -- Edward Rochester, the central male figure in Charlotte Brontë's novel, Jane Eyre (1847). He is a strange and moody man for whom Jane works as governess to his beautiful little daughter. The presence of Rochester's insane wife is not realized until the day he plans to marry Jane when the poor mad woman's existence is made public, thus preventing the ceremony. A year later, after much suffering for them both, they are finally united. [BH P]

5737 Rockies -- the vast mountain range extending from Montana to New Mexico in the western U. S. The range of which the Rockies are a part extends through Central and South America in an almost unbroken chain as the Rockies in North America, the Sierras in Central and the Andes in South America. [SP 15]

5738 Rockingham -- a Yorkshire earthenware and pottery factory founded in about 1745 by Edward Butler. In 1806, William Brameld took over and founded Brameld and Co. which existed until 1842. A great quantity of excellent if somewhat ornate china was made. See also Brameld, John Wager. [BH E2]

5739 Rodolph -- the title appears as that of a major work when, in fact, "Rodolph the Wild" is "The Second Fytte" of T. L. Beddoes'* The Improvisatore, a long poem in three "fyttes". The Improvisatore, with some other poems, appeared in 1821, printed at Oxford. The first and third "fyttes" are, respectively, "Albert and Emily", and "Leopold". The whole of the poem is larded with graphic details of death, hell, murder, and the corruption of the grave. [HHC 1]

5740 Roger -- Dawson. See the genealogical table at the back of UD [UD 13]

5741 Rogers -- PW's assumed name in "Cave of Ali Baba" wherein he "dies" for two years in order to destroy a theft ring called The Society*. Rogers had been a Wimsey family servant who had died overseas. PW simply assumed the man's identity and infiltrated the group. To The Society he is known as Number 21. [ab]

5742 Rogers -- a garage proprietor at Castle Douglas* who reported some mysterious doings to the police during their investigation of Sandy Campbell's* death [FRH 16]

5743 Rogers -- the commissionaire or attendant at the Bellona Club*. PW exchanges pleasantries with him. [BC 4]

5744 Rogers -- Reggie Pomfret's* accomplice in the spree that led to his being caught dumping Miss Cattermole* back into Shrewsbury College* after hours and drunk [GN 7]

5745 Rogers, Mrs. -- wife of the Bellona Club* attendant [BC 4]

5746 Rogers and Peabody -- a fictitious gentlemen's clothing firm in Wilvercombe* [HHC 32]

5747 Roget -- the thesaurus, originally compiled by Peter Mark Roget. PW uses one in the solution of Meleager Finch's* crossword puzzle. [umw]

5748 Roland -- a reference to the dashing and rather reckless hero of the French Medieval chanson de geste, the Song of Roland*. The name is applied to PW. [BC 8]

5749 "Roll on thou deep and dark blue ocean, roll." -- the line is from Lord Byron's (1788-1824) Childe Harold's Pilgrimage, Canto IV, 179, 1. The line is usually written as: "Roll on, thou deep and dark blue Ocean--roll!" In the circumstances where PW cites this line the next line is of greater interest and irony: "Ten thousand fleets sweep over thee in vain . . . ." [FRH 24]

5750 rolled round and round -- see whatsinames [MMA 15]

5751 Rollers [the] -- a line of rollers up which boats are pushed to move them to a higher [or lower] water level as at a weir and where locks would be unnecessary or impractical. At Oxford

ROLAND AT RONCESVALLES

From a thirteenth-century window of stained glass in Chartres Cathedral. At the right Roland sounding his horn; at the left Roland endeavoring to break his sword Durendal.

#5748

Roland at Roncesvalles, from a 13th C. window in stained glass at Chartres Cathedral. At the right Roland is sounding his horn; at the left he is attempting to break the sword Durendal.

they are at the southern end of the University Parks, not at King's Mill. [GN 12]

5752 Rolls-Royce [Rolls] -- advertised, with justification, as the greatest car in the world, the Rolls-Royce has been manufactured in England since 1904 by the firm established by Charles S. Rolls (1877-1910) and Frederick H. Royce (1863-1933). They now also manufacture the Bentley automobile. The aircraft engines that bear the Rolls-Royce name are manufactured by a separate firm. The Rolls name is synonymous with elegance, great wealth, comfort, and unmatched craftsmanship. In 1905, one model sold for $1300; today a price of over $100,000 is more the norm for many models. PW remains loyal to his Daimlers*, however. [te/FRH 1/SP 13]

5753 Roman ruins -- as DLS claims that all locales in HHC are fictitious, these ruins are also fictitious. However, there were Roman incursions into southwest England, the largest being at _Isca Dumnoniorum_, now Exeter, where a large fortress was maintained. There are, however, no Roman ruins that match the geographical features that DLS has described here. [HHC 1]

5754 Roman vest -- a piece of black material worn with a clerical collar by a clergyman to cover that part of the shirt that would otherwise show above the waistcoat. It is a misnomer in that it is no more associated with the Roman Church than with the Anglican. [BH 5]

5755 Romanée Conti -- the great Grand Cru wine produced in the Vosne-Romanée region of Burgundy. It is one of the most famous and expensive of all the Burgundy wines. [BC 21]

5756 Romano's -- a real restaurant at 399 The Strand, but it no longer exists [GN 11]

5757 Romanov -- the last imperial dynasty in Russia. The family ruled from 1598 until Czar Nicholas II was deposed in March of 1917. For many years after Nicholas's removal as Emperor and his subsequent death, all sorts of people claimed the throne. One of the most poignant of these claims revolved around Nicholas's daughter, Anastasia, who is supposed to have survived the massacre that killed the family. There is no indication that any of the Czar's family survived. [HHC 34]

5758 _romans-policier_ -- French for police or detective novels [HHC 7]

5759 Rome -- the Church of Rome, Roman Catholicism [NT 2]

5760 "Rome prizes most her citizens . . ." -- see leapt into the gulf [BH 14]

5761 _Romeo and Juliet_ -- William Shakespeare's famous romantic tragedy about the starcrossed lovers, probably written in 1595 [UD 23/BH 7]

5762 Romford -- a town to the northeast of London about 15 miles. It is the location of Brotherhood's, Ltd. and the famous cricket* match. [MMA 17]

5763 Romish Convent -- a Roman Catholic convent. The passage reflects the lingering fear, especially in Northern Ireland, that relates Roman Catholicism with political instability. The fear is rooted in the reigns of Henry VIII, Edward VI, and Mary I, and was amplified during the reigns of Charles II and James II, 100 years later. [UD 12]

5764 Roncevaux -- or Roncevalles, a pass in the Pyrenees Mountains where a rear guard of Charlemagne's army was ambushed and defeated in 778 by a band of Basque mountaineers. In such romances as _Le Chanson de Roland_, the Basques become Moslems and Charlemagne returns with the army, defeats the Moslems soundly, and, thus, wins a great victory for Christianity. [GN 17/BH E2]

5765 Ronnie -- the name of an Eton* student mentioned in a conversation overheard by HV in the lounge of the Hotel Resplendent* in Wilvercombe* [HHC 3]

5766 rood screen -- a screen, usually elaborately carved or designed, and, if properly done, surmounted by a rood, or crucifix, bearing the figure of Christ crucified. It separates the nave from the choir or chancel of a church. [bc/NT 2]

5767 rooks -- an Old World bird, _Cor-_

CALEDONIA
Boderia Aestuaria
(Firth of Forth)
WALL OF ANTONINUS
OCEANUS
GERMANICUS
WALL OF HADRIAN
Tina Fl.
(Tyne)
Ituna Aest.
(Solway Firth)
Caer Leul
(Carlisle)
Scoti
HIBERNIA
OCEANUS HIBERNICUS
Moricambe Aest.
(Morecambe B.)
Brigantes
Eboracum
(York)
Mancunium
(Manchester)
Abus Fl.
(Humber)
Mona
(Anglesey)
Lindum
(Lincoln)
Segontium
(Caernarvon)
Deva
(Chester)
Metaris Aest.
(The Wash)
Coritani
OCEANUS VERGIVIUS
Viriconium
(Wroxeter)
Ratae
(Leicester)
Venta Icenorum
(Caistor)
Iceni
St. David's Head
Glevum
(Gloucester)
Verulamium
(St. Albans)
Camulodunum
(Colchester)
LONDINIUM
(London)
Isca Silurum
(Caerleon upon Usk)
Sabrina Aest.
Aquae Solis
(Bath)
Calleva Atrebatum
(Silchester)
Rutupiae
(Richborough)
Venta Belgarum
(Winchester)
Portus Dubrae
Belgae
Atrebates
Cantii
Isca
(Exeter)
Anderida
(Pevensey)
Vectis Ins
(Isle of Wight)
The Saxon Shore
OCEANUS BRITANNICUS
WATLING ST.
FOSSE WAY
IRMIN ST.
AKEMAN ST.
ROMAN BRITAIN
ROMAN MILES
0 25 50 75
ENGLISH MILES
0 15 30 60

#5753

vus frugliegus, black, about the size of a crow, as noisy, and as much a pest [NT 7/GN 11]

5768 "The Rosamunde" -- a short story by French author Julian [Julien] Sermet, an obscure writer of the late 1800's [NT 17]

5769 Rose and Crown -- a pub in Stapley* [CW 11]

5770 Rose and Crown -- a pub that may, from the context, formerly have existed in London at Seven Dials* [MMA 12]

5771 rose madder -- a bright and deep rose-red hue, a sort of "hot pink" to rich maroon depending on how it is mixed. Straight out of the tube it is the rich maroon shade reminiscent of the old and very deeply colored roses. [FRH 2]

5772 Rosenbaum's shows -- the producer of burlesques and pantomimes (not dumb shows) for whom Mrs. Lefranc* once worked [HHC 15]

5773 Rosencrantz -- a producer (?) in the talent agency offices of Isaac Sullivan* who is looking for actors to play in his production of Worm That Turned* [HHC 23]

5774 Roses Round the Door -- a fictitious play [HHC 23]

5775 Rosie -- the daughter of the railway gatekeeper at Darley Halt's* level crossing* [HHC 12]

5776 Rosie -- the elder of the Thoday's* two daughters [NT 6]

5777 "Rosie's Weekly Bits" -- with Aunt Judith, fictitious. The inspiration is probably taken from a then popular weekly, Titbits, an information and gossip publication that is still available. [BC 7]

5778 Ross Island -- see Ross Light [FRH 21]

5779 Ross Light -- a light for mariners on Little Ross Island on the West side of the mouth of Kirkcudbright Bay [FRH 19]

5780 Ross, P. C. -- the constable assigned to work with Sgt. Dalziel* during the investigation of the death of Sandy Campbell* [FRH 2]

5781 Rossetti -- Dante Gabriel Rossetti (1828-82), English artist and poet whose work included various translations from Italian poets including Dante*. See also Pre-Raphaelite Brotherhood. [FRH 13]

5782 Rossiter, Miss -- one of the secretaries in the copywriting department at Pym's Publicity* [MMA 1]

5783 Rotherhithe -- a community on the South side of the Thames, down river from London. It is suggested to PW that if anyone leaks information about The Society* to the police, the body of the talker will be found floating in the Thames there. The area remains a maze of docks and mills, but is now a most respectable district. [ab]

5784 rouble[s] -- or ruble, the official Russian unit of currency [CW 5]

5785 Rouen -- a city in northern France approximately thirty-eight miles East of Le Havre on the Seine, down river from Paris. Arthur Prendergast and Mrs. Fielding are located there. [te/aq]

5786 Rouge Dragon -- see College of Arms [CW 14]

5787 Round Pond -- the large pond in Kensington Gardens* that is not round--it is a sort of oval with pretensions patterned after Italianate designs for gardens dating from the Renaissance and later. [MMA 17]

5788 Round Table rule -- PW is alluding in this sentence to Tennyson's* Idylls of the King, "Guinevere, l. 472:

"To love one maiden only, cleave to her . . . ."

[BH 10]

5789 Round the World -- one of the basic fancy maneuvers done with a yo-yo [MMA 6]

5790 Roundabout [curling like the road to] -- the allusion is to G. K. Chesterton's poem, "The Road to Roundabout", lines 7 and 13-16:

"And so the roads they twist and squirm . . .
And I should say they wound about
To find the town of Roundabout,
The merry town of Roundabout,
That makes the world go round."

The word roundabout is also applied,

infrequently, to what is known as a merry-go-round in North America. [FRH 2]

5791 roundabouts -- merry-go-rounds; see above [SP 9]

5792 rounds -- going down the scale from the high toned bells to the low toned bells [NT 1]

5793 Rouse Case -- the reference is to one Arthur Alfred Rouse, a fancy goods travelling salesman of Buxted Rd., North Finchley, who, on November 6, 1930, killed an unknown man to whom he had given a ride. Rouse left the body in his car alongside the Northampton-Hardingstone Rd. He destroyed both the body and the car in a fire.

Rouse was questioned by locals about the fire shortly after it had begun and coolly told them he thought it must be a local bonfire. The body was burned beyond recognition and was never identified, but an examination of the car was conducted in a garage. Rouse was found guilty of murder on February 1, 1931, at the Northamptonshire Assizes and was sentenced to death by Mr. Justice Talbot. The jury returned its verdict after deliberating for only about fifteen minutes. He was executed at Bedford Prison at 8:00 A. M. on March 30, 1931. [te]

5794 rove-over lines -- wandering, run-on lines in poetry [GN 13]

5795 the Row -- Rotten Row, the horseback riding lane or circuit in Hyde Park* that extends from Hyde Park Corner to Kensington Gardens. The origin of the name is obscure and uncertain. [MMA 19]

5796 rowan-tree -- the Eurasian Sorbus aucuparia, a member of the rose family and a cousin to the American mountain ash [FRH 2]

5797 Rowe, Jimmy -- publican at the Blue Dragon*, a neighborhood pub near where the George Fentiman's* live. As presented here, it is fictitious. [BC 18]

5798 Royal Automobile Club -- the R. A. C. is headquartered at 83 Pall Mall* and offers an extensive array of services to member motorists including the information posts as alluded to in "Cat in the Bag". [cb/CW 14]

5799 Royal Commission -- usually an ad hoc committee appointed by the government in Letters Patent* to investigate a particular issue or problem. The Commission reports to the Home Secretary* who presents the report to Parliament and the Commission is disbanded with the exception of those that are Standing Commissions such as that on Ancient Monuments.

The one referred to in FRH was created in 1929 to investigate reports that a girl who had been arrested and charged with an offense had been bullied by the police for five hours. The Royal Commission was formed after a local tribunal failed to agree on just what had happened. Previous Royal Commissions regarding the police were formed in 1836-9, 1855, and 1906-8. After 1929, the next one was not appointed until 1960. [FRH 7]

5800 Royal Enclosure at Ascot -- that part of the Ascot racecourse reserved for use by royalty, admission to which is obtained only upon application to the Lord Chamberlain. [MMA 3/GN 4]

5801 Royal Family -- the reference is to the present family, the Windsors, and the penchant of Queen Mary for rather ornately frilled bodices on her dresses and turban hats of elaborate design. [UD 11]

5802 Royal Free Hospital -- located on Gray's Inn Rd., Holborn** between Clerkenwell and King's Cross in a Classical style building dating, in parts, from 1842, and originally built as the Light Horse Volunteer Barracks. Mary Whittaker* trained there. [UD 1]

5803 Royal Gallery -- the room immediately to the left of the Lords' Chambers at the Victoria Tower (the one opposite Big Ben*) end of the Houses of Parliament* is the Prince's Chamber. Next in line is the Royal Gallery, then the King's (Queen's) Robing Room*. As the Royal Gallery and Prince's Chamber form a long processional route for the sovereign when opening Parliament, the effect is almost one long room. [CW 6]

5804 Royal Oak -- a fictitious pub in the Pagford* area, the name alluding to an oak in which Charles II hid from Cromwell's men after the battle of Worcester in 1651 [BH 11]

ROTTEN ROW, HYDE PARK.

#5795 Rotten Row, Hyde Park, London.

5805 Royal Prerogative -- royalty enjoys certain rights that others do not. For instance, in England no member of the Royal Family can be arrested on a civil charge unless he consents to it. In this sense, however, it is meant more generally to mean prerogative of rank. [GN 17]

5806 royal proxy bedding his master's bride -- in earlier times when travel was slow, it was the custom for a monarch to send a royal envoy to the home of his intended bride whom he had never seen. The envoy would marry the woman as a proxy for his master. The marriage would be consummated symbolically in some discreet fashion. These actions would cement the marriage as if it had been conducted with all the principals in attendance, thus giving it the weight of law. [BH 4]

5807 Royal Sunbeam Cycle -- a reference to either the Sunbeam* bicycles or motorcycles manufactured in the first half of this century. The motorcycles were noted racers and often contended successfully with Norton* and Indian machines. The 1924 "Roadster" motorcycle, for instance, displaced 347cc and cost about $315.00 U. S. The bicycles cost propotionally less. [WB 10]

5808 Royal Yacht Club at Cowes -- formed in 1815, it became the Royal Yacht Squadron in 1833 after the Prince Regent became George IV in 1820. The Prince was the Squadron's most illustrious member. Cowes is at the mouth of the River Medina on the North coast of the Isle of Wight on the Solent, and is the center of yachting in Britain. [MMA 3]

5809 Royalty [ought to have been] -- the reference is to the punctuality of royalty in general. If one receives an invitation or a royal command for some function, one may assume that it will start at the stated time and that those in attendance should be present at that time. Royalty are not kept waiting. [qs]

5810 Rozier, Aristide -- the commissaire de police in Chateau-Thierry* from whom PW receives every cooperation and courtesy. He is fictitious. [NT 8]

5811 Ruat coelum! -- Latin for, "Let the heavens fall!" in the sense of submission to Divine will as well as in the literal sense [BH 5]

5812 rubbidge -- see Mrs. Gamp [GN 3]

5813 rubber solution -- an adhesive [MMA 19]

5814 Rubens -- Peter Paul Rubens (1577-1640), a master artist of the Flemish school noted for being prolific and for having a rich and robust style [ab]

5815 rudder lines -- the cables used to control the rudder on a scull*. They would normally be handled by the coxswain. [GN 12]

5816 Ruddle, Bert -- Mrs. Ruddle's* son. He is not presented in any detail. [BH 1]

5817 Ruddle, Martha -- mother of Bert Ruddle*, she is the cleaning lady at Talboys*. She had worked for Mr. Noakes* and continues on as an "aide" to Bunter after the Wimseys buy the house. She is abrupt and crude and is the cause of Bunter's nearly becoming apoplectic when she dusts all those "dirty" bottles of port, an '08 Cockburn! She lives next door to the house and was known to HV when Harriet was a little girl. [BH 1]

5818 rudeness [to see through] -- PW is referring to St. Augustine's* autobiography, The Confessions, written about 1600 years ago. Outside of the Bible, especially Paul's "Letters", probably no other work has had so great an impact on the development of Christian thought. Specifically, PW is alluding to Book I, Ch. 18. At that point, Augustine is considering his education when a youth. He writes (translation by R. S. Pine-Coffin): "But was it surprising that I was lured into these fruitless pastimes and wandered away from you, my God? I was expected to model myself upon men who were disconcerted by the rebukes they received if they used outlandish words or strange idioms [rudeness, from the Latin barbarismus for foreign or rude speech] to tell of some quite harmless thing they might have done, but revelled in the applause they earned for the fine flow of well-ordered and nicely balanced phrases with which they described their own acts of indecency."

From this, Saint Augustine goes on to build his whole theory of sin and his explanation of it in later parts of the autobiography. The theory is, interestingly, drawn from Aristotle and states that the public will accept almost any sin or aberration if the sinner gets up and makes a beautiful speech about it. Such an approach is, however, as Augustine points out very carefully, a logical fallacy, a distraction: No amount of beautiful speech can eradicate a sin. [MMA 15]

5819 Rudge in the Arcade -- a fictitious firm in the Burlington Arcade* [MMA 3]

5820 Rue Auguste Léopold -- a street in Paris that supposedly intersects with the Rue de la Paix* in the Opera Quarter. It is apparently a DLS invention as no such street could be located. [CW 5]

5821 Rue de la Paix -- a famous street in Paris beginning at the Rue de Rivoli opposite the Jardin de Tuileries, crossing the Rue Faubourg St. Honoré, the Place Vendôme, and continuing on to the Opéra, almost due North of the Louvre. The street is located in the Opera Quarter of Paris and is home to that fabled jeweller, Cartier, as well as many other exclusive shops, making it a synonym for luxury and elegance. [CW 5]

5822 Rue St. Honoré -- a famous major street in Paris on the Right Bank. It is basically a continuation of the Faubourg St. Honoré that begins at the Rue Royale and runs southward to join the Avénue de l'Opéra just North of the Louvre. [CW 5]

5823 rug -- a heavy blanket used in older cars and carriages to supplement poor or to suffice with nonexistent heating systems. In summer they served as useful ground cover at picnics. [BH 1]

5824 Rugby -- a market town and famous railway junction in central England that is perhaps better known for the public school* there which created Rugby football in 1823. The school was founded in 1567. [UD 20/FRH 14/MMA 10]

5825 Rugby Tavern -- a tavern given as being on the corner of Great James and Chapel Sts. The intersection is fictitious. Both streets are real, but they never intersect. However, there is a Rugby St. that intersects with Great James St., and there is a Rugby Tavern there, so that may be what DLS had in mind. [NT 16]

5826 rule of three -- a mathematical process used to find a fourth number when three are known. The first is of the same relation to the second as the third is to the unknown fourth. It is also known as the "golden rule" or the "rule of proportion". It is a simple algebraic analogy. [HHC 25]

5827 Rules -- London's oldest restaurant and oyster bar at 34-5 Maiden Lane, East of Charing Cross and North of and parallel to The Strand**. It was established in 1798 by Benjamin Rule and features caricatures and prints recalling the law, theatre, and artists. [SP 15]

5828 "Rules for Change-Making on Four Bells" -- there are a great many rulebooks, pamphlets, and essays on change-ringing for different numbers of bells. This particular one was not identified. [NT 11]

5829 Rumm, Bill -- the quiet one of the two burglars who is helped by PW to see the error of his ways and who teaches PW how to pick locks, etc. His redemption and subsequent usefulness to PW is shown extensively in SP wherein he teaches Joan Murchison* how to get into a deed box*. His nickname is "Blindfold Bill" and it is said that, "he was the most accomplished burglar and safe-breaker in the three kingdoms [England, Scotland and Wales]". His disquisition on the evils of gelignite is marvellous. He appears at the PW-HV wedding in his Salvation Army uniform. See also Bill. [SP 13]

5830 Rumpelmeyer's -- the restaurant where the Dowager Duchess* takes HV for tea to perk her up after a fit of depression over the financial arrangement she must make with PW as HV has always had to work for her money. This fashionable restaurant at 10 St. James's St. no longer exists. [BH P]

5831 run a corner in wheat in Chicago -- a market maneuver wherein someone buys all or almost all of a stock or commodity to force the price up. If

one has a monopoly, then one may charge whatever the purchasers will bear. It is a dangerous speculative operation that requires a great deal of both money and nerve. Apparently Mr. Milligan has both. [WB 7]

5832 Ruritania -- the mythical European kingdom central to the adventure novels of Anthony Hope [Hawkins] (1863-1933): The Prisoner of Zenda, Rupert of Hentzau, and The Heart of Princess Osra. The name Ruritania has become synonymous with romantic court adventures featuring confused identities, intrigue, duels, etc. [HHC 4/GN 4]

5833 Rushworth[s] -- Naomi, an artist, and her unnamed mother, friends of Marjory Phelps*. Naomi is now "into" the study of glands (see Dr. Voronoff), a currently popular topic in Chelsea* circles. [BC 10]

5834 Russell, Bob -- the undertaker in Fenchurch St. Paul* [NT 4]

5835 Russell, Mary -- see Thoday, Mary [NT 2]

5836 Russell Square -- one of the largest squares in central London's Bloomsbury* district, named for landowning Russell family to which the Dukes of Bedford belonged. The Square is bordered on the West by the University of London and the British Museum. Sir Julian Freke* was headed for #24 Russell Square when Parker gave him the cab that he had ordered for himself. [WB 10]

5837 Ruyslaender, Henry -- a diamond merchant, and jealous husband. He does not appear in the story. [pj]

5838 Ruyslaender, Mrs. -- the wife of Henry Ruyslaender* and victim of blackmail. PW resorts to some rather unusual tactics to dispense justice poetically in his successful plan to save the lady from disgrace and divorce. [pj]

5839 Ryder's Heath -- a fictitious location. See Shelly Head. [UD 20]

(S)

5840 S. A. -- an abbreviation (to observe modesty?) for sex appeal [HHC 3]

5841 SCR -- see Senior Common Room [GN 1]

5842 sa maitresse -- French for "his mistress" [HHC 7]

5843 Sabine maiden, captured -- the reference is to the legendary rape of the Sabine virgins, ca. 753 B. C. Romulus tricked the male Sabine population into leaving and sent the male population of Rome, in desperate need of wives, to help themselves to the women. The vision of PW as one of these maidens is amusing, but even more so when one considers his captors. [BC 15]

5844 Sabaoth -- the number 2 bell at Fenchurch St. Paul*, it is only slightly heavier (about 800 pounds) than little Gaude*. She is a new bell in the ring and is tuned to ring B. She was cast in 1887. The word "sabaoth" appears in Romans 9:29 and James 5:4 as "the Lord of Sabaoth", or "hosts". In that usage, "hosts" refers to all of the forces at God's disposal in His universe. The concept is clarified in Psalm 89:6-8. [NT 1]

5845 sackbut -- the old version of the modern trombone [SP 13]

5846 sachet -- a small bag or pouch, in this case for pajamas, but more usually of smaller size and containing a perfumed powder of dried flowers used to scent closets, drawers, etc., lavender being a favorite [FRH 18]

5847 Sacrament [to a dying parishoner] -- when a priest, through anointing and prayer, bestows spiritual help and the hope of bodily health on someone who is seriously ill, he is administering a Sacrament (there are six others), sometimes still referred to as Extreme Unction. The rite is for all who are seriously ill, not just for the dying. The Biblical precedent for this sacrament is in the Epistle of James 5:14-16. [CW 3/NT 2]

5848 Sacred Heart with its French text . . . Corpus Christi -- one of the various illustrations of the Sacred

Heart of Jesus with a printed French text on the reverse. There is no text of a specific nature in the Church of England, so we must assume a text of sentimental piety to match the picture. The special observance for the Sacred Heart is especially French in nature, it having been initiated there by Saint Mary Margaret Alacoque in the 1600's. The feast did not become general in the Roman Catholic Church until 1856. [UD 22]

5849 sacrilege -- gross profanation of anything sacred to God [NT 6]

5850 sacristan -- an officer of a church in charge of the sacristy and its ceremonial equipment. The term is also used to refer to a sexton. The latter sense is the more common when used as Miss Climpson* does in this case. [UD 22]

5851 sacristy -- a room separate from the sanctuary of a church but adjacent to it where the priest's vestments and other paraphernalia, elements for the Eucharist, etc., are stored [UD 22]

5852 sad sea waves [to weep by the] -- a typical construction of epic poetry which utilizes alliteration widely for its aural effect. The line is suggestive of Homer's Odyssey, but could as easily be from any epic. It is probably a PW paraphrase of something from Homer. [HHC 9]

5853 saddle of mutton -- a cut from a sheep to be roasted and including the backbone and both loins or parts of them and weighing up to ten pounds [CW 10/BC 5/MMA 4]

5854 saddlebag chairs -- usually upholstered in cloth or supple leather, the chair was made in imitation of or with genuine Asian camel saddlebags. True saddlebag chairs had upholstery of carpeting in direct imitation of the camel bags, but Cathcart's* were rendered in crimson leather. [CW 5]

5855 Sadducee attitude -- the Sadducees were a Jewish party of mostly priestly aristocracy who questioned and rejected any doctrine not in the Law. Such an attitude would reject anything not in the Law or not proved. PW is reflecting on Parker's habit of not readily accepting the obvious inferences without some tangible proof-- a not unreasonable attitude for a police officer. [CW 2]

5856 saecular -- a variant of secular used in GN to refer to the apparent agelessness of the beech trees in question [GN 12]

5857 safe as houses -- houses means churches here, from house of worship. The expression is apparently of recent origin, not having appeared in print prior to 1859 when it was recorded in Cornwallis's New World, i, 79. [WB 9/MMA 5/NT 19/GN 12]

5858 safe bind, safe find -- Miss Twitterton* and Mr. Puffett* are quoting from Thomas Tusser's (1524?-80) Five Hundred Points of Good Husbandry, Ch. 56, the section on "Washing":

"Dry sun, dry wind;
Safe bind, safe find."

The phrase also appears, later, in Shakespeare's The Merchant of Venice, II, v, 53, with "fast" instead of "safe". There is no conscious effort to quote here, however, the phrase long being popular colloquially. [BH 6]

5859 Saffron Walden -- a town in Essex about 14 miles southeast of Cambridge [BH 11]

5860 Sahib and all that -- sahib is an Urdu word from Arabic which originally meant friend. During the period of British control of India it meant "sir" and was used to address any European or Indian with either military or social status. Cathcart fitted this precisely--he had money, a commission, he could shoot, ride, and do all the things one has come to expect of the colonial of the period. In general, a term of respect. [CW 1/BC 9]

5861 St. Albans -- a city approximately twenty miles North of London, site of the Roman town of Verulamium. The present name derives from St. Alban, a 4th C. Christian martyr. [BC 18]

5862 St. Aldate's -- the name of one segment of the main North-South street through the center of old Oxford. Christ Church College and the Oxford Town Hall are on St. Aldate's St. [GN 3]

5863 St. Andrews -- in Fife, Scotland, a resort and university town

famous as the home of both John Knox and golf. Knox preached his first sermon at Holy Trinity Church on South St. in 1547. The capital of golfdom is located at the Royal and Ancient Golf Club where the rules of modern golf and the first eighteen-hole course were originated in 1754. The British Open and other great matches are played there. [FRH 13]

5864 St. Andrew's -- DLS is probably referring to St. George's, Queen's Square, Bloomsbury. The nearest St. Andrew's is in Holborn, some distance away. [NT 11]

5865 St. Augustine -- of Hippo (345-430), teacher of rhetoric at Milan where he was converted from his heretical beliefs by the work of St. Ambrose of Milan who baptised him. He later entered the priesthood and became Bishop of Hippo in North Africa. His Confessions and City of God have had more influence on Western thought and the Church than any works other than the Bible. He is celebrated on August 28. He is not to be confused with St. Augustine of Canterbury who, as emissary of Pope Gregory I, brought Christianity to England, first converting King Ethelbert of Kent. That St. Augustine founded his mission at Canterbury and died in 604. His feast is celebrated on May 26. [CW 9/MMA 15]

5866 St. Clement Danes -- designed by Christopher Wren in 1682, it was destroyed in 1941 and was rebuilt and dedicated to the Royal Air Force in 1955-58. Other air forces are honored there as well. The church is on an "island" in The Strand* just outside the Law Courts*. The bells of St. Clement's are associated with oranges and lemons in the nursery rhyme because of the fruit barges that landed nearby. Samuel Johnson* worshipped there. [MMA 12]

5867 St. Cross Church -- a very ancient and small church on St. Cross Rd., Oxford, across the street from the Balliol College cricket ground where DLS located her fictitious Shrewsbury* College. The church is chapel to St. Catherine's College as well as being a parish church. The structure is very old, parts dating from the 12th C. [BH P]

5868 St. Cross Lodge -- a gate lodge at the St. Cross Rd. side of the fictitious Shrewsbury College* [GN 1]

5869 St. Cross Rd. -- a real street running to the North from and at right angles to Holywell St. in Oxford. It is on the East side of the fictitious Shrewsbury College* [GN 1]

5870 St. Cuthbert's St. -- in Kirkcudbright*. It is only natural that there should be such a street there as the town's name is a corruption of the saint's name--Kirk-cuthbert--a reference to the man who converted much of Scotland to Christianity. [FRH 13]

5871 St. Denis, Cedric -- a pen name used by Alfred Morecambe* when writing plays for his wife [HHC 32]

5872 St. Edfrith's -- Miss Climpson* has a friend who is a vicar* at this church in Holborn*. As there is no saint of that name, the church must be fictitious. [UD 4]

5873 St. Enoch Station -- the main railway terminus in Glasgow when the Glasgow and South Western Railway was operating. By 1930, that railway had merged with others to form the London, Midland and Scottish Railway which is now a part of British Rail. Glasgow Central Station is now used, St. Enoch's having been closed. [FRH 10]

5874 St. Gengulphus -- a reference to "The Lay of St. Gengulphus", a poem from the Ingoldsby Legends by Richard Harris Barham. The author claims that this is the full name of the saint whom we remember in the phrase "By Jingo!" The quotation, "Good gracious!", etc., is found in line 283 of the poem which comically recounts how the fictitious Gengulphus earned his sainthood. [FRH 7]

5875 St. George -- a reference to the patron saint of England and a popular pub name as in The George and Dragon. (He is popularly portrayed in the act of slaying a dragon.) He has been known in England since at least the 8th C., but gained special attention there when he appeared in a mass vision to the troops of Richard I during the Crusades. He replaced Edward the Confessor as patron saint during the reign of Edward III. [BC 7]

5876 Saint George -- see Viscount St. George [GN 8/BH P]

5877 St. George's -- a church on Hanover Square* in London. Constructed in 1721-24 as the area was developed, it remains an integral part of the neighborhood. The interior is white with gold detail work, and is noted for the fashionable weddings held there. Among these weddings were those of Benjamin Disraeli and Theodore Roosevelt. The church is at the intersection of St. George's St. and Hanover Square. [HHC 4/BH P]

5878 St. George's Square -- a street in Pimlico* which runs in a northerly direction from the Thames at Grosvenor Rd. to Belgrave Rd. The street is entitled to its status as a square because it is split by a wide parklike median. Miss Climpson* has a flat on this street at number 97A. [UD 3]

5879 St. Giles' -- a broad main street in "old" Oxford [GN 12]

5880 St. Giles's Circus -- in central London, the intersection of Oxford and New Oxford Sts.** with Charing Cross and Tottenham Court Rds.** [WB 6]

5881 St. Ives -- a town to the North and West of Cambridge. It is now a part of Cambridgeshire, but was formerly in Huntingdonshire. That latter county was absorbed into the former during the reorganization of local governments in the 1970's. The town is on the River Great Ouse and is named after St. Ivo. It was the home of Oliver Cromwell*. [HHC 17/NT 18]

5882 St. James's St. -- a London street running northwest from Pall Mall at St. James's Palace to Piccadilly [UD 23]

5883 St. John -- see Feast of St. John [UD 19]

5884 St. John-ad-Portam-Latinum -- the Latin version of St. John before the Latin Gate*, the church at Duke's Denver*. This is the church that Alfred Thipps was working on when he found the nude corpse in his bathtub. [NT 1]

5885 St. John Before the Latin Gate -- according to tradition, St. John the Evangelist was boiled in oil by Domitian, but he survived the ordeal which took place near the Latin Gate of ancient Rome's southeast quarter about a quarter of a mile from the Baths of Caracalla. The story continues, by way of Tertullian, that St. John not only survived, but his health was improved by the experience. The church at Duke's Denver* apparently is named to honor and to remember that event. Other versions of the story suggest that John was tortured by the Proconsul at Ephesus, not by Domitian. Whichever version is true, there is now a church in Rome honoring St. John that is located on the Via Latina not far from the Latin Gate or the Baths of Caracalla. The one in DLS's reference refers to the Saint's Day, May 6--St. John ante Portam Latinum in the Anglican calendar, so the church antedates the Reformation and follows Roman Catholic naming practices. [WB 4]

5886 St. John of Jerusalem -- the apostle St. John of the gospels to whom the Order of St. John of Jerusalem is dedicated [WB 8]

5887 St. John's -- adjacent to Balliol and Trinity Colleges on St. Giles' and Broad Sts. in central Oxford, the College was founded, like Trinity, during the reign of "Bloody" Mary in 1555 as a thank offering for her drive to return to the "true" religion, Roman Catholicism. The gardens referred to by PW occupy about five acres and are described as the closest thing in Oxford to a genuine English "Country House" garden with its richly varied beds. [SP 11]

5888 St. John's College -- Cambridge, founded in 1511 with benefactions from Lady Margaret Beaufort and under the direction of John Fisher. A statue of Lady Shrewsbury stands in the College's Second Court. Among its favorite famous alumni are Roger Ascham, Robert Herrick, John Herschel, William Wordsworth, and Louis Leakey. [GN 3]

5889 St. John's Gardens -- see St. John's [GN 14]

5890 St. John's wort -- a family of herbs and shrubs with showy yellow flowers. The St. John in question is St. John the Baptist. [NT 3]

5891 Saint-Lazare, Gare -- see Gare

Saint Lazare [mt/aq]

5892 St. Luke's Hospital -- the teaching hospital in Battersea* alluded to as the location of Sir Julian Freke's* teaching and medical work. He is a surgeon and neurologist there, teaches anatomy, among other things, and does research in psychopathology and physical disorders at the hospital's laboratories. DLS's hospital is fictitious as presented, but it is obvious that she had St. John's in mind. There are two St. Luke's in London--one might assume so as St. Luke is the patron saint of doctor's, goldsmiths, and sculptors--but they are situated elsewhere in London and are nowhere near Battersea. [WB 1]

5893 St. Luke's House -- the home of Sir Julian Freke*. It is connected directly to the hospital. [WB 6]

5894 St. Margaret's -- in Westminster*, was orginally built by Edward the Confessor in the 11th C. It has been rebuilt and altered many times. One of the stained glass windows is a gift from Ferdinand and Isabella commemorating the marriage of their daughter, Catherine, to Prince Arthur. By the time it arrived, however, Arthur was dead and Catherine was betrothed to his younger brother, the future Henry VIII. The church is the chapel for the House of Commons which is just across the Old Palace Yard. Next door is Westminster Abbey. [MMA 12]

5895 St. Martin-in-the-Field's [crypt of] -- a church located on Trafalgar Square in central London. The original medieval church was surrounded by fields and was remodelled by James Gibbs in the 18th C. to its present Neo-classical appearance. The quasi-Greek temple effect was not well received at first, but the structure eventually became a model for other churches. The crypt contains an 18th C. whipping post among other artifacts, but is better known as a shelter for the homeless, a tradition begun by WW I Army chaplain H. R. L. Sheppard who wanted a place for servicemen and others who were stranded. [HHC 30]

5896 St. Martin's-le-Grand -- PW is referring to the Post Office on that street just North of St. Paul's Cathedral [MMA 17]

5897 St. Mary-le-Strand -- a baroque miniature designed by James Gibbs from 1714-17. Like St. Clement Danes, it is on an "island" in the middle of the street just opposite King's College and Somerset House* on The Strand*. [MMA 12]

5898 St. Michael's, Coventry -- the parish church for Coventry* which is better known as Coventry Cathedral (from 1919). It was built in the 14th and 15th centuries, but was destroyed by German bombs on November 14, 1940. Only the shell now remains, a memorial to that raid and to the dead of WW II. A new St. Michael's was built adjacent to the ruin of the original. [NT 1]

5899 Saint Onesimus -- the church in Leahampton* attended by Miss Climpson*. It is named for Onesimus who died ca. A. D. 90. His feast day is February 16. Paul's Epistle to Philemon relates Onesimus's story, including his martyrdom. While the saint is real, this particular church is fictitious. [UD 4]

5900 St. Pancras -- a railway terminus in the North of London built in 1864 by the Midland Railway. While not very close to the center of London, it is as close as was permitted at the time of its construction. Designed by Sir George Gilbert Scott, it remains as built, a unique mixture of medieval Gothic in brick and Italian terracotta. The upper stories of the station housed a hotel. [WB 3]

5901 St. Paul's Cathedral -- in central London within The City*. The present church may be the fourth or fifth on the site and was designed by Christopher Wren. The foundation stone was laid on June 21, 1675, and it was completed in 1708 when Wren was 75. He was buried within the cathedral in 1723, and his inscription reads: "Si monumentum requiris circumspice", or "Reader, if you seek his monument, look around you." The cathedral is 500 feet long, 242 feet wide across the transepts, and 365 feet high to the top of the cross on the dome. The building encloses 78,000 square feet. [NT 20/BH E2]

5902 St. Peter Mancroft -- in Norwich,

St. Martin's in the Fields, Trafalgar Square.

#5895 St. Martin's in the Fields, Trafalgar Square, London.

#5901 St. Paul's Cathedral, London

#5901 The nave, St. Paul's Cathedral, London.

Norfolk, on St. Peter's St. It is the finest of Norwich's churches apart from the Cathedral. St. Peter's is an outstanding example of Perpendicular* architecture and its ring of bells celebrated the defeat of the Spanish Armada in 1588. On May 2, 1715, the bells completed the first known complete peal of 5,040 changes in three hours and eighteen minutes. The same bells are still in regular use. [NT 1]

5903 Saint-Saens, Camille -- the French composer (1835-1921) who was a true prodigy with perfect pitch. He gave his first recital at age ten. [ie]

5904 St. Simon's -- the parish church in North Fellcote*. It is amusing to recall that St. Simon may have been a member of the Zealots*, those extreme nationalists who eventually brought about the revolt against the Romans in 70 A. D. which led to the destruction of Jerusalem, because the church's pastor, the Reverend Nathaniel Foulis*, is victimized by a modern zealot in the person of George Goyles*. It was St. Luke who called Simon the Zealot. [CW 3]

5905 St. Simon's Eau -- eau, or water, from the French, applies here, but the canal or stream is apparently fictitious. [NT 7]

5906 St. Stephen's -- St. Stephen's Porch and Hall form the major public entry to the Houses of Parliament on the side of the building opposite the Thames River and about midway along the building's length. [CW 19]

5907 St. Thingummy on the gridiron -- St. Lawrence, according to legend, was roasted alive on a gridiron* at the order of the Roman emperor Valerian in A. D. 258. Pope Sixtus had been killed, and Lawrence, a Deacon of Rome, was ordered to bring the treasures of the Church to Valerian. Lawrence brought the poor and sick who had been helped by alms. Not amused, Valerian had him killed. Contrary to the legend, however, Lawrence was probably beheaded. [BH E2]

5908 Sainte-Croix, Duc de (in Rouen*) -- a friend of PW's with whom he plans to spend a few days, but the events of the story force postponement of the visit [aq]

5909 sal volatile -- a strong solution of ammonium carbonate in ammonia water, alcohol, or, possibly, both. It is useful as a smelling salt for those who feel faint. [CW 1]

5910 sale Boche -- French for, "dirty Boche". See Boche. [NT 8]

5911 Salic Law -- an ancient law code of the Salian Franks, written in Latin, and extant in various critical revisions in the 5th, 8th, and 9th centuries. PW is using the term here in its common meaning as excluding females from inheritance. Such exclusion would also exclude inheritance through a female line. It is the basis for the law of the French monarchy that excluded females from succession. It is this law that was cited to prevent Edward III from claiming the French throne through his mother's lineage--she was the daughter of Philip IV of France. The French courts gave the crown to Philip of Valois, a nephew of Philip IV, in 1328. Edward took no action until 1340, when he proclaimed himself king of France, thus starting the Hundred Years' War which featured that famous encounter with Joan of Arc, the battles of Agincourt, Poitiers, and Crécy, and the sieges of Orléans and Calais. [HHC 32]

5912 Salient -- in WW I, with a capital "S", DLS is referring to the area around Ypres* in Belgium which, from 1914 almost to the end of the War, was the focus of much brutal fighting. A salient is a convexity in the front line that leaves the defender exposed to fire on three sides. [HHC 4/NT 2]

5913 saline injections -- salt water injections. The human body is mostly water and has a need for salt, an electrolyte, so such injections would help keep a body's fluid levels at a proper point and would delay or slow the process of dehydration which would weaken the body and allow a more rapid spread of a disease. [WB 13]

5914 Salisbury -- an ancient city 83 miles southwest of London noted for its magnificent 13th C. Cathedral and surrounding buildings. The Cathedral library has one of four surviving copies of the Magna Charta, that of William of Longespée, Earl of Salisbury, who was buried in the Cathedral

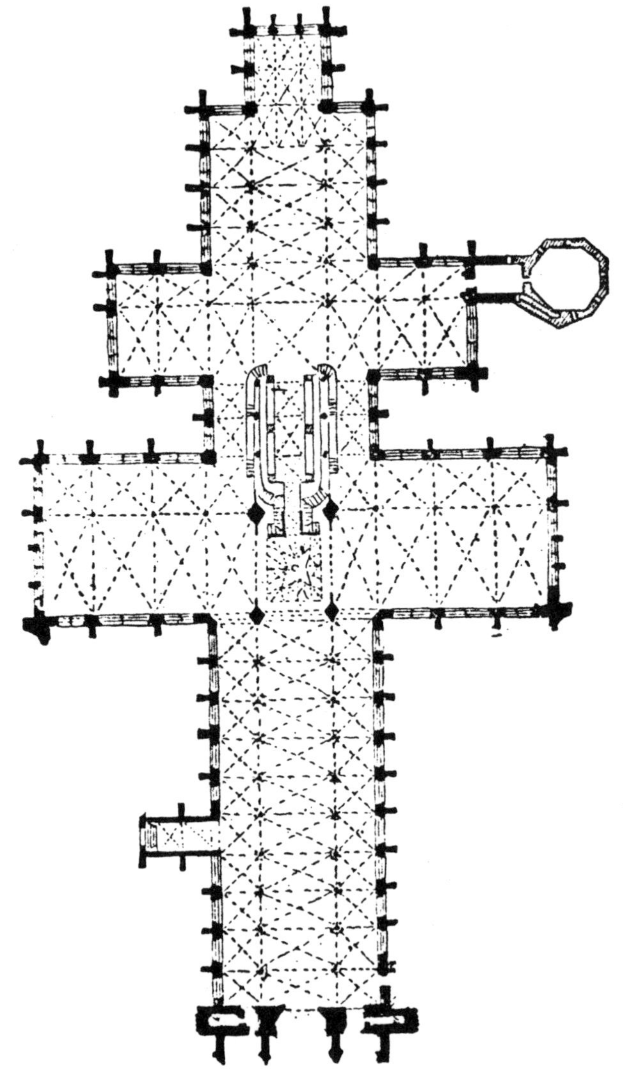

PLAN OF SALISBURY CATHEDRAL, ENGLAND

Note the double transepts.

5914

The floorplan for Salisbury Cathedral; note the double transepts. The dotted lines are indications of the plan of the vaulting for the ceiling.

in 1226. DLS attended the Godolphin School in Salisbury prior to her entry into Somerville College, Oxford. [WB 5]

5915 Salle des Pas Perdus -- French for "waiting room". The phrase translates literally as the room of the lost steps. [aq]

5916 Sallie in our alley . . . -- PW is punning on Henry Carey's (1693?-1743) poem, "Sally in Our Alley":
"Of all the girls that are so smart
There's none like pretty Sally,
She is the darling of my heart,
And she lives in our alley."
[NT 6]

5917 sallies -- the colorful handholds on a bell rope. One could not pull a bell rope for long without getting cuts and slivers from the hemp from which the rope is made. Hence, the sallies protect the ringers' hands and absorb perspiration as well. They are often colorfully striped, but those at Fenchurch St. Paul* are scarlet. [NT 1]

5918 salmis [of game] -- a thick, well-seasoned stew of the ragout group made from game birds roasted until they are about done. Their cooking is completed in the stew. Both red and white wine, one or the other, may be used in its preparation. [ie/WB 4]

5919 saloon -- British English for a sedan of large size. It may have either two or four doors. [bc/te/FRH 8/MMA 4]

5920 saloon-bar -- the more elegant room in a pub or hotel for beverage and, sometimes, food service. It offers a more refined atmosphere than that of the public bar; something like a lounge in U. S. parlance. [SP 10]

5921 Salvation Army -- a religious organization started in 1865 by Gen. William Booth as a Christian Mission. It became the Salvation Army in 1878, assuming a sort of religious militarism in that the group affected uniforms and otherwise capitalized on the "Army" aspect of the title. They are a revivalist fundamental group that performs a wide range of charitable duties around the world. After Bill Rumm's* encounter with PW in "Dragon's Head", he joins the Salvation Army and attends PW's wedding in uniform--much to the horror of the Duchess of Denver*, PW's sister-in-law. [MMA 15/BH P]

5922 salver -- a small tray, usually silver, used by a waiter or other servant to serve drinks or to deliver messages; also placed in an entry hall to receive the calling cards of visitors [ae/NT 4]

5923 Sam -- possibly a reference to the unnamed burglar who assisted Bill Rumm* in the attempt to burgle PW's flat; otherwise he is unknown [SP 13]

5924 Sam Weller face -- the character is from Charles Dickens's* Pickwick Papers and is Mr. Pickwick's devoted servant. He is presented as a cheerful, loquacious, resourceful, and humorous character with an endless supply of appropriate stories. He is considered to be one of Dickens's greatest creations. [BC 4]

5925 Sambo and Rastas -- Raustus in one edition; blackface minstrel performers made up with burnt cork and curly fright wigs to resemble stereotypical comic Blacks. The names have become common parlance for any such blackface performers. [UD 11]

5926 Sambourne, Mark -- a guest at the Christmas party given by Sir Charles Deverill* and a bridge* player with PW, Lady Hermione Creethorpe*, and Mrs. Wrayburn*. Sambourne had to pay PW and Lady Hermione about $30 (£5/17/6) as the game was for small stakes and he lost. [qs]

5927 samovar -- a usually elaborate Russian device for storing hot water for tea. They sometimes have their own heaters rather than just being a large storage container for heated water. [SP 8]

5928 Samson, beard of -- see beard of Samson [FRH 29]

5929 sanctuary -- the most holy place in a religious building; the location of the altar in Christian houses of worship [NT 2]

5930 SANCTUS•SANCTUS•SANCTUS•DOMINUS•DEUS•SABAOTH -- Latin for, "Holy, Holy, Holy, Lord God of Hosts". The inscription refers to Isaiah 6:3 or to Revelations 4:8, and is the text of the

Te Deum Laudamus. The inscription is on the bell Sabaoth*. [NT 4]

5931 Sanderton, Sir John -- Bunter's employer before his service in WW I. Sir John is fictitious. [BH E2]

5932 Sand Green -- or Sandgreen, a beachside village on Fleet Bay about four miles South of Gatehouse-of-Fleet* [FRH 14]

5933 Sands, Mr. -- Meleager Finch's* solicitor* [umw]

5934 The Sands of Crime -- one of HV's detective novels [GN 1]

5935 Sandy Point -- one place where Insp. Umpelty* thinks Paul Alexis's* body might turn up when the tide goes out. It is fictitious. [HHC 4]

5936 The Sandyford Mystery -- a reference to the comfortable home at #17 Sandyford Place in Glasgow's West End where, in the summer of 1862, there lived one old James Fleming, his son, John, John's family, and the usual coterie of servants. John and the younger members of the family were upright Victorian citizens in every sense of the word Victorian. Old James, either 78 or 87 years of age--that fact remains in dispute--was a dirty, drunken lecher, a moral derelict who became senile when it suited him to do so. In 1852, he had fathered a bastard and had been censured by the Kirk session of the Anderson United Presbyterian Church, of which he was the eldest member, on a charge of fornication. Ten years later, on Friday, July 4, 1862, the younger Flemings left for a weekend in the country, leaving Old James and the servants at home, alone.

That night, during one of his drinking bouts, this one in the company of a servant, Jessie Macpherson, and a former servant, Jessie McLachlan, Jessie Macpherson died brutally. She was hacked to death with a meat cleaver. James Fleming was arrested, but was released when McLachlan was charged with the murder. She held that the old man had done it.

Thus, the chief witness for the defense was also the chief witness for the Crown. Further, the judge, Lord Deas, was so obviously biased in his handling of the case that general public outrage was expressed all the way to the Commons. The death sentence was, as a result, commuted to life in prison, but McLachlan was paroled after fifteen years. The truth of the situation will never be known, but the evidence seems to point overwhelmingly toward Old James as the murderer with McLachlan as accessory. [BH]

5937 Sanfect -- a disinfectant product invented by DLS for use here [MMA 4]

5938 sang froid -- calmness under pressure; imperturbability [HHC 1]

5939 Sanger's Circus -- a popular show run by John Sanger (1816-89) and his brother, George, of Somerset. The show appeared every winter in London, either at the Agricultural Hall or at Astley's Amphitheatre, and it toured the country in the summer. It no longer exists. [UD 4]

5940 sanitary inspector -- a local government official who looked after public health hygiene generally. Such persons are now called Environmental Health Officers. [BH 11]

5941 Sans-culotte, Jacques -- the name PW applies to Jacques Lerouge*. The name seems to translate into Lerouge's having been caught "with his pants down", a reference to his failure as a female impersonator. However, the name derives also from the French revolution when it was applied to the extremists of the working classes, "the rabble" as opposed to the aristocracy, and who wore trousers, not culottes, the then fashionable knee-length pants. In either case the phrase is apt. [aq]

5942 sappers -- military field engineers who tunnel, lay and disarm mines and bombs, and build various military structures [WB 8]

5943 Sargent -- John Singer Sargent (1856-1925), the American portrait artist who had apparently done a portrait of Alice Wetherall* in her earlier and happier days. He also did one of PW at age twenty-one that PW dislikes because it is too honest. That painting hangs at Bredon Hall*. [ie/BH E2]

5944 sarsnet [red] -- a very fine quality, soft silk material, in this case, red [BH E2]

5945 Sassenachs -- a term used by the Scots, who are of Gaelic and Celtic stock, to refer to the English who are of Anglo-Saxon stock and are, therefore, considered separate and distinct [ss]

5946 Satyricon -- a prose satirical romance by the Roman author Petronius*, only part of which has survived. The work is a part prose, part verse description of the sometimes obscene, usually Rabelaisian adventures of two rogues, Encolpius and Ascyltus, and their boy, Giton, as they travel about in southern Italy during the reign of Nero. One of the more famous episodes is the description of Trimalchio's banquet. [dh]

5947 Saul smote the Philistines -- an allusion to I Samuel 17. This is the story of how the Israelites slew the Philistines* led by Goliath. After David slew the giant, the victory for Saul was an easy one. [MMA 18]

5948 Saunders -- a laboratory assistant to Sir James Lubbock* [BC 7]

5949 Saunders, Mr. -- the sales agent at Sparkes and Crisp* who helped John Ferguson* with his magneto problems. He is remarkable for his "private" business lunches. [FRH 21]

5950 Saunders, Sergeant -- one of the police officers at Wilvercombe* [HHC 3]

5951 sauterne -- more usually given as Sauterne(s), a rich, sweet, smooth wine, golden in color. It is the white wine of the Bordeaux (Sauternes) region of France. [mt/BC 21]

5952 Savidgery -- PW tweaks a local police sergeant about his possibly overzealous interrogation procedures with the comment, "No Savidgery." The phrase refers to the case of Irene Savidge, 22, and Sir Henry Money, 57, who were arrested in Hyde Park by plainclothes officers for some unspecified "offense to public decency" supposedly observed by the two officers. Miss Savidge was a friend of the Money family and Lady Money posted bail for both. The police were careless in their charges and in gathering the names of witnesses, of whom there were several, generally making a botch of things. With the lack of witnesses it appears that the police resorted to strong-arm tactics to get a confession. The case was dismissed for lack of evidence, the police had to pay court costs, and they were reprimanded for excessive use of force against Sir Henry in particular. The case made quite a stir in late April and early May of 1928. [im]

5953 Savile Club -- an exclusive men's club on Brook St., London, just East of Grosvenor Square* in Mayfair*. PW is not a member. [WB 1]

5954 Savile Row -- along with Sackville St., it is the center of London's custom tailoring business. Savile Row is just North of Piccadilly Circus* just West of and roughly parallel to Regent St.* PW's suits are from an unspecified tailor on Savile Row. [UD 7/SP 15]

5955 savory -- a light salt or piquant (never sweet) dish served at the end of a meal as a digestive [BC 7]

5956 Savoy -- near Waterloo Bridge and between the Victoria Embankment and The Strand is an area famous for the luxury hotel, The Savoy (where PW takes Ann Dorland* for dinner), and the Savoy Theatre built by Richard D'Oyly Carte for Gilbert and Sullivan operas. The name Savoy dates from the 1240's, but the present complex dates only from the 1880's. [BC 1]

5957 sawbones -- slang for a surgeon [WB 9]

5958 Saxon monosyllables -- the reference is to the root language of English, Anglo-Saxon, that is noted for its short words--ox, ghost, house, etc. It is interesting to note that most of our modern common words are from the Anglo-Saxon while thing relating to government are from the French and things relating to theology are from Latin. [HHC 5]

5959 Say When! -- a fictitious theatrical endeavor, probably a musical revue [MMA 19]

5960 Sayers, Tom -- an English boxer (1826-65) whose career lasted from 1849 to 1860. He was a bricklayer by profession. [NT 1]

5961 scabious -- any of the plants, genus Scabiosa Erigeron or Arte-

mesia, also called fleabane for their supposed ability to drive away fleas. The pink-flowered Scabiosa columbaria is probably intended as it is the only species that grows near the sea. [HHC 1]

5962 scale of thirty-two notes to the octave -- a reference to the quarter and sixth tones of Czech composer Alois Haba (1893-1973). However, Englishman John Foulds (1880-1939) and the more famous Arnold Schoenberg had both experimented with quarter tones and dispensing with the octave much earlier. [SP 8]

5963 scansion -- the process of dividing lines of poetry into metrical feet by locating the accented words or syllables, the unaccented ones, and then determining the underlying rhythm of the poem. The most common metrical foot in English is the iambus wherein one foot consists of two syllables, the first unaccented, the second accented. [GN 13]

5964 Scarlatti, Domenico -- Giuseppe Domenico Scarlatti was born in Naples, Italy, in 1685, and died in Madrid, Spain, in 1757. Son of the composer Alessandro Scarlatti, he is known for his keyboard pieces, especially some 600 sonatas* and other pieces for the harpsichord. Their performance requires considerable technical skill. [WB 3]

5965 scarlet and ermine -- the dominant color and fur used in the robes worn by English royalty and peers [CW 11]

5966 scarlet and French grey -- a reference to the colors in the hood of an Oxford D.Litt. or D.Sc. degree. In this case, Dr. Baring* is likely the former. The gown would be scarlet. Academicals for doctorates are usually quite colorful. [GN 1]

5967 scarlet-vermilion -- a vermilion of a redder tint than usual; a somewhat deeper hue than light cadmium red. It is a commanding color sometimes loosely referred to as Chinese red. [FRH 12]

5968 scarp -- a steep wall of stone left either by erosion or by geologic faulting [FRH 2]

5969 Scatterblood, Mr. -- the nickname assumed by Bredon Wimsey* when he and PW carry out their assault on Miss Quirk's* nerves. It is apparently a fictitious name used when he and his father are engaged in their wilder activities. It suggests a combination of Captain Hook from Peter Pan and one of the nastier types from an N. C. Wyeth pirate painting--something melodramatically and extravagantly wicked and sinful. There is also a slight connection to Blackbeard* as that pirate's flag, a Jolly Roger, featured four red drops of blood in the lower right hand corner and that pirate is probably not to be outdone for extravagant sinfulness. [t]

5970 scene about the strawberries -- it is in Richard III, III, iv, 34ff. The conversation is between Richard as Gloucester and the Bishop of Ely. [HHC 23]

5971 sceptre -- any of a variety of batons or staffs carried by royalty to symbolize their authority and rule [qs]

5972 Schlitzers -- the artistic couple who are friends of PW and Marjorie Phelps* and who are "feuding" but who cannot end their marriage because neither has enough money to get a studio of his or her own. Olga is apparently quite hot-tempered. [BC 10]

5973 Schloss Johannisberger -- Castle Johannisberger, an aristocrat of the great German white wines of the Rhine valley. To obtain this title, the grapes must be picked from those grown in the precincts of the castle itself on the slopes above the Rhine about twelve miles West of Mainz. [mt]

5974 scholar -- an English college student whose expenses are paid by the college foundation. The student may be poor, but not necessarily, and is simply the recipient of a scholarship. [GN 1]

5975 scholar's gown -- the typical knee-length academic gown with full sleeves but no decorations as are found on masters' and doctors' gowns [GN 5]

5976 Schools -- the all-or-nothing final examinations for the BA degree at Oxford. Once these are completed successfully, one is automati-

cally eligible for the MA after having met certain relatively minor requirements. [GN 5]

5977 schooner -- usually a two-masted sailing vessel rigged with fore-and-aft sails, but it may have up to seven masts and still be called a schooner if the sails are rigged fore-and-aft [HHC 9]

5978 Schubert, Franz Peter -- a Viennese composer, Schubert wrote songs, symphonies, sonatas, etc., but gained fame only late in his short life (1797-1828) [ie]

5979 Schuster-Slatt, Sadie -- the "strident" former Shrewsbury College* student--she never graduated --who has climbed on the bandwagon of unnatural selection. She has become involved with the League for the Encouragement of Matrimonial Fitness*. [GN 2]

5980 schwärmerei -- German for excessive or unwholesome sentiment in some matter; exaggerated sentimental or emotional attachment [UD 22]

5981 schwärmerisch -- the adjective form of the preceding entry [UD 16]

5982 scone -- a muffin or quick bread usually made of oatmeal or barley flour, rolled out, cut into rounds, quartered, and baked on a griddle [UD 5]

5983 Scoot -- secretary to John P. Milligan*, the American financier and railroad magnate [WB 4]

5984 Scotch blood -- an extension, by allusion, of the supposed Scottish predilection to stinginess. In this case, PW is suggesting that Parker* must have Scotch blood because of his refusal to accept anything short of absolute proof; reluctance to accept circumstantial evidence is suitable behavior for a police officer. [WB 4]

5985 Scotch thistle -- see Pembroke [GN 13]

5986 Scotland, recovery of civil debts -- see civil debts contracted elsewhere [BH 10]

5987 Scotland Yard -- the nickname of the location, wherever it happens to be, of the London Metropolitan Police and of the force, itself. The headquarters of the force originally stood (1842-1890) on a street in Whitehall where, in 970, King Edgar gave a palace to Kenneth II of Scotland, hence, Scotland Yard. The name stuck and, when, in 1890, New Scotland Yard was opened in Westminster* on the Thames embankment, only the "New" was added by way of a change. In more recent times a second New Scotland Yard was built on Victoria St. in central London where "The Yard" is presently headquartered, not far from Westminster Abbey. [passim]

5988 Scotland Yard, head of -- Mr. David Wicks* mentions that PW goes fishing with "the head of Scotland Yard" who at the time of the story, 1923, would have been Brigadier General Horwood. See also #4173. [WB 5]

5989 Scott Flying Squirrel -- a brand of motorcycle manufactured in England from 1909 to 1950. First built by Alfred Angus Scott, he applied a water-cooled two-stroke engine to the machines and gained world-wide fame for them as excellent motorcycles. [cb]

5990 Scottish Bar -- while England and Scotland have legal systems that are very similar in many ways, they are not identical and are not arranged so that a lawyer in one is automatically a lawyer in the other. They have separate legal processes and unique terminology. Furthermore, the verdicts and penalties are differentiated as well. [ss]

5991 scour -- to dig out or deepen a river bed by means of a more rapid flow of water, a feat usually accomplished by straightening the riverbed [NT 16]

5992 scour of the burn -- a place along a riverbank that has been washed out or deepened by the action of moving water. A burn is a small river or stream. [FRH 2]

5993 scout -- a servant whose duty is to take care of the basic housekeeping needs of Oxford's students [GN 1]

5994 scouted the idea [theory] -- to reject with scorn an idea or statement [ae/HHC 17]

5995 scratch, bring him up to -- to

bring someone up to an established standard; to eliminate any handicap or hindrance. It is usually a sporting term. [qs]

5996 scratch team -- one assembled "from scratch" to meet a specific challenge; not a standing team [MMA 10]

5997 screamer -- printing jargon for an exclamation point (!) [MMA 8]

5998 screen -- see rood screen [NT 2]

5999 screens -- sight screens, white panels placed behind the bowler in cricket* to allow the batsman to have a better view of the pitched ball. It is not a requirement of the Laws of Cricket, but most grounds have them at each end of the pitch, usually mounted on wheels for ease of placement. [MMA 18]

6000 screw -- an unhealthy horse or, by connection, a broken-winded horse that ran and lost, its condition being an excuse for backing a loser [GN 10]

6001 Scrooger, old -- one of the physicians and a teacher of anatomy at St. Luke's* Hospital [WB 10]

6002 Scruggs -- the dog at the Dog and Gun*. The local children pester Hugh Farren* to immortalize Scruggs on the pub's sign, but he is the wrong type of dog. [FRH 20]

6003 scull -- or sculler, a racing boat with shorter and more efficient oars (sculls) designed to allow one person to operate both oars. If designed for two people, it is called a "pair". [GN 11]

6004 sculling test -- a test of one's abilities in handling the oars of a racing scull*. Oxford and Cambridge are famous for their teams and for their annual competition in sculling. [GN 5]

6005 sculls -- racing oars, the blades of which are slightly curved for a more efficient push against the water and, hence, greater speed. They are slightly smaller to allow one person to wield two oars comfortably. [GN 11]

6006 scunner -- see ta'en a scunner [UD 3]

6007 sea-anemone -- an animal (order Actinaria), a polyp, of bright colors and having tentacles that resemble flowers. They capture things gently with the tentacles which then numb the prey to make it docile for eating. [BH 20]

6008 seagreen incorruptible -- PW describes Bunter thus. The allusion is to Carlyle's* History of the French Revolution, Part II, book iv, Ch. 4, and refers to Robespierre. See also #5100. [BH 17]

6009 Seahampton -- a fictitious community about fifty miles from Wilvercombe* and where Col. Belfridge's* razors went after he gave them to his gardener who didn't want them [HHC 8]

6010 seal-ring -- a signet-ring* [MMA 5]

6011 sealing up that bottle of burgundy -- a direct reference to the Bravo case* [SP 22]

6012 seals, fixing the -- replacing the various lead or paper seals and notices used by police and other governmental agencies to shut off an area from any use by anyone other than those authorized to conduct an investigation. The object is to protect one and all from the possible destruction of evidence, etc. [CW 5]

6013 séance[s] -- a spiritualist gathering to contact spirits of the deceased, usually with the help of a medium* [SP 18/MMA 4]

6014 seapink -- also called "thrift" or "statice", it is Armeria maritima [HHC 1]

6015 The Search -- by C. P. Snow* is a novel about a scientist who distorts evidence in order to support his research [GN 12]

6016 Second -- British universities offer first, second, and third degree honors, below them comes the ordinary pass degree [GN 1]

6017 The Second Brother -- by T. L. Beddoes*, is a play of political intrigue and fighting between two brothers, the second and third brothers of the ducal family of Ferrara, after their elder brother died leaving no heir. Marcello, the second brother, takes the title and Orazio, the third brother, is supposedly banished. We then find Orazio a prisoner of Marcello

who has set himself up as a demigod, The play is incomplete, work on it having been abandoned in 1825. [HHC 2/BH 14]

6018 second law of thermodynamics -- this is summarized by the Kelvin-Planck statement: "It is impossible to construct a device that operates in a cycle and produces no other effect than the production of work and exchange of heat with a single reservoir." It is the law that negates the possibility of a perpetual motion machine because it is impossible to do some form of work, undo it, and do it again with the same reservoir of energy. For example, one may not burn gasoline to drive a car and have any expectation of retaining a full tank. Once the energy reservoir is emptied, no further work can be done. [HHC 22]

6019 second "Our Father" -- a shortened version of the Lord's Prayer recited after the Creed at Anglican matins. It is said as that prayer is written, but stops at "deliver us from evil." [NT 22]

6020 Second-Year play -- a bachelor's degree at an Oxford college requires three years of study. At the end of each year, many colleges stage a play or other entertainment. In this case, the play was J. M. Barrie's _Quality Street_, a sentimental comedy in period costume that is considered one of his finer works. [GN 1]

6021 _seconde_ -- French for, "second-class" as in passenger coaches, etc. [mt]

6022 Secret Society -- an otherwise nameless organization being discussed by some of PW's travelling companions [nf]

6023 Seddon case -- the reference is to the trial of Mr. and Mrs. Frederick Seddon in 1911. He was an insurance agent of a greedy and miserly nature who rented rooms to a Miss Barrow who was apparently every bit as mean as Seddon. Miss Barrow died, leaving her money to Seddon in an annuity.

Seddon gave her a pauper's funeral, her relatives had her exhumed, and the autopsy found arsenic. The source of the arsenic was never determined, but it was assumed to have come from some arsenical fly papers that had been soaked in water. Mrs. Seddon was acquitted, but he was found guilty and sentenced to death by Mr. Justice Bucknill who was moved to tears when Seddon revealed that he, too, was a Freemason during a speech he made to the court before sentencing. [CW 7/SP 2]

6024 see a man there--about a dog -- or about a horse. This is a catchphrase referring to taking care of personal business that one does not care to share in detail; a euphemism [GN 18]

6025 "See the conquering hero comes" -- the phrase is used in at least two places. As, "See, the conquering hero comes", the line appears in part iii of Thomas Morell's _Joshua_, and as, "See, the conqu'ring hero comes", it is the title of a famous chorus from G. F. Handel's oratorio, _Judas Maccabaeus_ as derived from _Joshua_ with _Morell's_ help. [MMA 8]

6026 seedy-cake -- or seed-cake. A plain cake flavored with (usually) caraway seed and sweetened and formerly popular for afternoon tea, fall festivals, etc. [BH 1]

6027 "Seeking the bubble reputation" -- PW is citing Jacques' famous "All the world's a stage" speech from _As You Like It_, II, vii, 139ff. The image creates a picture of perhaps foolhardy bravery to earn a reputation that may be destroyed easily. [HHC 31]

6028 Seidlitz powder -- a laxative made of Rochelle salts, sodium bicarbonate, and tartaric acid named after mineral waters of the village of Seidlitz, Bohemia, which have a similar effect [aq]

6029 Segrave bade farewell to Brooklands -- the reference is to Major Sir Henry O'Neal DeHane Segrave (1896-1930) who set several land speed records at the Brooklands* race track. At this time, Sir Henry had just returned from a triumph at Daytona, Florida, never doing any racing of consequence at Brooklands after that. He died on Lake Windermere while trying to break the water speed record. [UD 19]

6030 Seine-et-Marne -- see department

6031 Selby, Miss Margaret -- one of

PW's neighbors in Kirkcudbright*. Bunter takes pleasure in helping her with various household chores. See also Cochran, Miss. [FRH 5]

6032 Select Committee -- a special committee of the Lords who would work with the Lord Chancellor and the Lord High Steward** to arrange the trial of a peer--Gerald, Duke of Denver*. Such a trial would be impossible now as the process was eliminated in 1948. [CW 6]

6033 Selfridge[s] [Mr.] -- London's largest department store, erected in 1908 by the American, Gordon Selfridge. It is noted for its wide range of merchandise and services, including an antique shop. The store is on Oxford St.* [BC 10/SP 5/HHC 22]

6034 Selkirk Arms -- on Old High St. in Kirkcudbright*. It has twenty-seven rooms and is still open for guests. [FRH 15]

6035 Sellon, Joe -- P. C. Sellon. He is a young constable, is married, and he patrols the Paggleham* area. He is an alert but foolish young man whose judgmental errors harm seriously his work as a policeman. He is, however, anxious to learn and strives to do a good job. He later moves to Canada with his family and is replaced as constable by Jack Baker*. [t/BH 1]

6036 Sellon, Mrs. -- P. C. Sellon's* rather distraught and worn wife. She is expecting their second child, but that is not the central cause of her distress. [BH 11]

6037 semi-toilette -- semi-formal dress [MMA 10]

6038 semi-tones -- the tone at a half-step, the smallest interval in a standard scale [SP 8]

6039 Semite -- also Shemite; descendants of Shem, the eldest son of Noah. They are Caucasions and include the Jews and the Arabs. In ancient times, Babylonians, Assyrians, Phoenicians, and other Middle Eastern peoples were included. [WB 2]

6040 "Send him back again . . ." -- from a letter, part in verse and part in prose, written by T. L. Beddoes* to one B. W. Proctor, Esq., 14 Southampton Row, Russel[l] Square, London. The letter is dated at Göttengen, Germany, on March 7, 1826, while Beddoes was a student at the university there. The quote is from lines 69 and 70 of the verse segment of the letter. The "him" being addressed is death, and the next three lines are:

"For death is more 'a jest' than life: you see
Contempt grows quick from familiarity.
I owe this wisdom to Anatomy--"

Beddoes was studying medicine. [HHC 8]

6041 Senior Common Room -- the center for coffee and much social life at an English college. It is open only to senior members of the college, that is, those who are either faculty or graduates of the college and their guests. [GN 1]

6042 Senior Member of this University -- a graduate or faculty member at Oxford as opposed to an undergraduate [GN 1]

6043 Senior Student -- an undergraduate who is roughly equivalent to the president of the student body; a liason between students and faculty [GN 5]

6044 Senior Wrangler -- at Cambridge University the title denotes pre-eminence among those who took first class honors in the Mathematical Tripos*, the one placed first among the wranglers [NT 12]

6045 sens dessus dessous -- French for, "upside down", but suggesting topsy-turvy [CW 5]

6046 sent down -- to be asked to leave a college for some serious infraction of its rules. One may be sent down for a specific period of time or permanently. [GN 7]

6047 sepia -- a brownish-gray color. As an ink it most likely refers to ink made from the self-defense spray of cuttlefish [BC 3]

6048 septic poisoning -- blood poisoning with the release of pus [BH E2]

6049 seraphic -- angelic. Mr. Ingleby* is keeping his metaphor straight--he had earlier referred to the Misses Rossiter and Parton** as guardian angels. [MMA 1]

6050 seraphim -- sometimes seraphin.

Generally, another class of angel often mentioned concurrently with cherubim*. Isaiah describes them as having six wings, hands and feet, and a voice that one assumes is human. They are described by that prophet as hovering above the throne of God, but they are the first, or lowest, order of heavenly beings. [WB 7/NT 2]

6051 serge -- a twilled fabric of a durable nature having a smooth surface and a pronounced diagonal ribbing on the front and back. The fabric develops a lustre with use. [CW 9/FRH 1/HHC 1]

6052 sergeant -- Bunter's military rank during WW I, also a police rank* [passim]

6053 Sergeant -- the otherwise unidentified person at Pym's Publicity* who leads the errand boys in their morning exercises [MMA 3]

6054 Sergeant-at-Arms -- a sort of bailiff for the Houses of Parliament [CW 12]

6055 sergeant-major -- the highest rank of noncommissioned officer in the Army. To have the air of one would be seen as militarily correct, in command. Loosely, it refers to one who assumes command without necessarily having been asked to do so. [FRH 1/NT 1/GN 17]

6056 serial rights -- the right to publish a work serially; over a period of time in installments in periodic publications. Most of Charles Dickens's* works were published in that fashion. [GN 11]

6057 seriatim -- in a series [UD 6]

6058 Sermet, Julia[or e]n -- see "The Rosamunde" [NT 20]

6059 "'Serpent, I say again!' repeated the Pigeon . . ." -- the exchange is from Lewis Carroll's Alice in Wonderland**, Ch. V, "Advice from a Caterpillar", and is between Alice and a pigeon shortly after Alice has eaten a piece of the caterpillar's magic mushroom, causing her neck to grow to great length while the rest of her body retains its usual proportions. Her neck does resemble a serpent for a time, but only in its length. [BH 13]

6060 Serpent's Fang -- a fictitous novel. The author is not identified. [GN 11]

6061 serpentine -- see not serpentine at all [UD 4]

6062 Serpentine -- a large lake in Hyde Park* used for sailing, rowing, and swimming. It was created from a dammed stream in the early 1700's. [im]

6063 Servant's Hall -- the collective name for the dining and recreation area of a large home as set aside for the servants' use [NT 6]

6064 service [in] -- employed as a servant [UD 12]

6065 service flat -- one with which service is supplied, the service normally including cleaning, bedmaking, and porterage, but not serving food or drink [UD 7]

6066 "Service in Advertising" -- the title of Mr. Pym's* "sermon" to those who have recently joined the agency's staff. It has been known to scare people into quitting the job. At its best, the speech is dull. [MMA 3]

6067 servitore -- Italian for, "waiter" [GN 11]

6068 sesquipedalian[s] -- given to the use of long words [HHC 25]

6069 sestet -- a six line stanza. In some sonnet forms it is the second part of the sonnet and functions as a response of some sort to a problem or a question posed in the first eight lines of the poem, the octave*. [GN 11]

6070 set -- a group of adjoined rooms or a small apartment. At English universities most of the faculty live "in college" with the students. A student would have a room of his or her own while most of the unmarried faculty would enjoy the privilege of a small suite of perhaps four or five rooms. [GN 4]

6071 "set the springe for his woodcock" -- see "springe, set the" [BC 13/BH 18]

6072 settle -- a solid, high-backed wooden bench with arms, the base of which may also function as a chest or storage area [CW 4]

6073 Settlement work -- a community social work effort as through a local settlement, outreach house, or mission [GN 3]

6074 Seven Dials -- formerly an open space in the parish of St. Giles-in-the-Fields from which seven streets radiate. At one time there was a column in the center with seven sundials, one for each of the seven streets. It was removed in 1773. Monmouth, Mercer, and Earlham Sts. now divide the square for six of the seven streets, the seventh being Shorts Gardens. [MMA 12]

6075 £750 -- the sum PW paid for his purchases at the Brocklebury* sale. Bunter did the bidding for PW while the latter investigated the nude corpse in Mr. Thipps's* bathtub. The sum is approximately equal to U. S. $3000, a most considerable sum for the day, equivalent to about $30,000 today. [WB 2]

6076 704 -- the number of changes* in the touch*. The same applies to other such number references (as 804) [NT 1]

6077 seven sharps -- see key of seven sharps [BC 3]

6078 Seven Sisters window -- in York Minster there is one of the glories of the medieval glassmakers art, the Five Sisters Windows. Why DLS added two sisters is a puzzle. She may have had any of several things in mind, including "The Seven Sisters" chalk cliffs in Kent. The Five Sisters windows are five tall lancets at the end of the North transept of the Minster. They are done en grisaille, or in a whitish glass with only a touch of jewel-bright color here and there. The quality of the glass is frequently compared to that at Chartres and is considered the best in England. [CW 11]

6079 7/6 -- seven shillings and six pence. See British Monetary Units. [SP 6]

6080 seven white cats -- a sign of great magic. Seven is a powerful number in magic and numerology, white is good magic, and cats are traditional familiars. Such a sight would be considered powerful indicators of magic to those who believe. [ie]

6081 Severn and Thames -- see Mirabelle, Countess of Severn and Thames [BH P]

6082 Sèvres -- a fine quality porcelain, often highly decorated, made in Sèvres, France. Pieces made there often acquire great value. [WB 2]

6083 Sexton Blake -- see Blake, Sexton [MMA 6]

6084 shabby tigers -- the phrase that starts PW and HV off on their run of tiger allusions is from Ralph Hodgson's poem, "The Bells of Heaven", a plea for kindness to all animals. [BH 1]

6085 "The shadow of a great rock . . ." -- see "Peter, what a rock you are!" [GN 14]

6086 Shaftesbury Avenue -- one of central London's major streets, it runs roughly northeast from Piccadilly Circus across Charing Cross Rd.* to New Oxford St. and is named for the philanthropist,the Earl of Shaftesbury. [WB 4/HHC 22]

6087 shafts -- the two long pieces of wood between which a horse is hitched to draw a cart, wagon, or coach [CW 11]

6088 shag -- a fine cut coarse tobacco favored by Sherlock Holmes* [HHC 4]

6089 Shakespeare First Quarto -- the question here is which play? Many of Shakespeare's plays were published in quarto, sometimes in as many as five or six versions. The first folio is the first collection of his plays and has been photographically reproduced in facsimile to make this rare and valuable book available to more scholars and enthusiasts. [GN 6]

6090 "Shakespeare says . . ." -- see "put his crime off . . ." [HHC 10]

6091 Shale, Betty -- daughter of John Shale* and niece of Sir Septimus Shale [np]

6092 Shale, Henry -- son of John Shale* and nephew of Sir Septimus Shale* [np]

6093 Shale, John -- brother of Sir Sep-

timus Shale [np]

6094 Shale, Lady Septimus -- wife of Sir Septimus Shale*, it is she who is so fascinated by things modern while her husband seems to be thoroughly Victorian. He suffers her interior decorating while she suffers his Dickensian Christmas fetes. The arrangement seems to be an amicable one. [np]

6095 Shale, Margharita -- daughter of Sir Septimus Shale* and owner of the fabulous pearl necklace that is central to the action of the story [np]

6096 Shale, Sir Septimus -- PW's host and a great lover of the traditional Christmas celebration with huge meals and lots of games. One such gathering figures prominently in the story. [np]

6097 "shall I call thee bird or but a wandering voice" -- PW is being humorous, but the telephone operator fails to grasp his humor. The line is from Wordsworth's* "To the Cuckoo: O Blithe Newcomer!", and the full lines are:
"O Cuckoo! Shall I call thee bird
Or but a wandering voice?"
They are lines 3 and 4 in the poem. [UD 9]

6098 "Shall I make spirits fetch me . . ." -- HV switches from Shakespeare to Marlowe's Dr. Faustus for this quote. It is from I, i, 78-9. [BH 18]

6099 Shalott, Lady of -- she is Elaine, the maid of Astolat, and is the heroine of Alfred, Lord Tennyson's* poem, "The Lady of Shalott". PW's reference is to lines 116-17 of that poem. Tennyson says that the curse is upon her if she looks down to Camelot. She therefore has to watch the highway by means of a mirror, and this cracks when she sees Lancelot reflected in it as he passes by. In a different context, PW alludes to Elaine's constant spinning and weaving, a reference to Mrs. Farren's artistic pursuits, and to the fact that neither woman has a "loyal knight and true" (1. 22). Both are cursed to love faithless "knights". [t/FRH 6]

6100 shambles -- a slaughterhouse or meat market [NT 5]

6101 Shandy, Mrs. -- the reference is to Laurence Sterne's (1713-68) novel, The Life and Opinions of Tristram Shandy. Mr. Shandy does as PW does, he keeps all sorts of things in his mind at once--a situation that would be a mad jumble to most people. However, HV's comment about shocking Mrs. Shandy is unclear--the connection to Sterne's character is incomplete in the allusion. See also #6844. [BH 5]

6102 shanks -- the legs from the knees to the ankles [UD 12]

6103 share coupons -- separable warrants or certificates for the dividends payable on the shares or debentures to which they relate [UD 10]

6104 sharrer -- a corruption of charabanc*, considered low or vulgar in the sense of its being used only by the uneducated [NT 4]

6105 Shaw, Miss -- the modern language tutor at Shrewsbury College* [GN 1]

6106 Shaw, You agree with -- see You agree with Shaw [MMA 17]

6107 she is no better than she should be -- perhaps a reference to IV, iii, of The Coxcomb, a play by Francis Beaumont and John Fletcher. The line, "You are no better than you should be," appears there. The play is a romantic comedy first acted in 1612. As "He's just--nae better than he should be," the line appears in Burns's "A Dedication to Gavin Hamilton", 1. 26. In all likelihood the phrase first appears in print in Pasquil's Jests of 1604, but it is certainly much older than that. It expresses one's doubts about the moral character of another, and is negative in the assessment. [SP 18]

6108 Sheba, no more spirit in her than the Queen of -- the line is a reference to I Kings 10:5. After Sheba had tested Solomon and had seen him in all his glory, "There was no more spirit in her" to test him further. [BC 13]

6109 Sheeny -- a sharp fellow, a Jewish dealer. The term is not now considered an appropriate descriptor. [WB 10]

6110 Sheffield -- in South Yorkshire, a major industrial center noted for

its steel and silver plate products. Sheffield cutlery is particularly well known. [UD 20/BC 8]

6111 Sheffield blade -- cutlery is almost synonymous with Sheffield as the trade was established there well before Chaucer's time and a Sheffield blade is mentioned as being carried by the miller in "The Reeve's Tale" in The Canterbury Tales. Even today, Sheffield's Master Cutler is second only to the mayor in that city. It is a world-famous center for knives, scissors, and fine blades of all sorts. [HHC 14]

6112 Sheffield plate -- ingots of a copper alloy on to which silver is fused. The ingots were then rolled and treated as one metal. The process was developed in the middle of the 18th C. by Thomas Boulsover, a cutler of Sheffield. True Sheffield plate is now highly prized by collectors and should not be confused with electroplated imitations. [cf/CW 10]

6113 Sheila -- the glamorous but neglected wife in HV's novel, Death 'twixt Wind and Water [GN 19]

6114 shekel -- an ancient Hebrew unit of weight equal to approximately 252 grains troy; any coin of that weight [WB 4]

6115 shell shock -- any of a variety of psychoneurotic conditions appearing in soldiers, especially from WW I and later. Neurasthenia* and nightmares are common symptoms of shell shock. [BC 18]

6116 Shelley, Percy Bysshe -- English poet (1792-1822) of the Romantic period. Other than Queen Mab, a rebellious, youthful work written when he was eighteen, Shelley is noted for his odes and lyrics such as "Ode to the West Wind" and "To a Skylark", among many others. His magnificent lyric drama is Prometheus Unbound. His wife, Mary Wollstonecraft Shelley, was an early, prominent women's rights advocate and wrote Frankenstein.

6117 Shelly Head -- a fictitious location on England's South coast. It could be either Beachy Head, about ten miles from Brighton, or Hengistbury Head, near Bournemouth, but the geography created by DLS leaves certain identification impossible. [UD 20]

6118 Shelly Point -- a fishing community near Wilvercombe* [HHC 10]

6119 "Shenandoah" -- the beautiful anonymous ballad beginning, "Oh Shenandoah, I long to hear you . . . ." It was originally a sea chantey, the words to which have become so garbled as to have no real meaning today. [BH 5]

6120 Shepherd Market -- a small residential area between Piccadilly and Curzon St. in the immediate vicinity of the Bellona Club* (The Naval and Military Club). The area is named for architect Edward Shepherd who opened a general food market there and added small homes. [BC 5]

6121 shepherd's pie -- a great way to use up leftover beef, lamb, or mutton. It is a meat and vegetable pie in gravy that uses mashed potatoes for a crust instead of pastry. [NT 2]

6122 Sheraton bureaux -- bureau is most likely used here in the sense of a writing desk having drawers and a slanted, drop front writing surface in the Sheraton style, one marked by straight lines, graceful proportions, and lightness of appearance [SP 18]

6123 Sheringham, Roger -- a fictional detective created by Anthony Berkeley [Cox] (1893-1970). Known originally for his offensive behavior, his popularity required that his offensiveness be toned down. He appears in a variety of novels, one of the most famous being The Poisoned Chocolates Case where he comes up with the wrong solution to the puzzle. [HHC 33]

6124 Sherlock -- PW is referred to by allusion to the great Sherlock Holmes* in many situations, but he applies the name to HV in HHC [bc/BC 6/FRH 7/HHC 4]

6125 Sherlock Holmes says -- see "we shall look imposing enough . . ." [SP 20]

6126 Sherlock Holmes would say . . . -- see "I see nothing at all" [SP 20]

6127 shibboleths -- catch words or phrases, distinctive language usage that identifies a particular group. The word is Hebrew and was used by Jephthah as a test to distinguish

his troops from those of the Ephraimites who could not pronounce the Hebrew "sh" sound. The story is in Judges 12:4-6. From that, the word has come to mean any test-word or situation meant to separate or identify. [UD 16/ GN 10]

6128 shilling -- a British coin worth twelve old pence*. See British Monetary Units. [passim]

6129 shindy -- an uproar [UD 3]

6130 shingle -- a very coarse gravel or detritus worn smooth by wave action and found at the point where the tide reaches its highest point on a beach [HHC 1]

6131 shingled or bingled -- a shingle was a particular short women's hair cut that followed the "bob"* in popularity in the mid-1920's. The bingle was a mixture of the bob and the shingle which followed them in popularity. All three were variations on a short cut with little hair on the neck and some specific styling over the temples. They were a response to the popularity of the cloche hat. [FRH 13]

6132 ship-shape and Bristol fashion -- neat, tidy, and in good order. The phrase appears in R. H. Dana's novel, Two Years Before the Mast (1840), and probably antedates that. [UD 2]

6133 Shipway -- William, author of The Campanalogia: or Universal Instructor in the Art of Ringing: In Three Parts. The book is an extensive catalogue of the different kinds of peal and how to ring them. [NT 2]

6134 Shootering -- a fictitious community to the East and South of Little Doddering* [bc]

6135 shooting box -- a small country home adjacent to a hunting area and used as a base for short hunting forays. To most people Riddlesdale Lodge* hardly constitutes a small country home, but when compared to an estate of the magnitude of Duke's Denver*, small is appropriate as a descriptor. [CW 1]

6136 short hairs [got me by the] -- a rather blunt expression meaning to have been trapped in an uncompromisingly difficult situation. The hairs in question are either those of the nape of the neck or of the genital region, usually the latter. [GN 9]

6137 shot its bolt -- see bolt [GN 6]

6138 Shotover -- Shotover Country Park, about two and a half miles East of Oxford. The Park's steep approach road affords a view over most of Oxford. [GN 11]

6139 shoulder -- the point at the top of a bell that marks the transition from horizontal to vertical [NT 3]

6140 shove ha'penny -- a variation on an early form of shuffleboard that is also called shovegroat and shovelboard. A tabletop board game quickly set up or taken down, it needs only a few coins and a flat surface. The game is played much as shuffleboard would be, the object being to shove the playing discs from one end of the playing area to the other, the ends being marked off as "beds". A turn consists of five coins and the winner is the first to get three coins in each of the nine beds without having any coins on the dividing lines. Darts have largely replaced it in popularity. [MMA 4]

6141 shrammed -- a dialectical word for numbed [CW 11]

6142 Shrewsbury College -- the fictitious nondenominational college created by DLS for GN. If real, it would be located on Balliol's Cricket Ground. HV is a graduate. Shrewsbury is generally thought to be a view of the real Somerville College, DLS's alma mater at Oxford. See also Oxford Colleges and Shrewsbury, Mary Countess of. [GN AN/BH P]

6143 Shrewsbury, Earl of -- a descendant of John Talbot, 1st Earl of Shrewsbury, famous for his leadership during the Hundred Years' War and for his connection with Joan of Arc. The Earl in question is the 7th Earl, Gilbert Talbot, who died in 1616. That Earl married Mary Cavendish in 1568 at the same time his father, George, the 6th Earl, married Elizabeth Hardwick, Gilbert's mother-in-law. See also Bess of Hardwick. [GN 3]

6144 Shrewsbury, Mary Countess of -- Mary Cavendish (1555-1632), daughter of Bess of Hardwick*. She married

Gilbert Talbot, 7th Earl of Shrewsbury (see item 6143), her mother's stepson. She was a strong supporter of St. John's College, Cambridge, and is the lady in whose honor DLS named her fictitious Shrewsbury College at Oxford. She was as strong a lady as her mother and spent about a year in the Tower of London on suspicion of having helped in the flight of her niece, Arabella Stuart, a complicity which angered the Crown. See also Bess of Hardwick. [GN 3]

6145 A Shropshire Lad -- a collection of poems by A. E. Housman* set in the English countryside and marked by irony and youthful disillusionment. They show a strong influence from English ballads and classical verse. [SP 20]

6146 shuffling off this mortal thingummy -- PW's slightly irreverent reference to the famous line from Hamlet's "To be, or not to be" soliloquy in III, i, 66ff:

"For in that sleep of death what dreams may come
When we have shuffled off this mortal coil,
Must give us pause." [SP 10]

6147 Shulamite -- PW alludes to The Song of Solomon, 6:13: "Return, return, O Shulamite; return, return, that we may look upon thee." See also "black but comely". [BH 4]

6148 Sicily -- the large island province of Italy located in the Mediterranean at the toe of the "boot" of the Italian peninsula [BC 13]

6149 side wickets -- gates to the side of a level crossing* that could be used by pedestrians who would not need to have the entire gate opened, thus saving the gatekeeper extra and unnecessary work [HHC 2]

6150 Sidebotham, Mr. -- an employee of Pym's Publicity* who is not otherwise identified [MMA 6]

6151 sidesmen -- helpers at a church service; ushers, greeters, or assistants to distribute required material [NT 2]

6152 Sidgwick, Captain -- an officer in PW's unit with whom PW is still in contact [GN 17]

6153 Sidney, Sir Philip -- English poet (1554-86) and foremost among the typically Elizabethan gentlemen courtiers. He was a soldier, humanist, and man of letters. He died as the result of the treatment for a bullet wound received during an attack on a convoy near Zutphen in the Netherlands. At that battle he is reputed to have given his water supply to a dying foot soldier with the words, "Thy necessity is greater than mine." [GN 1/BH E2]

6154 Sie haben sich so weit darin eingeheimnisst. -- German for, "They have involved themselves most deeply in self-deception (or self-mystification)." The quotation, if it is one, is so nonspecific as to defy locating exactly. [WB 6]

6155 "Siegfried: 'What does this mean?'" -- from II, iv, 75-6 of T. L. Beddoes' Death's Jest Book**. The passage refers to the fact that Isbrand has removed Duke Melveric's wife's body from her grave and has substituted that of the murdered Wolfram. The action becomes significant later in the play when Melveric conjures the return of what he thinks will be his wife and gets his murder victim instead. [UD 20]

6156 "Sigh no more ladies" -- the opening line from a song in Shakespeare's Much Ado About Nothing, II, iii, 65ff. It is sung by Balthazar, an attendant to Don Pedro. [MMA 19]

6157 sign my name across the stamps -- until recently, receipts in England had to bear two pence in cancelled stamps to be valid. Cancellation could be done at a post office or, as in this case, could be done by the signatory receiving the goods, money, or whatever. [UD 3]

6158 signet ring -- a ring, often rather large and heavy, having an engraved flat top surface carved in deep relief. The engraved design usually is either a coat of arms or ornate initials and would be used to seal letters, legal documents, etc., by pressing the ring's design into sealing wax on the document or envelope, thus leaving a version of the design in relief. [BH P]

6159 A Silent Witness -- a 1914 novel

by R. Austin Freeman* that features a body which disappears when help arrives [BC 18]

6160 Silkanette Hosiery -- the company for which Pamela Dean* works. It is fictitious. [MMA 3]

6161 Silver King -- the brand of golf ball supposedly used when Henry Strachan* received his black eye. They were a brand of high quality golf balls popular at the time as manufactured by the Silvertown and Gutta Percha Co., Ltd., in London's East End. The firm later became the Silvertown Co., Ltd. The golf balls were manufactured until about 1950. [FRH 4]

6162 Simcox -- the real estate agent who handled the sale of Talboys* to the Wimseys [BH 1]

6163 Simmonds -- the Brotherhood's* employee who is known as a "demon bowler" (pitcher) on their cricket* team [MMA 18]

6164 Simms-Gaythorpe, Mr. -- another PW pseudonym, this one used when he calls on Nurse Forbes* [UD 9]

6165 Simon -- see Wimsey, Simon [BH E2]

6166 Simonetta, La Bella -- the reference is to Simonetta Vespucci, the blond, blue-eyed; ivory-skinned beauty who was the favorite female model of the great Italian Renaissance artist, Sandro Botticelli. She married into the Vespucci family and was cousin to Amerigo Vespucci who gave America his name. Subject of poems; mistress to Giuliano, the younger brother of Lorenzo de Medici; Queen of Beauty at one of Florence's great pageants, her death at age twenty-two caused general mourning in that great city.

To see her today, look at Botticelli's Birth of Venus or Primavera and know why her beauty captivated. She bore illegitimate children through her liason with Guiliano de Medici, hence the reference to "descended somehow or other". [WB 3]

6167 Simons, Mr. -- an affected acquaintance of the Dowager Duchess* who pretended not be be Jewish for the sake of convenience [WB 3]

6168 Simons, Lewis -- Olga Kohn's* fiancé. Understandably jealous of her beauty, he is at least reasonable to deal with. [HHC 22]

6169 Simpkins, J. -- the courier who is riding the Norton* motorcycle and who carries the grisly package which he understandably wishes to dispose of anonymously [cb]

6170 Simpson -- a people's warden and resident of Little Doddering* [bc]

6171 Simpson -- Sir Reuben Levy's* new butler [WB 5]

6172 Simpson -- manservant to Mr. Murbles* at his quarters in Staple Inn* [CW 10]

6173 Simpson, Bill -- what William Bright* claims is his real name, but it is another of his aliases [HHC 14]

6174 Simpson -- an alias of Arthur Robinson [GN 19]

6175 Simpson's in The Strand -- established in 1828 and a favorite stop for Sherlock Holmes*, it is one of London's more famous traditional restaurants with a variety of dining rooms on two floors. They do carve joints of meat on large, heated carving trolleys or carts taken to the table. It used to be a tradition in British restaurants and pubs to have certain rooms or areas reserved for ladies and their escorts--it being considered indiscreet at best for them to be out alone, and as late as 1977, Simpson's restricted the ladies to the upstairs dining room, the ground floor being reserved for men at lunchtime. Simpson's is at 100 The Strand, WC 2. [MMA 4]

6176 simulacrum -- a semblance of something, a trace of it [MMA 11]

6177 Sinclair, May -- English novelist (1865-1946) who experimented with the form and who employed Freudian psychology in her works. She is best known for Mary Olivier (1919). [BC 18]

6178 sine die -- Latin for, "without an appointed day (or date)"; indefinitely or until needed again [NT 4/BH 11]

6179 Sing Sing -- the maximum security state prison on the Hudson River in New York State at Ossining. It is the only prison in the United States

with a major railroad running through it, making it, perhaps, unique in the world. The prison has its own cemetery and the apparatus necessary for the execution of criminals by electrocution. Julius and Ethel Rosenburg are among the more famous inmates to have died there. [NT 14]

6180 the single eye, directed to the object -- the reference to motes and beams is taken from Matthew 7:1-5, part of the Sermon on the Mount, especially verse 5: "Thou hypocrite, first cast out the beam out of thine own eye; and then shalt thou see clearly to cast out the mote out of thy brother's eye." For the remainder, see, "If thine eye be single." [GN 4]

6181 singles -- when one pair of bells change places as opposed to a bob or a dodge** when two pairs change places [NT 1]

6182 singleted -- see singlets [GN 15]

6183 singleton -- a single card of a given suit; the term is commonly used in bridge* [MMA 6]

6184 singlets -- undershirts [MMA 4]

6185 Sir Eglamore achieving his first dragon -- Sir Eglamore is a chivalrous knight and staunch supporter of the courts of love. He appears in Shakespeare's _Two Gentlemen of Verona_ specifically for the purpose of helping Silvia, one of the heroines, to escape to find Valentine, her true love. While he makes no specific mention of dragons, he is presented as one who would not hesitate to assault one to protect his lady in her attempt to reach her lover. [UD BN]

6186 Sir Hubert -- see Hubert, Sir [GN 15]

6187 _Sir John Magill's Last Journey_ -- a novel by Freeman Wills Crofts* which is a typical Crofts railway timetable puzzle set in the western part of Wigtownshire* and in Northern Ireland with references to Portpatrick, Stranraer**, and Belfast. It is interesting to note that Strachan recommends it to the police. [FRH 21]

6188 Sir Roger [dance] -- a very ancient and well-known dance wherein couples form two long lines facing each other. The couple at one end forms an arch and the others dance through, the last couple through forming another arch, etc., until all have been involved. There are several versions, but all have the same general pattern. The dance is associated with _The Spectator_ of Addison and Steele as they deliberately linked the dance with their fictitious character, Sir Roger de Coverley, who claimed that it was named for his great-grandfather. [qs]

6189 Sister -- a nurse in an English hospital. More specifically, however, the term refers to a head nurse or one in charge of a ward. There is no necessary connection to religion as a nurse need not be a nun to be a sister in this sense. The word refers to "sisterhood" as in "sisterhood of nursing". [GN 10]

6190 sister [St. George's] -- see Wimsey, Winifred [GN 9]

6191 Sister Anne -- the sister of Bluebeard's last wife who kept watch until their brothers saved them at the last moment [HHC 12]

6192 Sister in a black habit -- see black habit [UD 19]

6193 six-and-six [acceptance would have meant] -- George Fentiman* is mentally expressing his relief at not having to go buy the whiskey as he did not want to spend the minimum six shillings and six pence to get some. See also British Monetary Units. [BC 7]

6194 six tailors -- there are nine for a man, six for a woman. The tailors are teller-strokes or tolling bells rung in groups of three strokes. One is reminded of John Donne's "Meditation 17, 'The Tolling of the Bells'", and its famous line, "Any man's death diminishes me because I am involved in mankind, and therefore never send to know for whom the bell tolls; it tolls for thee . . . ." [NT 2]

6195 sixpence -- a British coin about the size of a dime and worth six old pence. See British Monetary Units. [WB 10/MMA 1]

6196 Sixth Form -- roughly equivalent to a mix of 12th grade and college work in the U. S. It is to prepare a student for the Advanced Level exams, usually taken in three subjects, that may be used for college entrance.

[UD BN]

6197 sixties -- DLS means, of course, the 1860's [SP 6]

6198 skelloch -- Scots dialect for a loud, shrill cry, yell, or scream [ss/FRH 7]

6199 skelp her ower the lug -- an archaic and dialectal expression meaning to strike her over the ear or on the head [FRH 11]

6200 Skimpole, Harold -- a character in Charles Dickens's* Bleak House (1852). Skimpole is an amateur artist who is always borrowing from his friends. [WB 2]

6201 skite [too much] -- skite is a dialectical term meaning either to run off or to void excrement, i. e. to shit. There is also a connection with "blatherskite"*. In any sense the comment is offensive. [FRH 1]

6202 skittled his leg stump -- see cricket [MMA 18]

6203 Skipton, Bill -- a poacher and general mischief-maker in the Paggleham* area [BH 11]

6204 Skriner -- a well-known picture dealer and dinner guest in the home of Sir Reuben Levy*; he is fictitious [WB 5]

6205 Skrymes -- a bidder on books at auctions PW has attended and who, because of PW's acuity at bidding, bears enmity toward PW for that success. His lordship seems to derive a certain perverse pleasure from making Skrymes suffer at such auctions, so the animosity is probably well earned. [ss]

6206 Skye -- the large Highland island off Scotland's West coast. It is steeped in history and remains the center of the Clan McLeod at Dunvegan Castle. The island is associated with Bonnie Prince Charlie (Prince Charles Edward Stuart) who stayed on the island briefly as a fugitive after the disastrous Battle of Culloden in 1746. [FRH 13]

6207 Skyre Burn -- a stream which runs southeast into Fleet Bay [FRH 21]

6208 slam -- see bridge

6209 "slashing trade that" -- see Farrar, Dean [SP 5]

6210 slate [entered it all on the] -- a running (perhaps daily) record or account of purchases or debits akin to the expression, "put it on my tab" [GN 6]

6211 Slater, Mary -- a pseudonym used by HV when purchasing arsenic in preparation for writing the detective novel which features in the investigation of her involvement with the death of Philip Boyes* [SP 1]

6212 Slater person -- the Duchess is referring to the case of a German Jew named George Slater, convicted in May of 1909 of having murdered an old lady for her jewelry. Sir Arthur Conan Doyle finally got Slater freed when it was proved that two key witnesses had been paid to perjure themselves to convict Slater. Slater was freed in 1927 and was paid £6000 for his ordeal. His strange lack of gratitude was shown when he refused to repay Doyle for the considerable expenses he had encountered on Slater's behalf. [SP 3]

6213 slaughter of the innocents -- the reference is to Herod's order to kill all children in Bethlehem and the surrounding areas who were two years of age or younger. See Matthew 2:16. [GN 17]

6214 Slav -- any person from central Europe or the northern Balkan regions speaking a Slavic language [WB 11]

6215 The Sleeping Athlete -- a work of sculpture planned by Eric Loder* [cf]

6216 Sleuths Incorporated -- a private detective firm hired by PW to assist him in his pursuit of the elusive Mr. Oliver*. The firm is fictitious. [BC 10]

6217 slice off the tee -- a bit of golfing jargon. The tee is the little wooden peg used only on the first stroke at a given hole during the round. To "slice" is to drive the ball to the right instead of straight ahead. A "hook" would be to drive to the left. Neither is desirable unless done intentionally for some reason. [FRH 13]

6218 slider -- a device used with a

stay* to support the bell just beyond top dead center so that it rests in the inverted position. To give a single note, the bell has to swing freely round and come to rest against the opposite side of the stay. The note will then give its full tone. [NT 3]

6219 Sliders [Steel Office Tables] -- one of the fictitious firms created by DLS for the story [MMA 1]

6220 Sligo, Prof. -- the fictitious scientist under whom Dr. Penberthy* had studies glands. See Dr. Voronoff. [BC 16]

6221 sling -- not a slingshot, but a cloth or leather pouch with two thongs or strings attached. A stone or marble in the pouch can be hurled with murderous force by someone trained in its use. Goliath is testimony to its dangers. [MMA 5]

6222 Sloane Square murderer -- an unidentified and fictitious person whose boots PW found in the Underground* [aq]

6223 slopin[g] off -- slang for making off, going away, etc. [CW 3]

6224 slops -- British slang for police. The word is a shortened form of "ecilop", or police spelled backward. [ab]

6225 sloth -- a capital sin and one of the seven deadly sins, the others being pride, avarice, lust, gluttony, envy, and anger. The first four are listed as sins which pervert legitimate goals. Sloth, envy, and anger are sins which deny the pursuit of legitimate goals. [CW 2]

6226 slow-combustion stoves -- stoves the drafts of which are carefully regulated to burn fuel more slowly and, thus more efficiently [NT 1]

6227 slow hunt -- see hunting course [NT 1]

6228 Sludge the Medium -- the reference is to "Mr. Sludge, the 'Medium'", a poem by Robert Browning* first published in 1864 in Dramatis Personae. In the poem, Sludge, a detected cheat, is made to confess and defend his activity as a fraudulent medium. However, he manages to place a fair amount of the blame on the gullibility, stupidity, or ignorance of his customers. [WB 6]

6229 slugs -- lead spacers used in typesetting to make blank spaces and to fill between segments of the form so that the type will be held tightly in place; or the line of type itself as set by a linotype machine, also cast in lead [CW 15]

6230 Slumbermalt -- part of the fictitious Nutrax family of patent medicines advertised by Pym's Publicity* [MMA 1]

6231 slump -- a reference to the Great Depression, the world-wide economic crash of 1929 and the subsequent period of hardship that lasted until WW II began [MMA 2]

6232 small bells -- those bells of higher tone are smaller than those of deep tone and, in change-ringing*, are the one designated by the smaller numbers [NT 2]

6233 small bone of the leg -- the fibula [MMA 10]

6234 small-cord -- twine [BH 20]

6235 smaller the fall -- or downhill slope. A river on flat land will be sluggish and deposit its silt along the way, thus clogging the stream. A sharp fall is needed to keep a swift current moving to prevent clogging the stream bed. [NT 16]

6236 Smayle, Mr. -- one of the staff members at Pym's Publicity. He is the group manager* for Dairyfields Ltd.* [MMA 1]

6237 smell of the lamp -- the reference is to Laurence Sterne's Tristram Shandy*, Ch. 23, where it is written, "I should have no objection to this method, but that I think it must smell too strong of the lamp." The passage refers to lamp in the sense of laborious, nocturnal study, and carries with it the idea of strained or unnatural results. HV was reading Tristram Shandy at the beginning of the novel. [HHC 25]

6238 Smith, Mr. -- a student at Queen's College. See Oxford Colleges. [GN 8]

6239 Smith, Mrs. -- a resident of Kensington and a cousin to Mrs. Ven-

ables* [NT 4]

6240 Smith, A. L. -- Arthur Lionel Smith (1850-1924), Fellow and Lecturer at Trinity College, Oxford, 1874-79, Tutor of Modern History at Balliol in 1879, Fellow of Balliol in 1882, Dean in 1907 (two years before PW went up) and Master of Balliol from 1916. He was educated at Christ's Hospital and at Balliol. Among his works is _Church and State in the Middle Ages_ (Ford Lectures, 1905 and 1913). He may be the "charming old tutor" mentioned in GN, Ch. 15. [GN 14]

6241 Smith, George Joseph -- see brides-in-the-bath [WB 10/UD 8/ BH 5]

6242 Smith, Greg -- landlord at the Bridge and Bottle* pub in Riddlesdale*. He is described as surly and unpleasant, but also as one who serves good drink. [CW 11]

6243 Smith, Joe -- one of the natives of the Wilvercombe* area and who is thought, wrongly, to have been a candidate as the corpse after HV finds the body on the rocks [HHC 2]

6244 Smith, John -- see Beck, Adolf [WB 2]

6245 Smith, John -- like John Doe, a name for one unknown or wishing to remain unidentified as the Viscount St. George* certainly would have wished to do. There is also a possible connection to the Adolf Beck* situation. [GN 10]

6246 Smith, Madeleine [Hamilton] -- (1836-1928) an unpleasant and altogether too forward a young woman for Edinburgh in the mid-1850's. The daughter of a prosperous merchant, Madeleine saw a French clerk, Pierre Emile L'Angelier, and contrived to meet him. By 1856, their flirtation had become an affair, but neither of them had any money. She then met William Minnoch, a prosperous merchant, and tried to break off her affair with L'Angelier.

L'Angelier refused to end their liason and produced some of her torrid love letters for use as blackmail. The Frenchman was found dead in March of 1857, and the autopsy revealed 88 (!) grains of arsenic in his body. Madeleine was brought to trial and a verdict of Not Proven* was returned, mostly because there was no absolute link between her and Pierre on the day that he consumed the poison. She later married a physician and divorced him. Her second marriage, to George Wardle, an artist, lasted. She died in the U. S. in April of 1928, at the age of 92. [SP 2]

6247 Smith-Hartington -- an otherwise unidentified employee of the _Morning Yell_* [cf]

6248 Smith-Lemesurier, Mrs. -- the pathetic widow of an African civil servant who "sacrifices" her reputation to provide an alibi for Jock Graham* with whom she fancies she is having an affair [FRH 18]

6249 smoking room -- modern readers must remember that smoking was considered differently than it is today, so after dinner the gentlemen would retire there for conversation. The ladies could smoke in some circumstances, but not as openly as is done today. [CW 1]

6250 snapping [lead] -- a difficult maneuver performed by the treble* bell at lead or behind** requiring that the ringer strike only one blow and leave that place without returning to complete a whole pull, or two blows [NT 1]

6251 sneck -- see door-sneck [ss]

6252 Sneezes, Rich as -- see Rich as Sneezes [SP 9]

6253 Snell-Wilmington, Mrs. -- the fictitious author of that fictitious work of fiction, _Passion-flower Pie_* [GN 11]

6254 Snettisley -- a fictitious community in the Pagford/Paggleham** area [BH 11]

6255 snick of the flying bails -- see cricket [MMA 18]

6256 Snoates, Robert -- a fictitious person created by DLS perhaps to suggest her feelings toward such poetry as Snoates is supposed to have written. It may also be a snide comment about Edith Sitwell's _Façade_, set to music by William Walton and first performed in 1923, the year of the action in CW. The eighth poem in Sitwell's collection is entitled "Trio for Two Cats and a Trombone", a title in keeping with

Snoates's efforts. [CW 7]

6257 Snoot, Miss -- the schoolmistress and organist at Fenchurch St. Paul* [NT 2]

6258 Snow, C[harles] P[ercy] -- (b. 1905) an English scientist, novelist, essayist, and administrator educated at Cambridge* University. The zenith of Snow's career as a novelist came in the 1950's, but his The Two Cultures and a Second Look were widely popular on American college campuses in the 1960's. Snow was knighted in 1957 for administrative work he had done for the British government. [GN 12]

6259 The snow white horsepower -- PW is meandering literarily. The horsepower section of the line is probably his own, but may be an allusion to Matthew Arnold's (1822-88) "The Forsaken Merman", l. 6, "Now the wild white horses play". The blue bonnet part is a reference to Ch. 25 of Sir Walter Scott's (1771-1832) The Monastery. In that chapter Scott resorts to poetry, one line of which reads: "All the Blue Bonnets are bound for the border." [UD 11]

6260 Snowden, Mr. -- Philip, 1st Viscount Snowden of Ickornshaw (1864-1937), English economist and politician who served as Chancellor of the Exchequer under Ramsey MacDonald* in the 1924 Labour government. He stood for high taxes, free trade, the gold standard, and repaying the war debt to the U. S. He wanted to help the people in any way that would not upset the economic or political basis of the nation. [HHC 22]

6261 Snupshed, Professor -- a creation of one of PW's flights of fancy whom PW identifies as a colleague [WB 5]

6262 Snype, Dalilah -- a letterwriter who dislikes PW despite his money, and who does not think the Wimsey-Vane marriage will last [BH P]

6263 "So here I'll watch the night and wait . . ." -- the line is from A. E. Housman's* A Shropshire Lad*, poem IX, stanza 7:

"So here I'll watch the night and wait
To see the morning shine,
When he will hear the stroke of eight
And not the stroke of nine . . ."

The opening line of the poem is, "There sleeps in Shrewsbury jail tonight . . . ." [BH E3]

6264 Soames -- a house servant at Duke's Denver* [WB 9]

6265 soap and pickles lords -- peers created in recognition of some outstanding service to the British nation and usually in reference to some business or other notable economic achievement. Of late, such titles are not usually hereditary. [CW 15]

6266 Sobranies -- a popular brand of English cigarette still widely available around the world. PW is known to have smoked them on at least one occasion. [pj/UD 3]

6267 Socialist[s] -- an advocate or practitioner of socialism, that doctrine which favors the nationalization of the economic life of a nation within the framework of a strong central government for the administration of various programs for health, insurance, etc.; an intermediate step between free enterprise and communism. [CW 2/BC 8/FRH 10/HHC 26]

6268 Society -- an unspecified organization whose meeting was attended by Pomfret, Rogers, and Cattermole**, and, from all appearance, which does not seem to be strictly academic in nature. There are many Oxford clubs and organizations with the word society in the name somewhere. [GN 7]

6269 The Society -- "the crook society" that PW spends two years trying to destroy. PW has himself declared legally dead, joins the group under an alias, and destroys it from within, but not before many robberies have been committed, some controlled by PW, including one of his flat at 110A Piccadilly. The diamond tiara stolen from the Dowager Duchess* is commented on as, "a very ugly tiara--no real loss to anyone with decent taste." One wonders what the Dowager Duchess thought of it. The time placement of the story within the PW canon is contradictory, suggesting that it may be apocryphal. [ab]

6270 "Society is at the mercy . . . ." -- see Pearson, Edmund [UD 8]

6271 Socrates -- the Greek philosopher

(470?-399 B. C.) whose work is recounted for us through the writings of Plato. Socrates never wrote down his own material, so anything we have of "his" is as interpreted by Plato. His favorite method of discourse was to pose a question and, by further questioning, force the examination of as much of the problem as time would allow or until the group could agree on the "truth" of a response to the original question. This teaching technique is still referred to as the Socratic method. [GN 8]

6272 Socrates' slave -- the reference is to Plato's dialogue, Meno, wherein Socrates is talking with Menon and Anytos about whether or not virtue can be taught. As a part of that dialogue, Socrates calls on a slave boy to determine if he is being taught something or if he is remembering it, and Socrates demonstrates that the slave boy knew things without ever having been taught them. [WB 10]

6273 soda-mint lozenges -- stomach sweeteners on the order of a magnesia tablet (milk of magnesia) [BC 3]

6274 soda-siphon -- what Sherlock Holmes* calls a gasogene, a very sturdy glass (or sometimes today of metal) bottles with various control valves on top. One fills it with water and charges it with a carbon-dioxide cylinder, and then enjoys fresh soda water for drinking or for mixing with whiskey or brandy. [MMA 5]

6275 sodium flame [ghastly effects of] -- elemental sodium is too dangerous, so some sodium salt would be used. Easily combustible, they would provide a bright yellow flame of considerable intensity. The effects would, indeed, be ghastly. [ie]

6276 soeur -- French for, "sister" [CW 13]

6277 Soho -- an area in London long associated with nightlife, cabarets, etc. It centers on Soho Square and is roughly bounded by New Oxford St., Charing Cross Rd., Shaftesbury Ave., and Regent St. in central London due North of Westminster. The area was well known to DLS and she had PW and Parker meet Dr. Carr* at the Au Bon Bourgeois* restaurant there to start their adventures in UD. The area is noted for its many and varied foreign restaurants. [UD 1/BC 20/SP 14/GN 4]

6278 Sol -- the sun. Cuthbert Conyers* was playing with the terms of astrology, making puns about the nature of his hidden treasure. The sun and Leo are associated with gold, but Cuthbert was more concerned with the effect of sunlight on his lake and the "new" islands it contained. [dh]

6279 solar plexus -- the exposed segment of the diaphragm at the base of the breast bone and just above the stomach. It is the locus of several nerve bundles, and a blow there is at least temporarily disabling and has come to mean any such blow, whether physical or emotional. [GN 8]

6280 Sole Colbert -- a preparation for fillets of sole where they are coated with lemon juice, flour, pepper, salt, egg, and bread crumbs and then fried over high heat in a small amount of butter sauce flavored with lemon, parsley, and scallions. [BC 7]

6281 Solent quoque hujus insulae cultores -- PW manages a good spur-of-the-moment translation of the medieval Latin when he reads the passage as, "It is the custom of the dwellers in this island . . . ." The passage is from the Cosmographia Universalis*. [dh]

6282 solicitor -- a general practitioner of the law, a lawyer who handles the day-to-day routine of legal business. For specialist advice or for representation in the High Court he refers to a barrister*. Even then, the solicitor still has to be in court to work with the client as the barrister may only work with the solicitor who acts as an intermediary. [passim]

6283 "The Solitary Cyclist" -- a Sherlock Holmes story first anthologized in The Return of Sherlock Holmes [BH 10]

6284 Solomon [as many wives as] [as wise as] -- that good and wise king of the Old Testament who is reputed to have had as many as 1000 wives (or 700 wives and 300 concubines). He is also known to have been a great and wise judge as is related in the story of the two women who claimed the same baby that is recounted in I Kings 3:

16-28. [MMA 17/GN 17]

6285 Solomons, Mr. -- the representative from Moss & Isaacs* who has come in haste to try to beat Mr. MacBride* to any claim on the furniture in Talboys* that William Noakes* might have owned [BH 18]

6286 solute chlorinated lime -- a combination of lime and chlorine dissolved together in pure water; one of the usual reagents for distinguishing arsenic from antimony [SP 20]

6287 solvitur ambulando -- Latin for the concept that the problem is to be solved by action; work it out by experimentation [CW 15]

6288 Some Notes on the Pathological Aspects of Genius -- see publications, Sir Julian Freke [WB 8]

6289 "Some say thy fault is youth, some wantonness" -- the lines are from Shakespeare's Sonnet XCVI, lines 1-4. The poem continues in lines 9-12 as:

"How many lambs might the stern wolf betray,
If like a lamb he could his looks translate!
How many gazers mightst thou lead away,
If thou wouldst use the strength of all thy state!"

[GN 10]

6290 Somebody laid claim to a marquisate -- the reference is too vague for absolute identification, but it appears that with so many other accurate references that it is probable that DLS had some such incident in mind [UD 19]

6291 Somerset -- the large southwestern English county which forms, roughly, the northern part of the peninsula that ends in Devon and Cornwall [MMA 12]

6292 Somerset House -- formerly the palace of the Duke of Somerset and, later, a succession of queens. Demolished in the late 1700's, it was replaced by the present building which retained the name. It used to house the Revenue Department, the major Probate Registry, and the registry for births, deaths, and marriages. PW and Miss Climpson* make frequent use of its resources for their research. The building is located on the Victoria Embankment near the northeast end of Waterloo Bridge. [ss/im/UD 3/GN 19]

6293 Somerville -- DLS's alma mater at Oxford (she attended from 1912 to 1915, but did not receive her degree until October 14, 1920, when she was among the first women to be granted degrees from Oxford), one of the earliest of the Oxford colleges for women, opened in 1879. It fronts on Woodstock Rd. with the Radcliffe Infirmary, Little Clarendon St., and Kingston Rd. forming the other boundaries. Across Kingston Rd. from the college is the Oxford University Press building. Miss Meteyard* is a graduate of Somerville, but more famous real graduates include, in addition to DLS, Iris Murdoch, Vera Brittain, and the United Kingdom's first female Prime Minister, Margaret Thatcher. It is generally accepted that Somerville is the model for the fictitious Shrewsbury College* in GN and BH as the similarities between the two are most striking. [MMA 1/GN 2]

6294 Something about a body in a belfry -- a reference to the events recounted in NT [GN 11]

6295 "Sometimes you are tempted to ask yourself . . ." -- the game in question is not known, but may be "Who Am I?", also called "Botticelli", a game wherein one player pretends to be someone out of history or literature and the other players have to guess who is being portrayed through a series of questions which must be answerable with either a yes or a no response. "Who Am I?" also seems to fit in with the tenor of the advertisement. [MMA 19]

6296 Somme, Second Battle of -- a reference to the major German offensive along the Somme River area of the Western Front in early 1918 [BC 2]

6297 sonata -- an instrumental composition usually of three or four movements, from the Italian for sounded of played as opposed to cantata for vocalized music. The basic structure is to state a theme or themes, develop it or them, and then recapitulate. The form evolved from a collection of dance tunes in one key. [WB 3]

6298 Song of Roland -- the famous medieval French narrative poem

(chanson de geste) translated by DLS in verse form. It tells of the great deeds and exploits of the trusting, impetuous, and straightforward hero, Roland, and of his friend, Oliver, the less impetuous of the two. The tale is over 4000 lines long and was written in the middle of the 11th C., probably in Brittany. Roland and Oliver are great knights in service to Charlemagne in his drive to force the Saracens from Spain. See also "Four Sons of Aymon".

6299 Song of Songs -- another name for the Old Testament book Song of Solomon. The book is alluded to in "Uncle Meleager's Will", and, when PW suggests a passage from that book, Bunter supplies the quote from 8:6. When PW later suggests to HV that she start reading the book, he is being cute and naughty as the book is a love idyll traditionally ascribed to Solomon, but erroneously so. It is claimed to be an allegory of the mystical union between God and his people (or Christ and His Church) more than an Oriental love poem, but, whichever, it is one of the more sensually beautiful books of the Bible. [umw/fr/UD 16/HHC 16]

6300 sonnet -- a poem which, by definition, must have fourteen lines of ten syllables per line, and which must be end-rhymed according to one of several accepted patterns, the most common of which were created by Petrarch, Shakespeare, Spenser, and Milton. The first part of the poem will pose some sort of question or problem which is addressed in either the sestet or the couplet at the end of the poem. [GN 11]

6301 Sophy, Aunt -- Aggie Twitterton's* aunt, the one who presented a cruet to "grandpa and grandma" as a wedding gift. It is impossible to sort out the relationships accurately as we do not know if the people are maternal or paternal relatives. [BH 9]

6302 Sopo -- a brand name of soap created by DLS to provide work for Pym's Publicity* [MMA 3]

6303 soporific -- anything that causes drowsiness or that leads to sleep [CW 1/NT 2]

6304 "Sorrow vanquished, labour ended, Jordan passed." -- the reference here is to the fifth of seven stanzas of the hymn "Art Thou Weary" by John M. Neale (1818-66) with music by Henry W. Baker (1821-77). The full stanza reads: "If I still hold closely to Him, what hath He at Last? 'Sorrow vanquished, labour ended, Jordan passed.'" Neale's source is 8th C. Greek. The hymn is number 254 in <u>Hymns A & M</u>* and number 193 in <u>The Methodist Hymnal</u> of 1935. [UD 11]

6305 <u>sot[t]o voce</u> -- Italian for speaking in a hushed or quiet voice [BH 5]

6306 <u>soufflé glacé</u> -- a cold, fluffy, lemon-flavored dessert enjoyed by PW and Ann Dorland* [BC 21]

6307 "The Soul's Awakening" -- a picture hanging in the parlor at Talboys* before PW and HV have had a chance to redecorate. The title suggests the typical Victorian didactic parlor painting reproduction meant to be morally uplifting in an obvious and sentimental manner. [BH 12]

6308 sound and fury -- an allusion to Shakespeare's <u>Macbeth</u>, V, v, 27. The line comes at the end of Macbeth's "Tomorrow, and tomorrow, and tomorrow" soliloquy wherein he states:

> " . . . it [life] is a tale
> Told by an idiot, full of sound and fury,
> Signifying nothing."

In SP the reference is not to life, but to Miss Murchison's* actions. [SP 14]

6309 soundbow -- the point where the clapper strikes on the inside of a bell near the mouth [NT 4]

6310 soupçon -- a suspicion, pinch, trace, or touch of something; any unspecified minute quantity [SP 9]

6311 South Audley St. -- a street in the Mayfair* section of the West End* near Hyde Park* which runs from Curzon St. to Grosvenor Square*. It is a very fashionable and expensive section of London. PW and HV establish their home in Town on Audley Square*, an enclave off South Audley St., and Mrs. Forrest* has a home (flat) there. [hp/UD 7]

6312 South Avenue -- a street in Pagford* [BH 11]

6313 South Kensington Station -- an Underground* station just South of the Victoria and Albert Museum in the suburb of South Kensington (South of Kensington Gardens) [MMA 15]

6314 South Parks Rd. -- an East-West road in Oxford connecting Parks Rd. with St. Cross Rd. A footpath goes on to Parson's Pleasure*. [GN 18]

6315 South Seas -- South Pacific islands, many of which were controlled by Great Britain prior to WW II [WB 11]

6316 South Wind -- a novel by Norman Douglas (1868-1952) in the form of a discussion of ideas such as Aldous Huxley's Point Counter Point. Douglas's work is a bold "assault upon conventional moral standards . . . .". [CW 2]

6317 Southampton -- Britain's principal South coast seaport and, with Liverpool, one of her two major passenger vessel ports. It is also one of the major cross-Channel ports with regular service to Le Havre, France. [UD 23/BC 11/ BH 2]

6318 Southampton Row -- a street connecting Russell Square in Bloomsbury* with Kingsway* at High Holborn*. Pym's Publicity* is located on Southampton Row. The real Benson's where DLS worked and after which she patterned Pym's was located at 75 Kingsway. [SP 1/MMA 2]

6319 Southend -- or Southend-on-Sea is a popular resort East of London on the North side of the mouth of the Thames River. It is in Essex and features a fine variety of entertainment opportunities for vacationers. [cb/ im/NT 20]

6320 Southern -- the Southern Railway was formed in 1923 by the amalgamation of the London and South Western, the L. B. & S. C.*, and others. It ran to the South and West of London, but is now part of British Rail. [UD 6]

6321 Southerner[s] -- Englishmen from the South [CW 9/FRH 20]

6322 Southron -- Scots dialect for an Englishman. The Scottish borderline for Southerner* is a bit further North than an Englishman's would be. [FRH 1]

6323 Southwark -- the location of a one time royal "burh" or citadel. It was the South Work, hence its name. It is also called The Borough from its former status as a royal "burh". It is an area of great antiquity which is mentioned prominently in Chaucer and Shakespeare. It is directly across the Thames from The City*. In earlier times the district was distinctly seamy, but changing times and moral attitudes have changed all that. Robert Duckworthy was born in that area of London. [im]

6324 Soviet Club -- a Marxist/Leninist club in London. PW visits there and is shot by Lady Mary's former intended, George Goyles*. He also meets Hannah Marryat* there. PW dislikes the place not so much because of having been shot near there, but because the food is so bad. As given here, it is fictitious, but could be any such club that flourished in the 1920's and 30's when it was popular in some circles to hold socialist and communist views a bit too vocally. The club DLS created is located on Gerrard St. which is also the location of the real Detection Club which DLS helped to found. Julian Perkins is also a member of the Soviet Club, but it is hard to imagine a less likely radical. [umw/CW 7/HHC 25]

6325 sovereign in the streets of Aberdeen -- the Scots are stereotypically known for their frugality, so for one to find a sovereign in the stated circumstances would have to be at least providential. PW notes that the Aberdonians are frugal even by Scottish standards. See also British Monetary Units. [HHC 13]

6326 Sowerton, Mr. and Mrs. [old] -- locals in the Paggleham* area who attend William Noakes's* funeral [BH 19]

6327 Spanish Fleet -- the famous Armada of 1588 which was defeated by the English aided by their faster, more maneuverable ships. As a result, over sixty ships of the original 130, and some 9000 of the 30,000 troops were lost. The bulk of the action took place from July 29 to August 7 of 1588. [MMA 15]

6328 Spanish poplar -- one of the rapidly growing deciduous trees,

genus Populus, and related to the aspen, cottonwood, and Lombardy poplar. They are often called tulip trees. [CW 2]

6329 spanner -- a wrench [dh/UD 20/ FRH 11]

6330 Sparkes -- a person, not further identified, who functions as an officer of the court of inquest regardin the body found in the belfry at Fenchurch St. Paul* [NT 4]

6331 Sparkes and Crisp -- an automobile and motorcycle sales and repair firm in Glasgow. John Ferguson* takes his auto's magneto* there for repairs. The firm is fictitious. [FRH 13]

6332 Sparkler, Edmund -- a character in Dickens's* Little Dorrit* who marries Fanny, Dorrit's sister. He is a minor character. [UD 6]

6333 Sparkletone -- an "invigorating vegetable" laxative. It is fictitious. [MMA 16]

6334 Sparkling Pompayne -- one of the Brotherhood's, Ltd., family of nonalcoholic fruit drinks. The name "pompayne" is a pun drawn from the French for "apple" (pomme) with a phonetic spelling of the ending of champagne; hence, some sort of sparkling apple juice. [MMA 4]

6335 "Speak the speech I pray you . . ." -- PW is quoting from Hamlet, III, ii, 1ff, the famous advice to the players speech [BH 16]

6336 speaking at lead -- the first bell to speak in a sequence of changes. See lead. [NT 2]

6337 special constable -- an ordinary citizen, especially sworn to help in some special way, whose rights and responsibilities as a law officer relate only to the duties for which he was sworn and to no other police function. The office was created by statute in 1673 and was regularized by the Special Constables Act of 1831. They were used in the Fenian "disturbances" of 1867, and again in the railway strike of 1911. In 1939, there were 130,000 "specials", of whom some 2600 were serving as full-time PC's in 1940. They are not paid, but may receive an expense allowance. Their main function today is to help with crowd control. [NT 8]

6338 special intention -- a prayer said for someone or something specifically rather than a general prayer as for confession [UD 19]

6339 special license -- a marriage license that shortcuts the usual requirements of banns being read for three consecutive Sundays and then followed by the phrase "If anybody here present knows just cause or impediment why these two persons should not be joined in Holy Matrimony, ye are now to declare it." Jane Eyre has fiction's most famous response to that challenge. Such licenses are granted solely by the authority of the Archbishop of Canterbury. [HHC 19]

6340 special subject -- the study of a limited historical period or topic that is examined in Schools* as one of the required papers [GN 15]

6341 The Spectator -- the weekly periodical started in 1828 by R. S. Rintoul. It espoused the cause of "educated radicalism". The magazine shares its name with the famous series of essays by Addison and Steele, but the two are separated by over a hundred years, the earlier essays having been published between 1711 and 1712. Today the journal is an independent review of politics, current affairs, literature, and the arts with offices at 56 Doughty St., London. [NT 4]

6342 speedwell eyes -- the speedwell (Veronica officinalis) is a perennial European herb with bluish flowers; hence, Mrs. Smith-Lemesurier* has eyes of that shade of blue [FRH 18]

6343 Spencer, George John -- the 2nd Earl Spencer (1758-1834), a member of the Commons from 1780-82, he moved to the Lords on the death of his father in 1783. He served as First Lord of the Admiralty from 1794 to 1801 and is remembered particularly for having given Horatio Nelson his first command. From 1806-07 he was secretary of state for the Home Department. His private library, the result of his intense interest in bibliophily, was considered one of the finest private libraries in Europe and was rich in 15th C. items including 58 Caxtons!

Most of his library is now in the John Rylands library in Manchester,

England, having been sold to Mrs. Rylands in 1892 by the 6th Earl Spencer. Mrs. Rylands, in turn, made it a memorial to her husband. The Spencers are the family of HRH Diana, Princess of Wales, and are descendants of both Henry VII and the 1st Duke of Marlborough. [WB 1]

6344 Spender, Mr. -- an employee of Pym's Publicity*, he is in charge of vouchers* [MMA 6]

6345 Spenlow [young] -- an otherwise unidentified member of the de Momerie* crowd [MMA 9]

6346 Spenser, Edmund -- English poet (1552?-99) and a relative of the Earls Spencer*. With Shakespeare and Milton, he is remembered as one of the very greatest of English poets. He is most known for <u>The Fairie Queen</u>, an allegorical epic; "Shepherd's Calendar"; and his sonnet sequence, <u>Amoretti</u>. [GN 8]

6347 sphinx-like -- mysterious or puzzling; given to riddles as in the story of Oedipus and the sphinx [BC 7]

6348 spifflicates -- or spiflicates; a word of fanciful origin meaning to confound, confuse, and destroy, the result of rough or coarse handling. To be spifflicated also means to be drunk. [HHC 34]

6349 Spiller, Mr. -- a garage mechanic in West Felpham* [nf]

6350 Spilsbury, Dr. Sir Bernard Henry -- the Home Office pathologist (1877-1947) made famous at the trials of Dr. Hawley Harvey Crippen* and, later, as principal Crown witness in the Brides-in-the-Bath* case. He was soon established as the "doctor-detective" prototype for modern fiction. He was knighted for his work in 1923. His passion for exacting detail, his prodigious memory, and his quiet assurance when testifying brought him success, fame, and the respect of juries for his objectivity. DLS probably patterned her fictional Dr. Lubbock* after Sir Bernard. [CW 6]

6351 Spinner -- the nickname of a Brotherhood's* cricketer who is otherwise unidentified [MMA 18]

6352 Spinster's Splash -- DLS's version of "Dame's Delight", a swimming place for women and children near Parson's Pleasure* in Oxford [GN 17]

6353 spirited away like the lady in the Ingoldsby Legends -- the reference is probably to the "Legend" entitled, "Mrs. Botherby's Story: The Leech of Folkestone". Unlike most of the <u>Ingoldsby Legends</u>*, "The Leech" is in prose and recounts the tale of a love triangle in which the husband fortuitously outwits his wife and her lover, the family doctor, or leech, as they attempt to kill him. The doctor attempts the murder with black magic and potions while a charlatan aids the husband with white magic.

The doctor is killed when some of his black magic backfires upon the intervention of the charlatan, and the wife disappears, apparently "spirited away". There are a number of parallels to the plot of <u>Whose Body?</u>, and PW fills one of his roles as a curious intruder and righter of wrongs, a strong element of the "Ingoldsby" story. [WB 2]

6354 Spiritualist Press -- a publishing company located at 23 Great Queen St., London. It is now, however, known as the Psychic Press, Ltd., and is at that same address. [SP 16]

6355 spoliation of the Abbey -- plundering of the abbey. See also Cromwell, Oliver, and break up the images. [NT 4]

6356 spondaic cadence -- a spondee is a poetic foot of two syllables, both of which are accented. Hence, a spondaic cadence would be a commanding, heavy, hard-driving pattern to hear and one that would be, of necessity, demanding of attention if read with a stern tone as PW would have done. [ie]

6357 Spooner, Dr. -- the Rev. Dr. William Archibald Spooner (1844-1930), an English clergyman and educator who spent his working life at New College, Oxford. He was ordained in 1875. His fame rests mostly upon his somewhat exaggerated reputation for "spoonerisms" or metathesis, the unwitting transposition of beginning sounds. One of his most famous utterances is, "Kinquering congs their titles take" delivered when announcing the hymn in Chapel in 1879. His taste in nightclothes is unknown. There is a pos-

sible connection to the nursery rhyme "Wee Willie Winkie" where town rhymes with gown. In one illustrated version at least, there seems to have been a connection with Dr. Spooner, but Lady Mary's remark is so casual as to make positive identification unlikely. [SP 12]

6358 sported oak -- university slang for a shut door, but the implication is that the occupant is either out or does not wish to be disturbed. See item #4844. [GN 8]

6359 spread-eagled the . . . stumps -- see cricket [MMA 18]

6360 to spread the tail of vanity -- this is most likely a PW allusion to the peacock as a symbol of vanity and not a quotation from anything in particular. Shakespeare and others use the allusion, but such references antedate that period by a good deal. [GN 14]

6361 spring lock -- or night latch or spring latch lock; a lock with a beveled bolt which can be forced easily unless there are other precautions built in [BH 8]

6362 "springe for his woodcock, set the" -- a springe is a snare to catch small game. A woodcock is a small, fast bird known for its explosive and erratic flight pattern. It is also rather tasty. Such a trap would be easier than trying to shoot the bird as they are small and are very difficult targets. Shooting one is more a matter of luck than of skill. References appear in Hamlet, I, iii, and V, ii. [BC 13/BH 18]

6363 springs, top of -- an especially high tide about the times of the new and full moons when the earth, moon, and sun are in line and exert maximum gravitational pull. Top of the springs would be the highest point reached by the tide. [HHC 1]

6364 sprung [rhythm] -- a term coined by poet Gerard Manley Hopkins* to explain his difficult-to-scan lines wherein the individual feet always have the first syllable accented, but there is no consistent number of unaccented syllables--there may be none, or two, or whatever he wants to use as in "The Starry Night":

"Lo̅ok ăt tĥe | stārs! | lo̅ok, |
lo̅ok ŭp ăt tĥe skīes!"

In this system, the (-) marks the stressed syllables and the (˘) marks the unstressed syllables. [GN 13]

6365 the Square -- see Grosvenor Square [hp]

6366 square-leg -- see cricket [MMA 18]

6367 Squeers, Mr. [Wackford] -- the allusion is to the bullying and ignorant, grasping and conceited schoolmaster of Dotheboys Hall, Wackford Squeers. He starves his students and steals their money in Charles Dickens's* Nicholas Nickleby. The principle is stated variously in the early chapters of the novel. The allusion that precedes the reference to the principle appears in Ch. 8 of the novel. [BH 18]

6368 The Squeezed Lemon -- a fictitious novel [GN 11]

6369 squelched -- the action of water making the sound created when subjected to sudden pressure or intermittent pressure (OED). Humans have been known to make similar sounds under similar conditions. [CW 12]

6370 squib -- a small firecracker or a broken larger one that only burns with a fizz and would fail to impress. A damp one would be notably quiet. [UD BN]

6371 Squills, Jacqueline -- a divorced author who maliciously puts her ex-husband in the pillory in her latest novel, Gas Filled Bulbs. Fortunately, one suspects, both she and the novel are fictitious. [GN 11]

6372 squish -- English university slang for marmalade [CW 2]

6373 squit -- a stupid, silly, diminutive, and insignificant person [SP 12]

6374 Stab and end the creature--to the heft! -- apparently not a quotation, but simply an allusion to the climax of a bullfight, the matador's coup de grâce to the bull, the object being to have the animal drop dead at his feet [SP 8]

6375 The Stag at Bay -- the pub where

the last cocaine delivery is made and where the ring's drug distribution system came to an end. It is apparently fictitious as DLS was careful not to use the names of real places in situations that would cause embarrassment. [MMA 19]

6376 Stage Charities -- no particular charity is implied here. Miss Climpson* tends to think in capital letters. [SP 19]

6377 staggie [like playing at] -- the reference is to "stag tick", a form of tag popular between the World Wars that requires a large number of children to play--twenty or more is recommended. All players save "It" line up and at the shout of "Cross!" from "It" run to some other agreed upon point such as across a street. Any runners tagged by "It" have to join hands with that person, the first one tagged forming the opposite end of a line of tagged persons. "It" and the first tagged are always the ends of the line formed, later persons tagged joining the line in the middle. Only the two end persons may tag others, so as the line grows, the whole game becomes rather more difficult. Tagging may be done only when the line is unbroken. [GN 9]

6378 stags of Jesus -- a reference to the stags on the heraldic crest of Jesus College, Oxford. See also Oxford colleges. [GN 13]

6379 Stalky -- see I gloat, as Stalky says. [FRH 13]

6380 Stamford -- in Lincolnshire, a very ancient town with extensive historical connections starting in 1215 when Earl Warenne gathered the barons there prior to their meeting with King John at Runnymede. William Cecil, Lord Burghley*, established his home there in 1553; it is now open to the public. DLS's Col. Belfridge* lives there. [HHC 6]

6381 Stamford Royal -- one of Col. Belfridge's* best dogs [HHC 8]

6382 stanchion -- as used here it refers to an iron brace attached to the main roof beams and to the upper end of the chimney stack. While they may be quite ornamental, their function is to provide support. [WB 4]

6383 stand -- stop [NT 1]

6384 Standing-Stone Pool -- a pool in the Water of Fleet* directly behind the cottages rented by Sandy Campbell and John Ferguson**. Jock Graham* liked to fish there not so much because the fishing was good, but because it irritated Campbell. [FRH 3]

6385 Stanford in C -- Sir Charles Villiers Stanford's (1852-1924) setting of the canticles in C major. The Magnificat and Nunc Dimittis in C (1909) is probably the part of the service referred to in BH, and would be sung at evening prayer. Stanford was a prolific composer of church music, but was widely known for secular music as well. He was knighted in 1902. [BH 5]

6386 Stanley, Mr. -- an employee of Pym's Publicity* who is not further identified [MMA 10]

6387 Stanislaus -- the pianist who rode the escalators in the Piccadilly Tube Station for five days to "absorb the tone-values" in order to compose the work he is playing when PW and Marjorie Phelps* visit the Kropotkys'* home [SP 8]

6388 Stanniforth, Mr. -- the sacristan or sexton at St. Onesimus* church in Leahampton* [UD 22]

6389 Staple Inn -- on Holborn* in proximity to the great Inns of Court*, Lincoln's and Gray's. Staple Inn was one of the Inns of Chancery* where students began their law studies if excluded from one of the Inns of Court. It is now a part of Gray's Inn, and its building, dating from 1586 but often restored, is among the few survivors of the Great Fire of September, 1666. The building is now occupied by the Institute of Actuaries. Mr. Murbles's* rooms, overlooking the formal garden, would have been on the South side of the building. [CW 10/UD 6/BC 7]

6390 Stapley -- fourteen miles from Riddlesdale Lodge*, it is the closest town of any size. It is from here that the police and a physician are brought to begin the investigation into the death of Denis Cathcart*. In this context the town is fictitous. [CW 1]

6391 Star -- PW is referring to The

#6389 Staple Inn, London.

Star, formerly one of London's many evening newspapers [WB 2]

6392 Star of Quebec -- an apparently fictitious ship for which Lloyd's Registry of Shipping has no record whatever [UD 8]

6393 The Stars Look Down -- a novel by A[rchibald] J[oseph] Cronin (1896-1981), a Scottish novelist and physician. The novel in question, published in 1935, is considered to be one of his best, and deals with a Northumberland miner's ambitious rise to Parliament. Cronin is perhaps best remembered for The Citadel (1937), and The Keys of the Kingdom (1942). [BH P]

6394 start[ing] two hares -- a hunting reference suggesting the confusion attendant when a hunter or his dogs flushes two hares at the same time. The question is which one should be chased or shot. The confusion often allows both to escape; hence, any situation where confusion will result from trying to chase two divergent trails at once. [WB 5/UD 6]

6395 starting handle -- the crank located at the bottom of the front of the engine block on older cars prior to successful electric starters. The location is sometimes indicated by a hole at the base of the radiator casing shell through which the detachable handle would be engaged with the crankshaft. They were usually difficult to work and could result in injury when used carelessly. [HHC 12]

6396 starvation -- one will die from the lack of fluids faster than from the lack of food [NT 4]

6397 state of the margins -- the condition of both the inner and the outer margins. It must be determined if the margins are smooth or if they are chipped and worn; if the inner margins or gutters are solidly bound in, etc. Such conditions would be important to a collector as determiners of value for a given book. [dh]

6398 State school -- a public school in the American sense of that phrase, one supported by local and state public tax revenues and open to all. In New York State public schools are regulated and financed in part by the State, but each district is an autonomous unit with a locally elected school board in direct supervision of school policies, etc. The one in question here is on New York City's East Side, an expression generally reserved for the East side of Manhattan Island, a focal point for various minority groups. [HHC 5]

6399 Station Hotel -- at Windle*. English railroad stations frequently have hotels attached or nearby for late arriving passengers or for those who have a long layover. Miss Climpson* chooses to spend her first night in Windle at the hotel because of the lateness of the hour of her arrival there. [SP 16]

6400 Station Hotel -- there has never been a Station Hotel in the docks vicinity (Pier Head or Prince's Landing Stage) in Liverpool*. There was, however, a large and comfortable hotel at the Exchange Station, the Station Hotel, that had a foyer area large enough to accommodate the action that DLS describes. It was, however, a half mile from the riverfront. One must, therefore, assume that DLS used poetic license to move the hotel to suit her purposes in this story. [UD 11]

6401 statutory dressing gown -- a reference to Sherlock Holmes's appearance when he thinks out a case. Holmes's gown is a "mouse" color, but PW's is mauve silk. [SP 20]

6402 "statutum est quod Juniores Senioribus debitam et congruam . . ." --Latin for, "[the] statute is that Juniors should exhibit to the Seniors appropriate respect in private as in public." The passage is a shortened version of Title XV, Section I, Paragraph 1 of Statuta Universitatis Oxoniensis (1963 ed.). This particular statute dates from 1636 with amendments in 1838. [GN 1]

6403 Staunton men -- see chess [sf]

6404 Stavesacre, Lady -- a sister to an early (Elizabethan) Duke of Denver who is reputed to have slapped Sir Francis Bacon's* face, reason unknown [BH E2]

6405 stay -- the vertical timber or bar that is attached to the beam (headstock) from which a bell is suspended when hung for change-ringing*.

Its purpose is to help prevent the bell from being overthrown*.

6406 Stedman['s] -- a reference to any of the change-ringing* patterns designed by or after those of Fabian Stedman, a Cambridge printer and ringer of the late 1600's. While it is not known if he invented the whole wheel system that allows change-ringing to work (the practice of fastening the bell rope to a wheel rather than to the clapper or to some other sort of suspension device, thus allowing greater control over the bell's action), but he did originate the study of mathematical possibilities involved in having the bells change places or sequence as they are rung. His books on the subject are Tintinnalogia--or the Art of Ringing (1668), and Campanologia (1677), and are considered as the origin and foundation of British bell ringing. [NT 1]

6407 Stefan -- see Mr. Petrovinsky [hp]

6408 Steinitz gambit -- an opening procedure to establish positional advantage in chess developed by the Austrian chess master Wilhelm Steinitz (1836-1900). He was a superb defensive player who developed the technique of restraint of play to blunt the opponent's opening attack. He kept his position closed and more defendable, thereby destroying any opening initiative by the attacker. The danger and difficulty mentioned by DLS arises from the fact that pressure and tension build persistently from the start, thus demanding careful play from the outset. In particular, the opening moves are a variation of the Vienna Opening and go as follows:

1. P-K4; P-K4
2. Kt-QB3; Kt-QB3
3. P-B4; P x P
4. P-Q4; etc.

The Steinitz gambit was introduced by Steinitz in his game against Gustave Neumann in a tournament in Dundee in 1867. Steinitz won in thirty-three moves. From 1872 to 1894, Steinitz was considered the best player in the world. [sf]

6409 steps -- a reference to the movements back and forth within the combinations rung that a given bell might have to make to ring in the proper sequence from course* to course [NT 1]

6410 Stepney -- that area of London's East End adjacent to the Thames on the North side in the London and West India Docks area. It is, perhaps, more famous as it includes the Whitechapel area made infamous by Jack the Ripper. The area has traditionally been depressed and overcrowded, but is not now the cesspool of humanity it was in the later 1800's. [UD 13]

6411 stereos -- a metal plate containing all elements of an advertisement or other item to be printed. The original is set up with individual letters, wood-block carvings, or whatever; a matrix is made of this original which then serves as the mold from which the stereo is cast. Stereotyping vastly increased the speed with which a newspaper page could be laid out, thus increasing the amount of illustrated material possible per paper. [MMA 1]

6412 stereotypers -- those responsible for making stereos* [MMA 4]

6413 Sterne, Mrs. -- Henry Weldon's* housekeeper/dairymaid at Fourways, his farm [HHC 22]

6414 Steve -- in BC, the line, "Oh, I get you Steve." is perhaps a reference to Steve Donoghue, a champion jockey of the day. The expression, "Come on, Steve" was current at the time. [BC 6]

6415 Stevenage -- a large town on the Great North Rd.* through which PW and HV pass on their way to Duke's Denver*. Since 1935, it has expanded greatly to accommodate London's overspill population. [BH E2]

6416 Stevens, Miss -- Shrewsbury College's* bursar* at the time of HV's visit there for the annual gaudy [GN 1]

6417 Stevensonian manner -- possibly a reference to R. L. Stevenson's novel, The Wrong Box, wherein a body is shipped all over to prevent discovery of the death. The situation, while macabre, is presented in such a way as to make it absurdly funny. [UD 1]

6418 Stevenson's romance -- the novel The Wrong Box. See Finsbury, Michael. [WB 13]

6419 steward -- a servant or other employee in whom certain household and supervisory duties have been entrusted [GN 9]

6420 Steward, Lord High -- since the time of Henry IV*, an appointed position created to oversee, supervise, and organize such affairs as coronations, royal weddings, jubilees, and funerals. Prior to 1948 when the practice was discontinued, he would also have arranged any trials of peers before the House of Lords. The position reverts to the Crown when the function is complete. The position of Lord High Steward is, in modern times, usually assigned to the Lord Chancellor*. [CW 5]

6421 the Stewartry -- a territorial division in Scotland established in 1748. The name derives from the fact that the areas so called were under the jurisdiction of a Royal Steward, or magistrate, appointed by the king to administer Crown lands. The term applies only in Scotland, and then in a limited way. The only county-sized areas involved were Orkney and Shetland and the locale of FRH, Kirkcudbrightshire and Galloway. The term now loosely applies to that general area of Scotland where the Stewards formerly held forth, especially in the Galloway* area where their influence is still felt strongly. [FRH 3]

6422 sticking plaster -- adhesive tape or a Band-Aid type device [nf/ MMA 6/GN 4]

6423 stickleback -- any member of a family of small scaleless fishes having free spines standing in front of the dorsal fin [np]

6424 stick o'grass -- asparagus [im]

6425 stile -- a wooden or stone step arranged to allow easy access to either side of a fence [SP 5]

6426 Still harping on my Bunter . . . -- there is a possible connection here to Hamlet, II, ii, 186ff, in Polonius's speech to Hamlet in the "Fishmonger scene": " . . . still harping on my daughter . . . and truly in my youth I suffered much extremity for love . . . ." [BH 10]

6427 stillroom maid -- a woman in charge, originally, of the room where perfumes, liquers, etc., were prepared in stills. Later, these rooms came to be used for the preparation of preserves, coffee, tea, etc. [UD 12]

6428 Stilton -- a cheese made in Leicestershire and sold to travellers on the Great North Road* at Stilton which made it famous. It is a rich, waxy cheese having a blue-green edible mold and a wrinkled rind. [WB 5]

6429 Stock Exchange -- located on Old Broad St. in The City* near the Bank of England and the Royal Exchange. It is the center of England's dealings in stocks and shares. [WB 5]

6430 stocking-ladders -- a "run" in a pair of silk stockings. "Ladders" is, however, more accurate as a description as the runs do resemble ladders. [np]

6431 Stokes -- a fellow whom Col. Belfridge* thought might be known to PW. He is not. [HHC 8]

6432 Stokes, Mary -- the former close college friend of HV's who had implored her to attend the Shrewsbury College* Gaudy, thus involving her in the events of the search for the College's poltergeist*. She has married Mr. H. Attwood. [GN 1]

6433 stole -- the long, narrow neckpiece that hangs around a clergyman's neck and down either side of the front of his gown. They are usually in the appropriate ecclesiastical color for the given church season (green for Pentecost, etc.), are often rather ornate, and generally terminate in fringe. [NT 2]

6434 stolen a march -- to gain upon or surpass, a military expression [HHC 20]

6435 Stoll -- originally the London Opera House, opened in 1911, it became The Stoll when Sir Oswald Stoll bought it and ran it as a music hall. For many years, including part of the WW I era, it was a movie theatre as mentioned by Robert Duckworthy*. The theatre was located on Kingsway*. [im]

6436 stone -- a unit of weight equal to

fourteen pounds [BH 7]

6437 Stone Cottage -- the name of Thomas Macpherson's* home in Gatehouse-of-Fleet* which PW visits twice in his search for the elusive diamonds [ss]

6438 stooks -- sheaves or bundles stood on end in the field. It was so wet that corn (cereal grain, not corn as in North America) sprouted after harvesting [NT 18]

6439 stoop to conquer -- the allusion refers to the title of Oliver Goldsmith's comedy, She Stoops to Conquer, and to Kate Hardcastle's line in Act IV, "I'll still preserve the character in which I stooped to conquer . . .", and to her dual role as Kate, the daughter of the master of the house, and as barmaid at the "inn". The situation PW hopes to create parallels that of Kate Hardcastle--he wants to play two roles at once: that of himself and that of a lounge lizard*. [HHC 31]

6440 Storey, Philip -- Dahlia Dallmeyers'* husband and murderer. PW and Parker* arrest him just as he is about to sail for the U. S. He is given away when Simpkins* remembers his "weak" and prominent eyes and an unusual crescent-shaped scar under his left eye. [cb]

6441 stout -- the heavy, dark-brown beer peculiar to the British Isles. It is made with roasted malt and a fairly high concentration of hops. [NT 11]

6442 Strachan -- an M. D. from Gatehouse-of-Fleet* who sets Robert Ferguson's* broken knee [ss]

6443 Strachan, Henry [Harry] -- a member of the local group at Gatehouse* and Kirkcudbright*. He is secretary for the local golf club, is married, has a daughter, and does portrait paintings and illustrations. He is thirty-eight, and he, too, has quarrelled with Campbell*. [FRH 1]

6444 Straddles -- the bursar* at Shrewsbury College* prior to Miss Stevens's* tenure. She has moved on to the position of treasurer at Brontë College*. [GN 2]

6445 strafe -- military action, a fierce punishment of the enemy by firepower. The word is military slang derived from the German, "Gott strafe England", a common wartime expression or salutation in Germany meaning, "God punish England". Hence, "strafe" came into English meaning any sort of military punishment inflicted by firepower on the enemy. Of late (WW II and after) the verb has come to mean to fire machine guns, rockets, etc., at the ground from an aircraft. [GN 17]

6446 straight flush -- see poker [MMA 14]

6447 The Strand -- one of London's major East-West streets. It begins at Trafalgar Square and runs roughly East and North to Temple Bar*. It was built to connect the seat of government at Westminster with the mercantile and military centers of The City*, and along its path the medieval aristocracy built its palaces on the banks of the Thames. Fleet St.* is, essentially, a continuation of The Strand to St. Paul's Cathedral and The City. [SP 6/HHC 30]

6448 The Strand Corner House -- one of four "Corner House" restaurants of the Lyons* chain, this one on The Strand* in London. Being so prominently located in the capital, it boasts several refinements of interior decorating, including the Mirror Hall where Robert Duckworthy* had one of his unfortunately confusing episodes. [im]

6449 "'strange and mystical' transmigration of silk worms . . ." -- the string of quotations HV reads at this point are all from Religio Medici* by Sir Thomas Browne. That work is broken into a wide variety of subparts such as "Nature doeth nothing in vain", "of sleep", and "of marriage and harmony". DLS has simply lifted various quotes from the work to illustrate HV's thoughts. [GN 15]

6450 "A stranger with thee . . ." -- from Psalm 39 as presented in The Book of Common Prayer [NT 5]

6451 Stranraer -- the port town at the head of Loch Ryan on the North Channel. It is still served by regular rail service which connects with the auto-ferry steamer to Larne*, Northern Ireland, about twenty miles to the West. [FRH 2]

6452 Stratford -- a London suburb at the junction of the roads to Newmarket and to Southend. This is not the Stratford associated with William Shakespeare which is on the Avon in Warwickshire some ninety-two miles northwest of London. [MMA 19]

6453 Strathallen and Begg, Earl of -- one of the peers at the trial of the Duke of Denver. He is fictitious. [CW 14]

6454 "stravaiguin aboot" -- an archaic dialectical expression for, "wandering aimlessly about" [FRH 11]

6455 strawberries -- see scene about the strawberries [HHC 23]

6456 strawberry leaves -- a reference to the ornamentation on a ducal coronet, eight strawberry leaves. They are arranged around the top edge of the coronet's base circlet, are on a vertical axis, and are, thus, silhouetted against the crimson cap insert. [GN 8]

6457 Strawberry, Walton -- a fictitious person (author ?) mentioned as having some connection with the "Book of the Moment"* crowd [GN 11]

6458 streaky rashers -- fatty slices of bacon from the belly of the pig as opposed to the choicer back bacon [BH 4]

6459 streamers -- a poster usually measuring about four inches by thirty-six inches. They are meant to be displayed in windows or on shop shelves. [MMA 17]

6460 stress-shift -- a shift in the emphasis or stress given a syllable or word in poetry from one foot or line to another [GN 11]

6461 Striding Hall -- the ancestral home of the Striding family that had been purchased by Mr. Creech*, disrupting Mr. Mellilow's retirement plans [sf]

6462 Stroheim -- Erich von Stroheim (1885-1957), the brilliant director of epic films who was frustrated in most of his attempts at directing by supervisors who did not understand what he was trying to accomplish with the medium. Nevertheless, what he did remains in cinematic history as work without parallel. Most notable is, perhaps, Greed, a film version of Frank Norris's novel, McTeague. Even though Greed is a vastly shortened version of Stroheim's work, it remains a true cinematic masterwork. As an actor, Stroheim, born in Austria, is famous for his portrayals of exceptionally cruel Prussian officers. He was so good at such roles that he became known as "the man you love to hate". [GN 17]

6463 stroke -- see apoplexy or bow and stroke [NT 2/GN 11]

6464 strop a razor -- to put a finished edge on a razor with a flexible leather strap, one side for rough work, the other for finish work. The use of a strop indicates that the razor already has an edge that is properly ground and set, the strop being used for maintaining such an edge. [CW 4]

6465 strychnine -- a poison used as a heart stimulant and as a rat poison. In the latter applications it works well on both the two-and four-legged varieties. HV is known to have purchased some as part of her research into poisons for one of her novels. [cf/WB 13/UD 19/BC 19/SP 1/GN 19]

6466 stud book -- listings of the peerage and landed gentry families such as Burke's or Debrett's; a useful catalogue for those persons who seek titles, wealth, or both. The term is borrowed from horse breeding. [GN 8]

6467 The Student of Prague -- the English name for the German five-reel horror film, Der Student von Prague (1913). The movie was produced by Paul Wegener, directed by Stellan Rye, and starred Wegener, Lyda Salmanova, and Fritz Weidemann. Bioscop released the film in Europe. The U. S. title was A Bargain With Satan. Robert Duckworthy* remembers seeing the film as a youngster and being terrified by it, but DLS has her dates confused here. Duckworthy could not have been seven or eight in 1913 or 14 when he could have seen the film and then serve in WW I as a conscript. The movie would have been frightening as it is a mixture of Faust*, doppelgängers*, and the Golem* myths. [im]

6468 stumer -- also stumor, slang for a forged or dishonored check; a sham, false [CW 2]

6469 Stupid and dangerous, like Desdemona -- the reference is to Othello's wife in Shakespeare's tragedy. One normally thinks of her as the beautiful and innocent victim of the outrages plotted by Iago and carried out by Othello in his fits of blind jealousy. However, her blind devotion and stupid refusal to deal with her husband's irrational behavior openly, preferring to suffer, is at least somewhat responsible for the tragic situation which results. There is a certain parallel to Mrs. Farren*. [FRH 6]

6470 Stygian blackness -- hellish blackness; blackness in the extreme. Stygian is the adjective form of Styx, the river in the Greek infernal regions. [GN 9]

6471 Stygian cloud -- a black cloud from hell [BH 5]

6472 Styria -- a province in Austria's southeastern corner; its capital is Graz. It has been relatively common for natives in a variety of central European areas to eat arsenic at one time or another, as much as a daily dose of thirty-one grains (six or seven times the normal fatal dosage). The object is to help build up endurance for mountain climbing. [SP 22]

6473 "Suam quisque homo rem meminit." -- PW's inscription on the lost chimney pot that is found. It is Latin for, "Everyone remembers his own concerns." The line is from Plautus's* Mercator (The Merchant), V, iv, 51, one of his minor plays. [BH 14]

6474 Sub-Warden -- a deputy to the Warden* at an English college. Miss Lydgate* is Sub-Warden at Shrewsbury College*. [GN 5]

6475 subfusc -- from the Latin, subfuscus, meaning dark, dusky, drab. The term also refers to academic dress. See also full academicals. [HHC 30/GN 1]

6476 subjective case -- or nominative case; that group of nouns or pronouns that function as the subject of a sentence or of a clause in some languages such as Latin [BH 18]

6477 submerged tenth -- the ten percent of the population that are always in direst poverty [BC 10]

6478 subordinate clause -- an adverbial or adjectival clause so named because it depends upon or is subordinate to some other part of the sentence for its complete meaning. They are also known as dependent clauses. [CW 7]

6479 subscription [card] -- any cause for which a monetary collection is taken; the card upon which the names, etc., of donors have been recorded [UD 22/MMA 1]

6480 substitution -- generally, the process of substituting some letter, number, or symbol for the letters and numbers of a plaintext message according to some prearranged system so as to hide the plaintext message from those who are not intended to read it [HHC 26]

6481 succès d'estime -- French for a success that earns more honor than profit [SP 6]

6482 "Such lily-livered meek humanity." -- a perfect description of Julian Perkins*. The line appears in the second, or "Gamma", version of T. L. Beddoes' Death's Jest Book**, I, i, 269. Isbrand is speaking, berating Wolfram for having lost his sense of vengeance. [HHC 24]

6483 suck up to -- an ugly phrase used to describe the ugly action of hypocritically paying attention to someone in the expectation of reward [HHC 13]

6484 sucking Socialists -- one expects that the Dowager Duchess* had no kind thoughts in mind, so we may probably assume with safety that she had infantile, immature, or naive, as in sucking pig, in mind [CW 9]

6485 Suffering refines the character -- perhaps PW is thinking of H. W. Longfellow's poem, "The Light of the Stars" where we find:
"Know how sublime a thing it is
To suffer and be strong."
However, the concept is an ancient one that finds expression in the works of the Greeks and Romans. [HHC 21]

6486 Sugg, Inspector -- the police officer who, in the early stories, is the object of PW's mockery for his ineptitude. However, by the end of CW, Sugg helpfully bundles PW, Freddy

Arbuthnot*, and Parker* into taxis so that their drunken revelry won't embarrass them or their families. Sugg's slowness is shown by the rapidity with which Parker comes to outrank him, but any enmity between the three men is gone by the time of UD. At the time of NT it is reported that he has retired to the country (1930). [ab/WB 1/CW 19/UD 2/NT 4]

6487 Suggery [purest] -- denseness, obtuseness, naiveté of thought; a reflection on Insp. Sugg* [WB 10]

6488 suggified -- a word coined by PW in WB as a pun on Insp. Sugg's* name. It seems to mean to be made a fool of; to have erred grievously; to have become dense like Insp. Sugg. [WB 3]

6489 "Sugg of the evening . . ." -- PW is chortling his own version of a line from Alice in Wonderland, Ch. 10, "Soup of the evening, beautiful soup!", to poke fun at Parker's* colleague, Insp. Sugg*. Carroll was, in his own right, poking fun at James M. Sayles's poem, "Star of the Evening". [WB 2]

6490 Suite -- Handel* wrote a wide range of music including "The Water Music" and "Music for the Royal Fireworks" that are suites. It is probably one of these as they were popular, in Sir Hamilton Harty's reorchestration, between the wars, but it may be other of Handel's music presented as a suite. [HHC 20]

6491 Sullivan, Isaac J. -- the fictitious theatrical agent through whom PW and Insp. Umpelty* finally manage to trace Morecambe* [HHC 23]

6492 "summer-time on Bredon" -- the reference is to A. E. Housman's* A Shropshire Lad*, poem XXI, "Bredon Hill", the first line of which is, "In summertime on Bredon". Bredon Hill is a rounded mound, 961 feet high, northeast of Tewkesbury, which commands a fine view of the surrounding counties. The poem tells of a love ended by the death of the prospective bride before the wedding. [MMA 1]

6493 Summers -- Col. Belfridge's* gardener and helper with the dogs bred by the colonel [HHC 8]

6494 Sunbeam -- a popular brand of bicycle, motorcycle, and car of good quality. The firm no longer exists. [FRH 10]

6495 Sunday Chronicle -- of the various British major papers having the word "chronicle" as part of their title, none published a Sunday edition. It is, therefore, fictitious. [FRH 22]

6496 Sunday Shriek -- a fictitious newspaper. See Bunt, Sir Roger. [cf]

6497 Sundays after Trinity -- the Sunday after Whitsunday and before Corpus Christi is Trinity Sunday, now called Pentecost*. Following it comes the long string of the Sundays after Pentecost until the church year begins agains with the First Sunday in Advent. [UD 22]

6498 Super -- short for superintendent. See Police Ranks. [BH 7]

6499 superficies -- the external or superficial aspects of something [BH 7]

6500 Superintendent -- see Police Ranks [passim]

6501 Superintendent at Stapley -- Insp. Craikes's* supervisor and the chief police officer at Stapley* [CW 2]

6502 supralapsarian -- a Calvinist doctrine holding that it is divinely ordained for some people to achieve eternal life and for others to achieve eternal death. This divine rule is supposed to have been ordained before the creation and fall. [HHC 25]

6503 Sûreté -- the closest thing in France to a central, national police agency. It is roughly a cross between Scotland Yard and the FBI, and is a criminal investigation agency with branches all over France. It does not issue parking tickets. [aq/CW 3/NT 8]

6504 Surface, Mr. Joseph -- the hypocritical brother in R. B. Sheridan's The School for Scandal. Surface's comment to Lady Teazle, to which PW alludes, relates to his unscrupulous attempts to seduce her. P. C. Burt is innocent of drinking on duty as his sergeant thinks, so PW offers him some wine with the questionable logic that if you are suspected of doing something, you might as well do it. [hp]

6505 surgery lamp -- the light kept burning in a doctor's office (surgery) even after he and his family have retired for the night. It indicates to late-comers where to go so as not to disturb the rest of the household. [BH 1]

6506 surplice[d choir] -- a surplice is an overgarment, knee-length, white, and loosely fitting, that is worn at an Anglican church service (other denominations use them as well) by clergymen, acolytes, and members of the choir [NT 2/BH 19]

6507 Surrey -- one of the counties bordering on Greater London (the Home Counties) and situated South of the Thames [im]

6508 Susan -- Tyler, Mrs. Hodges'* daughter [BH 4]

6509 Susie's Snippets -- a fictitious magazine doubtless intended to suggest the real Titbits; a sort of cheap gossip weekly. Madame Crystal suggests an astrology column wherein witchcraft, voodoo, etc., might be considered. [SP 21]

6510 Susannah -- the name of Tom Drewett's* sailboat. Under no circumstances could it be mistaken for any sort of luxury vessel. [FRH 19]

6511 Suzanne [Legros] -- the wife of "Jean Legros"*; the protective and devoted wife who finally identifies her husband, Deacon* [NT 7]

6512 Swaffham, Lady -- an acquaintance of the Wimsey family with whom PW is to lunch. The name is likely a reference to the community of Swaffham in Norfolk, not far from the location of the fictitious Duke's Denver*. Her ladyship is also fictitious. [WB 7]

6513 Swain, Mr. -- one of the cab drivers who drove Gen. Fentiman* on November 10th [BC 8]

6514 Swamp Drove -- a road in the parish of Fenchurch St. Paul*. For "drove", see Diggs's Drove. [NT 18]

6515 Swan -- see White Swan [MMA 12]

6516 Swan vesta -- a brand of match. See also vesta. [FRH 2]

6517 Swan and Edgar -- one of London's more famous clothing centers, it was located on Piccadilly at the Circus, and on Regent St. at the intersection of those famous thoroughfares. In the typical travel brochure photograph of the Statue of Eros at Piccadilly Circus, Swan and Edgar is usually in the background at the northwest corner of the Circus. The store closed in January of 1982, a victim of out-of-date merchandising attitudes and a West End address that never attracted enough West End customers. [CW 19]

6518 swank -- to show off [FRH 22]

6519 swans -- see all the swans in England [GN 13]

6520 sweep -- a sweepstakes as in the Irish Sweep* [MMA 1]

6521 sweep [behaving like a] [feel a] -- slang for behaving or feeling like a dirty or disreputable person [BC 8/GN 9]

6522 "Sweeping through the gates . . ." -- the chorus of hymn 285 in The Salvation Army Song Book. Bill Rumm is a member of the Salvation Army. The line refers to the New Testament book of Revelation, 7:14: "These are they which came out of great tribulation, and have washed their robes, and made them white in the blood of the Lamb."

The concept is an ancient one in the Judeo-Christian tradition and refers to the blood of sacrificial lambs which was sprinkled on those who made the offering. The blood is symbolic of life, and represents God's gift of life given to please God, and is, therefore, pleasing to God. It derives from God's instructions at the time of Passover. [SP 13]

6523 sweet omelette -- an omelette served as a sweet and possibly flavored with jam or fruit [SP 1]

6524 "Sweet Cupid, Ripen Her Desire" -- a song (#VII) in William Corkine's (15??-16??) Ayres, to Sing and Play To The Lute and Basse Violl, London, 1610. The anonymous lyric reads:

"Sweet Cupid, ripen her desire,
Thy joyful harvest may begin;
If age, approach a little nigher,
'Twill be too late to get it in.

"Cold winter storms lay standing corn,
Which once too ripe will never rise,
And lovers wish themselves unborn

When all their joys lie in their
eyes.

"Then, sweet, let us embrace and
kiss.
Shall beauty shale upon the
ground?
If age bereave us of this bliss,
Then will no more such spot be
found."

HV's blush seems well-founded. [GN 19]

6525 sweet-shop -- a catch-all phrase for a small store selling candies and snacks, chocolate, mineral water, etc., and often combined with the functions of a newsstand and tobacconist [SP 1]

6526 Sweetapple, Mrs. -- the housekeeper at Duke's Denver* who knows everything about all the family portraits. It is to her that PW suggests HV go for more information about them. [BH E2]

6527 Sweeting -- a woman who kept pigs and who lived in the cottage behind Talboys* now occupied by Mrs. Ruddle* [BH 1]

6528 swept and garnished -- see "Its evil spirit cast out", and parable of the swept and garnished house [BH E3]

6529 Swift, Miss -- a Shrewsbury College* student [GN 21]

6530 Swinburne, Algernon Charles -- English (Victorian) poet and dramatist (1837-1909) and author of such disparate works as "An Interlude", and Atalanta in Calydon. See also, Chesterton says . . . . [FRH 22]

6531 swine fever -- African swine fever, a viral disease that attacks pigs in Africa and Europe. It is unrelated to North American swine fever which is also called hog cholera. [BH 11]

6532 swipe 'em up -- to hit the pitched ball in a cricket* match, but without any sense of placement, thus making it easy for the fielders to put the batsman out by catching the ball before it touches the ground [MMA 10]

6533 Swiveller, Dick -- a character in Dickens's* The Old Curiosity Shop (1841). A disreputable but jovial sort, the sentence, "May we ne'er lack a friend or a bottle to give him" is typical of something Swiveller would say. However, the line belongs to Captain Cuttle in Dombey and Son, Ch. 15: "May we never want a friend in need, nor a bottle to give him." The line also appears in HHC, rather thoroughly overhauled by PW, as, "May we ne'er lack a friend or a story to give him." As PW is addressing Sally Hardy*, a bottle would have been as appropriate. [UD 6/HHC 11]

6534 swots -- he/she works hard at his/her studies [GN 12]

6535 Sydney -- the capital city of the state of New South Wales, Australia [cf]

6536 syllogism -- a formal deductive argument in three statements or premises such as:

All men are mortal.
John is a man.
Therefore, John is mortal.

Such arguments are tricky and must adhere to certain specific rules. Also, they must be able to withstand separate tests of their validity and truth before they can be accepted as a logical part of an argument. [HHC 21]

6537 Sylvester-Quicke, Amaranth -- the recipient of Mrs. Dalilah Snype's letter in the "Prothalamion" of BH. That letter assails PW, but seems to be meant to soothe Miss Sylvester-Quicke's feelings as it is implied that she had had designs on PW herself. The Dowager Duchess* suspects so too, even suggesting that it was she who reminded the national press of the Vane-Boyes* mess of six years earlier as recounted in SP. [BH P]

6538 Sylvia -- a granddaughter to the Dowager Duchess of Medway* who is to be married "in a fortnight's time to that stupid son of Attenbury's". [aq]

6539 syncope -- pronounced as sin-koh-pee with the accent on the first syllable, it is a partial or complete temporary suspension of breathing and blood flow caused by a form of cerebral anemia. It can be but need not always be fatal. [UD 8/BC 15]

6540 syntax -- that area of the study of grammar dealing with how words and phrases are put together as sentences; the study of the underlying logical assumptions of any language

system [CW 7]

6541 syphon -- see soda siphon [ie/WB 13/UD 7]

6542 Szleposky, Miss -- a student at Shrewsbury College* [GN 6]

(T)

6543 Tabbitt, Sam -- one of the errand boys at Pym's Publicity* [MMA 7]

6544 tabernacle -- an ornamental niche or storage place, usually on the altar or near it, housing various elements for communion [bc]

6545 Tabernacle Mission -- a Nonconformist* group doing what Bishop Lambert* considered to be "very valuable work" in the West Indies* area [UD 13]

6546 tacking [up into the wind] -- the method used to make forward progress in a sailboat when the wind is not coming from somewhere behind the vessel. It involves zigzagging back and forth to advance in the desired direction. One covers a greater distance, but it does allow a greater speed. [HHC 1]

6547 ta'en a scunner -- Scots dialect for, "taken a scunner against", that is, taking or developing a loathing disgust [UD 3]

6548 Tailor Paul -- the bell with the lowest note or tone in the ring at Fenchurch St. Paul*. It was cast in what is known as the Bell-Field adjacent to the church building in 1614. It is the largest of the bells in that ring and weighs a bit over two tons. It is tuned to C. [NT 1]

6549 Take care of the knots . . . -- a clever reworking of the old proverb, "Take care of the pence and the pounds will take care of themselves." Lewis Carroll's* version of the line appears in Ch. 9, "The Mock Turtle's Story", in Alice in Wonderland as: "Take care of the sense and the sounds will take care of themselves." [NT 6]

6550 "Take her up tenderly, lift her with care." -- while PW is lifting the bell ropes from the well in the churchyard, he quotes Thomas Hood's (1799-1845) poem, "The Bridge of Sighs":

"One more Unfortunate
Weary of breath,
Rashly importunate
Gone to her death!

"Take her up tenderly,
Lift her with care;

Fashion'd so slenderly,
Young, and so fair!" [NT 6]

6551 take the wrong turning -- to do an illegal or immoral thing--a variation on the idea of turning away from the proper pathway of a righteous life [GN 3]

6552 "Take thou this flower to strew upon his grave . . ." -- the line is from T. L. Beddoes' Death's Jest Book**, V, iv, 240-45. Isbrand has just learned of Sibylla's death when he speaks these lines. The "his" in the citation is "her" in the play. [HHC 34]

6553 taking middle -- see cricket [MMA 18]

6554 Talbot -- a British automobile manufactured from 1903 to 1938. The firm produced saloons* and sport models of a lower price range, the 14 h.p. model being a popular one throughout the late 1920's and early 1930's. The firm was absorbed by the British Leyland company which still uses the name on some models. [FRH 16]

6555 Talboys -- the name of the last of the PW short stories (1942) and the name of PW's country cottage purchased at the time of his marriage to HV. In BH it is described as "Elizabethan, very pretty", and is located in Hertfordshire near HV's childhood home.

The house holds various pleasant associations for HV and she is genuinely excited and pleased that she and PW will honeymoon there. One of her stronger concerns upon the discovery of Mr. Noakes's* corpse in the cellar and the attendant unpleasantries which follow is that those events do not spoil any positive feelings PW might have for the house.

Much needs to be done to improve and modernize the house and, by the time of the action in "Talboys", PW's architect friend, Mr. Thipps*, has completed those changes. It is to be noted that while the house was made more comfortable and suitable for a modern family, PW was careful not to alter the essential beauty and character of the original structure. He even went so far as to attempt to locate and purchase the original chimney pots that had been sold off by the previous owner, the unfortunate Mr. Noakes. [t/BH P]

6556 "talk of many things" -- see "time has come to talk . . ." [FRH 6]

6557 talkie -- a motion picture with sound, still a novelty in the early 1930's [HHC 30/MMA 11]

6558 Tallboy, James [Jim] -- a more senior staff member at Pym's Publicity*, he is a group-manager* for the Nutrax account. He seems pleasant, if distant, but, as MMA unfolds, it becomes obvious that his life is not as ordered as it would outwardly appear to be. He plays cricket* very well, but is not in the same league as is PW. [MMA 4]

6559 tam o'shanter -- a hat of Scottish origin with a tight headband and a circular, flat crown wider than the headband by three or four inches. They are knit of wool and are decorated with a pom-pom on top. [CW 7]

6560 Tanganyika -- now a part of Tanzania, so named after gaining independence and uniting with Zanzibar. It was formerly a German colony, German East Africa, and, after WW I, was mandated to Great Britain who granted independence in 1961. With Kenya and Uganda, Tanzania comprises East Africa and borders on the Indian Ocean. In "Cave of Ali Baba", PW is reported as having been killed there while hunting big game. [ab]

6561 tanner -- slang for a sixpence. See British Monetary Units.

6562 tantalus -- a case for holding decanters so the contents are visible but are inaccessible without a key. The allusion is to Greek mythology and the character Tantalus who is punished eternally in Hades with hunger and thirst while standing in water up to his chin and with a bough of fruit over his head. Every time he tries to eat or drink, the water or fruit is removed from his reach. [WB 13]

6563 Tapestry Room -- one of the major guest rooms at the Dower House, Duke's Denver* [BH E2]

6564 Tarbaby -- the reference is to the "Brer Rabbit" stories of American writer Joel Chandler Harris (1848-1908) in his Uncle Remus: His Songs and His

Sayings, first published as a collection in 1881. The Tarbaby is a creature made by Brer Fox and Brer Bear to catch Brer Rabbit. Rabbit gets mad when it won't answer him, hits it, and gets trapped as planned. However, true to form, Brer Rabbit talks his way out of the predicament. The stories are traditional to southern U. S. Blacks and are accurate in their period dialogue. Some of the stories were further made popular in Walt Disney's feature film, Song of the South. [WB 5]

6565 Tarff -- the station stop near Ringford named for the Tarff Water [FRH 5]

6566 tarradiddle -- a variant of taradiddle, defined by the OED as a trifling falsehood; a fib [CW 7]

6567 Tarrant, Miss -- the socialist friend of Lady Mary* from nursing and social work days in WW I. She invites PW to dinner and a speech at the Soviet Club* where he at last encounters George Goyles*. [CW 7]

6568 tartar -- a formidable and unexpectedly irritable person [UD 9]

6569 tartar emetic -- a poisonous salt containing antimony* that has a sweetish metallic taste. It is used to induce vomiting (emesis) and to treat amoebic diseases. [SP 20]

6570 Tasker, Mr. -- the name given as a reference by Stephen Driver* when he asked Ezra Wilderspin* for work [NT 4]

6571 The Tatler -- a journal established in 1709 by Addison and Steele (early essays by the founders are now required reading in typical English literature courses) and still publishing. It is an illustrated society paper featuring biographical profiles, fashion news, and information about the arts. [WB 9]

6572 Taunton -- a town in Somerset and the county town. The great hall of the restored Norman castle was the scene of Judge Jeffreys's* Bloody Assizes, vengeance against the followers of the Duke of Monmouth for their attempt to rid England of James II because of his Roman Catholic religious beliefs. [HHC 24]

6573 Tavistock St. -- a short street on the South edge of Covent Garden*, two blocks North of and parallel to The Strand*. The name comes from a title of the Russell (see Russell Square) family. Bunter likely used Burleigh St. to get to The Strand. [HHC 30]

6574 Taylor -- a reference to Alfred Swain Taylor's (1806-80) The Principles and Practice of Medical Jurisprudence (1865). The work was popular with early detective fiction writers, not the least of whom was R. Austin Freeman. [BC 15/FRH 16/BH 12]

6575 Taylor, John -- a famous bell-founder who moved to Loughborough* from Oxford* and established a bell foundry there in 1858. His name has since become famous for the quality of the bells his firm manufactures. The company he formed has cast many bells including the 37,483 lbs. (about 18.75 tons) "Great Paul" for St. Paul's Cathedral in London in 1882. [NT 4]

6576 Taylor, Mrs. -- Dr. Pritchard's* mother-in-law whom he murdered. He was hanged for the crime in 1865. [UD 1]

6577 Te Deum -- fully, Te Deum laudamus, Latin for, "We praise thee, O God". This ancient hymn of praise is part of the worship service in the Roman Catholic and in many Protestant churches. It was composed by Niceta, Bishop of Remesia in Dacia at the end of the 4th C. [BH 5]

6578 tea -- the drink served with a light snack at a midmorning or midafternoon work break. It is served each work day between 3:15 and 3:45 P. M. at Pym's Publicity*. [MMA 2]

6579 Teach, Cap'n -- pirate captain Edward Teach, better known as Blackbeard*, who was killed in 1718. He started his career as a privateer--a pirate with a legal license to be one--and went on to ignore governmental limitations and go into business for himself. He died in action.

Bredon Wimsey* addresses PW as Cap'n Teach during their assault on Miss Quirk's* nerves. Teach's notoriety is still so great and his appearance in fiction so pervasive

that he has almost become the archetypal pirate. PW and Bredon are certainly using his romantic image more than his real one here. [t]

6580 "Tears, Idle Tears" -- a poem by Alfred, Lord Tennyson* that appears in The Princess, a half-serious, half-burlesque narrative poem. "Tears" is one of the several songs which appear therein. The narrative considers normal human emotions versus artificial attempts to suppress them, but "Tears" is a lyric addressed to a longing for the past. [MMA 13]

6581 Teazle, Lady -- a character in R. B. Sheridan's The School for Scandal. She is the target of Joseph Surface's* attempts at seduction. [hp]

6582 Tebbutt, Mrs. -- the landlady at the Wheatsheaf pub in Fenchurch St. Paul* and wife of Tom Tebbutt* [NT 1]

6583 Tebbutt, Miss Eliza -- the woman on the South Kensington Underground Station* platform who claims that Horace Mountjoy* did not fall to his death under the train wheels, but was pushed [MMA 16]

6584 Tebbutt, Tom -- the landlord at the Wheatsheaf pub. He has influenza at the time of the opening of NT. [NT 1]

6585 Teesdalia nudicaulis -- more commonly known as pepper cress, rock cress, or shepherd's cress, a harmless plant named for Yorkshire botanist Robert Teesdale [BH 15]

6586 Teddy -- see Edwards, Joan [BH P]

6587 Telegraph -- see Daily Telegraph [GN 10]

6588 teleological -- the doctrine or study of ends or final causes, that there is a mind, will, or force behind and motivating all things [CW 3]

6589 "Tell me what you eat and I will tell you what you are." -- one of the more famous aphorisms from Brillat-Savarin's* famous book, The Physiology of Taste [UD 7]

6590 "Tell that to the Marines" -- a shortened version of the phrase, "Tell it to the Horse Marines", an absurd concept to suit an absurd assertion [MMA 10]

6591 Temple, Mr. -- a person identified only as having a five handicap at St. Andrews* which would make him a very good golfer indeed. He was a guest of Bob Anderson's* at the Thursday night get-together attended by PW. [FRH 13]

6592 The Temple -- a collection of buildings located North of the Victoria Embankment* and South of The Strand* which houses two of the four Inns of Court*, the Inner and Middle Temples. The name derives from the Knights Templars who built on the site in 1185. It has been a center for legal education since 1346.

6593 Temple Bar -- The City's* western barrier since the Middle Ages and the point where the sovereign pauses to receive and return the Pearl Sword from the Lord Mayor whenever entering The City in State. There is now a memorial pillar at the place where the gate was located until 1880, and atop the pillar is a griffin, emblem of The City. It is the junction of Fleet St. and The Strand**. The original gate is now in a park in Hertfordshire. [MMA 12]

6594 Temple Station -- an Underground* station which serves the area of the Inns of Court* [cf]

6595 Templeton, Mr. -- the pseudonym used by PW when he calls on Mrs. Forrest* at her flat [UD 7]

6596 Templeton, Robert -- HV's detective hero in her works of fiction. He is described in some detail in Ch. 1 of HHC. [HHC 1/BH E1]

6597 Templeton Scholar -- an otherwise unidentified fictitious academic honor at Shrewsbury College* [GN 7]

6598 Tempsford -- a small community approximately forty-five miles North of western London. See Motorcycle Race. [cb]

6599 ten-centime piece -- a French coin valued at one-tenth of a franc [NT 7]

6600 £10,000 -- in the early part of this century, pre-WW I, roughly $48,700 U. S., a very considerable sum [CW 1]

6601 "Tendebantque manus ripae ulterioris amorae." -- PW is reciting line 314, book iv, of Vergil's Aeneid, and has stated, "Their hands outstretched in yearning for the farther shore." The shore in question is on the opposite side of the River Styx. Those who are yearning are the unburied dead who must serve a one-hundred year penance before they may cross into Hades. The quote is most appropriate for the situation PW faces in "Incredible Elopement". Ryland Vaughan* manages a mangled version of the citation as well. [ie/SP 8]

6602 Tennyson, Alfred -- 1st Baron Tennyson (1809-92), author of such poems as Idylls of the King, "Ulysses", "In Memoriam", and "The Charge of the Light Brigade". He was appointed Poet Laureate of England in 1850, elevated to the peerage in 1884, and was buried in Westminster Abbey. [UD 9/MMA 13/BH 7]

6603 tenor -- not as in singing; a tenor bell has the lowest tone of a ring or set of bells [NT 1]

6604 tenterhooks -- special nails used for hanging and stretching tapestries or other fabric hangings. They may also be used to hang other objects. To be "on tenterhooks" is used colloquially to mean being in a state of great mental suspense. [BH E2]

6605 term-time -- any one of the three semesters during which undergraduates are required to be in residence at their college. The terms at Oxford are Michaelmas, Hilary, and Trinity in that order. [GN 2]

6606 terminus ad quem -- Latin for, "the end (or limit) to which"; a finishing point or end limit [BC 4/GN 5]

6607 terminus a quo -- Latin for, "the end (or limit) from which"; the starting point or beginning limit [GN 5]

6608 terms -- used here to refer to the premises or statements of a logical argument as in a syllogism* [BH 20]

6609 Terrace, House of Commons -- it borders the Thames and is a favorite place for Members of Parliament and their guests to take tea in the summertime [MMA 10]

6610 Terrington, Mrs. -- a metal-working artist and guest of Bob Anderson* at the Thursday evening gathering attended by PW [FRH 13]

6611 testamentary disposition [proper] -- disposal of one's property through a properly drawn and valid will [BC 3]

6612 testator[trix] -- a person who, at his or her death, leaves in force a valid will. The different endings indicate the Latin for male or female, a male being a testator. [ab/UD 8/SP 13/NT 16]

6613 Tewke and Peabody -- a firm to which Norman Urquhart* had addressed a letter, the shorthand notes for which give Miss Murchison* some pretended difficulty. The firm is unknown, presumably fictitious. [SP 20]

6614 "That I may be certified" -- from Psalm 39 as presented in The Book of Common Prayer [NT 5]

6615 "That one word, my dear Watson . . ." -- from the Sherlock Holmes story, "The Crooked Man", at the end of the story. The preceding paragraph reads:
"'There's one thing,' said I, as we walked down to the station; 'if the husband's name was James, and the other was Henry, what was this talk about David?'"
At this point the quoted paragraph appears, concluding with the line, "'It was evidently a term of reproach.'" The reference is to the story of David, Uriah, and Bathsheba in II Samuel 11. [CW 13]

6616 "That will ask some tears in the true performing . . ." -- from A Midsummer-Night's Dream, I, ii, 26ff. The speech is Bottom's in the first scene involving the rustic drama group. [BH P]

6617 their eyes met and hers fell -- see Lancelot and Guinevere [BH 9]

6618 "Then downwards from the steep hill's edge . . ." -- the two lines PW recites are ll. 45-6 of William Wordsworth's* poem, "Lucy Gray or Solitude". What Parker* uses as a response are ll. 53-6 of the same poem, but his memory is not as accurate as

PW's. In l. 53, "earthy" should be "snowy"; "footsteps" in l. 54 should be "footmarks" and is followed by a comma; and "farther" in l. 56 should be "further". The missing six lines read"

"And through the broken hawthorne
hedge,
And by the long stone wall . . .
And then an open field they crossed:
The marks were still the same;
They tracked them on, nor never lost;
And to the bridge they came."

All of this is similar to the situation in which PW and Parker find themselves, however, the poem is based on a real incident of a little girl who dies in a snowstorm, a situation of pathos and not at all sinister or mysterious as is the Riddlesdale Lodge* problem. [CW 2]

6619 "then saw I that there was a way to hell . . ." -- the reference is to John Bunyan's* Pilgrim's Progress, part I [GN 14]

6620 Theobald's Rd. -- a London street that extends from Southampton Row to Gray's Inn Rd.** [FRH 7/SP 5/MMA 7]

6621 theorizing ahead of my data -- Sherlock Holmes uses this line or words like them in several places. PW has in mind the Sherlockian dictum that, "It is a capital mistake to theorize before one has data. Insensibly one begins to twist facts to suit theories, instead of theories to suit facts." The passage as stated here is from A Study in Scarlet. [GN 15]

6622 Theotokou -- see cist graves at Theotokou [GN 3]

6623 "There Ain't Nobody Loves Me" -- a dance tune that is not further identifiable. DLS may have had in mind some other song such as "I Ain't Got Nobody", or "Somebody Loves Me", among other possibilities. [ab]

6624 "there are always wheels within wheels" -- Mrs. Venables* alludes to Ezekiel 10:10 by way of Ch. 40 of Dickens's* Pickwick Papers. She is suggesting that problems may be more complex than first thought. [NT 12]

6625 "There are more things . . ." -- the line concludes, "Horatio, Than are dreamt of in your philosophy." It is from Hamlet, I, v, 166-7. [BH 9]

6626 -- There are points about him which seem suggestive . . ." -- Sherlock Holmes uses phrases similar to the one PW uses here in all sorts of places. The allusion may be to "A Case of Identity": "The point about the signature is very suggestive--in fact, we may call it conclusive." [HHC 10]

6627 There, as the poet ungrammatically observes, let them lay . . ." -- the poet in question is Lord Byron* in what is claimed by some to be the most famous solecism in English poetry. The reference is to Childe Harold's Pilgrimage, Canto IV, stanza 180, l. 1620: "And dashest him again to earth--there let him lay." It should be "lie", but Byron was not one to worry about such things. The part about the goose and the golden eggs is an addition from Aesop. [BH 9]

6628 "There is a little, hairy, green-eyed snake" -- Ziba, the Moorish sorcerer, speaks these lines in his plot to kill Isbrand in V, ii, 61-65, of T. L. Beddoes' Death's Jest Book [HHC 18]

6629 "There is nothing good or evil save in the will." -- the line is from Epictetus* and is found in his Discourses, book iii, chapter 10, section 18 [UD 19]

6630 "There was an old man of Whitehaven" -- this is the first line of a limerick written by Edward Lear appearing in his The Book of Nonsense (1846):

"There was an old man of Whitehaven
Who danced a quadrille with a raven;
But they said--'It's absurd,
To encourage this bird!'
So they smashed that Old Man of
Whitehaven."

Lear is chiefly remembered for his collections of such nonsense. [WB 4]

6631 "There's a fellow . . ." -- the passage printed as the chapter heading quote is the entire poetic fragment entitled, "A Ruffian" by T. L. Beddoes* [HHC 11]

6632 "There's many a slip . . ." -- the first modern reference to this line (which concludes "twixt the cup and the lip") appears in Richard Harris Barham's "Lady Rohesia", a short story recounting the death of Lady Rohesia Ingoldsby (see The Ingoldsby Legends). The earliest appearance seems to be in

Homer's Odyssey, book 22, ll. 8-18, where Odysseus shoots an arrow into Antinoos's neck just as the latter is about to drink a cup of wine. That scene occurs just as Odysseus discloses his return to Ithaca to the suitors. [FRH 13]

6633 "There's not a crime . . ." -- see Aurora Leigh [UD 19]

6634 There's nothing like a mother's instinct . . . -- an unidentifiable idea as it has probably been around as a bit of folk propaganda from the inception of motherhood. It is a convenient if false bit of rationalization. [HHC 21]

6635 thermodynamics -- see second law of thermodynamics [HHC 22]

6636 Thermopylae -- the famous battle of the Persian Wars (500-499 B. C.). The Spartan army met the Persians (480 B. C.) under Xerxes at the pass of Thermopylae, but they were betrayed by Ephiates. The Spartans withdrew leaving 300 men under Leonidas to face Xerxes' entire army. The 300 fought until all were dead. When news of the defeat was heard, the Athenian navy sought shelter at Salamis, but encountered the Persians there and routed them in one of history's greatest naval battles. [GN 17]

6637 "These hangman's hands . . ." -- PW alludes to Macbeth, II, ii, 28-9. See "One cried, 'God bless us!'" [BH 17]

6638 "They all wrote down on their slates . . ." -- the allusion is to Alice in Wonderland*, Ch. 12. The lines are: "The jury all wrote down on their slates, 'She doesn't believe there's an atom of meaning in it.'" [SP 1]

6639 They also serve who only serve writs . . . -- PW renders his own version of line 14 of John Milton's Sonnet XVI, "On His Blindness": "They also serve who only stand and wait." [BH 6]

6640 They are coming, my own, my sweet . . . -- PW recites his version of some lines from Tennyson's* Maud, a long monodrama containing some of the poet's best lyrics, including the famous "Come into the garden, Maud". PW alludes to Part I, section XXII, stanza xi, which reads:

"She is coming, my own, my sweet;
Were it ever so airy a tread,
My heart would hear her and beat,
Were it earth in an earthy bed;
My dust would hear her and beat,
Had I lain for a century dead;
Would start and tremble under her feet,
And blossom in purple and red."

[SP 3]

6641 They can't even cut me . . . -- PW here uses "cut" as a pun in the sense of giving him a social rebuff by ignoring him [SP 21]

6642 "They do best who, if they cannot but admit love . . ." -- the line is from "Of Love" by Sir Francis Bacon* in an essay written in 1625 [GN 3]

6643 They're artificial--they smell of the lamp. -- see smell of the lamp [HHC 25]

6644 "Things done without example . . ." -- the lines are from Shakespeare's King Henry VIII, I, ii, 90-1. The speech begins:

HVIIIR: "Things done well,
And with a care exempt themselves from fear;
Things done without example, in their issue
Are to be feared. Have you a precedent
Of this commission? I believe, not any.
We must not rend our subjects from our laws,
And stick them in our will."

The King is responding to the news that a new tax has been levied of which he was unaware and which he shrewdly concludes was of Wolsey's doing. His concern stems from the fact that the populace is expressing their displeasure with the new tax, an amazing one-sixth of their total wealth. [UD 14]

6645 Thingummy -- see O Turpitude . . . [UD 23]

6646 Thingummy, Dr. -- PW's nickname for Dr. Thorpe* [CW 5]

6647 Thingumtight, Dr. -- a PW invention to illustrate one of Sir Impey Biggs's* courtroom appearances wherein that barrister* cited all sorts of medical evidence on the theory that if one cannot convince, then

one should confuse [WB 2]

6648 Thipps, Alfred [Alf] -- the quiet, small, nervous, and balding little architect who finds a naked corpse in his bathtub at the beginning of WB. He has been engaged to supervise the work to repair the roof for the parish church at Duke's Denver*. PW comes to respect and like this odd man, probably for his knowledge of period architecture and his skill in working with such special problems, and later hires him to renovate Talboys, a labor of love for which PW would have sought only the most competent person. [WB 1/[BH E1]

6649 Thipps, Mrs. Georgiana -- the doughty and hard of hearing mother of Alfred Thipps*, and fellow victim of the nude corpse in the bathtub problem. She is that delightful sort of elderly person who is quite capable of riding roughshod over those who do not treat her with the respect she deserves. [WB 3]

6650 third degree in the Gallic manner [apply the] -- in France, preliminary questioning of a suspect, once arrested, is conducted by a juge d'instruction (examining magistrate) among others. The third degree Parker* suggests derives from the reputation of the French police at that time as they tended to treat anyone who did not "conform" as an "enemy". [UD 6]

6651 third duke -- PW refers to the third duke as Peter, but one suspects he was distracted or was being careless on purpose during his conversation with Mr. Milligan*. According to C. W. Scott-Giles in The Wimsey Family, Earl Peter, 6th Earl of Denver, was created 1st Duke by Henry VII in the late 1480's. The second duke was Richard, the third, Roger. However, the third Baron de Wimsey was a Peter. See Wimsey genealogy. [WB 4]

6652 Third International [Comintern] -- the Communist International organized by the Bolsheviks in 1919 to coordinate communist movements around the world. All labor unions were included as members and were originally to work to establish the political and economic superiority of communism. The United Front refers to the idea that all member communist societies would be controlled from Moscow, and that all would follow the same Marxist/Leninist/Stalinist dogmas as issued by Moscow. The idea did not work. [umw/CW 7]

6653 Third Year -- the last year in most English university degree programs. It should be noted, however, that most "high school" courses in England last a year longer than those in the U. S. [GN 1]

6654 Third Year Play -- a friendly spoof prepared by graduating students at Oxford colleges. The aim is to review the three years' events and people in a gently satirical manner for the enjoyment of all. [GN 5]

6655 thirds -- the third position in the changing sequence. In rounds* the thirds position would be occupied by the third bell in the ring, but during the change pattern, depending on which one is used, almost any other bell could occupy the thirds position. When referring to the ringing pattern, as in "cascading thirds", the sequence would be 1 3 5 2 4 6, etc. [NT 1]

6656 Thirty-foot Drain -- a fictitious drainage ditch created by DLS after the real Sixteen-foot Drain which drains the Middle Level, the area between the Rivers Nene and Great Ouse [NT 1]

6657 thirty pieces of silver -- a reference to the price paid Judas by the priests for betraying Jesus. See Matthew 26 and 27. [BC 18]

6658 38-B -- a central London bus route, the B indicating a shorter variation of the regular route of a 38 bus [WB 1]

6659 thirty-two presents at once -- a reference to the chess pieces that figure so prominently in Lewis Carroll's Through the Looking Glass**. In that story the plot follows, rather closely, standard chess moves and the pieces are red and white, as are the pieces in HV's set. [GN 19]

6660 "This is the dead land . . ." -- this passage is from T. S. Eliot's* "The Hollow Men". The first stanza quoted is from Section III of the poem, 11. 39-44 there; the second is from Section V, 11. 72-76. The poem was in part inspired by Joseph Conrad's Heart of Darkness and both works consider the hollowness of modern man--hol-

low in the sense of lacking moral or spiritual depth. [BH 19]

6661 "This is the oft-wished hour . . ." -- from T. L. Beddoes' Death's Jest Book**, I, iii, 1-2. Wolfram is speaking to Sibylla. [HHC 16]

6662 "Tho marking him with melting eyes" -- from Edmund Spenser's* The Shepheardes Calendar, a long bucolic poem with a separate segment for each month of the year. The lines quoted are from "May", ll. 207ff. [GN 8]

6663 Thoday, James -- first mate on the Hannah Brown*, a merchantman out of Hull*, and brother of William Thoday* [NT 1]

6664 Thoday, Mary [Russell/Deacon] -- wife first to Jeff Deacon*, the butler/thief at the Red House in Fenchurch St. Paul**, she married Will Thoday* when Deacon was pronounced dead after escaping from jail. She was born into the Russell family, locals in Fenchurch St. Paul, became housemaid to the Thorpes and met Deacon at the Red House. She married him at the end of 1913. It is not precisely stated when she married Will Thoday, but it is 1920 if we accept that NT takes place in 1930. [NT 2]

6665 Thoday, Old John -- father of Will and James Thoday** [NT 3]

6666 Thoday, William [Will] -- a highly regarded member of the community at Fenchurch St. Paul*, he is a member of the bell-ringing group there, but a bout with influenza* prevents his helping with the great New Year's peal of 1929-30, so PW fills in for him. The name Thoday is still to be seen on tombstones in the churchyard at Bluntisham where DLS spent much of her youth, her father having been pastor there. Members of the Thoday family attended the 1981 seminar of the DLS Society. [NT 1]

6667 Thomas -- see Wimsey, Thomas [BH E2]

6668 Thomas, Jimmy [Mr.] -- James Henry Thomas (1874-1949), trade union leader and politician whose career started with the railway union and led to his becoming a prominent labor leader in 1911 during the strike that brought trade-unionism to prominence in the Labour movement. The railway porter's anger (FRH) is an expression of disgust with Thomas's support of Ramsay MacDonald. Thomas was one of only four ministers to support MacDonald. His subsequent action in joining MacDonald's National Government so embittered the unions that his own Railway Union censured him bitterly by depriving him of union membership even to the point of denying him his retirement pension. [FRH 10/HHC 22]

6669 Thomas, Mr. -- Nobby Cranton's referent for Batty Thomas* before he finds out just what "Mr. Thomas" is [NT 4]

6670 Thompson case -- a reference to the Thompson-Bywaters case of October, 1922, handled by the famous Chief Inspector Frederick Porter Wensley. On Wednesday, October 14, Percy Thompson was stabbed to death as he and his wife, Edith, were walking along a dark street after having attended a show at the Criterion*. Edith, aged 28, and her "lover", one Frederick Bywaters, a steward on the P & O liner Morea, had carried on a torrid romance by mail even though he was a full eight years her junior. She burned his letters, but he had a suitcase full of hers, and one of them said: "Don't forget what we talked of in the tearoom. I'll still risk and try if you will . . . ."

The two were confronted about Thompson's death separately, their stories broke down, and they both confessed, Bywaters in an attempt to protect Mrs. Thompson. While it is true that she did not wield the knife, she had helped by giving encouragement to the plot to commit murder. The December, 1922, trial lasted five days, the jury was out for just over two hours, and both were found guilty. The decision to find her guilty was thought to be influenced by the jury's dislike of extramarital affairs. They were hanged on the morning of January 9, 1923, he at Pentonville, she at Holloway*.

F. Tennyson Jesse wrote a novel, called A Pin to See the Peepshow (1934), about the case. It draws its title from a children's show where the "heroine" met her future lover. The story was also treated in fiction by E. M. Delafield in "Messalina of the Suburbs" (1924), by Francis Iles in As

for the Woman (1939), and in a play, Spellbound (1927), by Frank Vosper. The latter title is not related to the Alfred Hitchcock film of the same name. [BC 19]

6671 Thorndyke, Dr. -- Dr. John Evelyn Thorndyke, the fictitious medico-legal detective genius created by R. Austin Freeman*. The great doctor lives at No. 5A King's Bench Walk, the Inner Temple, London. Also residing there are Christopher Jervis and Nathaniel Polton, his aide and laboratory assistant, respectively. Thorndyke may be patterned after the real Dr. Alfred Swain Taylor*, the great medico-legal expert of the late 1800's.

Thorndyke appears in a series of distinguished short stories and novels which provide, in the "inverted" stories, one of the two major contributions to the evolution of the classic detective story not made by Poe*. The inverted story, first appearing in The Singing Bone (1912), observes the criminal in action and then pits the detective against him, thus allowing the reader to observe the crime from both points of view. Agatha Christie, in The Murder of Roger Ackroyd, made famous the other contribution. All other "rules" were established by Poe in the 1840's. [HHC 1]

6672 Thorne, Harry -- a "notoriously rotten" driver and a member of the de Momerie* crowd [MMA 9]

6673 Thorpe, Dr. -- the closest physician to Riddlesdale Lodge*, he lives in Stapley*. It is he who pronounces Denis Cathcart* dead. [CW 1]

6674 Thorpe, Sir Charles -- the master at the Red House when the Wilbraham emeralds* were stolen. He is Sir Henry's father and Hilary's grandfather. [NT 2]

6675 Thorpe, Edward -- brother to Sir Henry Thorpe, Hilary's father. He assumes guardianship over Hilary after her parents' deaths, but he is not a welcome prospect as far as she is concerned. [NT 5]

6676 Thorpe, Sir Henry -- father of Hilary Thorpe* and, until his death in 1930, master of the Red House in Fenchurch St. Paul*. It was at his wedding to Lady Thorpe in April of 1914, that the Wilbraham emeralds* were stolen. [NT 2]

6677 Thorpe, Hilary -- daughter of Sir Henry* and Lady Thorpe*, she aspires to a career in writing and, suddenly finding herself independent, she is encouraged by PW as her trustee to follow her dream and go to Oxford*. She and PW establish a warm friendship and her help is instrumental in reslov-ing part of the complexities of the story's plot. [NT 2]

6678 Thorpe, Lady -- wife of Sir Henry* and mother of Hilary*, she dies of influenza on New Year's Day, 1930, at the beginning of the novel's action [NT 2]

6679 Thorpe, Sir Martin -- Hilary Thorpe's* great-great-grandfather [NT 3]

6680 Thorpe, Sir Richard -- Hilary's* great-grandfather who died in 1883. The bell Dimity* was presented to Fenchurch St. Paul* in his memory. [NT 4]

6681 "Thou art no more a servant, but a son" -- part of the Epistle for the first Sunday after Christmas (December 29, 1929). The passage is from Galatians 4:7. [NT 9]

6682 "Thou blind man's mark . . ." -- the first six lines of the octave to a sonnet by Sir Philip Sidney*. The line cited is used as the title as Sidney did not otherwise title the poem. [GN 1]

6683 "Thou canst not, Love, disgrace me half so ill" -- the quotation is from Shakespeare's Sonnet 89, ll. 5-12. The first line is, "Say that thou didst forsake me for some fault . . ." [GN 4]

6684 "thou foster child of Silence and slow Time" -- PW is wasting his quote on Mrs. Ruddle* who would not recognize it, only thinking that PW is a bit peculiar. The line is from Keats' "Ode on a Grecian Urn":

"Thou still unravished bride of quietness,
Thou foster-child of silence and slow time."

There is no mystery why PW chose to ignore the line preceeding the one he quotes. [BH 9]

6685 "Thou has appealed unto Caesar . . ." -- this is from Acts 25:12,

but as "Hast thou . . ." [BH 12]

6686 "Thou has set our misdeed . . ." -- the line is from the Coverdale translation of Psalm 90:8 as it is presented in The Book of Common Prayer. The KJV reads: "Thou has set our iniquities before thee, our secret sins in the light of thy countenance." [NT 5]

6687 "Thou shalt pronounce this hideous thing . . ." -- see Myrc, John [NT 3]

6688 "Though after my skin . . ." -- from the Service for the Burial of the Dead in The Book of Common Prayer. The lines are from Job 19:26. [NT 5]

6689 "Though their injunction be . . ." -- Supt. Kirk* is quoting from King Lear, III, iv, 155ff. The speech is Gloucester's and is a part of the "mad" scene. [BH 18]

6690 thraldom of British good form -- a reference to the fact that the British cultural tradition is poorly equipped for the expression of sympathy in an open and sincere manner [WB 11]

6691 Thrale, Mr. -- a notorious taskmaster in the printing department of Pym's Publicity* [MMA 17]

6692 three alphabet thirteen letter lock -- see cipher lock [ab]

6693 three-color folder -- a pamphlet or brochure printed using three colors of ink [MMA 4]

6694 Three Feathers -- a pub in Darley* visited by Haviland Martin*. The pub's name alludes to the badge of the Prince of Wales, three feathers over the motto "Ich Dien", "I serve". [HHC 10]

6695 300 gold sovereigns -- £300. A sovereign was a gold coin equal to a pound sterling. Britain left the gold standard on September 21, 1931, and the U. S. followed suit in 1933. After leaving the gold standard, gold coins were no longer legal tender. See British Monetary Units. [HHC 11]

6696 three-leaf clover -- a yo-yo maneuver which, when executed, follows a pattern resembling its name [MMA 17]

6697 three no trumps -- a bid in bridge which, depending on the bidding convention being used, can signal a variety of things to the other players. See also bridge. [MMA 6]

6698 three third returns -- given wrongly as "three singles to returns" in some editions, the reference is to railway tickets, here meaning three round trip tickets in third class, the cheaper of the two classes then in use on all trains other than boat trains [FRH 14]

6699 Threep, Dr. Noel -- a member of the governing Council of Shrewsbury College* and who is most notably remembered for his popping shirt front. He is fictitious. [GN 13]

6700 "Thrift, thrift, Horatio." -- the line is from Hamlet, I, ii, 180, and continues:

" . . . the funeral bak'd meats
Did coldly furnish forth the marriage tables." [BH 13]

6701 Thrill Magazine -- HV wrote three stories for this magazine, earning 40 guineas (see British Monetary Units) each, to earn the money to buy PW his wedding present, the Donne manuscript. The magazine is fictitious. [BH 14]

6702 Thripsey -- a community to the East and South of Little Doddering*. It is fictitious as presented here. [bc]

6703 "throat they cut from ear to ear" -- the line is from William Webb's ballad of about the year 1839:

"His throat they cut from ear to ear,
His brains they punched in,
His name was Mr. William Weare,
Wot lived in Lyon's Inn."

The poem, "Ballad", is credited to Webb in the ODQ, but that volume lists other possible authors, the matter being in dispute. [HHC 1]

6704 Throgmorton -- the Rev. Constantine is vicar* of St. John-ad-Portinam-Latinum* at Duke's Denver*. Mrs. Throgmorton is the vicar's wife. It is she who calls PW's mother, the Dowager Duchess*, to tell of the body found in Mr. Thipps's* bathtub, thus starting the events recounted in the story. [WB 1/WB 4]

6705 Throgmorton St. -- the street

that extends from the northeast corner of the Bank of England* to Old Broad St. at the Stock Exchange* in The City*. The Hon. Freddy Arbuthnot* has offices there. [GN 13]

6706 Through the Looking Glass -- the second of Lewis Carroll's* supposed nonsense stories and the sequel to Alice in Wonderland. In the sequel, Alice passes through a mirror to have adventures with members of a chess set, Humpty-Dumpty, Tweedledum and Tweedledee, and others. There is a great deal of careful logic beneath what appears at a superficial glance to be a grand collection of silliness. [GN 19/BH P]

6707 Through the Wall -- a 1909 novel by the American journalist, novelist, and playwright, Cleveland Moffett (1863-1926). The book was, for a long time, considered a cornerstone book in detective fiction. It no longer holds such a place of preeminence. [BC 18]

6708 "thrown her bonnet over the windmill" -- a colloquial expression meaning that Suzanne had gone to bed with Legros* [NT 8]

6709 thrush -- a disorder in the feet of hoofed animals including horses. It is caused by standing in wet and unclean stalls. [SP 12]

6710 Thunderclap -- the socialist weekly newspaper for which George Goyles* worked. It is fictitious as presented in CW, but DLS may have had in mind the Clarion as it is the most likely candidate from among the six noteworthy socialist weeklies of the day. [CW 9]

6711 Thunderer -- a nickname for The Times* [HHC 4]

6712 thurifer -- one who carries the thurifer or censer in a religious service; the censer itself. The word is Latin for incense-bearing. [bc/BC 13]

6713 "Thus she there wayted untill eventyde . . ." -- the passage is stanza 55, section XVII of Spenser's* The Fairie Queen, an allegorical poem of great magnitude and concept. It is considered Spenser's greatest work. [GN 21]

6714 Thus spake Zarathustra -- PW alludes to Friedrich Nietzsche's Also Sprach Zarathustra, that philosophical treatise of immense impact on the 20th C., that appeared in full form in the early 1890's after Nietzsche had become quite insane and had no idea what was going on. It is this work that states that God is dead--at least in any cultural sense--and that it is now up to mankind to raise itself above the animal and the typically human; man must become "the superman" (or übermencsh or overman). God is dead in the spiritual or cultural sense as mankind has become separated from God as He is presented in the Bible. A complete misinterpretation of Nietzsche's ideas fed Hitler's demented schemes and has led permanently to an erroneous association between Hitler and the philosopher. While his ideas are most unsettling, they deserve to be read for themselves. [BH 13]

6715 thyroid -- an excess of thyroxin, produced in the thyroid gland (located in the neck), can cause hyperactivity, but other effects will be noticed as well. These include nervousness, high blood pressure, rapid pulse, loss of weight, sweatiness, etc. [ie/GN 16]

6716 tibia -- the larger of the two lower leg bones, the other being the fibula. They connect the knee and the ankle. [MMA 2]

6717 tiddler -- a slang name for any small fish or small person [NT 6]

6718 Tiens! -- French for, "Really!", or, "You don't say so!" [NT 8]

6719 tig -- to play, tease, or annoy in a frolicsome manner from the game "tig", or "touch me if you can", a form of tag. [GN 12]

6720 Tighe, Hamilton -- a character in "The Legend of Hamilton Tighe" a poem in The Ingoldsby Legends* by Thomas Ingoldsby, a pseudonym of Richard Harris Barham (1788-1845). In his poem, Tighe's head is removed quickly by a well-aimed cannon ball. He then wanders the earth, carrying his head along, haunting those he had known when alive, particularly those who were in some way connected with his death. PW alludes to Tighe in his ghostly manifestation. [fr]

6721 tightened a peg -- the pegs

#6720 Hamilton Tighe, from an illustration for the 1864, New York, edition of The Ingoldsby Legends.

are the keylike devices used to control the tension of the strings on violins and other string instruments. To tighten one would increase the tension and raise the tonal quality. [HHC 3]

6722 tiles, out on the -- a night out to obtain sexual gratification [FRH 17]

6723 Timbuctoo -- or Timbuktu among other spellings, a caravan stop and important trading center in the southern Sahara. In PW's time it was a part of French West Africa, but it is now a part of the nation of Mali. [FRH 25]

6724 "time has come to talk of many things . . ." -- the reference is to lines in "The Walrus and the Carpenter" from Ch. 4 of Through the Looking Glass* [FRH 6]

6725 "'Time is,' quoth the Brazen Head . . ." -- a reference to the fabled Brazen Head made by Roger Bacon (ca. 1214-94), English philosopher, scientist, alchemist, and, in his later life, a Franciscan monk. The story states that if Bacon heard the head speak, then his projects would be successful; if not, they would fail. While Bacon slept, his familiar, Miles, is supposed to have heard the head speak: "Time is." A half hour later it said, "Time was"; and a half hour past that it said, "Time [is] past". It then fell down and was broken to smithereens. [GN 4]

6726 The Times -- of London. One of the world's most famous and respected newspapers, it is published six days a week. The Sunday Times is a separate paper usually owned by the same company. Until May of 1966, it ran personal and want ads on the front page rather than news, and a certain loyal readership developed who followed the strange variety of messages printed there. It was often used as a means of sending secret coded messages. The paper was founded in 1785 as The Daily Universal Register; it has been known as The Times since 1788. It is now an institution that inspires awe among journalists everywhere and which command the attention of world readers. [passim]

6727 Times Atlas -- the great multi-volume atlas and gazeteer published by The Times. Victor Dean* was carrying one of its volumes (or the single volume edition) when he was murdered. [BC 5/MMA 1]

6728 Times Literary Supplement -- an exhaustive review of the latest publications, both popular and scholarly, issued weekly by The Times*. It is an invaluable reference tool and guide for scholars and general readers alike. [WB 5]

6729 Times Book Club -- a book club that was run by The Times through its Literary Supplement* [t]

6730 timid mumbo-jumbo of the superstitious Corinthians -- St. Paul had a variety of problems establishing the Church in Corinth. First, he had to overcome the various pagan practices, especially in the worship of Aphrodite wherein virgins sacrificed their virginity as part of the rites. Also, Corinth was a Roman provincial capital and a great trading center. The result of these and other factors was to create a reputation for Corinth as a center for luxury and license. Therefore, St. Paul's tone in the Epistles to the Corinthians is frequently either admonitory or rather condescending as a parent might be to an overly recalcitrant child. Sir Julian Freke* is suggested as having a similar attitude when he takes his oath at the coroner's inquest. [WB 6]

6731 Timmins, Miss -- the aunt to Mrs. Budge's* maid at the time of the action (1927) of the story [UD 11]

6732 Timms's -- the Timms boatyard was a real place, probably on the site of the present Cherwell* Boat House. There may have been more than one, however. [GN 12]

6733 tincture of oranges -- alcohol and orange flavoring oil used by Dr. Grainger* to make his prescription for Philip Boyes* more palatable [SP 1]

6734 "Tinker, tailor . . ." -- a children's nursery rhyme for "fortune-telling" akin to "Who shall I marry?" [NT 5]

6735 tinned -- canned. The English emphasize the tin part of tin can while North Americans emphasize the

can part. [CW 11/MMA 3]

6736 tintack -- a thumb-tack [BH 1]

6737 Tir-nan-Og -- the Gaelic land of Eternal Childhood, akin to Peter Pan's Never-Never Land. Tir-nan-Og is located to the West of Ireland under the sea and appears in an Irish folk tale wherein Ossian, prince of Ireland, goes there to marry Nia, daughter of the imaginary land's king. Eventually he longs to see home and, though warned he will die of old age, returns, like Rip Van Winkle, to find all his old friends dead. [GN 11]

6738 "'Tis but an empty cipher." -- from T. L. Beddoes' The Bride's Tragedy**, III, ii, 47. Floribel speaks to Lenora, her mother, about Hesperus, Floribel's love. The subject is her life when Hesperus is not there to brighten it. [HHC 25]

6739 "'Tis not so deep as a well . . ." -- the line is part of Mercutio's speech in Romeo and Juliet, III, i, 99-106, that bitterly punning and witty commentary upon his impending death after being stabbed by Tybalt [UD 23]

6740 "'Tis not the balm, the sceptre and the ball . . ." -- from Shakespeare's King Henry V, IV, i, 277ff. The lines are from the middle of a long soliloquy on the eve of Agincourt--a not inauspicious comparison for Sir Impey Biggs* to use at that moment in the Duke's trial. [CW 18]

6741 'Tis Pity She's a Whore -- see "Why, how now friends!" [BH 12]

6742 "'Tis proper to all melancholy men . . ." -- the passage is from Robert Burton's The Anatomy of Melancholy** [GN 2]

6743 "'Tis the Last Judgment's fire . . ." -- PW is quoting from lines 65ff of Robert Browning's poem, "Childe Roland to the Dark Tower Came", with "Nature" speaking:

"'Tis the Last Judgement's fire must
cure this place,
Calcine its clods, and set my prisoners free . . ."

Of this poem, G. K. Chesterton wrote, "It is the hint of an entirely new and curious type of poetry, the poetry of the shabby and hungry aspect of the earth itself. He [Browning] insists upon celebrating the poetry of mean landscapes." PW could hardly say more. [MMA 15]

6744 tithe -- a contribution of one-tenth of one's earnings to the church. The practice dates from early times, the tenth, or tithe, at that time referring to the produce of the land. Such payments usually went to the bishop who distributed them to the clergy, but eventually each parish's tithes went directly to the clergyman of that parish. Payment of tithes in England became law in 900, and came in three types: Profits from produce, profits from labor, and a combination of the first two. Great tithes were paid on major crops, etc.; small tithes were paid on such things as the earnings from the sale of some chickens. Tithes were paid to an appropriator who had the responsibility of providing the parish with a clergyman. If the appropriator also happened to be the parish priest, he was entitled to all of the tithe income and was called a rector. Otherwise, a "hired" priest was called a vicar, a distinction which remains in name only. A parish could have both a rector and a vicar in which case the former got the great tithes and the latter got the small.

Eventually all tithes in England became fixed by legislation, as dependent upon the price of corn (i. e. cereal grain, not corn as in the U. S. which is maize in Europe), so that one paid an annual fee in relation to that year's corn price. In 1918, Parliament stabilized the price of corn for seven years. In 1925, efforts were made to remove all tithe rent charges, efforts that were furthered in the 1936 Tithe Act. The result was a fund created to eliminate the tithe through a series of tithe redemption stocks and real estate annuities, the interest from which has replaced the direct tithe entirely. The real estate taxes paid to the government--those that remain--will disappear by 1996. Hence, a tithe is a tax paid to the government for use by the Church. No wonder Mr. Venables'* confusion over "render unto Caesar" is so vexing to him. Much of the reform of tithing was through the efforts of DLS's Somerville friend, Doreen Rash (née Wallace) and her husband. She is represented in GN as

Catherine Freemantle* (Bendick), "the Derby winner making shift with a coal cart." That comment left a strain on their friendship ever afterward.

One must remember that the Church of England is not dependent upon the government for financial support--the opposite is true as the government took the Church's wealth and doles it out in the form of the Queen Anne's Bounty*. As with any church, the Church of England is still dependent upon parish donations for the bulk of its operating revenues. [HHC 12/NT 9/GN 3]

6745 Tithe Sermon -- not a standard title in reference to any particular sermon, but probably referring to a sermon preached on that topic (see tithes) which would have been preached after the harvest in the autumn [NT 9]

6746 title -- in bibliophily this refers to the title page. Any old book without one would be considered seriously defective if it originally had one, but not all old books do. As a collector, PW would have to know which did and which did not. Such information would be found in bibliographies as they provide detailed descriptions of the first and subsequent editions. [dh]

6747 Titterton, Miss -- a house guest at Duke's Denver* during the Christmas season of 1929. She seems to be more concerned with the possibility of not having more of HV's detective novels than she is about that lady's guilt or innocence. [SP 12]

6748 Tittums -- see consecutive fifths of Tittums [NT 1]

6749 Titus Andronicus -- see "I know thou art religious . . . ." [UD 22]

6750 to leg for three -- see cricket [MMA 18]

6751 "To speak the truth and boldy rebuke vice." -- the line is a reference to the entry in The Book of Common Prayer, the office for the feast of St. John the Baptist: "Constantly speak the truth, boldly rebuke vice, and patiently suffer for the truth's sake." [UD 22]

6752 "To the place from which you came . . ." -- part of the ritualized pronouncement of death used at a sentencing in an English court. The exact wording may vary, but not by much. Capital punishment is no longer practiced in Great Britain except under military law and for treason. [MMA 11]

6753 "The toad beneath the harrow . . ." -- PW is citing lines from Rudyard Kipling's "Padgett, M. P.", and they are:

"The toad beneath the harrow knows
Exactly where each tooth-point goes;
The butterfly upon the road
Preaches contentment to that toad."

[GN 17]

6754 Toby jugs -- ceramic jugs of various sizes made to resemble in most cases an old man wearing a three-cornered hat and buckled shoes and carrying a tankard and a pipe [GN 19]

6755 toff -- slang for either a dandy or a gentleman [dh]

6756 toffee -- a candy made from sugar and butter boiled together and available in various flavors. It is virtually the same thing as taffy, but tends to be somewhat stiffer. [t/HHC 12]

6757 Tolbooth -- a combination town hall, customs house (where necessary or relevant), jail, and, sometimes, guildhall. The term is generally restricted to use in Scotland and is derived from tool booth, meaning customs stop originally. The one in Kirkcudbright* has a notable spire topped by a weathervane featuring a 17th C. sailing ship and is prominently visible from the surrounding area. [FRH 7/HHC 15]

6758 Tollbooth Spire -- see Tolbooth [FRH 20]

6759 Tolley, Mr. -- an investigator from the company which manufactured Arthur Prendergast's* automobile [te]

6760 Tom, Cousin -- Insp. Macpherson's* cousin who is apparently knowledgeable concerning electricity [FRH 8]

6761 Tom Boy Toffee -- one of the fictitious products advertised by Pym's Publicity*. It was the center of a special campaign built around a crick-

et* theme at the time of the novel. [MMA 1]

6762 "Tom, Tom, the piper's son" -- one version of the famous old nursery rhyme and, in this form, dating from about 1795 [MMA 9]

6763 Tom Tower -- at Christ Church College, Oxford, on St. Aldate's* St. The Tower, cupola-topped, was designed by Sir Christopher Wren in 1681, and in it is a six and one-quarter ton bell, Great Tom, which is rung 101 times each evening at 9:05 (which is 9:00 by the Oxford meridian), once for each member of the College's original foundation. It is supposed to be a curfew for the students, but in the breach more than the observance. [GN 9]

6764 Tomaso -- the halfwit servant to Standish Wetherall* who is assigned the responsibility of making certain that Alice Wetherall* does not leave the house [ie]

6765 Tomkins, Miss -- secretary to Lady Shale* [np]

6766 Tomlin -- a servant in the London home of the Duke of Denver* [MMA 11]

6767 Tompkin, Mr. -- the reception clerk at Pym's Publicity*, and the person responsible for the staff register [MMA 10]

6768 Tongland -- a village at the southern end of Tongland Loch and about three miles North of Kirkcudbright. There is now an electrical generating station in the village. [FRH 14]

6769 Tongland Rd. -- the road between Gatehouse* and Tongland* [FRH 5]

6770 "tongue nor heart cannot conceive . . ." -- see "O horror, horror, horror . . . ." [FRH 22]

6771 "Too late, too late, you cannot enter now." -- the quote is from Tennyson's* "Guinevere", line 168, which is usually written, "Too late, too late! ye cannot enter now." The poem is a part of _The Idylls of the King_, a retelling, in a series of poems, of the Arthur, Lancelot, and Guinevere legends. [SP 3]

6772 "Too old, by heaven, Let still . . ." -- Supt. Kirk* quotes _Twelfth Night_, II, iv, 29ff. The speech is that of Orsino, Duke of Illyria. [BH 18]

6773 "too vulgar big" -- the allusion is to Rudyard Kipling's _Just So Stories_, "How the Leopard Changed His Spots" [HHC 19]

6774 Toobin, Sugar -- a fictitious person who is suing the _Daily Headline_* for libel [GN 11]

6775 toom -- Scots dialect for empty [FRH 6]

6776 Toop, Sergeant-Major -- PW's sergeant-major during WW I who, at the time of GN, is married to a small woman who might as well be the sergeant's Field Marshall [GN 17]

6777 Toothshine -- a fictitious brand of tooth cleaner [MMA 10]

6778 Tooting -- an area in southwest London about three miles due South of Battersea* between Wandsworth and Tooting Bec Commons [UD 9]

6779 Tooting Bec -- a residential area adjacent to Tooting Bec Common in southwest London [BC 6]

6780 Topham, Mr. -- the owner of some land rented by Mr. Mortimer* for raising horse and cattle fodder [bc]

6781 torch -- a flashlight [bc/WB 2/NT 1]

6782 Torquemada -- not Tomaso Torquemada of Spanish Inquisition fame, but a creator of crossword puzzles, acrostics, and brain-teasers for the British press which, in their way, are every bit as tormenting as some of his namesake's devices [MMA 3]

6783 _Torrismond_ -- an unfinished play by T. L. Beddoes*, written in 1824. The action, as completed, hinges on problems within the family of the Duke of Ferrara and includes various subplots that center on revenge and intrigue within the Duke's retinue of advisers and courtiers. [HHC 22]

6784 tortoise stoves -- a cast-iron, free-standing, slow-burning stove very popular prior to central heating. They were made by C. Portaway & Son for the Nokes Foundry, Ltd., at the Tortoise Works, Halstead, Essex. [FRH 1]

TOM TOWER.

#6763 Tom Tower, Christ Church College, Oxford.

6785 Tortue Vrai -- real turtle soup. It is difficult to obtain today and virtually impossible to make at home. It is the soup course for PW's dinner with Ann Dorland*. [BC 21]

6786 Tory -- a loyal supporter of King, country, and church, an alternative name for the Conservative Party whose policies lie to the right politically. "Tory", meaning an Irish Roman Catholic bandit, was later applied by Hanoverians to the supporters of the Stuart regime. The former were, in turn, called "whigs" after a term for the Scottish Covenanters who opposed Charles I. The Whigs were radicals who became the Liberals. [umw/CW 9]

6787 Tottenham Court Rd. -- basically an extension of Charing Cross Rd.* in central London. It begins at St. Giles's Circus* and continues in a northerly direction to Euston Rd. where Hampstead Rd. begins. Tottenham Court Rd. was formerly known as the center of the British furniture retailing industry. [WB 6/HHC 24/GN 1/BH 7]

6788 touch -- in change-ringing* a sequence in whatever manner of not more than 5,040 changes* [NT 1]

6789 touch of 96 -- a touch* of 96 changes*. At Fenchurch St. Paul* that would mean ringing each bell once for each of the 96 different changes planned so that a total of 768 notes would have been struck [NT 1]

6790 touch wood -- the "ancient pagan rite" is probably drawn from the Druids, but its origins are lost in time. [NT 3]

6791 Toule and Jollop, Messrs. -- the proprietors of the firm that manufactures Nutrax, Maltogene, and other patent medicines. They are fictitious. [MMA 4]

6792 tout -- one who solicits business, especially a bookmaker's spy who is assigned to reconnoitre the stables, jockeys' lounges, etc., for information that will help the bookie set his odds [MMA 12]

6793 tout ça impressione trop -- French for, "everything leaves a strong impression" [WB 11]

6794 tow -- flaxen, very light yellow, often used to describe a very blond child as in "towhead" [BH 4]

6795 Tower -- the Tower of London, that great Norman keep and the surrounding fortifications on the Thames at the North end of Tower Bridge [GN 3]

6796 Tower Hill, beheaded on -- a low hill adjacent to the Tower of London and the site of many executions, usually on the charge of treason. The scaffold stood on Trinity Square at the top of the hill; Sir Thomas More and the poet the, Earl of Surrey, being among the many who died there before public executions were outlawed. The executions of royalty were not public, but were carried out on Tower Green within the precincts of the Tower itself. [CW 2]

6797 "Towery City, and branchy between towers . . ." -- the passage is from Gerard Manley Hopkins's (1844-89) poem, "Duns Scotus' Oxford", ll. 1-3 [GN 23]

6798 Towkington, Mr. -- a barrister* specializing in wills, the laws regarding inheritance, and other matters relative to probate who is consulted by PW, Parker, and Mr, Murbles** to clarify some fine points of the new inheritance laws. He resided in Gray's Inn* and is a connoisseur of port. [UD 14]

6799 Town -- a colloquialism for London [passim]

6800 Trabbs, Mrs. -- the chambermaid on the staff at the block of flats where Horace Mountjoy* lived [MMA 15]

6801 tracery -- the term usually applies to the ornate carving of interwoven and interconnected lines on solid surfaces or as openwork. Here it refers to the lead strips in a stained-glass window. [NT 3]

6802 "The track was slippery with spouting blood." -- line 302 of "Rodolph"* at the point where the title character is about to enter one of literature's more graphically described charnel houses. Poe would have loved it. [HHC 1]

6803 Trafalgar Square -- the intersection of Pall Mall, The Mall, Whitehall, and The Strand** in West

THE TOWER OF LONDON

#6795 The Tower of London.

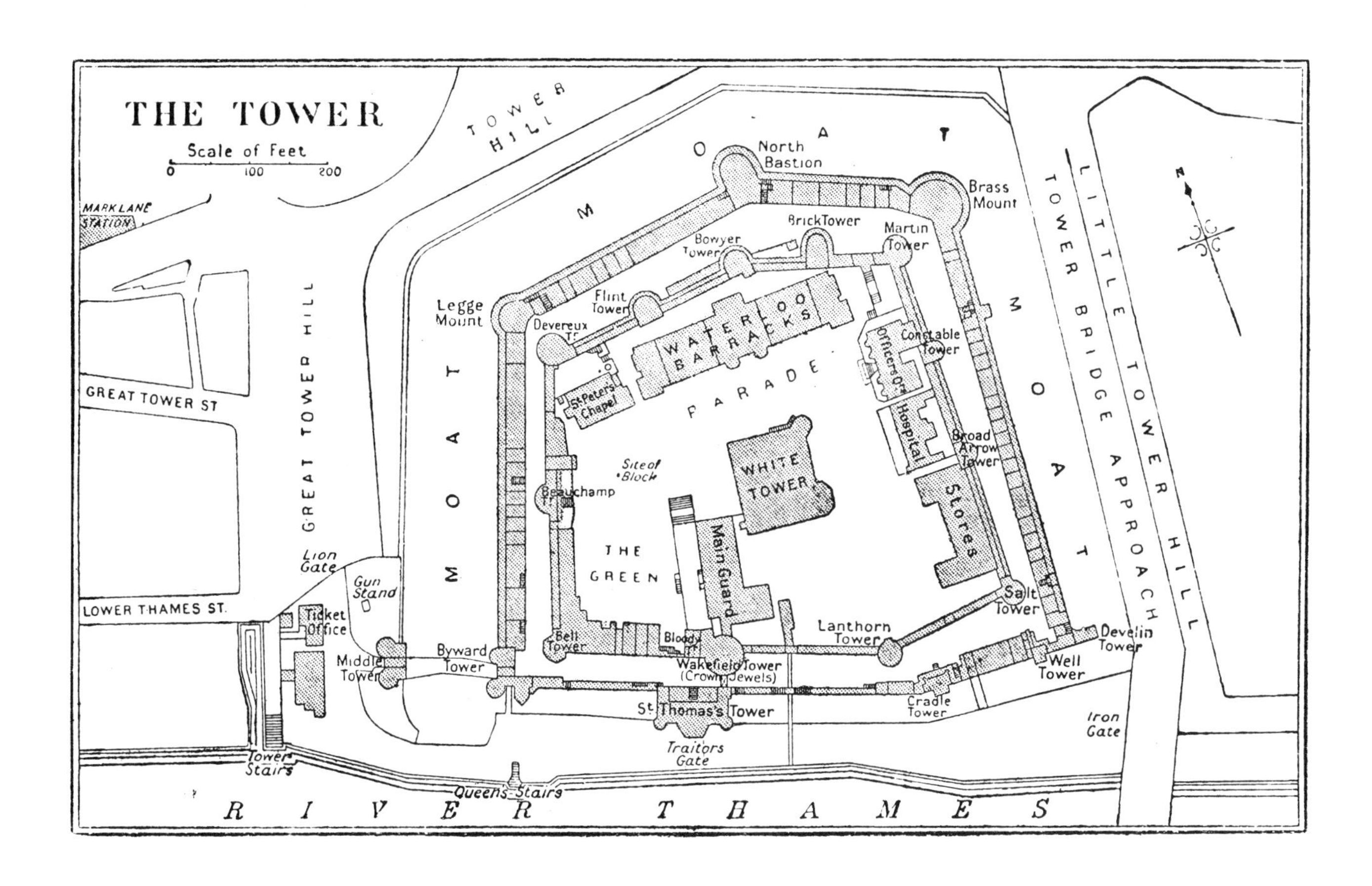
THE TOWER
Scale of Feet
0 100 200
TOWER HILL
MARK LANE STATION
GREAT TOWER ST
GREAT TOWER HILL
LOWER THAMES ST.
Lion Gate
Gun Stand
Ticket Office
Middle Tower
Byward Tower
MOAT
Legge Mount
North Bastion
Brass Mount
Brick Tower
Martin Tower
Bowyer Tower
Flint Tower
Devereux T.
WATERLOO BARRACKS
St Peter's Chapel
PARADE
Constable Tower
Officers Qrs
Hospital
Broad Arrow Tower
Site of Block
WHITE TOWER
Beauchamp T.
THE GREEN
Main Guard
Stores
Salt Tower
Lanthorn Tower
Bell Tower
Bloody T.
Wakefield Tower (Crown Jewels)
St Thomas's Tower
Traitors Gate
Cradle Tower
Well Tower
Develin Tower
Iron Gate
Tower Stairs
Queens Stairs
TOWER BRIDGE APPROACH
LITTLE TOWER HILL
RIVER THAMES

#6795

central London just North of the government offices in Westminster. The square was designed by Nash in the early 19th C. and is named for Admiral Lord Nelson's great victory over the French and Spanish fleets at Trafalgar. The Nelson monument on the South side of the Square is a fluted column of granite 145 feet tall. The statue of Nelson on top is 17' 4½" tall, three times Nelson's actual height, and the bronze pedestal decorations were cast from French cannons. [MMA 19]

6804 <u>The Trail of the Purple Python</u> -- many snakes appear in titles, some pythons, some purple, but no purple pythons. The trail is so well hidden that one must assume that the title is fictitious. [HHC 15]

6805 "Train up a child . . ." -- Mrs. Gulliver* doesn't quite get the quotation correct. It is from Proverbs 22:6: "Train up a child in the way he should go: and when he is old he will not depart from it." [UD 6]

6806 Trajan's Column -- a tall marble column in Rome commemorating the victories of Spanish-born Roman emperor Trajan (Marcus Ulpius Trajānus) who ruled from 98-117 A. D. The column is unique for its lettering and for the spiral treatment of the events depicted in the relief carved into it. [GN 6]

6807 tram -- a streetcar [CW 19]

6808 "Tramp, tramp, tramp along the land . . ." -- the reference is to Sir Walter Scott's poem, "William and Helen" and is usually written:

"Tramp! tramp! along the land they rode,
Splash! Splash along the sea."

[HHC 16]

6809 Transitional -- the term is used here to refer to the transition from Gothic "Decorated" to Gothic "Perpendicular"* periods [NT 1]

6810 transmogrify[ied] -- to change or alter, thereby creating a humorous or grotesque result [CW 11]

6811 traps -- baggage, personal belongings [bc/NT 3]

6812 travellers' samples -- salesman's free samples or demonstration samples [MMA 20]

6813 treacly voice -- from treacle, molasses, hence a tone of voice that is, at once, too heavily sweet and cloying [t]

6814 Treasury notes -- money; paper currency issued between 1914 and 1928 when Bank of England notes replaced them [CW 4]

6815 Treaty of Berlin -- PW must have in mind the Treaty of Frankfurt of 1871 that ended the Franco-Prussian War* with hideously repressive terms that laid the foundation for World Wars I and II. If Krasky married Louise** (see HHC, Ch. XXXII) in 1871, then the reference has to be to that treaty. The nearest thing to a Treaty of Berlin is Bismarck's famous Congress of Berlin, but that, and the subsequent treaty, weren't a consideration in 1871 as they date from 1878. The Russians would certainly have wanted observers--even low-level ones--at Frankfurt even if the results of the German unification were immediately obvious to them (the results becoming painfully obvious in WW I). [HHC 32]

6816 Treaty of Paris -- of 1856. Russia invaded Turkish territory in 1853 and France and England declared war in support of Turkey, defeating the Russian forces. The Paris Congress and the resultant treaty imposed harsh punishments on Russia including the termination of Russia's protectorate over Rumania. In 1871, Russia, at a conference in London, rejected much of the Treaty, especially those clauses that had refused her permission to fortify or to have warships on the Black Sea. This little war is more familiarly known as the Crimean War. [HHC 32]

6817 treble [bell] -- the bell with the highest tone in a set or ring of bells. At Fenchurch St. Paul* it is little Gaude*, the #1 bell. [NT 1]

6818 Treble Bob -- a change-ringing* method in which the treble bell* follows a dodging* course with relatively frequent maneuvering. See also Kent Treble Bob Major. [NT 1]

6819 Tredgold, Mr. -- the vicar* at St. Onesimus* church, Leahampton*. He provides significant moral and spiritual guidance for both Miss Climpson* and PW. It is interesting to note that despite the High Church* atmosphere at Leahampton, it is Mr. Tredgold, not

THE ADMIRALTY ARCH AND TRAFALGAR SQUARE

#6803 Trafalgar Square with the Admiralty Arch in the foreground, St. Martin's in the Field Church directly above the Nelson Monument.

Father Tredgold. Even though such a distinction was dated even in 1927, as Mr. Tredgold he was identifying himself as a secular priest, not a monastic one. The former is attached to a diocese, the latter to a monastic order. The distinction is no longer made. [UD 4]

6820 trench foot -- a disorder caused by continuous overexposure to cold and wet conditions. It resembles frostbite. [NT 7]

6821 _très comme il faut_ -- French for, "very proper" as in well-bred [CW 5]

6822 _très correct_ -- French for "most polite"; correct or proper in one's manners [CW 5]

6823 _très gentil_ -- French for, "very nice", or "very kind", a pleasant man [CW 5]

6824 Trevor, Mr. -- the squire at Lopsley*, a village about thirty miles from Paggleham* in the parish where PW finds one of Talboys' chimney pots being used as a support for a sundial [BH 14]

6825 Trevor, Rev./Mr. -- vicar at Heathbury*, near Wilvercombe*; host, with his wife, to Mrs. Morecambe* [HHC 20]

6826 "The Trial of Florence Maybrick" -- one of the titles in _Notable British Trials_*. See also, _Maybrick, Florence_. [SP 20]

6827 Trichinopoly -- the capital of Trichinopoly province, the state of Madras, India, known for the manufacture of cigars and after which a brand of cigar is named. These cigars were the only ones manufactured within the British Empire and enjoyed considerable popularity once their strong flavor was calmed somewhat by advanced agricultural methods and the use of lighter wrappers from Java and Sumatra. PW, in BC, mentions that one "polluted" some Cockburn* port and the person who committed such a barbarism would never be invited to one of his functions again. It is intimated that the man's suicide was connected to his criminal treatment of the port. However, this is not to be taken as a condemnation of cigars, only a condemnation of the mixture of good cigars with good port--they should be enjoyed separately. [cf/BC 3]

6828 tried for murder two years ago -- a reference to her trial for the murder of Philip Boyes* as related in SP [HHC 3]

6829 trifle -- a sweet or pudding made of sponge cake, jam or Jell-o, custard, and macaroons soaked in sherry and topped with cream [NT 19]

6830 Trigg, J. F. -- a solicitor* of Bedford Row* who was visited by a mysterious and handsome lady, a Miss Grant*, who questioned him with regard to inheritances under the new Property Act (1925)* [UD 17]

6831 Trimbles, Joey -- his studio is the "stronghold" of the literary group to which HV is attached. It is the second stop on the trip through Bohemia* taken by PW under the guidance of Marjorie Phelps*. [SP 8]

6832 Trimmer -- the Shrewsbury College* graduate who rather nervily wore a yellow dress under her academic gown. At the time of GN she has become involved in mental healing. See also full academicals. [GN 1]

6833 Trimmer's Lane -- the street in Stapley* on which Gooch* lived [CW 11]

6834 Trinidad -- the large island just off the coast of Venezuela and the mouth (delta) of the Orinoco River. It was given independence by Britain and is now part of the nation of Trinidad and Tobago. Simon Dawson* wound up there after his escapade as a privateer. [UD 13]

6835 Trinity -- the last of the eight Sundays of the Easter celebration in western Christian churches. Its universal acceptance dates from 1334 when Pope John XXII ordered its observance. It is a celebration of God's tripartite nature as Father, Son, and Holy Spirit. The Sundays after Trinity are now the Sundays after Pentecost* and are renumbered as such. [UD 22]

6836 Trinity -- the Christian churches --or most of them--believe in the tripartite nature of God as Father, Son, and Holy Spirit (Ghost) [GN 13]

6837 Trinity -- Trinity College, Oxford, right next door to Balliol*

on Broad St., it is described as a "pretty muddle of buildings". It is medieval in origin, having been built to serve the Benedictine priory of Durham, but dates from 1555 in its present form as the College of the Holy and Undivided Trinity. Sir Thomas Pope re-established the college in that year after the dissolution of the monasteries in 1544. Mr. Ingleby* is a graduate. See also Oxford Colleges. [FRH 19/MMA 1]

6838 Trinity College -- the largest at Cambridge University* and founded by Henry VIII in 1546. Francis Bacon, Byron, and Tennyson are numbered among its more illustrious graduates. [WB 8/MMA 1]

6839 Trinity Term -- the third term of the three academic sessions in an Oxford school year. See term-time. [GN 9]

6840 Tripes à la Mode de Caen -- tripe, the lining of the first of the four stomachs of an ox, prepared with onions, carrots, leeks, a bouquet garni, garlic, salt, pepper, and allspice. Additional flavoring comes from an ox foot, beef fat, and, often, cider that is sometimes fortified with calvados (apple spirit). The ingredients are arranged in an earthenware casserole, hermetically sealed by paste, and cooked in a slow oven for ten to twelve hours. Only the tripe and the gravy are served, the remainder of the cooking ingredients are discarded as they are inedible. [UD 1]

6841 Tripos -- a final examination for the B. A. honors degree at Cambridge University. It is applicable to all disciplines. [CW 18]

6842 tripper -- slang for vacationer of the more exuberant type; short for day-tripper [HHC 1]

6843 Tristan -- PW is off to the British Museum* to collate or study critically a 12th C. manuscript of Tristan--the Tristram or Tristan of Malory, Wagner, and Tennyson whose life was governed by an unending love for Iseult (Ysold, Isolde, or Isolt). The story is told in many versions, and it cannot be determined which one PW may have in mind. [UD 3]

6844 Tristram Shandy -- HV is carrying a pocket-sized edition of the novel by Laurence Sterne. It purports to be an account of the life of Tristram Shandy, but its chaotic structure prevents the autobiography from ever reaching completion. It is an expression of Sterne's belief in John Locke's theory regarding the irrationality of the interrelation of ideas. [HHC 1]

6845 "tristius haud illis monstrum nec saevior ulla" -- the lines are a description of the harpies* from Vergil's Aeneid, Book III, ll. 281ff. (of the Allen Mandelbaum translation):

"No monster is more malevolent than these,
No scourge of gods or pestilence more savage
Ever rose from the Stygian waves.
These birds may wear the face of virgins,
But their bellies drip with a disgusting discharge,
And their hands are talons and their features pale and famished." [GN 8]

6846 Trivett -- Frimpton's* local constable [bc]

6847 Trivett, Joyce -- a friend and guest of Henry Shale* at Sir Septimus Shale's* Christmas gathering [np]

6848 trop emotionné -- see métier d'époux [BH 19]

6849 Trotman, Miss -- a student of Shrewsbury College* [GN 8]

6850 trotters -- pigs' feet [SP 13]

6851 Trotters -- one of PW's acquaintances at the Foreign Office*. The name is a nickname probably meant to poke fun at or be an irreverent reference to his surname. [HHC 26]

6852 Trouble shared is trouble halved. -- an old maxim possibly based on Balthasar Gracian's Oráculo Manual of 1648, as he had written, in maxim 258, "Search out someone to share your troubles." Similar ideas appear in the works of the ancient Greeks as well, however. [FRH 9]

6853 trout casts -- see cast [FRH 2]

6854 Troy -- see Fall of Troy [GN 17]

6855 Troyte -- C. A. W. Troyte was a change-ringer and noted author on

change-ringing* techniques of the late 1800's. His work is still highly regarded, especially his Change Ringing published in London in 1869. [NT 1]

6856 Troyte on Change-ringing -- see Troyte [NT 4]

6857 "Truce gentle love, a parly now I crave . . . ." -- the line is from Michael Drayton's Sonnet 63 from Idea in Sixty-Three Sonnets. The closing couplet of the poem is:
"I send defiance, since, if overthrown,
Thou vanquishing, the conquest is mine own." [GN 14]

6858 true bill -- an indictment endorsed by the majority of jurors on a grand jury who found sufficient reason to warrant the criminal prosecution stated in the indictment. The phrase is also used to mean "genuine article". [CW 6/BC 11]

6859 True, O God -- see "True, O King (Queen)" [BH 10]

6860 "True, O King (Queen). Live for ever." -- PW quotes Daniel when Darius delivers him from the lion's den in Daniel 6:21: "Then said Daniel unto the king, O king, live for ever." The "true" is PW's alteration--he adds Daniel 3:24 to the main phrase from 6:21. [t/CW 2/HHC 9]

6861 True, Ronnie -- a pathetic imposter who, in March of 1922, killed a prostitute to get her valuables, such as they were. He was found guilty and sentenced to be executed, but was later found to be insane, thus preventing his execution under British law. He was sent to Broadmoor and died there, at age 61, almost thirty years after the murder. He had been a model prisoner. [BC 18]

6862 Truegood, Oswald -- Betty Shale's* fiancé [np]

6863 Trufoot's -- HV's publisher at the time of the action in SP. They are fictitious. [SP 1]

6864 trug -- a measure for wheat equal to two-thirds of a bushel; the basket or container holding that amount. The term also applies to a shallow wooden garden basket holding a trug and used to carry flowers and vegetables. [NT 3]

6865 Trumpe-Harte, Hon. Mrs. -- recipient of a letter expressing surprise at the PW-HV marriage; she is someone who apparently knows the Wimseys. [BH P]

6866 truncheon -- a policeman's billy-club [NT 8]

6867 trunk call -- a long-distance telephone call [HHC 20/BH P]

6868 trunnions -- a pair of gudgeons* supporting a shaft that allow it to tilt or swing freely [NT 3]

6869 trust deeds -- deeds of conveyance by which a trust (a confidence in another to whom is assigned legal ownership of property to be held or used for the benefit of someone else) is established and its conditions defined [SP 5]

6870 Trust House -- a hotel in Wilvercombe* where Julian Perkins* had stayed before his accident near Seahampton*. Trust Houses was a chain of middle-priced family hotels of good value found all over England that have since amalgamated with restauranteur Charles Forte as Trust Houses Forte Hotels. [HHC 24]

6871 trustee -- one legally empowered and entrusted with the management of someone else's funds, property, etc. [SP 14]

6872 truth -- the tonal quality of a bell--that it sounds the note that that it was meant to sound exactly on pitch. Tailor Paul* is a bell with notable "truth" as it sounds a clear "C". [NT 4]

6873 truth in advertising -- there was no such law in 1933, but there are now regulations in food and drug laws regarding how words may or may not be used in advertisements, especially in regard to claims of purity, etc. [MMA 5]

6874 Truth in advertising is like leaven . . . -- the reference is to Matthew 16:6 and Mark 8:15. Leaven there, the leaven of the Sadducees and Pharisees, refers, as does PW to hypocrisy, scrupulosity, and placing the letter before the spirit of the law or whatever. [MMA 5]

6875 try Roman -- see A busman's honeymoon. [BH 7]

6876 Tsar Nicholas I -- see Nicholas I [HHC 29]

6877 Tsarevitch -- the Russian crown prince or the designated successor to the czar [HHC 29]

6878 Tu m'enivres! -- French for, "You intoxicate me!" in the sense of to excite or to arouse, etc. [BH 1]

6879 Tube entrance -- see Piccadilly Tube station [MMA 2]

6880 tubular chimes -- hollow brass tubes of a certain diameter, the length of which determines what note they will sound when tuned and properly struck [NT 2]

6881 Tucker, Phoebe -- a history student at Shrewsbury College* who had married an archaeologist, Mr. Bancroft*, and was raising a family while digging at sites in Greece [GN 1]

6882 tuckings -- the loose end of a bell rope, especially the excess part of the rope left after having been adjusted for the height of the man pulling on it [NT 1]

6883 Tudor Building -- one of the older buildings on the Shrewsbury College* campus. It had housed the library until the new one was built. [GN 3]

6884 Tudor bonnets -- a reference to the caps worn with full academicals* which are indeed very ancient in their design [GN 1]

6885 tugs -- the leather straps and loops fastened to a horse and which support the shaft against which the horse pulls to move the wagon [CW 11]

6886 Tuke Holdsworth '08 -- a highly regarded variety of port wine. A bottle of '08 would be hard to come by now, but a bottle of a vintage year in the 1940's or 50's would be "harmless enough" today. One must appreciate Mr. Venables' concept of harmless. [NT 1]

6887 Tulliver, Tillie -- Mrs. Morecambe's* stage name before her marriage to Alfred Morecambe* [HHC 32]

6888 tumulos at Halos -- a Greek Dark Age (11th-9th centuries B. C.) burial site or mound at Halos, not far from the modern Volos in Thessaly. The word "halos" is Greek for threshing floor. [GN 3]

6889 tuneable and sound -- to have a bell tuneable it must be properly cast to specific dimensions and then be ground down to a specific note which it keeps, with minor additional tuning, for its useful life. Sound means to be free from defects; no cracks or flaws in the metal or the casting. [NT 1]

6890 Tupper's End -- where Wally Pratt* lives. It is one of the more distant points from the church in the parish of Fenchurch St. Paul*. It is fictitious. [NT 1]

6891 turbot [with sauce] -- a North Atlantic, European flatfish of delicate flavor and firm white flesh, highly regarded as an eating fish. The sauce is unspecified. [ae/SP 1/MMA 17]

6892 Turgeot, M. -- the manager of the Crédit Lyonnais* branch visited by Charles Parker* while investigating Denis Cathcart's* background [CW 5]

6893 Turkey carpet -- an "oriental" rug made in Turkey and featuring various geometric patterns imitating the more widely known Persian rugs. The Turks were, perhaps, more alert to the export market and made rugs for that purpose earlier than most other sources of "oriental" carpets. [CW 10]

6894 Turkish Abdullahs -- cigarettes of good quality, thick and oval in shape. They are still available. [MMA 15]

6895 Turkish coffee -- a very thick and sweet brew made from coffee ground to a powder. It is served in demitasse cups. [SP 1]

6896 Turkish delight -- in Turkish, lokum, a thick, gooey confection cut into cubes and dusted with sugar or a sugar and starch mixture to keep the blocks separate [SP 1]

6897 Turks -- a general term referring to cigarettes made from Turkish tobacco [MMA 15]

6898 Turl -- a narrow street connecting Broad and High Streets** in Oxford [GN 11]

6899 turn [whole and half] -- particular maneuvers of the observation bell. In the following list of changes

(in Stedman's Triples), whole and half turns are marked:

```
   3 4 7 5 6 1 2
   3 7 4 6 5 1 2
  †7 3 4 5 6 1 2
  †7 4 3 6 5 2 1
   4‡7 5 3 6 1 2   Course End
  †7 4 5 3 1 6 2
  †7 5 4 1 3 2 6
   5 7 4 3 1 6 2
   5 4 7 1 3 2 6
   4 5 7 3 1 6 2
   4‡7 5 1 3 2 6   Course End
  ‡7 4 1 5 2 3 6
   4‡7 1 2 5 6 3
   4 1 7 5 2 3 6
```

The five lines marked with a dagger (†) indicate the point at which a whole turn is made. Note that the #7 bell is in firsts position for two strokes, in seconds for one and returns to firsts for two more strokes before continuing on its course. When it returns to firsts place at the double dagger (‡), it is executing a half turn. [NT 11]

6900 Turn again Whittington -- PW addresses this line to his mount, Polly Flinders, and the rest of it is, "Lord Mayor of London". As a young boy from Gloucestershire, Dick Whittington ran away from his London employment because of abuse. He started for home, but soon fancied he heard the Bow Bells of Cheapside ringing the verse quoted here as he stood on Highgate Hill. He returned to London and eventually became the Lord Mayor and an important benefactor of The City*. He died in 1423. [bc]

6901 turned out the monks -- see Henry VIII [NT 3]

6902 Turner, William -- see "Often they were gone to bed . . ." [GN 6]

6903 Turvey Bessie -- mother to the child who saw Mr. Newcombe's* mare running around loose the day after Paul Alexis* was found slain [HHC 16]

6904 "Tuscany [like the ranks of]" -- the line is from Thomas Babington, Baron Macaulay's (1800-59) <u>Lays of Ancient Rome</u>, in "Horatius", section ix. The line is:

"And even the ranks of Tuscany
Could scarce forbear to cheer."

Macaulay's inspiration was likely drawn from Livy's history of Rome, <u>Ab Urbe Condita Libri</u>, Book II, which survives only in fragments. [FRH 28]

6905 <u>The Twaddler</u> -- a newspaper of PW's creation. Bunter* is somehow supposed to make himself look like a photographer from this paper. [BC 5]

6906 twaddling -- a verb form of twaddle or twattle, a dialectical expression meaning any kind of idle, meaningless, or silly chatter or conversation. PW uses the word disarmingly to describe his own patter. [im]

6907 Tweall, Miss -- one of the guests at the boarding house in Windle* where Miss Climpson* stays while working for PW [SP 18]

6908 Tweedle, Mr. -- the chemist who identifies Hector Puncheon's* "bicarbonate of soda" for what it really is--cocaine* [MMA 12]

6909 Tweedling Parva -- the fictitious home of the equally fictitious Rev. Arthur Boyes*. The location is not specified as to county, but it is somewhere in the general vicinity of London. [SP 6]

6910 <u>Twelfth Night</u> -- <u>Or What You Will</u>, Shakespeare's comedy of about 1600. The story concerns spurned love, mistaken identities, women disguised as men, etc. The funniest parts of the play, however, belong to the minor characters, Sir Toby Belch, Sir Andrew Aguecheek, Malvolio, Maria and Feste. The basic plot involves the love of Duke Orsino for Olivia. [BH 18]

6911 Twentyman's Teas -- a firm created by DLS to provide work for the staff at Pym's Publicity* [MMA 3]

6912 twine willow-wreaths . . . -- PW is joking at Parker's expense. A willow-wreath or garland is the symbol of grief for a lost loved one. In this instance, Parker's case against HV is being destroyed so PW suggests that Parker is going into mourning over that. The reference in BH is to all the young women who will no longer be able to catch PW as a husband, so those hapless women are being grieved for. [SP 4/BH P]

6913 Twitterton, Aggie -- Mr. Noakes's* niece, a middle-aged spinster who keeps hens and plays the organ in the

church at Paggleham*. She is presented as a naive woman of simple tastes, is somewhat neurotic, and is rather pathetic in her insecurity. She is a tragicomic figure whose surname adequately describes her surface behavior. [BH 1]

6914 Twitterton, Dick -- Aggie Twitterton's* father, the cowherd who married the schoolmistress, thus giving his daughter her "airs" of gentility [BH 10]

6915 Twitterton, Gladys -- a typist at Crichton's* advertising agency who tells Salcombe Hardy* about an oil painting of Coreggio Plant*, the victim of a particularly brutal crime. The painting, by Thomas Crowder*, proves so interesting and valuable to PW's investigation that he buys it. Miss Twitterton's name proves to be whimsically Dickensian as, when PW takes her to lunch, she does seem to twitter rather than talk. PW's fame and suave manner might have something to do with that. [nf]

6916 Two and thirty chessmen baked in a pie -- a deliberate misquotation from the nursery rhyme, "Sing-a-Song-of-Sixpence". The pie actually contains five and twenty blackbirds. [GN 20]

6917 two centuries in successive innings -- see cricket [MMA 18]

6918 two double-faults running -- a reference to tennis. In lawn tennis, a double fault costs the erring player the point for failure to deliver either permitted serve. In certain circumstances, such failure could cost the player the game. [MMA 1]

6919 £200 -- Bunter's annual salary, approximately $800 at the time, a princely sum for a manservant in the 1920's or 30's when such a salary would not have been uncommon for white collar workers and some professionals. The salary is even more noteworthy when one considers that Bunter does not have to provide his own room and board. [WB 2]

6920 two-innings match -- see cricket [MMA 18]

6921 2LO -- the call sign of a London medium wave (361.4 meters) broadcasting station dating from about 1922. Bunter tunes in to get the weather forecast as PW flies across the Atlantic on his return from New York with the information he needs to free his brother of the charge of murdering Denis Cathcart*. See also Chief Engineer at 2LO. [aq/CW 15]

6922 "two ladies lived in a bower . . ." -- PW is alluding to an anonymous ballad called "Binnorie". The lines to which he refers are usually written as:

"There were two sisters sat in a bour;
Binnorie, O Binnorie!
There came a knight to be their wooer,
By the bonnie milldams o'Binnorie." [SP 8]

6923 "Two minds with but a single thought . . ." -- the lines are taken freely from Friedrich Halm's (Franz von Münch-Bellinghausen, 1806-71) <u>Der Sohn der Wildness</u>, Act II, as translated by Maria Lovell (1803-77) in <u>Ingomar the Barbarian</u>:

"<u>What love is, if thou</u> wouldst be taught,
Thy heart must teach alone,--
Two souls with but a single thought,
Two hearts that beat as one." [HHC 14]

6924 "Two strings to the bow for use . ." -- HV alludes in part to a line from Henry Fielding's (1707-54) <u>Love in Several Masques</u>, V, xiii, "Yes, <u>I had two strings to my</u> bow, both golden ones, agad! and both cracked." [BH 18]

6925 two third singles to Euston -- railway jargon meaning the purchase of two third-class, one-way tickets to London's Euston Station [FRH 14]

6926 <u>The Two Tickets Puzzle</u> -- a novel <u>by J. J. Connington*.</u> The story features railways, stations, and a problem with two tickets, the return halves of round trips. DLS used several of Connington's premises in FRH, but, generally, improved on them as FRH is more thoroughly developed as a novel. It is interesting to note that PW sees a copy of this book during his investigations. In the U. S., the title is <u>The Two Ticket Puzzle</u>. [FRH 27]

6927 Twynholm -- a small village to the

North and West of Kirkcudbright* about two and a half miles [FRH 25]

6928 Tyburn -- the place near the northeast corner of Hyde Park (near the site of the Marble Arch*) where, until 1783, criminals were hanged. The name comes from Tybourne, a stream or bourne that once flowed in the open there. The name of the district that is located there now, St. Marylebone*, is derived in part from Tybourne as the same stream provided the name of the district in its original form: Mary-le-bourne. [BH E3]

6929 tyke -- a low, churlish, clumsy or eccentric person. In Scotland the word means as above and takes on the extra connotation of a bitch mongrel of lowest degree; a thoroughly contemptible person. "Yorkshire tyke" is slang for Yorkshireman. [CW 4/ FRH 1]

6930 Tyler -- Susan Hodges' (see #3248) second husband's surname [BH 4]

6931 Tywnholm -- a typographical error in some editions. See #6927. [FRH 25]

(!J)

6932 U. P. -- up, but spelled out for emphasis. Freddy Arbuthnot* uses the expression "all U. P." to refer to a financial deal that has fallen apart. [WB 4]

6933 'Uggins -- Huggins, the disagreeable sort who disliked PW as Major Wimsey. Padgett* taught Huggins proper respect for his company officer. [GN 17]

6934 ukase -- a proclamation or edict [GN 12]

6935 Ulsterwoman -- a woman of Ulster, the northeastern of the four Irish provinces; most there of Scottish descent [FRH 1]

6936 ultramarine #2 -- a rich, bright blue of vivid hue that has strong hints of purple in it [FRH 2]

6937 ult. -- ultimo, Latin for, in full, ultimo mense, of or occurring in the previous month [CW 13]

6938 ultramontane -- those who prefer greater or absolute papal supremacy over diocesan or even national authority. Usually applied to Roman Catholics, PW sees some similarity to Church of England High Church* types. [UD 19]

6939 Ulysses -- or Odysseus, the great archetypal wanderer of Homer's epic poem, The Odyssey [NT 1]

6940 Umpelty, Insp. -- the officer of the Wilvercombe* police in charge of the investigation into the death of Paul Alexis*. At first a bit comic, he settles down and eventually accepts the help of HV and PW with some enthusiasm. [HHC 3]

6941 un jeune homme très rangé -- French for a well ordered, tidy person of regular habits, in this case, a young man [CW 5]

6942 "Un lion est une mâchiore et non pas une creniére." -- French for, "A lion is a jawbone and not merely a mane." The quote is from Émile Faguet* [umw]

6943 Un peu d'audace, que diable! . . . -- French for, "A little boldness, what the devil! . . ." [BH 18]

6944 Uncle Buthie -- see Buthie, Uncle and Arbuthnot, Freddy [SP 12]

6945 Uncle Lorne's dream -- see LeFanu for information about Wylder's Hand. The passage is in Chapter 48 of that book and is, indeed, structured like that of the letter Hilary Thorpe* found and later sent to PW. In both cases the ravings of a madman are suspected, in LeFanu's novel they are a fact--Uncle Lorne is quite out of touch with reality. [NT 9]

6946 Uncle Pandarus -- PW's nickname for his uncle, Paul Delagardie*. The reference is to the Pandarus of Greek legend. In the original he is depicted as an admirable man much honored, but in medieval romances and later he is portrayed as a despicable pimp. He appears in Boccaccio's Filostrato, Chaucer's Troilus and Criseyde, and Shakespeare's Troilus and Cressida. Shakespeare's is the least flattering portrait of the man. In that play he shamelessly procures Cressida for Troilus. His name has entered the language as "pander"--one who secures sexual services for another. [BH P]

6947 Uncle Roger -- a former captain of the guard (unspecified as to which one) who is now one of the Wimsey family ghosts at Bredon Hall.* Poor Uncle Roger suffers from Helen's* thoughtlessness as she put a new guest bathroom right where he likes to walk and the Dowager Duchess is concerned--he has been looking quite "foggy" of late because of the damp heat. He is probably not the same person as Lord Roger*. [BH E2]

6948 Uncle Ugly -- a nickname PW applies to himself while in his guise as Death Bredon*. It refers to his services as a social arbiter after the fashion of newspaper columnists. [MMA 13]

6949 "under a spreading chestnut tree" -- PW alludes to the opening lines of Henry Wadsworth Longfellow's poem, "The Village Blacksmith":

"Under the spreading chestnut tree
The village smithy stands;
The smith, a mighty man is he . . ."

The smithy is the building, the smith is the man who works there. [HHC 16]

6950 Underground -- the popular name in London for what is known as a subway in North America [passim]

6951 Underwood -- a community to the East and South of Little Doddering*. The name is a corruption of Highwood, a locality in Essex. [bc]

6952 undistributed middle -- the logical fallacy of categorical syllogisms (see syllogisms) wherein the middle term (insects in the example given below) is not properly used in the syllogism. It is a fallacy of structure, not content. For example:

All bees are insects.
All gnats are insects.
Therefore, all gnats are bees.

The problem here is that both bees and gnats are insects and neither premise succeeds in connecting bees with gnats as asserted in the conclusion. [HHC 21]

6953 une jolie blonde -- French for, "a pretty blonde". The article and the "e" at the end of "blonde" indicate that the subject is female. [CW 5]

6954 une vie reglée -- see métier d'époux [BH 19]

6955 unearned increment -- an increase in property value independent of and unrelated to any effort of the property owner; an element of supply and demand economics [CW 9]

6956 "Unfinished" Symphony -- Franz Peter Schubert's great B-Minor Symphony, only two movements of which exist complete. Schubert gave the symphony to one Anselm Hüttenbrenner to deliver to the Graz Musical Society as a thank you from Schubert who had just been elected to membership in that group. What happened after that is unknown for certain, but the last two movements have never been found. [SP 13]

6957 unit system -- a form of mass production where subassemblies or "units" of an item are easily added or replaced if damaged. The concept continues in the form of wall "units" of standard dimensions that are manufactured by several different firms. Desks, bars, entertainment centers, chests of drawers, bookshelves, etc., are all a part of such systems. Many other industries have

capitalized on the concept as well. [MMA 7]

6958 the Union -- the Oxford Union Society, a University debating organization founded in 1823. It is located in St. Michael's St., Oxford. Some of England's greatest leaders got their start with this organization. [UD BN]

6959 Unitarians -- Christians who do not believe in the Trinity*. The English movement dates from 1773. [GN 2]

6960 United Front -- see Third International [CW 7]

6961 University College -- one of the several colleges at Oxford University. The two are separate and distinct. See Oxford Colleges. [GN 13]

6962 University Sermon -- a sermon delivered on Sundays during term-time* at the Church of St. Mary the Virgin on the High St. and adjacent to the South side of the Radcliffe Camera* in the central part of the older quarter of the city. The church is Oxford's parish church but works closely with the University and is a noted landmark. [GN 14]

6963 unjust steward -- in this passage old Hezekiah Lavender* is alluding to and quoting from Luke 16:1-13, the rather difficult Parable of the Unjust Steward. The idea of the passage is to enforce the concept that wealth is ours only for a short time and is meant to be used unselfishly for others and for the advancement of God's kingdom. "Wealth" here can mean any sort of wealth or gift. If it is not used properly, then it is used for evil in some degree. The unjust steward was quick, but he was unjust or "evil" all the same and he was "given the sack". The parable concludes with the famous line, "Ye cannot serve God and mammon." [NT 4]

6964 unsported -- university slang for an open outer door [UD 14]

6965 "Up above the world so high . . ." -- the reference is to Lewis Carroll's Alice in Wonderland**, Ch. 7, at the Mad Hatter's tea party. The line is from Carroll's version of Jane Taylor's poem, "The Star", more commonly known as "Twinkle, Twinkle, Little Star". His parody goes:
"Twinkle, twinkle, little bat!
How I wonder what you're at!
Up above the world you fly!
Like a teatray in the sky." [SP 5]

6966 upper forms -- a form is the English equivalent of a school grade. In this case, at age ten, the upper forms would include sixth grade in an American school, but the level of work expected would most likely be a year or so beyond that of an American school. [dh]

6967 "upstairs, downstairs, in my lady's chamber--" -- from the famous nursery rhyme, "Goosey, goosey, gander", that appeared as early as 1784 in Gammer Gurton's Garland, a play. [BH 7]

6968 Upwell Church -- a few miles North of DLS's home at Christchurch in the Fens, the church does have an angel roof and gallery like that described by her as once having been in Fenchurch St. Paul*. Mr. Venables'* had the gallery removed as unnecessary. [NT 12]

6969 Urquhart, Charles -- son of Josiah and Mary Hubbard Urquhart** and father of Norman Urquhart*. He, too, was a solicitor* and he had handled Cremorna Garden's* affairs before his son took over those duties. [SP 11]

6970 Urquhart, Josiah -- husband of Mary Hubbard*; grandfather to Norman Urquhart, he was engaged in the Nottingham* lace trade [SP 11]

6971 Urquhart, Norman -- the cousin of Philip Boyes* and an attorney (solicitor*). Boyes moved in with Urquhart after breaking with HV, and it was in Urquhart's home that Boyes died. Urquhart is described as being very fair of complexion with slicked-down hair. He does not encourage confidence in some people. [SP 1]

(V)

6972 V. A. D. hospital -- a hospital run by a Voluntary Aid Detachment. See V. A. D. work. [UD BN]

6973 V. A. D. work -- services performed by a Voluntary Aid Detachment, a quasi-military group organized to do hospital auxiliary work and social work during WW I. Inspired by Florence Nightingale, society ladies became anxious to help in wartime nursing. They were active in both World wars and, as volunteers, were granted officer status. They were usually the wives and daughters of serving officers or the equivalent. Regularly trained nurses of the Queen Alexandra's Imperial Nursing Yeomanry looked down upon the V. A. D. workers as unqualified and tended to use them as bottle washers. During WW II such volunteer groups were merged into the (Women's) Auxiliary Territorial Service and lost their officer status. Much of the difficulty in accepting V. A. D. workers stemmed from the fact that they were almost exclusively from the upper classes and, as such, did not know how to work properly or were thought of as not taking the work seriously. Lady Mary's shallowness of character at the time of her service would tend to support that attitude. [CW 6]

6974 _Vade in pace._ -- Latin for, "Go in peace." It is a benediction of sorts. [GN 4]

6975 vademecum -- a handbook or ready reference manual. PW applies the word to his favorite walking stick which is marked off in inches to do double duty as a yardstick. [WB 2]

6976 "_vagula, blandula_" -- this Latin reference is to a poem by the Emperor Hadrian which he composed shortly before his death on July 10, 138 A. D. It is, fully:

"_Animula, vagula, blandula,_
Hospes comesque corporis
Quae nunc abibis in loca,
Pallidula, rigida, nudula,
Nec ut soles dabis jocos."

Any sort of exact translation is almost impossible because of the extensive use of diminutives which are not directly translatable. However, an English approximation is:

"Little soul, pretty one, gentle one,
My body's guest and companion,
Who now will leave me for places
Pallid, stiff, and bare,
Never again will you make fun as was your custom."

This emotional and whimsical little poem is Hadrian's farewell to his soul. The first line of the poem or fragments of it--as in the citation here--appear frequently in classical literature, and the poem has become something of a _cause célèbre_ among students of Latin. Its challenge as a translation drill is indicated by the existence of at least one anthology of attempts to render the poem into English. [BH 14]

6977 "vainly accuse the fury of guns . . ." -- see "'strange and mystical' transmigration of silk worms . . ." [GN 15]

6978 Vainsé -- pronounced as vain-say, it is the Frenchman's attempt to pronounce Wimsey. They think the same thing about what most speakers of English do to French. As Professor Higgins says in _My Fair Lady_, "The French don't care what they do actually, as long as they pronounce it properly." [NT 8]

6979 Valbesch -- a Frenchman's attempt to pronounce Walbeach; see above [NT 8]

6980 valet -- as a noun it means a gentleman's personal manservant, but as a verb it means to perform the duties of such a manservant [WB 9]

6981 _Valete_ -- see Conjuring banter [ie]

6982 Valetta -- DLS's footnote is to a reference in J. Dixon Mann's* _Forensic Medicine and Toxicology_, p. 378, in the section on "Arsenic-eating". She has, however, remembered the name incorrectly. One Max Cloetta reported in the German _Archive fer Experimental Pathology_ how it is possible for someone to become immune to arsenious oxide (arsenic) by ingesting ever larger doses over a two year period. Cloetta also discovered why such huge doses were possible: If arsenic is ingested dissolved in water, even minute quantities are fatal, but eaten without liquid and taken in ever larger doses, an "immunity" is built up

in the digestive tract. Such immunity is, however, local. If liquid is taken soon after eating the solid arsenic, the dose becomes toxic. The immunity applies only to the intestinal tract. Cloetta's experiment involved dogs and was reported in 1906. [SP 22]

6983 Vallombrosa -- a valley about twenty miles East of Florence, Italy, and which is mentioned by John Milton in Paradise Lost, i, 301ff:
"His Legions, Angel Forms, who lay intrans'd
Thick as Autumnal Leaves that strow the Brooks
In Vallombrosa, where th' Etrurian shades
High overarch't imbowr . . . ."
The valley is also lauded by Dante and Ariosto. [SP 8/NT 12/GN 4]

6984 vamp[s] -- the top of the front of a pair of shoes or boots. In this case, the "vamps" are of crocodile and the remainder of the shoes' uppers are of white suede. [MMA 10]

6985 vamp[ing] -- to seduce in a lavishly obvious and outrageous manner. The word is a derivative of "vampire". [HHC 18/GN 18]

6986 Van Hoogstraaten -- see Hoogstraaten [hp]

6987 Van Humperdinck, Cornelius -- the man who replaced Denis Cathcart* in Simone Vonderaa's* affections(?). She moved to New York to be with him. [CW 16]

6988 Van Leyden's Sluice -- fictitious as described, it functions for the River Wale as the real Denver Sluice* functions for the River Great Ouse. The name is a deliberate corruption of the name of the Dutch engineer, Vermuyden, who was hired to drain the fens by Charles II. See also fen country. [NT 2]

6989 Vance, Philo -- a creation of S. S. Van Dine, the pseudonym of Willard Huntingdon Wright (1888-1939). Vance appears in a series of novels all having the title formula of The "X" Murder Case, as with The Bishop Murder Case, thought by many to be the best of his works. Vance's behavior is so pompous and affected that PW seems to be homey and down-to-earth by comparison. Perhaps the most famous reaction to Vance was Ogden Nash's:
"Philo Vance
Needs a kick in the pance." [HHC 33]

6990 Vancouver -- in British Columbia, Canada [cf]

6991 vandal -- an allusion to the northern European tribe, the Vandals, a ferocious group, from which our modern words vandal and vandalize are derived. In this case, though, the reference is not to minor, mindless destruction, but to an act considered to be barbaric in its enormity and in its heinous qualities. [NT 2]

6992 Vandyck -- Sir Anthony (1599-1641), a Flemish painter who worked mostly in England after having been called there to be court painter to Charles I. He achieved great popularity for his portraits. [BH E2]

6993 Vane, Harriet -- introduced to DLS's readers in SP as a writer of detective stories whose latest work deals with death by arsenical poisoning. That work is completed in Holloway Gaol* while she awaits the conclusion of her trial for the murder by arsenical poisoning of Philip Boyes*. She is described as intelligent, but not particularly attractive, yet PW is absolutely besotted by her and proposes to her upon first being introduced. She is still incarcerated at the time and quite understandably refuses him.

Harriet was left to her own devices shortly after her graduation from Oxford as both her parents had died, leaving her "penniless" and in urgent need of a means of support. For that latter reason she had not returned to Oxford since her college days there, and returned only at the specific request of one of her college friends. At the end of the adventures that result from that visit (in GN), she finally accepts PW's proposal. They are married in BH. See also Wimsey, Harriet Vane. [hp/t/SP 1/HHC 1/GN 1/BH P]

6994 Vane, Henry, M. D. -- HV's father, a physician of Great Pagford*, Herts.* It is not known when Mrs. Vane died, but the doctor died soon after Harriet's graduation from Oxford, leaving her quite penniless and alone. It is from this that she took to writing detective stories to ear a liv-

ing. [BH P]

6995 Vane novels -- the titles of HV's detective novels that are known to us are: The Sands of Crime, Death in the Pot, Murder by Degrees, The Fountain Pen Mystery, and Death 'twixt Wind and Water [SP/HHC/GN]

6996 Varden -- a professional athlete turned movie star who is the guest of Masterman* at the Egotists' Club*. He is rescued from an unusual fate by PW. He is also fictitious. [cf]

6997 Varden's Great Unknown -- PW. See above. [cf]

6998 Varus -- Publius Quintilius Varus, a Roman general commanded by the emperor to introduce Roman culture and language into the area of Germany recently conquered by Drusus. In his initial effort to do so, his three legions were overwhelmed and destroyed by a horde of Germans under Arminius (Hermann) at a pass of the Saltus Teutoburgiensis. Varus took his own life. The eagles refer to the Roman Imperial Standards that Varus's legions would have carried. The scene of the battle was visited by Germanicus and his army in 16 A. D., seven years after Varus's defeat, to bury the dead, about 20,000 legionaries. [BH 14]

6999 Vatican -- the reference here is to the Vatican Library, a magnificent collection of treasures of incunabula* and printed material, the extent of which is not fully known even to the librarians as it has never been fully catalogued. [WB 1]

7000 Vaughan, Ryland -- Philip Boyes's* close friend and confidant who vacations with him at Harlech*. Vaughan is named Boyes's literary executor. [SP 1]

7001 "vaulting ambition . . ." -- the allusion is to Macbeth, I, vii, 27. The entire sentence is:

"I have no spur
To prick the sides of my intent, but only
Vaulting ambition, which o'erleaps itself
And falls on the other." [GN 19]

7002 Vavasour, Miss Ethel -- the rather demanding and forward young woman who assaults the quiet precincts of Pym's Publicity* with her demands to see Mr. Tallboy*, and with good reason: He has been avoiding her, she is pregnant, and there is already a Mrs. Tallboy. [MMA 13]

7003 Vavasour, Maurice -- the name of the "agent" who needs "Russian types for the provinces" and who contacts Isaac Sullivan's* talent agency for suitable persons and takes a photograph of Olga Kohn* for consideration. The Vavasour name is an alias. [HHC 23]

7004 vegetable marrers [marrows] -- Mr. Puffett* means a long summer squash with a smooth skin, the color of which ranges from a creamy white to a deep green. He had won a prize at a local fair with his one year. [t/NT 3]

7005 Vehmgericht -- a medieval secret tribunal found especially in Westphalia in what is now part of East Germany [MMA 4]

7006 Venables, Agnes -- wife to the Rev. Mr. Venables*, she is an exceptional woman who seems to take her husband's forgetfulness, unexpected guests, floods, and all manner of distraction in her stride. DLS portrays her as a loving and very capable woman, the perfect counter to her husband. [NT 1]

7007 Venables, Rev. Theodore -- the loving, lovable, gentle, forgetful, and scholarly man who is rector* at Fenchurch St. Paul*. He tenderly guides his flock, cares for them, and supervises their community's collective life with a real devotion to his duties. He also provides an ecclesiastical balance to PW's secular investigations. Although elderly, Mr. Venables is sprightly and alert. In all, he is one of DLS's more delightful characterizations. [NT 1]

7008 Venice -- the northern Italian city famous for its canals, cathedral, pigeons, and, formerly, for its empire and its wealth [BC 11]

7009 Venite -- a chant composed of parts of Psalms 95 and 96. It is from the 94th Psalm in the Vulgate which starts "Venite exultemus Domino" and forms the opening psalm or canticle at matins or morning prayer. [NT 12]

7010 Venus of Milo -- the famous statue

#7007 Ian Carmichael (left) as PW with Donald Eccles as Mr. Venables in the BBC production of NT. They are working on the solution to the famous change-ringing cipher. BBC copyright photograph.

in the Louvre in Paris of the woman of robust good health and Rubenesque proportions who has lost most of her arms and who is draped only from the hips down. She is the standard classic Greek representation of the female form. [BC 19]

7011 Vera incessu patuit dean? -- Latin for, "By her gait (walk) the true dean was revealed?" The line is a pun on Vergil's "Vera incessu patuit dea" in which we may substitute goddess for dean. The line is from The Aeneid, I, 405. [GN 16]

7012 verbena -- a plant (herb) cultivated for its scented leaves which are widely used in soaps, ointments, or cooking. PW likes to bathe in verbena scented water. [umw/WB 5]

7013 verger -- an official of a large church who would function as sacristan, tour guide, etc., and, in England, one who carries a bishop's symbols of office; an attendant [CW 11]

7014 "Verges: You have always been called . . ." -- from Shakespeare's comedy, Much Ado About Nothing, III, iii, 64. [BH E1]

7015 Vergil -- also Virgil; Publius Vergilius Maro (70-19 B. C.). Author of the Eclogues, Georgics, and Aeneid, along with a variety of lesser works, he is remembered chiefly today for The Aeneid. His work reflects perfection of verse forms and he remains highly regarded for the quality of his poetical structures.

7016 Vergilian hexameters -- Vergil* wrote The Aeneid in a verse form requiring that each line have six accented syllables, the remaining six syllables being unaccented. Ten syllables per line is the norm in English poetry. [GN 8]

7017 Verhaeren -- Émile (1855-1916), a Belgian poet who was known for his power as a vers libre poet who became the poet patriot of the people and culture of Flanders. He is the author of "Le Carillon", or "The Bell". [NT 8]

7018 vermiform appendix -- vermiform refers to the wormlike appearance of the appendix, that three-to four-inch long, narrow, blind tube attached to the lower right section of the large intestine [WB 10]

7019 vermilion -- a vivid red-orange color also called cinnabar or Chinese red [FRH 2]

7020 Verneuil-sur-Eure -- a village on the East-West branch of the River Eure, approximately sixty-seven miles West of Paris; PW's destination and the home of M. le Comte de Reuil*. See also Paris-Évreux Express. [mt]

7021 veronal -- or Veronal, the trade name for barbital, a white crystalline sedative. It is addictive. A dose of thirty grains (0.06249 ounce) could be fatal if consumed entirely as five grains was the usual dose. It is no longer available. [UD 18/SP 8]

7022 Verry's -- a restaurant at 233 Regent St., but it is listed as Verrey's in the directories. In the 1930's it was given as being at 229 Regent St. [UD 7]

7023 versifying in the manner of the old man sitting on the gate . . . --PW's reference is to a poem in Ch. 7 of Through the Looking Glass*. In response to the question, "Come tell me how you live!", the old man in question replies:

" . . . I hunt for haddock's eyes
Among the heather bright,
And work them into waistcoat-buttons
In the silent night."

The situation is certainly appropriate for PW's search for the weapon apparently used to kill Campbell*. Agatha Christie's account of her travels with her archaeologist husband, Max Mallowan, is also titled Come Tell Me How You Live. [FRH 13]

7024 vertical breeze up -- see got the wind up [NT 14]

7025 vertigo -- a disordered state marked by giddiness and dizziness and frequently associated with open stairways, ladders, and other high, open places [MMA 2]

7026 A very conceited, metaphysical conclusion! -- PW's is a very conceited, metaphysical statement. A conceit in that sense refers to a metaphor (analogy) that gives rise to a highly intellectual analogy quite beyond the one stated. What PW has done is to observe the conceit in the poem and then pun on the word in his observation of the device. See also

metaphysics. [GN 18]

7027 Vespers -- see Evensong [UD 22]

7028 vesta -- a short friction match designed for smokers and made by Swan. There was also a version made of waxed cotton instead of wood. [bc/ FRH 2]

7029 vestry -- a room of a church where vestments are kept and put on and where sacred articles are housed; a sacristy [bc]

7030 veto -- see House of Lord's veto [aq]

7031 vetted -- examined for approval. The word originates from veterinarian, but applies to anything that needs verification for approval by close examination. [BC 21/HHC 11]

7032 Veuve Cliquot -- a product of one of the great champagne houses of Reims, East and slightly North of Paris. In the early 1800's the widow Cliquot discovered the method for removing the sediment laid down during in-bottle fermentation of the wine without removing the bubbles at the same time. [UD 7]

7033 vi et armis -- Latin for, "by strength (force) and by arms". It is the punning motto of the Armstrong family. [HHC 16]

7034 viaduct -- from the train station at Gatehouse-of-Fleet*, the viaduct in question would be the one across the Big Water of Fleet, approximately one and one-half miles to the northeast [FRH 3]

7035 Vibart, Harry -- a guest at the Christmastime party given by Sir Charles Deverill*. He is one of the targets of Charmian Grayle's* obvious flirting. His costume for the affair is that of a polo* player. [qs]

7036 Vibart, Mr. -- one of the art department staff at Pym's Publicity* [MMA 10]

7037 vicar -- in the Anglican church a priest who does not receive the tithes* from his parish. Some parish priests were called rectors*, but since the abolition of tithes, there is no distinction between the two. [qs/bc/t/ UD 4/SP 15/HHC 12/BH 2]

7038 vicarage -- the residence of a vicar* [bc]

7039 Vice-Chancellor -- the person, usually the head of one of the colleges, who is elected to function as the executive of the University for a term of four years. It is he who does the real work, the Chancellor being a figurehead. [GN 1]

7040 Vickey, Mr. -- owner of a farm or estate called Five Elms near Paglehams*. Mrs. Ruddle's husband worked there before his death. [BH 1]

7041 Victoria -- queen of Great Britain, the Colonies, and Empress of India. She reigned from 1837 to 1901. The influence of her reign is still felt strongly throughout the world and her name as an adjective is still in use to describe the moral/ social/ethical attitudes of her reign. [UD 14/GN 3]

7042 Victoria -- Victoria Station, a major London railway terminus in Westminster near Buckingham Palace. It was originally two stations belonging to the London South Western and the London, Chatham, and Dover Railways. It is now a part of the British Railways Southern Region. [WB 5/GN 4]

7043 Victoria -- in an effort to emulate railroads and their fabulous named express and luxury trains, airlines often named their aircraft. This is one such case. If assigned to a particular route and schedule, as a train might be, the airlines could then advertise that fact for its snob appeal. Some airlines continue the practice of naming certain aircraft, but it has been discontinued for the most part. [CW 1]

7044 Viennese singer -- a reference to one of PW's early amours. The woman sang lieder and was, apparently, highly suited to PW's musical talents. [GN 8]

7045 Villa Bianca -- Italian for "White House", Mr. Probyn's* home in Fiesole*, Italy [UD 12]

7046 Villar Villar -- a cigar. See below. [WB 2]

7047 Villar y Villar -- a brand of cigar* that was produced by the Cuban branch of the American Cigarette and Cigar Co., Inc. Only the very best

MEDALLION OF QUEEN VICTORIA
(1837—1901)

#7041 A medallion of Victoria R. I., 1837-1901.

Cuban tobacco was used, and, depending on the size and shape of the cigar, the price during the 1920's and 30's would have ranged from $.15 to $.50 in the U. S., possibly as much as a shilling or more in Great Britain. The Cuban manufacturing branch was the A. de Villar y Villar, Fabrica de Tabacos y Cigarros, Havana. It is apparently one of PW's favorites. [aq/WB 2/CW 3/UD 6]

7048 Vimy Ridge -- a flat-topped little ridge only about 400 feet above sea level, but it was important because it commanded the flat ground on either side of it. The area saw heavy fighting throughout WW I. [CW 15]

7049 vin de Bourgogne -- French for, "wine of Burgundy", an area famous for its wines, but this one is not identified other than as being "tolerable" [NT 8]

7050 Vines, Miss -- a reviewer's misspelling of Vane [GN 11]

7051 Virginia cigarette -- a cigarette, brand unspecified, made with tobacco from Virginia in the U. S. [MMA 16]

7052 "Virginity is such a fine picture . . ." -- from The Anatomy of Melancholy* by Robert Burton** [GN 5]

7053 viridian -- or chrome green, a rich, bright green of a darker hue. It verges on black when it comes out of the tube, but it is startlingly bright when cut with white or a painting medium. [FRH 2]

7054 viridical communications -- or veridical. The OED cites F. W. H. Myers, a spiritualist, with the definition for the entry as: "The truth-telling, or, as we may call them, veridical hallucinations which do, in fact, coincide with some crisis in the life of the person whose image is seen; also truthful, verifiable. [SP 16]

7055 viscount -- the next to the lowest rank in the English peerage* [dh/BC 3]

7056 Viscount St. George -- PW's nephew, son of Gerald, the Duke of Denver* and his wife, Helen*. At the time he is introduced to us he is ten years of age, a fairly typical youngster despite his mother. By the time of GN he is at Christ Church College, Oxford**. He is known as St. George because the eldest sons of peers are generally known by one of their father's lesser titles until they inherit the first title in their own right. Such use applies only to the eldest son, however, as all other sons are given courtesy titles only, like Lord Peter Wimsey who is, in fact, a commoner. St. George is also a Gerald Wimsey. [dh/GN 8]

7057 vitamin B -- a family of similar organic compounds including thiamine, riboflavin, niacin, pyridoxine, pantothenic acid, folic acid, and vitamin B-12. With the exception of B-12, they are water soluble and are found in yeast. [fr]

7058 Vitruvius -- Marcus Vitruvius Pollio (ca. 50-26 B. C.) served under Julius Caesar and wrote a ten-part discussion of architecture and all related arts and sciences called De Architectura. The work had a strong influence on Renaissance architecture as it is the only surviving classical work on the subject. [dh]

7059 viva voce exams [vivas] -- oral exams as in defense of an honors paper or of a thesis or dissertation [GN 13]

7060 voice identification, electronic -- in "Cave of Ali Baba" DLS uses an ingenious method of electronic voice identification to open a secret part of PW's safe. Reference to such a device showed great foresight and technical understanding for only recently have such things been made as reasonably effective and safe controls. [ab]

7061 "Voice that Breathed o'er Eden" -- the reference is to a poem by John Keble (1792-1866) who was noted for his gentle, spiritual verse. This poem was later set to music and became popular at weddings. The comment made by PW in SP is most apt given the poem's title. In BH, PW uses the word "Eden" to wander off into a word game that begins with reference to the fact that British statesman Anthony Eden was the Minister to the League of Nations. [CW 14/SP 6/BH P]

7062 Voltaire -- François Marie Arouet (1694-1778), the great French

philosopher and man of letters. He is the author of Candide and the Dictionnaire philosophique, among other works. His writings are marked by disrespect for existing institutions and a healthy contempt for authority. He did not make the comment PW wonders about in UD. See "Was it Voltaire who said . . . ?" [UD 11]

7063 volte-face -- an about face as with the marching maneuver [CW 18]

7064 Volucria -- a trans-Atlantic liner aboard which Wimsey and Parker arrest Philip Storey* for murder. While the "ia" suffix is suggestive of the Cunard liners, Lloyd's Registry of Shipping has no listing for a Volucria. [cb]

7065 voluntary -- a musical piece, sometimes an improvisation, played on an organ at the choice of the organist in that church, usually before or after the service, but sometimes at the offertory [GN 8]

7066 Vonderaa, Simone -- Denis Cathcart's* mistress. Correspondence between them helps initiate the sequence of events that unfold at Riddlesdale Lodge*. It is to interview her that PW makes his famous trip to New York City and the subsequent dangerous flight back to England in an effort to save his brother from the gallows. [CW 17]

7067 Voragine, James de [Blessed] -- a Dominican friar (ca. 1230-98), later archbishop of Genoa, who wrote the Legenda aurea, or Golden Legend*, a Latin anthology of readings for the Christian year which included a history of Genoa as well. He was born at Varazza, near Genoa, and died in that city. He taught theology and Scripture and was a popular preacher, but his attempts to resolve the disputes between the Guelphs and Ghibellines regarding the question of Papal versus Imperial domination of Europe failed. He was beatified in 1816. [WB 1]

7068 "The Vorm is a good Vorm, Sullivan . . ." -- nowhere does Shakespeare have anyone say quite what Mr. Rosencrantz utters--the closest being in Antony and Cleopatra when, in V, ii, 240ff., Cleopatra commits suicide with the "worm of Nilus". It is referred to as the "pretty" worm, and, later, "she makes very good report of the worm . . . the worm's an odd worm," etc. Cleopatra's worm is good for its part as PW is good for his, the difference being that PW refuses to play along. Nevertheless, both PW and Cleopatra's worms are relatively painless: PW politely and firmly refuses the acting job while the worm of Nilus performs as advertised. [HHC 23]

7069 Vorodin, Alexis Gregorovitch -- given as Paul Alexis's* father in the fake genealogy [HHC 32]

7070 Vorodin, Pavlo Alexeivitch -- see Alexis, Paul [HHC 32]

7071 Voronoff, Dr. -- Serge Voronoff (1866-1951), a French surgeon and physiologist who did research leading to the publication of his claim that he could rejuvenate older men with transplants of sexual glands from young animals. He applied his theories to retarded people as well, recommending the use of monkey thyroid glands. His Rejuvenation by Grafting was fist published in English in 1925.

One is reminded of a parallel situation in the U. S. with "Dr." John R. Brinkley who advertised "goat gland" rejuvenation operations on his radio station, KFKB, in Milford, Kansas. He also prescribed drugs over the air through a chain of stores which carried his special concoctions. The Federal Communications Commission and the American Medical Association teamed up and finally put Brinkley out of business in 1930 by revoking his broadcasting license.

While totally mistaken, the glandular rejuvenation scheme created quite a stir during the 1920's. [BC 16]

7072 vouchers -- a documentary record of a business transaction. At Pym's Publicity* that would be a rather large storage area where past advertising campaigns, magazines, newspapers, etc., would be kept for future reference. [MMA 5]

7073 voyons, madame, voyons -- French for, "Let us see, madam, let us see" [NT 8]

7074 Vrilovitch's "Ecstasy on the Letter Z" -- a "musical" composition that is "pure vibration with no antiquated pattern in it." It is ficti-

tious, but may be construed almost as a reference before its time to electronic music. [SP 8]

7075 vulcanite -- a durable, hard, rubber product made by combining rubber, sulfur, and other additives in the presence of heat and pressure. It was frequently used to house electrical apparatus in home appliances and automobiles and in the manufacture of telephone receiver housings and fountain pens. [WB 3]

7076 vulgari-sateur -- sometimes not hyphenated, it is French for, "popularizer" or "popular exponent"; a vulgarizer in the sense of to make popular or common [MMA 14]

7077 Vulgate -- a version of the Bible, particularly St. Jerome's Latin version completed in A. D. 405. It is the authorized text of the Roman Catholic Church as revised by order of Pope Clement VIII, 1592-1605. [umw]

(W)

7078 W. C. [1] -- see West Central office [MMA 1/NT 4]

7079 W. P. B. -- waste-paper basket [GN 5]

7080 "Wad the gods the giftie gie us" -- PW misquotes Robert Burns's "To a Louse". The lines are:
"O wad some Pow'r the giftie gie us
To see oursels as others see us!"
[im]

7081 wafer -- a thin disc of adhesive paste with coloring added and used as a seal [CW 3]

7082 Wages of Sin -- the phrase is an allusion to Paul's Epistle to the Romans, 6:23. In full it is: "For the wages of sin is death; but the gift of God is eternal life through Jesus Christ our Lord." That segment of the Epistle deals with deliverance from sin. [SP 9]

7083 Waggett -- the local butcher mentioned as one who might have stolen Mr. Puffett's* peaches [t]

7084 Waggett, George -- the son of the local butcher mentioned above, and the one generally credited with being a particular troublemaker and instigator of deviltry [t]

7085 Wainwright, Henry -- on Saturday, September 11, 1875, Wainwright attempted to carry two large, smelly bundles some distance from where they had been stored to a point where a cab could be hired. He was aided by an employee, Alfred Stokes, by no means a boy, who carried both bundles for some of the distance.

While waiting for Wainwright to find a cab, Stokes opened one parcel and saw a severed human hand. The cab arrived, and Wainwright loaded the bundles, driving off in the company of an acquaintance he had met on the way back. Stokes gave chase and finally convinced a policeman that he was telling the truth. The cab was stopped and Wainwright was arrested on the spot.

One successful ruse Wainwright employed in covering up the murder of Harriet Lane, his mistress, was the use of a friend's name--Edward Frieake

--in a claim that they had gone to Europe together, leaving Wainwright behind.

Of the murder, the poet Algernon Charles Swinburne commented, " . . . a vulgar and clumsy murder, utterly inartistic and discreditable to the merest amateur." Lord Chief Justice, Sir Alexander James Cockburn commented, "You cannot carry with any degree of safety, either in a cab or by any other mode, a dead body along the streets of London." Indeed! [WB 13]

7086 waist -- see item #1211 [NT 4]

7087 Waitin' for kisses in the gloamin'? -- gloaming is twilight or dusk; a time, not a place. Sir Harry Lauder sang a song about it ("Roamin' in the Gloamin'"), and Meta Orred wrote a poem about it ("In the Gloaming"). Of the two, Orred's is the more subtly passionate. [BH 15]

7088 waits -- persons who go door-to-door singing carols at Christmastime, frequently in anticipation of small monetary or food rewards. In this instance, they were specifically requested to appear by Sir Charles Deverill* to entertain his guests, so their expectation of some reward would be appropriate. [qs]

7089 "Wake Duncan with thy knocking?" -- from Macbeth, II, ii, 74. Macbeth has just returned to his rooms after killing Duncan, his king. The knocking refers to the famous "Knocking at the Gate" scene with the drunken porter, a scene famous in its own right, but made additionally so by Thomas De Quincey's essay, "On the Knocking at the Gate in Macbeth". [FRH 22/BH 1]

7090 wake the whole zoo -- to arouse the "beast" in someome; to excite one's lusts and passions [BH 1]

7091 Walbeach -- a fictitious town sharing some of the qualities of both King's Lynn and Wisbech in the fens country [NT 1]

7092 Wale -- see River Wale [NT 2]

7093 Wale Conservancy Board -- a fictitious water agency typical of those in the fen country [NT 7]

7094 Walea -- a fictitious fen town to the West of Fenchurch St. Paul*; a corruption of Manea, a real village in that area [NT 2]

7095 Wales, Prince of -- see Prince of Wales [CW 9/BH 4]

7096 Walker, Johnny -- see Johnny Walker [BC 7]

7097 Wallace -- one of the parish families at Fenchurch St. Paul*. They are easily offended and seem to switch religious allegiance to register those offenses. [NT 3]

7098 Wallace, Mr. -- an alias used by Joseph Ferguson* when buying diamonds from Nathan Abrahams*. He paid as much as £7,000 for each of the twelve matched diamonds, something in excess of a third of a million dollars at that time. [ss]

7099 Wallace, Edgar -- Richard Horatio Edgar Wallace (1875-1932), the prolific English author of thrillers which sometimes feature his hero, J. G. Reeder. He was one of the early 20th century's most widely read authors. The reference in SP to his detective work probably alludes to his efforts in 1927 or 1928 when he was asked by the authorities in Düsseldorf, Germany, to help them solve a series of particularly brutal sex murders. The murderer was Peter Kürten, a psychopath who eventually gave himself up. He was guillotined on July 2, 1931. Wallace's "detective" work, in a less literal sense, also applied to his work as a newspaper reporter and as a policeman. His plots and characterization are not strong, but the underworld jargon is first-rate. [BC 18/SP 3/HHC 3/MMA 1/GN 12/BH 7]

7100 wallah[s] -- in Anglo-Indian use, a worker, agent, or executive concerned with some particular thing; for instance, a legal wallah would be a lawyer. [BC 11/UD 9/HHC 19/MMA 7]

7101 The Wallet of Kai-Lung -- a collection of short stories by Ernest Bramah, a pseudonym of Ernest Bramah Smith (1868-1942). The Wallet was first published in 1900, and its mock-Chinese idiom had readers convinced, wrongly, that Smith had spent years in the Orient. Kai-Lung is an itinerant Chinese storyteller whose tales and turns of irony are considered Bramah's greates work and they

were popular on both sides of the Atlantic. He also created Max Carrados, the first blind detective. [CW 1/SP 4/GN 15/BH 7]

7102 Walmisley, Supt. -- the local police superintendent who meets PW and Parker* when they go to investigate the scene of Bertha Gotobed's* murder in Epping Forest* [UD 6]

7103 Walmisley-Hubbard -- the fictitious automobile sales dealership for which George Fentiman* hopes to work regularly [BC 9]

7104 Waln, Nora -- an American writer (1895-1964) of Quaker heritage who married an Englishman and spent most of her adult life in England when not travelling. Her work was well received by critics, but she chose to do most of her writing in short magazine pieces rather than in larger works such as her The House of Exile (1933). That work focuses on the time she spent with a Chinese family. It is a sympathetic portrait of that family, of Chinese life, and of the political turmoil of the period. [NT 7]

7105 Walters -- the motorcyclist who chased Simpkins* to return a rather ghastly parcel. Upon discovering its contents there is no wonder why he should be so anxious to get rid of it. He is riding the Scott* cycle. [cb]

7106 Walters -- another of William Bright's* aliases [HHC 14]

7107 Walton, Izaak -- an English author (1593-1683) most remembered for his treatise on the joys of fishing, The Compleat Angler. It is uncertain, but PW may be punning on a brand of bottled beer not now known. [BH 19]

7108 wame -- Scottish dialect for stomach, or, in a humorous sense, the belly. The word derives from womb. [ss/FRH 6]

7109 wandering Jew -- a legendary character condemned to wander until Christ's second coming. The wandering is punishment for his having persecuted and tormented Christ on His way to Calvary. The character was extremely popular in the Middle Ages and has been made popular in more recent times, especially in Eugène Sue's The Wandering Jew (Le Juif errant) of 1845. PW uses the term in reference to the missing Sir Reuben Levy*, but in a jocular and offhand fashion. [WB 3]

7110 Wandsworth Common -- a common ground, now a park, South of the Thames in Wandsworth, a London administrative district that now includes Battersea*. [WB 13]

7111 Wapley -- the location of William Grimbold's* home. It is located on the Great North Rd.* near Baldock* according to DLS, but no Wapley exists in that area, so one is forced to assume that the name is coincidentally the same as that of a village in the County of Avon. [ae]

7112 Wapping -- a London precinct adjacent to the East side of the Tower of London. While now quite reformed, it was one of London's most notorious and dangerous areas including, as it does, some of the extensive docks area. [MMA 16]

7113 War Memorial -- a monument erected to the memory of the War dead near the Murray Arms* in Gatehouse-of-Fleet*. It is immediately noticed as one enters the town from the East. [FRH 11]

7114 War Memorial -- the one at Little Doddering* would also be a memorial to war dead, but it is not further described [bc]

7115 War Office -- originally the office of the Secretary-at-War, but from 1870 to 1964, the W. O. was controlled by the Secretary of State for War and had responsibility for the Army only. From April 1, 1964, the Ministry of Defense has controlled all military matters for all of the military services. [HHC 26]

7116 War Tribunals -- a reference to the tribunals held for conscientious objectors to war service. Their grounds for consideration were based on active membership in religions (sometimes previously unheard-of) the tenets of which forbade armed service. The reference is, obviously, to WW I, but such conscientious objection has been noted in all modern wars. [UD 11]

7117 Warbeck, Perkin -- the imposter (1474-99) who claimed he was Richard, Duke of York, son of Edward IV. In 1497 he claimed the throne as

Richard IV, was taken prisoner and hanged after confessing his hoax in 1499 after two escape attempts. In reality, he was the son of one John Osbeck or De Werbecque, controller of Tournay. The Richard, Duke of York, that Warbeck impersonated was none other than one of the princes in the Tower who died, supposedly, at the order of Richard III. [HHC 32]

7118 Warboys, Lord -- a fellow student of Lord St. George's* at Christ Church College, Oxford. He and the title are fictitious. [GN 9]

7119 warden -- a churchwarden* [HHC 12]

7120 Warden -- another name for head or senior administrator of a college [GN 1/BH P]

7121 warder -- a prison guard [CW 11/ SP 4/NT 2]

7122 Wardour St. -- a North-South street in Soho* that extends from Oxford St.* across Shaftesbury Ave.* to Coventry St. [HHC 22]

7123 wardrobe -- any tall cabinet, closet, or small room designed to store clothes. In many cases it is a freestanding piece of furniture of considerable size. [WB 6]

7124 wards -- see barrels and wards [SP 13]

7125 Warner, Mrs. -- a resident of Paggleham*, long deceased, who had had "terrible rheumatism in her hands." HV recalls her as she and PW drive through the hamlet. [BH 1]

7126 warren -- see free warren [MMA 6]

7127 Warren -- the photographer working with Salcombe Hardy* who is also employed by the Evening Views* newspaper [nf]

7128 Warwickshire -- Shakespeare's home county in the western Midlands of England. Agatha Dawson* and Clara Whittaker* ran a horse farm there. The name is pronounced as warrick•shr. [UD 8]

7129 "Was it Voltaire who said . . .?" -- The answer is no. The comment is attributed to Francesco Caraccioli (1752-99), and is more precisely stated as: "In England there are sixty different religions, and only one sauce." [UD 11]

7130 "Was this the face that launched a thousand ships?" -- this famous line is from Christopher Marlowe's Dr. Faustus, Part I, line 1328. The section continues: "And burnt the topless towers of Ilium?" [BC 9]

7131 The Wash -- a large bay opening into the North Sea on England's East coast. The Rivers Witham, Welland, Nene, and Great Ouse empty into it. It is surrounded by the counties of Norfolk and Lincolnshire. The South side of The Wash is marked by shallow salt flats and mud banks that make the area unsafe for navigation without navigation channels being dug to allow safe passage at low tide. [NT 16]

7132 Wash Cut -- the mouth of the fictitious River Wale* from Walbeach* to The Wash*. The description matches that of the real River Great Ouse from King's Lynn to The Wash. [NT 7]

7133 wash-hand apparatus -- probably a separate stand with a bowl and water jug, towel, soap, etc., for washing the hands [BC 6]

7134 wash-house copper -- see copper [NT 19]

7135 wash our hands like Pilate -- a reference to Pontius Pilate's washing his hands to disassociate himself from the Jews' demand for Jesus's execution. The incident appears in Matthew 27:24 as well as in other places in the Gospels. [GN 17]

7136 washes [of the 100-foot level] -- washes are low-lying tracts of land that are set aside as areas to be flooded and are usually dotted with pools of standing water or marshes. They are flooded when it is necessary to reduce the water pressure in fenland drainage canals. The reference here is probably to the 100-Foot Wash or Drain between the Old and New Bedford Rivers*. Level here means a system of drainage and is not a reference to elevation. [HHC 22/NT 1]

7137 Watchett, Timothy -- the loquacious and helpful landlord of the Rose and Crown* pub in Stapley*. He is well-liked locally. [CW 11]

7138 water-bottle -- a carafe for drinking water with matching glass usually made to have the glass inverted over the mouth of the carafe to serve as a sort of cover or stopper. There is no suggestion of a hot-water bottle. [SP 20]

7139 water-bottle [emptying the bedroom] -- a reference to the Bravo case* [SP 21]

7140 Water-fly -- the name of a scull* used by the Misses Stevens and Edwards** [GN 12]

7141 water polo -- Nina Hartford* dresses to play water polo as her costume for the masquerade party given by Sir Charles Deverill*. Her choice is described as sensible, but more appropriate for a less ample lady. The game is played in a pool twenty to thirty yards long by twenty yards wide with an inflated ball of twenty-seven to twenty-eight inches circumference. [qs]

7142 Waterloo -- referred to variously as the Battle of (1815); the railroad terminus in London named in honor of the Battle; or, in reference to the first, having met one's supreme challenge and defeat. Waterloo Station is South of the Thames opposite the Houses of Parliament and would be the arrival point for trains departing from Southampton for London. The station is mentioned in aq/mt/te/WB 7/UD 22/BC 11; while the Battle is mentioned in UD 13/HHC 11.

7143 Waterloo year -- 1815; a reference to the antiquity of the gun brought to clear the chimneys at Talboys* [BH 5]

7144 Waterman pen -- a brand of fountain pen formerly used widely around the world. It is no longer readily available in the U. S. At one time it was advertised as being functional in any position, a feat most pens cannot claim even now. [FRH 22]

7145 watermanship -- boat-handling skill, grace, and poise [GN 14]

7146 Waters, Edith -- a pseudonym used by HV when purchasing arsenical weed killer during research for a detective novel featuring poisoning with arsenic. Her action in making the purchase forms a major portion of the evidence against her at her trial for the murder of Philip Boyes*. [SP 1]

7147 Waters, Miss -- a second-year student who reads French at Shrewsbury College* [GN 5]

7148 Waters, Michael -- the twenty-eight-year-old landscape painter with whom Sandy Campbell* had the unsightly barroom brawl the night before his murder was discovered [FRH 1]

7149 Watson -- a servant to Sir Charles Deverill*. He is likely the household's butler. See also Watson, Dr. John H. [qs]

7150 Watson at St. Stephen -- the incumbent at Fenchurch St. Stephen*, the parish that adjoins Fenchurch St. Paul* [NT 18]

7151 Watson, Dr. John H. -- Sherlock Holmes's* assistant and one of Great Britain's masters of understatement. As PW points out, Watson is famous for his ability to observe but without reasoning from his observations. P. C. Burt* has something of the same problem. PW sometimes downgrades himself from Sherlock to Watson when he has made an error of some sort, but when he addresses HV as his Watson at a later point, he is not intending any slight. In MMA, Watson's "incompetent zeal" is mentioned. The allusion in BH is to the fact that Watson has had more experience with women than has Holmes, a reference to _The Sign of Four_, Ch. 2, when Watson says, "In an experience of women which extends over many nations and three separate continents, I have never looked upon a face which gave a clearer promise of a refined and sensitive nature [than Mary Morstan's]." [hp/WB 4/FRH 7/HHC 16/MMA 5/BH 18]

7152 Watson, John -- a carrier or delivery man of Stapley* [CW 11]

7153 Watts, William -- the dissecting room attendant at St. Luke's Hospital* [WB 6]

7154 waxen image -- a reference to the voodoo practice of making an image of a person, often in wax, and then doing things to it in the belief that the sympathetic magic will do the same things to the person represented by the image [SP 21]

7155 We both have got a body . . . -- PW has reworked the song inspired by Ralph (pronounced Rafe) Rackstraw in Act II of Gilbert and Sullivan's H. M. S. Pinafore:

"For he might have been a Roosian,
A French, or Turk, or Proosian,
Or perhaps Ital-ian!
But in spite of all temptations
To belong to other nations,
He remains an Englishman!" [WB 2]

7156 "We brought nothing into this world . . ." -- part of the service for the Burial of the Dead in The Book of Common Prayer [NT 5]

7157 "we shall look imposing enough . . ." -- a strung-together series of quotations, a PW commonplace. The Sherlock Holmes segment, "I think that we are sufficiently imposing to strike terror into the guilty breast," appears in "The Adventure of the Three Students" as Holmes is arranging the crucial interview with Bannister. The triple steel part is from Shakespeare's Henry VI, Part II, III, ii, 232, in the line, "Thrice is he armed who hath his quarrel just." That also appears in "The Disappearance of Lady Frances Carfax", another Holmes adventure. PW has also apparently brought to mind Book II, line 568 of Milton's Paradise Lost:

" . . . Arm th'obdur'd breast
With stubborn patience as with triple steel."

Holmes never used those lines, but that wouldn't stop PW from tacking them on to a Holmes quote. [BC 14]

7158 "we shall not look upon his like again" -- the line is from Hamlet, I, ii, 187. Hamlet refers to his late father. [BH 18]

7159 "We'll have it gentle and the elements . . ." -- Supt. Kirk* quotes, indirectly, from Julius Caesar, V, v, 73ff:

"His life was gentle, and the elements
So mixed in him, that Nature might stand up
And say to all the world, 'This was a man!'" [BH 18]

7160 Weare, Dr. -- the physician who treated Philip Boyes* during one of his gastric attacks [SP 1]

7161 Weare, Samuel -- see "throat they cut from ear to ear" [HHC 1]

7162 Weary Traveller -- one of the pubs near Little Doddering*. It is fictitious. [bc]

7163 Webster, John -- see "Dost thou know what reputation is?" [BH 9]

7164 Wedderburn, Mr. -- one of the employees at Pym's Publicity*, he is the group-secretary* for the Nutrax account [MMA 7]

7165 "Wedding March" -- the one from Lohengrin* is the familiar one known as "Here Comes the Bride". It is usually played as the processional if used. The recessional march used as often is from Felix Mendelssohn's* A Midsummer Night's Dream. [NT 17]

7166 Wedgwood -- the famous English pottery and porcelain manufacturer especially famous for the unglazed, colored "Jasperware" with overlays of classical ornamentation and other motifs [GN 21]

7167 Weekes, Mr. -- the gentleman, probably advertising editor, at the Morning Star* who refused to print the Nutrax advertisement as submitted, thereby triggering a most unfortunate sequence of events [MMA 8]

7168 Weeks -- the vicar* for the parish of Little Doddering* who was followed in the office by the Rev. Mr. Hancock*. He was a canon*. [bc]

7169 "Weeping late and weeping early . . ." -- the quotation is from Tennyson's poem, "The Lord of Burleigh", line 89, where it is written, "Weeping late and early." [MMA 19]

7170 Weirdale -- a fictitious valley. As DLS did not know the Yorkshire dales at all well, it is even difficult to speculate about what localities, if any, she might have had in mind. [CW 3]

7171 Weldon, Mrs. Flora -- the middle-aged widow who becomes engaged to Paul Alexis*. The nature of the relationship is central to the plot of HHC. Mrs. Weldon is a lonely and vulnerable person who clings pathetically to what little happiness she can find. [HHC 5]

7172 Weldon, Henry -- Flora Weldon's* son and one of the major suspects in HHC. His sudden change from quarrelsome son to concerned and solicitous

son arouses considerable suspicion. [HHC 12]

7173 Weldon, John [George] -- Mrs. Weldon's* late husband and a prosperous farmer who left her well off and left the farm in excellent condition for their son, Henry*. The question is, what was her husband's name? In Ch. V he is John, but in Ch. XVII he is George. [HHC 5]

7174 Well, one must face up to things . . . -- a hopelessly bad music hall type of joke. Perhaps mercifully, its author is unknown. [NT 6]

7175 Weller, Sam -- see Sam Weller face [BC 4]

7176 Wellington Ave. -- a street in Leahampton* presumably named for the great military hero, the Duke of Wellington [UD 5]

7177 Wellington St. -- there are at least three Wellington Sts. in Greater London, which of them Ginger Potts* had in mind is not known. The one in central London connects Bow St. with The Strand*. [MMA 7]

7178 Wells -- the reference is to Herbert George Wells (1866-1946), a prolific English novelist and journalist. He is most famous for his speculative fiction such as The Time Machine and The War of the Worlds. He wrote various other novels now less well remembered than his science fiction. His Outline of History, still a highly regarded work, is a useful survey of world history. In any regard, his science fiction is, in some instances, proving to be science fact. [im/BC 18]

7179 Wellwater, Lord -- the fictitious friend of the Wimsey family and an officer of the Foreign Office (F. O.) who distracts the press who came to report on the PW-HV wedding. His ploy of releasing an important statement on the situation in Abyssinia* gives the newlyweds a chance to escape without being pestered by the newshounds. [BH P]

7180 Welney Wash -- Welney is a small village on the Old Bedford River a little more than halfway toward the North end of the river and Denver Sluice*. Hence, Welney Wash is that section of land adjacent to Welney and set aside for flooding in times of emergency. See washes of the 100 foot level. Welney is about eight miles East and slightly South of March*. [NT 2]

7181 Weltschmerz -- German for, "melancholia", a vague distraction or dissatisfaction with "things"; pessimism, world sadness [SP 15]

7182 Welwyn -- a village on the Great North Road* approximately two miles North of Welwyn Garden City and about twenty-five miles from central London [ae]

7183 Welwyn Garden City -- a model architect-designed town near the Great North Road* about twenty-three miles North of the central portion of London [ae]

7184 Wensleydale -- an English hard, crumbly cheese peculiar to Yorkshire* and named for the region where it was first made. It is pale in color and delicate of flavor. [WB 5]

7185 went down -- to leave college honorably as opposed to sent down* [GN 1]

7186 west [went, go] -- slang for death or to die [CW 19/NT 3]

7187 Wesleyan Chapel -- the church serving the needs of the Wesleyan (low church/fundamental) Methodists in Pagford* [BH 11]

7188 West Central office [District] -- the post office on New Oxford St. and High Holborn which lends its name to the WC area of London's postal code system as in SW, EC, etc. [UD 23/MMA 12]

7189 West Coast -- the western coast of England and Wales [nf]

7190 West End -- in London, the most popular shopping and entertainment area. It centers, roughly, on Piccadilly Circus* and includes Regent, Bond, and Oxford Streets; Selfridge's, the famous department store; Hyde Park Corner, and other attractions. PW lives in the West End when in London, one of the most expensive and exclusive residential area. [passim]

7191 West End Club -- any of the several private and special interest clubs in the West End* such as White's or the Army and Navy Club [CW 7]

7192 West-end practitioner -- the reference is to the smooth "bed-side manner" of Harley St.* physicians and others of that type [BC 2]

7193 West Felpham -- mentioned as the location of a busy yacht club and summer resort, it is fictitious. See also East Felpham. [nf]

7194 West Indies -- the Caribbean archipelago extending from Cuba eastward and South toward Venezuela. It includes the Bahamas and the Greater and Lesser Antilles Islands. [WB 9/ UD 12]

7195 West, Mrs. -- postmistress at Fenchurch St. Paul* [NT 4]

7196 West, Tommy -- one of the school children at Fenchurch St. Paul*. He has a broken arm at the time of this story. [NT 6]

7197 Western Electric -- a worldwide telegraph transmission and equipment manufacturing service dating from the beginning of the century and presently located at 46 Mount St., London. Varden's* reference is to the firm's service to Australia and the western Pacific area. [cf]

7198 Westlock, Hannah -- the maid in Norman Urquhart's* Woburn Square* residence. She gives the "impression of being a sensible and observant witness." [SP 1]

7199 Westlock, Sir John -- an owner of a pair of Mr. Endicott's* razors [HHC 6]

7200 Westminster -- the governmental area of London centering on the Houses of Parliament and Downing St., where, at #10, the Prime Minister resides. The War Office, old New Scotland Yard*, and the Admiralty, among other governmental offices, are all located in this area. [CW 12/UD 6/ MMA 10]

7201 Westminster Bridge -- the bridge across the Thames at the opposite ends of which are the Houses of Parliament* and the County Hall, headquarters of the Greater London Council, part of London's local government structure [CW 19]

7202 Westminster chimes -- the famous chimes that strike the quarter, half, three-quarter, and hour marks at the clock tower of the Houses of Parliament. They are used traditionally in mantel and floor clocks. It is probable that if a clock is advertised as a chiming one and if the chimes are not identified otherwise, then the clock will strike the Westminster chimes. See also Big Ben. [MMA 19]

7203 Westmorland -- formerly a county in the northwest of England encompassing much of what Wordsworth immortalized as the "Lake District", it is now a part of Cumbria [FRH 20/SP 7]

7204 Weston -- an assistant commissionaire at the Bellona Club* who is unable to help PW determine when, exactly, General Fentiman* had entered the Club. He had recently replaced an attendant named Briggs. [BC 4]

7205 Westshire -- there is not, nor has there been, any such county in England or Wales. A play on Thomas Hardy's "Wessex" might be a possible source of DLS's inspiration. [nf]

7206 Westshire Tigers -- a fictitious football (soccer) team for which Jem Pollock* hopes to play [HHC 22]

7207 Wetherall, Alice -- the wife and victim of Standish Wetherall*. DLS ascribes her symptoms to a "congenital thyroid deficiency", and the description she provides would indicate a severely acute condition. Treatment is relatively simple and successful using thyroxin or other thyroid derivatives. [ie]

7208 Wetherall, Hiram -- Standish Wetherall's* father, an automobile magnate of considerable wealth who left his son in a very comfortable financial state [ie]

7209 Wetherall, Standish -- the fiendishly cruel American physician who takes his wife, Alice, to the Pyrenees Mountains* and there deprives her of the thyroid medicine she needs to lead a normal life. His motivation is jealousy and in that regard he makes Browning's Duke in "My Last Duchess" seem gentlemanly and kind by comparison. Wetherall is wealthy thanks to the estate left him by his father. [ie]

7210 Wetherby, Duke of -- a fictitious peer who owns one of Mr. Endicott's* fine razors [HHC 6]

7211 Wetherby, George -- landlord at The Bull* in Brough* [FRH 20]

7212 Wetherby, Mrs. -- wife to George, as above [FRH 20]

7213 Wetheridge -- the perennially complaining member of the Bellona Club* [BC 2]

7214 whack -- a slang term used to mean one's cut of the take; loot [ab]

7215 Whang in the gold -- a perfect shot; at the center of the target in archery which is yellow, or gold if preferred [GN 15]

7216 "What! all my pretty chickens and their dam?" -- when PW finds out what has happened to his Cockburn '96*, he retreats to one of the most heart-rending and poignant lines from Macbeth in IV, iii, 218, MacDuff's reaction when he learns that Macbeth has had MacDuff's entire family slaughtered. [BH 16]

7217 "What! all that water . . ." -- see Brinvilliers, Marquise de [UD 19]

7218 "What I like about Clive" -- a poem by E. C. Bentley* in a form called a clerihew after Edmund CLERIHEW Bentley who invented the form. Its structure is rigid, humorous, and at least somewhat biographical in that the subject's name must be mentioned in the first line. [CW 10]

7219 "what, in our 'ouse" -- the allusion is to Lady Macbeth's reaction to the "news" of Duncan's murder in II, iii, 93, of Macbeth: "Woe, alas! what, in our house?" [SP 9]

7220 what is the verse about the struck eagle . . . -- the verse is:

"Twas thine own genius gave the final blow,
And help'd to plant the wound that laid thee low:
So the struck eagle, stretch'd upon the plain,
No more through rolling clouds to soar again,
View'd his own feather on the fatal dart,
And wing'd the shaft that quiver'd in his heart . . ."

The lines are by George Gordon, Lord Byron* in "English Bards and Scotch Reviewers", ll. 839ff. [NT 11]

7221 "'What is truth?' said jesting Pilate" -- the original of this line appears in John 18:38, but PW is quoting the essayist, Francis Bacon, in "Of Truth". The rest of the quote is, "and would not stay for an answer." The irony here is that PW didn't want to know the answer either, at least not concerning the conclusion of the story. [nf]

7222 what-not [bamboo] -- a curio cabinet made of bamboo with open shelves. Bamboo enjoyed a great vogue in all sorts of occasional furniture during the early part of the century. [BH 2]

7223 "What oft was thought . . ." -- the passage is from Pope's* "An Essay on Criticism":

"True wit is nature to advantage dressed,
What oft was thought, but ne'er so well expressed."

The lines are 296-7 in the poem. [CW 9]

7224 what suits Holland -- a reference to the fact that Dutch engineers used the techniques that were successful there when they attempted to drain the fens in England. They were not, however, as successful in England as they had been in Holland as gravity drainage only helped in part, and, eventually had to be assisted by pumping. [NT 7]

7225 what the Leopard called "too vulgar big" -- see "too vulgar big" [HHC 9]

7226 "What's done cannot be undone." -- the sentence appears in Hamlet, King Lear, and Julius Caesar, but the latter, in IV, ii, 9 is the closest to PW's words [NT 11]

7227 What's Hecuba's bank balance . . . -- Mr. Ingleby* is giving a very free rendering of a line from Hamlet and the title hero's "O, what a rogue and peasant slave am I" soliloquy, II, ii, 576ff. The particular lines are 585-6, but usually appear as:

"What's Hecuba to him or he to Hecuba
That he should weep for her?"

[MMA 17]

7228 "What's this? Did you not see a white convulsion . . ." -- the

lines are from a fragment of poetry by T. L. Beddoes* entitled "Doubt", ll. 1-3. [HHC 15]

7229 whatsinames -- bats, hands, or patters of wood used to shape butter into ornamental balls for use at the table when one wanted a little touch of elegance. Also, butter would never have been served in a block--between the Wars it was always carved up in some decorative way. From this practice derives the tongue twister: "Betty put a bit o'better butter on a patter." [MMA 17]

7230 wheat and oats -- the Dowager Duchess* has in mind the card game Pit, a great icebreaker for more informal gatherings. She uses conversation about the game adroitly to accomplish--without the cards--exactly the purpose of the game itself. The object of the game is to gain control of all the cards of one type: oats, wheat, corn, etc. The name of the game comes from the names of the various sections or pits on the floor of a commodities exchange where a given item is being traded and sold. When played alertly, the game takes on some of the nature of a commodities exchange, becoming rather noisy and cut-throat in a friendly way. [WB 7]

7231 Wheatsheaf public-house -- the inn at Fenchurch St. Paul* where PW and Bunter meet the Rev. Mr. Venables*. The inn is on the outskirts of the village just South of Russell's Bridge over the Thirty-foot Drain*. [NT 1]

7232 wheel-cipher -- a cipher created by the rotation of wheels, each wheel with a complete alphabet on its rim, the wheels fixed on a shaft or spindle. There could be as many as twenty-five, thirty, or more such discs on the shaft with a knob at one end to tighten them in place. When one wishes to send a message, it is spelled out in a row. If the message to be sent is "DLS wrote exciting novels", simply rotate the discs, starting at the left, to obtain

"XDLSWROTEEXCITINGNOVELSQZ"

on a twenty-five disc device. The prefix "X" and the suffix "QZ" are nulls used to fill out the available spaces. All one has to do then is to copy off a jumbled row from any of the twenty-five other rows of nonsense. The recipient then simply takes the message, arranges it on a machine identical to the sender's, and then looks for one row that makes sense.

This is a simple format to use but is difficult to break because each message is keyed on a different letter or letters. President Thomas Jefferson invented the device sometime during the 1790's and figured, correctly, that a machine with thirty-six discs would provide combinations to 36 factorial, or 371,993,326,789,901,217,467,999,448,150,835,200,000,000 possible combinations! For a complete consideration of codes and ciphers, their history and operating principles, see David Kahn's The Codebreakers, Macmillan, 1967. [HHC 26]

7233 wheels -- for change-ringing* it is essential that the ringer have control over the bell that simply suspending it from a moveable beam does not allow. The bell is suspended from an axle on one end of which is a wheel. The rope is attached to the wheel which controls the speed and degree of arc of the bell's swing. This also allows control over the order in which one bell of a ring is struck. [NT 1]

7234 wheels within wheels -- see "there are always wheels within wheels" [NT 12]

7235 Whemmeling Fell -- a notable high spot on the moor between Riddlesdale Lodge* and Grider's Hole*. The word "whemmel" means to upset or overturn, a state of confusion, while "fell" means a hill, mountain, or moorland ridge that is usually waste land but may be pasturage. Hence, this fictitious place is "topsy-turvy hill", an appropriate description of the location. [CW 4]

7236 "When found, make note of." -- the line is Captain Cuttle's in Charles Dickens's* David Copperfield, Ch. 15. Untile 1923, the line was the motto of the periodical Notes and Queries, an organ for the exchange of information and ideas for those engaged in research in the arts and sciences. [BH 7]

7237 "When I am from him . . ." -- see "'strange and mystical' transmigration of silk worms . . . ." [GN 15]

7238 "When lo! by Break of Morning" -- see Morley's Canzonets for Two Voices [GN 19]

7239 "when you have eliminated the impossible . . ." -- this frequently expressed Holmesian maxim is also called The Law of Improbable Truth and is stated in various ways throughout the Holmes canon [SP 8]

7240 "Where Alph . . ." -- these are lines 3-5 of Samuel Taylor Coleridge's "Kubla Khan", a fragmentary but lovely oriental dream picture written in the summer of 1797. The name Alph may be a reference to Alpheus, a Greek mythological river god. [WB 8]

7241 "Where and oh where is she?" -- the question is reminiscent of Dorothea Johnson's (1762-1816) poem, "The Blue Bells of Scotland":

"Oh where, and Oh! where is your
Highland laddie gone?
He's gone to fight the French . . ."

[NT 6]

7242 "Where got'st thou that goose look . . ." -- see "O horror, horror, horror" [FRH 22]

7243 "Where the carcase is . . ." -- PW is quoting Matthew 24:28 (KJV). The carcase is a man dead in sin, the eagles are Christ as judge. [HHC 4]

7244 where the lords of creation fear to tread -- the description of Mrs. Hodges* alludes to Alexander Pope's "An Essay on Criticism", line 625:

"For fools rush in where angels fear
to tread." [BH 10]

7245 "Where there is no love . . ." -- this quotation may be from Ovid's Ars Amatoria, but the precise source of this translation was not found. It could be a DLS misquotation as the concepts expressed appear in several places in Ovid's work in one form or another. [ie]

7246 "Where thy treasure is . . ." -- PW is quoting from Matthew 6:21, a version of the Parable of the Unjust Steward that also appears in Luke 16:1-13 [NT 10]

7247 "Where's Death and his sweetheart?" -- the lines are sung by skeletal figures in a dance of death (see The Dance of Machabree) in V, iv, 22ff. of T. L. Beddoes' Death's Jest Book**. The song is sung in a ruined Gothic cathedral at midnight. [HHC 3]

7248 whether it is better to be happy or virtuous -- the allusion is to Plato's Republic, the end of Book I, the discussion of virtue, vice, happiness and unhappiness, justice and injustice [GN 9]

7249 Which is Impossible -- the conclusion Euclid used when some proposition proved contrary to logic or observable natural laws [HHC 26]

7250 Whifflets -- a fictitious brand of cigarette that provided PW with his greatest advertising coup while working at Pym's Publicity* [MMA 3]

7251 Whiffling Round Britain -- the brilliant advertising coup created by PW which features collecting coupons from Whifflets cigarettes and saving them toward vacations, etc. One is reminded of DLS's own work with the "Mustard Club"*. [MMA 15]

7252 "while memory holds her seat" -- the line is from Hamlet, I, v, 96:

" . . . Remember thee!
Ay, thou poor ghost while memory
holds a seat
In this distracted globe. Remember
thee!
Yea, from the table of my memory
I'll wipe away all trivial fond
records,
All saws of books, all forms, all
pressures past,
That youth and observation copied
there."

The passage is part of Hamlet's response to the charges of his father's ghost. [HHC 22]

7253 Whiskey, Mr. -- see Mr. Petrovinsky [hp]

7254 whist-drive -- whist is an early version of bridge* and a whist-drive would be a progressive party, i. e. one moving from table to table for the purpose of playing whist. The purpose is to provide opportunities to change opponents from time to time. [BH 8]

7255 white bands -- see cassock [and bands] [GN 23]

7256 The White City -- the stadium

built in 1908 for the Olympic games held in North London near Wormwood Scrubs. The stadium is at the intersection of Westway and Wood Lane. [UD 19/BC 3/MMA 12]

7257 White Hart -- one of the better hotels on St. John St., Salisbury*, some way from PW's destination in Milford Hill* [WB 5]

7258 White Label -- Dewar's White Label Scotch whiskey, one of the better ones available. It is a light scotch blended by John Dewar and Sons, Ltd., of Perth, Scotland. It is 86.8 proof. [nf]

7259 white linen -- a reference to the heroines in Gothic romances who are generally dressed in white linen nightgowns, go places where they should not, and are deliberately pushed to the point of mental collapse by some crazed relative who wants her inheritance, boyfriend, or whatever for him or herself [GN 7]

7260 white linen and pipe-clay -- a reference to absolute whiteness of clothing and the requisite neatness and attention to detail when wearing such clothing. The pipe-clay refers to the fine white clay formerly used by soldiers to keep their uniform trousers, etc., white. [GN 14]

7261 White Queen -- in Lewis Carroll's* Through the Looking Glass (1872 the White Queen is one of several unusual characters. She can remember both the past and the future and, as PW reminds us, can "believe as many as six impossible things before breakfast". PW is alluding to Mr. Mellilow's* dream. See also hair dresser to the White Queen. [sf/NT 1]

7262 White Rabbit -- from Lewis Carroll's* Alice in Wonderland*, that perennially excited and babbling creature whom Alice follows down the hole to begin her adventures [BH 20]

7263 White Stag -- while there may have been or may now be a White Stag pub, it is not likely that DLS had a real place in mind given the circumstances. The use of a realistic name for a fictitious place is more typical of her approach when something unpleasant is to be associated with that place. [MMA 16]

7264 white staves -- staves carried by high ranking officers of the College of Arms* to indicate the rank of their office and to differentiate among the various officers of the College. See also Gentleman Usher of the Black Rod. Such staves are also carried by members of the Privy Council, the Lord Chamberlain, the Household Treasurer, and others. [CW 12]

7265 White Stoat -- possible a real pub, but more likely a fictitious one given the circumstances. DLS tried to avoid linking real places with unpleasantries. [MMA 16]

7266 White Swan -- there are no less than ten establishments in London with the name White Swan, one of which is a Chinese restaurant (at the time of this writing). It may, however, be assumed that DLS chose the name only because it sounded like a suitable name for a pub. She studiously avoided linking real places with illegal operations when some embarrassment might result. [MMA 12]

7267 White's -- a club established in 1693 from a coffeehouse of the same name. It is the oldest London club and is Tory in its politics. It is located on St. James's St. just South of Piccadilly. [WB 8]

7268 Whitechapel -- an area in Eastern London bordering on The City* to the West and including formerly an area of some of London's worst slums and zones of criminal activity. It was the area where Jack the Ripper operated and has been the scene of countless stories of evil, including those of Thomas Burke and Sax Rohmer. The district has been the center for all sorts of minorities from the Jews to various Oriental and central European groups. Sherlock Holmes was found in opium dens in Whitechapel on more than one occasion. It had the reputation of being the place one would go to find any sort of nefarious activity one could wish. Social reform, urban renewal, and improved policing of the area have stripped Whitechapel of its former "colorful" character and it is now entirely respectable. [dh/HHC 30/BH 6]

7269 Whitechapel Rd. -- a section of that major thoroughfare beginning

#7262 The White Rabbit from an illustration by John Tenniel.

at the center of The City* and extending outward to the North and East. Starting as Lombard St., it becomes, in turn, Fenchurch St., Aldgate, Whitechapel High St., Whitechapel Rd., Mile End Rd., etc. Its name is drawn, in this instance, from the section of London through which it travels (see above). Bill Rumm's home is located along it down an unidentifiable side street. [SP 13]

7270 Whitehall [1212] -- a London telephone exchange named for the former Tudor and Stuart palace along the Thames. Most of the palace was destroyed in a fire in 1698, but the Banqueting House still stands on the street called Whitehall in Westminster. The telephone number for Scotland Yard used to be Whitehall 1212, much more memorable than the present 230-1212. [MMA 15]

7271 Whitehall touch -- the drive to economy, often in the extreme and frequently silly; false economy [MMA 1]

7272 Whitehaven -- a community on the northwest coast of England on the Irish Sea just South of Solway Firth. It is mentioned in a limerick by Edward Lear and is where PW landed at the end of his famous trans-Atlantic flight to save his brother from the gallows. [CW 17]

7273 Whitehead, Mr. -- a banker, bank officer, perhaps lawyer (?), who will bring the Medway diamonds to the home of the Dowager Duchess of Medway* prior to her granddaughter's wedding [aq]

7274 Whit-Monday -- it follows Whit-Sunday, the seventh Sunday after Easter, also known as Pentecost*. In the Christian Church it is the day the Holy Spirit descended to the Disciples. It happened to be on a Jewish feast day celebrating fifty days from the second day of Passover. The word "whit" is for white from the custom of wearing white baptismal robes at the Feast of Pentecost. [nf]

7275 Whitsuntide -- the Christian Feast of Pentecost*. It is the Sunday falling on the fiftieth day after Easter. Whitsuntide refers to the Sunday and the two following days, formerly the English summer holidays which began the summer season. [UD 6]

7276 Whittaker -- see the genealogical chart at the back of UD [UD 4]

7277 Whittaker, Rev. Charles -- Mary Whittaker's father. See item 7276. [UD 8]

7278 Whittaker, Clara -- Mary Whittaker's* maiden great-aunt on her father's side. Clara and Agatha Dawson* ran a horse ranch together for many years. [UD 8]

7279 Whittaker, James -- the husband of Harriet Dawson*. See item 7276. [UD 8]

7280 Whittaker, Mary -- great-niece to Agatha Dawson*, a nurse, and subject of much investigative interest by PW, Parker*, and Miss Climpson* [UD 4]

7281 Whittington, Fr. -- the priest PW encounters at the "glandular rejuvenation party" given by the Rushworths*. The gentleman seems to be very carefully attuned to the current scientific theories and their potential importance to his line of work. [BC 16]

7282 Whittington -- see "Turn again, Whittington". [bc]

7283 "who dragged whom, how many times . . ." -- PW is referring to Book XXII of Homer's <u>Iliad</u> wherein the battle between Achilles and Hector is described. Achilles kills Hector and drags his body around the walls of Troy. Hector's ankles are pinned together and are tied to Achilles' chariot. The outrage is repeated on several occasions when Achilles drags the corpse around Patroclus's funeral pyre. [MMA 3]

7284 who goes there? France . . . -- PW is using the standard challenge and response format of military identification. The challenge is issued by a guard on duty, the response, which had best be prompt and correct, is given by the person challenged. In this example, France refers to the shoe with the French heel*. [GN 21]

7285 "Who hast exalted thine only son . . ." -- fully, "who hast exalted thine only Son Jesus Christ with great triumph unto thy kingdom in heaven . . .". The quotation is from the collect for the Sunday after Ascension Day. A

collect is a one sentence prayer, and there are three said regularly at matins or evensong: There is a collect for the day which is the same for that day every year, and two collects which are always the same, one for peace and one for grace. Collects are frequently chanted by the minister. [NT 12]

7286 "Who is Sylvia?" -- a famous song from Shakespeare's Two Gentlemen of Verona, IV, ii. The song opens:
"Who is Sylvia [Silvia]? What is she
That all our swains commend her?
Holy, fair, and wise is she;
The heaven such grace did lend her,
That she might admired be." [UD 7]

7287 Who Put Back the Clock -- Hawkshaw the Detective, in addition to appearing in Bullivant's The Ticket of Leave Man (see Hawkshaw) became the pseudonym of John Arthur Fraser. No such title as the one cited here appears anywhere, so we must assume that PW has adapted the situation to one typically found in such detective/ romance novels. [BH 14]

7288 "who saw him die?" -- the reference is to that rather morbid nursery poem, "Who Killed Cock Robin?" from Tommy Thumb's Pretty Song Book (ca. 1744) [MMA 5]

7289 Who's Who -- the English annual biographical dictionary first produced in 1849 and now with many imitators throughout the world, including PW. PW would not have to check his version for Sir Julian Freke*, however, as the commercial version would be most adequate. In FRH, PW suggests that the police check it to see if any of their suspects is a particularly good athlete, and Miss Meteyard* uses it in MMA to verify her suspicions about the real identity of Death Bredon*. [WB 8/ FRH 22/MMA 17]

7290 Who's Who -- not the volumes as mentioned above, but PW's own creation containing "biographies of the most unexpected people, and the most unexpected facts about the most obvious people." This is very similar to Sherlock Holmes's collection of notebooks although it seems likely that PW's would be neater as Bunter is in charge of them. Either set of notebooks would be most desirable to the modern detective bibliophile. [aq]

7291 whole blood -- siblings who share the same parents as opposed to half brothers or sisters who share only one parent [UD 14]

7292 whole pull -- two notes struck, one on the head (forward) stroke and one on the back stroke. The bell has gone 360° twice so that the rope and sally* are back where they started from. [NT 12]

7293 whole treble -- the full length of a newspaper page covering three columns [MMA 1]

7294 whole turn -- see turn [NT 11]

7295 Whoosh Vacuum-cleaner -- a product advertised through the efforts of Pym's Publicity*. The machine is fictitious. [MMA 3]

7296 "Why, how now friends! what saucy mates are you . . ." -- the lines are from John Ford's* (1586-1639?) 'Tis Pity She's a Whore, first performed in about 1633 when it was published. The play is a tragedy centering on incest, murder, and revenge. The citation is from III, ix, the Cardinal's speech. Little is known of Ford other than that he was a lawyer and that some of his works have been lost. [BH 12]

7297 why they rather choose to have a weight -- PW alludes to Shakespeare's The Merchant of Venice*, IV, i, 40ff:
"You'll ask me, why I rather choose to have
A weight of carrion flesh than to receive
Three thousand ducats . . . ."
The speaker is Shylock. [BH 18]

7298 Why We Behave Like Humans -- a study by the American anthropologist George Amos Dorsey (1868-1931), published in the U. S. in 1925 and in England in 1928. It, along with some of his other works, proved to be widely popular at the time. Dorsey was attached to the Field Museum in Chicago and is known more for his studies of American Indians. [BC 18]

7299 Whybrow, Mr. -- the surgeon who tended to the Viscount St. George's wounds after his automobile

accident [GN 10]

7300 Wick -- an important fishing town and county town in the extreme North of Scotland noted for herring curing. It is on the North Sea side of Scotland in what was County Caithness, now the Highland Region. [FRH 1]

7301 Wicked Simon -- see Dawson, Simon [UD 12]

7302 wicket-keeper -- see cricket [MMA 10]

7303 Wicks, David -- the younger partner in the law firm of Crimplesham* and Wicks, Solicitors* of Salisbury* [WB 5]

7304 widdershins -- or withershins; backwards, in reverse order, counter-clockwise [bc/CW 3/NT 2]

7305 The Widow's Tears -- a play by George Chapman*. It is an unpleasant, bitter, cynical play based on the story of the matron widow of Ephesus who is discovered weeping at the tomb of her recently deceased husband. The soldier who discovers her induces her to take food and then to become his lover. Chapman uses the version related in Petronius's Satyricon* as a basis for his play, but plots it powerfully, makes it misogynystic in the extreme, and focuses on the negative aspects of lust. A harsh comedy, there is no appeal to pity or fear. [UD 6]

7306 Wigtown Bay -- the large bay composed of the estuaries of the Rivers Cree and Fleet** which open into the larger portion of the Bay to the South [FRH 19]

7307 Wigtownshire -- a former county, now part of Dumfries and Galloway, which extended West of the River Cree from Wigtown to Bargrennan and South from Bargrennan to near the mouth of of Loch Ryan** [FRH 2]

7308 Wilbraham emeralds -- the fine emeralds that comprised the magnificent necklace stolen from Mrs. Wilbraham in April of 1914 while she was visiting at the Red House* in Fenchurch St. Paul*. They are the elusive focus of attention for much of the action of the story. [NT 2]

7309 Wilbraham, Mrs. -- the eccentric, perverse, and unforgiving old lady whose emerald necklace creates much of the difficulty mentioned above [NT 2]

7310 Wilde, J[ames] -- a ringer and composer of some considerable repute who died in 1877. He was one of several change-ringers* of the Wilde family of Cheshire. [NT 18]

7311 Wilderspin, Ezra -- the blacksmith in Fenchurch St. Paul*, and one of their bellringers. Ironically, he has the smallest, or treble, bell, yet he is the largest of the men ringing. [NT 1]

7312 Wilderspin, George -- Ezra's* son who helps repair PW's Daimler* after the accident at Frog's Bridge* [NT 2]

7313 Wilfred -- the name of an Oxford student mentioned in a conversation overheard by HV at the Hotel Resplendent in Wilvercombe* [HHC 3]

7314 Wilfrid -- a character in HV's Death 'twixt Wind and Water with whom HV is having difficulty evolving a proper characterization. PW is reminded of the Daily Mirror cartoon, "Pip Squeak", in which Wilfrid was a rabbit. [GN 15]

7315 Wilkes -- the groom at Riddlesdale Lodge* [CW 11]

7316 Wilkes, Mr. -- the gentleman, probably the layout editor at the Morning Star*, who established the deadline for the rewrite of the Nutrax* ad [MMA 8]

7317 "The will! the will! We will hear Caesar's will!" -- the line is from Julius Caesar*, III, ii, 145, and follows Antony's famous funeral oration, "Friends, Romans, countrymen . . . ." [UD 10]

7318 will-o'-the-wisp -- any goal one is deceived into chasing [BC 14]

7319 Willett Memorial Sundial -- a sundial presented to Shrewsbury College* in memory of someone named Willett who, one assumes, had some strong connection with the College [GN 5]

7320 William -- Lady Dormer's* footman [BC 17]

7321 William and Mary [bedstead] -- King William and Queen Mary ruled jointly after the forced departure of Mary's father, James II, from the throne of England. After Mary's death

in 1694, William Henry, Prince of Orange, ruled until 1702 as William III. The furniture of the period was a natural development from the Caroline period and may be considered an extension of it. The furniture tended to be dark, large, heavy, and ornate. The living and dining furniture often appears hard and uncomfortable, but the bedsteads were often masterpieces of ornamental art, especially in the support posts for the carved canopy curtain rails and for the canopy frames themselves. The styles changed abruptly to the simple curved elegance that marked the reign of William III's successor, Queen Anne. [BH P]

7322 William -- a footman* in PW's household after his marriage to HV [hp]

7323 William IV -- King of England from 1830 to 1837. Queen Victoria followed him to the throne. [CW 14]

7324 Williams -- a patient of Arthur Prendergast's* who, conveniently for Prendergast, is from Australia [te]

7325 Williams -- the other worker who sleeps, as does Frank Crutchley*, over Mr. Hancock's* garage in Great Pagford*. It is he who helps provide Crutchley's alibi for the time of William Noakes's* death. [BH 8]

7326 Williams, Mrs. -- a neighbor of Miss Climpson's* at St. George's Square* who had borrowed Miss Climpson's last penny stamps [UD 3]

7327 Williams, Nurse -- the nurse who attended Philip Boyes* just before his death. While an astute professional, she did not handle her concern regarding Boyes' death at all well. [SP 2]

7328 Williams, William -- Gladys Horrocks'* boyfriend and escort to the Plumbers' and Glaziers' Ball. Williams is a glazier. [WB 6]

7329 Williamson -- a cloakroom attendant at the Bellona Club*. He is the one described as having the "Sam Weller face"*. [BC 4]

7330 Willis [Alec] -- one of the copywriting staff at Pym's Publicity*. He is romantically driven toward Pamela Dean*, but is too much of a priggish stuffed shirt to win her until PW takes him in hand and gives him a few pointers bluntly stated. He had been a close friend of Victor Dean's before Dean turned unpleasant. [MMA 1]

7331 Willis, George -- Paggleham's* grocer and purveyor to the Wimsey family when they are at Talboys* [BH 4]

7332 willow and leather -- a reference to the bat and ball as used in cricket* [MMA 10]

7333 willow-pussy cloth -- a soft, rich fabric in that light, silvery-gray color associated with the blooms of the pussywillow [UD 9]

7334 willow-wreaths -- see twine willow-wreaths . . . [SP 4/BH P]

7335 Willy -- Gaffer Gander's* grandson who had given the old gentleman a good quality radio [HHC 26]

7336 Wilson, Annie -- a scout* at Shrewsbury College*. She works to support herself and her two children now that her husband has died. [GN 3]

7337 "Wilt thou love, cherish . . ." -- part of the traditional wedding service [SP 20]

7338 Wiltshire, Duke of -- one of the peers at the trial of the Duke of Denver*. He is fictitious. [CW 14]

7339 Wiltshire Downs -- the reference is most likely to northern Wiltshire and that area just to the South of the Thames known as Marlborough Downs. The area is due West of London. The Downs feature a rolling chalk landscape with dramatic wooded high points. [BC 20]

7340 Wilvercombe -- a fictitious town on the southwest coast of England. It is futile to speculate about any relationships to real places as DLS deliberately worked to obscure such relationships in her effort to create a fictional locale. [HHC 1]

7341 Wilvercombe case -- a reference to the events recorded in HHC [GN 2]

7342 Wilvercombe Sanitary Steam Laundry -- the fictitious company that laundered Paul Alexis's* belongings [HHC 4]

7343 Wimbledon Common -- not to be con-

fused with Wimbledon Park near where the tennis championships are played, the Common is South of London's western regions immediately East of Richmond Park. Arthur Prendergast's* home is located near there. [te/UD 15]

7344 Wimbles -- PW's nickname among his acquaintances at the Foreign Office* [HHC 26]

7345 Wimsey, Bredon Delagardie Peter -- mentioned at his birth as recorded in "Haunted Policeman" (1936) and again in "Talboys" (1942) as a central figure. He is PW and HV's first son. [hp/t/UD BN]

7346 Wimsey genealogy --
the Sieur de Guimsey (?) of France
Roger de Guimsey (fl. ca. 1066) was the eldest of three sons who earned the family lands in Norfolk as a gift from William the Conqueror
Fulk de Guimsey -- son of Roger, he got the manor at Denver (the real Denver, not DLS's creation)
Fulk de Guimsey -- eldest son of Fulk. The second son, Roger, founded the line of Irish Wimseys.
Peter de Guimsey -- the eldest son of Fulk, Jr., fl. ca. 1200
Roger de Wimsey
Gerald, 1st Baron de Wimsey, d. 1300
Roger, 2nd Baron de Wimsey
Peter, 3rd Baron de Wimsey and Roger's eldest, dsp*
Ralph, 4th Baron de Wimsey, Roger's second son
Gerald, 5th Baron de Wimsey, Ralph's son, built Denver Castle (torn down during the Civil War) b. 1307, d. 1370, married Margaret, daughter and heiress of Sir Thomas Bredon
Ralph, 6th Baron de Wimsey, 1st Earl of Denver, d. 1405. Ralph's third son, Peter is the earliest family connection for the 1st Duke, 2nd Creation (see Charles)
Gerald, 2nd Earl, eldest son of Ralph, dsp*
Ralph, 3rd Earl, second son of Ralph, dsp*
Roger, 4th Earl of Denver
Gerald, 5th Earl of Denver
Peter, 6th Earl of Denver, d. 1499 as 1st Duke of Denver, created by Henry VII in the late 1480's after the battle at Bosworth Field that put Henry Tudor on the throne as Henry VII
Richard, 2nd Duke of Denver
Roger, 3rd Duke of Denver
Gerald, 4th Duke of Denver (fl. ca. 1558 ff.)
Henry, 5th Duke of Denver (the one PW calls "greedy" in BH)
Christian, 6th Duke of Denver; his daughter married her cousin, Col. John Wimsey, and from this union the Dukes of the Second Creation are descended
Paul, 7th Duke of Denver; he was created Knight of the Garter and Hereditary Keeper of the Privy Stair
Peter, 8th Duke of Denver, is Paul's half brother and the 1st Viscount St. George
George, 9th Duke of Denver
Thomas, 10th Duke of Denver; d. ca. 1775
George, 11th Duke of Denver
William, 12th Duke of Denver, dsp*, the title reverted to the Crown
Charles, 13th Duke of Denver; he was created Duke and Viscount in 1820 and is rightly titled 1st Duke of the Second Creation, but the original numbering has been retained as if the succession had not been broken
George, 14th Duke of Denver, 2nd Duke of the 2nd Creation
Mortimer Gerald, 15th Duke of Denver and 3rd Duke of the Second Creation who died in 1911 of a broken neck, the result of a fall from a horse when hunting. He is PW's father. His widow is the wonderfully charming Dowager Duchess.
Gerald Christian, 16th Duke of Denver and 4th Duke of the Second Creation. He is PW's older brother.

Mortimer Gerald, the 15th Duke, married Honoria Lucasta Delagardie, and their children were Gerald, Peter, and Mary. Gerald married Helen, the cold prude, and they had Gerald, the Viscount St. George*, and Winifred, about whom we know nothing. PW married Harriet Vane and had Bredon, Roger, and Paul. Mary married Chief Insp. Charles Parker* and had Charles Peter and Mary Lucasta. For more complete details, see The Wimsey Family by C. W. Scott-Giles.

7347 Wimsey, Gerald -- see Viscount St. George

7348 Wimsey, Gerald Christian -- Viscount St. George, Duke of Denver, Peer of the United Kingdom of Great

Britain and Ireland, brother of PW and Lady Mary, and Duke during all of the PW stories. He is basically a decent and dull sort of man who has a great deal of money and who runs a good farm. He is not at all like PW, and is even known to have rebuked PW mildly for his interest in detection, a position one suspects is changed by the events of CW. His well-intentioned stuffiness appears again in the form of his objections to Lady Mary's marriage to Charles Parker*, but PW controls that situation, too. One suspects that he doesn't like HV very well either, but it is his wife, Helen, who is the opposition in that marriage. [passim]

7349 Wimsey, Gerald de [original] -- PW is referring to Gerald, 1st Baron Wimsey, the first titled Wimsey. The title was granted by Edward I in 1289 for services to the Crown. Gerald died in 1300. However, as the Siege of Acre took place between 1189 and 1191, PW is mistaken, but understandably so. In a letter to C. W. Scott-Giles in February, 1936, DLS explains that, "It seems more likely, however, that the incident occurred during one of the later crusades and was transferred to the earlier date by the antiquarian enthusiasm of the family chronicler." The reference should be to Fulk de Guimsey, great-grandfather to the Gerald mentioned. See Wimsey genealogy. [SP 21]

7350 Wimsey, Dr. Gervase -- Dean* of St. Paul's, London, and a martyr under Queen Mary I, the devoutly Roman Catholic daughter of Henry VIII and of his first wife, Catherine of Aragon. Mary ruled from 1553 - 1558. [BH E2]

7351 Wimsey, Harriet Deborah [Vane] -- as PW's wife, HV appears in only two of the short stories, the last two, and in the last novel, BH. The couple have three sons, no other children are mentioned, and seem thoroughly happy with their domestic life together. She and PW were married on October 8, 1935, in Oxford. She is the only daughter of the late Henry Vane, M. D., of Great Pagford*, Hertfordshire, and the late Mrs. Vane. Her escape from the gallows is recounted in SP; her work in helping to solve the murder of Paul Alexis* is detailed in HHC. She flatly refuses PW's proposals of marriage in both books. GN is very much HV's novel, and the reluctance to deal with PW's proposals is still there until they have had a chance to function as equals, a situation provided by the cloistered nature of Shrewsbury College* where HV is the insider and PW is the visitor, and encouraged by some astute advice to HV from Miss de Vine*. GN concludes happily with one of literature's most famous proposals of marriage. See also items 4748 and 5250. [hp/t/SP 1/HHC 1/BH P]

7352 Wimsey, Helen -- the Duchess of Denver, Gerald's wife, mother of Gerald and Winifred Wimsey. She and PW are not on good terms with one another, his reference to her as "straitlaced" being one of the kinder ones. She is described as the one who does not like to let her emotions show and who, therefore, does not give an impression of open warmth and friendliness. One is left with the feeling that she is cold and distant. The Duke apparently thinks so, too. In SP she is presented in the same light, but with the added dimension of priggishness, a character trait that is allowed to blossom fully in BH with its companion, snobbishness. [passim]

7353 Wimsey, Henry -- the brother of Gervase Wimsey* and 5th Duke of Denver. "Greed was one of his leading characteristics." These brothers follow the Wimsey tradition of having someone in each camp during times of civil and political unrest. Gervase died a martyr to Mary I's Catholicism while Henry raised her banner in Norfolk. This trait helped assure the family's survival. [BH E2]

7354 Wimsey, Lady Mary -- "Polly", sister to Gerald and PW and daughter of Mortimer Gerald and Honoria Lucasta Delagardie Wimsey**. She has violet-blue eyes, blonde hair, is tall and slender, and attempted to do some nursing work as a volunteer during WW I. It was at this time that she developed her rather confused socialist leanings as a result of her liason with George Goyles*, a romance that was terminated at her brother's command--or at least he thought it had been terminated at his command. She then took up with Denis Cathcart*, but upon his death and the subsequent demonstration of Goyles's true colors, she begins to notice PW's

good friend, Charles Parker*. By the time of SP, she and Parker are in love and PW clears the way for their marriage. Their marriage appears to be a loving and stable one, and they have two children, Charles Peter and Mary Lucasta. They live at 12A Great Ormond St.*, Parker's old bachelor flat, but they have expanded it into a maisonette*. She helps PW with his investigations in MMA, an outgrowth of the delightful encounter with his nephew, young "Peterkin". [CW 1 and passim]

7355 Wimsey, Matthew -- PW's poor cousin who "works" at Duke's Denver* and who is preparing a family history of the Wimseys in a leisurely fashion. PW does respect Matthew's knowledge about all the "antiquarian stuff" at Bredon Hall*. [BH E2]

7356 Wimsey, Mortimer -- "mad as a hatter and founded a new religion with himself as its only follower." Lord Mortimer Wimsey is the famous "Hermit of the Wash" who liked to be addressed as "Ichthus". He wore only fish skins to preserve modesty and had shoulder-length yellow hair, bleached that color from its constant exposure to the sun. He was known among the locals as "Old Scaley". He died ca. 1815 in an attempt to swim out into The Wash* to a vision of Jesus. His delusion was that he honestly thought himself to be one of the fish netted by St. Peter, and, ironically, his body was found by a fisherman netting fish on The Wash. [BH E2]

7357 Wimsey, Mortimer Gerald Bredon -- the 15th Duke of Denver and 3rd Duke of the Second Creation. He was born ca. 1855 and died in 1911, the victim of a fall from a horse while hunting. He is the father of Gerald, the 16th Duke, PW, and Lady Mary. His wife is Honoria Lucasta, the Dowager Duchess. [aq/UD BN]

7358 Wimsey, Paul -- the third (?) son of PW and HV who is mentioned only in "Talboys" and in "The Wimsey Papers" where he is called the second son. He is probably named for PW's favorite uncle, Paul Delagardie*. [t]

7359 Wimsey, Lord Peter Death Bredon -- unlike Sherlock Holmes, there is very little left to question about PW. His Who's Who* entry is provided for us as is a biographical sketch by his uncle, Paul Delagardie* (both are available in copies of UD), so a detailed biographical sketch here is superfluous. Some notes are, however, appropriate here to fill in details not specifically addressed in the canon. First, PW's two middle names are pronounced in ways that their spelling does not indicate. Death is pronounced to rhyme with teeth, and Bredon has the emphasis on the first syllable with a long "e" as "breedun". Also, a detailed family history has been prepared by the late C. W. Scott-Giles from his correspondence with DLS and is entitled The Wimsey Family. This little volume is an invaluable aid to a fuller understanding of just who and what PW is and greatly aids our general understanding of the history of the Wimsey family as is hinted at in the tour of Bredon Hall in BH. Lastly, Mr. G. A. Lee, a fellow member of the Dorothy L. Sayers Historical and Literary Society has prepared "The Wimsey Saga: A Chronology" which is reproduced in part here. The "Saga" is the perfect guide to what happened when in the PW canon.

Date	Event and Source
1890	PW born, BN, Who's Who entry
1895	Lady Mary born, CW
1903	HV born, HHC/SP
1911	death of PW's father, Gerald becomes 16th Duke, BN
1918	(October) PW badly wounded at Caudry, Cpl. Padgett* saves his life BN/CW/GN
1919	(January) Mervyn Bunter becomes PW's manservant, BH
1921	case of the Attenbury emeralds (diamonds) [not written up], BN/WB/CW
1921	(summer) case of the Footsteps That Ran, LPVB
1922	(November) the murder of Sir Reuben Levy, WB
1923	(October 13) Gerald, 16th Duke of Denver, accused of the mur-
to	der of Denis Cathcart*, CW
1924	(January) Gerald acquitted of murder charge at trial in the House of Lords, CW
1922	HV at Shrewsbury College, Oxford; earns First in English in 1925, GN
1927	(April to June 29) case of Mary

#7359 Ian Carmichael as PW in the BBC production of CW. BBC copyright photograph.

Whittaker, total eclipse of the sun, UD

1927 (November) murder of General Fentiman*, Parker* promoted to Det. Chief Insp., BC

1928 (March) HV living with Philip Boyes, SP

1929 (February) HV and Philip Boyes separate, SP

1929 (June 23) poisoning of Philip Boyes, HV accused of his murder, SP

1929 (December 13[?]) HV's first trial concluded with a hung jury, SP

1929 (December 30 [?]) Parker engaged to Lady Mary Wimsey, SP

1929 to 1930 (December 31) PW's first visit to Fenchurch St. Paul*, notable peal rung (to January 1), NT

1930 (January 12[?]) HV acquitted of murder of Philip Boyes, SP

1930 (April-May) case of the corpse in the churchyard, NT

1930 (summer[?]) Parker and Lady Mary wed, HHC

1930 (August) case of the murdered artist, FRH

1930 to 1931 (December 24) solution to the case of the corpse in the churchyard, NT

1931 (June 18-July 8) the Wilvercombe* murder case, HHC

1931 (July[?]) HV abroad, GN

1932 (June) HV returns to England, GN

1933 to 1933 (May 25) murder at Pym's Publicity* and destruction of drug smuggling ring (July), MMA

1934 (June) HV at Shrewsbury College* for the Gaudy, GN

1935 (March to May) case of the college poltergeist; PW and HV engaged, GN

1935 (October 8-11) PW and HV marry, eventful honeymoon at Talboys, visit to Denver Ducis, BH

1936 (January[?]) execution of Pagglеham* murderer, BH

1936 (November[?]) birth of Bredon Wimsey, first son of PW and HV, hp/sf

1942 (September) case of the missing peaches; PW and HV now have three sons, t

7360 Wimsey, Roger -- see Uncle Roger [BH E2]

7361 Wimsey, Roger -- PW and HV's second (?) son. It is unclear if Roger is the second son or Paul. [t]

7362 Wimsey, Lord Roger -- according to PW, an "acceptable Wimsey" who wrote poetry and who died young. He was a friend of Sir Philip Sidney's*. It is not likely that Lord Roger and Uncle Roger are one in the same. [BH E2]

7363 Wimsey, Lady Sarah -- an earlier Wimsey who "married into the Severn-and-Thameses", and who is represented at Bredon Hall* by a piece of china on which she had done a painting. See also Mirabelle, Countess of Severn and Thames. [BH E2]

7364 Wimsey, Simon -- one of the elusive Wimseys who is reputed to have been a pirate. Not even Matthew Wimsey* knows much about him. DLS seems to have had a fondness for piratical miscreants named Simon (see Dawson, Simon) as there is one in UD as well. At least the piratical Dawson's descendants helped restore the family name, something that can't be said for all of the Wimseys. [BH E2]

7365 Wimsey, Susan -- see Lady Susan [BH E2]

7366 Wimsey, Thomas -- the tenth of the Wimsey dukes, who died ca. 1775. PW describes him as "that awful ill-tempered-looking brute." [BH E2]

7367 Wimsey, Winifred -- daughter of the 16th Duke, PW's brother, and Helen, she is mentioned in a letter on "The Wimsey Chin" published by DLS in <u>The Times</u> in 1937. She is never mentioned in the stories and novels other than as "my sister" in a comment by Lord St. George*. [GN 9]

7368 Wimsey's Standard Poets -- see "O Turpitude . . ." [UD 23]

7369 Winbottle, Mrs. -- the housekeeper and charlady at Miss Climpson's* apartment building on St. George's Sq.* [UD 3]

7370 Winchester -- an ancient city and once capital of Saxon England. There is a famous cathedral and public school*, technically England's oldest having been founded in 1382 by William of Wykeham, and much of historic interest dating back to William the Conqueror. The city is a few miles North and slightly East of Southampton in Hampshire. PW's dentist, Dr. Lamplough*, went to school at Winchester. [te/UD

20/MMA 10]

7371 Winchester -- a character in HV's novel, <u>Death 'twixt Wind and Water</u>

7372 wind -- see put[s] the wind up [HHC 3/GN 12]

7373 wind -- see punch in the wind [MMA 4]

7374 windchest -- the pressurized air reservoir that forces air through the pipes of an organ when a key is depressed on the keyboard or pedal work of a nonelectric instrument [NT 2]

7375 Winderpane -- Windowpane, one of PW's nicknames from his days in the Army; a reference to his monocle [GN 17]

7376 winding sheet -- grave clothes or shroud [BH P]

7377 Windle -- a fictitious place probably patterned after Kendal, known for the manufacture of shoes and boots, in the Lake District of north-western England [SP 7]

7378 Windon St. -- a street in Stapley* [CW 11]

7379 window-bill -- an advertisement meant for display in a shop window [MMA 17]

7380 windscreen-wiper -- a windshield wiper [GN 5]

7381 windward -- in the direction from which the wind is blowing [NT 1]

7382 windy -- a shortened variation on "got the wind up"*; to become alarmed [NT 14]

7383 wine of the country -- the local drink. In Scotland, Scotch whis-key, blended or unblended, light or dark, would be the proper choice. [FRH 1]

7384 Wingate, Mr. -- Master of the Chelsea* workhouse where the body came from that was found in Mr. Thipps's* bathtub [WB 12]

7385 Winsor and Newton -- Britain's best known suppliers of equip-ment, etc., to artists, still located at 51 Rathbone Place, London, W1 [FRH 12]

7386 Winter Gardens -- an entertainment center in Wilvercombe*, it may have featured a glass-enclosed room (conser-vatory) probably inspired by the Crys-tal Palace* or the Paris Conservatoire. [HHC 10]

7387 Winter, George -- a person mur-dered by Black Ralph of Herriot-ting** in 1674. The spot is marked by Dead Man's Post* and the whole business is fictitious. [bc]

7388 Winter, Mrs. Lucy -- William Grimbold's longtime friend and mistress, a recent widow [ae]

7389 Winterbottom, Det. Insp. -- the police officer assigned to inves-tigate the murder of Coreggio Plant*. The Insp. receives considerable help from PW, but their solutions to the crime differ. In a rather remarkable conclusion, PW admits a preference for Winterbottom's solution. [nf]

7390 Winterlake, Mr. -- an otherwise unidentifiable author of a book on the Earl of Essex. He and his book are fictitious. [GN 1]

7391 Winthrop, Theodore -- his mansion is burglarized by The Society* [ab]

7392 Wintrington -- a millionaire patient of Sir Julian Freke*. He controlled the finances of five coun-tries and had attempted suicide. [WB 11]

7393 wireless -- the now archaic term for radio and the attendant trans-mission and reception apparatus. The medium was in its infancy when DLS wrote most of the PW stories. [np/HHC 12]

7394 Wisbech -- a flourishing market town, the center of a rich flower and fruit growing area. It ranks next to Cambridge for architectural interest in the area. The town is on the River Nene on the A47 route to the East and North of Peterborough. [NT 12]

7395 With her sallie cut short . . . -- PW has created his own version of an "anonymous little ditty" that was popular as a college song at the turn of the century and later. The title is "Where, Oh Where, Has My Little Dog Gone", but it is the dog's ears that are cut short and its tail that is cut long. [NT 6]

7396 "With my good sword I plough . .

." -- from "Hybrias the Cretan"* [BH 5]

7397 "With the big sugar nippers . . ." -- this not-quite-accurate quotation is from the Rev. Richard Harris Barham's "A Lay of St. Gengulphus", 1. 79. Gengulphus is murdered and the criminals dismember him:

"Thus, limb from limb, they dismembered him
So entirely, that e'en when they came to his wrists
With those great sugar-nippers they nipp'd off his 'flippers',
As the Clerk, very flippantly, term'd his fists."

Barham would have us believe that it is from the fictitious St. Gengulphus that our expression "By Jingo!" derives. See also The Ingoldsby Legends. [NT 17]

7398 "With vollies of eternal babble" -- from Samuel Butler's* Hudibras*, Part 3, Canto 2, line 453 [UD 5]

7399 Wither [George] -- English poet and essayist (1588-1667), a convert to Puritanism and a military participant for that cause during the Civil War [UD 17]

7400 withers -- the ridge between the shoulder bones of a horse [HHC 26]

7401 Withers -- a valet on the staff of the block of flats where Horace Mountjoy* lived [MMA 15]

7402 Withers, George -- a resident of Paggleham* who Mrs. Ruddle* thinks stole Aggie Twitterton's* hens. Given the fact that Mrs. Ruddle's son was a suspect in the matter does not make her an unbiased source. [BH 1]

7403 Withers, P. C. -- a constable who walks the beat near that of P. C. Burt* [hp]

7405 Wodehouse, P. G. -- Pelham Grenville Wodehouse (1881-1975) was one of the great English 20th C. humorous writers of stories and novels. His creation of the omni-capable butler/ valet, Jeeves, ranks as one of light literature's more inspired events. PW does resemble strongly the fair and somewhat silly-looking Bertie Wooster* whom Wodehouse had Jeeves protect, but the resemblance is only superficial even if intentional. Among Wodehouse's efforts are: Leave it to Psmith, The Inimitable Jeeves, and The Code of the Woosters, all early works that DLS would have known. Wodehouse was knighted in 1975. [UD 6/MMA 1]

7406 Wolsey's great unfinished quadrangle -- Thomas, Cardinal Wolsey (1475?-1530) arranged to take over various monastic structures in Oxford and began what he called Cardinal College. After his fall from the grace of Henry VIII, the College became Christ Church College, but the cloisters meant to enclose the quadrangle were never completed. [GN 8]

7407 "The women also looked pale and wan." -- this chapter heading quotation is from Part II of Bunyan's Pilgrim's Progress* which recounts Christiana's progress to the Celestial City. The reference is a reflection upon Lady Mary's self-induced difficulties and upon Mrs. Grimethorpe's* ugly circumstances induced by her husband's insane jealousy of her exotic beauty. Both women appear in Ch. IV of CW. The quote is taken from that part of Bunyan's story where Christiana, her children, and Mercy enter the Valley of the Shadow of Death in the company of Mr. Great-Heart, their protector and conductor. The paragraph reads:

"When they were entered upon this valley, they thought that they heard a groaning as of dying men--a very great groaning. They thought also that they did hear words of lamentation, spoken as of some in extreme torment. These things made the boys to quake, the women also looked pale and wan; but their guide bid them be of good comfort." [CW 4]

7408 Women in Love -- a novel (1920) by D. H. Lawrence*. The book is a philosophical consideration of Lawrence's beliefs regarding the nature of sensual relationships in modern society. [BC 18]

7409 women in the Gospels [They do what they can like the] -- those women, while often funtioning as important catalysts, rarely initiate action. They are supporters and facilitators, but they are also generally kept out of the main stream of action. It is to be noted that none of Jesus's Disciples

was female. [BC 16]

7410 Women's College -- see Shrewsbury College [BH P]

7411 Women's Institute -- The National Federation of Women's Institutes was founded in 1915 to improve and develop conditions of rural life. There is a branch at Fenchurch St. Paul and in Paggleham**. By 1978, there were over 400,000 members in almost 9300 branches. Activities are social, educational, and practical, but not political. The organization is patterned after a model developed in Canada and now administers country markets (with an annual turnover of a million pounds) and a small residential college. [NT 4/BH 14]

7412 Woodbines [packet of] -- cigarettes of the Wills Woodbine brand, the classic cheap, small cigarette. They are still available. [NT 4]

7413 woodcock -- see "springe for his . . ." [BC 13]

7414 Woodhurst, Mr. -- an employee of Pym's Publicity* who is not otherwise identified [MMA 6]

7415 Woodley, Babs -- one of the de Momerie crowd who goes berserk at one of their Friday night entertainments when the cocaine fails to arrive [MMA 9]

7416 woodlouse -- any one of several small, wingless insects of the order Corrodentia. They live under bark, in walls, and among old books and papers. [CW 13]

7417 Woodstock Rd. -- a North-South road in central Oxford. St. Giles's St. splits at the War Memorial, becoming Woodstock Rd. on the West and Banbury Rd. on the East. Somerville College, DLS's alma mater, is on Woodstock Rd. It leads to Woodstock where Winston Churchill was born at Blenheim Palace. [GN 18]

7418 Woodstock typewriter -- a machine first marketed in 1914 and later taken over by the R. C. Allen Corp., manufacturers of various business machines. The company was one of the first to introduce an electric machine during the 1920's, but only the keys were electrically operated, not the carriage return. The Allen Co. reintroduced the Woodstock in 1953--low demand and WW II had forced it out of the market for a while. They are no longer produced. [SP 11]

7419 Woodward -- General Fentiman's* manservant [BC 6]

7420 Woolf, [Adeline] Virginia -- English novelist, essayist and critic (1882-1941). She belonged to the Bloomsbury* Group, writers who met from 1906 on, and she was a contemporary of James Joyce. Like Joyce, she experimented with style and language in her work, especially in the use of the interior monologue and stream-of-consciousness techniques. To the Lighthouse is, perhaps, her most famous effort. [BC 18]

7421 Woollcott, Rev. Christopher -- a former rector at Fenchurch St. Paul*, author of History of the Bells of Fenchurch St. Paul. Both he and the book are fictitious. [NT 2]

7422 Woolsack -- the usual seat of the Lord Chancellor* in the House of Lords. It is armless and backless and is a large square bag of wool covered with red cloth. Thought to have been adopted during the reign of Edward III (1327-77) as a reminder of the importance of wool and the wool trade to England, "Woolsack" has since come to be an allusive nickname for the office of Lord Chancellor as well. [aq]

7423 Woolworth, Mr. -- the famous variety store chain founded by Frank W. Woolworth. The chain was, during the early and middle part of the 20th C., one of the most successful of the low-priced variety store firms. They are still in business, but the English stores are now operated by a different company under the Woolworth name. [HHC 31/MMA 7/BH 6]

7424 Wooster, Bertie -- the quintessential "silly ass" Englishman, a creation of P. G. Wodehouse*. There are many parallels between Wooster and PW, very likely deliberate ones, but the monocle, the fatuous language, and the appearance of naive innocence are especially notable. Wooster's valet is Jeeves, and Bunter is of a similar mold. Such characterizations were immensely popular during the 1920's and 30's in England. For a perfectly Woosterian exchange in the PW canon,

read the last five paragraphs of chapter 31 in HHC. [MMA 1]

7425 wopses -- a mispronunciation of wasps [BH 15]

7426 "The word, and nought else . . ." -- HV is quoting from "The Iliad", a poem by minor British poet Humbert Wolfe (1886-1940), 11. 3-8. The poem reflects perfectly the sentiment expressed by Mrs. Bendick* immediately prior to HV's quotation. Wolfe's poem seems to have been published not long before the action of GN's early chapters (1934). [GN 3]

7427 Worcester, martlets of -- see martlets of Worcester [GN 13]

7428 Worde, Wynkyn de -- the better known name of Jan van Wynkyn, an assistant to William Caxton* from 1477 who assumed control of Caxton's business in 1491 after the latter's death. At least 700 works are known to have been printed by de Worde, but his probably only represents half of his output. He was first to print music in England with movable type, and made the first use of Italic type in England. Therefore, the 1493 "Golden Legend"* sought by PW in WB is one of his earliest works after succeeding to Caxton's business. It is the third English edition and is among his most notable accomplishments as a printer.

7429 "Words, words, words" -- intentionally or otherwise, PW is quoting Hamlet's famous response (II, ii, 194) to Polonius's question, "What do you read, my Lord?" in the famous "fishmonger" scene when Hamlet feigns insanity for the old man's benefit or confusion [GN 14]

7430 The words of Mercury . . . -- PW is observing that the discussion of messages, hence Mercury, that relate to their investigations are far less pleasant than the songs, hence Apollo, they had enjoyed together in the antique shop [GN 20]

7431 Wordsworth -- William Wordsworth, the great English Romantic poet (1770-1850). His publication, in 1798, of Lyrical Ballads is considered a turning point in English poetry. His more famous works include "Lines Written Above Tintern Abbey", "The Prelude" and "Intimations of Immortality". [CW 2/UD 9]

7432 workhouse -- a center established to house and to provide work for the unemployed poor of a specific area. In 1922, J. J. Clarke wrote in Social Administration that, "The workhouse or institution . . . is the foundation of all indoor relief." [WB 9]

7433 world and time enough -- an allusion of Andrew Marvell's (1621-78) "To His Coy Mistress":

"Had we but world enough and time,
This coyness, Lady, were no crime."

[BH 4]

7434 "world without end, Amen" -- the conclusion to the Gloria Patri. One common musical setting for this hymn of praise is by Charles Meineke (1782-1850). [NT 5/BH 10]

7435 Worm That Turned -- a play for which Mr. Rosencrantz* tried to cast PW as the lead. PW must have shown great promise as he was offered £500 a week to take the role--an astronomical sum at the time. [HHC 23]

7436 Worplesham -- the "Worplesham" business refers to the case involving Insp. Sugg's* somewhat limited talents while PW and Parker are becoming involved with the Dawson problem. The reference is a DLS creation and the place is fictitous. [UD 2]

7437 Wort, Dr. Jabez K. -- an American diplomat of considerable rank mentioned by Sir Reuben Levy* in his diary as having been a dinner guest in the Levy home [WB 5]

7438 Worth's -- a famous Parisian fashion house established by an Englishman, Charles Frederick Worth, born in Bourne, Lincolnshire, in 1825. Worth was self-made, had worked for Swan and Edgar* in London for a time, and then went to Paris in 1846 to join the couturiers Gagelin & Opigez. He was the first man to take up dress designing and was a favorite of the Empress Eugenie. A Worth wedding dress was a design which would not necessarily be bought at a Worth salon (not store), but could be fitted by Worth-approved couturiers. [BH P]

7439 Worthing -- located on the coast of West Sussex South of London, it is a popular seaside resort twelve miles from Brighton. Part of Mrs.

Prendergast's* family lived there. [te]

7440 Worthington -- a famous British beer and ale, still available [BC 4/FRH 1]

7441 Worthington, Lady -- an apparently sharp-tongued lady toward whom Bunter is not favorably disposed. He feels that PW earn his nobleman's income just having to put up with her at dinner while keeping his "undoubted powers of repartee" tightly reigned. [WB 2]

7442 "A worthless life" -- the speech is Athulf's in IV, iii, 6-7 of T. L. Beddoes' Death's Jest Book**. Athulf has a short soliloquy under Amala's windows and these lines are a part of it. He is referring to his own life. [HHC 7]

7443 Wrayburn, Mrs. -- the niece of Lady Hermione Creethorpe* and bridge partner for Mark Sambourne*. Her costume for Sir Charles Deverill's* Christmas costume party is meant to represent a backgammon* board. [qs]

7444 Wrayburn, Mrs. Rosanna -- the very old and incapacitated great-aunt to Norman Urquhart* and Philip Boyes*. The terms of her will provide the motive for SP. In her youth she had been very rebellious and notorious, having gone on the stage as Cremorna Garden*, earning a good deal more than a reputation for herself. [SP 7]

7445 "The Wreck of the Hesperus" -- the poem by American writer Henry Wadsworth Longfellow (1807-1882), long a favorite for reciting at school functions as it has all of the favorite Victorian emotions and would be a certain hit at such events. It would, of course, have been accompanied by all the standard elocutionary posturings then popular. [GN 17]

7446 Wren, Jenny -- the business name of Fanny Cleaver in Dickens's Our Mutual Friend. She was a tiny girl, but deformed, and worked as a doll's dressmaker. She was, however, shrewd and was able to support her father and herself. While Sylvia Marriott's* comments are not quite Dickensian in style, they do get the point across. [SP 8]

7447 Wrigley, Miss -- a former member of the Senior Common Room at Shrewsbury College*. See also SCR. [GN 8]

7448 Wrinching, Sir Wigmore -- the fictitious Attorney-General who prosecutes the Duke of Denver* at the Duke's trial in the House of Lords [CW 14]

7449 Writer to the Signet in Edinburgh -- originally a clerk* who prepared documents for authentication by application of the Royal or Privy seal or signet, today he is a solicitor* who draws up Crown writs, charters, and other legal documents and who conducts cases in the Court of Session where civil cases are heard. As Edinburgh is Scotland's capital, such a court would necessarily be located there. In Scotland, the Society of Writers to His (or Her) Majesty's Signet would be the bar association open only to those who have passed the appropriate examinations. [ss]

7450 Writtle, Marchioness of -- her famous diamond necklace was found in the Lord Chancellor's Woolsack** as a result of some of PW's "silly" questions [aq]

7451 The Wrong Box -- a "detective" story built around some black humor. It is by R. L. Stevenson. See Finsbury, Michael. [HHC 13]

7452 wrong side of the blanket -- a euphemism for illegitimate [HHC 32]

7453 Wyck -- as presented, a fictitious community to the East and South of Little Doddering* [bc]

7454 Wylder's Hand -- a mystery novel (1864) by J. Sheridan LeFanu* [NT 9]

7455 Wyndham's -- the Hon. Freddy Arbuthnot's* club, The Wyndham Club, at 13 St. James's Square was founded in 1828. It was later amalgamated with the Marlborough Club* to become the Marlborough-Wyndham. [WB 2]

(X-Y-Z)

7456 Y. M. C. A. -- Young Men's Christian Association, a service organization known throughout the western world for clean, inexpensive housing, food, and, frequently, athletic facilities. It is nonsectarian, emphasizing mostly its efforts to provide clean and decent residential facilities. Recently, however, there has been a growing emphasis on "family centers" with recreation, craft, and counselling programs,etc. [WB 9]

7457 Yale -- a brand of lock devised by Linus Yale, Jr., of Connecticut. It is the standard form of lock in much of the world. The basic design is that of the pin-tumbler variety and, because it is relatively secure in relation to its modest price, it has gained and held the public's trust. [WB 2]

7458 Yale things -- not the lock as above, which is a mortise lock*, but the dead-bolt variety housed in a cast metal case fastened to the inside surface of the door. It is not as secure as the mortise lock. [BH 8]

7459 yard arm -- either end of a yard on a square-rigged ship, a yard being a spar at right angles to a mast and used to support a sail. The reference here to "hanged from a yard arm" is accurate in that yard arms were most convenient for that purpose. [t]

7460 Ye Cosye Corner -- one of the fictitious tea shops in Windle* frequented by Miss Climpson* during her search for the nurse/companion to Rosanna Wrayburn*. "Ye" should be pronounced as "the". [SP 16]

7461 Ye Olde Worlde Tudor Tea-Shoppe -- a PW creation in reference to a possible place to stop for tea with HV. The comment about synthetic pastries is, perhaps, meant to be critical of the shop's name as such constructions are, themselves, synthetic contrivances meant to suggest great age to an unsuspecting public. [GN 19]

7462 "Ye'll no fickle Tammas Yownie." -- this quote is from John Buchan, Baron Tweedsmuir's (1875-1940) novel, Huntingtower (1922), at the end of Ch. 14. Yownie is one of a gang of boys called "The Gorbals Diehards", and the line is used by the gang's leader, Dugal Crombie, to praise Yownie. "Fickle" is used here to mean to puzzle or to fluster. [GN 17]

7463 yellow-dog dingo -- the phrase alludes to the line in Kipling's "Sing-Song of Old Man Kangaroo": "Old Man Kangaroo first, Yellow-Dog Dingo behind", from the Just So Stories. Specifically it refers to Canis dingo, the red-brown wild dog of Australia. "Yellow-dog Dingo" is just a redoubling of effort to suggest a cur, a mongrel, or a street-wise animal. [MMA 7]

7464 Yellow Peril -- most likely a fictitious pub given both the name and the circumstances. The name refers to the vast population of Orientals and the attitude toward them quite popular even today, although slighly less xenophobic names are used at present. The term "yellow peril" was popularized by that sensationalist author of the Fu Manchu stories, Sax Rohmer. [MMA 16]

7465 Yelsall Manor -- in Norfolk*, it is the fictitious home of Dr. Conyers* [dh]

7466 Yelverton Arms -- another of the pubs, fictitious, that is suspected of being a part of the cocaine* smuggling system described [MMA 17]

7467 Yeomen -- Gilbert and Sullivan's* The Yeomen of the Guard which opened at the Savoy on October 3, 1888. This opera is different from the others in that it is tragic and involves more realistic people in a most real setting, the Tower of London. [SP 5]

7468 York -- the well-preserved medieval city in Yorkshire, a focal point of English history for almost 2000 years. Its cathedral, the largest in England, is a glory of stained glass, and has recently undergone extensive repair and renovation. York Minster* is the cathedral for the only other Anglican archbishop outside Canterbury. [GN 18]

7469 York and Lancaster -- probably a fictitious pub* given the situation. The name refers to the Wars of the Roses and to the two family factions involved. The wars were ended by Henry Tudor, later Henry VII, at Bosworth Field in 1485. [MMA 16]

7470 York Assizes -- see assizes [CW 6]

7471 York hams -- one of the well-known English hams, the others being Bradenham*, Suffolk, and Wiltshire. York hams are cured with dry salt, are lightly smoked, and matured for several months. The tender pink meat has a mild flavor. [BC 8]

7472 York Minster -- England's largest Gothic cathedral, dating from the 13th C., retains the name "minster" which is the Anglo-Saxon word for a large church. It is 524 feet long by 249 feet wide at the transept. The tower is 234 feet high. The Minster features over 100 stained glass windows, some dating from about 1150, and reputed to be the oldest glass in England. It is second only to Chartres for its magnificent glass. See also Seven Sisters. [CW 11]

7473 York University -- such a university did not exist when DLS was alive. There is one now, but it dates from 1963, and DLS had died in 1957. [GN 17]

7474 Yorker -- see cricket [MMA 3]

7475 Yorkshire -- originally a part of the ancient Saxon kingdom of Northumbria and, prior to 1974, divided into the North, East, and West Ridings. It now consists of North, West, and South Yorkshire, North Humberside, and Cleveland. [CW 1/MMA 18]

7476 "You agree with Shaw . . ." -- Mr. Ingleby* is alluding to George Bernard Shaw's play, Man and Superman, a part of which, though not meant to be acted, is called The Revolutionist's Handbook. In the section on "Beating Children", the first of two maxims states: "If you strike a child, take care that you strike it in anger, even at the risk of maiming it for life. A blow in cold blood neither can nor should be forgiven." [MMA 17]

7477 "You are an adept in these chamber-passions" -- Adalmar addresses Athulf in II, iii, 146-48 of T. L. Beddoes' Death's Jest Book**. The speech continues:

" . . . I never knew before
The meaning of this love. But one has taught me,
It is a heaven wandering among men,
The spirit of gone Eden haunting earth." [HHC 15]

7478 "You are my garden of beautiful roses . . ." -- this may be a typical Edwardian drawing room ballad in the spirit of Eric Coates's "You are my rose", or "Love's garden of roses" by Haydn Wood. However, it may also be a misquotation from Tennyson's* Idylls of the King, "Pelleas and Ettarre":

"A rose, but one, none other rose had I,
A rose, one rose, and this was wondrous fair,
One rose, a rose that gladdened earth and sky,
One rose, my rose, that sweetened all mine air--"

Whatever the source, PW is again being hard on Insp. Sugg* as the lines suggest that Sugg's behavior is the antidote to PW's making foolish errors in judgment. [WB 3]

7479 you b____ fool -- see bloody [CW 18]

7480 "You can't escape the fierce light . . ." -- this is an allusion to the "Dedication" of Tennyson's* The Idylls of the King, ll. 24ff:

"Wearing the white flower of a blameless life,
Before a thousand peering littlenesses,
In that fierce light which beats upon a throne,
And blackens every blot." [BH 7]

7481 "You have always been called a merciful man . . ." -- the lines are from Much Ado About Nothing, III, iii, 64ff. in an exchange between Dogberry, Verges, and the Watch [BH E1]

7482 "You have got the wrong man . . . ." -- Parker* is quoting Dr. Thorndyke's comment as it appears in "Pandora's Box" which first appeared as part of a collection in The Magic Casket (1927): "Thorndyke regarded the agitated detective with a quiet smile. 'My comments, Miller,' said he, 'can be put in a nut-shell.'" The paragraph concludes with the sentence cited. [HHC 33]

7483 "you in your small corner and I in mine" -- the line is from a hymn, "Jesus Bids Us Shine", and forms

the last line of the hymn's three stanzas. The entire first verse is:

"Jesus bids us shine with a clear pure light,
Like a little candle burning in the night;
In this world of darkness we must shine--
You in your small corner, and I in mine." [CW 7]

7484 "You Jack o'Di'monds . . ." -- Mark Sambourne* quotes these lines from an anonymous Anglo-American folk song called "Jack of Diamonds" or "Jack o' Di'monds". It has many variant forms including songs entitled "Rye Whiskey", "Drunkard's Hiccups", and "Clinch Mountain". If the verses are easily adapted, the tune is even more so, being a version of the tune group sometimes referred to as the "Toddlen Hame" family. The music is often arranged to feature some virtuoso fiddle playing with a left-hand pizzicato meant to suggest a hiccough. The piece has appeared in a variety of recordings, so which version DLS might have had in mind is impossible to determine. [qs]

7485 You know my methods, Bunter. -- PW is quoting Sherlock Holmes almost directly. The sentence appears as cited (subsitute Watson for Bunter) in The Memoirs in "The Crooked Man" and in nearly identical form in "The Musgrave Ritual." [BH 3]

7486 "You not alone . . ." -- the lines are the first two verses of Michael Drayton's* Idea in Sixty-Three Sonnets, sonnet 11 (1619). The concluding couplet is:

"You doe bewitch Me, O that I could flie
From my Selfe You, or from your owne Self I."

[GN 4]

7487 "You paid your money . . ." -- the line apparently first appeared in Punch, X, p. 16, 1846, as, "You pays your money and you takes your choice." [NT 5]

7488 "You're a better man than I am, Gunga Din." -- PW is quoting from Rudyard Kipling's* poem, "Gunga Din", which relates the story of a native boy in India who brought water to wounded British troops. [BH 5]

7489 "young lady of Riga" -- the line is from an anonymous limerick:

"There was a young lady of Riga,
Who rode with a smile on a tiger;
They returned from the ride
With the lady inside,
And a smile on the face of the tiger." [HHC 23]

7490 Young Lochinvar -- the reference is to Lochinvar, hero of the fifth canto of Sir Walter Scott's "Marmion". In the narrative, Ellen, Lochinvar's beloved, is to be married to "a laggard in love and a dastard in war" when Lochinvar arrives to carry her off on his horse. [CW 9]

7491 Young Men in Love -- a novel by Michael Arlen* and published in 1927. It is one of Arlen's typically flippant society farces. [UD 15]

7492 your grace -- the proper form of address when speaking to a duke or duchess, or to an archbishop. Such a greeting is formal, but is the only correct one until authorized to use something less formal. [WB 1/CW 1]

7493 Yownie, Tammas -- see "Ye'll no fickle Tammas Yownie." [GN 17]

7494 Ypres -- also Ieper; a town in Belgium some thirty miles southwest of Bruges. It was the scene of three major battles in WW I. The first was in October-November of 1914, the second in April-May of 1915, and the third in July-November of 1917. All were costly in lives lost, but the third battle was especially so. It was at the second battle that the Germans introduced the use of poison gas warfare when they used chlorine gas to open an offensive against the Allies. PW saw action near there with his rifle brigade. See also Ytres. [pj]

7495 Yquem, Chateau -- see Chateau Yquem [mt/CW 6]

7496 Ytres -- also Ittre; a small village on the Canal du Nord in France, some seven miles southeast of Bapaume. In "Image in the Mirror" the reference to Ypres* is a typographical error and should be Ytres. The latter was occupied by the Germans until about September 8, 1918, when the British Third Army captured it. The story refers to Caudry* which was captured on

October 10, 1918, a month after Ytres, so the CCS* could very likely have been located in the latter town [im]

7497 Yule Log -- a large log burned at Christmas and traditionally lit by a fragment of the previous year's log. It is an ancient tradition especially popular during the Middle Ages. [qs/np]

7498 Zambesi -- a steamship which would have originated its voyage at Durban, East London, Port Elizabeth, or Cape Town, South Africa, but, most likely the latter. The destination seems to have been Southampton*. Lloyd's Register of Shipping lists a Zambesi, a salvage steamer built in 1914. In the 1930's it was owned by the Holland-Afrika Lijn, Amsterdam, a part of the larger firm N. V. Vereeigde Nederlandische Scheepvaartmaatschapi who provided services to various parts of Africa and the U. K. Even though it seems unlikely that Mr. Ruyslaender*, a successful diamond merchant, would book passage on such a vessel, all sorts of reasons may be given for his having done so. However, it is more likely a coincidence that DLS should have chosen this particular name for the ship in the story. [pj]

7499 Zeppelins -- the huge, lighter-than-air airships used by the German army and navy in WW I. They could carry, for the times, huge bomb loads, and could inflict great damage in their raids. Zeppelins were rigid frame airships named for their inventor, Count Ferdinand von Zeppelin. His first was produced in 1900. They are not to be confused with blimps which do not have a rigid frame. [NT 2]

7500 Zeus -- the youngest son of the Titan Cronos whom he overthrew to become chief of the Greek gods [UD 6]

7501 Zion -- Bill Rumm* is referring to the songs of heaven; religious music. He is not referring to Zion in the usual sense of Israel and her people. [SP 13]

7502 Zoo -- Padgett* is unclear as to which zoo, but it is probably the London Zoo at Regent's Park when one notes that he was the assistant camel-hand [GN 6]

7503 Zucchero -- or Zuccaro, two Italian painters: Taddeo (1529-66), and Federigo (1542-1609). The legend that Federigo painted many portraits in England does not have basis in fact. He did do one of Elizabeth I and one of the Earl of Leicester, but only the drawings for them are known today. [BH E2]

Addenda

7504 "Go to, go to . . . ." -- PW is quoting almost exactly from Macbeth, V, i, 51, the Doctor's speech to the gentlewoman who has reported to him the behavior of Lady Macbeth, and from V, i, 68ff., one of Lady Macbeth's ramblings about earlier events in the play. This is all a part of the famous sleepwalking scene. [FRH 22]

7505 Bourgois -- the concierge* at the apartment building in Paris where Denis Cathcart* kept a flat [CW 5]

7506 A little benzene* rids us of this guilt. -- PW echoes Lady Macbeth in II, ii, 67 of Macbeth. The line there is, "A little water clears us of this deed . . . ." [FRH 27]

7507 hangman . . . . They published his diary the other day. -- the reference is to Hans Schmidt, the hangman at Nuremburg, Germany, during the later 1500's. His diary was published, as edited by Albrecht Keller, in 1928, under the title A Hangman's Diary. [bc]

7508 The Curse of Scotland -- many of the chapter titles of BC refer to card games, especially bridge*. In this case, however, the relationship is not to bridge, but to a bit of British history. The nine of diamonds is often called "The Curse of Scotland" as it is reputed that the order for the Massacre of Glencoe, 1692, was written on such a card. Troops from the Campbells, traditional enemies of the Macdonalds, were quartered with the Macdonalds, fell upon their hosts, and attempted a slaughter. Most escaped, but thirty-eight Macdonalds died. The massacre was ordered as punishment because the Chief of the Macdonalds had not taken an oath of allegiance to William III and Mary before the stated deadline date. [BC 7]

7509 viridarium -- a green court or pleasure garden, literally a "place of greenness". Not exactly a greenhouse or a conservatory, it is more likely a sort of courtyard with, in England, a glazed roof as a possibility because of the cooler climate. [umw]

The Lord Peter Wimsey Companion

Bibliography, Index and Gazetteer

Selected Bibliography

Abrams, M. H., et al., eds., The Norton Anthology of English Literature. New York: W. W. Norton & Co., Inc., 1982.

Adams, Gordon, Manager of the Psychic Press, Ltd., London. Correspondence dated 15 April 1982.

Allen, Reginald, ed., The First Night Gilbert and Sullivan. New York: The Heritage Press, 1958.

Altick, Richard D., Victorian Studies in Scarlet. New York: W. W. Norton & Co., Inc., 1970.

The Annual Register, or A View of the History, Politics, and Literature for the Year 1760, 5th ed. London: J. Dodsley, 1793.

Apperson, G. L., English Proverbs and Proverbial Phrases. London: J. M. Dent, 1929.

Archer, J., Information Officer, County Legal Dept., Greater Manchester Council, Manchester, England. Correspondence dated 23 April 1982.

Arlott, James, et al., Illustrated Guide to Britain. London: Drive Publications, Ltd., 1978.

Arlott, John, The Oxford Companion to Sports and Games. New York: Oxford University Press, 1975.

Auden, W. H., ed., The Oxford Book of Light Verse. New York: Oxford University Press, 1970.

Baedecker's Travel Guide: England/Scotland, 1906.

Bailey, Adrian, The Cooking of the British Isles. New York: Time-Life Books, 1971.

Baker, A. E., A Concordance to the Poetical and Dramatic Works of Alfred, Lord Tennyson. London: Routledge & Kegan Paul, Ltd., 1965.

Bald, R. C., ed., Six Elizabethan Plays. New York: Houghton Mifflin Co., 1963.

Barham, Rev. Richard Harris, The Ingoldsby Legends 2 vols. New York: W. J. Widdleton, 1864.

Baring-Gould, S., H. F. Sheppard, and F. W. Russell, Songs of the West (Devon and Cornwall). London: Methuen, n. d.

Barnhart, Clarence L., and William D. Halsey, The New Century Cyclopedia of Names. New York: Appleton-Century-Crofts, 1954

Bartholomew, John, ed., The Times Atlas of the World, Vol. III, Northern Europe, Mid-Century Edition. Boston: Houghton Mifflin, 1955.

________, The Times World Gazeteer, Mid-Century Edition. Boston: Houghton Mifflin, 1955.

Bartis, Peter T., Folklife Researcher, American Folklife Center, The Library of Congress, Washington, D. C. Correspondence dated 17 December 1981.

Bartlett, John, Familiar Quotations. Boston: Little Brown, 1955.

Barzun, Jacques, and Wendell Hertig Taylor, A Catalogue of Crime. New York: Harper and Row, 1971.

Bate, Walter Jackson, ed., Criticism: The Major Texts. New York: Harcourt, Brace, and Co., 1952.

Baugh, Albert C., et al., eds., A Literary History of England. New York: Appleton-Century-Crofts, 1948.

Beaman, Bruce R., The Sherlock Holmes Book of Quotations. Bloomington, Indiana: Gaslight Publications, 1980.

Bedford, Peter M., M. I. P. R., Director of Tourism and Entertainments, Borough of Eastbourne, Eastbourne, Sussex, England. Correspondence dated 29 April 1982.

Benét, William Rose, The Reader's Encyclopedia. New York: Thomas Y. Crowell Co., 1965.

Berry, George R., The Classic Greek Dictionary. Chicago: Follett, 1962.

Bickmore, D. P., and M. A. Shaw, The Atlas of Britain and Northern Ireland. Oxford: The Clarendon Press, 1963.

Blom, Eric, ed., Grove's Dictionary of Music and Musicians, 5th Ed. New York: St. Martin's Press, 1960.

Bowen, Ezra, ed., This Fabulous Century, 1920-1930, Vol. III. New York: Time-Life Books, 1969.

Brabazon, James, Dorothy L. Sayers. New York: Scribner's, 1981.

Bradbury, Malcolm, et al., eds., The Penguin Companion to American Literature. New York: McGraw Hill, 1971.

Brewer, Rev. E. C., Brewer's Dictionary of Phrase and Fable. New York: Harper

and Row, 1965.

________, The Historic Note-book. Detroit, Michigan: Gale Research Co., 1966.

________, The Reader's Handbook. Detroit, Michigan: Gale Research Co., 1966.

Buck, Percy, The Oxford Song Book, 2 vols. New York: Oxford University Press, 1962.

Buckley, Jerome H., and George B. Woods, eds., Poetry of the Victorian Period. Fair Lawn, New Jersey: Scott, Foresman and Co., 1965.

Bullock, L. G. Historical Map of England and Wales. Edinburgh: John Bartholomew & Son, Ltd., 1969.

________, Historical Map of Scotland. Edinburgh: John Bartholomew & Son, Ltd., no date.

Burnham, Mary, ed., Cumulative Book Index: 1928-1932. New York: H. W. Wilson Co., 1933.

Businessman's London Map. Edinburgh: John Bartholomew & Son, Ltd., 1976.

Cady, Michael, ed., The Book of London. Basingstoke, Hants., England: The Automobile Association, 1979.

Cagle, William R., Lilly Librarian, The Lilly Library, Indiana University, Bloomington, Indiana. Correspondence dated 30 September 1981.

Camp, John, "Bell Ringing in Britain", British History Illustrated, Vol. 3, No. 6 (February/March, 1977), pp. 8ff.

Castiglione, Baldesar, The Book of the Courtier. (Translated by Charles S. Singleton.) Garden City, New York: Doubleday and Co., 1959.

Chambers, E. K., The Medieval Stage, 2 vols. New York: Oxford University Press, 1963.

Chaytor, H. J., From Script to Print: An Introduction to Medieval Vernacular Literature. New York: October House, 1967.

Chesterton, G. K., The Collected Poems of G. K. Chesterton. New York: Dodd Mead, 1932.

Child, F. J., ed., English and Scottish Popular Ballads. Boston: Houghton-Mifflin Co., 1904.

Cole, Ruth Martin, ed., Britannica World Atlas. Chicago: Encyclopedia Britannica, Inc., 1968.

Cook, Chris, and Brendan Keith, British Historical Facts: 1830-1900. New York: St. Martin's, 1975.

Copi, Irving M., Introduction to Logic. New York: Macmillan, 1961.

Cowie, L. W., and John Selwyn Gummer, The Christian Calendar. Springfield, Massachusetts: G. &. C. Merriam, 1974.

Craig, Hardin, The Complete Works of Shakespeare. Fair Lawn, New Jersey: Scott, Foresman, & Co., 1961.

Cram, George F., Cram's Unrivaled Atlas of the World. New York: Geo. F. Cram, 1900.

Cross, F. L., and E. A. Livingston, eds., The Oxford Dictionary of the Christian Church. New York: Oxford University Press, 1974.

Crowley, Ellen T., ed., Acronyms, Initialisms, & Abbreviations Dictionary, 6th Ed., Detroit, Michigan: Gale Research Co., 1978.

Cruden, Alexander M., Cruden's Complete Concordance to the Old and New Testaments. Grand Rapids, Michigan: Zondervan Publishing House, 1980.

Daiches, David, The Penguin Companion to English Literature. New York: McGraw-Hill, 1971.

Dars, Celestine, Images of Deception. Oxford: Phaidon Press, Ltd., 1979

Day, David, Publicity Manager, Negretti and Zambra, Ltd., Stockdale, Aylesbury, Bucks., England. Correspondence dated 30 September 1981.

Deutsch, Babette, Poetry Handbook: A Dictionary of Terms. New York: Funk and Wagnalls, 1974.

Dickens, Charles, Pickwick Papers. New York: New American Library, 1964.

Donner, H. W., ed., The Works of Thomas Lovell Beddoes. London: Humphrey Milford (for Oxford University Press), 1935. This volume contains all of Beddoes' work in all versions in which they are known to exist.

The Dorothy L. Sayers Society, "Tour of the Fens". Witham, Essex, England: The Dorothy L. Sayers Society, 1980.

________, "Tour of London". Witham, Essex, England: The Dorothy L. Sayers Society, 1980.

________, "Tour of Oxford". Witham, Essex, England: The Dorothy L. Sayers Society, 1980.

________, "Tour of Galloway". Witham, Essex, England: The Dorothy L. Sayers Society, 1981.

Dubois, Marguerite-Marie, et al., eds., Larousse Modern French-English Dictionary. New York: McGraw-Hill, 1960.

Dummelow, Rev. J. R., M. A., The One Volume Bible Commentary. New York: Macmillan, 1974.

Dunn, Esther Cloudman, ed., Eight Famous Elizabethan Plays. New York: Random House, 1950.

Eagle, Dorothy, and Hilary Carnell, eds., The Oxford Literary Guide to the British Isles. New York: Oxford University Press, 1977.

Ellis, Havelock, ed., Christopher Marlowe: Five Plays. New York: Hill and Wang, 1956.

Esposito, Brigadier General Vincent J., U. S. A. (ret.), ed., The West Point Atlas of American Wars, 2 vols. New York: Frederick Praeger, 1964.

Farmer, John S., and W. E. Henley, Slang and Its Analogues. New York: Kraus Reprint Corp., 1965.

Fiedler, Leslie, Freaks. New York: Touchstone Books, 1978.

Fillmore, Stanley, ed., The Life Book of Christmas, 3 vols. New York: Time, Inc., 1963.

Fishbein, Morris, et al., eds., The New Illustrated Medical and Health Encyclopedia, 4 vols. New York: H. S. Stuttman Co., Inc., 1970.

Fox-Davies, Arthur Charles, A Complete Guide to Heraldry. New York: Bonanza Books, 1978.

________, Heraldry Explained. Newton Abbot, Devon, England: David & Charles, Ltd., 1971.

Fowler, Harold N. (translator), Plato ("The Statesman"). The Loeb Classical Library. Cambridge, Massachusetts: Harvard University Press, 1962.

Freeman, William, Dictionary of Fictional Characters. Boston: The Writer, Inc., 1974.

Freeman-Grenville, G. S. P., Atlas of British History. London: Rex Collings, 1979.

________, The Queen's Lineage From A. D. 495 to the Silver Jubilee of Her Majesty Queen Elizabeth II. London: Rex Collings, 1977.

Gaillard, Dawson, Dorothy L. Sayers. New York: Frederick Unger Publishing Co., 1981.

Gardner, Martin, The Annotated Alice. New York: New American Library, 1974. (This work contains the complete texts of Alice in Wonderland and Through the Looking Glass by Lewis Carroll, notes, commentary and an introduction by Martin Gardner.)

Georgano, G. N., ed., The Complete Encyclopedia of Motorcars, 1885 to the Present. New York: E. P. Dutton Co., 1973.

Gilbert, Colleen B., A Bibliography of the Works of Dorothy L. Sayers. New York: Macmillan Press, 1978.

Goethe, Johann Wolfgang von, Wilhelm Meister's Apprenticeship and Travels. (Translated by Thomas Carlyle.) Boston: D. Estes, 1839(?).

Goldsmith, Oliver, She Stoops to Conquer. Woodbury, New York: Barron's Educational Series, 1958.

Great Britain and Ireland (Map #986). London: Michelin Tyre Co., Ltd., 1978.

Green, Martin, Children of the Sun: A Narrative of "Decadence" in England After 1918. New York: Wideview Books, 1980.

Grossman, Harold J., Grossman's Guide to Wines, Spirits, and Beers. New York: Scribner's, 1964.

Gurney, E. H., Reference Handbook for Readers, Students and Teachers of English History. Boston: Ginn & Co., 1890.

Haggart, Stanley, and Darwin Porter, Frommer's 1981-82 Guide to Paris. New York: Simon & Schuster, 1981.

Haller, Margaret, The Book Collector's Fact Book. New York: Arco Publishing Co., Inc., 1976.

Hamilton, Edith, Mythology. New York: New American Library, 1962.

Hannay, Margaret P., ed., As Her Whimsey Took Her. Kent, Ohio: Kent State University Press, 1979.

Harmon, Robert B., and Margaret A. Burger, An

Annotated Guide to the Works of Dorothy L. Sayers. New York: Garland Publishing Co., 1977. (Garland Reference Library of the Humanities, Vol. 80)

Hart, James D., The Oxford Companion to American Literature. New York: Oxford University Press, 1956.

Hartnoll, Phyllis, The Oxford Companion to the Theatre. New York: Oxford University Press, 1964.

Harvey, Sir Paul, The Oxford Companion to Classical Literature. New York: Oxford University Press, 1962.

________, The Oxford Companion to English Literature. New York: Oxford University Press, 1962.

________, and J. E. Heseltine, The Oxford Companion to French Literature. New York: Oxford University Press, 1959.

Hayward, John, ed., The Oxford Book of Nineteenth Century Verse. New York: Oxford University Press, 1965.

Heyworth, Peter, The Oxford Guide to Oxford. New York: Oxford University Press, 1981.

Historical Map of London. Edinburgh: John Bartholomew & Son, Ltd., no date.

Hone, Ralph E., Dorothy L. Sayers: A Literary Biography. Kent, Ohio: Kent State University Press, 1979.

Hood, Jean, Information Officer, Shipping Information Services, Lloyd's Registry of Shipping, London. Correspondence 15 July and 10 September 1981.

Hoppe, E. O. London. Boston: Hale, Cushman, and Flint, no date.

Houfe, Simon, The Dictionary of British Book Illustrators and Caricaturists, 1800-1914. Woodbridge, Sullolk, England: Baron Publishing, 1978.

Hubin, Allen J., The Bibliography of Crime Fiction 1749-1975. Del Mar, California: Publisher's Inc., 1979.

Ireland, N. O., Index to Scientists of the World. Boston: F. W. Faxon Co., 1962.

Ison, Leonora and Walter, English Architecture Through the Ages. New York: Coward McCann, 1967.

Jabbour, Alan, Director, American Folklife Center, The Library of Congress, Washington, D. C. Correspondence dated 3 November 1981.

Jacobs, Jay, ed., The Horizon Book of Great Cathedrals. New York: American Heritage Publishing Co., Inc., 1968.

Johnson, Allen, et al., eds., Dictionary of American Biography. New York: Charles Scribner's Sons, 1957.

Johnson, Hugh, The World Atlas of Wine. New York: Simon & Schuster, 1977.

Josephy, Alvin M., Jr., ed., The American Heritage History of World War I. New York: American Heritage Publishing Co., Inc., 1964.

Kay, F. George, London: A Rand McNally Pocket Guide. New York: Rand McNally, 1980.

Kenner, Hugh, ed., Seventeenth Century Poetry. New York: Holt, Rinehart and Winston, Inc., 1964.

Kielty, Bernardine, Masters of Painting. Garden City, New York: Doubleday and Co., 1964.

Knight, Marion A., and Mertice M. James, Book Review Digest (1926). New York: H. W. Wilson Co., 1927.

Lamson, Roy, and Hallett Smith, eds., Renaissance England. New York: W. W. Norton & Co., Inc., 1956.

Langer, William L., An Encyclopedia of World History, 4th Ed. Boston: Houghton Mifflin Co., 1968.

Latham, Edward, Dictionary of Names, Nicknames, and Surnames of Persons, Places, and Things. Detroit, Michigan: Gale Research Co., 1966.

Lee, Geoffrey, "Notes on an Impromptu Concert: Gaudy Night, Chapter 19". Witham, Essex, England: The Dorothy L. Sayers Society, no date.

Lee, Geoffrey, John Morris, and Philip Scowcroft, "The Chronology of Lord Peter Wimsey". Witham, Essex, England: The Dorothy L. Sayers Society, 1983.

Lewis, Charlton T., and Charles Short, A Latin Dictionary. New York: Oxford University Press, 1975.

Linton, David, ed., Benn's Press Directory, 1972, 2 vols. London: Benn Publications Ltd., 1979.

Llewellin, Philip, and Ann Saunders, Book of British Towns. New York: W. W. Norton & Co., Inc., 1979.

London, Michelin Green Guide Series. London: Michelin Tyre Co., Ltd., 1980.

London A-Z Street Atlas and Index. London: Geographer's A-Z Map Co., Ltd., no date.

London to and Through (map). Edinburgh: John Bartholomew & Son, 1977.

Loomis, Stanley, A Crime of Passion. New York: Avon Books, 1973.

Lucie-Smith, Edward, Cultural Calendar of the 20th Century. Oxford: Phaidon Press, Ltd., 1979.

Lustgarten, Edgar, The Illustrated Story of Crime. New York: Harper & Row, 1977.

Mankowitz, Wolf, and Reginald G. Haggar, The Concise Encyclopedia of English Pottery and Porcelain. New York: Frederick A. Praeger, 1968.

Mann, John Dixon, M. D., F. R. C. P., Forensic Medicine and Toxicology, 6th Ed. London: Charles Griffin and Co., 1922.

Mason, Mercia, Blue Guide: Oxford and Cambridge. New York: W. W. Norton & Co., 1982.

Massie, Robert K., Nicholas and Alexandra. New York: Dell, 1969.

Mawson, C. O., and Charles Berlitz, Dictionary of Foreign Terms. New York: Barnes & Noble, 1975.

Maxtone-Graham, John, The Only Way to Cross. New York: Collier Books, 1978.

McMurtrie, Douglas C., The Book. New York: Oxford University Press, 1943.

Montagné, Prosper, Larousse Gastronomique. New York: Crown Publishers, 1961.

Montaigne, Michèle de, Essays and Selected Writings. A bilingual edition translated and edited by Donald M. Frame. New York: St. Martin's Press, 1963.

Moorehead, Alan, The Russian Revolution. New York: Bantam Books, 1959.

Moran, Thomas Francis, The Theory and Practice of the English Government. Chatauqua, New York: The Chatauqua Press, 1903.

Morehead, Albert H, and Geoffrey Mott-Smith, Hoyle's Rules of Games. New York: New York: New American Library, 1958.

Morris, William, The Collected Works of William Morris. London: Longmans Green, 1910.

Morris, William, ed., The American Heritage Dictionary of the English Language. New York: American Heritage Co., Inc., 1969.

Murray, James A. H., et al., eds., The Oxford English Dictionary. New York: Oxford University Press, 1976.

Murray, Jane, The Kings and Queens of England: A Tourist Guide. New York: Scribner's, 1974.

Neubecker, Ottfried, Heraldry. New York: McGraw Hill, 1976.

Neumann, Werner, Sämpliche von Johann Sebastian Bach Vertonte Texte. Leipzig: V. E. B. Deutscher Verlag für Musik, 1974.

Newell, Gordon, Ocean Liners of the 20th Century. New York: Bonanza Books, 1963.

Nixon, Paul (translator), Plautus. Vol. III, The Loeb Classical Library. Cambridge, Massachusetts: Harvard University Press, 1963.

Nock, O. S., Great Steam Locomotives of All Time. London: Blandford Press, 1976.

________, Steam Railways of Britain. London: Blandford Press, 1967.

________, World Atlas of Railways. New York: Mayflower Books, 1979.

O'Neill, Peter, Business Manager, Creative Department, Ogilvy and Mather (Advertising Agency). Correspondence dated 8 July 1982.

Opie, Iona, and Peter Opie, Children's Games in Street and Playground. London: Oxford University Press, 1969.

Osborne, Harold, ed., The Oxford Companion to Art. New York: Oxford University Press, 1971.

The Oxford Dictionary of Quotations. New York: Oxford University Press, 1959.

The Oxford Book of English Proverbs, 3rd Ed. London: Oxford University Press, 1970.

Paget, Julian, The Pageantry of England. London: Michael Joseph Ltd., 1979.

Palmer, A. W., A Dictionary of Modern History: 1789-1945. Baltimore, Maryland: Penguin Books, 1971.

Palmer, Alan, Kings and Queens of England. London: Octopus Books, 1976.

Palmer's Index to the Times Newspaper: (London) 1927. Nendeln, Lichtenstein: Kraus Reprint Ltd., 1966.

Panek, Leroy Lad, Watteau's Shepherds: The Detective Novel in Britain, 1914-1940. Bowling Green, Ohio: The Popular Press, 1979.

Parker, Derek and Julia Parker, The Compleat Astrologer. New York: McGraw-Hill, 1971.

Partridge, Eric, A Dictionary of Slang and Unconventional English. New York: The Macmillan Co., 1970.

Phyfe, William H. P., 5000 Facts and Fancies. Detroit, Michigan: Gale Research Co., 1966.

Pollard, A. W., and G. R. Redgrave, A Short Title Catalogue of Books Printed in England, Scotland and Ireland And English Books Printed Abroad, 1475-1640. London: The Bibliographical Society, 1969.

Quiller-Couch, Sir Arthur, ed., The Oxford Book of Ballads. New York: Oxford University Press, 1963.

________, The Oxford Book of Victorian Verse. New York: Oxford University Press, 1955.

Randal, Don Michael, Harvard Concise Dictionary of Music. Cambridge, Massachusetts: Harvard University Press, 1978.

The Reader's Digest Complete Atlas of the British Isles. London: Reader's Digest Association, 1965.

Reynolds, Barbara, ed., The Cambridge Italian Dictionary. Cambridge: Cambridge University Press, 1962.

Roadbook of Britain. London: Charles Letts and Co., Ltd., 1977.

Roughead, William, Classic Crimes. New York: Vintage Books, 1977.

Rouse, W. H. D. (translator), Great Dialogues of Plato. New York: New American Library, 1956.

Rowse, A. L., The Annotated Shakespeare, 3 vols. New York: Clarkson N. Potter, 1978.

Ryan, Elizabeth Bond, and William J. Eakins, The Lord Peter Wimsey Cookbook. New Haven, Connecticut: Ticknor & Fields, 1981.

Rydbeck, Margareta E., "Though It Be Madness There is Method In It". Unpublished paper, Varnamo, Sweden, April 1970.

Sadie, Stanley, ed., The New Grove Dictionary of Music and Musicians. Washington, D. C.: Grove's Dictionaries of Music, Inc., 1980.

Sayers, Dorothy L., Busman's Honeymoon. New York: Avon Books, 1968.

________, Clouds of Witness. New York: Avon Books, 1966.

________, Five Red Herrings. New York: Avon Books, 1968.

________, Gaudy Night. New York: Avon Books, 1968.

________, Have His Carcase. New York: Avon Books, 1968.

________, Lord Peter, James Sandoe, ed. New York: Equinox Books, 1972.

________, Murder Must Advertise. New York: Avon Books, 1968.

________, The Nine Tailors. New York: Harbrace Paperback Library, no date.

________, Strong Poison. New York: Avon Books, 1969.

________, Unnatural Death. New York: Avon Books, 1964.

________, The Unpleasantness at the Bellona Club. New York: Avon Books, 1963.

________, Whose Body?. New York: Avon Books, 1961.

Schmidt, Alexander, Shakespeare Lexicon and Quotation Dictionary, 2 vols. New York: Dover Publications, 1971.

Schmeider, Wolfgang, Thematisch-Systematisches Verzeichnis der Musikalishen Werke von Johann Sebastian Bach (Bach-Werke-Verzeichnis/BWV). Leipzig: V. E. B. Breitkopf & Härtel Musik-Verlag, 1971.

Schonberg, Harold C., The Lives of the Great Composers. New York: W. W. Norton Co., 1970.

Scott, Sir Walter, The Complete Poetical Works of Sir Walter Scott, Cambridge Edition, edited by Horace E. Scudder. Boston: Houghton Mifflin, 1900.

Scott-Giles, C. W., The Wimsey Family. London: Victor Gollancz, Ltd., 1977.

Scowcroft, Philip L., "Sidelights on Sayers". Witham, Essex, England: The Dorothy L. Sayers Society, 1981.

Sears, Minnie Earl, Song Index. New York: H. W. Wilson Co., 1926.

Selman, R. R., The First World War. New York: Criterion Books, 1962.

Sévigné, Marie de Rabutin-Chantal, Marquise de,

Lettres, vol. 2. Paris: Gallimard, 1960.

Shipway, William, The Campanalogia: Or Universal Instructor in the Art of Ringing: In Three Parts. London: Sherwood Neely and Jones, 1816.

A Short Military History of World War I: Atlas. West Point, New York: United States Military Academy, 1954.

Simon, André L., et al., eds., Wines of the World. New York: McGraw-Hill, 1968.

Sisam, Celia, The Oxford Book of Medieval Verse. New York: Oxford University Press, 1973.

Skeat, Rev. W. W., A Concise Etymological Dictionary of the English Language. New York: Capricorn Books, 1963.

Sloan, Kenneth J., F. R. G. S., Head, Geography Dept., La Sagesse High School, Grassendale, Liverpool, England. Correspondence dated 1 March 1982.

Smith, Goldwin, A History of England. New York: Scribner's, 1957.

Songs and Sonnets of Pierre de Ronsard. (Curtis Hidden Page, translator and editor.) Boston: Houghton Mifflin, 1924.

Spence, Lewis, An Encyclopedia of Occultism. Hyde Park, New York: University Books, 1960.

Spiller, Robert E., et al., eds., Literary History of the United States: History. New York: Macmillan, 1963.

Steinberg, S. H., and I. H. Evans, et al., eds., Steinberg's Dictionary of British History. New York: St. Martin's Press, 1971.

Steinbrunner, Chris, and Otto Penzler, Encyclopedia of Mystery and Detection. New York: McGraw-Hill, 1976.

Steiner, Rudolf, The Steinerbooks Dictionary of the Psychic, Mystic, Occult. Blauvelt, New York: Rudolf Steiner Publications, 1973.

Stephen, Sir Leslie, and Sir Sidney Lee, eds., Dictionary of National Biography. New York: Oxford University Press, 1882.

Stevenson, Burton, Stevenson's Home Book of Quotations. New York: Dodd Mead, 1964.

Sunnocks, Anne, ed., The Encyclopedia of Chess. New York: St. Martin's Press, 1970.

Swinson, Arthur, ed., A Register of the Regiments and Corps of the British Army. London: Archive Press, 1972.

Symons, Julian, Crime: A Pictorial History of Crime, 1840 to the Present. New York: Bonanza Books, 1966.

Terry, Charles Sanford, Joh. Seb. Bach Cantata Texts Sacred and Secular. London: The Holland Press, 1964.

Thomas, Clayton W., ed., Taber's Cyclopedic Medical Dictionary. Philadelphia: F. A. Davis Co., 1981.

Thompson, Stith, and John Gassner, eds., Our Heritage of World Literature. New York: Holt, Rinehart and Winston, 1961.

Thomson, Sir Basil, The Story of Scotland Yard. New York: The Literary Guild, 1936.

Thorlby, Anthony, ed., The Penguin Companion to European Literature. New York: McGraw-Hill, 1969.

Thrall, William Flint, Addison Hibbard, and C. Hugh Holman, A Handbook to Literature. New York: The Odyssey Press, 1962.

The Times. London: The Times Co., 1900ff., passim.

Tracy, Jack, The Encyclopedia Sherlockiana. New York: Avon Books, 1979.

Traill, H. D., and J. S. Mann, eds., Social England, 6 vols. New York: Greenwood Press, Publishers, 1969.

Trollope, J. Armiger, The College Youths. Woking, England: "The Ringing World" Office, 1937.

Troyte, Charles A. W., Change Ringing. London: Wells Gardner, Darton & Co., 1869.

VanWijk, H. L. Gerth, A Dictionary of Plant Names. Amsterdam, The Netherlands: A. Asher & Co., 1962.

Villon, François, The Complete Works of François Villon, translated by Anthony Bonner. New York: David McKay and Co., Inc., 1960,

Walsh, William, Handbook of Literary Curiosities. Detroit, Michigan: Gale Research Co., 1966.

________, Heroes and Heroines of Literature. Detroit, Michigan: Gale Research Co., 1966.

Wavell, A. P., Other Men's Flowers. New York: G. P. Putnam's Sons, 1945.

Wekerlin, J. B., Bergerettes. Boston: Ditson, 1913.

Willings Press Guide: 1980. East Grimstead, West Sussex, England: Thomas Skinner Directories, 1980.

Wilson, Colin, A Casebook of Murder. London: Mayflower Books, 1971.

Winn, Dilys, Murder Ink. New York: Workman Publishing Co., Inc., 1977.

________, Murderess Ink. New York: Workman Publishing Co., Inc., 1979.

Winterich, John T., and David A. Randall, A Primer of Book Collecting. New York: Bell Publishing Co., 1966.

Wykes, Alan, "The English Club", British History Illustrated, Vol. 1, No. 5 (December, 1974), pp. 44-51.

Index

All numbers in the index refer to the consecutively numbered entry items, NOT to page numbers.

Each short story entry item is listed after the abbreviation for that story. The novels are broken down by chapters, so any entry numbers following the chapter abbreviations relate only to that chapter. All short story and novel abbreviations are listed in the Introduction.

The Short Stories

MT: 234, 255, 420, 421, 749, 810, 1186, 1188, 1243, 1369, 1473, 1474, 1485, 1495, 1887, 1998, 2092, 2111, 2239, -247, 2271, 2660, 2661, 2662, 2895, 2896, 3245, 3255, 3311, 3459, 3477, 3571, 3640, 3840, 3854, 4294, 4417, 4493, 4506, 4799, 5022, 5036, 5147, 5174, 5193, 5397, 5401, 5538, 5663, 5700, 5891, 5951, 5973, 6021, 7020, 7142, 7495.

NP: 53, 191, 199, 866, 1224, 1384, 1404, 1469, 1592, 1682, 1841, 1843, 1867, 1871, 2040, 2167, 2208, 2431, 3200, 3360, 3422, 4304, 4555, 4608, 4770, 4858, 5010, 5284, 5408, 5659, 6091, 6092, 6093, 6094, 6095, 6096, 6423, 6430, 6765, 6847, 6862, 7393, 7497.

PJ: 99, 143, 234, 314, 599, 660, 672, 1079, 3704, 3739, 3990, 4205, 4274, 4384, 4707, 4993, 5166, 5299, 5521, 5837, 5838, 6266, 7494, 7498.

QS: 374, 380, 543, 544, 586, 730, 837, 861, 1104, 1107, 1111, 1258, 1448, 1599, 1616, 1745, 1830, 1859, 1860, 1866, 1914, 1962, 2420, 2455, 2533, 2550, 2837, 2907, 3105, 3243, 3253, 3382, 3651, 3923, 4208, 4624, 4852, 4886, 5020, 5207, 5267, 5316, 5321, 5360, 5677, 5809, 5926, 5971, 5995, 6188, 7035, 7037, 7088, 7141, 7149, 7443, 7484, 7497.

SS: 18, 24, 25, 481, 484, 594, 640, 813, 826, 985, 1146, 1260, 1262, 1658, 1770, 1945, 1947, 2042, 2357, 2359, 2448, 2592, 2684, 2770, 2771, 2776, 2828, 2940, 3114, 3381, 3481, 3633, 3703, 3709, 3778, 3779, 3881, 3957, 4054, 4177, 4199, 4360, 4471, 4603, 4719, 4853, 5052, 5084, 5233, 5375, 5671, 5945, 5990, 6198, 6205, 6251, 6292, 6437, 6442, 7098, 7108, 7449.

SF: 1258, 1271, 1413, 1465, 1614, 2123, 2163, 2308, 2330, 2472, 2575, 2758, 2948, 3031, 3361, 3765, 4385, 4386, 4545, 5374, 5626, 6403, 6408, 6461, 7261.

T: 45, 396, 604, 734, 1207, 1429, 1641, 1663, 1705, 2010, 2180, 2322, 2919, 2998, 2999, 3004, 3480, 3597, 3630, 3658, 3837, 4085, 4200, 4202, 4295, 4560, 4664, 5404, 5446, 5489, 5490, 5516, 5574, 5969, 6035, 6099, 6555, 6579, 6729, 6756, 6813, 6860, 6993, 7004, 7037, 7083, 7084, 7345, 7351, 7358, 7361, 7459.

TE: 46, 65, 128, 565, 590, 705, 1117, 1154, 1377, 1735, 1806, 1858, 2061, 2372, 2455, 2619, 2622, 2766, 3086, 3379, 3479, 3604, 3631, 3853, 4201, 4325, 4667, 5240, 5343, 5402, 5403, 5526, 5752, 5785, 5793, 5919, 6759, 7142, 7324, 7343, 7370, 7439.

UMW: 37, 98, 133, 234, 316, 492, 1152, 1734, 1894, 1953, 2283, 2387, 2757, 2879, 2931, 3460, 3461, 4238, 4305, 4365, 4511, 4840, 5005, 5423, 5450, 5519, 5537, 5631, 5747, 5933, 6299 6324, 6652, 6786, 6942, 7012, 7077, 7509.

The Novels

Whose Body?

WB 1: 90, 466, 477, 479, 879, 959, 1156, 1196, 1315, 1442, 1445, 1498, 1754, 1830, 1902, 2075, 2102, 2118, 2226, 2466, 2468, 2532, 2583, 2766, 2822, 2852, 2937, 3086, 3302, 3305, 4105, 4125, 4229, 4497, 4640, 4734, 5039, 5050, 5193, 5227, 5429, 5553, 5643, 5650, 5892, 5953, 5957, 6343, 6486, 6648, 6658, 6704, 6999, 7067, 7428.

WB 2: 39, 173, 362, 510, 599, 860, 915, 1024, 1076, 1238, 1250, 1259, 1334, 1907, 1960, 2203, 2333, 2495, 2750, 2768, 3316, 3365, 3617, 3972, 3976, 3981, 4251, 4334, 4394, 4729, 4757, 5040, 5258, 5717, 6039, 6050, 6075, 6082, 6200, 6244, 6353, 6391, 6489, 6647, 6781, 6919, 6975, 7046, 7047, 7155, 7441, 7455, 7457.

WB 3: 92, 223, 224, 250, 312, 315, 398, 491, 538, 1086, 1124, 1125, 1155, 1169, 1328, 1500, 1974, 2133, 2413, 2615, 2821, 2823, 3091, 3417, 3488, 3529, 3547, 3852, 3979, 4086, 4215, 4368, 4642, 5100, 5137, 5219, 5221, 5344, 5354, 5355, 5532, 5900, 5964, 6166, 6167, 6297, 6488, 6649, 7075, 7109, 7478.

WB 4: 181, 234, 235, 242, 464, 499, 1210, 1282, 1323, 1378, 1428, 1496, 1539, 2484, 2877, 2906, 3373, 3484, 3496, 3497, 3509, 3963, 3975, 4068, 4293, 4452, 4506, 4717, 4740, 4872, 5030, 5120, 5304, 5417, 5585, 5709, 5885, 5918, 5983, 5984, 6086, 6114, 6382, 6630, 6651, 6704, 6932, 7151.

WB 5: 56, 121, 202, 213, 366, 368, 385, 402, 478, 740, 743, 884, 938, 1052, 1138, 1139, 1143, 1307, 1371, 1541, 1636, 1637, 1702, 1715, 1724, 1864, 2155, 2197, 2240, 2674, 2725, 2820, 2918, 2978, 3081, 3137, 3185, 3484, 3642, 3809, 4007, 4242, 4374, 4446, 4463, 4521, 4983, 4985, 5125, 5154, 5184, 5191, 5268, 5914, 5968, 6171, 6204, 6261, 6394, 6428, 6429, 6564, 6278, 7012, 7042, 7184, 7257, 7303, 7437.

WB 6: 95, 624, 792, 842, 994, 1151, 1174, 1316, 1889, 2137, 2217, 2398, 2506, 2842, 2957, 2996, 3259, 3489, 3691, 3728, 3935, 3974, 4532, 4856, 4984, 5276, 5642, 5880, 5893, 6154, 6228, 6730, 6787, 7123, 7153, 7328.

WB 7: 208, 251, 654, 1254, 1255, 1508, 1675, 1771, 2001, 2165, 2190, 2480, 2565, 2580, 2637, 3960, 4265, 4859, 5140, 5289, 5398, 5485, 5511, 5607, 5729, 5831, 6512, 7142, 7230.

WB 8: 3, 123, 831, 1047, 1612, 1712, 1980,

2206, 2273, 2274, 2582, 2584, 2623, 2979, 2980, 3099, 3705, 3706, 3707, 3790, 4224, 4927, 4978, 5886, 5942, 6288, 6838, 7240, 7267, 7289.

WB 9: 68, 369, 629, 677, 810, 1010, 1026, 1071, 1222, 1247, 1251, 1400, 1692, 3037, 3177, 4173, 4518, 5347, 5567, 5857, 6264, 6571, 6980, 7194, 7432, 7456.

WB 10: 525, 609, 675, 835, 1249, 1605, 1694, 1964, 2262, 2350, 2705, 3027, 3179, 3869, 4037, 4287, 4542, 4615, 5013, 5215, 5216, 5325, 5436, 5688, 5807, 5836, 6001, 6109, 6195, 6241, 6272, 6487, 7018.

WB 11: 1159, 1179, 1181, 2172, 2215, 2953, 3131, 3249, 4182, 4217, 4492, 4681, 5095, 5384, 5482, 5593, 6214, 6315, 6690, 6793, 7392.

WB 12: 878, 1425, 2455, 3003, 3281, 3968, 4131, 4332, 4933, 7384.

WB 13: 303, 564, 858, 2392, 3356, 4264, 4973, 5913, 6418, 6465, 6541, 6562, 7085, 7110.

Clouds of Witness

CW 1: 234, 431, 472, 480, 1031, 1135, 1136, 1298, 1494, 1549, 1582, 1598, 1806, 2021, 2258, 2451, 2574, 2726, 3074, 3310, 3320, 3708, 4232, 4274, 4275, 4469, 4502, 4504, 4510, 4736, 4779, 4835, 4862, 5172, 5173, 5498, 5704, 5705, 5860, 5909, 6135, 6249, 6303, 6390, 6600, 6673, 7043, 7101, 7354, 7475, 7492.

CW 2: 49, 50, 51, 71, 82, 84, 127, 162, 314, 315, 393, 599, 664, 673, 729, 791, 1229, 1308, 1519, 1590, 1620, 2004, 2115, 2361, 2825, 2826, 3816, 3821, 4092, 4094, 4260, 4383, 4422, 4521, 4589, 4776, 4780, 4920, 5311, 5364, 5536, 5855, 6225, 6267, 6316, 6328, 6372, 6468, 6501, 6618, 6795, 6860, 7431.

CW 3: 299, 454, 566, 784, 964, 1266, 1514, 1610, 1774, 1803, 1830, 1967, 2521, 2608, 2633, 2694, 2800, 3075, 3761, 3894, 3959, 4037, 4038, 4777, 4792, 4812, 4946, 5493, 5685, 5716, 5847, 5904, 6223, 6503, 6588, 7047, 7081, 7170, 7304.

CW 4: 457, 722, 941, 960, 1156, 1451, 1482, 1924, 2292, 2364, 2450, 2778, 2838, 2937, 2949, 2963, 2964, 3051, 3315, 3366, 3372, 3394, 3485, 3495, 3557, 3743, 4083, 4126, 4213, 4375, 4711, 4781, 4782, 5158, 5219, 5483, 5506, 5702, 6072, 6464, 6814, 6929, 7235, 7407.

CW 5: 8, 69, 748, 774, 775, 865, 1017, 1032, 1047, 1202, 1233, 1240, 1427, 1458, 1480, 1817, 2045, 2191, 2379, 2427, 2557, 2729, 3009, 3155, 3176, 3418, 3523, 3921, 3934, 4091, 4218, 4291, 4444, 4903, 5115, 5205, 5259, 5382, 5449, 5554, 5577, 5666, 5697, 5722, 5784, 5820, 5821, 5822, 5854, 6012, 6045, 6420, 6646, 6821, 6822, 6823, 6892, 6941, 6853, 7505.

CW 6: 179, 200, 302, 1206, 1243, 1259, 2142, 2251, 2665, 2774, 2855, 2974, 3393, 3516, 3806, 4088, 4322, 5440, 5803, 6032, 6350, 6858, 6973, 7470, 7495.

CW 7: 651, 810, 1227, 1417, 1467, 2114, 2730, 2873, 2879, 3152, 3675, 3892, 4173, 4533, 4694, 5459, 6023, 6256, 6324, 6478, 6540, 6559, 6566, 6567, 6652, 6960, 7191, 7483.

CW 8: 1226, 3373, 5002, 5193.

CW 9: 103, 170, 527, 706, 711, 909, 1260, 1342, 1675, 2212, 2321, 2469, 2570, 2734, 3490, 3696, 3800, 3823, 3824, 4055, 4254, 4258, 4460, 4478, 4564, 4674, 4710, 4925, 5335, 5428, 5540, 5640, 5865, 6051, 6321, 6484, 6710, 6786, 6955, 7223, 7490.

CW 10: 163, 843, 993, 1634, 1903, 1940, 1977, 2331, 2516, 2698, 3136, 3261, 3540, 3840, 3889, 4790, 5227, 5542, 5853, 6112, 6172, 6389, 6893, 7218.

CW 11: 117, 289, 578, 742, 832, 838, 890, 1004, 1137, 1215, 1378, 1402, 1497, 1727, 1928, 2002, 2136, 2335, 2733, 2833, 2968, 3198, 3257, 3323, 3561, 3601, 3652, 4041, 4044, 4046, 4103, 4405, 4756, 4769, 4783, 4808, 4841, 4870, 4915, 4944, 4977, 5194, 5208, 5337, 5369, 5686, 5769, 5965, 6078, 6087, 6141, 6242, 6810, 6833, 6885, 7013, 7121, 7137, 7152, 7315, 7378, 7472.

CW 12: 1012, 1381, 1668, 2864, 3227, 3338, 3395, 3510, 3568, 3671, 4104, 4766, 5111, 5567, 5688, 5691, 6054, 6369, 7200, 7264.

CW 13: 4, 11, 108, 678, 1022, 1285, 1332, 1479, 1881, 2225, 2316, 2414, 2558, 3590, 4062, 4063, 4389, 4544, 4774, 4860, 4861, 5109, 5134, 5135, 5415, 5520, 6276, 6615, 6937, 7416.

CW 14: 134, 138, 428, 445, 533, 593, 633, 728, 914, 926, 1173, 1189, 1358, 1359, 1432, 1731, 2074, 2144, 2235, 2419, 2672, 2709, 2721, 2783, 2918, 2924, 3206, 3643, 3704, 3757, 3764, 3768, 3905, 3931, 4050, 4093, 4873, 5581, 5627, 5786, 5798, 6453, 7061, 7323, 7338, 7448.

CW 15: 429, 539, 625, 660, 1166, 1531, 2141, 2898, 2971, 3154, 3186, 3312, 3769, 4128, 4965, 5412, 5606, 5681, 6229, 6265, 6287, 6921, 7048.

CW 16: 47, 404, 509, 987, 1176, 1853, 3015, 3566, 3588, 3836, 4600, 4702, 5143, 6987.

CW 17: 347, 717, 850, 3586, 4180, 4685, 7066, 7272.

CW 18: 568, 672, 727, 1079, 1182, 1264, 1852, 2808, 3441, 3476, 4744, 4758, 5586, 5594, 5608, 5732, 6740, 6841, 7063, 7479.

CW 19: 675, 751, 1383, 1538, 2014, 2149, 3328, 4155, 4677, 5009, 5048, 5049, 5645, 5906, 6486, 6517, 6807, 7186, 7201.

Unnatural Death

UD BN: 262, 315, 431, 546, 1713, 1805, 1831, 2110, 2111, 2226, 2386, 2397, 2913, 3099, 4293, 4800, 6185, 6196, 6370, 6958, 6972, 7357.

UD 1: 232, 319, 686, 883, 1001, 1098, 1188, 1670, 1703, 1811, 2747, 3051, 3160, 4397, 4526, 5080, 5193, 5425, 5440, 5648, 5656, 5802, 6277, 6417, 6576, 6840.

UD 2: 145, 1013, 1069, 3122, 3303, 4166, 4435, 4449, 4849, 5706, 6132, 6486, 7436.

UD 3: 6, 249, 473, 870, 1014, 1172, 1191, 1618, 1624, 2103, 2439, 2440, 2561, 3376, 3644, 3750, 4075, 4372, 4273, 4499, 4802, 4804, 4951, 5225, 5290, 5302, 5345, 5611, 5878, 6006, 6129, 6157, 6292, 6547, 6843, 7326, 7369.

UD 4: 154, 296, 361, 597, 1098, 1141, 1361, 1665, 1775, 1776, 2289, 2583, 2866, 2868, 2975, 3003, 3071, 3617, 3752, 3856, 3911, 4338, 4711, 4793, 5182, 5220, 5872, 5899, 5939, 6061, 6819, 7037, 7276, 7280.

UD 5: 97, 731, 1007, 1045, 1284, 1839, 2008, 2201, 2389, 2390, 2491, 3080, 3346, 3372, 3715, 3834, 3955, 4598, 5033, 5105, 5426, 5466, 5982, 7176, 7398.

UD 6: 5, 326, 635, 671, 801, 1221, 1437, 1537, 1657, 1734, 1735, 1900, 2194, 2238, 2256, 2862, 2995, 3081, 3150, 3400, 3522, 3840, 3845, 4000, 4028, 4083, 4155, 4173, 4346, 4438, 4589, 4741, 4905, 5091, 5172, 5328, 5381, 6057, 6320, 6332, 6389, 6394, 6533, 6650, 6805, 7047, 7102, 7200, 7275, 7305, 7405, 7500.

UD 7: 311, 856, 859, 876, 1459, 1558, 2039, 2297, 2508, 2513, 3801, 3952, 4044, 4151, 4152, 4609, 4709, 4931, 5650, 5663, 5954, 6065, 6311, 6589, 6595, 7022, 7032, 7286.

UD 8: 256, 338, 464, 928, 979, 1511, 1647, 1747, 2259, 3092, 3423, 3518, 4313, 4591, 4679, 5008, 5067, 5104, 6241, 6270, 6392, 6539, 6612, 7128, 7277, 7278, 7279.

UD 9: 1225, 2893, 4001, 4144, 4953, 6097, 6164, 6568, 6602, 6778, 7100, 7333, 7431.

UD 10: 783, 1302, 1418, 2764, 2865, 3695, 5386, 6103, 7317.

UD 11: 64, 370, 490, 803, 920, 964, 1168, 1394, 1428, 1583, 1645, 1777, 1920, 1937, 2207, 2454, 2546, 2635, 3401, 3770, 3808, 3904, 4037, 4259, 4894, 4906, 5083, 5212, 5213, 5545, 5801, 5925, 6259, 6304, 6400, 6731, 7062, 7116, 7129.

UD 12: 457, 618, 645, 825, 978, 1395, 1648, 1778, 1913, 2086, 2374, 2634, 2832, 2994, 3254, 3795, 3847, 4433, 4934, 5023, 5244, 5297, 5387, 5451, 5644, 5763, 6064, 6102, 6427, 7045, 7194, 7301.

UD 13: 442, 2204, 2568, 3082, 4472, 4764, 4949, 5320. 5400, 5413, 5444, 5718, 5740, 6410, 6545, 6834, 7142.

UD 14: 41, 673, 2023, 2116, 2180, 2235, 2901, 2909, 3116, 3177, 3238, 4596, 4699, 4844, 4873, 5006, 5132, 5462, 5561, 5612, 6644, 6798, 6964, 7041, 7291.

UD 15: 231, 252, 741, 1169, 1303, 1820, 1876, 2185, 2791, 2915, 3330, 3534, 3766, 4457, 5472, 7343, 7491.

UD 16: 580, 1669, 1792, 3133, 3591, 3725, 4290, 4458, 4843, 4940, 5199, 5981, 6127, 6299.

UD 17: 52, 160, 234, 379, 515, 675, 1472, 1503, 2266, 2910, 3250, 3256, 4010, 4703, 5002, 5252, 6830, 7399.

UD 18: 1320, 1402, 2385, 2825, 2885, 2899, 3052, 3053, 4072, 4251, 4363, 5014, 5175, 7021.

UD 19: 111, 269, 336, 480, 626, 864, 889, 910, 1071, 1195, 1271, 1290, 1607, 1666, 1696, 1710, 1751, 1877, 1891, 2122, 2175, 2186, 2328, 2549, 2720, 2809, 2814, 3014, 3049, 3205, 3206, 3306, 3324, 3375, 3425, 3487, 3645, 4126, 4207, 4301, 4825, 4959, 4980, 4985, 4987, 5223, 5883, 6029, 6192, 6290, 6338, 6465, 6629, 6633, 6938, 7217, 7256.

UD 20: 2, 96, 511, 631, 789, 1040, 1730, 1732, 1733, 1814, 1950, 1970, 2045, 2469, 3129, 3294, 3348, 3912, 4434, 4682, 4705, 5054, 5603, 5824, 5839, 6110, 6117, 6155, 6329, 7370.

UD 21: 9, 177, 236, 497, 503, 860, 1291, 1708, 1808, 2319, 2578, 2629, 2936.

UD 22: 346, 426, 834, 1078, 1440, 1483, 1491, 1546, 2189, 2234, 2551, 2799, 2990, 3411, 3833, 3859, 3873, 4473, 4865, 5127, 5395, 5465, 5848, 5850, 5851, 5980, 6388, 6479, 6497, 6749, 6751, 6835, 7027, 7142.

UD 23: 33, 118, 595, 614, 620, 1554, 1865, 1898, 2094, 2150, 2340, 2542, 3086, 4833,

5217, 5357, 5761, 5882, 6317, 6645, 6739, 7188, 7368.

The Unpleasantness at the Bellona Club

BC 1: 254, 546, 721, 1164, 1635, 2235, 2351, 2352, 2354, 2886, 3214, 4225, 4274, 4276, 4518, 4521, 4891, 4938, 5024, 5122, 5499, 5662, 5956.

BC 2: 1192, 1380, 1461, 1689, 1955, 1971, 2353, 3004, 4680, 5354, 6296, 7192, 7213.

BC 3: 528, 1014, 1191, 1400, 1679, 1954, 1956, 2488, 2538, 2612, 3053, 3486, 3703, 3731, 4010, 4075, 4241, 4248, 4589, 5053, 5441, 6047, 6077, 6273, 6611, 6827, 7055, 7256.

BC 4: 846, 2937, 3086, 4229, 4340, 5193, 5743, 5745, 5924, 6606, 7175, 7204, 7329, 7440.

BC 5: 320, 1460, 2566, 4410, 4425, 4615, 4768, 4798, 5202, 5242, 5294, 5853, 6120, 6727, 6905.

BC 6: 418, 1676, 2366, 2388, 2609, 2687, 3554, 4718, 4901, 6124, 6414, 6719, 7133, 7419.

BC 7: 221, 269, 332, 610, 682, 1247, 1401, 1630, 1673, 1699, 1835, 2393, 2885, 3648, 3723, 3987, 4047, 4126, 4127, 4191, 4306, 4406, 4467, 4585, 4633, 5379, 5777, 5875, 5948, 5955, 6193, 6280, 6347, 6389, 7096, 7508.

BC 8: 253, 1153, 1228, 1438, 1898, 2230, 2232, 2789, 2921, 3219, 4204, 4348, 4559, 4900, 5041, 5652, 5748, 6513, 6521, 7471.

BC 9: 359, 498, 500, 993, 1083, 4231, 4282, 4561, 5860, 7103, 7130.

BC 10: 444, 585, 1227, 1328, 2126, 2185, 2260, 2373, 2723, 3241, 3370, 4857, 4898, 5178, 5833, 5972, 6033, 6216, 6477.

BC 11: 1199, 3119, 3278, 3729, 5136, 5366, 6317, 6858, 7008, 7100, 7142.

BC 12: 1603, 2438, 3095, 4525.

BC 13: 1031, 1163, 1239, 1336, 1511, 2286, 2469, 2505, 2918, 3272, 3300, 3310, 4646, 4666, 4750, 4902, 4990, 5008, 5550, 5559, 6071, 6108, 6148, 6362, 6712, 7413.

BC 14: 282, 476, 1875, 1879, 2459, 3083, 4837, 5204, 6125, 7157, 7318.

BC 15: 250, 422, 459, 672, 1732, 1734, 1907, 2433, 2548, 2768, 3079, 3375, 4312, 4336, 4817, 5176, 5473, 5843, 6539, 6574.

BC 16: 777, 1343, 1362, 2624, 2626, 2857, 3487, 3799, 3922, 4647, 4713, 4991, 5026, 5164, 5230, 5247, 5334, 6220, 7071, 7281, 7409.

BC 17: 136, 261, 957, 2055, 3682, 4190, 4474, 4673, 5180, 5539, 7320.

BC 18: 357, 523, 559, 570, 573, 785, 876, 1329, 1475, 1493, 1694, 1754, 1755, 1768, 1978, 2062, 2578, 2598, 2646, 3080, 3369, 3579, 3580, 3663, 3734, 3892, 3998, 4058, 4167, 4174, 4186, 4192, 4261, 4584, 4711, 4762, 4945, 5051, 5106, 5116, 5153, 5329, 5421, 5651, 5698, 5731, 5797, 5861, 6110, 6115, 6159, 6177, 6267, 6657, 6707, 6861, 7178, 7298, 7408, 7420.

BC 19: 146, 2295, 2769, 2927, 4020, 6465, 6670, 7010, 7099.

BC 20: 1258, 1639, 1685, 1697, 1833, 1836, 1926, 1933, 1990, 2591, 4165, 5082,6277, 7339.

BC 21: 1268, 1360, 2290, 2383, 3350, 4792, 5324, 5755, 5951, 6306, 6785, 7031.

BC 22: 195, 2314.

BC 23: 1534, 5004.

Strong Poison

SP 1: 34, 40, 54, 234, 269, 317, 360, 430, 490, 589, 599, 797, 853, 899, 977, 1252, 1290, 1361, 1550, 1711, 1772, 1830, 1966, 2060, 2349, 2676, 2681, 2752, 2887, 2933, 2992, 2994, 3079, 3084, 3134, 3595, 3736, 3861, 3988, 4097, 4126, 4302, 4713, 4873, 4897, 4917, 5140, 5170, 5380, 5416, 5473, 5484, 6211, 6318, 6465, 6523, 6525, 6638, 6733, 6863, 6891, 6895, 6971, 6993, 7000, 7146, 7160, 7198, 7351, 7404.

SP 2: 256, 500, 675, 1193, 2498, 2885, 6023, 6246, 7327.

SP 3: 158, 238, 299, 1293, 1357, 1475, 1476, 1978, 2560, 3009, 3406, 4064, 4183, 6212, 6640, 6771, 7099.

SP 4: 414, 1002, 1650, 1651, 1660, 1797, 3133, 3206, 3268, 3708, 3997, 6912, 7101, 7121, 7334.

SP 5: 39, 506, 640, 660, 855, 901, 1145, 1220, 2253, 2278, 2285, 2303, 2727, 3123, 3212, 4369, 4433, 4554, 4924, 5081, 5293, 5392, 5731, 6033, 6209, 6425, 6620, 6869, 6965, 7181, 7467.

SP 6: 753, 796, 1118, 1423, 1809, 2656, 2793, 2965, 4401, 5193, 5227, 5269, 5534, 5596, 6079, 6197, 6447, 6481, 6909, 7061.

SP 7: 225, 515, 1824, 2258, 3469, 3489, 4021, 4498, 7203, 7377, 7444.

Five Red Herrings

Have His Carcase

5572, 6533, 6631, 6695, 7031, 7142.

HHC 12: 425, 536, 689, 1627, 1905, 1959, 1994, 2083, 2147, 2341, 2697, 2843, 2888, 2892, 2985, 3010, 3222, 3334, 3365, 3407, 3647, 4143, 4447, 4706, 4768, 5319, 5340, 5530, 5541, 5571, 5579, 5583, 5678, 5775, 6191, 6395, 6744, 6756, 7037, 7119, 7172, 7393.

HHC 13: 820, 1097, 1518, 2187, 2392, 2411, 2476, 5611, 6325, 6483, 7451.

HHC 14: 4235, 4251, 4330, 4789, 5602, 5615, 6111, 6923.

HHC 15: 81, 83, 130, 201, 582, 760, 771, 1093, 1177, 1277, 1396, 1726, 1857, 1983, 3558, 3688, 3815, 3825, 3893, 4221, 4515, 4565, 4578, 4848, 5018, 5431, 5434, 5772, 6757, 6804, 7228, 7477.

HHC 16: 140, 157, 169, 680, 1320, 1324, 1389, 1850, 1909, 1981, 1988, 2018, 2537, 2698, 2715, 2777, 2815, 2844, 2905, 2945, 3335, 3355, 3412, 3600, 3871, 3985, 4193, 4617, 4838, 6299, 6661, 6808, 6903, 6949, 7033, 7106, 7151.

HHC 17: 3187, 3452, 3531, 3915, 4048, 4158, 4764, 4823, 5547, 5881, 5994.

HHC 18: 518, 675, 837, 6628, 6985.

HHC 19: 562, 713, 993, 1481, 2199, 2807, 3941, 4278, 4288, 4528, 6339, 6773 7100.

HHC 20: 76, 522, 1567, 1600, 2120, 2445, 2848, 3063, 3723, 3938, 4184, 4392, 4509, 4515, 4567, 4868, 4937, 5332, 5665, 6434, 6490, 6825, 6867.

HHC 21: 305, 1096, 1392, 1502, 1547, 1923, 1929, 1949, 2159, 2355, 3440, 3478, 3599, 3740, 5088, 5163, 5479, 6485, 6536, 6634, 6952.

HHC 22: 107, 403, 591, 1194, 1951, 2544, 2571, 2595, 2788, 3252, 3797, 3910, 3966, 4009, 4535, 4709, 5017, 5273, 5621, 5649, 6018, 6033, 6086, 6168, 6260, 6413, 6635, 6668, 6783, 7122, 7136, 7252.

HHC 23: 58, 271, 857, 921, 925, 2182, 2881, 3301, 3435, 4040, 4239, 4553, 5169, 5190, 5697, 5773, 5774, 5970, 6455, 6491, 7003, 7068, 7435, 7489.

HHC 24: 1038, 1559, 3520, 3812, 4114, 4652, 5050, 6482, 6572, 6787, 6870.

HHC 25: 1025, 1271, 1910, 4255, 4487, 4488, 5308, 5309, 5310, 5826, 6068, 6237, 6324, 6502, 6643, 6738.

HHC 26: 289, 953, 1385, 1441, 1447, 1875, 2067, 2499, 2653, 2713, 3022, 3128, 3732, 4014, 4043, 4117, 4316, 4627, 4871, 5266, 5591, 6267, 6480, 6851, 7115, 7232, 7249, 7335, 7344, 7400.

HHC 27: 3000, 3111, 3794, 3918, 7206.

HHC 28: 1088, 1283, 2460, 3298, 3409, 4714.

HHC 29: 93, 768, 1237, 1296, 2890, 2956, 3467, 4721, 5090, 6876, 6877.

HHC 30: 794, 870, 872, 919, 1225, 2461, 2831, 2922, 2992, 3126, 3256, 3372, 3680, 3702, 3772, 3845, 3851, 3937, 4073, 4513, 4619, 5638, 5895, 6447, 6475, 6557, 6573, 7268.

HHC 31: 31, 1257, 1459, 2722, 2784, 2818, 3012, 3014, 3201, 3429, 3456, 3992, 4116, 4829, 5659, 6027, 6439, 7423.

HHC 32: 151, 284, 572, 781, 987, 1235, 1716, 1782, 2109, 2398, 2555, 2556, 2680, 2755, 2891, 3357, 3802, 3817, 3924, 3965, 4113, 4115, 4382, 4517, 4722, 4890, 4930, 5035, 5037, 5746, 5871, 5911, 6815, 6816, 6887, 7069, 7070, 7117, 7452.

HHC 33: 548, 2158, 2177, 2585, 3584, 4210, 4807, 5690, 6123, 6989, 7482.

HHC 34: 192, 1662, 3019, 3585, 3748, 4919, 5757, 6348, 6552.

Murder Must Advertise

MMA 1: 103, 105, 288, 300, 382, 458, 615, 628, 822, 1275, 1520, 1560, 1736, 1750, 1765, 1800, 1805, 1813, 1850, 1888, 2128, 2129, 2130, 2143, 2235, 2458, 2461, 2648, 2669, 2678, 2786, 2846, 2918, 2938, 2982, 3027, 3028, 3066, 3098, 3482, 3494, 3660, 3888, 4008, 4059, 4154, 4206, 4421, 4610, 4611, 4646, 4816, 4838, 4962, 5021, 5064, 5409, 5468, 5481, 5494, 5572, 5782, 6049, 6195, 6219, 6230, 6236, 6293, 6411, 6479, 6492, 6520, 6727, 6761, 6837, 6838, 6918, 7078, 7099, 7271, 7293, 7330, 7405, 7424.

MMA 2: 38, 308, 394, 675, 926, 996, 1248, 1537, 1580, 1642, 1799, 2151, 2270, 2279, 2539, 2577, 2861, 3007, 3546, 3573, 3936, 4419, 4785, 5195, 5226, 5238, 5525, 5566, 6231, 6318, 6578, 6716, 6879, 7025.

MMA 3: 89, 259, 701, 703, 745, 829, 855, 951, 1134, 1309, 1468, 1728, 1784, 1785, 2301, 2529, 2589, 2836, 3316, 3359, 4045, 4786, 4801, 4966, 5097, 5243, 5391, 5482, 5493, 5504, 5507, 5524, 5800, 5808, 5819, 6053, 6066, 6160, 6302, 6735, 6782, 6911, 7250, 7283, 7295, 7474.

MMA 4: 142, 433, 605, 666, 684, 726, 735, 776, 809, 892, 950, 964, 1009, 1033, 1103, 1422, 1553, 1578, 1672, 1753, 1863, 1873, 2054,

The Nine Tailors

Gaudy Night

1205, 1253, 1386, 1403, 1439, 1463, 1555, 1577, 1788, 1798, 1932, 1935, 1987, 2164, 2188, 2209, 2337, 2378, 2399, 2432, 2453, 2590, 2613, 2691, 2724, 2984, 3023, 3048, 3147, 3148, 3202, 3210, 3216, 3288, 3425, 3437, 3530, 3551, 3555, 3562, 3582, 3674, 3698, 3846, 3948, 4081, 4146, 4194, 4197, 4198, 4251, 4262, 4263, 4286, 4315, 4345, 4369, 4388, 4391, 4491, 4538, 4604, 4650, 4701, 4751, 4892, 4977, 4985, 5046, 5087, 5123, 5146, 5148, 5270, 5351, 5457, 5471, 5617, 5696, 5697, 5841, 5868, 5869, 5934, 5966, 5974, 5993, 6016, 6020, 6041, 6042, 6105, 6153, 6402, 6416, 6432, 6475, 6653, 6682, 6787, 6832, 6881, 6884, 6993, 7039, 7120, 7185, 7390.

GN 2: 63, 382, 415, 460, 556, 579, 880, 885, 991, 1501, 1931, 2345, 2346, 2347, 2429, 2510, 2573, 2576, 2627, 2803, 3170, 3284, 3204, 3209, 3282, 4036, 4348, 5092, 5096, 5255, 5360, 5406, 5496, 5979, 6444, 6605, 6742, 6959, 7341.

GN 3: 66,85, 185, 193, 330, 367, 377, 448, 554, 567, 576, 741, 886, 1232, 1279, 1365, 1725, 1850, 1908, 2034, 2073, 2091, 2135, 2579, 2652, 2880, 2928, 2931, 3038, 3044, 3076, 3088, 3326, 3331, 3726, 3909, 4207, 4289, 4299, 4326, 4448, 4658, 4986, 4994, 5007, 5141, 5342, 5445, 5463, 5512, 5523, 5561, 5630, 5812, 5862, 5888, 6073, 6143, 6144, 6551, 6622, 6642, 6744, 6795, 6883, 6888, 7041, 7059, 7336, 7426.

GN 4: 28, 55, 60, 194, 269, 295, 306, 427, 454, 558, 840, 1027, 1077, 1331, 1529, 1838, 1890, 2089, 2111, 2138, 2178, 2179, 2313, 2327, 2360, 2603, 2725, 2805, 2992, 3004, 3236, 3443, 3536, 3575, 3758, 3828, 3830, 3835, 3955, 4227, 4331, 4433, 4796, 4811, 4845, 4947, 5061, 5133, 5193, 5317, 5361, 5427, 5464, 5676, 5800, 5832, 6070, 6180, 6277, 6683, 6725, 6974, 6983, 7042, 7486.

GN 5: 119, 222, 989, 1144, 1218, 1278, 1361, 1433, 1462, 1528, 2020, 2079, 2139, 2307, 2444, 2745, 2845, 2930, 3347, 3673, 4019, 4069, 4160, 4481, 4483, 4581, 4686, 4775, 5057, 5359, 5555, 5594, 5674, 5975, 5976, 6004, 6043, 6450, 6474, 6606, 6607, 6654, 7052, 7079, 7147, 7319, 7380.

GN 6: 475, 720, 732, 898, 1419, 1446, 1897, 2467, 3514, 3527, 3552, 3567, 3659, 3720, 3994, 4243, 4252, 4569, 4866, 5059, 5278, 5558, 6089, 6137, 6210, 6542, 6806, 6902, 7502.

GN 7: 494, 719, 849, 891, 1564, 1855, 1995, 2032, 2153, 2174, 2210, 2287, 2545, 2683, 2712, 2811, 3125, 3167, 3233, 3287, 3741, 3843, 3864, 3896, 3899, 4011, 4187, 4249, 4450, 4618, 4826, 4827, 4971, 5060, 5183, 5272, 5322, 5365, 5379, 5454, 5600, 5744, 6046, 6268, 6597, 7259.

GN 8: 57, 110, 186, 281, 417, 660, 679, 882, 900, 936, 1017, 1080, 1085, 1298, 1299, 1434, 1523, 1688, 1620, 1714, 1758, 1816, 2338, 2531, 2732, 2875, 3020, 3090, 3199, 3203, 3226, 3244, 3246, 3257, 3419, 3655, 3689, 3692, 3694, 3697, 3798, 4307, 4362, 4399, 4406, 4821, 4887, 4921, 5074, 5192, 5876, 6238, 6271, 6279, 6346, 6358, 6456, 6466, 6662, 6845, 6849, 7016, 7044, 7056, 7065, 7406, 7447.

GN 9: 333, 371, 692, 1274, 1440, 1450, 1756, 1901, 2021, 2043, 2184, 2200, 2343, 2735, 2806, 2859, 3169, 3177, 3276, 3320, 3493, 3563, 3614, 3745, 3946, 3957, 3970, 4724, 6136, 6190, 6377, 6419, 6470, 6521, 6763, 6839, 7118, 7248, 7367.

GN 10: 395, 647, 954, 1058, 1110, 1406, 1722, 1729, 1731, 2250, 2382, 2509, 2748, 2790, 2851, 3295, 4311, 4338, 4759, 4888, 4910, 5316, 5356, 5362, 5726, 6000, 6127, 6189, 6245, 6289, 6587, 7299.

GN 11: 62, 229, 234, 246, 435, 501, 644, 754, 755, 787, 799, 1047, 1094, 1223, 1256, 1281, 1301, 1368, 1569, 1695, 1723, 1810, 2015, 2051, 2208, 2226, 2363, 2398, 2436, 2511, 2614, 2647, 2664, 2675, 2798, 2925, 3099, 3180, 3609, 3636, 3763, 3919, 4102, 4418, 4426, 4480, 4726, 4855, 4893, 4964, 5004, 5056, 5069, 5162, 5229, 5422, 5499, 5503, 5573, 5588, 5589, 5756, 5767, 6003, 6005, 6056, 6060, 6067, 6069, 6138, 6253, 6294, 6300, 6368, 6371, 6457, 6460, 6463, 6737, 6774, 6898, 7050.

GN 12: 125, 279, 873, 1030, 1060, 1127, 1340, 1414, 1518, 1589, 1602, 2105, 2119, 2254, 2255, 2348, 2400, 2536, 2610, 2761, 2903, 3197, 3746, 3791, 3844, 3878, 4018, 4281, 4430, 4459, 4579, 4605, 4698, 4708, 5047, 5452, 5453, 5456, 5590, 5751, 5815, 5856, 5857, 5879, 6015, 6258, 6293, 6534, 6719, 6732, 6934, 7099, 7140.

GN 13: 59, 114, 273, 287, 616, 874, 949, 1545, 1561, 1783, 1794, 2951, 3304, 3498, 3587, 3699, 3735, 4017, 4065, 4196, 4317, 4364, 4415, 4416, 4590, 4625, 4693, 4928, 4963, 5118, 5189, 5236, 5368, 5385, 5794, 5963, 5985, 6364, 6378, 6519, 6699, 6705, 6836, 6961, 7427.

GN 14: 112, 183, 245, 258, 294, 416, 419, 493, 592, 642, 772, 858, 963, 1039, 1114, 1586, 1627, 1628, 1761, 1779, 1982, 2473, 2646, 3432, 3454, 3618, 3625, 3662, 3716, 3891, 4022, 4318, 4471, 4620, 4700, 4976, 5032, 5101, 5156, 5239, 5646, 5694, 5889, 6085, 6240, 6360, 6619, 6857, 6962, 7145, 7260, 7429.

GN 15: 10, 103, 126, 168, 226, 228, 327, 584, 715, 738, 786, 862, 908, 999, 1129, 1171, 1212, 1280, 1687, 1829, 1940, 2171, 2312, 2371, 2433, 3164, 3173, 3337, 3345, 3391, 3436, 3445, 3504, 3708, 4119, 4172, 4476, 4742, 4998, 5188,

5650, 6182, 6186, 6340, 6449, 6621, 6977, 7101, 7215, 7237, 7314, 7371.

GN 16: 1101, 1760, 2607, 3191, 3471, 4390, 4562, 5150, 6715, 7011.

GN 17: 155, 167, 171, 244, 250, 546, 655, 670, 1068, 1148, 1245, 1294, 1312, 1351, 1593, 1644, 1743, 1748, 1812, 1904, 2031, 2148, 2157, 2163, 2269, 2294, 2318, 2424, 2471, 2502, 2640, 2698, 2929, 2931, 3016, 3144, 3232, 3332, 3354, 3404, 3519, 3747, 3866, 4034, 4062, 4122, 4532, 4551, 4637, 4738, 4942, 5121, 5218, 5246, 5248, 5261, 5616, 5620, 5764, 5805, 6055, 6152, 6213, 6284, 6352, 6445, 6462, 6636, 6753, 6776, 6854, 6933, 7135, 7375, 7445, 7462, 7473, 7493.

GN 18: 211, 641, 1326, 1477, 1513, 2223, 2659, 2795, 3157, 3319, 3428, 3916, 4066, 4223, 4882, 5034, 5131, 6024, 6314, 6985, 7026, 7417, 7468.

GN 19: 278, 674, 918, 984, 1258, 1396, 1411, 1505, 1562, 1585, 1680, 2066, 2146, 2241, 2243, 2284, 2625, 2743, 2796, 2941, 3353, 4120, 4308, 4484, 4520, 4716, 4805, 4834, 5130, 5348, 5623, 5733, 5735, 6113, 6174, 6292, 6465, 6524, 6659, 6706, 6754, 7001, 7238, 7461.

GN 20: 116, 156, 581, 675, 769, 1128, 1236, 1346, 2426, 2489, 2655, 2893, 3525, 3714, 3943, 4226, 4228, 4253, 4669, 6916, 7430.

GN 21: 152, 694, 982, 1667, 1681, 1791, 2052, 2446, 2520, 2586, 3034, 3224, 3333, 3526, 3925, 4079, 4527, 4657, 4672, 5209, 5443, 5527, 6529, 6713, 7166, 7284.

GN 22: 863, 2185, 3548, 3668, 3742, 4665, 4828.

GN 23: 113, 409, 461, 487, 980, 1053, 1478, 2181, 2794, 3872,4690, 4748, 5249, 5250, 6797, 7255.

Busman's Honeymoon

BH P: 25, 27, 72, 122, 237, 321, 325, 386, 504, 530, 693, 729, 858, 960, 982, 983, 1003, 1055, 1200, 1204, 1267, 1278, 1286, 1304, 1306, 1361, 1366, 1373, 1566, 1788, 1798, 1830, 1831, 1844, 1875, 1895, 1935, 1940, 1986, 1997, 2105, 2272, 2406, 2562, 2813, 2817, 2919, 2977, 3068, 3097, 3146, 3163, 3177, 3182, 3275, 3349, 3448, 3451, 3503, 3577, 3583, 3614, 3838, 3878, 3910, 3945, 4067, 4099, 4100, 4141, 4146, 4161, 4315, 4320, 4392, 4394, 4413, 4433, 4466, 4476, 4495, 4504, 4589, 4610, 4731, 4755, 4787, 4873, 4985, 5015, 5086, 5333, 5394, 5439, 5447, 5467, 5503, 5656, 5736, 5830, 5867, 5876, 5877, 5921, 6081, 6142, 6158, 6262, 6393, 6537, 6555, 6586, 6616, 6706, 6865, 6867, 6912, 6946, 6993, 6994, 7061, 7179, 7321, 7334, 7351, 7376, 7410, 7438.

BH 1: 220, 347, 471, 542, 575, 700, 1016, 1338, 1717, 1735, 1757, 2017, 2180, 2220, 2226, 2415, 2494, 2513, 2851, 3374, 3386, 3654, 3669, 3870, 4095, 4744, 4995, 4997, 5157, 5652, 5816, 5817, 5823, 6026, 6035, 6084, 6162, 6505, 6527, 6736, 6878, 6913, 7040, 7089, 7090, 7125, 7402.

BH 2: 296, 405, 502, 524, 545, 551, 740, 916, 1000, 1797, 1995, 2104, 2889, 3183, 3309, 3387, 3539, 3598, 3791, 3900, 5055, 7037, 7222.

BH 3: 637, 1005, 2173, 2192, 2329, 3389, 3439, 3450, 3576, 3880, 4788, 5028, 5635, 7485.

BH 4: 268, 384, 621, 877, 997, 1064, 1170, 1408, 1420, 1512, 1556, 1643, 2035, 2288, 2657, 2658, 3181, 3248, 3277, 3327, 3388, 3421, 3628, 3865, 4106, 4117, 4147, 4220, 4537, 4595, 4671, 4840, 4918, 5011, 5027, 5065, 5203, 5214, 5371, 5428, 5446, 5490, 5806, 6147, 6458, 6508, 6794, 6930, 7331, 7433.

BH 5: 102, 148, 153, 198, 264, 421, 507, 528, 752, 956, 1158, 1314, 1470, 1544, 1677, 1975, 2198, 2202, 2212, 2245, 2668, 2841, 3036, 3057, 3206, 3225, 3284, 3371, 3717, 3956, 4168, 4195, 4337, 4342, 4414, 4566, 4743, 4809, 4820, 4935, 5298, 5461, 5576, 5715, 5754, 5811, 6101, 6119, 6241, 6305, 6385, 6471, 6577, 7143, 7396, 7488.

BH 6: 86, 218, 280, 399, 515, 789, 821, 954, 2775, 3021, 3958, 3973, 4170, 4187, 4281, 4381, 4532, 5570, 5858, 6639, 7268, 7423.

BH 7: 274, 377, 464, 649, 704, 806, 995, 1002, 1074, 1089, 1109, 1128, 1206, 1604, 1663, 1707, 1785, 1932, 2101, 2224, 2282, 2377, 2587, 2636, 2849, 2908, 3100, 3168, 3339, 3413, 3472, 3475, 3708, 1777, 3818, 3827, 4003, 4087, 4088, 4110, 4178, 4226, 4552, 4658, 4727, 4791, 4795, 4803, 5079, 5208, 5302, 5543, 5718, 5654, 5728, 5761, 6008, 6436, 6498, 6499, 6602, 6787, 6875, 6967, 7099, 7101, 7236, 7480.

BH 8: 241, 356, 627, 656, 960, 2339, 2487, 2564, 2718, 2744, 3296, 3433, 3603, 3630, 3733, 3775, 4244, 4407, 4457, 4508, 4539, 5099, 5368, 5489, 5514, 6361, 7254, 7325, 7458.

BH 9: 334, 1217, 1670, 1944, 1958, 2022, 3043, 3528, 3611, 3683, 3849, 3858, 4033, 4134, 4233, 4432, 4490, 4649, 5288, 5655, 6301, 6617, 6625, 6627, 6684, 7163.

BH 10: 210, 310, 365, 397, 1337, 1372, 1978, 2029, 2280, 2325, 2717, 2987, 3229, 3453, 3626, 3713, 3954, 4078, 4121, 4327, 4447, 4836, 5062, 5144, 5265, 5314, 5488, 5628, 5788, 5986, 6283, 6426, 6859, 6914, 7244, 7434.

ENGLAND & WALES.
ENGLISH MILES.
Sites of Battles.
SCOTLAND
NORTH SEA
IRISH SEA
ENGLISH CHANNEL
Bristol Channel
St. Georges Channel
IRELAND
North Channel
I. OF MAN
ANGLESEY
LIVERPOOL
LONDON
EDINBURGH
I. OF WIGHT
West Longitude
East Longitude

SCOTLAND
SCALE OF MILES
0 10 20 30 40
Railroads
Submarine Cables
Canals
Size of type indicates relative importance of places
A T L A N T I C
O C E A N
N O R T H S E A
E N G L A N D
I R E L A N D
N O R T H C H A N N E L
Orkney Islands
Shetland Islands
ATLANTIC OCEAN
NORTH SEA
SCALE OF MILES
0 10 20 30
Outer Hebrides or Long Island
THE MINCH
LITTLE MINCH
GULF OF THE HEBRIDES
SOLWAY FIRTH
SUTHERLAND
CAITHNESS
ROSS & CROMARTY
INVERNESS
NAIRN
ELGIN
BANFF
ABERDEEN
KINCARDINE
FORFAR
PERTH
FIFE
KINROSS
CLACKMANNAN
STIRLING
DUMBARTON
ARGYLL
BUTE
RENFREW
LANARK
LINLITHGOW
EDINBURGH
HADDINGTON
BERWICK
PEEBLES
SELKIRK
ROXBURGH
AYR
DUMFRIES
KIRKCUDBRIGHT
WIGTOWN
ABERDEEN
DUNDEE
EDINBURGH
GLASGOW
Perth
Inverness
Peterhead
Montrose
Arbroath
Leith
Greenock
Paisley
Kilmarnock
Dumfries
Hawick
Belfast
Londonderry
Skye
Mull
Arran
Jura
Islay
Tiree
Coll
Harris
South Uist
Barra
Longitude 5° West from 4° Greenwich
7° 6° 5° 4° 3° 2°
58° 57° 56° 55°

EC
FARRINGDON & HIGH HOLBORN
HOLBORN
GENERAL POST OFFICE
HOLBORN VIADUCT STA.
LUDGATE HILL
BANK
Bunhill Fields
Artillery Ground
CANNON ST. STATION
LONDON BRIDGE STATION
EMBANKMENT
Temple Pier
Waterloo Pier
WATERLOO BRIDGE
Barclays Brewery
Guy's Hospital
UNION ST.
PEABODY SQUARE
BOROUGH ROAD
Bethlem
BRICKLAYERS ARMS STATION
THE TOWER
TOWER BRIDGE

HOUSES OF PARLIAMENT
WHITEHALL
CONSTITUTION HILL
SERPENTINE RIVER
KENSINGTON GARDENS
EXHIBITION ROAD
QUEENS GATE
SLOANE STREET
CADOGAN PLA.
VICTORIA & ALBERT MUSEUM